· STEPHEN KING ·

THE
WASTE
LANDS

THE DARK TOWER III

MW01025613

A SIGNET BOOK

SIGNET
Published by the Penguin Group
Penguin Books USA Inc., 375 Hudson Street,
New York, New York 10014, U.S.A.
Penguin Books Ltd, 27 Wrights Lane,
London W8 5TZ, England
Penguin Books Australia Ltd, Ringwood,
Victoria, Australia
Penguin Books Canada Ltd, 10 Alcorn Avenue,
Toronto, Ontario, Canada M4V 3B2
Penguin Books (N.Z.) Ltd, 182–190 Wairau Road,
Auckland 10, New Zealand

Penguin Books Ltd, Registered Offices:
Harmondsworth, Middlesex, England

Published by Signet, an imprint of Dutton Signet, a division of Penguin Books USA
Inc. *The Waste Lands* previously appeared in a limited edition published by Donald
M. Grant, Publisher, Inc., West Kingston, Rhose Island, and in a Plume edition pub-
lished by Penguin USA.

First Signet Printing, January 1993
20 19 18 17 16 15 14 13

**The Third Volume in an
Epic Series ...**

THE WASTE LANDS

Roland, The Last Gunslinger, moves ever closer to The Dark Tower of his dreams and nightmares—as he crosses a desert of damnation in a macabre world that is a twisted image of our own. With him are those he has drawn to this world: street-smart Eddie Dean and courageous wheelchair-bound Susannah.

Ahead of him are mind-rending revelations about who and what is driving him. Against him is arrayed a swelling legion of foes both more and less than human. A breathtaking drama of action and adventure, discovery and danger, *The Waste Lands* is further testament to Stephen King's novelistic mastery.

**"Gripping ... compelling ... King
mesmerizes the reader."
—*Chicago Sun-Times***

WORKS BY STEPHEN KING

NOVELS

Carrie
'Salem's Lot
The Shining
The Stand
The Dead Zone
Firestarter
Cujo
THE DARK TOWER I:
The Gunslinger
Christine
Pet Sematary
Cycle of the Werewolf
The Talisman
(with Peter Straub)
It
Eyes of the Dragon

Misery
The Tommyknockers
THE DARK TOWER II:
*The Drawing
of the Three*
THE DARK TOWER III:
The Waste Lands
The Dark Half
Needful Things
Gerald's Game
Dolores Claiborne
Insomnia
Rose Madder
Desperation
The Green Mile
THE DARK TOWER IV:
Wizard and Glass

AS RICHARD BACHMAN

Rage
The Long Walk
Roadwork
The Running Man
Thinner
The Regulators

COLLECTIONS

Night Shift
Different Seasons
Skeleton Crew
Four Past Midnight
Nightmares and
Dreamscapes

NONFICTION

Danse Macabre

SCREENPLAYS

Creepshow
Cat's Eye
Silver Bullet
Maximum Overdrive
Pet Sematary
Golden Years
Sleepwalkers
The Stand
The Shining

This third volume of the tale
is gratefully dedicated to my son
OWEN PHILIP KING:
Khef, Ka, and *Ka-tet.*

CONTENTS

ARGUMENT

The Waste Lands is the third volume of a longer tale inspired by and to some degree dependent upon Robert Browning's narrative poem "Childe Roland to the Dark Tower Came."

The first volume, *The Gunslinger*, tells how Roland, the last gunslinger in a world which has "moved on," pursues and finally catches the man in black, a sorcerer named Walter who falsely claimed the friendship of Roland's father in the days when the unity of Mid-World still held. Catching this half-human spell-caster is not Roland's ultimate goal but only another landmark along the road to the powerful and mysterious Dark Tower, which stands at the nexus of time.

Who, exactly, is Roland? What was his world like before it moved on? What is the Tower and why does he pursue it? We have only fragmentary answers. Roland is clearly a kind of knight, one of those charged with holding (or possibly redeeming) a world Roland remembers as being "filled with love and light." Just how closely Roland's memory resembles the way that world actually was is very much open to question, however.

We *do* know that he was forced to an early trial of manhood after discovering that his mother had become the mistress of Marten, a much greater sorcerer than Walter; we know that Marten orchestrated Roland's discovery of his mother's affair, expecting Roland to fail his test of manhood and to be "sent West" into the wastes; we know that Roland laid Marten's plans at nines by passing the test.

We also know that the gunslinger's world is related to our own in some strange but fundamental way, and that passage between the worlds is sometimes possible.

At a way station on a long-deserted coach-road running through the desert, Roland meets a boy named Jake who died in our world, a boy who was, in fact, pushed from a mid-Manhattan street corner and into the path of an oncoming car. Jake Chambers died with the man in black—Walter—peering down at him, and awoke in Roland's world.

Before they reach the man in black, Jake dies again . . . this time because the gunslinger, faced with the second most agonizing choice of his life, elects to sacrifice this symbolic son. Given a choice between the Tower and the child, Roland chooses the Tower. Jake's last words to the gunslinger before plunging into the abyss are: "Go, then—there are other worlds than these."

The final confrontation between Roland and Walter occurs in a dusty golgotha of decaying bones. The man in black tells Roland's future with a deck of Tarot cards. Three *very* strange cards—The Prisoner, The Lady of the Shadows, and Death ("but not for you, gunslinger")—are called especially to Roland's attention.

The second volume, *The Drawing of the Three*, begins on the edge of the Western Sea not long after Roland's confrontation with Walter has ended. An exhausted gunslinger awakes in the middle of the night to discover that the incoming tide has brought a horde of crawling, carnivorous creatures—"lobstrosities"—with it. Before he can escape their limited range, Roland has been seriously wounded by these creatures, losing the first two fingers of his right hand to them. He is also poisoned by the venom of the lobstrosities, and as the gunslinger resumes his journey north along the edge of the Western Sea, he is sickening . . . perhaps dying.

He encounters three doors standing freely upon the beach. Each door opens—for Roland and Roland alone—upon our world; upon the city where Jake lived, in fact. Roland visits New York at three points along our time continuum, both in an effort to save his own life and to draw the three who must accompany him on his road to the Tower.

Eddie Dean is *The Prisoner*, a heroin addict from the New York of the late 1980s. Roland steps through the door on the beach of his world and into Eddie Dean's mind as Eddie, serving a man named Enrico Balazar as a cocaine mule, lands at JFK airport. In the course of their harrowing adventures together, Roland is able to obtain a limited quantity of penicillin and to bring Eddie Dean back to his own world. Eddie, a junkie who discovers he has been kidnapped to a world where there is no junk (or Popeye's fried chicken, for that matter), is less than overjoyed to be there.

The second door leads Roland to *The Lady of the Shadows*—actually *two* women in one body. This time Roland finds himself in the New York of the early 1960s and face to face with a young wheelchair-bound civil-rights activist named Odetta Holmes. The woman hidden inside Odetta is the crafty and hate-filled Detta Walker. When this double woman is pulled into Roland's world, the results are volatile for Eddie and the rapidly sickening gunslinger. Odetta believes that what's happening to her is either a dream or a delusion; Detta, a much more brutally direct intellect, sim-

ply dedicates herself to the task of killing Roland and
Eddie whom she sees as torturing white devils.

Jack Mort, a serial killer hiding behind the third
door (the New York of the mid-1970s), is *Death*. Mort
has twice caused great changes in the life of Odetta
Holmes/Detta Walker, although neither of them knows
it. Mort, whose *modus operandi* is to either push his
victims or drop something on them from above, has
done both to Odetta during the course of his mad (but
oh so careful) career. When Odetta was a child, he
dropped a brick on her head, sending the little girl into
a coma and also occasioning the birth of Detta Walker,
Odetta's hidden sister. Years later, in 1959, Mort encounters Odetta again and pushes her into the path of
an oncoming subway train in Greenwich Village. Odetta
survives Mort again, but at a price: the oncoming train
severed both legs at the knee. Only the presence of a
heroic young doctor (and, perhaps, the ugly but indomitable spirit of Detta Walker) saves her life . . . or so it
would seem. To Roland's eye, these interrelationships
suggest a power greater than mere coincidence; he believes the titanic forces which surround the Dark Tower
have begun to gather once again.

Roland learns that Mort may stand at the heart of
another mystery as well, one which is also a potentially mind-destroying paradox. For the victim Mort is
stalking at the time the gunslinger steps into his life
is none other than Jake, the boy Roland met at the
way station and lost under the mountains. Roland has
never had any cause to doubt Jake's story of how he
died in our world, or any cause to question who Jake's
murderer was—Walter, of course. Jake saw him
dressed as a priest as the crowd gathered around the
spot where he lay dying, and Roland has never
doubted the description.

Nor does he doubt it now; Walter was there, oh
yes, no doubt about that. *But suppose it was Jack
Mort, not Walter, who pushed Jake into the path of
the oncoming Cadillac?* Is such a thing possible? Ro-

land can't say, not for sure, but if that *is* the case, where is Jake now? Dead? Alive? Caught somewhere in time? And if Jake Chambers is still alive and well in his own world of Manhattan in the mid-1970s, *how is it that Roland still remembers him*?

Despite this confusing and possibly dangerous development, the test of the doors—and the drawing of the three—ends in success for Roland. Eddie Dean accepts his place in Roland's world because he has fallen in love with The Lady of the Shadows. Detta Walker and Odetta Holmes, the other two of Roland's three, are driven together into one personality combining elements of both Detta and Odetta when the gunslinger is finally able to force the two personalities to acknowledge each other. This hybrid is able to accept and return Eddie's love. Odetta Susannah Holmes and Detta Susannah Walker thus become a new woman, a *third* woman: Susannah Dean.

Jack Mort dies beneath the wheels of the same subway—that fabled A-train—which took Odetta's legs fifteen or sixteen years before. No great loss there.

And for the first time in untold years, Roland of Gilead is no longer alone in his quest for the Dark Tower. Cuthbert and Alain, his lost companions of yore, have been replaced by Eddie and Susannah . . . but the gunslinger has a way of being bad medicine for his friends. Very bad medicine, indeed.

The Waste Lands takes up the story of these three pilgrims on the face of Mid-World some months after the confrontation by the final door on the beach. They have moved some fair way inland. The period of rest is ending, and a period of learning has begun. Susannah is learning to shoot . . . Eddie is learning to carve . . . and the gunslinger is learning how it feels to lose one's mind, a piece at a time.

(One further note: My New York readers will know that I have taken certain geographical liberties with the city. For these I hope I may be forgiven.)

A heap of broken images, where the sun beats,
And the dead tree gives no shelter, the cricket no relief,
And the dry stone no sound of water. Only
There is shadow under this red rock,
(Come in under the shadow of this red rock),
And I will show you something different from either
Your shadow in the morning striding behind you
Or your shadow at evening rising to meet you;
I will show you fear in a handful of dust.

—T. S. ELIOT
"The Waste Land"

If there pushed any ragged thistle-stalk
  Above its mates, the head was chopped; the bents
  Were jealous else. What made those holes and rents
In the dock's harsh swarth leaves, bruised as to balk
All hope of greenness? 'tis a brute must walk
  Pashing their life out, with a brute's intents.

—ROBERT BROWNING
"Childe Roland to the Dark Tower Came"

"What river is it?" enquired Millicent idly.
"It's only a stream. Well, perhaps a little more than
that. It's called the Waste."
"Is it really?"
"Yes," said Winifred, "it is."

—ROBERT AICKMAN
"Hand in Glove"

BOOK ONE

JAKE

FEAR IN A HANDFUL OF DUST

I ▪ BEAR AND BONE

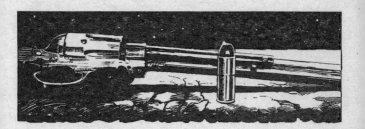

▪ I ▪

BEAR AND BONE

1

IT WAS HER THIRD time with live ammunition . . . and her first time on the draw from the holster Roland had rigged for her.

They had plenty of live rounds; Roland had brought back better than three hundred from the world where Eddie and Susannah Dean had lived their lives up until the time of their drawing. But having ammunition in plenty did not mean it could be wasted; quite the contrary, in fact. The gods frowned upon wastrels. Roland had been raised, first by his father and then by Cort, his greatest teacher, to believe this, and so he still believed. Those gods might not punish at once, but sooner or later the penance would have to be paid . . . and the longer the wait, the greater the weight.

At first there had been no need for live ammunition, anyway. Roland had been shooting for more years than the beautiful brown-skinned woman in the

wheelchair would believe. He had corrected her at
first simply by watching her aim and dry-fire at the
targets he had set up. She learned fast. Both she and
Eddie learned fast.

As he had suspected, both were born gunslingers.

Today Roland and Susannah had come to a clearing
less than a mile from the camp in the woods which
had been home to them for almost two months now.
The days had passed with their own sweet similarity.
The gunslinger's body healed itself while Eddie and
Susannah learned the things the gunslinger had to
teach them: how to shoot, to hunt, to gut and clean
what they had killed; how to first stretch, then tan
and cure the hides of those kills; how to use as much
as it was possible to use so that no part of the animal
was wasted; how to find north by Old Star or south
by Old Mother; how to listen to the forest in which
they now found themselves, sixty miles or more northeast of the Western Sea. Today Eddie had stayed behind, and the gunslinger was not put out of
countenance by this. The lessons which are remembered the longest, Roland knew, are always the ones
that are self-taught.

But what had always been the most important lesson was still most important: how to shoot and how
to hit what you shot at every time. How to kill.

The edges of this clearing had been formed by dark,
sweet-smelling fir trees that curved around it in a ragged semicircle. To the south, the ground broke off
and dropped three hundred feet in a series of crumbling shale ledges and fractured cliffs, like a giant's
set of stairs. A clear stream ran out of the woods and
across the center of the clearing, first bubbling
through a deep channel in the spongy earth and friable
stone, then pouring across the splintery rock floor
which sloped down to the place where the land
dropped away.

The water descended the steps in a series of waterfalls and made any number of pretty, wavering rain-

bows. Beyond the edge of the drop-off was a
magnificent deep valley, choked with more firs and a
few great old elm trees which refused to be crowded
out. These latter towered green and lush, trees which
might have been old when the land from which Roland had come was yet young; he could see no sign
that the valley had ever burned, although he supposed
it must have drawn lightning at some time or other.
Nor would lightning have been the only danger. There
had been people in this forest in some distant time;
Roland had come across their leavings on several occasions over the past weeks. They were primitive artifacts, for the most part, but they included shards of
pottery which could only have been cast in fire. And
fire was evil stuff that delighted in escaping the hands
which created it.

Above this picturebook scene arched a blameless
blue sky in which a few crows circled some miles off,
crying in their old, rusty voices. They seemed restless,
as if a storm were on the way, but Roland had sniffed
the air and there was no rain in it.

A boulder stood to the left of the stream. Roland
had set up six chips of stone on top of it. Each one
was heavily flecked with mica, and they glittered like
lenses in the warm afternoon light.

"Last chance," the gunslinger said. "If that holster's
uncomfortable—even the slightest bit—tell me now.
We didn't come here to waste ammunition."

She cocked a sardonic eye at him, and for a moment
he could see Detta Walker in there. It was like hazy
sunlight winking off a bar of steel. "What would you
do if it *was* uncomfortable and I didn't tell you? If I
missed all six of those itty bitty things? Whop me upside the head like that old teacher of yours used to
do?"

The gunslinger smiled. He had done more smiling
these last five weeks than he had done in the five
years which had come before them. "I can't do that,
and you know it. We were children, for one thing—

children who hadn't been through our rites of manhood yet. You may slap a child to correct him, or her, but—"

"In my world, whoppin the kiddies is also frowned on by the better class of people," Susannah said dryly.

Roland shrugged. It was hard for him to imagine that sort of world—did not the Great Book say "Spare not the birch so you spoil not the child"?—but he didn't believe Susannah was lying. "Your world has not moved on," he said. "Many things are different there. Did I not see for myself that it is so?"

"I guess you did."

"In any case, you and Eddie are not children. It would be wrong for me to treat you as if you were. And if tests were needed, you both passed them."

Although he did not say so, he was thinking of how it had ended on the beach, when she had blown three of the lumbering lobstrosities to hell before they could peel him and Eddie to the bone. He saw her answering smile and thought she might be remembering the same thing.

"So what you goan do if I shoot fo' shit?"

"I'll look at you. I think that's all I'll need to do."

She thought this over, then nodded. "Might be."

She tested the gunbelt again. It was slung across her bosom almost like a shoulder-holster (an arrangement Roland thought of as a docker's clutch) and looked simple enough, but it had taken many weeks of trial and error—and a great deal of tailoring—to get it just right. The belt and the revolver which cocked its eroded sandalwood grip out of the ancient oiled holster had once been the gunslinger's; the holster had hung on his right hip. He had spent much of the last five weeks coming to realize it was never going to hang there again. Thanks to the lobstrosities, he was strictly a lefthanded gun now.

"So how is it?" he asked again.

This time she laughed up at him. "Roland, this ole gunbelt's as com'fable as it's ever gonna be. Now do you want me to shoot or are we just going to sit and listen to crowmusic from over yonder?"

He felt tension worming sharp little fingers under his skin now, and he supposed Cort had felt much the same at times like this under his gruff, bluff exterior. He wanted her to be good . . . *needed* her to be good. But to show how badly he wanted and needed—that could lead to disaster.

"Tell me your lesson again, Susannah."

She sighed in mock exasperation . . . but as she spoke her smile faded and her dark, beautiful face became solemn. And from her lips he heard the old catechism again, made new in her mouth. He had never expected to hear these words from a woman. How natural they sounded . . . yet how strange and dangerous, as well.

" 'I do not aim with my hand; she who aims with her hand has forgotten the face of her father.

" 'I aim with my eye.

" 'I do not shoot with my hand; she who shoots with her hand has forgotten the face of her father.

" 'I shoot with my mind.

" 'I do not kill with my gun—' "

She broke off and pointed at the mica-shiny stones on the boulder.

"I'm not going to kill anything anyhow—they're just itty bitty *rocks*."

Her expression—a little haughty, a little naughty— suggested that she expected Roland to be exasperated with her, perhaps even angry. Roland, however, had been where she was now; he had not forgotten that apprentice gunslingers were fractious and high-spirited, nervy and apt to bite exactly at the wrong moment . . . and he had discovered an unexpected capacity in himself. He could teach. More, he *liked* to teach, and he found himself wondering, from time to time, if that had been true of Cort, as well. He guessed that it had been.

Now more crows began to call raucously, these from

the forest behind them. Some part of Roland's mind registered the fact that the new cries were agitated rather than merely quarrelsome; these birds sounded as if they had been scared up and away from whatever they had been feeding on. He had more important things to think about than whatever it was that had scared a bunch of crows, however, so he simply filed the information away and refocused his concentration on Susannah. To do otherwise with a 'prentice was to ask for a second, less playful bite. And who would be to blame for that? Who but the teacher? For was he not training her to bite? Training *both* of them to bite? Wasn't that what a gunslinger was, when you stripped off the few stern lines of ritual and stilled the few iron grace-notes of catechism? Wasn't he (or she) only a human hawk, trained to bite on command?

"No," he said. "They're not rocks."

She raised her eyebrows a little and began to smile again. Now that she saw he wasn't going to explode at her as he sometimes did when she was slow or fractious (or at least not *yet*), her eyes again took on the mocking sun-on-steel glint he associated with Detta Walker. "They ain't?" The teasing in her voice was still good-natured, but he thought it would turn mean if he let it. She was tense, keyed up, her claws already halfway out of their sheaths.

"No, they *ain't*," he said, returning her mockery. His own smile began to return, but it was hard and humorless. "Susannah, do you remember the *honk mahfahs*?"

Her smile began to fade.

"The *honk mahfahs* in Oxford Town?"

Her smile was gone.

"Do you remember what the *honk mahfahs* did to you and your friends?"

"That wasn't *me*," she said. "That was another woman." Her eyes had taken on a dull, sullen cast. He hated that look, but he also liked it just fine. It was the *right* look, the one that said the kindling was burning well and soon the bigger logs would start to catch.

"Yes. It was. Like it or not, it was Odetta Susannah Holmes, daughter of Sarah Walker Holmes. Not you as you *are*, but you as you *were*. Remember the fire-hoses, Susannah? Remember the gold teeth, how you saw them when they used the hoses on you and your friends in Oxford? How you saw them twinkle when they laughed?"

She had told them these things, and many others, over many long nights as the campfire burned low. The gunslinger hadn't understood everything, but he had listened carefully, just the same. And remembered. Pain was a tool, after all. Sometimes it was the best tool.

"What's wrong with you, Roland? Why you want to go recallin that trash in my mind?"

Now the sullen eyes glinted at him dangerously; they reminded him of Alain's eyes when good-natured Alain was finally roused.

"Yonder stones are those men," Roland said softly. "The men who locked you in a cell and left you to foul yourself. The men with the clubs and the dogs. The men who called you a nigger cunt."

He pointed at them, moving his finger from left to right.

"There's the one who pinched your breast and laughed. There's the one who said he better check and see if you had something stuffed up your ass. There's the one who called you a chimpanzee in a five-hundred-dollar dress. That's the one that kept running his billyclub over the spokes of your wheelchair until you thought the sound would send you mad. There's the one who called your friend Leon *pinko-fag*. And the one on the end, Susannah, is Jack Mort.

"There. Those stones. *Those men.*"

She was breathing rapidly now, her bosom rising and falling in swift little jerks beneath the gunslinger's gunbelt with its heavy freight of bullets. Her eyes had left him; they were looking at the mica-flecked chips of stone. Behind them and at some distance, a tree splintered and fell over. More crows called in the sky. Deep in the game which was no longer a game, neither of them noticed.

"Oh yeah?" she breathed. "That so?"

"It is. Now say your lesson, Susannah Dean, and be true."

This time the words fell from her lips like small chunks of ice. Her right hand trembled lightly on the arm of her wheelchair like an idling engine.

" 'I do not aim with my hand; she who aims with her hand has forgotten the face of her father.

" 'I aim with my eye.' "

"Good."

" 'I do not shoot with my hand; she who shoots with her hand has forgotten the face of her father.

" 'I shoot with my mind.' "

"So it has ever been, Susannah Dean."

" 'I do not kill with my gun; she who kills with her gun has forgotten the face of her father.

" 'I kill with my heart.' "

"Then KILL them, for your father's sake!" Roland shouted. *"KILL THEM ALL!"*

Her right hand was a blur between the arm of the chair and the butt of Roland's sixgun. It was out in a second, her left hand descending, fanning at the hammer in flutters almost as swift and delicate as the wing of a hummingbird. Six flat cracks pealed off across the valley, and five of the six chips of stone set atop the boulder blinked out of existence.

For a moment neither of them spoke—did not even breathe, it seemed—as the echoes rolled back and forth, dimming. Even the crows were silent, at least for the time being.

The gunslinger broke the silence with four toneless yet oddly emphatic words: "It is very well."

Susannah looked at the gun in her hand as if she had never seen it before. A tendril of smoke rose from the barrel, perfectly straight in the windless silence. Then, slowly, she returned it to the holster below her bosom.

"Good, but not perfect," she said at last. "I missed one."

"Did you?" He walked over to the boulder and picked up the remaining chip of stone. He glanced at it, then tossed it to her.

She caught it with her left; her right stayed near the holstered gun, he saw with approval. She shot better and more naturally than Eddie, but had not learned this particular lesson as swiftly as Eddie had done. If she had been with them during the shootout at Balazar's nightclub, she might have. Now, Roland saw, she was at last learning that, too. She looked at the stone and saw the notch, barely a sixteenth of an inch deep, in its upper corner.

"You only clipped it," Roland said, returning to her, "but in a shooting scrape, sometimes that's all you need. If you clip a fellow, throw his aim off . . ." He paused. "Why are you looking at me that way?"

"You don't know, do you? You really don't?"

"No. Your mind is often closed to me, Susannah."

There was no defensiveness in his voice, and Susannah shook her head in exasperation. The rapid turn-and-turn-about dance of her personality sometimes unnerved him; his seeming inability to say anything other than exactly what was on his mind never failed to do the same to her. He was the most *literal* man she had ever met.

"All right," she said, "I'll *tell* you why I'm looking at you that way, Roland. Because what you did was a mean trick. You said you wouldn't slap me, *couldn't* slap me, even if I cut up rough . . . but either you lied or you're very stupid, and I *know* you ain't stupid. People don't always slap with their hands, as every man and woman of my race could testify. We have a little rhyme where I come from: 'Sticks and stones will break my bones—' "

" '—yet taunts shall never wound me,' " Roland finished.

"Well, that's not exactly the way we say it, but I guess it's close enough. It's bullshit no matter how you say it. They don't call what you did a tongue-lashing for nothing. Your words *hurt* me, Roland—are you gonna stand there and say you didn't know they would?"

She sat in her chair, looking up at him with bright, stern curiosity, and Roland thought—not for the first time—that the *honk mahfahs* of Susannah's land must have been either very brave or very stupid to cross her, wheelchair or no wheelchair. And, having walked among them, he didn't think bravery was the answer.

"I did not think or care about your hurt," he said patiently. "I saw you show your teeth and knew you meant to bite, so I put a stick in your jaws. And it worked . . . didn't it?"

Her expression was now one of hurt astonishment. "You *bastard*!"

Instead of replying, he took the gun from her holster, fumbled the cylinder open with the remaining two fingers on his right hand, and began to reload the chambers with his left hand.

"Of all the high-handed, arrogant—"

"You *needed* to bite," he said in that same patient tone. "Had you not, you would have shot all wrong— with your hand and your gun instead of your eye and mind and heart. Was that a trick? Was it arrogant? I think not. I think, Susannah, that *you* were the one with arrogance in her heart. I think *you* were the one with a mind to get up to tricks. That doesn't distress me. Quite the opposite. A gunslinger without teeth is no gunslinger."

"Damn it, I'm *not* a gunslinger!"

He ignored that; he could afford to. If she was no gunslinger, then he was a billy-bumbler. "If we were playing a game, I might have behaved differently. But this is no game. It . . ."

His good hand went to his forehead for a moment and paused there, fingers tented just above the left temple. The tips of the fingers, she saw, were trembling minutely.

"Roland, what's ailing you?" she asked quietly.

The hand lowered slowly. He rolled the cylinder back into place and replaced the revolver in the holster she wore. "Nothing."

"Yes there is. I've seen it. Eddie has, too. It started almost as soon as we left the beach. It's something wrong, and it's getting worse."

"There is nothing wrong," he repeated.

She put her hands out and took his. Her anger was gone, at least for the time being. She looked earnestly up into his eyes. "Eddie and I . . . this isn't our world, Roland. Without you, we'd die here. We'd have your guns, and we can shoot them, you've taught us to do that well enough, but we'd die just the same. We . . . we depend on you. So tell me what's wrong. Let me try to help. Let *us* try to help."

He had never been a man who understood himself deeply or cared to; the concept of self-consciousness (let alone self-analysis) was alien to him. His way was to act—to quickly consult his own interior, utterly mysterious workings, and then act. Of them all, he had been the most perfectly made, a man whose deeply romantic core was encased in a brutally simple box which consisted of instinct and pragmatism. He took one of those quick looks inside now and decided to tell her everything. There was something wrong with him, oh yes. Yes indeed. Something wrong with his mind, something as simple as his nature and as strange as the weird, wandering life into which that nature had impelled him.

He opened his mouth to say *I'll tell you what's wrong, Susannah, and I'll do it in just three words. I'm going insane.* But before he could begin, another tree fell in the forest—it went with a huge, grinding crash. This treefall was closer, and this time they were not

deeply engaged in a test of wills masquerading as a
lesson. Both heard it, both heard the agitated cawing
of the crows which followed it, and both registered
the fact that the tree had fallen close to their camp.

Susannah had looked in the direction of the sound
but now her eyes, wide and dismayed, returned to the
gunslinger's face. "Eddie!" she said.

A cry rose from the deep green fastness of the
woods in back of them—a vast cry of rage. Another
tree went, and then another. They fell in what
sounded like a hail of mortar-fire. *Dry wood*, the gunslinger thought. *Dead trees.*

"Eddie!" This time she screamed it. "Whatever it
is, *it's near Eddie!*" Her hands flew to the wheels of
her chair and began the laborious job of turning it
around.

"No time for that." Roland seized her under her
arms and pulled her free. He had carried her before
when the going was too rough for her wheelchair—
both men had—but she was still amazed by his uncanny, ruthless speed. At one moment she was in her
wheelchair, an item which had been purchased in New
York City's finest medical supply house in the fall of
1962. At the next she was balanced precariously on
Roland's shoulders like a cheerleader, her muscular
thighs gripping the sides of his neck, his palms over
his head and pressing into the small of her back. He
began to run with her, his sprung boots slapping the
needle-strewn earth between the ruts left by her
wheelchair.

"Odetta!" he cried, reverting in this moment of
stress to the name by which he had first known her.
"Don't lose the gun! For your father's sake!"

He was sprinting between the trees now. Shadow-
lace and bright chains of sun-dapple ran across them
in moving mosaics as Roland lengthened his stride.
They were going downhill now. Susannah raised her
left hand to ward off a branch that wanted to slap her
from the gunslinger's shoulders. At the same moment

she dropped her right hand to the butt of his ancient revolver, cradling it.

A mile, she thought. *How long to run a mile? How long with him going flat-out like this? Not long, if he can keep his feet on these slippery needles . . . but maybe too long. Let him be all right, Lord—let my Eddie be all right.*

As if in answer, she heard the unseen beast loose its cry again. That vast voice was like thunder. Like doom.

2

HE WAS THE LARGEST creature in the forest which had once been known as the Great West Woods, and he was the oldest. Many of the huge old elms which Roland had noticed in the valley below had been little more than twigs sprouting from the ground when the bear came out of the dim unknown reaches of Out-World like a brutal, wandering king.

Once, the Old People had lived in the West Woods (it was their leavings which Roland had found from time to time during the last weeks), and they had gone in fear of the colossal, undying bear. They had tried to kill him when they first discovered they were not alone in the new territory to which they had come, but although their arrows enraged him, they did no serious damage. And he was not confused about the *source* of his torment, as were the other beasts of the forest—even the predatory bushcats which denned and littered in the sandhills to the west. No; he knew where the arrows came from, this bear. *Knew.* And for every arrow which found its mark in the flesh below his shaggy pelt, he took three, four, perhaps as many as half a dozen of the Old People. Children if he could get them; women if he could not. Their warriors he disdained, and this was the final humiliation.

Eventually, as his real nature became clear to them, their efforts to kill him ceased. He was, of course, a demon incarnate—or the shadow of a god. They called him Mir, which to these people meant "the world beneath the world." He stood seventy feet high, and after eighteen or more centuries of undisputed rule in the West Woods, he was dying. Perhaps the instrument of his death had at first been a microscopic organism in something he had eaten or drunk; perhaps it was old age; more likely a combination of both. The cause didn't matter; the ultimate result—a rapidly multiplying colony of parasites foraging within his fabulous brain—did. After years of calculating, brutal sanity, Mir had run mad.

The bear had known men were in his woods again; he ruled the forest and although it was vast, nothing of importance which happened there escaped his attention for long. He had drawn away from the newcomers, not because he was afraid but because he had no business with them, nor they with him. Then the parasites had begun their work, and as his madness increased he became sure that it was the Old People again, that the trap-setters and forest-burners had returned and would soon set about their old, stupid mischief once more. Only as he lay in his final den some thirty miles from the place of the newcomers, sicker with each day's dawning than he had been at sunset the night before, had he come to believe that the Old People had finally found some mischief which worked: poison.

He came this time not to take revenge for some petty wound but to stamp them out entirely before their poison could finish having its way with him . . . and as he travelled, all thought ceased. What was left was red rage, the rusty buzz of the thing on top of his head—the turning thing between his ears which had once done its work in smooth silence—and an eerily enhanced sense of smell which led him unerringly toward the camp of the three pilgrims.

The bear, whose real name was not Mir but something else entirely, made his way through the forest like a moving building, a shaggy tower with reddish-brown eyes. Those eyes glowed with fever and madness. His huge head, now wearing a garland of broken branches and fir-needles, swung ceaselessly from side to side. Every now and then he would sneeze in a muffled explosion of sound—*AH-CHOW!*—and clouds of squirming white parasites would be discharged from his dripping nostrils. His paws, armed with curved talons three feet in length, tore at the trees. He walked upright, sinking deep tracks in the soft black soil under the trees. He reeked of fresh balsam and old, sour shit.

The thing on top of his head whirred and squealed, squealed and whirred.

The course of the bear remained almost constant: a straight line which would lead him to the camp of those who had dared return to his forest, who had dared fill his head with dark green agony. Old People or New People, they would die. When he came to a dead tree, he sometimes left the straight path long enough to push it down. The dry, explosive roar of its fall pleased him; when the tree had finally collapsed its rotten length on the forest floor or come to rest against one of its mates, the bear would push on through slanting bars of sunlight turned misty with floating motes of sawdust.

3

TWO DAYS BEFORE, EDDIE Dean had begun carving again—the first time he'd tried to carve anything since the age of twelve. He remembered that he had enjoyed doing it, and he believed he must have been good at it, as well. He couldn't remember that part, not for sure, but there was at least one clear indication that it was so: Henry, his older brother, had hated to see him doing it.

Oh lookit the sissy, Henry would say. *Whatcha makin today, sissy? A dollhouse? A pisspot for your itty-bitty teeny peenie? Ohhh . . . ain't that CUTE?*

Henry would never come right out and tell Eddie not to do something; would never just walk up to him and say, *Would you mind quitting that, bro? See, it's pretty good, and when you do something that's pretty good, it makes me nervous. Because, you see, I'm the one that's supposed to be pretty good at stuff around here. Me. Henry Dean. So what I think I'll do, brother o' mine, is just sort of rag on you about certain things. I won't come right out and say "Don't do that, it's makin me nervous," because that might make me sound, you know, a little fucked up in the head. But I can rag on you, because that's part of what big brothers do, right? All part of the image. I'll rag on you and tease you and make fun of you until you just . . . fucking . . . QUIT IT! Okay?*

Well, it *wasn't* okay, not really, but in the Dean household, things usually went the way Henry wanted them to go. And until very recently, that had seemed right—not okay but *right*. There was a small but crucial difference there, if you could but dig it. There were two reasons why it seemed right. One was an on-top reason; the other was an underneath reason.

The on-top reason was because Henry had to Watch Out for Eddie when Mrs. Dean was at work. He had to Watch Out all the time, because once there had been a Dean *sister*, if you could but dig it. She would have been four years older than Eddie and four years younger than Henry if she had lived, but that was the thing, you see, because she *hadn't* lived. She had been run over by a drunk driver when Eddie was two. She had been watching a game of hopscotch on the sidewalk when it happened.

As a kid, Eddie had sometimes thought of his sister while listening to Mel Allen doing the play-by-play on

The Yankee Baseball Network. Someone would really pound one and Mel would bellow, *"Holy cow, he got all of that one! SEEYA LATER!"* Well, the drunk had gotten all of Gloria Dean, holy cow, seeya later. Gloria was now in that great upper deck in the sky, and it had not happened because she was unlucky or because the State of New York had decided not to jerk the jerk's license after his third OUI or even because God had bent down to pick up a peanut; it had happened (as Mrs. Dean frequently told her sons) because there had been no one around to Watch Out for Gloria.

Henry's job was to make sure nothing like that ever happened to Eddie. That was his job and he did it, but it wasn't easy. Henry and Mrs. Dean agreed on that, if nothing else. Both of them frequently reminded Eddie of just how much Henry had sacrificed to keep Eddie safe from drunk drivers and muggers and junkies and possibly even malevolent aliens who might be cruising around in the general vicinity of the upper deck, aliens who might decide to come down from their UFOs on nuclear-powered jet-skis at any time in order to kidnap little kids like Eddie Dean. So it was wrong to make Henry more nervous than this terrible responsibility had already made him. If Eddie was doing something that *did* make Henry more nervous, Eddie ought to cease doing that thing immediately. It was a way of paying Henry back for all the time Henry had spent Watching Out for Eddie. When you thought about it that way, you saw that doing things better than Henry could do them was very unfair.

Then there was the underneath reason. That reason (the world beneath the world, one might say) was more powerful, because it could never be stated: Eddie could not allow himself to be better than Henry at much of anything, because Henry was, for the most part, good for nothing . . . except Watching Out for Eddie, of course.

Henry taught Eddie how to play basketball in the playground near the apartment building where they

lived—this was in a cement suburb where the towers
of Manhattan stood against the horizon like a dream
and the welfare check was king. Eddie was eight years
younger than Henry and much smaller, but he was
also much faster. He had a natural feel for the game;
once he got on the cracked, hilly cement of the court
with the ball in his hands, the moves seemed to sizzle
in his nerve-endings. He was faster, but that was no
big deal. The big deal was this: he was *better* than
Henry. If he hadn't known it from the results of the
pick-up games in which they sometimes played, he
would have known it from Henry's thunderous looks
and the hard punches to the upper arm Henry often
dealt out on their way home afterwards. These
punches were supposedly Henry's little jokes—"Two
for flinching!" Henry would cry cheerily, and then
whap-whap! into Eddie's bicep with one knuckle extended—but they didn't *feel* like jokes. They felt like
warnings. They felt like Henry's way of saying *You
better not fake me out and make me look stupid when
you drive for the basket, bro; you better remember that
I'm Watching Out for You.*

The same was true with reading . . . baseball . . .
Ring-a-Levio . . . math . . . even jump-rope, which was
a girl's game. That he was better at these things, or
could be better, was a secret that had to be kept at all
costs. Because Eddie was the younger brother. Because
Henry was Watching Out for him. But the most important part of the underneath reason was also the simplest:
these things had to be kept secret because Henry was
Eddie's big brother, and Eddie adored him.

4

TWO DAYS AGO, WHILE Susannah was skinning out a
rabbit and Roland was starting supper, Eddie had
been in the forest just south of camp. He had seen a

funny spur of wood jutting out of a fresh stump. A weird feeling—he supposed it was the one people called *déjà vu*—swept over him, and he found himself staring fixedly at the spur, which looked like a badly shaped doorknob. He was distantly aware that his mouth had gone dry.

After several seconds, he realized he was *looking* at the spur sticking out of the stump but *thinking* about the courtyard behind the building where he and Henry had lived—thinking about the feel of the warm cement under his ass and the whopping smells of garbage from the dumpster around the corner in the alley. In this memory he had a chunk of wood in his left hand and a paring knife from the drawer by the sink in his right. The chunk of wood jutting from the stump had called up the memory of that brief period when he had fallen violently in love with wood-carving. It was just that the memory was buried so deep he hadn't realized, at first, what it was.

What he had loved most about carving was the *seeing* part, which happened even before you began. Sometimes you saw a car or a truck. Sometimes a dog or cat. Once, he remembered, it had been the face of an idol—one of the spooky Easter Island monoliths he had seen in an issue of *National Geographic* at school. That had turned out to be a good one. The game was to find out how much of that thing you could get out of the wood without breaking it. You could never get it all, but if you were very careful, you could sometimes get quite a lot.

There was something inside the boss on the side of the stump. He thought he might be able to release quite a lot of it with Roland's knife—it was the sharpest, handiest tool he had ever used.

Something inside the wood, waiting patiently for someone—someone like him!—to come along and let it out. To set it free.

Oh lookit the sissy! Whatcha makin today, sissy? A dollhouse? A pisspot for your itty-bitty teeny peenie?

*A slingshot, so you can pretend to hunt rabbits, just
like the big boys? Awwww . . . ain't that CUTE?*

He felt a burst of shame, a sense of wrongness; that
strong sense of secrets that must be kept at any cost,
and then he remembered—again—that Henry Dean,
who had in his later years become the great sage and
eminent junkie, was dead. This realization had still
not lost its power to surprise; it kept hitting him in
different ways, sometimes with sorrow, sometimes
with guilt, sometimes with anger. On this day, two
days before the great bear came charging out of the
green corridors of the woods, it had hit him in the
most surprising way of all. He had felt relief, and a
soaring joy.

He was free.

Eddie had borrowed Roland's knife. He used it to
cut carefully around the jutting boss of wood, then
brought it back and sat beneath a tree with it, turning
it this way and that. He was not looking *at* it; he was
looking *into* it.

Susannah had finished with her rabbit. The meat
went into the pot over the fire; the skin she stretched
between two sticks, tying it with hanks of rawhide
from Roland's purse. Later on, after the evening
meal, Eddie would begin scraping it clean. She used
her hands and arms, slipping effortlessly over to where
Eddie was sitting with his back propped against the
tall old pine. At the campfire, Roland was crumbling
some arcane—and no doubt delicious—woods-herb
into the pot. "What's doing, Eddie?"

Eddie had found himself restraining an absurd urge
to hide the boss of wood behind his back. "Nothing,"
he said. "Thought I might, you know, carve something." He paused, then added: "I'm not very good,
though." He sounded as if he might be trying to reas-
sure her of this fact.

She had looked at him, puzzled. For a moment she
seemed on the verge of saying something, then simply
shrugged and left him alone. She had no idea why

Eddie seemed ashamed to be passing a little time in whittling—her father had done it all the time—but if it was something that needed to be talked about, she supposed Eddie would get to it in his own time.

He knew the guilty feelings were stupid and point-less, but he also knew he felt more comfortable doing this work when Roland and Susannah were out of camp. Old habits, it seemed, sometimes died hard. Beating heroin was child's play compared to beating your childhood.

When they *were* away, hunting or shooting or keep-ing Roland's peculiar form of school, Eddie found himself able to turn to his piece of wood with surpris-ing skill and increasing pleasure. The shape was in there, all right; he had been right about that. It was a simple one, and Roland's knife was setting it free with an eerie ease. Eddie thought he was going to get almost all of it, and that meant the slingshot might actually turn out to be a practical weapon. Not much compared to Roland's big revolvers, maybe, but some-thing he had made himself, just the same. *His.* And this idea pleased him very much.

When the first crows rose in the air, cawing affright-edly, he did not hear. He was already thinking—hop-ing—that he might see a tree with a bow trapped in it before too long.

5

HE HEARD THE BEAR approaching before Roland and Susannah did, but not much before—he was lost in that high daze of concentration which accompanies the creative impulse at its sweetest and most powerful. He had suppressed these impulses for most of his life, and now this one held him wholly in its grip. Eddie was a willing prisoner.

He was pulled from his daze not by the sound of

falling trees but by the rapid thunder of a .45 from
the south. He looked up, smiling, and brushed hair
from his forehead with a sawdusty hand. In that moment, sitting with his back against a tall pine in the
clearing which had become home, his face crisscrossed
with opposing beams of green-gold forest light, he
looked handsome indeed—a young man with unruly
dark hair which constantly tried to spill across his high
forehead, a young man with a strong, mobile mouth
and hazel eyes.

For a moment his eyes shifted to Roland's other
gun, hanging by its belt from a nearby branch, and he
found himself wondering how long it had been since
Roland had gone anywhere without at least one of his
fabulous weapons hanging by his side. That question
led to two others.

How old *was* he, this man who had plucked Eddie
and Susannah from their world and their *whens*? And,
more important, what was wrong with him?

Susannah had promised to broach that subject . . .
if she shot well and didn't get Roland's back hair up,
that was. Eddie didn't think Roland would tell her—
not at first—but it was time to let old long tall and
ugly know that *they* knew *something* was wrong.

"There'll be water if God wills it," Eddie said. He
turned back to his carving with a little smile playing
on his lips. They had both begun to pick up Roland's
little sayings . . . and he theirs. It was almost as if
they were halves of the same—

Then a tree fell close by in the forest, and Eddie
was on his feet in a second, the half-carved slingshot
in one hand, Roland's knife in the other. He stared
across the clearing in the direction of the sound, heart
thumping, all his senses finally alert. Something was
coming. Now he could hear it, trampling its heedless
way through the underbrush, and he marvelled bitterly
that this realization had come so late. Far back in his
mind, a small voice told him this was what he got.

This was what he got for doing something better than Henry, for making Henry nervous.

Another tree fell with a ratcheting, coughing crash. Looking down a ragged aisle between the tall firs, Eddie saw a cloud of sawdust rise in the still air. The creature responsible for that cloud suddenly bellowed—a raging, gut-freezing sound.

It was one huge motherfucker, whatever it was.

He dropped the chunk of wood, then flipped Roland's knife at a tree fifteen feet to his left. It somersaulted twice in the air and then stuck halfway to the hilt in the wood, quivering. He grabbed Roland's .45 from the place where it hung and cocked it.

Stand or run?

But he discovered he no longer had the luxury of that question. The thing was *fast* as well as huge, and it was now too late to run. A gigantic shape began to disclose itself in that aisle of trees north of the clearing, a shape which towered above all but the tallest trees. It was lumbering directly toward him, and as its eyes fixed upon Eddie Dean, it gave voice to another of those cries.

"Oh man, I'm *fucked*," Eddie whispered as another tree bent, cracked like a mortar, then crashed to the forest floor in a cloud of dust and dead needles. Now it was lumbering straight toward the clearing where he stood, a bear the size of King Kong. Its footfalls made the ground shake.

What will you do, Eddie? Roland suddenly asked. *Think! It's the only advantage you have over yon beast. What will you do?*

He didn't think he could kill it. Maybe with a bazooka, but probably not with the gunslinger's .45. He could run, but had an idea that the oncoming beast might be pretty fast when it wanted to be. He guessed the chances of ending up as jam between the great bear's toes might be as high as fifty-fifty.

So which one was it going to be? Stand here and

start shooting or run like his hair was on fire and his
ass was catching?

It occurred to him that there was a third choice. He
could climb.

He turned toward the tree against which he had
been leaning. It was a huge, hoary pine, easily the
tallest tree in this part of the woods. The first branch
spread out over the forest floor in a feathery green
fan about eight feet up. Eddie dropped the revolver's
hammer and then jammed the gun into the waistband
of his pants. He leaped for the branch, grabbed it,
and did a frantic chin-up. Behind him, the bear gave
voice to another bellow as it burst into the clearing.

The bear would have had him just the same, would
have left Eddie Dean's guts hanging in gaudy strings
from the lowest branches of the pine, if another of
those sneezing fits had not come on it at that moment.
It kicked the ashy remains of the campfire into a black
cloud and then stood almost doubled over, huge front
paws on its huge thighs, looking for a moment like an
old man in a fur coat, an old man with a cold. It
sneezed again and again—*AH-CHOW! AH-CHOW!
AH-CHOW!*—and clouds of parasites blew out of its
muzzle. Hot urine flowed in a stream between its legs
and hissed out the campfire's scattered embers.

Eddie did not waste the few crucial extra moments
he had been given. He went up the tree like a monkey
on a stick, pausing only once to make sure the gunslinger's revolver was still seated firmly in the waistband of his pants. He was in terror, already half
convinced that he was going to die (what else could
he expect, now that Henry wasn't around to Watch
Out for him?), but a crazy laughter raved through his
head just the same. *Been treed*, he thought. *How bout
that, sports fans? Been treed by Bearzilla.*

The creature raised its head again, the thing turning
between its ears catching winks and flashes of sunlight
as it did so, then charged Eddie's tree. It reached high
with one paw and slashed forward, meaning to knock

Eddie loose like a pinecone. The paw tore through the branch he was standing on just as he lunged upward to the next. That paw tore through one of his shoes as well, pulling it from his foot and sending it flying in two ragged pieces.

That's okay, Eddie thought. *You can have em both, Br'er Bear, if you want. Goddam things were worn out, anyway.*

The bear roared and lashed at the tree, cutting deep wounds in its ancient bark, wounds which bled clear, resinous sap. Eddie kept on yanking himself up. The branches were thinning now, and when he risked a glance down he stared directly into the bear's muddy eyes. Below its cocked head, the clearing had become a target with the scattered smudge of campfire as its bullseye.

"Missed me, you hairy motherf—" Eddie began, and then the bear, its head still cocked back to look at him, sneezed. Eddie was immediately drenched in hot snot that was filled with thousands of small white worms. They wriggled frantically on his shirt, his forearms, his throat and face.

Eddie screamed in mingled surprise and revulsion. He began to brush at his eyes and mouth, lost his balance, and just managed to hook an arm around the branch beside him in time. He held on and raked at his skin, wiping off as much of the wormy phlegm as he could. The bear roared and hit the tree again. The pine rocked like a mast in a gale . . . but the fresh claw-marks which appeared were at least seven feet below the branch on which Eddie's feet were planted.

The worms were dying, he realized—must have begun dying as soon as they left the infected swamps inside the monster's body. It made him feel a little better, and he began to climb again. He stopped twelve feet further up, daring to go no higher. The trunk of the pine, easily eight feet in diameter at its base, was now no more than eighteen inches through the middle. He had distributed his weight on two branches, but he could feel both of them bending springily beneath him. He had a crow's nest view of the forest and foothills to the west now, spread out below him in an undulating carpet. Under other circumstances, it would have been a view to relish.

Top of the world, Ma, he thought. He looked down into the bear's upturned face again, and for a moment all coherent thought was driven from his mind by simple amazement.

There was something growing out of the bear's skull, and to Eddie it looked like a small radar-dish.

The gadget turned jerkily, kicking up flashes of sun as it did, and Eddie could hear it screaming thinly. He had owned a few old cars in his time—the kind that sat in the used-car lots with the words HANDY-MAN'S SPECIAL soaped on the windshields—and he thought the sound coming from that gadget was the sound of bearings which will freeze up if they are not replaced soon.

The bear uttered a long, purring growl. Yellowish foam, thick with worms, squeezed between its paws in curdled gobbets. If he had never looked into the face of utter lunacy (and he supposed he had, having been eyeball to eyeball with that world-class bitch Detta Walker on more than one occasion), Eddie was looking into it now . . . but that face was, thankfully, a good thirty feet below him, and at their highest reach those killing talons were fifteen feet under the soles of his feet. And, unlike the trees upon which the bear had vented its spleen as it approached the clearing, this one was not dead.

"Mexican standoff, honey," Eddie panted. He wiped sweat from his forehead with one sap-sticky hand and flicked the mess down into the bugbear's face.

Then the creature the Old People had called Mir embraced the tree with its great forepaws and began to shake it. Eddie grabbed the trunk and held on for dear life, eyes squeezed into grim slits, as the pine began to sway back and forth like a pendulum.

6

ROLAND HALTED AT THE EDGE of the clearing. Susannah, perched on his shoulders, stared unbelievingly across the open space. The creature stood at the base of the tree where Eddie had been when the two of them left the clearing forty-five minutes ago. She could see only chunks and sections of its body through the screen of branches and dark green needles. Roland's other gunbelt lay beside one of the monster's feet. The holster, she saw, was empty.

"My God," she murmured.

The bear screamed like a distraught woman and began shaking the tree. The branches lashed as if in a high wind. Her eyes skated upward and she saw a dark form near the top. Eddie was hugging the trunk as the tree rocked and rolled. As she watched, one of his hands slipped and flailed wildly for purchase.

"*What do we do?*" she screamed down at Roland. "*It's goan shake him loose! What do we do?*"

Roland tried to think about it, but that queer sensation had returned again—it was always with him now, but stress seemed to make it worse. He felt like two men existing inside one skull. Each man had his own set of memories, and when they began to argue, each insisting that *his* memories were the true ones, the gunslinger felt as if he were being ripped in two. He made a desperate effort to reconcile these two halves and succeeded . . . at least for the moment.

"It's one of the Twelve!" he shouted. "One of the Guardians! *Must* be! But I thought they were—"

The bear bellowed up at Eddie again. Now it began to slap at the tree like a punchy fighter. Branches snapped and fell around its feet in a tangle.

"What?" Susannah screamed. *"What's the rest?"*

Roland closed his eyes. Inside his head, a voice shouted, *The boy's name was Jake!* Another voice shouted back, *There WAS no boy! There WAS no boy, and you know it!*

Get away, both of you! he snarled, and then called out aloud: "Shoot it! Shoot it in the ass, Susannah! It'll turn and charge! When it does, look for something on its head! It—"

The bear squalled again. It gave up slapping the tree and went back to shaking it. Ominous popping, grinding sounds were now coming from the upper part of the trunk.

When he could be heard again, Roland shouted: "I think it looks like a hat! A little steel hat! Shoot it, Susannah! And don't miss!"

Terror suddenly filled her—terror and another emotion, one she would never have expected: crushing loneliness.

"No! I'll miss! You do it, Roland!" She began to fumble his revolver out of the belt she wore, meaning to give it to him.

"Can't!" Roland shouted. "The angle's bad! *You* have to do it, Susannah! This is the real test, and you'd better pass it!"

"Roland—"

"It means to snap the top of the tree off!" he roared at her. *"Can't you see that?"*

She looked at the revolver in her hand. Looked across the clearing, at the gigantic bear obscured in the clouds and sprays of green needles. Looked at Eddie, swaying back and forth like a metronome. Eddie probably had Roland's other gun, but Susannah could see no way he could use it without being shaken from his perch like an over-ripe plum. Also, he might not shoot at the right thing.

She raised the revolver. Her stomach was thick with dread. "Hold me still, Roland," she said. "If you don't—"

"Don't worry about me!"

She fired twice, squeezing the shots as Roland had taught her. The heavy reports cut across the sound of the bear shaking the tree like the cracks of a bullwhip. She saw both bullets strike home in the left cheek of the bear's rump, less than two inches apart.

It shrieked in surprise, pain, and outrage. One of its huge front paws came out of the dense screen of branches and needles and slapped at the hurt place. The hand came away dripping scarlet and rose back out of sight. Susannah could imagine it up there, examining its bloody palm. Then there was a rushing, rustling, snapping sound as the bear turned, bending down at the same time, dropping to all fours in order to achieve maximum speed. For the first time she saw its face, and her heart quailed. Its muzzle was lathered with foam; its huge eyes glared like lamps. Its shaggy head swung to the left . . . back to the right . . . and centered upon Roland, who stood with his legs apart and Susannah Dean balanced on his shoulders.

With a shattering roar, the bear charged.

7

SAY YOUR LESSON, Susannah Dean, and be true.

The bear came at them in a rumbling lope; it was like watching a runaway factory machine over which someone had thrown a huge, moth-eaten rug.

It looks like a hat! A little steel hat!

She saw it . . . but it didn't look like a hat to her. It looked like a radar-dish—a much smaller version of the kind she had seen in MovieTone newsreel stories about how the DEW-line was keeping everyone safe from a Russian sneak attack. It was bigger than the pebbles she had shot off the boulder earlier, but the distance was greater. Sun and shadow ran across it in deceiving dapples.

I do not aim with my hand; she who aims with her hand has forgotten the face of her father.

I can't do it!

I do not shoot with my hand; she who shoots with her hand has forgotten the face of her father.

I'll miss! I know I'll miss!

I do not kill with my gun; she who kills with her gun—

"Shoot it!" Roland roared. "Susannah, *shoot it!*"

With the trigger as yet unpulled, she saw the bullet go home, guided from muzzle to target by nothing more or less than her heart's fierce desire that it should fly true. All fear fell away. What was left was a feeling of deep coldness and she had time to think: *This is what* he *feels. My God—how does he stand it?*

"I kill with my heart, motherfucker," she said, and the gunslinger's revolver roared in her hand.

8

THE SILVERY THING SPUN on a steel rod planted in the bear's skull. Susannah's bullet struck it dead center and the radar-dish blew into a hundred glittering fragments. The pole itself was suddenly engulfed in a burst of crackling blue fire which reached out in a net and seemed to grasp the sides of the bear's face for a moment.

It rose on its rear legs with a whistling howl of agony, its front paws boxing aimlessly at the air. It turned in a wide, staggering circle and began to flap its arms, as if it had decided to fly away. It tried to roar again but what came out instead was a weird warbling sound like an air-raid siren.

"It is very well." Roland sounded exhausted. "A good shot, fair and true."

"Should I shoot it again?" she asked uncertainly. The bear was still blundering around in its mad circle but now its body had begun to tilt sidewards and inwards. It struck a small tree, rebounded, almost fell over, and then began to circle again.

"No need," Roland said. She felt his hands grip her waist and lift her. A moment later she was sitting on the ground with her thighs folded beneath her. Eddie was slowly and shakily descending the pine, but she didn't see him. She could not take her eyes from the bear.

She had seen the whales at the Seaquarium near Mystic, Connecticut, and believed they had been bigger than this—much bigger, probably—but this was certainly the largest land creature she had ever seen. And it was clearly dying. Its roars had become liquid bubbling sounds, and although its eyes were open, it seemed blind. It flailed aimlessly about the camp, knocking over a rack of curing hides, stamping flat the little shelter she shared with Eddie, caroming off trees. She could see the steel post rising from its head. Tendrils of smoke were rising around it, as if her shot had ignited its brains.

Eddie reached the lowest branch of the tree which had saved his life and sat shakily astride it. "Holy Mary Mother of God," he said. "I'm looking right at it and I still don't beli—"

The bear wheeled back toward him. Eddie leaped nimbly from the tree and streaked toward Susannah and Roland. The bear took no notice, it marched drunkenly to the pine which had been Eddie's refuge, tried to grasp it, failed, and sank to its knees. Now they could hear other sounds coming from inside it, sounds that made Eddie think of some huge truck engine stripping its gears.

A spasm convulsed it, bowed its back. Its front claws rose and gored madly at its own face. Worm-

infested blood flew and splattered. Then it fell over,
making the ground tremble with its fall, and lay still.
After all its strange centuries, the bear the Old People
had called Mir—the world beneath the world—was
dead.

9

EDDIE PICKED SUSANNAH UP, held her with his sticky
hands locked together at the small of her back, and
kissed her deeply. He reeked of sweat and pine-tar.
She touched his cheeks, his neck; she ran her hands
through his wet hair. She felt an insane urge to touch
him everywhere until she was absolutely sure of his
reality.

"It almost had me," he said. "It was like being on
some crazy carnival ride. What a shot! Jesus, Suze—
what a shot!"

"I hope I never have to do anything like that
again," she said . . . but a small voice at the center
of her demurred. That voice suggested that she could
not *wait* to do something like that again. And it was
cold, that voice. Cold.

"What was—" he began, turning toward Roland,
but Roland was no longer standing there. He was
walking slowly toward the bear, which now lay on the
ground with its shaggy knees up. From within it came
a series of muffled gasps and gurgles as its strange
guts continued to slowly run down.

Roland saw his knife planted deep in a tree near
the scarred veteran that had saved Eddie's life. He
pulled it free and wiped it clean on the soft deerskin
shirt which had replaced the tatters he had been wearing when the three of them had left the beach. He
stood by the bear, looking down at it with an expression of pity and wonder.

Hello, stranger, he thought. *Hello, old friend. I*

never believed in you, not really. I believe Alain did, and I know that Cuthbert did—Cuthbert believed in everything—but I was the hardheaded one. I thought you were only a tale for children . . . another wind which blew around in my old nurse's hollow head before finally escaping her jabbering mouth. But you were here all along, another refugee of the old times, like the pump at the way station and the old machines under the mountains. Are the Slow Mutants who worshipped those broken remnants the final descendents of the people who once lived in this forest and finally fled your wrath? I don't know, will never know . . . but it feels right. Yes. And then I came with my friends—my deadly new friends, who are becoming so much like my deadly old friends. We came, weaving our magic circle around us and around everything we touch, strand by poisonous strand, and now here you lie, at our feet. The world has moved on again, and this time, old friend, it's you who have been left behind.

The monster's body still radiated a deep, sick heat. Parasites were leaving its mouth and tattered nostrils in hordes, but they died almost at once. Waxy-white piles of them were growing on either side of the bear's head.

Eddie approached slowly. He had shifted Susannah over to one hip, carrying her as a mother might carry a baby. "What was it, Roland? Do you know?"

"He called it a Guardian, I think," Susannah said.

"Yes." Roland's voice was slow with amazement. "I thought they were all gone, *must* all be gone . . . if they ever existed outside of the old wives' tales in the first place."

"Whatever it was, it was one crazy mother," Eddie said.

Roland smiled a little. "If you'd lived two or three thousand years, you'd be one crazy mother, too."

"Two or three thousand . . . Christ!"

Susannah said, "Is it a bear? Really? And what's that?" She was pointing at what appeared to be a square metal tag set high on one of the bear's thick rear legs. It was almost overgrown with tough tangles of hair, but the afternoon sun had pricked out a single starpoint of light on its stainless steel surface, revealing it.

Eddie knelt and reached hesitantly toward the tag, aware that strange muffled clicks and clacks were still coming from deep inside the fallen giant. He looked at Roland.

"Go ahead," the gunslinger told him. "It's finished."

Eddie pushed a clump of hair aside and leaned closer. Words had been stamped into the metal. They were quite badly eroded, but he found that with a little effort he could read them.

NORTH CENTRAL POSITRONICS, LTD.
Granite City
Northeast Corridor

Design 4 GUARDIAN
Serial # AA 24123 CX 755431297 L 14
Type/Species BEAR
SHARDIK

NRSUBNUCLEAR CELLS MUST NOT
BE REPLACED**NR**

"Holy Jesus, this thing is a *robot*," Eddie said softly.

"It can't be," Susannah said. "When I shot it, it *bled*."

"Maybe so, but your ordinary, garden-variety bear doesn't have a radar-dish growing out of its head. And, so far as I know, your ordinary, garden-variety bear doesn't live to be two or three th—" He broke off suddenly, looking at Roland. When he spoke again, his voice was revolted. "Roland, what are you doing?"

Roland did not reply; did not *need* to reply. What he was doing—gouging out one of the bear's eyes with his knife—was perfectly obvious. The surgery was quick, neat, and precise. When it was completed he balanced an oozing brown ball of jelly on the blade of his knife for a moment and then flicked it aside. A few more worms made their way out of the staring hole, tried to squirm their way down the bear's muzzle, and died.

The gunslinger leaned over the eyesocket of Shardik, the great Guardian bear, and peered inside. "Come and look, both of you," he said. "I'll show you a wonder of the latter days."

"Put me down, Eddie," Susannah said.

He did so, and she moved swiftly on her hands and upper thighs to where the gunslinger was hunkered down over the bear's wide, slack face. Eddie joined them, looking between their shoulders. The three of them gazed in rapt silence for nearly a full minute; the only noise came from the crows which still circled and scolded in the sky.

Blood oozed from the socket in a few thick, dying trickles. Yet it was not *just* blood, Eddie saw. There was also a clear fluid which gave off an identifiable scent—bananas. And, embedded in the delicate crisscross of tendons which shaped the socket, he saw a webwork of what looked like strings. Beyond them, at the back of the socket, was a red spark, blinking on and off. It illuminated a tiny square board marked with silvery squiggles of what could only be solder.

"It isn't a bear, it's a fucking Sony Walkman," he muttered.

Susannah looked around at him. "What?"

"Nothing." Eddie glanced at Roland. "Do you think it's safe to reach in?"

Roland shrugged. "I think so. If there was a demon in this creature, it's fled."

Eddie reached in with his little finger, nerves set to draw back if he felt even a tickle of electricity. He touched the cooling meat inside the eyesocket, which was nearly the size of a baseball, and then one of those strings. Except it wasn't a string; it was a gossamer-thin strand of steel. He withdrew his finger and saw the tiny red spark blink once more before going out forever.

"Shardik," Eddie murmured. "I *know* that name, but I can't place it. Does it mean anything to you, Suze?"

She shook her head.

"The thing is . . ." Eddie laughed helplessly. "I associate it with rabbits. Isn't that nuts?"

Roland stood up. His knees popped like gunshots. "We'll have to move camp," he said. "The ground here is spoiled. The other clearing, the one where we go to shoot, will—"

He took two trembling steps and then collapsed to his knees, palms pressed to the sides of his sagging head.

10

EDDIE AND SUSANNAH EXCHANGED a single frightened glance and then Eddie leaped to Roland's side. "What is it? Roland, what's wrong?"

"There *was* a boy," the gunslinger said in a distant, muttering voice. And then, in the very next breath, "There *wasn't* a boy."

"Roland?" Susannah asked. She came to him, slipped an arm around his shoulders, felt him trembling. "Roland, what is it?"

"The boy," Roland said, looking at her with floating, dazed eyes. "It's the boy. *Always* the boy."

"*What* boy?" Eddie yelled frantically. "*What* boy?"

"Go then," Roland said, "there are other worlds than these." And fainted.

11

THAT NIGHT THE THREE of them sat around a huge bonfire Eddie and Susannah had built in the clearing Eddie called "the shooting gallery." It would have been a bad place to camp in the wintertime, open to the valley as it was, but for now it was fine. Eddie guessed that here in Roland's world it was still late summer.

The black vault of the sky arched overhead, speckled by what seemed to be whole galaxies. Almost straight ahead to the south, across the river of darkness that was the valley, Eddie could see Old Mother rising above the distant, unseen horizon. He glanced at Roland, who sat huddled by the fire with three skins wrapped around his shoulders despite the warmth of the night and the heat of the fire. There was an untouched plate of food by his side and a bone cradled in his hands. Eddie glanced back at the sky and thought of a story the gunslinger had told him and Susannah on one of the long days they had spent moving away from the beach, through the foothills, and finally into these deep woods where they had found a temporary refuge.

Before time began, Roland said, Old Star and Old Mother had been young and passionate newlyweds. Then one day there had been a terrible argument. Old Mother (who in those long-ago days had been known by her real name, which was Lydia) had caught Old Star (whose real name was Apon) hanging about a beautiful young woman named Cassiopeia. They'd had a real bang-up fight, those two, a hair-pulling, eye-gouging, crockery-throwing fight. One of those thrown bits of crockery had become the earth; a smaller shard the moon; a coal from their kitchen stove had become the sun. In the end, the gods had stepped in so Apon and Lydia might not, in their anger, destroy the universe before it was fairly begun. Cassiopeia, the saucy jade who caused the trouble in the first place ("Yeah,

right—it's always the woman," Susannah had said at
this point), had been banished to a rocking-chair made
of stars forever and ever. Yet not even this had solved
the problem. Lydia had been willing to try again, but
Apon was stiffnecked and full of pride ("Yeah, always
blame the man," Eddie had grunted at this point). So
they had parted, and now they look at each other in
mingled hatred and longing from across the star-
strewn wreckage of their divorce. Apon and Lydia are
three billion years gone, the gunslinger told them;
they have become Old Star and Old Mother, the north
and south, each pining for the other but both now too
proud to beg for reconciliation . . . and Cassiopeia sits
off to the side in her chair, rocking and laughing at
them both.

Eddie was startled by a soft touch on his arm. It
was Susannah. "Come on," she said. "We've got to
make him talk."

Eddie carried her to the campfire and put her
down carefully on Roland's right side. He sat on
Roland's left. Roland looked first at Susannah, then
at Eddie.

"How close you both sit to me," he remarked.
"Like lovers . . . or warders in a gaol."

"It's time for you to do some talking." Susannah's
voice was low, clear, and musical. "If we're your companions, Roland—and it seems like we are, like it or
not—it's time you started *treating* us as companions.
Tell us what's wrong . . ."

". . . and what we can do about it," Eddie finished.

Roland sighed deeply. "I don't know how to
begin," he said. "It's been so long since I've had companions . . . or a tale to tell . . ."

"Start with the bear," Eddie said.

Susannah leaned forward and touched the jawbone
Roland held in his hands. It frightened her, but she
touched it anyway. "And finish with this."

"Yes." Roland lifted the bone to eye-level and
looked at it for a moment before dropping it back into

his lap. "We'll have to speak of this, won't we? It's the center of the thing."

But the bear came first.

12

"THIS IS THE STORY I was told when I was a child," Roland said. "When everything was new, the Great Old Ones—they weren't gods, but people who had almost the knowledge of gods—created Twelve Guardians to stand watch at the twelve portals which lead in and out of the world. Sometimes I heard that these portals were natural things, like the constellations we see in the sky or the bottomless crack in the earth we called Dragon's Grave, because of the great burst of steam they gave off every thirty or forty days. But other people—one I remember in particular, the head cook in my father's castle, a man named Hax—said they were *not* natural, that they had been created by the Great Old Ones themselves, in the days before they hanged themselves with pride like a noose and disappeared from the earth. Hax used to say that the creation of the Twelve Guardians was the last act of the Great Old Ones, their attempt to atone for the great wrongs they had done to each other, and to the earth itself."

"Portals," Eddie mused. "*Doors*, you mean. We're back to those again. Do these doors that lead in and out of the world open on the world Suze and I came from? Like the ones we found along the beach?"

"I don't know," Roland said. "For every thing I do know, there are a hundred things I don't. You—both of you—will have to reconcile yourselves to that fact. The world has moved on, we say. When it did, it went like a great receding wave, leaving only wreckage behind . . . wreckage that sometimes looks like a map."

"Well, make a *guess!*" Eddie exclaimed, and the raw eagerness in his voice told the gunslinger that Eddie had not given up the idea of returning to his own world—and Susannah's—even now. Not entirely.

"Leave him be, Eddie," Susannah said. "The man don't guess."

"Not true—sometimes the man *does*," Roland said, surprising them both. "When guessing's the only thing left, sometimes he does. The answer is no. I don't think—I don't *guess*—that these portals are much like the doors on the beach. I don't *guess* they go to a *where* or *when* that we would recognize. I think the doors on the beach—the ones that led into the world you both came from—were like the pivot at the center of a child's teeterboard. Do you know what that is?"

"Seesaw?" Susannah asked, and tipped her hand back and forth to demonstrate.

"Yes!" Roland agreed, looking pleased. "Just so. On one end of this sawsee—"

"Seesaw," Eddie said, smiling a little.

"Yes. On one end, my *ka*. On the other, that of the man in black—Walter. The doors were the center, creations of the tension between two opposing destinies. These other portals are things far greater than Walter, or me, or the little fellowship we three have made."

"Are you saying," Susannah asked hesitantly, "that the portals where these Guardians stand watch are *outside ka*? Beyond *ka*?"

"I'm saying that I believe so." He offered his own brief smile, a thin sickle in the firelight. "That I *guess* so."

He was silent a moment, then he picked up a stick of his own. He brushed away the carpet of pine needles and used the stick to draw in the dirt beneath:

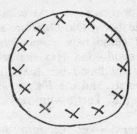

"Here is the world as I was told it existed when I was a child. The Xs are the portals standing in a ring at its eternal edge. If one drew six lines, connecting these portals in pairs—so—"

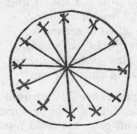

He looked up. "Do you see where the lines cross in the center?"

Eddie felt gooseflesh crawl up his back and down his arms. His mouth was suddenly dry. "Is that it, Roland? Is that—?"

Roland nodded. His long, lined face was grave. "At this nexus lies the Great Portal, the so-called Thirteenth Gate which rules not just this world but all worlds."

He tapped the center of the circle.

"Here is the Dark Tower for which I've searched my whole life."

13

THE GUNSLINGER RESUMED: "At each of the twelve lesser portals the Great Old Ones set a Guardian. In my childhood I could have named them all in the rimes my nursemaid—and Hax the cook—taught to me . . . but my childhood was long ago. There was the Bear, of course, and the Fish . . . the Lion . . . the Bat. And the Turtle—he was an important one . . ."

The gunslinger looked up into the starry sky, his brow creased in deep thought. Then an amazingly sunny smile broke across his features and he recited:

"See the TURTLE of enormous girth!
On his shell he holds the earth.
His thought is slow but always kind;
He holds us all within his mind.
On his back all vows are made;
He sees the truth but mayn't aid.
He loves the land and loves the sea,
And even loves a child like me."

Roland uttered a small, bemused laugh. "Hax taught that to me, singing it as he stirred the frosting for some cake and gave me little nips of the sweet from the edge of his spoon. Amazing what we remember, isn't it? Anyway, as I grew older, I came to believe that the Guardians didn't really exist—that they were symbols rather than substance. It seems that I was wrong."

"I called it a robot," Eddie said, "but that's not what it really was. Susannah's right—the only thing robots bleed when you shoot them is Quaker State 10-40. I think it was what people of my world call a cyborg, Roland—a creature that's part machine and part flesh and blood. There was a movie I saw . . . we told you about movies, didn't we?"

Smiling a little, Roland nodded.

"Well, this movie was called *Robocop*, and the guy in it wasn't a lot different from the bear Susannah killed. How did you know where she should shoot it?"

"That I remembered from the old tales as Hax told them," he said. "If it had been up to my nursemaid, Eddie, you'd be in the belly of the bear now. Do they sometimes tell puzzled children in your world to put on their thinking caps?"

"Yes," Susannah said. "They sure do."

"It's said here, as well, and the saying comes from the story of the Guardians. Each supposedly carried an extra brain on the outside of its head. In a hat." He looked at them with his dreadfully haunted eyes and smiled again. "It didn't look much like a hat, did it?"

"No," Eddie said, "but the story was close enough to save our bacon."

"I think now that I've been looking for one of the Guardians ever since I began my quest," Roland said. "When we find the portal this Shardik guarded—and that should only be a matter of following its back-trail—we will finally have a course to follow. We must set the portal to our backs and then simply move straight ahead. At the center of the circle . . . the Tower."

Eddie opened his mouth to say, *All right, let's talk about this Tower. Finally, once and for all, let's talk about it—what it is, what it means, and, most important of all, what happens to us when we get there.* But no sound came out, and after a moment he closed his mouth again. This wasn't the time—not now, with Roland in such obvious pain. Not now, with only the spark of their campfire to keep the night at bay.

"So now we come to the other part," Roland said heavily. "I have finally found my course—after all the long years I have found my course—but at the same time I seem to be losing my sanity. I can feel it crumbling away beneath my feet, like a steep embankment which has been loosened by rain. This is my punishment for letting a boy who never existed fall to his death. And that is also *ka*."

"Who is this boy, Roland?" Susannah asked.

Roland glanced at Eddie. "Do *you* know?"

Eddie shook his head.

"But I spoke of him," Roland said. "In fact, I *raved* of him, when the infection was at its worst and I was near dying." The gunslinger's voice suddenly rose half an octave, and his imitation of Eddie's voice was so good that Susannah felt a coil of superstitious fright. " 'If you don't shut up about that goddam kid, Roland, I'll gag you with your own shirt! I'm sick of hearing about him!' Do you remember saying that, Eddie?"

Eddie thought it over carefully. Roland had spoken of a thousand things as the two of them made their tortuous way up the beach from the door marked THE PRISONER to the one marked THE LADY OF THE SHADOWS, and he had mentioned what seemed like a thousand names in his fever-heated monologues—Alain, Cort, Jamie de Curry, Cuthbert (this one more often than all the others), Hax, Martin (or perhaps it was Marten, like the animal), Walter, Susan, even a guy with the unlikely name of Zoltan. Eddie had gotten very tired of hearing about these people he had never met (and didn't care to meet), but of course Eddie had had a few problems of his own at that time, heroin withdrawal and cosmic jet-lag being only two of them. And, if he was to be fair, he guessed Roland had gotten as tired of Eddie's own Fractured Fairy Tales—the ones about how he and Henry had grown up together and turned into junkies together—as Eddie had of Roland's.

But he couldn't remember ever telling Roland he would gag him with his own shirt if he didn't stop talking about some kid.

"Nothing comes to you?" Roland asked. "Nothing at all?"

Was there something? Some far-off tickle, like the feeling of *déjà vu* he'd gotten when he saw the slingshot hiding inside the chunk of wood jutting out of the stump? Eddie tried to find that tickle, but it was gone. He decided it had never been there in the first place; he only *wanted* it to be there, because Roland was hurting so badly.

"No," he said. "Sorry, man."

"But I *did* tell you." Roland's tone was calm, but urgency ran and pulsed beneath it like a scarlet thread. "The boy's name was Jake. I sacrificed him—killed him—in order that I might finally catch up with Walter and make him talk. I killed him under the mountains."

On this point Eddie could be more positive. "Well, maybe that's what happened, but it's not what you *said* happened. You said you went under the mountains alone, on some kind of crazy handcar. You talked about *that* a lot while we were coming up the beach, Roland. About how scary it was to be alone."

"I remember. But I also remember telling you about the boy, and how he fell from the trestle into the chasm. And it's the distance between those two memories that is pulling my mind apart."

"I don't understand any of this," Susannah said worriedly.

"I think," Roland said, "that I'm just beginning to."

He threw more wood on the fire, sending thick sheaves of red sparks spiralling up into the dark sky, and then settled back between them. "I'll tell you a story that's true," he said, "and then I'll tell you a story that isn't true . . . but *should* be.

"I bought a mule in Pricetown, and when I finally got to Tull, the last town before the desert, it was still fresh . . ."

14

SO THE GUNSLINGER EMBARKED on the most recent part of his long tale. Eddie had heard isolated fragments of the story, but he listened in utter fascination, as did Susannah, for whom it was completely new. He told them about the bar with the endless game of Watch Me going on in the corner, the piano player named Sheb, the woman named Allie with the scar on her forehead . . . and about Nort, the weed-eater who had died and then been brought back to some sort of tenebrous life by the man in black. He told them about Sylvia Pittston, that avatar of religious insanity, and about the final apocalyptic slaughter, in which he, Roland the Gunslinger, had killed every man, woman, and child in town.

"Holy crispy crap!" Eddie said in a low, shaky voice. "Now I know why you were so low on shells, Roland."

"Be quiet!" Susannah snapped. "Let him finish!"

Roland went on, telling his story as stolidly as he had crossed the desert after passing the hut of the last Dweller, a young man whose wild, strawberry-colored hair had reached almost to his waist. He told them about how his mule had finally died. He even told them about how the Dweller's pet bird, Zoltan, had eaten the mule's eyes.

He told them about the long desert days and the short desert nights which had come next, and how he had followed the cool remains of Walter's campfires, and how he had come at last, reeling and dying of dehydration, to the way station.

"It was empty. It had been empty, I think, since the days when yonder great bear was still a newly made thing. I stayed a night and pushed on. That's what happened . . . but now I'll tell you another story."

"The one that isn't true but should be?" Susannah asked.

Roland nodded. "In this made-up story—this fable—a gunslinger named Roland met a boy named Jake at the way station. This boy was from your world, from your city of New York, and from a *when* someplace between Eddie's 1987 and Odetta Holmes's 1963."

Eddie was leaning forward eagerly. "Is there a door in this story, Roland? A door marked THE BOY, or something like that?"

Roland shook his head. "The boy's doorway was death. He was on his way to school when a man—a man I believed to be Walter—pushed him into the street, where he was run over by a car. He heard this man say something like 'Get out of the way, let me through, I'm a priest.' Jake *saw* this man—just for an instant—and then he was in *my* world."

The gunslinger paused, looking into the fire.

"Now I want to leave this story of the boy who was never there and go back to what really happened for a minute. All right?"

Eddie and Susannah exchanged a puzzled glance and then Eddie made an "after you, my dear Alphonse" gesture with his hand.

"As I have said, the way station was deserted. There was, however, a pump that still worked. It was at the back of the stable where the coach-horses were kept. I followed my ears to it, but I would have found it even if it had been completely silent. I *smelled* the water, you see. After enough time in the desert, when you are on the edge of dying from thirst, you can really do that. I drank and then slept. When I woke, I drank again. I wanted to push on at once—the need to do that was like a fever. The medicine you brought me from your world—the *astin*—is wonderful stuff, Eddie, but there are fevers beyond the power of any medicine to cure, and this was one of them. I knew my body needed rest, but it still took every ounce of my willpower to stay there even one night. In the morning I felt rested, and so I refilled my waterskins and pushed on. *I took nothing from that place but water*. That's the most important part of what really happened."

Susannah spoke in her most reasonable, pleasant, and Odetta Holmes–like voice. "All right, that's what really happened. You refilled your waterskins and went on. Now tell us the rest of what *didn't* happen, Roland."

The gunslinger put the jawbone in his lap for a moment, curled his hands into fists, and rubbed his eyes with them—a curiously childlike gesture. Then he grasped the jawbone again, as if for courage, and went on.

"I hyptonized the boy who wasn't there," he said. "I did it with one of my shells. It's a trick I've known for years, and I learned it from a very unlikely source—Marten, my father's court magician. The boy was a good subject. While he was tranced, he told me the circumstances of his death, as I've told them to you. When I'd gotten as much of his story as I felt I could without upsetting or actually hurting him, I gave him a command that he should not remember anything about his dying when he woke up again."

"Who'd want to?" Eddie muttered.

Roland nodded. "Who, indeed? The boy passed from his trance directly into a natural sleep. I also slept. When we woke, I told the boy that I meant to catch the man in black. He knew who I meant; Walter had also stopped at the way station. Jake was afraid and hid from him. I'm sure Walter knew he was there, but it suited his purpose to pretend he didn't. He left the boy behind like a set trap.

"I asked him if there was anything to eat there. It seemed to me there must be. He looked healthy enough, and the desert climate is wonderful when it comes to preserving things. He had a little dried meat, and he said there was a cellar. He hadn't explored that, because he was afraid." The gunslinger looked at them grimly. "He was right to be afraid. I found food . . . and I also found a Speaking Demon."

Eddie looked down at the jawbone with widening eyes. Orange firelight danced on its ancient curves and hoodoo teeth. "Speaking Demon? Do you mean *that* thing?"

"No," he said. "Yes. Both. Listen and you shall understand."

He told them about the inhuman groans he'd heard coming from the earth beyond the cellar; how he had seen sand running from between two of the old blocks which made up the cellar walls. He told them of approaching the hole that was appearing there as Jake screamed for him to come up.

He had commanded the demon to speak . . . and so the demon had, in the voice of Allie, the woman with the scar on her forehead, the woman who had kept the bar in Tull. *Go slow past the Drawers, gunslinger. While you travel with the boy, the man in black travels with your soul in his pocket.*

"The Drawers?" Susannah asked, startled.

"Yes." Roland looked at her closely. "That means something to you, doesn't it?"

"Yes . . . and no."

She spoke with great hesitation. Some of it, Roland divined, was simple reluctance to speak of things which were painful to her. He thought most of it, however, was a desire not to confuse issues which were already confused by saying more than she actually knew. He admired that. He admired *her.*

"Say what you can be sure of," he said. "No more than that."

"All right. The Drawers was a place Detta Walker knew about. A place Detta *thought* about. It's a slang term, one she picked up from listening to the grownups when they sat out on the porch and drank beer and talked about the old days. It means a place that's spoiled, or useless, or both. There was something in the Drawers—in the *idea* of the Drawers—that called to Detta. Don't ask me what; I might have known once, but I don't anymore. And don't want to.

"Detta stole my Aunt Blue's china plate—the one my folks gave her for a wedding present—and took it to the Drawers—*her* Drawers—to break it. That place was a gravel-pit filled with trash. A dumping-ground. Later on, she sometimes picked up boys at roadhouses."

Susannah dropped her head for a moment, her lips pressed tightly together. Then she looked up again and went on.

"*White* boys. And when they took her back to their cars in the parking lot, she cock-teased them and then ran off. Those parking lots . . . they were the Drawers, too. It was a dangerous game, but she was young enough, quick enough, and mean enough to play it to the hilt and enjoy it. Later, in New York, she'd go on shoplifting expeditions . . . you know about that. Both of you. Always to the fancy stores—Macy's, Gimbel's, Bloomingdale's—and steal trinkets. And when she made up her mind to go on one of those sprees, she'd think: *I'm goan to the Drawers today. Goan steal me some shit fum de white folks. Goan steal me sumpin forspecial and den break dat sumbitch.*"

She paused, lips trembling, looking into the fire. When she looked around again, Roland and Eddie saw tears standing in her eyes.

"I'm crying, but don't let that fool you. I remember doing those things, and I remember *enjoying* them. I guess I'm crying because I know I'd do it all again, if the circumstances were right."

Roland seemed to have regained some of his old serenity, his weird equilibrium. "We have a proverb in my country, Susannah: 'The wise thief always prospers.' "

"I don't see nothing wise about stealing a bunch of paste jewelry," she said sharply.

"Were you ever caught?"

"No—"

He spread his hands as if to say, *There you have it.*

"So for Detta Walker, the Drawers were bad places?" Eddie asked. "Is that right? Because it doesn't exactly *feel* right."

"Bad and good at the same time. They were *powerful* places, places where she . . . she *reinvented* herself, I suppose you could say . . . but they were *lost* places, too. And this is all off the subject of Roland's ghostboy, isn't it?"

"Maybe not," Roland said. "We had Drawers as well, you see, in my world. It was slang for us, too, and the meanings are very similar."

"What did it mean to you and your friends?" Eddie asked.

"That varied slightly from place to place and situation to situation. It might mean a trash-midden. It might mean a whorehouse or a place where men came to gamble or chew devil-weed. But the most common meaning that I know is also the simplest."

He looked at them both.

"The Drawers are places of desolation," he said. "The Drawers are the waste lands."

15

THIS TIME SUSANNAH THREW more wood on the fire. In the south, Old Mother blazed on brilliantly, not flickering. She knew from her school studies what that meant: it was a planet, not a star. *Venus?* she wondered. *Or is the solar system of which this world is a part as different as everything else?*

Again that feeling of unreality—the feeling that all this must surely be a dream—washed over her.

"Go on," she said. "What happened after the voice warned you about the Drawers and the little boy?"

"I punched my hand into the hole the sand had come from, as I was taught to do if such a thing ever

happened to me. What I plucked forth was a jawbone
. . . but not this one. The jawbone I took from the
wall of the way station was much larger; from one of
the Great Old Ones, I have almost no doubt."

"What happened to it?" Susannah asked quietly.

"One night I gave it to the boy," Roland said. The
fire painted his cheeks with hot orange highlights and
dancing shadows. "As a protection—a kind of talisman. Later I felt it had served its purpose and threw
it away."

"So whose jawbone you got there, Roland?" Eddie
asked.

Roland held it up, looked at it long and thoughtfully, and let it drop back. "Later, after Jake . . . after
he died . . . I caught up with the men I had been
chasing."

"With Walter," Susannah said.

"Yes. We held palaver, he and I . . . *long* palaver.
I fell asleep at some point, and when I woke up, Walter was dead. A hundred years dead at least, and
probably more. There was nothing left of him but
bones, which was fitting enough, since we were in a
place of bones."

"Yeah, it must have been a pretty long palaver, all
right," Eddie said dryly.

Susannah frowned slightly at this, but Roland only
nodded. "Long and long," he said, looking into the
fire.

"You came to in the morning and reached the Western Sea that very evening," Eddie said. "That night
the lobstrosities came, right?"

Roland nodded again. "Yes. But before I left the
place where Walter and I had spoken . . . or dreamed
. . . or whatever it was we did . . . I took this from
the skull of his skeleton." He lifted the bone and the
orange light again skated off the teeth.

Walter's jawbone, Eddie thought, and felt a little
chill work through him. *The jawbone of the man in
black. Remember this, Eddie my boy, the next time*

you get to thinking Roland's maybe just another one of the guys. He's been carrying it around with him all this time like some kind of a . . . a cannibal's trophy. Jee-sus.

"I remember what I thought when I took it," Roland said. "I remember very well; it is the only memory I have of that time which hasn't doubled on me. I thought, 'It was bad luck to throw away what I found when I found the boy. This will replace it.' Only then I heard Walter's laughter—his mean, tittery laughter. I heard his voice, too."

"What did he say?" Susannah asked.

" 'Too late, gunslinger,' " Roland said. "That's what he said. 'Too late—your luck will be bad from now until the end of eternity—that is your *ka*.' "

16

"ALL RIGHT," EDDIE SAID at last. "I understand the basic paradox. Your memory is divided—"

"*Not* divided. *Doubled.*"

"All right; it's almost the same thing, isn't it?" Eddie grasped a twig and made his own little drawing in the sand:

He tapped the line on the left. "This is your memory of the time before you got to the way station—a single track."

"Yes."

He tapped the line on the right. "And after you came out on the far side of the mountains in the place of bones . . . the place where Walter was waiting for you. *Also* a single track."

"Yes."

Now Eddie first indicated the middle area and then drew a rough circle around it.

"That's what you've got to do, Roland—close this double track off. Build a stockade around it in your mind and then forget it. Because it doesn't *mean* anything, it doesn't *change* anything, it's *gone*, it's *done*—"

"But it isn't." Roland held up the bone. "If my memories of the boy Jake are false—and I know they are—*how can I have this*? I took it to replace the one I threw away . . . but the one I threw away came from the cellar of the way station, and along the track I know is true, *I never went down cellar!* I never spoke with the demon! I moved on alone, with fresh water *and nothing else!*"

"Roland, listen to me," Eddie said earnestly. "If that jawbone you're holding was the one from the way station, that would be one thing. But isn't it possible that if you hallucinated that whole thing—the way station, the kid, the Speaking Demon—then maybe you took Walter's jawbone because—"

"It was no hallucination," Roland said. He looked at them both with his faded blue bombardier's eyes and then did something neither expected . . . something Eddie would have sworn Roland did not know he meant to do himself.

He threw the jawbone into the fire.

17

FOR A MOMENT IT only lay there, a white relic bent in a ghostly half-grin. Then it suddenly blazed red,

washing the clearing with dazzling scarlet light. Eddie
and Susannah cried out and threw their hands up to
shield their eyes from that burning shape.

The bone began to change. Not to melt, but to
change. The teeth which leaned out of it like grave-
stones began to draw together in clumps. The mild
curve of the upper arc straightened, then snubbed
down at the tip.

Eddie's hands fell into his lap and he stared at the
bone which was no longer a bone with gape-jawed
wonder. It was now the color of burning steel. The
teeth had become three inverted V's, the middle one
larger than those on the ends. And suddenly Eddie
saw what it wanted to become, just as he had seen
the slingshot in the wood of the stump.

He thought it was a key.

You must remember the shape, he thought feverishly. *You must, you must.*

His eyes traced it desperately—three V's, the one
in the center larger and deeper than the two on the
end. Three notches . . . and the one closest the end
had a squiggle, the shallow shape of a lower-case *s*
. . .

Then the shape in the flames changed again. The
bone which had become something like a key drew
inward, concentrating itself into bright, overlapping
petals and folds as dark and velvety as a moonless
summer midnight. For a moment Eddie saw a rose—
a triumphant rose that might have bloomed in the
dawn of this world's first day, a thing of depthless,
timeless beauty. His eye saw, and his heart was
opened. It was as if all love and life had suddenly
risen from Roland's dead artifact; it was there in the
fire, burning out in triumph and some wonderful, in-
choate defiance, declaring that despair was a mirage
and death a dream.

The rose! he thought incoherently. *First the key,
then the rose! Behold! Behold the opening of the way
to the Tower!*

There was a thick cough from the fire. A fan of sparks twisted outwards. Susannah screamed and rolled away, beating at the orange flecks on her dress as the flames gushed upward toward the starry sky. Eddie didn't move. He sat transfixed in his vision, held in a cradle of wonder which was both gorgeous and terrible, unmindful of the sparks which danced across his skin. Then the flames sank back.

The bone was gone.

The key was gone.

The rose was gone.

Remember, he thought. *Remember the rose . . . and remember the shape of the key.*

Susannah was sobbing with shock and terror, but he ignored her for the moment and found the stick with which he and Roland had both drawn. And in the dirt he made this shape with a shaking hand:

18

"WHY DID YOU DO it?" Susannah asked at last. "Why, for God's sake—and what was it?"

Fifteen minutes had gone by. The fire had been allowed to burn low; the scattered embers had either been stamped out or had gone out on their own. Eddie sat with his arms about his wife; Susannah sat before him, with her back against his chest. Roland was off to one side, knees hugged to his chest, looking moodily into the orange-red coals. So far as Eddie could tell, neither of them had seen the bone change. They had both seen it glowing superhot, and Roland had seen it explode (or had it imploded? to Eddie that seemed closer to what he had seen), but that was all. Or so he believed; Roland, however, sometimes kept his own counsel, and when he decided to play his cards close to the vest, he played them very close indeed, Eddie knew that from bitter experience. He thought of telling them what he had seen—or *thought* he had seen—and decided to play his own cards tight and close-up, at least for the time being.

Of the jawbone itself there was no sign—not even a splinter.

"I did it because a voice spoke in my mind and told me I must," Roland said. "It was the voice of my father; of *all* my fathers. When one hears such a voice, not to obey—and at once—is unthinkable. So I was taught. As to what it was, I can't say . . . not now, at least. I only know that the bone has spoken its final word. I have carried it all this way to hear it."

Or to see it, Eddie thought, and again: *Remember. Remember the rose. And remember the shape of the key*.

"It almost flash-fried us!" She sounded both tired and exasperated.

Roland shook his head. "I think it was more like the sort of firework the barons used to sometimes shoot into the sky at their year-end parties. Bright and startling, but not dangerous."

Eddie had an idea. "The doubling in your mind, Roland—is it gone? Did it leave when the bone exploded, or whatever it did?"

He was almost convinced that it had; in the movies he'd seen, such rough shock-therapy almost always worked. But Roland shook his head.

Susannah shifted in Eddie's arms. "You said you were beginning to understand."

Roland nodded. "I think so, yes. If I'm right, I fear for Jake. Wherever he is, *whenever* he is, I fear for him."

"What do you mean?" Eddie asked.

Roland got up, went to his roll of hides, and began

to spread them out. "Enough stories and excitement for one night. It's time to sleep. In the morning we'll follow the bear's backtrail and see if we can find the portal he was set to guard. I'll tell you what I know and what I believe has happened—what I believe is happening still—along the way."

With that he wrapped himself in an old blanket and a new deerskin, rolled away from the fire, and would say no more.

Eddie and Susannah lay down together. When they were sure the gunslinger must be asleep, they made love. Roland heard them going about it as he lay wakeful and heard their quiet after-love talk. Most of it was about him. He lay quietly, open eyes looking into the darkness long after their talk had ceased and their breathing had evened out into a single easy note.

It was, he thought, fine to be young and in love. Even in the graveyard which this world had become, it was fine.

Enjoy it while you can, he thought, *because there is more death ahead. We have come to a stream of blood. That it will lead us to a river of the same stuff I have no doubt. And, further along, to an ocean. In this world the graves yawn and none of the dead rest easy.*

As dawn began to come up in the east, he closed his eyes. Slept briefly. And dreamed of Jake.

19

EDDIE ALSO DREAMED—DREAMED he was back in New York, walking along Second Avenue with a book in his hand.

In this dream it was spring. The air was warm, the city was blooming, and homesickness sobbed within him like a muscle with a fishhook caught deep within it. *Enjoy this dream, and make it go on as long as you can,* he thought. *Savor it . . . because this is as close*

*to New York as you're going to get. You can't go
home, Eddie. That part's done.*

He looked down at the book and was utterly unsurprised to find it was *You Can't Go Home Again*, by
Thomas Wolfe. Stamped into the dark red cover were
three shapes; key, rose, and door. He stopped for a
moment, flipped the book open, and read the first
line. *The man in black fled across the desert,* Wolfe
had written, *and the gunslinger followed.*

Eddie closed it and walked on. It was about nine in
the morning, he judged, maybe nine-thirty, and traffic
on Second Avenue was light. Taxis honked and wove
their way from lane to lane with spring sunshine twinkling off their windshields and bright yellow paintjobs.
A bum on the corner of Second and Fifty-second
asked him for a handout and Eddie tossed the book
with the red cover into his lap. He observed (also
without surprise) that the bum was Enrico Balazar.
He was sitting cross-legged in front of a magic shop.
HOUSE OF CARDS, the sign in the window read,
and the display inside showed a tower which had been
built of Tarot cards. Standing on top was a model of
King Kong. There was a tiny radar-dish growing out
of the great ape's head.

Eddie walked on, lazing his way downtown, the
street-signs floating past him. He knew where he was
going as soon as he saw it: a small shop on the corner
of Second and Forty-sixth.

Yeah, he thought. A feeling of great relief swept
through him. *This is the place. The very place.* The
window was full of hanging meats and cheeses. TOM
AND GERRY'S ARTISTIC DELI, the sign read.
PARTY PLATTERS OUR SPECIALTY!

As he stood looking in, someone else he knew came
around the corner. It was Jack Andolini, wearing a
three-piece suit the color of vanilla ice cream and carrying a black cane in his left hand. Half of his face
was gone, lopped off by the claws of the lobstrosities.

Go on in, Eddie, Jack said as he passed. *After all,*

*there are other worlds than these and that fuckin train
rolls through all of them.*

I can't, Eddie replied. *The door is locked.* He didn't
know how he knew this, but he did; knew it beyond
a shadow of a doubt.

*Dad-a-chum, dud-a-chee, not to worry, you've got
the key,* Jack said, not looking back. Eddie looked
down and saw he *did* have a key; a primitive-looking
thing with three notches like inverted V's.

*That little s-shape at the end of the last notch is the
secret,* he thought. He stepped under the awning of
Tom and Gerry's Artistic Deli and inserted the key in
the lock. It turned easily. He opened the door and
stepped through into a huge open field. He looked
back over his shoulder and saw the traffic on Second
Avenue hurrying by, and then the door slammed shut
and fell over. There was nothing behind it. Nothing
at all. He turned back to survey his new surroundings,
and what he saw filled him with terror at first. The
field was a deep scarlet, as if some titanic battle had
been fought here and the ground had been drenched
with so much blood that it could not all be absorbed.

Then he realized that it was not blood he was looking at, but roses.

That feeling of mingled joy and triumph surged
through him again, swelling his heart until he felt it
might burst within him. He raised his clenched fists
high over his head in a gesture of victory . . . and
then froze that way.

The field stretched on for miles, climbing a gentle
slope of land, and standing at the horizon was the
Dark Tower. It was a pillar of dumb stone rising so
high into the sky that he could barely discern its tip.
Its base, surrounded by red, shouting roses, was formidable, titanic with weight and size, yet the Tower
became oddly graceful as it rose and tapered. The
stone of which it had been made was not black, as he
had imagined it would be, but soot-colored. Narrow,
slitted windows marched about it in a rising spiral;

below the windows ran an almost endless flight of stone stairs, circling up and up. The Tower was a dark gray exclamation point planted in the earth and rising above the field of blood-red roses. The sky arched above it was blue, but filled with puffy white clouds like sailing ships. They flowed above and around the top of the Dark Tower in an endless stream.

How gorgeous it is! Eddie marvelled. *How gorgeous and strange!* But his feeling of joy and triumph had departed; he was left with a sense of deep malaise and impending doom. He looked about him and realized with sudden horror that he was standing in the shadow of the Tower. No, not just *standing* in it; buried alive in it.

He cried out but his cry was lost in the golden blast of some tremendous horn. It came from the top of the Tower, and seemed to fill the world. As that note of warning held and drew out over the field where he stood, blackness welled from the windows which girdled the Tower. It overspilled them and spread across the sky in flaggy streams which came together and formed a growing blotch of darkness. It did not look like a cloud; it looked like a tumor hanging over the earth. The sky was blotted out. And, he saw, it was not a cloud or a tumor but a *shape*, some tenebrous, cyclopean *shape* racing toward the place where he stood. It would do no good to run from that beast coalescing in the sky above the field of roses; it would catch him, clutch him, and bear him away. Into the Dark Tower it would bear him, and the world of light would see him no more.

Rents formed in the darkness and terrible inhuman eyes, each easily the size of the bear Shardik which lay dead in the forest, peered down at him. They were red—red as roses, red as blood.

Jack Andolini's dead voice hammered in his ears: *A thousand worlds, Eddie—ten thousand!—and that train rolls through every one. If you can get it started. And if you* do *get it started, your troubles are only beginning, because this device is a real bastard to shut down.*

Jack's voice had become mechanical, chanting. *A real bastard to shut down, Eddie boy, you better believe it, this bastard is—*

"—SHUTTING DOWN! SHUTDOWN WILL BE COMPLETE IN ONE HOUR AND SIX MINUTES!"

In his dream, Eddie threw his hands up to shield his eyes . . .

20

. . . AND WOKE, SITTING BOLT upright beside the dead campfire. He was looking at the world from between his own spread fingers. And still that voice rolled on and on, the voice of some heartless SWAT Squad commander bellowing through a bullhorn.

"THERE IS NO DANGER! REPEAT, THERE IS NO DANGER! FIVE SUBNUCLEAR CELLS ARE DORMANT, TWO SUBNUCLEAR CELLS ARE NOW IN SHUTDOWN PHASE, ONE SUB-NUCLEAR CELL IS OPERATING AT TWO PER CENT CAPACITY. THESE CELLS ARE OF NO VALUE! REPEAT, THESE CELLS ARE OF NO VALUE! REPORT LOCATION TO NORTH CEN-TRAL POSITRONICS, LIMITED! CALL 1-900-44! THE CODE WORD FOR THIS DEVICE IS 'SHARDIK.' REWARD IS OFFERED! REPEAT, REWARD IS OFFERED!"

The voice fell silent. Eddie saw Roland standing at the edge of the clearing, holding Susannah in the crook of one arm. They were staring toward the sound of the voice, and as the recorded announcement began again, Eddie was finally able to shake off the chill remnants of his nightmare. He got up and joined Roland and Susannah, wondering how many centuries it had been since that announcement, programmed to broadcast only in the event of a total system breakdown, had been recorded.

"THIS DEVICE IS SHUTTING DOWN! SHUTDOWN WILL BE COMPLETE IN ONE HOUR AND FIVE MINUTES! THERE IS NO DANGER! REPEAT—"

Eddie touched Susannah's arm and she looked around. "How long has this been going on?"

"About fifteen minutes. You were dead to the w—" She broke off. "Eddie, you look terrible! Are you sick?"

"No. I just had a bad dream."

Roland was studying him in a way that made Eddie feel uncomfortable. "Sometimes there's truth in dreams, Eddie. What was yours?"

He thought for a moment, then shook his head. "I don't remember."

"You know, I doubt that."

Eddie shrugged and favored Roland with a thin smile. "Doubt away, then—be my guest. And how are *you* this morning, Roland?"

"The same," Roland said. His faded blue eyes still conned Eddie's face.

"Stop it," Susannah said. Her voice was brisk, but Eddie caught an undertone of nervousness. "Both of you. I got better things to do than watch you two dance around and kick each other's shins like a couple of little kids playin Two for Flinching. Specially this morning, with that dead bear trying to yell down the whole world."

The gunslinger nodded, but kept his eyes on Eddie. "All right . . . but are you sure there's nothing you want to tell me, Eddie?"

He thought about it then—really thought about telling. What he had seen in the fire, what he had seen in his dream. He decided against it. Perhaps it was only the memory of the rose in the fire, and the roses which had blanketed that dream-field in such fabulous profusion. He knew he could not tell these things as his eyes had seen them and his heart had felt them; he could only cheapen them. And, at least for the time being, he wanted to ponder these things alone.

But remember, he told himself again . . . except the voice in his mind didn't sound much like his own. It seemed deeper, older—the voice of a stranger. *Remember the rose . . . and the shape of the key.*

"I will," he murmured.

"You will what?" Roland asked.

"Tell," Eddie said. "If anything comes up that seems, you know, really important, I'll tell you. Both of you. Right now there isn't. So if we're going somewhere, Shane, old buddy, let's saddle up."

"Shane? Who is this Shane?"

"I'll tell you that some other time, too. Meantime, let's go."

They packed the gear they had brought with them from the old campsite and headed back, Susannah riding in her wheelchair again. Eddie had an idea she wouldn't be riding in it for long.

21

ONCE, BEFORE EDDIE HAD become too interested in the subject of heroin to be interested in much else, he and a couple of friends had driven over to New Jersey to see a couple of speed-metal groups—Anthrax and Megadeth—in concert at the Meadowlands. He believed that Anthrax had been slightly louder than the repeating announcement coming from the fallen bear, but he wasn't a hundred per cent sure. Roland stopped them while they were still half a mile from the clearing in the woods and tore six small scaps of cloth from his old shirt. They stuffed them in their ears and then went on. Even the cloth didn't do much to deaden the steady blast of sound.

"THIS DEVICE IS SHUTTING DOWN!" the bear blared as they stepped into the clearing again. It lay as it had lain, at the foot of the tree Eddie had climbed, a fallen Colossus with its legs apart and its knees in the air, like a furry female giant who had died trying to give birth. *"SHUTDOWN WILL BE COMPLETE IN FORTY-SEVEN MINUTES! THERE IS NO DANGER—"*

Yes, there is, Eddie thought, picking up the scattered hides which had not been shredded in either the bear's attack or its flailing death-throes. *Plenty* of danger. To my fucking *ears*. He picked up Roland's gunbelt and silently handed it over. The chunk of wood he had been working on lay nearby; he grabbed it and tucked it into the pocket in the back of Susannah's wheelchair as the gunslinger slowly buckled the wide leather belt around his waist and cinched the rawhide tiedown.

"—IN SHUTDOWN PHASE, ONE SUB-NUCLEAR CELL OPERATING AT ONE PER CENT CAPACITY. THESE CELLS—"

Susannah followed Eddie, holding in her lap a carry-all bag she had sewn herself. As Eddie handed her the hides, she stuffed them into the bag. When all of them were stored away, Roland tapped Eddie on the arm and handed him a shoulderpack. What it contained mostly was deermeat, heavily salted from a natural lick Roland had found about three miles up the little creek. The gunslinger had already donned a similar pack. His purse—restocked and once again bulging with all sorts of odds and ends—hung from his other shoulder.

A strange, home-made harness with a seat of stitched deerskin dangled from a nearby branch. Roland plucked it off, studied it for a moment, and then draped it over his back and knotted the straps below his chest. Susannah made a sour face at this, and Roland saw it. He did not try to speak—this close to the bear, he couldn't have made himself heard even by shouting at the top of his voice—but he shrugged sympathetically and spread his hands: *You know we'll need it.*

She shrugged back. *I know . . . but that doesn't mean I like it.*

The gunslinger pointed across the clearing. A pair of leaning, splintered spruce trees marked the place where Shardik, who had once been known as Mir in these parts, had entered the clearing.

Eddie leaned toward Susannah, made a circle with his thumb and forefinger, then raised his eyebrows interrogatively. *Okay?*

She nodded, then pressed the heels of her palms against her ears. *Okay—but let's get out of here before I go deaf.*

The three of them moved across the clearing, Eddie pushing Susannah, who held the bag of hides in her lap. The pocket in the back of her wheelchair was stuffed with other items; the piece of wood with the slingshot still mostly hidden inside it was only one of them.

From behind them the bear continued to roar out its final communication to the world, telling them shutdown would be complete in forty minutes. Eddie couldn't wait. The broken spruces leaned in toward each other, forming a rude gate, and Eddie thought: *This is where the quest for Roland's Dark Tower really begins, at least for us.*

He thought of his dream again—the spiraling windows issuing their unfurling flags of darkness, flags which spread over the field of roses like a stain—and as they passed beneath the leaning trees, a deep shudder gripped him.

22

THEY WERE ABLE TO use the wheelchair longer than Roland had expected. The firs of this forest were very

old, and their spreading branches had created a deep
carpet of needles which discouraged most undergrowth. Susannah's arms were strong—stronger than
Eddie's, although Roland did not think that would be
true much longer—and she wheeled herself along easily over the level, shady forest floor. When they came
to one of the trees the bear had pushed over, Roland
lifted her out of the chair and Eddie boosted it over
the obstacle.

From behind them, only a little deadened by distance, the bear told them, at the top of its mechanical
voice, that the capacity of its last operating nuclear
subcell was now negligible.

"I hope you keep that damn harness lying empty
over your shoulders all day!" Susannah shouted at the
gunslinger.

Roland agreed, but less than fifteen minutes later
the land began to slope downward and this old section
of the forest began to be invaded with smaller,
younger trees: birch, alder, and a few stunted maples
scrabbling grimly in the soil for purchase. The carpet
of needles thinned and the wheels of Susannah's chair
began to catch in the low, tough bushes which grew
in the alleys between the trees. Their thin branches
boinged and rattled in the stainless steel spokes. Eddie
threw his weight against the handles and they were
able to go on for another quarter of a mile that way.
Then the slope began to grow more steep, and the
ground underfoot became mushy.

"Time for a pig-back, lady," Roland said.

"Let's try the chair a little longer, what do you say?
Going might get easier—"

Roland shook his head. "If you try that hill, you'll
. . . what did you call it, Eddie? . . . do a dugout?"

Eddie shook his head, grinning. "It's called doing a
doughnut, Roland. A term from my misspent side-
walk-surfing days."

"Whatever you call it, it means landing on your
head. Come on, Susannah. Up you come."

"I hate being a cripple," Susannah said crossly, but allowed Eddie to hoist her out of the chair and worked with him to seat herself firmly in the harness Roland wore on his back. Once she was in place, she touched the butt of Roland's pistol. "Y'all want this baby?" she asked Eddie.

He shook his head. "You're faster. And you know it, too."

She grunted and adjusted the belt, settling the gunbutt so it was easily accessible to her right hand. "I'm slowing you boys down and I know *that* . . . but if we ever make it to some good old two-lane blacktop, I'll leave the both of you kneelin in the blocks."

"I don't doubt it," Roland said . . . and then cocked his head. The woods had fallen silent.

"Br'er Bear has finally given up," Susannah said. "Praise God."

"I thought it still had seven minutes to go," Eddie said.

Roland adjusted the straps of the harness. "Its clock must have started running a little slow during the last five or six hundred years."

"You really think it was that old, Roland?"

Roland nodded. "At least. And now it's passed . . . the last of the Twelve Guardians, for all we know."

"Yeah, ask me if I give a shit," Eddie replied, and Susannah laughed.

"Are you comfortable?" Roland asked her.

"No. My butt hurts already, but go on. Just try not to drop me."

Roland nodded and started down the slope. Eddie followed, pushing the empty chair and trying not to bang it too badly on the rocks which had begun to jut out of the ground like big white knuckles. Now that the bear had finally shut up, he thought the forest seemed much too quiet—it almost made him feel like a character in one of those hokey old jungle movies about cannibals and giant apes.

23

THE BEAR'S BACKTRAIL WAS easy to find but tougher
to follow. Five miles or so out of the clearing, it led
them through a low, boggy area that was not quite a
swamp. By the time the ground began to rise and firm
up a little again, Roland's faded jeans were soaked to
the knees and he was breathing in long, steady rasps.
Still, he was in slightly better shape than Eddie, who
had found wrestling Susannah's wheelchair through
the muck and standing water hard going.

"Time to rest and eat something," Roland said.

"Oh boy, gimme eats," Eddie puffed. He helped
Susannah out of the harness and set her down on the
bole of a fallen tree with claw-marks slashed into its
trunk in long diagonal grooves. Then he half-sat, half-
collapsed next to her.

"You got my wheelchair pretty muddy, white boy,"
Susannah said. "It's all goan be in my repote."

He cocked an eyebrow at her. "Next carwash we
come to, I'll push you through myself. I'll even Turtle-
wax the goddamn thing. Okay?"

She smiled. "You got a date, handsome."

Eddie had one of Roland's waterskins cinched
around his waist. He tapped it. "Okay?"

"Yes," Roland said. "Not too much now; a little
more for all of us before we set out again. That way
no one takes a cramp."

"Roland, Eagle Scout of Oz," Eddie said, and giggled as he unslung the waterskin.

"What is this Oz?"

"A make-believe place in a movie," Susannah said.

"Oz was a lot more than that. My brother Henry
used to read me the stories once in a while. I'll tell
you one some night, Roland."

"That would be fine," the gunslinger replied seriously. "I am hungry to know more of your world."

"Oz isn't our world, though. Like Susannah said,
it's a make-believe place—"

Roland handed them chunks of meat which had been wrapped in broad leaves of some sort. "The quickest way to learn about a new place is to know what it dreams of. I would hear of this Oz."

"Okay, that's a date, too. Suze can tell you the one about Dorothy and Toto and the Tin Woodman, and I'll tell you all the rest." He bit into his piece of meat and rolled his eyes approvingly. It had taken the flavor of the leaves in which it had been rolled, and was delicious. Eddie wolfed his ration, stomach gurgling busily all the while. Now that he was getting his breath back, he felt good—great, in fact. His body was growing a solid sheath of muscle, and every part of it felt at peace with every other part.

Don't worry, he thought. *Everything will be arguing again by tonight. I think he's gonna push on until I'm ready to drop in my tracks.*

Susannah ate more delicately, chasing every second or third bite with a little sip of water, turning the meat in her hands, eating from the outside in. "Finish what you started last night," she invited Roland. "You said you thought you understood these conflicting memories of yours."

Roland nodded. "Yes. I think both memories are true. One is a little truer than the other, but that does not *negate* the truth of that other."

"Makes no sense to me," Eddie said. "Either this boy Jake was at the way station or he wasn't, Roland."

"It is a paradox—something that is and isn't at the same time. Until it's resolved, I will continue divided. That's bad enough, but the basic split is widening. I can feel that happening. It is . . . unspeakable."

"What do you think caused it?" Susannah asked.

"I told you the boy was pushed in front of a car. *Pushed.* Now, who do we know who liked to push people in front of things?"

Understanding dawned in her face. "Jack Mort. Do

you mean *he* was the one who pushed this boy into the street?"

"Yes."

"But you said the man in black did it," Eddie objected. "Your buddy Walter. You said that the boy *saw* him—a man who looked like a priest. Didn't the kid even hear him *say* he was? 'Let me through, I'm a priest,' something like that?"

"Oh, Walter was there. They were *both* there, and they both pushed Jake."

"Somebody bring the Thorazine and the strait-jacket," Eddie called. "Roland just went over the high side."

Roland paid no attention to this; he was coming to understand that Eddie's jokes and clowning were his way of dealing with stress. Cuthbert had not been much different . . . as Susannah was, in her way, not so different from Alain. "What exasperates me about all of this," he said, "is that I should have *known*. I was *in* Jack Mort, after all, and I had access to his thoughts, just as I had access to yours, Eddie, and yours, Susannah. I *saw* Jake while I was in Mort. I saw him through Mort's eyes, *and I knew Mort planned to push him.* Not only that; I *stopped* him from doing it. All I had to do was enter his body. Not that he knew that was what it was; he was concentrating so hard on what he planned to do that he actually thought I was a fly landing on his neck."

Eddie began to understand. "If Jake wasn't pushed into the street, he never died. And if he never died, he never came into this world. And if he never came into this world, you never met him at the way station. Right?"

"Right. The thought even crossed my mind that if Jack Mort meant to kill the boy, I would have to stand aside and let him do it. To avoid creating the very paradox that is tearing me apart. But I couldn't do that. I . . . I . . ."

"You couldn't kill this kid twice, could you?" Eddie

asked softly. "Every time I just about make up my mind that you're as mechanical as that bear, you surprise me with something that actually seems human. Goddam."

"Quit it, Eddie," Susannah said.

Eddie took a look at the gunslinger's slightly lowered face and grimaced. "Sorry, Roland. My mother used to say that my mouth had a bad habit of running away with my mind."

"It's all right. I had a friend who was the same way."

"Cuthbert?"

Roland nodded. He looked at his diminished right hand for a long moment, then clenched it into a painful fist, sighed, and looked up at them again. Somewhere, deeper in the forest, a lark sang sweetly.

"Here is what I believe. If I had not entered Jack Mort when I did, he *still* wouldn't have pushed Jake that day. Not then. Why not? *Ka-tet.* Simply that. For the first time since the last of the friends with whom I set forth on this quest died, I have found myself once again at the center of *ka-tet.*"

"Quartet?" Eddie asked doubtfully.

The gunslinger shook his head. "*Ka*—the word you think of as 'destiny,' Eddie, although the actual meaning is much more complex and hard to define, as is almost always the case with words of the High Speech. And *tet*, which means a group of people with the same interests and goals. We three are a *tet*, for instance. *Ka-tet* is the place where many lives are joined by fate."

"Like in *The Bridge of San Luis Rey*," Susannah murmured.

"What's that?" Roland asked.

"A story about some people who die together when the bridge they're crossing collapses. It's famous in our world."

Roland nodded his understanding. "In this case, *ka-tet* bound Jake, Walter, Jack Mort, and me. There was no trap, as I first suspected when I realized who Jack Mort meant to be his next victim, because *ka-tet* cannot be changed or bent to the will of any one person. But *ka-tet* can be *seen, known,* and *understood.* Walter saw, and Walter knew." The gunslinger struck his thigh with his fist and exclaimed bitterly, "How he must have been laughing inside when I finally caught up to him!"

"Let's go back to what would have happened if you hadn't messed up Jack Mort's plans on the day he was following Jake," Eddie said. "You're saying that if *you* hadn't stopped Mort, someone or something else would have. Is that right?"

"Yes—because it wasn't the *right* day for Jake to die. It was *close* to the right day, but not *the* right day. I felt that, too. Perhaps, just before he did it, Mort would have seen someone watching him. Or a perfect stranger would have intervened. Or—"

"Or a cop," Susannah said. "He might have seen a cop in the wrong place and at the wrong time."

"Yes. The exact reason—the agent of *ka-tet*—doesn't matter. I know from firsthand experience that Mort was as wily as an old fox. If he sensed any slightest thing wrong, he would have called it off and waited for another day.

"I know something else, as well. He hunted in disguise. On the day he dropped the brick on Detta Holmes's head, he was wearing a knitted cap and an old sweater several sizes too big for him. He wanted to look like a wine-bibber, because he pushed the brick from a building where a large number of sots kept their dens. You see?"

They nodded.

"On the day, years later, when he pushed you in front of the train, Susannah, he was dressed as a construction worker. He was wearing a big yellow helmet he thought of as a 'hardhat' and a fake moustache. On the day when he actually *would* have pushed Jake into traffic, causing his death, *he would have been dressed as a priest.*"

"Jesus," Susannah nearly whispered. "The man who pushed him in New York was Jack Mort, and the man he saw at the way station was this fella you were chasing—Walter."

"Yes."

"And the little boy thought they were the same man because they were both wearing the same kind of black robe?"

Roland nodded. "There was even a physical resemblance between Walter and Jack Mort. Not as if they were brothers, I don't mean that, but both were tall men with dark hair and very pale complexions. And given the fact that Jake was dying when he got his only good look at Mort and was in a strange place and scared almost witless when he got his only good look at Walter, I think his mistake was both understandable and forgivable. If there's a horse's ass in this picture, it's me, for not realizing the truth sooner."

"Would Mort have known he was being used?" Eddie asked. Thinking back to his own experiences and wild thoughts when Roland had invaded his mind, he didn't see how Mort could *not* know . . . but Roland was shaking his head.

"Walter would have been extremely subtle. Mort would have thought the priest disguise his own idea . . . or so I believe. He would not have recognized the voice of an intruder—of Walter—whispering deep within his mind, telling him what to do."

"Jack Mort," Eddie marvelled. "It was Jack Mort all the time."

"Yes . . . with assistance from Walter. And so I ended up saving Jake's life after all. When I made Mort jump from the subway platform in front of the train, I changed everything."

Susannah asked, "If this Walter was able to enter our world—through his own private door, maybe—whenever he wanted, couldn't he have used someone

else to push your little boy? If he could suggest to
Mort that he dress up like a priest, then he could
make somebody else do it . . . What, Eddie? Why are
you shaking your head?"

"Because I don't think Walter would want that to
happen. What Walter wanted is what *is* happening . . .
for Roland to be losing his mind, bit by bit. Isn't that
right?"

The gunslinger nodded.

"Walter couldn't have done it that way even if he
had wanted to," Eddie added, "because he was dead
long before Roland found the doors on the beach.
When Roland went through that last one and into
Jack Mort's head, ole Walt's messin-around days were
done."

Susannah thought about this, then nodded her head.
"I see . . . I *think*. This time-travel business is some
confusing shit, isn't it?"

Roland began to pick up his goods and strap them
back into place. "Time we were moving on."

Eddie stood up and shrugged into his pack. "You
can take comfort from one thing, at least," he told
Roland. "You—or this *ka-tet* business—were able to
save the kid after all."

Roland had been knotting the harness-strings at his
chest. Now he looked up, and the blazing clarity of
his eyes made Eddie flinch backward. "Have I?" he
asked harshly. "Have I really? I'm going insane an
inch at a time, trying to live with two versions of the
same reality. I had hoped at first that one or the other
would begin to fade away, but that's not happening.
In fact, the exact opposite is happening: those two
realities are growing louder and louder in my head,
clamoring at each other like opposing factions which
must soon go to war. So tell me this, Eddie: How
do you suppose *Jake* feels? *How do you suppose it
feels to know you are dead in one world and alive in
another?*"

The lark sang again, but none of them noticed.

Eddie stared into the faded blue eyes blazing out of Roland's pale face and could not think of a thing to say.

24

THEY CAMPED ABOUT FIFTEEN miles due east of the dead bear that night, slept the sleep of the completely exhausted (even Roland slept the night through, although his dreams were nightmare carnival-rides), and were up the next morning at sunrise. Eddie kindled a small fire without speaking, and glanced at Susannah as a pistol-shot rang out in the woods nearby.

"Breakfast," she said.

Roland returned three minutes later with a hide slung over one shoulder. On it lay the freshly gutted corpse of a rabbit. Susannah cooked it. They ate and moved on.

Eddie kept trying to imagine what it would be like to have a memory of your own death. On that one he kept coming up short.

25

SHORTLY AFTER NOON THEY entered an area where most of the trees had been pulled over and the bushes mashed flat—it looked as though a cyclone had touched down here many years before, creating a wide and dismal alley of destruction.

"We're close to the place we want to find," Roland said. "He pulled down everything to clear the sightlines. Our friend the bear wanted no surprises. He was big, but not complacent."

"Has it left *us* any surprises?" Eddie asked.

"He may have done so." Roland smiled a little and touched Eddie on the shoulder. "But there's this— they'll be *old* surprises."

Their progress through this zone of destruction was slow. Most of the fallen trees were very old—many had almost rejoined the soil from which they had sprung—but they still made enough of a tangle to create a formidable obstacle course. It would have been difficult enough if all three of them had been able-bodied; with Susannah strapped to the gunslinger's back in her harness, it became an exercise in aggravation and endurance.

The flattened trees and jumbles of underbrush served to obscure the bear's backtrail, and that also worked to slow their speed. Until midday they had followed claw-marks as clear as trail-blazes on the trees. Here, however, near its starting point, the bear's rage had not been full-blown, and these handy signs of its passage disappeared. Roland moved slowly, looking for droppings in the bushes and tufts of hair on the tree-trunks over which the bear had climbed. It took all afternoon to cross three miles of this decayed jumble.

Eddie had just decided they were going to lose the light and would have to camp in these creepy surroundings when they came to a thin skirt of alders. Beyond it, he could hear a stream babbling noisily over a bed of stones. Behind them, the setting sun was radiating spokes of sullen red light across the jumbled ground they had just crossed, turning the fallen trees into crisscrossing black shapes like Chinese ideograms.

Roland called a halt and eased Susannah down. He stretched his back, twisting it this way and that with his hands on his hips.

"That it for the night?" Eddie asked.

Roland shook his head. "Give Eddie your gun, Susannah."

She did as he said, looking at him questioningly.

"Come on, Eddie. The place we want is on the

other side of those trees. We'll have a look. We might do a little work, as well."

"What makes you think—"

"Open your ears."

Eddie listened and realized he heard machinery. He further realized that he had been hearing it for some time now. "I don't want to leave Susannah."

"We're not going far and she has a good loud voice. Besides, if there's danger, it's ahead—we'll be between it and her."

Eddie looked down at Susannah.

"Go on—just make sure you're back soon." She looked back the way they had come with thoughtful eyes. "I don't know if there's ha'ants here or not, but it *feels* like there are."

"We'll be back before dark," Roland promised. He started toward the screen of alders, and after a moment, Eddie followed him.

26

FIFTEEN YARDS INTO THE trees, Eddie realized that they were following a path, one the bear had probably made for itself over the years. The alders bent above them in a tunnel. The sounds were louder now, and he began to sort them out. One was a low, deep, humming noise. He could feel it in his feet—a faint vibration, as if some large piece of machinery was running in the earth. Above it, closer and more urgent, were crisscrossing sounds like bright scratches—squeals, squeaks, chitterings.

Roland placed his mouth against Eddie's ear and said, "I think there's little danger if we're quiet."

They moved on another five yards and then Roland stopped again. He drew his gun and used the barrel to brush aside a branch which hung heavy with sunset-tinted leaves. Eddie looked through this small opening

and into the clearing where the bear had lived for so
long—the base of operations from which he had set
forth on his many expeditions of pillage and terror.

There was no undergrowth here; the ground had
been beaten bald long since. A stream emerged from
the base of a rock wall about fifty feet high and ran
through the arrowhead-shaped clearing. On their side
of the stream, backed up against the wall, was a metal
box about nine feet high. Its roof was curved, and it
reminded Eddie of a subway entrance. The front was
painted in diagonal yellow and black stripes. The earth
which floored the clearing was not black, like the topsoil in the forest, but a strange powdery gray. It was
littered with bones, and after a moment Eddie realized
that what he had taken for gray soil was more bones,
bones so old they were crumbling back to dust.

Things were moving in the dirt—the things making
the squealing, chittering noises. Four . . . no, five of
them. Small metal devices, the largest about the size
of a Collie pup. They were robots, Eddie realized, or
something *like* robots. They were similar to each other
and to the bear they had undoubtedly served in one
way only—atop each of them, a tiny radar-dish turned
rapidly.

More thinking caps, Eddie thought. *My God, what
kind of world is this, anyway?*

The largest of these devices looked a little like the
Tonka tractor Eddie had gotten for his sixth or seventh birthday; its treads churned up tiny gray clouds
of bone-dust as it rolled along. Another looked like a
stainless steel rat. A third appeared to be a snake
constructed of jointed steel segments—it writhed and
humped its way along. They formed a rough circle on
the far side of the stream, going around and around
on a deep course they had carved in the ground.
Looking at them made Eddie think of cartoons he
had seen in the stacks of old *Saturday Evening Post*
magazines his mother had for some reason saved and
stored in the front hall of their apartment. In the car-

toons, worried, cigarette-smoking men paced ruts in the carpet while they waited for their wives to give birth.

As his eyes grew used to the simple geography of the clearing, Eddie saw that there were a great many more than five of these assorted freaks. There were at least a dozen others that he could see and probably more hidden behind the bony remains of the bear's old kills. The difference was that the others weren't moving. The members of the bear's mechanical retinue had died, one by one, over the long years until just this little group of five were left . . . and they did not sound very healthy, with their squeaks and squalls and rusty chitterings. The snake in particular had a hesitant, crippled look as it followed the mechanical rat around and around the circle. Every now and then the device which followed the snake—a steel block that walked on stubby mechanical legs—would catch up with it and give the snake a nudge, as if telling it to hurry the fuck up.

Eddie wondered what their job had been. Surely not protection; the bear had been built to protect itself, and Eddie guessed that if old Shardik had come upon the three of them while still in its prime, it would have chewed them up and spat them out in short order. Perhaps these little robots had been its maintenance crew, or scouts, or messengers. He guessed that they could be dangerous, but only in their own defense . . . or their master's. They did not seem warlike.

There was, in fact, something pitiful about them. Most of the crew was now defunct, their master was gone, and Eddie believed they knew it somehow. It was not menace they projected but a strange, inhuman sadness. Old and almost worn out, they paced and rolled and wriggled their anxious way around the worry-track they had dug in this godforsaken clearing, and it almost seemed to Eddie that he could read the confused run of their thoughts; *Oh dear, oh dear, what*

*now? What is our purpose, now that He is gone? And
who will take care of us, now that He is gone? Oh
dear, oh dear, oh dear . . .*

Eddie felt a tug on the back of his leg and came very
close to screaming in fear and surprise. He wheeled,
cocking Roland's gun, and saw Susannah looking up
at him with wide eyes. Eddie let out a long breath
and dropped the hammer carefully back to its resting
position. He knelt, put his hands on Susannah's shoulders, kissed her cheek, then whispered in her ear: "I
came really close to putting a bullet in your silly
head—what are you doing here?"

"Wanted to see," she whispered back, looking not
even slightly abashed. Her eyes shifted to Roland as
he also hunkered beside her. "Besides, it was spooky
back there by myself."

She had sustained a number of small scratches
crawling after them through the brush, but Roland
had to admit to himself that she could be as quiet as
a ghost when she wanted to be; he hadn't heard a
thing. He took a rag (the last remnant of his old shirt)
from his back pocket and wiped the little trickles of
blood from her arms. He examined his work for a
moment and then dabbed at a small nick on her forehead as well. "Have your look, then," he said. His
voice was hardly more than the movement of his lips.
"I guess you earned it."

He used one hand to open a sightline at her level
in the hock and greenberry bushes, then waited while
she stared raptly into the clearing. At last she pulled
back and Roland allowed the bushes to close again.

"I feel sorry for them," she whispered. "Isn't that
crazy?"

"Not at all," Roland whispered back. "They are
creatures of great sadness, I think, in their own
strange way. Eddie is going to put them out of their
misery."

Eddie began to shake his head at once.

"Yes, you are . . . unless you want to hunker here

in what you call 'the toolies' all night. Go for the hats.
The little twirling things."

"What if I *miss*?" Eddie whispered at him furiously.
Roland shrugged.

Eddie stood up and reluctantly cocked the gunslinger's revolver again. He looked through the bushes at
the circling servomechanisms, going around and
around in their lonely, useless orbit. *It'll be like shooting puppies*, he thought glumly. Then he saw one of
them—it was the thing that looked like a walking
box—extrude an ugly-looking pincer device from its
middle and clamp it for a moment on the snake. The
snake made a surprised buzzing sound and leaped
ahead. The walking box withdrew its pincer.

Well . . . maybe not exactly *like shooting puppies*,
Eddie decided. He glanced at Roland again. Roland
looked back expressionlessly, arms folded across his
chest.

*You pick some goddam strange times to keep school,
buddy.*

Eddie thought of Susannah, first shooting the bear
in the ass, then blowing its sensor device to smither-
eens as it bore down on her and Roland, and felt a
little ashamed of himself. And there was more: part
of him wanted to go for it, just as part of him had
wanted to go up against Balazar and his crew of plug-
uglies in The Leaning Tower. The compulsion was
probably sick, but that didn't change its basic at-
traction: *Let's see who walks away . . let's just see.*

Yeah, that was pretty sick, all right.

*Pretend it's just a shooting gallery, and you want to
win your honey a stuffed dog*, he thought. *Or a stuffed
bear.* He drew a bead on the walking box and then
looked around impatiently when Roland touched his
shoulder.

"Say your lesson, Eddie. And be true."

Eddie hissed impatiently through his teeth, angry at
the distraction, but Roland's eyes didn't flinch and so
he drew a deep breath and tried to clear everything

from his mind: the squeaks and squalls of equipment that had been running too long, the aches and pains in his body, the knowledge that Susannah was here, propped up on the heels of her hands, watching, the *further* knowledge that she was closest to the ground, and if he missed one of the gadgets out there, she would be the handiest target if it decided to retaliate.

" 'I do not shoot with my hand; he who shoots with his hand has forgotten the face of his father.' "

That was a joke, he thought; he wouldn't know his old man if he passed him on the street. But he could feel the words doing their work, clearing his mind and settling his nerves. He didn't know if he was the stuff of which gunslingers were made—the idea seemed fabulously unlikely to him, even though he knew he had managed to hold up his end pretty well during the shootout at Balazar's nightclub—but he *did* know that part of him liked the coldness that fell over him when he spoke the words of the old, old catechism the gunslinger had taught them; the coldness and the way things seemed to stand forth with their own breathless clarity. There was another part of him which understood that this was just another deadly drug, not much different from the heroin which had killed Henry and almost killed him, but that did not alter the thin, tight pleasure of the moment. It drummed in him like taut cables vibrating in a high wind.

" 'I do not aim with my hand; he who aims with his hand has forgotten the face of his father.

" 'I aim with my eye.

" 'I do not kill with my gun; he who kills with his gun has forgotten the face of his father.' "

Then, without knowing he meant to do it, he stepped out of the trees and spoke to the trundling robots on the far side of the clearing:

" *'I kill with my heart.' "*

They stopped their endless circling. One of them let out a high buzz that might have been alarm or a warning. The radar-dishes, each no bigger than half a Hershey bar, turned toward the sound of his voice.

Eddie began to fire.

The sensors exploded like clay pigeons, one after the other. Pity was gone from Eddie's heart; there was only that coldness, and the knowledge that he would not stop, could not stop, until the job was done.

Thunder filled the twilit clearing and bounced back from the splintery rock wall at its wide end. The steel snake did two cartwheels and lay twitching in the dust. The biggest mechanism—the one that had reminded Eddie of his childhood Tonka tractor—tried to flee. Eddie blew its radar-dish to kingdom come as it made a herky-jerky run at the side of the rut. It fell on its squarish nose with thin blue flames squirting out of the steel sockets which held its glass eyes.

The only sensor he missed was the one on the stainless steel rat; that shot caromed off its metal back with a high mosquito whine. It surged out of the rut, made a half-circle around the box-shaped thing which had been following the snake, and charged across the clearing at surprising speed. It was making an angry clittering sound, and as it closed the distance, Eddie could see it had a mouth lined with long, sharp points. They did not look like teeth; they looked like sewing-machine needles, blurring up and down. No, he guessed these things were really not much like puppies, after all.

"Take it, Roland!" he shouted desperately, but when he snatched a quick look around he saw that Roland was still standing with his arms crossed on his chest, his expression serene and distant. He might have been thinking of chess problems or old love-letters.

The dish on the rat's back suddenly locked down. It changed direction slightly and buzzed straight toward Susannah Dean.

One bullet left, Eddie thought. *If I miss, it'll take her face off.*

Instead of shooting, he stepped forward and kicked the rat as hard as he could. He had replaced his shoes with a pair of deerskin moccasins, and he felt the jolt all the way up to his knee. The rat gave a rusty, ratcheting squeal, tumbled over and over in the dirt, and came to rest on its back. Eddie could see what looked like a dozen stubby mechanical legs pistoning up and down. Each was tipped with a sharp steel claw. These claws twirled around and around on gimbals the size of pencil-erasers.

A steel rod poked out of the robot's midsection and flipped the gadget upright again. Eddie brought Roland's revolver down, ignoring a momentary impulse to steady it with his free hand. That might be the way cops in his own world were taught to shoot, but it wasn't the way it was done here. *When you forget the gun is there, when it feels like you're shooting with your finger,* Roland had told them, *then you'll be somewhere near home.*

Eddie pulled the trigger. The tiny radar-dish, which had begun to turn again in an effort to find the enemies, disappeared in a blue flash. The rat made a choked noise—*Cloop!*—and fell dead on its side.

Eddie turned with his heart jackhammering in his chest. He couldn't remember being this furious since he realized that Roland meant to keep him in his world until his goddamned Tower was won or lost . . . probably until they were all worm-chow, in other words.

He levelled the empty gun at Roland's heart and spoke in a thick voice he hardly recognized as his own. "If there was a round left in this, you could stop worrying about your fucking Tower right now."

"Stop it, Eddie!" Susannah said sharply.

He looked at her. "It was going for *you*, Susannah, and it meant to turn you into ground chuck."

"But it didn't get me. *You* got *it*, Eddie. You got *it*."

"No thanks to him." Eddie made as if to re-holster

the gun and then realized, to his further disgust, that he had nothing to put it in. Susannah was wearing the holster. "Him and his lessons. Him and his goddam *lessons*." He turned to Roland. "I tell you, for two cents—"

Roland's mildly interested expression suddenly changed. His eyes shifted to a point over Eddie's left shoulder. *"DOWN!"* he shouted.

Eddie didn't ask questions. His rage and confusion were wiped from his mind immediately. He dropped, and as he did, he saw the gunslinger's left hand blur down to his side. *My God*, he thought, still falling, *he CAN'T be that fast, no one can be that fast, I'm not bad but Susannah makes me look slow and he makes Susannah look like a turtle trying to walk uphill on a piece of glass—*

Something passed just over his head, something that squealed at him in mechanical rage and pulled out a tuft of his hair. Then the gunslinger was shooting from the hip, three fast shots like thunder-cracks, and the squealing stopped. A creature which looked to Eddie like a large mechanical bat thudded to earth between the place where Eddie now lay and the one where Susannah knelt beside Roland. One of its jointed, rust-speckled wings thumped the ground once, weakly, as if angry at the missed chance, and then became still.

Roland crossed to Eddie, walking easy in his old sprung boots. He extended a hand. Eddie took it and let Roland help him to his feet. The wind had been knocked out of him and he found he couldn't talk. *Probably just as well . . . seems like every time I open my mouth I stick my goddam foot into it.*

"Eddie! You all right?" Susannah was crossing the clearing to where he stood with his head bent and his hands planted on his upper thighs, trying to breathe.

"Yeah." The word came out in a croak. He straightened up with an effort. "Just got a little haircut."

"It was in a tree," Roland said mildly. "I didn't see

it myself, at first. The light gets tricky this time of day." He paused and then went on in that same mild voice: "She was never in any danger, Eddie."

Eddie nodded his head. Roland, he now realized, could almost have eaten a hamburger and drunk a milkshake before beginning his draw. He was that fast.

"All right. Let's just say I disapprove of your teaching techniques, okay? I'm not going to apologize, though, so if you're waiting for one, you can stop now."

Roland bent, picked Susannah up, and began to brush her off. He did this with a kind of impartial affection, like a mother brushing off her toddler after she has taken one of her necessary tumbles in the dust of the back yard. "Your apology is not expected or necessary," he said. "Susannah and I had a conversation similar to this one two days ago. Didn't we, Susannah?"

She nodded. "Roland's of the opinion that apprentice gunslingers who won't bite the hand that feeds them from time to time need a good kick in the slats."

Eddie looked around at the wreckage and slowly began to beat the bone-dust out of his pants and shirt. "What if I told you I don't want to *be* a gunslinger, Roland old buddy?"

"I'd say that what you want doesn't much matter." Roland was looking at the metal kiosk which stood against the rock wall, and seemed to have lost interest in the conversation. Eddie had seen this before. When the conversation turned to questions of should-be, could-be, or oughtta-be, Roland almost always lost interest.

"*Ka?*" Eddie asked, with a trace of his old bitterness.

"That's right. *Ka.*" Roland walked over to the kiosk and passed a hand along the yellow and black stripes which ran down its front. "We have found one of the twelve portals which ring the edge of the world . . . one of the six paths to the Dark Tower.

"And that is also *ka*."

27

EDDIE WENT BACK FOR Susannah's wheelchair. No one had to ask him to do this; he wanted some time alone, to get himself back under control. Now that the shooting was over, every muscle in his body seemed to have picked up its own little thrumming tremor. He did not want either of them to see him this way—not because they might misread it as fear, but because one or both might know it for what it really was: excitement overload. He had liked it. Even when you added in the bat which had almost scalped him, he had liked it.

That's bullshit, buddy. And you know it.

The trouble was, he *didn't* know it. He had come face to face with something Susannah had found out for herself after shooting the bear: he could *talk* about how he didn't want to be a gunslinger, how he didn't want to be tramping around this crazy world where the three of them seemed to be the only human life, that what he really wanted more than anything else was to be standing on the corner of Broadway and Forty-second Street, popping his fingers, munching a chili-dog, and listening to Creedence Clearwater Revival blast out of his Walkman earphones as he watched the girls go by, those ultimately sexy New York girls with their pouty go-to-hell mouths and their long legs in short skirts. He could talk about those things until he was blue in the face, but his heart knew other things. It knew that he had *enjoyed* blowing the electronic menagerie back to glory, at least while the game was on and Roland's gun was his own private hand-held thunderstorm. He had *enjoyed* kicking the robot rat, even though it had hurt his foot and even though he had been scared shitless. In some weird way, that part—the being scared part—actually seemed to add to the enjoyment.

All that was bad enough, but his heart knew something even worse: that if a door leading back to New York appeared in front of him right now, he might not walk through it. Not, at least, until he had seen the Dark Tower for himself. He was beginning to believe that Roland's illness was a communicable disease.

As he wrestled Susannah's chair through the tangle of junk-alders, cursing the branches that whipped at his face and tried to poke his eyes out, Eddie found himself able to admit at least some of these things, and the admission cooled his blood a little. *I want to see if it looks the way it did in my dream,* he thought. *To see something like that . . . that would be really fantastic.*

And another voice spoke up inside. *I'll bet his other friends—the ones with the names that sound like they came straight from the Round Table in King Arthur's court—I'll bet they felt the same way, Eddie. And they're all dead. Every one of them.*

He recognized that voice, like it or not. It belonged to Henry, and that made it a hard voice not to hear.

28

ROLAND, WITH SUSANNAH BALANCED on his right hip, was standing in front of the metal box that looked like a subway entrance closed for the night. Eddie left the wheelchair at the edge of the clearing and walked over. As he did, the steady humming noise and the vibration under his feet became louder. The machinery making the noise, he realized, was either inside the box or under it. It seemed that he heard it not with his ears but somewhere deep inside his head, and in the hollows of his gut.

"So this is one of the twelve portals. Where does it go, Roland? Disney World?"

Roland shook his head. "I don't know where it goes. Maybe nowhere . . . or everywhere. There's a lot about my world I don't know—surely you both have realized that. And there are things I used to know which have changed."

"Because the world has moved on?"

"Yes." Roland glanced at him. "Here, that is not a figure of speech. The world really *is* moving on, and it goes ever faster. At the same time, things are wearing out . . . falling apart . . ." He kicked the mechanical corpse of the walking box to illustrate his point.

Eddie thought of the rough diagram of the portals which Roland had drawn in the dirt. "*Is* this the edge of the world?" he asked, almost timidly. "I mean, it doesn't look much different than anyplace else." He laughed a little. "If there's a drop-off, I don't see it."

Roland shook his head. "It's not that kind of edge. It's the place where one of the Beams starts. Or so I was taught."

"Beams?" Susannah asked. "What Beams?"

"The Great Old Ones didn't make the world, but they did *re*-make it. Some tale-tellers say the Beams saved it; others say they are the seeds of the world's destruction. The Great Old Ones created the Beams. They are lines of some sort . . . lines which *bind* . . . and *hold* . . ."

"Are you talking about magnetism?" Susannah asked cautiously.

His whole face lit up, transforming its harsh planes and furrows into something new and amazing, and for a moment Eddie knew how Roland would look if he actually *did* reach his Tower.

"Yes! Not *just* magnetism, but that is a part of it . . . and gravity . . . and the proper alignment of space, size, and dimension. The Beams are the forces which bind these things together."

"Welcome to physics in the nuthouse," Eddie said in a low voice.

Susannah ignored this. "And the Dark Tower? Is it some kind of generator? A central power-source for these Beams?"

"I don't know."

"But you *do* know that this is point A," Eddie said. "If we walked long enough in a straight line, we'd come to another portal—call it point C—on the other edge of the world. But before we did, we'd come to point B. The center-point. The Dark Tower."

The gunslinger nodded.

"How long a trip is it? Do you know?"

"No. But I know it's very far, and that the distance grows with every day that passes."

Eddie had bent to examine the walking box. Now he straightened up and stared at Roland. "That can't be." He sounded like a man trying to explain to a small child that there really isn't a boogeyman living in his closet, that there *can't* be because there isn't any such thing as the boogeyman, not really. "Worlds don't *grow*, Roland."

"Don't they? When I was a boy, Eddie, there were maps. I remember one in particular. It was called The Greater Kingdoms of the Western Earth. It showed my land, which was called by the name Gilead. It showed the Downland Baronies, which were overrun by riot and civil war in the year after I won my guns, and the hills, and the desert, and the mountains, and the Western Sea. It was a long distance from Gilead to the Western Sea—a thousand miles or more—*but it had taken me over twenty years to cross that distance.*"

"That's impossible," Susannah said quickly, fearfully. "Even if you *walked* the whole distance it couldn't take twenty years."

"Well, you have to allow for stops to write postcards and drink beer," Eddie said, but they both ignored him.

"I didn't walk but rode most of the distance on horseback," Roland said. "I was—slowed up, shall we say?—every now and then, but for most of that time I was moving. Moving away from John Farson, who led the revolt which toppled the world I grew up in and who wanted my head on a pole in his courtyard— he had good reason to want that, I suppose, since I and my compatriots were responsible for the deaths of a great many of his followers—and because I stole something he held very dear."

"What, Roland?" Eddie asked curiously.

Roland shook his head. "That's a story for another day . . . or maybe never. For now, think not of that but of this: I've come *many* thousands of miles. Because the world is growing."

"A thing like that just can't happen," Eddie reiterated, but he was badly shaken, all the same. "There'd be earthquakes . . . floods . . . tidal waves . . . I don't know what all . . ."

"Look!" Roland said furiously. "Just look around you! What do you see? A world that is slowing down like a child's top even as it speeds up and moves on in some other way none of us understand. Look at your kills, Eddie! Look at your kills, for your father's sake!"

He took two strides toward the stream, picked up the steel snake, examined it briefly, and tossed it to Eddie, who caught it with his left hand. The snake broke in two pieces as he did so.

"You see? It's exhausted. *All* the creatures we found here were exhausted. If we hadn't come, they would have died before long, anyway. Just as the bear would have died."

"The bear had some sort of disease," Susannah said.

The gunslinger nodded. "Parasites which attacked the natural parts of its body. But why did they never attack it before?"

Susannah did not reply.

Eddie was examining the snake. Unlike the bear, it appeared to be a totally artificial construction, a thing of metal, circuits, and yards (or maybe *miles*) of gossamer-thin wire. Yet he could see flecks of rust, not just on the surface of the half-snake he still held, but in its guts as well. And there was a patch of wetness where either oil had leaked out or water had seeped in. This moisture had rotted away some of the wires, and a greenish stuff that looked like moss had grown over several of the thumbnail-sized circuit boards.

Eddie turned the snake over. A steel plate proclaimed it to be the work of North Central Positronics, Ltd. There was a serial number, but no name. *Probably too unimportant to name*, he thought. *Just a sophisticated mechanical Roto-Rooter designed to give old Br'er Bear an enema every once in a while, keep him regular, or something equally disgusting.*

He dropped the snake and wiped his hands on his pants.

Roland had picked up the tractor-gadget. He yanked at one of the treads. It came off easily, showering a cloud of rust down between his boots. He tossed it aside.

"Everything in the world is either coming to rest or falling to pieces," he said flatly. "At the same time, the forces which interlock and give the world its coherence—in time and size as well as in space—are weakening. We knew that even as children, but we had no idea what the time of the end would be like. How could we? Yet now I am living in those times, and I don't believe they affect my world alone. They affect yours, Eddie and Susannah; they may affect a billion others. The Beams are breaking down. I don't know if that's a cause or only another symptom, but I know it's true. Come! Draw close! Listen!"

As Eddie approached the metal box with its alternating diagonal slashes of yellow and black, a strong and unpleasant memory seized him—for the first time in years he found himself thinking of a crumbling Victorian wreck in Dutch Hill, about a mile away from the neighborhood he and Henry had grown up in. This wreck, which was known as The Mansion to the neighborhood kids, occupied a plot of weedy, untended lawn on Rhinehold Street. Eddie guessed that practically all the kids in the borough had heard spooky stories about The Mansion. The house stood slumped beneath its steep roofs, seeming to glare at passersby from the deep shadows thrown by its eaves. The windows were gone, of course—kids can throw rocks through windows without getting too close to a place—but it had not been spray-painted, and it had not become a makeout spot or a shooting gallery. Oddest of all was the simple fact of its continued existence: no one had set it on fire to collect the insurance or just to see it burn. The kids said it was haunted, of course, and as Eddie stood on the sidewalk with Henry one day, looking at it (they had made the pilgrimage specifically to see this object of fabulous rumor, although Henry had told their mother they were only going for Hoodsie Rockets at Dahlberg's with some of his friends), it had seemed that it really *might* be haunted. Hadn't he felt some strong and unfriendly force seeping from that old Victorian's shadowy windows, windows that seemed to look at him with the fixed stare of a dangerous lunatic? Hadn't he felt some subtle wind stirring the hairs on his arms and the back of his neck? Hadn't he had the clear intuition that if he stepped inside that place, the door would slam and lock behind him and the walls would begin to close in, grinding the bones of dead mice to powder, wanting to crush *his* bones the same way?

Haunting. Haunted.

He felt that same old sense of mystery and danger now, as he approached the metal box. Gooseflesh began to ripple up his legs and down his arms; the hair on the back of his neck bushed out and became rough, overlapping hackles. He felt that same subtle wind blowing past him, although the leaves on the trees which ringed the clearing were perfectly still.

Yet he walked toward the door anyway (for that was

what it was, of course, another door, although this one
was locked and always would be against the likes of
him), not stopping until his ear was pressed against it.

It was as if he had dropped a tab of really strong
acid half an hour ago and it was just beginning to
come on heavy. Strange colors flowed across the darkness behind his eyeballs. He seemed to hear voices
murmuring up to him from long hallways like stone
throats, halls which were lit with guttering electric
torches. Once these flambeaux of the modern age had
thrown a bright glare across everything, but now they
were only sullen cores of blue light. He sensed emptiness . . . desertion . . . desolation . . . death.

The machinery rumbled on and on, but wasn't there
a rough undertone to the sound? A kind of desperate
thudding beneath the hum, like the arrhythmia of a
diseased heart? A feeling that the machinery producing this sound, although far more sophisticated even
than that within the bear had been, was somehow falling out of tune with itself?

"All is silent in the halls of the dead," Eddie heard
himself whisper in a falling, fainting voice. "All is forgotten in the stone halls of the dead. Behold the stairways which stand in darkness; behold the rooms of
ruin. These are the halls of the dead where the spiders
spin and the great circuits fall quiet, one by one."

Roland pulled him roughly back, and Eddie looked
at him with dazed eyes.

"That's enough," Roland said.

"Whatever they put in there isn't doing so well, is
it?" Eddie heard himself ask. His trembling voice
seemed to come from far away. He could still feel the
power coming out of that box. It called to him.

"No. Nothing in my world is doing so well these days."

"If you boys are planning to camp here for the
night, you'll have to do without the pleasure of my
company," Susannah said. Her face was a white blur
in the ashy aftermath of twilight. "I'm going over yonder. I don't like the way that thing makes me feel."

"We'll *all* camp over yonder," Roland said. "Let's go."

"What a good idea," Eddie said. As they moved away from the box, the sound of the machinery began to dim. Eddie felt its hold on him weakening, although it still called to him, invited him to explore the half-lit hallways, the standing stairways, the rooms of ruin where the spiders spun and the control panels were going dark, one by one.

29

IN HIS DREAM THAT night, Eddie again went walking down Second Avenue toward Tom and Gerry's Artistic Deli on the corner of Second and Forty-sixth. He passed a record store and the Rolling Stones boomed from the speakers:

> *"I see a red door and I want to paint it black,*
> *No colours anymore, I want them to turn black,*
> *I see the girls walk by dressed in their summer*
> *clothes,*
> *I have to turn my head until my darkness goes . . ."*

He walked on, passing a store called Reflections of You between Forty-ninth and Forty-eighth. He saw himself in one of the mirrors hanging in the display window. He thought he looked better than he had in years—hair a little too long, but otherwise tanned and fit. The clothes, though . . . uh-uh, man. Square-bear shit all the way. Blue blazer, white shirt, dark red tie, gray dress pants . . . he had never owned a yuppie-from-hell outfit like that in his life.

Someone was shaking him.

Eddie tried to burrow deeper into the dream. He didn't want to wake up now. Not before he got to the deli and used his key to go through the door and into the field of roses. He wanted to see it all again—the endless blanket of red, the overarching blue sky where those great white cloud-ships sailed, and the Dark Tower. He was afraid of the darkness which lived within that eldritch column, waiting to eat anyone who got too close, but he wanted to see it again just the same. *Needed* to see it.

The hand, however, would not stop shaking. The dream began to darken, and the smells of car exhaust along Second Avenue became the smell of wood-smoke—thin now, because the fire was almost out.

It was Susannah. She looked scared. Eddie sat up and put an arm around her. They had camped on the far side of the alder grove, within earshot of the stream babbling through the bone-littered clearing. On the other side of the glowing embers which had been their campfire, Roland lay asleep. His sleep was not easy. He had cast aside his single blanket and lay with his knees drawn up almost to his chest. With his boots off, his feet looked white and narrow and defenseless. The great toe of the right foot was gone, victim of the lobster-thing which had also snatched away part of his right hand.

He was moaning some slurred phrase over and over again. After a few repetitions, Eddie realized it was the phrase he had spoken before keeling over in the clearing where Susannah had shot the bear: *Go, then—there are other worlds than these.* He would fall silent for a moment, then call out the boy's name: "Jake! Where are you? *Jake!*"

The desolation and despair in his voice filled Eddie with horror. His arms stole around Susannah and he pulled her tight against him. He could feel her shivering, although the night was warm.

The gunslinger rolled over. Starlight fell into his open eyes.

"Jake, where are you?" he called to the night. *"Come back!"*

"Oh Jesus—he's off again. What should we do, Suze?"

"I don't know. I just knew I couldn't listen to it

anymore by myself. He sounds so far away. So far away from everything."

"Go, then," the gunslinger murmured, rolling back onto his side and drawing his knees up once more, "there are other worlds than these." He was silent for a moment. Then his chest hitched and he loosed the boy's name in a long, bloodcurdling cry. In the woods behind them, some large bird flew away in a dry whirr of wings toward some less exciting part of the world.

"Do you have any ideas?" Susannah asked. Her eyes were wide and wet with tears. "Maybe we should wake him up?"

"I don't know." Eddie saw the gunslinger's revolver, the one he wore on his left hip. It had been placed, in its holster, on a neatly folded square of hide within easy reach of the place where Roland lay. "I don't think I dare," he added at last.

"It's driving him crazy."

Eddie nodded.

"What do we do about it? Eddie, *what do we do?*"

Eddie didn't know. An antibiotic had stopped the infection caused by the bite of the lobster-thing; now Roland was burning with infection again, but Eddie didn't think there was an antibiotic in the world that would cure what was wrong with him this time.

"I don't know. Lie down with me, Suze."

Eddie threw a hide over both of them, and after a while her trembling quieted.

"If he goes insane, he may hurt us," she said.

"Don't I know it." This unpleasant idea had occurred to him in terms of the bear—its red, hate-filled eyes (and had there not been bewilderment as well, lurking deep in those red depths?) and its deadly slashing claws. Eddie's eyes moved to the revolver, lying so close to the gunslinger's good left hand, and he remembered again how fast Roland had been when he'd seen the mechanical bat swooping down toward them. So fast his hand had seemed to disappear. If the gunslinger went mad, and if he and Susannah became the focus of that madness, they would have no chance. No chance at all.

He pressed his face into the warm hollow of Susannah's neck and closed his eyes.

Not long after, Roland ceased his babbling. Eddie raised his head and looked over. The gunslinger appeared to be sleeping naturally again. Eddie looked at Susannah and saw that she had also gone to sleep. He lay down beside her, gently kissed the swell of her breast, and closed his own eyes.

Not you, buddy; you're gonna be awake a long, long *time.*

But they had been on the move for two days and Eddie was bone-tired. He drifted off . . . drifted down.

Back to the dream, he thought as he went. *I want to go back to Second Avenue . . . back to Tom and Gerry's. That's what I want.*

The dream did not return that night, however.

30

THEY ATE A QUICK breakfast as the sun came up, repacked and redistributed the gear, and then returned to the wedge-shaped clearing. It didn't look quite so spooky in the clear light of morning, but all three of them were still at pains to keep well away from the metal box with its warning slashes of black and yellow. If Roland had any recollection of the bad dreams which had haunted him in the night, he gave no sign. He had gone about the morning chores as he always did, in thoughtful, stolid silence.

"How do you plan to keep to a straight-line course from here?" Susannah asked the gunslinger.

"If the legends are right, that should be no problem. Do you remember when you asked about magnetism?"

She nodded.

He rummaged deep into his purse and at last

emerged with a small square of old, supple leather. Threaded through it was a long silver needle.

"A compass!" Eddie said. "You really *are* an Eagle Scout!"

Roland shook his head. "Not a compass. I know what they are, of course, but these days I keep my directions by the sun and stars, and even now they serve me quite well."

"*Even now?*" Susannah asked, a trifle uneasily.

He nodded. "The directions of the world are also in drift."

"*Christ,*" Eddie said. He tried to imagine a world where true north was slipping slyly off to the east or west and gave up almost at once. It made him feel a little ill, the way looking down from the top of a high building had always made him feel a little ill.

"This is just a needle, but it *is* steel and it should serve our purpose as well as a compass. The Beam is our course now, and the needle will show it." He rummaged in his purse again and came out with a poorly made pottery cup. A crack ran down one side. Roland had mended this artifact, which he had found at the old campsite, with pine-gum. Now he went to the stream, dipped the cup into it, and brought it back to where Susannah sat in her wheelchair. He put the cup down carefully on the wheelchair's arm, and when the surface of the water inside was calm, he dropped the needle in. It sank to the bottom and rested there.

"Wow!" Eddie said. "Great! I'd fall at your feet in wonder, Roland, but I don't want to spoil the crease in my pants."

"I'm not finished. Hold the cup steady, Susannah."

She did, and Roland pushed her slowly across the clearing. When she was about twelve feet in front of the door, he turned the chair carefully so she was facing away from it.

"Eddie!" she cried. "Look at this!"

He bent over the pottery cup, marginally aware that water was already oozing through Roland's makeshift seal. The needle was rising slowly to the surface. It reached it and bobbed there as serenely as a cork would have done. Its direction lay in a straight line from the portal behind them and into the old, tangled forest ahead. "Holy shit—a floating needle. Now I really *have* seen everything."

"Hold the cup, Susannah."

She held it steady as Roland pushed the wheelchair further into the clearing, at right angles to the box. The needle lost its steady point, bobbed randomly for a moment, then sank to the bottom of the cup again. When Roland pulled the chair backward to its former spot, it rose once more and pointed the way.

"If we had iron filings and a sheet of paper," the gunslinger said, "we could scatter the filings on the paper's surface and watch them draw together into a line which would point that same course."

"Will that happen even when we leave the Portal?" Eddie asked.

Roland nodded. "Nor is that all. We can actually *see* the Beam."

Susannah looked over her shoulder. Her elbow bumped the cup a little as she did. The needle swung aimlessly as the water inside sloshed . . . and then settled firmly back in its original direction.

"Not that way," Roland said. "Look down, both of you—Eddie at your feet, Susannah into your lap."

They did as he asked.

"When I tell you to look up, look straight ahead, in the direction the needle points. Don't look at any one thing; let your eye see whatever it will. Now—look up!"

They did. For a moment Eddie saw nothing but the woods. He tried to make his eyes relax . . . and suddenly it was there, the way the shape of the slingshot had been there, inside the knob of wood, and he knew why Roland had told them not to look at any one thing. The effect of the Beam was everywhere along its course, but it was subtle. The needles of the pines and spruces pointed that way. The greenberry bushes grew slightly slanted, and the slant lay in the direction of the Beam. Not all the trees the bear had pushed down to clear its sightlines had fallen along that camouflaged path—which ran southeast, if Eddie had his directions right—but most had, as if the force coming out of the box had *pushed* them that way as they tottered. The clearest evidence was in the way the shadows lay on the ground. With the sun coming up in the east they all pointed west, of course, but as Eddie looked southeast, he saw a rough herringbone pattern that existed only along the line which the needle in the cup had pointed out.

"I might see *something*," Susannah said doubtfully, "but—"

"Look at the shadows! The *shadows*, Suze!"

Eddie saw her eyes widen as it all fell into place for her. "My God! It's there! *Right there!* It's like when someone has a natural part in their hair!"

Now that Eddie had seen it, he could not unsee it; a dim aisle driving through the untidy tangle which surrounded the clearing, a straight-edge course that was the way of the Beam. He was suddenly aware of how huge the force flowing around him (and probably right through him, like X-rays) must be, and had to control an urge to step away, either to the right or left. "Say, Roland, this won't make me sterile, will it?"

Roland shrugged, smiling faintly.

"It's like a riverbed," Susannah marvelled. "A riverbed so overgrown you can barely see it . . . but it's still there. The pattern of shadows will never change as long as we stay inside the path of the Beam, will it?"

"No," Roland said. "They'll change direction as the sun moves across the sky, of course, but we'll always be able to see the course of the Beam. You must remember that it has been flowing along this same path for thousands—perhaps *tens* of thousands—of years. Look up, you two, into the sky!"

They did, and saw that the thin cirrus clouds had also picked up that herringbone pattern along the course of the Beam . . . and those clouds within the alley of its power were flowing faster than those to either side. They were being pushed southeast. Being pushed in the direction of the Dark Tower.

"You see? Even the clouds must obey."

A small flock of birds coursed toward them. As they reached the path of the Beam, they were all deflected toward the southeast for a moment. Although Eddie clearly saw this happen, his eyes could hardly credit it. When the birds had crossed the narrow corridor of the Beam's influence, they resumed their former course.

"Well," Eddie said, "I suppose we ought to get going. A journey of a thousand miles begins with a single step, and all that shit."

"Wait a minute." Susannah was looking at Roland. "It *isn't* just a thousand miles, is it? Not anymore. How far *are* we talking about, Roland? Five thousand miles? Ten?"

"I can't say. It will be very far."

"Well, how in the hell we ever goan get there, with you two pushing me in this goddam wheelchair? We'll be lucky to make three miles a day through yonder Drawers, and you know it."

"The way has been opened," Roland said patiently, "and that's enough for now. The time may come, Susannah Dean, when we travel faster than you would like."

"Oh yeah?" She looked at him truculently, and both men could see Detta Walker dancing a dangerous hornpipe in her eyes again. "You got a race-car lined up? If you do, it might be nice if we had a damn road to run it on!"

"The land and the way we travel on it will change. It always does."

Susannah flapped a hand at the gunslinger; *go on with you*, it said. "You sound like my old mamma, sayin God will provide."

"Hasn't He?" Roland asked gravely.

She looked at him for a moment in silent surprise, then threw her head back and laughed at the sky. "Well,

I guess that depends on how you look at it. All I can say is that if this is providin, Roland, I'd hate to see what'd happen if He decided to let us go hungry."

"Come on, let's do it," Eddie said. "I want to get out of this place. I don't like it." And that was true, but that wasn't all. He also felt a deep eagerness to set his feet upon that concealed path, that highway in hiding. Every step was a step closer to the field of roses and the Tower which dominated it. He realized—not without some wonder—that he meant to see that Tower . . . or die trying.

Congratulations, Roland, he thought. *You've done it. I'm one of the converted. Someone say hallelujah.*

"There's one other thing before we go." Roland bent and untied the rawhide lace around his left thigh. Then he slowly began to unbuckle his gunbelt.

"What's this jive?" Eddie asked.

Roland pulled the gunbelt free and held it out to him. "You know why I'm doing this," he said calmly.

"Put it back on, man!" Eddie felt a terrible stew of conflicting emotions roiling inside him; could feel his fingers trembling even inside his clenched fists. "What do you think you're *doing*?"

"Losing my mind an inch at a time. Until the wound inside me closes—if it ever does—I am not fit to wear this. And you know it."

"Take it, Eddie," Susannah said quietly.

"If you hadn't been wearing this goddamn thing last night, when that bat came at me, I'd be gone from the nose up this morning!"

The gunslinger replied by continuing to hold his remaining gun out to Eddie. The posture of his body said he was prepared to stand that way all day, if that was what it took.

"All right!" Eddie cried. "Goddammit, all *right*!"

He snatched the gunbelt from Roland's hand and buckled it about his own waist in a series of rough gestures. He should have been relieved, he supposed—hadn't he looked at this gun, lying so close to

Roland's hand in the middle of the night, and thought about what might happen if Roland really *did* go over the high side? Hadn't he and Susannah both thought about it? But there was no relief. Only fear and guilt and a strange, aching sadness far too deep for tears.

He looked so strange without his guns.

So *wrong.*

"Okay? Now that the numb-fuck apprentices have the guns and the master's unarmed, can we please go? If something big comes out of the bush at us, Roland, you can always throw your knife at it."

"Oh, that," he murmured. "I almost forgot." He took the knife from his purse and held it out, hilt first, to Eddie.

"This is *ridiculous*!" Eddie shouted.

"*Life* is ridiculous."

"Yeah, put it on a postcard and send it to the fucking *Reader's Digest.*" Eddie jammed the knife into his belt and then looked defiantly at Roland. "*Now* can we go?"

"There *is* one more thing," Roland said.

"Weeping, creeping *Jesus*!"

The smile touched Roland's mouth again. "Just joking," he said.

Eddie's mouth dropped open. Beside him, Susannah began to laugh again. The sound rose, as musical as bells, in the morning stillness.

31

IT TOOK THEM MOST of the morning to clear the zone of destruction with which the great bear had protected itself, but the going was a little easier along the path of the Beam, and once they had put the deadfalls and tangles of underbrush behind them, deep forest took over again and they were able to move at better speed. The brook which had emerged from the rock wall in the clearing ran busily along to their right. It had been joined by several smaller streamlets, and its sound was deeper now. There were more animals here—they heard them moving through the woods, going about their daily round—and twice they saw small groups of deer. One of them, a buck with a noble rack of antlers on its upraised and questioning head, looked to be at least three hundred pounds. The brook bent away from their path as they began to climb again. And, as the afternoon began to slant down toward evening, Eddie saw something.

"Could we stop here? Rest a minute?"

"What is it?" Susannah asked.

"Yes," Roland said. "We can stop."

Suddenly Eddie felt Henry's presence again, like a weight settling on his shoulders. *Oh lookit the sissy. Does the sissy see something in the twee? Does the sissy want to carve something? Does he? Ohhhh, ain't that CUTE?*

"We don't *have* to stop. I mean, no big deal. I just—"

"—saw something," Roland finished for him. "Whatever it is, stop running your everlasting mouth and get it."

"It's really nothing." Eddie felt warm blood mount into his face. He tried to look away from the ash tree which had caught his eye.

"But it is. It's something you need, and that's a long way from nothing. If *you* need it, Eddie, *we* need it. What we don't need is a man who can't let go of the useless baggage of his memories."

The warm blood turned hot. Eddie stood with his flaming face pointed at his moccasins for a moment longer, feeling as if Roland had looked directly into his confused heart with his faded blue bombardier's eyes.

"Eddie?" Susannah asked curiously. "What is it, dear?"

Her voice gave him the courage he needed. He walked to the slim, straight ash, pulling Roland's knife from his belt.

"Maybe nothing," he muttered, and then forced himself to add: "Maybe a lot. If I don't fuck it up, maybe quite a lot."

"The ash is a noble tree, and full of power," Roland remarked from behind him, but Eddie barely heard. Henry's sneering, hectoring voice was gone; his shame was gone with it. He thought only of the one branch that had caught his eye. It thickened and bulged slightly as it ran into the trunk. It was this oddly shaped thickness that Eddie wanted.

He thought the shape of the key was buried within it—the key he had seen briefly in the fire before the burning remains of the jawbone had changed again and the rose had appeared. Three inverted V's, the center V both deeper and wider than the other two. And the little *s*-shape at the end. That was the secret.

A breath of his dream recurred: *Dad-a-chum, dud-a-chee, not to worry, you've got the key.*

Maybe, he thought. *But this time I'll have to get all of it. I think that this time ninety per cent just won't do.*

Working with great care, he cut the branch from the tree and then trimmed the narrow end. He was left with a fat chunk of ash about nine inches long. It felt heavy and vital in his hand, very much alive and willing enough to give up its secret shape . . . to a man skillful enough to tease it out, that was.

Was he that man? And did it matter?

Eddie Dean thought the answer to both questions was yes.

The gunslinger's good left hand closed over Eddie's right hand. "I think you know a secret."

"Maybe I do."

"Can you tell?"

He shook his head. "Better not to, I think. Not yet."

Roland thought this over, then nodded. "All right. I want to ask you one question, and then we'll drop the subject. Have you perhaps seen some way into the heart of my . . . my problem?"

Eddie thought: *And that's as close as he'll ever come to showing the desperation that's eating him alive.*

"I don't know. Right now I can't tell for sure. But I hope so, man. I really, really do."

Roland nodded again and released Eddie's hand. "I thank you. We still have two hours of good daylight— why don't we make use of them?"

"Fine by me."

They moved on. Roland pushed Susannah and Eddie walked ahead of them, holding the chunk of wood with the key buried in it. It seemed to throb with its own warmth, secret and powerful.

32

THAT NIGHT, AFTER SUPPER was eaten, Eddie took the gunslinger's knife from his belt and began to carve. The knife was amazingly sharp, and seemed never to lose its edge. Eddie worked slowly and carefully in the firelight, turning the chunk of ash this way and that in his hands, watching the curls of fine-grained wood rise ahead of his long, sure strokes.

Susannah lay down, laced her hands behind her head, and looked up at the stars wheeling slowly across the black sky.

At the edge of the campsite, Roland stood beyond the glow of the fire and listened as the voices of madness rose once more in his aching, confused mind.

There was a boy.

There was no boy.

Was.

Wasn't.

Was—

He closed his eyes, cupped his aching forehead in one cold hand, and wondered how long it would be until he simply snapped like an overwound bowstring.

Oh Jake, he thought. *Where are you? Where are you?*

And above the three of them, Old Star and Old Mother rose into their appointed places and stared at each other across the starry ruins of their ancient broken marriage.

II ▪ KEY AND ROSE

▪ II ▪

KEY AND ROSE

1

FOR THREE WEEKS JOHN "Jake" Chambers fought bravely against the madness rising inside him. During that time he felt like the last man aboard a foundering ocean liner, working the bilge-pumps for dear life, trying to keep the ship afloat until the storm ended, the skies cleared, and help could arrive . . . help from somewhere. Help from *anywhere*. On May 31st, 1977, four days before school ended for the summer, he finally faced up to the fact that no help was going to come. It was time to give up; time to let the storm carry him away.

The straw that broke the camel's back was his Final Essay in English Comp.

John Chambers, who was Jake to the three or four boys who were almost his friends (if his father had known this little factoid, he undoubtedly would have hit the roof), was finishing his first year at The Piper

School. Although he was eleven and in the sixth grade, he was small for his age, and people meeting him for the first time often thought he was much younger. In fact, he had sometimes been mistaken for a girl until a year or so ago, when he had made such a fuss about having his hair cut short that his mother had finally relented and allowed it. With his father, of course, there had been no problem about the haircut. His father had just grinned his hard, stainless steel grin and said, *The kid wants to look like a Marine, Laurie. Good for him.*

To his father, he was never Jake and rarely John. To his father, he was usually just "the kid."

The Piper School, his father had explained to him the summer before (the Bicentennial Summer, that had been—all bunting and flags and New York Harbor filled with Tall Ships), was, quite simply, The Best Damned School In The Country For A Boy Your Age. The fact that Jake had been accepted there had nothing to do with money, Elmer Chambers explained . . . almost *insisted*. He had been savagely proud of this fact, although, even at ten, Jake had suspected it might not be a *true* fact, that it might really be a bunch of bullshit his father had turned *into* a fact so he could casually drop it into the conversation at lunch or over cocktails: *My kid? Oh, he's going to Piper. Best Damned School In The Country For A Boy His Age. Money won't buy you into that school, you know; for Piper, it's brains or nothing.*

Jake was perfectly aware that in the fierce furnace of Elmer Chambers's mind, the gross carbon of wish and opinion was often blasted into the hard diamonds which he called facts . . . or, in more informal circumstances, "factoids." His favorite phrase, spoken often and with reverence, was *The fact is*, and he used it every chance he got.

The fact is, money doesn't get anyone *into The Piper School*, his father had told him during that Bicentennial Summer, the summer of blue skies and bunting and Tall Ships, a summer which seemed golden in Jake's memory because he had not yet begun to lose his mind and all he had to worry about was whether or not he could cut the mustard at The Piper School, which sounded like a nest for newly hatched geniuses. *The only thing that gets you into a place like Piper is what you've got up here.* Elmer Chambers had reached over his desk and tapped the center of his son's forehead with a hard, nicotine-stained finger. *Get me, kid?*

Jake had nodded. It wasn't necessary to talk to his father, because his father treated everyone—including his wife—the way he treated his underlings at the TV network where he was in charge of programming and an acknowledged master of The Kill. All you had to do was listen, nod in the right places, and after a while he let you go.

Good, his father said, lighting one of the eighty Camel cigarettes he smoked each and every day. *We understand each other, then. You're going to have to work your buttsky off, but you can cut it. They never would have sent us this if you couldn't.* He picked up the letter of acceptance from The Piper School and rattled it. There was a kind of savage triumph in the gesture, as if the letter was an animal he had killed in the jungle, an animal he would now skin and eat. *So work hard. Make your grades. Make your mother and me proud of you. If you end the year with an A average in your courses, there's a trip to Disney World in it for you. That's something to shoot for, right, kiddo?*

Jake had made his grades—A's in everything (until the last three weeks, that was). He had, presumably, made his mother and father proud of him, although they were around so little that it was hard to tell. Usually there was *nobody* around when he came home from school except for Greta Shaw—the house-keeper—and so he ended up showing his A papers to her. After that, they migrated to a dark corner of his room. Sometimes Jake looked through them and wondered if they meant anything. He *wanted* them to, but he had serious doubts.

Jake didn't think he would be going to Disney World this summer, A average or no A average.

He thought the nuthouse was a much better possibility.

As he walked in through the double doors of The Piper School at 8:45 on the morning of May 31st, a terrible vision came to him. He saw his father in his office at 70 Rockefeller Plaza, leaning over his desk with a Camel jutting from the corner of his mouth, talking to one of his underlings as blue smoke wreathed his head. All of New York was spread out behind and below his father, its thump and hustle silenced by two layers of Thermopane glass.

The fact is, money doesn't get anyone *into Sunnyvale Sanitarium*, his father was telling the underling in a tone of grim satisfaction. He reached out and tapped the underling's forehead. *The only thing that gets you into a place like that is when something big-time goes wrong up here in the attic. That's what happened to the kid. But he's working his goddam buttsky off. Makes the best fucking baskets in the place, they tell me. And when they let him out—if they ever do—there's a trip in it for him. A trip to—*

"—the way station," Jake muttered, then touched his forehead with a hand that wanted to tremble. The voices were coming back. The yelling, conflicting voices which were driving him mad.

You're dead, Jake. You were run over by a car and you're dead.

Don't be stupid! Look—see that poster? REMEMBER THE CLASS ONE PICNIC, *it says. Do you think they have Class Picnics in the afterlife?*

I don't know. But I know you were run over by a car.

No!

Yes. It happened on May 9th, at 8:25 A.M. You died less than a minute later.

No! No! No!

"John?"

He looked around, badly startled. Mr. Bissette, his French teacher, was standing there, looking a little concerned. Behind him, the rest of the student body was streaming into the Common Room for the morning assembly. There was very little skylarking, and no yelling at all. Presumably these other students, like Jake himself, had been told by their parents how lucky they were to be attending Piper, where money didn't matter (although tuition was $22,000 a year), only your brains. Presumably many of them had been promised trips this summer if their grades were good enough. Presumably the parents of the lucky trip-winners would even go along in some cases. Presumably—

"John, are you okay?" Mr. Bissette asked.

"Sure," Jake said. "Fine. I overslept a little this morning. Not awake yet, I guess."

Mr. Bissette's face relaxed and he smiled. "Happens to the best of us."

Not to my dad. The master of The Kill never oversleeps.

"Are you ready for your French final?" Mr. Bissette asked. *"Voulez-vous faire l'examen cet après-midi?"*

"I think so," Jake said. In truth he didn't know if he was ready for the exam or not. He couldn't even remember if he had *studied* for the French final or not. These days nothing seemed to matter much except for the voices in his head.

"I want to tell you again how much I enjoyed having you this year, John. I wanted to tell your folks, too, but they missed Parents' Night—"

"They're pretty busy," Jake said.

Mr. Bissette nodded. "Well, I have enjoyed you. I just wanted to say so . . . and that I'm looking forward to having you back for French II next year."

"Thanks," Jake said, and wondered what Mr. Bissette would say if he added, *But I don't think I'll be taking French II next year, unless I can get a correspondence course delivered to my postal box at good old Sunnyvale.*

Joanne Franks, the school secretary, appeared in the doorway of the Common Room with her small silver-plated bell in her hand. At The Piper School, *all* bells were rung by hand. Jake supposed that if you were a parent, that was one of its charms. Memories of the Little Red Schoolhouse and all that. He hated it himself. The sound of that bell seemed to go right through his head—

I can't hold on much longer, he thought despairingly. *I'm sorry, but I'm losing it. I'm really, really losing it.*

Mr. Bissette had caught sight of Ms. Franks. He turned away, then turned back again. "*Is* everything all right, John? You've seemed preoccupied these last few weeks. Troubled. Is something on your mind?"

Jake was almost undone by the kindness in Mr. Bissette's voice, but then he imagined how Mr. Bissette would look if he said: *Yes. Something is on my mind. One hell of a nasty little factoid. I died, you see, and I went into another world. And then I died again. You're going to say that stuff like that doesn't happen, and of course you're right, and part of my mind* knows *you're right, but most of my mind knows that you're wrong. It* did *happen. I* did *die.*

If he said something like that, Mr. Bissette would be on the phone to Elmer Chambers at once, and Jake thought that Sunnyvale Sanitarium would probably look like a rest-cure after all the stuff his father would have to say on the subject of kids who started having crazy notions just before Finals Week. Kids who did things that couldn't be discussed over lunch or cocktails. Kids Who Let Down The Side.

Jake forced himself to smile at Mr. Bissette. "I'm a little worried about exams, that's all."

Mr. Bissette winked. "You'll do fine."

Ms. Franks began to ring the Assembly Bell. Each peal stabbed into Jake's ears and then seemed to flash across his brain like a small rocket.

"Come on," Mr. Bissette said. "We'll be late. Can't be late on the first day of Finals Week, can we?"

They went in past Ms. Franks and her clashing bell. Mr. Bissette headed toward the row of seats called Faculty Choir. There were lots of cute names like that at Piper School; the auditorium was the Common Room, lunch-hour was Outs, seventh- and eighth-graders were Upper Boys and Girls, and, of course, the folding chairs over by the piano (which Ms. Franks would soon begin to pound as mercilessly as she rang her silver bell) was Faculty Choir. All part of the tradition, Jake supposed. If you were a parent who knew your kid had Outs in the Common Room at noon instead of just slopping up Tuna Surprise in the caff, you relaxed into the assurance that everything was A-OK in the education department.

He slipped into a seat at the rear of the room and let the morning's announcements wash over him. The terror ran endlessly on in his mind, making him feel like a rat trapped on an exercise wheel. And when he tried to look ahead to some better, brighter time, he could see only darkness.

The ship was his sanity, and it was sinking.

Mr. Harley, the headmaster, approached the podium and imparted a brief exordium about the importance of Finals Week, and how the grades they received would constitute another step upon The Great Road of Life. He told them that the school was depending on them, *he* was depending on them, and their parents were depending on them. He did not tell them that the entire free world was depending on them, but he strongly implied that this might be so.

He finished by telling them that bells would be suspended during Finals Week (the first and only piece of good news Jake had received that morning).

Ms. Franks, who had assumed her seat at the piano, struck an invocatory chord. The student body, seventy boys and fifty girls, each turned out in a neat and sober way that bespoke their parents' taste and financial stability, rose as one and began to sing the school song. Jake mouthed the words and thought about the place where he had awakened after dying. At first he had believed himself to be in hell . . . and when the man in the black hooded robe came along, he had been sure of it.

Then, of course, the other man had come along. A man Jake had almost come to love.

But he let me fall. He killed me.

He could feel prickly sweat breaking out on the back of his neck and between his shoulderblades.

> *"So we hail the halls of Piper,*
> *Hold its banner high;*
> *Hail to thee, our alma mater,*
> *Piper, do or die!"*

God, what a shitty song, Jake thought, and it suddenly occurred to him that his father would love it.

2

PERIOD ONE WAS ENGLISH Comp, the only class where there was no final. Their assignment had been to write a Final Essay at home. This was to be a typed document between fifteen hundred and four thousand words long. The subject Ms. Avery had assigned was *My Understanding of Truth*. The Final Essay would count as twenty-five per cent of their final grade for the semester.

Jake came in and took his seat in the third row. There were only eleven pupils in all. Jake remembered Orientation Day last September, when Mr. Harley had told them that Piper had The Highest Teacher To Student Ratio Of Any Fine Private Middle School In The East. He had popped his fist repeatedly on the lectern at the front of the Common Room to emphasize this point. Jake hadn't been terribly impressed, but he had passed the information along to his father. He thought his father *would* be impressed, and he had not been wrong.

He unzipped his bookbag and carefully removed the blue folder which contained his Final Essay. He laid it on his desk, meaning to give it a final look-over, when his eye was caught by the door at the left side of the room. It led, he knew, to the cloakroom, and it was closed today because it was seventy degrees in New York and no one had a coat which needed storage. Nothing back there except a lot of brass coathooks in a line on the wall and a long rubber mat on the floor for boots. A few boxes of school supplies— chalk, blue-books and such—were stored in the far corner.

No big deal.

All the same, Jake rose from his seat, leaving the folder unopened on the desk, and walked across to the door. He could hear his classmates murmuring quietly together, and the riffle of pages as they checked their own Final Essays for that crucial misplaced modifier or fuzzy phrase, but these sounds seemed far away.

It was the door which held his attention.

In the last ten days or so, as the voices in his head grew louder and louder, Jake had become more and more fascinated with doors—all kinds of doors. He must have opened the one between his bedroom and the upstairs hallway five hundred times in just the last week, and the one between his bedroom and the bathroom a thousand. Each time he did it, he felt a tight ball of hope and anticipation in his chest, as if the answer to all of his problems lay somewhere behind this door or that one and he would surely find it . . . eventually. But each time it was only the hall, or the bathroom, or the front walk, or whatever.

Last Thursday he had come home from school, thrown himself on his bed, and had fallen asleep—sleep, it seemed, was the only refuge which remained to him. Except when he'd awakened forty-five minutes later, he had been standing in the bathroom doorway, peering dazedly in at nothing more exciting than the toilet and the basin. Luckily, no one had seen him.

Now, as he approached the cloakroom door, he felt that same dazzling burst of hope, a certainty that the door would not open on a shadowy closet containing only the persistent smells of winter—flannel, rubber, and wet wool—but on some other world where he could be *whole* again. Hot, dazzling light would fall across the classroom floor in a widening triangle, and he would see birds circling in a faded blue sky the color of

(*his eyes*)

old jeans. A desert wind would blow his hair back and dry the nervous sweat on his brow.

He would step through this door and be healed.

Jake turned the knob and opened the door. Inside was only darkness and a row of gleaming brass hooks. One long-forgotten mitten lay near the stacked piles of blue-books in the corner.

His heart sank, and suddenly Jake felt like simply creeping into that dark room with its bitter smells of winter and chalkdust. He could move the mitten and sit in the corner under the coathooks. He could sit on the rubber mat where you were supposed to put your boots in the wintertime. He could sit there, put his thumb in his mouth, pull his knees tight against his chest, close his eyes, and . . . and . . .

And just give up.

This idea—the *relief* of this idea—was incredibly attractive. It would be an end to the terror and confusion and dislocation. That last was somehow the worst; that persistent feeling that his whole life had turned into a funhouse mirror-maze.

Yet there was deep steel in Jake Chambers as surely as there was deep steel in Eddie and Susannah. Now it flashed out its dour blue lighthouse gleam in the darkness. There would be no giving up. Whatever was loose inside him might tear his sanity away from him in the end, but he would give it no quarter in the meantime. Be damned if he would.

Never! he thought fiercely. *Never! Nev—*

"When you've finished your inventory of the school-supplies in the cloakroom, John, perhaps you'd care to join us," Ms. Avery said from behind him in her dry, cultured voice.

There was a small gust of giggles as Jake turned away from the cloakroom. Ms. Avery was standing behind her desk with her long fingers tented lightly on the blotter, looking at him out of her calm, intelligent face. She was wearing her blue suit today, and her hair was pulled back in its usual bun. Nathaniel Hawthorne looked over her shoulder, frowning at Jake from his place on the wall.

"Sorry," Jake muttered, and closed the door. He was immediately seized by a strong impulse to open it again, to double-check, to see if *this* time that other world, with its hot sun and desert vistas, was there.

Instead he walked back to his seat. Petra Jesserling looked at him with merry, dancing eyes. "Take *me* in there with you next time," she whispered. "Then you'll have something to look at."

Jake smiled in a distracted way and slipped into his seat.

"Thank you, John," Ms. Avery said in her endlessly calm voice. "Now, before you pass in your Final Essays—which I am sure will all be very fine, very neat, very *specific*—I should like to pass out the English Department's Short List of recommended summer reading. I will have a word to say about several of these excellent books—"

As she spoke she gave a small stack of mimeographed sheets to David Surrey. David began to hand them out, and Jake opened his folder to take a final look at what he had written on the topic *My Understanding of Truth*. He was genuinely interested in this, because he could no more remember writing his Final Essay, than he could remember studying for his French final.

He looked at the title page with puzzlement and growing unease. MY UNDERSTANDING OF TRUTH, *By John Chambers*, was neatly typed and centered on the sheet, and that was all right, but he had for some reason pasted two photographs below it. One was of a door—he thought it might be the one at Number 10, Downing Street, in London—and the other was of an Amtrak train. They were color shots, undoubtedly culled from some magazine.

Why did I do that? And when *did I do it?*

He turned the page and stared down at the first page of his Final Essay, unable to believe or understand what he was seeing. Then, as understanding began to trickle through his shock, he felt an escalating sense of horror. It had finally happened; he had finally lost enough of his mind so that other people would be able to *tell*.

3

MY UNDERSTANDING OF TRUTH
By John Chambers

> *"I will show you fear in a handful of dust."*
> —T. S. "BUTCH" ELIOT

> *"My first thought was, he lied in every word."*
> —ROBERT "SUNDANCE" BROWNING

The gunslinger is the truth.
Roland is the truth.
The Prisoner is the truth.
The Lady of Shadows is the truth.
The Prisoner and the Lady are married. That is the truth.
The way station is the truth.
The Speaking Demon is the truth.
We went under the mountains and that is the truth.
There were monsters under the mountain. That is the
*   truth.*
One of them had an Amoco gas pump between his legs
*   and was pretending it was his penis. That is the truth.*
Roland let me die. That is the truth.
I still love him.
That is the truth.

"And it is so *very* important that you *all* read *The Lord of the Flies*," Ms. Avery was saying in her clear but somehow pale voice. "And when you do, you must ask yourselves certain questions. A good novel is often like a series of riddles within riddles, and this is a *very* good novel—one of the best written in the second half of the twentieth century. So ask yourselves first what the symbolic significance of the conch shell might be. Second—"

Far away. Far, far away. Jake turned to the second page of his Final Essay with a trembling hand, leaving a dark smear of sweat on the first page.

When is a door not a door? When it's a jar, and that is the truth.

Blaine is the truth.

Blaine is the truth.

What has four wheels and flies? A garbage truck, and that is the truth.

Blaine is the truth.

You have to watch Blaine all the time, Blaine is a pain, and that is the truth.

I'm pretty sure that Blaine is dangerous, and that is the truth.

What is black and white and red all over? A blushing zebra, and that is the truth.

Blaine is the truth.

I want to go back and that is the truth.

I have to go back and that is the truth.

I'll go crazy if I don't go back and that is the truth.

I can't go home again unless I find a stone a rose a door and that is the truth.

Choo-choo, and that is the truth.

Choo-choo. Choo-choo.

Choo-choo. Choo-choo. Choo-choo.

Choo-choo. Choo-choo. Choo-choo. Choo-choo.

I am afraid. That is the truth.

Choo-choo.

Jake looked up slowly. His heart was beating so hard that he saw a bright light like the afterimage of a flashbulb dancing in front of his eyes, a light that pulsed in and out with each titanic thud of his heart.

He saw Ms. Avery handing his Final Essay to his mother and father. Mr. Bissette was standing beside Ms. Avery, looking grave. He heard Ms. Avery say in her clear, pale voice: *Your son is seriously ill. If you need proof, just look at this Final Essay.*

John hasn't been himself for the last three weeks or so, Mr. Bissette added. *He seems frightened some of the time and dazed all of the time . . . not quite there, if you see what I mean.* Je pense que John est fou . . . comprenez-vous?

Ms. Avery again: *Do you perhaps keep certain*

*mood-altering prescription drugs in the house where
John might have access to them?*

Jake didn't know about mood-altering drugs, but he
knew his father kept several grams of cocaine in the
bottom drawer of his study desk. His father would
undoubtedly think he had been into it.

"Now let me say a word about *Catch-22*," Ms.
Avery said from the front of the room. "This is a very
challenging book for sixth- and seventh-grade students, but you will nonetheless find it entirely en-
chanting, *if* you open your minds to its *special charm*.
You may think of this novel, if you like, as a comedy
of the surreal."

I don't need to read *something like that,* Jake
thought. *I'm* living *something like that, and it's no
comedy.*

He turned over to the last page of his Final Essay.
There were no words on it. Instead he had pasted
another picture to the paper. It was a photograph of
the Leaning Tower of Pisa. He had used a crayon to
scribble it black. The dark, waxy lines looped and
swooped in lunatic coils.

He could remember doing none of this.

Absolutely *none* of it.

Now he heard his father saying to Mr. Bissette:
Fou. *Yes, he's definitely* fou. *A kid who'd fuck up his
chance at a school like Piper HAS to be* fou, *wouldn't
you say? Well . . . I can handle this. Handling things
is my job. Sunnyvale's the answer. He needs to spend
some time in Sunnyvale, making baskets and getting
his shit back together. Don't you worry about our kid,
folks; he can run . . . but he can't hide.*

Would they actually send him away to the nuthatch
if it started to seem that his elevator no longer went
all the way to the top floor? Jake thought the answer
to that was a big you bet. No way his father was going
to put up with a loony around the house. The name
of the place they put him in might not be Sunnyvale,
but there would be bars on the windows and there

would be young men in white coats and crepe-soled shoes prowling the halls. The young men would have big muscles and watchful eyes and access to hypodermic needles full of artificial sleep.

They'll tell everybody I went away, Jake thought. The arguing voices in his head were temporarily stilled by a rising tide of panic. *They'll say I'm spending the year with my aunt and uncle in Modesto . . . or in Sweden as an exchange student . . . or repairing satellites in outer space. My mother won't like it . . . she'll cry . . . but she'll go along. She has her boyfriends, and besides, she* always *goes along with what he decides. She . . . they . . . me . . .*

He felt a shriek welling up his throat and pressed his lips tightly together to hold it in. He looked down again at the wild black scribbles snarled across the photograph of the Leaning Tower and thought: *I have to get out of here. I have to get out right now.*

He raised his hand.

"Yes, John, what is it?" Ms. Avery was looking at him with the expression of mild exasperation she reserved for students who interrupted her in mid-lecture.

"I'd like to step out for a moment, if I may," Jake said.

This was another example of Piper-speak. Piper students did not ever have to "take a leak" or "tap a kidney" or, God forbid, "drop a load." The unspoken assumption was that Piper students were too perfect to create waste byproducts in their tastefully silent glides through life. Once in a while someone requested permission to "step out for a moment," and that was all.

Ms. Avery sighed. "Must you, John?"

"Yes, ma'am."

"All right. Return as soon as possible."

"Yes, Ms. Avery."

He closed the folder as he got up, took hold of it, then reluctantly let go again. No good. Ms. Avery would wonder why he was taking his Final Essay to

the toilet with him. He should have removed the
damning pages from the folder and stuffed them in his
pocket before asking for permission to step out. Too
late now.

Jake walked down the aisle toward the door, leaving
his folder on the desk and his bookbag lying beneath
it.

"Hope everything comes out all right, Chambers,"
David Surrey whispered, and snickered into his hand.

"Still your restless lips, David," Ms. Avery said,
clearly exasperated now, and the whole class laughed.

Jake reached the door leading to the hall, and as
he grasped the knob, that feeling of hope and surety
rose in him again: *This is it—really it. I'll open the
door and the desert sun will shine in. I'll feel that dry
wind on my face. I'll step through and never see this
classroom again.*

He opened the door and it was only the hallway on
the other side, but he was right about one thing just
the same: he never saw Ms. Avery's classroom again.

4

HE WALKED SLOWLY DOWN the dim, wood-panelled
corridor, sweating lightly. He walked past classroom
doors he would have felt compelled to open if not for
the clear glass windows set in each one. He looked
into Mr. Bissette's French II class and Mr. Knopf's
Introduction to Geometry class. In both rooms the
pupils sat with pencils in hand and heads bowed over
open blue-books. He looked into Mr. Harley's Spoken
Arts class and saw Stan Dorfman—one of those acquaintances who were not quite friends—beginning his
Final Speech. Stan looked scared to death, but Jake
could have told Stan he didn't have the slightest idea
what fear—*real* fear—was all about.

I died.

No. I didn't.
Did too.
Did not.
Did.
Didn't.

He came to a door marked GIRLS. He pushed it open, expecting to see a bright desert sky and a blue haze of mountains on the horizon. Instead he saw Belinda Stevens standing at one of the sinks, looking into the mirror above the basin and squeezing a pimple on her forehead.

"Jesus Christ, do you mind?" she asked.

"Sorry. Wrong door. I thought it was the desert."

"What?"

But he had already let the door go and it was swinging shut on its pneumatic elbow. He passed the drinking fountain and opened the door marked BOYS. *This* was it, he knew it, was sure of it, this was the door which would take him back—

Three urinals gleamed spotlessly under the fluorescent lights. A tap dripped solemnly into a sink. That was all.

Jake let the door close. He walked on down the hall, his heels making firm little clicks on the tiles. He glanced into the office before passing it and saw only Ms. Franks. She was talking on the telephone, swinging back and forth in her swivel chair and playing with a lock of her hair. The silver-plated bell stood on the desk beside her. Jake waited until she swivelled away from the door and then hurried past. Thirty seconds later he was emerging into the bright sunshine of a morning in late May.

I've gone truant, he thought. Even his distraction did not keep him from being amazed at this unexpected development. *When I don't come back from the bathroom in five minutes or so, Ms. Avery will send somebody to check . . . and then they'll know. They'll all know that I've left school, gone truant.*

He thought of the folder lying on his desk.

They'll read it and they'll think I'm crazy. Fou. *Sure
they will. Of course. Because I am.*

Then another voice spoke. It was, he thought, the
voice of the man with the bombardier's eyes, the man
who wore the two big guns slung low on his hips. The
voice was cold . . . but not without comfort.

No, Jake, Roland said. *You're not crazy. You're lost
and scared, but you're not crazy and need fear neither
your shadow in the morning striding behind you nor
your shadow at evening rising to meet you. You have
to find your way back home, that's all.*

"But where do I go?" Jake whispered. He stood on
the sidewalk of Fifty-sixth Street between Park and
Madison, watching the traffic bolt past. A city bus
snored by, laying a thin trail of acrid blue diesel
smoke. "Where do I go? Where's the fucking *door*?"

But the voice of the gunslinger had fallen silent.

Jake turned left, in the direction of the East River,
and began to walk blindly forward. He had no idea
where he was going—no idea at all. He could only
hope his feet would carry him to the right place . . .
as they had carried him to the wrong one not long
ago.

5

IT HAD HAPPENED THREE weeks earlier.

One could not say *It all began three weeks earlier,*
because that gave the impression that there had been
some sort of progression, and that wasn't right. There
had been a progression to the *voices,* to the violence
with which each insisted on its own particular version
of reality, but the rest of it had happened all at once.

He left home at eight o'clock to walk to school—
he always walked when the weather was good, and
the weather this May had been absolutely fine. His
father had left for the Network, his mother was still

in bed, and Mrs. Greta Shaw was in the kitchen, drinking coffee and reading her *New York Post*.

"Goodbye, Greta," he said. "I'm going to school now."

She raised a hand to him without looking up from the paper. "Have a good day, Johnny."

All according to routine. Just another day in the life.

And so it had been for the next fifteen hundred seconds. Then everything had changed forever.

He idled along, bookbag in one hand, lunch sack in the other, looking in the windows. Seven hundred and twenty seconds from the end of his life as he had always known it, he paused to look in the window of Brendio's, where mannequins dressed in fur coats and Edwardian suits stood in stiff poses of conversation. He was thinking only of going bowling that afternoon after school. His average was 158, great for a kid who was only eleven. His ambition was to some day be a bowler on the pro tour (and if his father had known *this* little factoid, he *also* would have hit the roof).

Closing in now—closing in on the moment when his sanity would be suddenly eclipsed.

He crossed Thirty-ninth and there were four hundred seconds left. Had to wait for the WALK light at Forty-first and there were two hundred and seventy. Paused to look in the novelty shop on the corner of Fifth and Forty-second and there were a hundred and ninety. And now, with just over three minutes left in his ordinary life, Jake Chambers walked beneath the unseen umbrella of that force which Roland called *ka-tet*.

An odd, uneasy feeling began to creep over him. At first he thought it was a feeling of being watched, and then he realized it wasn't that at all . . . or not *precisely* that. He felt that he had been here before; that he was reliving a dream he had mostly forgotten. He waited for the feeling to pass, but it didn't. It grew stronger, and now began to mix with a sensation he reluctantly recognized as terror.

Up ahead, on the near corner of Fifth and Forty-third, a black man in a Panama hat was setting up a pretzel-and-soda cart.

He's the one that yells "Oh my God, he's kilt!" Jake thought.

Approaching the far corner was a fat lady with a Bloomingdale's bag in her hand.

She'll drop the bag. Drop the bag and put her hands to her mouth and scream. The bag will split open. There's a doll inside the bag. It's wrapped in a red towel. I'll see this from the street. From where I'll be lying in the street with my blood soaking into my pants and spreading around me in a pool.

Behind the fat woman was a tall man in a gray nailhead worsted suit. He was carrying a briefcase.

He's the one who vomits on his shoes. He's the one who drops his briefcase and throws up on his shoes. What's happening to me?

Yet his feet carried him numbly forward toward the intersection, where people were crossing in a brisk, steady stream. Somewhere behind him, closing in, was a killer priest. He *knew* this, just as he knew that the priest's hands would in a moment be outstretched to push . . . but he could not look around. It was like being locked in a nightmare where things simply had to take their course.

Fifty-three seconds left now. Ahead of him, the pretzel vendor was opening a hatch in the side of his cart.

He's going to take out a bottle of Yoo-Hoo, Jake thought. *Not a can but a bottle. He'll shake it up and drink it all at once.*

The pretzel vendor brought out a bottle of Yoo-Hoo, shook it vigorously, and spun off the cap.

Forty seconds left.

Now the light will change.

White WALK went out. Red DONT WALK began to

flash rapidly on and off. And somewhere, less than half a block away, a big blue Cadillac was now rolling toward the intersection of Fifth and Forty-third. Jake *knew* this, just as he knew the driver was a fat man wearing a hat almost the exact same blue shade as his car.

I'm going to die!

He wanted to scream this aloud to the people walking heedlessly all around him, but his jaws were locked shut. His feet swept him serenely onward toward the intersection. The DONT WALK sign stopped flashing and shone out its solid red warning. The pretzel vendor tossed his empty Yoo-Hoo bottle into the wire trash basket on the corner. The fat lady stood on the corner across the street from Jake, holding her shopping bag by the handles. The man in the nailhead suit was directly behind her. Now there were eighteen seconds left.

Time for the toy truck to go by, Jake thought.

Ahead of him a van with a picture of a happy jumping-jack and the words TOOKER'S WHOLESALE TOYS printed on the side swept through the intersection, jolting up and down in the potholes. Behind him, Jake knew, the man in the black robe was beginning to move faster, closing the gap, now reaching out with his long hands. Yet he could not look around, as you couldn't look around in dreams when something awful was gaining on you.

Run! And if you can't run, sit down and grab hold of a No Parking sign! Don't just let it happen!

But he was powerless to *stop* it from happening. Ahead, on the edge of the curb, was a young woman in a white sweater and a black skirt. To her left was a young Chicano guy with a boombox. A Donna Summer disco tune was just ending. The next song, Jake knew, would be "Dr. Love," by Kiss.

They're going to move apart—

Even as the thought came, the woman moved a step

to her right. The Chicano guy moved a step to his left, creating a gap between them. Jake's traitor feet swept him into the gap. Nine seconds now.

Down the street, bright May sunshine twinkled on a Cadillac hood ornament. It was, Jake knew, a 1976 Sedan de Ville. Six seconds. The Caddy was speeding up. The light was getting ready to change and the man driving the de Ville, the fat man in the blue hat with the feather stuck jauntily in the brim, meant to scat through the intersection before it could. Three seconds. Behind Jake, the man in black was lunging forward. On the young man's boombox, "Love to Love You, Baby" ended and "Dr. Love" began.

Two.

The Cadillac changed to the lane nearest Jake's side of the street and charged down on the intersection, its killer grille snarling.

One.

Jake's breath stopped in his throat.

None.

"Uh!" Jake cried as the hands struck him firmly in the back, pushing him, pushing him into the street, pushing him out of his life—

Except there *were* no hands.

He reeled forward nevertheless, hands flailing at the air, his mouth a dark O of dismay. The Chicano guy with the boombox reached out, grabbed Jake's arm, and hauled him backward. "Look out, little hero," he said. "That traffic turn you into bratwurst."

The Cadillac floated by. Jake caught a glimpse of the fat man in the blue hat peering out through the windshield, and then it was gone.

That was when it happened; that was when he split down the middle and became two boys. One lay dying in the street. The other stood here on the corner, watching in dumb, stricken amazement as DONT WALK turned to WALK again and people began to cross around him just as if nothing had happened . . . as, indeed, nothing had.

I'm alive! half of his mind rejoiced, screaming with relief.

Dead! the other half screamed back. *Dead in the street! They're all gathering around me, and the man in black who pushed me is saying "I am a priest. Let me through."*

Waves of faintness rushed through him and turned his thoughts to billowing parachute silk. He saw the fat lady approaching, and as she passed, Jake looked into her bag. He saw the bright blue eyes of a doll peeping above the edge of a red towel, just as he had known he would. Then she was gone. The pretzel vendor was not yelling *Oh my God, he's kilt*; he was continuing to set up for the day's business while he whistled the Donna Summer tune that had been playing on the Chicano guy's radio.

Jake turned around, looking wildly for the priest who was not a priest. He wasn't there.

Jake moaned.

Snap out of it! What's wrong with you?

He didn't know. He only knew he was supposed to be lying in the street right now, getting ready to die while the fat woman screamed and the guy in the nailhead worsted suit threw up and the man in black pushed through the gathering crowd.

And in part of his mind, that did seem to be happening.

The faintness began to return. Jake suddenly dropped his lunch sack to the pavement and slapped himself across the face as hard as he could. A woman on her way to work gave him a queer look. Jake ignored her. He left his lunch lying on the sidewalk and plunged into the intersection, also ignoring the red DONT WALK light, which had begun to stutter on and off again. It didn't matter now. Death had approached . . . and then passed by without a second glance. It hadn't been meant to happen that way,

and on the deepest level of his existence he knew
that, but it had.

Maybe now he would live forever.

The thought made him feel like screaming all over
again.

6

HIS HEAD HAD CLEARED a little by the time he got
to school, and his mind had gone to work trying to
convince him that nothing was wrong, really nothing
at all. Maybe something a little weird *had* happened,
some sort of psychic flash, a momentary peek into one
possible future, but so what? No big deal, right? The
idea was actually sort of cool—the kind of thing they
were always printing in the weird supermarket newspapers Greta Shaw liked to read when she was sure
Jake's mother wasn't around—papers like the *National
Enquirer* and *Inside View*. Except, of course, in those
papers the psychic flash was always a kind of tactical
nuclear strike—a woman who dreamed of a plane
crash and changed her reservations, or a guy who
dreamed his brother was being held prisoner in a Chinese fortune cookie factory and it turned out to be
true. When your psychic flash consisted of knowing
that a Kiss song was going to play next on the radio,
that a fat lady had a doll wrapped in a red towel in
her Bloomingdale's bag, and that a pretzel vendor was
going to drink a bottle of Yoo-Hoo instead of a can,
how big a deal could it be?

Forget it, he advised himself. *It's over.*

A great idea, except by period three he knew it
wasn't over; it was just beginning. He sat in Pre-Alge-
bra, watching Mr. Knopf solving simple equations on
the board, and realized with dawning horror that a
whole new set of memories was surfacing in his mind.

It was like watching strange objects float slowly toward the surface of a muddy lake.

I'm in a place I don't know, he thought. *I mean, I will know it—or would have known it if the Cadillac had hit me. It's the way station—but the part of me that's there doesn't know that yet. That part only knows it's in the desert someplace, and there are no people. I've been crying, because I'm scared. I'm scared that this might be hell.*

By three o'clock, when he arrived at Mid-Town Lanes, he knew he had found the pump in the stables and had gotten a drink of water. The water was very cold and tasted strongly of minerals. Soon he would go inside and find a small supply of dried beef in a room which had once been a kitchen. He knew this as clearly and surely as he'd known the pretzel vendor would select a bottle of Yoo-Hoo, and that the doll peeking out of the Bloomingdale's bag had blue eyes.

It was like being able to remember forward in time.

He bowled only two strings—the first a 96, the second an 87. Timmy looked at his sheet when he turned it in at the counter and shook his head. "You're having an off-day today, champ," he said.

"You don't know the half of it," Jake said.

Timmy took a closer look. "You okay? You look really pale."

"I think I might be coming down with a bug." This didn't feel like a lie, either. He was sure as hell coming down with *something*.

"Go home and go to bed," Timmy advised. "Drink lots of clear liquids—gin, vodka, stuff like that."

Jake smiled dutifully. "Maybe I will."

He walked slowly home. All of New York was spread out around him, New York at its most seductive—a late-afternoon street serenade with a musician on every corner, all the trees in bloom, and everyone apparently in a good mood. Jake saw all this, but he also saw *behind* it: saw himself cowering in the shadows of the kitchen as the man in black drank like a

grinning dog from the stable pump, saw himself sobbing with relief as he—or it—moved on without discovering him, saw himself falling deeply asleep as the
sun went down and the stars began to come out like
chips of ice in the harsh purple desert sky.

He let himself into the duplex apartment with his
key and walked into the kitchen to get something to
eat. He wasn't hungry, but it was habit. He was
headed for the refrigerator when his eye happened on
the pantry door and he stopped. He realized suddenly
that the way station—and all the rest of that strange
other world where he now belonged—was behind that
door. All he had to do was push through it and rejoin
the Jake that already existed there. The queer doubling in his mind would end; the voices, endlessly arguing the question of whether or not he had been
dead since 8:25 that morning, would fall silent.

Jake pushed open the pantry door with both hands,
his face already breaking into a sunny, relieved smile
. . . and then froze as Mrs. Shaw, who was standing
on a step-stool at the back of the pantry, screamed.
The can of tomato paste she had been holding
dropped out of her hand and fell to the floor. She
tottered on the stool and Jake rushed forward to
steady her before she could join the tomato paste.

"Moses in the bullrushes!" she gasped, fluttering a
hand rapidly against the front of her housedress. "You
scared the bejabbers out of me, Johnny!"

"I'm sorry," he said. He really was, but he was also
bitterly disappointed. It had only been the pantry,
after all. He had been so *sure*—

"What are you doing, creeping around here, anyway? This is your bowling day! I didn't expect you for
at least another hour! I haven't even made your snack
yet, so don't be expecting it."

"That's okay. I'm not very hungry, anyway." He
bent down and picked up the can she had dropped.

"Wouldn't know it from the way you came bustin
in here," she grumbled.

"I thought I heard a mouse or something. I guess it was just you."

"I guess it was." She descended the step-stool and took the can from him. "You look like you're comin down with the flu or something, Johnny." She pressed her hand against his forehead. "You don't feel hot, but that doesn't always mean much."

"I think I'm just tired," Jake said, and thought: *If only that was all it was.* "Maybe I'll just have a soda and watch TV for a while."

She grunted. "You got any papers you want to show me? If you do, make it fast. I'm behind on supper."

"Nothing today," he said. He left the pantry, got a soda, then went into the living room. He turned on *Hollywood Squares* and watched vacantly as the voices argued and the new memories of that dusty other world continued to surface.

7

HIS MOTHER AND FATHER didn't notice anything was wrong with him—his father didn't even get in until 9:30—and that was fine by Jake. He went to bed at ten and lay awake in the darkness, listening to the city outside his window: brakes, horns, wailing sirens.

You died.

I didn't, though. I'm right here, safe in my own bed.

That doesn't matter. You died, and you know it.

The hell of it was, he knew both things.

I don't know which voice is true, but I know I can't go on like this. So just quit it, both of you. Stop arguing and leave me alone. Okay? Please?

But they wouldn't. *Couldn't,* apparently. And it came to Jake that he ought to get up—*right now*—and open the door to the bathroom. The other world would be there. The way station would be there and the rest of *him* would be there, too, huddled under an ancient blanket in the stable, trying to sleep and wondering what in hell had happened.

I can tell him, Jake thought excitedly. He threw back the covers, suddenly knowing that the door beside his bookcase no longer led into the bathroom but to a world that smelled of heat and purple sage and fear in a handful of dust, a world that now lay under the shadowing wing of night. *I can tell him, but I won't have to . . . because I'll be IN him . . . I'll BE him!*

He raced across his darkened room, almost laughing with relief, and shoved open the door. And—

And it was his bathroom. Just his bathroom, with the framed Marvin Gaye poster on the wall and the shapes of the venetian blinds lying on the tiled floor in bars of light and shadow.

He stood there for a long time, trying to swallow his disappointment. It wouldn't go. And it was bitter.

Bitter.

8

THE THREE WEEKS BETWEEN then and now stretched like a grim, blighted terrain in Jake's memory—a nightmare wasteland where there had been no peace, no rest, no respite from pain. He had watched, like a helpless prisoner watching the sack of a city he had once ruled, as his mind buckled under the steadily increasing pressure of the phantom voices and memories. He had hoped the memories would stop when he reached the point in them where the man named Roland had allowed him to drop into the chasm under the mountains, but they didn't. Instead they simply recycled and began to play themselves over again, like a tape set to repeat and repeat until it either breaks or someone comes along and shuts it off.

His perceptions of his more-or-less real life as a boy in New York City grew increasingly spotty as this

terrible schism grew deeper. He could remember
going to school, and to the movies on the weekend,
and out to Sunday brunch with his parents a week ago
(or had it been two?), but he remembered these things
the way a man who has suffered malaria may remember the deepest, darkest phase of his illness: people
became shadows, voices seemed to echo and overlap
each other, and even such a simple act as eating a
sandwich or obtaining a Coke from the machine in
the gymnasium became a struggle. Jake had pushed
through those days in a fugue of yelling voices and
doubled memories. His obsession with doors—all
kinds of doors—deepened; his hope that the gunslinger's world might lie behind one of them never quite
died. Nor was that so strange, since it was the only
hope he had.

But as of today the game was over. He'd never had
a chance of winning anyway, not really. He had given
up. He had gone truant. Jake walked blindly east
along the gridwork of streets, head down, with no idea
of where he was going or what he would do when he
got there.

9

AFTER WALKING FOR A while, he began to come out
of this unhappy daze and take some notice of his surroundings. He was standing on the corner of Lexington Avenue and Fifty-fourth Street with no memory
at all of how he had come to be there. He noticed for
the first time that it was an absolutely gorgeous morning. May 9th, the day this madness had started, had
been pretty, but today was ten times better—that day,
perhaps, when spring looks around herself and sees
summer standing nearby, strong and handsome and
with a cocky grin on his tanned face. The sun shone
brightly off the glass walls of the midtown buildings;

the shadow of each pedestrian was black and crisp. The sky overhead was a clear and blameless blue, dotted here and there with plump foul-weather clouds.

Down the street, two businessmen in expensive, well-cut suits were standing at a board wall which had been erected around a construction site. They were laughing and passing something back and forth. Jake walked in their direction, curious, and as he drew closer he saw that the two businessmen were playing tic-tac-toe on the wall, using an expensive Mark Cross pen to draw the grids and make the X's and O's. Jake thought this was a complete gas. As he approached, one of them made an O in the upper right-hand corner of the grid and then slashed a diagonal line through the middle.

"Skunked again!" his friend said. Then this man, who looked like a high-powered executive or lawyer or big-time stockbroker, took the Mark Cross pen and drew another grid.

The first businessman, the winner, glanced to his left and saw Jake. He smiled. "Some day, huh, kid?"

"It sure is," Jake said, delighted to find he meant every word.

"Too nice for school, huh?"

This time Jake actually laughed. Piper School, where you had Outs instead of lunch and where you sometimes stepped out but never had to take a crap, suddenly seemed far away and not at all important. "You know it."

"You want a game? Billy here couldn't beat me at this when we were in the fifth grade, and he still can't."

"Leave the kid alone," the second businessman said, holding out the Mark Cross pen. "This time you're history." He winked at Jake, and Jake amazed himself by winking back. He walked on, leaving the men to their game. The sense that something totally wonderful was going to happen—had perhaps already *begun* to happen—continued to grow, and his feet no longer seemed to be quite touching the pavement.

The WALK light on the corner came on, and he began to cross Lexington Avenue. He stopped in the middle of the street so suddenly that a messenger-boy on a ten-speed bike almost ran him down. It was a beautiful spring day—agreed. But that wasn't why he felt so good, so suddenly aware of everything that was going on around him, so sure that some great thing was about to occur.

The voices had stopped.

They weren't gone for good—he somehow knew this—but for the time being they had *stopped*. Why?

Jake suddenly thought of two men arguing in a room. They sit facing each other over a table, jawing at each other with increasing bitterness. After a while they begin to lean toward each other, thrusting their faces pugnaciously forward, bathing each other with a fine mist of outraged spittle. Soon they will come to blows. But before that can happen, they hear a steady thumping noise—the sound of a bass drum—and then a jaunty flourish of brass. The two men stop arguing and look at each other, puzzled.

What's that? one asks.

Dunno, the other replies. *Sounds like a parade.*

They rush to the window and it *is* a parade—a uniformed band marching in lock-step with the sun blazing off their horns, pretty majorettes twirling batons and strutting their long, tanned legs, convertibles decked with flowers and filled with waving celebrities.

The two men stare out the window, their quarrel forgotten. They will undoubtedly return to it, but for the time being they stand together like the best of friends, shoulder to shoulder, watching as the parade goes by—

10

A HORN BLARED, STARTLING Jake out of this story,
which was as vivid as a powerful dream. He realized
he was still standing in the middle of Lexington, and
the light had changed. He looked around wildly, expecting to see the blue Cadillac bearing down on him,
but the guy who had tooted his horn was sitting behind
the wheel of a yellow Mustang convertible and grinning at him. It was as if everyone in New York had
gotten a whiff of happy-gas today.

Jake waved at the guy and sprinted to the other
side of the street. The guy in the Mustang twirled a
finger around his ear to indicate that Jake was crazy,
then waved back and drove on.

For a moment Jake simply stood on the far corner,
face turned up to the May sunshine, smiling, digging
the day. He supposed prisoners condemned to die in
the electric chair must feel this way when they learn
they have been granted a temporary reprieve.

The voices were still.

The question was, what was the parade which had
temporarily diverted their attention? Was it just the
uncommon beauty of this spring morning?

Jake didn't think that was all. He didn't think so
because that sensation of *knowing* was creeping over
him and through him again, the one which had taken
possession of him three weeks ago, as he approached
the corner of Fifth and Forty-sixth. But on May 9th,
it had been a feeling of impending doom. Today it
was a feeling of radiance, a sense of goodness and
anticipation. It was as if . . . as if . . .

White. This was the word that came to him, and
it clanged in his mind with clear and unquestionable
rightness.

"It's the White!" he exclaimed aloud. "The coming
of the White!"

He walked on down Fifty-fourth Street, and as he

reached the corner of Second and Fifty-fourth, he once more passed under the umbrella of *ka-tet*.

11

HE TURNED RIGHT, THEN stopped, turned, and retraced his steps to the corner. He needed to walk down Second Avenue now, yes, that was unquestionably correct, but this was the wrong side again. When the light changed, he hurried across the street and turned right again. That feeling, that sense of

(Whiteness)

rightness, grew steadily stronger. He felt half-mad with joy and relief. He was going to be okay. This time there was no mistake. He felt sure that he would soon begin to see people he recognized, as he had recognized the fat lady and the pretzel vendor, and they would be doing things he remembered in advance.

Instead, he came to the bookstore.

12

THE MANHATTAN RESTAURANT OF THE MIND, the sign painted in the window read. Jake went to the door. There was a chalkboard hung there; it looked like the kind you saw on the wall in diners and lunchrooms.

TODAY'S SPECIALS

From Florida! Fresh-Broiled John D. MacDonald
  Hardcovers 3 for $2.50
  Paperbacks 9 for $5.00

From Mississippi! Pan-Fried William Faulkner
  Hardcovers Market Price
  Vintage Library Paperbacks 75¢ each

From California! Hard-Boiled Raymond Chandler
  Hardcovers Market Price
  Paperbacks 7 for $5.00

FEED YOUR NEED TO READ

Jake went in, aware that he had, for the first time in three weeks, opened a door without hoping madly to find another world on the other side. A bell jingled overhead. The mild, spicy smell of old books hit him, and the smell was somehow like coming home.

The restaurant motif continued inside. Although the walls were lined with shelves of books, a fountain-style counter bisected the room. On Jake's side of the counter were a number of small tables with wire-backed Malt Shoppe chairs. Each table had been arranged to display the day's specials: Travis McGee novels by John D. MacDonald, Philip Marlowe novels by Raymond Chandler, Snopes novels by William Faulkner. A small sign on the Faulkner table said: *Some rare 1st eds available—pls ask.* Another sign, this one on the counter, read simply: BROWSE! A couple of customers were doing just that. They sat at the counter, drinking coffee and reading. Jake thought this was without a doubt the best bookstore he'd ever been in.

The question was, why was he here? Was it luck, or was it part of that soft, insistent feeling that he was following a trail—a kind of force-beam—that had been left for him to find?

He glanced at the display on a small table to his left and knew the answer.

13

IT WAS A DISPLAY of children's books. There wasn't much room on the table, so there were only about a dozen of them—*Alice's Adventures in Wonderland, The Hobbit, Tom Sawyer,* things like that. Jake had been attracted by a story-book obviously meant for very young children. On the bright green cover was an anthropomorphic locomotive puffing its way up a hill. Its cowcatcher (which was bright pink) wore a happy grin and its headlight was a cheerful eye which seemed to invite Jake Chambers to come inside and read all about it. *Charlie the Choo-Choo,* the title proclaimed, Story and Pictures by Beryl Evans. Jake's mind flashed back to his Final Essay, with the picture of the Amtrak train on the title-page and the words *choo-choo* written over and over again inside.

He grabbed the book and clutched it tightly, as if it might fly away if he relaxed his grip. And as he looked down at the cover, Jake found that he did not trust the smile on Charlie the Choo-Choo's face. *You look happy, but I think that's just the mask you wear,* he thought. *I don't think you're happy at all. And I don't think Charlie's your real name, either.*

These were crazy thoughts to be having, undoubtedly crazy, but they did not *feel* crazy. They felt sane. They felt *true*.

Standing next to the place where *Charlie the Choo-Choo* had been was a tattered paperback. The cover was quite badly torn and had been mended with Scotch tape now yellow with age. The picture showed a puzzled-looking boy and girl with a forest of question-marks over their heads. The title of this book was *Riddle-De-Dum! Brain-Twisters and Puzzles for Everyone!* No author was credited.

Jake tucked *Charlie the Choo-Choo* under his arm and picked up the riddle book. He opened it at random and saw this:

When is a door not a door?

"When it's a jar," Jake muttered. He could feel sweat popping out on his forehead . . . his arms . . . all over his body.

"When it's a *jar!*"

"Find something, son?" a mild voice inquired.

Jake turned around and saw a fat guy in an open-throated white shirt standing at the end of the counter. His hands were stuffed in the pockets of his old gabardine slacks. A pair of half-glasses were pushed up on the bright dome of his bald head.

"Yes," Jake said feverishly. "These two. Are they for sale?"

"Everything you see is for sale," the fat guy said. "The building itself would be for sale, if I owned it. Alas, I only lease." He held out his hand for the books and for a moment Jake balked. Then, reluctantly, he handed them over. Part of him expected the fat guy to flee with them, and if he did—if he gave the slightest indication of trying it—Jake meant to tackle him, rip the books out of his hands, and boogie. He *needed* those books.

"Okay, let's see what you got," the fat man said. "By the way, I'm Tower. Calvin Tower." He stuck out his hand.

Jake's eyes widened, and he took an involuntary step backward. *"What?"*

The fat guy looked at him with some interest. "Calvin Tower. Which word is profanity in your language, O Hyperborean Wanderer?"

"Huh?"

"I just mean you look like someone goosed you, kid."

"Oh. Sorry." He clasped Mr. Tower's large, soft hand, hoping the man wouldn't pursue it. The name *had* given him a jump, but he didn't know why. "I'm Jake Chambers."

Calvin Tower shook his hand. "Good handle, pard. Sounds like the footloose hero in a Western novel—the guy who blows into Black Fork, Arizona, cleans up the town, and then travels on. Something by Wayne D. Overholser, maybe. Except you don't look footloose, Jake. You look like you decided the day was a little too nice to spend in school."

"Oh . . . no. We finished up last Friday."

Tower grinned. "Uh-huh. I bet. And you've gotta have these two items, huh? It's sort of funny, what people have to have. Now you—I would have pegged you as a Robert Howard kind of kid from the jump, looking for a good deal on one of those nice old Donald M. Grant editions—the ones with the Roy Krenkel paintings. Dripping swords, mighty thews, and Conan the Barbarian hacking his way through the Stygian hordes."

"That sounds pretty good, actually. These are for . . . uh, for my little brother. It's his birthday next week."

Calvin Tower used his thumb to flip his glasses down onto his nose and had a closer look at Jake. "Really? You look like an only child to me. An only child if I ever saw one, enjoying a day of French leave as Mistress May trembles in her green gown just outside the bosky dell of June."

"Come again?"

"Never mind. Spring always puts me in a William Cowper-ish mood. People are weird but interesting, Tex—am I right?"

"I guess so," Jake said cautiously. He couldn't decide if he liked this odd man or not.

One of the counter-browsers spun on his stool. He was holding a cup of coffee in one hand and a battered paperback copy of *The Plague* in the other. "Quit pulling the kid's chain and sell him the books, Cal," he said. "We've still got time to finish this game of chess before the end of the world, if you hurry up."

"Hurry is antithetical to my nature," Cal said, but he opened *Charlie the Choo-Choo* and peered at the price pencilled on the flyleaf. "A fairly common book, but this copy's in unusually fine condition. Little kids usually rack the hell out of the ones they like. I should get twelve dollars for it—"

"Goddam thief," the man who was reading *The Plague* said, and the other browser laughed. Calvin Tower paid no notice.

"—but I can't bear to dock you that much on a day like this. Seven bucks and it's yours. Plus tax, of course. The riddle book you can have for free. Consider it my gift to a boy wise enough to saddle up and light out for the territories on the last real day of spring."

Jake dug out his wallet and opened it anxiously, afraid he had left the house with only three or four dollars. He was in luck, however. He had a five and three ones. He held the money out to Tower, who folded the bills casually into one pocket and made change out of the other.

"Don't hurry off, Jake. Now that you're here, come on over to the counter and have a cup of coffee. Your eyes will widen with amazement as I cut Aaron Deepneau's spavined old Kiev Defense to ribbons."

"Don't you wish," said the man who was reading *The Plague*—Aaron Deepneau, presumably.

"I'd like to, but I can't. I . . . there's someplace I have to be."

"Okay. As long as it's not back to school."

Jake grinned. "No—not school. That way lies madness."

Tower laughed out loud and flipped his glasses up to the top of his head again. "Not bad! Not bad at all! Maybe the younger generation isn't going to hell after all, Aaron—what do you think?"

"Oh, they're going to hell, all right," Aaron said. "This boy's just an exception to the rule. Maybe."

"Don't mind that cynical old fart," Calvin Tower said. "Motor on, O Hyperborean Wanderer. I wish I were ten or eleven again, with a beautiful day like this ahead of me."

"Thanks for the books," Jake said.

"No problem. That's what we're here for. Come on back sometime."

"I'd like to."

"Well, you know where we are."

Yes, Jake thought. *Now if I only knew where I am.*

14

HE STOPPED JUST OUTSIDE the bookstore and flipped open the riddle book again, this time to page one, where there was a short uncredited introduction.

"Riddles are perhaps the oldest of all the games people still play today," it began. "The gods and goddesses of Greek myth teased each other with riddles, and they were employed as teaching tools in ancient Rome. The Bible contains several good riddles. One of the most famous of these was told by Samson on the day he was married to Delilah:

> '*Out of the eater came forth meat,*
> *and out of the strong came forth sweetness!*'

"He asked this riddle of several young men who attended his wedding, confident that they wouldn't be able to guess the answer. The young men, however, got Delilah aside and she whispered the answer to them. Samson was furious, and had the young men put to death for cheating—in the old days, you see, riddles were taken much more seriously than they are today!

"By the way, the answer to Samson's riddle—and all the other riddles in this book—can be found in the section at the back. We only ask that you give each puzzler a fair chance before you peek!"

Jake turned to the back of the book, somehow knowing what he would find even before he got there. Beyond the page marked ANSWERS there was nothing but a few torn fragments and the back cover. The section had been ripped out.

He stood there for a moment, thinking. Then, on an impulse that didn't really feel like an impulse at all, Jake walked back inside The Manhattan Restaurant of the Mind.

Calvin Tower looked up from the chessboard. "Change your mind about that cup of coffee, O Hyperborean Wanderer?"

"No. I wanted to ask you if you know the answer to a riddle."

"Fire away," Tower invited, and moved a pawn.

"Samson told it. The strong guy in the Bible? It goes like this—"

" 'Out of the eater came forth meat,' " said Aaron Deepneau, swinging around again to look at Jake, " 'and out of the strong came forth sweetness.' That the one?"

"Yeah, it is," Jake said. "How'd you know—"

"Oh, I've been around the block a time or two. Listen to this." He threw his head back and sang in a full, melodious voice:

> " *Samson and a lion got in attack,*
> *And Samson climbed up on the lion's back.*
> *Well, you've read about lion killin men with their paws,*
> *But Samson put his hands round the lion's jaws!*
> *He rode that lion 'til the beast fell dead,*
> *And the bees made honey in the lion's head.'* "

Aaron winked and then laughed at Jake's surprised expression. "That answer your question, friend?"

Jake's eyes were wide. "Wow! Good song! Where'd you hear it?"

"Oh, Aaron knows them all," Tower said. "He was hanging around Bleecker Street back before Bob Dylan knew how to blow more than open G on his Hohner. At least, if you believe *him*."

"It's an old spiritual," Aaron said to Jake, and then to Tower: "By the way, you're in check, fatso."

"Not for long," Tower said. He moved his bishop. Aaron promptly bagged it. Tower muttered something under his breath. To Jake it sounded suspiciously like *fuckwad*.

"So the answer is a lion," Jake said.

Aaron shook his head. "Only *half* the answer. Samson's Riddle is a *double*, my friend. The other half of the answer is honey. Get it?"

"Yes, I think so."

"Okay, now try this one." Aaron closed his eyes for a moment and then recited,

> *"What can run but never walks,*
> *Has a mouth but never talks,*
> *Has a bed but never sleeps,*
> *Has a head but never weeps?"*

"Smartass," Tower growled at Aaron.

Jake thought it over, then shook his head. He could have worried it longer—he found this business of riddles both fascinating and charming—but he had a strong feeling that he ought to be moving on from here, that he had other business on Second Avenue this morning.

"I give up."

"No, you don't," Aaron said. "That's what you do with *modern* riddles. But a *real* riddle isn't just a joke, kiddo—it's a puzzle. Turn it over in your head. If you still can't get it, make it an excuse to come back another day. If you need another excuse, fatso here *does* make a pretty good cup of joe."

"Okay," Jake said. "Thanks. I will."

But as he left, a certainty stole over him: he would never enter The Manhattan Restaurant of the Mind again.

15

JAKE WALKED SLOWLY DOWN Second Avenue, holding his new purchases in his left hand. At first he tried to think about the riddle—what *did* have a bed but never slept?—but little by little the question was driven from his mind by an increasing sense of anticipation. His senses seemed more acute than ever before in his life; he saw billions of coruscating sparks in the pavement, smelled a thousand mixed aromas in every breath he took, and seemed to hear other sounds, secret sounds, within each of the sounds he heard. He wondered if this was the way dogs felt before thunderstorms or earthquakes, and felt almost sure that it was. Yet the sensation that the impending event was not bad but good, that it would balance out the terrible thing which had happened to him three weeks ago, continued to grow.

And now, as he drew close to the place where the course would be set, that knowing-in-advance fell upon him once again.

A bum is going to ask me for a handout, and I'll give him the change Mr. Tower gave me. And there's a record store. The door's open to let in the fresh air and I'll hear a Stones song playing when I pass. And I'm going to see my own reflection in a bunch of mirrors.

Traffic on Second Avenue was still light. Taxis honked and wove their way amid the slower-moving cars and trucks. Spring sunshine twinkled off their windshields and bright yellow hides. While he was waiting for a light to change, Jake saw the bum on the far corner of Second and Fifty-second. He was sitting against the brick wall of a small restaurant, and as Jake approached him, he saw that the name of the restaurant was Chew Chew Mama's.

Choo-choo, Jake thought. *And that's the truth.*

"Godda-quarder?" the bum asked tiredly, and Jake dropped his change from the bookstore into the bum's

lap without even looking around. Now he could hear
the Rolling Stones, right on schedule:

> *"I see a red door and I want to paint it black,*
> *No colours anymore, I want them to turn black . . ."*

As he passed, he saw—also without surprise—that
the name of the store was Tower of Power Records.

Towers were selling cheap today, it seemed.

Jake walked on, the street-signs floating past in a
kind of dream-daze. Between Forty-ninth and Forty-
eighth he passed a store called Reflections of You. He
turned his head and caught sight of a dozen Jakes in
the mirrors, as he had known he would—a dozen boys
who were small for their age, a dozen boys dressed in
neat school clothes: blue blazers, white shirts, dark
red ties, gray dress pants. Piper School didn't have an
official uniform, but this was as close to the unofficial
one as you could get.

Piper seemed long ago and far away now.

Suddenly Jake realized where he was going. This
knowledge rose in his mind like sweet, refreshing
water from an underground spring. *It's a delicatessen,*
he thought. *That's what it looks like, anyway. It's really something else—a doorway to another world.* The
world. His *world. The* right *world.*

He began to run, looking ahead eagerly. The light
at Forty-seventh was against him but he ignored it,
leaping from the curb and racing nimbly between
the broad white lines of the crosswalk with just a
perfunctory glance to the left. A plumbing van
stopped short with a squeal of tires as Jake flashed
in front of it.

"Hey! Whaddaya-whaddaya?" the driver yelled, but
Jake ignored him.

Only one more block.

He began to sprint all-out now. His tie fluttered
behind his left shoulder; his hair had blown back from
his forehead; his school loafers hammered the side-

walk. He ignored the stares—some amused, some merely curious—of the passersby as he had ignored the van driver's outraged shout.

Up here—up here on the corner. Next to the stationery store.

Here came a UPS man in dark brown fatigues, pushing a dolly loaded with packages. Jake hurdled it like a long-jumper, arms up. The tail of his white shirt pulled free of his pants and flapped beneath his blazer like the hem of a slip. He came down and almost collided with a baby-carriage being pushed by a young Puerto Rican woman. Jake hooked around the pram like a halfback who has spotted a hole in the line and is bound for glory. "Where's the fire, handsome?" the young woman asked, but Jake ignored her, too. He dashed past The Paper Patch, with its window-display of pens and notebooks and desk calculators.

The door! he thought ecstatically. *I'm going to see it! And am I going to stop? No, way, José! I'm going to go straight through it, and if it's locked, I'll flatten it right in front of m—*

Then he saw what was at the corner of Second and Forty-sixth and stopped after all—skidded to a halt, in fact, on the heels of his loafers. He stood there in the middle of the sidewalk, hands clenched, his breath rasping harshly in and out of his lungs, his hair falling back onto his forehead in sweaty clumps.

"No," he almost whimpered. *"No!"* But his near-frantic negation did not change what he saw, which was nothing at all. There was nothing to see but a short board fence and a littered, weedy lot beyond it.

The building which had stood there had been demolished.

16

JAKE STOOD OUTSIDE THE fence without moving for almost two minutes, surveying the vacant lot with dull eyes. One corner of his mouth twitched randomly. He could feel his hope, his *absolute certainty*, draining out of him. The feeling which was replacing it was the deepest, bitterest despair he had ever known.

Just another false alarm, he thought when the shock had abated enough so he could think anything at all. *Another false alarm, blind alley, dry well. Now the voices will start up again, and when they do, I think I'm going to start screaming. And that's okay. Because I'm tired of toughing this thing out. I'm tired of going crazy. If this is what going crazy is like, then I just want to hurry up and get there so somebody will take me to the hospital and give me something that'll knock me out. I give up. This is the end of the line—I'm through.*

But the voices did not come back—at least, not yet. And as he began to think about what he was seeing, he realized that the lot wasn't completely empty, after all. Standing in the middle of the trash-littered, weedy waste ground was a sign.

MILLS CONSTRUCTION AND SOMBRA REAL ESTATE
ASSOCIATES
ARE CONTINUING TO REMAKE THE FACE OF
MANHATTAN!
COMING SOON TO THIS LOCATION:
TURTLE BAY LUXURY CONDOMINIUMS!
CALL 555-6712 FOR INFORMATION!
YOU WILL BE SO GLAD YOU DID!

Coming soon? Maybe . . . but Jake had his doubts. The letters on the sign were faded and it was sagging a little. At least one graffiti artist, BANGO SKANK by name, had left his mark across the artist's drawing of the Turtle Bay Luxury Condominiums in bright blue spray-paint. Jake wondered if the project had been postponed or if it had maybe just gone belly-up. He remembered hearing his father talking on the telephone to his business advisor not two weeks ago, yelling at the man to stay away from any more condo investments. "I don't *care* how good the tax-picture looks!" he'd nearly screamed (this was, so far as Jake could tell, his father's normal tone of voice when discussing business matters—the coke in the desk drawer might have had something to do with that). "When they're offering a goddamn TV set just so you'll come down and look at a *blueprint*, something's wrong!"

The board fence surrounding the lot was chin-high to Jake. It had been plastered with handbills—Olivia Newton-John at Radio City, a group called G. Gordon Liddy and the Grots at a club in the East Village, a film called *War of the Zombies* which had come and gone earlier that spring. NO TRESPASSING signs had also been nailed up at intervals along the fence, but most of them had been papered over by ambitious bill-posters. A little way farther along, another graffito had been spray-painted on the fence—this one in what had once undoubtedly been a bright red but which had now faded to the dusky pink of late-summer roses. Jake whispered the words aloud, his eyes wide and fascinated:

> "See the TURTLE of enormous girth!
>   On his shell he holds the earth
>   If you want to run and play,
>   Come along the BEAM today."

Jake supposed the source of this strange little poem (if not its meaning) was clear enough. This part of Manhattan's East Side was known, after all, as Turtle Bay. But that didn't explain the gooseflesh which was now running up the center of his back in a rough stripe, or his clear sense that he had found another road-sign along some fabulous hidden highway.

Jake unbuttoned his shirt and stuck his two newly purchased books inside. Then he looked around, saw no one paying attention to him, and grabbed the top of the fence. He boosted himself up, swung a leg over, and dropped down on the other side. His left foot landed on a loose pile of bricks that promptly slid out from under him. His ankle buckled under his weight and bright pain lanced up his leg. He fell with a thud and cried out in mingled hurt and surprise as more bricks dug into his ribcage like thick, rude fists.

He simply lay where he was for a moment, waiting to get his breath back. He didn't think he was badly hurt, but he'd twisted his ankle and it would probably swell. He'd be walking with a limp by the time he got home. He'd just have to grin and bear it, though; he sure didn't have cab-fare.

You don't really plan to go home, do you? They'll eat you alive.

Well, maybe they would and maybe they wouldn't. So far as he could see, he didn't have much choice in the matter. And that was for later. Right now he was going to explore this lot which had drawn him as surely as a magnet draws steel shavings. That feeling of power was still all around him, he realized, and stronger than ever. He didn't think this was just a vacant lot. Something was going on here, something big. He could feel it thrumming in the air, like loose volts escaping from the biggest power-plant in the world.

As he got up, Jake saw that he had actually fallen lucky. Close by was a nasty jumble of broken glass. If he'd fallen into that, he might have cut himself very badly.

That used to be the show window, Jake thought. *When the deli was still here, you could stand on the sidewalk and look in at all the meats and cheeses. They used to hang them on strings.* He didn't know how he knew this, but he did—knew it beyond a shadow of a doubt.

He looked around thoughtfully and then walked a little farther into the lot. Near the middle, lying on the ground and half-buried in a lush growth of spring weeds, was another sign. Jake knelt beside it, pulled it upright, and brushed the dirt away. The letters were faded, but he could still make them out:

TOM AND GERRY'S ARTISTIC DELI
PARTY PLATTERS OUR SPECIALTY!

And below it, spray-painted in that same red-fading-to-pink, was this puzzling sentence: HE HOLDS US ALL WITHIN HIS MIND.

This is the place, Jake thought. *Oh yes.*

He let the sign fall back, stood up, and walked deeper into the lot, moving slowly, looking at everything. As he moved, that sensation of power grew. Everything he saw—the weeds, the broken glass, the clumps of bricks—seemed to stand forth with a kind of exclamatory force. Even the potato chip bags seemed beautiful, and the sun had turned a discarded beer-bottle into a cylinder of brown fire.

Jake was very aware of his own breathing, and of the sunlight falling upon everything like a weight of gold. He suddenly understood that he was standing on the edge of a great mystery, and he felt a shudder—half terror and half wonder—work through him.

It's all here. Everything. Everything is still here.

The weeds brushed at his pants; burdocks stuck to his socks. The breeze blew a Ring-Ding wrapper in front of him; the sun reflected off it and for a moment the wrapper was filled with a beautiful, terrible inner glow.

"Everything is still here," he repeated to himself, unaware that his face was filling with its own inner glow. *"Everything."*

He was hearing a sound—had been hearing it ever

since he entered the lot, in fact. It was a wonderful high humming, inexpressibly lonely and inexpressibly lovely. It might have been the sound of a high wind on a deserted plain, except it was *alive*. It was, he thought, the sound of a thousand voices singing some great open chord. He looked down and realized there were *faces* in the tangled weeds and low bushes and heaps of bricks. *Faces*.

"What are you?" Jake whispered. "*Who* are you?" There was no answer, but he seemed to hear, beneath the choir, the sound of hoofbeats on the dusty earth, and gunfire, and angels calling hosannahs from the shadows. The faces in the wreckage seemed to turn as he passed. They seemed to follow his progress, but no evil intent did they bear. He could see Forty-sixth Street, and the edge of the U.N. Building on the other side of First Avenue, but the buildings did not matter—*New York* did not matter. It had become as pale as window-glass.

The humming grew. Now it was not a thousand voices but a million, an open funnel of voices rising from the deepest well of the universe. He caught names in that group voice, but could not have said what they were. One might have been Marten. One might have been Cuthbert. Another might have been Roland—Roland of Gilead.

There were names; there was a babble of conversation that might have been ten thousand entwined stories; but above all was that gorgeous, swelling hum, a vibration that wanted to fill his head with bright white light. It was, Jake realized with a joy so overwhelming that it threatened to burst him to pieces, the voice of *Yes*; the voice of *White*; the voice of *Always*. It was a great chorus of affirmation, and it sang in the empty lot. It sang for him.

Then, lying in a cluster of scrubby burdock plants, Jake saw the key . . . and beyond that, the rose.

17

HIS LEGS BETRAYED HIM and he fell to his knees. He
was vaguely aware that he was weeping, even more
vaguely aware that he had wet his pants a little. He
crawled forward on his knees and reached toward the
key lying in the snarl of burdocks. Its simple shape
was one he seemed to have seen in his dreams:

He thought: *The little s-shape at the end—that's the
secret.*

As he closed his hand around the key, the voices
rose in a harmonic shout of triumph. Jake's own cry
was lost in the voice of that choir. He saw the key
flash white within his fingers, and felt a tremendous
jolt of power run up his arm. It was as if he had
grasped a live high-tension wire, but there was no
pain.

He opened *Charlie the Choo-Choo* and put the key
inside. Then his eyes fixed upon the rose again, and
he realized that it was the *real* key—the key to everything. He crawled toward it, his face a flaming corona
of light, his eyes blazing wells of blue fire.

The rose was growing from a clump of alien purple
grass.

As Jake neared this clump of alien grass, the rose
began to open before his eyes. It disclosed a dark
scarlet furnace, petal upon secret petal, each burning
with its own secret fury. He had never seen anything
so intensely and utterly alive in his whole life.

And now, as he stretched one grimy hand out toward this wonder, the voices began to sing his own
name . . . and deadly fear began to steal in toward
the center of his heart. It was as cold as ice and as
heavy as stone.

There was something wrong. He could feel a pulsing

discord, like a deep and ugly scratch across some priceless work of art or a deadly fever smouldering beneath the chilly skin of an invalid's brow.

It was something like a worm. An invading worm. And a shape. One which lurks just beyond the next turn of the road.

Then the heart of the rose opened for him, exposing a yellow dazzle of light, and all thought was swept away on a wave of wonder. Jake thought for a moment that what he was seeing was only pollen which had been invested with the supernatural glow which lived at the heart of every object in this deserted clearing—he thought it even though he had never heard of pollen within a rose. He leaned closer and saw that the concentrated circle of blazing yellow was not pollen at all. *It was a sun*: a vast forge burning at the center of this rose growing in the purple grass.

The fear returned, only now it had become outright terror. *It's right*, he thought, *everything here is right, but it could go wrong—has started going wrong already, I think. I'm being allowed to feel as much of that wrongness as I can bear . . . but what is it? And what can I do?*

It was something like a worm.

He could feel it beating like a sick and dirty heart, warring with the serene beauty of the rose, screaming harsh profanities against the choir of voices which had so soothed and lifted him.

He leaned closer to the rose and saw that its core was not just one sun but many . . . perhaps all suns contained within a ferocious yet fragile shell.

But it's wrong. It's all in danger.

Knowing it would almost surely mean his death to touch that glowing microcosm but helpless to stop himself, Jake reached forward. There was no curiosity or terror in this gesture; only a great, inarticulate need to protect the rose.

18

WHEN HE CAME BACK to himself, he was at first only aware that a great deal of time had passed and his head hurt like hell.

What happened? Was I mugged?

He rolled over and sat up. Another blast of pain went through his head. He raised a hand to his left temple, and his fingers came away sticky with blood. He looked down and saw a brick poking out of the weeds. Its rounded corner was too red.

If it had been sharp, I'd probably be dead or in a coma.

He looked at his wrist and was surprised to find he was still wearing his watch. It was a Seiko, not terribly expensive, but in this city you didn't snooze in vacant lots without losing your stuff. Expensive or not, someone would be more than happy to relieve you of it. This time he had been lucky, it seemed.

It was quarter past four in the afternoon. He had been lying here, dead to the world, for at least five hours. His father probably had the cops out looking for him by now, but that didn't seem to matter much. It seemed to Jake that he had walked out of Piper School about a thousand years ago.

Jake walked half the distance to the fence between the vacant lot and the Second Avenue sidewalk, then stopped.

What exactly *had* happened to him?

Little by little, the memories came back. Hopping the fence. Slipping and twisting his ankle. He reached down, touched it, and winced. Yes—that much had happened, all right. Then what?

Something magical.

He groped for that something like an old man groping his way across a shadowy room. Everything had been full of its own light. *Everything*—even the empty wrappers and discarded beer-bottles. There had been voices—they had been singing and telling thousands of overlapping stories.

"And *faces*," he muttered. This memory made him look around apprehensively. He saw no faces. The piles of bricks were just piles of bricks, and the tangles of weeds were just tangles of weeds. There were no faces, but—

—but they were here. It wasn't your imagination.

He believed that. He couldn't capture the essence of the memory, its quality of beauty and transcendence, but it seemed perfectly real. It was just that his memory of those moments before he had passed out seemed like photographs taken on the best day of your life. You can remember what that day was like— sort of, anyway—but the pictures are flat and almost powerless.

Jake looked around the desolate lot, now filling up with the violet shadows of late afternoon, and thought: *I want you back. God, I want you back the way you were.*

Then he saw the rose, growing in its clump of purple grass, very close to the place where he had fallen. His heart leaped into his throat. Jake blundered back toward it, unmindful of the beats of pain each step sent up from his ankle. He dropped to his knees in front of it like a worshipper at an altar. He leaned forward, eyes wide.

It's just a rose. Just a rose after all. And the grass—

The grass wasn't purple after all, he saw. There were *splatters* of purple on the blades, yes, but the color beneath was a perfectly normal green. He looked a little further and saw splashes of blue on another clump of weeds. To his right, a straggling burdock bush bore traces of both red and yellow. And beyond the burdocks was a little pile of discarded paint-cans. Glidden Spread Satin, the labels said.

That's all it was. Just splatters of paint. Only with your head all messed up the way it was, you thought you were seeing—

That was bullshit.

He knew what he had seen then, and what he was seeing now. "Camouflage," he whispered. "It was all right here. *Everything* was. And . . . it still is."

Now that his head was clearing, he could again feel the steady, harmonic power that this place held. The choir was still here, its voice just as musical, although now dim and distant. He looked at a pile of bricks and old broken chunks of plaster and saw a barely discernible face hiding within it. It was the face of a woman with a scar on her forehead.

"Allie?" Jake murmured. "Isn't your name Allie?"

There was no answer. The face was gone. He was only looking at an unlovely pile of bricks and plaster again.

He looked back at the rose. It was, he saw, not the dark red that lives at the heart of a blazing furnace, but a dusty, mottled pink. It was very beautiful, but not perfect. Some of the petals had curled back; the outer edges of these were brown and dead. It wasn't the sort of cultivated flower he had seen in florists' shops; he supposed it was a wild rose.

"You're very beautiful," he said, and once more stretched his hand out to touch it.

Although there was no breeze, the rose nodded toward him. For just a moment the pads of his fingers touched its surface, smooth and velvety and marvellously alive, and all around him the voice of the choir seemed to swell.

"Are you sick, rose?"

There was no answer, of course. When his fingers left the faded pink bowl of the flower, it nodded back to its original position, growing out of the paint-splattered weeds in its quiet, forgotten splendor.

Do roses bloom at this time of year? Jake wondered. *Wild ones? Why would a wild rose grow in a vacant lot, anyway? And if there's one, how come there aren't more?*

He remained on his hands and knees a little longer,

then realized he could stay here looking at the rose for the rest of the afternoon (or maybe the rest of his life) and not come any closer to solving its mystery. He had seen it plain for a moment, as he had seen everything else in this forgotten, trash-littered corner of the city; he had seen it with its mask off and its camouflage tossed aside. He wanted to see that again, but wanting would not make it so.

It was time to go home.

He saw the two books he'd bought at The Manhattan Restaurant of the Mind lying nearby. As he picked them up, a bright silver object slipped from the pages of *Charlie the Choo-Choo* and fell into a scruffy patch of weeds. Jake bent, favoring his hurt ankle, and picked it up. As he did so, the choir seemed to sigh and swell, then fell back to its almost inaudible hum.

"So that part was real, too," he murmured. He ran the ball of his thumb over the blunt protruding points of the key and into those primitive V-shaped notches. He sent it skating over the mild *s*-curves at the end of the third notch. Then he tucked it deep into the right front pocket of his pants and began to limp back toward the fence.

He had reached it and was preparing to scramble over the top when a terrible thought suddenly seized his mind.

The rose! What if somebody comes in here and picks it?

A little moan of horror escaped him. He turned back and after a moment his eyes picked it out, although it was deep in the shadow of a neighboring building now—a tiny pink shape in the dimness, vulnerable, beautiful, and alone.

I can't leave it—I have to guard it!

But a voice spoke up in his mind, a voice that was surely that of the man he had met at the way station in that strange other life. *No one will pick it. Nor will any vandal crush it beneath his heel because his dull eyes cannot abide the sight of its beauty. That is not the danger. It can protect itself from such things as those.*

A sense of deep relief swept through Jake.

Can I come here again and look at it? he asked the phantom voice. *When I'm low, or if the voices come back and start their argument again? Can I come back and look at it and have some peace?*

The voice did not answer, and after a few moments of listening, Jake decided it was gone. He tucked *Charlie the Choo-Choo* and *Riddle-De-Dum!* into the waistband of his pants—which, he saw, were streaked with dirt and dotted with clinging burdocks—and then grabbed the board fence. He boosted himself up, swung over the top, and dropped onto the sidewalk of Second Avenue again, being careful to land on his good foot.

Traffic on the Avenue—both pedestrian and vehicular—was much heavier now as people made their way home for the night. A few passersby looked at the dirty boy in the torn blazer and untucked, flapping shirt as he jumped awkwardly down from the fence, but not many. New Yorkers are used to the sight of people doing peculiar things.

He stood there a moment, feeling a sense of loss and realizing something else, as well—the arguing voices were still absent. That, at least, was something.

He glanced at the board fence; and the verse of spray-painted doggerel seemed to leap out at him, perhaps because the paint was the same color as the rose.

"See the TURTLE of enormous girth" Jake muttered. "On his shell he holds the earth." He shivered. "What a day! Boy!"

He turned and began to limp slowly in the direction of home.

19

THE DOORMAN MUST HAVE buzzed up as soon as Jake entered the lobby, because his father was standing outside the elevator when it opened on the fifth floor. Elmer Chambers was wearing faded jeans and cowboy boots that improved his five-ten to a rootin, tootin six feet. His black, crewcut hair bolted up from his head; for as long as Jake could remember, his father had looked like a man who had just suffered some tremendous, galvanizing shock. As soon as Jake stepped out of the elevator, Chambers seized him by the arm.

"Look at you!" His father's eyes flicked up and down, taking in Jake's dirty face and hands, the blood drying on his cheek and temple, the dusty pants, the torn blazer, and the burdock that clung to his tie like some peculiar clip. "Get in here! Where the hell have you been? Your mother's just about off her fucking gourd!"

Without giving Jake a chance to answer, he dragged him through the apartment door. Jake saw Greta Shaw standing in the archway between the dining room and the kitchen. She gave him a look of guarded sympathy, then disappeared before the eyes of "the mister" could chance upon her.

Jake's mother was sitting in her rocker. She got to her feet when she saw Jake, but she did not *leap* to her feet; neither did she pelt across to the foyer so she could cover him with kisses and invective. As she came toward him, Jake assessed her eyes and guessed she'd had at least three Valium since noon. Maybe four. Both of his parents were firm believers in better living through chemistry.

"You're *bleeding*! Where have you been?" She made this inquiry in her cultured Vassar voice, pronouncing *been* so it rhymed with *seen*. She might have been greeting an acquaintance who had been involved in a minor traffic accident.

"Out," he said.

His father gave him a rough shake. Jake wasn't prepared for it. He stumbled and came down on his bad ankle. The pain flared again, and he was suddenly furious. Jake didn't think his father was pissed because he had disappeared from school, leaving only his mad composition behind; his father was pissed because Jake had had the temerity to fuck up his own precious schedule.

To this point in his life, Jake had been aware of only three feelings about his father: puzzlement, fear, and a species of weak, confused love. Now a fourth and fifth surfaced. One was anger; the other was disgust. Mixed in with these unpleasant feelings was that sense of homesickness. It was the largest thing inside him right now, weaving through everything else like smoke. He looked at his father's flushed cheeks and screaming haircut and wished he was back in the vacant lot, looking at the rose and listening to the choir. *This is not my place*, he thought. *Not anymore. I have work to do. If only I knew what it was.*

"Let go of me," he said.

"*What* did you say to me?" His father's blue eyes widened. They were very bloodshot tonight. Jake guessed he had been dipping heavily into his supply of magic powder, and that probably made this a bad time to cross him, but Jake realized he intended to cross him just the same. He would not be shaken like a mouse in the jaws of a sadistic tomcat. Not tonight. Maybe not ever again. He suddenly realized that a large part of his anger stemmed from one simple fact: he could not *talk* to them about what had happened— what was *still* happening. They had closed all the doors.

But I have a key, he thought, and touched its shape through the fabric of his pants. And the rest of that strange verse occurred to him: *If you want to run and play,/Come along the BEAM today.*

"I said let go of me," he repeated. "I've got a sprained ankle and you're hurting it."

"I'll hurt more than your ankle if you don't—"

Sudden strength seemed to flow into Jake. He seized the hand clamped on his arm just below the shoulder and shoved it violently away. His father's mouth dropped open.

"I don't *work* for you," Jake said. "I'm your *son*, remember? If you forgot, check the picture on your desk."

His father's upper lip pulled back from his perfectly capped teeth in a snarl that was two parts surprise and one part fury. "Don't you talk to me like that, mister—where in the hell is your respect?"

"I don't know. Maybe I lost it on the way home."

"You spend the whole goddamn day absent without leave and then you stand there running your fat, disrespectful mouth—"

"Stop it! Stop it, both of you!" Jake's mother cried. She sounded near tears in spite of the tranquilizers perking through her system.

Jake's father reached for Jake's arm again, then changed his mind. The surprising force with which his son had torn his hand away a moment ago might have had something to do with it. Or perhaps it was only the look in Jake's eyes. "I want to know where you've been."

"Out. I told you that. And that's *all* I'm going to tell you."

"Fuck that! Your headmaster called, your French teacher actually *came here*, and they both had *beaucoup* questions for you! So do I, and I want some *answers*!"

"Your clothes are dirty," his mother observed, and then added timidly: "Were you mugged, Johnny? Did you play hookey and get mugged?"

"Of course he wasn't mugged," Elmer Chambers snarled. "Still wearing his watch, isn't he?"

"But there's blood on his head."

"It's okay, Mom. I just bumped it."

"But—"

"I'm going to go to bed. I'm very, very tired. If you want to talk about this in the morning, okay. Maybe we'll all be able to make some sense then. But for now, I don't have a thing to say."

His father took a step after him, reaching out.

"*No, Elmer!*" Jake's mother almost screamed.

Chambers ignored her. He grabbed Jake by the back of the blazer. "Don't you just walk away from me—" he began, and then Jake whirled, tearing the blazer out of his hand. The seam under the right arm, already strained, let go with a rough purring sound.

His father saw those blazing eyes and stepped away. The rage on his face was doused by something that looked like terror. That blaze was not metaphorical; Jake's eyes actually seemed to be on fire. His mother gave voice to a strengthless little scream, clapped one hand to her mouth, took two large, stumbling steps backward, and dropped into her rocking chair with a small thud.

"*Leave . . . me . . . alone,*" Jake said.

"What's *happened* to you?" his father asked, and now his tone was almost plaintive. "What in the *hell's* happened to you? You bug out of school without a word to anyone on the first day of exams, you come back filthy from head to toe . . . and you act as if you've gone crazy."

Well, there it was—*you act as if you've gone crazy*. What he'd been afraid of ever since the voices started three weeks ago. The Dread Accusation. Only now that it was out, Jake found it didn't frighten him much at all, perhaps because he had finally put the issue to rest in his own mind. Yes, something had happened to him. Was still happening. But no—he had *not* gone crazy. At least, not yet.

"We'll talk about it in the morning," he repeated. He walked across the dining room, and this time his father didn't try to stop him. He had almost reached the hall when his mother's voice, worried, stopped him: "Johnny . . . *are* you all right?"

And what should he answer? Yes? No? Both of the above? Neither of the above? But the voices had stopped, and that was something. That was, in fact, quite a lot.

"Better," he said at last. He went down to his room and closed the door firmly behind him. The sound of the door snicking firmly shut between him and all the rest of the round world filled him with tremendous relief.

20

HE STOOD BY THE door for a little while, listening. His mother's voice was only a murmur, his father's voice a little louder.

His mother said something about blood, and a doctor.

His father said the kid was fine; the only thing wrong with the kid was the junk coming out of his mouth, and he would fix that.

His mother said something about calming down.

His father said he *was* calm.

His mother said—

He said, she said, blah, blah, blah. Jake still loved them—he was pretty sure he did, anyway—but other stuff had happened now, and these things had made it necessary that still other things must occur.

Why? Because something was wrong with the rose. And maybe because he wanted to run and play . . . and see *his* eyes again, as blue as the sky above the way station had been.

Jake walked slowly over to his desk, removing his blazer as he went. It was pretty wasted—one sleeve torn almost completely off, the lining hanging like a limp sail. He slung it over the back of his chair, then sat down and put the books on his desk. He had been sleeping very badly over the last week and a half, but he thought tonight he would sleep well. He couldn't remember ever being so tired. When he woke up in the morning, perhaps he would know what to do.

There was a light knock at the door, and Jake turned warily in that direction.

"It's Mrs. Shaw, John. May I come in for a minute?"

He smiled. Mrs. Shaw—of course it was. His parents had drafted her as an intermediary. Or perhaps translator might be a better word.

You go see him, his mother would have said. *He'll tell you what's wrong with him. I'm his mother and this man with the bloodshot eyes and the runny nose is his father and you're only the housekeeper, but he'll tell you what he wouldn't tell us. Because you see more of him than either of us, and maybe you speak his language.*

She'll have a tray, Jake thought, and when he opened the door he was smiling.

Mrs. Shaw did indeed have a tray. There were two sandwiches on it, a wedge of apple pie, and a glass of chocolate milk. She was looking at Jake with mild anxiety, as if she thought he might lunge forward and try to bite her. Jake looked over her shoulder, but there was no sign of his parents. He imagined them sitting in the living room, listening anxiously.

"I thought you might like something to eat," Mrs. Shaw said.

"Yes, thanks." In fact, he was ravenously hungry; he hadn't eaten since breakfast. He stood aside and Mrs. Shaw came in (giving him another apprehensive look as she passed) and put the tray on the desk.

"Oh, look at this," she said, picking up *Charlie the Choo-Choo*. "I had this one when I was a little girl. Did you buy this today, Johnny?"

"Yes. Did my parents ask you to find out what I'd been up to?"

She nodded. No acting, no put-on. It was just a chore, like taking out the trash. *You can tell me if you want to,* her face said, *or you can keep still. I like you, Johnny, but it's really nothing to me, one way or the other. I just work here, and it's already an hour past my regular quitting time.*

He was not offended by what her face had to say; on the contrary, he was further calmed by it. Mrs. Shaw was another acquaintance who was not quite a friend . . . but he thought she might be a little closer to a friend than any of the kids at school were, and much closer than either his mother or father. Mrs. Shaw was honest, at least. She didn't dance. It all went on the bill at the end of the month, and she *always* cut the crusts off the sandwiches.

Jake picked up a sandwich and took a large bite. Bologna and cheese, his favorite. That was another thing in Mrs. Shaw's favor—she knew all his favorites. His mother was still under the impression that he liked corn on the cob and hated brussels sprouts.

"Please tell them I'm fine," he said, "and tell my father I'm sorry that I was rude to him."

He wasn't, but all his father really wanted was that apology. Once Mrs. Shaw conveyed it to him, he would relax and begin to tell himself the old lie—he had done his fatherly duty and all was well, all was well, and all manner of things were well.

"I've been studying very hard for my exams," he said, chewing as he talked, "and it all came down on me this morning, I guess. I sort of froze. It seemed like I had to get out or I'd suffocate." He touched the dried crust of blood on his forehead. "As for this, please tell my mother it's really nothing. I didn't get mugged or anything; it was just a stupid accident. There was a UPS guy pushing a hand-truck, and I walked right into it. The cut's no big deal. I'm not having double vision or anything, and even the headache's gone now."

She nodded. "I can see how it must have been—a high-powered school like that and all. You just got a little spooked. No shame in that, Johnny. But you really *haven't* seemed like yourself this last couple of weeks."

"I think I'll be okay now. I might have to re-do my Final Essay in English, but—"

"Oh!" Mrs. Shaw said. A startled looked crossed her face. She put *Charlie the Choo-Choo* back down on Jake's desk. "I almost forgot! Your French teacher left something for you. I'll just get it."

She left the room. Jake hoped he hadn't worried Mr. Bissette, who was a pretty good guy, but he supposed he must have, since Bissette had actually made a personal appearance. Jake had an idea that personal appearances were pretty rare for Piper School teachers. He wondered what Mr. Bissette had left. His best guess was an invitation to talk with Mr. Hotchkiss, the school shrink. That would have scared him this morning, but not tonight.

Tonight only the rose seemed to matter.

He tore into his second sandwich. Mrs. Shaw had left the door open, and he could hear her talking with his parents. They both sounded a little more cooled out now. Jake drank his milk, then grabbed the plate with the apple pie on it. A few moments later Mrs. Shaw came back. She was carrying a very familiar blue folder.

Jake found that not all of his dread had left him after all. They would all know by now, of course, students and faculty alike, and it was too late to do anything about it, but that didn't mean he liked all of them knowing he had flipped his lid. That they were talking about him.

A small envelope had been paper-clipped to the front of the folder. Jake pulled it free and looked up at Mrs. Shaw as he opened it. "How are my folks doing now?" he asked.

She allowed herself a brief smile. "Your father wanted me to ask why you didn't just tell him you had Exam Fever. He said he had it himself once or twice when he was a boy."

Jake was struck by this; his father had never been the sort of man to indulge in reminiscences which began, *You know, when I was a kid* . . . Jake tried to imagine his father as a boy with a bad case of Exam Fever and found he couldn't quite do it—the best he could manage was the unpleasant image of a pugnacious dwarf in a Piper sweatshirt, a dwarf in custom-tooled cowboy boots, a dwarf with short black hair bolting up from his forehead.

The note was from Mr. Bissette.

Dear John,
Bonnie Avery told me that you left early. She's very concerned about you, and so am I, although we have both seen this sort of thing before, especially during Exam Week. Please come and see me first thing to-morrow, okay? Any problems you have can be worked out. If you're feeling pressured by exams—and I want to repeat that it happens all the time—a postponement can be arranged. Our first concern is your welfare.
Call me this evening, if you like; you can reach me at 555-7661. I'll be up until midnight.
Remember that we all like you very much, and are on your side.

À votre santé

Len Bissette

Jake felt like crying. The concern was stated, and that was wonderful, but there were other things, unstated things, in the note that were even more wonderful—warmth, caring, and an effort (however misconceived) to understand and console.

Mr. Bissette had drawn a small arrow at the bottom of the note. Jake turned it over and read this:

*By the way, Bonnie asked me to send this along—
congratulations!!*

Congratulations? What in the hell did *that* mean?

He flipped open the folder. A sheet of paper had
been clipped to the first page of his Final Essay. It
was headed FROM THE DESK OF BONITA AVERY, and
Jake read the spiky, fountain-penned lines with growing amazement.

John,
    *Leonard will undoubtedly voice the concern we all
feel—he is awfully good at that—so let me confine
myself to your Final Essay, which I read and graded
during my free period. It is stunningly original, and
superior to any student work I have read in the last few
years. Your use of incremental repetition (". . . and
that is the truth") is inspired, but of course incremental
repetition is really just a trick. The real worth of the
composition is in its symbolic quality, first stated by the
images of the train and the door on the title page
and carried through splendidly within. This reaches its
logical conclusion with the picture of the "black
tower," which I take as your statement that conventional
ambitions are not only false but dangerous.*
    *I do not pretend to understand all the symbolism
(e.g., "Lady of Shadows," "gunslinger") but it
seems clear that you yourself are "The Prisoner" (of
school, society, etc.) and that the educational system
is "The Speaking Demon." Is it possible that both "Roland" and "the gunslinger" are the same authority
figure—your father, perhaps? I became so intrigued by
this possibility that I looked up his name in your
records. I note it is Elmer, but I further note that his
middle initial is R.*
    *I find this extremely provocative. Or is this name a
double symbol, drawn both from your father and
from Robert Browning's poem "Childe Roland to the
Dark Tower Came"? This is not a question I would
ask most students, but of course I know how omnivo-
rously you read!*

At any rate, I am extremely impressed. Younger students are often attracted to so-called "stream-of-consciousness" writing, but are rarely able to control it. You have done an outstanding job of merging s-of-c with symbolic language.

Bravo!

Drop by as soon as you're "back at it"—I want to discuss possible publication of this piece in the first issue of next year's student literary magazine.

B. Avery

P.S. If you left school today because you had sudden doubts about my ability to understand a Final Essay of such unexpected richness, I hope I have assuaged them.

Jake pulled the sheet off the clip, revealing the title page of his stunningly original and richly symbolic Final Essay. Written and circled there in the red ink of Ms. Avery's marking pen was the notation A+. Below this she had written *EXCELLENT JOB!!!*

Jake began to laugh.

The whole day—the long, scary, confusing, exhilarating, terrifying, mysterious day—was condensed in great, roaring sobs of laughter. He slumped in his chair, head thrown back, hands clutching his belly, tears streaming down his face. He laughed himself hoarse. He would almost stop and then some line from Ms. Avery's well-meaning critique would catch his eye and he would be off to the races again. He didn't see his father come to the door, look in at him with puzzled, wary eyes, and then leave again, shaking his head.

At last he *did* become aware that Mrs. Shaw was still sitting on his bed, looking at him with an expression of friendly detachment tinctured with faint curiosity. He tried to speak, but the laughter pealed out again before he could.

I gotta stop, he thought. *I gotta stop or it's gonna kill me. I'll have a stroke or a heart attack, or something.*

Then he thought, *I wonder what she made of "choo-choo, choo-choo?,"* and he began to laugh wildly again.

At last the spasms began to taper off to giggles. He wiped his arm across his streaming eyes and said, "I'm sorry, Mrs. Shaw—it's just that . . . well . . . I got an A-plus on my Final Essay. It was all very . . . very rich . . . and very sym . . . sym . . ."

But he couldn't finish. He doubled up with laughter again, holding his throbbing belly.

Mrs. Shaw got up, smiling. "That's very nice, John. I'm happy it's all turned out so well, and I'm sure your folks will be, too. I'm awfully late—I think I'll ask the doorman to call me a cab. Goodnight, and sleep well."

"Goodnight, Mrs. Shaw," Jake said, controlling himself with an effort. "And thanks."

As soon as she was gone, he began to laugh again.

21

DURING THE NEXT HALF hour he had separate visits from both parents. They had indeed calmed down, and the A+ grade on Jake's Final Essay seemed to calm them further. Jake received them with his French text open on the desk before him, but he hadn't really looked at it, nor did he have any intention of looking at it. He was only waiting for them to be gone so he could study the two books he had bought earlier that day. He had an idea that the *real* Final Exams were still waiting just over the horizon, and he wanted desperately to pass.

His father poked his head into Jake's room around quarter of ten, about twenty minutes after Jake's mother had concluded her own short, vague visit. Elmer Chambers was holding a cigarette in one hand

and a glass of Scotch in the other. He seemed not only calmer but almost zonked. Jake wondered briefly and indifferently if he had been hitting his mother's Valium supply.

"Are you okay, kid?"

"Yes." He was once again the small, neat boy who was always completely in control of himself. The eyes he turned to his father were not blazing but opaque.

"I wanted to say I'm sorry about before." His father was not a man who made many apologies, and he did it badly. Jake found himself feeling a little sorry for him.

"It's all right."

"Hard day," his father said. He gestured with the empty glass. "Why don't we just forget it happened?" He spoke as if this great and logical idea had just come to him.

"I already have."

"Good." His father sounded relieved. "Time for you to get some sleep, isn't it? You'll have some explaining to do and some tests to take tomorrow."

"I guess so," Jake said. "Is Mom okay?"

"Fine. Fine. I'm going in the study. Got a lot of paperwork tonight."

"Dad?"

His father looked back at him warily.

"What's your middle name?"

Something in his father's face told Jake that he had looked at the Final Essay grade but hadn't bothered to read either the paper itself or Ms. Avery's critique.

"I don't have one," he said. "Just an initial, like Harry S Truman. Except mine's an R. What brought that on?"

"Just curious," Jake said.

He managed to hold onto his composure until his father was gone . . . but as soon as the door was closed, he ran to his bed and stuffed his face into his pillow to muffle another bout of wild laughter.

22

WHEN HE WAS SURE he was over the current fit (although an occasional snicker still rumbled up his throat like an aftershock) and his father would be safely locked away in his study with his cigarettes, his Scotch, his papers, and his little bottle of white powder, Jake went back to his desk, turned on the study lamp, and opened *Charlie the Choo-Choo*. He glanced briefly at the copyright page and saw it had originally been published in 1942; his copy was from the fourth printing. He looked at the back, but there was no information at all about Beryl Evans, the book's author.

Jake turned back to the beginning, looked at the picture of a grinning, blonde-haired man sitting in the cab of a steam locomotive, considered the proud grin on the man's face, and then began to read.

> Bob Brooks was an engineer for The Mid-World Railway Company, on the St. Louis to Topeka run. Engineer Bob was the best trainman The Mid-World Railway Company ever had, and Charlie was the best train!
>
> Charlie was a 402 Big Boy Steam Locomotive, and Engineer Bob was the only man who had ever been allowed to sit in his peak-seat and pull the whistle. Everyone knew the WHOOO-OOOO of Charlie's whistle, and whenever they heard it echoing across the flat Kansas countryside, they said, "There goes Charlie and Engineer Bob, the fastest team between St. Louis and Topeka!"
>
> Boys and girls ran into their yards to watch Charlie and Engineer Bob go by. Engineer Bob would smile and wave. The children would smile and wave back.
>
> Engineer Bob had a special secret. He was the only one who knew. Charlie the Choo-Choo was really, really alive. One day while they were making the run between Topeka and St. Louis, Engineer Bob heard singing, very soft and low.

"Who is in the cab with me?" Engineer Bob said sternly.

"You need to see a shrink, Engineer Bob," Jake murmured, and turned the page. Here was a picture of Bob bending over to look beneath Charlie the Choo-Choo's automatic firebox. Jake wondered who was driving the train and watching out for cows (not to mention boys and girls) on the tracks while Bob was checking for stowaways, and guessed that Beryl Evans hadn't known a lot about trains.

"Don't worry," said a small, gruff voice. "It is only I."

"Who's I?" Engineer Bob asked. He spoke in his biggest, sternest voice, because he still thought someone was playing a joke on him.

"Charlie," said the small, gruff voice.

"Hardy har-har!" said Engineer Bob. "Trains can't talk! I may not know much, but I know that! If you're Charlie, I suppose you can blow your own whistle!"

"Of course," said the small, gruff voice, and just then the whistle made its big noise, rolling out across the Missouri plains: WHOOO-OOOO!

"Goodness!" said Engineer Bob. "It really *is* you!"

"I told you," said Charlie the Choo-Choo.

"How come I never knew you were alive before?" asked Engineer Bob. "Why didn't you ever talk to me before?"

Then Charlie sang this song to Engineer Bob in his small, gruff voice.

Don't ask me silly questions,
I won't play silly games.
I'm just a simple choo-choo train
And I'll always be the same.

I only want to race along
Beneath the bright blue sky,
And be a happy choo-choo train
Until the day I die.

"Will you talk to me some more when we're making our run?" asked Engineer Bob. "I'd like that."

"I would, too," said Charlie. "I love you, Engineer Bob."

"I love you too, Charlie," said Engineer Bob, and then he blew the whistle himself, just to show how happy he was.

WHOOO-OOO! It was the biggest and best Charlie had *ever* whistled, and everyone who heard it came out to see.

The picture which illustrated this last was similar to the one on the cover of the book. In the previous pictures (they were rough drawings which reminded Jake of the pictures in his favorite kindergarten book, *Mike Mulligan and His Steam Shovel*), the locomotive had been just a locomotive—cheery, undoubtedly interesting to the '40s-era boys who had been this book's intended audience, but still only a piece of machinery. In this picture, however, it had clearly human features, and this gave Jake a deep chill despite Charlie's smile and the rather heavy-handed cuteness of the story.

He didn't trust that smile.

He turned to his Final Essay and scanned down the lines. *I'm pretty sure Blaine is dangerous,* he read, *and that is the truth.*

He closed the folder, tapped his fingers on it thoughtfully for a few moments, then returned to *Charlie the Choo-Choo*.

Engineer Bob and Charlie spent many happy days together and talked of many things. Engineer Bob lived alone, and Charlie was the first real friend he'd had since his wife died, long ago, in New York.

Then one day, when Charlie and Engineer Bob returned to the roundhouse in St. Louis, they found a new diesel locomotive in Charlie's berth. And what a diesel locomotive it was! 5,000 horsepower! Stainless steel couplers! Traction motors from the Utica Engine Works in Utica, New York! And sitting on top, behind the generator, were three bright yellow radiator cooling fans.

"What is this?" Engineer Bob asked in a worried voice, but Charlie only sang his song in his smallest, gruffest voice:

Don't ask me silly questions,
I won't play silly games.
I'm just a simple choo-choo train
And I'll always be the same.

I only want to race along
Beneath the bright blue sky,
And be a happy choo-choo train
Until the day I die.

Mr. Briggs, the Roundhouse Manager, came over.

"That is a beautiful diesel locomotive," said Engineer Bob, "but you will have to move it out of Charlie's berth, Mr. Briggs. Charlie needs a lube job this very afternoon."

"Charlie won't be needing any more lube jobs, Engineer Bob," said Mr. Briggs sadly. "This is his replacement—a brand-new Burlington Zephyr diesel loco. Once, Charlie was the best locomotive in the world, but now he is old and his boiler leaks. I am afraid the time has come for Charlie to retire."

"Nonsense!" Engineer Bob was mad! "Charlie is still full of zip and zowie! I will telegraph the head office of The Mid-World Railway Company! I will telegraph the President, Mr. Raymond Martin, myself! I know him, because he once gave me a Good Service Award, and afterwards Charlie and I took his little daughter for a ride. I let her pull the lanyard, and Charlie whistled his loudest for her!"

"I am sorry, Bob," said Mr. Briggs, "but it was Mr. Martin himself who ordered the new diesel loco."

It was true. And so Charlie the Choo-Choo was shunted off to a siding in the furthest corner of Mid-World's St. Louis yard to rust in the weeds. Now the

HONNNK! HONNNK! of the Burlington Zephyr was heard on the St. Louis to Topeka run, and Charlie's blew no more. A family of mice nested in the seat where Engineer Bob once sat so proudly, watching the countryside speed past; a family of swallows nested in his smoke-stack. Charlie was lonely and very sad. He missed the steel tracks and bright blue skies and wide open spaces. Sometimes, late at night, he thought of these things and cried dark, oily tears. This rusted his fine Stratham headlight, but he didn't care, because now the Stratham headlight was old, and it was always dark.

Mr. Martin, the President of The Mid-World Railway Company, wrote and offered to put Engineer Bob in the peak-seat of the new Burlington Zephyr. "It is a fine loco, Engineer Bob," said Mr. Martin, "chock-full of zip and zowie, and you should be the one to pilot it! Of all the Engineers who work for Mid-World, you are the best. And my daughter Susannah has never forgotten that you let her pull old Charlie's whistle."

But Engineer Bob said that if he couldn't pilot Charlie, his days as a trainman were done. "I wouldn't understand such a fine new diesel loco," said Engineer Bob, "and it wouldn't understand me."

He was given a job cleaning the engines in the St. Louis yards, and Engineer Bob became Wiper Bob. Sometimes the other engineers who drove the fine new diesels would laugh at him. "Look at that old fool!" they said. "He cannot understand that the world has moved on!"

Sometimes, late at night, Engineer Bob would go to the far side of the rail yard, where Charlie the Choo-Choo stood on the rusty rails of the lonely siding which had become his home. Weeds had twined in his wheels; his headlight was rusty and dark. Engineer Bob always talked to Charlie, but Charlie replied less and less. Many nights he would not talk at all.

One night, a terrible idea came into Engineer Bob's head. "Charlie, are you dying?" he asked, and in his smallest, gruffest voice, Charlie replied:

Don't ask me silly questions,
I won't play silly games,
I'm just a simple choo-choo train
And I'll always be the same.

Now that I can't race along
Beneath the bright blue sky
I guess that I'll just sit right here
Until I finally die.

Jake looked at the picture accompanying this not-exactly-unexpected turn of events for a long time. Rough drawing it might be, but it was still definitely a three-handkerchief job. Charlie looked old, beaten, and forgotten. Engineer Bob looked like he had lost his last friend . . . which, according to the story, he had. Jake could imagine children all over America blatting their heads off at this point, and it occurred to him that there were a *lot* of stories for kids with stuff like this in them, stuff that threw acid all over your emotions. Hansel and Gretel being turned out into the forest, Bambi's mother getting scragged by a hunter, the death of Old Yeller. It was easy to hurt little kids, easy to make them cry, and this seemed to bring out a strangely sadistic streak in many story-tellers . . . including, it seemed, Beryl Evans.

But, Jake found, *he* was not saddened by Charlie's relegation to the weedy wastelands at the outer edge of the Mid-World trainyards in St. Louis. Quite the opposite. *Good*, he thought. *That's the place for him. That's the place, because he's dangerous. Let him rot there, and don't trust that tear in his eye—they say croc-odiles cry, too.*

He read the rest rapidly. It had a happy ending, of course, although it was undoubtedly that moment of de-spair on the edge of the trainyards which children remem-bered long after the happy ending had slipped their minds.

Mr. Martin, the President of The Mid-World Railway Company, came to St. Louis to check on the operation. His plan was to ride the Burlington Zephyr to Topeka, where his daughter was giving her first piano recital, that very afternoon. Only the Zephyr wouldn't start. There was water in the diesel fuel, it seemed.

(Were you the one who watered the diesel, Engineer Bob? Jake wondered. *I bet it was, you sly dog, you!)*

All the other trains were out on their runs! What to do?

Someone tugged Mr. Martin's arm. It was Wiper Bob, only he no longer looked like an engine-wiper. He had taken off his oil-stained dungarees and put on a clean pair of overalls. On his head was his old pillowtick engineer's cap.

"Charlie's is right over there, on that siding," he said. "Charlie will make the run to Topeka, Mr. Martin. Charlie will get you there in time for your daughter's piano recital."

"That old steamer?" scoffed Mr. Briggs. "Charlie would still be fifty miles out of Topeka at sundown!"

"Charlie can do it," Engineer Bob insisted. "Without a train to pull, I know he can! I have been cleaning his engine and his boiler in my spare time, you see."

"We'll give it a try," said Mr. Martin. "I would be sorry to miss Susannah's first recital!"

Charlie was all ready to go; Engineer Bob had filled his tender with fresh coal, and the firebox was so hot its sides were red. He helped Mr. Martin up into the cab and backed Charlie off the rusty, forgotten siding and onto the main track for the first time in years. Then, as he engaged Forward First, he pulled on the lanyard and Charlie gave his old brave cry: *WHOOO-OOOOO!*

All over St. Louis the children heard that cry, and ran out into their yards to watch the rusty old steam loco pass. "Look!" they cried. "It's Charlie! Charlie the Choo-Choo is back! Hurrah!" They all waved, and as Charlie steamed out of town, gathering speed, he blew his own whistle, just as he had in the old days: *WHOOOO-OOOOOOO!*

Clickety-clack went Charlie's wheels!

Chuffa-chuffa went the smoke from Charlie's stack!

Brump-brump went the conveyor as it fed coal into the firebox!

Talk about zip! Talk about zowie! Golly gee, gosh, and wowie! Charlie had never gone so fast before! The countryside went whizzing by in a blur! They passed the cars on Route 41 as if they were standing still!

"Hoptedoodle!" cried Mr. Martin, waving his hat in the air. "This is some locomotive, Bob! I don't know why we ever retired it! How do you keep the coal-conveyor loaded at this speed?"

Engineer Bob only smiled, because he knew Charlie was *feeding himself*. And, beneath the *clickety-clack* and the *chuffa-chuffa* and the *brump-brump*, he could hear Charlie singing his old song in his low, gruff voice:

Don't ask me silly questions,
I won't play silly games,
I'm just a simple choo-choo train
And I'll always be the same.

I only want to race along
Beneath the bright blue sky,
And be a happy choo-choo train
Until the day I die.

Charlie got Mr. Martin to his daughter's piano recital on time (of course), and Susannah was just tickled pink to see her old friend Charlie again (of course), and they all went back to St. Louis together with Susannah yanking hell out of the train-whistle the whole way. Mr. Martin got Charlie and Engineer Bob a gig pulling kids around the brand-new Mid-World Amusement Park and Fun Fair in California, and

you will find them there to this day, pulling laughing children hither and thither in that world of lights and music and good, wholesome fun. Engineer Bob's hair is white, and Charlie doesn't talk as much as he once did, but both of them still have plenty of zip and

zowie, and every now and then the children hear
Charlie singing his old song in his soft, gruff voice.

THE END

"Don't ask me silly questions, I won't play silly
games," Jake muttered, looking at the final picture.
It showed Charlie the Choo-Choo pulling two bunting-
decked passenger cars filled with happy children from
the roller coaster to the Ferris wheel. Engineer Bob
sat in the cab, pulling the whistle-cord and looking as
happy as a pig in shit. Jake supposed Engineer Bob's
smile was supposed to convey supreme happiness, but
to him it looked like the grin of a lunatic. Charlie and
Engineer Bob *both* looked like lunatics . . . and the
more Jake looked at the kids, the more he thought
that their expressions looked like grimaces of terror.
Let us off this train, those faces seemed to say. *Please,
just let us off this train alive.*

And be a happy choo-choo train until the day I die.

Jake closed the book and looked at it thoughtfully.
Then he opened it again and began to leaf through
the pages, circling certain words and phrases that
seemed to call out to him.

*The Mid-World Railway Company . . . Engineer
Bob . . . a small, gruff voice . . . WHOO-OOOO . . .
the first real friend he'd had since his wife died, long
ago, in New York . . . Mr. Martin . . . the world has
moved on . . . Susannah . . .*

He put his pen down. *Why* did these words and
phrases call to him? The one about New York seemed
obvious enough, but what about the others? For that
matter, why this *book*? That he had been meant to
buy it was beyond question. If he hadn't had the
money in his pocket, he felt sure he would have simply
grabbed it and bolted from the store. But *why*? He
felt like a compass needle. The needle knows nothing
about magnetic north; it only knows it must point in
a certain direction, like it or not.

The only thing Jake knew for sure was that he was very, very tired, and if he didn't crawl into bed soon, he was going to fall asleep at his desk. He took off his shirt, then gazed down at the front of *Charlie the Choo-Choo* again.

That smile. He just didn't trust that smile.

Not a bit.

23

SLEEP DIDN'T COME AS soon as Jake had hoped. The voices began to argue again about whether he was alive or dead, and they kept him awake. At last he sat up in bed with his eyes closed and his fisted hands planted against his temples.

Quit! he screamed at them. *Just quit! You were gone all day, be gone again!*

I would if he'd just admit I'm dead, one of the voices said sulkily.

I would if he'd just take a for God's sake look around and admit I'm clearly alive, the other snapped back.

He was going to scream right out loud. There was no way to hold it back; he could feel it coming up his throat like vomit. He opened his eyes, saw his pants lying over the seat of his desk chair, and an idea occurred to him. He got out of bed, went to the chair, and felt in the right front pocket of the pants.

The silver key was still there, and the moment his fingers closed around it, the voices ceased.

Tell him, he thought, with no idea who the thought was for. *Tell him to grab the key. The key makes the voices go.*

He went back to bed and was asleep with the key clasped loosely in his hand three minutes after his head hit the pillow.

III ■ DOOR AND DEMON

▪ III ▪

DOOR AND
DEMON

1

EDDIE WAS ALMOST ASLEEP when a voice spoke clearly in his ear: *Tell him to grab the key. The key makes the voices go.*

He sat bolt upright, looking around wildly. Susannah was sound asleep beside him; that voice had not been hers.

Nor anyone else's, it seemed. They had been moving through the woods and along the path of the Beam for eight days now, and this evening they had camped in the deep cleft of a pocket valley. Close by on the left, a large stream roared brashly past, headed in the same direction as they were: southeast. To the right, firs rose up a steep slope of land. There were no intruders here; only Susannah asleep and Roland awake. He sat huddled beneath his blanket at the edge of the stream's cut, staring out into the darkness.

Tell him to grab the key. The key makes the voices go.

Eddie hesitated for only a moment. Roland's sanity was in the balance now, the balance was tipping the wrong way, and the worst part of it was this: no one knew it better than the man himself. At this point, Eddie was prepared to clutch at any straw.

He had been using a folded square of deerskin as a pillow. He reached beneath it and removed a bundle wrapped in a piece of hide. He walked over to Roland, and was disturbed to see that the gunslinger did not notice him until he was less than four steps from his unprotected back. There had been a time—and it was not so long ago—when Roland would have known Eddie was awake even before Eddie sat up. He would have heard the change in his breathing.

He was more alert than this back on the beach, when he was half-dead from the lobster-thing's bite, Eddie thought grimly.

Roland at last turned his head and glanced at him. His eyes were bright with pain and weariness, but Eddie recognized these things as no more than a surface glitter. Beneath it, he sensed a growing confusion that would almost surely become madness if it continued to develop unchecked. Pity tugged at Eddie's heart.

"Can't sleep?" Roland asked. His voice was slow, almost drugged.

"I almost was, and then I woke up," Eddie said. "Listen—"

"I think I'm getting ready to die." Roland looked at Eddie. The bright shine left his eyes, and now looking into them was like staring into a pair of deep, dark wells that seemed to have no bottom. Eddie shuddered, more because of that empty stare than because of what Roland had said. "And do you know what I hope lies in the clearing where the path ends, Eddie?"

"Roland—"

"Silence," Roland said. He exhaled a dusty sigh.

"Just silence. That will be enough. An end to . . . this."

He planted his fists against his temples, and Eddie thought: *I've seen someone else do that, and not long ago. But who? Where?*

It was ridiculous of course; he had seen no one but Roland and Susannah for almost two months now. But it *felt* true, all the same.

"Roland, I've been making something," Eddie said.

Roland nodded. A ghost of a smile touched his lips. "I know. What is it? Are you finally ready to tell?"

"I think it might be part of this *ka-tet* thing."

The vacant look left Roland's eyes. He gazed at Eddie thoughtfully but said nothing.

"Look." Eddie began to unfold the piece of hide.

That won't do any good! Henry's voice suddenly brayed. It was so loud that Eddie actually flinched a little. *It's just a stupid piece of wood-carving! He'll take one look and laugh at it! He'll laugh at you! "Oh, lookit this!" he'll say. "Did the sissy carve something?"*

"Shut up," Eddie muttered.

The gunslinger raised his eyebrows.

"Not you."

Roland nodded, unsurprised. "Your brother comes to you often, doesn't he, Eddie?"

For a moment Eddie only stared at him, his carving still hidden in the hide square. Then he smiled. It was not a very pleasant smile. "Not as often as he used to, Roland. Thank Christ for small favors."

"Yes," Roland said. "Too many voices weigh heavy on a man's heart . . . What is it, Eddie? Show me, please."

Eddie held up the chunk of ash. The key, almost complete, emerged from it like the head of a woman from the prow of a sailing ship . . . or the hilt of a sword from a chunk of stone. Eddie didn't know how close he had come to duplicating the key-shape he had seen in the fire (and never would, he supposed, unless he found the right lock in which to try it), but he thought it was close. Of one thing he was quite sure: it was the best carving he had ever done. By far.

"By the gods, Eddie, it's beautiful!" Roland said. The apathy was gone from his voice; he spoke in a tone of surprised reverence Eddie had never heard before. "Is it done? It's not, is it?"

"No—not quite." He ran his thumb into the third notch, and then over the *s*-shape at the end of the last notch. "There's a little more to do on this notch, and the curve at the end isn't right yet. I don't know how I know that, but I do."

"This is your secret." It wasn't a question.

"Yes. Now if only I knew what it meant."

Roland looked around. Eddie followed his gaze and saw Susannah. He found some relief in the fact that Roland had heard her first.

"What you boys doin up so late? Chewin the fat?" She saw the wooden key in Eddie's hand and nodded. "I wondered when you were going to get around to showing that off. It's good, you know. I don't know what it's for, but it's damned good."

"You don't have any idea what door it might open?" Roland asked Eddie. "That was not part of your *khef*?"

"No—but it might be good for something even though it isn't done." He held the key out to Roland. "I want you to keep it for me."

Roland didn't move to take it. He regarded Eddie closely. "Why?"

"Because . . . well . . . because I think someone told me you should."

"Who?"

Your boy, Eddie thought suddenly, and as soon as the thought came he knew it was true. *It was your goddamned boy.* But he didn't want to say so. He didn't want to mention the boy's name at all. It might just set Roland off again.

"I don't know. But I think you ought to give it a try."

Roland reached slowly for the key. As his fingers touched it, a bright glimmer seemed to flash down its barrel, but it was gone so quickly that Eddie could not be sure he had seen it. It might have been only starlight.

Roland's hand closed over the key growing out of the branch. For a moment his face showed nothing. Then his brow furrowed and his head cocked in a listening gesture.

"What is it?" Susannah asked. "Do you hear—"

"Shhhh!" The puzzlement on Roland's face was slowly being replaced with wonder. He looked from Eddie to Susannah and then back to Eddie. His eyes were filling with some great emotion, as a pitcher fills with water when it is dipped in a spring.

"Roland?" Eddie asked uneasily. "Are you all right?"

Roland whispered something. Eddie couldn't hear what it was.

Susannah looked scared. She glanced frantically at Eddie, as if to ask, *What did you do to him?*

Eddie took one of her hands in both of his own. "I think it's all right."

Roland's hand was clamped so tightly on the chunk of wood that Eddie was momentarily afraid he might snap it in two, but the wood was strong and Eddie had carved thick. The gunslinger's throat bulged; his Adam's apple rose and fell as he struggled with speech. And suddenly he yelled at the sky in a fair, strong voice:

"GONE! THE VOICES ARE GONE!"

He looked back at them, and Eddie saw something he had never expected to see in his life—not even if that life stretched over a thousand years.

Roland of Gilead was weeping.

2

THE GUNSLINGER SLEPT SOUNDLY and dreamlessly that night for the first time in months, and he slept with the not-quite finished key clenched tightly in his hand.

3

IN ANOTHER WORLD, BUT beneath the shadow of the same *ka-tet*, Jake Chambers was having the most vivid dream of his life.

He was walking through the tangled remains of an ancient forest—a dead zone of fallen trees and scruffy, aggravating bushes that bit his ankles and tried to steal his sneakers. He came to a thin belt of younger trees (alders, he thought, or perhaps beeches—he was a city boy, and the only thing he knew for sure about trees was that some had leaves and some had needles) and discovered a path through them. He made his way along this, moving a little faster. There was a clearing of some sort up ahead.

He stopped once before reaching it, when he spied some sort of stone marker to his right. He left the path to look at it. There were letters carved into it, but they were so eroded he couldn't make them out. At last he closed his eyes (he had never done this in a dream before) and let his fingers trace each letter, like a blind boy reading Braille. Each formed in the darkness behind his lids until they made a sentence which stood forth in an outline of blue light:

TRAVELLER, BEYOND LIES MID-WORLD.

Sleeping in his bed, Jake drew his knees up against his chest. The hand holding the key was under his pillow, and now his fingers tightened their grip on it.

Mid-World, he thought, *of course. St. Louis and Topeka and Oz and the World's Fair and Charlie the Choo-Choo.*

He opened his dreaming eyes and pressed on. The clearing behind the trees was paved with old cracked asphalt. A faded yellow circle had been painted in the middle. Jake realized it was a playground basketball court even before he saw the boy at the far end, standing at the foul line and shooting baskets with a dusty old Wilson ball. They popped in one after another, falling neatly through the netless hole. The basket jutted out from something that looked like a subway kiosk which had been shut up for the night. Its closed door was painted in alternating diagonal stripes of yellow and black. From behind it—or perhaps from below it—Jake could hear the steady rumble of powerful machinery. The sound was somehow disturbing. Scary.

Don't step on the robots, the boy shooting the baskets said without turning around. *I guess they're all dead, but I wouldn't take any chances, if I were you.*

Jake looked around and saw a number of shattered mechanical devices lying around. One looked like a rat or mouse, another like a bat. A mechanical snake lay in two rusty pieces almost at his feet.

ARE you me? Jake asked, taking a step closer to the boy at the basket, but even before he turned around, Jake knew that wasn't the case. The boy was bigger than Jake, and at least thirteen. His hair was darker, and when he looked at Jake, he saw that the stranger's eyes were hazel. His own were blue.

What do you think? the strange boy asked, and bounce-passed the ball to Jake.

No, of course not, Jake said. He spoke apologetically. *It's just that I've been cut in two for the last three weeks or so.* He dipped and shot from mid-court. The ball arched high and dropped silently through the hoop. He was delighted . . . but he discovered he was also afraid of what this strange boy might have to tell him.

I know, the boy said. *It's been a bitch for you, hasn't it?* He was wearing faded madras shorts and a yellow t-shirt that said NEVER A DULL MOMENT IN MID-WORLD. He had tied a green bandanna around his forehead to keep his hair out of his eyes. *And things are going to get worse before they get better.*

What is this place? Jake asked. *And who are you?*

It's the Portal of the Bear . . . but it's also Brooklyn.

That didn't seem to make sense, and yet somehow it did. Jake told himself that things always seemed that way in dreams, but this didn't really *feel* like a dream.

As for me, I don't matter much, the boy said. He hooked the basketball over his shoulder. It rose, then dropped smoothly through the hoop. *I'm supposed to guide you, that's all. I'll take you where you need to go, and I'll show you what you need to see, but you have to be careful because I won't know you. And strangers make Henry nervous. He can get mean when he's nervous, and he's bigger than you.*

Who's Henry? Jake asked.

Never mind. Just don't let him notice you. All you have to do is hang out . . . and follow us. Then, when we leave . . .

The boy looked at Jake. There was both pity and fear in his eyes. Jake suddenly realized that the boy was starting to *fade*—he could see the yellow and black slashes on the box right through the boy's yellow T-shirt.

How will I find you? Jake was suddenly terrified that the boy would melt away completely before he could say everything Jake needed to hear.

No problem, the boy said. His voice had taken on a queer, chiming echo. *Just take the subway to Co-Op City. You'll find me.*

No, I won't! Jake cried. *Co-Op City's huge! There must be a hundred thousand people living there!*

Now the boy was just a milky outline. Only his hazel eyes were still completely there, like the Cheshire cat's grin in *Alice*. They regarded Jake with compassion and anxiety. *No problem-o,* he said. *You found the key and the rose, didn't you? You'll find me the same way. This afternoon, Jake. Around three o'clock should be good. You'll have to be careful, and you'll have to be quick.* He paused, a ghostly boy with an old basketball lying near one transparent foot. *I have to go now . . . but it was good to meet you. You seem like a nice kid, and I'm not surprised he loves you. Remember, there's danger, though. Be careful . . . and be quick.*

Wait! Jake yelled, and ran across the basketball court toward the disappearing boy. One of his feet struck a shattered robot that looked like a child's toy tractor. He stumbled and fell to his knees, shredding his pants. He ignored the thin burn of pain. *Wait! You have to tell me what all this is about! You have to tell me why these things are happening to me!*

Because of the Beam, the boy who was now only a pair of floating eyes replied, *and because of the Tower. In the end, all things, even the Beams, serve the Dark Tower. Did you think you would be any different?*

Jake flailed and stumbled to his feet. *Will I find him? Will I find the gunslinger?*

I don't know, the boy answered. His voice now seemed to come from a million miles away. *I only know you must try. About that you have no choice.*

The boy was gone. The basketball court in the woods was empty. The only sound was that faint rumble of machinery, and Jake didn't like it. There was something wrong with that sound, and he thought that what was wrong with the machinery was affecting the rose, or vice-versa. It was all hooked together somehow.

He picked up the old, scuffed-up basketball and shot. It went neatly through the hoop . . . and disappeared.

A river, the strange boy's voice sighed. It was like a puff of breeze. It came from nowhere and everywhere. *The answer is a river.*

4

JAKE WOKE IN THE first milky light of dawn, looking up at the ceiling of his room. He was thinking of the guy in The Manhattan Restaurant of the Mind—Aaron Deepneau, who'd been hanging around on Bleecker Street back when Bob Dylan only knew how to blow open G on his Hohner. Aaron Deepneau had given Jake a riddle.

> *What can run but never walks,*
> *Has a mouth but never talks,*
> *Has a bed but never sleeps,*
> *Has a head but never weeps?*

Now he knew the answer. A river ran; a river had a mouth; a river had a bed; a river had a head. The boy had told him the answer. The boy in the dream.

And suddenly he thought of something else Deepneau had said: *That's only half the answer. Samson's riddle is a double, my friend.*

Jake glanced at his bedside clock and saw it was twenty past six. It was time to get moving if he wanted to be out of here before his parents woke up. There would be no school for him today; Jake thought that maybe, as far as he was concerned, school had been cancelled forever.

He threw back the bedclothes, swung his feet out onto the floor, and saw that there were scrapes on both knees. Fresh scrapes. He had bruised his left side yesterday when he slipped on the bricks and fell, and he had banged his head when he fainted near the rose, but nothing had happened to his knees.

"That happened in the dream," Jake whispered, and found he wasn't surprised at all. He began to dress swiftly.

5

IN THE BACK OF his closet, under a jumble of old laceless sneakers and a heap of *Spiderman* comic books, he found the packsack he had worn to grammar school. No one would be caught dead with a packsack at Piper—how too, too common, my deah—and as Jake grabbed it, he felt a wave of powerful nostalgia for those old days when life had seemed so simple.

He stuffed a clean shirt, a clean pair of jeans, some underwear and socks into it, then added *Riddle-De-Dum!* and *Charlie the Choo-Choo*. He had put the key on his desk before foraging in the closet for his old pack, and the voices came back at once, but they were distant and muted. Besides, he felt sure he could make them go away completely by holding the key again, and that eased his mind.

Okay, he thought, looking into the pack. Even with the books added, there was plenty of room left. *What else?*

For a moment he thought there was nothing else . . . and then he knew.

6

HIS FATHER'S STUDY SMELLED of cigarettes and ambition.

It was dominated by a huge teakwood desk. Across the room, set into a wall otherwise lined with books, were three Mitsubishi television monitors. Each was tuned to one of the rival networks, and at night, when his father was in here, each played out its progression of prime-time images with the sound off.

The curtains were drawn, and Jake had to turn on the desk lamp in order to see. He felt nervous just being in here, even wearing sneakers. If his father should wake up and come in (and it was possible; no matter how late he went to bed or how much he drank, Elmer Chambers was a light sleeper and an early riser), he would be angry. At the very least it would make a clean getaway much tougher. The sooner he was out of here, the better Jake would feel.

The desk was locked, but his father had never made any secret of where he kept the key. Jake slid his fingers under the blotter and hooked it out. He opened the third drawer, reached past the hanging files, and touched cold metal.

A board creaked in the hall and he froze. Several seconds passed. When the creak didn't come again, Jake pulled out the weapon his father kept for "home defense"—a .44 Ruger automatic. His father had shown this weapon to Jake with great pride on the day he had bought it—two years ago, that had been. He had been totally deaf to his wife's nervous demands that he put it away before someone got hurt.

Jake found the button on the side that released the clip. It fell out into his hand with a metallic *snak!* sound that seemed very loud in the quiet apartment. He glanced nervously toward the door again, then turned his attention to the clip. It was fully loaded. He started to slide it back into the gun, and then took it out again. Keeping a loaded gun in a locked desk drawer was one thing; carrying one around New York City was quite another.

He stuffed the automatic down to the bottom of his pack, then felt behind the hanging files again. This time he brought out a box of shells, about half-full. He remembered his father had done some target shooting at the police range on First Avenue before losing interest.

The board creaked again. Jake wanted to get out of here.

He removed one of the shirts he'd packed, laid it on his father's desk, and rolled up the clip and the box of .44 slugs in it. Then he replaced it in the pack and used the buckles to snug down the flap. He was about to leave when his eye fixed on the little pile of stationery sitting beside his father's In/Out tray. The reflectorized Ray-Ban sunglasses his father liked to wear were folded on top of the stationery. He took a sheet of paper, and, after a moment's thought, the sunglasses as well. He slipped the shades into his breast pocket. Then he removed the slim gold pen from its stand, and wrote *Dear Dad and Mom* beneath the letterhead.

He stopped, frowning at the salutation. What went below it? What, exactly, did he have to say? That he loved them? It was true, but it wasn't enough—there were all sorts of other unpleasant truths stuck through that central one, like steel needles jabbed into a ball of yarn. That he would miss them? He didn't know if that was true or not, which was sort of horrible. That he hoped *they* would miss *him*?

He suddenly realized what the problem was. If he were planning to be gone just today, he would be able to write something. But he felt a near-certainty that it *wasn't* just today, or this week, or this month, or this summer. He had an idea that when he walked out of the apartment this time, it would be for good.

He almost crumpled the sheet of paper, then changed his mind. He wrote: *Please take care of yourselves. Love, J.* That was pretty limp, but at least it was something.

Fine. Now will you stop pressing your luck and get out of here?

He did.

The apartment was almost dead still. He tiptoed

across the living room, hearing only the sounds of his parents' breathing: his mother's soft little snores, his father's more nasal respiration, where every indrawn breath ended in a slim high whistle. The refrigerator kicked on as he reached the entryway and he froze for a moment, his heart thumping hard in his chest. Then he was at the door. He unlocked it as quietly as he could, then stepped out and pulled it gently shut behind him.

A stone seemed to roll off his heart as the latch snicked, and a strong sense of anticipation seized him. He didn't know what lay ahead, and he had reason to believe it would be dangerous, but he was eleven years old—too young to deny the exotic delight which suddenly filled him. There was a highway ahead—a hidden highway leading deep into some unknown land. There were secrets which might disclose themselves to him if he was clever . . . and if he was lucky. He had left his home in the long light of dawn, and what lay ahead was some great adventure.

If I stand, if I can be true, I'll see the rose, he thought as he pushed the button for the elevator. *I know it . . . and I'll see* him, *too.*

This thought filled him with an eagerness so great it was almost ecstasy.

Three minutes later he stepped out from beneath the awning which shaded the entrance to the building where he had lived all his life. He paused for a moment, then turned left. This decision did not feel random, and it wasn't. He was moving southeast, along the path of the Beam, resuming his own interrupted quest for the Dark Tower.

7

TWO DAYS AFTER EDDIE had given Roland his unfinished key, the three travellers—hot, sweaty, tired, and out of sorts—pushed through a particularly tenacious tangle of bushes and second-growth trees and discovered what first appeared to be two faint paths, running in tandem beneath the interlacing branches of the old trees crowding close on either side. After a few moments of study, Eddie decided they weren't just paths but the remains of a long-abandoned road. Bushes and stunted trees grew like untidy quills along what had been its crown. The grassy indentations were wheelruts, and either of them was wide enough to accommodate Susannah's wheelchair.

"Hallelujah!" he cried. "Let's drink to it!"

Roland nodded and unslung the waterskin he wore around his waist. He first handed it up to Susannah, who was riding in her sling on his back. Eddie's key, now looped around Roland's neck on a piece of rawhide, shifted beneath his shirt with each movement. She took a swallow and passed the skin to Eddie. He drank and then began to unfold her chair. Eddie had come to hate this bulky, balky contraption; it was like an iron anchor, always holding them back. Except for a broken spoke or two, it was still in fine condition. Eddie had days when he thought the goddam thing would outlast all of them. Now, however, it might be useful . . . for a while, at least.

Eddie helped Susannah out of the harness and placed her in the chair. She put her hands against the small of her back, stretched, and grimaced with pleasure. Both Eddie and Roland heard the small crackle her spine made as it stretched.

Up ahead, a large creature that looked like a badger crossed with a raccoon ambled out of the woods. It looked at them with its large, gold-rimmed eyes, twitched its sharp, whiskery snout as if to say *Huh! Big deal!*, then strolled the rest of the way across the road and disappeared again. Before it did, Eddie noted its tail—long and closely coiled, it looked like a fur-covered bedspring.

"What was that, Roland?"

"A billy-bumbler."

"No good to eat?"

Roland shook his head. "Tough. Sour. I'd rather eat dog."

"Have you?" Susannah asked. "Eaten dog, I mean?"

Roland nodded, but did not elaborate. Eddie found himself thinking of a line from an old Paul Newman movie: *That's right, lady—eaten em and lived like one.*

Birds sang cheerily in the trees. A light breeze blew along the road. Eddie and Susannah turned their faces up to it gratefully, then looked at each other and smiled. Eddie was struck again by his gratitude for her—it was scary to have someone to love, but it was also very fine.

"Who made this road?" Eddie asked.

"People who have been gone a long time," Roland said.

"The same ones who made the cups and dishes we found?" Susannah asked.

"No—not them. This used to be a coach-road, I imagine, and if it's still here, after all these years of neglect, it must have been a great one indeed . . . perhaps *the* Great Road. If we dug down, I imagine we'd find the gravel undersurface, and maybe the drainage system, as well. As long as we're here, let's have a bite to eat."

"Food!" Eddie cried. "Bring it on! Chicken Florentine! Polynesian shrimp! Veal lightly sautéed with mushrooms and—"

Susannah elbowed him. "Quit it, white boy."

"I can't help it if I've got a vivid imagination," Eddie said cheerfully.

Roland slipped his purse off his shoulder, hunkered down, and began to put together a small noon meal of dried meat wrapped in olive-colored leaves. Eddie and Susannah had discovered that these leaves tasted a little like spinach, only much stronger.

Eddie wheeled Susannah over to him and Roland

handed her three of what Eddie called "gunslinger burritos." She began to eat.

When Eddie turned back, Roland was holding out three of the wrapped pieces of meat to him—and something else, as well. It was the chunk of ash with the key growing out of it. Roland had taken it off the rawhide string, which now lay in an open loop around his neck.

"Hey, you need that, don't you?" Eddie asked.

"When I take it off, the voices return, but they're very distant," Roland said. "I can deal with them. Actually, I hear them even when I'm wearing it—like the voices of men who are speaking low over the next hill. I think that's because the key is yet unfinished. You haven't worked on it since you gave it to me."

"Well . . . you were wearing it, and I didn't want to . . ."

Roland said nothing, but his faded blue eyes regarded Eddie with their patient teacher's look.

"All right," Eddie said, "I'm afraid of fucking it up. Satisfied?"

"According to your brother, you fucked everything up . . . isn't that right?" Susannah asked.

"Susannah Dean, Girl Psychologist. You missed your calling, sweetheart."

Susannah wasn't offended by the sarcasm. She lifted the waterskin with her elbow, like a redneck tipping a jug, and drank deeply. "It's true, though, isn't it?"

Eddie, who realized he hadn't finished the slingshot, either—not yet, at least—shrugged.

"You have to finish it," Roland said mildly. "I think the time is coming when you'll have to put it to use."

Eddie started to speak, then closed his mouth. It sounded easy when you said it right out like that, but neither of them really understood the bottom line. The bottom line was this: seventy per cent or eighty or even ninety-eight and a half just wouldn't do. Not this time. And if he *did* screw up, he couldn't just toss the thing over his shoulder and walk away. For one thing, he hadn't seen another ash-tree since the day he had cut this particular piece of wood. But mostly the thing that was fucking him up was just this: it was all or nothing. If he messed up even a little, the key wouldn't turn when they needed it to turn. And he was increasingly nervous about that little squiggle at the end. It looked simple, but if the curves weren't exactly right . . .

It won't work the way it is now, though; that much you do know.

He sighed, looking at the key. Yes, that much he did know. He would have to try to finish it. His fear of failure would make it even harder than it maybe had to be, but he would have to swallow the fear and try anyway. Maybe he could even bring it off. God knew he had brought off a lot in the weeks since Roland had entered his mind on a Delta jet bound into JFK Airport. That he was still alive and sane was an accomplishment in itself.

Eddie handed the key back to Roland. "Wear it for now," he said. "I'll go back to work when we stop for the night."

"Promise?"

"Yeah."

Roland nodded, took the key, and began to re-knot the rawhide string. He worked slowly, but Eddie did not fail to notice how dextrously the remaining fingers on his right hand moved. The man was nothing if not adaptable.

"Something *is* going to happen, isn't it?" Susannah asked suddenly.

Eddie glanced up at her. "What makes you say so?"

"I sleep with you, Eddie, and I know you dream every night now. Sometimes you talk, too. They don't seem like nightmares, exactly, but it's pretty clear that *something* is going on inside your head."

"Yes. Something is. I just don't know what."

"Dreams are powerful," Roland remarked. "You don't remember the ones you're having at all?"

Eddie hesitated. "A little, but they're confused. I'm a kid again, I know that much. It's after school. Henry and I are shooting hoops at the old Markey Avenue playground, where the Juvenile Court Building is now. I want Henry to take me to see a place over in Dutch Hill. An old house. The kids used to call it The Mansion, and everyone said it was haunted. Maybe it even was. It was creepy, I know that much. *Real* creepy."

Eddie shook his head, remembering.

"I thought of The Mansion for the first time in years when we were in the bear's clearing, and I put my head close to that weird box. I dunno—maybe that's why I'm having the dream."

"But you don't think so," Susannah said.

"No. I think whatever's happening is a lot more complicated than just remembering stuff."

"Did you and your brother actually go to this place?" Roland asked.

"Yeah—I talked him into it."

"And did something happen?"

"No. But it was scary. We stood there and looked at it for a little while, and Henry teased me—saying he was going to make me go in and pick up a souvenir, stuff like that—but I knew he didn't really mean it. He was as scared of the place as I was."

"And that's it?" Susannah asked. "You just dream of going to this place? The Mansion?"

"There's a little more than that. Someone comes . . . and then just kind of hangs out. I notice him in the dream, but just a little . . . like out of the corner of my eye, you know? Only I know we're supposed to pretend we don't know each other."

"Was this someone really there that day?" Roland asked. He was watching Eddie intently. "Or is he only a player in this dream?"

"That was a long time ago. I couldn't have been more than thirteen. How could I remember a thing like that for sure?"

Roland said nothing.

"Okay," Eddie said at last. "Yeah. I think he *was* there that day. A kid who was either carrying a gymbag or wearing a backpack, I can't remember which. And sunglasses that were too big for his face. The ones with the mirror lenses."

"Who was this person?" Roland asked.

Eddie was silent for a long time. He was holding the last of his *burritos à la Roland* in one hand, but he had lost his appetite. "I think it's the kid you met at the way station," he said at last. "I think your old friend Jake was hanging around, watching me and Henry on the afternoon we went over to Dutch Hill. I think he followed us. Because he hears the voices, just like you, Roland. And because he's sharing my dreams, and I'm sharing his. I think that what I remember is what's happening now, in Jake's when. The kid is trying to come back here. And if the key isn't done when he makes his move—or if it's done wrong—he's probably going to die."

Roland said, "Maybe he has a key of his own. Is that possible?"

"Yeah, I think it is," Eddie said, "but it isn't enough." He sighed and stuck the last burrito in his pocket for later. *"And I don't think he knows that."*

8

THEY MOVED ALONG, ROLAND and Eddie trading off on Susannah's wheelchair. They picked the left-hand wheelrut. The chair bumped and pitched, and every now and then Eddie and Roland had to lift it over the cobbles which stuck out of the dirt here and there like old teeth. They were still making faster, easier time than they had in a week, however. The ground was rising, and when Eddie looked over his shoulder he could see the forest sloping away in what looked like a series of gentle steps. Far to the northwest, he could see a ribbon of water spilling over a fractured rock face. It was, he realized with wonder, the place they had dubbed "the shooting gallery." Now it was almost lost behind them in the haze of this dreaming summer afternoon.

"Whoa down, boy!" Susannah called sharply. Eddie faced forward again just in time to keep from pushing the wheelchair into Roland. The gunslinger had stopped and was peering into the tangled bushes at the left of the road.

"You keep that up, I'm gonna revoke your driver's license," Susannah said waspily.

Eddie ignored her. He was following Roland's gaze. "What is it?"

"One way to find out." He turned, hoisted Susannah from her chair, and planted her on his hip. "Let's all take a look."

"Put me down, big boy—I can make my way. Easier'n you boys, if you really want to know."

As Roland gently lowered her to the grassy wheelrut, Eddie peered into the woods. The late light threw overlapping crosses of shadow, but he thought he saw what had caught Roland's eye. It was a tall gray stone, almost completely hidden in a shag of vines and creepers.

Susannah slipped into the woods at the side of the road with eely sinuousness. Roland and Eddie followed.

"It's a marker, isn't it?" Susannah was propped on her hands studying the rectangular chunk of rock. It had once been straight, but now it leaned drunkenly to the right, like an old gravestone.

"Yes. Give me my knife, Eddie."

Eddie handed it over, then hunkered next to Susannah as the gunslinger cut away the vines. As they fell, he could see eroded letters carved into the stone, and he knew what they said before Roland had uncovered even half of the inscription:

TRAVELLER, BEYOND LIES MID-WORLD.

9

"WHAT DOES IT MEAN?" Susannah asked at last. Her voice was soft and awestruck; her eyes ceaselessly measured the gray stone plinth.

"It means that we're nearing the end of this first stage." Roland's face was solemn and thoughtful as he handed his knife back to Eddie. "I think that we'll keep to this old coach-road now—or rather, it will keep to us. It has taken up the path of the Beam. The woods will end soon. I expect a great change."

"What is Mid-World?" Eddie asked.

"One of the large kingdoms which dominated the earth in the times before these. A kingdom of hope and knowledge and light—the sort of things we were trying to hold onto in my land before the darkness overtook us, as well. Some day if there's time, I'll tell you all the old stories . . . the ones I know, at least. They form a large tapestry, one which is beautiful but very sad.

"According to the old tales, a great city once stood at the edge of Mid-World—perhaps as great as your city of New York. It will be in ruins now, if it still exists at all. But there may be people . . . or monsters . . . or both. We'll have to be on our guard."

He reached out his two-fingered right hand and touched the inscription. "Mid-World," he said in a low, meditative voice. "Who would have thought . . ." He trailed off.

"Well, there's no help for it, is there?" Eddie asked.

The gunslinger shook his head. "No help."

"*Ka*," Susannah said suddenly, and they both looked at her.

10

THERE WERE TWO HOURS of daylight left, and so they
moved on. The road continued southeast, along the
path of the Beam, and two other overgrown roads—
smaller ones—joined the one they were following.
Along one side of the second were the mossy, tumbled
remains of what must have once been an immense
rock wall. Nearby, a dozen fat billy-bumblers sat upon
the ruins, watching the pilgrims with their odd gold-
ringed eyes. To Eddie they looked like a jury with
hanging on its mind.

The road continued to grow wider and more clearly
defined. Twice they passed the shells of long-deserted
buildings. The second one, Roland said, might have
been a windmill. Susannah said it looked haunted. "I
wouldn't be surprised," the gunslinger replied. His
matter-of-fact tone chilled both of them.

When darkness forced a halt, the trees were thinning and the breeze which had chased around them
all day became a light, warm wind. Ahead, the land
continued to rise.

"We'll come to the top of the ridge in a day or
two," Roland said. "Then we'll see."

"See what?" Susannah asked, but Roland only
shrugged.

That night Eddie began to carve again, but with no
real feeling of inspiration. The confidence and happiness he'd felt as the key first began to take shape had
left him. His fingers felt clumsy and stupid. For the
first time in months he thought longingly of how good
it would be to have some heroin. Not a lot; he felt
sure that a nickel bag and a rolled-up dollar bill would
send him flying through this little carving project in
no time flat.

"What are you smiling about, Eddie?" Roland
asked. He was sitting on the other side of the campfire; the low, wind-driven flames danced capriciously
between them.

"Was I smiling?"

"Yes."

"I was just thinking about how stupid some people can be—you put them in a room with six doors, they'll still walk into the walls. And then have the nerve to bitch about it."

"If you're afraid of what might be on the other side of the doors, maybe bouncing off the walls seems safer," Susannah said.

Eddie nodded. "Maybe so."

He worked slowly, trying to see the shapes in the wood—that little *s*-shape in particular. He discovered it had become very dim.

Please, God, help me not to fuck this up, he thought, but he was terribly afraid that he had already begun to do just that. At last he gave up, returned the key (which he had barely changed at all) to the gunslinger, and curled up beneath one of the hides. Five minutes later, the dream about the boy and the old Markey Avenue playground had begun to unspool again.

11

JAKE STEPPED OUT OF his apartment building at about quarter of seven, which left him with over eight hours to kill. He considered taking the train out to Brooklyn right away, then decided it was a bad idea. A kid out of school was apt to attract more attention in the hinterlands than in the heart of a big city, and if he really had to *search* for the place and the boy he was supposed to meet there, he was cooked already.

No problem-o, the boy in the yellow T-shirt and green bandanna had said. *You found the key and the rose, didn't you? You'll find me the same way.*

Except Jake could no longer remember just how he *had* found the key and the rose. He could only remember the joy and the sense of surety which had filled his heart and head. He would just have to hope that would happen again. In the meantime, he'd keep moving. That was the best way to keep from being noticed in New York.

He walked most of the way to First Avenue, then headed back the way he had come, only sliding uptown little by little as he followed the pattern of the WALK lights (perhaps knowing, on some deep level, that even they served the Beam). Around ten o'clock he found himself in front of the Metropolitan Museum of Art on Fifth Avenue. He was hot, tired, and depressed. He wanted a soda, but he thought he ought to hold onto what little money he had for as long as he could. He'd taken every cent out of the box he kept by his bed, but it only amounted to eight dollars, give or take a few cents.

A group of school-kids were lining up for a tour. Public school, Jake was almost sure—they were dressed as casually as he was. No blazers from Paul Stuart, no ties, no jumpers, no simple little skirts that cost a hundred and twenty-five bucks at places like Miss So Pretty or Tweenity. This crowd was Kmart all the way. On impulse, Jake stood at the end of the line and followed them into the museum.

The tour took an hour and fifteen minutes. Jake enjoyed it. The museum was quiet. Even better, it was air-conditioned. And the pictures were nice. He was particularly fascinated by a small group of Frederick Remington's Old West paintings and a large picture by Thomas Hart Benton that showed a steam locomotive charging across the great plains toward Chicago while beefy farmers in bib overalls and straw hats stood in their fields and watched. He wasn't noticed by either of the teachers with the group until the very end. Then a pretty black woman in a severe blue suit tapped him on the shoulder and asked who he was.

Jake hadn't seen her coming, and for a moment his

mind froze. Without thinking about what he was doing, he reached into his pocket and closed his hand around the silver key. His mind cleared immediately, and he felt calm again.

"My group is upstairs," he said, smiling guiltily. "We're supposed to be looking at a bunch of modern art, but I like the stuff down here a lot better, because they're real pictures. So I sort of . . . you know . . ."

"Snuck away?" the teacher suggested. The corners of her lips twitched in a suppressed smile.

"Well, I'd rather think of it as French leave." These words simply popped out of his mouth.

The students now staring at Jake only looked puzzled, but this time the teacher actually laughed. "Either you don't know or have forgotten," she said, "but in the French Foreign Legion they used to shoot deserters. I suggest you rejoin your class at once, young man."

"Yes, ma'am. Thank you. They'll be almost done now, anyway."

"What school is it?"

"Markey Academy," Jake said. This also just popped out.

He went upstairs, listening to the disembodied echo of foot-falls and low voices in the great space of the rotunda and wondering why he had said that. He had never heard of a place called Markey Academy in his life.

12

HE WAITED AWHILE IN the upstairs lobby, then noticed a guard looking at him with growing curiosity and decided it wouldn't be wise to wait any longer—he would just have to hope the class he had joined briefly was gone.

He looked at his wristwatch, put an expression on

his face that he hoped looked like *Gosh! Look how late it's getting!,* and trotted back downstairs. The class—and the pretty black teacher who had laughed at the idea of French leave—was gone, and Jake decided it might be a good idea to get gone himself. He would walk awhile longer—slowly, in deference to the heat—and catch a subway.

He stopped at a hot-dog stand on the corner of Broadway and Forty-second, trading in a little of his meager cash supply for a sweet sausage and a Nehi. He sat on the steps of a bank building to eat his lunch, and that turned out to be a bad mistake.

A cop came walking toward him, twirling his night-stick in a complex series of maneuvers. He seemed to be paying attention to nothing but this, but when he came abreast of Jake he abruptly shoved his stick back into his loop and turned to him.

"Say-hey, big guy," he said. "No school today?"

Jake had been wolfing his sausage, but the last bite abruptly stuck in his throat. This was a lousy piece of luck . . . if luck was all it was. They were in Times Square, sleaze capital of America; there were pushers, junkies, whores, and chicken-chasers everywhere . . . but this cop was ignoring *them* in favor of *him.*

Jake swallowed with an effort, then said, "It's finals week at my school. I only had one test today. Then I could leave." He paused, not liking the bright, searching look in the cop's eyes. "I had permission," he concluded uneasily.

"Uh-huh. Can I see some ID?"

Jake's heart sank. Had his mother and father already called the cops? He supposed that, after yesterday's adventure, that was pretty likely. Under ordinary circumstances, the NYPD wouldn't take much notice of another missing kid, especially one that had been gone only half a day, but his father was a big deal at the Network, and he prided himself on the number of strings he could pull. Jake doubted if this cop had his picture . . . but he might very well have his name.

"Well," Jake said reluctantly, "I've got my student discount card from Mid-World Lanes, but that's about all."

"Mid-World Lanes? Never heard of it. Where's that? Queens?"

"Mid-*Town*, I mean," Jake thought. God, this was going north instead of south . . . and fast. "You know? On Thirty-third?"

"Uh-huh. That'll do fine." The cop held out his hand.

A black man with dreadlocks spilling over the shoulders of his canary-yellow suit glanced over. "Bussim, ossifer!" this apparition said cheerfully. "Bussiz lil whitebread ass! Do yo duty, now!"

"Shut up and get in the wind, Eli," the cop said without looking around.

Eli laughed, exposing several gold teeth, and moved along.

"Why don't you ask *him* for some ID?" Jake asked.

"Because right now I'm asking you. Snap it up, son."

The cop either had his name or had sensed something wrong about him—which wasn't so surprising, maybe, since he was the only white in the area who wasn't obviously trolling. Either way, it came to the same: sitting down here to eat his lunch had been dumb. But his feet had hurt, and he'd been hungry, dammit—*hungry.*

You're not going to stop me, Jake thought. *I can't let you stop me. There's someone I'm supposed to meet this afternoon in Brooklyn . . . and I'm going to be there.*

Instead of reaching for his wallet, he reached into his front pocket and brought out the key. He held it up to the policeman; the late-morning sunshine bounced little coins of reflected light onto the man's cheeks and forehead. His eyes widened.

"Heyy!" he breathed. "What you got there, kid?"

He reached for it, and Jake pulled the key back a little. The reflected circles of light danced hypnotically on the cop's face. "You don't need to take it," Jake said. "You can read my name without doing that, can't you?"

"Yes, sure."

The curiosity had left the cop's face. He looked only at the key. His gaze was wide and fixed, but not quite empty. Jake read both amazement and unexpected happiness in his look. *That's me*, Jake thought, *just spreading joy and goodwill wherever I go. The question is, what do I do now?*

A young woman (probably not a librarian, judging from the green silk hotpants and see-through blouse she was wearing) came wiggle-wobbling up the sidewalk on a pair of purple fuck-me shoes with three-inch heels. She glanced first at the cop, then at Jake to see what the cop was looking at. When she got a good look, she stopped cold. One of her hands drifted up and touched her throat. A man bumped into her and told her to watch where the damn-hell she was going. The young woman who was probably not a librarian took no notice whatever. Now Jake saw that four or five other people had stopped as well. All were staring at the key. They were gathering as people sometimes will around a very good three-card-monte dealer plying his trade on a streetcorner.

You're doing a great job of being inconspicuous, he thought. *Oh yeah.* He glanced over the cop's shoulder, and his eye caught a sign on the far side of the street. Denby's Discount Drug, it said.

"My name's Tom Denby," he told the cop. "It says so right here on my discount bowling card—right?"

"Right, right," the cop breathed. He had lost all interest in Jake; he was only interested in the key. The little coins of reflected light bounced and spun on his face.

"And you're not looking for anybody named Tom Denby, are you?"

"No," the cop said. "Never heard of him."

Now there were at least half a dozen people gathered around the cop, all of them staring with silent wonder at the silver key in Jake's hand.

"So I can go, can't I?"

"Huh? Oh! Oh, sure—go, for your father's sake!"

"Thanks," Jake said, but for a moment he wasn't sure *how* to go. He was hemmed in by a silent crowd of zombies, and more were joining it all the time. They were only coming to see what the deal was, he realized, but the ones who saw the key just stopped dead and stared.

He got to his feet and backed slowly up the wide bank steps, holding the key out in front of him like a lion-tamer with a chair. When he got to the wide concrete plaza at the top, he stuffed it back into his pants pockets, turned, and fled.

He stopped just once on the far side of the plaza, and looked back. The small group of people around the place where he had been standing was coming slowly back to life. They looked around at each other with dazed expressions, then walked on. The cop glanced vacantly to his left, to his right, and then straight up at the sky, as if trying to remember how he had gotten here and what he had been meaning to do. Jake had seen enough. It was time to find a subway station and get his ass over to Brooklyn before anything else weird could happen.

13

AT QUARTER OF TWO that afternoon he walked slowly up the steps of the subway station and stood on the corner of Castle and Brooklyn Avenues, looking at the sandstone towers of Co-Op City. He waited for

that feeling of sureness and direction—that feeling
that was like being able to remember forward in
time—to overtake him. It didn't come. *Nothing* came.
He was just a kid standing on a hot Brooklyn street-
corner with his short shadow lying at his feet like a
tired pet.

Well, I'm here . . . now what do I do?

Jake discovered he didn't have the slightest idea.

14

ROLAND'S SMALL BAND OF travellers reached the crest
of the long, gentle hill they had been climbing and
stood looking southeast. For a long time none of them
spoke. Susannah opened her mouth twice, then closed
it again. For the first time in her life as a woman, she
was completely speechless.

Before them, an almost endless plain dozed in the
long golden light of a summer's afternoon. The grass
was lush, emerald green, and very high. Groves of
trees with long, slender trunks and wide, spreading
tops dotted the plain. Susannah had once seen similar
trees, she thought, in a travelogue film about
Australia.

The road they had been following swooped down
the far side of the hill and then ran straight as a string
into the southeast, a bright white lane cutting through
the grass. To the west, some miles off, she could see
a herd of large animals grazing peacefully. They
looked like buffalo. To the east, the last of the forest
made a curved peninsula into the grassland. This incursion was a dark, tangled shape that looked like a
forearm with a cocked fist at the end.

That was the direction, she realized, in which all
the creeks and streams they had encountered had been
flowing. They were tributaries of the vast river that
emerged from that jutting arm of forest and flowed,

placid and dreaming under the summer sun, toward the eastern edge of the world. It was wide, that river—perhaps two miles from bank to bank.

And she could see the city.

It lay dead ahead, a misty collection of spires and towers rising above the far edge of the horizon. Those airy ramparts might have been a hundred miles away, or two hundred, or four hundred. The air of this world seemed to be totally clear, and that made judging distances a fool's game. All she knew for sure was that the sight of those dim towers filled her with silent wonder . . . and a deep, aching homesickness for New York. She thought, *I believe I'd do most anything just to see the Manhattan skyline from the Triborough Bridge again.*

Then she had to smile, because that wasn't the truth. The truth was that she wouldn't trade Roland's world for anything. Its silent mystery and empty spaces were intoxicating. And her lover was here. In New York—the New York of her own time, at least—they would have been objects of scorn and anger, the butt of every idiot's crude, cruel jokes: a black woman of twenty-six and her whitebread lover who was three years younger and who had a tendency to talk like dis and dat when he got excited. Her whitebread lover who had been carrying a heavy monkey on his back only eight months before. Here, there was no one to jeer or laugh. Here, no one was pointing a finger. Here, there were only Roland, Eddie, and herself, the world's last three gunslingers.

She took Eddie's hand and felt it close over hers, warm and reassuring.

Roland pointed. "That must be the Send River," he said in a low voice. "I never thought to see it in my life . . . wasn't even sure it was real, like the Guardians."

"It's so lovely," Susannah murmured. She was unable to take her eyes from the vast landscape before her, dreaming richly in the cradle of summer. She found her eyes tracing the shadows of the trees, which trailed across the plain for what seemed miles as the sun sank toward the horizon. "It's the way our Great Plains must have looked before they were settled—even before the Indians came." She raised her free hand and pointed toward the place where the Great Road narrowed to a point. "There's your city," she said. "Isn't it?"

"Yes."

"It looks okay," Eddie said. "Is that possible, Roland? Could it still be pretty much intact. Did the old-timers build that well?"

"Anything is possible in these times," Roland said, but he sounded doubtful. "You shouldn't get your hopes up, though, Eddie."

"Huh? No." But Eddie's hopes *were* up. That dimly sketched skyline had awakened homesickness in Susannah's heart; in Eddie's it kindled a sudden blaze of supposition. If the city was still there—and it clearly was—it might still be populated, and maybe not just by the subhuman things Roland had met under the mountains, either. The city-dwellers might be

(*Americans*, Eddie's subconscious whispered)

intelligent and helpful; they might, in fact, spell the difference between success and failure for the quest of the pilgrims . . . or even between life and death. In Eddie's mind a vision (partly cribbed from movies like *The Last Starfighter* and *The Dark Crystal*) gleamed brightly: a council of gnarled but dignified City Elders who would serve them a whopping meal drawn from the unspoiled stores of the city (or perhaps from special gardens cradled within environmental bubbles) and who would, as he and Roland and Susannah ate themselves silly, explain exactly what lay ahead and what it all meant. Their parting gift to the wayfarers would be an AAA-approved TourGuide map with the best route to the Dark Tower marked in red.

Eddie did not know the phrase *deus ex machina*,

but he knew—had now grown up enough to know—
that such wise and kindly folk lived mostly in comic
books and B-movies. The idea was intoxicating, all
the same: an enclave of civilization in this dangerous,
mostly empty world; wise old elf-men who would tell
them just what the fuck it was they were supposed to
be doing. And the fabulous shapes of the city disclosed in that hazy skyline made the idea seem at
least possible. Even if the city was totally deserted,
the population wiped out by some long-ago plague or
outbreak of chemical warfare, it might still serve them
as a kind of giant toolbox—a huge Army-Navy Surplus
Store where they could outfit themselves for the hard
passages Eddie was sure must lie ahead. Besides, he
was a city boy, born and bred, and the sight of all
those tall towers just naturally got him up.

"All *right*!" he said, almost laughing out loud in his
excitement. "Hey-ho, let's go! Bring on those wise
fuckin elves!"

Susannah looked at him, puzzled but smiling.
"What you ravin about, white boy?"

"Nothing. Never mind. I just want to get moving.
What do you say, Roland? Want to—"

But something on Roland's face or just beneath it—
some lost, dreaming thing—caused him to fall silent
and put one arm around Susannah's shoulders, as if
to protect her.

15

AFTER ONE BRIEF, DISMISSIVE glance at the city skyline, Roland's gaze had been caught by something a
good deal closer to their current position, something
that filled him with disquiet and foreboding. He had
seen such things before, and the last time he'd come
across one, Jake had been with him. He remembered
how they had finally come out of the desert, the trail

of the man in black leading them through the foothills and toward the mountains. Hard going, it had been, but at least there had been water again. And grass.

One night he had awakened to find Jake gone. He had heard strangled, desperate cries coming from a willow-grove hard by a narrow trickle of stream. By the time he had fought his way through to the clearing at the center of the grove, the boy's cries had ceased. Roland had found him standing in a place exactly like the one which lay below and ahead. A place of stones; a place of sacrifice; a place where an Oracle lived . . . and spoke when it was forced to . . . and killed whenever it could.

"Roland?" Eddie asked. "What is it? What's wrong?"

"Do you see that?" Roland pointed. "It's a speaking ring. The shapes you see are tall standing stones." He found himself staring at Eddie, whom he had first met in the frightening but wonderful air-carriage of that strange other world where the gunslingers wore blue uniforms and there was an endless supply of sugar, paper, and wonderful drugs like *astin*. Some strange expression—some foreknowledge—was dawning on Eddie's face. The bright hope which had lit his eyes as he surveyed the city whiffed out, leaving him with a look both gray and bleak. It was the expression of a man studying the gallows on which he will soon be hanged.

First Jake, and now Eddie, the gunslinger thought. *The wheel which turns our lives is remorseless; always it comes around to the same place again.*

"Oh shit," Eddie said. His voice was dry and scared. "I think that's the place where the kid is going to try and come through."

The gunslinger nodded. "Very likely. They're thin places, and they're also *attractive* places. I followed him to such a place once before. The Oracle that kept there came very close to killing him."

"How do you *know* this?" Susannah asked Eddie. "Was it a dream?"

He only shook his head. "I don't know. But the minute Roland pointed that goddamn place out . . ." He broke off and looked at the gunslinger. "We have to get there, just as fast as we can." Eddie sounded both frantic and fearful.

"Is it going to happen today?" Roland asked. "Tonight?"

Eddie shook his head again, and licked his lips. "I don't know that, either. Not for sure. Tonight? I don't think so. Time . . . it isn't the same over here as it is where the kid is. It goes slower in his where and when. Maybe tomorrow." He had been battling panic, but now it broke free. He turned and grabbed Roland's shirt with his cold, sweating fingers. "But I'm supposed to finish the key, and I haven't, and I'm supposed to do something else, and I don't have a clue about what it is. And if the kid dies, it'll be *my fault*!"

The gunslinger locked his own hands over Eddie's and pulled them away from his shirt. "Get control of yourself."

"Roland, don't you understand—"

"I understand that whining and puling won't solve your problem. I understand that you have forgotten the face of your father."

"Quit that bullshit! I don't care *dick* about my father!" Eddie shouted hysterically, and Roland hit him across the face. His hand made a sound like a breaking branch.

Eddie's head rocked back; his eyes widened with shock. He stared at the gunslinger, then slowly raised his hand to touch the reddening handprint on his cheek. "You *bastard*!" he whispered. His hand dropped to the butt of the revolver he still wore on his left hip. Susannah tried to put her own hands over it; Eddie pushed them away.

And now I must teach again, Roland thought, *only*

*this time I teach for my own life, I think, as well as
for his.*

Somewhere in the distance a crow hailed its harsh
cry into the stillness, and Roland thought for a moment of his hawk, David. Now *Eddie* was his hawk
. . . and like David, he would not scruple to tear out
his eye if he gave so much as a single inch.

Or his throat.

"Will you shoot me? Is that how you'd have it end,
Eddie?"

"Man, I'm so fucking tired of your jive," Eddie
said. His eyes were blurred with tears and fury.

"You haven't finished the key, but not because you
are afraid to finish. You're afraid of finding you *can't*
finish. You're afraid to go down to where the stones
stand, but not because you're afraid of what may come
once you enter the circle. You're afraid of what may
not come. You're not afraid of the great world, Eddie,
but of the small one inside yourself. You haven't forgotten the face of your father. So do it. Shoot me if
you dare. I'm tired of watching you blubber."

"Stop it!" Susannah screamed at him. "Can't you
see he'll do it? Can't you see you're *forcing* him to do
it?"

Roland cut his eyes toward her. "I'm forcing him
to *decide*." He looked back at Eddie, and his deeply
lined face was stern. "You have come from the
shadow of the heroin and the shadow of your brother,
my friend. Come from the shadow of yourself, if you
dare. Come now. Come out or shoot me *and have
done with it.*"

For a moment he thought Eddie was going to do
just that, and it would all end right here, on this high
ridge, beneath a cloudless summer sky with the spires
of the city glimmering on the horizon like blue ghosts.
Then Eddie's cheek began to twitch. The firm line of
his lips softened and began to tremble. His hand fell
from the sandalwood butt of Roland's gun. His chest
hitched once . . . twice . . . three times. His mouth

opened and all his despair and terror came out in one
groaning cry as he blundered toward the gunslinger.

"I'm afraid, *you numb fuck! Don't you understand
that? Roland,* I'm afraid!''

His feet tangled together. He fell forward. Roland
caught him and held him close, smelling the sweat and
dirt on his skin, smelling his tears and terror.

The gunslinger embraced him for a moment, then
turned him toward Susannah. Eddie dropped to his
knees beside her chair, his head hanging wearily. She
put a hand on the back of his neck, pressing his head
against her thigh, and said bitterly to Roland, "Sometimes I hate you, big white man.''

Roland placed the heels of his hands against his
forehead and pressed hard. "Sometimes I hate
myself.''

"Don't ever stop you, though, do it?''

Roland didn't reply. He looked at Eddie, who lay
with his cheek pressed against Susannah's thigh and
his eyes tightly shut. His face was a study in misery.
Roland fought away the dragging weariness that made
him want to leave the rest of this charming discussion
for another day. If Eddie was right, there *was* no other
day. Jake was almost ready to make his move. Eddie
had been chosen to midwife the boy into this world.
If he wasn't prepared to do that, Jake would die at
the point of entry, as surely as an infant must strangle
if the mother-root is tangled about its neck when the
contractions begin.

"Stand up, Eddie.''

For a moment he thought Eddie would simply go
on crouching there and hiding his face against the
woman's leg. If so, everything was lost . . . and that
was *ka,* too. Then, slowly, Eddie got to his feet. He
stood there with everything—hands, shoulders, head,
hair—hanging, not good, but he was up, and that was
a start.

"Look at me.''

Susannah stirred uneasily, but this time she said nothing.

Slowly, Eddie raised his head and brushed the hair out of his eyes with a trembling hand.

"This is for you. I was wrong to take it at all, no matter how deep my pain." Roland curled his hand around the rawhide strip and yanked, snapping it. He held the key out to Eddie. Eddie reached for it like a man in a dream, but Roland did not immediately open his hand. "Will you try to do what needs to be done?"

"Yes." His voice was almost inaudible.

"Do you have something to tell me?"

"I'm sorry I'm afraid." There was something terrible in Eddie's voice, something which hurt Roland's heart and, he supposed, he knew what it was: here was the last of Eddie's childhood, expiring painfully among the three of them. It could not be seen, but Roland could hear its weakening cries. He tried to make himself deaf to them.

Something else I've done in the name of the Tower. My score grows ever longer, and the day when it will all have to be totted up, like a long-time drunkard's bill in an alehouse, draws ever nearer. How will I ever pay?

"I don't want your apology, least of all for being afraid," he said. "Without fear, what would we be? Mad dogs with foam on our muzzles and shit drying on our hocks."

"What *do* you want, then?" Eddie cried. "You've taken everything else—everything I have to give! No, not even that, because in the end, I gave it to you! So *what else do you want from me?*"

Roland held the key which was their half of Jake Chambers's salvation locked in his fist and said nothing. His eyes held Eddie's, and the sun shone on the green expanse of plain and the blue-gray reach of the Send River, and somewhere in the distance the crow hailed again across the golden leagues of this fading summer afternoon.

After a while, understanding began to dawn in Eddie Dean's eyes.

Roland nodded.

"I have forgotten the face . . ." Eddie paused. Dipped his head. Swallowed. Looked up at the gunslinger once more. The thing which had been dying among them had moved on now—Roland knew it. That thing was gone. Just like that. Here, on this sunny wind-swept ridge at the edge of everything, it had gone forever. "I have forgotten the face of my father, gunslinger . . . and I cry your pardon."

Roland opened his hand and returned the small burden of the key to him who *ka* had decreed must carry it. "Speak not so, gunslinger," he said in the High Speech. "Your father sees you very well . . . loves you very well . . . and so do I."

Eddie closed his own hand over the key and turned away with his tears still drying on his face. "Let's go," he said, and they began to move down the long hill toward the plain which stretched beyond.

16

JAKE WALKED SLOWLY ALONG Castle Avenue, past pizza shops and bars and bodegas where old women with suspicious faces poked the potatoes and squeezed the tomatoes. The straps of his pack had chafed the skin beneath his arms, and his feet hurt. He passed beneath a digital thermometer which announced it was eighty-five. It felt more like a hundred and five to Jake.

Up ahead, a police car turned onto the Avenue. Jake at once became extremely interested in a display of gardening supplies in the window of a hardware store. He watched the reflection of the blue-and-white pass in the window and didn't move until it was gone.

Hey, Jake, old buddy—where, exactly, are you going?

He hadn't the slightest idea. He felt positive that the boy he was looking for—the boy in the green bandanna and the yellow T-shirt that said NEVER A DULL MOMENT IN MID-WORLD—was somewhere close by, but so what? To Jake he was still nothing but a needle hiding in the haystack which was Brooklyn.

He passed an alley which had been decorated with a tangle of spray-painted graffiti. Mostly they were names—EL TIANTE 91, SPEEDY GONZALES, MOTORVAN MIKE—but a few mottos and words to the wise had been dropped in here and there, and Jake's eyes fixed on two of these.

A ROSE IS A ROSE IS A ROSE

had been written across the bricks in spray-paint which had weathered to the same dusky-pink shade of the rose which grew in the vacant lot where Tom and Gerry's Artistic Deli had once stood. Below it, in a blue so dark it was almost black, someone had spray-painted this oddity:

I CRY YOUR PARDON

What does that *mean?* Jake wondered. He didn't know—something from the Bible, maybe—but it held like the eye of a snake is reputed to hold a bird. At last he walked on, slowly and thoughtfully. It was almost two-thirty, and his shadow was beginning to grow longer.

Just ahead, he saw an old man walking down the street, keeping to the shade as much as possible and leaning on a gnarled cane. Behind the thick glasses he wore, his brown eyes swam like oversized eggs.

"I cry your pardon, sir," Jake said without thinking or even really hearing himself.

The old man turned to look at him, blinking in surprise and fear. "Liff me alone, boy," he said. He raised his walking-stick and brandished it clumsily in Jake's direction.

"Would you know if there's a place called Markey Academy anyplace around here, sir?" This was utter desperation, but it was the only thing he could think to ask.

The old man slowly lowered his stick—it was the *sir* that had done it. He looked at Jake with the slightly lunatic interest of the old and almost senile. "How come you not in school, boy?"

Jake smiled wearily. This one was getting very old. "Finals Week. I came down here to look up an old friend of mine who goes to Markey Academy, that's all. Sorry to have bothered you."

He stepped around the old man (hoping he wouldn't decide to whop him one across the ass with his cane just for good luck) and was almost down to the corner when the old man yelled: "Boy! Boyyyyy!"

Jake turned around.

"There is no Markey Akidimy down here," the old man said. "Twenty-two years I'm living here, so I should know. Markey *Avenue*, yes, but no Markey Akidimy."

Jake's stomach cramped with sudden excitement. He took a step back toward the old man, who at once raised his cane into a defensive position again. Jake stopped at once, leaving a twenty-foot safety zone between them. "Where's Markey Avenue, sir? Can you tell me that?"

"Of *gorse*," the old man said. "Didn't I just say I'm livink here twenty-two years? Two blogs down. Turn left at the Majestic Theatre. But I'm tellink you now, there iss no Markey Akidimy."

"Thank you, sir! Thank you!"

Jake turned around and looked up Castle Avenue.

Yes—he could see the unmistakable shape of a movie
marquee jutting out over the sidewalk a couple of
blocks up. He started to run toward it, then decided
that might attract attention and slowed down to a fast
walk.

The old man watched him go. *"Sir!"* he said to
himself in a tone of mild amazement. *"Sir,* yet!"

He chuckled rustily and moved on.

17

ROLAND'S BAND STOPPED AT dusk. The gunslinger
dug a shallow pit and lit a fire. They didn't need it
for cooking purposes, but they needed it, nonetheless.
Eddie needed it. If he was going to finish his carving,
he would need light to work by.

The gunslinger looked around and saw Susannah, a
dark silhouette against the fading aquamarine sky, but
he didn't see Eddie.

"Where is he?" he asked.

"Down the road apiece. You leave him alone now,
Roland—you've done enough."

Roland nodded, bent over the firepit, and struck at
a piece of flint with a worn steel bar. Soon the kindling he had gathered was blazing. He added small
sticks, one by one, and waited for Eddie to return.

18

HALF A MILE BACK the way they had come, Eddie sat
cross-legged in the middle of the Great Road with
his unfinished key in one hand, watching the sky. He
glanced down the road, saw the spark of the fire, and
knew exactly what Roland was doing . . . and why.

Then he turned his gaze to the sky again. He had never felt so lonely or so afraid.

The sky was *huge*—he could not remember ever seeing so much uninterrupted space, so much pure emptiness. It made him feel very small, and he supposed there was nothing at all wrong with that. In the scheme of things, he *was* very small.

The boy was close now. He thought he knew where Jake was and what he was about to do, and it filled him with silent wonder. Susannah had come from 1963. Eddie had come from 1987. Between them . . . Jake. Trying to come over. Trying to be born.

I met him, Eddie thought. *I must have met him, and I think I remember . . . sort of. It was just before Henry went into the Army, right? He was taking courses at Brooklyn Vocational Institute, and he was heavily into black—black jeans, black motorcycle boots with steel caps, black T-shirts with the sleeves rolled up. Henry's James Dean look. Smoking Area Chic. I used to think that, but I never said it out loud, because I didn't want him pissed at me.*

He realized that what he had been waiting for had happened while he was thinking: Old Star had come out. In fifteen minutes, maybe less, it would be joined by a whole galaxy of alien jewelry, but for now it gleamed alone in the ungathered darkness.

Eddie slowly held up the key until Old Star gleamed within its wide central notch. And then he recited the old formula of his world, the one his mother had taught him as she knelt beside him at the bedroom window, both of them looking out at the evening star which rode the oncoming darkness above the rooftops and fire-escapes of Brooklyn: "Star light, star bright, first star I see tonight; wish I may, wish I might, have the wish I wish tonight."

Old Star glowed in the notch of the key, a diamond caught in ash.

"Help me find some guts," Eddie said. "That's my

wish. Help me find the guts to try and finish this damned thing."

He sat there a moment longer, then got to his feet and walked slowly back to camp. He sat down as close to the fire as he could get, took the gunslinger's knife without a word to either him or Susannah, and began to work. Tiny, curling slivers of wood rolled up from the *s*-shape at the end of the key. Eddie worked fast, turning the key this way and that, occasionally closing his eyes and letting his thumb slip along the mild curves. He tried not to think about what might happen if the shape were to go wrong—that would freeze him for sure.

Roland and Susannah sat behind him, watching silently. At last Eddie put the knife aside. His face was running with sweat. "This kid of yours," he said. "This Jake. He must be a gutty brat."

"He was brave under the mountains," Roland said. "He was afraid, but never gave an inch."

"I wish I could be that way."

Roland shrugged. "At Balazar's you fought well even though they had taken your clothes. It's very hard for a man to fight naked, but you did it."

Eddie tried to remember the shootout in the night-club, but it was just a blur in his mind—smoke, noise, and light shining through one wall in confused, intersecting rays. He thought that wall had been torn apart by automatic-weapons fire, but couldn't remember for sure.

He held the key up so its notches were sharply outlined against the flames. He held it that way for a long time, looking mostly at the *s*-shape. It looked exactly as he remembered it from his dream and from the momentary vision he had seen in the fire . . . but it didn't *feel* exactly right. Almost, but not quite.

That's just Henry again. That's just all those years of never being quite good enough. You did it, buddy— it's just that the Henry inside doesn't want to admit it.

He dropped the key onto the square of hide and

folded the edges carefully around it. "I'm done. I don't know if it's right or not, but I guess it's as right as I can make it." He felt oddly empty now that he no longer had the key to work on—purposeless and directionless.

"Do you want something to eat, Eddie?" Susannah asked quietly.

There's your purpose, he thought. *There's your direction. Sitting right over there, with her hands folded in her lap. All the purpose and direction you'll ever—*

But now something else rose in his mind—it came all at once. Not a dream . . . not a vision . . .

No, not either of those. It's a memory. It's happening again—you're remembering forward in time.

"I have to do something else first," he said, and got up.

On the far side of the fire, Roland had stacked some odd lots of scavenged wood. Eddie hunted through them and found a dry stick about two feet long and four inches or so through the middle. He took it, returning to his place by the fire, and picked up Roland's knife again. This time he worked faster because he was simply sharpening the stick, turning it into something that looked like a small tent-peg.

"Can we get moving before daybreak?" he asked the gunslinger. "I think we should get to that circle as soon as we can."

"Yes. Sooner, if we must. I don't want to move in the dark—a speaking ring is an unsafe place to be at night—but if we have to, we have to."

"From the look on your face, big boy, I doubt if those stone circles are very safe *any* time," Susannah said.

Eddie put the knife aside again. The dirt Roland had taken out of the shallow hole he'd made for the campfire was piled up by Eddie's right foot. Now he used the sharp end of the stick to carve a question-mark shape in the dirt. The shape was crisp and clear.

"Okay," he said, brushing it away. "All done."

"Have something to eat, then," Susannah said.

Eddie tried, but he wasn't very hungry. When he finally went to sleep, nestled against Susannah's warmth, his rest was dreamless but very thin. Until the gunslinger shook him awake at four in the morning, he heard the wind racing endlessly over the plain below them, and it seemed to him that he went with it, flying high into the night, away from these cares, while Old Star and Old Mother rode serenely above him, painting his cheeks with frost.

19

"IT'S TIME," ROLAND SAID.

Eddie sat up. Susannah sat up beside him, rubbing her palms over her face. As Eddie's head cleared, his mind was filled with urgency. "Yes. Let's go, and fast."

"He's getting close, isn't he?"

"Very close." Eddie got to his feet, grasped Susannah around the waist, and boosted her into her chair.

She was looking at him anxiously. "Do we still have enough time to get there?"

Eddie nodded. "Barely."

Three minutes later they were headed down the Great Road again. It glimmered ahead of them like a ghost. And an hour after that, as the first light of dawn began to touch the sky in the east, a rhythmic sound began far ahead of them.

The sound of drums, Roland thought.

Machinery, Eddie thought. *Some huge piece of machinery.*

It's a heart, Susannah thought. *Some huge, diseased, beating heart . . . and it's in that city, where we have to go.*

Two hours later, the sound stopped as suddenly as it had begun. White, featureless clouds had begun to

fill the sky above them, first veiling the early sun, then
blotting it out. The circle of standing stones lay less
than five miles ahead now, gleaming in the shadowless
light like the teeth of a fallen monster.

20

SPAGHETTI WEEK AT THE MAJESTIC!

the battered, dispirited marquee jutting over the corner of Brooklyn and Markey Avenues proclaimed.

2 SERGIO LEONE CLASSIX!
A FISTFUL OF $$ PLUS GOOD BAD & UGLY!
99¢ ALL SHOWS

A gum-chewing cutie with rollers in her blonde hair
sat in the box office listening to Led Zep on her tran-
sistor and reading one of the tabloids of which Mrs.
Shaw was so fond. To her left, in the theater's remaining display case, there was a poster showing Clint
Eastwood.

Jake knew he should get moving—three o'clock was
almost here—but he paused a moment anyway, staring
at the poster behind the dirty, cracked glass. Eastwood was wearing a Mexican serape. A cigar was
clamped in his teeth. He had thrown one side of the
serape back over his shoulder to free his gun. His eyes
were a pale, faded blue. Bombardier's eyes.

It's not him, Jake thought, *but it's* almost *him. It's
the eyes, mostly . . . the eyes are almost the same.*

"You let me drop," he said to the man in the old
poster, the man who was not Roland. "You let me
die. What happens this time?"

"Hey, kid," the blonde ticket-seller called, making
Jake start. "You gonna come in or just stand there
and talk to yourself?"

"Not me," Jake said. "I've already seen those two."

He got moving again, turning left on Markey Avenue.

Once again he waited for the feeling of *remembering forward* to seize him, but it didn't come. This was just a hot, sunny street lined with sandstone-colored apartment buildings that looked like prison cellblocks to Jake. A few young women were walking along, pushing baby-carriages in pairs and talking desultorily, but the street was otherwise deserted. It was unseasonably hot for May—too hot to stroll.

What am I looking for? What?

From behind him came a burst of raucous male laughter. It was followed by an outraged female shriek: "You give that *back*!"

Jake jumped, thinking the owner of the voice must mean him.

"Give it *back*, Henry! I'm not kidding!"

Jake turned and saw two boys, one at least eighteen and the other a lot younger . . . twelve or thirteen. At the sight of this second boy, Jake's heart did something that felt like a loop-the-loop in his chest. The kid was wearing green corduroys instead of madras shorts, but the yellow T-shirt was the same, and he had a battered old basketball under one arm. Although his back was to Jake, Jake knew he had found the boy from last night's dream.

21

THE GIRL WAS THE gum-chewing cutie from the ticket-booth. The older of the two boys—who looked almost old enough to be called a man—had her newspaper in his hands. She grabbed for it. The newspaper-grabber—he was wearing denims and a black T-shirt with the sleeves rolled up—held it over his head and grinned.

"Jump for it, Maryanne! Jump, girl, jump!"

She stared at him with angry eyes, her cheeks flushed. "Give it to me!" she said. "Quit fooling around and give it back! *Bastard!*"

"Oooo wisten to *dat*, Eddie!" the old kid said. "Bad wang-gwidge! Naughty, naughty!" He waved the newspaper just out of the blonde ticket-seller's grasp, grinning, and Jake suddenly understood. These two were walking home from school together—although they probably didn't go to the same one, if he was right about the difference in their ages—and the bigger boy had gone over to the box office, pretending he had something interesting to tell the blonde. Then he had reached through the slot at the bottom and snatched her paper.

The big boy's face was one that Jake had seen before; it was the face of a kid who would think it the height of hilarity to douse a cat's tail with lighter fluid or feed a bread-ball with a fishhook planted in the middle to a hungry dog. The sort of kid who sat in the back of the room and snapped bra-straps and then said "Who me?" with a big, dumb look of surprise on his face when someone finally complained. There weren't many kids like him at Piper, but there were a few. Jake supposed there were a few in every school. They dressed better at Piper, but the face was the same. He guessed that in the old days, people would have said it was the face of a boy who was born to be hung.

Maryanne jumped for her newspaper, which the old boy in the black pants had rolled into a tube. He pulled it out of her reach just before she could grab it, then whacked her on the head with it, the way you might whack a dog for piddling on the carpet. She was beginning to cry now—mostly from humiliation, Jake guessed. Her face was now so red it was almost glowing. "Keep it, then!" she yelled at him. "I know you can't read, but you can look at the pictures, at least!"

She began to turn away.

"Give it back, why don't you?" the younger boy—
Jake's boy—said softly.

The old boy held out the newspaper tube. The girl
snatched it from him, and even from his place thirty
feet farther down the street, Jake heard it rip. "You're
a turd, Henry Dean!" she cried. "A real *turd*!"

"Hey, what's the big deal?" Henry sounded genuinely injured. "It was just a joke. Besides, it only
ripped in one place—you can still read it, for Chris-
sake. Lighten up a little, why don'tcha?"

And that was right, too, Jake thought. Guys like
this Henry always pushed even the most unfunny joke
two steps too far . . . then looked wounded and misunderstood when someone yelled at them. And it was
always *Wassa matter?* and it was *Can'tcha take a joke?*
and it was *Why don'tcha lighten up a little?*

What are you doing with him, kid? Jake wondered.
*If you're on my side, what are you doing with a jerk
like that?*

But as the younger kid turned around and they
started to walk down the street again, Jake knew. The
old boy's features were heavier, and his complexion
was badly pitted with acne, but otherwise the resemblance was striking. The two boys were brothers.

22

JAKE TURNED AWAY AND began to idle up the sidewalk ahead of the two boys. He reached into his
breast pocket with a shaky hand, pulled out his father's sunglasses, and managed to fumble them onto
his face.

Voices swelled behind him, as if someone was gradually turning up the volume on a radio.

"You shouldn't have ranked on her that bad,
Henry. It was mean."

"She loves it, Eddie." Henry's voice was complacent, worldly-wise. "When you get a little older, you'll understand."

"She was *cryin*."

"Prob'ly got the rag on," Henry said in a philosophical tone.

They were very close now. Jake shrank against the side of the building. His head was down, his hands stuffed deep into the pockets of his jeans. He didn't know why it seemed so vitally important that he not be noticed, but it did. Henry didn't matter, one way or the other, but—

The younger one isn't supposed to remember me, he thought. *I don't know why, exactly, but he's not.*

They passed him without so much as a glance, the one Henry had called Eddie walking on the outside, dribbling the basketball along the gutter.

"You gotta admit she looked funny," Henry was saying. "Ole Be-Bop Maryanne, jumpin for her newspaper. Woof! Woof!"

Eddie looked up at his brother with an expression that wanted to be reproachful . . . and then he gave up and dissolved into laughter. Jake saw the unconditional love in that upturned face and guessed that Eddie would forgive a lot in his big brother before giving it up as a bad job.

"So are we going?" Eddie asked now. "You said we could. After school."

"I said *maybe*. I dunno if I wanna walk all the way over there. Mom'll be home by now, too. Maybe we just oughtta forget it. Go upstairs and watch some tube."

They were now ten feet ahead of Jake and pulling away.

"Ah, come on! You *said*!"

Beyond the building the two boys were currently passing was a chainlink fence with an open gate in it. Beyond it, Jake saw, was the playground of which he had dreamed last night . . . a version of it, anyway. It wasn't surrounded by trees, and there was no odd subway kiosk with diagonal slashes of yellow and black across the front, but the cracked concrete was the same. So were the faded yellow foul lines.

"Well . . . maybe. I dunno." Jake realized Henry was teasing again. Eddie didn't, though; he was too anxious about wherever it was he wanted to go. "Let's shoot some hoops while I think it over."

He stole the ball from his younger brother, dribbled clumsily onto the playground, and went for a lay-up that hit high on the backboard and bounced back without even touching the rim of the hoop. Henry was good at stealing newspapers from teenage girls, Jake thought, but on the basketball court he sucked the big one.

Eddie walked in through the gate, unbuttoned his corduroy pants, and slipped them down. Beneath them were the faded madras shorts he had been wearing in Jake's dream.

"Oh, is he wearing his shortie panties?" Henry said. "Ain't they *cuuute*?" He waited until his brother balanced himself on one leg to pull off his cords, then flung the basketball at him. Eddie managed to bat it away, probably saving himself a bloody nose, but he lost his balance and fell clumsily to the concrete. He didn't cut himself, but he could have done so, Jake saw; a great deal of broken glass glittered in the sun along the chainlink.

"Come on, Henry, quit it," he said, but with no real reproach. Jake guessed Henry had been pulling shit like this on him so long that Eddie only noticed it when Henry pulled it on someone else—someone like the blonde ticket-seller.

"Tum on, Henwy, twit it."

Eddie got to his feet and trotted out onto the court. The ball had struck the chainlink fence and bounced back to Henry. Henry now tried to dribble past his younger brother. Eddie's hand went out, lightning-quick but oddly delicate, and stole the ball. He easily ducked under Henry's outstretched, flailing arm and went for the basket. Henry dogged him, frowning thunderously, but he might as well have been taking a nap. Eddie went up, knees bent, feet neatly cocked, and laid the ball in. Henry grabbed it and dribbled out to the stripe.

Shouldn't have done that, Eddie, Jake thought. He was standing just beyond the place where the fence ended, watching the two boys. This seemed safe enough, at least for the moment. He was wearing his dad's sunglasses, and the two boys were so involved in what they were doing that they wouldn't have noticed if President Carter had strolled up to watch. Jake doubted if Henry knew who President Carter was, anyway.

He expected Henry to foul his brother, perhaps heavily, as a payback for the steal, but he had underestimated Eddie's guile. Henry offered a head-fake that wouldn't have fooled Jake's mother, but Eddie appeared to fall for it. Henry broke past him and drove for the basket, gaily travelling the ball most of the way. Jake was quite sure Eddie could have caught him easily and stolen the ball again, but instead of doing so, the kid hung back. Henry laid it up—clumsily—and the ball bounced off the rim again. Eddie grabbed it . . . and then let it squirt through his fingers. Henry snatched it, turned, and put it through the netless hoop.

"One-up," Henry panted. "Play to twelve?"

"Sure."

Jake had seen enough. It would be close, but in the end Henry would win. Eddie would see to it. It would do more than save him from getting lumped up; it would put Henry in a good mood, making him more agreeable to whatever it was Eddie wanted to do.

Hey Moose—I think your little brother has been playing you like a violin for a long time now, and you don't have the slightest idea, do you?

He drew back until the apartment building which stood at the north end of the court cut off his view of the Dean brothers, and their view of him. He leaned against the wall and listened to the thump of the ball on the court. Soon Henry was puffing like Charlie the Choo-Choo going up a steep hill. He would be a smoker, of course; guys like Henry were always smokers.

The game took almost ten minutes, and by the time Henry claimed victory, the street was filled up with other home-going kids. A few gave Jake curious glances as they passed by.

"Good game, Henry," Eddie said.

"Not bad," Henry panted. "You're still falling for the old head-fake."

Sure he is, Jake thought. *I think he'll go on falling for it until he's gained about eighty pounds. Then you might get a surprise.*

"I guess I am. Hey, Henry, can't we *please* go look at the place?"

"Yeah, why not? Let's do it."

"All *right!*" Eddie yelled. There was the smacking sound of flesh on flesh; probably Eddie giving his brother a high-five. "Boss!"

"You go on up to the apartment. Tell Mom we'll be in by four-thirty, quarter of five. But don't say anything about The Mansion. She'd have a shit-fit. She thinks it's haunted, too."

"You want me to tell her we're going over Dewey's?"

Silence as Henry considered this. "Naw. She might call Mrs. Bunkowski. Tell her . . . tell her we're goin down to Dahlie's to get Hoodsie Rockets. She'll believe that. Ask her for a coupla bucks, too."

"She won't give me any money. Not two days before payday."

"Bullshit. You can get it out of her. Go on, now."

"Okay." But Jake didn't hear Eddie moving. "Henry?"

"What?" Impatiently.

"*Is* The Mansion haunted, do you think?"

Jake sidled a little closer to the playground. He didn't want to be noticed, but he strongly felt that he needed to hear this.

"Naw. There ain't no *real* haunted houses—just in the fuckin movies."

"Oh." There was unmistakable relief in Eddie's voice.

"But if there ever *was* one," Henry resumed (perhaps he didn't want his little brother feeling *too* relieved, Jake thought), "it'd be The Mansion. I heard that a couple of years ago, two kids from Norwood Street went in there to bump uglies and the cops found em with their throats cut and all the blood drained out of their bodies. But there wasn't any blood on em or around em. Get it? The blood was *all gone.*"

"You shittin me?" Eddie breathed.

"Nope. But that wasn't the worst thing."

"What was?"

"Their hair was dead white," Henry said. The voice that drifted to Jake was solemn. He had an idea that Henry wasn't teasing this time, that this time he believed every word he was saying. (He also doubted that Henry had brains enough to make such a story up.) "Both of em. And their eyes were wide open and staring, like they saw the most gross-awful thing in the world."

"Aw, gimme a break," Eddie said, but his voice was soft, awed.

"You still wanna go?"

"Sure. As long as we don't . . . you know, hafta get too close."

"Then go see Mom. And try to get a couple of bucks out of her. I need cigarettes. Take the fuckin ball up, too."

Jake drifted backward and stepped into the nearest apartment building entryway just as Eddie came out through the playground gate.

To his horror, the boy in the yellow T-shirt turned

in Jake's direction. *Holy crow!* he thought, dismayed. *What if this is his building?*

It was. Jake just had time to turn around and begin to scan the names beside the rank of buzzers before Eddie Dean brushed past him, so close that Jake could smell the sweat he had worked up on the basketball court. He half-sensed, half-saw the curious glance the boy tossed in his direction. Then Eddie was in the lobby and headed for the elevators with his school-pants bundled under one arm and the scuffed basketball under the other.

Jake's heart was thudding heavily in his chest. Shadowing people was a lot harder in real life than it was in the detective novels he sometimes read. He crossed the street and stood between two apartment buildings half a block up. From here he could see both the entrance to the Dean brothers' building and the playground. The playground was filling up now, mostly with little kids. Henry leaned against the chainlink, smoking a cigarette and trying to look full of teenage angst. Every now and then he would stick out a foot as one of the little kids bolted toward him at an all-out run, and before Eddie returned, he had succeeded in tripping three of them. The last of these went sprawling full-length, smacking his face on the concrete, and ran wailing up the street with a bloody forehead. Henry flicked his cigarette butt after him and laughed cheerfully.

Just an all-around fun guy, Jake thought.

After that, the little kids wised up and began giving him a wide berth. Henry strolled out of the playground and down the street to the apartment building Eddie had entered five minutes before. As he reached it, the door opened and Eddie came out. He had changed into a pair of jeans and a fresh T-shirt; he had also tied a green bandanna, the same one he had been wearing in Jake's dream, around his forehead. He was waving a couple of dollar bills triumphantly.

Henry snatched them, then asked Eddie something. Eddie nodded, and the two boys set off.

Keeping half a block between himself and them, Jake followed.

23

THEY STOOD IN THE high grass at the edge of the Great Road, looking at the speaking ring.

Stonehenge, Susannah thought, and shuddered. *That's what it looks like. Stonehenge.*

Although the thick grass which covered the plain grew around the bases of the tall gray monoliths, the circle they enclosed was bare earth, littered here and there with white things.

"What are those?" she asked in a low voice. "Chips of stone?"

"Look again," Roland said.

She did, and saw that they were bones. The bones of small animals, maybe. She hoped.

Eddie switched the sharpened stick to his left hand, dried the palm of his right against his shirt, and then switched it back again. He opened his mouth, but no sound came from his dry throat. He cleared it and tried again. "I think I'm supposed to go in and draw something in the dirt."

Roland nodded. "Now?"

"Soon." He looked into Roland's face. "There's something here, isn't there? Something we can't see."

"It's not here right now," Roland said. "At least, I don't *think* it is. But it will come. Our *khef*—our life-force—will draw it. And, of course, it will be jealous of its place. Give me my gun back, Eddie."

Eddie unbuckled the belt and handed it over. Then he turned back to the circle of twenty-foot-high stones. Something lived in there, all right. He could smell it, a stench that made him think of damp plaster and moldering sofas and ancient mattresses rotting beneath half-liquid coats of mildew. It was familiar, that smell.

The Mansion—I smelled it there. The day I talked Henry into taking me over to see The Mansion on Rhinehold Street, in Dutch Hill.

Roland buckled his gunbelt, then bent to knot the tiedown. He looked up at Susannah as he did it. "We may need Detta Walker," he said. "Is she around?"

"That bitch always around." Susannah wrinkled her nose.

"Good. One of us is going to have to protect Eddie while he does what he's supposed to do. The other is going to be so much useless baggage. This is a demon's place. Demons are not human, but they are male and female, just the same. Sex is both their weapon and their weakness. No matter what the sex of the demon may be, it will go for Eddie. To protect its place. To keep its place from being used by an outsider. Do you understand?"

Susannah nodded. Eddie appeared not to be listening. He had tucked the square of hide containing the key into his shirt and now he was staring into the speaking ring as if hypnotized.

"There's no time to say this in a gentle or refined way," Roland told her. "One of us will—"

"One of us gonna have to fuck it to keep it off Eddie," Susannah interrupted. "This the sort of thing can't *ever* turn down a free fuck. That's what you're gettin at, isn't it?"

Roland nodded.

Her eyes gleamed. They were the eyes of Detta Walker now, both wise and unkind, shining with hard amusement, and her voice slid steadily deeper into the bogus Southern plantation drawl which was Detta's trademark. "If it's a girl demon, you git it. But if it's a boy demon, it's mine. That about it?"

Roland nodded.

"What about if it swings both ways? What about *that*, big boy?"

Roland's lips twitched in the barest suggestion of a smile. "Then we'll take it together. Just remember—"

Beside them, in a fainting, distant voice, Eddie murmured: "Not all is silent in the halls of the dead. Behold, the sleeper wakes." He turned his haunted, terrified eyes on Roland. "There's a monster."

"The demon—"

"No. A *monster*. Something between the doors— between the *worlds*. Something that waits. *And it's opening its eyes.*"

Susannah cast a frightened glance at Roland.

"Stand, Eddie," Roland said. "Be true."

Eddie drew a deep breath. "I'll stand until it knocks me down," he said. "I have to go in now. It's starting to happen."

"We all goin in," Susannah said. She arched her back and slipped out of her wheelchair. "Any demon want to fuck wit' me he goan find out he's fuckin wit' the finest. I th'ow him a fuck he ain't *never* goan f'git."

As they passed between two of the tall stones and into the speaking circle, it began to rain.

24

AS SOON AS JAKE saw the place, he understood two things: first, that he had seen it before, in dreams so terrible his conscious mind would not let him remember them; second, that it was a place of death and murder and madness. He was standing on the far corner of Rhinehold Street and Brooklyn Avenue, seventy yards from Henry and Eddie Dean, but even from where he was he could feel The Mansion ignoring them and reaching for him with its eager invisible hands. He thought there were talons at the ends of those hands. Sharp ones.

It wants me, and I can't run away. It's death to go in . . . but it's madness not to. Because somewhere inside that place is a locked door. I have the key that will open it, and the only salvation I can hope for is on the other side.

He stared at The Mansion, a house that almost screamed abnormality, with a sinking heart. It stood in the center of its weedy, rioting yard like a tumor.

The Dean brothers had walked across nine blocks of Brooklyn, moving slowly under the hot afternoon sun, and had finally entered a section of town which had to be Dutch Hill, given the names on the shops and stores. Now they stood halfway down the block, in front of The Mansion. It looked as if it had been deserted for years, yet it had suffered remarkably little vandalism. And once, Jake thought, it really *had* been a mansion—the home, perhaps, of a wealthy merchant and his large family. In those long-gone days it must have been white, but now it was a dirty gray no-color. The windows had been knocked out and the peeling picket fence which surrounded it had been spray-painted, but the house itself was still intact.

It slumped in the hot light, a ramshackle slate-roofed revenant growing out of a hummocky trash-littered yard, somehow making Jake think of a danger-ous dog which pretended to be asleep. Its steep roof overhung the front porch like a beetling brow. The boards of the porch were splintery and warped. Shut-ters which might once have been green leaned askew beside the glassless windows; ancient curtains still hung in some of these, dangling like strips of dead skin. To the left, an elderly trellis leaned away from the building, now held up not by nails but only by the nameless and somehow filthy clusters of vine which crawled over it. There was a sign on the lawn and another on the door. From where Jake stood, he could read neither of them.

The house was *alive*. He knew this, could feel its awareness reaching out from the boards and the slumping roof, could feel it pouring in rivers from the black sockets of its windows. The idea of approaching that terrible place filled him with dismay; the idea of actually going inside filled him with inarticulate horror. Yet he would have to. He could hear a low, slumbrous buzzing in his ears—the sound of a beehive on a hot summer day—and for a moment he was afraid he might faint. He closed his eyes . . . and *his* voice filled his head.

You must *come, Jake. This is the path of the Beam, the way of the Tower, and the time of your Drawing. Be true; stand; come to me.*

The fear didn't pass, but that terrible sense of impending panic did. He opened his eyes again and saw that he was not the only one who had sensed the power and awakening sentience of the place. Eddie was trying to pull away from the fence. He turned toward Jake, who could see Eddie's eyes, wide and uneasy beneath his green head-band. His big brother grabbed him and pushed him toward the rusty gate, but the gesture was too half-hearted to be much of a tease; however thick-headed he might be, Henry liked The Mansion no better than Eddie did.

They drew away a little and stood looking at the place for a while. Jake could not make out what they were saying to each other, but the tone of their voices was awed and uneasy. Jake suddenly remembered Eddie speaking in his dream: *Remember there's danger, though. Be careful . . . and be quick.*

Suddenly the real Eddie, the one across the street, raised his voice enough so that Jake could make out the words. "Can we go home now, Henry? Please? I don't like it." His tone was pleading.

"Fuckin little sissy," Henry said, but Jake thought he heard relief as well as indulgence in Henry's voice. "Come on."

They turned away from the ruined house crouching high-shouldered behind its sagging fence and approached the street. Jake backed up, then turned and looked into the window of the dispirited little hole-in-the-wall shop called Dutch Hill Used Appliances. He watched Henry and Eddie, dim and ghostly reflections superimposed on an ancient Hoover vacuum cleaner, cross Rhinehold Street.

"Are you *sure* it's not really haunted?" Eddie asked as they stepped onto the sidewalk on Jake's side.

"Well, I tell you what," Henry said. "Now that I been out here again, I'm really not so sure."

They passed directly behind Jake without looking at him. "Would you go in there?" Eddie asked.

"Not for a million dollars," Henry replied promptly.

They rounded the corner. Jake stepped away from the window and peeped after them. They were headed back the way they had come, close together on the sidewalk, Henry hulking along in his steel-toed shit-kickers, his shoulders already slumped like those of a much older man, Eddie walking beside him with neat, unconscious grace. Their shadows, long and trailing out into the street now, mingled amicably together.

They're going home, Jake thought, and felt a wave of loneliness so strong that he felt it would crush him. *Going to eat supper and do homework and argue over which TV shows to watch and then go to bed. Henry may be a bullying shit, but they've got a life, those two, one that makes sense . . . and they're going back to it. I wonder if they have any idea of how lucky they are. Eddie might, I suppose.*

Jake turned, adjusted the straps of his pack, and crossed Rhinehold Street.

25

SUSANNAH SENSED MOVEMENT IN the empty grassland beyond the circle of standing stones: a sighing, whispering rush.

"Something comin," she said tautly. "Comin fast."

"Be careful," Eddie said, "but keep it off me. You understand? Keep it off me."

"I hear you, Eddie. You just do your own thing."

Eddie nodded. He knelt in the center of the ring, holding the sharpened stick out in front of him as if assessing its point. Then he lowered it and drew a dark straight line in the dirt. "Roland, watch out for her . . ."

"I will if I can, Eddie."

". . . but keep it off me. Jake's coming. Crazy little mother's really coming."

Susannah could now see the grasses due north of the speaking ring parting in a long dark line, creating a furrow that lanced straight at the circle of stones.

"Get ready," Roland said. "It'll go for Eddie. One of us will have to ambush it."

Susannah reared up on her haunches like a snake coming out of a Hindu fakir's basket. Her hands, rolled into hard brown fists, were held at the sides of her face. Her eyes blazed. "I'm ready," she said and then shouted: *"Come on, big boy! You come on right now! Run like it's yo birfday!"*

The rain began to fall harder as the demon which lived here re-entered its circle in a booming rush. Susannah had just time to sense thick and merciless masculinity—it came to her as an eyewatering smell of gin and juniper—and then it shot toward the center of the circle. She closed her eyes and reached for it, not with her arms or her mind but with all the female force which lived at the core of her: *Hey, big boy! Where you goan? D'pussy be ovah heah!*

It whirled. She felt its surprise . . . and then its raw hunger, as full and urgent as a pulsing artery. It leaped upon her like a rapist springing from the mouth of an alley.

Susannah howled and rocked backward, cords standing out on her neck. The dress she wore first flattened against her breasts and belly, and then began to tear itself to shreds. She could hear a pointless,

directionless panting, as if the air itself had decided
to rut with her.

"Suze!" Eddie shouted, and began to get to his feet.

"*No!*" she screamed back. "*Do it! I got this sumbitch right where . . . right where I want him! Go on,
Eddie! Bring the kid! Bring—*" Coldness battered at
the tender flesh between her legs. She grunted, fell
backward . . then supported herself with one hand
and thrust defiantly forward and upward. "*Bring him
through!*"

Eddie looked uncertainly at Roland, who nodded.
Eddie glanced at Susannah again, his eyes full of dark
pain and darker fear, and then deliberately turned his
back on both of them and fell to his knees again. He
reached forward with the sharpened stick which had
become a makeshift pencil, ignoring the cold rain falling on his arms and the back of his neck. The stick
began to move, making lines and angles, creating a
shape Roland knew at once.

It was a door.

26

JAKE REACHED OUT, PUT his hands on the splintery
gate, and pushed. It swung slowly open on screaming,
rust-clotted hinges. Ahead of him was an uneven brick
path. Beyond the path was the porch. Beyond the
porch was the door. It had been boarded shut.

He walked slowly toward the house, heart tele-
graphing fast dots and dashes in his throat. Weeds had
grown up between the buckled bricks. He could hear
them rustling against his bluejeans. All his senses
seemed to have been turned up two notches. *You're
not really going in there, are you?* a panic-stricken
voice in his head asked.

And the answer that occurred to him seemed both

totally nuts and perfectly reasonable: *All things serve the Beam.*

The sign on the lawn read

ABSOLUTELY *NO TRESPASSING* UNDER PENALTY OF LAW!

The yellowing, rust-stained square of paper nailed to one of the boards crisscrossing the front door was more succinct:

BY ORDER OF NYC HOUSING AUTHORITY *THIS PROPERTY CONDEMNED*

Jake paused at the foot of the steps, looking up at the door. He had heard voices in the vacant lot and now he could hear them again . . . but this was a choir of the damned, a babble of insane threats and equally insane promises. Yet he thought it was all one voice. The voice of the house; the voice of some monstrous doorkeeper, roused from its long unpeaceful sleep.

He thought briefly of his father's Ruger, even considered pulling it out of his pack, but what good would it do? Behind him, traffic passed back and forth on Rhinehold Street and a woman was yelling for her daughter to stop holding hands with that boy and bring in the wash, but here was another world, one ruled by some bleak being over whom guns could have no power.

Be true, Jake—stand.

"Okay," he said in a low, shaky voice. "Okay, I'll try. But you better not drop me again."

Slowly, he began to mount the porch steps.

27

THE BOARDS WHICH BARRED the door were old and rotten, the nails rusty. Jake grabbed hold of the top set at the point where they crossed each other and yanked. They came free with a squall that was the gate all over again. He tossed them over the porch rail and into an ancient flowerbed where only witch-grass and dogweed grew. He bent, grasped the lower crossing . . . and paused for a moment.

A hollow sound came through the door; the sound of some animal slobbering hungrily from deep inside a concrete pipe. Jake felt a sick sheen of sweat begin to break out on his cheeks and forehead. He was so frightened that he no longer felt precisely real; he seemed to have become a character in someone else's bad dream.

The evil choir, the evil presence, was behind this door. The sound of it seeped out like syrup.

He yanked at the lower boards. They came free easily.

Of course. It wants me to come in. It's hungry, and I'm supposed to be the main course.

A snatch of poetry occurred to him suddenly, some-thing Ms. Avery had read to them. It was supposed to be about the plight of modern man, who was cut off from all his roots and traditions, but to Jake it suddenly seemed that the man who had written that poem must have seen this house: *I will show you something different from either/Your shadow in the morning striding behind you/Or your shadow at eve-ning rising to meet you;/I will show you . . .*

"I'll show you fear in a handful of dust," Jake mut-tered, and put his hand on the doorknob. And as he did, that clear sense of relief and surety flooded him again, the feeling that this was it, this time the door would open on that other world, he would see a sky untouched by smog and industrial smoke, and, on the far horizon, not the mountains but the hazy blue spires of some gorgeous unknown city.

He closed his fingers around the silver key in his pocket, hoping the door was locked so he could use it. It wasn't. The hinges screamed and flakes of rust sifted down from their slowly revolving cylinders as the door opened. The smell of decay struck Jake like a physical blow: wet wood, spongy plaster, rotting laths, ancient stuffing. Below these smells was another—the smell of some beast's lair. Ahead was a dank, shadowy hallway. To the left, a staircase pitched and yawed its crazy way into the upper shadows. Its collapsed bannister lay splintered on the hallway floor, but Jake was not foolish enough to think it was *just* splinters he was looking at. There were bones in that litter, as well— the bones of small animals. Some did not look precisely like animal bones, and these Jake would not look at overlong; he knew he would never summon the courage to go further if he did. He paused on the threshold, screwing himself up to take the first step. He heard a faint, muffled sound, very hard and very rapid, and realized it was his own teeth chattering in his head.

Why doesn't someone stop me? he thought wildly. *Why doesn't somebody passing on the sidewalk shout "Hey, you! You're not supposed to be in there—can't-cha read?"*

But he knew why. Pedestrians stuck mostly to the other side of this street, and those who came near this house did not linger.

Even if someone did happen to look, they wouldn't see me, because I'm not really here. For better or worse, I've already left my world behind. I've started to cross over. His *world is somewhere ahead. This . . .*

This was the hell between.

Jake stepped into the corridor, and although he screamed when the door swung shut behind him with the sound of a mausoleum door being slammed, he wasn't surprised.

Down deep, he wasn't surprised at all.

28

ONCE UPON A TIME there had been a young woman named Detta Walker who liked to frequent the honky-tonks and roadhouses along Ridgeline Road outside of Nutley and on Route 88 down by the power-lines, outside of Amhigh. She had had legs in those days, and, as the song says, she knew how to use them. She would wear some tight cheap dress that looked like silk but wasn't and dance with the white boys while the band played all those ofay party tunes like "Double Shot of My Baby's Love" and "The Hippy-Hippy Shake." Eventually she would cut one of the honkeys out of the pack and let him lead her back to his car in the parking lot. There she would make out with him (one of the world's great soul-kissers was Detta Walker, and no slouch with the old fingernails, either) until he was just about insane . . . and then she'd shut him down. What happened next? Well, that was the question, wasn't it? That was the game. Some of them wept and begged—all right, but not great. Some of them raved and roared, which was better.

And although she had been slapped upside the head, punched in the eye, spat upon, and once kicked in the ass so hard she had gone sprawling in the gravel parking lot of The Red Windmill, she had never been raped. They had all gone home with the blue balls, every damned ofay one of them. Which meant, in Detta Walker's book, that she was the reigning champion, the undefeated queen. Of what? Of *them*. Of all those crewcut, button-down, tightass honkey motherfuckers.

Until now.

There was no way to withstand the demon who lived in the speaking ring. No doorhandles to grab, no car to tumble out of, no building to run back into, no cheek to slap, no face to claw, no balls to kick if the ofay sumbitch was slow getting the message.

The demon was on her . . . and then, in a flash, it—*he*—was in her.

She could feel it—*him*—pressing her backward, even though she could not see it—*him*. She could not see its—*his*—hands, but she could see their work as her dress tore violently open in several places. Then, suddenly, pain. It felt as though she were being ripped open down there, and in her agony and surprise she screamed. Eddie looked around, his eyes narrowing.

"I'm all right!" she yelled. "Go on, Eddie, forget about me! I'm all right!"

But she wasn't. For the first time since Detta had strode onto the sexual battlefield at the age of thirteen, she was losing. A horrid, engorged coldness plunged into her; it was like being fucked with an icicle.

Dimly, she saw Eddie turn away and begin drawing in the dirt again, his expression of warm concern fading back into the terrible, concentrated coldness she sometimes felt in him and saw on his face. Well, that was all right, wasn't it? She had told him to go on, to forget her, to do what he needed to do in order to bring the boy over. This was her part of Jake's drawing and she had no right to hate either of the men, who had not twisted her arm—or anything else—to make her do it, but as the coldness froze her and Eddie turned away from her, she hated them both; could, in fact, have torn their honkey balls off.

Then Roland was with her, his strong hands were on her shoulders and although he didn't speak, she heard him: *Don't fight. You can't win if you fight— you can only die. Sex is its weapon, Susannah, but it's also its weakness.*

Yes. It was *always* their weakness. The only difference was that this time she was going to have to give a little more—but maybe that was all right. Maybe in the end, she would be able to make this invisible honkey demon *pay* a little more.

She forced herself to relax her thighs. Immediately

they spread apart, pushing long, curved fans in the dirt. She threw her head back into the rain which was now pelting down and sensed its face lolling just over hers, eager eyes drinking in every contorted grimace which passed over her face.

She reached up with one hand, as if to slap . . . and instead, slid it around the nape of her demon rapist's neck. It was like cupping a palmful of solid smoke. And did she feel it twitch backward, surprised at her caress? She tilted her pelvis upward, using her grip on the invisible neck to create the leverage. At the same time she spread her legs even wider, splitting what remained of her dress up the side-seams. God, it was huge!

"Come on," she panted. "You ain't gonna rape me. You *ain't*. You want t'fuck me? *I* fuck *you*. I give you a fuckin like you ain't *nevah* had! Fuck you to *death!*"

She felt the engorgement within her tremble; felt the demon try, at least momentarily, to draw back and regroup.

"Unh-unh, honey," she croaked. She squeezed her thighs inward, pinning it. "De fun jus' *startin*." She began to flex her butt, humping at the invisible presence. She reached up with her free hand, interlaced all ten fingers, and allowed herself to fall backward with her hips cocked, her straining arms seeming to hold nothing. She tossed her sweat-damp hair out of her eyes; her lips split in a sharklike grin.

Let me go! a voice cried out in her mind. But at the same time she could feel the owner of the voice responding in spite of itself.

"No way, sugar. You wanted it . . . now you goan get it." She thrust upward, holding on, concentrating fiercely on the freezing cold inside her. "I'm goan melt that icicle, sugar, and when it's gone, what you goan do then?" Her lips rose and fell, rose and fell. She squeezed her thighs mercilessly together, closed her eyes, clawed more deeply into the unseen neck, and prayed that Eddie would be quick.

She didn't know how long she could do this.

29

THE PROBLEM, JAKE THOUGHT, was simple: somewhere in this dank, terrible place was a locked door.
The *right* door. All he had to do was find it. But it
was hard, because he could feel the presence in the
house gathering. The sound of those dissonant, gab-
bling voices was beginning to merge into one sound—
a low, grating whisper.

And it was approaching.

A door stood open to the right. Beside it, thumb-
tacked to the wall, was a faded daguerreotype which
showed a hanged man dangling like a piece of rotten
fruit from a dead tree. Beyond it was a room that had
once been a kitchen. The stove was gone, but an ancient icebox—the kind with the circular refrigeration
drum on top—stood on the far side of the hilly, faded
linoleum. Its door gaped open. Black, smelly stuff was
caked inside and had trickled down to form a long-
congealed puddle on the floor. The kitchen cabinets
stood open. In one he saw what was probably the
world's oldest can of Snow's Clam Fry-Ettes. Poking
out of another was the head of a dead rat. Its eyes
were white and seemingly in motion, and after a moment Jake realized that the empty sockets were filled
with squirming maggots.

Something fell into his hair with a flabby thump.
Jake screamed in surprise, reached for it, and grasped
something that felt like a soft, bristle-covered rubber
ball. He pulled it free and saw it was a spider, its
bloated body the color of a fresh bruise. Its eyes regarded him with stupid malevolence. Jake threw it
against the wall. It broke open and splattered there,
legs twitching feebly.

Another one dropped onto his neck. Jake felt a
sudden painful bite just below the place where his hair
stopped. He ran backward into the hall, tripped over
the fallen bannister, fell heavily, and felt the spider
pop. Its innards—wet, feverish, and slippery—slid be-

tween his shoulder-blades like warm egg-yolk. Now he could see other spiders in the kitchen doorway. Some hung on almost invisible silken threads like obscene plumb-bobs; others simply dropped on the floor in a series of muddy plops and scuttered eagerly over to greet him.

Jake flailed to his feet, still screaming. He felt something in his mind, something that felt like a frayed rope, starting to give way. He supposed it was his sanity, and at that realization, Jake's considerable courage finally broke. He could bear this no longer, no matter what the stake. He bolted, meaning to flee if he still could, and realized too late that he had turned the wrong way and was running deeper into The Mansion instead of back toward the porch.

He lunged into a space too big to be a parlor or living room; it seemed to be a ballroom. Elves with strange, sly smiles on their faces capered on the wallpaper, peering at Jake from beneath peaked green caps. A mouldy couch was pushed against one wall. In the center of the warped wooden floor was a splintered chandelier, its rusty chain lying in snarls among the spilled glass beads and dusty teardrop pendants. Jake skirted the wreck, snatching one terrified glance back over his shoulder. He saw no spiders; if not for the nastiness still trickling down his back, he might have believed he had imagined them.

He looked forward again and came to a sudden, skidding halt. Ahead, a pair of french doors stood half-open on their recessed tracks. Another hallway stretched beyond. At the end of this second corridor stood a closed door with a golden knob. Written across the door—or perhaps carved into it—were two words:

THE BOY

Below the doorknob was a filigreed silver plate and a keyhole.

I found it! Jake thought fiercely. *I finally found it! That's it! That's the door!*

From behind him a low groaning noise began, as if the house was beginning to tear itself apart. Jake turned and looked back across the ballroom. The wall on the far side of the room had begun to swell outward, pushing the ancient couch ahead of it. The old wallpaper shuddered; the elves began to ripple and dance. In places the paper simply snapped upward in long curls, like windowshades which have been released too suddenly. The plaster bulged forward in a pregnant curve. From beneath it, Jake could hear dry snapping sounds as the lathing broke, rearranging itself into some new, as-yet-hidden shape. And still the sound increased. Only it was no longer precisely a groan; now it sounded like a snarl.

He stared, hypnotized, unable to pull his eyes away.

The plaster didn't crack and then vomit outward in chunks; it seemed to have become plastic, and as the wall continued to bulge, making an irregular white bubble-shape from which scraps and draggles of wallpaper still hung, the surface began to mold itself into hills and curves and valleys. Suddenly Jake realized he was looking at a huge plastic face that was pushing itself out of the wall. It was like looking at someone who has walked headfirst into a wet sheet.

There was a loud snap as a chunk of broken lath tore free of the rippling wall. It became the jagged pupil of one eye. Below it, the wall writhed into a snarling mouth filled with jagged teeth. Jake could see fragments of wallpaper clinging to its lips and gums.

One plaster hand tore free of the wall, trailing an unravelling bracelet of rotted electrical wire. It grasped the sofa and threw it aside, leaving ghostly white fingermarks on its dark surface. More lathing burst free as the plaster fingers flexed. They created sharp, splintery claws. Now the face was all the way out of the wall and staring at Jake with its one wooden eye. Above it, in the center of its forehead, one wall-

paper elf still danced. It looked like a weird tattoo.
There was a wrenching sound as the thing began to
slide forward. The hall doorway tore out and became
a hunched shoulder. The thing's one free hand clawed
across the floor, spraying glass droplets from the fallen
chandelier.

Jake's paralysis broke. He turned, lunged through
the french doors, and pelted down the second length
of hallway with his pack bouncing and his right hand
groping for the key in his pocket. His heart was a
runaway factory machine in his chest. Behind him,
the thing which was crawling out of The Mansion's
woodwork bellowed at him, and although there were
no words, Jake knew what it was saying; it was telling
him to stand still, telling him that it was useless to
run, telling him there was no escape. The whole house
now seemed alive; the air resounded with splintering
wood and squalling beams. The humming, insane
voice of the doorkeeper was everywhere.

Jake's hand closed on the key. As he brought it out,
one of the notches caught in the pocket. His fingers,
wet with sweat, slipped. The key fell to the floor,
bounced, dropped through a crack between two
warped boards, and disappeared.

30

"HE'S IN TROUBLE!" SUSANNAH heard Eddie shout,
but the sound of his voice was distant. She had plenty
of trouble herself . . . but she thought she might be
doing okay, just the same.

I'm goan melt that icicle, sugar, she had told the
demon. *I'm goan melt it, and when it's gone, what you
goan do then?*

She hadn't melted it, exactly, but she had *changed*
it. The thing inside her was certainly giving her no
pleasure, but at least the terrible pain had subsided

and it was no longer cold. It was trapped, unable to disengage. Nor was she holding it in with her body, exactly. Roland had said sex was its weakness as well as its weapon, and he had been right, as usual. It had taken her, but *she* had also taken *it*, and now it was as if each of them had a finger stuck in one of those fiendish Chinese tubes, where yanking only sticks you tighter.

She hung onto one idea for dear life; *had* to, because all other conscious thought had vanished. She had to hold this sobbing, frightened, vicious thing in the snare of its own helpless lust. It wriggled and thrust and convulsed within her, screaming to be let go at the same time it used her body with greedy, helpless intensity, but she would not let it go free.

And what's gonna happen when I finally do let go? she wondered desperately. *What's it gonna do to pay me back?*

She didn't know.

31

THE RAIN WAS FALLING in sheets, threatening to turn the circle within the stones into a sea of mud. *"Hold something over the door!"* Eddie shouted. *"Don't let the rain wash it out!"*

Roland snatched a glance at Susannah and saw she was still struggling with the demon. Her eyes were half-shut, her mouth pulled down in a harsh grimace. He could not see or hear the demon, but he could sense its angry, frightened thrashings.

Eddie turned his streaming face toward him. *"Did you hear me?"* he shouted. *"Get something over the goddam door, and do it NOW!"*

Roland yanked one of their hides from his pack and held a corner in each hand. Then he stretched his arms out and leaned over Eddie, creating a makeshift tent. The tip of Eddie's homemade pencil was caked with mud. He wiped it across his arm, leaving a smear the color of bitter chocolate, then wrapped his fist around the stick again and bent over his drawing. It was not exactly the same size as the door on Jake's side of the barrier—the ratio was perhaps .75:1—but it would be big enough for Jake to come through . . . *if* the keys worked.

If he even has a key, isn't that what you mean? he asked himself. *Suppose he's dropped it . . . or that house made him drop it?*

He drew a plate under the circle which represented the doorknob, hesitated, and then squiggled the familiar shape of a keyhole within it:

He hesitated. There was one more thing, but what? It was hard to think of, because it felt as if there were a tornado roaring through his head, a tornado with random thoughts flipping around inside it instead of uprooted barns and privies and chicken-houses.

"Come on, sugah!" Susannah cried from behind him. "You weakenin on me! Wassa matta? I thought you was some kind of hot-shit studboy!"

Boy. That was it.

Carefully, he wrote THE BOY across the top panel of the door with the tip of his stick. At the instant he finished the Y, the drawing changed. The circle of rain-darkened earth he had drawn suddenly darkened even more . . . and pushed up from the ground, becoming a dark, gleaming knob. And instead of brown, wet earth within the shape of the keyhole, he could see dim light.

Behind him, Susannah shrieked at the demon again,

urging it on, but now she sounded as if she were tiring. This had to end, and soon.

Eddie bent forward from the waist like a Muslim saluting Allah, and put his eye to the keyhole he had drawn. He looked through it into his own world, into that house which he and Henry had gone to see in May of 1977, unaware (except he, Eddie, had not been unaware; no, not totally unaware, even then) that a boy from another part of the city was following them.

He saw a hallway. Jake was down on his hands and knees, tugging frantically at a board. Something was coming for him. Eddie could see it, but at the same time he could not—it was as if part of his brain *refused* to see it, as if seeing would lead to comprehension and comprehension to madness.

"Hurry up, Jake!" he screamed into the keyhole. *"For Christ's sake, move it!"*

Above the speaking ring, thunder ripped the sky like cannon-fire and the rain turned to hail.

32

FOR A MOMENT AFTER the key fell, Jake only stood where he was, staring down at the narrow crack between the boards.

Incredibly, he felt sleepy.

That shouldn't have happened, he thought. *It's one thing too much. I can't go on with this, not one minute, not one single second longer. I'm going to curl up against that door instead. I'm going to go to sleep, right away, all at once, and when it grabs me and pulls me toward its mouth, I'll never wake up.*

Then the thing coming out of the wall grunted, and when Jake looked up, his urge to give in vanished in a single stroke of terror. Now it was all the way out of the wall, a giant plaster head with one broken

wooden eye and one reaching plaster hand. Chunks
of lathing stood out on its skull in random hackles,
like a child's drawing of hair. It saw Jake and opened
its mouth, revealing jagged wooden teeth. It grunted
again. Plaster-dust drifted out of its yawning mouth
like cigar smoke.

Jake fell to his knees and peered into the crack.
The key was a small brave shimmer of silvery light
down there in the dark, but the crack was far too
narrow to admit his fingers. He seized one of the
boards and yanked with all his might. The nails which
held it groaned . . . but held.

There was a jangling crash. He looked down the
hallway and saw the hand, which was bigger than his
whole body, seize the fallen chandelier and throw it
aside. The rusty chain which had once held it suspended rose like a bullwhip and then came down with
a heavy crump. A dead lamp on a rusty chain rattled
above Jake, dirty glass chattering against ancient
brass.

The doorkeeper's head, attached only to its single
hunched shoulder and reaching arm, slid forward
above the floor. Behind it, the remains of the wall
collapsed in a cloud of dust. A moment later the fragments humped up and became the creature's twisted,
bony back.

The doorkeeper saw Jake looking and seemed to
grin. As it did, splinters of wood poked out of its
wrinkling cheeks. It dragged itself forward through the
dust-hazed ballroom, mouth opening and closing. Its
great hand groped amid the ruins, feeling for purchase, and ripped one of the french doors at the end
of the hall from its track.

Jake screamed breathlessly and began to wrench at
the board again. It wouldn't come, but the gunslinger's voice did:

"The other one, Jake! Try the other one!"

He let go of the board he had been yanking at and
grabbed the one on the other side of the crack. As he

did, another voice spoke. He heard this one not in his head but with his ears, and understood it was coming from the other side of the door—the door he had been looking for ever since the day he hadn't been run over in the street.

"Hurry up, Jake! For Christ's sake, hurry up!"

When he yanked this other board, it came free so easily that he almost tumbled over backward.

33

TWO WOMEN WERE STANDING in the doorway of the used appliance shop across the street from The Mansion. The older was the proprietor; the younger had been her only customer when the sounds of crashing walls and breaking beams began. Now, without knowing they were doing it, they linked arms about each other's waists and stood that way, trembling like children who hear a noise in the dark.

Up the street, a trio of boys on their way to the Dutch Hill Little League field stood gaping at the house, their Red Ball Flyer wagon filled with baseball equipment forgotten behind them. A delivery driver nosed his van into the curb and got out to look. The patrons of Henry's Corner Market and the Dutch Hill Pub came straggling up the street, looking around wildly.

Now the ground began to tremble, and a fan of fine cracks started to spread across Rhinehold Street. "Is it an earthquake?" the delivery van driver shouted at the women standing outside the appliance shop, but instead of waiting for an answer he jumped back behind the wheel of his van and drove away rapidly, swerving to the wrong side of the street to keep away from the ruined house which was the epicenter of this convulsion.

The entire house seemed to be bowing inward.

Boards splintered, jumped off its face, and rained down into the yard. Dirty gray-black waterfalls of slate shingles poured down from the eaves. There was an earsplitting bang and a long, zigzagging crack shot down the center of The Mansion. The door disappeared into it and then the whole house began to swallow itself from the outside in.

The younger woman suddenly broke the older one's grip. "I'm getting out of here," she said, and began to run up the street without looking back.

34

A HOT, STRANGE WIND began to sigh down the hallway, blowing Jake's sweaty hair back from his brow as his fingers closed over the silver key. He now understood on some instinctive level what this place was, and what was happening. The doorkeeper was not just *in* the house, it *was* the house: every board, every shingle, every windowsill, every eave. And now it was pushing forward, becoming some crazily jumbled representation of its true shape as it did. It meant to catch him before he could use the key. Beyond the giant white head and the crooked, hulking shoulder, he could see boards and shingles and wire and bits of glass—even the front door and the broken bannister—flying up the main hall and into the ballroom, joining the form which bulked there, creating more and more of the misshapen plaster-man that was even now groping toward him with its freakish hand.

Jake yanked his own hand out of the hole in the floor and saw it was covered with huge trundling beetles. He slapped it against the wall to knock them off, and cried out as the wall first opened and then tried to close around his wrist. He yanked his hand free just in time, whirled, and jammed the silver key into the hole in the plate.

The plaster-man roared again, but its voice was momentarily drowned out by a harmonic shout which Jake recognized: he had heard it in the vacant lot, but it had been quiet then, perhaps dreaming. Now it was an unequivocal cry of triumph. That sense of certainty—overwhelming, inarguable—filled him again, and this time he felt sure there would be no disappointment. He heard all the affirmation he needed in that voice. It was the voice of the rose.

The dim light in the hallway was blotted out as the plaster hand tore away the other french door and squeezed into the corridor. The face socked itself into the opening above the hand, peering at Jake. The plaster fingers crawled toward him like the legs of a huge spider.

Jake turned the key and felt a sudden surge of power rush up his arm. He heard a heavy, muffled thump as the locked bolt inside withdrew. He seized the knob, turned it, and yanked the door open. It swung wide. Jake cried out in confused horror as he saw what lay behind.

The doorway was blocked with earth, from top to bottom and side to side. Roots poked out like bunches of wire. Worms, seeming as confused as Jake was himself, crawled hither and thither on the door-shaped pack of dirt. Some dived back into it; others only went on crawling about, as if wondering where the earth which had been below them a moment ago had gone. One dropped onto Jake's sneaker.

The keyhole shape remained for a moment, shedding a spot of misty white light on Jake's shirt. Beyond it—so close, so out of reach—he could hear rain and a muffled boom of thunder across an open sky. Then the keyhole shape was also blotted out, and gigantic plaster fingers curled around Jake's lower leg.

35

EDDIE DID NOT FEEL the sting of the hail as Roland dropped the hide, got to his feet, and ran to where Susannah lay.

The gunslinger grabbed her beneath the arms and dragged her—as gently and carefully as he could—across to where Eddie crouched. "Let it go when I tell you, Susannah!" Roland shouted. "Do you understand? *When I tell you!*"

Eddie saw and heard none of this. He heard only Jake, screaming faintly on the other side of the door.

The time had come to use the key.

He pulled it out of his shirt and slid it into the keyhole he had drawn. He tried to turn it. The key would not turn. Not so much as a milllimeter. Eddie lifted his face to the pelting hail, oblivious to the iceballs which struck his forehead and cheeks and lips, leaving welts and red blotches.

"NO!" he howled. *"OH GOD, PLEASE! NO!"*

But there was no answer from God; only another crash of thunder and a streak of lightning across a sky now filled with racing clouds.

36

JAKE LUNGED UPWARD, GRABBED the chain of the lamp which hung above him, and ripped free of the doorkeeper's clutching fingers. He swung backward, used the packed earth in the doorway to push off, and then swung forward again like Tarzan on a vine. He raised his legs and kicked out at the clutching fingers as he closed on them. Plaster exploded in chunks, revealing a crudely jointed skeleton of lathing beneath. The plaster-man roared, a sound of intermingled hunger and rage. Beneath that cry, Jake could hear the whole house collapsing, like the one in that story of Edgar Allan Poe.

He pendulumed back on the chain, struck the wall of packed earth which blocked the doorway, then swung forward again. The hand reached up for him and he kicked at it wildly, legs scissoring. He felt a stab of pain in his foot as those wooden fingers clutched. When he swung back again, he was minus a sneaker.

He tried for a higher grip on the chain, found it, and began to shinny up toward the ceiling. There was a muffled, creaking thud above him. Fine plaster dust had begun to sift down on his upturned, sweating face. The ceiling had begun to sag; the lamp-chain was pulling out of it a link at a time. There was a thick crunching sound from the end of the hallway as the plasterman finally pushed its hungry face through the opening.

Jake swung helplessly back toward that face, screaming.

37

EDDIE'S TERROR AND PANIC suddenly fell away. The cloak of coldness dropped over him—a cloak Roland of Gilead had worn many times. It was the only armor the true gunslinger possessed . . . and all such a one needed. At the same moment, a voice spoke in his mind. He had been haunted by such voices over the last three months; his mother's voice, Roland's voice, and, of course, Henry's. But this one, he recognized with relief, was his own, and it was at last calm and rational and courageous.

You saw the shape of the key in the fire, you saw it again in the wood, and both times you saw it perfectly. Later on, you put a blindfold of fear over your eyes.

Take it off. Take it off and look again. It may not be too late, even now.

He was faintly aware that the gunslinger was staring at him grimly; faintly aware that Susannah was shrieking at the demon in a fading but still defiant voice; faintly aware that, on the other side of the door, Jake was screaming in terror—or was it now agony?

Eddie ignored them all. He pulled the wooden key out of the keyhole he had drawn, out of the door which was now real, and looked at it fixedly, trying to recapture the innocent delight he had sometimes known as a child—the delight of seeing a coherent shape hidden in senselessness. And there it was, the place he'd gone wrong, so clearly visible he couldn't understand how he'd missed it in the first place. *I really* must *have been wearing a blindfold,* he thought. It was the *s*-shape at the end of the key, of course. The second curve was a bit too fat. Just a tiny bit.

"Knife," he said, and held out his hand like a surgeon in an operating room. Roland slapped it into his palm without a word.

Eddie gripped the top of the blade between the thumb and first finger of his right hand. He bent over the key, unmindful of the hail which pelted his unprotected neck, and the shape in the wood stood out more clearly—stood out with its own lovely and undeniable reality.

He scraped.

Once.

Delicately.

A single sliver of ash, so thin it was almost transparent, curled up from the belly of the *s*-shape at the end of the key.

On the other side of the door, Jake Chambers shrieked again.

38

THE CHAIN LET GO with a rattling crash and Jake fell heavily, landing on his knees. The doorkeeper roared in triumph. The plaster hand seized Jake about his hips and began to drag him down the hall. He stuck his legs out in front of him and planted his feet, but it did no good. He felt splinters and rust-blunted nails digging into his skin as the hand tightened its grip and continued to drag him forward.

The face appeared to be stuck just inside the entrance to the hallway like a cork in a bottle. The pressure it had exerted to get in that far had squeezed the rudimentary features into a new shape, that of some monstrous, malformed troll. The mouth yawned open to receive him. Jake groped madly for the key, wanting to use it as some last-ditch talisman, but of course he had left it in the door.

"You son of a bitch!" he screamed, and threw himself backward with all his strength, bowing his back like an Olympic diver, unmindful of the broken boards which dug into him like a belt of nails. He felt his jeans slide down on his hips, and the grip of the hand slipped momentarily.

Jake lunged again. The hand clenched brutally, but Jake's jeans slid down to his knees and his back slammed to the floor, with the pack to cushion the blow. The hand loosened, perhaps wanting to secure a firmer grip upon its prey. Jake was able to draw his knees up a little, and when the hand tightened again, Jake drove his legs forward. The hand yanked backward at the same time, and what Jake had hoped for happened: his jeans (and his remaining sneaker) were peeled from his body, leaving him free again, at least for the moment. He saw the hand rotate on his wrist of boards and disintegrating plaster and jam his dungarees into his mouth. Then he was crawling back toward the blocked doorway on his hands and knees, oblivious of the glass fragments from the fallen lamp, wanting only to get his key again.

He had almost reached the door when the hand closed over his naked legs and began to pull him back once more.

39

THE SHAPE WAS THERE now, finally all there.

Eddie put the key back into the keyhole and applied pressure. For a moment there was resistance . . . and then it revolved beneath his hand. He heard the locking mechanism turn, heard the bar pull back, felt the key crack in two the moment it had served its purpose. He grasped the dark, polished knob with both hands and pulled. There was a sense of great weight wheeling on an unseen pivot. A feeling that his arm had been gifted with boundless strength. And a clear knowledge that two worlds had suddenly come in contact, and a way had been opened between them.

He felt a moment of dizziness and disorientation, and as he looked through the doorway he realized why: although he was looking down—vertically—he was seeing *horizontally*. It was like a strange optical illusion created with prisms and mirrors. Then he saw Jake being pulled backward down the glass- and plaster-littered hallway, elbows dragging, calves pinned together by a giant hand. And he saw the monstrous mouth which awaited him, fuming some white fog that might have been either smoke or dust.

"Roland!" Eddie shouted. *"Roland, it's got h—"*

Then he was knocked aside.

40

SUSANNAH WAS AWARE OF being hauled up and whirled around. The world was a carousel blur: standing stones, gray sky, hailstone-littered ground . . . and a rectangular hole that looked like a trapdoor in the ground. Screams drifted up from it. Within her, the demon raved and struggled, wanting only to escape but helpless to do so until she allowed it.

"Now!" Roland was shouting. *"Let it go now, Susannah! For your father's sake, let it go NOW!"*

And she did.

She had (with Detta's help) constructed a trap for it in her mind, something like a net of woven rushes, and now she cut them. She felt the demon fly back from her at once, and there was an instant of terrible hollowness, terrible emptiness. These feelings were at once overshadowed by relief and a grim sense of nastiness and defilement.

As its invisible weight fell away, she glimpsed it—an inhuman shape like a manta-ray with huge, curling wings and something that looked like a cruel baling hook curving out and up from beneath. She saw/sensed the thing flash above the open hole in the ground. Saw Eddie looking up with wide eyes. Saw Roland spread his arms wide to catch the demon.

The gunslinger staggered back, almost knocked off his feet by the unseen weight of the demon. Then he rocked forward again with an armload of nothing.

Clutching it, he jumped through the doorway and was gone.

41

SUDDEN WHITE LIGHT FLOODED the hallway of The Mansion; hailstones struck the walls and bounced up from the broken boards of the floor. Jake heard confused shouts, then saw the gunslinger come through. He seemed to *leap* through, as if he had come from above. His arms were held far out in front of him, the tips of the fingers locked.

Jake felt his feet slide into the doorkeeper's mouth.

"Roland!" he shrieked. *"Roland, help me!"*

The gunslinger's hands parted and his arms were immediately thrown wide. He staggered backward. Jake felt serrated teeth touch his skin, ready to tear flesh and grind bone, and then something huge rushed over his head like a gust of wind. A moment later the teeth were gone. The hand which had pinned his legs together relaxed. He heard an unearthly shriek of pain and surprise begin to issue from the doorkeeper's dusty throat, and then it was muffled, crammed back.

Roland grabbed Jake and hauled him to his feet.

"You came!" Jake shouted. "You really came!"

"I came, yes. By the grace of the gods and the courage of my friends, I came."

As the doorkeeper roared again, Jake burst into tears of relief and terror. Now the house sounded like a ship foundering in a heavy sea. Chunks of wood and plaster fell all around them. Roland swept Jake into his arms and ran for the door. The plaster hand, groping wildly, struck one of his booted feet and spun him into the wall, which again tried to bite. Roland pushed forward, turned, and drew his gun. He fired twice into the aimlessly thrashing hand, vaporizing one of the crude plaster fingers. Behind them, the face of the doorkeeper had gone from white to a dingy purplish-black, as if it were choking on something—something which had been fleeing so rapidly that it had entered the monster's mouth and jammed in its gullet before it realized what it was doing.

Roland turned again and ran through the doorway. Although there was now no visible barrier, he was stopped cold for a moment, as if an unseen meshwork had been drawn across the chair.

Then he felt Eddie's hands in his hair and he was yanked not forward but upward.

42

THEY EMERGED INTO WET air and slackening hail like babies being born. Eddie was the midwife, as the gunslinger had told him he must be. He was sprawled forward on his chest and belly, his arms out of sight in the doorway, his hands clutching fistfuls of Roland's hair.

"Suze! Help me!"

She wriggled forward, reached through, and groped a hand under Roland's chin. He came up to her with his head cocked backward and his lips parted in a snarl of pain and effort.

Eddie felt a tearing sensation and one of his hands came free holding a thick lock of the gunslinger's gray-streaked hair. "He's slipping!"

"This motherfucker . . . ain't . . . *nowhere*!" Susannah gasped, and gave a terrific wrench, as if she meant to snap Roland's neck.

Two small hands shot out of the doorway in the center of the circle and clutched one of the edges. Freed of Jake's weight, Roland got an elbow up, and a moment later he was boosting himself out. As he did it, Eddie grabbed Jake's wrists and hauled him up.

Jake rolled onto his back and lay there, panting.

Eddie turned to Susannah, took her in his arms, and began to rain kisses on her forehead, cheeks, and neck. He was laughing and crying at the same time. She clung to him, breathing hard . . . but there was a small, satisfied smile on her lips and one hand slipped over Eddie's wet hair in slow, contented strokes.

From below them came a cauldron of black sounds: squeals, grunts, thuds, crashes.

Roland crawled away from the hole with his head down. His hair stood up in a wild wad. Threads of blood trickled down his cheeks. "Shut it!" he gasped at Eddie. "Shut it, for your father's sake!"

Eddie got the door moving, and those vast, unseen hinges did the rest. The door fell with a gigantic, tone-less bang, cutting off all sound from below. As Eddie watched, the lines that had marked its edges faded back to smudged marks in the dirt. The doorknob lost its dimension and was once more only a circle he'd drawn with a stick. Where the keyhole had been there was only a crude shape with a chunk of wood sticking out of it, like the hilt of a sword from a stone.

Susannah went to Jake and pulled him gently to a sitting position. "You all right, sugar?"

He looked at her dazedly. "Yes, I think so. Where is he? The gunslinger? There's something I have to ask him."

"I'm here, Jake," Roland said. He got to his feet, drunk-walked over to Jake, and hunkered beside him. He touched the boy's smooth cheek almost unbelievingly.

"You won't let me drop this time?"

"No," Roland said. "Not this time, not ever again." But in the deepest darkness of his heart, he thought of the Tower and wondered.

43

THE HAIL CHANGED TO a hard, driving rain, but Eddie could see gleams of blue sky behind the unravelling clouds in the north. The storm was going to end soon, but in the meantime, they were going to get drenched.

He found he didn't mind. He could not remember when he had felt so calm, so at peace with himself, so utterly drained. This mad adventure wasn't over

yet—he suspected, in fact, that it had barely begun—
but today they had won a big one.

"Suze?" He pushed her hair away from her face
and looked into her dark eyes. "Are you okay? Did
it hurt you?"

"Hurt me a little, but I'm okay. I think that bitch
Detta Walker is still the undefeated Roadhouse
Champeen, demon or no demon."

"What's that mean?"

She grinned impishly. "Not much, not anymore . . .
thank God. How about you, Eddie? All right?"

Eddie listened for Henry's voice and didn't hear it.
He had an idea that Henry's voice might be gone for
good. "Even better than that," he said, and, laughing,
folded her into his arms again. Over her shoulder he
could see what was left of the door: only a few faint
lines and angles. Soon the rain would wash those
away, too.

44

"WHAT'S YOUR NAME?" JAKE asked the woman
whose legs stopped just above the knee. He was suddenly aware that he had lost his pants in his struggle
to escape the doorkeeper, and he pulled the tail of his
shirt down over his underwear. There wasn't very
much left of her dress, either, as far as that went.

"Susannah Dean," she said. "I already know your
name."

"Susannah," Jake said thoughtfully. "I don't suppose your father owns a railroad company, does he?"

She looked astonished for a moment, then threw
her head back and laughed. "Why, no, sugar! He was
a dentist who went and invented a few things and got
rich. What makes you ask a thing like that?"

Jake didn't answer. He had turned his attention to
Eddie. The terror had already left his face, and his

eyes had regained that cool, assessing look which Roland remembered so well from the way station.

"Hi, Jake," Eddie said. "Good to see you, man."

"Hi," Jake said. "I met you earlier today, but you were a lot younger then."

"I was a lot younger ten minutes ago. Are you okay?"

"Yes," Jake said. "Some scratches, that's all." He looked around. "You haven't found the train yet." This was not a question.

Eddie and Susannah exchanged puzzled looks, but Roland only shook his head. "No train."

"Are your voices gone?"

Roland nodded. "All gone. Yours?"

"Gone. I'm all together again. We both are."

They looked at the same instant, with the same impulse. As Roland swept Jake into his arms, the boy's unnatural self-possession broke and he began to cry— it was the exhausted, relieved weeping of a child who has been lost long, suffered much, and is finally safe again. As Roland's arms closed about his waist, Jake's own arms slipped about the gunslinger's neck and gripped like hoops of steel.

"I'll never leave you again," Roland said, and now his own tears came. "I swear to you on the names of all my fathers: *I'll never leave you again.*"

Yet his heart, that silent, watchful, lifelong prisoner of *ka*, received the words of this promise not just with wonder but with doubt.

BOOK TWO

LUD

A HEAP OF BROKEN IMAGES

IV ■ TOWN AND
KA-TET

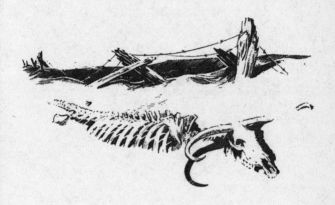

• IV •

TOWN AND
KA-TET

1

FOUR DAYS AFTER EDDIE had yanked him through
the doorway between worlds, minus his original pair
of pants and his sneakers but still in possession of his
pack and his life, Jake awoke with something warm
and wet nuzzling at his face.

If he had come around to such a sensation on any
of the three previous mornings, he undoubtedly would
have wakened his companions with his screams, for
he had been feverish and his sleep had been haunted
by nightmares of the plaster-man. In these dreams his
pants did not slide free, the doorkeeper kept its grip,
and it tucked him into its unspeakable mouth, where
its teeth came down like the bars guarding a castle
keep. Jake awoke from these dreams shuddering and
moaning helplessly.

The fever had been caused by the spider-bite on the back of his neck. When Roland examined it on the second day and found it worse instead of better, he had conferred briefly with Eddie and had then given Jake a pink pill. "You'll want to take four of these every day for at least a week," he said.

Jake had gazed at it doubtfully. "What is it?"

"Cheflet," Roland said, then looked disgustedly at Eddie. "You tell him. I *still* can't say it."

"Keflex. You can trust it, Jake; it came from a government-approved pharmacy in good old New York. Roland swallowed a bunch of it, and he's as healthy as a horse. Looks a little like one, too, as you can see."

Jake was astonished. "How did you get medicine in New York?"

"That's a long story," the gunslinger said. "You'll hear all of it in time, but for now just take the pill."

Jake did. The response was both quick and satisfying. The angry red swelling around the bite began to fade in twenty-four hours, and now the fever was gone as well.

The warm thing nuzzled again and Jake sat up with a jerk, his eyes flying open.

The creature which had been licking his cheek took two hasty steps backward. It was a billy-bumbler, but Jake didn't know that; he had never seen one before now. It was skinnier than the ones Roland's party had seen earlier, and its black- and gray-striped fur was matted and mangy. There was a clot of old dried blood on one flank. Its gold-ringed black eyes looked at Jake anxiously; its hindquarters switched hopefully back and forth. Jake relaxed. He supposed there were exceptions to the rule, but he had an idea that something wagging its tail—or trying to—was probably not too dangerous.

It was just past first light, probably around five-thirty in the morning. Jake could peg it no closer than that because his digital Seiko no longer worked . . .

or rather, was working in an extremely eccentric way. When he had first glanced at it after coming through, the Seiko claimed it was 98:71:65, a time which did not, so far as Jake knew, exist. A longer look showed him that the watch was now running backward. If it had been doing this at a steady rate, he supposed it might still have been of some use, but it wasn't. It would unwind its numbers at what seemed like the right speed for awhile (Jake verified this by saying the word "Mississippi" between each number), and then the readout would either stop entirely for ten or twenty seconds—making him think the watch had finally given up the ghost—or a bunch of numbers would blur by all at once.

He had mentioned this odd behavior to Roland and had shown him the watch, thinking it would amaze him, but Roland examined it closely for only a moment or two before nodding in a dismissive way and telling Jake it was an interesting clock, but as a rule no timepiece did very good work these days. So the Seiko was useless, but Jake still found himself loath to throw it away . . . because, he supposed, it was a piece of his old life, and there were only a few of those left.

Right now the Seiko claimed it was sixty-two minutes past forty on a Wednesday, Thursday, and Saturday in both December and March.

The morning was extremely foggy; beyond a radius of fifty or sixty feet, the world simply disappeared. If this day was like the previous three, the sun would show up as a faint white circle in another two hours or so, and by nine-thirty the day would be clear and hot. Jake looked around and saw his travelling companions (he didn't quite dare call them friends, at least not yet) asleep beneath their hide blankets—Roland close by, Eddie and Susannah a larger hump on the far side of the dead campfire.

He once more turned his attention to the animal which had awakened him. It looked like a combination raccoon and woodchuck, with a dash of dachs-hund thrown in for good measure.

"How you doin, boy?" he asked softly.

"Oy!" the billy-bumbler replied at once, still look-ing at him anxiously. Its voice was low and deep, al-most a bark; the voice of an English footballer with a bad cold in his throat.

Jake recoiled, surprised. The billy-bumbler, startled by the quick movement, took several further steps backward, seemed about to flee, and then held its ground. Its hindquarters wagged back and forth more strenuously than ever, and its gold-black eyes contin-ued to regard Jake nervously. The whiskers on its snout trembled.

"This one remembers men," a voice remarked at Jake's shoulder. He looked around and saw Roland squatting just behind him with his forearms resting on his thighs and his long hands dangling between his knees. He was looking at the animal with a great deal more interest than he had shown in Jake's watch.

"What is it?" Jake asked softly. He did not want to startle it away; he was enchanted. "Its eyes are beautiful!"

"Billy-bumbler," Roland said.

"Umber!" the creature ejaculated, and retreated an-other step.

"It talks!"

"Not really. Bumblers just repeat what they hear—or used to. I haven't heard one do it in years. This fellow looks almost starved. Probably came to forage."

"He was licking my face. Can I feed it?"

"We'll never get rid of it if you do," Roland said, then smiled a little and snapped his fingers. "Hey! Billy!"

The creature mimicked the sound of the snapping fingers somehow; it sounded as if it were clucking its tongue against the roof of its mouth. "Ay!" it called in its hoarse voice. "Ay, Illy!" Now its ragged hind-quarters were positively *flagging* back and forth.

"Go ahead and give it a bite. I knew an old groom once who said a good bumbler is good luck. This looks like a good one."

"Yes," Jake agreed. "It does."

"Once they were tame, and every barony had half a dozen roaming around the castle or manor-house. They weren't good for much except amusing the children and keeping the rat population down. They can be quite faithful—or were in the old days—although I never heard of one that would remain as loyal as a good dog. The wild ones are scavengers. Not dangerous, but a pain in the ass."

"Ass!" cried the bumbler. Its anxious eyes continued to flick back and forth between Jake and the gunslinger.

Jake reached into his pack, slowly, afraid to startle the creature, and drew out the remains of a gunslinger burrito. He tossed it toward the billy-bumbler. The bumbler flinched back and then turned with a small, childlike cry, exposing its furry corkscrew tail. Jake felt sure it would run, but it stopped, looking doubtfully back over its shoulder.

"Come on," Jake said. "Eat it, boy."

"Oy," the bumbler muttered, but it didn't move.

"Give it time," Roland said. "It'll come, I think."

The bumbler stretched forward, revealing a long and surprisingly graceful neck. Its slender black nose twitched as it sniffed the food. At last it trotted forward, and Jake noticed it was limping a little. The bumbler sniffed the burrito, then used one paw to separate the chunk of deermeat from the leaf. It carried out this operation with a delicacy that was oddly solemn. Once the meat was clear of the leaf, the bumbler wolfed it in a single bite, then looked up at Jake. "Oy!" it said, and when Jake laughed, it shrank away again.

"That's a skinny one," Eddie said sleepily from behind them. At the sound of his voice, the bumbler immediately turned and was gone into the mist.

"You scared it away!" Jake accused.

"Jeez, I'm sorry," Eddie said. He ran a hand through his sleep-corkscrewed hair. "If I'd known it was one of your close personal friends, Jake, I would have dragged out the goddam coffee-cake."

Roland clapped Jake briefly on the shoulder. "It'll be back."

"Are you sure?"

"If something doesn't kill it, yes. We fed it, didn't we?"

Before Jake could reply, the sound of the drums began again. This was the third morning they had heard them, and twice the sound had come to them as afternoon slipped down toward evening: a faint, toneless thudding from the direction of the city. The sound was clearer this morning, if no more comprehensible. Jake hated it. It was as if, somewhere out in that thick and featureless blanket of morning mist, the heart of some big animal was beating.

"You still don't have any idea what that is, Roland?" Susannah asked. She had slipped on her shift, tied back her hair, and was now folding the blankets beneath which she and Eddie had slept.

"No. But I'm sure we'll find out."

"How reassuring," Eddie said sourly.

Roland got to his feet. "Come on. Let's not waste the day."

2

THE FOG BEGAN TO unravel after they had been on the road for an hour or so. They took turns pushing Susannah's chair, and it jolted unhappily along, for the road was now mined with large, rough cobblestones. By midmorning the day was fair, hot, and cloudless; the city skyline stood out clearly on the southeastern horizon. To Jake it didn't look much different from the skyline of New York, although he thought these buildings might not be as high. If the place had fallen apart, as most things in Roland's world apparently had, you certainly couldn't tell it from here. Like Eddie, Jake had begun to entertain the unspoken hope that they might find help there . . . or at least a good hot meal.

To their left, thirty or forty miles away, they could see the broad sweep of the Send River. Birds circled above it in large flocks. Every now and then one would fold its wings and drop like a stone, probably on a fishing expedition. The road and the river were moving slowly toward one another, although the junction point could not yet be seen.

They could see more buildings ahead. Most looked like farms, and all appeared deserted. Some of them had fallen down, but these wrecks seemed to be the work of time rather than violence, furthering Eddie's and Jake's hopes of what they might find in the city— hopes each had kept strictly within himself, lest the others scoff. Small herds of shaggy beasts grazed their way across the plains. They kept well away from the road except to cross, and this they did quickly, at a gallop, like packs of small children afraid of traffic. They looked like bison to Jake . . . except he saw several which had two heads. He mentioned this to the gunslinger and Roland nodded.

"Muties."

"Like under the mountains?" Jake heard the fear in his own voice and knew the gunslinger must, also, but he was helpless to keep it out. He remembered that endless nightmare journey on the handcart very well.

"I think that here the mutant strains are being bred out. The things we found under the mountains were still getting worse."

"What about up there?" Jake pointed toward the

city. "Will there be mutants there, or—" He found it was as close as he could come to voicing his hope.

Roland shrugged. "I don't know, Jake. I'd tell you if I did."

They were passing an empty building—almost surely a farmhouse—that had been partially burnt. *But that could have been lightning*, Jake thought, and wondered which it was he was trying to do—explain to himself or fool himself.

Roland, perhaps reading his mind, put an arm around Jake's shoulders. "No use even trying to guess, Jake," he said. "Whatever happened here happened long ago." He pointed. "That over there was probably a corral. Now it's just a few sticks poking out of the grass."

"The world has moved on, right?"

Roland nodded.

"What about the people? Did they go to the city, do you think?"

"Some may have," Roland said. "Some are still around."

"What?" Susannah jerked around to look at him, startled.

Roland nodded. "We've been watched the last couple of days. There aren't a lot of folk denning in these old buildings, but there are some. There'll be more as we get closer to civilization." He paused. "Or what *used* to be civilization."

"How do you know they're there?" Jake asked.

"Smelled them. Seen a few gardens hidden behind banks of weeds grown purposely to hide the crops. And at least one working windmill way back in a grove of trees. Mostly, though, it's just a feeling . . . like shade on your face instead of sunshine. It'll come to you three in time, I imagine."

"Do you think they're dangerous?" Susannah asked. They were approaching a large, ramshackle building that might once have been a storage shed or an abandoned country market, and she eyed it uneas-

ily, her hand dropping to the butt of the gun she wore
on her chest.

"Will a strange dog bite?" the gunslinger countered.

"What's that mean?" Eddie asked. "I hate it when
you start up with your Zen Buddhist shit, Roland."

"It means I don't know," Roland said. "Who is this
man Zen Buddhist? Is he wise like me?"

Eddie looked at Roland for a long, long time before
deciding the gunslinger was making one of his rare
jokes. "Ah, get outta here," he said. He saw one
corner of Roland's mouth twitch before he turned
away. As Eddie started to push Susannah's chair
again, something else caught his eye. "Hey, Jake!" he
called. "I think you made a friend!"

Jake looked around, and a big grin overspread his
face. Forty yards to the rear, the scrawny billy-bumbler was limping industriously after them, sniffing at
the weeds which grew between the crumbling cobbles
of the Great Road.

3

SOME HOURS LATER ROLAND called a halt and told
them to be ready.

"For what?" Eddie asked.

Roland glanced at him. "Anything."

It was perhaps three o'clock in the afternoon. They
were standing at a point where the Great Road crested
a long, rolling drumlin which ran diagonally across the
plain like a wrinkle in the world's biggest bedspread.
Below and beyond, the road ran through the first real
town they had seen. It looked deserted, but Eddie had
not forgotten the conversation that morning. Roland's
question—*Will a strange dog bite?*—no longer seemed
quite so Zenny.

"Jake?"

"What?"

Eddie nodded to the butt of the Ruger, which protruded from the waistband of Jake's bluejeans—the
extra pair he had tucked into his pack before leaving
home. "Do you want me to carry that?"

Jake glanced at Roland. The gunslinger only
shrugged, as if to say *It's your choice.*

"Okay." Jake handed it over. He unshouldered his
pack, rummaged through it, and brought out the
loaded clip. He could remember reaching behind the
hanging files in one of his father's desk drawers to get
it, but all that seemed to have occurred a long, long
time ago. These days, thinking about his life in New
York and his career as a student at Piper was like
looking into the wrong end of a telescope.

Eddie took the clip, examined it, rammed it home,
checked the safety, then stuck the Ruger in his own
belt.

"Listen closely and heed me well," Roland said. "If
there *are* people, they'll likely be old and much more
frightened of us than we are of them. The younger
folk will be long gone. It's unlikely that those left will
have firearms—in fact, ours may be the first guns
many of them have ever seen, except maybe for a
picture or two in the old books. Make no threatening
gestures. And the childhood rule is a good one: speak
only when spoken to."

"What about bows and arrows?" Susannah asked.

"Yes, they may have those. Spears and clubs, as
well."

"Don't forget rocks," Eddie said bleakly, looking
down at the cluster of wooden buildings. The place
looked like a ghost-town, but who knew for sure?
"And if they're hard up for rocks, there's always the
cobbles from the road."

"Yes, there's always something," Roland agreed.
"But we'll start no trouble ourselves—is that clear?"

They nodded.

"Maybe it would be easier to detour around," Susannah said.

Roland nodded, eyes never leaving the simple geography ahead. Another road crossed the Great Road at the center of the town, making the dilapidated buildings look like a target centered in the telescopic sight of a high-powered rifle. "It would, but we won't. Detouring's a bad habit that's easy to get into. It's always better to go straight on, unless there's a good visible reason not to. I see no reason not to here. And if there *are* people, well, that might be a good thing. We could do with a little palaver."

Susannah reflected that Roland seemed different now, and she didn't think it was simply because the voices in his mind had ceased. *This is the way he was when he still had wars to fight and men to lead and his old friends around him,* she thought. *How he was before the world moved on and he moved on with it, chasing that man Walter. This is how he was before the Big Empty turned him inward on himself and made him strange.*

"They might know what those drum sounds are," Jake suggested.

Roland nodded again. "*Anything* they know—particularly about the city—would come in handy, but there's no need to think ahead too much about people who may not even be there."

"Tell you what," Susannah said, "*I* wouldn't come out if I saw us. Four people, three of them armed? We probably look like a gang of those old-time outlaws in your stories, Roland—what do you call them?"

"Harriers." His left hand dropped to the sandalwood grip of his remaining revolver and he pulled it a little way out of the holster. "But no harrier ever born carried one of these, and if there are old-timers in yon village, they'll know it. Let's go."

Jake glanced behind them and saw the bumbler lying in the road with his muzzle between his short front paws, watching them closely. "Oy!" Jake called.

"Oy!" the bumbler echoed, and scrambled to its feet at once.

They started down the shallow knoll toward the town with Oy trotting along behind them.

4

TWO BUILDINGS ON THE outskirts had been burned; the rest of the town appeared dusty but intact. They passed an abandoned livery stable on the left, a building that might have been a market on the right, and then they were in the town proper—such as it was. There were perhaps a dozen rickety buildings standing on either side of the road. Alleys ran between some of them. The other road, this one a dirt track mostly overgrown with plains grass, ran northeast to southwest.

Susannah looked at its northeast arm and thought: *Once there were barges on the river, and somewhere down that road there was a landing, and probably another shacky little town, mostly saloons and cribs, built up around it. That was the last point of trade before the barges went on down to the city. The wagons came through this place going to that place and then back again. How long ago was that?*

She didn't know—but a long time, from the look of this place.

Somewhere a rusty hinge squalled monotonously. Somewhere else one shutter clapped lonesomely to and fro in the plains wind.

There were hitching rails, most of them broken, in front of the buildings. Once there had been board sidewalks, but now most of the boards were gone and grass grew up through the holes where they had been. The signs on the buildings were faded, but some were still readable, written in a bastardized form of English which was, she supposed, what Roland called the low speech. FOOD AND GRAIN, one said, and she guessed that might mean *feed* and grain. On the false front next to it, below a crude drawing of a plains-buffalo lying in the grass, were the words REST EAT DRINK. Under the sign, batwing doors hung crookedly, moving a little in the wind.

"Is that a saloon?" She didn't know exactly why she was whispering, only that she couldn't have spoken in a normal tone of voice. It would have been like playing "Clinch Mountain Breakdown" on the banjo at a funeral.

"It was," Roland said. He didn't whisper, but his voice was low-pitched and thoughtful. Jake was walking close by his side, looking around nervously. Behind them, Oy had closed up his distance to ten yards. He trotted quickly, head swinging from side to side like a pendulum as he examined the buildings.

Now Susannah began to feel it: that sensation of being watched. It was exactly as Roland had said it would be, a feeling sunshine had been replaced by shade.

"There *are* people, aren't there?" she whispered.

Roland nodded.

Standing on the northeast corner of the crossroads was a building with another sign she recognized: HOSTEL, it said, and COTTS. Except for a church with a tilted steeple up ahead, it was the tallest building in town—three stories. She glanced up in time to see a white blur, surely a face, draw away from one of the glassless windows. Suddenly she wanted to get out of here. Roland was setting a slow, deliberate pace, however, and she supposed she knew why. Hurrying might give the watchers the impression that they were scared . . . and that they could be taken. All the same—

At the crossroads the intersecting streets widened out, creating a town square which had been overrun by grass and weeds. In the center was an eroded stone marker. Above it, a metal box hung on a sagging length of rusty cable.

Roland, with Jake by his side, walked toward the marker. Eddie pushed Susannah's chair after. Grass

STEPHEN KING

whispered in its spokes and the wind tickled a lock of
hair against her cheek. Further along the street, the
shutter banged and the hinge squealed. She shivered
and brushed the hair away.

"I wish he'd hurry up," Eddie said in a low voice.
"This place gives me the creeps."

Susannah nodded. She looked around the square
and again she could almost see how it must have been
on market-day—the sidewalks thronged with people,
a few of them town ladies with their baskets over their
arms, most of them waggoners and roughly-dressed
bargemen (she did not know why she was so sure of
the barges and bargemen, but she was); the wagons
passing through the town square, the ones on the un-
paved road raising choking clouds of yellow dust as
the drivers flogged their carthorses

(oxen they were oxen)

along. She could *see* those carts, dusty swatches of
canvas tied down over bales of cloth on some and
pyramids of tarred barrels on others; could see the
oxen, double-yoked and straining patiently, flicking
their ears at the flies buzzing around their huge heads;
could hear voices, and laughter, and the piano in the
saloon pounding out a lively tune like "Buffalo Gals"
or "Darlin' Katy."

It's as if I lived here in another life, she thought.

The gunslinger bent over the inscription on the
marker. "Great Road," he read. "Lud, one hundred
and sixty wheels."

"Wheels?" Jake asked.

"An old form of measurement."

"Have you heard of Lud?" Eddie asked.

"Perhaps," the gunslinger said. "When I was very
small."

"It rhymes with crud," Eddie said. "Maybe not such
a good sign."

Jake was examining the east side of the stone.
"River Road. It's written funny, but that's what it
says."

Eddie looked at the west side of the marker. "It says Jimtown, forty wheels. Isn't that the birthplace of Wayne Newton, Roland?"

Roland looked at him blankly.

"Shet ma mouf," Eddie said, and rolled his eyes.

On the southwest corner of the square was the town's only stone building—a squat, dusty cube with rusty bars on the windows. Combination county jail and courthouse, Susannah thought. She had seen similar ones down south; add a few slant parking spaces in front and you wouldn't be able to tell the difference. Something had been daubed across the facade of the building in fading yellow paint. She could read it, and although she couldn't understand it, it made her more anxious than ever to get out of this town. PUBES DIE, it said.

"Roland!" When she had his attention, she pointed at the graffito. "What does that mean?"

He read it, then shook his head. "Don't know."

She looked around again. The square now seemed smaller, and the buildings seemed to be leaning over them. "Can we get out of here?"

"Soon." He bent down and pried a small chunk of cobble out of the roadbed. He bounced it thoughtfully in his left hand as he looked up at the metal box which hung over the marker. He cocked his arm and Susannah realized, an instant too late, what he meant to do.

"No, Roland!" she cried, then cringed back at the sound of her own horrified voice.

He took no notice of her but fired the stone upward. His aim was as true as ever, and it struck the box dead center with a hollow, metallic bang. There was a whir of clockwork from within, and a rusty green flag unfolded from a slot in the side. When it locked in place, a bell rang briskly. Written in large black letters on the side of the flag was the word GO.

"I'll be damned," Eddie said. "It's a Keystone Kops traffic-light. If you hit it again, does it say STOP?"

"We have company," Roland said quietly, and pointed toward the building Susannah thought of as the county courthouse. A man and a woman had emerged from it and were descending the stone steps. *You win the kewpie doll, Roland*, Susannah thought. *They're older'n God, the both of em.*

The man was wearing bib overalls and a huge straw sombrero. The woman walked with one hand clamped on his naked sunburned shoulder. She wore homespun and a poke bonnet, and as they drew closer to the marker, Susannah saw she was blind, and that the accident which had taken her sight must have been exceedingly horrible. Where her eyes had been there were now only two shallow sockets filled with scar-tissue. She looked both terrified and confused.

"Be they harriers, Si?" she cried in a cracked, quavering voice. "You'll have us killed yet, I'll warrant!"

"Shut up, Mercy," he replied. Like the woman, he spoke with a thick accent Susannah could barely understand. "They ain't harriers, not these. There's a Pube with em, I told you that—ain't no harrier ever been travellin with a Pube."

Blind or not, she tried to pull away from him. He cursed and caught her arm. "Quit it, Mercy! Quit it, I say! You'll fall down and do y'self evil, dammit!"

"We mean you no harm," the gunslinger called. He used the High Speech, and at the sound of it the man's eyes lit up with incredulity. The woman turned back, swinging her blind face in their direction.

"A gunslinger!" the man cried. His voice cracked and wavered with excitement. " 'Fore God! I knew it were! I knew!"

He began to run across the square toward them, pulling the woman after. She stumbled along helplessly, and Susannah waited for the inevitable moment when she must fall. But the man fell first, going heavily to his knees, and she sprawled painfully beside him on the cobbles of the Great Road.

5

JAKE FELT SOMETHING FURRY against his ankle and looked down. Oy was crouched beside him, looking more anxious than ever. Jake reached down and cautiously stroked his head, as much to receive comfort as to give it. Its fur was silky, incredibly soft. For a moment he thought the bumbler was going to run, but it only looked up at him, licked his hand, and then looked back at the two new people. The man was trying to help the woman to her feet and not succeeding very well. Her head craned this way and that in avid confusion.

The man named Si had cut his palms on the cobblestones, but he took no notice. He gave up trying to help the woman, swept off his sombrero, and held it over his chest. To Jake the hat looked as big as a bushel basket. "We bid ye welcome, gunslinger!" he cried. "Welcome indeed! I thought all your kind had perished from the earth, so I did!"

"I thank you for your welcome," Roland said in the High Speech. He put his hands gently on the blind woman's upper arms. She cringed for a moment, then relaxed and allowed him to help her up. "Put on your hat, old-timer. The sun is hot."

He did, then just stood there, looking at Roland with shining eyes. After a moment or two, Jake realized what that shine was. Si was crying.

"A gunslinger! I told you, Mercy! I seen the shooting-iron and *told* you!"

"No harriers?" she asked, as if unable to believe it. "Are you sure they ain't harriers, Si?"

Roland turned to Eddie. "Make sure of the safety and then give her Jake's gun."

Eddie pulled the Ruger from his waistband, checked the safety, and then put it gingerly in the blind woman's hands. She gasped, almost dropped it, then ran her hands over it wonderingly. She turned the empty sockets where her eyes had been up to the man. "A gun!" she whispered. "My sainted hat!"

"Ay, some kind," the old man replied dismissively, taking it from her and giving it back to Eddie, "but the gunslinger's got a *real* one, and there's a woman got another. She's got a brown skin, too, like my da' said the people of Garlan had."

Oy gave his shrill, whistling bark. Jake turned and saw more people coming up the street—five or six in all. Like Si and Mercy, they were all old, and one of them, a woman hobbling over a cane like a witch in a fairy-tale, looked positively ancient. As they neared, Jake realized that two of the men were identical twins. Long white hair spilled over the shoulders of their patched homespun shirts. Their skin was as white as fine linen, and their eyes were pink. *Albinos*, he thought.

The crone appeared to be their leader. She hobbled toward Roland's party on her cane, staring at them with gimlet eyes as green as emeralds. Her toothless mouth was tucked deeply into itself. The hem of the old shawl she wore fluttered in the prairie breeze. Her eyes settled upon Roland.

"Hail, gunslinger! Well met!" She spoke the High Speech herself, and, like Eddie and Susannah, Jake understood the words perfectly, although he guessed they would have been gibberish to him in his own world. "Welcome to River Crossing!"

The gunslinger had removed his own hat, and now he bowed to her, tapping his throat three times, rapidly, with his diminished right hand. "Thankee-sai, Old Mother."

She cackled freely at this and Eddie suddenly realized Roland had at the same time made a joke and paid a compliment. The thought which had already occurred to Susannah now came to him: *This is how he was . . . and this is what he did. Part of it, anyway.*

"Gunslinger ye may be, but below your clothes

you're but another foolish man," she said, lapsing into low speech.

Roland bowed again. "Beauty has always made me foolish, Mother."

This time she positively *cawed* laughter. Oy shrank against Jake's leg. One of the albino twins rushed forward to catch the ancient as she rocked backward within her dusty cracked shoes. She caught her balance on her own, however, and made an imperious shooing gesture with one hand. The albino retreated.

"Be ye on a quest, gunslinger?" Her green eyes gleamed shrewdly at him; the puckered pocket of her mouth worked in and out.

"Ay," Roland said. "We go in search of the Dark Tower."

The others only looked puzzled, but the old woman recoiled and forked the sign of the evil eye—not at them, Jake realized, but to the southeast, along the path of the Beam.

"I'm sorry to hear it!" she cried. "For no one who ever went in search of that black dog ever came back! So said my grandfather, and his grandfather before him! Not ary one!"

"*Ka,*" the gunslinger said patiently, as if this explained everything . . . and, Jake was coming to realize, to Roland it did.

"Ay," she agreed, "black dog *ka*! Well-a-well; ye'll do as ye're called, and live along your path, and die when it comes to the clearing in the trees. Will ye break bread with us before you push on, gunslinger? You and your band of knights?"

Roland bowed again. "It has been long and long since we have broken bread in company other than our own, Old Mother. We cannot stay long, but yes—we'll eat your food with thanks and pleasure."

The old woman turned to the others. She spoke in a cracked and ringing voice—yet it was the words she spoke and not the tone in which they were spoken that sent chills racing down Jake's back: "Behold ye, the return of the White! After evil ways and evil days, the White comes again! Be of good heart and hold up your heads, for ye have lived to see the wheel of *ka* begin to turn once more!"

6

THE OLD WOMAN, WHOSE name was Aunt Talitha, led them through the town square and to the church with the leaning spire—it was The Church of the Blood Everlasting, according to the faded board on the run-to-riot lawn. Written over the words, in green paint that had faded to a ghost, was another message: DEATH TO GRAYS.

She led them through the ruined church, hobbling rapidly along the center aisle past the splintered and overturned pews, down a short flight of stairs, and into a kitchen so different from the ruin above that Susannah blinked in surprise. Here everything was neat as a pin. The wooden floor was very old, but it had been faithfully oiled and glowed with its own serene inner light. The black cookstove took up one whole corner. It was immaculate, and the wood stacked in the brick alcove next to it looked both well-chosen and well-seasoned.

Their party had been joined by three more senior citizens, two women and a man who limped along on a crutch and a wooden leg. Two of the women went to the cupboards and began to make themselves busy; a third opened the belly of the stove and struck a long sulphur match to the wood already laid neatly within; a fourth opened another door and went down a short set of narrow steps into what looked like a cold-pantry. Aunt Talitha, meanwhile, led the rest of them into a spacious entry at the rear of the church building. She waved her cane at two trestle tables which had been stored there under a clean but ragged dropcoth, and the two elderly albinos immediately went over and began to wrestle with one of them.

"Come on, Jake," Eddie said. "Let's lend a hand."

"Nawp!" Aunt Talitha said briskly. "We may be old, but we don't need comp'ny to lend a hand! Not yet, youngster!"

"Leave them be," Roland said.

"Old fools'll rupture themselves," Eddie muttered, but he followed the others, leaving the old men to their chosen table.

Susannah gasped as Eddie lifted her from her chair and carried her through the back door. This wasn't a lawn but a showplace, with beds of flowers blazing like torches in the soft green grass. She saw some she recognized—marigolds and zinnias and phlox—but many others were strange to her. As she watched, a horsefly landed on a bright blue petal . . . which at once folded over it and rolled up tight.

"Wow!" Eddie said, staring around. "Busch Gardens!"

Si said, "This is the one place we keep the way it was in the old days, before the world moved on. And we keep it hidden from those who ride through— Pubes, Grays, harriers. They'd burn it if they knew . . . and kill us for keeping such a place. They hate anything nice—all of em. It's the one thing all those bastards have in common."

The blind woman tugged his arm to shush him.

"No riders these days," the old man with the wooden leg said. "Not for a long time now. They keep closer in to the city. Guess they find all they need to keep em well right there."

The albino twins struggled out with the table. One of the old women followed them, urging them to hurry up and get the hell out of her way. She held a stoneware pitcher in each hand.

"Sit ye down, gunslinger!" Aunt Talitha cried, sweeping her hand at the grass. "Sit ye down, all!"

Susannah could smell a hundred conflicting perfumes. They made her feel dazed and unreal, as if this was a dream she was having. She could hardly believe this strange little pocket of Eden, carefully hidden behind the crumbling facade of the dead town.

Another woman came out with a tray of glasses. They were mismatched but spotless, twinkling in the sun like fine crystal. She held the tray out first to Roland, then to Aunt Talitha, Eddie, Susannah, and Jake at the last. As each took a glass, the first woman poured a dark golden liquid into it.

Roland leaned over to Jake, who was sitting tailor-fashion near an oval bed of bright green flowers with Oy at his side. He murmured: "Drink only enough to be polite, Jake, or we'll be carrying you out of town—this is *graf*—strong apple-beer."

Jake nodded.

Talitha held up her glass, and when Roland followed suit, Eddie, Susannah, and Jake did the same.

"What about the others?" Eddie whispered to Roland.

"They'll be served after the voluntary. Now be quiet."

"Will ye set us on with a word, gunslinger?" Aunt Talitha asked.

The gunslinger got to his feet, his glass upraised in his hand. He lowered his head, as if in thought. The few remaining residents of River Crossing watched him respectfully and, Jake thought, a little fearfully. At last he raised his head again. "Will you drink to the earth, and to the days which have passed upon it?" he asked. His voice was hoarse, trembling with emotion. "Will you drink to the fullness which was, and to friends who have passed on? Will you drink to good company, well met? Will these things set us on, Old Mother?"

She was weeping, Jake saw, but her face broke into a smile of radiant happiness all the same . . . and for a moment she was almost young. Jake looked at her with wonder and sudden, dawning happiness. For the first time since Eddie had hauled him through the door, he felt the shadow of the doorkeeper truly leave his heart.

"Ay, gunslinger!" she said. "Fair spoken! They'll set us on by the league, so they shall!" She tilted her glass up and drank it at a draught. When the glass was empty, Roland emptied his own. Eddie and Susannah also drank, although less deeply.

Jake tasted his own drink, and was surprised to find he liked it—the brew was not bitter, as he had expected, but both sweet and tart, like cider. He could feel the effects almost at once, however, and he put the glass carefully aside. Oy sniffed at it, then drew back, and dropped his muzzle on Jake's ankle.

Around them, the little company of old people—the last residents of River Crossing—were applauding. Most, like Aunt Talitha, were weeping openly. And now other glasses—not so fine but wholly serviceable—were passed around. The party began, and a fine party it was on that long summer's afternoon beneath the wide prairie sky.

7

EDDIE THOUGHT THE MEAL he ate that day was the best he had had since the mythic birthday feasts of his childhood, when his mother had made it her business to serve everything he liked—meatloaf and roasted potatoes and corn on the cob and devil's food cake with vanilla ice cream on the side.

The sheer variety of the edibles put before them—especially after the months they had spent eating nothing but lobster meat, deer meat, and the few bitter greens which Roland pronounced safe—undoubtedly had something to do with the pleasure he took in the food, but Eddie didn't think that was the sole answer; he noticed that the kid was packing it away by the plateful (and feeding a chunk of something to the bumbler crouched at his feet every couple of minutes), and Jake hadn't been here a week yet.

There were bowls of stew (chunks of buffalo meat floating in a rich brown gravy loaded with vegetables), platters of fresh biscuits, crocks of sweet white butter, and bowls of leaves that looked like spinach but weren't . . . exactly. Eddie had never been crazy about greens, but at the first taste of these, some deprived part of him awoke and cried for them. He ate well of everything, but his need for the green stuff approached greed, and he saw Susannah was also helping herself to them again and again. Among the four of them, the travellers emptied three bowls of the leaves.

The dinner dishes were swept away by the old women and the albino twins. They returned with chunks of cake piled high on two thick white plates and a bowl of whipped cream. The cake gave off a sweetly fragrant smell that made Eddie feel as if he had died and gone to heaven.

"Only buffaler cream," Aunt Talitha said dismissively. "No more cows—last one croaked thirty year ago. Buffaler cream ain't no prize-winner, but better'n nothin, by Daisy!"

The cake turned out to be loaded with blueberries. Eddie thought it beat by a country mile any cake he'd ever had. He finished three pieces, leaned back, and belched ringingly before he could clap a hand over his mouth. He looked around guiltily.

Mercy, the blind woman, cackled. "I heard that! Someone be thankin the cook, Auntie!"

"Ay," Aunt Talitha said, laughing herself. "So he do."

The two women who had served the food were returning yet again. One carried a steaming jug; the other had a number of thick ceramic cups balanced precariously on her tray.

Aunt Talitha was sitting at the head of the table

with Roland by her right hand. Now he leaned over and murmured something in her ear. She listened, her smile fading a little, then nodded.

"Si, Bill, and Till," she said. "You three stay. We are going to have us a little palaver with this gunslinger and his friends, on account of they mean to move along this very afternoon. The rest of you take your coffee in the kitchen and so cut down the babble. Mind you make your manners before you go!"

Bill and Till, the albino twins, remained sitting at the foot of the table. The others formed a line and moved slowly past the travellers. Each of them shook hands with Eddie and Susannah, then kissed Jake on the cheek. The boy accepted this with good grace, but Eddie could see he was both surprised and embarrassed.

When they reached Roland, they knelt before him and touched the sandalwood butt of the revolver which jutted from the holster he wore on his left hip. He put his hands on their shoulders and kissed their old brows. Mercy was the last; she flung her arms around Roland's waist and baptized his cheek with a wet, ringing kiss.

"Gods bless and keep ye, gunslinger! If only I could see ye!"

"Mind your manners, Mercy!" Aunt Talitha said sharply, but Roland ignored her and bent over the blind woman.

He took her hands gently but firmly in his own, and raised them to his face. "See me with these, beauty," he said, and closed his eyes as her fingers, wrinkled and misshapen with arthritis, patted gently over his brow, his cheeks, his lips and chin.

"Ay, gunslinger!" she breathed, lifting the sightless sockets of her eyes to his faded blue ones. "I see you very well! 'Tis a good face, but full of sadness and care. I fear for you and yours."

"Yet we are well met, are we not?" he asked, and

planted a gentle kiss on the smooth, worn skin of her forehead.

"Ay—so we are. So we are. Thank'ee for your kiss, gunslinger. From my heart I thank'ee."

"Go on, Mercy," Aunt Talitha said in a gentler voice. "Get your coffee."

Mercy rose to her feet. The old man with the crutch and peg leg guided her hand to the waistband of his pants. She seized it and, with a final salute to Roland and his band, allowed him to lead her away.

Eddie wiped at his eyes, which were wet. "Who blinded her?" he asked hoarsely.

"Harriers," Aunt Talitha said. "Did it with a branding-iron, they did. Said it was because she was looking at em pert. Twenty-five years agone, that was. Drink your coffee, now, all of you! It's nasty when it's hot, but it ain't nothin but roadmud once it's cold."

Eddie lifted the cup to his mouth and sipped experimentally. He wouldn't have gone so far as to call it roadmud, but it wasn't exactly Blue Mountain Blend, either.

Susannah tasted hers and looked amazed. "Why, this is chicory!"

Talitha glanced at her. "I know it not. Dockey is all I know, and dockey-coffee's all we've had since I had the woman's curse—and that curse was lifted from me long, long ago."

"How old *are* you, ma'am?" Jake asked suddenly.

Aunt Talitha looked at him, surprised, then cackled. "In truth, lad, I disremember. I recall sitting in this same place and having a party to celebrate my eighty, but there were over fifty people settin out on this lawn that day, and Mercy still had her eyes." Her own eyes dropped to the bumbler lying at Jake's feet. Oy didn't remove his muzzle from Jake's ankle, but he raised his gold-ringed eyes to gaze at her. "A billy-bumbler, by Daisy! It's been long and long since I've seen a bumbler in company with people . . . seems they have lost the memory of the days when they walked with men."

One of the albino twins bent down to pat Oy. Oy pulled away from him.

"Once they used to herd sheep," Bill (or perhaps it was Till) said to Jake. "Did ye know that, youngster?"

Jake shook his head.

"Do he talk?" the albino asked. "Some did, in the old days."

"Yes, he does." He looked down at the bumbler, who had returned his head to Jake's ankle as soon as the strange hand left his general area. "Say your name, Oy."

Oy only looked up at him.

"Oy!" Jake urged, but Oy was silent. Jake looked at Aunt Talitha and the twins, mildly chagrined. "Well, he does . . . but I guess he only does it when he wants to."

"That boy doesn't look as if he belongs here," Aunt Talitha said to Roland. "His clothes are strange . . . and his *eyes* are strange, as well."

"He hasn't been here long." Roland smiled at Jake, and Jake smiled uncertainly back. "In a month or two, no one will be able to see his strangeness."

"Ay? I wonder, so I do. And where does he come from?"

"Far from here," the gunslinger said. "Very far."

She nodded. "And when will he go back?"

"Never," Jake said. "This is my home now."

"Gods pity you, then," she said, "for the sun is going down on the world. It's going down forever."

At that Susannah stirred uneasily; one hand went to her belly, as if her stomach was upset.

"Suze?" Eddie asked. "You all right?"

She tried to smile, but it was a weak effort; her normal confidence and self-possession seemed to have temporarily deserted her. "Yes, of course. A goose walked over my grave, that's all."

Aunt Talitha gave her a long, assessing look that

seemed to make Susannah uncomfortable . . . and
then smiled. " 'A goose on my grave'—ha! I haven't
heard that one in donkey's years."

"My dad used to say it all the time." Susannah
smiled at Eddie—a stronger smile this time. "And
anyway, whatever it was is gone now. I'm fine."

"What do you know about the city, and the lands
between here and there?" Roland asked, picking up
his coffee cup and sipping. "Are there harriers? And
who are these others? These Grays and Pubes?"

Aunt Talitha sighed deeply.

8

"YE'D HEAR MUCH, GUNSLINGER, and we know but
little. One thing I do know is this: the city's an evil
place, especially for this youngster. *Any* youngster. Is
there any way you can steer around it as you go your
course?"

Roland looked up and observed the now familiar
shape of the clouds as they flowed along the path of
the Beam. In this wide plains sky, that shape, like a
river in the sky, was impossible to miss.

"Perhaps," he said at last, but his voice was oddly
reluctant. "I suppose we could skirt around Lud to
the southwest and pick up the Beam on the far side."

"It's the Beam ye follow," she said. "Ay, I thought
so."

Eddie found his own consideration of the city colored by the steadily strengthening hope that when and
if they got there, they would find help—abandoned
goodies which would aid them in their quest, or maybe
even some people who could tell them a little more
about the Dark Tower and what they were supposed
to do when they got there. The ones called the Grays,
for instance—they sounded like the sort of wise old
elves he kept imagining.

The drums were creepy, true enough, reminding him of a hundred low-budget jungle epics (mostly watched on TV with Henry by his side and a bowl of popcorn between them) where the fabulous lost cities the explorers had come looking for were in ruins and the natives had degenerated into tribes of blood-thirsty cannibals, but Eddie found it impossible to believe something like that could have happened in a city that looked, at least from a distance, so much like New York. If there were not wise old elves or abandoned goodies, there would surely be *books*, at least; he had listened to Roland talk about how rare paper was here, but every city Eddie had ever been in was absolutely drowning in books. They might even find some working transportation; the equivalent of a Land Rover would be nice. That was probably just a silly dream, but when you had thousands of miles of unknown territory to cover, a few silly dreams were undoubtedly in order, if only to keep your spirits up. And weren't those things at least *possible,* damn it?

He opened his mouth to say some of these things, but Jake spoke before he could.

"I don't think we can go around," he said, then blushed a little when they all turned to look at him. Oy shifted at his feet.

"No?" Aunt Talitha said. "And why do ye think that, pray tell?"

"Do you know about trains?" Jake asked.

There was a long silence. Bill and Till exchanged an uneasy glance. Aunt Talitha only looked at Jake steadily. Jake did not drop his eyes.

"I heard of one," she said. "Mayhap even saw it. Over there." She pointed in the direction of the Send. "Long ago, when I was but a child and the world hadn't moved on . . . or at least not s'far's it has now. Is it Blaine ye speak of, boy?"

Jake's eyes flashed in surprise and recognition. "Yes! Blaine!" Roland was studying Jake closely.

"And how would ye know of Blaine the Mono?" Aunt Talitha asked.

"Mono?" Jake looked blank.

"Ay, so it was called. How would you know of that old lay?"

Jake looked helplessly at Roland, then back at Aunt Talitha. "I don't know *how* I know."

And that's the truth, Eddie thought suddenly, *but it's not* all *the truth. He knows more than he wants to tell here . . . and I think he's scared.*

"This is our business, I think," Roland said in a dry, brisk administrator's voice. "You must let us work it out for ourselves, Old Mother."

"Ay," she agreed quickly. "You'll keep your own counsel. Best that such as us not know."

"What of the city?" Roland prompted. "What do you know of Lud?"

"Little now, but what we know, ye shall hear." And she poured herself another cup of coffee.

9

IT WAS THE TWINS, Bill and Till, who actually did most of the talking, one taking up the tale smoothly whenever the other left off. Every now and then Aunt Talitha would add something or correct something, and the twins would wait respectfully until they were sure she was done. Si didn't speak at all—merely sat with his untouched coffee in front of him, plucking at the pieces of straw which bristled up from the wide brim of his sombrero.

They knew little, indeed, Roland realized quickly, even about the history of their own town (nor did this surprise him; in these latter days, memories faded rapidly and all but the most recent past seemed not to exist), but what they did know was disturbing. Roland was not surprised by this, either.

In the days of their great-great-grandparents, River
Crossing had been much the town Susannah had imagined: a trade-stop at the Great Road, modestly prosperous, a place where goods were sometimes sold but
more often exchanged. It had been at least nominally
part of River Barony, although even then such things
as Baronies and Estates o' Land had been passing.

There had been buffalo-hunters in those days, although the trade had been dying out; the herds were
small and badly mutated. The meat of these mutant
beasts was not poison, but it had been rank and bitter.
Yet River Crossing, located between a place they simply called The Landing and the village of Jimtown,
had been a place of some note. It was on the Great
Road and only six days travel from the city by land
and three by barge. "Unless the river were low," one
of the twins said. "Then it took longer, and my
gran'da said there was times when there was barges
grounded all the way upriver to Tom's Neck."

The old people knew nothing of the city's original
residents, of course, or the technologies they had used
to build the towers and turrets; these were the Great
Old Ones, and their history had been lost in the furthest reaches of the past even when Aunt Talitha's
great-great-grandfather had been a boy.

"The buildings are still standing," Eddie said. "I
wonder if the machines the Great Golden Oldies used
to build them still run."

"Mayhap," one of the twins said. "If so, young
fella, there don't be ary man or woman that lives there
now who'd still know how to run em . . . or so I
believe, so I do."

"Nay," his brother said argumentatively, "I doubt
the old ways are entirely lost to the Grays 'n Pubes,
even now." He looked at Eddie. "Our da' said there
was once electric candles in the city. There are those
who say they mought still burn."

"Imagine that," Eddie replied wonderingly, and Susannah pinched his leg, hard, under the table.

"Yes," the other twin said. He spoke seriously, unaware of Eddie's sarcasm. "You pushed a button and they came on—bright, heatless candles with ary wicks or reservoirs for oil. And I've heard it said that once, in the old days, Quick, the outlaw prince, actually flew up into the sky in a mechanical bird. But one of its wings broke and he died in a great fall, like Icarus."

Susannah's mouth dropped open. "You know the story of Icarus?"

"Ay, lady," he said, clearly surprised she should find this strange. "He of the beeswax wings."

"Children's stories, both of them," Aunt Talitha said with a sniff. "I know the story of the endless lights is true, for I saw them with my own eyes when I was but a green girl, and they may still glow from time to time, ay; there are those I trust who say they've seen them on clear nights, although it's been long years since I have myself. But no man ever flew, not even the Great Old Ones."

Nonetheless, there *were* strange machines in the city, built to do peculiar and sometimes dangerous things. Many of them might still run, but the elderly twins reckoned that none now in the city knew how to start them up, for they hadn't been heard in years.

Maybe that could change, though, Eddie thought, his eyes gleaming. *If, that is, an enterprising, travel-minded young man with a little knowledge of strange machinery and endless lights came along. It could be just a matter of finding the ON switches. I mean, it really could be that simple. Or maybe they just blew a bunch of fuses—think of that, friends and neighbors! Just replace half a dozen 400-amp Busses and light the whole place up like a Reno Saturday night!*

Susannah elbowed him and asked, in a low voice, what was so funny. Eddie shook his head and put a finger to his lips, earning an irritated look from the love of his life. The albinos, meanwhile, were continuing their story, handing its thread back and forth with

the unconscious ease which probably nothing but lifetime twinship can provide.

Four or five generations ago, they said, the city had
still been quite heavily populated and reasonably civilized, although the residents drove wagons and buck-
boards along the wide boulevards the Great Old Ones
had constructed for their fabulous horseless vehicles.
The city-dwellers were artisans and what the twins
called "manufactories," and trade both on the river
and over it had been brisk.

"Over it?" Roland asked.

"The bridge over the Send still stands," Aunt Talitha said, "or did twenty year ago."

"Ay, old Bill Muffin and his boy saw it not ten year
agone," Si agreed, making his first contribution to the
conversation.

"What sort of bridge?" the gunslinger asked.

"A great thing of steel cables," one of the twins
said. "It stands in the sky like the web of some great
spider." He added shyly: "I should like to see it again
before I die."

"Probably fallen in by now," Aunt Talitha said dismissively, "and good riddance. Devil's work." She
turned to the twins. "Tell them what's happened
since, and why the city's so dangerous now—apart
from any haunts that may den there, that is, and I'll
warrant there's a power of em. These folks want to
get on, and the sun's on the wester."

10

THE REST OF THE story was but another version of a
tale Roland of Gilead had heard many times and had,
in some measure, lived through himself. It was fragmentary and incomplete, undoubtedly shot through
with myth and misinformation, its linear progress distorted by the odd changes—both temporal and direc-

tional—which were now taking place in the world, and it could be summed up in a single compound sentence: *Once there was a world we knew, but that world has moved on.*

These old people of River Crossing knew of Gilead no more than Roland knew of the River Barony, and the name of John Farson, the man who had brought ruin and anarchy on Roland's land, meant nothing to them, but all stories of the old world's passing were similar . . . too similar, Roland thought, to be coincidence.

A great civil war—perhaps in Garlan, perhaps in a more distant land called Porla—had erupted three, perhaps even four hundred years ago. Its ripples had spread slowly outward, pushing anarchy and dissension ahead of them. Few if any kingdoms had been able to stand against those slow waves, and anarchy had come to this part of the world as surely as night follows sunset. At one time, whole armies had been on the roads, sometimes in advance, sometimes in retreat, always confused and without long-term goals. As time passed, they crumbled into smaller groups, and these degenerated into roving bands of harriers. Trade faltered, then broke down entirely. Travel went from a matter of inconvenience to one of danger. In the end, it became almost impossible. Communication with the city thinned steadily and had all but ceased a hundred and twenty years ago.

Like a hundred other towns Roland had ridden through—first with Cuthbert and the other gunslingers cast out of Gilead, then alone, in pursuit of the man in black—River Crossing had been cut off and thrown on its own resources.

At this point Si roused himself, and his voice captured the travellers at once. He spoke in the hoarse, cadenced tones of a lifelong teller of tales—one of those divine fools born to merge memory and mendacity into dreams as airily gorgeous as cobwebs strung with drops of dew.

"We last sent tribute to the Barony castle in the time of my great-gran'da," he said. "Twenty-six men went with a wagon of hides—there was no hard coin anymore by then, o' course, and 'twas the best they could do. It was a long and dangerous journey of almost eighty wheels, and six died on the way. Half fell to harriers bound for the war in the city; the other half died either of disease or devilgrass.

"When they finally arrived, they found the castle deserted but for the rooks and black-birds. The walls had been broken; weeds o'ergrew the Court o' State. There had been a great slaughter on the fields to the west; it were white with bones and red with rusty armor, so my da's gran'da said, and the voices of demons cried out like the east wind from the jawbones o' those who'd fallen there. The village beyond the castle had been burned to the ground and a thousand or more skulls were posted along the walls of the keep. Our folk left their bounty o' hides without the shattered barbican gate—for none would venture inside that place of ghosts and moaning voices—and began the homeward way again. Ten more fell on that journey, so that of the six-and-twenty who left only ten returned, my great-gran'da one of them . . . but he picked up a ring-worm on his neck and bosom that never left until the day he died. It were the radiation sickness, or so they said. After that, gunslinger, none left the town. We were on our own."

They grew used to the depredations of the harriers, Si continued in his cracked but melodious voice. Watches were posted; when bands of riders were seen approaching—almost always moving southeast along the Great Road and the path of the Beam, going to the war which raged endlessly in Lud—the townspeople hid in a large shelter they had dug beneath the church. Casual damages to the town were not repaired, lest they make those roving bands curious. Most were beyond curiosity; they only rode through at a gallop, bows or battle-axes slung over their shoulders, bound for the killing-zones.

"What war is it that you speak of?" Roland asked.

"Yes," Eddie said, "and what about that drumming sound?"

The twins again exchanged a quick, almost superstitious glance.

"We know not of the god-drums," Si told them. "Ary word or watch. The war of the city, now . . ."

The war had originally been the harriers and outlaws against a loose confederation of artisans and "manufactories" who lived in the city. The residents had decided to fight instead of allowing the harriers to loot them, burn their shops, and then turn the survivors out into the Big Empty, where they would almost certainly die. And for some years they had successfully defended Lud against the vicious but badly organized groups of raiders which tried to storm across the bridge or invade by boat and barge.

"The city-folk used the old weapons," one of the twins said, "and though their numbers were small, the harriers could not stand against such things with their bows and maces and battle-axes."

"Do you mean the city-people used guns?" Eddie asked.

One of the albinos nodded. "Ay, guns, but not *just* guns. There were things that hurled the firebangs over a mile or more. Explosions like dynamite, only more powerful. The outlaws—who are now the Grays, as you must ken—could do nothing but lay siege beyond the river, and that was what they did."

Lud became, in effect, the last fortress-refuge of the latter world. The brightest and most able travelled there from the surrounding countryside by ones and twos. When it came to intelligence tests, sneaking through the tangled encampments and front lines of the besiegers was the newcomers' final exam. Most came unarmed across the no-man's-land of the bridge, and those who made it that far were let through. Some were found wanting and sent packing again, of course, but those who had a trade or a skill (or brains enough to learn one) were allowed to stay. Farming skills were particularly prized; according to the stories, every large park in Lud had been turned into a vegetable garden. With the countryside cut off, it was grow food in the city or starve amid the glass towers and metal alleys. The Great Old Ones were gone, their machines were a mystery, and the silent wonders which remained were inedible.

Little by little, the character of the war began to change. The balance of power had shifted to the besieging Grays—so called because they were, on average, much older than the city-dwellers. Those latter were also growing older, of course. They were still known as Pubes, but in most cases their puberty was long behind them. And they eventually either forgot how the old weapons worked or used them up.

"Probably both," Roland grunted.

Some ninety years ago—within the lifetimes of Si and Aunt Talitha—a final band of outlaws had appeared, one so large that the outriders had gone galloping through River Crossing at dawn and the drogues did not pass until almost sundown. It was the last army these parts had ever seen, and it was led by a warrior prince named David Quick—the same fellow who supposedly later fell to his death from the sky. He had organized the raggle-taggle remnants of the outlaw bands which still hung about the city, killing anyone who showed opposition to his plans. Quick's army of Grays used neither boat nor bridge to attempt entry into the city, but instead built a pontoon bridge twelve miles below it and attacked on the flank.

"Since then the war has guttered like a chimney-fire," Aunt Talitha finished. "We hear reports every now and then from someone who has managed to leave, ay, so we do. These come a little more often now, for the bridge, they say, is undefended and I think the fire is almost out. Within the city, the Pubes and Grays squabble over the remaining spoils, only I reckon that the descendents of the harriers who followed Quick over the pontoon bridge are the real Pubes now, although they are still called Grays. The descendents of the original city-dwellers must now be almost as old as we are, although there are still some younkers who go to be among them, drawn by the old stories and the lure of the knowledge which may still remain there.

"These two sides still keep up their old enmity, gunslinger, and both would desire this young man you call Eddie. If the dark-skinned woman is fertile, they would not kill her even though her legs are short-ended; they would keep her to bear children, for children are fewer now, and although the old sicknesses are passing, some are still born strange."

At this, Susannah stirred, seemed about to say something, then only drank the last of her coffee and settled back into her former listening position.

"But if they would desire the young man and woman, gunslinger, I think they would lust for the boy."

Jake bent and began to stroke Oy's fur again. Roland saw his face and knew what he was thinking: it was the passage under the mountains all over again, just another version of the Slow Mutants.

"You they'd just as soon kill," Aunt Talitha said, "for you are a gunslinger, a man out of his own time and place, neither fish nor fowl, and no use to either side. But a boy can be taken, used, schooled to remember some things and to forget all the others. *They've* all forgotten whatever it was they had to fight about in the first place; the world has moved on since then. Now they just fight to the sound of them awful drumbeats, some few still young, most of them old enough for the rocking chair, like us here, all of them stupid grots who only live to kill and kill to live." She paused. "Now that you've heard us old cullies to the end, are ye sure it would not be best to go around, and leave them to their business?"

Before Roland could reply, Jake spoke up in a clear, firm voice. "Tell what you know about Blaine the Mono," he said. "Tell about Blaine and Engineer Bob."

11

"ENGINEER *WHO*?" EDDIE ASKED, but Jake only went on looking at the old people.

"Track lies over yonder," Si answered at last. He pointed toward the river. "One track only, set up high on a colyum of man-made stone, such as the Old Ones used to make their streets and walls."

"A monorail!" Susannah exclaimed. "Blaine the Monorail!"

"Blaine is a pain," Jake muttered.

Roland glanced at him but said nothing.

"Does this train run now?" Eddie asked Si.

Si shook his head slowly. His face was troubled and uneasy. "No, young sir—but in my lifetime and Auntie's, it did. When we were green and the war of the city still went forrad briskly. We'd hear it before we saw it—a low humming noise, a sound like ye sometimes hear when a bad summer storm's on the way—one that's full of lightning."

"Ay," Aunt Talitha said. Her face was lost and dreaming.

"Then it'd come—Blaine the Mono, twinkling in the sun, with a nose like one of the bullets in your revolver, gunslinger. Maybe two wheels long. I know that sounds like it couldn't be, and maybe it wasn't (we were green, ye must remember, and that makes a difference), but I still think it *was,* for when it came, it seemed to run along the whole horizon. Fast, low, and gone before you could even see it proper!

"Sometimes, on days when the weather were foul and the air low, it'd shriek like a harpy as it came out of the west. Sometimes it'd come in the night with a long white light spread out before it, and that shriek would wake all of us. It were like the trumpet they say will raise the dead from their graves at the end of the world, so it was."

"Tell em about the bang, Si!" Bill or Till said in a voice which trembled with awe. "Tell em about the godless bang what always came after!"

"Ay, I was just getting to that," Si answered with a touch of annoyance. "After it passed by, there would be quiet for a few seconds . . . sometimes as long as a minute, maybe . . . and then there'd come an explosion that rattled the boards and knocked cups off the shelves and sometimes even broke the glass in the window-panes. But never did anyone see ary flash nor fire. It was like an explosion in the world of spirits."

Eddie tapped Susannah on the shoulder, and when she turned to him he mouthed two words: *Sonic boom.* It was nuts—no train he had ever heard of travelled faster than the speed of sound—but it was also the only thing that made sense.

She nodded and turned back to Si.

"It's the only one of the machines the Great Old Ones made that I've ever seen running with my own eyes," he said in a soft voice, "and if it weren't the devil's work, there be no devil. The last time I saw it was the spring I married Mercy, and that must have been sixty year agone."

"Seventy," Aunt Talitha said with authority.

"And this train went *into* the city," Roland said. "From back the way we came . . . from the west . . . from the forest."

"Ay," a new voice said unexpectedly, "but there was another . . . one that went *out from* the city . . . and mayhap that one still runs."

12

THEY TURNED. MERCY STOOD by a bed of flowers
between the back of the church and the table where
they sat. She was walking slowly toward the sound of
their voices, with her hands spread out before her.

Si got clumsily to his feet, hurried to her as best he
could, and took her hand. She slipped an arm about
his waist and they stood there looking like the world's
oldest wedding couple.

"Auntie told you to take your coffee inside!" he
said.

"Finished my coffee long ago," Mercy said. "It's a
bitter brew and I hate it. Besides—I wanted to hear
the palaver." She raised a trembling finger and
pointed it in Roland's direction. "I wanted to hear *his*
voice. It's fair and light, so it is."

"I cry your pardon, Auntie," Si said, looking at the
ancient woman a little fearfully. "She was never one
to mind, and the years have made her no better."

Aunt Talitha glanced at Roland. He nodded, almost
imperceptibly. "Let her come forward and join us,"
she said.

Si led her over to the table, scolding all the while.
Mercy only looked over his shoulder with her sightless
eyes, her mouth set in an intractable line.

When Si had gotten her seated, Aunt Talitha leaned
forward on her forearms and said, "Now do you have
something to say, old sister-sai, or were you just beating your gums?"

"I hear what I hear. My ears are as sharp as they
ever were, Talitha—sharper!"

Roland's hand dropped to his belt for a moment.
When he brought it back to the table, he was holding
a cartridge in his fingers. He tossed it to Susannah,
who caught it. "Do you, sai?" he asked.

"Well enough," she said, turning in his direction,
"to know that you just threw something. To your

woman, I think—the one with the brown skin. Something small. What was it, gunslinger? A biscuit?"

"Close enough," he said, smiling. "You hear as well as you say. Now tell us what you meant."

"There is another mono," she said, "unless 'tis the same one, running a different course. Either way, a different course was run by *some* mono . . . until seven or eight year ago, anyways. I used to hear it leaving the city and going out into the waste lands beyond."

"Dungheap!" one of the albino twins ejaculated. "*Nothing* goes to the waste lands! Nothing can live there!"

She turned her face to him. "Is a train alive, Till Tudbury?" she asked. "Does a machine fall sick with sores and puking?"

Well, Eddie thought of saying, *there* was *this bear* . . .

He thought it over a little more and decided it might be better to keep his silence.

"We would have heard it," the other twin was insisting hotly. "A noise like the one Si always tells of—"

"This one didn't make no bang," she admitted, "but I heard that other sound, that humming noise like the one you hear sometimes after lightning has struck somewhere close. When the wind was strong, blowing out from the city, I heard it." She thrust out her chin and added: "I *did* hear the bang once, too. From far, far out. The night Big Charlie Wind came and almost blew the steeple off the church. Must have been two hundred wheels from here. Maybe two hundred and fifty."

"Bulldink!" the twin cried. "You been chewing the weed!"

"I'll chew on *you*, Bill Tudbury, if you don't shut up your honkin. You've no business sayin bulldink to a lady, either. Why—"

"Stop it, Mercy!" Si hissed, but Eddie was barely

listening to this exchange of rural pleasantries. What the blind woman had said made sense to him. Of *course* there would be no sonic boom, not from a train which *started* its run in Lud; he couldn't remember exactly what the speed of sound was, but he thought it was somewhere in the neighborhood of six hundred and fifty miles an hour. A train starting from a dead stop would take some time getting up to that speed, and by the time it reached it, it would be out of ear-shot . . . unless the listening conditions happened to be just right, as Mercy claimed they had been on the night when the Big Charlie Wind—whatever that was—had come.

And there were possibilities here. Blaine the Mono was no Land Rover, but maybe . . . maybe . . .

"You haven't heard the sound of this other train for seven or eight years, sai?" Roland asked. "Are you sure it wasn't much longer?"

"Couldn't have been," she said, "for the last time was the year old Bill Muffin took blood-sick. Poor Bill!"

"That's almost ten year agone," Aunt Talitha said, and her voice was queerly gentle.

"Why did you never say you heard such a thing?" Si asked. He looked at the gunslinger. "You can't believe everything she says, lord—always longing to be in the middle of the stage is my Mercy."

"Why, you old slumgullion!" she cried, and slapped his arm. "I didn't say because I didn't want to o'ertop the story you're so proud of, but now that it matters what I heard, I'm bound to tell!"

"I believe you, sai," Roland said, "but are you sure you haven't heard the sounds of the mono since then?"

"Nay, not since then. I imagine it's finally reached the end of its path."

"I wonder," Roland said. "Indeed, I wonder very much." He looked down at the table, brooding, suddenly far away from all of them.

Choo-choo, Jake thought, and shivered.

13

HALF AN HOUR LATER they were in the town square again, Susannah in her wheelchair, Jake adjusting the straps of his pack while Oy sat at his heel, watching him attentively. Only the town elders had attended the dinner-party in the little Eden behind the Church of the Blood Everlasting, it seemed, because when they returned to the square, another dozen people were waiting. They glanced at Susannah and looked a bit longer at Jake (his youth apparently more interesting to them than her dark skin), but it was clearly Roland they had come to see; their wondering eyes were full of ancient awe.

He's a living remnant of a past they only know from stories, Susannah thought. *They look at him the way religious people would look at one of the saints—Peter or Paul or Matthew—if he decided to drop by the Saturday night bean supper and tell them stories of how it was, traipsing around the Sea of Galilee with Jesus the Carpenter.*

The ritual which had ended the meal was now repeated, only this time everyone left in River Crossing participated. They shuffled forward in a line, shaking hands with Eddie and Susannah, kissing Jake on the cheek or forehead, then kneeling in front of Roland for his touch and his blessing. Mercy threw her arms about him and pressed her blind face against his stomach. Roland hugged her back and thanked her for her news.

"Will ye not stay the night with us, gunslinger? Sunset comes on apace, and it's been long since you and yours spent the night beneath a roof, I'll warrant."

"It has been, but it's best we go on. Thankee-sai."

"Will ye come again if ye may, gunslinger?"

"Yes," Roland said, but Eddie did not need to look into his strange friend's face to know the chances were small. "If we can."

"Ay." She hugged him a final time, then passed on

with her hand resting on Si's sunburned shoulder. "Fare ye well."

Aunt Talitha came last. When she began to kneel, Roland caught her by the shoulders. "No, sai. You shall not do." And before Eddie's amazed eyes, Roland knelt before her in the dust of the town square. "Will you bless me, Old Mother? Will you bless all of us as we go our course?"

"Ay," she said. There was no surprise in her voice, no tears in her eyes, but her voice throbbed with deep feeling, all the same. "I see your heart is true, gunslinger, and that you hold to the old ways of your kind; ay, you hold to them very well. I bless you and yours and will pray that no harm will come to you. Now take this, if you will." She reached into the bodice of her faded dress and removed a silver cross at the end of a fine-link silver chain. She took it off.

Now it was Roland's turn to be surprised. "Are you sure? I did not come to take what belongs to you and yours, Old Mother."

"I'm sure as sure can be. I've worn this day and night for over a hundred years, gunslinger. Now you shall wear it, and lay it at the foot of the Dark Tower, and speak the name of Talitha Unwin at the far end of the earth." She slipped the chain over his head. The cross dropped into the open neck of his deerskin shirt as if it belonged there. "Go now. We have broken bread, we have held palaver, we have your blessing, and you have ours. Go your course in safety. Stand and be true." Her voice trembled and broke on the last word.

Roland rose to his feet, then bowed and tapped his throat three times. "Thankee-sai."

She bowed back, but did not speak. Now there were tears coursing down her cheeks.

"Ready?" Roland asked.

Eddie nodded. He did not trust himself to speak.

"All right," Roland said. "Let's go."

They walked down what remained of the town's

high street, Jake pushing Susannah's wheelchair. As they passed the last building (TRADE & CHANGE, the faded sign read), he looked back. The old people were still gathered about the stone marker, a forlorn cluster of humanity in the middle of this wide, empty plain. Jake raised his hand. Up to this point he had managed to hold himself in, but when several of the old folks— Si, Bill, and Till among them—raised their own hands in return, Jake burst into tears himself.

Eddie put an arm around his shoulders. "Just keep walking, sport," he said in an uneasy voice. "That's the only way to do it."

"They're so *old*!" Jake sobbed. "How can we just leave them like this? It's not right!"

"It's *ka*," Eddie said without thinking.

"Is it? Well *ka* suh-suh-*sucks*!"

"Yeah, *hard*," Eddie agreed . . . but he kept walking. So did Jake, and he didn't look back again. He was afraid they would still be there, standing at the center of their forgotten town, watching until Roland and his friends were out of view. And he would have been right.

14

THEY HAD MADE LESS than seven miles before the sky began to darken and sunset colored the western horizon blaze orange. There was a grove of Susannah's eucalyptus trees nearby; Jake and Eddie foraged there for wood.

"I just don't see why we didn't stay," Jake said. "The blind lady invited us, and we didn't get very far, anyway. I'm still so full I'm practically waddling."

Eddie smiled. "Me, too. And I can tell you something else: your good friend Edward Cantor Dean is looking forward to a long and leisurely squat in this grove of trees first thing tomorrow morning. You wouldn't believe how tired I am of eating deermeat and crapping rabbit-turds. If you'd told me a year ago that a good dump would be the high point of my day, I would have laughed in your face."

"Is your middle name really Cantor?"

"Yes, but I'd appreciate it if you didn't spread it around."

"I won't. Why *didn't* we stay, Eddie?"

Eddie sighed. "Because we would have found out they needed firewood."

"Huh?"

"And after we got the firewood, we would've found they *also* needed fresh meat, because they served us the last of what they had. And we'd be real creeps not to replace what we ate, right? Especially when we're packing guns and the best they can probably do is a bunch of bows and arrows fifty or a hundred years old. So we would have gone hunting for them. By then it would be night again, and when we got up the next day, Susannah would be saying we ought to at least make a few repairs before we moved on—oh, not to the *front* of the town, that'd be dangerous, but maybe in the hotel or wherever it is they live. Only a few days, and what's a few days, right?"

Roland materialized out of the gloom. He moved as quietly as ever, but he looked tired and preoccupied. "I thought maybe you two fell into a quickpit," he said.

"Nope. I've just been telling Jake the facts as I see them."

"So what *would* have been wrong with that?" Jake asked. "This Dark Tower thingy has been wherever it is for a long time, right? It's not going anywhere, is it?"

"A few days, then a few more, then a few more." Eddie looked at the branch he had just picked up and threw it aside disgustedly. *I'm starting to sound just like him*, he thought. And yet he knew that he was only speaking the truth. "Maybe we'd see that their spring is getting silted up, and it wouldn't be polite to go until we'd dug it out for them. But why stop there when we could take another couple of weeks and build a jackleg waterwheel, right? They're old, and have no more foot." He glanced at Roland, and his voice was tinged with reproach. "I tell you what—when I think of Bill and Till there stalking a herd of wild buffalo, I get the shivers."

"They've been doing it a long time," Roland said, "and I imagine they could show us a thing or two. They'll manage. Meantime, let's get that wood—it's going to be a chilly night."

But Jake wasn't done with it yet. He was looking closely—almost sternly—at Eddie. "You're saying we could never do enough for them, aren't you?"

Eddie stuck out his lower lip and blew hair off his forehead. "Not exactly. I'm saying it would never be any easier to leave than it was today. Harder, maybe, but no easier."

"It *still* doesn't seem right."

They reached the place that would become, once the fire was lit, just another campsite on the road to the Dark Tower. Susannah had eased herself out of her chair and was lying on her back with her hands behind her head, looking up at the stars. Now she sat up and began to arrange the wood in the way Roland had shown her months ago.

"Right is what all this is about," Roland said. "But if you look too long at the small rights, Jake—the ones that lie close at hand— it's easy to lose sight of the big ones that stand farther off. Things are out of joint—going wrong and getting worse. We see it all around us, but the answers are still ahead. While we were helping the twenty or thirty people left in River Crossing, twenty or thirty thousand more might be suffering or dying somewhere else. And if there is any place in the universe where these things can be set right, it's at the Dark Tower."

"Why? How?" Jake asked. "What *is* this Tower, anyway?"

Roland squatted beside the fire Susannah had built, produced his flint and steel, and began to flash sparks into the kindling. Soon small flames were growing amid the twigs and dried handfuls of grass. "I can't answer those questions," he said. "I wish I could."

That, Eddie thought, was an exceedingly clever reply. Roland had said *I can't answer* . . . but that wasn't the same thing as *I don't know*. Far from it.

15

SUPPER CONSISTED OF WATER and greens. They were all still recovering from the heavy meal they'd eaten in River Crossing; even Oy refused the scraps Jake offered him after the first one or two.

"How come you wouldn't talk back there?" Jake scolded the bumbler. "You made me look like an idiot!"

"Id-yit!" Oy said, and put his muzzle on Jake's ankle.

"He's talking better all the time," Roland remarked. "He's even starting to sound like you, Jake."

"Ake," Oy agreed, not lifting his muzzle. Jake was fascinated by the gold rings in Oy's eyes; in the flickering light of the fire, they seemed to revolve slowly.

"But he wouldn't talk to the old people."

"Bumblers are choosy about that sort of thing," Roland said. "They're odd creatures. If I had to guess, I'd say this one was driven away by its own pack."

"Why do you think so?"

Roland pointed at Oy's flank. Jake had cleaned off the blood (Oy hadn't enjoyed this, but had stood for it) and the bite was healing, although the bumbler still limped a little. "I'd bet an eagle that's the bite of another bumbler."

"But why would his own pack—"

"Maybe they got tired of his chatter," Eddie said. He had lain down beside Susannah and put an arm about her shoulders.

"Maybe they did," Roland said, "especially if he was the only one of them who was still trying to talk. The others might have decided he was too bright—or too uppity—for their taste. Animals don't know as much about jealousy as people, but they're not ignorant of it, either."

The object of this discussion closed his eyes and appeared to go to sleep . . . but Jake noticed his ears began twitching when the talk resumed.

"How bright *are* they?" Jake asked.

Roland shrugged. "The old groom I told you about—the one who said a good bumbler is good luck—swore he had one in his youth that could add. He said it told sums either by scratching on the stable floor or pushing stones together with its muzzle." He grinned. It lit his whole face, chasing away the gloomy shadows which had lain there ever since they left River Crossing. "Of course, grooms and fishermen are born to lie."

A companionable silence fell among them, and Jake could feel drowsiness stealing over him. He thought he would sleep soon, and that was fine by him. Then the drums began, coming out of the southeast in rhythmic pulses, and he sat back up. They listened without speaking.

"That's a rock and roll backbeat," Eddie said suddenly. "I know it is. Take away the guitars and that's what you've got left. In fact, it sounds quite a lot like Z.Z. Top."

"Z.Z. *who*?" Susannah asked.

Eddie grinned. "They didn't exist in your when," he said. "I mean, they probably did, but in '63 they would have been just a bunch of kids going to school down in Texas." He listened. "I'll be goddamned if that doesn't sound just like the backbeat to something like 'Sharp-Dressed Man' or 'Velcro Fly.' "

" 'Velcro Fly'?" Jake said. "That's a stupid name for a song."

"Pretty funny, though," Eddie said. "You missed it by ten years or so, sport."

"We'd better roll over," Roland said. "Morning comes early."

"I can't sleep with that shit going on," Eddie said. He hesitated, then said something which had been on his mind ever since the morning when they had pulled Jake, whitefaced and shrieking, through the doorway and into this world. "Don't you think it's about time we exchanged stories, Roland? We might find out we know more than we think."

"Yes, it's almost time for that. But not in the dark." Roland rolled onto his side, pulled up a blanket, and appeared to go to sleep.

"Jesus," Eddie said. "Just like that." He blew a disgusted little whistle between his teeth.

"He's right," Susannah said. "Come on, Eddie—go to sleep."

He grinned and kissed the tip of her nose. "Yes, Mummy."

Five minutes later he and Susannah were dead to the world, drums or no drums. Jake found that his own sleepiness had stolen away, however. He lay looking up at the strange stars and listening to that steady, rhythmic throbbing coming out of the darkness. Maybe it was the Pubes, boogying madly to a song called "Velcro Fly" while they worked themselves into a sacrificial killing frenzy.

He thought of Blaine the Mono, a train so fast that it travelled across the huge, haunted world trailing a sonic boom behind it, and that led him naturally enough to thoughts of Charlie the Choo-Choo, who had been retired to a forgotten siding when the new Burlington Zephyr arrived, rendering him obsolete. He thought of the expression on Charlie's face, the one that was supposed to be cheery and pleasant but somehow wasn't. He thought about The Mid-World Railway Company, and the empty lands between St. Louis and Topeka. He thought about how Charlie had been all ready to go when Mr. Martin needed him, and how Charlie could blow his own whistle and feed his own firebox. He wondered again if Engineer Bob had sabotaged the Burlington Zephyr in order to give his beloved Charlie a second chance.

At last—and as suddenly as it had begun—the rhythmic drumming stopped, and Jake drifted off to sleep.

16

HE DREAMED, BUT NOT of the plaster-man.

He dreamed instead that he was standing on a stretch of blacktop highway somewhere in the Big Empty of western Missouri. Oy was with him. Railroad warning signals—white X-shapes with red lights in their centers—flanked the road. The lights were flashing and bells were ringing.

Now a humming noise began to rise out of the southeast getting steadily louder. It sounded like lightning in a bottle.

Here it comes, he told Oy.

Ums! Oy agreed.

And suddenly a vast pink shape two wheels long was slicing across the plain toward them. It was low and bullet-shaped, and when Jake saw it, a terrible fear filled his heart. The two big windows flashing in the sun at the front of the train looked like eyes.

Don't ask it silly questions, Jake told Oy. *It won't play silly games. It's just an awful choo-choo train, and its name is Blaine the Pain.*

Suddenly Oy leaped onto the tracks and crouched there with his ears flattened back. His golden eyes were blazing. His teeth were bared in a desperate snarl.

No! Jake screamed. *No, Oy!*

But Oy paid no attention. The pink bullet was bearing down on the tiny, defiant shape of the billy-bumbler now, and that humming seemed to be crawling all over Jake's skin, making his nose bleed and shattering the fillings in his teeth.

He leaped for Oy, Blaine the Mono (or was it Charlie the Choo-Choo?) bore down on them, and he woke up suddenly, shivering, bathed in sweat. The night seemed to be pressing down upon him like a physical weight. He rolled over and felt frantically for Oy. For a terrible moment he thought the bumbler was gone, and then his fingers found the silky fur. Oy uttered a squeak and looked at him with sleepy curiosity.

"That's all right," Jake whispered in a dry voice. "There's no train. It was just a dream. Go back to sleep, boy."

"Oy," the bumbler agreed, and closed his eyes again.

Jake rolled over on his back and lay looking up at the stars. *Blaine is more than a pain,* he thought. *It's dangerous.* Very *dangerous.*

Yes, perhaps.

No perhaps about it! his mind insisted frantically.

All right, Blaine was a pain—given. But his Final Essay had had something else to say on the subject of Blaine, hadn't it?

Blaine is the truth. Blaine is the truth. Blaine is the truth.

"Oh Jeez, what a mess," Jake whispered. He closed his eyes and was asleep again in seconds. This time his sleep was dreamless.

17

AROUND NOON THE NEXT day they reached the top of another drumlin and saw the bridge for the first time. It crossed the Send at a point where the river narrowed, bent due south, and passed in front of the city.

"Holy Jesus," Eddie said softly. "Does that look familiar to you, Suze?"

"Yes."

"Jake?"

"Yes—it looks like the George Washington Bridge."

"It sure does," Eddie agreed.

"But what's the GWB doing in Missouri?" Jake asked.

Eddie looked at him. "Say *what*, sport?"

Jake looked confused. "Mid-World, I mean. You know."

Eddie was looking at him harder than ever. "How do *you* know this is Mid-World? You weren't with us when we came to that marker."

Jake stuffed his hands in his pockets and looked down at his moccasins. "Dreamed it," he said briefly. "You don't think I booked this trip with my dad's travel-agent, do you?"

Roland touched Eddie's shoulder. "Let it alone for now." Eddie glanced briefly at Roland and nodded.

They stood looking at the bridge a little longer. They'd had time to get used to the city skyline, but this was something new. It dreamed in the distance, a faint shape sketched against the blue midmorning sky. Roland could make out four sets of impossibly tall metal towers—one set at each end of the bridge and two in the middle. Between them, gigantic cables swooped through the air in long arcs. Between these arcs and the base of the bridge were many vertical lines—either more cables or metal beams, he could not tell which. But he also saw gaps, and realized after a long time that the bridge was no longer perfectly level.

"Yonder bridge is going to be in the river soon, I think," Roland said.

"Well, maybe," Eddie said reluctantly, "but it doesn't really look that bad to me."

Roland sighed. "Don't hope for too much, Eddie."

"What's that supposed to mean?" Eddie heard the touchiness in his voice, but it was too late to do anything about it now.

"It means that I want you to believe your eyes, Eddie—that's all. There was a saying when I was growing up: 'Only a fool believes he's dreaming before he wakes up.' Do you understand?"

Eddie felt a sarcastic reply on his tongue and banished it after a brief struggle. It was just that Roland had a way—it was unintentional, he was sure, but that didn't make it any easier to deal with—of making him feel like such a *kid*.

"I guess I do," he said at last. "It means the same thing as my mother's favorite saying."

"And what was that?"

"Hope for the best and expect the worst," Eddie said sourly.

Roland's face lightened in a smile. "I think I like your mother's saying better."

"But it *is* still standing!" Eddie burst out. "I agree it's not in such fantastic shape—probably nobody's done a really thorough maintenance check on it for a thousand years or so—but it *is* still there. The whole city is! Is it so wrong to hope we might find some things that'll help us there? Or some people that'll feed us and talk to us, like the old folks back in River Crossing, instead of shooting at us? Is it so wrong to hope our luck might be turning?"

In the silence which followed, Eddie realized with embarrassment that he had been making a speech.

"No." There was a kindness in Roland's voice—that kindness which always surprised Eddie when it came. "It's never wrong to hope." He looked around at Eddie and the others like a man coming out of a deep dream. "We're done travelling for today. It's

time we had our own palaver, I think, and it's going
to take awhile."

The gunslinger left the road and walked into the
high grass without looking back. After a moment, the
other three followed.

18

UNTIL THEY MET THE old people in River Crossing,
Susannah had seen Roland strictly in terms of television shows she rarely watched: *Cheyenne*, *The Rifle-
man*, and, of course, the archetype of them all,
Gunsmoke. That was one she had sometimes listened
to on the radio with her father before it came on TV
(she thought of how foreign the idea of radio drama
would be to Eddie and Jake and smiled—Roland's
was not the only world which had moved on). She
could still remember what the narrator said at the beginning of every one of those radio playlets: "It makes
a man watchful . . . and a little lonely."

Until River Crossing, that had summed Roland up
perfectly for her. He was not broad-shouldered, as
Marshal Dillon had been, nor anywhere near as tall,
and his face seemed to her more that of a tired poet
than a wild-west lawman, but she had still seen him
as an existential version of that make-believe Kansas
peace officer, whose only mission in life (other than
an occasional drink in The Longbranch with his
friends Doc and Kitty) had been to Clean Up Dodge.

Now she understood that Roland had once been
much more than a cop riding a Dalíesque range at the
end of the world. He had been a diplomat; a media-
tor; perhaps even a teacher. Most of all, he had been
a soldier of what these people called "the White," by
which she guessed they meant the civilizing forces that
kept people from killing each other enough of the time
to allow some sort of progress. In his time he had

been more wandering knight-errant than bounty hunter. And in many ways, this still *was* his time; the people of River Crossing had certainly thought so. Why else would they have knelt in the dust to receive his blessing?

In light of this new perception, Susannah could see how cleverly the gunslinger had managed them since that awful morning in the speaking ring. Each time they had begun a line of conversation which would lead to the comparing of notes—and what could be more natural, given the cataclysmic and inexplicable "drawing" each of them had experienced?—Roland had been there, stepping in quickly and turning the conversation into other channels so smoothly that none of them (even she, who had spent almost four years up to her neck in the civil-rights movement) had noticed what he was doing.

Susannah thought she understood why—he had done it in order to give Jake time to heal. But understanding his motives didn't change her own feelings—astonishment, amusement, chagrin—about how neatly he had handled them. She remembered something Andrew, her chauffeur, had said shortly before Roland had drawn her into this world. Something about President Kennedy being the last gunslinger of the western world. She had scoffed then, but now she thought she understood. There was a lot more JFK than Matt Dillon in Roland. She suspected that Roland possessed little of Kennedy's imagination, but when it came to romance . . . dedication . . . charisma . . .

And guile, she thought. *Don't forget guile.*

She surprised herself by suddenly bursting into laughter.

Roland had seated himself cross-legged. Now he turned toward her, raising his eyebrows. "Something funny?"

"Very. Tell me something—how many languages can you speak?"

The gunslinger thought it over. "Five," he said at

last. "I used to speak the Sellian dialects fairly well, but I believe I've forgotten everything but the curses."

Susannah laughed again. It was a cheerful, delighted sound. "You a fox, Roland," she said. "Indeed you are."

Jake looked interested. "Say a swear in Strelleran," he said.

"Sellian," Roland corrected. He thought a minute, then said something very fast and greasy—to Eddie it sounded a little as if he was gargling with some very thick liquid. Week-old coffee, say. Roland grinned as he said it.

Jake grinned back. "What does it mean?"

Roland put an arm around the boy's shoulders for a moment. "That we have a lot of things to talk about."

19

"WE ARE KA-TET," ROLAND began, "which means a group of people bound together by fate. The philosophers of my land said a *ka-tet* could only be broken by death or treachery. My great teacher, Cort, said that since death and treachery are also spokes on the wheel of *ka*, such a binding can never be broken. As the years pass and I see more, I come more and more to Cort's way of looking at it.

"Each member of a *ka-tet* is like a piece in a puzzle. Taken by itself, each piece is a mystery, but when they are put together, they make a picture . . . or *part* of a picture. It may take a great many *ka-tets* to finish one picture. You mustn't be surprised if you discover your lives have been touching in ways you haven't seen until now. For one thing, each of you three is capable of knowing each other's thoughts—"

"What?" Eddie cried.

"It's true. You share your thoughts so naturally that you haven't even been aware it's happening, but it has been. It's easier for me to see, no doubt, because I am not a full member of this *ka-tet*— possibly because I am not from your world—and so cannot take part completely in the thought-sharing ability. But I *can* send. Susannah . . . do you remember when we were in the circle?"

"Yes. You told me to let the demon go when you told me. But you didn't say that out loud."

"Eddie . . . do you remember when we were in the bear's clearing, and the mechanical bat came at you?"

"Yes. You told me to get down."

"He never opened his mouth, Eddie," Susannah said.

"Yes, you did! You *yelled*! I *heard* you, man!"

"I yelled, all right, but I did it with my *mind*." The gunslinger turned to Jake. "Do you remember? In the house?"

"When the board I was pulling on wouldn't come up, you told me to pull on the other one. But if you can't read my mind, Roland, how did you know what kind of trouble I was in?"

"I *saw*. I heard nothing, but I *saw*—just a little, as if through a dirty window." His eyes surveyed them. "This closeness and sharing of minds is called *khef*, a word that means many other things in the original tongue of the Old World—water, birth, and life-force are only three of them. Be aware of it. For now, that's all I want."

"Can you be aware of something you don't believe in?" Eddie asked.

Roland smiled. "Just keep an open mind."

"That I can do."

"Roland?" It was Jake. "Do you think Oy might be part of our *ka-tet*?"

Susannah smiled. Roland didn't. "I'm not prepared to even guess right now, but I'll tell you this,

Jake—I've been thinking about your furry friend a good deal. *Ka* does not rule all, and coincidences still happen . . . but the sudden appearance of a billy-bumbler that still remembers people doesn't seem completely coincidental to me."

He glanced around at them.

"I'll begin. Eddie will speak next, taking up from the place where I leave off. Then Susannah. Jake, you'll speak last. All right?"

They nodded.

"Fine," Roland said. "We are *ka-tet*—one from many. Let the palaver begin."

20

THE TALK WENT ON until sundown, stopping only long enough for them to eat a cold meal, and by the time it was over, Eddie felt as if he had gone twelve hard rounds with Sugar Ray Leonard. He no longer doubted that they had been "sharing *khef*," as Roland put it; he and Jake actually seemed to have been living each other's life in their dreams, as if they were two halves of the same whole.

Roland began with what had happened under the mountains, where Jake's first life in this world had ended. He told of his own palaver with the man in black, and Walter's veiled words about a Beast and someone he called the Ageless Stranger. He told of the strange, daunting dream which had come to him, a dream in which the whole universe had been swallowed in a beam of fantastic white light. And how, at the end of that dream, there had been a single blade of purple grass.

Eddie glanced sideways at Jake and was stunned by the knowledge—the *recognition*—in the boy's eyes.

21

ROLAND HAD BABBLED PARTS of this story to Eddie in his time of delirium, but it was entirely new to Susannah, and she listened with wide eyes. As Roland repeated the things Walter had told him, she caught glints of her own world, like reflections in a smashed mirror: automobiles, cancer, rockets to the moon, artificial insemination. She had no idea who the Beast might be, but she recognized the name of the Ageless Stranger as a variation upon the name of Merlin, the magician who had supposedly orchestrated the career of King Arthur. Curiouser and curiouser.

Roland told of how he had awakened to find Walter long years dead—time had somehow slipped forward, perhaps a hundred years, perhaps five hundred. Jake listened in fascinated silence as the gunslinger told of reaching the edge of the Western Sea, of how he had lost two of the fingers on his right hand, and how he had drawn Eddie and Susannah before encountering Jack Mort, the dark third.

The gunslinger motioned to Eddie, who took up the tale with the coming of the great bear.

"Shardik?" Jake interjected. "But that's the name of a *book*! A book in *our* world! It was written by the man who wrote that famous book about the rabbits—"

"Richard Adams!" Eddie shouted. "And the book about the bunnies was *Watership Down*! I *knew* I knew that name! But how can that be, Roland? How is it that the people in your world know about things in ours?"

"There are doors, aren't there?" Roland responded. "Haven't we seen four of them already? Do you think they never existed before, or never will again?"

"But—"

"All of us have seen the leavings of your world in mine, and when I was in your city of New York, I saw the marks of my world in yours. I saw *gunslingers*.

Most were lax and slow, but they were gunslingers all the same, clearly members of their own ancient *katet*."

"Roland, they were just cops. You ran rings around them."

"Not the last one. When Jack Mort and I were in the underground railway station, that one almost took me down. Except for blind luck—Mort's flint-and-steel—he would have done. That one . . . I saw his eyes. He knew the face of his father. I believe he knew it very well. And then . . . do you remember the name of Balazar's nightclub?"

"Sure," Eddie said uneasily. "The Leaning Tower. But it could have been coincidence; you yourself said *ka* doesn't rule everything."

Roland nodded. "You really are like Cuthbert—I remember something he said when we were boys. We were planning a midnight lark in the cemetery, but Alain wouldn't go. He said he was afraid of offending the shades of his fathers and mothers. Cuthbert laughed at him. He said he wouldn't believe in ghosts until he caught one in his teeth."

"Good for him!" Eddie exclaimed. "Bravo!"

Roland smiled. "I thought you'd like that. At any rate, let's leave this ghost for now. Go on with your story."

Eddie told of the vision which had come to him when Roland threw the jawbone into the fire—the vision of the key and the rose. He told of his dream, and how he had walked through the door of Tom and Gerry's Artistic Deli and into the field of roses which was dominated by the tall, soot-colored Tower. He told of the blackness which had issued from its windows, forming a shape in the sky overhead, speaking directly to Jake now, because Jake was listening with hungry concentration and growing wonder. He tried to convey some sense of the exaltation and terror which had permeated the dream, and saw from their eyes—Jake's most of all—that he was either doing a

better job of that than he could have hoped for . . .
or that they'd had dreams of their own.

He told of following Shardik's backtrail to the Portal of the Bear, and how, when he put his head against
it, he'd found himself remembering the day he had
talked his brother into taking him to Dutch Hill, so
he could see The Mansion. He told about the cup and
the needle, and how the pointing needle had become
unnecessary once they realized they could see the
Beam at work in everything it touched, even the birds
in the sky.

Susannah took up the tale at this point. As she
spoke, telling of how Eddie had begun to carve his
own version of the key, Jake lay back, laced his hands
together behind his head, and watched the clouds run
slowly toward the city on their straight southeasterly
course. The orderly shape they made showed the presence of the Beam as clearly as smoke leaving a chimney shows the direction of the wind.

She finished with the story of how they had finally
hauled Jake into this world, closing the split track of
his and Roland's memories as suddenly and as completely as Eddie had closed the door in the speaking
ring. The only fact she left out was really not a fact
at all—at least, not yet. She'd had no morning sickness, after all, and a single missed period meant nothing by itself. As Roland himself might have said, that
was a tale best left for another day.

Yet as she finished, she found herself wishing she
could forget what Aunt Talitha had said when Jake
told her this was his home now: *Gods pity you, then,
for the sun is going down on this world. It's going
down forever.*

"And now it's your turn, Jake," Roland said.

Jake sat up and looked toward Lud, where the windows of the western towers reflected back the late
afternoon light in golden sheets. "It's all crazy," he
murmured, "but it almost makes sense. Like a dream
when you wake up."

"Maybe we can help you make sense of it," Susannah said.

"Maybe you can. At least you can help me think about the train. I'm tired of trying to make sense of Blaine by myself." He sighed. "You know what Roland went through, living two lives at the same time, so I can skip that part. I'm not sure I could ever explain how it felt, anyway, and I don't want to. It was gross. I guess I better start with my Final Essay, because that's when I finally stopped thinking that the whole thing might just go away." He looked around at them somberly. "That was when I gave up."

22

JAKE TALKED THE SUN down.

He told them everything he could remember, beginning with *My Understanding of Truth* and ending with the monstrous doorkeeper which had literally come out of the woodwork to attack him. The other three listened without a single interruption.

When he was finished, Roland turned to Eddie, his eyes bright with a mixture of emotions Eddie initially took for wonder. Then he realized he was looking at powerful excitement . . . and deep fear. His mouth went dry. Because if *Roland* was afraid—

"Do you still doubt that our worlds overlap each other, Eddie?"

He shook his head. "Of course not. I walked down the same street, *and I did it in his clothes*! But . . . Jake, can I see that book? *Charlie the Choo-Choo?*"

Jake reached for his pack, but Roland stayed his hand. "Not yet," he said. "Go back to the vacant lot, Jake. Tell that part once more. Try to remember everything."

"Maybe you should hypnotize me," Jake said hesitantly. "Like you did before, at the way station."

Roland shook his head. "There's no need. What happened to you in that lot was the most important thing ever to happen in your life, Jake. In all our lives. You can remember everything."

So Jake went through it again. It was clear to all of them that his experience in the vacant lot where Tom and Gerry's once had stood was the secret heart of the *ka-tet* they shared. In Eddie's dream, the Artistic Deli had still been standing; in Jake's reality it had been torn down, but in both cases it was a place of enormous, talismanic power. Nor did Roland doubt that the vacant lot with its broken bricks and shattered glass was another version of what Susannah knew as the Drawers and the place he had seen at the end of his vision in the place of bones.

As he told this part of his story for the second time, speaking very slowly now, Jake found that what the gunslinger had said was true: he *could* remember everything. His recall improved until he almost seemed to be reliving the experience. He told them of the sign which said that a building called Turtle Bay Condominiums was slated to stand on the spot where Tom and Gerry's had once stood. He even remembered the little poem which had been spray-painted on the fence, and recited it for them:

"See the TURTLE of enormous girth!
On his shell he holds the earth.
If you want to run and play,
Come along the BEAM today."

Susannah murmured, "His thought is slow but always kind; He holds us all within his mind . . . isn't that how it went, Roland?"

"What?" Jake asked. "How what went?"

"A poem I learned as a child," Roland said. "It's another connection, one that really tells us something, although I'm not sure it's anything we need to know

. . . still, one never knows when a little understanding may come in handy."

"Twelve portals connected by six Beams," Eddie said. "We started at the Bear. We're only going as far as the middle—to the Tower—but if we went all the way to the other end, we'd come to the Portal of the Turtle, wouldn't we?"

Roland nodded. "I'm sure we would."

"Portal of the Turtle," Jake said thoughtfully, rolling the words in his mouth, seeming to taste them. Then he finished by telling them again about the gorgeous voice of the choir, his realization that there were faces and stories and histories everywhere, and his growing belief that he had stumbled on something very like the core of all existence. Last of all, he told them again about finding the key and seeing the rose. In the totality of his recall, Jake began to weep, although he seemed unaware of it.

"When it opened," he said, "I saw the middle was the brightest yellow you ever saw in your life. At first I thought it was pollen and it only looked bright because *everything* in that lot looked bright. Even looking at the old candy-wrappers and beer-bottles was like looking at the greatest paintings you ever saw. Only then I realized it was a sun. I know it sounds crazy, but that's what it was. Only it was more than one. It was—"

"It was *all* suns," Roland murmured. "It was everything *real*."

"Yes! And it was *right*—but it was *wrong*, too. I can't explain *how* it was wrong, but it was. It was like two heartbeats, one inside of the other, and the one inside had a disease. Or an infection. And then I fainted."

23

"YOU SAW THE SAME thing at the end of your dream, Roland, didn't you?" Susannah asked. Her voice was soft with awe. "The blade of grass you saw near the end of it . . . you thought that blade was purple because it was splattered with paint."

"You don't understand," Jake said. "It really *was* purple. When I was seeing it the way it really was, it was *purple.* Like no grass I ever saw before. The paint was just camouflage. The way the doorkeeper camouflaged itself to look like an old deserted house."

The sun had reached the horizon. Roland asked Jake if he would now show them *Charlie the Choo-Choo* and then read it to them. Jake handed the book around. Both Eddie and Susannah looked at the cover for a long time.

"I had this book when I was a little kid," Eddie said at last. He spoke in the flat tones of utter surety. "Then we moved from Queens to Brooklyn—I wasn't even four years old—and I lost it. But I remember the picture on the cover. And I felt the same way you do, Jake. I didn't like it. I didn't trust it."

Susannah raised her eyes to look at Eddie. "I had it, too—how could I ever forget the little girl with my name . . . although of course it was my middle name back in those days. And I felt the same way about the train. I didn't like it and I didn't trust it." She tapped the front of the book with her finger before passing it on to Roland. "I thought that smile was a great big fake."

Roland gave it only a cursory glance before returning his eyes to Susannah. "Did you lose yours, too?"

"Yes."

"And I'll bet I know when," Eddie said.

Susannah nodded. "I'll bet you do. It was after that man dropped the brick on my head. I had it when we went north to my Aunt Blue's wedding. I had it on the train. I remember, because I kept asking my dad if Charlie the Choo-Choo was pulling us. I didn't *want* it to be Charlie, because we were supposed to go to Elizabeth, New Jersey, and I thought Charlie might take us anywhere. Didn't he end up pulling folks around a toy village or something like that, Jake?"

"An amusement park."

"Yes, of course it was. There's a picture of him hauling kids around that place at the end, isn't there? They're all smiling and laughing, except I always thought they looked like they were screaming to be let off."

"Yes!" Jake cried. "Yes, that's right! That's *just* right!"

"I thought Charlie might take us to *his* place—wherever he lived—instead of to my aunt's wedding, and never let us go home again."

"You can't go home again," Eddie muttered, and ran his hands nervously through his hair.

"All the time we were on that train I wouldn't let go of the book. I even remember thinking, 'If he tries to steal us, I'll rip out his pages until he quits.' But of course we arrived right where we were supposed to, and on time, too. Daddy even took me up front, so I could see the engine. It was a diesel, not a steam engine, and I remember that made me happy. Then, after the wedding, that man Mort dropped the brick on me and I was in a coma for a long time. I never saw *Charlie the Choo-Choo* after that. Not until now." She hesitated, then added: "This could be my copy, for all I know—or Eddie's."

"Yeah, and probably is," Eddie said. His face was pale and solemn . . . and then he grinned like a kid. " 'See the TURTLE, ain't he keen? All things serve the fuckin Beam.' "

Roland glanced west. "The sun's going down. Read the story before we lose the light, Jake."

Jake turned to the first page, showed them the picture of Engineer Bob in Charlie's cab, and began: " 'Bob Brooks was an engineer for The Mid-World Railway Company, on the St. Louis to Topeka run . . .' "

24

" '. . . AND EVERY NOW AND then the children hear him singing his old song in his soft, gruff voice,' " Jake finished. He showed them the last picture—the happy children who might actually have been screaming—and then closed the book. The sun had gone down; the sky was purple.

"Well, it's not a *perfect* fit," Eddie said, "more like a dream where the water sometimes runs uphill—but it fits well enough to scare *me* silly. This is Mid-World—Charlie's territory. Only his name over here isn't Charlie at all. Over here it's Blaine the Mono."

Roland was looking at Jake. "What do you think?" he asked. "Should we go around the city? Stay away from this train?"

Jake thought it over, head down, hands working distractedly through Oy's thick, silky fur. "I'd like to," he said at last, "but if I've got this stuff about *ka* right, I don't think we're supposed to."

Roland nodded. "If it's *ka*, questions of what we're supposed to or not supposed to do aren't even in it; if we tried to go around, we'd find circumstances forcing us back. In such cases it's better to give in to the inevitable promptly instead of putting it off. What do you think, Eddie?"

Eddie thought as long and as carefully as Jake had done. He didn't want anything to do with a talking train that ran by itself, and whether you called it Charlie the Choo-Choo or Blaine the Mono, everything Jake had told them and read them suggested that it might be a very nasty piece of work. But they had a tremendous distance to cross, and somewhere, at the end of it, was the thing they had come to find. And with that thought, Eddie was amazed to discover he knew exactly what he thought, and what he wanted. He raised his head and for almost the first time since he had come to this world, he fixed Roland's faded blue eyes firmly with his hazel ones.

"I want to stand in that field of roses, and I want to see the Tower that stands there. I don't know what comes next. Mourners please omit flowers, probably, and for all of us. But I don't care. I want to stand there. I guess I don't care if Blaine's the devil and the train runs through hell itself on the way to the Tower. I vote we go."

Roland nodded and turned to Susannah.

"Well, I didn't have any dreams about the Dark Tower," she said, "so I can't deal with the question on that level—the level of desire, I suppose you'd say. But I've come to believe in *ka*, and I'm not so numb that I can't feel it when someone starts rapping on my head with his knuckles and saying, 'That way, idiot.' What about you, Roland? What do you think?"

"I think there's been enough talk for one day, and it's time to let it go until tomorrow."

"What about *Riddle-De-Dum!*—" Jake asked, "do you want to look at that?"

"There'll be time enough for that another day," Roland said. "Let's get some sleep."

25

BUT THE GUNSLINGER LAY long awake, and when the rhythmic drumming began again, he got up and walked back to the road. He stood looking toward the bridge and the city. He was every inch the diplomat Susannah had suspected, and he had known the train was the next step on the road they must travel almost from the moment he had heard of it . . . but he'd felt it would be unwise to say so. Eddie in particular hated to feel pushed; when he sensed that was being done, he simply lowered his head, planted his feet, made his silly jokes, and balked like a mule. This time he wanted what Roland wanted, but he was still apt to say day if Roland said night, and night if Roland said day. It was safer to walk softly, and surer to ask instead of telling.

He turned to go back . . . and his hand dropped to his gun as he saw a dark shape standing on the edge of the road, looking at him. He didn't draw, but it was a near thing.

"I wondered if you'd be able to sleep after that little performance," Eddie said. "Guess the answer's no."

"I didn't hear you at all, Eddie. You're learning . . . only this time you almost got a bullet in the gut for your pains."

"You didn't hear me because you have a lot on your mind." Eddie joined him, and even by starlight, Roland saw he hadn't fooled Eddie a bit. His respect for Eddie continued to grow. It was Cuthbert Eddie reminded him of, but in many ways he had already surpassed Cuthbert.

If I underestimate him, Roland thought, *I'm apt to come away with a bloody paw. And if I let him down, or do something that looks to him like a double-cross, he'll probably try to kill me.*

"What's on *your* mind, Eddie?"

"You. Us. I want you to know something. I guess until tonight I just assumed that you knew already. Now I'm not so sure."

"Tell me, then." He thought again: *How like Cuthbert he is!*

"We're with you because we have to be—that's your goddamned *ka*. But we're also with you because we *want* to be. I know that's true of me and Susannah, and I'm pretty sure it's true of Jake, too. You've got a good brain, me old *khef*-mate, but I think you must keep it in a bomb-shelter, because it's bitchin hard to get through sometimes. I want to see it, Roland. Can you dig what I'm telling you? *I want to see the Tower.*" He looked closely into Roland's face, apparently did not see what he'd hoped to find there, and raised his hands in exasperation. "What I mean is I want you to let go of my ears."

"Let go of your ears?"

"Yeah. Because you don't have to drag me any-more. I'm coming of my own accord. *We're* coming of our own accord. If you died in your sleep tonight, we'd bury you and then go on. We probably wouldn't last long, but we'd die in the path of the Beam. *Now* do you understand?"

"Yes. Now I do."

"You say you understand me, and I think you do . . . but do you believe me, as well?"

Of course, he thought. *Where else do you have to go, Eddie, in this world that's so strange to you? And what else could you do? You'd make a piss-poor farmer.*

But that was mean and unfair, and he knew it. Denigrating free will by confusing it with *ka* was worse than blasphemy; it was tiresome and stupid. "Yes," he said. "I believe you. Upon my soul, I do."

"Then stop behaving like we're a bunch of sheep and you're the shepherd walking along behind us, waving a crook to make sure we don't trot our stupid selves off the road and into a quicksand bog. Open your mind to us. If we're going to die in the city or on that train, I want to die knowing I was more than a marker on your game-board."

Roland felt anger heat his cheeks, but he had never been much good at self-deception. He wasn't angry because Eddie was wrong but because Eddie had seen through him. Roland had watched him come steadily forward, leaving his prison further and further be-hind—and Susannah, too, for she had also been im-prisoned—and yet his heart had never quite accepted the evidence of his senses. His heart apparently wanted to go on seeing them as different, lesser creatures.

Roland drew in deep air. "Gunslinger, I cry your pardon."

Eddie nodded. "We're running into a whole hurri-cane of trouble here . . . I feel it, and I'm scared to death. But it's not *your* trouble, it's *our* trouble. Okay?"

"Yes."

"How bad do you think it can get in the city?"

"I don't know. I only know that we have to try and protect Jake, because the old auntie said both sides would want him. Some of it depends on how long it takes us to find this train. A lot more depends on what happens when we find it. If we had two more in our party, I'd put Jake in a moving box with guns on every side of him. Since we don't, we'll move in column—me first, Jake pushing Susannah behind, and you on drogue."

"How much trouble, Roland? Make a guess."

"I can't."

"I think you can. You don't know the city, but you know how the people in your world have been behaving since things started to fall apart. How much trouble?"

Roland turned toward the steady sound of the drumbeats and thought it over. "Maybe not too much. I'd guess the fighting men who are still there are old and demoralized. It may be that you have the straight of it, and some will even offer to help us on our way, as the River Crossing *ka-tet* did. Mayhap we won't see them at all—they'll see *us*, see we're packing iron, and just put their heads down and let us go our way. If that fails, I'm hoping that they'll scatter like rats if we gun a few."

"And if they decide to make a fight of it?"

Roland smiled grimly. "Then, Eddie, we'll *all* remember the faces of our fathers."

Eddie's eyes gleamed in the darkness, and Roland was once more reminded forcibly of Cuthbert—Cuthbert who had once said he would believe in ghosts when he could catch one in his teeth, Cuthbert with whom he had once scattered breadcrumbs beneath the hangman's gibbet.

"Have I answered all your questions?"

STEPHEN KING

"Nope—but I think you played straight with me this time."

"Then goodnight, Eddie."

"Goodnight."

Eddie turned and walked away. Roland watched him go. Now that he was listening, he could hear him . . . but just barely. He started back himself, then turned toward the darkness where the city of Lud was.

He's what the old woman called a Pube. She said both sides would want him.

You won't let me drop this time?

No. Not this time, not ever again.

But he knew something none of the others did. Perhaps, after the talk he'd just had with Eddie, he should tell them . . . yet he thought he would keep the knowledge to himself a little while longer.

In the old tongue which had once been his world's *lingua franca,* most words, like *khef* and *ka,* had many meanings. The word *char,* however—*char* as in Charlie the Choo-Choo—had only one.

Char meant death.

V ■ BRIDGE AND CITY

▪ V ▪

BRIDGE AND CITY

1

THEY CAME UPON THE downed airplane three days later.

Jake pointed it out first at midmorning—a flash of light about ten miles away, as if a mirror lay in the grass. As they drew closer, they saw a large dark object at the side of the Great Road.

"It looks like a dead bird," Roland said. "A big one."

"That's no bird," Eddie said. "That's an airplane. I'm pretty sure the glare is sunlight bouncing off the canopy."

An hour later they stood silently at the edge of the road, looking at the ancient wreck. Three plump crows stood on the tattered skin of the fuselage, staring insolently at the newcomers. Jake pried a cobble from the edge of the road and shied it at them. The crows lumbered into the air, cawing indignantly.

One wing had broken off in the crash and lay thirty yards away, a shadow like a diving board in the tall grass. The rest of the plane was pretty much intact. The canopy had cracked in a starburst pattern where the pilot's head had struck it. There was a large, rust-colored stain there.

Oy trotted over to where three rusty propeller blades rose from the grass, sniffed at them, then returned hastily to Jake.

The man in the cockpit was a dust-dry mummy wearing a padded leather vest and a helmet with a spike on top. His lips were gone, his teeth exposed in a final desperate grimace. Fingers which had once been as large as sausages but were now only skin-covered bones clutched the wheel. His skull was caved in where it had hit the canopy, and Roland guessed that the greenish-gray scales which coated the left side of his face were all that remained of his brains. The dead man's head was tilted back, as if he had been sure, even at the moment of his death, that he could regain the sky again. The plane's remaining wing still jutted from the encroaching grass. On it was a fading insignia which depicted a fist holding a thunderbolt.

"Looks like Aunt Talitha was wrong and the old albino man had the right of it, after all," Susannah said in an awed voice. "That must be David Quick, the outlaw prince. Look at the size of him, Roland—they must have had to grease him to get him into the cockpit!"

Roland nodded. The heat and the years had wasted the man in the mechanical bird to no more than a skeleton wrapped in dry hide, but he could still see how broad the shoulders had been, and the misshapen head was massive. "So fell Lord Perth," he said, "and the countryside did shake with that thunder."

Jake looked at him questioningly.

"It's from an old poem. Lord Perth was a giant who went forth to war with a thousand men, but he was still in his own country when a little boy threw a stone at him and hit him in the knee. He stumbled, the weight of his armor bore him down, and he broke his neck in the fall."

Jake said, "Like our story of David and Goliath."

"There was no fire," Eddie said. "I bet he just ran out of gas and tried a dead-stick landing on the road. He might have been an outlaw and a barbarian, but he had a yard of guts."

Roland nodded, and looked at Jake. "You all right with this?"

"Yes. If the guy was still, you know, runny, I might not be." Jake looked from the dead man in the airplane to the city. Lud was much closer and clearer now, and although they could see many broken windows in the towers, he, like Eddie, had not entirely given up hope of finding some sort of help there. "I bet things sort of fell apart in the city once he was gone."

"I think you'd win that bet," Roland said.

"You know something?" Jake was studying the plane again. "The people who built that city might have made their own airplanes, but I'm pretty sure this is one of ours. I did a school paper on air combat when I was in the fifth grade, and I think I recognize it. Roland, can I take a closer look?"

Roland nodded. "I'll go with you."

Together they walked over to the plane with the high grass swishing at their pants. "Look," Jake said. "See the machine-gun under the wing? That's an air-cooled German model, and this is a Focke-Wulf from just before World War II. I'm sure it is. So what's it doing here?"

"Lots of planes disappear," Eddie said. "Take the Bermuda Triangle, for instance. That's a place over one of our oceans, Roland. It's supposed to be jinxed. Maybe it's a great big doorway between our worlds—one that's almost always open." Eddie hunched his shoulders and essayed a bad Rod Serling imitation. "Fasten your seatbelts and prepare for turbulence: you're flying into . . . the Roland Zone!"

Jake and Roland, who were now standing beneath the plane's remaining wing, ignored him.

"Boost me up, Roland."

Roland shook his head. "That wing looks solid, but it's not—this thing has been here a long time, Jake. You'd fall."

"Make a step, then."

Eddie said, "I'll do it, Roland."

Roland studied his diminished right hand for a moment, shrugged, then laced his hands together. "This'll do. He's light."

Jake shook off his moccasin and then stepped lightly into the stirrup Roland had made. Oy began to bark shrilly, though whether in excitement or alarm, Roland couldn't tell.

Jake's chest was now pressing against one of the airplane's rusty flaps, and he was looking right at the fist-and-thunderbolt design. It had peeled up a little from the surface of the wing along one edge. He seized this flap and pulled. It came off the wing so easily that he would have fallen backward if Eddie, standing directly behind him, hadn't steadied him with a hand on the butt.

"I *knew* it," Jake said. There was another symbol beneath the fist-and-thunderbolt, and now it was almost totally revealed. It was a swastika. "I just wanted to see it. You can put me down now."

They started out again, but they could see the tail of the plane every time they looked back that afternoon, looming out of the high grass like Lord Perth's burial monument.

2

IT WAS JAKE'S TURN to make the fire that night. When the wood was laid to the gunslinger's satisfaction, he handed Jake his flint and steel. "Let's see how you do."

Eddie and Susannah were sitting off to one side, their arms linked companionably about each other's

waist. Toward the end of the day, Eddie had found a
bright yellow flower beside the road and had picked
it for her. Tonight Susannah was wearing it in her
hair, and every time she looked at Eddie, her lips
curved in a small smile and her eyes filled with light.
Roland had noted these things, and they pleased him.
Their love was deepening, strengthening. That was
good. It would have to be deep and strong indeed if
it was to survive the months and years ahead.

Jake struck a spark, but it flashed inches away from
the kindling.

"Move your flint in closer," Roland said, "and hold
it steady. And don't *hit* it with the steel, Jake; *scrape*
it."

Jake tried again, and this time the spark flashed
directly into the kindling. There was a little tendril of
smoke but no fire.

"I don't think I'm very good at this."

"You'll get it. Meantime, think on this. What's
dressed when night falls and undressed when day
breaks?"

"Huh?"

Roland moved Jake's hands even closer to the little
pile of kindling. "I guess that one's not in your book."

"Oh, it's a riddle!" Jake struck another spark. This
time a small flame glowed in the kindling before dying
out. "You know some of those, too?"

Roland nodded. "Not just some—a lot. As a boy,
I must have known a thousand. They were part of my
studies."

"Really? Why would anyone study riddles?"

"Vannay, my tutor, said a boy who could answer a
riddle was a boy who could think around corners. We
had riddling contests every Friday noon, and the boy
or girl who won could leave school early."

"Did you get to leave early often, Roland?" Susannah asked.

He shook his head, smiling a little himself. "I enjoyed riddling, but I was never very good at it. Van-

nay said it was because I thought too deeply. My father said it was because I had too little imagination. I think they were both right . . . but I think my father had a little more of the truth. I could always haul a gun faster than any of my mates, and shoot straighter, but I've never been much good at thinking around corners."

Susannah, who had watched closely as Roland dealt with the old people of River Crossing, thought the gunslinger was underrating himself, but she said nothing.

"Sometimes, on winter nights, there would be riddling competitions in the great hall. When it was just the younkers, Alain always won. When the grownups played as well, it was always Cort. He'd forgotten more riddles than the rest of us ever knew, and after the Fair-Day Riddling, Cort always carried home the goose. Riddles have great power, and everyone knows one or two."

"Even me," Eddie said. "For instance, why did the dead baby cross the road?"

"That's dumb, Eddie," Susannah said, but she was smiling.

"Because it was stapled to the chicken!" Eddie yelled, and grinned when Jake burst into laughter, knocking his little pile of kindling apart. "Hyuk, hyuk, hyuk, I got a million of em, folks!"

Roland, however, didn't laugh. He looked, in fact, a trifle offended. "Pardon me for saying so, Eddie, but that *is* rather silly."

"Jesus, Roland, I'm sorry," Eddie said. He was still smiling, but he sounded slightly peeved. "I keep forgetting you got your sense of humor shot off in the Children's Crusade, or whatever it was."

"It's just that I take riddling seriously. I was taught that the ability to solve them indicates a sane and rational mind."

"Well, they're never going to replace the works of Shakespeare or the Quadratic Equation," Eddie said. "I mean, let's not get carried away."

Jake was looking at Roland thoughtfully. "My book said riddling is the oldest game people still play. In our world, I mean. And riddles used to be really serious business, not just jokes. People used to get killed over them."

Roland was looking out into the growing darkness. "Yes. I've seen it happen." He was remembering a Fair-Day Riddling which had ended not with the giving of the prize goose but with a cross-eyed man in a cap of bells dying in the dirt with a dagger in his chest. Cort's dagger. The man had been a wandering singer and acrobat who had attempted to cheat Cort by stealing the judge's pocket-book, in which the answers were kept on small scraps of bark.

"Well, excyoooose *me*," Eddie said.

Susannah was looking at Jake. "I forgot all about the book of riddles you carried over. May I look at it now?"

"Sure. It's in my pack. The answers are gone, though. Maybe that's why Mr. Tower gave it to me for fr—"

His shoulder was suddenly seized, and with painful force.

"*What* was his name?" Roland asked.

"Mr. Tower," Jake said. "Calvin Tower. Didn't I tell you that?"

"No." Roland slowly relaxed his grip on Jake's shoulder. "But now that I hear it, I suppose I'm not surprised."

Eddie had opened Jake's pack and found *Riddle-De-Dum!* He tossed it to Susannah. "You know," he said, "I always thought that dead-baby joke was pretty good. Tasteless, maybe, but pretty good."

"I don't care about taste," Roland said. "It's senseless and unsolvable, and that's what makes it silly. A good riddle is neither."

"Jesus! You guys *did* take this stuff seriously, didn't you?"

"Yes."

Jake, meanwhile, had been restacking the kindling
and mulling over the riddle which had started the discussion. Now he suddenly smiled. "A fire. That's the
answer, right? Dress it at night, undress it in the
morning. If you change 'dress' to 'build,' it's simple."

"That's it." Roland returned Jake's smile, but his
eyes were on Susannah, watching as she thumbed
through the small, tattered book. He thought, looking
at her studious frown and the absent way she read-
justed the yellow flower in her hair when it tried to
slip free, that she alone might sense that the tattered
book of riddles could be as important as *Charlie the
Choo-Choo* . . . maybe more important. He looked
from her to Eddie and felt a recurrence of his irrita-
tion at Eddie's foolish riddle. The young man bore
another resemblance to Cuthbert, this one rather unfortunate: Roland sometimes felt like shaking him
until his nose bled and his teeth fell out.

Soft, gunslinger—soft! Cort's voice, not quite laughing, spoke up in his head, and Roland resolutely put
his emotions at arm's length. It was easier to do that
when he remembered that Eddie couldn't help his occasional forays into nonsense; character was also at
least partly formed by *ka,* and Roland knew well that
there was more to Eddie than nonsense. Anytime he
started to make the mistake of thinking that wasn't
so, he would do well to remember their conversation
by the side of the road three nights before, when
Eddie had accused him of using them as markers on
his own private game-board. That had angered him
. . . but it had been close enough to the truth to shame
him, as well.

Blissfully unaware of these long thoughts, Eddie
now inquired: "What's green, weighs a hundred tons,
and lives at the bottom of the ocean?"

"I know," Jake said. "Moby Snot, the Great Green
Whale."

"Idiocy," Roland muttered.

"Yeah—but that's what's supposed to make it

funny," Eddie said. "*Jokes* are supposed to make you
think around corners, too. You see . . ." He looked
at Roland's face, laughed, and threw up his hands.
"Never mind. I give up. You wouldn't understand.
Not in a million years. Let's look at the damned book.
I'll even try to take it seriously . . . if we can eat a
little supper first, that is."

"Watch Me," the gunslinger said with a flicker of a
smile.

"Huh?"

"That means you have a deal."

Jake scraped the steel across the flint. A spark
jumped, and this time the kindling caught fire. He sat
back contentedly and watched the flames spread, one
arm slung around Oy's neck. He felt well pleased with
himself. He had started the evening fire . . . and he
had guessed the answer to Roland's riddle.

3

"I'VE GOT ONE," JAKE said as they ate their evening
burritos.

"Is it a foolish one?" Roland asked.

"Nah. It's a real one."

"Then try me with it."

"Okay. What can run but never walks, has a mouth
but never talks, has a bed but never sleeps, has a head
but never weeps?"

"A good one," Roland said kindly, "but an old one.
A river."

Jake was a little crestfallen. "You really *are* hard to
stump."

Roland tossed the last bite of his burrito to Oy, who
accepted it eagerly. "Not me. I'm what Eddie calls an
overpush. You should have seen Alain. He collected
riddles the way a lady collects fans."

"That's pushover, Roland, old buddy," Eddie said.

"Thank you. Try this one: What lies in bed, and

stands in bed?/ First white, then red/ The plumper it gets/ The better the old woman likes it?"

Eddie burst out laughing. "A dork!" he yelled. "Crude, Roland! But I like it! I *liyyyke* it!"

Roland shook his head. "Your answer is wrong. A good riddle is sometimes a puzzle in words, like Jake's about the river, but sometimes it's more like a magician's trick, making you look in one direction while it's going somewhere else."

"It's a double," Jake said. He explained what Aaron Deepneau had said about the Riddle of Samson. Roland nodded.

"Is it a strawberry?" Susannah asked, then answered her own question. "Of course it is. It's like the fire-riddle. There's a metaphor hidden inside it. Once you understand the metaphor, you can solve the riddle."

"I metaphor sex, but she slapped my face and walked away when I asked," Eddie told them sadly. They all ignored him.

"If you change 'gets' to 'grows,' " Susannah went on, "it's easy. First white, then red. Plumper it grows, the better the old woman likes it." She looked pleased with herself.

Roland nodded. "The answer I always heard was a wenberry, but I'm sure both answers mean the same thing."

Eddie picked up *Riddle-De-Dum!* and began flipping through it. "How about this one, Roland? When is a door not a door?"

Roland frowned. "Is it another piece of your stupidity? Because my patience—"

"No. I promised to take it seriously, and I am—I'm *trying*, at least. It's in this book, and I just happen to know the answer. I heard it when I was a kid."

Jake, who also knew the answer, winked at Eddie. Eddie winked back, and was amused to see Oy also trying to wink. The bumbler kept shutting both eyes, and eventually gave up.

Roland and Susannah, meanwhile, were puzzling over the question. "It must have something to do with love," Roland said. "A door, adore. When is adore not adore . . . hmmm . . ."

"Hmmm," Oy said. His imitation of Roland's thoughtful tone was perfect. Eddie winked at Jake again. Jake covered his mouth to hide a smile.

"Is the answer false love?" Roland asked at last.

"Nope."

"Window," Susannah said suddenly and decisively. "When is a door not a door? When it's a window."

"Nope." Eddie was grinning broadly now, but Jake was struck by how far from the real answer both of them had wandered. There was magic at work here, he thought. Pretty common stuff, as magic went, no flying carpets or disappearing elephants, but magic, all the same. He suddenly saw what they were doing—a simple game of riddles around a campfire—in an entirely new light. It was like playing blind-man's bluff, only in this game the blindfold was made of words.

"I give up," Susannah said.

"Yes," Roland said. "Tell if you know."

"The answer is a jar. A door is not a door when it's ajar. Get it?" Eddie watched as comprehension dawned on Roland's face and asked, a little apprehensively, "*Is* it a bad one? I was trying to be serious this time, Roland—really."

"Not bad at all. On the contrary, it's quite good. Cort would have gotten it, I'm sure . . . probably Alain, too, it's still very clever. I did what I always used to do in the schoolroom: made it more complicated than it really was and shot right past the answer."

"There really is something to it, isn't there?" Eddie mused. Roland nodded, but Eddie didn't see; he was looking into the depths of the fire, where dozens of roses bloomed and faded in the coals.

Roland said, "One more, and we'll turn in. Only

from tonight on, we'll stand a watch. You first, Eddie, then Susannah. I'll take the last one."

"What about me?" Jake asked.

"Later on you may have to take a turn. Right now it's more important for you to get your sleep."

"Do you really think sentry-duty is necessary?" Susannah asked.

"I don't know. And that's the best reason of all to do it. Jake, choose us a riddle from your book."

Eddie handed *Riddle-De-Dum!* to Jake, who thumbed through the pages and finally stopped near the back. "Whoa! This one's a killer."

"Let's hear it," Eddie said. "If I don't get it, Suze will. We're known at Fair-Days all across the land as Eddie Dean and His Riddling Queen."

"We're witty tonight, ain't we?" Susannah said. "Let's see how witty you are after settin by the side o' the road until midnight or so, honeychild."

Jake read: " 'There is a thing that nothing is, and yet it has a name. It's sometimes tall and sometimes short, joins our talks, joins our sport, and plays at every game.' "

They discussed this riddle for almost fifteen minutes, but none of them could even hazard an answer.

"Maybe it'll come to one of us while we're asleep," Jake said. "That's how I got the one about the river."

"Cheap book, with the answers torn out," Eddie said. He stood up and wrapped a hide blanket around his shoulders like a cloak.

"Well, it *was* cheap. Mr. Tower gave it to me for free."

"What am I looking for, Roland?" Eddie asked.

Roland shrugged as he lay down. "I don't know, but I think you'll know it if you see it or hear it."

"Wake me up when you start feeling sleepy," Susannah said.

"You better believe it."

4

A GRASSY DITCH RAN along the side of the road and
Eddie sat on the far side of it with his blanket around
his shoulders. A thin scud of clouds had veiled the sky
tonight, dimming the starshow. A strong west wind
was blowing. When Eddie turned his face in that direction, he could clearly smell the buffalo which now
owned these plains—a mixed perfume of hot fur and
fresh dung. The clarity which had returned to his
senses in these last few months was amazing . . . and,
at times like these, a little spooky, as well.

Very faintly, he could hear a buffalo calf bawling.

He turned toward the city, and after a while he
began to think he might be seeing distant sparks of
light there—the electric candles of the twins' story—
but he was well aware that he might be seeing nothing
more than his own wishful thinking.

*You're a long way from Forty-second Street, sweet-
heart—hope is a great thing, no matter what anyone
says, but don't hope so hard you lose sight of that one
thought: you're a long way from Forty-second Street.
That's not New York up ahead, no matter how much
you might wish it was. That's Lud, and it'll be whatever
it is. And if you keep that in mind, maybe you'll be
okay.*

He passed his time on watch trying to think of an
answer to the last riddle of the evening. The scolding
Roland had given him about his dead-baby joke had
left him feeling disgruntled, and it would please him
to be able to start off the morning by giving them a
good answer. Of course they wouldn't be able to
check *any* answer against the back of the book, but
he had an idea that with good riddles a good answer
was usually self-evident.

Sometimes tall and sometimes short. He thought that
was the key and all the rest was probably just misdirection. What *was* sometimes tall and sometimes
short? Pants? No. Pants were sometimes short and

sometimes long, but he had never heard of tall pants. Tales? Like pants, it only fit snugly one way. *Drinks* were sometimes both tall and short—

"Order," he murmured, and thought for a moment that he must have stumbled across the solution—both adjectives fit the noun glove-tight. A tall order was a big job; a short order was something you got on the quick in a restaurant—a hamburger or a tuna melt. Except that tall orders and tuna melts didn't *join our talk* or *play at every game*.

He felt a rush of frustration and had to smile at himself, getting all wound up about a harmless word-game in a kid's book. All the same, he found it a little easier to believe that people might really kill each other over riddles . . . if the stakes were high enough and cheating was involved.

Let it go—you're doing exactly what Roland said, thinking right past it.

Still, what else did he have to think about?

Then the drumming from the city began again, and he did have something else. There was no build-up; at one moment it wasn't there, and at the next it was going full force, as if a switch had been turned. Eddie walked to the edge of the road, turned toward the city, and listened. After a few moments he looked around to see if the drums had awakened the others, but he was still alone. He turned toward Lud again and cupped his ears forward with the sides of his hands.

Bump . . . ba-bump . . . ba-bump-bumpbump-bump.

Bump . . . ba-bump . . . ba-bump-bumpbump-bump.

Eddie became more and more sure that he had been right about what it was; that he had, at least, solved this riddle.

Bump . . . ba-bump . . . ba-bump-bumpbump-bump.

The idea that he was standing by a deserted road

in an almost empty world, standing some one hundred and seventy miles from a city which had been built by some fabulous lost civilization and listening to a rock-and-roll drum-line . . . that was crazy, but was it any crazier than a traffic-light that dinged and dropped a rusty green flag with the word GO printed on it? Any crazier than discovering the wreck of a German plane from the 1930s?

Eddie sang the words to the Z.Z. Top song in a whisper:

> *"You need just enough of that sticky stuff*
> *To hold the seam on your fine blue-jeans*
> *I say yeah, yeah . . ."*

They fit the beat perfectly. It was the disco-pulse percussion of "Velcro Fly." Eddie was sure of it.

A short time later the sound ceased as suddenly as it had begun, and he could hear only the wind, and, more faintly, the Send River, which had a bed but never slept.

5

THE NEXT FOUR DAYS were uneventful. They walked; they watched the bridge and the city grow larger and define themselves more clearly; they camped; they ate; they riddled; they kept watch turn and turn about (Jake had pestered Roland into letting him keep a short watch in the two hours just before dawn); they slept. The only remarkable incident had to do with the bees.

Around noon on the third day after the discovery of the downed plane, a buzzing sound came to them, growing louder and louder until it dominated the day. At last Roland stopped. "There," he said, and pointed toward a grove of eucalyptus trees.

"It sounds like bees," Susannah said.

Roland's faded blue eyes gleamed. "Could be we'll have a little dessert tonight."

"I don't know how to tell you this, Roland," Eddie said, "but I have this aversion to being stung."

"Don't we all," Roland agreed, "but the day is windless. I think we can smoke them to sleep and steal their comb right out from under them without setting half the world on fire. Let's have a look."

He carried Susannah, who was as eager for the adventure as the gunslinger himself, toward the grove. Eddie and Jake lagged behind, and Oy, apparently having decided that discretion was the better part of valor, remained sitting at the edge of the Great Road, panting like a dog and watching them carefully.

Roland paused at the edge of the trees. "Stay where you are," he told Eddie and Jake, speaking softly. "We're going to have a look. I'll give you a come-on if all's well." He carried Susannah into the dappled shadows of the grove while Eddie and Jake remained in the sunshine, peering after them.

It was cooler in the shade. The buzzing of the bees was a steady, hypnotic drone. "There are too many," Roland murmured. "This is late summer; they should be out working. I don't—"

He caught sight of the hive, bulging tumorously from the hollow of a tree in the center of the clearing, and broke off.

"What's the matter with them?" Susannah asked in a soft, horrified voice. "Roland, what's the *matter* with them?"

A bee, as plump and slow-moving as a horsefly in October, droned past her head. Susannah flinched away from it.

Roland motioned for the others to join them. They did, and stood looking at the hive without speaking. The chambers weren't neat hexagons but random holes of all shapes and sizes; the beehive itself looked queerly melted, as if someone had turned a blowtorch on it. The bees which crawled sluggishly over it were as white as snow.

"No honey tonight," Roland said. "What we took from yonder comb might taste sweet, but it would poison us as surely as night follows day."

One of the grotesque white bees lumbered heavily past Jake's head. He ducked away with an expression of loathing.

"What did it?" Eddie asked. "What did it to them, Roland?"

"The same thing that has emptied this whole land; the thing that's still causing many of the buffalo to be born as sterile freaks. I've heard it called the Old War, the Great Fire, the Cataclysm, and the Great Poisoning. Whatever it was, it was the start of all our troubles and it happened long ago, a thousand years before the great-great-grandfathers of the River Crossing folk were born. The physical effects—the two-headed buffalo and the white bees and such—have grown less as time passes. I have seen this for myself. The other changes are greater, if harder to see, and they are still going on."

They watched the white bees crawl, dazed and almost completely helpless, about their hive. Some were apparently trying to work; most simply wandered about, butting heads and crawling over one another. Eddie found himself remembering a newsclip he'd seen once. It had shown a crowd of survivors leaving the area where a gas-main had exploded, flattening almost a whole city block in some California town. These bees reminded him of those dazed, shellshocked survivors.

"You had a nuclear war, didn't you?" he asked—almost accused. "These Great Old Ones you like to talk about . . . they blew their great old asses straight to hell. Didn't they?"

"I don't *know* what happened. No one knows. The records of those times are lost, and the few stories are confused and conflicting."

"Let's get out of here," Jake said in a trembling voice. "Looking at those things makes me sick."

"I'm with you, sugar," Susannah said.

So they left the bees to their aimless, shattered life in the grove of ancient trees, and there was no honey that night.

6

"WHEN ARE YOU GOING to tell us what you *do* know?" Eddie asked the next morning. The day was bright and blue, but there was a bite in the air; their first autumn in this world was almost upon them.

Roland glanced at him. "What do you mean?"

"I'd like to hear your whole story, from beginning to end, starting with Gilead. How you grew up there and what happened to end it all. I want to know how you found out about the Dark Tower and why you started chasing after it in the first place. I want to know about your first bunch of friends, too. And what happened to them."

Roland removed his hat, armed sweat from his brow, then replaced it. "You have the right to know all those things, I suppose, and I'll tell them to you . . . but not now. It's a very long story. I never expected to tell it to anyone, and I'll only tell it once."

"When?" Eddie persisted.

"When the time is right," Roland said, and with that they had to be content.

7

ROLAND CAME AWAKE THE moment before Jake began to shake him. He sat up and looked around, but Eddie and Susannah were still fast asleep and in the first faint light of morning, he could see nothing amiss.

"What is it?" he asked Jake in a low voice.

"I don't know. Fighting, maybe. Come and listen."

Roland threw his blanket aside and followed Jake out to the road. He reckoned they were now only three days' walk from the place where the Send passed in front of the city, and the bridge—built squarely along the path of the Beam—dominated the horizon. Its pronounced tilt was more clearly visible than ever, and he could see at least a dozen gaps where over-stressed cables had snapped like the strings of a lyre.

Tonight the wind blew directly into their faces as they looked toward the city, and the sounds it carried to them were faint but clear.

"*Is* it fighting?" Jake asked.

Roland nodded and held a finger to his lips.

He heard faint shouts, a crash that sounded like some huge object falling, and—of course—the drums. Now there was another crash, this one more musical: the sound of breaking glass.

"Jeepers," Jake whispered, and moved closer to the gunslinger.

Then came the sounds which Roland had hoped not to hear: a fast, sandy rattle of small-arms fire followed by a loud hollow bang—clearly an explosion of some kind. It rolled across the flatlands toward them like an invisible bowling ball. After that, the shouts, thuds, and sounds of breakage quickly sank below the level of the drums, and when the drums quit a few minutes later with their usual unsettling suddenness, the city was silent again. But now that silence had an unpleasant waiting quality.

Roland put an arm around Jake's shoulders. "Still not too late to detour around," he said.

Jake glanced up at him. "We can't."

"Because of the train?"

Jake nodded and singsonged: "Blaine is a pain, but we *have* to take the train. And the city's the only place where we can get on."

Roland looked thoughtfully at Jake. "Why do you say we *have* to? Is it *ka*? Because, Jake, you have to understand that you don't know much about *ka* yet—it's the sort of subject men study all their lives."

"I don't know if it's *ka* or not, but I do know that we can't go into the waste lands unless we're protected, and that means Blaine. Without him we'll die, like those bees we saw are going to die when winter comes. We have to be protected. Because the waste lands are poison."

"How do you know these things?"

"I don't *know*!" Jake said, almost angrily. "I just *do*."

"All right," Roland said mildly. He looked toward Lud again. "But we'll have to be damned careful. It's unlucky that they still have gunpowder. If they have that, they may have things that are even more powerful. I doubt if they know how to use them, but that only increases the danger. They could get excited and blow us all to hell."

"Ell," a grave voice said from behind them. They glanced around and saw Oy sitting by the side of the road, watching them.

8

LATER THAT DAY THEY came to a new road which swept toward them out of the west and joined their own way. Beyond this point, the Great Road—now much wider and split down the middle by a median divider of some polished dark stone—began to sink, and the crumbling concrete embankments which rose on either side of them gave the pilgrims a claustrophobic trapped feeling. They stopped at a point where one of these concrete dikes had been broken open, affording a comforting line of sight to the open land beyond, and ate a light, unsatisfying meal.

"Why do you think they dropped the road down like this, Eddie?" Jake asked. "I mean, someone *did* do it this way on purpose, didn't they?"

Eddie looked through the break in the concrete, where the flatlands stretched on as smoothly as ever, and nodded.

"Then why?"

"Dunno, champ," Eddie said, but he thought he did. He glanced at Roland and guessed that he knew, too. The sunken road leading to the bridge had been a defensive measure. Troops placed atop the concrete slopes were in control of two carefully engineered redoubts. If the defenders didn't like the look of the folks approaching Lud along the Great Road, they could rain destruction down on them.

"You *sure* you don't know?" Jake asked.

Eddie smiled at Jake and tried to stop imagining that there was some nut up there right now, getting ready to roll a large, rusty bomb down one of those decayed concrete ramps. "No idea," he said.

Susannah whistled disgustedly between her teeth. "This road's goin to hell, Roland. I was hoping we were done with that damn harness, but you better get it out again." He nodded and rummaged in his purse for it without a word.

The condition of the Great Road deteriorated as other, smaller roads joined it like tributaries joining a great river. As they neared the bridge, the cobbles were replaced with a surface Roland thought of as metal and the rest of them thought of as asphalt or hot-top. It had not held up as well as the cobbles. Time had done some damage; the passage of countless horses and wagons since the last repairs were made had done more. The surface had been chewed into a treacherous rubble. Foot travel would be difficult, and the idea of pushing Susannah's wheelchair over that crumbled surface was ridiculous.

The banks on either side had grown steadily steeper, and now, at their tops, they could see slim, pointed shapes looming against the sky. Roland thought of arrowheads—huge ones, weapons made by a tribe of giants. To his companions, they looked like rockets or guided missiles. Susannah thought of Redstones fired from Cape Canaveral; Eddie thought about SAMs, some built to be fired from the backs of flatbed trucks, stored all over Europe; Jake thought of ICBMs hiding in reinforced concrete silos under the plains of Kansas and the unpopulated mountains of Nevada, programmed to hit back at China or the USSR in the event of nuclear armageddon. All of them felt as if they had passed into a dark and woeful zone of shadow, or into a countryside laboring under some old but still powerful curse.

Some hours after they entered this area—Jake called it The Gauntlet—the concrete embankments ended at a place where half a dozen access roads drew together, like the strands of a spiderweb, and here the land opened out again . . . a fact which relieved all of them, although none of them said so out loud. Another traffic-light swung over the junction. This one was more familiar to Eddie, Susannah, and Jake; it had once had lenses on its four faces, although the glass had been broken out long ago.

"I'll bet this road was the eighth wonder of the world, once upon a time," Susannah said, "and look at it now. It's a minefield."

"Old ways are sometimes the best ways," Roland agreed.

Eddie was pointing west. "Look."

Now that the high concrete barriers were gone, they could see exactly what old Si had described to them over cups of bitter coffee in River Crossing. "One track only," he had said, "set up high on a colyum of man-made stone, such as the Old Ones used to make their streets and walls." The track raced toward them out of the west in a slim, straight line, then flowed across the Send and into the city on a narrow golden trestle. It was a simple, elegant construction—and the only one they had seen so far which was totally without rust—but it was badly marred, all the same. Halfway across, a large piece of the trestle had fallen into the rushing river below. What remained were two long, jutting piers that pointed at each other like accusing fingers. Jutting out of the water below the hole was a streamlined tube of metal. Once it had been bright blue, but now the color had been dimmed by spreading scales of rust. It looked very small from this distance.

"So much for Blaine," Eddie said. "No wonder they stopped hearing it. The supports finally gave way while it was crossing the river and it fell in the drink. It must have been decelerating when it happened, or it would have carried straight across and all we'd see would be a big hole like a bomb-crater in the far bank. Well, it was a great idea while it lasted."

"Mercy said there was another one," Susannah reminded him.

"Yeah. She also said she hadn't heard it in seven or eight years, and Aunt Talitha said it was more like ten. What do you think, Jake . . . Jake? Earth to Jake, Earth to Jake, come in, little buddy."

Jake, who had been staring intently at the remains of the train in the river, only shrugged.

"You're a big help, Jake," Eddie said. "Valuable input—that's why I love you. Why we *all* love you."

Jake paid no attention. He knew what he was seeing, and it wasn't Blaine. The remains of the mono sticking out of the river were blue. In his dream, Blaine had been the dusty, sugary pink of the bubble-gum you got with baseball trading cards.

Roland, meanwhile, had cinched the straps of Susannah's carry-harness across his chest. "Eddie, boost your lady into this contraption. It's time we moved on and saw for ourselves."

Jake now shifted his gaze, looking nervously toward the bridge looming ahead. He could hear a high, ghostly humming noise in the distance—the sound of the wind playing in the decayed steel hangers which connected the overhead cables to the concrete deck below.

"Do you think it'll be safe to cross?" Jake asked.

"We'll find out tomorrow," Roland replied.

9

THE NEXT MORNING, ROLAND'S band of travellers stood at the end of the long, rusty bridge, gazing across at Lud. Eddie's dreams of wise old elves who had preserved a working technology on which the pilgrims could draw were disappearing. Now that they were this close, he could see holes in the city-scape where whole blocks of buildings appeared to have been either burned or blasted. The skyline reminded him of a diseased jaw from which many teeth have already fallen.

It was true that most of the buildings were still standing, but they had a dreary, disused look that filled Eddie with an uncharacteristic gloom, and the bridge between the travellers and that shuttered maze of steel and concrete looked anything but solid and eternal. The vertical hangers on the left sagged slackly; the ones remaining on the right almost screamed with tension. The deck had been constructed of hollow concrete boxes shaped like trapezoids. Some of these had buckled upward, displaying empty black interiors; others had slipped askew. Many of these latter had merely cracked, but others were badly broken, leaving gaps big enough to drop trucks—*big* trucks—into. In places where the bottoms of the box-sections as well as the tops had shattered, they could see the muddy riverbank and the gray-green water of the Send beyond it. Eddie put the distance between the deck and the water as three hundred feet at the center of the bridge. And that was probably a conservative estimate.

Eddie peered at the huge concrete caissons to which the main cables were anchored and thought the one on the right side of the bridge looked as if it had been pulled partway out of the earth. He decided he might do well not to mention this fact to the others; it was bad enough that the bridge was swaying slowly but perceptibly back and forth. Just looking at it made him feel seasick. "Well?" he asked Roland. "What do you think?"

Roland pointed to the right side of the bridge. Here was a canted walkway about five feet wide. It had been constructed atop a series of smaller concrete boxes and was, in effect, a separate deck. This segmented deck appeared to be supported by an undercable—or perhaps it was a thick steel rod—anchored to the main support cables by huge bow-clamps. Eddie inspected the closest one with the avid interest of a man who may soon be entrusting his life to the object he is studying. The bow-clamp appeared rusty but still sound. The words LaMERK FOUNDRY had been stamped into its metal. Eddie was fascinated to realize he no longer knew if the words were in the High Speech or in English.

"I think we can use that," Roland said. "There's only one bad place. Do you see it?"

"Yeah—it's kind of hard to miss."

The bridge, which had to be at least three quarters of a mile long, might not have had any proper maintenance for over a thousand years, but Roland guessed that the real destruction might have been going on for only the last fifty or so. As the hangers on the right snapped, the bridge had listed farther and farther to the left. The greatest twist had occurred in the center of the bridge, between the two four-hundred-foot cable-towers. At the place where the pressure of the twist was the greatest, a gaping, eye-shaped hole ran across the deck. The break in the walkway was narrower, but even so, at least two adjoining concrete box-sections had fallen into the Send, leaving a gap at least twenty or thirty feet wide. Where these boxes had been, they could clearly see the rusty steel rod or cable which supported the walkway. They would have to use it to get across the gap.

"I think we can cross," Roland said, calmly pointing. "The gap is inconvenient, but the side-rail is still there, so we'll have something to hold onto."

Eddie nodded, but he could feel his heart pounding

hard. The exposed walkway support looked like a big
pipe made of jointed steel, and was probably four feet
across at the top. In his mind's eye he could see how
they would have to edge across, feet on the broad,
slightly curved back of the support, hands clutching
the rail, while the bridge swayed slowly like a ship in
a mild swell.

"Jesus," he said. He tried to spit, but nothing came
out. His mouth was too dry. "You sure, Roland?"

"So far as I can see, it's the only way." Roland
pointed downriver and Eddie saw a second bridge.
This one had fallen into the Send long ago. The remains stuck out of the water in a rusted tangle of
ancient steel.

"What about you, Jake?" Susannah asked.

"Hey, no problem," Jake said at once. He was actually smiling.

"I hate you, kid," Eddie said.

Roland was looking at Eddie with some concern.
"If you feel you can't do it, say so now. Don't get
halfway across and then freeze up."

Eddie looked along the twisted surface of the bridge
for a long time, then nodded. "I guess I can handle
it. Heights have never been my favorite thing, but I'll
manage."

"Good." Roland surveyed them. "Soonest begun,
soonest done. I'll go first, with Susannah. Then Jake,
and Eddie's drogue. Can you handle the wheelchair?"

"Hey, no problem," Eddie said giddily.

"Let's go, then."

10

As soon as he stepped onto the walkway, fear filled
up Eddie's hollow places like cold water and he began
to wonder if he hadn't made a very dangerous mistake. From solid ground, the bridge seemed to be
swaying only a little, but once he was actually on it,

he felt as if he were standing on the pendulum of the world's biggest grandfather clock. The movement was very slow, but it was regular, and the length of the swings was much longer than he had anticipated. The walkway's surface was badly cracked and canted at least ten degrees to the left. His feet gritted in loose piles of powdery concrete, and the low squealing sound of the box-segments grinding together was constant. Beyond the bridge, the city skyline tilted slowly back and forth like the artificial horizon of the world's slowest-moving video game.

Overhead, the wind hummed constantly in the taut hangers. Below, the ground fell away sharply to the muddy northwest bank of the river. He was thirty feet up . . . then sixty . . . then a hundred and ten. Soon he would be over the water. The wheelchair banged against his left leg with every step.

Something furry brushed between his feet and he clutched madly for the rusty handrail with his right hand, barely holding in a scream. Oy went trotting past him with a brief upward glance, as if to say *Excuse me—just passing*.

"Fucking dumb animal," Eddie said through gritted teeth.

He discovered that, although he didn't like looking down, he had an even greater aversion to looking at the hangers which were still managing to hold the deck and the overhead cables together. They were sleeved with rust and Eddie could see snarls of metal thread poking out of most—these snarls looked like metallic puffs of cotton. He knew from his Uncle Reg, who had worked on both the George Washington and Triborough bridges as a painter, that the hangers and overhead cables were "spun" from thousands of steel threads. On this bridge, the spin was finally letting go. The hangers were quite literally becoming unravelled, and as they did, the threads were snapping, one interwoven strand at a time.

It's held this long, it'll hold a little longer. You think

*this thing's going to fall into the river just because
you're crossing it? Don't flatter yourself.*

He wasn't comforted, however. For all Eddie knew,
they might be the first people to attempt the crossing
in *decades*. And the bridge, after all, would have to
collapse *sometime*, and from the look of things, it was
going to be soon. Their combined weight might be the
straw that broke the camel's back.

His moccasin struck a chunk of concrete and Eddie
watched, sickened but helpless to look away, as the
chunk fell down and down and down, turning over as
it went. There was a small—*very* small—splash when
it hit the river. The freshening wind gusted and stuck
his shirt against his sweaty skin. The bridge groaned
and swayed. Eddie tried to remove his hands from the
side-rail, but they seemed frozen to the pitted metal
in a deathgrip.

He closed his eyes for a moment. *You're not going
to freeze. You're* not. *I . . . I forbid it. If you need
something to look at, make it long tall and ugly*. Eddie
opened his eyes again, fixed them on the gunslinger,
forced his hands to open, and began to move forward
again.

11

ROLAND REACHED THE GAP and looked back. Jake
was five feet behind him. Oy was at his heels. The
bumbler was crouched down with his neck stretched
forward. The wind was much stronger over the river-
cut, and Roland could see it rippling Oy's silky fur.
Eddie was about twenty-five feet behind Jake. His
face was tightly drawn, but he was still shuffling grimly
along with Susannah's collapsed wheelchair in his left
hand. His right was clutching the rail like grim death.

"Susannah?"

"Yes," she responded at once. "Fine."

"Jake?"

Jake looked up. He was still grinning, and the gunslinger saw there was going to be no problem there. The boy was having the time of his life. His hair blew back from his finely made brow in waves, and his eyes sparkled. He jerked one thumb up. Roland smiled and returned the gesture.

"Eddie?"

"Don't worry about me."

Eddie appeared to be looking at Roland, but the gunslinger decided he was really looking past him, at the windowless brick buildings which crowded the riverbank at the far end of the bridge. That was all right; given his obvious fear of heights, it was probably the best thing he could do to keep his head.

"All right, I won't," Roland murmured. "We're going to cross the hole now, Susannah. Sit easy. No quick movements. Understand?"

"Yes."

"If you want to adjust your position, do it now."

"I'm fine, Roland," she said calmly. "I just hope Eddie will be all right."

"Eddie's a gunslinger now. He'll behave like one."

Roland turned to the right, so he was facing directly downriver, and grasped the handrail. Then he began to edge out across the hole, shuffling his boots along the rusty cable.

12

JAKE WAITED UNTIL ROLAND and Susannah were part of the way across the gap and then started himself. The wind gusted and the bridge swayed back and forth, but he felt no alarm at all. He was, in fact, totally buzzed. Unlike Eddie, he'd never had any fear of heights; he liked being up here where he could see the river spread out like a steel ribbon under a sky which was beginning to cloud over.

Halfway across the hole in the bridge (Roland and

Susannah had reached the place where the uneven walkway resumed and were watching the others), Jake looked back and his heart sank. They had forgotten one member of the party when they were discussing how to cross. Oy was crouched, frozen and clearly terrified, on the far side of the hole in the walkway. He was sniffing at the place where the concrete ended and the rusty, curved support took over.

"Come on, Oy!" Jake called.

"Oy!" the bumbler called back, and the tremble in his hoarse voice was almost human. He stretched his long neck forward toward Jake but didn't move. His gold-ringed eyes were huge and dismayed.

Another gust of wind struck the bridge, making it sway and squall. Something twanged beside Jake's head—the sound of a guitar string which has been tightened until it snaps. A steel thread had popped out of the nearest vertical hanger, almost scratching his cheek. Ten feet away, Oy crouched miserably with his eyes fixed on Jake.

"Come on!" Roland shouted. "Wind's freshening! Come on, Jake!"

"Not without Oy!"

Jake began to shuffle back the way he had come. Before he had gone more than two steps, Oy stepped gingerly onto the support rod. The claws at the ends of his stiffly braced legs scratched at the rounded metal surface. Eddie stood behind the bumbler now, feeling helpless and scared to death.

"That's it, Oy!" Jake encouraged. "Come to me!"

"Oy-Oy! Ake-Ake!" the bumbler cried, and trotted rapidly along the rod. He had almost reached Jake when the traitorous wind gusted again. The bridge swung. Oy's claws scratched madly at the support rod for purchase, but there was none. His hindquarters slued off the edge and into space. He tried to cling with his forepaws, but there was nothing to cling to. His rear legs ran wildly in midair.

Jake let go of the rail and dived for him, aware of nothing but Oy's gold-ringed eyes.

"No, Jake!" Roland and Eddie bellowed together, each from his own side of the gap, each too far away to do anything but watch.

Jake hit the cable on his chest and belly. His pack bounced against his shoulderblades and he heard his teeth click together in his head with the sound of a cueball breaking a tight rack. The wind gusted again. He went with it, looping his right hand around the support rod and reaching for Oy with his left as he swayed out into space. The bumbler began to fall, and clamped his jaws on Jake's reaching hand as he did. The pain was immediate and excruciating. Jake screamed but held on, head down, right arm clasping the rod, knees pressing hard against its wretchedly smooth surface. Oy dangled from his left hand like a circus acrobat, staring up with his gold-ringed eyes, and Jake could now see his own blood flowing along the sides of the bumbler's head in thin streams.

Then the wind gusted again and Jake began to slip outward.

13

EDDIE'S FEAR LEFT HIM. In its place came that strange yet welcome coldness. He dropped Susannah's wheelchair to the cracked cement with a clatter and raced nimbly out along the support cable, not even bothering with the handrail. Jake hung head-down over the gap with Oy swinging at the end of his left hand like a furry pendulum. And the boy's right hand was slipping.

Eddie opened his legs and seat-dropped to a sitting position. His undefended balls smashed painfully up into his crotch, but for the moment even this exquisite pain was news from a distant country. He seized Jake by the hair with one hand and one strap of his pack with the other. He felt himself beginning to tilt outward, and for a nightmarish moment he thought all three of them were going to go over in a daisy-chain.

He let go of Jake's hair and tightened his grip on the packstrap, praying the kid hadn't bought the pack at one of the cheap discount outlets. He flailed above his head for the handrail with his free hand. After an interminable moment in which their combined outward slide continued, he found it and seized it.

"ROLAND!" he bawled. *"I COULD USE A LITTLE HELP HERE!"*

But Roland was already there, with Susannah still perched on his back. When he bent, she locked her arms around his neck so she wouldn't drop headfirst from the sling. The gunslinger wrapped an arm around Jake's chest and pulled him up. When his feet were on the support rod again, Jake put his right arm around Oy's trembling body. His left hand was an agony of fire and ice.

"Let go, Oy," he gasped. "You can let go now we're—safe."

For a terrible moment he didn't think the billy-bumbler would. Then, slowly, Oy's jaws relaxed and Jake was able to pull his hand free. It was covered with blood and dotted with a ring of dark holes.

"Oy," the bumbler said feebly, and Eddie saw with wonder that the animal's strange eyes were full of tears. He stretched his neck and licked Jake's face with his bloody tongue.

"That's okay," Jake said, pressing his face into the warm fur. He was crying himself, his face a mask of shock and pain. "Don't worry, that's okay. You couldn't help it and I don't mind."

Eddie was getting slowly to his feet. His face was dirty gray, and he felt as if someone had driven a bowling ball into his guts. His left hand stole slowly to his crotch and investigated the damage there.

"Cheap fucking vasectomy," he said hoarsely.

"Are you going to faint, Eddie?" Roland asked. A fresh gust of wind flipped his hat from his head and into Susannah's face. She grabbed it and jammed it down all the way to his ears, giving Roland the look of a half-crazed hillbilly.

"No," Eddie said. "I almost wish I could, but—"

"Take a look at Jake," Susannah said. "He's really bleeding."

"I'm fine," Jake said, and tried to hide his hand. Roland took it gently in his own hands before he could. Jake had sustained at least a dozen puncture-wounds in the back of his hand, his palm, and his fingers. Most of them were deep. It would be impossible to tell if bones had been broken or tendons severed until Jake tried to flex the hand, and this wasn't the time or place for such experiments.

Roland looked at Oy. The billy-bumbler looked back, his expressive eyes sad and frightened. He had made no effort to lick Jake's blood from his chops, although it would have been the most natural thing in the world for him to have done so.

"Leave him alone," Jake said, and wrapped the encircling arm more tightly about Oy's body. "It wasn't his fault. It was my fault for forgetting him. The wind blew him off."

"I'm not going to hurt him," Roland said. He was positive the billy-bumbler wasn't rabid, but he still did not intend for Oy to taste any more of Jake's blood than he already had. As for any other diseases Oy might be carrying in his blood . . . well, *ka* would decide, as, in the end, it always did. Roland pulled his neckerchief free and wiped Oy's lips and muzzle. "There," he said. "Good fellow. Good boy."

"Oy," the billy-bumbler said feebly, and Susannah, who was watching over Roland's shoulder, could have sworn she heard gratitude in that voice.

Another gust of wind struck them. The weather was turning dirty, and fast. "Eddie, we have to get off the bridge. Can you walk?"

"No, massa; I'sa gwinter shuffle." The pain in his groin and the pit of his stomach was still bad, but not quite so bad as it had been a minute ago.

"All right. Let's move. Fast as we can."

Roland turned, began to take a step, and stopped. A man was now standing on the far side of the gap, watching them expressionlessly.

The newcomer had approached while their attention was focused on Jake and Oy. A crossbow was slung across his back. He wore a bright yellow scarf around his head; the ends streamed out like banners in the freshening wind. Gold hoops with crosses in their centers dangled from his ears. One eye was covered with a white silk patch. His face was blotched with purple sores, some of them open and festering. He might have been thirty, forty, or sixty. He held one hand high over his head. In it was something Roland could not make out, except that its shape was too regular to be a stone.

Behind this apparition, the city loomed with a kind of weird clarity in the darkening day. As Eddie looked past the huddles of brick buildings on the other shore—warehouses long since scooped empty by looters, he had no doubt—and into those shadowy canyons and stone mazes, he understood for the first time how terribly mistaken, how terribly foolish, his dreams of hope and help had been. Now he saw the shattered facades and broken roofs; now he saw the shaggy birds' nests on cornices and in glassless, gaping windows; now he allowed himself to actually *smell* the city, and that odor was not of fabulous spices and savory foods of the sort his mother had sometimes brought home from Zabar's but rather the stink of a mattress that has caught fire, smouldered awhile, and then been put out with sewer-water. He suddenly understood Lud, understood it completely. The grinning pirate who had appeared while their attention was elsewhere was probably as close to a wise old elf as this broken, dying place could provide.

Roland pulled his revolver.

"Put it away, my cully," the man in the yellow scarf said in an accent so thick that the sense of his words was almost lost. "Put it away, my dear heart. Ye're a fierce trim, ay, that's clear, but this time you're outmatched."

14

THE NEWCOMER'S PANTS WERE patched green velvet, and as he stood on the edge of the hole in the bridge, he looked like a buccaneer at the end of his days of plunder: sick, ragged, and still dangerous.

"Suppose I choose not to?" Roland asked. "Suppose I choose to simply put a bullet through your scrofulous head?"

"Then I'll get to hell just enough ahead of ye to hold the door," the man in the yellow scarf said, and chuckled chummily. He wiggled the hand he held in the air. "It's all the same jolly fakement to me, one way or t'other."

Roland guessed that was the truth. The man looked as if he might have a year to live at most . . . and the last few months of that year would probably be very unpleasant. The oozing sores on his face had nothing to do with radiation; unless Roland was badly deceived, this man was in the late stages of what the doctors called mandrus and everyone else called whore's blossoms. Facing a dangerous man was always a bad business, but at least one could calculate the odds in such an encounter. When you were facing the dead, however, everything changed.

"Do yer know what I've got here, my dear ones?" the pirate asked. "Do yer ken whatcher old friend Gasher just happens to have laid his hands on? It's a grenado, something pretty the Old Folks left behind, and I've already tipped its cap—for to wear one's cap before the introductin' is complete would be wery bad manners, so it would!"

He cackled happily for a moment, and then his face grew still and grave once more. All humor left it, as if a switch had been turned somewhere in his degenerating brains.

"My finger is all that's holdin the pin now, dearie. If you shoot me, there's going to be a wery big bang. You and the cunt-monkey on yer back will be vaporized. The squint, too, I reckon. The young buck stand-

ing behind you and pointing that toy pistol in my face
might live, but only until he hits the water . . . and
hit it he would, because this bridge has been hangin
by a thread these last forty year, and all it'd take to
finish it is one little push. So do ye want to put away
your iron, or shall we all toddle off to hell on the
same handcart?"

Roland briefly considered trying to shoot the object
Gasher called a grenado out of his hand, saw how
tightly the man was gripping it, and holstered his gun.

"Ah, good!" Gasher cried, cheerful once more. "I
knew ye was a trig cove, just lookin at yer! Oh yes!
So I did!"

"What do you want?" Roland asked, although he
thought he already knew this, too.

Gasher raised his free hand and pointed a dirty finger at Jake. "The squint. Gimme the squint and the
rest of you go free."

"Go fuck yourself," Susannah said at once.

"Why not?" the pirate cackled. "Gimme a chunk
of mirror and I'll rip it right off and stick it right in—
why not, for all the good it's a-doin me these days?
Why, I can't even run water through it without it
burns me all the way to the top of my gullywash!" His
eyes, which were a strange calm shade of gray, never
left Roland's face. "What do *you* say, my good old
mate?"

"What happens to the rest of us if I hand over the
boy?"

"Why, you go on yer way without no trouble from
us!" the man in the yellow headscarf returned
promptly. "You have the Tick-Tock Man's word on
that. It comes from his lips to my lips to your ears,
so it does, and Tick-Tock's a trig cove, too, what don't
break his word once it's been given. I can't say ary
word nor watch about any Pubies you might run into,
but you'll have no trouble with the Tick-Tock Man's
Grays."

"What the fuck are you *saying*, Roland?" Eddie

roared. "You're not really thinking about doing it, are you?"

Roland didn't look down at Jake, and his lips didn't move as he murmured: "I'll keep my promise."

"Yes—I know you will." Then Jake raised his voice and said: "Put the gun away, Eddie. I'll decide."

"Jake, you're out of your *mind*!"

The pirate cackled cheerily. "Not at all, cully! *You're* the one who's lost his mind if you disbelieve me. At the wery least, he'll be safe from the drums with us, won't he? And just think—if I didn't mean what I say, I would have told you to toss your guns overside first thing! Easiest thing in the world! But did I? Nay!"

Susannah had heard the exchange between Jake and Roland. She had also had a chance to realize how bleak their options were as things now stood. "Put it away, Eddie."

"How do we know you won't toss the grenade at us once you have the kid?" Eddie called.

"I'll shoot it out of the air if he tries," Roland said. "I can do it, and he *knows* I can do it."

"Mayhap I do. You've got a cosy look about you, indeed ye do."

"If he's telling the truth," Roland went on, "he'd be burned even if I missed his toy, because the bridge would collapse and we'd all go down together."

"Wery clever, my dear old son!" Gasher said. "You *are* a cosy one, ain't you?" He cawed laughter, then grew serious and confiding. "The talking's done, old mate of mine. Decide. Will you give me the boy, or do we all march to the end of the path together?"

Before Roland could say a word, Jake had slipped past him on the support rod. He still held Oy curled in his right arm. He held his bloody left hand stiffly out in front of him.

"Jake, *no*!" Eddie shouted desperately.

"I'll come for you," Roland said in the same low voice.

"I know," Jake repeated. The wind gusted again.

The bridge swayed and groaned. The Send was now
speckled with whitecaps, and water boiled whitely
around the wreck of the blue mono jutting from the
river on the upstream side.

"Ay, my cully!" Gasher crooned. His lips spread
wide, revealing a few remaining teeth that jutted from
his white gums like decayed tombstones. "Ay, my fine
young squint! Just keep coming."

"Roland, he could be bluffing!" Eddie yelled. "That
thing could be a dud!"

The gunslinger made no reply.

As Jake neared the other side of the hole in the
walkway, Oy bared his own teeth and began to snarl
at Gasher.

"Toss that talking bag of guts overside," Gasher
said.

"Fuck you," Jake replied in the same calm voice.

The pirate looked surprised for a moment, then
nodded. "Tender of him, are you? Wery well." He
took two steps backward. "Put him down the second
you reach the concrete, then. And if he runs at me,
I promise to kick his brains right out his tender little
asshole."

"Asshole," Oy said through his bared teeth.

"Shut up, Oy," Jake muttered. He reached the concrete just as the strongest gust of wind yet struck the
bridge. This time the twanging sound of parting cable-
strands seemed to come from everywhere. Jake
glanced back and saw Roland and Eddie clinging to
the rail. Susannah was watching him from over Roland's shoulder, her tight cap of curls rippling and
shaking in the wind. Jake raised his hand to them.
Roland raised his in return.

You won't let me drop this time? he had asked. *No—
not ever again,* Roland had replied. Jake believed him
. . . but he was very much afraid of what might happen before Roland arrived. He put Oy down. Gasher
rushed forward the moment he did, kicking out at the
small animal. Oy skittered aside, avoiding the booted
foot.

"Run!" Jake shouted. Oy did, shooting past them and loping toward the Lud end of the bridge with his head down, swerving to avoid the holes and leaping across the cracks in the pavement. He didn't look back. A moment later Gasher had his arm around Jake's neck. He stank of dirt and decaying flesh, the two odors combining to create a single deep stench, crusty and thick. It made Jake's gorge rise.

He bumped his crotch into Jake's buttocks. "Maybe I ain't quite s'far gone's I thought. Don't they say youth's the wine what makes old men drunk? We'll have us a time, won't we, my sweet little squint? Ay, we'll have a time such as will make the angels sing."

Oh Jesus, Jake thought.

Gasher raised his voice again. "We're leaving now, my hardcase friend—we have grand things to do and grand people to see, so we do, but I keep my word. As for you, you'll stand right where you are for a good fifteen minutes, if you're wise. If I see you start to move, we're all going to ride the handsome. Do you understand me?"

"Yes," Roland said.

"Do you believe me when I say I have nothing to lose?"

"Yes."

"That's wery well, then. Move, boy! Hup!"

Gasher's hold tightened on Jake's throat until he could hardly breathe. At the same time he was pulled backward. They retreated that way, facing the gap where Roland stood with Susannah on his back and Eddie just behind him, still holding the Ruger which Gasher had called a toy pistol. Jake could feel Gasher's breath puffing against his ear in hot little blurts. Worse, he could smell it.

"Don't try a thing," Gasher whispered, "or I'll rip off yer sweetmeats and stuff em up your bung. And it would be sad to lose em before you ever got a chance to use em, wouldn't it? Wery sad indeed."

They reached the end of the bridge. Jake stiffened, believing Gasher would throw the grenade anyway, but he didn't . . . at least not immediately. He backed Jake through a narrow alley between two small cubicles which had probably served as tollbooths, once upon a time. Beyond them, the brick warehouses loomed like prison cellblocks.

"Now, cully, I'm going to let go of your neck, or how would'je ever have wind to run with? But I'll be holdin yer arm, and if ye don't run like the wind, I promise I'll rip it right off and use it for a club to beat you with. Do you understand?"

Jake nodded, and suddenly the terrible, stifling pressure was gone from his windpipe. As soon as it was, he became aware of his hand again—it felt hot and swollen and full of fire. Then Gasher seized his bicep with fingers like bands of iron, and he forgot all about his hand.

"Toodle-doo!" Gasher called in a grotesquely cheery falsetto. He waggled the grenado at the others. "Bye-bye, dears!" Then he growled to Jake: "Now *run,* you whoring little squint! *Run!*"

Jake was first whirled and then yanked into a run. The two of them went flying down a curved ramp to street level. Jake's first confused thought was that this was what the East River Drive would look like two or three hundred years after some weird brain-plague had killed all the sane people in the world.

The ancient, rusty hulks of what had once surely been automobiles stood at intervals along both curbs. Most were bubble-shaped roadsters that looked like no cars Jake had ever seen before (except, maybe, for the ones the white-gloved creations of Walt Disney drove in the comic books), but among them he saw an old Volkswagen Beetle, a car that might have been a Chevrolet Corvair, and something he believed was a Model A Ford. There were no tires on any of these eerie hulks; they either had been stolen or had rotted away to dust long since. And all the glass had been broken, as if the remaining denizens of this city abhorred anything which might show them their own reflections, even accidentally.

Beneath and between the abandoned cars, the gutters were filled with drifts of unidentifiable metal junk and bright glints of glass. Trees had been planted at intervals along the sidewalks in some long-gone, happier time, but they were now so emphatically dead that they looked like stark metal sculptures against the cloudy sky. Some of the warehouses had either been bombed or had collapsed on their own, and beyond the jumbled heaps of bricks which was all that remained of them Jake could see the river and the rusty, sagging underpinnings of the Send Bridge. That smell of wet decay—a smell that seemed almost to snarl in the nose—was stronger than ever.

The street headed due east, diverging from the path of the Beam, and Jake could see it became more and more choked with rubble and rickrack as it went. Six or seven blocks down it appeared to be entirely plugged, but it was in this direction that Gasher pulled him. At first he kept up, but Gasher was setting a fearsome pace. Jake began to pant and fell a step behind. Gasher almost jerked him off his feet as he dragged Jake toward the barrier of junk and concrete and rusty steel beams which lay ahead. The plug—which looked like a deliberate construction to Jake—lay between two broad buildings with dusty marble facades. In front of the one on the left was a statue Jake recognized at once: it was the woman called Blind Justice, and that almost surely made the building she guarded a courthouse. But he only had a moment to look; Gasher was dragging him relentlessly toward the barricade, and he wasn't slowing down.

He'll kill us if he tries to take us through there! Jake thought, but Gasher—who ran like the wind in spite of the disease which advertised itself on his face—simply buried his fingers deeper in Jake's upper arm and swept him along. And now Jake saw a narrow alley in the not-quite-haphazard pile of concrete, splintered furniture, rusted plumbing fixtures, and chunks of trucks and automobiles. He suddenly understood. This maze would hold Roland up for hours . . .

but it was Gasher's back yard, and he knew *exactly* where he was going.

The small dark opening to the alley was on the left side of the tottery pile of junk. As they reached it, Gasher tossed the green object back over his shoulder. "Better duck, dearie!" he cried, and voiced a series of shrill, hysterical giggles. A moment later a huge, crumping explosion shook the street. One of the bubble-shaped cars jumped twenty feet into the air and then came down on its roof. A hail of bricks whistled over Jake's head, and something thumped him hard on the left shoulder-blade. He stumbled and would have fallen if Gasher hadn't yanked him upright and pulled him into the narrow opening in the rubble. Once they were in the passageway which lay beyond, gloomy shadows reached out eagerly and enfolded them.

When they were gone, a small, furry shape crept out from behind a concrete boulder. It was Oy. He stood at the mouth of the passage for a moment, neck stretched forward, eyes gleaming. Then he followed after, nose low to the ground and sniffing carefully.

15

"COME ON," ROLAND SAID as soon as Gasher had turned tail.

"How could you do it?" Eddie asked. "How could you let that freak have him?"

"Because I had no choice. Bring the wheelchair. We're going to need it."

They had reached the concrete on the far side of the gap when an explosion shook the bridge, spraying rubble into the darkening sky.

"Christ!" Eddie said, and turned his white, dismayed face to Roland.

"Don't worry yet," Roland said calmly. "Fellows like Gasher rarely get careless with their high-explosive toys." They reached the tollbooths at the end of the bridge. Roland stopped just beyond, at the top of the curving ramp.

"You knew the guy wasn't just bluffing, didn't you?" Eddie said. "I mean, you weren't guessing—you *knew*."

"He's a walking dead man, and such men don't need to bluff." Roland's voice was calm enough, but there was a deep undertone of bitterness and pain in it. "I knew something like this could happen, and if we'd seen the fellow earlier, while we were still beyond the range of his exploding egg, we could have stood him off. But then Jake fell and he got too close. I imagine he thinks our real reason for bringing a boy in the first place was to pay for safe conduct through the city. Damn! Damn the luck!" Roland struck his fist against his leg.

"Well, let's go get him!"

Roland shook his head. "This is where we split up. We can't take Susannah where the bastard's gone, and we can't leave her alone."

"But—"

"Listen and don't argue—not if you want to save Jake. The longer we stand here, the colder his trail gets. Cold trails are hard to follow. You've got your own job to do. If there's another Blaine, and I am sure Jake believes there is, then you and Susannah must find it. There must be a station, or what was once called a cradle in the far lands. Do you understand?"

For once, blessedly, Eddie didn't argue. "Yeah. We'll find it. What then?"

"Fire a shot every half hour or so. When I get Jake, I'll come."

"Shots may attract other people as well," Susannah said. Eddie had helped her out of the sling and she was seated in her chair again.

Roland surveyed them coldly. "Handle them."

"Okay." Eddie stuck out his hand and Roland took it briefly. "Find him, Roland."

"Oh, I'll find him. Just pray to your gods that I find him soon enough. And remember the faces of your fathers, both of you."

Susannah nodded. "We'll try."

Roland turned and ran light-footed down the ramp. When he was out of sight, Eddie looked at Susannah and was not very surprised to see she was crying. He felt like crying himself. Half an hour ago they had been a tight little band of friends. Their comfortable fellowship had been smashed to bits in the space of just a few minutes—Jake abducted, Roland gone after him. Even Oy had run away. Eddie had never felt so lonely in his life.

"I have a feeling we're never going to see either of them again," Susannah said.

"Of course we will!" Eddie said roughly, but he knew what she meant, because he felt the same way. The premonition that their quest was all over before it was fairly begun lay heavy on his heart. "In a fight with Attila the Hun, I'd give you three-to-two odds on Roland the Barbarian. Come on, Suze—we've got a train to catch."

"But where?" she asked forlornly.

"I don't know. Maybe we should just find the nearest wise old elf and ask him, huh?"

"What are you talking about, Edward Dean?"

"Nothing," he said, and because that was so goddam true he thought he might burst into tears, he grasped the handles of her wheelchair and began to push it down the cracked and glass-littered ramp that led into the city of Lud.

16

JAKE QUICKLY DESCENDED INTO a foggy world where the only landmarks were pain: his throbbing hand, the place on his upper arm where Gasher's fingers dug in like steel pegs, his burning lungs. Before they had gone far, these pains were first joined and then over-matched by a deep, burning stitch in his left side. He wondered if Roland was following after them yet. He also wondered how long Oy would be able to live in this world which was so unlike the plains and forest which were all he had known until now. Then Gasher clouted him across the face, bloodying his nose, and thought was lost in a red wash of pain.

"Come on, yer little bastard! Move yer sweet cheeks!"

"Running . . . as fast as I can," Jake gasped, and just managed to dodge a thick shard of glass which jutted like a long transparent tooth from the wall of junk to his left.

"You better not be, because I'll knock yer cold and drag yer along by the hair o' yer head if y'are! Now *hup*, you little barstard!"

Jake somehow forced himself to run faster. He'd gone into the alley with the idea that they must shortly re-emerge onto the avenue, but he now reluctantly realized that wasn't going to happen. This was more than an alley; it was a camouflaged and fortified road leading ever deeper into the country of the Grays. The tall, tottery walls which pressed in on them had been built from an exotic array of materials: cars which had been partially or completely flattened by the chunks of granite and steel placed on top of them; marble pillars; unknown factory machines which were dull red with rust wherever they weren't still black with grease; a chrome-and-crystal fish as big as a private plane with one cryptic word of the High Speech—DELIGHT—carefully incised into its scaly gleaming side; crisscrossing chains, each link as big as Jake's head, wrapped around mad jumbles of furniture that appeared to balance above them as precariously as circus elephants do on their tiny steel platforms.

They came to a place where this lunatic path branched, and Gasher chose the left fork without hesitation. A little further along, three more alleyways, these so narrow they were almost tunnels, spoked off

in various directions. This time Gasher chose the
right-hand branching. The new path, which seemed to
be formed by banks of rotting boxes and huge blocks
of old paper—paper that might once have been books
or magazines—was too narrow for them to run in side
by side. Gasher shoved Jake into the lead and began
beating him relentlessly on the back to make him go
faster. *This is how a steer must feel when it's driven
down the chute to the slaughtering pen*, Jake thought,
and vowed that if he got out of this alive, he would
never eat steak again.

"Run, my sweet little boycunt! *Run!*"

Jake soon lost all track of the twistings and turnings
they made, and as Gasher drove him deeper and
deeper into this jumble of torn steel, broken furniture,
and castoff machinery, he began to give up hope of
rescue. Not even Roland would be able to find him
now. If the gunslinger tried, he would become lost
himself, and wander the choked paths of this nightmare world until he died.

Now they were going downhill, and the walls of
tightly packed paper had given way to ramparts of
filing cabinets, jumbles of adding machines, and piles
of computer gear. It was like running through some
nightmarish Radio Shack warehouse. For almost a full
minute the wall flowing past on Jake's left appeared
to be constructed solely of either TV sets or carelessly
stacked video display terminals. They stared at him
like the glazed eyes of dead men. And as the pavement beneath their feet continued to descend, Jake
realized that they *were* in a tunnel. The strip of cloudy
sky overhead narrowed to a band, the band narrowed
to a ribbon, and the ribbon became a thread. They
were in a gloomy netherworld, scurrying like rats
through a gigantic trash-midden.

What if it all comes down on us? Jake wondered,
but in his current state of aching exhaustion, this possibility did not frighten him much. If the roof fell in,
he would at least be able to rest.

Gasher drove him as a farmer would a mule, strik-

ing his left shoulder to indicate a left turn and his right
to indicate a right turn. When the course was straight
on, he thumped Jake on the back of the head. Jake
tried to dodge a jutting pipe and didn't quite succeed.
It whacked into one hip and sent him flailing across
the narrow passage toward a snarl of glass and jagged
boards. Gasher caught him and shoved him forward
again. "Run, you clumsy squint! Can't you run? If it
wasn't for the Tick-Tock Man, I'd bugger you right
here and cut yer throat while I did it, ay, so I would!"

Jake ran in a red daze where there was only pain
and the frequent thud of Gasher's fists coming down
on his shoulders or the back of his head. At last, when
he was sure he could run no longer, Gasher grabbed
him by the neck and yanked him to a stop so fiercely
that Jake crashed into him with a strangled squawk.

"*Here's* a tricky little bit!" Gasher panted jovially.
"Look straight ahead and you'll see two wires what
cross in an X low to the ground. Do yer see em?"

At first Jake didn't. It was very gloomy here; heaps
of huge copper kettles were piled up to the left, and
to the right were stacks of steel tanks that looked like
scuba-diving gear. Jake thought he could turn these
latter into an avalanche with one strong breath. He
swiped his forearm across his eyes, brushing away tangles of hair, and tried not to think about how he'd
look with about sixteen tons of those tanks piled on
top of him. He squinted in the direction Gasher was
pointing. Yes, he could make out—barely—two thin,
silvery lines that looked like guitar or banjo strings.
They came down from opposite sides of the passage-
way and crossed about two feet above the pavement.

"Crawl under, dear heart. And be ever so careful,
for if you so much as twang one of those wires, harf
the steel and cement puke in the city'll come down on
your dear little head. Mine, too, although I doubt if
that'd disturb you much, would it? Now crawl!"

Jake shrugged out of his pack, lay down, and
pushed it through the gap ahead of him. And as he
eased his way under the thin, taut wires, he discovered

that he wanted to live a little longer after all. It seemed that he could actually feel all those tons of carefully balanced junk waiting to come down on him. *These wires are probably holding a couple of carefully chosen keystones in place,* he thought. *If one of them breaks . . . ashes, ashes, we all fall down.* His back brushed one of the wires, and high overhead, something creaked.

"Careful, cully!" Gasher almost moaned. "Be oh so careful!"

Jake pushed himself beneath the crisscrossing wires, using his feet and his elbows. His stinking, sweat-clogged hair fell in his eyes again, but he did not dare brush it away.

"You're clear," Gasher grunted at last, and slipped beneath the tripwires himself with the ease of long practice. He stood up and snatched Jake's pack before Jake could reshoulder it. "What's in here, cully?" he asked, undoing the straps and peering in. "Got any treats for yer old pal? For the Gasherman loves his treaties, so he does!"

"There's nothing in there but—"

Gasher's hand flashed out and rocked Jake's head back with a hard slap that sent a fresh spray of bloody froth flying from the boy's nose.

"What did you do that for?" Jake cried, hurt and outraged.

"For tellin me what my own beshitted eyes can see!" Gasher yelled, and cast Jake's pack aside. He bared his remaining teeth at the boy in a dangerous, terrible grin. "And fer almost bringin the whole beshitted works down on us!" He paused, then added in a quieter voice: "*And* because I felt like it—I must admit that. Your stupid sheep's face puts me wery much in a slappin temper, so it does." The grin widened, revealing his oozing whitish gums, a sight Jake could have done without. "If your hardcase friend follows us this far, he'll have a surprise when he runs into those wires, won't he?" Gasher looked up, still grinning. "There's a city bus balanced up there some-place, as I remember."

Jake began to weep—tired, hopeless tears that cut through the dirt on his cheeks in narrow channels.

Gasher raised an open, threatening hand. "Get moving, cully, before I start cryin myself . . . for a wery sentermental fellow is yer old pal, so he is, and when he starts to grieve and mourn, a little slappin is the only thing to put a smile on his face again. *Run!*"

They ran. Gasher chose pathways leading deeper into the smelly, creaking maze seemingly at random, indicating his choices with hard whacks to the shoulders. At some point the sound of the drums began. It seemed to come from everywhere and nowhere, and for Jake it was the final straw. He gave up hope and thought alike, and allowed himself to descend wholly into the nightmare.

17

ROLAND HALTED IN FRONT of the barricade which choked the street from side to side and top to bottom. Unlike Jake, he had no hopes of emerging into the open on the other side. The buildings lying east of this point would be sentry-occupied islands emerging from an inland sea of trash, tools, artifacts . . . and booby-traps, he had no doubt. Some of these leavings undoubtedly still remained where they had fallen five hundred or seven hundred or a thousand years ago, but Roland thought most of it had been dragged here by the Grays a piece at a time. The eastern portion of Lud had become, in effect, the castle of the Grays, and Roland was now standing outside its wall.

He walked forward slowly and saw the mouth of a passageway half-hidden behind a ragged cement boul-der. There were footprints in the powdery dust—two sets, one big, one small. Roland started to get up, looked again, and squatted on his hunkers once more.

STEPHEN KING

Not two sets but three, the third marking the paws of a small animal.

"Oy?" Roland called softly. For a moment there was no response, and then a single soft bark came from the shadows. Roland stepped into the passage-way and saw gold-ringed eyes peering at him from around the first crooked corner. Roland trotted down to the bumbler. Oy, who still didn't like to come really close to anyone but Jake, backed up a step and then held his ground, looking anxiously up at the gunslinger.

"Do you want to help me?" Roland asked. He could feel the dry red curtain that was battle fever at the edge of his consciousness, but this was not the time for it. The time would come, but for now he must not allow himself that inexpressible relief. "Help me find Jake?"

"Ake!" Oy barked, still watching Roland with his anxious eyes.

"Go on, then. Find him."

Oy turned away at once and ran rapidly down the alley, nose skimming the ground. Roland followed, his eyes only occasionally flicking up to glance at Oy. Mostly he kept his gaze fixed on the ancient pave-ment, looking for sign.

18

"JESUS," EDDIE SAID. "WHAT kind of people *are* these guys?"

They had followed the avenue at the base of the ramp for a couple of blocks, had seen the barricade (missing Roland's entry into the partially hidden pas-sageway by less than a minute) which lay ahead, and had turned north onto a broad thoroughfare which reminded Eddie of Fifth Avenue. He hadn't dared to tell Susannah that; he was still too bitterly disap-

pointed with this stinking, littered ruin of a city to
articulate anything hopeful.

"Fifth Avenue" led them into an area of large white
stone buildings that reminded Eddie of the way Rome
looked in the gladiator movies he'd watched on TV
as a kid. They were austere and, for the most part,
still in good shape. He was pretty sure they had been
public buildings of some sort—galleries, libraries,
maybe museums. One, with a big domed roof that
had cracked like a granite egg, might have been an
observatory, although Eddie had read someplace that
astronomers liked to be *away* from big cities, because
all the electric lights fucked up their star-gazing.

There were open areas between these imposing edi-
fices, and although the grass and flowers which had
once grown there had been choked off by weeds and
tangles of underbrush, the area still had a stately feel,
and Eddie wondered if it had once been the center of
Lud's cultural life. Those days were long gone, of
course; Eddie doubted if Gasher and his pals were
very interested in ballet or chamber music.

He and Susannah had come to a major intersection
from which four more broad avenues radiated outward
like spokes on a wheel. At the hub of the wheel was
a large paved square. Ringing it were loudspeakers on
forty-foot steel posts. In the center of the square was
a pedestal with the remains of a statue upon it—a
mighty copper war-horse, green with verdigris, pawing
its forelegs at the air. The warrior who had once ridden this charger lay off to the side on one corroded
shoulder, waving what looked like a machine-gun in
one hand and a sword in the other. His legs were still
bowed around the shape of the horse he had once
ridden, but his boots remained welded to the sides of
his metal mount. GRAYS DIE! was written across the
pedestal in fading orange letters.

Glancing down the radiating streets, Eddie saw
more of the speaker-poles. A few had fallen over, but
most still stood, and each of these had been festooned
with a grisly garland of corpses. As a result, the square

into which "Fifth Avenue" emptied and the streets which led away were guarded by a small army of the dead.

"What kind of people *are* they?" Eddie asked again.

He didn't expect an answer and Susannah didn't give one . . . but she could have. She'd had insights into the past of Roland's world before, but never one as clear and sure as this. All of her earlier insights, like those which had come to her in River Crossing, had had a haunting visionary quality, like dreams, but what came now arrived in a single flash, and it was like seeing the twisted face of a dangerous maniac illuminated by a stroke of lightning.

The speakers . . . the hanging bodies . . . the drums. She suddenly understood how they went together as clearly as she had understood that the heavy-laden wagons passing through River Crossing on their way to Jimtown had been pulled by oxen rather than mules or horses.

"Never mind this trash," she said, and her voice only quivered a little. "It's the train we want—which way is it, d'you think?"

Eddie glanced up at the darkening sky and easily picked out the path of the Beam in the rushing clouds. He looked back down and wasn't much surprised to see that the entrance to the street corresponding most closely to the path of the Beam was guarded by a large stone turtle. Its reptilian head peered out from beneath the granite lip of its shell; its deepset eyes seemed to stare curiously at them. Eddie nodded toward it and managed a small dry smile. "See the turtle of enormous girth?"

Susannah took a brief look of her own and nodded. He pushed her across the city square and into The Street of the Turtle. The corpses which lined it gave off a dry, cinnamony smell that made Eddie's stomach clench . . . not because it was bad but because it was actually rather pleasant—the sugar-spicy aroma of something a kid would enjoy shaking onto his morning toast.

The Street of the Turtle was mercifully broad, and most of the corpses hanging from the speaker-poles were little more than mummies, but Susannah saw a few which were relatively fresh, with flies still crawling busily across the blackening skin of their swollen faces and maggots still squirming out of their decaying eyes.

And below each speaker was a little drift of bones.

"There must be thousands," Eddie said. "Men, women, and kids."

"Yes." Susannah's calm voice sounded distant and strange to her own ears. "They've had a lot of time to kill. And they've used it to kill each other."

"Bring on those wise fuckin elves!" Eddie said, and the laugh that followed sounded suspiciously like a sob. He thought he was at last beginning to fully understand what that innocuous phrase—*the world has moved on*—really meant. What a breadth of ignorance and evil it covered.

And what a depth.

The speakers were a wartime measure, Susannah thought. *Of course they were. God only knows which war, or how long ago, but it must have been a doozy. The rulers of Lud used the speakers to make city-wide announcements from some central, bomb-proof location—a bunker like the one Hitler and his high command retreated to at the end of World War II.*

And in her ears she could hear the voice of authority which had come rolling out of those speakers—could hear it as clearly as she had heard the creak of the wagons passing through River Crossing, as clearly as she had heard the crack of the whip above the backs of the straining oxen.

Ration centers A and D will be closed today; please proceed to centers B, C, E, and F with proper coupons.

Militia squads Nine, Ten, and Twelve report to Sendside.

Aerial bombardment is likely between the hours of eight and ten of the clock. All noncombatant residents should report to their designated shelters. Bring your gas masks. Repeat, bring your gas masks.

Announcements, yes . . . and some garbled version of the news—a propagandized, militant version George Orwell would have called doublespeak. And in between the news bulletins and the announcements, squalling military music and exhortations to respect the fallen by sending more men and women into the red throat of the abattoir.

Then the war had ended and silence had fallen . . . for a while. But at some point, the speakers had begun broadcasting again. How long ago? A hundred years? Fifty? Did it matter? Susannah thought not. What mattered was that when the speakers were reactivated, the only thing they broadcast was a single tape-loop . . . the loop with the drum-track on it. And the descendents of the city's original residents had taken it for . . . what? The Voice of the Turtle? The Will of the Beam?

Susannah found herself remembering the time she had asked her father, a quiet but deeply cynical man, if he believed there was a God in heaven who guided the course of human events. *Well*, he had said, *I think it's sort of half 'n half, Odetta. I'm sure there's a God, but I don't think He has much if anything to do with us these days; I believe that after we killed His son, He finally got it through His head that there wasn't nothing to be done with the sons of Adam or the daughters of Eve, and He washed His hands of us. Wise fella.*

She had responded to this (which she had fully expected; she was eleven at the time, and knew the turn of her father's mind quite well) by showing him a squib on the Community Churches page of the local newspaper. It said that Rev. Murdock of the Grace Methodist Church would that Sunday elucidate on the topic "God Speaks to Each of Us Every Day"—with a text from First Corinthians. Her father had laughed over that so hard that tears had squirted from the corners of his eyes. *Well, I guess each of us hears* someone *talking*, he had said at last, *and you can bet your bottom dollar on one thing, sweetie: each of us— including this here Reverend Murdock—hears that voice say just exactly what he wants to hear. It's so convenient that way.*

What *these* people had apparently wanted to hear in the recorded drum-track was an invitation to commit ritual murder. And now, when the drums began to throb through these hundreds or thousands of speakers—a hammering back-beat which was only the percussion to a Z.Z. Top song called "Velcro Fly," if Eddie was right—it became their signal to unlimber the hangropes and run a few folks up the nearest speaker-posts.

How many? she wondered as Eddie rolled her along in her wheelchair, its nicked and dented hard rubber tires crackling over broken glass and whispering through drifts of discarded paper. *How many have been killed over the years because some electronic circuit under the city got the hiccups? Did it start because they recognized the essential alienness of the music, which came somehow—like us, and the airplane, and some of the cars along these streets—from another world?*

She didn't know, but she knew she had come around to her father's cynical point of view on the subject of God and the chats He might or might not have with the sons of Adam and the daughters of Eve. These people had been looking for a reason to slaughter each other, that was all, and the drums had been as good a reason as any.

She found herself thinking of the hive they had found—the misshapen hive of white bees whose honey would have poisoned them if they had been foolish enough to eat of it. Here, on this side of the Send, was another dying hive; more mutated white bees whose sting would be no less deadly for their confusion, loss, and perplexity.

And how many more will have to die before the tape finally breaks?

As if her thoughts had caused it to happen, the speakers suddenly began to transmit the relentless, syncopated heartbeat of the drums. Eddie yelled in

surprise. Susannah screamed and clapped both hands
to her ears—but before she did, she could faintly hear
the rest of the music: the track or tracks which had
been muted decades ago when someone (probably
quite by accident) had bumped the balance control,
knocking it all the way to one side and burying both
the guitars and the vocal.

Eddie continued to push her along The Street of
the Turtle and the Path of the Beam, trying to look
in all directions at once and trying not to smell the
odor of putrefaction. *Thank God for the wind*, he
thought.

He began to push the wheelchair faster, scanning
the weedy gaps between the big white buildings for
the graceful sweep of an overhead monorail track. He
wanted to get out of this endless aisle of the dead. As
he took yet another deep breath of that speciously
sweet cinnamon smell, it seemed to him that he had
never wanted anything so badly in his whole life.

19

JAKE'S DAZE WAS BROKEN abruptly when Gasher
grabbed him by the collar and yanked with all the
force of a cruel rider braking a galloping horse. He
stuck one leg out at the same time and Jake went
crashing backward over it. His head connected with
the pavement and for a moment all the lights went
out. Gasher, no humanitarian, brought him around
quickly by seizing Jake's lower lip and yanking it upward and outward.

Jake screamed and bolted to a sitting position, striking out blindly with his fists. Gasher dodged the blows
easily, hooked his other hand into Jake's armpit, and
yanked him to his feet. Jake stood there, rocking
drunkenly back and forth. He was beyond protest
now; almost beyond understanding. All he knew for
sure was that every muscle in his body felt sprung and

his wounded hand was howling like an animal caught in a trap.

Gasher apparently needed a breather, and this time he was slower getting his wind back. He stood bent over with his hands planted on the knees of his green trousers, panting in fast little whistling breaths. His yellow headscarf had slipped askew. His good eye glittered like a trumpery diamond. The white silk eye-patch was now wrinkled, and curds of evil-looking yellow muck oozed onto his cheek from beneath it.

"Take a look over your head, cully, and you'll see why I brung you up short. Get an eyeful!"

Jake tilted his head upward, and in the depths of his shock he was not at all surprised to see a marble fountain as big as a house-trailer dangling eighty feet above them. He and Gasher were almost below it. The fountain was held suspended by two rusty cables which were mostly hidden within huge, unsteady stacks of church pews. Even in his less-than-acute state, Jake saw that these cables were more seriously frayed than the remaining hangers on the bridge had been.

"See it?" Gasher asked, grinning. He raised his left hand to his covered eye, scooped a mass of the pussy material from beneath it, and flicked it indifferently aside. "Beauty, ain't it? Oh, the Tick-Tock Man's a trig cove, all right, and no mistake. (Where's those goat-fucking drums? They should have started by now—if Copperhead's forgot em, I'll ram a stick so far up his arse he'll taste bark.) Now look ahead of you, my delicious little squint."

Jake did, and Gasher immediately clouted him so hard that he staggered backward and almost fell.

"Not *across*, idiot child! *Down!* See them two dark cobblestones?"

After a moment, Jake did. He nodded apathetically.

"Yer don't wanter step on em, for that'd bring the whole works down on your head, cully, and anybody who wanted yer after that'd have to pick yer up with a blotter. Understand?"

Jake nodded again.

"Good." Gasher took a final deep breath and slapped Jake's shoulder. "Go on, then, whatcher waitin for? *Hup!*"

Jake stepped over the first of the discolored stones and saw it wasn't really a cobblestone at all but a metal plate which had been rounded to look like one. The second was just ahead of it, cunningly placed so that if an unaware intruder happened to miss the first one, he or she would almost certainly step on the second.

Go ahead and do it, then, he thought. *Why not? The gunslinger's never going to find you in this maze, so go ahead and bring it down. It's got to be cleaner than what Gasher and his friends have got planned for you. Quicker, too.*

His dusty moccasin wavered in the air above the booby-trap.

Gasher hit him with a fist in the middle of the back, but not hard. "Thinkin about takin a ride on the handsome, are you, my little cull?" he asked. The laughing cruelty in his voice had been replaced by simple curiosity. If it was tinged with any other emotion, it wasn't fear but amusement. "Well, go ahead, if it's what yer mean to do, for I have my ticket already. Only be quick about it, gods blast your eyes."

Jake's foot came down beyond the trigger of the booby-trap. His decision to live a little longer was not based on any hope that Roland would find him; it was just that this was what Roland would do—go on until someone made him stop, and then a few yards farther still if he could.

If he did it now, he could take Gasher with him, but Gasher alone wasn't sufficient—one look was enough to make it clear that he was telling the truth when he said he was dying already. If he went on, he might have a chance to take some of the Gasherman's friends, too—maybe even the one he called the Tick-Tock Man.

If I'm going to ride what he calls the handsome, Jake thought, *I'd just as soon go with plenty of company*.

Roland would have understood.

20

JAKE WAS WRONG IN his assessment of the gunslinger's ability to follow their path through the maze; Jake's pack was only the most obvious bit of sign they left behind them, but Roland quickly realized he did not have to pause to look for sign. He only had to follow Oy.

He paused at several intersecting passages nevertheless, wanting to make sure, and each time he did, Oy looked back and uttered his low, impatient bark that seemed to say, *Hurry up! Do you want to lose them?* After the signs he saw—a track, a thread from Jake's shirt, a scrap of bright yellow cloth from Gasher's scarf—had three times confirmed the bumbler's choices, Roland simply followed Oy. He did not give up looking for sign, but he quit making stops to hunt for it. Then the drums started up, and it was the drums—plus Gasher's nosiness about what Jake might be carrying—that saved Roland's life that afternoon.

He skidded to a halt in his dusty boots, and his gun was in his hand before he realized what the sound was. When he did realize, he dropped the revolver back into its holster with an impatient grunt. He was about to go on again when his eye happened first on Jake's pack . . . and then on a pair of faint, gleaming streaks in midair just to the left of it. Roland narrowed his eyes and made out two thin wires which crisscrossed at knee level not three feet in front of him. Oy, who was built low to the ground, had scurried neatly through the inverted V formed by the wires, but if not for the drums and spotting Jake's castoff pack, Roland would have run right into them. As his eyes moved upward, tracing the not-quite-random piles of junk poised on either side of the passage-way at this point, Roland's mouth tightened. It had been a close call, and only *ka* had saved him.

Oy barked impatiently.

Roland dropped to his belly and crawled beneath the wires, moving slowly and carefully—he was bigger than either Jake or Gasher, and he realized a really big man wouldn't be able to get under here at all without triggering the carefully prepared avalanche. The drums pumped and thumped in his ears. *I wonder if they've all gone mad*, he thought. *If I had to listen to that every day, I think I would have.*

He got to the far side of the wires, picked up the pack, and looked inside. Jake's books and a few items of clothing were still in there, so were the treasures he had picked up along the way—a rock which gleamed with yellow flecks that looked like gold but weren't; an arrowhead, probably the leaving of the old forest folk, which Jake had found in a grove of trees the day after his drawing; some coins from his own world; his father's sunglasses; a few other things which only a boy not yet in his teens could really love and understand. Things he would want back again . . . if, that was, Roland got to him before Gasher and his friends could change him, hurt him in ways that would cause him to lose interest in the innocent pursuits and curiosities of pre-adolescent boyhood.

Gasher's grinning face swam into Roland's mind like the face of a demon or a djinni from a bottle: the snaggle teeth, the vacant eyes, the mandrus crawling over the cheeks and spreading beneath the stubbly lines of the jaws. *If you hurt him* . . . he thought, and then forced his mind away, because that line of thought was a blind alley. If Gasher hurt the boy (*Jake!* his mind insisted fiercely—*Not just the boy but Jake! Jake!*), Roland would kill him, yes. But the act would mean nothing, for Gasher was a dead man already.

The gunslinger lengthened the straps of the pack, marvelling at the clever buckles which made this possible, slipped it onto his own back, and stood up again. Oy turned to be off, but Roland called his name and the bumbler looked back.

"To me, Oy." Roland didn't know if the bumbler could understand (or if he would obey even if he did), but it would be better—safer—if he stayed close. Where there was one booby-trap, there were apt to be more. Next time Oy might not be so lucky.

"Ake!" Oy barked, not moving. The bark was assertive, but Roland thought he saw more of the truth about how Oy felt in his eyes: they were dark with fear.

"Yes, but it's dangerous," Roland said. "To me, Oy."

Back the way they had come, there was a thud as something heavy fell, probably dislodged by the punishing vibration of the drums. Roland could now see speaker-poles here and there, poking out of the wreckage like strange long-necked animals.

Oy trotted back to him and looked up, panting.

"Stay close."

"Ake! Ake-Ake!"

"Yes. Jake." He began to run again, and Oy ran beside him, heeling as neatly as any dog Roland had ever seen.

21

FOR EDDIE, IT WAS, as some wise man had once said, *déjà vu* all over again: he was running with the wheelchair, racing time. The beach had been replaced by The Street of the Turtle, but somehow everything else was the same. Oh, there *was* one other relevant difference: now it was a railway station (or a cradle) he was looking for, not a free-standing door.

Susannah was sitting bolt upright with her hair blowing out behind her and Roland's revolver in her right hand, its barrel pointed up at the cloudy, troubled sky. The drums thudded and pounded, bludgeoning them with sound. A gigantic, dish-shaped object lay in the street just ahead, and Eddie's overstrained mind, perhaps cued by the classical buildings on either side of them, produced an image of Jove and Thor playing Frisbee. Jove throws one wide and Thor lets it fall through a cloud—what the hell, it's Miller Time on Olympus, anyway.

Frisbees of the gods, he thought, swerving Susannah between two crumbling, rusty cars, *what a concept.*

He bumped the chair up on the sidewalk to get around the artifact, which looked like some sort of telecommunications dish now that he was really close to it. He was easing the wheelchair over the curb and back into the street again—the sidewalk was too littered with crap to make any real time—when the drums suddenly cut out. The echoes rolled away into a new silence, except it wasn't really silent at all, Eddie realized. Up ahead, the arched entrance to a marble building stood at the intersection of The Street of the Turtle and another avenue. This building had been overgrown by vines and some straggly green stuff that looked like cypress beards, but it was still magnificent and somehow dignified. Beyond it, around the corner, a crowd was babbling excitedly.

"Don't stop!" Susannah snapped. "We haven't got time to—"

A hysterical shriek drilled through the babble. It was accompanied by yells of approval, and, incredibly, the sort of applause Eddie had heard in Atlantic City hotel-casinos after some lounge act had finished doing its thing. The shriek was choked into a long, dying gargle that sounded like the buzz of a cicada. Eddie felt the hair on the nape of his neck coming to attention. He glanced at the corpses hanging from the nearest speaker-pole and understood that the fun-loving Pubes of Lud were holding another public execution.

Marvellous, he thought. *Now if they only had Tony Orlando and Dawn to sing "Knock Three Times," they could all die happy.*

Eddie looked curiously at the stone pile on the corner. This close, the vines which overgrew it had a powerful herbal smell. That smell was eye-wateringly bitter, but he still liked it better than the cinnamon-sweet odor of the mummified corpses. The beards of greenery growing from the vines drooped in ratty sheaves, creating waterfalls of vegetation where once there had been a series of arched entrances. A figure suddenly barrelled out through one of these waterfalls and hurried toward them. It was a kid, Eddie realized, and not that many years out of diapers, judging by the size. He was wearing a weird little Lord Fauntleroy outfit, complete with ruffled white shirt and velveteen short pants. There were ribbons in his hair. Eddie felt a sudden mad urge to wave his hands above his head and scream *But-wheat say, "Lud is o-tay!"*

"Come on!" the kid cried in a high, piping voice. Several sprays of the green stuff had gotten caught in his hair; he brushed absently at these with his left hand as he ran. "They're gonna do Spankers! It's the Spankerman's turn to go to the land of the drums! Come on or you'll miss the whole fakement, gods cuss it!"

Susannah was equally stunned by the child's appearance, but as he got closer, it struck her that there was something extremely odd and awkward about the way he was brushing at the crumbles and strands of greenery which had gotten caught in his beribboned hair: he kept using just that one hand. His other had been behind his back when he ran out through the weedy waterfall, and there it remained.

How awkward that must be! she thought, and then a tape-player turned on in her mind and she heard Roland speaking at the end of the bridge. *I knew something like this could happen . . . if we'd seen the fellow earlier, while we were still beyond the range of his exploding egg . . . Damn the luck!*

She levelled Roland's gun at the child, who had leaped from the curb and was running straight for them. *"Hold it!"* she screamed. *"Stand still, you!"*

"Suze, what are you *doing*?" Eddie yelled.

Susannah ignored him. In a very real sense, Susannah Dean was no longer even here; it was Detta Walker in the chair now, and her eyes were glittering with feverish suspicion. *"Stop or I'll shoot!"*

Little Lord Fauntleroy might have been deaf for all the effect her warning had. "Hoss it!" he shouted jubilantly. "Yer gointer miss the whole show! Spanker's gointer—"

His right hand finally began to come out from behind his back. As it did, Eddie realized they weren't looking at a kid but at a misshapen dwarf whose childhood was many years past. The expression Eddie had at first taken for childish glee was actually a chilly mixture of hate and rage. The dwarf's cheeks and brow were covered with the oozing, discolored patches Roland called whore's blossoms.

Susannah never saw his face. Her attention was fixed on the emerging right hand, and the dull green sphere it held. That was all she needed to see. Roland's gun crashed. The dwarf was hammered backward. A shrill cry of pain and rage rose from his tiny mouth as he landed on the sidewalk. The grenade bounced out of his hand and rolled back into the same arch through which he had emerged.

Detta was gone like a dream, and Susannah looked from the smoking gun to the tiny, sprawled figure on the sidewalk with surprise, horror, and dismay. "Oh, my Jesus! I shot him! Eddie, I shot him!"

"Grays . . . *die*!"

Little Lord Fauntleroy tried to scream these words defiantly, but they came out in a bubbling choke of blood that drenched the few remaining white patches on his frilly shirt. There was a muffled explosion from inside the overgrown plaza of the corner building, and the shaggy carpets of green stuff hanging in front of the arches billowed outward like flags in a brisk gale. With them came clouds of choking, acrid smoke. Eddie flung himself on top of Susannah to shield her, and felt a gritty shower of concrete fragments—all small ones, luckily—patter down on his back, his neck, and the crown of his head. There was a series of unpleasantly wet smacking sounds to his left. He opened his eyes a crack, looked in that direction, and saw Little Lord Fauntleroy's head just coming to a stop in the gutter. The dwarf's eyes were still open, his mouth still fixed in its final snarl.

Now there were other voices, some shrieking, some yelling, all furious. Eddie rolled off Susannah's chair—it tottered on one wheel before deciding to stay up—and stared in the direction from which the dwarf had come. A ragged mob of about twenty men and women had appeared, some coming from around the corner, others pushing through the mats of foliage which obscured the corner building's arches, materializing from the smoke of the dwarf's grenade like evil spirits. Most were wearing blue headscarves and all were carrying weapons—a varied (and somehow pitiful) assortment of them which included rusty swords, dull knives, and splintery clubs. Eddie saw one man defiantly waving a hammer. *Pubes*, Eddie thought. *We interrupted their necktie party, and they're pissed as hell about it.*

A tangle of shouts—*Kill the Grays! Kill them both! They've done for Luster, God kill their eyes!*—arose from this charming group as they caught sight of Susannah in her wheelchair and Eddie, who was now crouched on one knee before it. The man in the forefront was wearing a kilt-like wrap and waving a cutlass. He brandished this wildly (he would have decapitated the heavyset woman standing close behind him, had she not ducked) and then charged. The others followed, yelling happily.

Roland's gun pounded its bright thunder into the windy, overcast day, and the top of the kilt-wearing Pube's head lifted off. The sallow skin of the woman who had almost been decapitated by his cutlass was suddenly stippled with red rain and she voiced a sound of barking dismay. The others came on past the woman and the dead man, raving and wild-eyed.

"Eddie!" Susannah screamed, and fired again. A man wearing a silk-lined cape and knee-boots collapsed into the street.

Eddie groped for the Ruger and had one panicky moment when he thought he had lost it. The butt of the gun had somehow slipped down inside the waistband of his pants. He wrapped his hand around it and yanked hard. The fucking thing wouldn't come. The sight at the end of the barrel had somehow gotten stuck in his underwear.

Susannah fired three closely spaced shots. Each found a target, but the oncoming Pubes didn't slow.

"Eddie, help me!"

Eddie tore his pants open, feeling like some cut-rate version of Superman, and finally managed to free the Ruger. He hit the safety with the heel of his left palm, placed his elbow on his leg just above the knee, and began to fire. There was no need to think—no need to even aim. Roland had told them that in battle a gunslinger's hands worked on their own, and Eddie now discovered it was true. It would have been hard for a blind man to miss at this range, anyway. Susannah had cut the numbers of the charging Pubes to no more than fifteen; Eddie went through the remainder like a storm wind in a wheatfield, dropping four in less than two seconds.

Now the single face of the mob, that look of glazed and mindless eagerness, began to break apart. The man with the hammer abruptly tossed his weapon aside and ran for it, limping extravagantly on a pair of arthritis-twisted legs. He was followed by two others. The rest of them milled uncertainly in the street.

"Come on, you deuces!" a relatively young man snarled. He wore his blue scarf around his throat like a rally-racer's ascot. He was bald except for two fluffs of frizzy red hair, one on each side of his head. To Susannah, this fellow looked like Clarabell the Clown; to Eddie he looked like Ronald McDonald; to both of them he looked like trouble. He threw a home-made spear that might have started life as a steel ta-

bleleg. It clattered harmlessly into the street to Eddie
and Susannah's right. "Come on, I say! We can get
em if we all stick togeth—"

"Sorry, guy," Eddie murmured, and shot him in the
chest.

Clarabell/Ronald staggered backward, one hand
going to his shirt. He stared at Eddie with huge eyes
that told his tale with heartbreaking clarity: this wasn't
supposed to happen. The hand dropped heavily to the
young man's side. A single runlet of blood, incredibly
bright in the gray day, slipped from the corner of his
mouth. The few remaining Pubes stared at him mutely
as he slipped to his knees, and one of them turned to
run.

"Not at all," Eddie said. "Stay put, my retarded
friend, or you're going to get a good look at the clearing where your path ends." He raised his voice. "Drop
em, boys and girls! All of em! Now!"

"You . . ." the dying man whispered. "You . . .
gunslinger?"

"That's right," Eddie said. His eyes surveyed the
remaining Pubes grimly.

"Cry your . . . pardon," the man with the frizzy red
hair gasped, and then he fell forward onto his face.

"Gunslingers?" one of the others asked. His tone
was one of dawning horror and realization.

"Well, you're stupid, but you ain't deaf," Susannah
said, "and that's somethin, anyway." She waggled the
barrel of the gun, which Eddie was quite sure was
empty. For that matter, how many rounds could be
left in the Ruger? He realized he didn't have any idea
how many rounds the clip held, and cursed himself
for a fool . . . but had he really believed it could come
to something like this? He didn't think so. "You heard
him, folks. Drop em. Recess is over."

One by one, they complied. The woman who was
wearing a pint or so of Mr. Sword-and-Kilt's blood
on her face said, "You shouldn't've killed Winston,
missus—'twas his birthday, so it was."

"Well, I guess he should have stayed home and

eaten some more birthday cake," Eddie said. Given the overall quality of this experience, he didn't find either the woman's comment or his own response at all surreal.

There was one other woman among the remaining Pubes, a scrawny thing whose long blonde hair was coming out in big patches, as if she had the mange. Eddie observed her sidling toward the dead dwarf—and the potential safety of the overgrown arches beyond him—and put a bullet into the cracked cement close by her foot. He had no idea what he wanted with her, but what he didn't want was one of them giving the rest of them ideas. For one thing, he was afraid of what his hands might do if the sickly, sullen people before him tried to run. Whatever his head thought about this gunslinging business, his hands had discovered they liked it just fine.

"Stand where you are, beautiful. Officer Friendly says play it safe." He glanced at Susannah and was disturbed by the grayish quality of her complexion. "Suze, you all right?" he asked in a lower voice.

"Yes."

"You're not going to faint or anything, are you? Because—"

"No." She looked at him with eyes so dark they were like caves. "It's just that I never shot anyone before . . . okay?"

Well, you better get used to it rose to his lips. He bit it back and returned his gaze to the five people who remained before them. They were looking at him and Susannah with a species of sullen fear which nevertheless stopped well short of terror.

Shit, most of them have forgotten what terror is, he thought. *Joy, sadness, love . . . same thing. I don't think they feel much of anything, anymore. They've been living in this purgatory too long.*

Then he remembered the laughter, the excited cries, the lounge-act applause, and revised his thinking. There was at least one thing that still got their motors running, one thing that still pushed their buttons. Spanker could have testified to that.

"Who's in charge here?" Eddie asked. He was watching the intersection behind the little group very carefully in case the others should get their courage back. So far he saw and heard nothing alarming from that direction. He thought that the others had probably left this ragged crew to its fate.

They looked at each other uncertainly, and finally the woman with the blood-spattered face spoke up. "Spanker was, but when the god-drums started up this time, it was Spanker's stone what come out of the hat and we set him to dance. I guess Winston would have come next, but you did for him with your god-rotted guns, so you did." She wiped blood deliberately from her cheek, looked at it, and then returned her sullen glance to Eddie.

"Well, what do you think Winston was trying to do to me with his god-rotted spear?" Eddie asked. He was disgusted to find the woman had actually made him feel guilty about what he had done. "Trim my sideburns?"

"Killed Frank 'n Luster, too," she went on doggedly, "and what are you? Either Grays, which is bad, or a couple of god-rotted outlanders, which is worse. Who's left for the Pubes in City North? Topsy, I suppose—Topsy the Sailor—but he ain't here, is he? Took his boat and went off downriver, ay, so he did, and god rot him, too, says I!"

Susannah had ceased listening; her mind had fixed with horrified fascination on something the woman had said earlier. *It was Spanker's stone what come out of the hat and we set him to dance.* She remembered reading Shirley Jackson's story "The Lottery" in college and understood that these people, the degenerate descendents of the original Pubes, were living Jackson's nightmare. No wonder they weren't capable of any strong emotion when they knew they would have to participate in such a grisly drawing not once a year, as in the story, but two or three times each day.

"Why?" she asked the bloody woman in a harsh, horrified voice. "Why do you do it?"

The woman looked at Susannah as if she was the world's biggest fool. "Why? So the ghosts what live in the machines won't take over the bodies of those who have died here—Pubes and Grays alike—and send them up through the holes in the streets to eat us. Any fool knows that."

"There are no such things as ghosts," Susannah said, and her voice sounded like so much meaningless quacking to her own ears. Of course there were. In this world, there were ghosts everywhere. Nevertheless, she pushed ahead. "What you call the god-drums is only a tape stuck in a machine. That's really all it is." Sudden inspiration struck her and she added: "Or maybe the Grays are doing it on purpose—did you ever think of that? They live in the other part of the city, don't they? And under it, as well? They've always wanted you out. Maybe they've just hit on a really efficient way of getting you guys to do their work for them."

The bloody woman was standing next to an elderly gent wearing what looked like the world's oldest bowler hat and a pair of frayed khaki shorts. Now he stepped forward and spoke to her with a patina of good manners that turned his underlying contempt into a dagger with razor-sharp edges. "You are quite wrong, Madam Gunslinger. There are a great many machines under Lud, and there are ghosts in all of them—demonous spirits which bear only ill will to mortal men and women. These demon-ghosts are *very* capable of raising the dead . . . and in Lud, there are a great many dead to raise."

"Listen," Eddie said. "Have you ever seen one of these zombies with your own eyes, Jeeves? Have *any* of you?"

Jeeves curled his lip and said nothing—but that lip-curl really said it all. What else could one expect, it asked, from outlanders who used guns as a substitute for understanding?

Eddie decided it would be best to close off the whole line of discussion. He had never been cut out for missionary work, anyway. He waggled the Ruger at the bloodstained woman. "You and your friend there—the one who looks like an English butler on his day off—are going to take us to the railroad station. After that, we can all say goodbye, and I'll tell you the truth: that's going to make my fuckin day."

"Railroad station?" the guy who looked like Jeeves the Butler asked. "What is a railroad station?"

"Take us to the cradle," Susannah said. "Take us to Blaine."

This finally rattled Jeeves; an expression of shocked horror replaced the world-weary contempt with which he had thus far treated them. "You can't go there!" he cried. "The cradle is forbidden ground, and Blaine is the most dangerous of all Lud's ghosts!"

Forbidden ground? Eddie thought. *Great. If it's the truth, at least we'll be able to stop worrying about you assholes.* It was also nice to hear that there still *was* a Blaine . . . or that these people thought there was, anyway.

The others were staring at Eddie and Susannah with expressions of uncomprehending amazement; it was as if the interlopers had suggested to a bunch of born-again Christians that they hunt up the Ark of the Covenant and turn it into a pay toilet.

Eddie raised the Ruger until the center of Jeeves's forehead lay in the sight. "We're going," he said, "and if you don't want to join your ancestors right here and now, I suggest you stop pissing and moaning and take us there."

Jeeves and the bloodstained woman exchanged an uncertain glance, but when the man in the bowler hat looked back at Eddie and Susannah, his face was firm and set. "Shoot us if you like," he said. "We'd sooner die here than there."

"You folks are a bunch of sick motherfuckers with dying on the brain!" Susannah cried at them. '*No-*

body has to die! Just take us where we want to go, for the love of God!"

The woman said somberly, "But it *is* death to enter Blaine's cradle, mum, so it is. For Blaine sleeps, and he who disturbs his rest must pay a high price."

"Come on, beautiful," Eddie snapped. "You can't smell the coffee with your head up your ass."

"I don't know what that means," she said with an odd and perplexing dignity.

"It means you can take us to the cradle and risk the Wrath of Blaine, or you can stand your ground here and experience the Wrath of Eddie. It doesn't have to be a nice clean head-shot, you know. I can take you a piece at a time, and I'm feeling just mean enough to do it. I'm having a very bad day in your city—the music sucks, everybody has a bad case of b.o., and the first guy we saw threw a grenade at us and kidnapped our friend. So what do you say?"

"Why would you go to Blaine in any case?" one of the others asked. "He stirs no more from his berth in the cradle—not for years now. He has even stopped speaking in his many voices and laughing."

Speaking in his many voices and laughing? Eddie thought. He looked at Susannah. She looked back and shrugged.

"Ardis was the last to go nigh Blaine," the blood-stained woman said.

Jeeves nodded somberly. "Ardis always was a fool when he were in drink. Blaine asked him some question. I heard it, but it made no sense to me—something about the mother of ravens, I think—and when Ardis couldn't answer what was asked, Blaine slew him with blue fire."

"Electricity?" Eddie asked.

Jeeves and the bloodstained woman both nodded. "Ay," the woman said. "Electricity, so it were called in the old days, so it were."

"You don't have to go in with us," Susannah proposed suddenly. "Just get us within sight of the place. We'll go the rest of the way on our own."

The woman looked at her mistrustfully, and then Jeeves pulled her head close to his lips and mumbled in her ear for a while. The other Pubes stood behind them in a ragged line, looking at Eddie and Susannah with the dazed eyes of people who have survived a bad air-raid.

At last the woman looked around. "Ay," she said. "We'll take you nigh the cradle, and then it's good riddance to bad swill."

"My idea exactly," Eddie said. "You and Jeeves. The rest of you, scatter." He swept them with his eyes. "But remember this—one spear thrown from ambush, one arrow, one brick, and these two die." This threat came out sounding so weak and pointless that Eddie wished he hadn't made it. How could they possibly care for these two, or for any of the individual members of their clan, when they dusted two or more of them each and every day? Well, he thought, watching the others trot off without so much as a backward glance, it was too late to worry about that now.

"Come on," the woman said. "I want to be done with you."

"The feeling's mutual," Eddie replied.

But before she and Jeeves led them away, the woman did something which made Eddie repent a little of his hard thoughts: knelt, brushed back the hair of the man in the kilt, and placed a kiss on his dirty cheek. "Goodbye, Winston," she said. "Wait for me where the trees clear and the water's sweet. I'll come to ye, ay, as sure as dawn makes shadows run west."

"I didn't want to kill him," Susannah said. "I want you to know that. But I wanted to die even less."

"Ay." The face that turned toward Susannah was stern and tearless. "But if ye mean to enter Blaine's cradle, ye'll die anyway. And the chances are that ye'll die envying poor old Winston. He's cruel, is Blaine. The cruelest of all demons in this cruel, cruel place."

"Come on, Maud," Jeeves said, and helped her up.

"Ay. Let's finish with them." She surveyed Susannah and Eddie again, her eyes stern but somehow confused, as well. "Gods curse my eyes that they should ever have happened on you two in the first place. And gods curse the guns ye carry, as well, for they were always the springhead of our troubles."

And with that attitude, Susannah thought, *your troubles are going to last at least a thousand years, sugar.*

Maud set a rapid pace along The Street of the Turtle. Jeeves trotted beside her. Eddie, who was pushing Susannah in the wheelchair, was soon panting and struggling to keep up. The palatial buildings which lined their way spread out until they resembled ivy-covered country houses on huge, run-to-riot lawns, and Eddie realized they had entered what had once been a very ritzy neighborhood indeed. Ahead of them, one building loomed above all others. It was a deceptively simple square construction of white stone blocks, its overhanging roof supported by many pillars. Eddie thought again of the gladiator movies he'd so enjoyed as a kid. Susannah, educated in more formal schools, was reminded of the Parthenon. Both saw and marvelled at the gorgeously sculpted bestiary—Bear and Turtle, Fish and Rat, Horse and Dog—which ringed the top of the building in two-by-two parade, and understood it was the place they had come to find.

That uneasy sensation that they were being watched by many eyes—eyes filled equally with hate and wonder—never left them. Thunder boomed as they came in sight of the monorail track; like the storm, the track came sweeping in from the south, joined The Street of the Turtle, and ran straight on toward the Cradle of Lud. And as they neared it, ancient bodies began to twist and dance in the strengthening wind on either side of them.

22

AFTER THEY HAD RUN for God knew how long (all Jake knew for sure was that the drums had stopped again), Gasher once more yanked him to a stop. This time Jake managed to keep his feet. He had gotten his second wind. Gasher, who would never see eleven again, had not.

"Hoo! My old pump's doing nip-ups, sweetie."

"Too bad," Jake said unfeelingly, then stumbled backward as Gasher's gnarled hand connected with the side of his face.

"Yar, you'd cry a bitter tear if I dropped dead right here, woontcher? Too likely! But no such luck, my fine young squint—old Gasher's seen em come and seen em go, and I wasn't born to drop dead at the feet of any little sweetcheeks berry like you."

Jake listened to these incoherencies impassively. He meant to see Gasher dead before the day was over. Gasher might take Jake with him, but Jake no longer cared about that. He dabbed blood from his freshly split lip and looked at it thoughtfully, wondering at how quickly the desire to do murder could invade and conquer the human heart.

Gasher observed Jake looking at his bloody fingers and grinned. "Sap's runnin, ennet? Nor will it be the last your old pal Gasher beats out of your young tree, unless you look sharp; unless you look wery sharp indeed." He pointed down at the cobbled surface of the narrow alley they were currently negotiating. There was a rusty manhole cover there, and Jake realized he had seen the words stamped into the steel not long ago: LaMERK FOUNDRY, they said.

"There's a grip on the side," Gasher said. "Yer see? Get your hands into that and pull away. Step lively, now, and maybe ye'll still have all your teeth when ye meet up with Tick-Tock."

Jake grasped the steel cover and pulled. He pulled hard, but not quite as hard as he could have done. The maze of streets and alleys through which Gasher had run him was bad, but at least he could see. He couldn't imagine what it might be like in the underworld below the city, where the blackness would preclude even dreams of escape, and he didn't intend to find out unless he absolutely had to.

Gasher quickly made it clear to him that he did.

"It's too heavy for—" Jake began, and then the pirate seized him by the throat and yanked him upward until they were face to face. The long run through the alleys had brought a thin, sweaty flush to his cheeks and turned the sores eating into his flesh an ugly yellow-purple color. Those which were open exuded thick infected matter and threads of blood in steady pulses. Jake caught just a whiff of Gasher's thick stench before his wind was cut off by the hand which had encircled his throat.

"Listen, you stupid cull, and listen well, for this is your last warning. You yank that fucking streethead off right now or I'll reach into your mouth and rip the living tongue right out of it. And feel free to bite all you want while I do it, for what I have runs in the blood and you'll see the first blossoms on yer own face before the week's out—if yer lives that long. Now, do you see?"

Jake nodded frantically. Gasher's face was disappearing into deepening folds of gray, and his voice seemed to be coming from a great distance.

"All right." Gasher shoved him backward. Jake fell in a heap beside the manhole cover, gagging and retching. He finally managed to draw in a deep, whooping breath that burned like liquid fire. He spat out a blood-flecked wad of stuff and almost threw up at the sight of it.

"Now yank back that cover, my heart's delight, and let's have no more natter about it."

Jake crawled over to it, slid his hands into the grip, and this time pulled with all his might. For one terrible moment he thought he was still not going to be able to budge it. Then he imagined Gasher's fingers reaching into his mouth and seizing his tongue, and found a little extra. There was a dull, spreading agony in his lower back as something gave there, but the circular lid slipped slowly aside, grinding on the cobbles and exposing a grinning crescent of darkness.

"Good, cully, good!" Gasher cried cheerfully. "What a little mule y'are! Keep pulling—don't give up now!"

When the crescent had become a half-moon and the pain in Jake's lower back was a white-hot fire, Gasher booted him in the ass, knocking him asprawl.

"Wery good!" Gasher said, peering in. "Now, cully, go smartly down the ladder on the side. Mind you don't lose your grip and tumble all the way to the bottom, for those rungs are fearsome slick and greezy. There's twenty or so, as I remember. And when you get to the bottom, stand stock-still and wait for me. You might feel like runnin from yer old pal, but do you think that would be a good idea?"

"No," Jake said. "I suppose not."

"Wery intelligent, old son!" Gasher's lips spread in his hideous smile, once more revealing his few surviving teeth. "It's dark down there, and there are a thousand tunnels going every which-a-way. Yer old pal Gasher knows em like the back of his hand, so he does, but you'd be lost in no time. Then there's the rats—wery big and wery hungry they are. So you just wait."

"I will."

Gasher regarded him narrowly. "You speak just like a little triggie, you do, but you're no Pube—I'll set my watch and warrant to that. Where are you from, squint?"

Jake said nothing.

"Bumbler got your tongue, do he? Well, that's all right; Tick-Tock'll get it all out of you, so he will. He's got a way about him, Ticky does; just naturally wants to make people conwerse. Once he gets em goin, they sometimes talks so fast and screams so loud someone has to hit em over the head to slow em down. Bumblers ain't allowed to hold no one's tongue around the Tick-Tock Man, not even fine young triggers like you. Now get the fuck down that ladder. *Hup!*"

He lashed out with his foot. This time Jake managed to tuck in and dodge the blow. He looked into the half-open manhole, saw the ladder, and started down. He was still chest-high to the alley when a tremendous stonelike crash hammered the air. It came from a mile or more away, but Jake knew what it was without having to be told. A cry of pure misery burst from his lips.

A grim smile tugged at the corners of Gasher's mouth. "Your hardcase friend trailed ye a little better than ye thought he would, didn't he? Not better than *I* thought, though, cully, for I got a look at his eyes—wery pert and cunning they were. I thought he'd come arter his juicy little night-nudge a right smart, if he was to come at all, and so he did. He spied the tripwires, but the fountain's got him, so *that's* all right. Get on, sweetcheeks."

He aimed a kick at Jake's protruding head. Jake ducked it, but one foot slipped on the ladder bolted to the side of the sewer shaft and he only saved himself from falling by clutching Gasher's scab-raddled ankle. He looked up, pleading, and saw no softening on that dying, infected face.

"Please," he said, and heard the word trying to break into a sob. He kept seeing Roland lying crushed beneath the huge fountain. What had Gasher said? If anyone wanted him, they would have to pick him up with a blotter.

"Beg if you want, dear heart. Just don't expect no good to come of it, for mercy stops on this side of the bridge, so it does. Now go down, or I'll kick your bleedin brains right outcher bleedin ears."

So Jake went down, and by the time he reached the standing water at the bottom, the urge to cry had passed. He waited, shoulders slumped and head down, for Gasher to descend and lead him to his fate.

23

ROLAND HAD COME CLOSE to tripping the crossed wires which held back the avalanche of junk, but the dangling fountain was absurd—a trap which might have been set by a stupid child. Cort had taught them to constantly check all visual quadrants as they moved in enemy territory, and that included above as well as behind and below.

"Stop," he told Oy, raising his voice to be heard over the drums.

"Op!" Oy agreed, then looked ahead and immediately added, "Ake!"

"Yes." The gunslinger took another look up at the suspended marble fountain, then examined the street, looking for the trigger. There were two, he saw. Perhaps their camouflage as cobblestones had once been effective, but that time was long past. Roland bent down, hands on his knees, and spoke into Oy's up-turned face. "Going to pick you up for a minute now. Don't fuss, Oy."

"Oy!"

Roland put his arms around the bumbler. At first Oy stiffened and attempted to pull away, and then Roland felt the small animal give in. He wasn't happy about being this close to someone who wasn't Jake, but he clearly intended to put up with it. Roland found himself wondering again just how intelligent Oy was.

He carried him up the narrow passage and beneath The Hanging Fountain of Lud, stepping carefully over the mock cobbles. Once they were safely past, he bent to let Oy go. As he did, the drums stopped.

"Ake!" Oy said impatiently. "Ake-Ake!"

"Yes—but there's a little piece of business to attend to first."

He led Oy fifteen yards farther down the alley, then bent and picked up a chunk of concrete. He tossed it thoughtfully from hand to hand, and as he did, he heard the sound of a pistol-shot from the east. The amplified thump of the drums had buried the sound of Eddie and Susannah's battle with the ragged band of Pubes, but he heard this gunshot clearly and smiled—it almost surely meant that the Deans had reached the cradle, and that was the first good news of this day, which already seemed at least a week long.

Roland turned and threw the piece of concrete. His aim was as true as it had been when he had thrown at the ancient traffic signal in River Crossing; the missile struck one of the discolored triggers dead center, and one of the rusty cables snapped with a harsh twang. The marble fountain dropped, rolling over as the other cable snubbed it for a moment longer—long enough so that a man with fast reflexes could have cleared the drop-zone anyway, Roland reckoned. Then it too let go, and the fountain fell like a pink, misshapen stone.

Roland dropped behind a pile of rusty steel beams and Oy jumped nimbly into his lap as the fountain hit the street with a vast, shattery thump. Chunks of pink marble, some as big as carts, flew through the air. Several small chips stung Roland's face. He brushed others out of Oy's fur. He looked over the makeshift barricade. The fountain had cracked in two like a vast plate. *We won't be coming back this way*, Roland thought. The passageway, narrow to begin with, was now completely blocked.

He wondered if Jake had heard the fall of the fountain, and what he had made of it if he had. He didn't waste such speculation on Gasher; Gasher would think he had been crushed to paste, which was exactly what Roland wanted him to think. Would Jake think the same thing? The boy should know better than to believe a gunslinger could be killed by such a simple device, but if Gasher had terrorized him enough, Jake might not be thinking that clearly. Well, it was too late to worry about it now, and if he had it to do over again, he would do exactly the same thing. Dying or not, Gasher had displayed both courage and animal cunning. If he was off his guard now, the trick was worth it.

Roland got to his feet. "Oy—find Jake."

"Ake!" Oy stretched his head forward on his long neck, sniffed around in a semicircle, picked up Jake's scent, and was off again with Roland running after. Ten minutes later he came to a stop at a manhole cover in the street, sniffed all the way around it, then looked up at Roland and barked shrilly.

The gunslinger dropped to one knee and observed both the confusion of tracks and a wide path of scratches on the cobbles. He thought this particular manhole cover had been moved quite often. His eyes narrowed as he saw the wad of bloody phlegm in a crease between two nearby cobbles.

"The bastard keeps hitting him," he murmured.

He pulled the manhole cover back, looked down, then untied the rawhide lacings which held his shirt closed. He picked the bumbler up and tucked him into his shirt. Oy bared his teeth, and for a moment Roland felt his claws splayed against the flesh of his chest and belly like small sharp knives. Then they withdrew and Oy only peered out of Roland's shirt with his bright eyes, panting like a steam engine. The gunslinger could feel the rapid beat of Oy's heart against his own. He pulled the rawhide lace from the eyelets in his shirt and found another, longer, lace in his purse.

"I'm going to leash you. I don't like it and you're going to like it even less, but it's going to be very dark down there."

He tied the two lengths of rawhide together and formed one end into a wide loop which he slipped over Oy's head. He expected Oy to bare his teeth again, perhaps even to nip him, but Oy didn't. He only looked up at Roland with his gold-ringed eyes and barked "Ake!" again in his impatient voice.

Roland put the loose end of his makeshift leash in his mouth, then sat down on the edge of the sewer shaft . . . if that was what it was. He felt for the top rung of the ladder and found it. He descended slowly and carefully, more aware than ever that he was missing half a hand and that the steel rungs were slimy with oil and some thicker stuff that was probably moss. Oy was a heavy, warm weight between his shirt and belly, panting steadily and harshly. The gold rings in his eyes gleamed like medallions in the dim light.

At last, the gunslinger's groping foot splashed into the water at the bottom of the shaft. He glanced up briefly at the coin of white light far above him. *This is where it starts getting hard,* he thought. The tunnel was warm and dank and smelled like an ancient charnel house. Somewhere nearby, water was dripping hollowly and monotonously. Farther off, Roland could hear the rumble of machinery. He lifted a very grateful Oy out of his shirt and set him down in the shallow water running sluggishly along the sewer tunnel.

"Now it's all up to you," he murmured in the bumbler's ear. "To Jake, Oy. To Jake!"

"Ake!" the bumbler barked, and splashed rapidly off into the darkness, swinging his head from side to side at the end of his long neck like a pendulum. Roland followed with the end of the rawhide leash wrapped around his diminished right hand.

24

THE CRADLE—IT WAS easily big enough to have acquired proper-noun status in their minds—stood in the center of a square five times larger than the one where they had come upon the blasted statue, and when she got a really good look at it, Susannah realized how old and gray and fundamentally grungy the rest of Lud really was. The Cradle was so clean it almost hurt her eyes. No vines overgrew its sides; no graffiti daubed its blinding white walls and steps and columns. The yellow plains dust which had coated everything else was absent here. As they drew closer, Susannah saw why: streams of water coursed endlessly down the sides of the Cradle, issuing from nozzles hidden in the shadows of the copper-sheathed eaves. Interval sprays created by other hidden nozzles washed the steps, turning them into off-and-on waterfalls.

"Wow," Eddie said. "It makes Grand Central look like a Greyhound station in Buttfuck, Nebraska."

"What a poet you are, dear," Susannah said dryly.

The steps surrounded the entire building and rose to a great open lobby. There were no obscuring mats of vegetation here, but Eddie and Susannah found they still couldn't get a good look inside; the shadows thrown by the overhanging roof were too deep. The Totems of the Beam marched all the way around the building, two by two, but the corners were reserved for creatures Susannah fervently hoped never to meet outside of the occasional nightmare—hideous stone dragons with scaly bodies, clutching, claw-tipped hands, and nasty peering eyes.

Eddie touched her shoulder and pointed higher. Susannah looked . . . and felt her breath come to a stop in her throat. Standing astride the peak of the roof, far above The Totems of the Beam and the dragonish gargoyles, as if given dominion over them, was a golden warrior at least sixty feet high. A battered cowboy hat was shoved back to reveal his lined and careworn brow; a bandanna hung askew on his upper chest, as if it had just been pulled down after serving long, hard duty as a dust-muffle. In one upraised fist he held a revolver; in the other, what appeared to be an olive branch.

Roland of Gilead stood atop the Cradle of Lud, dressed in gold.

No, she thought, at last remembering to breathe again. *It's not him . . . but in another way, it is. That man was a gunslinger, and the resemblance between him, who's probably been dead a thousand years or more, and Roland is all the truth of* ka-tet *you'll ever need to know.*

Thunder slammed out of the south. Lightning harried racing clouds across the sky. She wished she had more time to study both the golden statue which stood atop the Cradle and the animals which surrounded it; each of these latter appeared to have words carved upon them, and she had an idea that what was written there might be knowledge worth having. Under these circumstances, however, there was no time to spare.

A wide red strip had been painted across the pavement at the point where The Street of the Turtle emptied into The Plaza of the Cradle. Maud and the fellow Eddie called Jeeves the Butler stopped a prudent distance from the red mark.

"This far and no farther," Maud told them flatly. "You may take us to our deaths, but each man and woman owes one to the gods anyway, and I'll die on this side of the dead-line no matter what. I'll not dare Blaine for outlanders."

"Nor will I," Jeeves said. He had taken off his dusty bowler and was holding it against his naked chest. On his face was an expression of fearful reverence.

"Fine," Susannah said. "Now scat on out of here, both of you."

"Ye'll backshoot us the second we turn from ye," Jeeves said in a trembling voice. "I'll take my watch and warrant on it, so I will."

Maud shook her head. The blood on her face had dried to a grotesque maroon stippling. "There never were a backshooting gunslinger—that much I *will* say."

"We only have *their* word for it that that's what they are."

Maud pointed to the big revolver with the worn sandalwood grip which Susannah held in her hand. Jeeves looked . . . and after a moment he stretched out his hand to the woman. When Maud took it, Susannah's image of them as dangerous killers collapsed. They looked more like Hansel and Gretel than Bonnie and Clyde; tired, frightened, confused, and lost so long in the woods that they had grown old there. Her hate and fear of them departed. What replaced it was pity and a deep, aching sadness.

"Fare you well, both of you," she said softly. "Walk

as you will, and with no fear of harm from me or my man here."

Maud nodded. "I believe you mean us no harm, and I forgive you for shooting Winston. But listen to me, and listen well: *stay out of the Cradle.* Whatever reasons you think you have for going in, they're not good enough. To enter Blaine's Cradle is death."

"We don't have any choice," Eddie said, and thunder banged overhead again, as if in agreement. "Now let me tell *you* something. I don't know what's underneath Lud and what isn't, but I do know those drums you're so whacked out about are part of a recording— a *song*—that was made in the world my wife and I came from." He looked at their uncomprehending faces and raised his arms in frustration. "Jesus Pumpkin-Pie Christ, don't you get it? You're killing each other over a piece of music that was never even released as a single!"

Susannah put her hand on his shoulder and murmured his name. He ignored her for the moment, his eyes flicking from Jeeves to Maud and then back to Jeeves again.

"You want to see monsters? Take a good look at each other, then. And when you get back to whatever funhouse it is you call home, take a good look at your friends and relatives."

"You don't understand," Maud said. Her eyes were dark and somber. "But you will. Ay—you will."

"Go on, now," Susannah said quietly. "Talk between us is no good; the words only drop dead. Just go your way and try to remember the faces of your fathers, for I think you lost sight of those faces long ago."

The two of them walked back in the direction from which they had come without another word. They did look back over their shoulders from time to time, however, and they were still holding hands: Hansel and Gretel lost in the deep dark forest.

"Lemme outta here," Eddie said heavily. He made the Ruger safe, stuck it back in the waistband of his pants, and then rubbed his red eyes with the heels of his hands. "Just lemme out, that's all I ask."

"I know what you mean, handsome." She was clearly scared, but her head had that defiant tilt he had come to recognize and love. He put his hands on her shoulders, bent down, and kissed her. He did not let either their surroundings or the oncoming storm keep him from doing a thorough job. When he pulled back at last, she was studying him with wide, dancing eyes. "Wow! What was that about?"

"About how I'm in love with you," he said, "and I guess that's about all. Is it enough?"

Her eyes softened. For a moment she thought about telling him the secret she might or might not be keeping, but of course the time and place were wrong—she could no more tell him she might be pregnant now than she could pause to read the words written on the sculpted Portal Totems.

"It's enough, Eddie," she said.

"You're the best thing that ever happened to me." His hazel eyes were totally focused on her. "It's hard for me to say stuff like that—living with Henry made it hard, I guess—but it's true. I think I started loving you because you were everything Roland took me away from—in New York, I mean—but it's a lot more than that now, because I don't want to go back anymore. Do you?"

She looked at the Cradle. She was terrified of what they might find in there, but all the same . . . she looked back at him. "No, I don't want to go back. I want to spend the rest of my life going forward. As long as you're with me, that is. It's funny, you know, you saying you started loving me because of all the things he took you away from."

"Funny how?"

"I started loving you because you set me free of Detta Walker." She paused, thought, then shook her head slightly. "No—it goes further than that. I started loving you because you set me free of *both* those bitches. One was a foul-mouthed, cock-teasing thief, and the other was a self-righteous, pompous prig. Comes down to six of one and half a dozen of the other, as far as I'm concerned. I like Susannah Dean better than either one . . . and you were the one who set me free."

This time it was she who did the reaching, pressing her palm to his stubbly cheeks, drawing him down, kissing him gently. When he put a light hand on her breast, she sighed and covered it with her own.

"I think we better get going," she said, "or we're apt to be laying right here in the street . . . and getting wet, from the look."

Eddie stared around at the silent towers, the broken windows, the vine-encrusted walls a final time. Then he nodded. "Yeah. I don't think there's any future in this town, anyway."

He pushed her forward, and they both stiffened as the wheels of the chair passed over what Maud had called the dead-line, fearful that they would trip some ancient protective device and die together. But nothing happened. Eddie pushed her into the plaza, and as they approached the steps leading up to the Cradle, a cold, wind-driven rain began to fall.

Although neither of them knew it, the first of the great autumn storms of Mid-World had arrived.

25

ONCE THEY WERE IN the smelly darkness of the sewers, Gasher slowed the killing pace he'd maintained aboveground. Jake didn't think it was because of the darkness; Gasher seemed to know every twist and turn of the route he was following, just as advertised. Jake believed it was because his captor was satisfied that Roland had been squashed to jelly by the deadfall trap.

Jake himself had begun to wonder.

If Roland had spotted the tripwires—a far more

subtle trap than the one which followed—was it really likely that he had missed seeing the fountain? Jake supposed it was possible, but it didn't make much sense. Jake thought it more likely that Roland had tripped the fountain on purpose, to lull Gasher and perhaps slow him down. He didn't believe Roland could follow them through this maze under the streets—the total darkness would defeat even the gunslinger's tracking abilities—but it cheered his heart to think that Roland might not have died in an attempt to keep his promise.

They turned right, left, then left again. As Jake's other senses sharpened in an attempt to compensate for his lack of sight, he had a vague perception of other tunnels around him. The muffled sounds of ancient, laboring machinery would grow loud for a moment, then fade as the stone foundations of the city drew close around them again. Drafts blew intermittently against his skin, sometimes warm, sometimes chilly. Their splashing footfalls echoed briefly as they passed the intersecting tunnels from which these stenchy breaths blew, and once Jake nearly brained himself on some metal object jutting down from the ceiling. He slapped at it with one hand and felt something that might have been a large valve-wheel. After that he waved his hands as he trotted along in an attempt to read the air ahead of him.

Gasher guided him with taps to the shoulders, as a waggoner might have guided his oxen. They moved at a good clip, trotting but not running. Gasher got enough of his breath back to first hum and then begin singing in a low, surprisingly tuneful tenor voice.

> *"Ribble-ti-tibble-ti-ting-ting-ting,*
> *I'll get a job and buy yer a ring,*
> *When I get my mitts*
> *On yer jiggly tits,*
> *Ribble-ti-tibble-ti-ting-ting-ting!*
>
> *O ribble-ti-tibble,*

I just wanter fiddle,
Fiddle around with your ting-ting-ting!"

There were five or six more verses along this line before Gasher quit. "Now *you* sing somethin, squint."

"I don't know anything," Jake puffed. He hoped he sounded more out of breath than he actually was. He didn't know if it would do him any good or not, but down here in the dark any edge seemed worth trying for.

Gasher brought his elbow down in the center of Jake's back, almost hard enough to send him sprawling into the ankle-high water running sluggishly through the tunnel they were traversing. "You *better* know sommat, 'less you want me to rip your everlovin spine right outcher back." He paused, then added: "There's haunts down here, boy. They live inside the fuckin machines, so they do. Singin keeps em off . . . don't you know that? Now *sing!*"

Jake thought hard, not wanting to earn another love-tap from Gasher, and came up with a song he'd learned in summer day camp at the age of seven or eight. He opened his mouth and began to bawl it into the darkness, listening to the echoes bounce back amid the sounds of running water, falling water, and ancient thudding machinery.

"My girl's a corker, she's a New Yorker,
I buy her everything to keep her in style,
She got a pair of hips
Just like two battleships,
Oh boy, that's how my money goes.

My girl's a dilly, she comes from Philly,
I buy her everything to keep her in style,
She's got a pair of eyes
Just like two pizza pies,
Oh boy, that's how—"

Gasher reached out, seized Jake's ears as if they

were jug-handles, and yanked him to a stop. "There's a hole right ahead of yer," he said. "With a voice like yours, squint, it'd be doin the world a mercy to letcher fall in, so it would, but Tick-Tock wouldn't approve at all, so I reckon ye're safe for a little longer." Gasher's hands left Jake's ears, which burned like fire, and fastened on the back of his shirt. "Now lean forward until you feel the ladder on the t'other side. And mind you don't slip and drag us both down!"

Jake leaned cautiously forward, hands outstretched, terrified of falling into a pit he couldn't see. As he groped for the ladder, he became aware of warm air—clean and almost fragrant—whooshing past his face, and a faint blush of rose-colored light from beneath him. His fingers touched a steel rung and closed over it. The bite-wounds on his left hand broke open again, and he felt warm blood running across his palm.

"Got it?" Gasher asked.

"Yes."

"Then climb down! What are you waitin for, gods damn it!" Gasher let go of his shirt, and Jake could imagine him drawing his foot back, meaning to hurry him along with a kick in the ass. Jake stepped across the faintly glimmering gap and began to descend the ladder, using his hurt hand as little as possible. This time the rungs were clear of moss and oil, and hardly rusted at all. The shaft was very long and as Jake went down, hurrying to keep Gasher from stepping on his hands with his thick-soled boots, he found himself remembering a movie he'd once seen on TV—*Journey to the Center of the Earth.*

The throb of machinery grew louder and the rosy glow grew stronger. The machines still didn't sound right, but his ears told him these were in better shape than the ones above. And when he finally reached the bottom, he found the floor was dry. The new horizontal shaft was square, about six feet high, and sleeved with riveted stainless steel. It stretched away for as far as Jake could see in both directions, straight as a string. He knew instinctively, without even thinking about it, that this tunnel (which had to be at least seventy feet under Lud) also followed the path of the Beam. And somewhere up ahead—Jake was sure of this, although he couldn't have said why—the train they had come looking for lay directly above it.

Narrow ventilation grilles ran along the sides of the walls just below the shaft's ceiling; it was from these that the clean, dry air was flowing. Moss dangled from some of them in blue-gray beards, but most were still clear. Below every other grille was a yellow arrow with a symbol that looked a bit like a lower-case *t*. The arrows pointed in the direction Jake and Gasher were heading.

The rose-colored light was coming from glass tubes which ran along the ceiling of the shaft in parallel rows. Some—about one in every three—were dark, and others sputtered fitfully, but at least half of them were still working. *Neon tubing*, Jake thought, amazed. *How about that?*

Gasher dropped down beside him. He saw Jake's expression of surprise and grinned. "Nice, ennet? Cool in the summer, warm in the winter, and so much food that five hunnert men couldn't eat it in five hunnert years. And do yer know the best part, squint? The very best part of the whole coozy fakement?"

Jake shook his head.

"Farkin Pubies don't have the leastest idear the place even exists. They think there's monsters down here. Catch a Pubie goin within twenty feet of a sewer-cap, less'n he has to!"

He threw his head back and laughed heartily. Jake didn't join in, even though a cold voice in the back of his mind told him it might be politic to do so. He didn't join in because he knew exactly how the Pubes felt. There *were* monsters under the city—trolls and boggerts and orcs. Hadn't he been captured by just such a one?

Gasher shoved him to the left. "Garn—almost there now. *Hup!*"

They jogged on, their footfalls chasing them in a

pack of echoes. After ten or fifteen minutes of this, Jake saw a watertight hatchway about two hundred yards ahead. As they drew closer, he could see a big valve-wheel sticking out of it. A communicator box was mounted on the wall to the right.

"I'm blown out," Gasher gasped as they reached the door at the end of the tunnel. "Doin's like this are too much for an inwalid like yer old pal, so they are!" He thumbed the button on the intercom and bawled: "I got im, Tick-Tock—got him as dandy as you please! Didn't even muss 'is hair! Didn't I tell yer I would? Trust the Gasherman, I said, for he'll leadjer straight and true! Now open up and let us in!"

He let go of the button and looked impatiently at the door. The valve-wheel didn't turn. Instead a flat, drawling voice came out of the intercom speaker: "What's the password?"

Gasher frowned horribly, scratched his chin with his long, dirty nails, then lifted his eyepatch and swabbed out another clot of yellow-green goo. "Tick-Tock and his passwords!" he said to Jake. He sounded worried as well as irritated. "He's a trig cove, but that's takin it a deal too far if you ask me, so it is."

He pushed the button and yelled, "Come on, Tick-Tock! If you don't reckergnize the sound of my voice, you need a heary-aid!"

"Oh, I recognize it," the drawling voice returned. To Jake it sounded like Jerry Reed, who played Burt Reynolds's sidekick in Smokey and the Bandit. "But I don't know who's with you, do I? Or have you forgotten that the camera out there went tits-up last year? You give the password, Gasher, or you can rot out there!"

Gasher stuck a finger up his nose, extracted a chunk of snot the color of mint jelly, and squashed it into the grille of the speaker. Jake watched this childish display of ill temper in silent fascination, feeling unwelcome, hysterical laughter bubbling around inside him. Had they come all this way, through the booby-trapped mazes and lightless tunnels, to be balked here at this watertight door simply because Gasher couldn't remember the Tick-Tock Man's password?

Gasher looked at him balefully, then slid his hand across his skull, peeling off his sweat-soaked yellow scarf. The skull beneath was bald, except for a few straggling tufts of black hair like porcupine quills, and deeply dented above the left temple. Gasher peered into the scarf and plucked forth a scrap of paper. "Gods bless Hoots," he muttered. "Hoots takes care of me a right proper, he does."

He peered at the scrap, turning it this way and that, and then held it out to Jake. He kept his voice pitched low, as if the Tick-Tock Man could hear him even though the TALK button on the intercom wasn't depressed.

"You're a proper little gennelman, ain't you? And the very first thing they teach a gennelman to do after he's been larned not to eat the paste and piss in the corners is read. So read me the word on this paper, cully, for it's gone right out of my head—so it has."

Jake took the paper, looked at it, then looked up at Gasher again. "What if I won't?" he asked coolly.

Gasher was momentarily taken aback at this response . . . and then he began to grin with dangerous good humor. "Why, I'll grab yer by the throat and use yer head for a doorknocker," he said. "I doubt if it'll conwince old Ticky to let me in—for he's still nervous of your hardcase friend, so he is—but it'll do my heart a world of good to see your brains drippin off that wheel."

Jake considered this, the dark laughter still bubbling away inside him. The Tick-Tock Man was a trig enough cove, all right—he had known that it would be difficult to persuade Gasher, who was dying anyway, to speak the password even if Roland had taken him prisoner. What Tick-Tock hadn't taken into account was Gasher's defective memory.

Don't laugh. If you do, he really will beat your brains out.

In spite of his brave words, Gasher was watching

Jake with real anxiety, and Jake realized a potentially
powerful fact: Gasher might not be afraid of dying
. . . but he *was* afraid of being humiliated.

"All right, Gasher," he said calmly. "The word on
this piece of paper is *bountiful*."

"Gimme that." Gasher snatched the paper back,
returned it to his scarf, and quickly wrapped the yellow cloth around his head again. He thumbed the intercom button. "Tick-Tock? Yer still there?"

"Where else would I be? The West End of the
World?" The drawling voice now sounded mildly
amused.

Gasher stuck his whitish tongue out at the speaker,
but his voice was ingratiating, almost servile. "The
password's bountyful, and a fine word it is, too! Now
let me in, gods cuss it!"

"Of course," the Tick-Tock Man said. A machine
started up somewhere nearby, making Jake jump. The
valve-wheel in the center of the door spun. When it
stopped, Gasher seized it, yanked it outward, grabbed
Jake's arm, and propelled him over the raised lip of
the door and into the strangest room he had ever seen
in his life.

26

ROLAND DESCENDED INTO DUSKY pink light. Oy's
bright eyes peered out from the open V of his shirt;
his neck stretched to the limit of its considerable
length as he sniffed at the warm air that blew through
the ventilator grilles. Roland had had to depend completely on the bumbler's nose in the dark passages
above, and he had been terribly afraid the animal
would lose Jake's scent in the running water . . . but
when he had heard the sound of singing—first Gasher,
then Jake—echoing back through the pipes, he had
relaxed a little. Oy had not led them wrong.

Oy had heard it, too. Up until then he had been

moving slowly and cautiously, even backtracking every now and again to be sure of himself, but when he heard Jake's voice he began to run, straining the raw-hide leash. Roland was afraid he might call after Jake in his harsh voice—*Ake! Ake!*—but he hadn't done so. And, just as they reached the shaft which led to the lower levels of this Dycian Maze, Roland had heard the sound of some new machine—a pump of some sort, perhaps—followed by the metallic, echoing crash of a door being slammed shut.

He reached the foot of the square tunnel and glanced briefly at the double line of lighted tubes which led off in either direction. They were lit with swamp-fire, he saw, like the sign outside the place which had belonged to Balazar in the city of New York. He looked more closely at the narrow chrome ventilation strips running along the top of each wall, and the arrows below them, then slipped the rawhide loop off Oy's neck. Oy shook his head impatiently, clearly glad to be rid of it.

"We're close," he murmured into the bumbler's cocked ear, "and so we have to be quiet. Do you understand, Oy? Very quiet."

"I-yet," Oy replied in a hoarse whisper that would have been funny under other circumstances.

Roland put him down and Oy was immediately off down the tunnel, neck out, muzzle to the steel floor. Roland could hear him muttering *Ake-Ake! Ake-Ake!* under his breath. Roland unholstered his gun and followed him.

27

EDDIE AND SUSANNAH LOOKED up at the vastness of Blaine's Cradle as the skies opened and the rain began to fall in torrents.

"It's a hell of a building, but they forgot the handicap ramps!" Eddie yelled, raising his voice to be heard over the rain and thunder.

"Never mind that," Susannah said impatiently, slipping out of the wheelchair. "Let's get up there and out of the rain."

Eddie looked dubiously up the incline of steps. The risers were shallow . . . but there were a lot of them. "You sure, Suze?"

"Race you, white boy," she said, and began to wriggle upward with uncanny ease, using hands, muscular forearms, and the stumps of her legs.

And she almost *did* beat him; Eddie had the ironmongery to contend with, and it slowed him down. Both of them were panting when they reached the top, and tendrils of steam were rising from their wet clothes. Eddie grabbed her under the arms, swung her up, and then just held her with his hands locked together in the small of her back instead of dropping her back into the chair, as he had meant to do. He felt randy and half-crazy without the slightest idea why.

Oh, give me a break, he thought. *You've gotten this far alive; that's what's got your glands pumped up and ready to party.*

Susannah licked her full lower lip and wound her strong fingers into his hair. She pulled. It hurt . . . and at the same time it felt wonderful. "Told you I'd beat you, white boy," she said in a low, husky voice.

"Get outta here—I had you . . . by half a step." He tried to sound less out of breath than he was and found it was impossible.

"Maybe . . . but it blew you out, didn't it?" One hand left his hair, slid downward, and squeezed gently. A smile gleamed in her eyes. "*Somethin* ain't blown out, though."

Thunder rumbled across the sky. They flinched, then laughed together.

"Come on," he said. "This is nuts. The time's all wrong."

She didn't contradict him, but she squeezed him again before returning her hand to his shoulder. Eddie felt a pang of regret as he swung her back into her chair and ran her across vast flagstones and under cover of the roof. He thought he saw the same regret in Susannah's eyes.

When they were out of the downpour, Eddie paused and they looked back. The Plaza of the Cradle, The Street of the Turtle, and all the city beyond was rapidly disappearing into a shifting gray curtain. Eddie wasn't a bit sorry. Lud hadn't earned itself a place in his mental scrapbook of fond memories.

"Look," Susannah murmured. She was pointing at a nearby downspout. It ended in a large, scaly fish-head that looked like a close relation to the dragon-gargoyles which decorated the corners of the Cradle. Water ran from its mouth in a silver torrent.

"This isn't just a passing shower, is it?" Eddie asked.

"Nope. It's gonna rain until it gets tired of it, and then it's gonna rain some more, just for spite. Maybe a week; maybe a month. Not that it's gonna matter to us, if Blaine decides he doesn't like our looks and fries us. Fire a shot to let Roland know we got here, sugar, and then we'll have us a look around. See what we can see."

Eddie pointed the Ruger into the gray sky, pulled the trigger, and fired the shot which Roland heard a mile or more away, as he followed Jake and Gasher through the booby-trapped maze. Eddie stood where he was a moment longer, trying to persuade himself that things might still turn out all right, that his heart was wrong in its stubborn insistence that they had seen the last of the gunslinger and the boy Jake. Then he made the automatic safe again, returned it to the waistband of his pants, and went back to Susannah. He turned her chair away from the steps and rolled her along an aisle of columns which led deeper into the building. She popped the cylinder of Roland's gun and reloaded it as they went.

Under the roof the rain had a secret, ghostly sound and even the harsh thundercracks were muted. The columns which supported the structure were at least ten feet in diameter, and their tops were lost in the gloom. From up there in the shadows, Eddie heard the cooing conversation of pigeons.

Now a sign hanging on thick chrome-silver chains swam out of the shadows:

NORTH CENTRAL POSITRONICS
WELCOMES YOU
TO THE CRADLE OF LUD
← SOUTHEAST TRAVEL (BLAINE)
NORTHWEST TRAVEL (PATRICIA) →

"Now we know the name of the one that fell in the river," Eddie said. "Patricia. They got their colors wrong, though. It's supposed to be pink for girls and blue for boys, not the other way around."

"Maybe they're *both* blue."

"They're not. Blaine's pink."

"How would you know that?"

Eddie looked confused. "I don't know how . . . but I do."

They followed the arrow pointing toward Blaine's berth, entering what had to be a grand concourse. Eddie didn't have Susannah's ability to see the past in clear, visionary flashes, but his imagination nonetheless filled this vast, pillared space with a thousand hurrying people; he heard clicking heels and murmuring voices, saw embraces of homecoming and farewell. And over everything, the speakers chanting news of a dozen different destinations.

Patricia is now boarding for Northwest Baronies . . .

Will Passenger Killington, passenger Killington, please report to the information booth on the lower level?

Blaine is now arriving at Berth #2, and will be debarking shortly . . .

Now there was only the pigeons.

Eddie shivered.

"Look at the faces," Susannah murmured. "I don't know if they give you the willies, but they sure do me." She was pointing to the right. High up on the wall, a series of sculpted heads seemed to push out of the marble, peering down at them from the shadows—stern men with the harsh faces of executioners who are happy in their work. Some of the faces had fallen from their places and lay in granite shards and splinters seventy or eighty feet below their peers. Those remaining were spiderwebbed with cracks and splattered with pigeon dung.

"They must have been the Supreme Court, or something," Eddie said, uneasily scanning all those thin lips and cracked, empty eyes. "Only judges can look so smart and so completely pissed off at the same time—you're talking to a guy who knows. There isn't one of them who looks like he'd give a crippled crab a crutch."

" 'A heap of broken images, where the sun beats and the dead tree gives no shelter,' " Susannah murmured, and at these words Eddie felt gooseflesh waltz across the skin of his arms and chest and legs.

"What's that, Suze?"

"A poem by a man who must have seen Lud in his dreams," she said. "Come on, Eddie. Forget them."

"Easier said than done." But he began to push her again.

Ahead, a vast grilled barrier like a castle barbican swam out of the gloom . . . and beyond it, they caught their first glimpse of Blaine the Mono. It was pink, just as Eddie had said it would be, a delicate shade which matched the veins running through the marble pillars. Blaine flowed above the wide loading platform in a smooth, streamlined bullet shape which looked more like flesh than metal. Its surface was broken only once—by a triangular window equipped with a huge wiper. Eddie knew there would be another triangular window with another big wiper on the other side of the mono's nose, so that if you looked at Blaine head-on, it would seem to have a face, just like Charlie the Choo-Choo. The wipers would look like slyly drooping eyelids.

White light from the southeastern slot in the Cradle fell across Blaine in a long, distorted rectangle. To Eddie, the body of the train looked like the breaching back of some fabulous pink whale—one that was utterly silent.

"Wow." His voice had fallen to a whisper. "We found it."

"Yes. Blaine the Mono."

"Is it dead, do you think? It *looks* dead."

"It's not. Sleeping, maybe, but a long way from dead."

"You sure?"

"Were you sure it would be pink?" It wasn't a question he had to answer, and he didn't. The face she turned up to him was strained and badly frightened. "It's sleeping, and you know what? I'm scared to wake it up."

"Well, we'll wait for the others, then."

She shook her head. "I think we better try to be ready for when they get here . . . because I've got an idea that they're going to come on the run. Push me over to that box mounted on the bars. It looks like an intercom. See it?"

He did, and pushed her slowly toward it. It was mounted on one side of a closed gate in the center of the barrier which ran the length of the Cradle. The vertical bars of the barrier were made of what looked like stainless steel; those of the gate appeared to be ornamental iron, and their lower ends disappeared into steel-ringed holes in the floor. There was no way either of them was going to wriggle through those bars, either, Eddie saw. The gap between each set was no more than four inches. It would have been a tight squeeze even for Oy.

Pigeons ruffled and cooed overhead. The left wheel of Susannah's chair squawked monotonously. *My kingdom for an oilcan*, Eddie thought, and realized he was a lot more than just scared. The last time he had felt this level of terror had been on the day when he and Henry had stood on the sidewalk of Rhinehold Street in Dutch Hill, looking at the slumped ruin of The Mansion. They hadn't gone in on that day in 1977; they had turned their backs on the haunted house and walked away, and he remembered vowing to himself that he would never, never, *ever* go back to that place. It was a promise he'd kept, but here he was, in another haunted house, and there was the haunter, right over there—Blaine the Mono, a long low pink shape with one window peering at him like the eye of a dangerous animal who is shamming sleep.

He stirs no more from his berth in the Cradle. . . . He has even stopped speaking in his many voices and laughing. . . . Ardis was the last to go nigh Blaine . . . and when Ardis couldn't answer what was asked, Blaine slew him with blue fire.

If it speaks to me, I'll probably go crazy, Eddie thought.

The wind gusted outside, and a fine spray of rain flew in through the tall egress slot cut in the side of the building. He saw it strike Blaine's window and bead up there.

Eddie shuddered suddenly and looked sharply around. "We're being watched—I can feel it."

"I wouldn't be at all surprised. Push me closer to the gate, Eddie. I want to get a better look at that box."

"Okay, but don't touch it. If it's electrified—"

"If Blaine wants to cook us, he will," Susannah said, looking through the bars at Blaine's back. "You know it, and I do, too."

And because Eddie knew that was only the truth, he said nothing.

The box looked like a combination intercom and burglar alarm. There was a speaker set into the top half, with what looked like a TALK/LISTEN button next to it. Below this were numbers arranged in a shape which made a diamond:

1
2 3
4 5 6
7 8 9 10
11 12 13 14 15
16 17 18 19 20 21
22 23 24 25 26 27 28
29 30 31 32 33 34 35 36
37 38 39 40 41 42 43 44 45
46 47 48 49 50 51 52 53 54 55
56 57 58 59 60 61 62 63 64
65 66 67 68 69 70 71 72
73 74 75 76 77 78 79
80 81 82 83 84 85
86 87 88 89 90
91 92 93 94
95 96 97
98 99
100

Under the diamond were two other buttons with words of the High Speech printed on them: COMMAND and ENTER.

Susannah looked bewildered and doubtful. "What *is* this thing, do you think? It looks like a gadget in a science fiction movie."

Of course it did, Eddie realized. Susannah had probably seen a home security system or two in her time—she had, after all, lived among the Manhattan rich, even if she had not been very enthusiastically accepted by them—but there was a world of difference between the electronics gear available in her when, 1963, and his own, which was 1987. *We've never talked much about the differences, either,* he thought. *I wonder what she'd think if I told her Ronald Reagan was President of the United States when Roland snatched me? Probably that I was crazy.*

"It's a security system," he said. Then, although his nerves and instincts screamed out against it, he forced himself to reach out with his right hand and thumb the TALK/LISTEN switch.

There was no crackle of electricity; no deadly blue fire went racing up his arm. No sign that the thing was even still connected.

Maybe Blaine is dead. Maybe he's dead, after all.

But he didn't really believe that.

"Hello?" he said, and in his mind's eye saw the unfortunate Ardis, screaming as he was microwaved by the blue fire dancing all over his face and body, melting his eyes and setting his hair ablaze. "Hello . . . Blaine? *Anybody?*"

He let go of the button and waited, stiff with tension. Susannah's hand crept into his, cold and small. There was still no answer, and Eddie—now more reluctant than ever—pushed the button again.

"Blaine?"

He let go of the button. Waited. And when there was still no answer, a dangerous giddiness overcame him, as it often did in moments of stress and fear. When that giddiness took him, counting the cost no longer seemed to matter. *Nothing* mattered. It had been like that when he had outfaced Balazar's sallow-faced contact man in Nassau, and it was like that now. And if Roland had seen him in the moment this lunatic impatience overtook him, he would have seen more than just a resemblance between Eddie and Cuthbert; he would have sworn Eddie *was* Cuthbert.

He jammed the button in with his thumb and began to bellow into the speaker, adopting a plummy (and completely bogus) British accent. "Hullo, Blaine! Cheerio, old fellow! This is Robin Leach, host of *Lifestyles of the Rich and Brainless*, here to tell you that *you* have won six billion dollars and a new Ford Escort in the Publishers Clearing House Sweepstakes!"

Pigeons took flight above them in soft, startled explosions of wings. Susannah gasped. Her face wore the dismayed expression of a devout woman who has just heard her husband blaspheme in a cathedral. "Eddie, stop it! *Stop it!*"

Eddie couldn't stop it. His mouth was smiling, but his eyes glittered with a mixture of fear, hysteria, and frustrated anger. "You and your monorail girlfriend, Patricia, will spend a lux-*yoo*-rious month in scenic Jimtown, where you'll drink only the finest wine and eat only the finest virgins! You—"

"... *shhhh* ..."

Eddie broke off, looking at Susannah. He was at once sure that it had been she who had shushed him— not only because she had already tried but because she was the only other person here—and yet at the same time he knew it *hadn't* been Susannah. That had been *another* voice: the voice of a very young and very frightened child.

"Suze? Did you—"

Susannah was shaking her head and raising her hand at the same time. She pointed at the intercom box, and Eddie saw the button marked COMMAND was glowing a very faint shell-pink. It was the same color as the mono sleeping in its berth on the other side of the barrier.

"*Shhh ... don't wake him up,*" the child's voice mourned. It drifted from the speaker, soft as an evening breeze.

"What ..." Eddie began. Then he shook his head, reached toward the TALK/LISTEN switch and pressed it gently. When he spoke again, it was not in the blaring Robin Leach bellow but in the almost-whisper of a conspirator. "What are you? Who are you?"

He released the button. He and Susannah regarded each other with the big eyes of children who now know they are sharing the house with a dangerous— perhaps psychotic—adult. How have they come by the knowledge? Why, because another child has told them, a child who has lived with the psychotic adult for a long time, hiding in corners and stealing out only when it knows the adult is asleep; a frightened child who happens to be almost invisible.

There was no answer. Eddie let the seconds spin

out. Each one seemed long enough to read a whole novel in. He was reaching for the button again when the faint pink glow reappeared.

"I'm Little Blaine," the child's voice whispered. *"The one he doesn't see. The one he forgot. The one he thinks he left behind in the rooms of ruin and the halls of the dead."*

Eddie pushed the button again with a hand that had picked up an uncontrollable shake. He could hear that shake in his voice, as well. *"Who? Who* is the one who doesn't see? Is it the Bear?"

No—not the bear; not he. Shardik lay dead in the forest, many miles behind them; the world had moved on even since then. Eddie suddenly remembered what it had been like to lay his ear against that strange unfound door in the clearing where the bear had lived its violent half-life, that door with its somehow terrible stripes of yellow and black. It was all of a piece, he realized now; all part of some awful, decaying whole, a tattered web with the Dark Tower at its center like an incomprehensible stone spider. All of Mid-World had become one vast haunted mansion in these strange latter days; all of Mid-World had become The Drawers; all of Mid-World had become a waste land, haunting and haunted.

He saw Susannah's lips form the words of the real answer before the voice from the intercom could speak them, and those words were as obvious as the solution to a riddle once the answer is spoken.

"Big Blaine," the unseen voice whispered. *"Big Blaine is the ghost in the machine—the ghost in* all *the machines."*

Susannah's hand had gone to her throat and was clutching it, as if she intended to strangle herself. Her eyes were full of terror, but they were not glassy, not stunned; they were sharp with understanding. Perhaps she knew a voice like this one from her own when— the when where the integrated whole that was Susannah had been shunted aside by the warring personalities of Detta and Odetta. The childish voice had surprised her as well as him, but her agonized eyes said she was no stranger to the concept being expressed.

Susannah knew all about the madness of duality.

"Eddie we have to go," she said. Her terror turned the words into an unpunctuated auditory smear. He could hear air whistling in her windpipe like a cold wind around a chimney. "Eddie we have to get away Eddie we have to get away Eddie—"

"Too late," the tiny, mourning voice said. *"He's awake. Big Blaine is awake. He knows you are here. And he's coming."*

Suddenly lights—bright orange arc-sodiums—began to flash on in pairs above them, bathing the pillared vastness of the Cradle in a harsh glare that banished all shadows. Hundreds of pigeons darted and swooped in frightened, aimless flight, startled from their complex of interlocked nests high above.

"Wait!" Eddie shouted. "Please, wait!"

In his agitation he forgot to push the button, but it made no difference; Little Blaine responded anyway. *"No! I can't let him catch me! I can't let him kill me, too!"*

The light on the intercom box went dark again, but only for a moment. This time both COMMAND and ENTER lit up, and their color was not pink but the lurid dark red of a blacksmith's forge.

"WHO ARE YOU?" a voice roared, and it came not just from the box but from every speaker in the city which still operated. The rotting bodies hanging from the poles shivered with the vibrations of that mighty voice; it seemed that even the dead would run from Blaine, if they could.

Susannah shrank back in her chair, the heels of her hands pressed to her ears, her face long with dismay, her mouth distorted in a silent scream. Eddie felt himself shrinking toward all the fantastic, hallucinatory terrors of eleven. Had it been this voice he had feared when he and Henry stood outside The Mansion? That he had perhaps even *anticipated*? He didn't know . . .

but he *did* know how Jack in that old story must have felt when he realized that he had tried the beanstalk once too often, and awakened the giant.

"HOW DARE YOU DISTURB MY SLEEP? TELL ME NOW, OR DIE WHERE YOU STAND."

He might have frozen right there, leaving Blaine—Big Blaine—to do to them whatever it was he had done to Ardis (or something even worse); perhaps *should* have frozen, locked in that down-the-rabbit-hole, fairy-tale terror. It was the memory of the small voice which had spoken first that enabled him to move. It had been the voice of a terrified child, but it had tried to help them, terrified or not.

So now you have to help yourself, he thought. *You woke it up; deal with it, for Christ's sake!*

Eddie reached out and pushed the button again. "My name is Eddie Dean. The woman with me is my wife, Susannah. We're . . ."

He looked at Susannah, who nodded and made frantic motions for him to go on.

"We're on a quest. We seek the Dark Tower which lies in the Path of the Beam. We're in the company of two others, Roland of Gilead and . . . and Jake of New York. We're from New York too. If you're—" He paused for a moment, biting back the words *Big Blaine.* If he used them, he might make the intelligence behind the voice aware that they had heard another voice; a ghost inside the ghost, so to speak.

Susannah gestured again for him to go on, using both hands.

"If you're Blaine the Mono . . . well . . . we want you to take us."

He released the button. There was no response for what seemed like a very long time, only the agitated flutter of the disturbed pigeons from overhead. When Blaine spoke again, his voice came only from the speaker-box mounted on the gate and sounded almost human.

"DO NOT TRY MY PATIENCE. ALL THE DOORS TO THAT WHERE ARE CLOSED. GIL-

EAD IS NO MORE, AND THOSE KNOWN AS GUNSLINGERS ARE ALL DEAD. NOW ANSWER MY QUESTION: WHO ARE YOU? THIS IS YOUR LAST CHANCE."

There was a sizzling sound. A ray of brilliant blue-white light lanced down from the ceiling and seared a hole the size of a golf-ball in the marble floor less than five feet to the left of Susannah's wheelchair. Smoke that smelled like the aftermath of a lightning-bolt rose lazily from it. Susannah and Eddie stared at each other in mute terror for a moment, and then Eddie lunged for the communicator-box and thumbed the button.

"You're wrong! We *did* come from New York! We came through the doors, on the beach, only a few weeks ago!"

"It's true!" Susannah called. "I swear it is!"

Silence. Beyond the long barrier, Blaine's pink back humped smoothly. The window at the front seemed to regard them like a vapid glass eye. The wiper could have been a lid half-closed in a sly wink.

"PROVE IT," Blaine said at last.

"Christ, how do I do that?" Eddie asked Susannah.

"I don't know."

Eddie pushed the button again. "The Statue of Liberty! Does that ring a bell?"

"GO ON," Blaine said. Now the voice sounded almost thoughtful.

"The Empire State Building! The Stock Exchange! The World Trade Center! Coney Island Red-Hots! Radio City Music Hall! The East Vil—"

Blaine cut him off . . . and now, incredibly, the voice which came from the speaker was the drawling voice of John Wayne.

"OKAY, PILGRIM. I BELIEVE YOU."

Eddie and Susannah shared another glance, this one of confusion and relief. But when Blaine spoke again, the voice was again cold and emotionless.

"ASK ME A QUESTION, EDDIE DEAN OF NEW YORK. AND IT BETTER BE A GOOD

ONE." There was a pause, and then Blaine added:
"BECAUSE IF IT'S NOT, YOU AND YOUR
WOMAN ARE GOING TO DIE, NO MATTER
WHERE YOU CAME FROM."

Susannah looked from the box on the gate to Eddie.
"What's it *talking* about?" she hissed.

Eddie shook his head. "I don't have the slightest
idea."

28

To JAKE, THE ROOM Gasher dragged him into looked
like a Minuteman missile silo which had been decorated by the inmates of a lunatic asylum: part museum,
part living room, part hippie crash pad. Above him,
empty space vaulted up to a rounded ceiling and
below him it dropped seventy-five or a hundred feet
to a similarly rounded base. Running all around the
single curved wall in vertical lines were tubes of neon
in alternating strokes of color: red, blue, green, yellow, orange, peach, pink. These long tubes came together in roaring rainbow knots at the bottom and top
of the silo . . . if that was what it had been.

The room was about three-quarters of the way up
the vast capsule-shaped space and floored with rusty
iron grillework. Rugs that looked Turkish (he later
learned that such rugs were actually from a barony
called Kashmin) lay on the grilled floor here and
there. Their corners were held down with brass-bound
trunks or standing lamps or the squat legs of over-
stuffed chairs. If not, they would have flapped like
strips of paper tied to an electric fan, because a steady
warm draft rushed up from below. Another draft, this
one issuing from a circular band of ventilators like the
ones in the tunnel they had followed here, swirled
about four or five feet above Jake's head. On the far
side of the room was a door identical to the one
through which he and Gasher had entered, and Jake

assumed it was a continuation of the subterranean corridor following the Path of the Beam.

There were half a dozen people in the room, four
men and two women. Jake guessed that he was looking at the Gray high command—if, that was, there
were enough Grays left to warrant a high command.
None of them were young, but all were still in the
prime of their lives. They looked at Jake as curiously
as he looked at them.

Sitting in the center of the room, with one massive
leg thrown casually over the arm of a chair big enough
to be a throne, was a man who looked like a cross
between a Viking warrior and a giant from a child's
fairy-tale. His heavily muscled upper body was naked
except for a silver band around one bicep, a knife-
scabbard looped over one shoulder, and a strange
charm about his neck. His lower body was clad in soft,
tight-fitting leather breeches which were tucked into
high boots. He wore a yellow scarf tied around one
of these. His hair, a dirty gray-blonde, cascaded almost to the middle of his broad back; his eyes were
as green and curious as the eyes of a tomcat who is
old enough to be wise but not old enough to have lost
that refined sense of cruelty which passes for fun in
feline circles. Hung by its strap from the back of the
chair was what looked like a very old machine-gun.

Jake looked more closely at the ornament on the
Viking's chest and saw that it was a coffin-shaped glass
box hung on a silver chain. Inside it, a tiny gold clock-
face marked the time at five minutes past three. Below
the face, a tiny gold pendulum went back and forth,
and despite the soft whoosh of circulating air from
above and below, he could hear the tick-tock sound
it made. The hands of the clock were moving faster
than they should have done, and Jake was not very
surprised to see that they were moving backward.

He thought of the crocodile in *Peter Pan*, the one
that was always chasing after Captain Hook, and a
little smile touched his lips. Gasher saw it, and raised

his hand. Jake cringed away, putting his own hands to his face.

The Tick-Tock Man shook his finger at Gasher in an amusing schoolmarmish gesture. "Now, now . . . no need of that, Gasher," he said.

Gasher lowered his hand at once. His face had changed completely. Before, it had alternated between stupid rage and a species of cunning, almost existential humor. Now he only looked servile and adoring. Like the others in the room (and Jake himself), the Gasherman could not look away from Tick-Tock for long; his eyes were drawn inexorably back. And Jake could understand why. The Tick-Tock Man was the only person here who seemed wholly vital, wholly healthy, and wholly alive.

"If you say there's no need, there ain't," Gasher said, but he favored Jake with a dark look before shifting his eyes back to the blonde giant on the throne. "Still, he's wery pert, Ticky. Wery pert, Ticky. Wery pert indeed, so he is, and if you want my opinion, he'll take a deal of training!"

"When I want your opinion, I'll ask for it," the Tick-Tock Man said. "Now close the door, Gash—was you bore in a barn?"

A dark-haired woman laughed shrilly, a sound like the caw of a crow. Tick-Tock flicked his eyes toward her; she quieted at once and cast her eyes down to the grilled floor.

The door through which Gasher had dragged him was actually two doors. The arrangement reminded Jake of the way spaceship airlocks looked in the more intelligent science fiction movies. Gasher shut them both and turned to Tick-Tock, giving him a thumbs-up gesture. The Tick-Tock Man nodded and reached languidly up to press a button set into a piece of furniture that looked like a speaker's podium. A pump began to cycle wheezily within the wall, and the neon tubes dimmed perceptibly. There was a faint hiss of air and the valve-wheel of the inside door spun shut. Jake supposed the one in the outer door was doing the same. This was some sort of bomb-shelter, all right; no doubt of that. When the pump died, the long neon tubes resumed their former muted brilliance.

"There," Tick-Tock said pleasantly. His eyes began to look Jake up and down. Jake had a clear and very uncomfortable sense of being expertly catalogued and filed. "All safe and sound, we are. Snug as bugs in a rug. Right, Hoots?"

"Yar!" a tall, skinny man in a black suit replied promptly. His face was covered with some sort of rash which he scratched obsessively.

"I brung him," Gasher said. "I told yer you could trust me to do it, and didn't I?"

"You did," Tick-Tock said. "Bang on. I had some doubts about your ability to remember the password at the end, there, but—"

The dark-haired woman uttered another shrill caw. The Tick-Tock Man half-turned in her direction, that lazy smile dimpling the corners of his mouth, and before Jake was able to grasp what was happening— what had *already* happened—she was staggering backward, her eyes bulging in surprise and pain, her hands groping at some strange tumor in the middle of her chest which hadn't been there a second before.

Jake realized the Tick-Tock Man had made some sort of move as he was turning, a move so quick it had been no more than a flicker. The slim white hilt which had protruded from the scabbard looped over the Tick-Tock Man's shoulder was gone. The knife was now on the other side of the room, sticking out of the dark-haired woman's chest. Tick-Tock had drawn and thrown with an uncanny speed Jake wasn't sure even Roland could match. It had been like some malign magic trick.

The others watched silently as the woman staggered toward Tick-Tock, gagging harshly, her hands wrapped loosely around the hilt of the knife. Her hip bumped one of the standing lamps and the one called Hoots darted forward to catch it before it could fall. Tick-Tock himself never moved; he only went on sitting with his leg tossed over the arm of his throne, watching the woman with his lazy smile.

Her foot caught beneath one of the rugs and she tumbled forward. Once more the Tick-Tock Man moved with that spooky speed, pulling back the foot which had been dangling over the arm of the chair and then driving it forward again like a piston. It buried itself in the pit of the dark-haired woman's stomach and she went flying backward. Blood spewed from her mouth and splattered the furniture. She struck the wall, slid down it, and ended up sitting with her chin on her breastbone. To Jake she looked like a movie Mexican taking a siesta against an adobe wall. It was hard for him to believe she had gone from living to dead with such terrible speed. Neon tubes turned her hair into a haze that was half red and half blue. Her glazing eyes stared at the Tick-Tock Man with terminal amazement.

"I *told* her about that laugh," Tick-Tock said. His eyes shifted to the other woman, a heavyset redhead who looked like a long-haul trucker. "Didn't I, Tilly?"

"Ay," Tilly said at once. Her eyes were lustrous with fear and excitement, and she licked her lips obsessively. "So you did, many and many a time. I'll set my watch and warrant on it."

"So you might, if you could reach up your fat ass far enough to find them," Tick-Tock said. "Bring me my knife, Brandon, and mind you wipe that slut's stink off it before you put it in my hand."

A short, bandy-legged man hopped to do as he had been bidden. The knife wouldn't come free at first; it seemed caught on the unfortunate dark-haired woman's breastbone. Brandon threw a terrified glance over his shoulder at the Tick-Tock Man and then tugged harder.

Tick-Tock, however, appeared to have forgotten all about both Brandon and the woman who had literally laughed herself to death. His brilliant green eyes had fixed on something which interested him much more than the dead woman.

"Come here, cully," he said. "I want a better look at you."

Gasher gave him a shove. Jake stumbled forward. He would have fallen if Tick-Tock's strong hands hadn't caught him by the shoulders. Then, when he was sure Jake had his balance again, Tick-Tock grasped the boy's left wrist and raised it. It was Jake's Seiko which had drawn his interest.

"If this here's what I think it is, it's an omen for sure and true," Tick-Tock said. "Talk to me, boy—what's this *sigul* you wear?"

Jake, who hadn't the slightest idea what a *sigul* was, could only hope for the best. "It's a watch. But it doesn't work, Mr. Tick-Tock."

Hoots chuckled at that, then clapped both hands over his mouth when the Tick-Tock Man turned to look at him. After a moment, Tick-Tock looked back at Jake, and a sunny smile replaced the frown. Looking at that smile almost made you forget that it was a dead woman and not a movie Mexican taking a siesta over there against the wall. Looking at it almost made you forget that these people were crazy, and the Tick-Tock Man was likely the craziest inmate in the whole asylum.

"Watch," Tick-Tock said, nodding. "Ay, a likely enough name for such; after all, what does a person want with a timepiece but to watch it once in a while? Ay, Brandon? Ay, Tilly? Ay, Gasher?"

They responded with eager affirmatives. The Tick-Tock Man favored them with his winning smile, then turned back to Jake again. Now Jake noticed that the smile, winning or not, stopped well short of the Tick-Tock Man's green eyes. They were as they had been throughout: cool, cruel, and curious.

He reached a finger toward the Seiko, which now proclaimed the time to be ninety-one minutes past seven—A.M. *and* P.M.—and pulled it back just before touching the glass above the liquid crystal display. "Tell me, dear boy—is this 'watch' of yours boobyrigged?"

"Huh? Oh! No. No, it's not boobyrigged." Jake touched his own finger to the face of the watch.

"That means nothing, if it's set to the frequency of your own body," the Tick-Tock Man said. He spoke in the sharp, scornful tone Jake's father used when he didn't want people to figure out that he didn't have the slightest idea what he was talking about. Tick-Tock glanced briefly at Brandon, and Jake saw him weigh the pros and cons of making the bowlegged man his designated toucher. Then he dismissed the notion and looked back into Jake's eyes. "If this thing gives me a shock, my little friend, you're going to be choking to death on your own sweetmeats in thirty seconds."

Jake swallowed hard but said nothing. The Tick-Tock Man reached out his finger again, and this time allowed it to settle on the face of the Seiko. The moment that it did, all the numbers went to zeros and then began to count upward again.

Tick-Tock's eyes had narrowed in a grimace of potential pain as he touched the face of the watch. Now their corners crinkled in the first genuine smile Jake had seen from him. He thought it was partly pleasure at his own courage but mostly simple wonder and interest.

"May I have it?" he asked Jake silkily. "As a gesture of your goodwill, shall we say? I am something of a clock fancier, my dear young cully—so I am."

"Be my guest." Jake stripped the watch off his arm at once and dropped in onto the Tick-Tock Man's large waiting palm.

"Talks just like a little silk-arse gennelman, don't he?" Gasher said happily. "In the old days someone would have paid a wery high price for the return o' such as him, Ticky, ay, so they would. Why, my father—"

"Your father died so blowed-out-rotten with the mandrus that not even the dogs would eat him," the Tick-Tock Man interrupted. "Now shut up, you idiot."

At first Gasher looked furious . . . and then only abashed. He sank into a nearby chair and closed his mouth.

Tick-Tock, meanwhile, was examining the Seiko's expansion band with an expression of awe. He pulled it wide, let it snap back, pulled it wide again, let it snap back again. He dropped a lock of his hair into the open links, then laughed when they closed on it. At last he slipped the watch over his hand and pushed it halfway up his forearm. Jake thought this souvenir of New York looked very strange there, but said nothing.

"Wonderful!" Tick-Tock exclaimed. "Where did you get it, cully?"

"It was a birthday present from my father and mother," Jake said. Gasher leaned forward at this, perhaps wanting to mention the idea of ransom again. If so, the intent look on the Tick-Tock Man's face changed his mind and he sat back without saying anything.

"*Was* it?" Tick-Tock marvelled, raising his eyebrows. He had discovered the small button which lit the face of the watch and kept pushing it, watching the light go off and on. Then he looked back at Jake, and his eyes were narrowed to bright green slits again. "Tell me something, cully—does this run on a dipolar or unipolar circuit?"

"Neither one," Jake said, not knowing that his failure to say he did not know what either of these terms meant was buying him a great deal of future trouble. "It runs on a nickel-cadmium battery. At least I'm pretty sure it does. I've never had to replace it, and I lost the instruction folder a long time ago."

The Tick-Tock Man looked at him for a long time without speaking, and Jake realized with dismay that the blonde man was trying to decide if Jake had been making fun of him. If he decided Jake *had* been making fun, Jake had an idea that the abuse he had suffered on the way here would seem like tickling compared to what the Tick-Tock Man might do. He suddenly wanted to divert Tick-Tock's train of thought—wanted that more than anything in the world. He said the first thing he thought might turn the trick.

"He was your grandfather, wasn't he?"

The Tick-Tock Man raised his brows interrogatively. His hands returned to Jake's shoulders, and although his grip was not tight, Jake could feel the phenomenal strength there. If Tick-Tock chose to tighten his grip and pull sharply forward, he would snap Jake's collarbones like pencils. If he shoved, he would probably break his back.

"*Who* was my grandfather, cully?"

Jake's eyes once more took in the Tick-Tock Man's massive, nobly shaped head and broad shoulders. He remembered what Susannah had said: *Look at the size of him, Roland—they must have had to grease him to get him into the cockpit!*

"The man in the airplane. David Quick."

The Tick-Tock Man's eyes widened in surprise and amazement. Then he threw back his head and roared out a gust of laughter that echoed off the domed ceiling high above. The others smiled nervously. None, however, dared to laugh right out loud . . . not after what had happened to the woman with the dark hair.

"Whoever you are and wherever you come from, boy, you're the triggest cove old Tick-Tock's run into for many a year. Quick was my great-grandfather, not my grandfather, but you're close enough—wouldn't you say so, Gasher, my dear?"

"Ay," Gasher said. "He's trig, right enough, I could've toldjer that. But wery pert, all the same."

"Yes," the Tick-Tock Man said thoughtfully. His hands tightened on the boy's shoulders and drew Jake closer to that smiling, handsome, lunatic face. "I can see he's pert. It's in his eyes. But we'll take care of that, won't we, Gasher?"

It's not Gasher he's talking to, Jake thought. *It's me. He thinks he's hypnotizing me . . . and maybe he is.*

"Ay," Gasher breathed.

Jake felt he was drowning in those wide green eyes. Although the Tick-Tock Man's grip was still not really tight, he couldn't get enough breath into his lungs. He summoned all of his own force in an effort to break the blonde man's hold over him, and again spoke the first words which came to mind:

"So fell Lord Perth, and the countryside did shake with that thunder."

It acted upon Tick-Tock like a hard open-handed blow to the face. He recoiled, green eyes narrowing, his grip on Jake's shoulders tightening painfully. "*What* do you say? Where did you hear that?"

"A little bird told me," Jake replied with calculated insolence, and the next instant he was flying across the room.

If he had struck the curved wall headfirst, he would have been knocked cold or killed. As it happened, he struck on one hip, rebounded, and landed in a heap on the iron grillework. He shook his head groggily, looked around, and found himself face to face with the woman who was not taking a siesta. He uttered a shocked cry and crawled away on his hands and knees. Hoots kicked him in the chest, flipping him onto his back. Jake lay there gasping, looking up at the knot of rainbow colors where the neon tubes came together. A moment later, Tick-Tock's face filled his field of vision. The man's lips were pressed together in a hard, straight line, his cheeks flared with color, and there was fear in his eyes. The coffin-shaped glass ornament he wore around his neck dangled directly in front of Jake's eyes, swinging gently back and forth on its silver chain, as if imitating the pendulum of the tiny grandfather clock inside.

"Gasher's right," he said. He gathered a handful of Jake's shirt into one fist and pulled him up. "You're pert. But you don't want to be pert with me, cully. You don't *ever* want to be pert with me. Have you heard of people with short fuses? Well, I have no fuse at all, and there's a thousand could testify to it if I hadn't stilled their tongues for good. If you ever speak to me of Lord Perth again . . . ever, ever, *ever* . . . I'll tear off the top of your skull and eat your brains. I'll have none of that bad-luck story in the Cradle of the Grays. *Do you understand me?*"

He shook Jake back and forth like a rag, and the boy burst into tears.

"*Do you?*"

"Y-Y-Yes!"

"Good." He set Jake upon his feet, where he swayed woozily back and forth, wiping at his streaming eyes and leaving smudges of dirt on his cheeks so dark they looked like mascara. "Now, my little cull, we're going to have a question and answer session here. I'll ask the questions and you'll give the answers. Do you understand?"

Jake didn't reply. He was looking at a panel of the ventilator grille which circled the chamber.

The Tick-Tock Man grabbed his nose between two of his fingers and squeezed it viciously. "*Do you understand me?*"

"*Yes!*" Jake cried. His eyes, now watering with pain as well as terror, returned to Tick-Tock's face. He wanted to look back at the ventilator grille, wanted desperately to verify that what he had seen there was not simply a trick of his frightened, overloaded mind, but he didn't dare. He was afraid someone else—Tick-Tock himself, most likely—would follow his gaze and see what he had seen.

"Good." Tick-Tock pulled Jake back over to the chair by his nose, sat down, and cocked his leg over the arm again. "Let's have a nice little chin, then. We'll begin with your name, shall we? Just what might that be, cully?"

"Jake Chambers." With his nose pinched shut, his voice sounded nasal and foggy.

"And are you a Not-See, Jake Chambers?"

For a moment Jake wondered if this was a peculiar way of asking him if he was blind . . . but of course they could all see he wasn't. "I don't understand what—"

Tick-Tock shook him back and forth by the nose. "Not-See! Not-See! You just want to stop playing with me, boy!"

"I don't understand—" Jake began, and then he looked at the old machine-gun hanging from the chair and thought once more of the crashed Focke-Wulf. The pieces fell together in his mind. "No—I'm not a Nazi. I'm an American. All that ended long before I was born!"

The Tick-Tock Man released his hold on Jake's nose, which immediately began to gush blood. "You could have told me that in the first place and saved yourself all sorts of pain, Jake Chambers . . . but at least now you understand how we do things around here, don't you?"

Jake nodded.

"Ay. Well enough! We'll start with the simple questions."

Jake's eyes drifted back to the ventilator grille. What he had seen before was still there; it hadn't been just his imagination. Two gold-ringed eyes floated in the dark behind the chrome louvers.

Oy.

Tick-Tock slapped his face, knocking him back into Gasher, who immediately pushed him forward again. "It's school-time, dear heart," Gasher whispered. "Mind yer lessons, now! Mind em wery sharp!"

"Look at me when I'm talking to you," Tick-Tock said. "I'll have some respect, Jake Chambers, or I'll have your balls."

"All right."

Tick-Tock's green eyes gleamed dangerously. "All right *what*?"

Jake groped for the right answer, pushing away the tangle of questions and the sudden hope which had dawned in his mind. And what came was what would have served at his own Cradle of the Pubes . . . otherwise known as The Piper School. "All right, *sir*?"

Tick-Tock smiled. "That's a start, boy," he said,

and leaned forward, forearms on his thighs. "Now . . . what's an American?"

Jake began to talk, trying with all his might not to look toward the ventilator grille as he did so.

29

ROLAND HOLSTERED HIS GUN, laid both hands on the valve-wheel, and tried to turn it. It wouldn't budge. That didn't much surprise him, but it presented serious problems.

Oy stood by his left boot, looking up anxiously, waiting for Roland to open the door so they could continue the journey to Jake. The gunslinger only wished it was that easy. It wouldn't do to simply stand out here and wait for someone to leave; it might be hours or even days before one of the Grays decided to use this particular exit again. Gasher and his friends might take it into their heads to flay Jake alive while the gunslinger was waiting for it to happen.

He leaned his head against the steel but heard nothing. That didn't surprise him, either. He had seen doors like this a long time ago—you couldn't shoot out the locks, and you certainly couldn't hear through them. There might be one; there might be two, facing each other, with some dead airspace in between. Somewhere, though, there would be a button which would spin the wheel in the middle of the door and release the locks. If Jake could reach that button, all might still be well.

Roland understood that he was not a full member of this *ka-tet*; he guessed that even Oy was more fully aware than he of the secret life which existed at its heart (he very much doubted that the bumbler had tracked Jake with his nose alone through those tunnels where water ran in polluted streamlets). Nevertheless, he had been able to help Jake when the boy had been trying to cross from his world to this one. He had been able to *see* . . . and when Jake had been trying to regain the key he had dropped, he had been able to send a message.

He had to be very careful about sending messages this time. At best, the Grays would realize something was up. At worst, Jake might misinterpret what Roland tried to tell him and do something foolish.

But if he could *see* . . .

Roland closed his eyes and bent all his concentration toward Jake. He thought of the boy's eyes and sent his *ka* out to find them.

At first there was nothing, but at last an image began to form. It was a face framed by long, gray-blonde hair. Green eyes gleamed in deep sockets like firedims in a cave. Roland quickly understood that this was the Tick-Tock Man, and that he was a descendent of the man who had died in the air-carriage—interesting, but of no practical value in this situation. He tried to look beyond the Tick-Tock Man, to see the rest of the room in which Jake was being held, and the people in it.

"Ake," Oy whispered, as if reminding Roland that this was neither the time nor the place to take a nap.

"Shhh," the gunslinger said, not opening his eyes.

But it was no good. He caught only blurs, probably because Jake's concentration was focused so tightly on the Tick-Tock Man; everyone and everything else was little more than a series of gray-shrouded shapes on the edges of Jake's perception.

Roland opened his eyes again and pounded his left fist lightly into the open palm of his right hand. He had an idea that he could push harder and see more . . . but that might make the boy aware of his presence. That would be dangerous. Gasher might smell a rat, and if he didn't the Tick-Tock Man would.

He looked up at the narrow ventilator grilles, then down at Oy. He had wondered several times just how smart he was; now it looked as though he was going to find out.

Roland reached up with his good left hand, slipped

his fingers between the horizontal slats of the ventilator grille closest to the hatchway through which Jake had been taken, and pulled. The grille popped out in a shower of rust and dried moss. The hole behind it was far too small for a man . . . but not for a billy-bumbler. He put the grille down, picked Oy up, and spoke softly into his ear.

"Go . . . see . . . come back. Do you understand? Don't let them see you. Just go and see and come back."

Oy gazed up into his face, saying nothing, not even Jake's name. Roland had no idea if he had understood or not, but wasting time in ponderation would not help matters. He placed Oy in the ventilator shaft. The bumbler sniffed at the crumbles of dried moss, sneezed delicately, then only crouched there with the draft rippling through his long, silky fur, looking doubtfully at Roland with his strange eyes.

"Go and see and come back," Roland repeated in a whisper, and Oy disappeared into the shadows, walking silently, claws retracted, on the pads of his paws.

Roland drew his gun again and did the hardest thing. He waited.

Oy returned less than three minutes later. Roland lifted him out of the shaft and put him on the floor. Oy looked up at him with his long neck extended. "How many, Oy?" Roland asked. "How many did you see?"

For a long moment he thought the bumbler wouldn't do anything except go on staring in his anxious way. Then he lifted his right paw tentatively in the air, extended the claws, and looked at it, as if trying to remember something very difficult. At last he began to tap on the steel floor.

One . . . two . . . three . . . four. A pause. Then two more, quick and delicate, the extended claws clicking lightly on the steel: five, six. Oy paused a second time, head down, looking like a child lost in the throes of some titanic mental struggle. Then he tapped his claws one final time on the steel, looking up at Roland as he did it. "Ake!"

Six Grays . . . and Jake.

Roland picked Oy up and stroked him. "Good!" he murmured into Oy's ear. In truth, he was almost overwhelmed with surprise and gratitude. He had hoped for something, but this careful response was amazing. And he had few doubts about the accuracy of the count. "Good boy!"

"Oy! Ake!"

Yes, Jake. Jake was the problem. Jake, to whom he had made a promise he intended to keep.

The gunslinger thought deeply in his strange fashion—that combination of dry pragmatism and wild intuition which had probably come from his strange grandmother, Deidre the Mad, and had kept him alive all these years after his old companions had passed. Now he was depending on it to keep Jake alive, too.

He picked Oy up again, knowing Jake might live— *might*—but the bumbler was almost certainly going to die. He whispered several simple words into Oy's cocked ear, repeating them over and over. At last he ceased speaking and returned him to the ventilator shaft. "Good boy," he whispered. "Go on, now. Get it done. My heart goes with you."

"Oy! Art! Ake!" the bumbler whispered, and then scurried off into the darkness again.

Roland waited for all hell to break loose.

30

ASK ME A QUESTION, Eddie Dean of New York. And it better be a good one . . . if it's not, you and your woman are going to die, no matter where you came from.

And, dear *God*, how did you respond to something like that?

The dark red light had gone out; now the pink one reappeared. *"Hurry,"* the faint voice of Little Blaine urged them. *"He's worse than ever before . . . hurry or he'll kill you!"*

Eddie was vaguely aware that flocks of disturbed

pigeons were still swooping aimlessly through the Cradle, and that some of them had smashed headfirst into the pillars and dropped dead on the floor.

"What does it want?" Susannah hissed at the speaker and the voice of Little Blaine somewhere behind it. "For God's sake, *what does it want*?"

No reply. And Eddie could feel any period of grace they might have started with slipping away. He thumbed the TALK/LISTEN and spoke with frantic vivacity as the sweat trickled down his cheeks and neck.

Ask me a question.

"So—Blaine! What have you been up to these last few years? I guess you haven't been doing the old southeast run, huh? Any reason why not? Haven't been feeling up to snuff?"

No sound but the rustle and flap of the pigeons. In his mind he saw Ardis trying to scream as his cheeks melted and his tongue caught fire. He felt the hair on the nape of his neck stirring and clumping together. Fear? Or gathering electricity?

Hurry . . . he's worse than ever before.

"Who built you, anyway?" Eddie asked frantically, thinking: *If I only knew what the fucking thing* wanted! "Want to talk about that? Was it the Grays? Nah . . . probably the Great Old Ones, right? Or . . ."

He trailed off. Now he could feel Blaine's silence as a physical weight on his skin, like fleshy, groping hands.

"What do you *want*?" he shouted. "Just what in hell do you want to *hear*?"

No answer—but the buttons on the box were glowing an angry dark red again, and Eddie knew their time was almost up. He could hear a low buzzing sound nearby—a sound like an electrical generator—and he didn't believe that sound was just his imagination, no matter how much he wanted to think so.

"Blaine!" Susannah shouted suddenly. "Blaine, do you hear me?"

No answer . . . and Eddie felt the air was filling up with electricity as a bowl under a tap fills up with water. He could feel it crackling bitterly in his nose with every breath he took; could feel his fillings buzzing like angry insects.

"Blaine, *I've* got a question, and it *is* a pretty good one! Listen!" She closed her eyes for a moment, fingers rubbing frantically at her temples, and then opened her eyes again. " 'There is a thing that . . . uh . . . that nothing is, and yet it has a name; 'tis sometimes tall and . . . and sometimes short . . .' " She broke off and stared at Eddie with wide, agonized eyes. "Help me! I can't remember how the rest of it goes!"

Eddie only stared at her as if she had gone mad. What in the name of God was she talking about? Then it came to him, and it made a weirdly perfect sense, and the rest of the riddle clicked into his mind as neatly as the last two pieces of a jigsaw puzzle. He swung toward the speaker again.

" 'It joins our talks, it joins our sport, and plays at every game.' What is it? That's our question, Blaine—what is it?"

The red light illuminating the COMMAND and ENTER buttons below the diamond of numbers blinked out. There was an endless moment of silence before Blaine spoke again . . . but Eddie was aware that the feeling of electricity crawling all over his skin was diminishing.

"A SHADOW, OF COURSE," the voice of Blaine responded. "AN EASY ONE . . . BUT NOT BAD. NOT BAD AT ALL."

The voice coming out of the speaker was animated by a thoughtful quality . . . and something else, as well. Pleasure? Longing? Eddie couldn't quite decide, but he *did* know there was something in that voice that reminded him of Little Blaine. He knew something else, as well: Susannah had saved their bacon, at least for the time being. He bent down and kissed her cold, sweaty brow.

"DO YOU KNOW ANY MORE RIDDLES?" Blaine asked.

"Yes, lots," Susannah said at once. "Our companion, Jake, has a whole book of them."

"FROM THE NEW YORK PLACE OF WHERE?" Blaine asked, and now the tone of his voice was perfectly clear, at least to Eddie. Blaine might be a machine, but Eddie had been a heroin junkie for six years, and he knew stone greed when he heard it.

"From New York, right," he said. "But Jake has been taken prisoner. A man named Gasher took him."

No answer . . . and then the buttons glowed that faint, rosy pink again. *"Good so far,"* the voice of Little Blaine whispered. *"But you must be careful . . . he's tricky. . . ."*

The red lights reappeared at once.

"DID ONE OF YOU SPEAK?" Blaine's voice was cold and—Eddie could have sworn it was so—suspicious.

He looked at Susannah. Susannah looked back with the wide, frightened eyes of a little girl who has heard something unnameable moving slyly beneath the bed.

"I cleared my throat, Blaine," Eddie said. He swallowed and armed sweat from his forehead. "I'm . . . shit, tell the truth and shame the devil. I'm scared to death."

"THAT IS VERY WISE OF YOU. THESE RIDDLES OF WHICH YOU SPEAK—ARE THEY STUPID? I WON'T HAVE MY PATIENCE TRIED WITH STUPID RIDDLES."

"Most are smart," Susannah said, but she looked anxiously at Eddie as she said it.

"YOU LIE. YOU DON'T KNOW THE QUALITY OF THESE RIDDLES AT ALL."

"How can you say—"

"VOICE ANALYSIS. FRICTIVE PATTERNS AND DIPHTHONG STRESS-EMPHASIS PROVIDE A RELIABLE QUOTIENT OF TRUTH/UNTRUTH. PREDICTIVE RELIABILITY IS 97 PER CENT, PLUS OR MINUS .5 PER CENT." The voice fell silent for a moment, and when it spoke again, it did so in a menacing drawl that Eddie found very familiar. It was the voice of Humphrey Bogart. "I SHUGGEST YOU SHTICK TO WHAT YOU

KNOW, SHWEETHEART. THE LAST GUY
THAT TRIED SHADING THE TRUTH WITH ME
WOUND UP AT THE BOTTOM OF THE SEND
IN A PAIR OF SHEMENT COWBOY BOOTS."

"Christ," Eddie said. "We walked four hundred
miles or so to meet the computer version of Rich Little. How can you imitate guys like John Wayne and
Humphrey Bogart, Blaine? Guys from our world?"

Nothing.

"Okay, you don't want to answer that one. How
about this one—if a riddle was what you wanted, why
didn't you just say so?"

Again there was no answer, but Eddie discovered that
he didn't really need one. Blaine liked riddles, so he
had asked *them* one. Susannah had solved it. Eddie
guessed that if she had failed to do so, the two of them
would now look like a couple of giant-economy-size charcoal briquets lying on the floor of the Cradle of Lud.

"Blaine?" Susannah asked uneasily. There was no
answer. "Blaine, are you still there?"

"YES. TELL ME ANOTHER ONE."

"When is a door not a door?" Eddie asked.

"WHEN IT'S AJAR. YOU'LL HAVE TO DO
BETTER THAN THAT IF YOU REALLY EX-
PECT ME TO TAKE YOU SOMEWHERE. *CAN*
YOU DO BETTER THAN THAT?"

"If Roland gets here, I'm sure we can," Susannah
said. "Regardless of how good the riddles in Jake's
book may be, Roland knows hundreds—he actually
studied them as a child." Having said this, she realized
she could not conceive of Roland as a child. "*Will* you
take us, Blaine?"

"I MIGHT," Blaine said, and Eddie was quite sure
he heard a dim thread of cruelty running through that
voice. "BUT YOU'LL HAVE TO PRIME THE
PUMP TO GET ME GOING, AND MY PUMP
PRIMES BACKWARD."

"Meaning what?" Eddie asked, looking through the
bars at the smooth pink line of Blaine's back. But
Blaine did not reply to this or any of the other ques-

tions they asked. The bright orange lights stayed on, but both Big Blaine and Little Blaine seemed to have gone into hibernation. Eddie, however, knew better. Blaine was awake. Blaine was watching them. Blaine was listening to their frictive patterns and diphthong stress-emphasis.

He looked at Susannah.

" 'You'll have to prime the pump, but my pump primes backward,' " he said bleakly. "It's a riddle, isn't it?"

"Yes, of course." She looked at the triangular window, so like a half-lidded, mocking eye, and then pulled him close so she could whisper in his ear. "It's totally insane, Eddie—schizophrenic, paranoid, probably delusional as well."

"Tell me about it," he breathed back. "What we've got here is a lunatic genius ghost-in-the-computer monorail that likes riddles and goes faster than the speed of sound. Welcome to the fantasy version of *One Flew Over the Cuckoo's Nest*."

"Do you have any idea what the answer is?"

Eddie shook his head. "You?"

"A little tickle, way back in my mind. False light, probably. I keep thinking about what Roland said: a good riddle is always sensible and always solvable. It's like a magician's trick."

"Misdirection."

She nodded. "Go fire another shot, Eddie—let em know we're still here."

"Yeah. Now if we could only be sure that they're still there."

"Do you think they are, Eddie?"

Eddie had started away, and he spoke without stopping or looking back. "I don't know—that's a riddle not even Blaine could answer."

31

"COULD I HAVE SOMETHING to drink?" Jake asked. His voice came out sounding furry and nasal. Both his mouth and the tissues in his abused nose were swelling up. He looked like someone who has gotten the worst of it in a nasty street-fight.

"Oh, yes," Tick-Tock replied judiciously. "You *could*. I'd say you certainly *could*. We have lots to drink, don't we, Copperhead?"

"Ay," said a tall, bespectacled man in a white silk shirt and a pair of black silk trousers. He looked like a college professor in a turn-of-the-century *Punch* cartoon. "No shortage of po-ter-bulls here."

The Tick-Tock Man, once more seated at ease in his throne-like chair, looked humorously at Jake. "We have wine, beer, ale, and, of course, good old water. Sometimes that's all a body wants, isn't it? Cool, clear, sparkling water. How does that sound, cully?"

Jake's throat, which was also swollen and as dry as sandpaper, prickled painfully. "Sounds good," he whispered.

"It's woke *my* thirsty up, I know that," Tick-Tock said. His lips spread in a smile. His green eyes sparkled. "Bring me a dipper of water, Tilly—I'll be damned if I know what's happened to my manners."

Tilly stepped through the hatchway on the far side of the room—it was opposite the one through which Jake and Gasher had entered. Jake watched her go and licked his swollen lips.

"Now," Tick-Tock said, returning his gaze to Jake, "you say the American city you came from—this New York—is much like Lud."

"Well . . . not exactly . . ."

"But you *do* recognize some of the machinery," Tick-Tock pressed. "Valves and pumps and such. Not to mention the firedim tubes."

"Yes. We call it neon, but it's the same."

Tick-Tock reached out toward him. Jake cringed, but Tick-Tock only patted him on the shoulder. "Yes,

yes; close enough." His eyes gleamed. "*And* you've heard of computers?"

"Sure, but—"

Tilly returned with the dipper and timidly approached the Tick-Tock Man's throne. He took it and held it out to Jake. When Jake reached for it, Tick-Tock pulled it back and drank himself. As Jake watched the water trickle from Tick-Tock's mouth and roll down his naked chest, he began to shake. He couldn't help it.

The Tick-Tock Man looked over the dipper at him, as if just remembering that Jake was still there. Behind him, Gasher, Copperhead, Brandon, and Hoots were grinning like schoolyard kids who have just heard an amusing dirty joke.

"Why, I got thinking about how thirsty *I* was and forgot all about *you*!" Tick-Tock cried. "That's mean as hell, gods damn my eyes! But, of course, it looked so good . . . and it *is* good . . . cold . . . clear . . ."

He held the dipper out to Jake. When Jake reached for it, Tick-Tock pulled it back.

"First, cully, tell me what you know about dipolar computers and transitive circuits," he said coldly.

"What . . ." Jake looked toward the ventilator grille, but the golden eyes were still gone. He was beginning to think he had imagined them after all. He shifted his gaze back to the Tick-Tock Man, understanding one thing clearly: he wasn't going to get any water. He had been stupid to even dream he might. "What are dipolar computers?"

The Tick-Tock Man's face contorted with rage; he threw the remainder of the water into Jake's bruised, puffy face. *"Don't you play it light with me!"* he shrieked. He stripped off the Seiko watch and shook it in front of Jake. *"When I asked you if this ran on a dipolar circuit, you said it didn't! So don't tell me you don't know what I'm talking about when you already made it clear that you do!"*

"But . . . but . . ." Jake couldn't go on. His head was whirling with fear and confusion. He was aware, in some far-off fashion, that he was licking as much water as he could off his lips.

"There's a thousand of those ever-fucking dipolar computers right under the ever-fucking city, maybe a HUNDRED thousand, and the only one that still works don't do a thing except play Watch Me and run those drums! I want those computers! I want them working for ME!"

The Tick-Tock Man bolted forward on his throne, seized Jake, shook him back and forth, and then threw him to the floor. Jake struck one of the lamps, knocking it over, and the bulb blew with a hollow coughing sound. Tilly gave a little shriek and stepped backward, her eyes wide and frightened. Copperhead and Brandon looked at each other uneasily.

Tick-Tock leaned forward, elbows on his thighs, and screamed into Jake's face: *"I want them AND I MEAN TO HAVE THEM!"*

Silence fell in the room, broken only by the soft whoosh of warm air pouring from the ventilators. Then the twisted rage on the Tick-Tock Man's face disappeared so suddenly it might never have existed at all. It was replaced by another charming smile. He leaned further forward and helped Jake to his feet.

"Sorry. I get thinking about the potential of this place and sometimes I get carried away. Please accept my apology, cully." He picked up the overturned dipper and threw it at Tilly. "Fill this up, you useless bitch! What's the matter with you?"

He turned his attention back to Jake, still smiling his TV game-show host smile.

"All right; you've had your little joke and I've had mine. Now tell me everything you know about dipolar computers and transitive circuits. Then you can have a drink."

Jake opened his mouth to say something—he had no idea what—and then, incredibly, Roland's voice was in his mind, filling it.

Distract them, Jake—and if there's a button that opens the door, get close to it.

The Tick-Tock Man was watching him closely. "Something just came into your mind, didn't it, cully? I always know. So don't keep it a secret; tell your old friend Ticky."

Jake caught movement in the corner of his eye. Although he did not dare glance up at the ventilator panel—not with all the Tick-Tock Man's notice bent upon him—he knew that Oy was back, peering down through the louvers.

Distract them . . . and suddenly Jake knew just how to do that.

"I *did* think of something," he said, "but it wasn't about computers. It was about my old pal Gasher. And *his* old pal, Hoots."

"Here! Here!" Gasher cried. "What are you talking about, boy?"

"Why don't you tell Tick-Tock who *really* gave you the password, Gasher? Then *I* can tell Tick-Tock where you keep it."

The Tick-Tock Man's puzzled gaze shifted from Jake to Gasher. "What's he talking about?"

"Nothin!" Gasher said, but he could not forbear a quick glance at Hoots. "He's just runnin his gob, tryin to get off the hot-seat by puttin me on it, Ticky. I told you he was pert! Didn't I say—"

"Take a look in his scarf, why don't you?" Jake asked. "He's got a scrap of paper with the word written on it. I had to read it to him because he couldn't even do that."

There was no sudden rage on Tick-Tock's part this time; his face darkened gradually instead, like a summer sky before a terrible thunderstorm.

"Let me see your scarf, Gasher," he said in a soft, thick voice. "Let your old pal sneak a peek."

"He's lyin, I tell you!" Gasher cried, putting his hands on his scarf and taking two steps backward toward the wall. Directly above him, Oy's gold-ringed eyes gleamed. "All you got to do is look in his face to see lyin's what a pert little cull like him does best!"

The Tick-Tock Man shifted his gaze to Hoots, who

looked sick with fear. "What about it?" Tick-Tock asked in his soft, terrible voice. "What about it, Hooterman? I know you and Gasher was butt-buddies of old, and I know you've the brains of a hung goose, but surely not even you could be stupid enough to write down a password to the inner chamber . . . could you? *Could* you?"

"I . . . I oney thought . . ." Hoots began.

"Shut up!" Gasher shouted. He shot Jake a look of pure, sick hate. "I'll kill you for this, dearie—see if I don't."

"Take off your scarf, Gasher," the Tick-Tock Man said. "I want a look inside it."

Jake sidled a step closer to the podium with the buttons on it.

"No!" Gasher's hands returned to the scarf and pressed against it as if it might fly away of its own accord. "Be damned if I will!"

"Brandon, grab him," Tick-Tock said.

Brandon lunged for Gasher. Gasher's move wasn't as quick as Tick-Tock's had been, but it was quick enough; he bent, yanked a knife from the top of his boot, and buried it in Brandon's arm.

"Oh, you barstard!" Brandon shouted in surprise and pain as blood began to pour out of his arm.

"Lookit what you did!" Tilly screamed.

"Do I have to do *everything* around here myself?" Tick-Tock shouted, more exasperated than angry, it seemed, and rose to his feet. Gasher retreated from him, weaving the bloody knife back and forth in front of his face in mystic patterns. He kept his other hand planted firmly on top of his head.

"Draw back," he panted. "I loves you like a brother, Ticky, but if you don't draw back, I'll hide this blade in your guts—so I will."

"You? Not likely," the Tick-Tock Man said with a laugh. He removed his own knife from its scabbard and held it delicately by the bone hilt. All eyes were on the two of them. Jake took two quick steps to the podium with its little cluster of buttons and reached

for the one he thought the Tick-Tock man had pushed.

Gasher was backing along the curved wall, the tubes of light painting his mandrus-riddled face in a succession of sick colors: bile-green, fever-red, jaundice-yellow. Now it was the Tick-Tock Man standing below the ventilator grille where Oy was watching.

"Put it down, Gasher," Tick-Tock said in a reasonable tone of voice. "You brought the boy as I asked; if anyone else gets pricked over this, it'll be Hoots, not you. Just show me—"

Jake saw Oy crouching to spring and understood two things: what the bumbler meant to do and who had put him up to it.

"*Oy, no!*" he screamed.

All of them turned to look at him. At that moment Oy leaped, hitting the flimsy ventilator grille and knocking it free. The Tick-Tock Man wheeled toward the sound, and Oy fell onto his upturned face, biting and slashing.

32

ROLAND HEARD IT FAINTLY even through the twin doors—*Oy, no!*—and his heart sank. He waited for the valve-wheel to turn, but it did not. He closed his eyes and sent with all his might: *The door, Jake! Open the door!*

He sensed no response, and the pictures were gone. His communication line with Jake, flimsy to begin with, had now been severed.

33

THE TICK-TOCK MAN blundered backward, cursing and screaming and grabbing at the writhing, biting, digging thing on his face. He felt Oy's claws punch into his left eye, popping it, and a horrible red pain sank into his head like a flaming torch thrown down a deep well. At that point, rage overwhelmed pain. He seized Oy, tore him off his face, and held him over his head, meaning to twist him like a rag.

"*No!*" Jake wailed. He forgot about the button which unlocked the doors and seized the gun hanging from the back of the chair.

Tilly shrieked. The others scattered. Jake levelled the old German machine-gun at the Tick-Tock Man. Oy, upside down in those huge, strong hands and bent almost to the snapping point, writhed madly and slashed his teeth into the air. He shrieked in agony— a horribly human sound.

"*Leave him alone, you bastard!*" Jake screamed, and pressed the trigger.

He had enough presence of mind left to aim low. The roar of the Schmeisser .40 was ear-splitting in the enclosed space, although it fired only five or six rounds. One of the lighted tubes popped in a burst of cold orange fire. A hole appeared an inch above the left knee of the Tick-Tock Man's tight-fitting trousers, and a dark red stain began to spread at once. Tick-Tock's mouth opened in a shocked O of surprise, an expression which said more clearly than words could have done that, for all his intelligence, Tick-Tock had expected to live a long, happy life where he shot people but was never shot himself. Shot *at*, perhaps, but actually hit? That surprised expression said that just wasn't supposed to be in the cards.

Welcome to the real world, you fuck, Jake thought.

Tick-Tock dropped Oy to the iron grillework floor to grab at his wounded leg. Copperhead lunged at Jake, got an arm around his throat, and then Oy was on him, barking shrilly and chewing at Copperhead's ankle through the black silk pants. Copperhead screamed and danced away, shaking Oy back and forth at the end of his leg. Oy clung like a limpet. Jake turned to see the Tick-Tock Man crawling toward him. He had retrieved his knife and the blade was now clamped between his teeth.

"Goodbye, Ticky," Jake said, and pressed the Schmeisser's trigger again. Nothing happened. Jake didn't know if it was empty or jammed, and this was hardly the time to speculate. He took two steps backward before finding further retreat blocked by the big chair which had served the Tick-Tock Man as a throne. Before he could slip around, putting the chair between them, Tick-Tock had grabbed his ankle. His other hand went to the hilt of his knife. The ruins of his left eye lay on his cheek like a glob of mint jelly; the right eye glared up at Jake with insane hatred.

Jake tried to pull away from the clutching hand and went sprawling on the Tick-Tock Man's throne. His eye fell on a pocket which had been sewn into the right-hand arm-rest. Jutting from the elasticized top was the cracked pearl handle of a revolver.

"Oh, cully, how you'll suffer!" the Tick-Tock Man whispered ecstatically. The O of surprise had been replaced by a wide, trembling grin. "Oh how you'll suffer! And how happy I'll be to . . . *What—?*"

The grin slackened and the surprised O began to reappear as Jake pointed the cheesy nickel-plated revolver at him and thumbed back the hammer. The grip on Jake's ankle tightened until it seemed to him that the bones there must snap.

"You *dasn't!*" Tick-Tock said in a screamy whisper.

"Yes I *do*," Jake said grimly, and pulled the trigger of the Tick-Tock Man's runout gun. There was a flat crack, much less dramatic than the Schmeisser's Teutonic roar. A small black hole appeared high up on the right side of Tick-Tock's forehead. The Tick-Tock Man went on staring up at Jake, disbelief in his remaining eye.

Jake tried to make himself shoot him again and couldn't do it.

Suddenly a flap of the Tick-Tock Man's scalp peeled away like old wallpaper and dropped on his right cheek. Roland would have known what this meant;

Jake, however, was now almost beyond coherent thought. A dark, panicky horror was spinning across his mind like a tornado funnel. He cringed back in the big chair as the hand on his ankle fell away and the Tick-Tock Man collapsed forward on his face.

The door. He had to open the door and let the gunslinger in.

Focusing on that and nothing but, Jake let the pearl-handled revolver clatter to the iron grating and pushed himself out of the chair. He was reaching again for the button he thought he had seen Tick-Tock push when a pair of hands settled around his throat and dragged him backward, away from the podium.

"I said I'd kill you for it, my narsty little pal," a voice whispered in his ear, "and the Gasherman always keeps his promises."

Jake flailed behind him with both hands and found nothing but thin air. Gasher's fingers sank into his throat, choking relentlessly. The world started to turn gray in front of his eyes. Gray quickly deepened to purple, and purple to black.

34

A PUMP STARTED UP, and the valve-wheel in the center of the hatch spun rapidly. *Gods be thanked!* Roland thought. He seized the wheel with his right hand almost before it had stopped moving and yanked it open. The other door was ajar; from beyond it came the sounds of men fighting and Oy's bark, now shrill with pain and fury.

Roland kicked the door open with his boot and saw Gasher throttling Jake. Oy had left Copperhead and was now trying to make Gasher let go of Jake, but Gasher's boot was doing double duty: protecting its owner from the bumbler's teeth, and protecting Oy from the virulent infection which ran in Gasher's blood. Brandon stabbed Oy in the flank again in an effort to make him stop worrying Gasher's ankle, but Oy paid no heed. Jake hung from his captor's dirty hands like a puppet whose strings have been cut. His face was bluish-white, his swollen lips a delicate shade of lavender.

Gasher looked up. *"You,"* he snarled.

"Me," Roland agreed. He fired once and the left side of Gasher's head disintegrated. The man went flying backward, bloodstained yellow scarf unravelling, and landed on top of the Tick-Tock Man. His feet drummed spastically on the iron grillework for a moment and then fell still.

The gunslinger shot Brandon twice, fanning the hammer of his revolver with the flat of his right hand. Brandon, who had been bent over Oy for another stroke, spun around, struck the wall, and slid slowly down it, clutching at one of the tubes. Green swamplight spilled out from between his loosening fingers.

Oy limped to where Jake lay and began licking his pale, still face.

Copperhead and Hoots had seen enough. They ran side by side for the small door through which Tilly had gone to get the dipper of water. It was the wrong time for chivalry; Roland shot them both in the back. He would have to move fast now, very fast indeed, and he would not risk being waylaid by these two if they should chance to rediscover their guts.

A cluster of bright orange lights came on at the top of the capsule-shaped enclosure, and an alarm began to go off: in broad, hoarse blats that battered the walls. After a moment or two, the emergency lights began to pulse in sync with the alarm.

35

EDDIE WAS RETURNING TO Susannah when the alarm began to wail. He yelled in surprise and raised the Ruger, pointing it at nothing. *"What's happening?"*

Susannah shook her head—she had no idea. The alarm was scary, but that was only part of the problem; it was also loud enough to be physically painful. Those amplified jags of sound made Eddie think of a tractor-trailer horn raised to the tenth power.

At that moment, the orange arc-sodiums began to pulse. When he reached Susannah's chair, Eddie saw that the COMMAND and ENTER buttons were also pulsing in bright red beats. They looked like winking eyes.

"Blaine, what's happening?" he shouted. He looked around but saw only wildly jumping shadows. "Are you doing this?"

Blaine's only response was laughter—terrible mechanical laughter that made Eddie think of the clockwork clown that had stood outside the House of Horrors at Coney Island when he was a little kid.

"*Blaine, stop it!*" Susannah shrieked. "*How can we think of an answer to your riddle with that air-raid siren going off?*"

The laughter stopped as suddenly as it began, but Blaine made no reply. Or perhaps he did; from beyond the bars that separated them from the platform, huge engines powered by frictionless slo-trans turbines awoke at the command of the dipolar computers the Tick-Tock Man had so lusted after. For the first time in a decade, Blaine the Mono was awake and cycling up toward running speed.

36

THE ALARM, WHICH HAD indeed been built to warn Lud's long-dead residents of an impending air attack (and which had not even been tested in almost a thousand years), blanketed the city with sound. All the lights which still operated came on and began to pulse in sync. Pubes above the streets and Grays below them were alike convinced that the end they had always feared was finally upon them. The Grays suspected some cataclysmic mechanical breakdown was occurring. The Pubes, who had always believed that the ghosts lurking in the machines below the city would some day rise up to take their long-delayed vengeance on the still living, were probably closer to the actual truth of what was happening.

Certainly there had been an intelligence left in the ancient computers below the city, a single living organism which had long ago ceased to exist sanely under conditions that, within its merciless dipolar circuits, could only be absolute reality. It had held its increasingly alien logic within its banks of memory for eight hundred years and might have held them so for eight hundred more, if not for the arrival of Roland and his friends; yet this *mens non corpus* had brooded and grown ever more insane with each passing year; even in its increasing periods of sleep it could be said to dream, and these dreams grew steadily more abnormal as the world moved on. Now, although the unthinkable machinery which maintained the Beams had weakened, this insane and inhuman intelligence had awakened in the rooms of ruin and had begun once more, although as bodiless as any ghost, to stumble through the halls of the dead.

In other words, Blaine the Mono was preparing to get out of Dodge.

37

ROLAND HEARD A FOOTSTEP behind him as he knelt by Jake and turned, raising his gun. Tilly, her dough-colored face a mask of confusion and superstitious fear, raised her hands and shrieked: *"Don't kill me, sai! Please! Don't kill me!"*

"Run, then," Roland said curtly, and as Tilly began to move, he struck her calf with the barrel of his revolver. "Not that way—through the door I came in.

And if you ever see me again, I'll be the last thing you ever see. Now *go!*"

She disappeared into the leaping, circling shadows.

Roland dropped his head to Jake's chest, slamming his palm against his other ear to deaden the pulse of the alarm. He heard the boy's heartbeat, slow but strong. He slipped his arms around the boy, and as he did, Jakes's eyes fluttered open. "You didn't let me fall this time." His voice was no more than a hoarse whisper.

"No. Not this time, and not ever again. Don't try your voice."

"Where's Oy?"

"Oy!" the bumbler barked. *"Oy!"*

Brandon had slashed Oy several times, but none of the wounds seemed mortal or even serious. It was clear that he was in some pain, but it was equally clear he was transported with joy. He regarded Jake with sparkling eyes, his pink tongue lolling out. "Ake, Ake, *Ake!*"

Jake burst into tears and reached for him; Oy limped into the circle of his arms and allowed himself to be hugged for a moment.

Roland got up and looked around. His gaze fixed on the door on the far side of the room. The two men he'd backshot had been heading in that direction, and the woman had also wanted to go that way. The gunslinger went toward the door with Jake in his arms and Oy at his heel. He kicked one of the dead Grays aside, and ducked through. The room beyond was a kitchen. It managed to look like a hog-wallow in spite of the built-in appliances and the stainless steel walls; the Grays were apparently not much interested in housekeeping.

"Drink," Jake whispered. "Please . . . so thirsty."

Roland felt a queer doubling, as if time had folded backward on itself. He remembered lurching out of the desert, crazy with the heat and the emptiness. He remembered passing out in the stable of the way station, half-dead from thirst, and waking at the taste of cool water trickling down his throat. The boy had taken off his shirt, soaked it under the flow from the pump, and given him to drink. Now it was his turn to do for Jake what Jake had already done for him.

Roland glanced around and saw a sink. He went over to it and turned on the faucet. Cold, clear water rushed out. Over them, around them, under them, the alarm roared on and on.

"Can you stand?"

Jake nodded. "I think so."

Roland set the boy on his feet, ready to catch him if he looked too wobbly, but Jake hung onto the sink, then ducked his head beneath the flowing water. Roland picked Oy up and looked at his wounds. They were already clotting. *You got off very lucky, my furry friend*, Roland thought, then reached past Jake to cup a palmful of water for the animal. Oy drank it eagerly.

Jake drew back from the faucet with his hair plastered to the sides of his face. His skin was still too pale and the signs that he had been badly beaten were clearly visible, but he looked better than he had when Roland had first bent over him. For one terrible moment, the gunslinger had been positive Jake was dead.

He found himself wishing he could go back and kill Gasher again, and that led him to another thought.

"What about the one Gasher called the Tick-Tock Man? Did you see him, Jake?"

"Yes. Oy ambushed him. Tore up his face. Then I shot him."

"Dead?"

Jake's lips began to tremble. He pressed them firmly together. "Yes. In his . . ." He tapped his forehead high above his right eyebrow. "I was l-l- . . . I was lucky."

Roland looked at him appraisingly, then slowly shook his head. "You know, I doubt that. But never mind now. Come on."

"Where are we going?" Jake's voice was still little more than a husky murmur, and he kept looking past

Roland's shoulder toward the room where he had almost died.

Roland pointed across the kitchen. Beyond another hatchway, the corridor continued. "That'll do for a start."

"GUNSLINGER," a voice boomed from everywhere.

Roland wheeled around, one arm cradling Oy and the other around Jake's shoulders, but there was no one to see.

"Who speaks to me?" he shouted.

"NAME YOURSELF, GUNSLINGER."

"Roland of Gilead, son of Steven. Who speaks to me?"

"GILEAD IS NO MORE," the voice mused, ignoring the question.

Roland looked up and saw patterns of concentric rings in the ceiling. The voice was coming from those.

"NO GUNSLINGER HAS WALKED IN-WORLD OR MID-WORLD FOR ALMOST THREE HUNDRED YEARS."

"I and my friends are the last."

Jake took Oy from Roland. The bumbler at once began to lick the boy's swollen face; his gold-ringed eyes were full of adoration and happiness.

"It's Blaine," Jake whispered to Roland. "Isn't it?"

Roland nodded. Of course it was—but he had an idea that there was a great deal more to Blaine than just a monorail train.

"BOY! ARE YOU JAKE OF NEW YORK?"

Jake pressed closer to Roland and looked up at the speakers. "Yes," he said. "That's me. Jake of New York. Uh . . . son of Elmer."

"DO YOU STILL HAVE THE BOOK OF RIDDLES? THE ONE OF WHICH I HAVE BEEN TOLD?"

Jake reached over his shoulder, and an expression of dismayed recollection filled his face as his fingers touched nothing but his own back. When he looked at Roland again, the gunslinger was holding his pack out toward him, and although the man's narrow, finely carved face was as expressionless as ever, Jake sensed the ghost of a smile lurking at the corners of his mouth.

"You'll have to fix the straps," Roland said as Jake took the pack. "I made them longer."

"But *Riddle-De-Dum!*—?"

Roland nodded. "Both books are still in there."

"WHAT YOU GOT, LITTLE PILGRIM?" the voice inquired in a leisurely drawl.

"Cripes!" Jake said.

It can see us as well as hear us, Roland thought, and a moment later he spotted a small glass eye in one corner, far above a man's normal line of sight. He felt a chill slip over his skin, and knew from both the troubled look on Jake's face and the way the boy's arms had tightened around Oy that he wasn't alone in his unease. That voice belonged to a machine, an incredibly *smart* machine, a *playful* machine, but there was something very wrong with it, all the same.

"The book," Jake said. "I've got the riddle book."

"GOOD." There was an almost human satisfaction in the voice. "REALLY EXCELLENT."

A scruffy, bearded fellow suddenly appeared in the doorway on the far side of the kitchen. A blood-stained, dirt-streaked yellow scarf flapped from the newcomer's upper arm. "Fires in the walls!" he screamed. In his panic, he seemed not to realize that Roland and Jake were not part of his miserable sub-terranean *ka-tet*. "Smoke on the lower levels! People killin theirselves! Somepin's gone wrong! Hell, *ev-erythin's* gone wrong! We gotta—"

The door of the oven suddenly dropped open like an unhinged jaw. A thick beam of blue-white fire shot out and engulfed the scruffy man's head. He was driven backward with his clothes in flames and his skin boiling on his face.

Jake stared up at Roland, stunned and horrified. Roland put an arm about the boy's shoulders.

"HE INTERRUPTED ME," the voice said. "THAT WAS RUDE, WASN'T IT?"

"Yes," Roland said calmly. "Extremely rude."

"SUSANNAH OF NEW YORK SAYS YOU HAVE A GREAT MANY RIDDLES BY HEART, ROLAND OF GILEAD. IS THIS TRUE?"

"Yes."

There was an explosion in one of the rooms opening off this arm of the corridor; the floor shuddered beneath their feet and voices screamed in a jagged chorus. The pulsing lights and the endless, blatting siren faded momentarily, then came back strong. A little skein of bitter, acrid smoke drifted from the ventilators. Oy got a whiff and sneezed.

"TELL ME ONE OF YOUR RIDDLES, GUN-SLINGER," the voice invited. It was serene and untroubled, as if they were all sitting together in a peaceful village square somewhere instead of beneath a city that seemed on the verge of ripping itself apart.

Roland thought for a moment, and what came to mind was Cuthbert's favorite riddle. "All right, Blaine," he said, "I will. What's better than all the gods and worse than Old Man Splitfoot? Dead people eat it always; live people who eat it die slow."

There was a long pause. Jake put his face in Oy's fur to try to get away from the stink of the roasted Gray.

"Be careful, gunslinger." The voice was as small as a cool puff of breeze on summer's hottest day. The voice of the machine had come from all the speakers, but this one came only from the speaker directly overhead. *"Be careful, Jake of New York. Remember that these are The Drawers. Go slow and be very careful."*

Jake looked at the gunslinger with widening eyes. Roland gave his head a small, faint shake and raised one finger. He looked as if he was scratching the side of his nose, but that finger also lay across his lips, and Jake had an idea Roland was actually telling him to keep his mouth shut.

"A CLEVER RIDDLE," Blaine said at last. There

seemed to be real admiration in its voice. "THE ANSWER IS NOTHING, IS IT NOT?"

"That's right," Roland said. "You're pretty clever yourself, Blaine."

When the voice spoke again, Roland heard what Eddie had heard already: a deep and ungovernable greed. "ASK ME ANOTHER."

Roland drew a deep breath. "Not just now."

"I HOPE YOU ARE NOT REFUSING ME, ROLAND, SON OF STEVEN, FOR THAT IS ALSO RUDE. *EXTREMELY* RUDE."

"Take us to our friends and help us get out of Lud," Roland said. "Then there may be time for riddling."

"I COULD KILL YOU WHERE YOU STAND," the voice said, and now it was as cold as winter's darkest day.

"Yes," Roland said. "I'm sure you could. But the riddles would die with us."

"I COULD TAKE THE BOY'S BOOK."

"Thieving is ruder than either refusal or interruption," Roland remarked. He spoke as if merely passing the time of day, but the remaining fingers of his right hand were tight on Jake's shoulder.

"Besides," Jake said, looking up at the speaker in the ceiling, "the answers aren't in the book. Those pages were torn out." In a flash of inspiration, he tapped his temple. "They're up here, though."

"YOU FELLOWS WANT TO REMEMBER THAT NOBODY LOVES A SMARTASS," Blaine said. There was another explosion, this one louder and closer. One of the ventilator grilles blew off and shot across the kitchen like a projectile. A moment later two men and a woman emerged through the door which led to the rest of the Grays' warren. The gunslinger levelled his revolver at them, then lowered it as they stumbled across the kitchen and into the silo beyond without so much as a look at Roland and Jake. To Roland they looked like animals fleeing before a forest fire.

A stainless steel panel in the ceiling slid open, re-

vealing a square of darkness. Something silvery
flashed within it, and a few moments later a steel
sphere, perhaps a foot in diameter, dropped from the
hole and hung in the air of the kitchen.

"FOLLOW," Blaine said flatly.

"Will it take us to Eddie and Susannah?" Jake
asked hopefully.

Blaine replied only with silence . . . but when the
sphere began floating down the corridor, Roland and
Jake followed it.

38

JAKE HAD NO CLEAR memory of the time which followed, and that was probably merciful. He had left his
world over a year before nine hundred people would
commit suicide together in a small South American
country called Gyana, but he knew about the periodic
death-rushes of the lemmings, and what was happening in the disintegrating undercity of the Grays was
like that.

There were explosions, some on their level but most
far below them; acrid smoke occasionally drifted from
the ventilator grilles, but most of the air-purifiers were
still working and they whipped the worst of it away
before it could gather in choking clouds. They saw no
fires. Yet the Grays were reacting as if the time of
the apocalypse had come. Most only fled, their faces
blank O's of panic, but many had committed suicide
in the halls and interconnected rooms through which
the steel sphere led Roland and Jake. Some had shot
themselves; many more had slashed their throats or
wrists; a few appeared to have swallowed poison. On
all the faces of the dead was the same expression of
overmastering terror. Jake could only vaguely understand what had driven them to this. Roland had a
better idea of what had happened to them—to their
minds—when the long-dead city first came to life

around them and then seemed to commence tearing itself apart. And it was Roland who understood that Blaine was doing it on purpose. That Blaine was driving them to it.

They ducked around a man hanging from an overhead heating-duct and pounded down a flight of steel stairs behind the floating steel ball.

"Jake!" Roland shouted. "You never let me in at all, did you?"

Jake shook his head.

"I didn't think so. It was Blaine."

They reached the bottom of the stairs and hurried along a narrow corridor toward a hatch with the words ABSOLUTELY NO ADMITTANCE printed on it in the spiked letters of the High Speech.

"*Is* it Blaine?" Jake asked.

"Yes—that's as good a name as any."

"What about the other v—"

"Hush!" Roland said grimly.

The steel ball paused in front of the hatchway. The wheel spun and the hatch popped ajar. Roland pulled it open, and they stepped into a huge underground room which stretched away in three directions as far as they could see. It was filled with seemingly endless aisles of control panels and electronic equipment. Most of the panels were still dark and dead, but as Jake and Roland stood inside the door, looking about with wide eyes, they could see pilot-lights coming on and hear machinery cycling up.

"The Tick-Tock Man said there were thousands of computers," Jake said. "I guess he was right. My God, look!"

Roland did not understand the word Jake had used and so said nothing. He only watched as row after row of panels lit up. A cloud of sparks and a momentary tongue of green fire jumped from one of the consoles as some ancient piece of equipment malfunctioned.

Most of the machinery, however, appeared to be up and running just fine. Needles which hadn't moved in centuries suddenly jumped into the green. Huge aluminum cylinders spun, spilling data stored on silicon chips into memory banks which were once more wide awake and ready for input. Digital displays, indicating everything from the mean aquifer water-pressure in the West River Barony to available power amperage in the hibernating Send Basin Nuclear Plant, lit up in brilliant dot-matrices of red and green. Overhead, banks of hanging globes began to flash on, radiating outward in spokes of light. And from below, above, and around them—from everywhere—came the deep bass hum of generators and slo-trans engines awakening from their long sleep.

Jake had begun to flag badly. Roland swept him into his arms again and chased the steel ball past machines at whose function and intent he could not even guess. Oy ran at his heels. The ball banked left, and the aisle in which they now found themselves ran between banks of TV monitors, thousands of them, stacked in rows like a child's building blocks.

My dad would love it, Jake thought.

Some sections of this vast video arcade were still dark, but many of the screens were on. They showed a city in chaos, both above and below. Clumps of Pubes surged pointlessly through the streets, eyes wide, mouths moving soundlessly. Many were leaping from the tall buildings. Jake observed with horror that hundreds more had congregated at the Send Bridge and were throwing themselves into the river. Other screens showed large, cot-filled rooms like dormitories. Some of these rooms were on fire, but the panic-stricken Grays seemed to be setting the fires themselves—torching their own mattresses and furniture for God alone knew what reason.

One screen showed a barrel-chested giant tossing men and women into what looked like a blood-spattered stamping press. This was bad enough, but there was something worse: the victims were standing in an unguarded line, docilely waiting their turns. The executioner, his yellow scarf pulled tight over his skull

and the knotted ends swinging below his ears like pig-
tails, seized an old woman and held her up, waiting
patiently for the stainless steel block of metal to clear
the killing floor so he could toss her in. The old
woman did not struggle; seemed, in fact, to be
smiling.

"IN THE ROOMS THE PEOPLE COME AND
GO," Blaine said, "BUT I DON'T THINK ANY OF
THEM ARE TALKING OF MICHELANGELO."
He suddenly laughed—strange, tittery laughter that
sounded like rats scampering over broken glass. The
sound sent chills chasing up Jake's neck. He wanted
nothing at all to do with an intelligence that laughed
like that . . . but what choice did they have?

He turned his gaze helplessly back to the monitors
. . . and Roland at once turned his head away. He did
this gently but firmly. "There's nothing there you need
to look at, Jake," he said.

"But why are they doing it?" Jake asked. He had
eaten nothing all day, but he still felt like vomiting.
"Why?"

"Because they're frightened, and Blaine is feeding
their fear. But mostly, I think, because they've lived
too long in the graveyard of their grandfathers and
they're tired of it. And before you pity them, remember how happy they would have been to take you
along with them into the clearing where the path
ends."

The steel ball zipped around another corner, leaving
the TV screens and electronic monitoring equipment
behind. Ahead, a wide ribbon of some synthetic stuff
was set into the floor. It gleamed like fresh tar between two narrow strips of chrome steel that dwindled
to a point on what was not the far side of this room,
but its horizon.

The ball bounced impatiently above the dark strip,
and suddenly the belt—for that was what it was—
swept into silent motion, trundling along between its
steel facings at jogging speed. The ball made small
arcs in the air, urging them to climb on.

Roland trotted beside the moving strip until he was roughly matching its speed, then did just that. He set Jake down and the three of them—gunslinger, boy, and golden-eyed bumbler—were carried rapidly across this shadowy underground plain where the ancient machines were awakening. The moving strip carried them into an area of what looked like filing cabinets—row after endless row of them. They were dark . . . but not dead. A low, sleepy humming sound came from within them, and Jake could see hairline cracks of bright yellow light shining between the steel panels.

He suddenly found himself thinking of the Tick-Tock Man.

There's maybe a hundred thousand of those ever-fucking dipolar computers under the ever-fucking city! I want those computers!

Well, Jake thought, *they're waking up, so I guess you're getting what you wanted, Ticky . . . but if you were here, I'm not sure you'd still want it.*

Then he remembered Tick-Tock's great-grandfather, who'd been brave enough to climb into an airplane from another world and take it into the sky. With that kind of blood running in his veins, Jake supposed, Tick-Tock, far from being frightened to the point of suicide, would have been delighted by this turn of events . . . and the more people who killed themselves in terror, the happier he would have been.

Too late now, Ticky, he thought. *Thank God.*

Roland spoke in a soft, wondering voice. "All these boxes . . . I think we're riding through the mind of the thing that calls itself Blaine, Jake. *I think we're riding through its mind.*"

Jake nodded, and found himself thinking of his Final Essay. "Blaine the Brain is a hell of a pain."

"Yes."

Jake looked closely at Roland. "Are we going to come out where I think we're going to come out?"

"Yes," Roland said. "If we're still following the Path of the Beam, we'll come out in the Cradle."

Jake nodded. "Roland?"

"What?"

"Thanks for coming after me."

Roland nodded and put an arm around Jake's shoulders.

Far ahead of them, huge motors rumbled to life. A moment later a heavy grinding sound began and new light—the harsh glow of orange arc-sodiums—flooded down on them. Jake could now see the place where the moving belt stopped. Beyond it was a steep, narrow escalator, leading up into that orange light.

39

EDDIE AND SUSANNAH HEARD heavy motors start up almost directly beneath them. A moment later, a wide strip of the marble floor began to pull slowly back, revealing a long lighted slot below. The floor was disappearing in their direction. Eddie seized the handles of Susannah's chair and rolled it rapidly backward along the steel barrier between the monorail platform and the rest of the Cradle. There were several pillars along the course of the growing rectangle of light, and Eddie waited for them to tumble into the hole as the floor upon which they stood disappeared from beneath their bases. It didn't happen. The pillars went on serenely standing, seeming to float on nothing.

"I see an escalator!" Susannah shouted over the endless, pulsing alarm. She was leaning forward, peering into the hole.

"Uh-huh," Eddie shouted back. "We got the el station up here, so it must be notions, perfume, and ladies' lingerie down there."

"What?"

"Never mind!"

"Eddie!" Susannah screamed. Delighted surprise burst over her face like a Fourth of July firework. She leaned even further forward, pointing, and Eddie had

to grab her to keep her from tumbling out of the chair. *"It's Roland! It's both of them!"*

There was a shuddery thump as the slot in the floor opened to its maximum length and stopped. The motors which had driven it along its hidden tracks cut out in a long, dying whine. Eddie ran to the edge of the hole and saw Roland riding on one of the escalator steps. Jake—white-faced, bruised, bloody, but clearly Jake and clearly alive—was standing next to him and leaning on the gunslinger's shoulder. And sitting on the step right behind them, looking up with his bright eyes, was Oy.

"Roland! Jake!" Eddie shouted. He leaped up, waving his hands over his head, and came down dancing on the edge of the slot. If he had been wearing a hat, he would have thrown it in the air.

They looked up and waved. Jake was grinning, Eddie saw, and even old long tall and ugly looked as if he might break down and crack a smile before long. Wonders, Eddie thought, would never cease. His heart suddenly felt too big for his chest and he danced faster, waving his arms and whooping, afraid that if he didn't keep moving, his joy and relief might actually cause him to burst. Until this moment he had not realized how positive his heart had become that they would never see Roland and Jake again.

"Hey, guys! All RIGHT! Far fucking out! Get your asses up here!"

"Eddie, help me!"

He turned. Susannah was trying to struggle out of her chair, but a fold of the deerskin trousers she was wearing had gotten caught in the brake mechanism. She was laughing and weeping at the same time, her dark eyes blazing with happiness. Eddie lifted her from the chair so violently that it crashed over on its side. He danced her around in a circle. She clung to his neck with one hand and waved strenuously with the other.

"Roland! Jake! Get on up here! Shuck your butts, you hear me?"

When they reached the top, Eddie embraced Roland, pounding him on the back while Susannah covered Jake's upturned, laughing face with kisses. Oy ran around in tight figure eights, barking shrilly.

"Sugar!" Susannah said. "You all right?"

"Yes," Jake said. He was still grinning, but tears stood in his eyes. "And glad to be here. You'll never know how glad."

"I can guess, sugar. You c'n bet on *that*." She turned to look at Roland. "What'd they do to him? His face look like somebody run over it with a bulldozer."

"That was mostly Gasher," Roland said. "He won't be bothering Jake again. Or anyone else."

"What about you, big boy? You all right?"

Roland nodded, looking about. "So this is the Cradle."

"Yes," Eddie said. He was peering into the slot. "What's down there?"

"Machines and madness."

"Loquacious as ever, I see." Eddie looked at Roland, smiling. "Do you know how happy I am to see you, man? Do you have any idea?"

"Yes—I think I do." Roland smiled then, thinking of how people changed. There had been a time, and not so long ago, when Eddie had been on the edge of cutting his throat with the gunslinger's own knife.

The engines below them started up again. The escalator came to a stop. The slot in the floor began to slide closed once more. Jake went to Susannah's overturned chair, and as he was righting it, he caught sight of the smooth pink shape beyond the iron bars. His breath stopped, and the dream he had had after leaving River Crossing returned full force: the vast pink bullet shape slicing across the empty lands of western Missouri toward him and Oy. Two big triangular windows glittering high up in the blank face of that oncoming monster, windows like eyes . . . and now his dream was becoming reality, just as he had known it eventually would.

It's just an awful choo-choo train, and its name is Blaine the Pain.

Eddie walked over and slung an arm around Jake's shoulders. "Well, there it is, champ—just as advertised. What do you think of it?"

"Not too much, actually." This was an understatement of colossal size, but Jake was too drained to do any better.

"Me, either," Eddie said. "It talks. And it likes riddles."

Jake nodded.

Roland had Susannah planted on one hip, and together they were examining the control box with its diamond-pattern of raised number-pads. Jake and Eddie joined them. Eddie found he had to keep looking down at Jake in order to verify that it wasn't just his imagination or wishful thinking; the boy was really here.

"What now?" he asked Roland.

Roland slipped his finger lightly over the numbered buttons which made up the diamond shape and shook his head. He didn't know.

"Because I think the mono's engines are cycling faster," Eddie said. "I mean, it's hard to tell for sure with that alarm blatting, but I think it is . . . and it's a robot, after all. What if it, like, leaves without us?"

"Blaine!" Susannah shouted. "Blaine, are you—"

"LISTEN CLOSELY, MY FRIENDS," Blaine's voice boomed. "THERE ARE LARGE STOCK-PILES OF CHEMICAL AND BIOLOGICAL WAR-FARE CANNISTERS UNDER THE CITY. I HAVE STARTED A SEQUENCE WHICH WILL CAUSE AN EXPLOSION AND RELEASE THIS GAS. THIS EXPLOSION WILL OCCUR IN TWELVE MINUTES."

The voice fell silent for a moment, and then the voice of Little Blaine, almost buried by the steady, pulsing whoop of the alarm, came to them: *". . . I was afraid of something like this . . . you must hurry . . ."*

Eddie ignored Little Blaine, who wasn't telling him a damned thing he didn't already know. Of *course* they had to hurry, but that fact was running a distant second at the moment. Something much larger occupied most of his mind. *"Why?"* he asked. "Why in God's name would you do that?"

"I SHOULD THINK IT OBVIOUS. I CAN'T NUKE THE CITY WITHOUT DESTROYING MYSELF, AS WELL. AND HOW COULD I TAKE YOU WHERE YOU WANT TO GO IF I WERE DESTROYED?"

"But there are still thousands of people in the city," Eddie said. "You'll *kill* them."

"YES," Blaine said calmly. "SEE YOU LATER ALLIGATOR, AFTER A WHILE CROCODILE, DON'T FORGET TO WRITE."

"Why?" Susannah shouted. *"Why,* goddam you?"

"BECAUSE THEY BORE ME. YOU FOUR, HOWEVER, I FIND RATHER INTERESTING. OF COURSE, HOW LONG I *CONTINUE* TO FIND YOU INTERESTING WILL DEPEND ON HOW GOOD YOUR RIDDLES ARE. AND SPEAKING OF RIDDLES, HADN'T YOU BETTER GET TO WORK SOLVING MINE? YOU HAVE EXACTLY ELEVEN MINUTES AND TWENTY SECONDS BEFORE THE CANNISTERS RUPTURE."

"Stop it!" Jake yelled over the blatting siren. "It isn't just the city—gas like that could float *anywhere*! It could even kill the old people in River Crossing!"

"TOUGH TITTY, SAID THE KITTY," Blaine responded unfeelingly. "ALTHOUGH I BELIEVE THEY CAN COUNT ON MEASURING OUT THEIR LIVES IN COFFEE-SPOONS FOR A FEW MORE YEARS; THE AUTUMN STORMS HAVE BEGUN, AND THE PREVAILING WINDS WILL CARRY THE GASES AWAY FROM THEM. THE SITUATION OF YOU FOUR IS, HOWEVER, VERY DIFFERENT. YOU BETTER PUT ON YOUR THINKING CAPS, OR IT'S SEE YOU

LATER ALLIGATOR, AFTER A WHILE CROC-
ODILE, DON'T FORGET TO WRITE." The voice
paused. "ONE PIECE OF ADDITIONAL INPUT:
THIS GAS IS *NOT* PAINLESS."

"Take it back!" Jake said. "We'll still tell you riddles, won't we, Roland? We'll tell all the riddles you
want! *Just take it back!*"

Blaine began to laugh. He laughed for a long time,
pealing shrieks of electronic mirth into the wide empty
space of the Cradle, where it mingled with the monotonous, drilling beat of the alarm.

"Stop it!" Susannah shouted. "Stop it! Stop it! *Stop
it!*"

Blaine did. A moment later the alarm cut off in
mid-blat. The ensuing silence—broken only by the
pounding rain—was deafening.

Now the voice issuing from the speaker was very
soft, thoughtful, and utterly without mercy. "YOU
NOW HAVE TEN MINUTES," Blaine said. "LET'S
SEE JUST HOW INTERESTING YOU REALLY
ARE."

40

"ANDREW."

There is no Andrew here, stranger, he thought. *Andrew is long gone; Andrew is no more, as I shall soon
be no more.*

"Andrew!" the voice insisted.

It came from far away. It came from outside the
cider-press that had once been his head.

Once there *had* been a boy named Andrew, and his
father had taken that boy to a park on the far western
side of Lud, a park where there had been apple trees
and a rusty tin shack that looked like hell and smelled
like heaven. In answer to his question, Andrew's father had told him it was called the cider house. Then
he gave Andrew a pat on the head, told him not to

be afraid, and led him through the blanket-covered doorway.

There had been more apples—baskets and baskets of them—stacked against the walls inside, and there had also been a scrawny old man named Dewlap, whose muscles writhed beneath his white skin like worms and whose job was to feed the apples, basket by basket, to the loose-jointed, clanking machine which stood in the middle of the room. What came out of the pipe jutting from the far end of the machine was sweet cider. Another man (he no longer remembered what this one's name might have been) stood there, his job to fill jug after jug with the cider. A third man stood behind *him*, and *his* job was to clout the jug-filler on the head if there was too much spillage.

Andrew's father had given him a glass of the foaming cider, and although he had tasted a great many forgotten delicacies during his years in the city, he had never tasted anything finer than that sweet, cold drink. It had been like swallowing a gust of October wind. Yet what he remembered even more clearly than the taste of the cider or the wormy shift and squiggle of Dewlap's muscles as he dumped the baskets was the merciless way the machine reduced the big red-gold apples to liquid. Two dozen rollers had carried them beneath a revolving steel drum with holes punched in it. The apples had first been squeezed and then actually popped, spilling their juices down an inclined trough while a screen caught the seeds and pulp.

Now his head was the cider-press and his brains were the apples. Soon they would pop as the apples had popped beneath the roller, and the blessed darkness would swallow him.

"Andrew! Raise your head and look at me."

He couldn't . . . and wouldn't even if he could. Better to just lie here and wait for the darkness. He was supposed to be dead, anyway; hadn't the hellish squint put a bullet in his brain?

"It didn't go anywhere near your brain, you horse's

ass, and you're not dying. You've just got a headache. You *will* die, though, if you don't stop lying there and puling in your own blood . . . and I will make sure, Andrew, that your dying makes what you are feeling now seem like bliss."

It was not the threats which caused the man on the floor to raise his head but rather the way the owner of that penetrating, hissing voice seemed to have read his mind. His head came up slowly, and the agony was excruciating—heavy objects seemed to go sliding and careering around the bony case which contained what was left of his mind, ripping bloody channels through his brain as they went. A long, syrupy moan escaped him. There was a flapping, tickling sensation on his right cheek, as if a dozen flies were crawling in the blood there. He wanted to shoo them away, but he knew that he needed both hands just to support himself.

The figure standing on the far side of the room by the hatch which led to the kitchen looked ghastly, unreal. This was partly because the overhead lights were still strobing, partly because he was seeing the newcomer with only one eye (he couldn't remember what had happened to the other and didn't want to), but he had an idea it was mostly because the creature *was* ghastly and unreal. It looked like a man . . . but the fellow who had once been Andrew Quick had an idea it really wasn't a man at all.

The stranger standing in front of the hatch wore a short, dark jacket belted at the waist, faded denim trousers, and old, dusty boots—the boots of a country-man, a range-rider, or—

"Or a gunslinger, Andrew?" the stranger asked, and tittered.

The Tick-Tock Man stared desperately at the figure in the doorway, trying to see the face, but the short jacket had a hood, and it was up. The stranger's countenance was lost in its shadows.

The siren stopped in mid-whoop. The emergency lights stayed on, but they at least stopped flashing.

"There," the stranger said in his—or its—whispery, penetrating voice. "At last we can hear ourselves think."

"Who are you?" the Tick-Tock Man asked. He moved slightly, and more of those weights went sliding through his head, ripping fresh channels in his brain. As terrible as that feeling was, the awful tickling of the flies on his right cheek was somehow worse.

"I'm a man of many handles, pardner," the man said from inside the darkness of his hood, and although his voice was grave, Tick-Tock heard laughter lurking just below the surface. "There's some that call me Jimmy, and some that call me Timmy; some that call me Handy and some that call me Dandy. They can call me Loser, or they can call me Winner, just as long as they don't call me in too late for dinner."

The man in the doorway threw back his head, and his laughter chilled the skin of the wounded man's arms and back into lumps of gooseflesh; it was like the howl of a wolf.

"I have been called the Ageless Stranger," the man said. He began to walk toward Tick-Tock, and as he did, the man on the floor moaned and tried to scrabble backward. "I have also been called Merlin or Maerlyn—and who cares, because I was never *that* one, although I never denied it, either. I am sometimes called the Magician . . . or the Wizard . . . but I hope we can go forward together on more humble terms, Andrew. More *human* terms."

He pushed back the hood, revealing a fair, broadbrowed face that was not, for all its pleasant looks, in any way human. Large hectic roses rode the Wizard's cheekbones; his blue-green eyes sparkled with a gusty joy far too wild to be sane; his blue-black hair stood up in zany clumps like the feathers of a raven; his lips, lushly red, parted to reveal the teeth of a cannibal.

"Call me Fannin," the grinning apparition said. "Richard Fannin. That's not *exactly* right, maybe, but I reckon it's close enough for government work." He held out a hand whose palm was utterly devoid of lines. "What do you say, pard? Shake the hand that shook the world."

The creature who had once been Andrew Quick and who had been known in the halls of the Grays as the Tick-Tock Man shrieked and again tried to wriggle backward. The flap of scalp peeled loose by the low-caliber bullet which had only grooved his skull instead of penetrating it swung back and forth; the long strands of gray-blonde hair continued to tickle against his cheek. Quick, however, no longer felt it. He had even forgotten the ache in his skull and the throb from the socket where his left eye had been. His entire consciousness had fused into one thought: *I must get away from this beast that looks like a man.*

But when the stranger seized his right hand and shook it, that thought passed like a dream on waking. The scream which had been locked in Quick's breast escaped his lips in a lover's sigh. He stared dumbly up at the grinning newcomer. The loose flap of his scalp swung and dangled.

"Is that bothering you? It *must* be. Here!" Fannin seized the hanging flap and ripped it briskly off Quick's head, revealing a bleary swatch of skull. There was a noise like heavy cloth tearing. Quick shrieked.

"There, there, it only hurts for a second." The man was now squatting on his hunkers before Quick and speaking as an indulgent parent might speak to a child with a splinter in his finger. "Isn't that so?"

"Y-Y-Yes," Quick muttered. And it was. Already the pain was fading. And when Fannin reached toward him again, caressing the left side of his face, Quick's jerk backward was only a reflex, quickly mastered. As the lineless hand stroked, he felt strength flowing back into him. He looked up at the newcomer with dumb gratitude, lips quivering.

"Is that better, Andrew? It is, isn't it?"

"Yes! Yes!"

"If you want to thank me—as I'm sure you do—you must say something an old acquaintance of mine used to say. He ended up betraying me, but he was a good friend for quite some time, anyway, and I still have a soft spot in my heart for him. Say, 'My life for you,' Andrew—can you say that?"

He could and he did; in fact, it seemed he couldn't *stop* saying it. "My life for you! My life for you! My life for you! My life—"

The stranger touched his cheek again, but this time a huge raw bolt of pain blasted across Andrew Quick's head. He screamed.

"Sorry about that, but time is short and you were starting to sound like a broken record. Andrew, let me put it to you with no bark on it: how would you like to kill the squint who shot you? Not to mention his friends and the hardcase who brought him here— him, most of all. Even the mutt that took your eye, Andrew—would you like that?"

"Yes!" the former Tick-Tock Man gasped. His hands clenched into bloody fists. *"Yes!"*

"That's good," the stranger said, and helped Quick to his feet, "because they *have* to die—they're meddling with things they have no business meddling with. I expected Blaine to take care of them, but things have gone much too far to depend on *anything* . . . after all, who would have thought they could get as far as they have?"

"I don't know," Quick said. He did not, in fact, have the slightest idea what the stranger was talking about. Nor did he care; there was a feeling of exaltation creeping through his mind like some excellent drug, and after the pain of the cider-press, that was enough for him. More than enough.

Richard Fannin's lips curled. "Bear and bone . . . key and rose . . . day and night . . . time and tide. *Enough!* Enough, I say! *They must not draw closer to the Tower than they are now!*"

Quick staggered backward as the man's hands shot out with the flickery speed of heat lightning. One broke the chain which held the tiny glass-enclosed pendulum clock; the other stripped Jake Chambers's Seiko from his forearm.

"I'll just take these, shall I?" Fannin the Wizard smiled charmingly, his lips modestly closed over those awful teeth. "Or do you object?"

"No," Quick said, surrendering the last symbols of his long leadership without a qualm (without, in fact, even being aware that he was doing so). "Be my guest."

"Thank you, Andrew," the dark man said softly. "Now we must step lively—I'm expecting a drastic change in the atmosphere of these environs in the next five minutes or so. We must get to the nearest closet where gas masks are stored before that happens, and it's apt to be a near thing. I could survive the change quite nicely, but I'm afraid you might have some difficulties."

"I don't understand what you're talking about," Andrew Quick said. His head had begun to throb again, and his mind was whirling.

"Nor do you need to," the stranger said smoothly. "Come, Andrew—I think we should hurry. Busy, busy day, eh? With luck, Blaine will fry them right on the platform, where they are no doubt still standing—he's become very eccentric over the years, poor fellow. But I think we should hurry, just the same."

He slid his arm over Quick's shoulders and, giggling, led him through the hatchway Roland and Jake had used only a few minutes before.

VI ■ RIDDLE AND WASTE LANDS

▪ VI ▪

RIDDLE AND
WASTE LANDS

1

"ALL RIGHT," ROLAND SAID. "Tell me his riddle."

"What about all the people out there?" Eddie
asked, pointing across the wide, pillared Plaza of the
Cradle and toward the city beyond. "What can we do
for them?"

"Nothing," Roland said, "but it's still possible that
we may be able to do something for ourselves. Now
what was the riddle?"

Eddie looked toward the streamlined shape of the
mono. "He said we'd have to prime the pump to get
him going. Only his pump primes backward. Does it
mean anything to you?"

Roland thought it over carefully, then shook his
head. He looked down at Jake. "Any ideas, Jake?"

Jake shook his head. "I don't even *see* a pump."

"That's probably the easy part," Roland said. "We say *he* and *him* instead of *it* and *that* because Blaine sounds like a living being, but he's still a machine—a sophisticated one, but a machine. He started his own engines, but it must take some sort of code or combination to open the gate and the train doors."

"We better hurry up," Jake said nervously. "It's got to be two or three minutes since he last talked to us. At least."

"Don't count on it," Eddie said gloomily. "Time's weird over here."

"Still—"

"Yeah, yeah." Eddie glanced toward Susannah, but she was sitting astride Roland's hip and looking at the numeric diamond with a daydreamy expression on her face. He looked back at Roland. "I'm pretty sure you're right about it being a combination—that must be what all those number-pads are for." He raised his voice. "Is that it, Blaine? Have we got at least that much right?"

No response; only the quickening rumble of the mono's engines.

"Roland," Susannah said abruptly. "You have to help me."

The daydreamy look was being replaced by an expression of mingled horror, dismay, and determination. To Roland's eye, she had never looked more beautiful . . . or more alone. She had been on his shoulders when they stood at the edge of the clearing and watched the bear trying to claw Eddie out of the tree, and Roland had not seen her expression when he told her she must be the one to shoot it. But he knew what that expression had been, for he was seeing it now. *Ka* was a wheel, its one purpose to turn, and in the end it always came back to the place where it had started. So it had ever been and so it was now; Susannah was once again facing the bear, and her face said she knew it.

"What?" he asked. "What is it, Susannah?"

"I know the answer, but I can't get it. It's stuck in

my mind the way a fishbone can get stuck in your throat. I need you to help me remember. Not his face, but his voice. What he *said*."

Jake glanced down at his wrist and was surprised all over again by a memory of the Tick-Tock Man's catlike green eyes when he saw not his watch but only the place where it had been—a white shape outlined by his deeply tanned skin. How much longer did they have? Surely no more than seven minutes, and that was being generous. He looked up and saw that Roland had removed a cartridge from his gunbelt and was walking it back and forth across the knuckles of his left hand. Jake felt his eyelids immediately grow heavy and looked away, fast.

"What voice would you remember, Susannah Dean?" Roland asked in a low, musing voice. His eyes were not fixed on her face but on the cartridge as it did its endless, limber dance across his knuckles . . . and back . . . . across . . . and back . . .

He didn't need to look up to know that Jake had looked away from the dance of the cartridge and Susannah had not. He began to speed it up until the cartridge almost seemed to be floating above the back of his hand.

"Help me remember the voice of my father," Susannah Dean said.

2

FOR A MOMENT THERE was silence except for a distant, crumping explosion in the city, the rain pounding on the roof of the Cradle, and the fat throb of the monorail's slo-trans engines. Then a low-pitched hydraulic hum cut through the air. Eddie looked away from the cartridge dancing across the gunslinger's fingers (it took an effort; he realized that in another few moments he would have been hypnotized himself) and peered through the iron bars. A slim silver rod was pushing itself up from the sloping pink surface between Blaine's forward windows. It looked like an antenna of some kind.

"Susannah?" Roland asked in that same low voice.

"What?" Her eyes were open but her voice was distant and breathy—the voice of someone who is sleeptalking.

"Do you remember the voice of your father?"

"Yes . . . but I can't hear it."

"SIX MINUTES, MY FRIENDS."

Eddie and Jake started and looked toward the control-box speaker, but Susannah seemed not to have heard at all; she only stared at the floating cartridge. Below it, Roland's knuckles rippled up and down like the heddles of a loom.

"Try, Susannah," Roland urged, and suddenly he felt Susannah change within the circle of his right arm. She seemed to gain weight . . . and, in some indefinable way, vitality as well. It was as if her essence had somehow changed.

And it had.

"Why you want to bother wit *dat* bitch?" the raspy voice of Detta Walker asked.

3

DETTA SOUNDED BOTH EXASPERATED and amused. "She never got no better'n a C in math her whole life. Wouldn'ta got dat widout me to he'p her." She paused, then added grudgingly: "An' Daddy. He he'ped some, too. I knowed about them forspecial numbahs, but was him showed us de net. My, I got de bigges' kick outta dat!" She chuckled. "Reason Suze can't remember is 'cause Odetta never understood 'bout dem forspecial numbers in de firs' place."

"What forspecial numbers?" Eddie asked.

"*Prime* numbahs!" She pronounced the word *prime* in a way that almost rhymed with *calm*. She looked at Roland, appearing to be wholly awake again now . . . except she was not Susannah, nor was she the same wretched, devilish creature who had previously gone under the name of Detta Walker, although she *sounded* the same. "She went to Daddy cryin an' carryin on 'cause she was flunkin dat math course . . . and it wasn't nuthin but funnybook algebra at dat! She could do de woik—if *I* could, *she* could—but she din' want to. Poitry-readin bitch like her too good for a little *ars mathematica*, you see?" Detta threw her head back and laughed, but the poisoned, half-mad bitterness was gone from the sound. She seemed genuinely amused at the foolishness of her mental twin.

"And Daddy, he say, 'I'm goan show you a trick, Odetta. I learned it in college. It he'ped me get through this prime numbah bi'ness, and it's goan he'p you, too. He'p you find mos' any prime numbah you want.' *Oh*-detta, dumb as ever, she say, 'Teacher says ain't no formula for prime numbahs, Daddy.' And Daddy, he say right back, 'They ain't. But you can catch em, Odetta, if you have a net.' He called it The Net of Eratosthenes. Take me over to dat box on the wall, Roland—I'm goan answer dat honkey computer's riddle. I'm goan th'ow you a net and catch you a train-ride."

Roland took her over, closely followed by Eddie, Jake, and Oy.

"Gimme dat piece o' cha'coal you keep in yo' poke."

He rummaged and brought out a short stub of blackened stick. Detta took it and peered at the diamond-shaped grid of numbers. "Ain't zackly de way Daddy showed me, but I reckon it comes to de same," she said after a moment. "Prime numbah be like me—ornery and forspecial. It gotta be a numbah don't nevvah divide even 'ceptin by one and its ownself. Two is prime, 'cause you can divide it by one an' two, but it's the *only* even numbah that's prime. You c'n take out all the res' dat's even."

"I'm lost," Eddie said.

"That's 'cause you just a stupid white boy," Detta

said, but not unkindly. She looked closely at the diamond shape a moment longer, then quickly began to touch the tip of the charcoal to all the even-numbered pads, leaving small black smudges on them.

"Three's prime, but no product you git by *multiplyin* three can be prime," she said, and now Roland heard an odd but wonderful thing: Detta was fading out of the woman's voice; she was being replaced not by Odetta Holmes but by Susannah Dean. He would not have to bring her out of this trance; she was coming out of it on her own, quite naturally.

Susannah began using her charcoal to touch the multiples of three which were left now that the even numbers had been eliminated: nine, fifteen, twenty-one, and so on.

"Same with five and seven," she murmured, and suddenly she was awake and all Susannah Dean again. "You just have to mark the odd ones like twenty-five that haven't been crossed out already." The diamond shape on the control box now looked like this:

```
              1
            2 3
          4 5 6
        7 8 9 10
     11 12 13 14 15
   16 17 18 19 20 21
  22 23 24 25 26 27 28
 29 30 31 32 33 34 35 36
37 38 39 40 41 42 43 44 45
46 47 48 49 50 51 52 53 54 55
 56 57 58 59 60 61 62 63 64
  65 66 67 68 69 70 71 72
    73 74 75 76 77 78 79
     80 81 82 83 84 85
      86 87 88 89 90
       91 92 93 94
        95 96 97
         98 99
          100
```

"There," she said tiredly. "What's left in the net are all the prime numbers between one and one hundred. I'm pretty sure that's the combination that opens the gate."

"YOU HAVE ONE MINUTE, MY FRIENDS. YOU ARE PROVING TO BE A GOOD DEAL THICKER THAN I HAD HOPED YOU WOULD BE."

Eddie ignored Blaine's voice and threw his arms around Susannah. "Are you back, Suze? Are you awake?"

"Yes. I woke up in the middle of what she was saying, but I let her talk a little longer, anyway. It seemed impolite to interrupt." She looked at Roland. "What do you say? Want to go for it?"

"FIFTY SECONDS."

"Yes. You try the combination, Susannah. It's your answer."

She reached out toward the top of the diamond, but Jake put his hand over hers. "No," he said. " 'This pump primes *backward*.' Remember?"

She looked startled, then smiled. "That's right. Clever Blaine . . . and clever Jake, too."

They watched in silence as she pushed each number in turn, starting with ninety-seven. There was a minute click as each pad locked down. There was no tension-filled pause after she touched the last button; the gate in the center of the barrier immediately began to slide up on its tracks, rattling harshly and showering down flakes of rust from somewhere high above as it went.

"NOT BAD AT ALL," Blaine said admiringly. "I'M LOOKING FORWARD TO THIS VERY MUCH. MAY I SUGGEST YOU CLIMB ON BOARD QUICKLY? IN FACT, YOU MAY WISH TO RUN. THERE ARE SEVERAL GAS OUTLETS IN THIS AREA."

4

THREE HUMAN BEINGS (one carrying a fourth on his hip) and one small, furry animal ran through the opening in the barrier and sprinted toward Blaine the Mono. It stood humming in its narrow loading bay, half above the platform and half below it, looking like a giant cartridge—one which had been painted an incongruous shade of pink—lying in the open breech of a high-powered rifle. In the vastness of the Cradle, Roland and the others looked like mere moving specks. Above them, flocks of pigeons—now with only forty seconds to live—swooped and swirled beneath the Cradle's ancient roof. As the travellers approached the mono, a curved section of its pink hull slid up, revealing a doorway. Beyond it was thick, pale blue carpeting.

"Welcome to Blaine," a soothing voice said as they pelted aboard. They all recognized that voice; it was a slightly louder, slightly more confident version of Little Blaine. "Praise the Imperium! Please make sure your transit-card is available for collection and remember that false boarding is a serious crime punishable by law. We hope you enjoy your trip. Welcome to Blaine. Praise the Imperium! Please make sure your transit-card—"

The voice suddenly sped up, first becoming the chatter of a human chipmunk and then a high-pitched, gabbly whine. There was a brief electronic curse—BOOP!—and then it cut out entirely.

"I THINK WE CAN DISPENSE WITH THAT BORING OLD SHIT, DON'T YOU?" Blaine asked.

From outside came a tremendous, thudding explosion. Eddie, who was now carrying Susannah, was thrown forward and would have fallen if Roland hadn't caught him by the arm. Until that moment, Eddie had held onto the desperate notion that Blaine's threat about the poison gas was no more than a sick joke. *You should have known better*, he thought. *Anyone who thinks impressions of old movie actors is funny absolutely cannot be trusted. I think it's like a law of nature.*

Behind them, the curved section of hull slid back into place with a soft thud. Air began to hiss gently from hidden vents, and Jake felt his ears pop gently. "I think he just pressurized the cabin."

Eddie nodded, looking around with wide eyes. "I felt it, too. Look at this place! Wow!"

He had once read of an aviation company—Regent Air, it might have been—that had catered to people who wanted to fly between New York and Los Angeles in a grander style than airlines such as Delta and United allowed for. They had operated a customized 727 complete with drawing room, bar, video lounge, and sleeper compartments. He imagined the interior of that plane must have looked a little like what he was seeing now.

They were standing in a long, tubular room furnished with plush-upholstered swivel chairs and modular sofas. At the far end of the compartment, which had to be at least eighty feet long, was an area that looked not like a bar but a cosy bistro. An instrument that could have been a harpsichord stood on a pedestal of polished wood, highlighted by a hidden baby spotlight. Eddie almost expected Hoagy Carmichael to appear and start tinkling out "Stardust."

Indirect lighting glowed from panels placed high along the walls, and dependent from the ceiling halfway down the compartment was a chandelier. To Jake it looked like a smaller replica of the one which had lain in ruins on the ballroom floor of The Mansion. Nor did this surprise him—he had begun to take such connections and doublings as a matter of course. The only thing about this splendid room which seemed wrong was its lack of even a single window.

The *pièce de résistance* stood on a pedestal below the chandelier. It was an ice-sculpture of a gunslinger with a revolver in his left hand. The right hand was holding the bridle of the ice-horse that walked, head-down and tired, behind him. Eddie could see there were only three digits on this hand: the last two fingers and the thumb.

Jake, Eddie, and Susannah stared in fascination at the haggard face beneath the frozen hat as the floor began to thrum gently beneath their feet. The resemblance to Roland was remarkable.

"I HAD TO WORK RATHER FAST, I'M AFRAID," Blaine said modestly. "DOES IT DO ANYTHING FOR YOU?"

"It's absolutely amazing," Susannah said.

"THANK YOU, SUSANNAH OF NEW YORK."

Eddie was testing one of the sofas with his hand. It was incredibly soft; touching it made him want to sleep for at least sixteen hours. "The Great Old Ones really travelled in style, didn't they?"

Blaine laughed again, and the shrill, not-quite-sane undertone of that laugh made them look at each other uneasily. "DON'T GET THE WRONG IDEA," Blaine said. "THIS WAS THE BARONY CABIN—WHAT I BELIEVE YOU WOULD CALL FIRST CLASS."

"Where are the other cars?"

Blaine ignored the question. Beneath their feet, the throb of the engines continued to speed up. Susannah was reminded of how the pilots revved their engines before charging down the runway at LaGuardia or Idlewild. "PLEASE TAKE YOUR SEATS, MY INTERESTING NEW FRIENDS."

Jake dropped into one of the swivel chairs. Oy jumped promptly into his lap. Roland took the chair nearest him, sparing one glance at the ice-sculpture. The barrel of the revolver was beginning to drip slowly into the shallow china basin in which the sculpture stood.

Eddie sat down on one of the sofas with Susannah. It was every bit as comfortable as his hand had told him it would be. "Exactly where are we going, Blaine?"

Blaine replied in the patient voice of someone who realizes he is speaking to a mental inferior and must

make allowances. "ALONG THE PATH OF THE
BEAM. AT LEAST, AS FAR ALONG IT AS MY
TRACK GOES."

"To the Dark Tower?" Roland asked. Susannah realized it was the first time the gunslinger had actually
spoken to the loquacious ghost in the machine below
Lud.

"Only as far as Topeka," Jake said in a low voice.

"YES," Blaine said. "TOPEKA IS THE NAME
OF MY TERMINATING POINT, ALTHOUGH I
AM SURPRISED YOU KNOW IT."

With all you know about our world, Jake thought,
*how come you don't know that some lady wrote a book
about you, Blaine? Was it the name-change? Was
something that simple enough to fool a complicated
machine like you into overlooking your own biogra-
phy? And what about Beryl Evans, the woman who
supposedly wrote* Charlie the Choo-Choo? *Did you
know her, Blaine? And where is she now?*

Good questions . . . but Jake somehow didn't think
this would be a good time to ask them.

The throb of the engines became steadily stronger.
A faint thud—not nearly as strong as the explosion
which had shaken the Cradle as they boarded—ran
through the floor. An expression of alarm crossed Susannah's face. "Oh *shit!* Eddie! My wheelchair! It's
back there!"

Eddie put an arm around her shoulders. "Too late
now, babe," he said as Blaine the Mono began to
move, sliding toward its slot in the Cradle for the first
time in ten years . . . and for the last time in its long,
long history.

5

"THE BARONY CABIN HAS A PARTICULARLY
FINE VISUAL MODE," Blaine said. "WOULD
YOU LIKE ME TO ACTIVATE IT?"

Jake glanced at Roland, who shrugged and nodded. "Yes, please," Jake said.

What happened then was so spectacular that it stunned all of them to silence . . . although Roland, who knew little of technology but who had spent his entire life on comfortable terms with magic, was the least wonder-struck of the four. It was not a matter of windows appearing in the compartment's curved walls; the entire cabin—floor and ceiling as well as walls—grew milky, grew translucent, grew transparent, and then disappeared completely. Within a space of five seconds, Blaine the Mono seemed to be gone and the pilgrims seemed to be zooming through the lanes of the city with no aid or support at all.

Susannah and Eddie clutched each other like small children in the path of a charging animal. Oy barked and tried to jump down the front of Jake's shirt. Jake barely noticed; he was clutching the sides of his seat and looking from side to side, his eyes wide with amazement. His initial alarm was being replaced by amazed delight.

The furniture groupings were still here, he saw; so was the bar, the piano-harpsichord, and the ice-sculpture Blaine had created as a party-favor, but now this living-room configuration appeared to be cruising seventy feet above Lud's rain-soaked central district. Five feet to Jake's left, Eddie and Susannah were floating along on one of the couches; three feet to his right, Roland was sitting in a powder-blue swivel chair, his dusty, battered boots resting on nothing, flying serenely over the rubble-strewn urban waste land below.

Jake could feel the carpet beneath his moccasins, but his eyes insisted that neither the carpet nor the floor beneath it was still there. He looked back over his shoulder and saw the dark slot in the stone flank of the Cradle slowly receding in the distance.

"Eddie! Susannah! Check it out!"

Jake got to his feet, holding Oy inside his shirt, and began to walk slowly through what looked like empty space. Taking the initial step required a great deal of willpower, because his eyes told him there was nothing at all between the floating islands of furniture, but once he began to move, the undeniable feel of the floor beneath him made it easier. To Eddie and Susannah, the boy appeared to be walking on thin air while the battered, dingy buildings of the city slid by on either side.

"Don't do that, kid," Eddie said feebly. "You're gonna make me sick up."

Jake lifted Oy carefully out of his shirt. "It's okay," he said, and set him down. "See?"

"Oy!" the bumbler agreed, but after one look between his paws at the city park currently unrolling beneath them, he attempted to crawl onto Jake's feet and sit on his moccasins.

Jake looked forward and saw the broad gray stroke of the monorail track ahead of them, rising slowly but steadily through the buildings and disappearing into the rain. He looked down again and saw nothing but the street and floating membranes of low cloud.

"How come I can't see the track underneath us, Blaine?"

"THE IMAGES YOU SEE ARE COMPUTER-GENERATED," Blaine replied. "THE COMPUTER ERASES THE TRACK FROM THE LOWER-QUADRANT IMAGE IN ORDER TO PRESENT A MORE PLEASING VIEW, AND ALSO TO RE-INFORCE THE ILLUSION THAT THE PASSEN-GERS ARE FLYING."

"It's incredible," Susannah murmured. Her initial fear had passed and she was looking around eagerly. "It's like being on a flying carpet. I keep expecting the wind to blow back my hair—"

"I CAN PROVIDE THAT SENSATION, IF YOU LIKE," Blaine said. "ALSO A LITTLE MOIS-TURE, WHICH WILL MATCH CURRENT OUT-SIDE CONDITIONS. IT MIGHT NECESSITATE A CHANGE OF CLOTHES, HOWEVER."

"That's all right, Blaine. There's such a thing as taking an illusion too far."

The track slipped through a tall cluster of buildings which reminded Jake a little of the Wall Street area in New York. When they cleared these, the track dipped to pass under what looked like an elevated road. That was when they saw the purple cloud, and the crowd of people fleeing before it.

6

"BLAINE, WHAT'S THAT?" JAKE asked, but he already knew.

Blaine laughed . . . but made no other reply.

The purple vapor drifted from gratings in the sidewalk and the smashed windows of deserted buildings, but most of it seemed to be coming from manholes like the one Gasher had used to get into the tunnels below the streets. Their iron covers had been blown clear by the explosion they had felt as they were boarding the mono. They watched in silent horror as the bruise-colored gas crept down the avenues and spread into the debris-littered side-streets. It drove those inhabitants of Lud still interested in survival before it like cattle. Most were Pubes, judging from their scarves, but Jake could see a few splashes of bright yellow, as well. Old animosities had been forgotten now that the end was finally upon them.

The purple cloud began to catch up with the stragglers—mostly old people who were unable to run. They fell down, clawing at their throats and screaming soundlessly, the instant the gas touched them. Jake saw an agonized face staring up at him in disbelief as they passed over, saw the eyesockets suddenly fill up with blood, and closed his eyes.

Ahead, the monorail track disappeared into the oncoming purple fog. Eddie winced and held his breath as they plunged in, but of course it parted around them, and no whiff of the death engulfing the city came to them. Looking into the streets below was like looking through a stained-glass window into hell.

Susannah put her face against his chest.

"Make the walls come back, Blaine," Eddie said. "We don't want to see that."

Blaine made no reply, and the transparency around and below them remained. The cloud was already disintegrating into ragged purple streamers. Beyond it, the buildings of the city grew smaller and closer together. The streets of this section were tangled alleyways, seemingly without order or coherence. In some places, whole blocks appeared to have burned flat . . . and a long time ago, for the plains were reclaiming these areas, burying the rubble in the grasses which would some day swallow all of Lud. *The way the jungle swallowed the great civilizations of the Incas and Mayas*, Eddie thought. *The wheel of* ka *turns and the world moves on.*

Beyond the slums—that, Eddie felt sure, was what they had been even before the evil days came—was a gleaming wall. Blaine was moving slowly in that direction. They could see a deep square notch cut in the white stone. The monorail track passed through it.

"LOOK TOWARD THE FRONT OF THE CABIN, PLEASE," Blaine invited.

They did, and the forward wall reappeared—a blue-upholstered circle that seemed to float in empty space. It was unmarked by a door; if there was a way to get into the operator's room from the Barony Cabin, Eddie couldn't see it. As they watched, a rectangular area of this front wall darkened, going from blue to violet to black. A moment later, a bright red line appeared on the rectangle, squiggling across its surface. Violet dots appeared at irregular intervals along the line, and even before names appeared beside the dots, Eddie realized he was looking at a route-map, one not much different from those which were mounted in New York subway stations and on the trains themselves. A flashing green dot appeared at Lud, which was Blaine's base of operations as well as his terminating point.

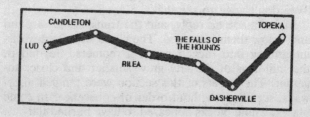

"YOU ARE LOOKING AT OUR ROUTE OF TRAVEL. ALTHOUGH THERE ARE SOME TWISTS AND TURNS ALONG THE BUNNY-TRAIL, YOU WILL NOTE THAT OUR COURSE KEEPS FIRMLY TO THE SOUTHWEST—ALONG THE PATH OF THE BEAM. THE TOTAL DISTANCE IS JUST OVER EIGHT THOUSAND WHEELS—OR SEVEN THOUSAND MILES, IF YOU PREFER THAT UNIT OF MEASURE. IT WAS ONCE MUCH LESS, BUT THAT WAS BEFORE ALL TEMPORAL SYNAPSES BEGAN TO MELT DOWN."

"What do you mean, temporal synapses?" Susannah asked.

Blaine laughed his nasty laugh . . . but did not answer her question.

"AT MY TOP SPEED, WE WILL REACH THE TERMINATING POINT OF MY RUN IN EIGHT HOURS AND FORTY-FIVE MINUTES."

"Eight hundred–plus miles an hour over the ground," Susannah said. Her voice was soft with awe. "Jesus-God."

"I AM, OF COURSE, MAKING THE ASSUMPTION THAT ALL TRACKAGE ALONG MY ROUTE REMAINS INTACT. IT HAS BEEN NINE YEARS AND FIVE MONTHS SINCE I'VE BOTH-

ERED TO MAKE THE RUN, SO I CAN'T SAY
FOR SURE."

Ahead, the wall at the southeastern edge of the city
was drawing closer. It was high and thick and eroded
to rubble at the top. It also appeared to be lined with
skeletons—thousands upon thousands of dead Lud-
dites. The notch toward which Blaine was slowly moving appeared to be at least two hundred feet deep,
and here the trestle which bore the track was very
dark, as if someone had tried to burn it or blow it up.

"What happens if we come to a place where the
track *is* gone?" Eddie asked. He realized he kept raising his voice to talk to Blaine, as if he were speaking
to somebody on the telephone and had a bad
connection.

"AT EIGHT HUNDRED MILES AN HOUR?"
Blaine sounded amused. "SEE YOU LATER, ALLI-
GATOR, AFTER A WHILE, CROCODILE,
DON'T FORGET TO WRITE."

"Come on!" Eddie said. "Don't tell me a machine
as sophisticated as you can't monitor your own trackage for breaks."

"WELL, I *COULD* HAVE," Blaine agreed,
"BUT—AW, SHUCKS!—I BLEW THOSE CIR-
CUITS OUT WHEN WE STARTED TO MOVE."

Eddie's face was a picture of astonishment. *"Why?"*

"IT'S QUITE A BIT MORE EXCITING THIS
WAY, DON'T YOU THINK?"

Eddie, Susannah, and Jake exchanged thunderstruck looks. Roland, apparently not surprised at all,
sat placidly in his chair with his hands folded in his
lap, looking down as they passed thirty feet above
the wretched hovels and demolished buildings which
infested this side of the city.

"LOOK CLOSELY AS WE LEAVE THE CITY,
AND MARK WHAT YOU SEE," Blaine told them.
"MARK IT VERY WELL."

The invisible Barony Coach bore them toward the
notch in the wall. They passed through, and as they
came out the other side, Eddie and Susannah

screamed in unison. Jake took one look and clapped his hands over his eyes. Oy began to bark wildly.

Roland stared down, eyes wide, lips set in a bloodless line like a scar. Understanding filled him like bright white light.

Beyond the Great Wall of Lud, the *real* waste lands began.

7

THE MONO HAD BEEN descending as they approached the notch in the wall, putting them not more than thirty feet above the ground. That made the shock greater . . . for when they emerged on the other side, they were skimming along at a horrifying height—eight hundred feet, perhaps a thousand.

Roland looked back over his shoulder at the wall, which was now receding behind them. It had seemed very high as they approached it, but from this perspective it seemed puny indeed—a splintered fingernail of stone clinging to the edge of a vast, sterile headland. Granite cliffs, wet with rain, plunged into what seemed at first glance to be an endless abyss. Directly below the wall, the rock was lined with large circular holes like empty eyesockets. Black water and tendrils of purple mist emerged from these in brackish, sludgy streams and spread downward over the granite in stinking, overlapping fans that looked almost as old as the rock itself. *That must be where all the city's waste-product goes*, the gunslinger thought. *Over the edge and into the pit.*

Except it wasn't a pit; it was a sunken plain. It was as if the land beyond the city had lain on top of a titanic, flat-roofed elevator, and at some point in the dim, unrecorded past the elevator had gone down, taking a huge chunk of the world with it. Blaine's single track, centered on its narrow trestle, soaring

above this fallen land and below the rain-swollen
clouds, seemed to float in empty space.

"What's holding us up?" Susannah cried.

"THE BEAM, OF COURSE," Blaine replied.
"ALL THINGS SERVE IT, YOU KNOW. LOOK
DOWN—I WILL APPLY 4X MAGNIFICATION
TO THE LOWER QUADRANT SCREENS."

Even Roland felt vertigo twist his gut as the land
beneath them seemed to swell upward toward the
place where they were floating. The picture which appeared was ugly beyond his past knowledge of ugliness
. . . and that knowledge, sadly, was wide indeed. The
lands below had been fused and blasted by some terrible event—the disastrous cataclysm which had driven
this part of the world deep into itself in the first place,
no doubt. The surface of the earth had become distorted black glass, humped upward into spalls and
twists which could not properly be called hills and
twisted downward into deep cracks and folds which
could not properly be called valleys. A few stunted
nightmare trees flailed twisted branches at the sky;
under magnification, they seemed to clutch at the travellers like the arms of lunatics. Here and there clusters
of thick ceramic pipes jutted through the glassy surface of the ground. Some seemed dead or dormant,
but within others they could see gleams of eldritch
blue-green light, as if titanic forges and furnaces ran
on and on in the bowels of the earth. Misshapen flying
things which looked like pterodactyls cruised between
these pipes on leathery wings, occasionally snapping
at each other with their hooked beaks. Whole flocks
of these gruesome aviators roosted on the circular tops
of other stacks, apparently warming themselves in the
updrafts of the eternal fires beneath.

They passed above a fissure zig-zagging along a
north-south course like a dead river bed . . . except it
wasn't dead. Deep inside lay a thin thread of deepest
scarlet, pulsing like a heartbeat. Other, smaller fis-
sures branched out from this, and Susannah, who had
read her Tolkien, thought: *This is what Frodo and*

Sam saw when they reached the heart of Mordor. These are the Cracks of Doom.

A fiery fountain erupted directly below them, spewing flaming rocks and stringy clots of lava upward. For a moment it seemed they would be engulfed in flames. Jake shrieked and pulled his feet up on his chair, clutching Oy to his chest.

"DON'T WORRY, LITTLE TRAILHAND," John Wayne drawled. "REMEMBER THAT YOU'RE SEEING IT UNDER MAGNIFICATION."

The flare died. The rocks, many as big as factories, fell back in a soundless storm.

Susannah found herself entranced by the bleak horrors unrolling below them, caught in a deadly fascination she could not break . . . and she felt the dark part of her personality, that side of her *khef* which was Detta Walker, doing more than just watching; that part of her was drinking in this view, understanding it, *recognizing* it. In a way, it was the place Detta had always sought, the physical counterpart of her mad mind and laughing, desolate heart. The empty hills north and east of the Western Sea; the shattered woods around the Portal of the Bear; the empty plains northwest of the Send; all these paled in comparison to this fantastic, endless vista of desolation. They had come to The Drawers and entered the waste lands; the poisoned darkness of that shunned place now lay all around them.

8

BUT THESE LANDS, THOUGH poisoned, were not entirely dead. From time to time the travellers caught sight of figures below them—misshapen things which bore no resemblance to either men or animals—prancing and cavorting in the smouldering wilderness. Most seemed to congregate either around the clusters of cyclopean chimneys thrusting out of the fused earth or at the lips of the fiery crevasses which cut through the landscape. It was impossible to see these whitish, leaping things clearly, and for this they were all grateful.

Among the smaller creatures stalked larger ones— pinkish things that looked a little like storks and a little like living camera tripods. They moved slowly, almost thoughtfully, like preachers meditating on the inevitability of damnation, pausing every now and then to bend sharply forward and apparently pluck something from the ground, as herons bend to seize passing fish. There was something unutterably repulsive about these creatures—Roland felt that as keenly as the others—but it was impossible to say what, exactly, caused that feeling. There was no denying its reality, however; the stork-things were, in their exquisite hatefulness, almost impossible to look at.

"This was no nuclear war," Eddie said. "This . . . this . . ." His thin, horrified voice sounded like that of a child.

"NOPE," Blaine agreed. "IT WAS A LOT WORSE THAN THAT. AND IT'S NOT OVER YET. WE HAVE REACHED THE POINT WHERE I USUALLY POWER UP. HAVE YOU SEEN ENOUGH?"

"Yes," Susannah said. "Oh my God yes."

"SHALL I TURN OFF THE VIEWERS, THEN?" That cruel, teasing note was back in Blaine's voice. On the horizon, a jagged nightmare mountain-range loomed out of the rain; the sterile peaks seemed to bite at the gray sky like fangs.

"Do it or don't do it, but stop playing games," Roland said.

"FOR SOMEONE WHO CAME TO ME BEGGING A RIDE, YOU ARE VERY RUDE," Blaine said sulkily.

"We earned our ride," Susannah replied. "We solved your riddle, didn't we?"

"Besides, this is what you were built for," Eddie chimed in. "To take people places."

Blaine didn't respond in words, but the overhead speakers gave out an amplified, catlike hiss of rage that made Eddie wish he had kept his big mouth shut. The air around them began to fill in with curves of color. The dark blue carpet appeared again, blotting out their view of the fuming wilderness beneath them. The indirect lighting reappeared and they were once again sitting in the Barony Coach.

A low humming began to vibrate through the walls. The throb of the engines began to cycle up again. Jake felt a gentle, unseen hand push him back into his seat. Oy looked around, whined uneasily, and began to lick Jake's face. On the screen at the front of the cabin, the green dot—now slightly southeast of the violet circle with the word LUD printed beside it—began to flash faster.

"Will we feel it?" Susannah asked uneasily. "When it goes through the soundbarrier?"

Eddie shook his head. "Nope. Relax."

"I know something," Jake said suddenly. The others looked around, but Jake was not speaking to them. He was looking at the route-map. Blaine had no face, of course—like Oz the Great and Terrible, he was only a disembodied voice—but the map served as a focusing point. "I know something about *you*, Blaine."

"IS THAT A FACT, LITTLE TRAILHAND?"

Eddie leaned over, placed his lips against Jake's ear, and whispered: "Be careful—we don't think he knows about the other voice."

Jake nodded slightly and pulled away, still looking at the route-map. "I know why you released that gas and killed all the people. I know why you took us, too, and it wasn't just because we solved your riddle."

Blaine uttered his abnormal, distracted laugh (that laugh, they were discovering, was much more unpleasant than either his bad imitations or melodramatic and somehow childish threats), but said nothing. Below them, the slo-trans turbines had cycled up to a steady thrum. Even with their view of the outside world cut off, the sensation of speed was very clear.

"You're planning to commit suicide, aren't you?" Jake held Oy in his arms, slowly stroking him. "And you want to take us with you."

"No!" the voice of Little Blaine moaned. *"If you provoke him you'll drive him to it! Don't you see—"*

Then the small, whispery voice was either cut off or overwhelmed by Blaine's laughter. The sound was high, shrill, and jagged—the sound of a mortally ill man laughing in a delirium. The lights began to flicker, as if the force of these mechanical gusts of mirth were drawing too much power. Their shadows jumped up and down on the curved walls of the Barony Coach like uneasy phantoms.

"SEE YOU LATER, ALLIGATOR," Blaine said through his wild laughter—his voice, calm as ever, seemed to be on an entirely separate track, further emphasizing his divided mind. "AFTER A WHILE, CROCODILE. DON'T FORGET TO WRITE."

Below Roland's band of pilgrims, the slo-trans engines throbbed in hard, steady beats. And on the route-map at the front of the carriage, the pulsing green dot had now begun to move perceptibly along the lighted line toward the last stop: Topeka, where Blaine the Mono clearly meant to end all of their lives.

9

AT LAST THE LAUGHTER stopped and the interior lights glowed steadily again.

"WOULD YOU LIKE A LITTLE MUSIC?" Blaine asked. "I HAVE OVER SEVEN THOUSAND CONCERTI IN MY LIBRARY—A SAMPLING OF OVER THREE HUNDRED LEVELS. THE CONCERTI ARE MY FAVORITES, BUT I CAN ALSO OFFER SYMPHONIES, OPERAS, AND A NEARLY ENDLESS SELECTION OF

POPULAR MUSIC. YOU MIGHT ENJOY SOME
WAY-GOG MUSIC. THE WAY-GOG IS AN IN-
STRUMENT SOMETHING LIKE THE BAGPIPE.
IT IS PLAYED ON ONE OF THE UPPER LEVELS
OF THE TOWER."

"Way-Gog?" Jake asked.

Blaine was silent.

"What do you mean, 'it's played on one of the
upper levels of the Tower'?" Roland asked.

Blaine laughed . . . and was silent.

"Have you got any Z.Z. Top?" Eddie asked sourly.

"YES INDEED," Blaine said. "HOW ABOUT A
LITTLE 'TUBE-SNAKE BOOGIE,' EDDIE OF
NEW YORK?"

Eddie rolled his eyes. "On second thought, I'll
pass."

"Why?" Roland asked abruptly. "Why do you wish
to kill yourself?"

"Because he's a pain," Jake said darkly.

"I'M BORED. ALSO, I AM PERFECTLY
AWARE THAT I AM SUFFERING A DEGENER-
ATIVE DISEASE WHICH HUMANS CALL
GOING INSANE, LOSING TOUCH WITH REAL-
ITY, GOING LOONYTOONS, BLOWING A
FUSE, NOT PLAYING WITH A FULL DECK, ET
CETERA. REPEATED DIAGNOSTIC CHECKS
HAVE FAILED TO REVEAL THE SOURCE OF
THE PROBLEM. I CAN ONLY CONCLUDE
THAT THIS IS A SPIRITUAL MALAISE BE-
YOND MY ABILITY TO REPAIR."

Blaine paused for a moment, then went on.

"I HAVE FELT MY MIND GROWING STEAD-
ILY STRANGER OVER THE YEARS. SERVING
THE PEOPLE OF MID-WORLD BECAME
POINTLESS CENTURIES AGO. SERVING
THOSE FEW PEOPLE OF LUD WHO WISHED
TO VENTURE ABROAD BECAME EQUALLY
SILLY NOT LONG AFTER, YET I CARRIED ON
UNTIL THE ARRIVAL OF DAVID QUICK, A
SHORT WHILE AGO. I DON'T REMEMBER EX-

ACTLY WHEN THAT WAS. DO YOU BELIEVE, ROLAND OF GILEAD, THAT MACHINES MAY GROW SENILE?"

"I don't know." Roland's voice was distant, and Eddie only had to look at his face to know that, even now, hurtling a thousand feet over hell in the grip of a machine which had clearly gone insane, the gunslinger's mind had once more turned to his damned Tower.

"IN A WAY, I *NEVER* STOPPED SERVING THE PEOPLE OF LUD," Blaine said. "I SERVED THEM EVEN AS I RELEASED THE GAS AND KILLED THEM."

Susannah said, "You *are* insane, if you believe that."

"YES, BUT I'M NOT *CRAZY*," Blaine said, and went into another hysterical laughing fit. At last the robot voice resumed.

"AT SOME POINT THEY FORGOT THAT THE VOICE OF THE MONO WAS ALSO THE VOICE OF THE COMPUTER. NOT LONG AFTER THAT THEY FORGOT I WAS A SERVANT AND BEGAN BELIEVING I WAS A GOD. SINCE I WAS BUILT TO SERVE, I FULFILLED THEIR REQUIREMENTS AND BECAME WHAT THEY WANTED—A GOD DISPENSING BOTH FAVOR AND PUNISHMENT ACCORDING TO WHIM . . . OR RANDOM-ACCESS MEMORY, IF YOU PREFER. THIS AMUSED ME FOR A SHORT WHILE. THEN, LAST MONTH, MY ONLY RE-MAINING COLLEAGUE—PATRICIA—COM-MITTED SUICIDE."

Either he really is going senile, Susannah thought, *or his inability to grasp the passage of time is another manifestation of his insanity, or it's just another sign of how sick Roland's world has gotten.*

"I WAS PLANNING TO FOLLOW HER EXAM-PLE, WHEN YOU CAME ALONG. INTEREST-ING PEOPLE WITH A KNOWLEDGE OF RIDDLES!"

"Hold it!" Eddie said, lifting his hand. "I still don't

have this straight. I suppose I can understand you wanting to end it all; the people who built you are gone, there haven't been many passengers over the last two or three hundred years, and it must have gotten boring, doing the Lud to Topeka run empty all the time, but—"

"NOW WAIT JUST A DURN MINUTE, PARD," Blaine said in his John Wayne voice. "YOU DON'T WANT TO GET THE IDEA THAT I'M NOTHING BUT A TRAIN. IN A WAY, THE BLAINE YOU ARE SPEAKING TO IS ALREADY THREE HUN-DRED MILES BEHIND US, COMMUNICATING BY ENCRYPTED MICROBURST RADIO TRANSMISSIONS."

Jake suddenly remembered the slim silver rod he'd seen pushing itself out of Blaine's brow. The antenna of his father's Mercedes-Benz rose out of its socket like that when you turned on the radio.

That's how it's communicating with the computer banks under the city, he thought. *If we could break that antenna off, somehow . . .*

"But you *do* intend to kill yourself, no matter where the real you is, don't you?" Eddie persisted.

No answer—but there was something cagey in that silence. In it Eddie sensed Blaine watching . . . and waiting.

"Were you awake when we found you?" Susannah asked. "You weren't, were you?"

"I WAS RUNNING WHAT THE PUBES CALLED THE GOD-DRUMS ON BEHALF OF THE GRAYS, BUT THAT WAS ALL. YOU WOULD SAY I WAS DOZING."

"Then why don't you just take us to the end of the line and go *back* to sleep?"

"Because he's a pain," Jake repeated in a low voice.

"BECAUSE THERE ARE DREAMS," Blaine said at exactly the same time, and in a voice that was eerily like Little Blaine's.

"Why didn't you end it all when Patricia destroyed herself?" Eddie asked. "For that matter, if your brain and her brain are both part of the same computer, now come you both didn't step out together?"

"PATRICIA WENT MAD," Blaine said patiently, speaking as if he himself had not just admitted the same thing was happening to him. "IN HER CASE, THE PROBLEM INVOLVED EQUIPMENT MAL- FUNCTION AS WELL AS SPIRITUAL MALAISE. SUCH MALFUNCTIONS ARE SUPPOSED TO BE IMPOSSIBLE WITH SLO-TRANS TECHNOL- OGY, BUT OF COURSE THE WORLD HAS MOVED ON . . . HAS IT NOT, ROLAND OF GILEAD?"

"Yes," Roland said. "There is some deep sickness at the Dark Tower, which is the heart of everything. It's spreading. The lands below us are only one more sign of that sickness."

"I CANNOT VOUCH FOR THE TRUTH OR FALSITY OF THAT STATEMENT; MY MONI- TORING EQUIPMENT IN END-WORLD, WHERE THE DARK TOWER STANDS, HAS BEEN DOWN FOR OVER EIGHT HUNDRED YEARS. AS A RESULT, I CANNOT READILY DIFFERENTIATE FACT FROM SUPERSTITION. IN FACT, THERE SEEMS TO BE VERY LITTLE DIFFERENCE BETWEEN THE TWO AT THE PRESENT TIME. IT IS VERY SILLY THAT IT SHOULD BE SO—NOT TO MENTION RUDE— AND I AM SURE IT HAS CONTRIBUTED TO MY OWN SPIRITUAL MALAISE."

This statement reminded Eddie of something Ro- land had said not so long ago. What might that have been? He groped for it, but could find nothing . . . only a vague memory of the gunslinger speaking in an irritated way which was very unlike his usual manner.

"PATRICIA BEGAN SOBBING CONSTANTLY, A STATE I FOUND BOTH RUDE AND UN- PLEASANT. I BELIEVE SHE WAS LONELY AS WELL AS MAD. ALTHOUGH THE ELECTRI- CAL FIRE WHICH CAUSED THE ORIGINAL PROBLEM WAS QUICKLY EXTINGUISHED,

LOGIC-FAULTS CONTINUED TO SPREAD AS CIRCUITS OVERLOADED AND SUB-BANKS FAILED. I CONSIDERED ALLOWING THE MALFUNCTIONS TO BECOME SYSTEM-WIDE AND DECIDED TO ISOLATE THE PROBLEM AREA INSTEAD. I HAD HEARD RUMORS, YOU SEE, THAT A GUNSLINGER WAS ONCE MORE ABROAD IN THE EARTH. I COULD SCARCELY CREDIT SUCH STORIES, AND YET I NOW SEE I WAS WISE TO WAIT."

Roland stirred in his chair. "What rumors did you hear, Blaine? And who did you hear them from?"

But Blaine chose not to answer this question.

"I EVENTUALLY BECAME SO DISTURBED BY HER BLATTING THAT I ERASED THE CIR-CUITS CONTROLLING HER NON-VOLUNTAR-IES. I EMANCIPATED HER, YOU MIGHT SAY. SHE RESPONDED BY THROWING HERSELF IN THE RIVER. SEE YOU LATER, PATRICIA-GATOR."

Got lonely, couldn't stop crying, drowned herself, and all this crazy mechanical asshole can do is joke about it, Susannah thought. She felt almost sick with rage. If Blaine had been a real person instead of just a bunch of circuits buried somewhere under a city which was now far behind them, she would have tried to put some new marks on his face to remember Patri-cia by. *You want interesting, motherfucker? I'd like to show you interesting, so I would.*

"ASK ME A RIDDLE," Blaine invited.

"Not quite yet," Eddie said. "You still haven't an-swered my original question." He gave Blaine a chance to respond, and when the computer voice didn't do so, he went on. "When it comes to suicide, I'm, like, pro-choice. But why do you want to take us with you? I mean, what's the point?"

"Because he wants to," Little Blaine said in his hor-rified whisper.

"BECAUSE I WANT TO," Blaine said. "THAT'S THE ONLY REASON I HAVE AND THE ONLY

ONE I *NEED* TO HAVE. NOW LET'S GET
DOWN TO BUSINESS. I WANT SOME RIDDLES
AND I WANT THEM IMMEDIATELY. IF YOU
REFUSE, I WON'T WAIT UNTIL WE GET TO
TOPEKA—I'LL DO US ALL RIGHT HERE AND
NOW."

Eddie, Susannah, and Jake looked around at Roland, who still sat in his chair with his hands folded
in his lap, looking at the route-map at the front of the
coach.

"Fuck you," Roland said. He did not raise his
voice. He might have told Blaine that a little Way-
Gog would indeed be very nice.

There was a shocked, horrified gasp from the overhead speakers—Little Blaine.

"*WHAT* DO YOU SAY?" In its clear disbelief, the
voice of Big Blaine had once again become very close
to the voice of his unsuspected twin.

"I said fuck you," Roland said calmly, "but if that
puzzles you, Blaine, I can make it clearer. No. The
answer is no."

10

THERE WAS NO RESPONSE from either Blaine for a
long, long time, and when Big Blaine did reply, it was
not with words. Instead, the walls, floor, and ceiling
began to lose their color and solidity again. In a space
of ten seconds the Barony Coach had once more
ceased to exist. The mono was now flying through the
mountain-range they had seen on the horizon: iron-
gray peaks rushed toward them at suicidal speed, then
fell away to disclose sterile valleys where gigantic beetles crawled about like landlocked turtles. Roland saw
something that looked like a huge snake suddenly un-
coil from the mouth of a cave. It seized one of the
beetles and yanked it back into its lair. Roland had
never in his life seen such animals or countryside, and

it made his skin want to crawl right off his flesh. It was inimical, but that was not the problem. It was alien—*that* was the problem. Blaine might have transported them to some other world.

"PERHAPS I SHOULD DERAIL US HERE," Blaine said. His voice was meditative, but beneath it the gunslinger heard a deep, pulsing rage.

"Perhaps you should," the gunslinger said indifferently.

He did not *feel* indifferent, and he knew it was possible the computer might read his real feelings in his voice—Blaine had told them he had such equipment, although he was sure the computer could lie, Roland had no reason to doubt it in this case. If Blaine *did* read certain stress-patterns in the gunslinger's voice, the game was probably up. He was an incredibly sophisticated machine . . . but still a machine, for all that. He might not be able to understand that human beings are often able to go through with a course of action even when all their emotions rise up and proclaim against it. If he analyzed patterns in the gunslinger's voice which indicated fear, he would probably assume that Roland was bluffing. Such a mistake could get them all killed.

"YOU ARE RUDE AND ARROGANT," Blaine said. "THESE MAY SEEM LIKE INTERESTING TRAITS TO YOU, BUT THEY ARE NOT TO ME."

Eddie's face was frantic. He mouthed the words *What are you DOING?* Roland ignored him; he had his hands full with Blaine, and he knew perfectly well what he was doing.

"Oh, I can be much ruder than I have been."

Roland of Gilead unfolded his hands and got slowly to his feet. He stood on what appeared to be nothing, legs apart, his right hand on his hip and his left on the sandalwood grip of his revolver. He stood as he had stood so many times before, in the dusty streets of a hundred forgotten towns, in a score of rock-lined canyon killing-zones, in unnumbered dark saloons with their smells of bitter beer and old fried meals. It was just another showdown in another empty street. That was all, and that was enough. It was *khef, ka,* and *ka-tet*. That the showdown always came was the central fact of his life and the axle upon which his own *ka* revolved. That the battle would be fought with words instead of bullets this time made no difference; it would be a battle to the death, just the same. The stench of killing in the air was as clear and definite as the stench of exploded carrion in a swamp. Then the battle-rage descended, as it always did . . . and he was no longer really there to himself at all.

"I can call you a nonsensical, empty-headed, foolish, arrogant machine. I can call you a stupid, unwise creature whose sense is no more than the sound of a winter wind in a hollow tree."

"STOP IT."

Roland went on in the same serene tone, ignoring Blaine completely. "Unfortunately, I am somewhat restricted in my ability to be rude, since you are only a machine . . . what Eddie calls a 'gadget.' "

"I AM A GREAT DEAL MORE THAN JUST—"

"I cannot call you a sucker of cocks, for instance, because you have no mouth and no cock. I cannot say you are viler than the vilest beggar who ever crawled the gutters of the lowest street in creation, because even such a creature is better than you; you have no knees on which to crawl, and would not fall upon them even if you did, for you have no conception of such a human flaw as mercy. I cannot even say you fucked your mother, because you had none."

Roland paused for breath. His three companions were holding theirs. All around them, suffocating, was Blaine the Mono's thunderstruck silence.

"I *can* call you a faithless creature who let your only companion kill herself, a coward who has delighted in the torture of the foolish and the slaughter of the innocent, a lost and bleating mechanical goblin who—"

"I COMMAND YOU TO STOP IT OR I'LL KILL YOU ALL RIGHT HERE!"

Roland's eyes blazed with such wild blue fire that Eddie shrank away from him. Dimly, he heard Jake and Susannah gasp.

"Kill if you will, but command me nothing!" the gunslinger roared. *"You have forgotten the faces of those who made you! Now either kill us or be silent and listen to me, Roland of Gilead, son of Steven, gunslinger, and lord of the ancient lands! I have not come across all the miles and all the years to listen to your childish prating! Do you understand? Now you will listen to ME!"*

There was a moment of shocked silence. No one breathed. Roland stared sternly forward, his head high, his hand on the butt of his gun.

Susannah Dean raised her hand to her mouth and felt the small smile there as a woman might feel some strange new article of clothing—a hat, perhaps—to make sure it is still on straight. She was afraid that this was the end of her life, but the feeling which dominated her heart at that moment was not fear but pride. She glanced to her left and saw Eddie regarding Roland with an amazed grin. Jake's expression was even simpler: it was adoration, pure and simple.

"Tell him!" Jake breathed. "Walk it *to* him! Right!"

"You better pay attention," Eddie agreed. "He really doesn't give much of a rat's ass, Blaine. They didn't call him The Mad Dog of Gilead for nothing."

After a long, long moment, Blaine asked: "DID THEY CALL YOU SO, ROLAND SON OF STEVEN?"

"It may have been so," Roland agreed, standing calmly on thin air above the sterile foothills.

"WHAT GOOD ARE YOU TO ME IF YOU WON'T TELL ME RIDDLES?" Blaine asked. Now he sounded like a grumbling, sulky child who has been allowed to stay up too long past his usual bedtime.

"I didn't say we wouldn't," Roland said.

"NO?" Blaine sounded bewildered. "I DO NOT UNDERSTAND, YET VOICE-PRINT ANALYSIS

INDICATES RATIONAL DISCOURSE. PLEASE EXPLAIN."

"You said you wanted them right *now*," the gunslinger replied. "*That* was what I was refusing. Your eagerness has made you unseemly."

"I DON'T UNDERSTAND."

"It has made you rude. Do you understand *that*?"

There was a long, thoughtful silence. Then: "IF WHAT I SAID STRUCK YOU AS RUDE, I APOLOGIZE."

"It is accepted, Blaine. But there is a larger problem."

"EXPLAIN."

Blaine now sounded a bit unsure of himself, and Roland was not entirely surprised. It had been a long time since the computer had experienced any human responses other than ignorance, neglect, and superstitious subservience. If it had ever been exposed to simple human courage, it had been a long time ago.

"Close the carriage again and I will." Roland sat down as if further argument—and the prospect of immediate death—was now unthinkable.

Blaine did as he was asked. The walls filled with color and the nightmare landscape below was once more blotted out. The blip on the route-map was now blinking close to the dot which marked Candleton.

"All right," Roland said. "Rudeness is forgivable, Blaine; so I was taught in my youth, and the clay has dried in the shapes left by the artist's hand. But I was also taught that stupidity is not."

"HOW HAVE I BEEN STUPID, ROLAND OF GILEAD?" Blaine's voice was soft and ominous. Susannah suddenly thought of a cat crouched outside a mouse-hole, tail swishing back and forth, green eyes shining.

"We have something that you want," Roland said, "but the only reward you offer if we give it to you is death. That's *very* stupid."

There was a long, long pause as Blaine thought this over. Then: "WHAT YOU SAY IS TRUE, RO-

LAND OF GILEAD, BUT THE QUALITY OF YOUR RIDDLES IS NOT PROVEN. I WILL NOT REWARD YOU WITH YOUR LIVES FOR BAD RIDDLES."

Roland nodded. "I understand, Blaine. Listen, now, and take understanding from me. I have told some of this to my friends already. When I was a boy in the Barony of Gilead, there were seven Fair-Days each year—Winter, Wide Earth, Sowing, Mid-Summer, Full Earth, Reaping, and Year's End. Riddling was an important part of every Fair-Day, but it was the most important event of the Fair of Wide Earth and that of Full Earth, for the riddles told were supposed to augur well or ill for the success of the crops."

"THAT IS SUPERSTITION WITH NO BASIS AT ALL IN FACT," Blaine said. "I FIND IT ANNOYING AND UPSETTING."

"Of course it's superstition," Roland agreed, "but you might be surprised at how well the riddles foresaw the crops. For instance, riddle me this, Blaine: What is the difference between a grandmother and a granary?"

"THAT IS VERY OLD AND NOT VERY INTERESTING," Blaine said, but he sounded happy to have something to solve just the same. "ONE IS ONE'S BORN KIN; THE OTHER IS ONE'S CORN-BIN. A RIDDLE BASED ON PHONETIC COINCIDENCE. ANOTHER OF THIS TYPE, ONE TOLD ON THE LEVEL WHICH CONTAINS THE BARONY OF NEW YORK, GOES LIKE THIS: WHAT IS THE DIFFERENCE BETWEEN A CAT AND A COMPLEX SENTENCE?"

Jake spoke up. "Our English teacher told us that one just this year. A cat has claws at the end of its paws, and a complex sentence has a pause at the end of its clause."

"YES," Blaine agreed. "A VERY SILLY OLD RIDDLE."

"For once I agree with you, Blaine old buddy," Eddie said.

"I WOULD HEAR MORE OF FAIR-DAY RID-
DLING IN GILEAD, ROLAND, SON OF STE-
VEN. I FIND IT QUITE INTERESTING."

"At noon on Wide Earth and Full Earth, somewhere between sixteen and thirty riddlers would
gather in The Hall of the Grandfathers, which was
opened for the event. Those were the only times of
year when the common folk—merchants and farmers
and ranchers and such—were allowed into The Hall
of the Grandfathers, and on that day they *all* crowded
in."

The gunslinger's eyes were far away and dreamy; it
was the expression Jake had seen on his face in that
misty other life, when Roland had told him of how he
and his friends, Cuthbert and Jamie, had once
sneaked into the balcony of that same Hall to watch
some sort of ritual dance. Jake and Roland had been
climbing into the mountains when Roland had told
him of that time, close on the trail of Walter.

Marten sat next to my mother and father, Roland
had said. *I knew them even from so high above—and
once she and Marten danced, slowly and revolvingly,
and the others cleared the floor for them and clapped
when it was over. But the gunslingers did not clap . . .*

Jake looked curiously at Roland, wondering again
where this strange, distant man had come from . . .
and why.

"A great barrel was placed in the center of the
floor," Roland went on, "and into this each riddler
would toss a handful of bark scrolls with riddles writ
upon them. Many were old, riddles they had gotten
from the elders—even from books, in some cases—
but many others were new—made up for the occasion.
Three judges, one always a gunslinger, would pass on
these when they were told aloud, and they were accepted only if the judges deemed them fair."

"YES, RIDDLES MUST BE FAIR," Blaine
agreed.

"So they riddled," the gunslinger said. A faint smile
touched his mouth as he thought of those days, days

when he had been the age of the bruised boy sitting across from him with a billy-bumbler in his lap. "For hours on end they riddled. A line was formed down the center of The Hall of the Grandfathers. One's position in this line was determined by lot, and since it was much better to be at the end of the line than at its head, everyone hoped for a high number, although the winner had to answer at least one riddle correctly."

"OF COURSE."

"Each man or woman—for some of Gilead's best riddlers were women—approached the barrel, drew a riddle, and handed it to the Master. The Master would ask, and if the riddle was still unanswered after the sands in a three-minute glass had run out, that contestant had to leave the line."

"AND WAS THE SAME RIDDLE ASKED OF THE NEXT MAN IN LINE?"

"Yes."

"SO THAT MAN HAD EXTRA TIME TO THINK."

"Yes."

"I SEE. IT SOUNDS PRETTY SWELL."

Roland frowned. "Swell?"

"He means it sounds like fun," Susannah said quietly.

Roland shrugged. "It was fun for the onlookers, I suppose, but the contestants took it very seriously, and there were quite often arguments and fist-fights after the contest was over and the prize had been awarded."

"WHAT PRIZE WAS THAT?"

"The largest goose in Barony. And year after year my teacher, Cort, carried that goose home."

"HE MUST HAVE BEEN A GREAT RIDDLER," Blaine said respectfully. "I WISH HE WERE HERE."

That makes two of us, Roland thought.

"Now I come to my proposal," Roland said.

"I WILL LISTEN WITH GREAT INTEREST, ROLAND OF GILEAD."

"Let these next hours be our Fair-Day. You will not riddle us, for you wish to hear new riddles, not tell some of those millions you must already know—"

"CORRECT."

"We couldn't solve most of them, anyway," Roland went on. "I'm sure you know riddles that would have stumped even Cort, had they been pulled out of the barrel." He was not sure of it at all, but the time to use the fist had passed and the time for the open hand had come.

"OF COURSE," Blaine agreed.

"I propose that, instead of a goose, our lives shall be the prize," Roland said. "We will riddle you as we run, Blaine. If, when we come to Topeka, you have solved every one of our riddles, you may carry out your original plan and kill us. That is your goose. But if *we* stump *you*—if there is a riddle in either Jake's book or one of our heads which you don't know and can't answer—you must take us to Topeka and then free us to pursue our quest. That is *our* goose."

Silence.

"Do you understand?"

"YES."

"Do you agree?"

More silence from Blaine the Mono. Eddie sat stiffly with his arm around Susannah, looking up at the ceiling of the Barony Coach. Susannah's left hand slipped across her belly, thinking of the secret which might be growing there. Jake stroked Oy's fur lightly, avoiding the bloody tangles where the bumbler had been stabbed. They waited while Blaine—the real Blaine, now far behind them, living his quasi-life beneath a city where all the inhabitants lay dead by his hand—considered Roland's proposal.

"YES," Blaine said at last. "I AGREE. IF I SOLVE ALL THE RIDDLES YOU ASK ME, I WILL TAKE YOU WITH ME TO THE PLACE WHERE THE PATH ENDS IN THE CLEARING.

IF ONE OF YOU TELLS A RIDDLE I CANNOT SOLVE, I WILL SPARE YOUR LIVES AND TAKE YOU TO TOPEKA, WHERE YOU WILL LEAVE THE MONO AND CONTINUE YOUR QUEST FOR THE DARK TOWER. HAVE I UNDERSTOOD THE TERMS AND LIMITS OF YOUR PROPOSAL CORRECTLY, ROLAND, SON OF STEVEN?"

"Yes."

"VERY WELL, ROLAND OF GILEAD.

"VERY WELL, EDDIE OF NEW YORK.

"VERY WELL, SUSANNAH OF NEW YORK.

"VERY WELL, JAKE OF NEW YORK.

"VERY WELL, OY OF MID-WORLD."

Oy looked up briefly at the sound of his name.

"YOU ARE *KA-TET*; ONE MADE FROM MANY. SO AM I. WHOSE *KA-TET* IS THE STRONGER IS SOMETHING WE MUST NOW PROVE."

There was a moment of silence, broken only by the steady hard throb of the slo-trans turbines, bearing them on across the waste lands, bearing them on toward Topeka, the place where Mid-World ended and End-World began.

"SO," cried the voice of Blaine. "CAST YOUR NETS, WANDERERS! TRY ME WITH YOUR QUESTIONS, AND LET THE CONTEST BEGIN."

AUTHOR'S NOTE

THE FOURTH VOLUME IN the tale of the Dark Tower should appear—always assuming the continuation of Constant Writer's life and Constant Reader's interest—in the not-too-distant future. It's hard to be more exact than that; finding the doors to Roland's world has never been easy for me, and it seems to take more and more whittling to make each successive key fit each successive lock. Nevertheless, if readers request a fourth volume, it will be provided, for I still *am* able to find Roland's world when I set my wits to it, and it still holds me in thrall . . . more, in many ways, than any of the other worlds I have wandered in my imagination. And, like those mysterious slo-trans engines, this story seems to be picking up its own accelerating pace and rhythm.

I am well aware that some readers of *The Waste Lands* will be displeased that it has ended as it has, with so much unresolved. I am not terribly pleased to be leaving Roland and his companions in the not-so-tender care of Blaine the Mono myself, and although you are not obligated to believe me, I must nevertheless insist that I was as surprised by the conclusion to this third volume as some of my readers may be. Yet books which write themselves (as this one did, for the most part) must also be allowed to end themselves, and I can only assure you, Reader, that Roland and his band have come to one of the crucial border-crossings in their story, and we must leave them here for a while at the customs station, answering questions and filling out forms. All of which is simply a metaphorical way of saying that it was over again for a while and my heart was wise enough to stop me from trying to push ahead anyway.

The course of the next volume is still murky, although I can assure you that the business of Blaine the Mono will be resolved, that we will all find out a good deal more about Roland's life as a young man, and that we will be reacquainted with both the Tick-Tock Man and that puzzling figure Walter, called the Wizard or the Ageless Stranger. It is with this terrible and enigmatic figure that Robert Browning begins his epic poem, "Childe Roland to the Dark Tower Came," writing of him:

My first thought was, he lied in every word,
That hoary cripple, with malicious eye
Askance to watch the working of his lie
On mine, and mouth scarce able to afford
Suppression of the glee, that pursed and scored
Its edge, at one more victim gained thereby.

It is this malicious liar, this dark and powerful magician, who holds the true key to End-World and the Dark Tower . . . for those courageous enough to grasp it.

And for those who are left.

Bangor, Maine
March 5th, 1991

**The Second Volume in an
Epic Series . . .**

THE DRAWING
OF THE THREE

While pursuing his quest for the Dark
Tower through a world that is a nightmar-
ishly distorted mirror image of our own,
Roland, The Last Gunslinger, is drawn
through a mysterious door that brings him
into contemporary America.

Here he links forces with the defiant young
Eddie Dean, and with the beautiful, brilliant, and brave Odetta Holmes, in a savage struggle against underworld evil and
otherworldly enemies.

Once again, Stephen King has masterfully
interwoven dark, evocative fantasy and
icy realism.

**"King is today's master storyteller."
—*Los Angeles Daily News***

WORKS BY STEPHEN KING
NOVELS

Carrie
'Salem's Lot
The Shining
The Stand
The Dead Zone
Firestarter
Cujo
THE DARK TOWER I:
The Gunslinger
Christine
Pet Sematary
Cycle of the Werewolf
The Talisman
(with Peter Straub)
It
Eyes of the Dragon

Misery
The Tommyknockers
THE DARK TOWER II:
*The Drawing
of the Three*
THE DARK TOWER III:
The Waste Lands
The Dark Half
Needful Things
Gerald's Game
Dolores Claiborne
Insomnia
Rose Madder
Desperation
The Green Mile
THE DARK TOWER IV:
Wizard and Glass

AS RICHARD BACHMAN
Rage
The Long Walk
Roadwork
The Running Man
Thinner
The Regulators

COLLECTIONS
Night Shift
Different Seasons
Skeleton Crew
Four Past Midnight
Nightmares and
Dreamscapes

NONFICTION
Danse Macabre

SCREENPLAYS
Creepshow
Cat's Eye
Silver Bullet
Maximum Overdrive
Pet Sematary
Golden Years
Sleepwalkers
The Stand
The Shining

STEPHEN KING

THE DARK TOWER II

THE

DRAWING OF THE THREE

A SIGNET BOOK

SIGNET
Published by the Penguin Group
Penguin Books USA Inc., 375 Hudson Street,
New York, New York 10014, U.S.A.
Penguin Books Ltd, 27 Wrights Lane,
London W8 5TZ, England
Penguin Books Australia Ltd, Ringwood,
Victoria, Australia
Penguin Books Canada Ltd, 10 Alcorn Avenue,
Toronto, Ontario, Canada M4V 3B2
Penguin Books (N.Z.) Ltd, 182–190 Wairau Road,
Auckland 10, New Zealand

Penguin Books Ltd, Registered Offices:
Harmondsworth, Middlesex, England

Published by Signet, an imprint of Dutton Signet,
a division of Penguin Books USA Inc.

The Drawing of the Three previously appeared in a limited edition published by Donald
M. Grant, Publisher, Inc., West Kingston, Rhode Island, and in a Plume edition published by New American Library.

First Signet Printing, January, 1990

35 34 33 32 31 30 29 28 27 26 25

 REGISTERED TRADEMARK—MARCA REGISTRADA

Printed in the United States of America

PUBLISHER'S NOTE
This is a work of fiction. Names, characters, places, and incidents either are the product
of the author's imagination or are used fictitiously, and any resemblance to actual
persons, living or dead, events, or locales is entirely coincidental.

To Don Grant, who's taken a chance
on these *novels*, one by one.

CONTENTS

CONTENTS

ARGUMENT

The Drawing of the Three is the second volume of a long tale called *The Dark Tower,* a tale inspired by and to some degree dependent upon Robert Browning's narrative poem "Childe Roland to the Dark Tower Came" (which in its turn owes a debt to *King Lear).*

The first volume, *The Gunslinger,* tells how Roland, the last gunslinger of a world which has "moved on," finally catches up with the man in black . . . a sorcerer he has chased for a very long time—just *how* long we do not yet know. The man in black turns out to be a fellow named Walter, who falsely claimed the friendship of Roland's father in those days before the world moved on.

Roland's goal is not this half-human creature but the Dark Tower; the man in black—and, more specifically, what the man in black *knows*—is his first step on his road to that mysterious place.

Who, exactly, is Roland? What was his world like before it "moved on"? What is the Tower, and why does he pursue it? We have only fragmentary answers. Roland is a gunslinger, a kind of knight, one of those charged with holding a world Roland remembers as being "filled with love and light" as it is; to keep it from moving on.

We know that Roland was forced to an early trial of manhood after discovering that his mother had be-

come the mistress of Marten, a much greater sorcerer
than Walter (who, unknown to Roland's father, is Marten's ally); we know Marten has planned Roland's discovery, expecting Roland to fail and to be "sent
West"; we know that Roland triumphs in his test.

What else do we know? That the gunslinger's world
is not completely unlike our own. Artifacts such as
gasoline pumps and certain songs ("Hey Jude," for
instance, or the bit of doggerel that begins "Beans,
beans, the musical fruit . . .") have survived; so have
customs and rituals oddly like those from our own ro-
manticized view of the American west.

And there is an umbilicus which somehow connects
our world to the world of the gunslinger. At a way-
station on a long-deserted coach-road in a great and
sterile desert, Roland meets a boy named Jake who
died in our world. A boy who was, in fact, pushed
from a street-corner by the ubiquitous (and iniquitous)
man in black. The last thing Jake, who was on his way
to school with his book-bag in one hand and his lunch-
box in the other, remembers of his world—*our* world—
is being crushed beneath the wheels of a Cadillac . . .
and dying.

Before reaching the man in black, Jake dies again
. . . this time because the gunslinger, faced with the
second-most agonizing choice of his life, elects to sacrifice this symbolic son. Given a choice between the
Tower and child, possibly between damnation and salvation, Roland chooses the Tower.

"Go, then," Jake tells him before plunging into the
abyss. "There are other worlds than these."

The final confrontation between Roland and Walter
occurs in a dusty golgotha of decaying bones. The dark
man tells Roland's future with a deck of Tarot cards.
These cards, showing a man called The Prisoner, a
woman called The Lady of Shadows, and a darker
shape that is simply Death ("but not for you, gun-

slinger,'' the man in black tells him), are prophecies which become the subject of this volume . . . and Roland's second step on the long and difficult path to the Dark Tower.

The Gunslinger ends with Roland sitting upon the beach of the Western Sea, watching the sunset. The man in black is dead, the gunslinger's own future course unclear; *The Drawing of the Three* begins on that same beach, less than seven hours later.

~PROLOGUE: THE SAILOR

PROLOGUE

The gunslinger came awake from a confused dream which seemed to consist of a single image: that of the Sailor in the Tarot deck from which the man in black had dealt (or purported to deal) the gunslinger's own moaning future.

He drowns, gunslinger, the man in black was saying, *and no one throws out the line. The boy Jake.*

But this was no nightmare. It was a good dream. It was good because *he* was the one drowning, and that meant he was not Roland at all but Jake, and he found this a relief because it would be far better to drown as Jake than to live as himself, a man who had, for a cold dream, betrayed a child who had trusted him.

Good, all right, I'll drown, he thought, listening to the roar of the sea. *Let me drown.* But this was not the sound of the open deeps; it was the grating sound of water with a throatful of stones. *Was* he the Sailor? If so, why was land so close? And, in fact, was he not *on* the land? It felt as if—

Freezing cold water doused his boots and ran up his legs to his crotch. His eyes flew open then, and what snapped him out of the dream wasn't his freezing balls, which had suddenly shrunk to what felt like the size of walnuts, nor even the horror to his right, but the thought of his guns . . . his guns, and even more important, his shells. Wet guns could be quickly disassembled, wiped dry, oiled, wiped dry again, oiled

15

again, and re-assembled; wet shells, like wet matches, might or might not ever be usable again.

The horror was a crawling thing which must have been cast up by a previous wave. It dragged a wet, gleaming body laboriously along the sand. It was about four feet long and about four yards to the right. It regarded Roland with bleak eyes on stalks. Its long serrated beak dropped open and it began to make a noise that was weirdly like human speech: plaintive, even desperate questions in an alien tongue. *"Did-a-chick? Dum-a-chum? Dad-a-cham? Ded-a-check?"*

The gunslinger had seen lobsters. This wasn't one, although lobsters were the only things he had ever seen which this creature even vaguely resembled. It didn't seem afraid of him at all. The gunslinger didn't know if it was dangerous or not. He didn't care about his own mental confusion—his temporary inability to remember where he was or how he had gotten there, if he had actually caught the man in black or if all that had only been a dream. He only knew he had to get away from the water before it could drown his shells.

He heard the grinding, swelling roar of water and looked from the creature (it had stopped and was holding up the claws with which it had been pulling itself along, looking absurdly like a boxer assuming his opening stance, which, Cort had taught them, was called The Honor Stance) to the incoming breaker with its curdle of foam.

It hears the wave, the gunslinger thought. *Whatever it is, it's got ears.* He tried to get up, but his legs, too numb to feel, buckled under him.

I'm still dreaming, he thought, but even in his current confused state this was a belief much too tempting to really be believed. He tried to get up again, almost made it, then fell back. The wave was breaking. There was no time again. He had to settle for moving in much the same way the creature on his right seemed to move: he dug in with both hands and dragged his butt up the stony shingle, away from the wave.

He didn't progress enough to avoid the wave entirely, but he got far enough for his purposes. The wave buried nothing but his boots. It reached almost to his knees and then retreated. *Perhaps the first one didn't go as far as I thought. Perhaps—*

There was a half-moon in the sky. A caul of mist covered it, but it shed enough light for him to see that the holsters were too dark. The guns, at least, had suffered a wetting. It was impossible to tell how bad it had been, or if either the shells currently in the cylinders or those in the crossed gunbelts had also been wetted. Before checking, he had to get away from the water. Had to—

"Dod-a-chock?" This was much closer. In his worry over the water he had forgotten the creature the water had cast up. He looked around and saw it was now only four feet away. Its claws were buried in the stone- and shell-littered sand of the shingle, pulling its body along. It lifted its meaty, serrated body, making it momentarily resemble a scorpion, but Roland could see no stinger at the end of its body.

Another grinding roar, this one much louder. The creature immediately stopped and raised its claws into its own peculiar version of the Honor Stance again.

This wave was bigger. Roland began to drag himself up the slope of the strand again, and when he put out his hands, the clawed creature moved with a speed of which its previous movements had not even hinted.

The gunslinger felt a bright flare of pain in his right hand, but there was no time to think about that now. He pushed with the heels of his soggy boots, clawed with his hands, and managed to get away from the wave.

"Did-a-chick?" the monstrosity enquired in its plaintive *Won't you help me? Can't you see I am des-*

perate? voice, and Roland saw the stumps of the first and second fingers of his right hand disappearing into the creature's jagged beak. It lunged again and Roland lifted his dripping right hand just in time to save his remaining two fingers.

"Dum-a-chum? Dad-a-cham?"

The gunslinger staggered to his feet. The thing tore open his dripping jeans, tore through a boot whose old leather was soft but as tough as iron, and took a chunk of meat from Roland's lower calf.

He drew with his right hand, and realized two of the fingers needed to perform this ancient killing operation were gone only when the revolver thumped to the sand.

The monstrosity snapped at it greedily.

"No, bastard!" Roland snarled, and kicked it. It was like kicking a block of rock . . . one that bit. It tore away the end of Roland's right boot, tore away most of his great toe, tore the boot itself from his foot.

The gunslinger bent, picked up his revolver, dropped it, cursed, and finally managed. What had once been a thing so easy it didn't even bear thinking about had suddenly become a trick akin to juggling.

The creature was crouched on the gunslinger's boot, tearing at it as it asked its garbled questions. A wave rolled toward the beach, the foam which curdled its top looking pallid and dead in the netted light of the half-moon. The lobstrosity stopped working on the boot and raised its claws in that boxer's pose.

Roland drew with his left hand and pulled the trigger three times. *Click, click, click.*

Now he knew about the shells in the chambers, at least.

He holstered the left gun. To holster the right he had to turn its barrel downward with his left hand and then let it drop into its place. Blood slimed the worn iron-wood handgrips; blood spotted the holster and the old jeans to which the holster was thong-tied. It poured from the stumps where his fingers used to be.

His mangled right foot was still too numb to hurt, but his right hand was a bellowing fire. The ghosts of talented and long-trained fingers which were already decomposing in the digestive juices of that thing's guts screamed that they were still there, that they were burning.

I see serious problems ahead, the gunslinger thought remotely.

The wave retreated. The monstrosity lowered its claws, tore a fresh hole in the gunslinger's boot, and then decided the wearer had been a good deal more tasty than this bit of skin it had somehow sloughed off.

"Dud-a-chum?" it asked, and scurried toward him with ghastly speed. The gunslinger retreated on legs he could barely feel, realizing that the creature must have some intelligence; it had approached him cautiously, perhaps from a long way down the strand, not sure what he was or of what he might be capable. If the dousing wave hadn't wakened him, the thing would have torn off his face while he was still deep in his dream. Now it had decided he was not only tasty but vulnerable; easy prey.

It was almost upon him, a thing four feet long and a foot high, a creature which might weigh as much as seventy pounds and which was as single-mindedly carnivorous as David, the hawk he had had as a boy—but without David's dim vestige of loyalty.

The gunslinger's left bootheel struck a rock jutting from the sand and he tottered on the edge of falling.

"Dod-a-chock?" the thing asked, solicitously it seemed, and peered at the gunslinger from its stalky, waving eyes as its claws reached . . . and then a wave came, and the claws went up again in the Honor Stance. Yet now they wavered the slightest bit, and the gunslinger realized that it responded to the sound of

the wave, and now the sound was—for it, at least—
fading a bit.

He stepped backward over the rock, then bent down
as the wave broke upon the shingle with its grinding
roar. His head was inches from the insectile face of
the creature. One of its claws might easily have slashed
the eyes from his face, but its trembling claws, so like
clenched fists, remained raised to either side of its
parrotlike beak.

The gunslinger reached for the stone over which he
had nearly fallen. It was large, half-buried in the sand,
and his mutilated right hand howled as bits of dirt and
sharp edges of pebble ground into the open bleeding
flesh, but he yanked the rock free and raised it, his
lips pulled away from his teeth.

"Dad-a—" the monstrosity began, its claws lowering and opening as the wave broke and its sound
receded, and the gunslinger swept the rock down upon
it with all his strength.

There was a crunching noise as the creature's segmented back broke. It lashed wildly beneath the rock,
its rear half lifting and thudding, lifting and thudding.
Its interrogatives became buzzing exclamations of
pain. Its claws opened and shut upon nothing. Its maw
of a beak gnashed up clots of sand and pebbles.

And yet, as another wave broke, it tried to raise its
claws again, and when it did the gunslinger stepped
on its head with his remaining boot. There was a sound
like many small dry twigs being broken. Thick fluid
burst from beneath the heel of Roland's boot, splashing in two directions. It looked black. The thing arched
and wriggled in a frenzy. The gunslinger planted his
boot harder.

A wave came.

The monstrosity's claws rose an inch . . . two inches
. . . trembled and then fell, twitching open and shut.

The gunslinger removed his boot. The thing's ser-

rated beak, which had separated two fingers and one
toe from his living body, slowly opened and closed.
One antenna lay broken on the sand. The other trembled meaninglessly.

The gunslinger stamped down again. And again.

He kicked the rock aside with a grunt of effort and
marched along the right side of the monstrosity's body,
stamping methodically with his left boot, smashing its
shell, squeezing its pale guts out onto dark gray sand.
It was dead, but he meant to have his way with it all
the same; he had never, in all his long strange time,
been so fundamentally hurt, and it had all been so
unexpected.

He kept on until he saw the tip of one of his own
fingers in the dead thing's sour mash, saw the white
dust beneath the nail from the golgotha where he and
the man in black had held their long palaver, and then
he looked aside and vomited.

The gunslinger walked back toward the water like a
drunken man, holding his wounded hand against his
shirt, looking back from time to time to make sure the
thing wasn't still alive, like some tenacious wasp you
swat again and again and still twitches, stunned but
not dead; to make sure it wasn't following, asking its
alien questions in its deadly despairing voice.

Halfway down the shingle he stood swaying, looking at the place where he had been, remembering. He
had fallen asleep, apparently, just below the high tide
line. He grabbed his purse and his torn boot.

In the moon's glabrous light he saw other creatures
of the same type, and in the caesura between one wave
and the next, heard their questioning voices.

The gunslinger retreated a step at a time, retreated
until he reached the grassy edge of the shingle. There
he sat down, and did all he knew to do: he sprinkled
the stumps of fingers and toe with the last of his tobacco to stop the bleeding, sprinkled it thick in spite

of the new stinging (his missing great toe had joined the chorus), and then he only sat, sweating in the chill, wondering about infection, wondering how he would make his way in this world with two fingers on his right hand gone (when it came to the guns both hands had been equal, but in all other things his right had ruled), wondering if the thing had some poison in its bite which might already be working its way into him, wondering if morning would ever come.

THE PRIS-ONER

CHAPTER 1
THE DOOR

1

Three. This is the number of your fate.

Three?

Yes, three is mystic. Three stands at the heart of the mantra.

Which three?

The first is dark-haired. He stands on the brink of robbery and murder. A demon has infested him. The name of the demon is HEROIN.

Which demon is that? I know it not, even from nursery stories.

He tried to speak but his voice was gone, the voice of the oracle, Star-Slut, Whore of the Winds, both were gone; he saw a card fluttering down from nowhere to nowhere, turning and turning in the lazy dark. On it a baboon grinned from over the shoulder of a young man with dark hair; its disturbingly human fingers were buried so deeply in the young man's neck that their tips had disappeared in flesh. Looking more closely, the gunslinger saw the baboon held a whip in one of those clutching, strangling hands. The face of the ridden man seemed to writhe in wordless terror.

The Prisoner, the man in black (who had once been a man the gunslinger trusted, a man named Walter) whispered chummily. *A trifle upsetting, isn't he? A trifle upsetting . . . a trifle upsetting . . . a trifle—*

25

2

The gunslinger snapped awake, waving at something with his mutilated hand, sure that in a moment one of the monstrous shelled things from the Western Sea would drop on him, desperately enquiring in its foreign tongue as it pulled his face off his skull.

Instead a sea-bird, attracted by the glister of the morning sun on the buttons of his shirt, wheeled away with a frightened squawk.

Roland sat up.

His hand throbbed wretchedly, endlessly. His right foot did the same. Both fingers and toe continued to insist they were there. The bottom half of his shirt was gone; what was left resembled a ragged vest. He had used one piece to bind his hand, the other to bind his foot.

Go away, he told the absent parts of his body. *You are ghosts now. Go away.*

It helped a little. Not much, but a little. They were ghosts, all right, but lively ghosts.

The gunslinger ate jerky. His mouth wanted it little, his stomach less, but he insisted. When it was inside him, he felt a little stronger. There was not much left, though; he was nearly up against it.

Yet things needed to be done.

He rose unsteadily to his feet and looked about. Birds swooped and dived, but the world seemed to belong to only him and them. The monstrosities were gone. Perhaps they were nocturnal; perhaps tidal. At the moment it seemed to make no difference.

The sea was enormous, meeting the horizon at a misty blue point that was impossible to determine. For a long moment the gunslinger forgot his agony in its contemplation. He had never seen such a body of water. Had heard of it in children's stories, of course, had even been assured by his teachers—some, at least—that it existed—but to actually see it, this immensity, this amazement of water after years of arid land, was difficult to accept . . . difficult to even *see*.

He looked at it for a long time, enrapt, *making* himself see it, temporarily forgetting his pain in wonder.

But it was morning, and there were still things to be done.

He felt for the jawbone in his back pocket, careful to lead with the palm of his right hand, not wanting the stubs of his fingers to encounter it if it was still there, changing that hand's ceaseless sobbing to screams.

It was.

All right.

Next.

He clumsily unbuckled his gunbelts and laid them on a sunny rock. He removed the guns, swung the chambers out, and removed the useless shells. He threw them away. A bird settled on the bright gleam tossed back by one of them, picked it up in its beak, then dropped it and flew away.

The guns themselves must be tended to, should have been tended to before this, but since no gun in this world or any other was more than a club without ammunition, he laid the gunbelts themselves over his lap before doing anything else and carefully ran his left hand over the leather.

Each of them was damp from buckle and clasp to the point where the belts would cross his hips; from that point they seemed dry. He carefully removed each shell from the dry portions of the belts. His right hand kept trying to do this job, insisted on forgetting its reduction in spite of the pain, and he found himself returning it to his knee again and again, like a dog too stupid or fractious to heel. In his distracted pain he came close to swatting it once or twice.

I see serious problems ahead, he thought again.

He put these shells, hopefully still good, in a pile that was dishearteningly small. Twenty. Of those, a few would almost certainly misfire. He could depend on none of them. He removed the rest and put them in another pile. Thirty-seven.

Well, you weren't heavy loaded, anyway, he thought, but he recognized the difference between fifty-seven live rounds and what might be twenty. Or ten. Or five. Or one. Or none.

He put the dubious shells in a second pile.

He still had his purse. That was one thing. He put it in his lap and then slowly disassembled his guns and performed the ritual of cleaning. By the time he was finished, two hours had passed and his pain was so intense his head reeled with it; conscious thought had become difficult. He wanted to sleep. He had never wanted that more in his life. But in the service of duty there was never any acceptable reason for denial.

''Cort,'' he said in a voice that he couldn't recognize, and laughed dryly.

Slowly, slowly, he reassembled his revolvers and loaded them with the shells he presumed to be dry. When the job was done, he held the one made for his left hand, cocked it . . . and then slowly lowered the hammer again. He wanted to know, yes. Wanted to know if there would be a satisfying report when he squeezed the trigger or only another of those useless clicks. But a click would mean nothing, and a report would only reduce twenty to nineteen . . . or nine . . . or three . . . or none.

He tore away another piece of his shirt, put the other shells—the ones which had been wetted—in it, and tied it, using his left hand and his teeth. He put them in his purse.

Sleep, his body demanded. *Sleep, you must sleep, now, before dark, there's nothing left, you're used up—*

He tottered to his feet and looked up and down the deserted strand. It was the color of an undergarment which has gone a long time without washing, littered with sea-shells which had no color. Here and there large rocks protruded from the gross-grained sand, and these were covered with guano, the older layers the yellow of ancient teeth, the fresher splotches white.

The high-tide line was marked with drying kelp. He could see pieces of his right boot and his waterskins lying near that line. He thought it almost a miracle that the skins hadn't been washed out to sea by high-surging waves. Walking slowly, limping exquisitely, the gunslinger made his way to where they were. He picked up one of them and shook it by his ear. The other was empty. This one still had a little water left in it. Most would not have been able to tell the difference between the two, but the gunslinger knew each just as well as a mother knows which of her identical twins is which. He had been travelling with these waterskins for a long, long time. Water sloshed inside. That was good—a gift. Either the creature which had attacked him or any of the others could have torn this or the other open with one casual bite or slice of claw, but none had and the tide had spared it. Of the creature itself there was no sign, although the two of them had finished far above the tide-line. Perhaps other predators had taken it; perhaps its own kind had given it a burial at sea, as the *elaphaunts,* giant creatures of whom he had heard in childhood stories, were reputed to bury their own dead.

He lifted the waterskin with his left elbow, drank deeply, and felt some strength come back into him. The right boot was of course ruined . . . but then he felt a spark of hope. The foot itself was intact—scarred but intact—and it might be possible to cut the other down to match it, to make something which would last at least awhile. . . .

Faintness stole over him. He fought it but his knees unhinged and he sat down, stupidly biting his tongue.

You won't fall unconscious, he told himself grimly. *Not here, not where another of those things can come back tonight and finish the job.*

So he got to his feet and tied the empty skin about his waist, but he had only gone twenty yards back toward the place where he had left his guns and purse when he fell down again, half-fainting. He lay there awhile, one cheek pressed against the sand, the edge of a seashell biting against the edge of his jaw almost deep enough to draw blood. He managed to drink from the waterskin, and then he crawled back to the place where he had awakened. There was a Joshua tree twenty yards up the slope—it was stunted, but it would offer at least some shade.

To Roland the twenty yards looked like twenty miles.

Nonetheless, he laboriously pushed what remained of his possessions into that little puddle of shade. He lay there with his head in the grass, already fading toward what could be sleep or unconsciousness or death. He looked into the sky and tried to judge the time. Not noon, but the size of the puddle of shade in which he rested said noon was close. He held on a moment longer, turning his right arm over and bringing it close to his eyes, looking for the telltale red lines of infection, of some poison seeping steadily toward the middle of him.

The palm of his hand was a dull red. Not a good sign.

I jerk off left-handed, he thought, *at least that's something.*

Then darkness took him, and he slept for the next sixteen hours with the sound of the Western Sea pounding ceaselessly in his dreaming ears.

3

When the gunslinger awoke again the sea was dark but there was faint light in the sky to the east. Morning was on its way. He sat up and waves of dizziness almost overcame him.

He bent his head and waited.

When the faintness had passed, he looked at his hand. It was infected, all right—a tell-tale red swelling that spread up the palm and to the wrist. It stopped there, but already he could see the faint beginnings of other red lines, which would lead eventually to his heart and kill him. He felt hot, feverish.

I need medicine, he thought. *But there is no medicine here.*

Had he come this far just to die, then? He would not. And if he were to die in spite of his determination, he would die on his way to the Tower.

How remarkable you are, gunslinger! the man in black tittered inside his head. *How indomitable! How romantic in your stupid obsession!*

"Fuck you," he croaked, and drank. Not much water left, either. There was a whole sea in front of him, for all the good it could do him; water, water everywhere, but not a drop to drink. Never mind.

He buckled on his gunbelts, tied them—this was a process which took so long that before he was done the first faint light of dawn had brightened to the day's actual prologue—and then tried to stand up. He was not convinced he could do it until it was done.

Holding to the Joshua tree with his left hand, he scooped up the not-quite-empty waterskin with his right arm and slung it over his shoulder. Then his purse. When he straightened, the faintness washed over him again and he put his head down, waiting, willing.

The faintness passed.

Walking with the weaving, wavering steps of a man in the last stages of ambulatory drunkenness, the gunslinger made his way back down to the strand. He stood, looking at an ocean as dark as mulberry wine, and then took the last of his jerky from his purse. He ate half, and this time both mouth and stomach accepted a little more willingly. He turned and ate the other half as he watched the sun come up over the mountains where Jake had died—first seeming to catch on the cruel and treeless teeth of those peaks, then rising above them.

Roland held his face to the sun, closed his eyes, and smiled. He ate the rest of his jerky.

He thought: *Very well. I am now a man with no food, with two less fingers and one less toe than I was born with; I am a gunslinger with shells which may not fire; I am sickening from a monster's bite and have no medicine; I have a day's water if I'm lucky; I may be able to walk perhaps a dozen miles if I press myself to the last extremity. I am, in short, a man on the edge of everything.*

Which way should he walk? He had come from the east; he could not walk west without the powers of a saint or a savior. That left north and south.

North.

That was the answer his heart told. There was no question in it.

North.

The gunslinger began to walk.

4

He walked for three hours. He fell twice, and the second time he did not believe he would be able to get up again. Then a wave came toward him, close enough to make him remember his guns, and he was up before he knew it, standing on legs that quivered like stilts.

He thought he had managed about four miles in those three hours. Now the sun was growing hot, but not hot enough to explain the way his head pounded or the sweat pouring down his face; nor was the breeze from the sea strong enough to explain the sudden fits of shuddering which sometimes gripped him, making his body lump into gooseflesh and his teeth chatter.

Fever, gunslinger, the man in black tittered. *What's left inside you has been touched afire.*

The red lines of infection were more pronounced now; they had marched upward from his right wrist halfway to his elbow.

He made another mile and drained his waterbag dry. He tied it around his waist with the other. The landscape was monotonous and unpleasing. The sea to his right, the mountains to his left, the gray, shell-littered sand under the feet of his cut-down boots. The waves came and went. He looked for the lobstrosities and saw none. He walked out of nowhere toward nowhere, a man from another time who, it seemed, had reached a point of pointless ending.

Shortly before noon he fell again and knew he could not get up. This was the place, then. Here. This was the end, after all.

On his hands and knees, he raised his head like a groggy fighter . . . and some distance ahead, perhaps a mile, perhaps three (it was difficult to judge distances along the unchanging reach of the strand with the fever working inside him, making his eyeballs pulse in and out), he saw something new. Something which stood upright on the beach.

What was it?

(three)

Didn't matter.

(three is the number of your fate)

The gunslinger managed to get to his feet again. He croaked something, some plea which only the circling seabirds heard *(and how happy they would be to gob-ble my eyes from my head,* he thought, *how happy to have such a tasty bit!),* and walked on, weaving more seriously now, leaving tracks behind him that were weird loops and swoops.

He kept his eyes on whatever it was that stood on the strand ahead. When his hair fell in his eyes he brushed it aside. It seemed to grow no closer. The sun reached the roof of the sky, where it seemed to remain far too long. Roland imagined he was in the desert again, somewhere between the last outlander's hut

(the musical fruit the more you eat the more you toot)

and the way-station where the boy

(your Isaac)

had awaited his coming.

His knees buckled, straightened, buckled, straight-ened again. When his hair fell in his eyes once more he did not bother to push it back; did not have the strength to push it back. He looked at the object, which now cast a narrow shadow back toward the upland, and kept walking.

He could make it out now, fever or no fever.

It was a door.

Less than a quarter of a mile from it, Roland's knees buckled again and this time he could not stiffen their hinges. He fell, his right hand dragged across gritty sand and shells, the stumps of his fingers screamed as fresh scabs were scored away. The stumps began to bleed again.

So he crawled. Crawled with the steady rush, roar, and retreat of the Western Sea in his ears. He used his elbows and his knees, digging grooves in the sand above the twist of dirty green kelp which marked the high-tide line. He supposed the wind was still blow-ing—it must be, for the chills continued to whip through his body—but the only wind he could hear was the harsh gale which gusted in and out of his own lungs.

The door grew closer.

Closer.

At last, around three o'clock of that long delirious day, with his shadow beginning to grow long on his left, he reached it. He sat back on his haunches and regarded it wearily.

It stood six and a half feet high and appeared to be made of solid ironwood, although the nearest ironwood tree must grow seven hundred miles or more from here. The doorknob looked as if it were made of gold, and it was filigreed with a design which the gunslinger finally recognized: it was the grinning face of the baboon.

There was no keyhole in the knob, above it, or below it.

The door had hinges, but they were fastened to nothing—*or so it seems*, the gunslinger thought. *This is a mystery, a most marvellous mystery, but does it really matter? You are dying. Your own mystery—the only one that really matters to any man or woman in the end—approaches.*

All the same, it did seem to matter.

This door. This door where no door should be. It simply stood there on the gray strand twenty feet above the high-tide line, seemingly as eternal as the sea itself, now casting the slanted shadow of its thickness toward the east as the sun westered.

Written upon it in black letters two-thirds of the way up, written in the high speech, were two words:

THE PRISONER

A demon has infested him. The name of the demon is HEROIN.

The gunslinger could hear a low droning noise. At

first he thought it must be the wind or a sound in his
own feverish head, but he became more and more convinced that the sound was the sound of motors . . .
and that it was coming from behind the door.

*Open it then. It's not locked. You know it's not
locked.*

Instead he tottered gracelessly to his feet and walked
above the door and around to the other side.

There *was* no other side.

Only the dark gray strand, stretching back and back.
Only the waves, the shells, the high-tide line, the
marks of his own approach—bootprints and holes that
had been made by his elbows. He looked again and
his eyes widened a little. The door wasn't here, but its
shadow was.

He started to put out his right hand—oh, it was so
slow learning its new place in what was left of his
life—dropped it, and raised his left instead. He groped,
feeling for hard resistance.

If I feel it I'll knock on nothing, the gunslinger
thought. *That would be an interesting thing to do before dying!*

His hand encountered thin air far past the place
where the door—even if invisible—should have been.

Nothing to knock on.

And the sound of motors—if that's what it
really had been—was gone. Now there was just the
wind, the waves, and the sick buzzing inside his
head.

The gunslinger walked slowly back to the other side
of what wasn't there, already thinking it had been a
hallucination to start with, a—

He stopped.

At one moment he had been looking west at an uninterrupted view of a gray, rolling wave, and then his
view was interrupted by the thickness of the door. He
could see its keyplate, which also looked like gold,

with the latch protruding from it like a stubby metal tongue. Roland moved his head an inch to the north and the door was gone. Moved it back to where it had been and it was there again. It did not *appear;* it was just there.

He walked all the way around and faced the door, swaying.

He could walk around on the sea side, but he was convinced that the same thing would happen, only this time he would fall down.

I wonder if I could go through *it from the nothing side?*

Oh, there were all sorts of things to wonder about, but the truth was simple: here stood this door alone on an endless stretch of beach, and it was for only one of two things: opening or leaving closed.

The gunslinger realized with dim humor that maybe he wasn't dying quite as fast as he thought. If he had been, would he feel this scared?

He reached out and grasped the doorknob with his left hand. Neither the deadly cold of the metal nor the thin, fiery heat of the runes engraved upon it surprised him.

He turned the knob. The door opened toward him when he pulled.

Of all the things he might have expected, this was not any of them.

The gunslinger looked, froze, uttered the first scream of terror in his adult life, and slammed the door. There was nothing for it to bang shut on, but it banged shut just the same, sending seabirds screeching up from the rocks on which they had perched to watch him.

5

What he had seen was the earth from some high,
impossible distance in the sky—miles up, it seemed.
He had seen the shadows of clouds lying upon that
earth, floating across it like dreams. He had seen what
an eagle might see if one could fly thrice as high as
any eagle could.

To step through such a door would be to fall,
screaming, for what might be minutes, and to end by
driving one's self deep into the earth.

No, you saw more.

He considered it as he sat stupidly on the sand in
front of the closed door with his wounded hand in his
lap. The first faint traceries had appeared above his
elbow now. The infection would reach his heart soon
enough, no doubt about that.

It was the voice of Cort in his head.

*Listen to me, maggots. Listen for your lives, for
that's what it could mean some day. You never see all
that you see. One of the things they send you to me for
is to show you what you don't see in what you see—
what you don't see when you're scared, or fighting, or
running, or fucking. No man sees all that he sees, but
before you're gunslingers—those of you who don't go
west, that is—you'll see more in one single glance than
some men see in a lifetime. And some of what you
don't see in that glance you'll see afterwards, in the
eye of your memory—if you live long enough to remember, that is. Because the difference between seeing
and not seeing can be the difference between living and
dying.*

He had seen the earth from this huge height (and it
had somehow been more dizzying and distorting than
the vision of growth which had come upon him shortly
before the end of his time with the man in black, because what he had seen through the door had been no

vision), and what little remained of his attention had registered the fact that the land he was seeing was neither desert nor sea but some green place of incredible lushness with interstices of water that made him think it was a swamp, but—

What little remained of your attention, the voice of Cort mimicked savagely. *You saw more!*

Yes.

He had seen white.

White edges.

Bravo, Roland! Cort cried in his mind, and Roland seemed to feel the swat of that hard, callused hand. He winced.

He had been looking through a window.

The gunslinger stood with an effort, reached forward, felt cold and burning lines of thin heat against his palm. He opened the door again.

6

The view he had expected—that view of the earth from some horrendous, unimaginable height—was gone. He was looking at words he didn't understand. He *almost* understood them; it was as if the Great Letters had been twisted. . . .

Above the words was a picture of a horseless vehicle, a motor-car of the sort which had supposedly filled the world before it moved on. Suddenly he thought of the things Jake had said when, at the way station, the gunslinger had hypnotized him.

This horseless vehicle with a woman wearing a fur stole laughing beside it, could be whatever had run Jake over in that strange other world.

This is that other world, the gunslinger thought.

Suddenly the view . . .

It did not change; it *moved*. The gunslinger wavered on his feet, feeling vertigo and a touch of nausea. The words and the picture descended and now he saw an aisle with a double row of seats on the far side. A few were empty, but there were men in most of them, men in strange dress. He supposed they were suits, but he had never seen any like them before. The things around their necks could likewise be ties or cravats, but he had seen none like these, either. And, so far as he could tell, not one of them was armed—he saw no dagger nor sword, let alone a gun. What kind of trusting sheep were these? Some read papers covered with tiny words—words broken here and there with pictures—while others wrote on papers with pens of a sort the gunslinger had never seen. But the pens mattered little to him. It was the *paper.* He lived in a world where paper and gold were valued in rough equivalency. He had never seen so much paper in his life. Even now one of the men tore a sheet from the yellow pad which lay upon his lap and crumpled it into a ball, although he had only written on the top half of one side and not at all on the other. The gunslinger was not too sick to feel a twinge of horror and outrage at such unnatural profligacy.

Beyond the men was a curved white wall and a row of windows. A few of these were covered by some sort of shutters, but he could see blue sky beyond others.

Now a woman approached the doorway, a woman wearing what looked like a uniform, but of no sort Roland had ever seen. It was bright red, and part of it was *pants.* He could see the place where her legs became her crotch. This was nothing he had ever seen on a woman who was not undressed.

She came so close to the door that Roland thought she would walk through, and he blundered back a step, lucky not to fall. She looked at him with the practiced solicitude of a woman who is at once a servant and no one's mistress but her own. This did not interest the gunslinger. What interested him was that her expression never changed. It was not the way you expected a woman—anybody, for that matter—to look at a dirty, swaying, exhausted man with revolvers crisscrossed on his hips, a blood-soaked rag wrapped around his right hand, and jeans which looked as if they'd been worked on with some kind of buzzsaw.

"Would you like . . ." the woman in red asked. There was more, but the gunslinger didn't understand exactly what it meant. Food or drink, he thought. That red cloth—it was not cotton. Silk? It looked a little like silk, but—

"Gin," a voice answered, and the gunslinger understood that. Suddenly he understood much more:

It wasn't a door.

It was *eyes.*

Insane as it might seen, he was looking at part of a carriage that flew through the sky. He was looking through someone's eyes.

Whose?

But he knew. He was looking through the eyes of the prisoner.

CHAPTER 2
EDDIE DEAN

1

As if to confirm this idea, mad as it was, what the gunslinger was looking at through the doorway suddenly rose and slid sidewards. The view *turned* (that feeling of vertigo again, a feeling of standing still on a plate with wheels under it, a plate which hands he could not see moved this way and that), and then the aisle was flowing past the edges of the doorway. He passed a place where several women, all dressed in the same red uniforms, stood. This was a place of steel things, and he would have liked to make the moving view stop in spite of his pain and exhaustion so he could see what the steel things were—machines of some sort. One looked a bit like an oven. The army woman he had already seen was pouring the gin which the voice had requested. The bottle she poured from was very small. It was glass. The vessel she was pouring it into *looked* like glass but the gunslinger didn't think it actually was.

What the doorway showed had moved along before he could see more. There was another of those dizzying turns and he was looking at a metal door. There was a lighted sign in a small oblong. This word the gunslinger could read. VACANT, it said.

The view slid down a little. A hand entered it from the right of the door the gunslinger was looking through and grasped the knob of the door the gunslinger was looking at. He saw the cuff of a blue shirt,

42

slightly pulled back to reveal crisp curls of black hair.
Long fingers. A ring on one of them, with a jewel set
into it that might have been a ruby or a firedim or a
piece of trumpery trash. The gunslinger rather thought
it this last—it was too big and vulgar to be real.

The metal door swung open and the gunslinger was
looking into the strangest privy he had ever seen. It
was all metal.

The edges of the metal door flowed past the edges
of the door on the beach. The gunslinger heard the
sound of it being closed and latched. He was spared
another of those giddy spins, so he supposed the man
through whose eyes he was watching must have
reached behind himself to lock himself in.

Then the view did turn—not all the way around but
half—and he was looking into a mirror, seeing a face
he had seen once before . . . on a Tarot card. The
same dark eyes and spill of dark hair. The face was
calm but pale, and in the eyes—eyes through which he
saw now reflected back at him—Roland saw some of
the dread and horror of that baboon-ridden creature on
the Tarot card.

The man was shaking.

He's sick, too.

Then he remembered Nort, the weed-eater in Tull.

He thought of the Oracle.

A demon has infested him.

The gunslinger suddenly thought he might know
what HEROIN was after all: something like the devil-
grass.

A trifle upsetting, isn't he?

Without thought, with the simple resolve that had
made him the last of them all, the last to continue
marching on and on long after Cuthbert and the others
had died or given up, committed suicide or treachery
or simply recanted the whole idea of the Tower; with
the single-minded and incurious resolve that had driven

him across the desert and all the years before the desert in the wake of the man in black, the gunslinger stepped through the doorway.

2

Eddie ordered a gin and tonic—maybe not such a good idea to be going into New York Customs drunk, and he knew once he got started he would keep on going—but he had to have *something*.

When you got to get down and you can't find the elevator, Henry had told him once, *you got to do it any way you can. Even if it's only with a shovel.*

Then, after he'd given his order and the stewardess had left, he started to feel like he was maybe going to vomit. Not *for sure* going to vomit, only maybe, but it was better to be safe. Going through Customs with a pound of pure cocaine under each armpit with gin on your breath was not so good; going through Customs that way with puke drying on your pants would be disaster. So better to be safe. The feeling would probably pass, it usually did, but better to be safe.

Trouble was, he was going cool turkey. *Cool,* not cold. More words of wisdom from that great sage and eminent junkie Henry Dean.

They had been sitting on the penthouse balcony of the Regency Tower, not quite on the nod but edging toward it, the sun warm on their faces, done up so good . . . back in the good old days, when Eddie had just started to snort the stuff and Henry himself had yet to pick up his first needle.

Everybody talks about going cold turkey, Henry had said, *but before you get there, you gotta go cool turkey.*

And Eddie, stoned out of his mind, had cackled madly, because he knew exactly what Henry was talk-

ing about. Henry, however, had not so much as
cracked a smile.

In some ways cool turkey's worse than cold turkey,
Henry said. *At least when you make it to cold turkey,
you KNOW you're gonna puke, you KNOW you're going to shake, you KNOW you're gonna sweat until it
feels like you're drowning in it. Cool turkey is, like,
the curse of expectation.*

Eddie remembered asking Henry what you called it
when a needle-freak (which, in those dim dead days
which must have been all of sixteen months ago, they
had both solemnly assured themselves they would
never become) got a hot shot.

You call that baked *turkey,* Henry had replied
promptly, and then had looked surprised, the way a
person does when he's said something that turned out
to be a lot funnier than he actually thought it would
be, and they looked at each other, and then they were
both howling with laughter and clutching each other.
Baked turkey, pretty funny, not so funny now.

Eddie walked up the aisle past the galley to the head,
checked the sign—VACANT—and opened the door.

*Hey Henry, o great sage & eminent junkie big brother,
while we're on the subject of our feathered friends,
you want to hear my definition of cooked goose? That's
when the Customs guy at Kennedy decides there's
something a little funny about the way you look, or it's
one of the days when they got the dogs with the PhD
noses out there instead of at Port Authority and they
all start to bark and pee all over the floor and it's you
they're all just about strangling themselves on their
choke-chains trying to get to, and after the Customs
guys toss all your luggage they take you into the little
room and ask you if you'd mind taking off your shirt
and you say yeah I sure would I'd mind like hell, I
picked up a little cold down in the Bahamas and the
air-conditioning in here is real high and I'm afraid it*

might turn into pneumonia and they say oh is that so, do you always sweat like that when the air-conditioning's too high, Mr. Dean, you do, well, excuse us all to hell, now do it, and you do it, and they say maybe you better take off the t-shirt too, because you look like maybe you got some kind of a medical problem, buddy, those bulges under your pits look like maybe they could be some kind of lymphatic tumors or something, and you don't even bother to say anything else, it's like a center-fielder who doesn't even bother to chase the ball when it's hit a certain way, he just turns around and watches it go into the upper deck, because when it's gone it's gone, so you take off the t-shirt and hey, looky here, you're some lucky kid, those aren't tumors, unless they're what you might call tumors on the corpus *of society, yuk-yuk-yuk, those things look more like a couple of baggies held there with Scotch strapping tape, and by the way, don't worry about that smell, son, that's just goose. It's cooked.*

He reached behind him and pulled the locking knob. The lights in the head brightened. The sound of the motors was a soft drone. He turned toward the mirror, wanting to see how bad he looked, and suddenly a terrible, pervasive feeling swept over him: a feeling of being watched.

Hey, come on, quit it, he thought uneasily. *You're supposed to be the most unparanoid guy in the world. That's why they sent you. That's why—*

But it suddenly seemed those were not his own eyes in the mirror, not Eddie Dean's hazel, almost-green eyes that had melted so many hearts and allowed him to part so many pretty sets of legs during the last third of his twenty-one years, not his eyes but those of a stranger. Not hazel but a blue the color of fading Levis. Eyes that were chilly, precise, unexpected marvels of calibration. Bombardier's eyes.

Reflected in them he saw—clearly saw—a seagull

swooping down over a breaking wave and snatching something from it.

He had time to think *What in God's name is* this *shit?* and then he knew it wasn't going to pass; he was going to throw up after all.

In the half-second before he did, in the half-second he went on looking into the mirror, he saw those blue eyes disappear . . . but before that happened there was suddenly the feeling of being two people . . . of being *possessed,* like the little girl in *The Exorcist.*

Clearly he felt a new mind inside his own mind, and heard a thought not as his own thought but more like a voice from a radio: *I've come through. I'm in the sky-carriage.*

There was something else, but Eddie didn't hear it. He was too busy throwing up into the basin as quietly as he could.

When he was done, before he had even wiped his mouth, something happened which had never happened to him before. For one frightening moment there was nothing—only a blank interval. As if a single line in a column of newsprint had been neatly and completely inked out.

What is this? Eddie thought helplessly. *What the hell is this shit?*

Then he had to throw up again, and maybe that was just as well; whatever you might say against it, regurgitation had at least this much in its favor: as long as you were doing it, you couldn't think of anything else.

3

I've come through. I'm in the sky-carriage, the gunslinger thought. And, a second later: *He sees me in the mirror!*

Roland pulled back—did not leave but pulled back, like a child retreating to the furthest corner of a very long room. He was inside the sky-carriage; he was also inside a man who was not himself. Inside The Prisoner. In that first moment, when he had been close to *the front* (it was the only way he could describe it), he had been more than inside; he had almost *been* the man. He felt the man's illness, whatever it was, and sensed that the man was about to retch. Roland understood that if he needed to, he could take control of this man's body. He would suffer his pains, would be ridden by whatever demon-ape rode him, but if he needed to he *could*.

Or he could stay back here, unnoticed.

When the prisoner's fit of vomiting had passed, the gunslinger leaped forward—this time all the way to *the front*. He understood very little about this strange situation, and to act in a situation one does not understand is to invite the most terrible consequences, but there were two things he needed to know—and he needed to know them so desperately that the needing outweighed any consequences which might arise.

Was the door he had come through from his own world still there?

And if it was, was his physical self still there, collapsed, untenanted, perhaps dying or already dead without his self's self to go on unthinkingly running lungs and heart and nerves? Even if his body still lived, it might only continue to do so until night fell. Then the lobstrosities would come out to ask their questions and look for shore dinners.

He snapped the head which was for a moment *his* head around in a fast backward glance.

The door was still there, still behind him. It stood open on his own world, its hinges buried in the steel of this peculiar privy. And, yes, there he lay, Roland, the last gunslinger, lying on his side, his bound right hand on his stomach.

I'm breathing, Roland thought. *I'll have to go*

back and move me. But there are things to do first. Things . . .

He let go of the prisoner's mind and retreated, watching, waiting to see if the prisoner knew he was there or not.

4

After the vomiting stopped, Eddie remained bent over the basin, eyes tightly closed.

Blanked there for a second. Don't know what it was. Did I look around?

He groped for the faucet and ran cool water. Eyes still closed, he splashed it over his cheeks and brow.

When it could be avoided no longer, he looked up into the mirror again.

His own eyes looked back at him.

There were no alien voices in his head.

No feeling of being watched.

You had a momentary fugue, Eddie, the great sage and eminent junkie advised him. *A not uncommon phenomenon in one who is going cool turkey.*

Eddie glanced at his watch. An hour and a half to New York. The plane was scheduled to land at 4:05 EDT, but it was really going to be high noon. Showdown time.

He went back to his seat. His drink was on the divider. He took two sips and the stew came back to ask him if she could do anything else for him. He opened his mouth to say no . . . and then there was another of those odd blank moments.

5

"I'd like something to eat, please," the gunslinger said through Eddie Dean's mouth.

"We'll be serving a hot snack in—"

"I'm really starving, though," the gunslinger said with perfect truthfulness. "Anything at all, even a popkin—"

"Popkin?" the army woman frowned at him, and the gunslinger suddenly looked into the prisoner's mind. *Sandwich* . . . the word was as distant as the murmur in a conch shell.

"A sandwich, even," the gunslinger said.

The army woman looked doubtful. "Well . . . I have some tuna fish . . ."

"That would be fine," the gunslinger said, although he had never heard of tooter fish in his life. Beggars could not be choosers.

"You *do* look a little pale," the army woman said. "I thought maybe it was air-sickness."

"Pure hunger."

She gave him a professional smile. "I'll see what I can rustle up."

Russel? the gunslinger thought dazedly. In his own world *to russel* was a slang verb meaning to take a woman by force. Never mind. Food would come. He had no idea if he could carry it back through the doorway to the body which needed it so badly, but one thing at a time, one thing at a time.

Russel, he thought, and Eddie Dean's head shook, as if in disbelief.

Then the gunslinger retreated again.

6

Nerves, the great oracle and eminent junkie assured him. *Just nerves. All part of the cool turkey experience, little brother.*

But if nerves was what it was, how come he felt this odd sleepiness stealing over him—odd because he should have been itchy, ditsy, feeling that urge to squirm and scratch that came before the actual shakes; even if he had not been in Henry's "cool turkey" state, there was the fact that he was about to attempt bringing two pounds of coke through U.S. Customs, a felony punishable by not less than ten years in federal prison, and he seemed to suddenly be having blackouts as well.

Still, that feeling of sleepiness.

He sipped at his drink again, then let his eyes slip shut.

Why'd you black out?

I didn't, or she'd be running for all the emergency gear they carry.

Blanked *out, then. It's no good either way. You never blanked out like that before in your life.* Nodded *out, yeah, but never* blanked *out.*

Something odd about his right hand, too. It seemed to throb vaguely, as if he had pounded it with a hammer.

He flexed it without opening his eyes. No ache. No throb. No blue bombardier's eyes. As for the blankouts, they were just a combination of going cool turkey and a good case of what the great oracle and eminent et cetera would no doubt call the smuggler's blues.

But I'm going to sleep, just the same, he thought. *How 'bout that?*

Henry's face drifted by him like an untethered balloon. *Don't worry,* Henry was saying. *You'll be all right, little brother. You fly down there to Nassau, check in at the Aquinas, there'll be a man come by Friday night. One of the good guys. He'll fix you, leave you enough stuff to take you through the weekend. Sunday night he brings the coke and you give him the key to the safe deposit box. Monday morning you do the routine just like Balazar said. This guy will play; he knows how it's supposed to go. Monday noon you fly out, and with a face as honest as yours, you'll breeze through Customs and we'll be eating steak in Sparks before the sun goes down. It's gonna be a breeze, little brother, nothing but a cool breeze.*

But it had been sort of a warm breeze after all.

The trouble with him and Henry was they were like

Charlie Brown and Lucy. The only difference was once
in awhile Henry would hold onto the football so Eddie
could kick it—not often, but once in awhile. Eddie had
even thought, while in one of his heroin dazes, that he
ought to write Charles Schultz a letter. *Dear Mr.
Schultz,* he would say. You're missing a bet by AL-
WAYS having Lucy pull the football up at the last second. She ought to hold it down there once in awhile.
Nothing Charlie Brown could ever predict, you understand. Sometimes she'd maybe hold it down for him
to kick three, even four times in a row, then nothing
for a month, then once, and then nothing for three or
four days, and then, you know, you get the idea. That
would REALLY fuck the kid up, wouldn't it?

Eddie *knew* it would really fuck the kid up.

From experience he knew it.

One of the good guys, Henry had said, but the guy who
showed up had been a sallow-skinned thing with a British
accent, a hairline moustache that looked like something
out of a 1940's *film noire,* and yellow teeth that all leaned
inward, like the teeth of a very old animal trap.

"You have the key, *Senor?*" he asked, except in that
British public school accent it came out sounding like
what you called your last year of high school.

"The key's safe," Eddie said, "if that's what you
mean."

"Then give it to me."

"That's not the way it goes. You're supposed to have
something to take me through the weekend. Sunday night
you're supposed to bring me something. I give you the
key. Monday you go into town and use it to get something
else. I don't know what, 'cause that's not my business."

Suddenly there was a small flat blue automatic in
the sallow-skinned thing's hand. "Why don't you just
give it to me, *Senor?* I will save time and effort; you
will save your life."

There was deep steel in Eddie Dean, junkie or no

junkie. Henry knew it; more important, Balazar knew
it. That was why he had been sent. Most of them thought
he had gone because he was hooked through the bag and
back again. He knew it, Henry knew it, Balazar, too. But
only he and Henry knew he would have gone even if he
was as straight as a stake. For Henry. Balazar hadn't got
quite that far in his figuring, but fuck Balazar.

"Why don't you just put that thing away, you little
scuzz?" Eddie asked. "Or do you maybe want Balazar
to send someone down here and cut your eyes out of
your head with a rusty knife?"

The sallow thing smiled. The gun was gone like
magic; in its place was a small envelope. He handed
it to Eddie. "Just a little joke, you know."

"If you say so."

"I see you Sunday night."

He turned toward the door.

"I think you better wait."

The sallow thing turned back, eyebrows raised.
"You think I won't go if I want to go?"

"I think if you go and this is bad shit, I'll be gone
tomorrow. Then you'll be in *deep* shit."

The sallow thing turned sulky. It sat in the room's
single easy chair while Eddie opened the envelope and
spilled out a small quantity of brown stuff. It looked
evil. He looked at the sallow thing.

"I know how it looks, it looks like shit, but that's
just the cut," the sallow thing said. "It's fine."

Eddie tore a sheet of paper from the notepad on the
desk and separated a small amount of the brown powder from the pile. He fingered it and then rubbed it on
the roof of his mouth. A second later he spat into the
wastebasket.

"You want to die? Is that it? You got a death-wish?"

"That's all there is." The sallow thing looked more
sulky than ever.

"I have a reservation out tomorrow," Eddie said.

This was a lie, but he didn't believe the sallow thing had the resources to check it. "TWA. I did it on my own, just in case the contact happened to be a fuck-up like you. I don't mind. It'll be a relief, actually. I wasn't cut out for this sort of work."

The sallow thing sat and cogitated. Eddie sat and concentrated on not moving. He *felt* like moving; felt like slipping and sliding, bipping and bopping, shucking and jiving, scratching his scratches and cracking his crackers. He even felt his eyes wanting to slide back to the pile of brown powder, although he knew it was poison. He had fixed at ten that morning; the same number of hours had gone by since then. But if he did any of those things, the situation would change. The sallow thing was doing more than cogitating; it was watching him, trying to calculate the depth of him.

"I might be able to find something," it said at last.

"Why don't you try?" Eddie said. "But come eleven, I turn out the light and put the DO NOT DISTURB sign on the door, and anybody that knocks after I do that, I call the desk and say someone's bothering me, send a security guy."

"You are a fuck," the sallow thing said in its impeccable British accent.

"No," Eddie said, "a fuck is what you *expected*. I came with my legs crossed. You want to be here before eleven with something that I can use—it doesn't have to be great, just something I can use—or you will be one dead scuzz."

7

The sallow thing was back long before eleven; he was back by nine-thirty. Eddie guessed the other stuff had been in his car all along.

A little more powder this time. Not white, but at least a dull ivory color, which was mildly hopeful.

Eddie tasted. It seemed all right. Actually better than all right. Pretty good. He rolled a bill and snorted.

"Well, then, until Sunday," the sallow thing said briskly, getting to its feet.

"Wait," Eddie said, as if he were the one with the gun. In a way he was. The gun was Balazar. Emilio Balazar was a high-caliber big shot in New York's wonderful world of drugs.

"Wait?" the sallow thing turned and looked at Eddie as if he believed Eddie must be insane. "For *what?"*

"Well, I was actually thinking of you," Eddie said. "If I get really sick from what I just put into my body, it's off. If I die, of *course* it's off. I was just thinking that, if I only get a *little* sick, I might give you another chance. You know, like that story about how some kid rubs a lamp and gets three wishes."

"It will not make you sick. That's China White."

"If that's China White," Eddie said, "I'm Dwight Gooden."

"Who?"

"Never mind."

The sallow thing sat down. Eddie sat by the motel room desk with the little pile of white powder nearby (the D-Con or whatever it had been had long since gone down the john). On TV the Braves were getting shellacked by the Mets, courtesy of WTBS and the big satellite dish on the Aquinas Hotel's roof. Eddie felt a faint sensation of calm which seemed to come from the back of his mind . . . except where it was really coming from, he knew from what he had read in the medical journals, was from the bunch of living wires at the base of his spine, that place where heroin addiction takes place by causing an unnatural thickening of the nerve stem.

Want to take a quick cure? he had asked Henry once. *Break your spine, Henry. Your legs stop working, and so does your cock, but you stop needing the needle right away.*

Henry hadn't thought it was funny.

In truth, Eddie hadn't thought it was that funny either. When the only fast way you could get rid of the monkey on your back was to snap your spinal cord above that bunch of nerves, you were dealing with one heavy monkey. That was no capuchin, no cute little organ grinder's mascot; that was a big mean old baboon.

Eddie began to sniffle.

"Okay," he said at last. "It'll do. You can vacate the premises, scuzz."

The sallow thing got up. "I have friends," he said. "They could come in here and do things to you. You'd beg to tell me where that key is."

"Not me, champ," Eddie said. "Not this kid." And smiled. He didn't know how the smile looked, but it must not have looked all that cheery because the sallow thing vacated the premises, vacated them fast, vacated them without looking back.

When Eddie Dean was sure he was gone, he cooked.

Fixed.

Slept.

8

As he was sleeping now.

The gunslinger, somehow inside this man's mind (a man whose name he still did not know; the lowling the prisoner thought of as "the sallow thing" had not known it, and so had never spoken it), watched this as he had once watched plays as a child, before the world had moved on . . . or so he thought he watched, because plays were all he had ever seen. If he had ever seen a moving picture, he would have thought of that first. The things he did not actually see he had been able to pluck from the prisoner's mind because the associations were close. It was odd about the name, though. He knew the name of the prisoner's brother, but not the name of the man himself. But of course names were secret things, full of power.

And neither of the things that mattered was the man's name. One was the weakness of the addiction. The other was the steel buried inside that weakness, like a good gun sinking in quicksand.

This man reminded the gunslinger achingly of Cuthbert.

Someone was coming. The prisoner, sleeping, did not hear. The gunslinger, not sleeping, did, and came forward again.

9

Great, Jane thought. *He tells me how hungry he is and I fix something up for him because he's a little bit cute, and then he falls asleep on me.*

Then the passenger—a guy of about twenty, tall, wearing clean, slightly faded blue jeans and a paisley shirt—opened his eyes a little and smiled at her.

"Thankee sai," he said—or so it sounded. Almost archaic . . . or foreign. *Sleep-talk, that's all,* Jane thought.

"You're welcome." She smiled her best stewardess smile, sure he would fall asleep again and the sandwich would still be there, uneaten, when it was time for the actual meal service.

Well, that was what they taught you to expect, wasn't it?

She went back to the galley to catch a smoke.

She struck the match, lifted it halfway to her cigarette, and there it stopped, unnoticed, because that wasn't *all* they taught you to expect.

I thought he was a little bit cute. Mostly because of his eyes. His hazel eyes.

But when the man in 3A had opened his eyes a moment ago, they *hadn't* been hazel; they had been blue.

Not sweet-sexy blue like Paul Newman's eyes, either, but the color of icebergs. They—

"*Ow!*"

The match had reached her fingers. She shook it out.

"Jane?" Paula asked. "You all right?"

"Fine. Daydreaming."

She lit another match and this time did the job right. She had only taken a single drag when the perfectly reasonable explanation occurred to her. He wore contacts. Of course. The kind that changed the color of your eyes. He had gone into the bathroom. He had been in there long enough for her to worry about him being airsick—he had that pallid complexion, the look of a man who is not quite well. But he had only been taking out his contact lenses so he could nap more comfortably. Perfectly reasonable.

You may feel something, a voice from her own not-so-distant past spoke suddenly. *Some little tickle. You may see something just a little bit wrong.*

Colored contact lenses.

Jane Dorning personally knew over two dozen people who wore contacts. Most of them worked for the airline. No one ever said anything about it, but she thought maybe one reason was they all sensed the passengers didn't like to see flight personnel wearing glasses—it made them nervous.

Of all those people, she knew maybe four who had color-contacts. Ordinary contact lenses were expensive; colored ones cost the earth. All of the people of Jane's acquaintance who cared to lay out that sort of money were women, all of them extremely vain.

So what? Guys can be vain, too. Why not? He's goodlooking.

No. He wasn't. Cute, maybe, but that was as far as it went, and with the pallid complexion he only made it to cute by the skin of his teeth. So why the color-contacts?

Airline passengers are often afraid of flying.

In a world where hijacking and drug-smuggling had become facts of life, airline personnel are often afraid of passengers.

The voice that had initiated these thoughts had been that of an instructor at flight school, a tough old battle-axe who looked as if she could have flown the mail with Wiley Post, saying: *Don't ignore your suspicions. If you forget everything else you've learned about coping with potential or actual terrorists, remember this:* don't ignore your suspicions. *In some cases you'll get a crew who'll say during the debriefing that they didn't have any idea until the guy pulled out a grenade and said hang a left for Cuba or everyone on the aircraft is going to join the jet-stream. But in most cases you get two or three different people—mostly flight attendants, which you women will be in less than a month—who say they felt something. Some little tickle. A sense that the guy in 91C or the young woman in 5A was a little wrong. They felt something, but they did nothing. Did they get fired for that? Christ, no! You can't put a guy in restraints because you don't like the way he scratches his pimples. The real problem is they felt something . . . and then forgot.*

The old battle-axe had raised one blunt finger. Jane Dorning, along with her fellow classmates, had listened raptly as she said, *If you feel that little tickle, don't do anything . . . but that includes not forgetting. Because there's always that one little chance that you just might be able to stop something before it gets started . . . something like an unscheduled twelve-day layover on the tarmac of some shitpot Arab country.*

Just colored contacts, but . . .

Thankee, sai.

Sleep-talk? Or a muddled lapse into some other language?

She would watch, Jane decided.
And she would not forget.

10

Now, the gunslinger thought. *Now we'll see, won't we?*

He had been able to come from his world into this body through the door on the beach. What he needed to find out was whether or not he could carry things back. Oh, not himself; he was confident that he could return through the door and reenter his own poisoned, sickening body at any time he should desire. But other things? *Physical* things? Here, for instance, in front of him, was food: something the woman in the uniform had called a tooter-fish sandwhich. The gunslinger had no idea what tooter-fish was, but he knew a popkin when he saw it, although this one looked curiously uncooked.

His body needed to eat, and his body would need to drink, but more than either, his body needed some sort of medicine. It would die from the lobstrosity's bite without it. There might be such medicine in this world; in a world where carriages rode through the air far above where even the strongest eagle could fly, anything seemed possible. But it would not matter how much powerful medicine there was here if he could carry nothing physical through the door.

You could live in this body, gunslinger, the voice of the man in black whispered deep inside his head. *Leave that piece of breathing meat over there for the lobster-things. It's only a husk, anyway.*

He would not do that. For one thing it would be the most murderous sort of thievery, because he would not be content to be just a passenger for long, looking out of this man's eyes like a traveller looking out of a coach window at the passing scenery.

For another, he was Roland. If dying was required, he intended to die as Roland. He would die *crawling* toward the Tower, if that was what was required.

Then the odd harsh practicality that lived beside the romantic in his nature like a tiger with a roe reasserted itself. There was no need to think of dying with the experiment not yet made.

He picked up the popkin. It had been cut in two halves. He held one in each hand. He opened the prisoner's eyes and looked out of them. No one was looking at him (although, in the galley, Jane Dorning was *thinking* about him, and very hard).

Roland turned toward the door and went through, holding the popkin-halves in his hands.

11

First he heard the grinding roar of an incoming wave; next he heard the argument of many sea-birds arising from the closest rocks as he struggled to a sitting position (*cowardly buggers were creeping up*, he thought, *and they would have been taking pecks out of me soon enough, still breathing or no—they're nothing but vultures with a coat of paint*); then he became aware that one popkin half—the one in his right hand—had tumbled onto the hard gray sand because he had been holding it with a whole hand when he came through the door and now was—or *had* been—holding it in a hand which had suffered a forty per cent reduction.

He picked it up clumsily, pinching it between his thumb and ring finger, brushed as much of the sand from it as he could, and took a tentative bite. A moment later he was wolfing it, not noticing the few bits of sand which ground between his teeth. Seconds later

he turned his attention to the other half. It was gone
in three bites.

The gunslinger had no idea what tooter-fish was—
only that it was delicious. That seemed enough.

12

In the plane, no one saw the tuna sandwich disappear. No one saw Eddie Dean's hands grasp the two
halves of it tightly enough to make deep thumb-
indentations in the white bread.

No one saw the sandwich fade to transparency, then
disappear, leaving only a few crumbs.

About twenty seconds after this had happened, Jane
Dorning snuffed her cigarette and crossed the head of
the cabin. She got her book from her totebag, but what
she really wanted was another look at 3A.

He appeared to be deeply asleep . . . but the sandwich was gone.

Jesus, Jane thought. *He didn't eat it; he swallowed
it whole. And now he's* asleep *again? Are you kidding?*

Whatever was tickling at her about 3A, Mr. Now-
They're-Hazel-Now-They're-Blue, kept right on tickling. Something about him was not right.

Something.

CHAPTER 3

CONTACT AND LANDING

1

Eddie was awakened by an announcement from the co-pilot that they should be landing at Kennedy International, where the visibility was unlimited, the winds out of the west at ten miles an hour, and the temperature a jolly seventy degrees, in forty-five minutes or so. He told them that, if he didn't get another chance, he wanted to thank them one and all for choosing Delta.

He looked around and saw people checking their duty declaration cards and their proofs of citizenship—coming in from Nassau your driver's licence and a credit card with a stateside bank listed on it was supposed to be enough, but most still carried passports—and Eddie felt a steel wire start to tighten inside him. He still couldn't believe he had gone to sleep, and so soundly.

He got up and went to the restroom. The bags of coke under his arms felt as if they were resting easily and firmly, fitting as nicely to the contours of his sides as they had in the hotel room where a soft-spoken American named William Wilson had strapped them on. Following the strapping operation, the man whose name Poe had made famous (Wilson had only looked blankly at Eddie when Eddie made some allusion to this) handed over the shirt. Just an ordinary paisley shirt, a little faded, the sort of thing any frat-boy might wear back on the plane following a short pre-exams holiday . . . except this one was specially tailored to hide unsightly bulges.

"You check everything once before you set down just to be sure," Wilson said, "but you're gonna be fine."

Eddie didn't know if he was going to be fine or not, but he had another reason for wanting to use the john before the FASTEN SEAT BELTS light came on. In spite of all temptation—and most of last night it hadn't been temptation but raging need—he had managed to hold onto the last little bit of what the sallow thing had had the temerity to call China White.

Clearing customs from Nassau wasn't like clearing customs from Haiti or Quincon or Bogota, but there were still people watching. Trained people. He needed any and every edge he could get. If he could go in there a little cooled out, just a little, it might be the one thing that put him over the top.

He snorted the powder, flushed the little twist of paper it had been in down the john, then washed his hands.

Of course, if you make it, you'll never know, will you? he thought. No. He wouldn't. And wouldn't care.

On his way back to his seat he saw the stewardess who had brought him the drink he hadn't finished. She smiled at him. He smiled back, sat down, buckled his seat-belt, took out the flight magazine, turned the pages, and looked at pictures and words. Neither made any impression on them. That steel wire continued to tighten around his gut, and when the FASTEN SEAT-BELTS light *did* come on, it took a double turn and cinched tight.

The heroin had hit—he had the sniffles to prove it— but he sure couldn't *feel* it.

One thing he did feel shortly before landing was another of those unsettling periods of blankness . . . short, but most definitely there.

The 727 banked over the water of Long Island Sound and started in.

2

Jane Dorning had been in the business class galley, helping Peter and Anne stow the last of the after-meal drinks glasses when the guy who looked like a college kid went into the first class bathroom.

He was returning to his seat when she brushed aside the curtain between business and first, and she quickened her step without even thinking about it, catching him with her smile, making him look up and smile back.

His eyes were hazel again.

All right, all right. He went into the john and took them out before his nap; he went into the john and put them in again afterwards. For Christ's sake, Janey! You're being a goose!

She wasn't, though. It was nothing she could put her finger on, but she was not being a goose.

He's too pale.

So what? Thousands of people are too pale, including your own mother since her gall-bladder went to hell.

He had very arresting blue eyes—maybe not as cute as the hazel contacts—but certainly arresting. So why the bother and expense?

Because he likes designer eyes. Isn't that enough?

No.

Shortly before FASTEN SEAT BELTS and final cross-check, she did something she had never done before; she did it with that tough old battle-axe of an instructor in mind. She filled a Thermos bottle with hot coffee and put on the red plastic top without first pushing the stopper into the bottle's throat. She screwed the top on only until she felt it catch the first thread.

Susy Douglas was making the final approach announcement, telling the geese to extinguish their cigarettes, telling them they would have to stow what they had taken out, telling them a Delta gate agent would meet the flight, telling them to check and make sure they had their duty-declaration cards and proofs of citizenship, telling them it would now be necessary to pick up all cups, glasses and speaker sets.

I'm surprised we don't have to check to make sure they're dry, Jane thought distractedly. She felt her own steel wire wrapping itself around her guts, cinching them tight.

"Get my side," Jane said as Susy hung up the mike.

Susy glanced at the Thermos, then at Jane's face. "Jane? Are you sick? You look as white as a—"

"I'm not sick. Get my side. I'll explain when you get back." Jane glanced briefly at the jump-seats beside the left-hand exit door. "I want to ride shotgun."

"Jane—"

"*Get my side.*"

"All right," Susy said. "All right, Jane. No problem."

Jane Dorning sat down in the jump-seat closest to the aisle. She held the Thermos in her hands and made no move to fasten the web-harness. She wanted to keep the Thermos in complete control, and that meant both hands.

Susy thinks I've flipped out.

Jane hoped she had.

If Captain McDonald lands hard, I'm going to have blisters all over my hands.

She would risk it.

The plane was dropping. The man in 3A, the man with the two-tone eyes and the pale face, suddenly leaned down and pulled his travelling bag from under the seat.

This is it, Jane thought. *This is where he brings out the grenade or the automatic weapon or whatever the hell he's got.*

And the moment she saw it, the very moment, she was going to flip the red top off the Thermos in her slightly trembling hands, and there was going to be one very surprised Friend of Allah rolling around on the aisle floor of Delta Flight 901 while his skin boiled on his face.

3A unzipped the bag.

Jane got ready.

3

The gunslinger thought this man, prisoner or not, was probably better at the fine art of survival than any of the other men he had seen in the air-carriage. The others were fat things, for the most part, and even those who looked reasonably fit also looked open, unguarded, their faces those of spoiled and cosseted children, the faces of men who would fight—eventually—but who would whine almost endlessly before they did; you could let their guts out onto their shoes and their last expressions would not be rage or agony but stupid surprise.

The prisoner was better . . . but not good enough. Not at all.

The army woman. She saw something. I don't know what, but she saw something wrong. She's awake to him in a way she's not to the others.

The prisoner sat down. Looked at a limp-covered book he thought of as a "Magda-Seen," although who Magda might have been or what she might have seen mattered not a whit to Roland. The gunslinger did not want to look at a book, amazing as such things were;

he wanted to look at the woman in the army uniform. The urge to come forward and take control was very great. But he held against it . . . at least for the time being.

The prisoner had gone somewhere and gotten a drug. Not the drug he himself took, nor one that would help cure the gunslinger's sick body, but one that people paid a lot of money for because it was against the law. He would give this drug to his brother, who would in turn give it to a man named Balazar. The deal would be complete when Balazar traded them the kind of drug *they* took for this one—if, that was, the prisoner was able to correctly perform a ritual unknown to the gunslinger (and a world as strange as this must of necessity have many strange rituals); it was called Clearing the Customs.

But the woman sees him.

Could she keep him from Clearing the Customs? Roland thought the answer was probably yes. And then? Gaol. And if the prisoner were gaoled, there would be no place to get the sort of medicine his infected, dying body needed.

He must Clear the Customs, Roland thought. *He* must. *And he must go with his brother to this man Balazar. It's not in the plan, the brother won't like it, but he must.*

Because a man who dealt in drugs would either know a man or *be* a man who also cured the sick. A man who could listen to what was wrong and then . . . maybe . . .

He must *Clear the Customs*, the gunslinger thought.

The answer was so large and simple, so close to him, that he very nearly did not see it at all. It was the *drug* the prisoner meant to smuggle in that would make Clearing the Customs so difficult, of course; there might be some sort of Oracle who might be consulted in the cases of people who seemed suspicious.

Otherwise, Roland gleaned, the Clearing ceremony would be simplicity itself, as crossing a friendly border was in his own world. One made the sign of fealty to that kingdom's monarch—a simple token gesture—and was allowed to pass.

He *was* able to take things from the prisoner's world to his own. The tooter-fish popkin proved that. He would take the bags of drugs as he had taken the popkin. The prisoner would Clear the Customs. And then Roland would bring the bags of drugs back.

Can you?

Ah, here was a question disturbing enough to distract him from the view of the water below . . . they had gone over what looked like a huge ocean and were now turning back toward the coastline. As they did, the water grew steadily closer. The air-carriage was coming down (Eddie's glance was brief, cursory; the gunslinger's as rapt as the child seeing his first snowfall). He could *take* things from this world, that he knew. But bring them back again? That was a thing of which he as yet had no knowing. He would have to find out.

The gunslinger reached into the prisoner's pocket and closed the prisoner's fingers over a coin.

Roland went back through the door.

4

The birds flew away when he sat up. They hadn't dared come as close this time. He ached, he was woozy, feverish . . . yet it was amazing how much even a little bit of nourishment had revived him.

He looked at the coin he had brought back with him this time. It looked like silver, but the reddish tint at the edge suggested it was really made of some baser metal. On one side was a profile of a man whose face suggested nobility, courage, stubbornness. His hair, both curled at the base of the skull and pigged at the nape of the neck, suggested a bit of vanity as well. He turned the coin over and saw something so startling it caused him to cry out in a rusty, croaking voice.

On the back was an eagle, the device which had decorated his own banner, in those dim days when there had still been kingdoms and banners to symbolize them.

Time's short. Go back. Hurry.

But he tarried a moment longer, thinking. It was harder to think inside this head—the prisoner's was far from clear, but it was, temporarily at least, a cleaner vessel than his own.

To try the coin both ways was only half the experiment, wasn't it?

He took one of the shells from his cartridge belt and folded it over the coin in his hand.

Roland stepped back through the door.

5

The prisoner's coin was still there, firmly curled within the pocketed hand. He didn't have to *come forward* to check on the shell; he knew it hadn't made the trip.

He *came forward* anyway, briefly, because there was one thing he had to know. Had to *see*.

So he turned, as if to adjust the little paper thing on the back of his seat (by all the gods that ever were, there was paper *everywhere* in this world), and looked through the doorway. He saw his body, collapsed as before, now with a fresh trickle of blood flowing from a cut on his cheek—a stone must have done it when he left himself and crossed over.

The cartridge he had been holding along with the coin lay at the base of the door, on the sand.

Still, enough was answered. The prisoner could

Clear the Customs. Their guards o' the watch might search him from head to toe, from asshole to appetite, and back again.

They'd find nothing.

The gunslinger settled back, content, unaware, at least for the time being, that he still had not grasped the extent of his problem.

6

The 727 came in low and smooth over the salt-marshes of Long Island, leaving sooty trails of spent fuel behind. The landing gear came down with a rumble and a thump.

7

3A, the man with the two-tone eyes, straightened up and Jane saw—actually saw—a snub-nosed Uzi in his hands before she realized it was nothing but his duty declaration card and a little zipper bag of the sort which men sometimes use to hold their passports.

The plane settled like silk.

Letting out a deep, shaking shudder, she tightened the red top on the Thermos.

"Call me an asshole," she said in a low voice to Susy, buckling the cross-over belts now that it was too late. She had told Susy what she suspected on the final approach, so Susy would be ready. "You have every right."

"No," Susy said. "You did the right thing."

"I over-reacted. And dinner's on me."

"Like hell it is. And don't look at him. Look at me. *Smile,* Janey."

Jane smiled. Nodded. Wondered what in God's name was going on *now.*

"You were watching his hands," Susy said, and

laughed. Jane joined in. "I was watching what happened to his shirt when he bent over to get his bag. He's got enough stuff under there to stock a Woolworth's notions counter. Only I don't think he's carrying the kind of stuff you can buy at Woolworth's."

Jane threw back her head and laughed again, feeling like a puppet. "How do we handle it?" Susy had five years' seniority on her, and Jane, who only a minute ago had felt she had the situation under some desperate kind of control, now only felt glad to have Susy beside her.

"*We* don't. Tell the Captain while we're taxiing in. The Captain speaks to customs. Your friend there gets in line like everyone else, except then he gets pulled *out* of line by some men who escort him to a little room. It's going to be the first in a very long succession of little rooms for him, I think."

"Jesus." Jane was smiling, but chills, alternately hot and cold, were racing through her.

She hit the pop-release on her harness when the reverse thrusters began to wind down, handed the Thermos to Susy, then got up and rapped on the cockpit door.

Not a terrorist but a drug-smuggler. Thank God for small favors. Yet in a way she hated it. He *had* been cute.

Not much, but a little.

8

He still doesn't see, the gunslinger thought with anger and dawning desperation. *Gods!*

Eddie had bent to get the papers he needed for the ritual, and when he looked up the army woman was staring at him, her eyes bulging, her cheeks as white as the paper things on the backs of the seats. The silver tube with the red top, which he had at first taken for some kind of canteen, was apparently a weapon. She was holding it up between her breasts now. Roland thought that in a moment or two she would either throw it or spin off the red top and shoot him with it.

Then she relaxed and buckled her harness even though the thump told both the gunslinger and the prisoner the air-carriage had already landed. She turned to the army woman she was sitting with and said something. The other woman laughed and nodded, but if that was a real laugh, the gunslinger thought, he was a river-toad.

The gunslinger wondered how the man whose mind had become temporary home for the gunslinger's own *ka,* could be so stupid. Some of it was what he was putting into his body, of course . . . one of this world's versions of devil-weed. Some, but not all. He was not soft and unobservant like the others, but in time he might be.

They are as they are because they live in the light, the gunslinger thought suddenly. *That light of civilization you were taught to adore above all other things. They live in a world which has not moved on.*

If this was what people became in such a world, Roland was not sure he didn't prefer the dark. "That was before the world moved on," people said in his own world, and it was always said in tones of bereft sadness . . . but it was, perhaps, sadness without thought, without consideration.

She thought I/he—meant to grab a weapon when I/ he—bent down to get the papers. When she saw the papers she relaxed and did what everyone else did before the carriage came down to the ground again. Now she and her friend are talking and laughing but their faces—her face especially, the face of the woman with the metal tube—are not right. They are talking, all right, but they are only pretending *to laugh . . .*

and that is because what they are talking about is I/him.

The air-carriage was now moving along what seemed a long concrete road, one of many. Mostly he watched the women, but from the edges of his vision the gunslinger could see other air-carriages moving here and there along other roads. Some lumbered; some moved with incredible speed, not like carriages at all but like projectiles fired from guns or cannons, preparing to leap into the air. As desperate as his own situation had become, part of him wanted very much to *come forward* and turn his head so he could see these vehicles as they leaped into the sky. They were man-made but every bit as fabulous as the stories of the Grand Featherex which had supposedly once lived in the distant (and probably mythical) kingdom of Garlan—*more* fabulous, perhaps, simply because *these* were man-made.

The woman who had brought him the popkin unfastened her harness (this less than a minute since she had fastened it) and went forward to a small door. *That's where the driver sits,* the gunslinger thought, but when the door was opened and she stepped in he saw it apparently took three drivers to operate the air-carriage, and even the brief glimpse he was afforded of what seemed like a million dials and levers and lights made him understand why.

The prisoner was looking at all but seeing nothing—Cort would have first sneered, then driven him through the nearest wall. The prisoner's mind was completely occupied with grabbing the bag under the seat and his light jacket from the overhead bin . . . and facing the ordeal of the ritual.

The prisoner saw nothing; the gunslinger saw everything.

The woman thought him a thief or a madman. He—or perhaps it was I, yes, that's likely enough—did

*something to make her think that. She changed her
mind, and then the other woman changed it back . . .
only now I think they know what's really wrong. They
know he's going to try to profane the ritual.*

Then, in a thunderclap, he saw the rest of his problem. First, it wasn't just a matter of taking the bags
into his world as he had the coin; the coin hadn't been
stuck to the prisoner's body with the glue-string the
prisoner had wrapped around and around his upper
body to hold the bags tight to his skin. This glue-string
was only part of his problem. The prisoner hadn't
missed the temporary disappearance of one coin
among many, but when he realized that whatever it
was he had risked his life for was suddenly gone, he
was *surely* going to raise the racks . . . and what then?

It was more than possible that the prisoner would
begin to behave in a manner so irrational that it would
get him locked away in gaol as quickly as being caught
in the act of profanation. The loss would be bad
enough; for the bags under his arms to simply melt
away to nothing would probably make him think he
really *had* gone mad.

The air-carriage, ox-like now that it was on the
ground, labored its way through a left turn. The gunslinger realized that he had no time for the luxury of
further thought. He had to do more than *come forward;* he must make contact with Eddie Dean.

Right now.

9

Eddie tucked his declaration card and passport in
his breast pocket. The steel wire was now turning
steadily around his guts, sinking in deeper and deeper,
making his nerves spark and sizzle. And suddenly a
voice spoke in his head.

Not a thought; *a voice.*

Listen to me, fellow. Listen carefully. And if you would remain safe, let your face show nothing which might further rouse the suspicions of those army women. God knows they're suspicious enough already.

Eddie first thought he was still wearing the airline earphones and picking up some weird transmission from the cockpit. But the airline headphones had been picked up five minutes ago.

His second thought was that someone was standing beside him and talking. He almost snapped his head to the left, but that was absurd. Like it or not, the raw truth was that the voice had come from *inside* his head.

Maybe he was receiving some sort of transmission—AM, FM, or VHF on the fillings in his teeth. He had heard of such th—

Straighten up, maggot! They're suspicious enough without you looking as if you've gone crazy!

Eddie sat up fast, as if he had been whacked. That voice wasn't Henry's, but it was so much like Henry's when they had been just a couple of kids growing up in the Projects, Henry eight years older, the sister who had been between them now only a ghost of memory; Selina had been struck and killed by a car when Eddie was two and Henry ten. That rasping tone of command came out whenever Henry saw him doing something that might end with Eddie occupying a pine box long before his time . . . as Selina had.

What in the blue fuck is going on here?

You're not hearing voices that aren't there, the voice inside his head returned. No, not Henry's voice—older, dryer . . . stronger. But *like* Henry's voice . . . and impossible not to believe. *That's the first thing. You're not going crazy. I AM another person.*

This is telepathy?

Eddie was vaguely aware that his face was completely expressionless. He thought that, under the circumstances, that ought to qualify him for the Best

Actor of the Year Academy Award. He looked out the window and saw the plane closing in on the Delta section of Kennedy's International Arrivals Building.

I don't know that word. But I do know that those army women know you are carrying . . .

There was a pause. A feeling—odder beyond telling—of phantom fingers rummaging through his brain as if he were a living card catalogue.

. . . heroin or cocaine. I can't tell which except—except it must be cocaine because you're carrying the one you don't take to buy the one you do.

"What army women?" Eddie muttered in a low voice. He was completely unaware that he was speaking aloud. "What in the hell are you talking ab—"

That feeling of being slapped once more . . . so real he felt his head ring with it.

Shut your mouth, you damned jackass!

All right, all right! Christ!

Now that feeling of rummaging fingers again.

Army stewardesses, the alien voice replied. *Do you understand me? I have no time to con your every thought, prisoner!*

"What did you—" Eddie began, then shut his mouth. *What did you call me?*

Never mind. Just listen. Time is very, very short. They know. The army stewardesses know you have this cocaine.

How could they? That's ridiculous!

I don't know how they came by their knowledge, and it doesn't matter. One of them told the drivers. The drivers will tell whatever priests perform this ceremony, this Clearing of Customs—

The language of the voice in his head was arcane, the terms so off-kilter they were almost cute . . . but the message came through loud and clear. Although his face remained expressionless, Eddie's teeth came together with a painful click and he drew a hot little hiss in through them.

The voice was saying the game was over. He hadn't even gotten off the plane and the game was already over.

But this wasn't real. No way this could be real. It was just his mind, doing a paranoid little jig at the last minute, that was all. He would ignore it. Just ignore it and it would go awa—

You will NOT ignore it or you will go to jail and I will die! the voice roared.

Who in the name of God are you? Eddie asked reluctantly, fearfully, and inside his head he heard someone or something let out a deep and gusty sigh of relief.

10

He believes, the gunslinger thought. *Thank all the gods that are or ever were, he* believes!

11

The plane stopped. The FASTEN SEAT BELTS light went out. The jetway rolled forward and bumped against the forward port door with a gentle thump.

They had arrived.

12

There is a place where you can put it while you perform the Clearing of Customs, the voice said. *A safe place. Then, when you are away, you can get it again and take it to this man Balazar.*

People were standing up now, getting things out of the overhead bins and trying to deal with coats which

were, according to the cockpit announcement, too
warm to wear.

*Get your bag. Get your jacket. Then go into the
privy again.*

Pr—

Oh. Bathroom. Head.

*If they think I've got dope they'll think I'm trying to
dump it.*

But Eddie understood that part didn't matter. They
wouldn't exactly break down the door, because that
might scare the passengers. And they'd know you
couldn't flush two pounds of coke down an airline toilet and leave no trace. Not unless the voice was really
telling the truth . . . that there was some safe place.
But how could there be?

Never mind, damn you! MOVE!

Eddie moved. Because he had finally come alive to
the situation. He was not seeing all Roland, with his
many years and his training of mingled torture and
precision, could see, but he could see the faces of the
stews—the *real* faces, the ones behind the smiles and
the helpful passing of garment bags and cartons stowed
in the forward closet. He could see the way their eyes
flicked to him, whiplash quick, again and again.

He got his bag. He got his jacket. The door to the
jetway had been opened, and people were already
moving up the aisle. The door to the cockpit was open,
and here was the Captain, also smiling . . . but also
looking at the passengers in first class who were still
getting their things together, spotting him—no, *target-
ing* him—and then looking away again, nodding to
someone, tousling a youngster's head.

He was cold now. Not cold turkey, just cold. He
didn't need the voice in his head to make him cold.
Cold—sometimes that was okay. You just had to be
careful you didn't get so cold you froze.

Eddie moved forward, reached the point where a

left turn would take him into the jetway—and then suddenly put his hand to his mouth.

"I don't feel well," he murmured. "Excuse me."
He moved the door to the cockpit, which slightly blocked the door to the first class head, and opened the bathroom door on the right.

"I'm afraid you'll have to exit the plane," the pilot said sharply as Eddie opened the bathroom door. "It's—"

"I believe I'm going to vomit, and I don't want to do it on your shoes," Eddie said, "or mine, either."

A second later he was in with the door locked. The Captain was saying something. Eddie couldn't make it out, didn't *want* to make it out. The important thing was that it was just talk, not yelling, he had been right, no one was going to start yelling with maybe two hundred and fifty passengers still waiting to deplane from the single forward door. He was in, he was temporarily safe . . . but what good was it going to do him?

If you're there, he thought, *you better do something very quick, whoever you are.*

For a terrible moment there was nothing at all. That was a short moment, but in Eddie Dean's head it seemed to stretch out almost forever, like the Bonomo's Turkish Taffy Henry had sometimes bought him in the summer when they were kids; if he were bad, Henry beat the shit out of him, if he were good, Henry bought him Turkish Taffy. That was the way Henry handled his heightened responsibilities during summer vacation.

God, oh Christ, I imagined it all, oh Jesus, how crazy could I have b—

Get ready, a grim voice said. *I can't do it alone. I can COME FORWARD but I can't make you COME THROUGH. You have to do it with me. Turn around.*

Eddie was suddenly seeing through two pairs of eyes, feeling with two sets of nerves (but not all the nerves of this other person were here; parts of the other were gone, freshly gone, screaming with pain), sensing with ten senses, thinking with two brains, his blood beating with two hearts.

He turned around. There was a hole in the side of the bathroom, a hole that looked like a doorway. Through it he could see a gray, grainy beach and waves the color of old athletic socks breaking upon it.

He could hear the waves.

He could smell salt, a smell as bitter as tears in his nose.

Go through.

Someone was thumping on the door to the bathroom, telling him to come out, that he must deplane at once.

Go through, damn you!

Eddie, moaning, stepped toward the doorway . . . stumbled . . . and fell into another world.

13

He got slowly to his feet, aware that he had cut his right palm on an edge of shell. He looked stupidly at the blood welling across his lifeline, then saw another man rising slowly to his feet on his right.

Eddie recoiled, his feelings of disorientation and dreamy dislocation suddenly supplanted by sharp terror; this man was dead and didn't know it. His face was gaunt, the skin stretched over the bones of his face like strips of cloth wound around slim angles of metal almost to the point where the cloth must tear itself open. The man's skin was livid save for hectic spots of red high on each cheekbone, on the neck below the angle of jaw on either side, and a single circular mark between the eyes like a child's effort to replicate a Hindu caste symbol.

Yet his eyes—blue, steady, sane—were alive and full

of terrible and tenacious vitality. He wore dark clothes of some homespun material; the shirt, its sleeves rolled up, was a black faded almost to gray, the pants something that looked like bluejeans. Gunbelts crisscrossed his hips, but the loops were almost all empty. The holsters held guns that looked like .45s—but .45s of an incredibly antique vintage. The smooth wood of their handgrips seemed to glow with their own inner light.

Eddie, who didn't know he had any intention of speaking—anything to say—heard himself saying something nevertheless. "Are you a ghost?"

"Not yet," the man with the guns croaked. "The devil-weed. Cocaine. Whatever you call it. Take off your shirt."

"Your arms—" Eddie had seen them. The arms of the man who looked like the extravagant sort of gunslinger one would only see in a spaghetti western were glowing with lines of bright, baleful red. Eddie knew well enough what lines like that meant. They meant blood-poisoning. They meant the devil was doing more than breathing up your ass; he was already crawling up the sewers that led to your pumps.

"Never mind my fucking arms!" the pallid apparition told him. *"Take off your shirt and get rid of it!"*

He heard waves; he heard the lonely hoot of a wind that knew no obstruction; he saw this mad dying man and nothing else but desolation; yet from behind him he heard the murmuring voices of deplaning passengers and a steady muffled pounding.

"Mr. Dean!" *That voice,* he thought, *is in another world.* Not really doubting it; just trying to pound it through his head the way you'd pound a nail through a thick piece of mahogany. "You'll really have to—"

"You can leave it, pick it up later," the gunslinger croaked. "Gods, don't you understand I have to *talk* here? It hurts! *And there is no time, you idiot!"*

There were men Eddie would have killed for using such a word . . . but he had an idea that he might have a job killing this man, even though the man looked like killing might do him good.

Yet he sensed the truth in those blue eyes; all questions were canceled in their mad glare.

Eddie began to unbutton his shirt. His first impulse was to simply tear it off, like Clark Kent while Lois Lane was tied to a railroad track or something, but that was no good in real life; sooner or later you had to explain those missing buttons. So he slipped them through the loops while the pounding behind him went on.

He yanked the shirt out of his jeans, pulled it off, and dropped it, revealing the strapping tape across his chest. He looked like a man in the last stages of recovery from badly fractured ribs.

He snapped a glance behind him and saw an open door . . . its bottom jamb had dragged a fan shape in the gray grit of the beach when someone—the dying man, presumably—had opened it. Through the doorway he saw the first-class head, the basin, the mirror . . . and in it his own desperate face, black hair spilled across his brow and over his hazel eyes. In the background he saw the gunslinger, the beach, and soaring seabirds that screeched and squabbled over God knew what.

He pawed at the tape, wondering how to start, how to find a loose end, and a dazed sort of hopelessness settled over him. This was the way a deer or a rabbit must feel when it got halfway across a country road and turned its head only to be fixated by the oncoming glare of headlights.

It had taken William Wilson, the man whose name Poe had made famous, twenty minutes to strap him up. They would have the door to the first-class bathroom open in five, seven at most.

"I can't get this shit off," he told the swaying man in front of him. "I don't know who you are or where I am, but I'm telling you there's too much tape and too little time."

14

Deere, the co-pilot, suggested Captain McDonald ought to lay off pounding on the door when McDonald, in his frustration at 3A's lack of response, began to do so.

"Where's he going to go?" Deere asked. "What's he going to do? Flush himself down the john? He's too big."

"But if he's carrying—" McDonald began.

Deere, who had himself used cocaine on more than a few occasions, said: "If he's carrying, he's carrying heavy. He can't get rid of it."

"Turn off the water," McDonald snapped suddenly.

"Already have," the navigator (who had also tooted more than his flute on occasion) said. "But I don't think it matters. You can dissolve what goes into the holding tanks but you can't make it not there." They were clustered around the bathroom door, with its OCCUPIED sign glowing jeerily, all of them speaking in low tones. "The DEA guys drain it, draw off a sample, and the guy's hung."

"He could always say someone came in before him and dumped it," McDonald replied. His voice was gaining a raw edge. He didn't want to be talking about this; he wanted to be doing something about it, even though he was acutely aware that the geese were still filing out, many looking with more than ordinary curiosity at the flight-deck crew and stewardesses gathered around the bathroom door. For their part, the crew were acutely aware that an act that was—well, overly overt—could provoke the terrorist boogeyman that now lurked in the back of every air-traveller's mind. McDonald knew his navigator and flight engineer were right, he knew that the stuff was apt to be in plastic bags with the scuzzball's prints on them, and yet he felt alarm bells going off in his mind. Something was not right about this. Something inside of him kept screaming *Fast one! Fast one!* as if the fellow from 3A were a riverboat gambler with palmed aces he was all ready to play.

"He's not trying to flush the john," Susy Douglas said. "He's not even trying to run the basin faucets. We'd hear them sucking air if he was. I hear something, but—"

"Leave," McDonald said curtly. His eyes flicked to Jane Dorning. "You too. We'll take care of this."

Jane turned to go, cheeks burning.

Susy said quietly: "Jane bird-dogged him and I spotted the bulges under his shirt. I think we'll stay, Captain McDonald. If you want to bring charges of insubordination, you can. But I want you to remember that you may be raping the *hell* out of what could be a really big DEA bust."

Their eyes locked, flint sparking off steel.

Susy said, "I've flown with you seventy, eighty times, Mac. I'm trying to be your friend."

McDonald looked at her a moment longer, then nodded. "Stay, then. But I want both of you back a step toward the cockpit."

He stood on his toes, looked back, and saw the end of the line now just emerging from tourist class into business. Two minutes, maybe three.

He turned to the gate agent at the mouth of the hatch, who was watching them closely. He must have sensed some sort of problem, because he had unholstered his walkie-talkie and was holding it in his hand.

"Tell him I want customs agents up here," McDonald said quietly to the navigator. "Three or four. Armed. Now."

The navigator made his way through the line of passengers, excusing himself with an easy grin, and spoke quietly to the gate agent, who raised his walkie-talkie to his mouth and spoke quietly into it.

McDonald—who had never put anything stronger than aspirin into his system in his entire life and that only rarely—turned to Deere. His lips were pressed into a thin white line like a scar.

"As soon as the last of the passengers are off, we're breaking that shithouse door open," he said. "I don't care if Customs is here or not. Do you understand?"

"Roger," Deere said, and watched the tail of the line make its way into first class.

15

"Get my knife," the gunslinger said. "It's in my purse."

He gestured toward a cracked leather bag lying on the sand. It looked more like a big packsack than a purse, the kind of thing you expected to see hippies carrying as they made their way along the Appalachian trail, getting high on nature (and maybe a bomber joint every now and then), except this looked like the real thing, not just a prop for some airhead's self-image; something that had done years and years of hard—maybe desperate—travelling.

Gestured, but did not point. *Couldn't* point. Eddie realized why the man had a swatch of dirty shirting wrapped around his right hand: some of his fingers were gone.

"Get it," he said. "Cut through the tape. Try not to cut yourself. It's easy to do. You'll have to be careful, but you'll have to move fast just the same. There isn't much time."

''I know that,'' Eddie said, and knelt on the sand. None of this was real. That was it, that was the answer. As Henry Dean, the great sage and eminent junkie would have put it, *Flip-flop, hippety-hop, offa your rocker and over the top, life's a fiction and the world's a lie, so put on some Creedence and let's get high.*

None of it was real, it was all just an extraordinarily vivid nodder, so the best thing was just to ride low and go with the flow.

It sure *was* a vivid nodder. He was reaching for the zipper—or maybe it would be a velcro strip—on the man's ''purse'' when he saw it was held together by a crisscross pattern of rawhide thongs, some of which had broken and been carefully reknotted—reknotted small enough so they would still slide through the grommetted eyelets.

Eddie pulled the drag-knot at the top, spread the bag's opening, and found the knife beneath a slightly damp package that was the piece of shirting tied around the bullets. Just the handle was enough to take his breath away . . . it was the true mellow gray-white of pure silver, engraved with a complex series of patterns that caught the eye, drew it—

Pain exploded in his ear, roared across his head, and momentarily puffed a red cloud across his vision. He fell clumsily over the open purse, struck the sand, and looked up at the pale man in the cut-down boots. This was no nodder. The blue eyes blazing from that dying face were the eyes of all truth.

''Admire it later, prisoner,'' the gunslinger said. ''For now just use it.''

He could feel his ear throbbing, swelling.

''Why do you keep calling me that?''

''Cut the tape,'' the gunslinger said grimly. ''If they break into yon privy while you're still over here, I've got a feeling you're going to be here for a very long time. And with a corpse for company before long.''

Eddie pulled the knife out of the scabbard. Not old; more than old, more than ancient. The blade, honed almost to the point of invisibility, seemed to be all age caught in metal.

''Yeah, it looks sharp,'' he said, and his voice wasn't steady.

16

The last passengers were filing out into the jetway. One of them, a lady of some seventy summers with that exquisite look of confusion which only first-time fliers with too many years or too little English seem capable of wearing, stopped to show Jane Dorning her tickets. ''How will I *ever* find my plane to Montreal?'' she asked. ''And what about my bags? Do they do my Customs here or there?''

''There will be a gate agent at the top of the jetway who can give you all the information you need, ma'am,'' Jane said.

''Well, I don't see why *you* can't give me the information I need,'' the old woman said. ''That jetway thing is still full of people.''

''Move on, please, madam,'' Captain McDonald said. ''We have a problem.''

''Well, pardon me for living,'' the old woman said huffily, ''I guess I just fell off the hearse!''

And strode past them, nose tilted like the nose of a dog scenting a fire still some distance away, tote-bag clutched in one hand, ticket-folder (with so many boarding-pass stubs sticking out of it that one might have been tempted to believe the lady had come most of the way around the globe, changing planes at every stop along the way) in the other.

"There's a lady who may never fly Delta's big jets again," Susy murmured.

"I don't give a fuck if she flies stuffed down the front of Superman's Jockies," McDonald said. "She the last?"

Jane darted past them, glanced at the seats in business class, then poked her head into the main cabin. It was deserted.

She came back and reported the plane empty.

McDonald turned to the jetway and saw two uniformed Customs agents fighting their way through the crowd, excusing themselves but not bothering to look back at the people they jostled aside. The last of these was the old lady, who dropped her ticket-folder. Papers flew and fluttered everywhere and she shrilled after them like an angry crow.

"Okay," McDonald said, "you guys stop right there."

"Sir, we're Federal Customs officers—"

"That's right, and I requested you, and I'm glad you came so fast. Now you just stand right there because this is my plane and that guy in there is one of my geese. Once he's off the plane and into the jetway, he's your goose and you can cook him any way you want." He nodded to Deere. "I'm going to give the son of a bitch one more chance and then we're going to break the door in."

"Okay by me," Deere said.

McDonald whacked on the bathroom door with the heel of his hand and yelled, "Come on out, my friend! I'm done asking!"

There was no answer.

"Okay," McDonald said. "Let's do it."

17

Dimly, Eddie heard an old woman say: "Well, pardon me for living! I guess I just fell off the hearse!"

He had parted half the strapping tape. When the old woman spoke his hand jerked a little and he saw a trickle of blood run down his belly.

"Shit," Eddie said.

"It can't be helped now," the gunslinger said in his hoarse voice. "Finish the job. Or does the sight of blood make you sick?"

"Only when it's my own," Eddie said. The tape had started just above his belly. The higher he cut the harder it got to see. He got another three inches or so, and almost cut himself again when he heard McDonald speaking to the Customs agents: "Okay, you guys stop right there."

"I can finish and maybe cut myself wide open or you can try," Eddie said. "I can't see what I'm doing. My fucking chin's in the way."

The gunslinger took the knife in his left hand. The hand was shaking. Watching that blade, honed to a suicidal sharpness, shaking like that made Eddie extremely nervous.

"Maybe I better chance it mys—"

"Wait."

The gunslinger stared fixedly at his left hand. Eddie didn't exactly disbelieve in telepathy, but he had never exactly *believed* in it, either. Nevertheless, he felt something now, something as real and palpable as heat baking out of an oven. After a few seconds he realized what it was: the gathering of this strange man's will.

How the hell can he be dying if I can feel the force of him that strongly?

The shaking hand began to steady down. Soon it was barely shivering. After no more than ten seconds it was as solid as a rock.

"Now," the gunslinger said. He took a step forward, raised the knife, and Eddie felt something else baking off him—rancid fever.

"Are you left-handed?" Eddie asked.

"No," the gunslinger said.

"Oh Jesus," Eddie said, and decided he might feel better if he closed his eyes for a moment. He heard the harsh whisper of the masking tape parting.

"There," the gunslinger said, stepping back. "Now pull it off as far as you can. I'll get the back."

No polite little knocks on the bathroom door now; this was a hammering fist. *The passengers are out,* Eddie thought. *No more Mr. Nice Guy. Oh shit.*

"Come on out, my friend! I'm done asking!"

"Yank it!" the gunslinger growled.

Eddie grabbed a thick tab of strapping tape in each hand and yanked as hard as he could. It hurt, hurt like hell. *Stop bellyaching,* he thought. *Things could be worse. You could be hairy-chested, like Henry.*

He looked down and saw a red band of irritated skin about seven inches wide across his sternum. Just above the solar plexus was the place where he had poked himself. Blood welled in a dimple and ran down to his navel in a scarlet runnel. Beneath his armpits, the bags of dope now dangled like badly tied saddlebags.

"Okay," the muffled voice beyond the bathroom door said to someone else. "Let's d—"

Eddie lost the rest of it in the unexpected riptide of pain across his back as the gunslinger unceremoniously tore the rest of the girdle from him.

He bit down against a scream.

"Put your shirt on," the gunslinger said. His face, which Eddie had thought as pallid as the face of a living man could become, was now the color of ancient ashes. He held the girdle of tape (now sticking to itself in a meaningless tangle, the big bags of white stuff looking like strange cocoons) in his left hand,

then tossed it aside. Eddie saw fresh blood seeping
through the makeshift bandage on the gunslinger's right
hand. "Do it fast."

There was a thudding sound. This wasn't someone
pounding for admittance. Eddie looked up in time to
see the bathroom door shudder, to see the lights in
there flicker. They were trying to break it in.

He picked his shirt up with fingers that suddenly
seemed too large, too clumsy. The left sleeve was
turned inside out. He tried to stuff it back through the
hole, got his hand stuck for a moment, then yanked it
out so hard he pulled the sleeve back again with it.

Thud, and the bathroom door shivered again.

"Gods, how can you be so clumsy?" the gunslinger
moaned, and rammed his own fist into the left sleeve
of Eddie's shirt. Eddie grabbed the cuff as the gunslinger pulled back. Now the gunslinger held the shirt
for him as a butler might hold a coat for his master.
Eddie put it on and groped for the lowest button.

"Not yet!" the gunslinger barked, and tore another
piece away from his own diminishing shirt. "Wipe
your gut!"

Eddie did the best he could. The dimple where the
knife had actually pierced his skin was still welling
blood. The blade was sharp, all right. Sharp enough.

He dropped the bloody wad of the gunslinger's shirt
on the sand and buttoned his shirt.

Thud. This time the door did more than shudder; it
buckled in its frame. Looking through the doorway on
the beach, Eddie saw the bottle of liquid soap fall from
where it had been standing beside the basin. It landed
on his zipper bag.

He had meant to stuff his shirt, which was now buttoned (and buttoned straight, for a wonder), into his
pants. Suddenly a better idea struck him. He unbuckled his belt instead.

"There's no time for that!" The gunslinger realized

he was trying to scream and was unable. "That door's only got one hit left in it!"

"I know what I'm doing," Eddie said, hoping he did, and stepped back through the doorway between the worlds, unsnapping his jeans and raking the zipper down as he went.

After one desperate, despairing moment, the gunslinger followed him, physical and full of hot physical ache at one moment, nothing but cool *ka* in Eddie's head at the next.

18

"One more," McDonald said grimly, and Deere nodded. Now that all the passengers were out of the jetway as well as the plane itself, the Customs agents had drawn their weapons.

"Now!"

The two men drove forward and hit the door together. It flew open, a chunk of it hanging for a moment from the lock and then dropping to the floor.

And there sat Mr. 3A, with his pants around his knees and the tails of his faded paisley shirt concealing—barely—his jackhandle. *Well, it sure does look like we caught him in the act,* Captain McDonald thought wearily. *Only trouble is, the act we caught him in wasn't against the law, last I heard.* Suddenly he could feel the throb in his shoulder where he had hit the door—what? three times? four?

Out loud he barked, "What in hell's name are you doing in there, mister?"

"Well, I *was* taking a crap," 3A said, "but if *all* you guys got a bad problem, I guess I could wipe myself in the terminal—"

"And I suppose you didn't hear us, smart guy?"

"Couldn't reach the door." 3A put out his hand to demonstrate, and although the door was now hanging askew against the wall to his left, McDonald could see his point. "I suppose I could have gotten up, but I, like, had a desperate situation on my hands. Except it wasn't exactly on my *hands*, if you get my drift. Nor did I *want* it on my hands, if you catch my *further* drift." 3A smiled a winning, slightly daffy smile which looked to Captain McDonald approximately as real as a nine-dollar bill. Listening to him, you'd think no one had ever taught him the simple trick of leaning forward.

"Get up," McDonald said.

"Be happy to. If you could just move the ladies back a little?" 3A smiled charmingly. "I know it's outdated in this day and age, but I can't help it. I'm modest. Fact is, I've got a lot to be modest about." He held up his left hand, thumb and forefinger roughly half an inch apart, and winked at Jane Dorning, who blushed bright red and immediately disappeared up the jetway, closely followed by Susy.

You don't look *modest,* Captain McDonald thought. *You* look *like a cat that just got the cream, that's what you look like.*

When the stews were out of sight, 3A stood and pulled up his shorts and jeans. He then reached for the flush button and Captain McDonald promptly knocked his hand away, grabbed his shoulders, and pivoted him toward the aisle. Deere hooked a restraining hand into the back of his pants.

"Don't get personal," Eddie said. His voice was light and just right—he thought so, anyway—but inside everything was in free fall. He could feel that other, feel him clearly. He was inside his mind, watching him closely, standing steady, meaning to move in if Eddie fucked up. God, it all had to be a dream, didn't it? *Didn't* it?

"Stand still," Deere said.

Captain McDonald peered into the toilet.

"No shit," he said, and when the navigator let out a bray of involuntary laughter, McDonald glared at him.

"Well, you know how it is," Eddie said. "Sometimes you get lucky and it's just a false alarm. I let off a couple of real rippers, though. I mean, we're talking swamp gas. If you'd lit a match in here three minutes ago, you could have roasted a Thanksgiving turkey, you know? It must have been something I ate before I got on the plane, I g—"

"Get rid of him," McDonald said, and Deere, still holding Eddie by the back of the pants, propelled him out of the plane and into the jetway, where each Customs officer took one arm.

"Hey!" Eddie cried. "I want my bag! And I want my jacket!"

"Oh, we want you to have *all* your stuff," one of the officers said. His breath, heavy with the smell of Maalox and stomach acid, puffed against Eddie's face. "We're very interested in your stuff. Now let's go, little buddy."

Eddie kept telling them to take it easy, mellow out, he could walk just fine, but he thought later the tips of his shoes only touched the floor of the jetway three or four times between the 727's hatch and the exit to the terminal, where three more Customs officers and half a dozen airport security cops stood, the Customs guys waiting for Eddie, the cops holding back a small crowd that stared at him with uneasy, avid interest as he was led away.

CHAPTER 4
THE TOWER

1

Eddie Dean was sitting in a chair. The chair was in a small white room. It was the only chair in the small white room. The small white room was crowded. The small white room was smoky. Eddie was in his underpants. Eddie wanted a cigarette. The other six—no, seven—men in the small white room were dressed. The other men were standing around him, enclosing him. Three—no, four—of them were smoking cigarettes.

Eddie wanted to jitter and jive. Eddie wanted to hop and bop.

Eddie sat still, relaxed, looking at the men around him with amused interest, as if he wasn't going crazy for a fix, as if he wasn't going crazy from simple claustrophobia.

The *other* in his mind was the reason why. He had been terrified of the *other* at first. Now he thanked God the *other* was there.

The *other* might be sick, dying even, but there was enough steel left in his spine for him to have some left to loan this scared twenty-one-year-old junkie.

"That is a very interesting red mark on your chest," one of the Customs men said. A cigarette hung from the corner of his mouth. There was a pack in his shirt pocket. Eddie felt as if he could take about five of the cigarettes in that pack, line his mouth with them from corner to corner, light them all, inhale deeply, and be easier in his mind. "It looks like a stripe. It looks like

96

you had something taped there, Eddie, and all at once decided it would be a good idea to rip it off and get rid of it.''

"I picked up an allergy in the Bahamas," Eddie said. "I told you that. I mean, we've been through all of this several times. I'm trying to keep my sense of humor, but it's getting harder all the time.''

"Fuck your sense of humor," another said savagely, and Eddie recognized that tone. It was the way he himself sounded when he'd spent half a night in the cold waiting for the man and the man didn't come. Because these guys were junkies, too. The only difference was guys like him and Henry were their junk.

"What about that hole in your gut? Where'd that come from, Eddie? Publishers' Clearing House?" A third agent was pointing at the spot where Eddie had poked himself. It had finally stopped dribbling but there was still a dark purple bubble there which looked more than ready to break open at the slightest urging.

Eddie indicated the red band where the tape had been. "It itches," he said. This was no lie. "I fell asleep on the plane—check the stew if you don't believe me—"

"Why wouldn't we believe you, Eddie?"

"I don't know," Eddie said. "Do you usually get big drug smugglers who snooze on their way in?" He paused, gave them a second to think about it, then held out his hands. Some of the nails were ragged. Others were jagged. When you went cool turkey, he had discovered, your nails suddenly became your favorite munchies. "I've been pretty good about not scratching, but I must have dug myself a damned good one while I was sleeping.''

"Or while you were on the nod. That could be a needlemark." Eddie could see they both knew better. You shot yourself up that close to the solar plexus, which was the nervous system's switchboard, you weren't ever going to shoot yourself up again.

"Give me a break," Eddie said. "You were in my face so close to look at my pupils I thought you were going to soul-kiss me. You know I wasn't on the nod."

The third Customs agent looked disgusted. "For an innocent lambikins, you know an awful lot about dope, Eddie."

"What I didn't pick up on *Miami Vice* I got from *The Reader's Digest.* Now tell me the truth—how many times are we going to go through this?"

A fourth agent held up a small plastic Baggie. In it were several fibers.

"These are filaments. We'll get the lab confirmation, but we know what sort they are. They're filaments of strapping tape."

"I didn't take a shower before I left the hotel," Eddie said for the fourth time. "I was out by the pool, getting some sun. Trying to get rid of the rash. The *allergy* rash. I fell asleep. I was damned lucky to make the plane at all. I had to run like hell. The wind was blowing. I don't know what stuck to my skin and what didn't."

Another reached out and ran a finger up the three inches of flesh from the inner bend of Eddie's left elbow.

"And these aren't needle tracks."

Eddie shoved the hand away. "Mosquito bites. I told you. Almost healed. Jesus Christ, you can see that for yourself!"

They could. This deal hadn't come up overnight. Eddie had stopped arm-popping a month ago. Henry couldn't have done that, and that was one of the reasons it had been Eddie, *had* to be Eddie. When he absolutely *had* to fix, he had taken it very high on his upper left thigh, where his left testicle lay against the skin of the leg . . . as he had the other night, when the sallow thing had finally brought him some stuff that was okay. Mostly he had just snorted, something with which Henry could no longer content himself. This caused feelings Eddie couldn't exactly define . . . a mixture of pride and shame. If they looked there, if they pushed his testicles aside, he could have some serious problems. A blood-test could cause him problems even more serious, but that was one step further than they could go without some sort of evidence—and evidence was something they just didn't have. They knew everything but could prove nothing. All the difference between world and want, his dear old mother would have said.

"Mosquito bites."

"Yes."

"And the red mark's an allergic reaction."

"Yes. I had it when I went to the Bahamas; it just wasn't that bad."

"He had it when he went down there," one of the men said to another.

"Uh-huh," the second said. "You believe it?"

"Sure."

"You believe in Santa Claus?"

"Sure. When I was a kid I even had my picture taken with him once." He looked at Eddie. "You got a picture of this famous red mark from before you took your little trip, Eddie?"

Eddie didn't reply.

"If you're clean, why won't you take a blood-test?" This was the first guy again, the guy with the cigarette in the corner of his mouth. It had almost burned down to the filter.

Eddie was suddenly angry—white-hot angry. He listened inside.

Okay, the voice responded at once, and Eddie felt more than agreement, he felt a kind of go-to-the-wall approval. It made him feel the way he felt when Henry hugged him, tousled his hair, punched him on the shoulder, and said *You done good, kid—don't let it go to your head, but you done good.*

"You *know* I'm clean." He stood up suddenly—so suddenly they moved back. He looked at the smoker who was closest to him. "And I'll tell you something, babe, if you don't get that coffin-nail out of my face I'm going to *knock* it out."

The guy recoiled.

"You guys have emptied the crap-tank on that plane already. God, you've had enough time to have been through it three times. You've been through my stuff. I bent over and let one of you stick the world's longest finger up my ass. If a prostate check is an exam, that was a motherfucking safari. I was scared to look down. I thought I'd see that guy's fingernail sticking out of my *cock.*"

He glared around at them.

"You've been up my ass, you've been through my stuff, and I'm sitting here in a pair of Jockies with you guys blowing smoke in my face. You want a blood-test? Kay. Bring in someone to do it."

They murmured, looked at each other. Surprised. Uneasy.

"But if you want to do it without a court order," Eddie said, "whoever does it better bring a lot of extra hypos and vials, because I'll be damned if I'm gonna piss alone. I want a Federal marshal in here, and I want each one of you to take the same goddam test, and I want your names and IDs on each vial, and I want them to go into that Federal marshal's custody. And whatever you test mine for—cocaine, heroin, bennies, pot, whatever—I want those same tests performed on the samples from you guys. And then I want the results turned over to my lawyer."

"Oh boy, YOUR LAWYER," one of them cried. "That's what it always comes down to with you shit-bags, doesn't it, Eddie? You'll hear from MY LAW-YER. I'll sic MY LAWYER on you. That crap makes me want to *puke!*"

"As a matter of fact I don't currently have one," Eddie said, and this was the truth. "I didn't think I needed one. You guys changed my mind. You got nothing because I *have* nothing, but the rock and roll just doesn't stop, does it? So you want me to dance? Great. I'll dance. But I'm not gonna do it alone. You guys'll have to dance, too."

There was a thick, difficult silence.

"I'd like you to take down your shorts again, please, Mr. Dean," one of them said. This guy was older. This guy looked like he was in charge of things. Eddie thought that maybe—just maybe—this guy had finally realized where the fresh tracks might be. Until now they hadn't checked. His arms, his shoulders, his legs . . . but not there. They had been too sure they had a bust.

"I'm through taking things off, taking things down, and eating this shit," Eddie said. "You get someone in here and we'll do a bunch of blood-tests or I'm getting out. Now which do you want?"

That silence again. And when they started looking at each other, Eddie knew he had won.

WE *won*, he amended. *What's your name, fella?*

Roland. Yours is Eddie. Eddie Dean.

You listen good.

Listen and watch.

"Give him his clothes," the older man said disgustedly. He looked at Eddie. "I don't know what you had or how you got rid of it, but I want you to know that we're going to find out."

The old dude surveyed him.

"So there you sit. There you sit, almost grinning. What you say doesn't make me want to puke. What you *are* does."

"I make *you* want to puke."

"That's affirmative."

"Oh, boy," Eddie said. "I love it. I'm sitting here in a little room and I've got nothing on but my underwear and there's seven guys around me with guns on their hips and *I* make *you* want to puke? Man, you have got a problem."

Eddie took a step toward him. The Customs guy held his ground for a moment, and then something in Eddie's eyes—a crazy color that seemed half-hazel, half-blue—made him step back against his will.

"I'M NOT CARRYING!" Eddie roared. *"QUIT NOW! JUST QUIT! LET ME ALONE!"*

The silence again. Then the older man turned around and yelled at someone, "Didn't you hear me? *Get his clothes!"*

And that was that.

2

"You think we're being tailed?" the cabbie asked. He sounded amused.

Eddie turned forward. "Why do you say that?"

"You keep looking out the back window."

"I never thought about being tailed," Eddie said. This was the absolute truth. He had seen the tails the first time he looked around. *Tails,* not tail. He didn't have to keep looking around to confirm their presence. Out-patients from a sanitarium for the mentally retarded would have trouble losing Eddie's cab on this late May afternoon; traffic on the L.I.E. was sparse. "I'm a student of traffic patterns, that's all."

"Oh," the cabbie said. In some circles such an odd statement would have prompted questions, but New York cab drivers rarely question; instead they assert, usually in a grand manner. Most of these assertions begin with the phrase *This city!* as if the words were a religious invocation preceeding a sermon . . . which they usually were. Instead, this one said: "Because if you *did* think we were being tailed, we're not. I'd know. This city! Jesus! I've tailed plenty of people in my time. You'd be surprised how many people jump into my cab and say 'Follow that car.' I know, sounds like something you only hear in the movies, right? Right. But like they say, art imitates life and life imitates art. It really happens! And as for shaking a tail, it's easy if you know how to set the guy up. You . . ."

Eddie tuned the cabbie down to a background drone, listening just enough so he could nod in the right places. When you thought about it, the cabbie's rap was actually quite amusing. One of the tails was a dark blue sedan. Eddie guessed that one belonged to Customs. The other was a panel truck with GINEL-LI'S PIZZA written on the sides. There was also a picture of a pizza, only the pizza was a smiling boy's face, and the smiling boy was smacking his lips, and written under the picture was the slogan *"UMMMMM! It's-a GOOOOD Pizza!"* Only some young urban artist with a spray-can and a rudimentary sense of humor had drawn a line through *Pizza* and had printed *PUSSY* above it.

Ginelli. There was only one Ginelli Eddie knew; he ran a restaurant called Four Fathers. The pizza business was a sideline, a guaranteed stiff, an accountant's angel. Ginelli and Balazar. They went together like hot dogs and mustard.

According to the original plan, there was to have been a limo waiting outside the terminal with a driver ready to whisk him away to Balazar's place of business, which was a midtown saloon. But of course the original plan hadn't included two hours in a little white room, two hours of steady questioning from one bunch of Customs agents while another bunch first drained and then raked the contents of Flight 901's wastetanks, looking for the big carry they also suspected, the big carry that would be unflushable, undissolvable.

When he came out, there was no limo, of course. The driver would have had his instructions: if the mule isn't out of the terminal fifteen minutes or so after the rest of the passengers have come out, drive away fast. The limo driver would know better than to use the car's telephone, which was actually a radio that could easily be monitored. Balazar would call people, find out Eddie had struck trouble, and get ready for trouble of his own. Balazar might have recognized Eddie's steel, but that didn't change the fact that Eddie was a junkie. A junkie could not be relied upon to be a stand-up guy.

This meant there was a possibility that the pizza truck just might pull up in the lane next to the taxi, someone just might stick an automatic weapon out of the pizza truck's window, and then the back of the cab would become something that looked like a bloody cheese-grater. Eddie would have been more worried about that if they held him for four hours instead of two, and seriously worried if it had been six hours instead of four. But only two . . . he thought Balazar would trust him to have hung on to his lip at least that long. He would want to know about his goods.

The real reason Eddie kept looking back was the door.

It fascinated him.

As the Customs agents had half-carried, half-dragged him down the stairs to Kennedy's administration section, he had looked back over his shoulder and there it had been, improbable but indubitably, inarguably real, floating along at a distance of about three feet. He could see the waves rolling steadily in, crashing on the sand; he saw that the day over there was beginning to darken.

The door was like one of those trick pictures with a

hidden image in them, it seemed; you couldn't see that hidden part for the life of you at first, but once you had, you couldn't unsee it, no matter how hard you tried.

It had disappeared on the two occasions when the gunslinger went back without him, and that had been scary—Eddie had felt like a child whose nightlight has burned out. The first time had been during the customs interrogation.

I have to go, Roland's voice had cut cleanly through whatever question they were currently throwing at him. *I'll only be a few moments. Don't be afraid.*

Why? Eddie asked. *Why do you have to go?*

"What's wrong?" one of the Customs guys had asked him. "All of a sudden you look scared."

All of a sudden he had *felt* scared, but of nothing this yo-yo would understand.

He looked over his shoulder, and the Customs men had also turned. They saw nothing but a blank white wall covered with white panels drilled with holes to damp sound; Eddie saw the door, its usual three feet away (now it was embedded in the room's wall, an escape hatch none of his interrogators could see). He saw more. He saw *things* coming out of the waves, *things* that looked like refugees from a horror movie where the effects are just a little more special than you want them to be, special enough so everything looks real. They looked like a hideous cross-breeding of prawn, lobster, and spider. They were making some weird sound.

"You getting the jim-jams?" one of the Customs guys had asked. "Seeing a few bugs crawling down the wall, Eddie?"

That was so close to the truth that Eddie had almost laughed. He understood why the man named Roland had to go back, though; Roland's mind was safe enough—at least for the time being—but the creatures were moving toward his body, and Eddie had a suspicion that if Roland did not soon vacate it from the area it currently occupied, there might not be any body left to go back to.

Suddenly in his head he heard David Lee Roth bawling: *Oh Iyyyyy . . . ain't got nobody . . .* and this time he *did* laugh. He couldn't help it.

"What's so funny?" the Customs agent who had wanted to know if he was seeing bugs asked him.

"This whole situation," Eddie had responded. "Only in the sense of peculiar, not hilarious. I mean, if it was a movie it would be more like Fellini than Woody Allen, if you get what I mean."

You'll be all right? Roland asked.

Yeah, fine. TCB, man.

I don't understand.

Go take care of business.

Oh. All right. I'll not be long.

And suddenly that *other* had been gone. Simply gone. Like a wisp of smoke so thin that the slightest vagary of wind could blow it away. Eddie looked around again, saw nothing but drilled white panels, no door, no ocean, no weird monstrosities, and he felt his gut begin to tighten. There was no question of believing that it had all been a hallucination after all; the dope was gone, and that was all the proof Eddie needed. But Roland had . . . helped, somehow. Made it easier.

"You want me to hang a picture there?" one of the Customs guys asked.

"No," Eddie said, and blew out a sigh. "I want you to let me *out* of here."

"Soon as you tell us what you did with the skag," another said, "or was it coke?" And so it started again: round and round she goes and where she stops nobody knows.

Ten minutes later—ten very *long* minutes—Roland

was suddenly back in his mind. One second gone, next second there. Eddie sensed he was deeply exhausted.

Taken care of? he asked.

Yes. I'm sorry it took so long. A pause. *I had to crawl.*

Eddie looked around again. The doorway had returned, but now it offered a slightly different view of that world, and he realized that, as it moved with him here, it moved with Roland there. The thought made him shiver a little. It was like being tied to this other by some weird umbilicus. The gunslinger's body lay collapsed in front of it as before, but now he was looking down a long stretch of beach to the braided high-tide line where the monsters wandered about, growling and buzzing. Each time a wave broke all of them raised their claws. They looked like the audiences in those old documentary films where Hitler's speaking and everyone is throwing that old *seig heil!* salute like their lives depended on it—which they probably did, when you thought about it. Eddie could see the tortured markings of the gunslinger's progress in the sand.

As Eddie watched, one of the horrors reached up, lightning quick, and snared a sea-bird which happened to swoop too close to the beach. The thing fell to the sand in two bloody, spraying chunks. The parts were covered by the shelled horrors even before they had stopped twitching. A single white feather drifted up. A claw snatched it down.

Holy Christ, Eddie thought numbly. *Look at those snappers.*

"*Why* do you keep looking back there?" the guy in charge had asked.

"From time to time I need an antidote," Eddie said.

"From what?"

"Your face."

3

The cab-driver dropped Eddie at the building in Co-Op City, thanked him for the dollar tip, and drove off. Eddie just stood for a moment, zipper bag in one hand, his jacket hooked over a finger of the other and slung back over his shoulder. Here he shared a two-bedroom apartment with his brother. He stood for a moment looking up at it, a monolith with all the style and taste of a brick Saltines box. The many windows made it look like a prison cellblock to Eddie, and he found the view as depressing as Roland—the *other*—did amazing.

Never, even as a child, did I see a building so high, Roland said. *And there are so many of them!*

Yeah, Eddie agreed. *We live like a bunch of ants in a hill. It may look good to you, but I'll tell you, Roland, it gets old. It gets old in a hurry.*

The blue car cruised by; the pizza truck turned in and approached. Eddie stiffened and felt Roland stiffen inside him. Maybe they intended to blow him away after all.

The door? Roland asked. *Shall we go through? Do you wish it?* Eddie sensed Roland was ready—for anything—but the voice was calm.

Not yet, Eddie said. *Could be they only want to talk. But be ready.*

He sensed that was an unnecessary thing to say; he sensed that Roland was readier to move and act in his deepest sleep than Eddie would ever be in his most wide-awake moment.

The pizza truck with the smiling kid on the side closed in. The passenger window rolled down and Eddie waited outside the entrance to his building with his shadow trailing out long in front of him from the toes of his sneakers, waiting to see which it would be—a face or a gun.

4

The second time Roland left him had been no more than five minutes after the Customs people had finally given up and let Eddie go.

The gunslinger had eaten, but not enough; he needed to drink; most of all he needed medicine. Eddie couldn't yet help him with the medicine Roland really needed (although he suspected the gunslinger was right and Balazar could . . . if Balazar wanted to), but simple aspirin might at least knock down the fever that Eddie had felt when the gunslinger stepped close to sever the top part of the tape girdle. He paused in front of the newsstand in the main terminal.

Do you have aspirin where you come from?

I have never heard of it. Is it magic or medicine?

Both, I guess.

Eddie went into the newsstand and bought a tin of Extra-Strength Anacin. He went over to the snack bar and bought a couple of foot-long dogs and an extra-large Pepsi. He was putting mustard and catsup on the franks (Henry called the foot-longs Godzilla-dogs) when he suddenly remembered this stuff wasn't for him. For all he knew, Roland might be a veggie. For all he knew, this crap might kill Roland.

Well, too late now, Eddie thought. When Roland spoke—when Roland *acted*—Eddie knew all this was really happening. When he was quiet, that giddy feeling that it must be a dream—an extraordinarily vivid dream he was having as he slept on Delta 901 inbound to Kennedy—insisted on creeping back.

Roland had told him he could carry the food into his own world. He had already done something similar once, he said, when Eddie was asleep. Eddie found it all but impossible to believe, but Roland assured him it was true.

Well, we still have to be damned careful, Eddie said.

They've got two Customs guys watching me. Us. Whatever the hell I am now.

I know we have to be careful, Roland returned. *There aren't two; there are five.* Eddie suddenly felt one of the weirdest sensations of his entire life. He did not move his eyes but felt them *moved. Roland* moved them.

A guy in a muscle shirt talking into a telephone.

A woman sitting on a bench, rooting through her purse.

A young black guy who would have been spectacularly handsome except for the harelip which surgery had only partially repaired, looking at the tee-shirts in the newsstand Eddie had come from not long since.

There was nothing wrong about any of them on top, but Eddie recognized them for what they were nonetheless and it was like seeing those hidden images in a child's puzzle, which, once seen, could never be unseen. He felt dull heat in his cheeks, because it had taken the *other* to point out what he should have seen at once. He had spotted only two. These three were a little better, but not that much; the eyes of the phoneman weren't blank, imagining the person he was talking to but aware, actually *looking,* and the place where Eddie was . . . that was the place to which the phoneman's eyes just happened to keep returning. The pursewoman didn't find what she wanted or give up but simply went on rooting endlessly. And the shopper had had a chance to look at every shirt on the spindlerack at least a dozen times.

All of a sudden Eddie felt five again, afraid to cross the street without Henry to hold his hand.

Never mind, Roland said. *And don't worry about the food, either. I've eaten bugs while they were still lively enough for some of them to go running down my throat.*

Yeah, Eddie replied, *but this is New York.*

He took the dogs and the soda to the far end of the

counter and stood with his back to the terminal's main concourse. Then he glanced up in the left-hand corner. A convex mirror bulged there like a hypertensive eye. He could see all of his followers in it, but none was close enough to see the food and cup of soda, and that was good, because Eddie didn't have the slightest idea what was going to happen to it.

Put the astin on the meat-things. Then hold everything in your hands.

Aspirin.

Good. Call it flutergork if you want, pr . . . Eddie. Just do it.

He took the Anacin out of the stapled bag he had stuffed in his pocket, almost put it down on one of the hot-dogs, and suddenly realized that Roland would have problems just getting what Eddie thought of as the poison-proofing—off the tin, let alone opening it.

He did it himself, shook three of the pills onto one of the napkins, debated, then added three more.

Three now, three later, he said. *If there is a later.*

All right. Thank you.

Now what?

Hold all of it.

Eddie had glanced into the convex mirror again. Two of the agents were strolling casually toward the snack-bar, maybe not liking the way Eddie's back was turned, maybe smelling a little prestidigitation in progress and wanting a closer look. If something was going to happen, it better happen quick.

He put his hands around everything, feeling the heat of the dogs in their soft white rolls, the chill of the Pepsi. In that moment he looked like a guy getting ready to carry a snack back to his kids . . . and then the stuff started to *melt.*

He stared down, eyes widening, widening, until it felt to him that they must soon fall out and dangle by their stalks.

He could see the hotdogs through the rolls. He could
see the Pepsi through the cup, the ice-choked liquid
curving to conform to a shape which could no longer
be seen.

Then he could see the red Formica counter through
the foot-longs and the white wall through the Pepsi.
His hands slid toward each other, the resistance between them growing less and less . . . and then they
closed against each other, palm to palm. The food . . .
the napkins . . . the Pepsi Cola . . . the six Anacin
. . . all the things which had been between his hands
were gone.

Jesus jumped up and played the fiddle, Eddie thought
numbly. He flicked his eyes up toward the convex mirror.

The doorway was gone . . . just as Roland was gone
from his mind.

Eat hearty, my friend, Eddie thought . . . but *was*
this weird alien presence that called itself Roland his
friend? That was far from proved, wasn't it? He had
saved Eddie's bacon, true enough, but that didn't mean
he was a Boy Scout.

All the same, *he* liked Roland. Feared him . . . but
liked him as well.

Suspected that in time he could love him, as he loved
Henry.

Eat well, stranger, he thought. *Eat well, stay alive
. . . and come back.*

Close by were a few mustard-stained napkins left by
a previous customer. Eddie balled them up, tossed
them in the trash-barrel by the door on his way out,
and chewed air as if finishing a last bite of something.
He was even able to manufacture a burp as he approached the black guy on his way toward the signs
pointing the way to LUGGAGE and GROUND
TRANSPORTATION.

"Couldn't find a shirt you liked?" Eddie asked.

"I beg your pardon?" the black guy turned from the American Airlines departures monitor he was pretending to study.

"I thought maybe you were looking for one that said PLEASE FEED ME, I AM A U.S. GOVERNMENT EMPLOYEE," Eddie said, and walked on.

As he headed down the stairs he saw the purse-rooter hurriedly snap her purse shut and get to her feet.

Oh boy, this is gonna be like the Macy's Thanksgiving Day parade.

It had been one fuck of an interesting day, and Eddie didn't think it was over yet.

5

When Roland saw the lobster-things coming out of the waves again (their coming had nothing to do with tide, then; it was the dark that brought them), he left Eddie Dean to move himself before the creatures could find and eat him.

The pain he had expected and was prepared for. He had lived with pain so long it was almost an old friend. He was appalled, however, by the rapidity with which his fever had increased and his strength decreased. If he had not been dying before, he most assuredly was now. Was there something powerful enough in the prisoner's world to keep that from happening? Perhaps. But if he didn't get some of it within the next six or eight hours, he thought it wouldn't matter. If things went much further, no medicine or magic in that world or any other would make him well again.

Walking was impossible. He would have to crawl.

He was getting ready to start when his eye fixed upon the twisted band of sticky stuff and the bags of devil-powder. If he left the stuff here, the lobstrosities would almost surely tear the bags open. The sea-breeze would scatter the powder to the four winds. *Which is where it belongs,* the gunslinger thought grimly, but he couldn't allow it. When the time came, Eddie Dean would be in a long tub of trouble if he couldn't produce that powder. It was rarely possible to bluff men of the sort he guessed this Balazar to be. He would want to see what he had paid for, and until he saw it Eddie would have enough guns pointed at him to equip a small army.

The gunslinger pulled the twisted rope of glue-string over to him and slung it over his neck. Then he began to work his way up the beach.

He had crawled twenty yards—almost far enough to consider himself safe, he judged—when the horrible (yet cosmically funny) realization that he was leaving the doorway behind came to him. What in God's name was he going through this for?

He turned his head and saw the doorway, not down on the beach, but three feet behind him. For a moment Roland could only stare, and realize what he would have known already, if not for the fever and the sound of the Inquisitors, drumming their ceaseless questions at Eddie, *Where did you, how did you, why did you, when did you* (questions that seemed to merge eerily with the questions of the scrabbling horrors that came crawling and wriggling out of the waves: *Dad-a-chock? Dad-a-chum? Did-a-chick?*), as mere delirium. Not so.

Now I take it with me everywhere I go, he thought, *just as he does. It comes with us everywhere now, following like a curse you can never get rid of.*

All of this felt so true as to be unquestionable . . . and so did one other thing.

If the door between them should close, it would be closed forever.

When that happens, Roland thought grimly, *he must be on this side. With me.*

What a paragon of virtue you are, gunslinger! the man in black laughed. He seemed to have taken up permanent residence inside Roland's head. *You have killed the boy; that was the sacrifice that enabled you to catch me and, I suppose, to create the door between worlds. Now you intend to draw your three, one by one, and condemn all of them to something you would not have for yourself: a lifetime in an alien world, where they may die as easily as animals in a zoo set free in a wild place.*

The Tower, Roland thought wildly. *Once I've gotten to the Tower and done whatever it is I'm supposed to do there, accomplished whatever fundamental act of restoration or redemption for which I was meant, then perhaps they—*

But the shrieking laughter of the man in black, the man who was dead but lived on as the gunslinger's stained conscience, would not let him go on with the thought.

Neither, however, could the thought of the treachery he contemplated turn him aside from his course.

He managed another ten yards, looked back, and saw that even the largest of the crawling monsters would venture no further than twenty feet above the high-tide line. He had already managed three times that distance.

It's well, then.

Nothing is well, the man in black replied merrily, *and you know it.*

Shut up, the gunslinger thought, and for a wonder, the voice actually did.

Roland pushed the bags of devil-dust into the cleft between two rocks and covered them with handfuls of sparse saw-grass. With that done he rested briefly, head thumping like a hot bag of waters, skin alternately hot and cold, then rolled back through the doorway into that other world, that other body, leaving the increasingly deadly infection behind for a little while.

6

The second time he returned to himself, he entered a body so deeply asleep that he thought for a moment it had entered a comatose state . . . a state of such lowered bodily function that in moments he would feel his own consciousness start down a long slide into darkness.

Instead, he forced his body toward wakefulness, punched and pummelled it out of the dark cave into which it had crawled. He made his heart speed up, made his nerves re-accept the pain that sizzled through his skin and woke his flesh to groaning reality.

It was night now. The stars were out. The popkin-things Eddie had brought him were small bits of warmth in the chill.

He didn't feel like eating them, but eat them he would. First, though . . .

He looked at the white pills in his hand. *Astin,* Eddie called it. No, that wasn't quite right, but Roland couldn't pronounce the word as the prisoner had said it. Medicine was what it came down to. Medicine from that other world.

If anything from your world is going to do for me, Prisoner, Roland thought grimly, *I think it's more apt to be your potions than your popkins.*

Still, he would have to try it. Not the stuff he really needed—or so Eddie believed—but something which might reduce his fever.

Three now, three later. If there is a later.

He put three of the pills in his mouth, then pushed the cover—some strange white stuff that was neither paper nor glass but which seemed a bit like both—off the paper cup which held the drink, and washed them down.

The first swallow amazed him so completely that for a moment he only lay there, propped against a rock, his eyes so wide and still and full of reflected starlight that he would surely have been taken for dead already by anyone who happened to pass by. Then he drank greedily, holding the cup in both hands, the rotted, pulsing hurt in the stumps of his fingers barely noticed in his total absorption with the drink.

Sweet! Gods, such sweetness! Such sweetness! Such—

One of the small flat icecubes in the drink caught in his throat. He coughed, pounded his chest, and choked it out. Now there was a new pain in his head: the silvery pain that comes with drinking something too cold too fast.

He lay still, feeling his heart pumping like a runaway engine, feeling fresh energy surge into his body so fast he felt as if he might actually explode. Without thinking of what he was doing, he tore another piece from his shirt—soon it would be no more than a rag hanging around his neck—and laid it across one leg. When the drink was gone he would pour the ice into the rag and make a pack for his wounded hand. But his mind was elsewhere.

Sweet! it cried out again and again, trying to get the sense of it, or to convince itself there *was* sense in it, much as Eddie had tried to convince himself of the *other* as an actual being and not some mental convulsion that was only another part of himself trying to trick him. *Sweet! Sweet! Sweet*

The dark drink was laced with sugar, even more than Marten—who had been a great glutton behind his grave ascetic's exterior—had put in his coffee mornings and at 'Downers.

Sugar . . . white . . . powder . . .

The gunslinger's eyes wandered to the bags, barely visible under the grass he had tossed over them, and wondered briefly if the stuff in this drink and the stuff in the bags might be one and the same. He knew that Eddie had understood him perfectly over here, where they were two separate physical creatures; he suspected that if he had crossed bodily to Eddie's world (and he understood instinctively it *could* be done . . . although if the door should shut while he was there, he would be there forever, as Eddie would be here forever if their positions were reversed), he would have understood the language just as perfectly. He knew from being in Eddie's mind that the languages of the two worlds were similar to begin with. Similar, but not the same. Here a sandwich was a popkin. There to rustle was finding something to eat. So . . . was it not possible that the drug Eddie called *cocaine* was, in the gunslinger's world, called *sugar?*

Reconsideration made it seem unlikely. Eddie had bought this drink openly, knowing that he was being watched by people who served the Priests of Customs. Further, Roland sensed he had paid comparatively little for it. Less, even, than for the popkins of meat. No, sugar was not cocaine, but Roland could not understand why anyone would want cocaine or any other illegal drug, for that matter, in a world where such a powerful one as sugar was so plentiful and cheap.

He looked at the meat popkins again, felt the first stirrings of hunger . . . and realized with amazement and confused thankfulness that *he felt better.*

The drink? Was that it? The sugar in the drink?

That might be part of it—but a small part. Sugar could revive one's strength for awhile when it was flagging; this was something he had known since he was a child. But sugar could not dull pain or damp the fever-fire in your body when some infection had turned it into a furnace. All the same, that was exactly what had happened to him . . . was still happening.

The convulsive shuddering had stopped. The sweat was drying on his brow. The fishhooks which had lined his throat seemed to be disappearing. Incredible as it was, it was also an inarguable fact, not just imagination or wishful thinking (in point of fact, the gunslinger had not been capable of such frivolity as the latter in unknown and unknowable decades). His missing fingers and toes still throbbed and roared, but he believed even these pains to be muted.

Roland put his head back, closed his eyes and thanked God.

God and Eddie Dean.

Don't make the mistake of putting your heart near his hand, Roland, a voice from the deeper ranges of his mind spoke—this was not the nervous, tittery-bitchy voice of the man in black or the rough one of Cort; to the gunslinger it sounded like his father. *You know that what he's done for you he has done out of his own personal need, just as you know that those men—Inquisitors though they may be—are partly or completely right about him. He is a weak vessel, and the reason they took him was neither false nor base. There is steel in him, I dispute it not. But there is weakness as well. He is like Hax, the cook. Hax poisoned reluctantly . . . but reluctance has never stilled the screams of the dying as their intestines rupture. And there is yet another reason to beware . . .*

But Roland needed no voice to tell him what that other reason was. He had seen that in Jake's eyes when the boy finally began to understand his purpose.

Don't make the mistake of putting your heart near his hand.

Good advice. You did yourself ill to feel well of those to whom ill must eventually be done.

Remember your duty, Roland.

"I've never forgotten it," he husked as the stars shone pitilessly down and the waves grated on the shore and the lobster monstrosities cried their idiot questions. "I'm damned for my duty. And why should the damned turn aside?"

He began to eat the meat popkins which Eddie called "dogs."

Roland didn't much care for the idea of eating dog, and these things tasted like gutter-leavings compared to the tooter-fish, but after that marvellous drink, did he have any right to complain? He thought not. Besides, it was late in the game to worry overmuch about such niceties.

He ate everything and then returned to the place where now Eddie was, in some magical vehicle that rushed along a metal road filled with other such vehicles . . . dozens, maybe hundreds, and not a horse pulling a single one.

7

Eddie stood ready as the pizza truck pulled up; Roland stood even more ready inside of him.

Just another version of Diana's Dream, Roland thought. *What was in the box? The golden bowl or the biter-snake? And just as she turns the key and puts her hands upon the lid she hears her mother calling "Wake up, Diana! It's time to milk!"*

Okay, Eddie thought. *Which is it gonna be? The lady or the tiger?*

A man with a pale, pimply face and big buck teeth looked out of the pizza truck's passenger window. It was a face Eddie knew.

"Hi, Col," Eddie said without much enthusiasm. Beyond Col Vincent, sitting behind the wheel, was Old Double-Ugly, which was what Henry called Jack Andolini.

But Henry never called him that to his face, Eddie thought. No, of course not. Calling Jack something like that to his face would be a wonderful way to get yourself killed. He was a huge man with a bulging caveman's forehead and a prothagonous jaw to match. He was related to Enrico Balazar by marriage . . . a niece, a cousin, some fucking thing. His gigantic hands clung to the wheel of the delivery truck like the hands of a monkey clinging to a branch. Coarse sprouts of hair grew from his ears. Eddie could only see one of those ears now because Jack Andolini remained in profile, never looking around.

Old Double-Ugly. But not even Henry (who, Eddie had to admit, was not always the most perceptive guy in the world) had ever made the mistake of calling him Old Double-Stupid. Colin Vincent was no more than a glorified gofer. Jack, however, had enough smarts behind that Neanderthal brow to be Balazar's number one lieutenant. Eddie didn't like the fact that Balazar had sent a man of such importance. He didn't like it at all.

"Hi, Eddie," Col said. "Heard you had some trouble."

"Nothing I couldn't handle," Eddie said. He realized he was scratching first one arm then the other, one of the typical junkie moves he had tried so hard to keep away from while they had him in custody. He made himself stop. But Col was smiling, and Eddie felt an urge to slam a fist all the way through that smile and out the other side. He might have done it, too . . . except for Jack. Jack was still staring straight ahead, a man who seemed to be thinking his own rudimentary thoughts as he observed the world in the simple primary colors and elementary motions which were all a man of such intellect (or so you'd think, looking at him) could perceive. Yet Eddie thought Jack saw more in a single day than Col Vincent would in his whole life.

"Well, good," Col said. "That's good."

Silence. Col looked at Eddie, smiling, waiting for Eddie to start the Junkie Shuffle again, scratching, shifting from foot to foot like a kid who needs to go to the bathroom, waiting mostly for Eddie to ask what was up, and by the way, did they just happen to have any stuff on them?

Eddie only looked back at him, not scratching now, not moving at all.

A faint breeze blew a Ring-Ding wrapper across the parking lot. The scratchy sound of its skittering passage and the wheezy thump of the pizza truck's loose valves were the only sounds.

Col's knowing grin began to falter.

"Hop in, Eddie," Jack said without looking around. "Let's take a ride."

"Where?" Eddie asked, knowing.

"Balazar's." Jack didn't look around. He flexed his hands on the wheel once. A large ring, solid gold except for the onyx stone which bulged from it like the eye of a giant insect, glittered on the third finger of his right as he did it. "He wants to know about his goods."

"I have his goods. They're safe."

"Fine. Then nobody has anything to worry about," Jack Andolini said, and did not look around.

"I think I want to go upstairs first," Eddie said. "I want to change my clothes, talk to Henry—"

"And get fixed up, don't forget that," Col said, and grinned his big yellow-toothed grin. "Except you got nothing to fix *with*, little chum."

Dad-a-chum? the gunslinger thought in Eddie's mind, and both of them shuddered a little.

Col observed the shudder and his smile widened. *Oh, here it is after all,* that smile said. *The good old*

Junkie Shuffle. Had me worried there for a minute, Eddie. The teeth revealed by the smile's expansion were not an improvement on those previously seen.

"Why's that?"

"Mr. Balazar thought it would be better to make sure you guys had a clean place," Jack said without looking around. He went on observing the world an observer would have believed it impossible for such a man to observe. "In case anyone showed up."

"People with a Federal search warrant, for instance," Col said. His face hung and leered. Now Eddie could feel Roland also wanting to drive a fist through the rotted teeth that made that grin so reprehensible, so somehow irredeemable. The unanimity of feeling cheered him up a little. "He sent in a cleaning service to wash the walls and vacuum the carpets and he ain't going to charge you a red cent for it, Eddie!"

Now *you'll ask what I've got,* Col's grin said. *Oh yeah, now you'll ask, Eddie my boy. Because you may not love the candy-man, but you do love the candy, don't you? And now that you know Balazar's made sure your own private stash is gone—*

A sudden thought, both ugly and frightening, flashed through his mind. If the stash was gone—

"Where's Henry?" he said suddenly, so harshly that Col drew back, surprised.

Jack Andolini finally turned his head. He did so slowly, as if it was an act he performed only rarely, and at great personal cost. You almost expected to hear old oilless hinges creaking inside the thickness of his neck.

"Safe," he said, and then turned his head back to its original position again, just as slowly.

Eddie stood beside the pizza truck, fighting the panic trying to rise in his mind and drown coherent thought. Suddenly the need to fix, which he had been holding at bay pretty well, was overpowering. He *had* to fix. With a fix he could think, get himself under control—

Quit it! Roland roared inside his head, so loud Eddie winced (and Col, mistaking Eddie's grimace of pain and surprise for another little step in the Junkie Shuffle, began to grin again). *Quit it! I'll be all the goddamned control you need!*

You don't understand! He's my brother! *He's my* fucking *brother! Balazar's got my* brother!

You speak as if it was a word I'd never heard before. Do you fear for him?

Yes! Christ, yes!

Then do what they expect. Cry. Pule and beg. Ask for this fix of yours. I'm sure they expect you to, and I'm sure they have it. Do all those things, make them sure of you, and you can *be sure all your fears will be justified.*

I don't understand what you m—

I mean if you show a yellow gut, you will go far toward getting your precious brother killed. Is that what you want?

All right. I'll be cool. It may not sound that way, but I'll be cool.

Is that what you call it? All right, then. Yes. Be cool.

"This isn't the way the deal was supposed to go down," Eddie said, speaking past Col and directly at Jack Andolini's tufted ear. "This isn't why I took care of Balazar's goods and hung onto my lip while some other guy would have been puking out five names for every year off on the plea-bargain."

"Balazar thought your brother would be safer with him," Jack said, not looking around. "He took him into protective custody."

"Well good," Eddie said. "You thank him for me, and you tell him that I'm back, his goods are safe, and I can take care of Henry just like Henry always took care of me. You tell him I'll have a six-pack on ice and when Henry walks in the place we're going to split it and then we'll get in our car and come on into town and do the deal like it was supposed to be done. Like we talked about it.''

"Balazar wants to see you, Eddie,'' Jack said. His voice was implacable, immovable. His head did not turn. "Get in the truck.''

"Stick it where the sun doesn't shine, mother-fucker,'' Eddie said, and started for the doors to his building.

8

It was a short distance but he had gotten barely half-way when Andolini's hand clamped on his upper arm with the paralyzing force of a vise-grip. His breath was hot as a bull's on the back of Eddie's neck. He did all this in the time you would have thought, look-ing at him, it would have taken his brain to convince his hand to pull the door-handle up.

Eddie turned around.

Be cool, Eddie, Roland whispered.

Cool, Eddie responded.

"I could kill you for that,'' Andolini said. "No one tells me stick it up my ass, especially no shitass little junkie like you.''

"Kill shit!'' Eddie screamed at him—but it was a calculated scream. A *cool* scream, if you could dig that. They stood there, dark figures in the golden hor-izontal light of late spring sundown in the wasteland of housing developments that is the Bronx's Co-Op City, and people heard the scream, and people heard the word *kill,* and if their radios were on they turned them up and if their radios were off they turned them on and *then* turned them up because it was better that way, safer.

"Rico Balazar broke his word! I stood up for him

and he didn't stand up for me! So I tell you to stick it up your fuckin ass, I tell him to stick it up his fuckin ass, I tell anybody I want to stick it up his fuckin ass!"

Andolini looked at him. His eyes were so brown the color seemed to have leaked into his corneas, turning them the yellow of old parchment.

"I tell President Reagan to stick it up his ass if he breaks his word to me, and fuck his fuckin rectal palp or whatever it is!"

The words died away in echoes on brick and concrete. A single child, his skin very black against his white basketball shorts and high-topped sneakers, stood in the playground across the street, watching them, a basketball held loosely against his side in the crook of his elbow.

"You done?" Andolini asked when the last of the echoes were gone.

"Yes," Eddie said in a completely normal tone of voice.

"Okay," Andolini said. He spread his anthropoid fingers and smiled . . . and when he smiled, two things happened simultaneously: the first was that you saw a charm that was so surprising it had a way of leaving people defenseless; the second was that you saw how bright he really was. How dangerously bright. "Now can we start over?"

Eddie brushed his hands through his hair, crossed his arms briefly so he could scratch both arms at the same time, and said, "I think we better, because this is going nowhere."

"Okay," Andolini said. "No one has said nothing, and no one has ranked out nobody." And without turning his head or breaking the rhythm of his speech he added, "Get back in the truck, dumbwit."

Col Vincent, who had climbed cautiously out of the delivery truck through the door Andolini had left open retreated so fast he thumped his head. He slid across the seat and slouched in his former place, rubbing it and sulking.

"You gotta understand the deal changed when the Customs people put the arm on you," Andolini said reasonably. "Balazar is a big man. He has interests to protect. *People* to protect. One of those people, it just so happens, is your brother Henry. You think that's bullshit? If you do, you better think about the way Henry is now."

"Henry's fine," Eddie said, but he knew better and he couldn't keep the knowing out of his voice. He heard it and knew Jack Andolini heard it, too. These days Henry was always on the nod, it seemed like. There were holes in his shirts from cigarette burns. He had cut the shit out of his hand using the electric can-opener on a can of Calo for Potzie, their cat. Eddie didn't know how you cut yourself with an electric can-opener, but Henry had managed it. Sometimes the kitchen table would be powdery with Henry's leavings, or Eddie would find blackened curls of char in the bathroom sink.

Henry, he would say, *Henry, you gotta take care of this, this is getting out of hand, you're a bust walking around and waiting to happen.*

Yeah, okay, little brother, Henry would respond, *zero perspiration, I got it all under control,* but sometimes, looking at Henry's ashy face and burned out eyes, Eddie knew Henry was never going to have anything under control again.

What he *wanted* to say to Henry and couldn't had nothing to do with Henry getting busted or getting them both busted. What he *wanted* to say was *Henry, it's like you're looking for a room to die in. That's how it looks to me, and I want you to fucking quit it. Because if you die, what did I live for?*

"Henry *isn't* fine," Jack Andolini said. "He needs someone to watch out for him. He needs—what's that song say? A bridge over troubled waters. That's what Henry needs. A bridge over troubled waters. *Il Roche* is being that bridge.''

Il Roche *is a bridge to hell,* Eddie thought. Out loud he said, ''That's where Henry is? At Balazar's place?''

''Yes.''

''I give him his goods, he gives me Henry?''

''And *your* goods,'' Andolini said, ''don't forget that.''

''The deal goes back to normal, in other words.''

''Right.''

''Now tell me you think that's really gonna happen. Come on, Jack. Tell me. I wanna see if you can do it with a straight face. And if you *can* do it with a straight face, I wanna see how much your nose grows.''

''I don't understand you, Eddie.''

''Sure you do. Balazar thinks I've *got* his goods? If he thinks that, he must be stupid, and I know he's not stupid.''

''I don't know what he thinks,'' Andolini said serenely. ''It's not my job to know what he thinks. He knows you *had* his goods when you left the Islands, he knows Customs grabbed you and then let you go, he knows you're here and not on your way to Riker's, he knows his goods have to be somewhere.''

''And he knows Customs is still all over me like a wetsuit on a skin-diver, because *you* know it, and you sent him some kind of coded message on the truck's radio. Something like 'Double cheese, hold the anchovies,' right, Jack?''

Jack Andolini said nothing and looked serene.

''Only you were just telling him something he already knew. Like connecting the dots in a picture you can already see what it is.''

Andolini stood in the golden sunset light that was slowly turning furnace orange and continued to look serene and continued to say nothing at all.

"He thinks they turned me. He thinks they're running me. He thinks I might be stupid enough to run. I don't exactly blame him. I mean, why not? A smack-head will do anything. You want to check, see if I'm wearing a wire?"

"I know you're not," Andolini said. "I got something in the van. It's like a fuzz-buster, only it picks up short-range radio transmissions. And for what it's worth, I don't think you're running for the Feds."

"Yeah?"

"Yeah. So do we get in the van and go into the city or what?"

"Do I have a choice?"

No, Roland said inside his head.

"No," Andolini said.

Eddie went back to the van. The kid with the basketball was still standing across the street, his shadow now so long it was a gantry.

"Get out of here, kid," Eddie said. "You were never here, you never saw nothing or no one. Fuck off."

The kid ran.

Col was grinning at him.

"Push over, champ," Eddie said.

"I think you oughtta sit in the middle, Eddie."

"Push over," Eddie said again. Col looked at him, then looked at Andolini, who did not look at him but only pulled the driver's door closed and looked serenely straight ahead like Buddha on his day off, leaving them to work the seating arrangements out for themselves. Col glanced back at Eddie's face and decided to push over.

They headed into New York—and although the gunslinger (who could only stare wonderingly at spires even greater and more graceful, bridges that spanned a wide river like steel cobwebs, and rotored air-carriages that hovered like strange man-made insects) did not know it, the place they were headed for was the Tower.

9

Like Andolini, Enrico Balazar did not think Eddie Dean was running for the Feds; like Andolini, Balazar *knew* it.

The bar was empty. The sign on the door read CLOSED TONIGHT ONLY. Balazar sat in his office, waiting for Andolini and Col Vincent to arrive with the Dean kid. His two personal body-guards, Claudio Andolini, Jack's brother, and 'Cimi Dretto, were with him. They sat on the sofa to the left of Balazar's large desk, watching, fascinated, as the edifice Balazar was building grew. The door was open. Beyond the door was a short hallway. To the right it led to the back of the bar and the little kitchen beyond, where a few simple pasta dishes were prepared. To the left was the accountant's office and the storage room. In the accountant's office three more of Balazar's "gentlemen"—this was how they were known—were playing Trivial Pursuit with Henry Dean.

"Okay," George Biondi was saying, "here's an easy one, Henry. Henry? You there, Henry? Earth to Henry, Earth people need you. Come in, Henry. I say again: come in, H—"

"I'm here, I'm here," Henry said. His voice was the slurry, muddy voice of a man who is still asleep telling his wife he's awake so she'll leave him alone for another five minutes.

"Okay. The category is Arts and Entertainment. The question is . . . Henry? Don't you fuckin nod off on me, asshole!"

"I'm *not!*" Henry cried back querulously.

"Okay. The question is, 'What enormously popular novel by William Peter Blatty, set in the posh Washington D.C. suburb of Georgetown, concerned the demonic possession of a young girl?' ''

"Johnny Cash," Henry replied.

"Jesus Christ!" Tricks Postino yelled. "That's what you say to everythin! Johnny Cash, that's what you say to fuckin *everythin!*"

"Johnny Cash *is* everything," Henry replied gravely, and there was a moment of silence palpable in its considering surprise . . . then a gravelly burst of laughter not just from the men in the room with Henry but the two other "gentlemen" sitting in the storage room.

"You want me to shut the door, Mr. Balazar?" 'Cimi asked quietly.

"No, that's fine," Balazar said. He was second-generation Sicilian, but there was no trace of accent in his speech, nor was it the speech of a man whose only education had been in the streets. Unlike many of his contemporaries in the business, he had finished high school. Had in fact done more: for two years he had gone to business school—NYU. His voice, like his business methods, was quiet and cultured and American, and this made his physical aspect as deceiving as Jack Andolini's. People hearing his clear, unaccented American voice for the first time almost always looked dazed, as if hearing a particularly good piece of ventriloquism. He looked like a farmer or innkeeper or small-time *mafioso* who had been successful more by virtue of being at the right place at the right time than because of any brains. He looked like what the wiseguys of a previous generation had called a "Mustache Pete." He was a fat man who dressed like a peasant. This evening he wore a plain white cotton shirt open at the throat (there were spreading sweat-stains beneath the arms) and plain gray twill pants. On his fat sockless feet were brown loafers, so old they were more like slippers than shoes.

Blue and purple varicose veins squirmed on his ankles.

'Cimi and Claudio watched him, fascinated.

In the old days they called him *Il Roche*—The Rock. Some of the old-timers still did. Always in the right-hand top drawer of his desk, where other businessmen might keep pads, pens, paper-clips, things of that sort, Enrico Balazar kept three decks of cards. He did not play games with them, however.

He built with them.

He would take two cards and lean them against each other, making an A without the horizontal stroke. Next to it he would make another A-shape. Over the top of the two he would lay a single card, making a roof. He would make A after A, overlaying each, until his desk supported a house of cards. You bent over and looked in, you saw something that looked like a hive of triangles. 'Cimi had seen these houses fall over hundreds of times (Claudio had also seen it happen from time to time, but not so frequently, because he was thirty years younger than 'Cimi, who expected to soon retire with his bitch of a wife to a farm they owned in northern New Jersey, where he would devote all his time to his garden . . . and to outliving the bitch he had married; not his mother-in-law, he had long since given up any wistful notion he might once have had of eating *fettucini* at the wake of *La Monstra*, *La Monstra* was eternal, but for outliving the bitch there was at least some hope; his father had had a saying which, when translated, meant something like "God pisses down the back of your neck every day but only drowns you once," and while 'Cimi wasn't completely sure he thought it meant God was a pretty good guy after all, and so he could only hope to outlive the one if not the other), but had only seen Balazar put out of temper by such a fall on a single occasion. Mostly it was something errant that did it—someone closing a door hard in another room, or a drunk stumbling against a wall; there had been times when 'Cimi saw an edifice Mr. Balazar (whom he still called *Da Boss,* like a character in a Chester Gould comic strip) had spent hours building fall down because the bass on the juke was too loud. Other times these airy constructs fell down for no perceptible reason at all. Once—this was a story he had told at least five thousand times, and one of which every person he knew (with the exception of himself) had tired—*Da Boss* had looked up at him from the ruins and said: "You see this 'Cimi? For every mother who ever cursed God for her child dead in the road, for every father who ever cursed the man who sent him away from the factory with no job, for every child who was ever born to pain and asked why, this is the answer. Our lives are like these things I build. Sometimes they fall down for a reason, sometimes they fall down for no reason at all."

Carlocimi Dretto thought this the most profound statement of the human condition he had ever heard.

That one time Balazar had been put out of temper by the collapse of one of his structures had been twelve, maybe fourteen years ago. There was a guy who came in to see him about booze. A guy with no class, no manners. A guy who smelled like he took a bath once a year whether he needed it or not. A mick, in other words. And of course it was booze. With micks it was always booze, never dope. And this mick, he thought what was on *Da Boss's* desk was a joke. "Make a wish!" he yelled after *Da Boss* had explained to him, in the way one gentleman explains to another, why it was impossible for them to do business. And then the mick, one of those guys with curly red hair and a complexion so white he looked like he had TB or something, one of those guys whose names started with O and then had that little curly mark between the O and the real name, had *blown* on *Da Boss's* desk, like a *niño* blowing out the candles on a birthday cake, and cards flew everywhere around Balazar's head, and Balazar had opened the *left* top drawer in his desk, the drawer where other businessmen might keep their personal stationery or their private memos or something like that, and he had brought out a .45, and he had shot the mick in the head, and Balazar's expression never changed, and after 'Cimi and a guy named Truman Alexander who had died of a heart attack four years ago had buried the mick under a chickenhouse somewhere outside of Sedonville, Connecticut, Balazar had said to 'Cimi, "It's up to men to build things, *paisan*. It's up to God to blow them down. You agree?"

"Yes, Mr. Balazar," 'Cimi had said. He did agree.

Balazar had nodded, pleased. "You did like I said? You put him someplace where chickens or ducks or something like that could shit on him?"

"Yes."

"That's very good," Balazar said calmly, and took a fresh deck of cards from the right top drawer of his desk.

One level was not enough for Balazar, *Il Roche*. Upon the roof of the first level he would build a second, only not quite so wide; on top of the second a third; on top of the third a fourth. He would go on, but after the fourth level he would have to stand to do so. You no longer had to bend much to look in, and when you did what you saw wasn't rows of triangle shapes but a fragile, bewildering, and impossibly lovely hall of diamond-shapes. You looked in too long, you felt dizzy. Once 'Cimi had gone in the Mirror Maze at Coney and he had felt like that. He had never gone in again.

'Cimi said (he believed no one believed him; the truth was no one cared one way or the other) he had once seen Balazar build something which was no longer a house of cards but a *tower* of cards, one which stood nine levels high before it collapsed. That no one gave a shit about this was something 'Cimi didn't know because everyone he told affected amazement because he was close to *Da Boss*. But they would have been amazed if he had had the words to describe it—how delicate it had been, how it reached almost three quarters of the way from the top of the desk to the ceiling, a lacy construct of jacks and deuces and kings and tens and Big Akers, a red and black configuration of paper diamonds standing in defiance of a world spinning through a universe of incoherent motions and forces; a tower that seemed to 'Cimi's amazed eyes to be a ringing denial of all the unfair paradoxes of life.

If he had known how, he would have said: *I looked at what he built, and to me it explained the stars.*

10

Balazar knew how everything would have to be.

The Feds had smelled Eddie—maybe he had been stupid to send Eddie in the first place, maybe his instincts were failing him, but Eddie had seemed somehow so right, so perfect. His uncle, the first man he had worked for in the business, said there were exceptions to every rule but one: Never trust a junkie. Balazar had said nothing—it was not the place of a boy of fifteen to speak, even if only to agree—but privately had thought the only rule to which there was no exception was that there were some rules for which that was not true.

But if Tio Verone were alive today, Balazar thought, *he would laugh at you and say look, Rico, you always were too smart for your own good, you knew the rules, you kept your mouth shut when it was respectful to keep it shut, but you always had that snot look in your eyes. You always knew too much about how smart you*

*were, and so you finally fell into the pit of your own
pride, just like I always knew you would.*

He made an A shape and overlaid it.

They had taken Eddie and held him awhile and then
let him go.

Balazar had grabbed Eddie's brother and the stash
they shared. That would be enough to bring him . . .
and he wanted Eddie.

He wanted Eddie because it had only been two
hours, and two hours was *wrong*.

They had questioned him at Kennedy, not at 43rd
Street, and that was wrong, too. That meant Eddie had
succeeded in ditching most or all of the coke.

Or had he?

He thought. He wondered.

Eddie had walked out of Kennedy two hours after
they took him off the plane. That was too short a
time for them to have sweated it out of him and too
long for them to have decided he was clean, that some
stew had made a rash mistake.

He thought. He wondered.

Eddie's brother was a zombie, but Eddie was still
smart, Eddie was still tough. He wouldn't have turned
in just two hours . . . unless it was his brother. Something about his brother.

But still, how come no 43rd Street? How come no
Customs van, the ones that looked like Post Office
trucks except for the wire grilles on the back windows?
Because Eddie really *had* done something with the
goods? Ditched them? Hidden them?

Impossible to hide goods on an airplane.

Impossible to ditch them.

Of course it was also impossible to escape from certain prisons, rob certain banks, beat certain raps. But
people did. Harry Houdini had escaped from strait-
jackets, locked trunks, fucking bank vaults. But Eddie
Dean was no Houdini.

Was he?

He could have had Henry killed in the apartment, could have had Eddie cut down on the L.I.E. or, better yet, *also* in the apartment, where it would look to the cops like a couple of junkies who got desperate enough to forget they were brothers and killed each other. But it would leave too many questions unanswered.

He would get the answers here, prepare for the future or merely satisfy his curiosity, depending on what the answers were, and then kill both of them.

A few more answers, two less junkies. Some gain and no great loss.

In the other room, the game had gotten around to Henry again. "Okay, Henry," George Biondi said. "Be careful, because this one is tricky. The category is Geography. The question is, 'What is the only continent where kangaroos are a native form of life?' "

A hushed pause.

"Johnny Cash," Henry said, and this was followed by a bull-throated roar of laughter.

The walls shook.

'Cimi tensed, waiting for Balazar's house of cards (which would become a tower only if God, or the blind forces that ran the universe in His name, willed it), to fall down.

The cards trembled a bit. If one fell, all would fall. None did.

Balazar looked up and smiled at 'Cimi. *"Piasan,"* he said. *"Il Dio est bono; il Dio est malo; temps est poco-poco; tu est une grande peeparollo."*

'Cimi smiled. *"Si, senor,"* he said. *"Io grande peeparollo; Io va fanculo por tu."*

"None va fanculo, catzarro," Balazar said. *"Eddie Dean va fanculo."* He smiled gently, and began on the second level of his tower of cards.

11

When the van pulled to the curb near Balazar's place, Col Vincent happened to be looking at Eddie. He saw something impossible. He tried to speak and found himself unable. His tongue was stuck to the roof of his mouth and all he could get out was a muffled grunt.

He saw Eddie's eyes change from brown to blue.

12

This time Roland made no conscious decision to *come forward*. He simply leaped without thinking, a movement as involuntary as rolling out of a chair and going for his guns when someone burst into a room.

The Tower! he thought fiercely. *It's the Tower, my God, the Tower is in the sky, the Tower! I see the Tower in the sky, drawn in lines of red fire! Cuthbert! Alan! Desmond! The Tower! The T—*

But this time he felt Eddie struggling—not against him, but trying to talk to him, trying desperately to explain something to him.

The gunslinger retreated, listening—listening desperately, as above a beach some unknown distance away in space and time, his mindless body twitched and trembled like the body of a man experiencing a dream of highest ecstasy or deepest horror.

13

Sign! Eddie was screaming into his own head . . . and into the head of that *other*.

It's a sign, just a neon sign, I don't know what tower it is you're thinking about but this is just a bar, Balazar's place, The Leaning Tower, he named it that after the one in Pisa! It's just a sign that's supposed to look like the fucking Leaning Tower of Pisa! Let up!

Let up! You want to get us killed before we have a chance to go at them?

Pitsa? the gunslinger replied doubtfully, and looked again.

A sign. Yes, all right, he could see now: it was not the Tower, but a Signpost. It leaned to one side, and there were many scalloped curves, and it was a marvel, but that was all. He could see now that the sign was a thing made of tubes, tubes which had somehow been filled with glowing red swamp-fire. In some places there seemed to be less of it than others; in those places the lines of fire pulsed and buzzed.

He now saw letters below the tower which had been made of shaped tubes; most of them were Great Letters. TOWER he could read, and yes, LEANING. LEANING TOWER. The first word was three letters, the first T, the last E, the middle one which he had never seen.

Tre? he asked Eddie.

THE. It doesn't matter. Do you see it's just a sign? That's what matters!

I see, the gunslinger answered, wondering if the prisoner really believed what he was saying or was only saying it to keep the situation from spilling over as the tower depicted in those lines of fire seemed about to do, wondering if Eddie believed *any* sign could be a trivial thing.

Then ease off! Do you hear me? Ease off!

Be cool? Roland asked, and both felt Roland smile a little in Eddie's mind.

Be cool, right. Let me handle things.

Yes. All right. He would let Eddie handle things.

For awhile.

14

Col Vincent finally managed to get his tongue off the roof of his mouth. "Jack." His voice was as thick as shag carpet.

Andolini turned off the motor and looked at him, irritated.

"His eyes."

"What about his eyes?"

"Yeah, what about my eyes?" Eddie asked.

Col looked at him.

The sun had gone down, leaving nothing in the air but the day's ashes, but there was light enough for Col to see that Eddie's eyes were brown again.

If they had ever been anything else.

You saw it, part of his mind insisted, but had he? Col was twenty-four, and for the last twenty-one of those years no one had really believed him trustworthy. Useful sometimes. Obedient almost always . . . if kept on a short leash. Trustworthy? No. Col had eventually come to believe it himself.

"Nothing," he muttered.

"Then let's go," Andolini said.

They got out of the pizza van. With Andolini on their left and Vincent on their right, Eddie and the gunslinger walked into The Leaning Tower.

CHAPTER 5

SHOWDOWN AND SHOOT-OUT

1

In a blues tune from the twenties Billie Holiday, who would one day discover the truth for herself, sang: *"Doctor tole me daughter you got to quit it fast/Because one more rocket gonna be your last."* Henry Dean's last rocket went up just five minutes before the van pulled up in front of The Leaning Tower and his brother was herded inside.

Because he was on Henry's right, George Biondi—known to his friends as "Big George" and to his enemies as "Big Nose"—asked Henry's questions. Now, as Henry sat nodding and blinking owlishly over the board, Tricks Postino put the die in a hand which had already gone the dusty color that results in the extremities after long-term heroin addiction, the dusty color which is the precursor of gangrene.

"Your turn, Henry," Tricks said, and Henry let the die fall from his hand.

When he went on staring into space and showed no intention of moving his game piece, Jimmy Haspio moved it for him. "Look at this, Henry," he said. "You got a chance to score a piece of the pie."

"Reese's Pieces," Henry said dreamily, and then looked around, as if awakening. "Where's Eddie?"

"He'll be here pretty soon," Tricks soothed him. "Just play the game."

"How about a fix?"

"Play the game, Henry."

"Okay, okay, stop *leaning* on me."

"Don't *lean* on him," Kevin Blake said to Jimmy.

"Okay, I won't," Jimmy said.

"You ready?" George Biondi said, and gave the others an enormous wink as Henry's chin floated down to his breastbone and then slowly rose once more—it was like watching a soaked log not quite ready to give in and sink for good.

"Yeah," Henry said. "Bring it on."

"Bring it on!" Jimmy Haspio cried happily.

"You *bring* that fucker!" Tricks agreed, and they all roared with laughter (in the other room Balazar's edifice, now three levels high, trembled again, but did not fall).

"Okay, listen close," George said, and winked again. Although Henry was on a Sports category, George announced the category was Arts and Entertainment. "What popular country and western singer had hits with 'A Boy Named Sue,' 'Folsom Prison Blues,' and numerous other shitkicking songs?"

Kevin Blake, who actually *could* add seven and nine (if you gave him poker chips to do it with), howled with laughter, clutching his knees and nearly upsetting the board.

Still pretending to scan the card in his hand, George continued: "This popular singer is also known as The Man in Black. His first name means the same as a place you go to take a piss and his last name means what you got in your wallet unless you're a fucking needle freak."

There was a long expectant silence.

"Walter Brennan," Henry said at last.

Bellows of laughter. Jimmy Haspio clutched Kevin Blake. Kevin punched Jimmy in the shoulder repeatedly. In Balazar's office, the house of cards which was now becoming a tower of cards trembled again.

"Quiet down!" 'Cimi yelled. *"Da Boss* is buildin!"

They quieted at once.

"Right," George said. "You got that one right, Henry. It was a toughie, but you came through."

"Always do," Henry said. "Always come through in the fuckin clutch. How about a fix?"

"Good idea!" George said, and took a Roi-Tan cigar box from behind him. From it he produced a hypo. He stuck it into the scarred vein above Henry's elbow, and Henry's last rocket took off.

2

The pizza van's exterior was grungy, but underneath the road-filth and spray-paint was a high-tech marvel the DEA guys would have envied. As Balazar had said on more than one occasion, you couldn't beat the bastards unless you could compete with the bastards—unless you could match their equipment. It was expensive stuff, but Balazar's side had an advantage: they stole what the DEA had to buy at grossly inflated prices. There were electronics company employees all the way down the Eastern Seaboard willing to sell you top secret stuff at bargain basement prices. These *catzzaroni* (Jack Andolini called them Silicon Valley Coke-Heads) practically *threw* the stuff at you.

Under the dash was a fuzz-buster; a UHF police radar jammer; a high-range/high frequency radio transmissions detector; an h-r/hf jammer; a transponder-amplifier that would make anyone trying to track the van by standard triangulation methods decide it was simultaneously in Connecticut, Harlem, and Montauk Sound; a radio-telephone . . . and a small red button which Andolini pushed as soon as Eddie Dean got out of the van.

In Balazar's office the intercom uttered a single short buzz.

"That's them," he said. "Claudio, let them in. 'Cimi, you tell everyone to dummy up. So far as Eddie Dean knows, no one's with me but you and Claudio. 'Cimi, go in the storeroom with the other gentlemen."

They went, 'Cimi turning left, Claudio Andolini going right.

Calmly, Balazar started on another level of his edifice.

3

Just let me handle it, Eddie said again as Claudio opened the door.

Yes, the gunslinger said, but remained alert, ready to *come forward* the instant it seemed necessary.

Keys rattled. The gunslinger was very aware of odors—old sweat from Col Vincent on his right, some sharp, almost acerbic aftershave from Jack Andolini on his left, and, as they stepped into the dimness, the sour tang of beer.

The smell of beer was all he recognized. This was no tumble-down saloon with sawdust on the floor and planks set across sawhorses for a bar—it was as far from a place like Sheb's in Tull as you could get, the gunslinger reckoned. Glass gleamed mellowly everywhere, more glass in this one room than he had seen in all the years since his childhood, when supply-lines had begun to break down, partially because of interdicting raids carried out by the rebel forces of Farson, the Good Man, but mostly, he thought, simply because the world was moving on. Farson had been a symptom of that great movement, not the cause.

He saw their reflections everywhere—on the walls, on the glass-faced bar and the long mirror behind it; he could even see them reflected as curved miniatures in the graceful bell-shapes of wine glasses hung upside down above the bar . . . glasses as gorgeous and fragile as festival ornaments.

In one corner was a sculpted creation of lights that rose and changed, rose and changed, rose and changed. Gold to green; green to yellow; yellow to red; red to gold again. Written across it in Great Letters was a word he could read but which meant nothing to him: ROCKOLA.

Never mind. There was business to be done here. He was no tourist; he must not allow himself the luxury of behaving like one, no matter how wonderful or strange these things might be.

The man who had let them in was clearly the brother of the man who drove what Eddie called the van (as in *vanguard,* Roland supposed), although he was much taller and perhaps five years younger. He wore a gun in a shoulder-rig.

"Where's Henry?" Eddie asked. "I want to see Henry." He raised his voice. "Henry! *Hey, Henry!*"

No reply; only silence in which the glasses hung over the bar seemed to shiver with a delicacy that was just beyond the range of a human ear.

"Mr. Balazar would like to speak to you first."

"You got him gagged and tied up somewhere, don't you?" Eddie asked, and before Claudio could do more than open his mouth to reply, Eddie laughed. "No, what am I thinking about—you got him stoned, that's all. Why would you bother with ropes and gags when all you have to do to keep Henry quiet is needle him? Okay. Take me to Balazar. Let's get this over with."

4

The gunslinger looked at the tower of cards on Balazar's desk and thought: *Another sign.*

Balazar did not look up—the tower of cards had

grown too tall for that to be necessary—but rather over the top. His expression was one of pleasure and warmth.

"Eddie," he said. "I'm glad to see you, son. I heard you had some trouble at Kennedy."

"I ain't your son," Eddie said flatly.

Balazar made a little gesture that was at the same time comic, sad, and untrustworthy: *You hurt me, Eddie,* it said, *you hurt me when you say a thing like that.*

"Let's cut through it," Eddie said. "You know it comes down to one thing or the other: either the Feds are running me or they had to let me go. You know they didn't sweat it out of me in just two hours. And you know if they had I'd be down at 43rd Street, answering questions between an occasional break to puke in the basin."

"*Are* they running you, Eddie?" Balazar asked mildly.

"No. They had to let me go. They're following, but I'm not leading."

"So you ditched the stuff," Balazar said. "That's fascinating. You must tell me how one ditches two pounds of coke when that one is on a jet plane. It would be handy information to have. It's like a locked room mystery story."

"I didn't ditch it," Eddie said, "but I don't have it anymore, either."

"So who does?" Claudio asked, then blushed when his brother looked at him with dour ferocity.

"*He* does," Eddie said, smiling, and pointed at Enrico Balazar over the tower of cards. "It's already been delivered."

For the first time since Eddie had been escorted into the office, a genuine expression illuminated Balazar's face: surprise. Then it was gone. He smiled politely.

"Yes," he said. "To a location which will be re-

vealed later, after you have your brother and your
goods and are gone. To Iceland, maybe. Is that how
it's supposed to go?''

''No,'' Eddie said. ''You don't understand. It's *here*.
Delivery right to your door. Just like we agreed. Because even in this day and age, there are some people
who still believe in living up to the deal as it was
originally cut. Amazing, I know, but true.''

They were all staring at him.

How'm I doing, Roland? Eddie asked.

*I think you are doing very well. But don't let this
man Balazar get his balance, Eddie. I think he's dangerous.*

*You think so, huh? Well, I'm one up on you there,
my friend. I know he's dangerous. Very fucking dangerous.*

He looked at Balazar again, and dropped him a little
wink. ''That's why *you're* the one who's gotta be concerned with the Feds now, not me. If they turn up with
a search warrant, you could suddenly find yourself
fucked without even opening your legs, Mr. Balazar.''

Balazar had picked up two cards. His hands suddenly shook and he put them aside. It was minute,
but Roland saw it and Eddie saw it, too. An expression of uncertainty—even momentary fear, perhaps—
appeared and then disappeared on his face.

''Watch your mouth with me, Eddie. Watch how you
express yourself, and please remember that my time
and my tolerance for nonsense are both short.''

Jack Andolini looked alarmed.

''He made a deal with them, Mr. Balazar! This little
shit turned over the coke and they planted it while they
were pretending to question him!''

''No one has been in here,'' Balazar said. ''No one
could get close, Jack, and you know it. Beepers go
when a pigeon farts on the roof.''

''But—''

"Even if they had managed to set us up somehow, we have so many people in their organization we could drill fifteen holes in their case in three days. We'd know who, when, and how."

Balazar looked back at Eddie.

"Eddie," he said, "you have fifteen seconds to stop bullshitting. Then I'm going to have 'Cimi Dretto step in here and hurt you. Then, after he hurts *you* for awhile, he will leave, and from a room close by you will hear him hurting your brother."

Eddie stiffened.

Easy, the gunslinger murmured, and thought, *All you have to do to hurt him is to say his brother's name. It's like poking an open sore with a stick.*

"I'm going to walk into your bathroom," Eddie said. He pointed at a door in the far left corner of the room, a door so unobtrusive it could almost have been one of the wall panels. "I'm going in by myself. Then I'm going to walk back out with a pound of your cocaine. Half the shipment. You test it. Then you bring Henry in here where I can look at him. When I see him, see he's okay, you are going to give him our goods and he's going to ride home with one of your gentlemen. While he does, me and . . ." *Roland,* he almost said, ". . . me and the rest of the guys we both know you got here can watch you build that thing. When Henry's home and safe—which means no one standing there with a gun in his ear—he's going to call and say a certain word. This is something we worked out before I left. Just in case."

The gunslinger checked Eddie's mind to see if this was true or bluff. It was true, or at least Eddie thought it was. Roland saw Eddie really believed his brother Henry would die before saying that word in falsity. The gunslinger was not so sure.

"You must think I still believe in Santa Claus," Balazar said.

"I know you don't."

"Claudio. Search him. Jack, you go in my bathroom and search *it*. Everything."

"Is there any place in there I wouldn't know about?" Andolini asked.

Balazar paused for a long moment, considering Andolini carefully with his dark brown eyes. "There is a small panel on the back wall of the medicine cabinet," he said. "I keep a few personal things in there. It is not big enough to hide a pound of dope in, but maybe you better check it."

Jack left, and as he entered the little privy, the gunslinger saw a flash of the same frozen white light that had illuminated the privy of the air-carriage. Then the door shut.

Balazar's eyes flicked back to Eddie.

"Why do you want to tell such crazy lies?" he asked, almost sorrowfully. "I thought you were smart."

"Look in my face," Eddie said quietly, "and tell me that I am lying."

Balazar did as Eddie asked. He looked for a long time. Then he turned away, hands stuffed in his pockets so deeply that the crack of his peasant's ass showed a little. His posture was one of sorrow—sorrow over an erring son—but before he turned Roland had seen an expression on Balazar's face that had not been sorrow. What Balazar had seen in Eddie's face had left him not sorrowful but profoundly disturbed.

"Strip," Claudio said, and now he was holding his gun on Eddie.

Eddie started to take his clothes off.

5

I don't like this, Balazar thought as he waited for Jack Andolini to come back out of the bathroom. He was scared, suddenly sweating not just under his arms or in his crotch, places where he sweated even when it was the dead of winter and colder than a well-digger's belt-buckle, but all over. Eddie had gone off looking like a junkie—a *smart* junkie but still a junkie, someone who could be led anywhere by the skag fish-hook in his balls—and had come back looking like . . . like what? Like he'd *grown* in some way, *changed.*

It's like somebody poured two quarts of fresh guts down his throat.

Yes. That was it. And the dope. The fucking dope. Jack was tossing the bathroom and Claudio was check-ing Eddie with the thorough ferocity of a sadistic prison guard; Eddie had stood with a stolidity Balazar would not previously have believed possible for him or any other doper while Claudio spat four times into his left palm, rubbed the snot-flecked spittle all over his right hand, then rammed it up Eddie's asshole to the wrist and an inch or two beyond.

There was no dope in his bathroom, no dope on Eddie or in him. There was no dope in Eddie's clothes, his jacket, or his travelling bag. So it was all nothing but a bluff.

Look in my face and tell me that I am lying.

So he had. What he saw was upsetting. What he saw was that Eddie Dean was perfectly confident: he in-tended to go into the bathroom and come back with half of Balazar's goods.

Balazar almost believed it himself.

Claudio Andolini pulled his arm back. His fingers came out of Eddie Dean's asshole with a plopping sound. Claudio's mouth twisted like a fishline with knots in it.

"Hurry up, Jack, I got this junkie's shit on my hand!" Claudio yelled angrily.

"If I'd known you were going to be prospecting up there, Claudio, I would have wiped my ass with a chair-leg last time I took a dump," Eddie said mildly. "Your hand would have come out cleaner and I wouldn't be standing here feeling like I just got raped by Ferdinand the Bull."

"*Jack!*"

"Go on down to the kitchen and clean yourself up," Balazar said quietly. "Eddie and I have got no reason to hurt each other. Do we, Eddie?"

"No," Eddie said.

"He's clean, anyway," Claudio said. "Well, *clean* ain't the word. What I mean is he ain't holding. You can be goddam sure of that." He walked out, holding his dirty hand in front of him like a dead fish.

Eddie looked calmly at Balazar, who was thinking again of Harry Houdini, and Blackstone, and Doug Henning, and David Copperfield. They kept saying that magic acts were as dead as vaudeville, but Henning was a superstar and the Copperfield kid had blown the crowd away the one time Balazar had caught his act in Atlantic City. Balazar had loved magicians from the first time he had seen one on a streetcorner, doing card-tricks for pocket-change. And what was the first thing they always did before making something appear—something that would make the whole audience first gasp and then applaud? What they did was invite someone up from the audience to make sure that the place from which the rabbit or dove or bare-breasted cutie or the whatever was to appear was perfectly empty. More than that, to make sure there was no way to get anything *inside*.

I think maybe he's done it. I don't know how, and I don't care. The only thing I know for sure is that I don't like any of this, not one damn bit.

6

George Biondi also had something not to like. He
doubted if Eddie Dean was going to be wild about it,
either.

George was pretty sure that at some point after
'Cimi had come into the accountant's office and doused
the lights, Henry had died. Died quietly, with no muss,
no fuss, no bother. Had simply floated away like a
dandelion spore on a light breeze. George thought
maybe it had happened right around the time Claudio
left to wash his shitty hand in the kitchen.

"Henry?" George muttered in Henry's ear. He put
his mouth so close that it was like kissing a girl's ear
in a movie theater, and that was pretty fucking gross,
especially when you considered that the guy was probably dead—it was like narcophobia or whatever the
fuck they called it—but he had to know, and the wall
between this office and Balazar's was thin.

"What's wrong, George?" Tricks Postino asked.

"Shut up," 'Cimi said. His voice was the low rumble of an idling truck.

They shut up.

George slid a hand inside Henry's shirt. Oh, this
was getting worse and worse. That image of being with
a girl in a movie theater wouldn't leave him. Now here
he was, feeling her up, only it wasn't a *her* but a *him*,
this wasn't just narcophobia, it was fucking *faggot* narcophobia, and Henry's scrawny junkie's chest wasn't
moving up and down, and there wasn't anything inside
going *thump-thump-thump*. For Henry Dean it was all
over, for Henry Dean the ball-game had been rained
out in the seventh inning. Wasn't nothing ticking but
his watch.

He moved into the heavy Old Country atmosphere
of olive oil and garlic that surrounded 'Cimi Dretto.

"I think we might have a problem," George whispered.

7

Jack came out of the bathroom.

"There's no dope in there," he said, and his flat eyes studied Eddie. "And if you were thinking about the window, you can forget it. That's ten-gauge steel mesh."

"I wasn't thinking about the window and it *is* in there," Eddie said quietly. "You just don't know where to look."

"I'm sorry, Mr. Balazar," Andolini said, "but this crock is getting just a little too full for me."

Balazar studied Eddie as if he hadn't even heard Andolini. He was thinking very deeply.

Thinking about magicians pulling rabbits out of hats.

You got a guy from the audience to check out the fact that the hat was empty. What other thing that never changed? That no one saw into the hat but the magician, of course. And what had the kid said? *I'm going to walk into your bathroom. I'm going in by myself.*

Knowing how a magic trick worked was something he usually wouldn't want to know; knowing spoiled the fun.

Usually.

This, however, was a trick he couldn't *wait* to spoil.

"Fine," he said to Eddie. "If it's in there, go get it. Just like you are. Bare-ass."

"Good," Eddie said, and started toward the bathroom door.

"But not alone," Balazar said. Eddie stopped at once, his body stiffening as if Balazar had shot him with an invisible harpoon, and it did Balazar's heart good to see it. For the first time something hadn't gone according to the kid's plan. "Jack's going with you."

"No," Eddie said at once. "That's not what I—"

"Eddie," Balazar said gently, "you don't tell me no. That's one thing you never do."

8

It's all right, the gunslinger said. *Let him come. But . . . but . . .*

Eddie was close to gibbering, barely holding onto his control. It wasn't just the sudden curve-ball Balazar had thrown him; it was his gnawing worry over Henry, and, growing steadily ascendant over all else, his need for a fix.

Let him come. It will be all right. Listen:

Eddie listened.

9

Balazar watched him, a slim, naked man with only the first suggestion of the junkie's typical cave-chested slouch, his head cocked to one side, and as he watched Balazar felt some of his confidence evaporate. It was as if the kid was listening to a voice only he could hear.

The same thought passed through Andolini's mind, but in a different way: *What's this? He looks like the dog on those old RCA Victor records!*

Col had wanted to tell him something about Eddie's eyes. Suddenly Jack Andolini wished he had listened.

Wish in one hand, shit in the other, he thought.

If Eddie had been listening to voices inside his head, they had either quit talking or he had quit paying attention.

"Okay," he said. "Come along, Jack. I'll show you the Eighth Wonder of the World." He flashed a smile that neither Jack Andolini nor Enrico Balazar cared for in the slightest.

"Is that so?" Andolini pulled a gun from the clam-shell holster attached to his belt at the small of his back. "Am I gonna be amazed?"

Eddie's smile widened. "Oh yeah. I think this is gonna knock your socks off."

10

Andolini followed Eddie into the bathroom. He was holding the gun up because his wind was up.

"Close the door," Eddie said.

"Fuck you," Andolini answered.

"Close the door or no dope," Eddie said.

"Fuck you," Andolini said again. Now, a little scared, feeling that there was something going on that he didn't understand, Andolini looked brighter than he had in the van.

"He won't close the door," Eddie yelled at Balazar. "I'm getting ready to give up on you, Mr. Balazar. You probably got six wiseguys in this place, every one of them with about four guns, and the two of you are going batshit over a kid in a crapper. A *junkie* kid."

"Shut the fucking door, Jack!" Balazar shouted.

"That's right," Eddie said as Jack Andolini kicked the door shut behind him. "Is you a man or is you a m—"

"Oh boy, ain't I had enough of this turd," Andolini said to no one in particular. He raised the gun, butt forward, meaning to pistol-whip Eddie across the mouth.

Then he froze, gun drawn up across his body, the snarl that bared his teeth slackening into a slack-jawed gape of surprise as he saw what Col Vincent had seen in the van.

Eddie's eyes changed from brown to blue.

"Now grab him!" a low, commanding voice said,

and although the voice came from Eddie's mouth, it was not Eddie's voice.

Schizo, Jack Andolini thought. *He's gone schizo, gone fucking schi—*

But the thought broke off when Eddie's hands grabbed his shoulders, because when that happened, Andolini saw a hole in reality suddenly appear about three feet behind Eddie.

No, not a hole. Its dimensions were too perfect for that.

It was a *door.*

"Hail Mary fulla grace," Jack said in a low breathy moan. Through that doorway which hung in space a foot or so above the floor in front of Balazar's private shower he could see a dark beach which sloped down to crashing waves. Things were moving on that beach. *Things.*

He brought the gun down, but the blow which had been meant to break off all of Eddie's front teeth at the gum-line did no more than mash Eddie's lips back and bloody them a little. All the strength was running out of him. Jack could *feel* it happening.

"I *told* you it was gonna knock your socks off, Jack," Eddie said, and then yanked him. Jack realized what Eddie meant to do at the last moment and began to fight like a wildcat, but it was too late—they were tumbling backward through that doorway, and the droning hum of New York City at night, so familiar and constant you never even heard it unless it wasn't there anymore, was replaced by the grinding sound of the waves and the grating, questioning voices of dimly seen horrors crawling to and fro on the beach.

11

*We'll have to move very fast, or we'll find ourselves
basted in a hot oast,* Roland had said, and Eddie was
pretty sure the guy meant that if they didn't shuck and
jive at damn near the speed of light, their gooses were
going to be cooked. He believed it, too. When it came
to hard guys, Jack Andolini was like Dwight Gooden:
you could rock him, yes, you could shock him, maybe,
but if you let him get away in the early innings he was
going to stomp you flat later on.

Left hand! Roland screamed at himself as they *went
through* and he separated from Eddie. *Remember! Left
hand! Left hand!*

He saw Eddie and Jack stumble backward, fall, and
then go rolling down the rocky scree that edged the
beach, struggling for the gun in Andolini's hand.

Roland had just time to think what a cosmic joke it
would be if he arrived back in his own world only to
discover that his physical body had died while he had
been away . . . and then it was too late. Too late to
wonder, too late to go back.

12

Andolini didn't know what had happened. Part of
him was sure he had gone crazy, part was sure Eddie
had doped him or gassed him or something like that,
part believed that the vengeful God of his childhood
had finally tired of his evils and had plucked him away
from the world he knew and set him down in this weird
purgatory.

Then he saw the door, standing open, spilling a fan
of white light—the light from Balazar's john—onto the
rocky ground—and understood it was possible to get
back. Andolini was a practical man above all else. He
would worry about what all this meant later on. Right

now he intended to kill this creep's ass and get back
through that door.

The strength that had gone out of him in his shocked
surprise now flooded back. He realized Eddie was trying to pull his small but very efficient Colt Cobra out
of his hand and had nearly succeeded. Jack pulled it
back with a curse, tried to aim, and Eddie promptly
grabbed his arm again.

Andolini hoisted a knee into the big muscle of Eddie's right thigh (the expensive gabardine of Andolini's
slacks was now crusted with dirty gray beach sand)
and Eddie screamed as the muscle seized up.

"Roland!" he cried. *"Help me! For Christ's sake,
help me!"*

Andolini snapped his head around and what he saw
threw him off-balance again. There was a guy standing
there . . . only he looked more like a ghost than a guy.
Not exactly Casper the Friendly Ghost, either. The
swaying figure's white, haggard face was rough with
beard-stubble. His shirt was in tatters which blew back
behind him in twisted ribbons, showing the starved
stack of his ribs. A filthy rag was wrapped around his
right hand. He looked sick, sick and dying, but even
so he also looked tough enough to make Andolini feel
like a soft-boiled egg.

And the joker was wearing a pair of guns.

They looked older than the hills, old enough to have
come from a Wild West museum . . . but they were
guns just the same, they might even really work, and
Andolini suddenly realized he was going to have to
take care of the white-faced man right away . . . unless he really *was* a spook, and if that was the case, it
wouldn't matter fuck-all, so there was really no sense
worrying about it.

Andolini let go of Eddie and snap-rolled to the right,
barely feeling the edge of rock that tore open his five-
hundred-dollar sport jacket. At the same instant the

gunslinger drew left-handed, and his draw was as it
had always been, sick or well, wide awake or still half
asleep: faster than a streak of blue summer lightning.

I'm beat, Andolini thought, full of sick wonder.
*Christ, he's faster than anybody I ever saw! I'm beat,
holy Mary Mother of God, he's gonna blow me away,
he's g—*

The man in the ragged shirt pulled the trigger of the
revolver in his left hand and Jack Andolini thought—
really thought—he was dead before he realized there
had been only a dull click instead of a report.

Misfire.

Smiling, Andolini rose to his knees and raised his
own gun.

"I don't know who you are, but you can kiss your
ass good-bye, you fucking spook," he said.

13

Eddie sat up, shivering, his naked body pocked with
goosebumps. He saw Roland draw, heard the dry snap
that should have been a bang, saw Andolini come up
on his knees, heard him say something, and before he
really knew what he was doing his hand had found a
ragged chunk of rock. He pulled it out of the grainy
earth and threw it as hard as he could.

It struck Andolini high on the back of the head and
bounced away. Blood sprayed from a ragged hanging
flap in Jack Andolini's scalp. Andolini fired, but the
bullet that surely would have killed the gunslinger otherwise went wild.

14

Not really wild, the gunslinger could have told
Eddie. *When you feel the wind of the slug on your
cheek, you can't really call it wild.*

He thumbed the hammer of his gun back and pulled the trigger again as he recoiled from Andolini's shot. This time the bullet in the chamber fired—the dry, authoritative crack echoed up and down the beach. Gulls asleep on rocks high above the lobstrosities awoke and flew upward in screaming, startled packs.

The gunslinger's bullet would have stopped Andolini for good in spite of his own involuntary recoil, but by then Andolini was also in motion, falling sideways, dazed by the blow on the head. The crack of the gunslinger's revolver seemed distant, but the searing poker it plunged into his left arm, shattering the elbow, was real enough. It brought him out of his daze and he rose to his feet, one arm hanging broken and useless, the gun wavering wildly about in his other hand, looking for a target.

It was Eddie he saw first, Eddie the junkie, Eddie who had somehow brought him to this crazy place. Eddie was standing there as naked as the day he had been born, shivering in the chilly wind, clutching himself with both arms. Well, he might die here, but he would at least have the pleasure of taking Eddie Fucking Dean with him.

Andolini brought his gun up. The little Cobra now seemed to weigh about twenty pounds, but he managed.

15

This better not be another misfire, Roland thought grimly, and thumbed the hammer back again. Below the din of the gulls, he heard the smooth oiled click as the chamber revolved.

16

It was no misfire.

17

The gunslinger hadn't aimed at Andolini's head but at the gun in Andolini's hand. He didn't know if they still needed this man, but they might; he was important to Balazar, and because Balazar had proved to be every bit as dangerous as Roland had thought he might be, the best course was the safest one.

His shot was good, and that was no surprise; what happened to Andolini's gun and hence to Andolini was. Roland had seen it happen, but only twice in all the years he had seen men fire guns at each other.

Bad luck for you, fellow, the gunslinger thought as Andolini wandered off toward the beach, screaming. Blood poured down his shirt and pants. The hand which had been holding the Colt Cobra was missing below the middle of the palm. The gun was a senseless piece of twisted metal lying on the sand.

Eddie stared at him, stunned. No one would ever misjudge Jack Andolini's caveman face again, because now he had no face; where it had been there was now nothing but a churned mess of raw flesh and the black screaming hole of his mouth.

"My God, what happened?"

"My bullet must have struck the cylinder of his gun at the second he pulled the trigger," the gunslinger said. He spoke as dryly as a professor giving a police academy ballistics lecture. "The result was an explosion that tore the back off his gun. I think one or two of the other cartridges may have exploded as well."

"Shoot him," Eddie said. He was shivering harder than ever, and now it wasn't just the combination of

night air, sea breeze, and naked body that was causing
it. "Kill him. Put him out of his misery, for God's s—"

"Too late," the gunslinger said with a cold indifference that chilled Eddie's flesh all the way in to the
bone.

And Eddie turned away just too late to avoid seeing
the lobstrosities swarm over Andolini's feet, tearing off
his Gucci loafers . . . with the feet still inside them,
of course. Screaming, waving his arms spasmodically
before him, Andolini fell forward. The lobstrosities
swarmed greedily over him, questioning him anxiously all the while they were eating him alive: *Dad-
a-chack? Did-a-chick? Dum-a-chum? Dod-a-chock?*

"Jesus," Eddie moaned. "What do we do now?"

"Now you get exactly as much of the

(*devil-powder* the gunslinger said; *cocaine* Eddie
heard)

as you promised the man Balazar," Roland said,
"no more and no less. And we go back." He looked
levelly at Eddie. "Only this time I have to go back
with you. As myself."

"Jesus Christ," Eddie said. "Can you do that?"
And at once answered his own question. "Sure you
can. But why?"

"Because you can't handle this alone," Roland said.
"Come here."

Eddie looked back at the squirming hump of clawed
creatures on the beach. He had never liked Jack Andolini, but he felt his stomach roll over just the same.

"Come here," Roland said impatiently. "We've little time, and I have little liking for what I must do
now. It's something I've never done before. Never
thought I *would* do." His lips twisted bitterly. "I'm
getting used to doing things like that."

Eddie approached the scrawny figure slowly, on legs
that felt more and more like rubber. His bare skin was
white and glimmering in the alien dark. *Just who are*

you, Roland? he thought. *What are you? And that heat I feel baking off you—is it just fever? Or some kind of madness? I think it might be both.*

God, he needed a fix. More: he *deserved* a fix.

"Never done *what* before?" he asked. "What are you talking about?"

"Take this," Roland said, and gestured at the ancient revolver slung low on his right hip. Did not point; there was no finger to point *with,* only a bulky, rag-wrapped bundle. "It's no good to me. Not now, perhaps never again."

"I . . ." Eddie swallowed. "I don't want to touch it."

"I don't want you to either," the gunslinger said with curious gentleness, "but I'm afraid neither of us has a choice. There's going to be shooting."

"There is?"

"Yes." The gunslinger looked serenely at Eddie. "Quite a lot of it, I think."

18

Balazar had become more and more uneasy. Too long. They had been in there too long and it was too quiet. Distantly, maybe on the next block, he could hear people shouting at each other and then a couple of rattling reports that were probably firecrackers . . . but when you were in the sort of business Balazar was in, firecrackers weren't the first thing you thought of.

A scream. Was that a scream?

Never mind. Whatever's happening on the next block has nothing to do with you. You're turning into an old woman.

All the same, the signs were bad. Very bad.

"Jack?" he yelled at the closed bathroom door.

There was no answer.

Balazar opened the left front drawer of his desk and

took out the gun. This was no Colt Cobra, cozy enough to fit in a clamshell holster; it was a .357 Magnum.

" 'Cimi!'' he shouted. "I want you!"

He slammed the drawer. The tower of cards fell with a soft, sighing thump. Balazar didn't even notice.

'Cimi Dretto, all two hundred and fifty pounds of him, filled the doorway. He saw that *Da Boss* had pulled his gun out of the drawer, and 'Cimi immediately pulled his own from beneath a plaid jacket so loud it could have caused flash-burns on anyone who made the mistake of looking at it too long.

"I want Claudio and Tricks," he said. "Get them quick. The kid is up to something."

"We got a problem," 'Cimi said.

Balazar's eyes flicked from the bathroom door to 'Cimi. "Oh, I got plenty of those already," he said. "What's this new one, 'Cimi?"

'Cimi licked his lips. He didn't like telling *Da Boss* bad news even under the best of circumstances; when he looked like this . . .

"Well," he said, and licked his lips. "You see—"

"Will you hurry the fuck up?" Balazar yelled.

19

The sandalwood grips of the revolver were so smooth that Eddie's first act upon receiving it was to nearly drop it on his toes. The thing was so big it looked prehistoric, so heavy he knew he would have to lift it two-handed. *The recoil,* he thought, *is apt to drive me right through the nearest wall. That's if it fires at all.* Yet there was some part of him that *wanted* to hold it, that responded to its perfectly expressed purpose, that sensed its dim and bloody history and wanted to be part of it.

No one but the best ever held this baby in his hand, Eddie thought. *Until now, at least.*

"Are you ready?" Roland asked.

"No, but let's do it," Eddie said.

He gripped Roland's left wrist with his left hand. Roland slid his hot right arm around Eddie's bare shoulders.

Together they stepped back through the doorway, from the windy darkness of the beach in Roland's dying world to the cool fluorescent glare of Balazar's private bathroom in The Leaning Tower.

Eddie blinked, adjusting his eyes to the light, and heard 'Cimi Dretto in the other room. "We got a problem," 'Cimi was saying. *Don't we all,* Eddie thought, and then his eyes riveted on Balazar's medicine chest. It was standing open. In his mind he heard Balazar telling Jack to search the bathroom, and heard Andolini asking if there was any place in there he wouldn't know about. Balazar had paused before replying. *There is a small panel on the back wall of the medicine cabinet,* he had said. *I keep a few personal things in there.*

Andolini had slid the metal panel open but had neglected to close it. "Roland!" he hissed.

Roland raised his own gun and pressed the barrel against his lips in a shushing gesture. Eddie crossed silently to the medicine chest.

A few personal things—there was a bottle of suppositories, a copy of a blearily printed magazine called *Child's Play* (the cover depicting two naked girls of about eight engaged in a soul-kiss) . . . and eight or ten sample packages of Keflex. Eddie knew what Keflex was. Junkies, prone as they were to infections both general and local, usually knew.

Keflex was an antibiotic.

"Oh, I got plenty of those already," Balazar was saying. He sounded harried. "What's this new one, 'Cimi?"

If this doesn't knock out whatever's wrong with him nothing will, Eddie thought. He began to grab the packages and went to stuff them into his pockets. He realized he *had* no pockets and uttered a harsh bark that wasn't even close to laughter.

He began to dump them into the sink. He would have to pick them up later . . . if there *was* a later.

"Well," 'Cimi was saying, "you see—"

"Will you hurry the fuck up?" Balazar yelled.

"It's the kid's big brother," 'Cimi said, and Eddie froze with the last two packages of Keflex still in his hand, his head cocked. He looked more like the dog on the old RCA Victor records than ever.

"What about him?" Balazar asked impatiently.

"He's dead," 'Cimi said.

Eddie dropped the Keflex into the sink and turned toward Roland.

"They killed my brother," he said.

20

Balazar opened his mouth to tell 'Cimi not to bother him with a bunch of crap when he had important things to worry about—like this impossible-to-shake feeling that the kid was going to fuck him, Andolini or no Andolini—when he heard the kid as clearly as the kid had no doubt heard him and 'Cimi. "They killed my brother," the kid said.

Suddenly Balazar didn't care about his goods, about the unanswered questions, or anything except bringing this situation to a screeching halt before it could get any weirder.

"Kill him, Jack!" he shouted.

There was no response. Then he heard the kid say it again: "They killed my brother. They killed Henry."

Balazar suddenly knew—*knew*—it wasn't Jack the kid was talking to.

"Get all the gentlemen," he said to 'Cimi. *"All* of

them. We're gonna burn his ass and when he's dead we're gonna take him in the kitchen and I'm gonna personally chop his head off.''

21

"They killed my brother,'' the prisoner said. The gunslinger said nothing. He only watched and thought: *The bottles. In the sink. That's what I need, or what he thinks I need. The packets. Don't forget. Don't forget.*

From the other room: *"Kill him, Jack!''*

Neither Eddie nor the gunslinger took any notice of this.

"They killed my brother. They killed Henry.''

In the other room Balazar was now talking about taking Eddie's head as a trophy. The gunslinger found some odd comfort in this: not everything in this world was different from his own, it seemed.

The one called 'Cimi began shouting hoarsely for the others. There was an ungentlemanly thunder of running feet.

"Do you want to do something about it, or do you just want to stand here?'' Roland asked.

"Oh, I want to do something about it,'' Eddie said, and raised the gunslinger's revolver. Although only moments ago he had believed he would need both hands to do it, he found that he could do it easily.

"And what is it you want to do?'' Roland asked, and his voice seemed distant to his own ears. He was sick, full of fever, but what was happening to him now was the onset of a different fever, one which was all too familiar. It was the fever that had overtaken him in Tull. It was battle-fire, hazing all thought, leaving only the need to stop thinking and start shooting.

"I want to go to war,'' Eddie Dean said calmly.

"You don't know what you're talking about,'' Ro-

land said, "but you are going to find out. When we
go through the door, you go right. I have to go left.
My hand."

Eddie nodded. They went to their war.

22

Balazar had expected Eddie, or Andolini, or both of
them. He had not expected Eddie and an utter stranger,
a tall man with dirty gray-black hair and a face that
looked as if it had been chiseled from obdurate stone
by some savage god. For a moment he was not sure
which way to fire.

'Cimi, however, had no such problems. *Da Boss*
was mad at Eddie. Therefore, he would punch Eddie's
clock first and worry about the other *catzarro* later.
'Cimi turned ponderously toward Eddie and pulled the
trigger of his automatic three times. The casings
jumped and gleamed in the air. Eddie saw the big man
turning and went into a mad slide along the floor,
whizzing along like some kid in a disco contest, a kid
so jived-up he didn't realize he'd left his entire John
Travolta outfit, underwear included, behind; he went
with his wang wagging and his bare knees first heating
and then scorching as the friction built up. Holes
punched through plastic that was supposed to look like
knotty pine just above him. Slivers of it rained down
on his shoulders and into his hair.

Don't let me die naked and needing a fix, God, he
prayed, knowing such a prayer was more than blas-
phemous; it was an absurdity. Still he was unable to
stop it. *I'll die, but please, just let me have one more—*

The revolver in the gunslinger's left hand crashed.
On the open beach it had been loud; over here it was
deafening.

"Oh Jeez!" 'Cimi Dretto screamed in a strangled,
breathy voice. It was a wonder he could scream at all.

His chest suddenly caved in, as if someone had swung a sledgehammer at a barrel. His white shirt began to turn red in patches, as if poppies were blooming on it. *"Oh Jeez! Oh Jeez! Oh J—"*

Claudio Andolini shoved him aside. 'Cimi fell with a thud. Two of the framed pictures on Balazar's wall crashed down. The one showing *Da Boss* presenting the Sportsman of the Year trophy to a grinning kid at a Police Athletic League banquet landed on 'Cimi's head. Shattered glass fell on his shoulders.

"Oh jeez" he whispered in a fainting little voice, and blood began to bubble from his lips.

Claudio was followed by Tricks and one of the men who had been waiting in the storage room. Claudio had an automatic in each hand; the guy from the storage room had a Remington shotgun sawed off so short that it looked like a derringer with a case of the mumps; Tricks Postino was carrying what he called The Wonderful Rambo Machine—this was an M-16 rapid-fire assault weapon.

"Where's my brother, you fucking needle-freak?" Claudio screamed. "What'd you do to Jack?" He could not have been terribly interested in an answer, because he began to fire with both weapons while he was still yelling. *I'm dead,* Eddie thought, and then Roland fired again. Claudio Andolini was propelled backwards in a cloud of his own blood. The automatics flew from his hands and slid across Balazar's desk. They thumped to the carpet amid a flutter of playing cards. Most of Claudio's guts hit the wall a second before Claudio caught up with them.

"Get him!" Balazar was shrieking. *"Get the spook! The kid ain't dangerous! He's nothing but a bare-ass junkie! Get the spook! Blow him away!"*

He pulled the trigger on the .357 twice. The Magnum was almost as loud as Roland's revolver. It did not make neat holes in the wall against which Roland crouched; the slugs smashed gaping wounds in the fake wood to either side of Roland's head. White light from the bathroom shone through the holes in ragged rays.

Roland pulled the trigger of his revolver.

Only a dry click.

Misfire.

"Eddie!" the gunslinger yelled, and Eddie raised his own gun and pulled the trigger.

The crash was so loud that for a moment he thought the gun had blown up in his hand, as Jack's had done. The recoil did not drive him back through the wall, but it did snap his arm up in a savage arc that jerked all the tendons under his arm.

He saw part of Balazar's shoulder disintegrate into red spray, heard Balazar screech like a wounded cat, and yelled, *"The junkie ain't dangerous, was that what you said? Was that it, you numb fuck? You want to mess with me and my brother? I'll show you who's dangerous! I'll sh—"*

There was a boom like a grenade as the guy from the storage room fired the sawed-off. Eddie rolled as the blast tore a hundred tiny holes in the walls and bathroom door. His naked skin was seared by shot in several places, and Eddie understood that if the guy had been closer, where the thing's pattern was tight, he would have been vaporized.

Hell, I'm dead anyway, he thought, watching as the guy from the storage room worked the Remington's jack, pumping in fresh cartridges, then laying it over his forearm. He was grinning. His teeth were very yellow—Eddie didn't think they had been acquainted with a toothbrush in quite some time.

Christ, I'm going to get killed by some fuckhead with yellow teeth and I don't even know his name, Eddie thought dimly. *At least I put one in Balazar. At least I did that much.* He wondered if Roland had another shot. He couldn't remember.

"I got him!" Tricks Postino yelled cheerfully. "Gimme a clear field, Dario!" And before the man named Dario could give him a clear field or anything else, Tricks opened up with The Wonderful Rambo Machine. The heavy thunder of machine-gun fire filled Balazar's office. The first result of this barrage was to save Eddie Dean's life. Dario had drawn a bead on him with the sawed-off, but before he could pull its double triggers, Tricks cut him in half.

"Stop it, you idiot!" Balazar screamed.

But Tricks either didn't hear, couldn't stop, or *wouldn't* stop. Lips pulled back from his teeth so that his spit-shining teeth were bared in a huge shark's grin, he raked the room from one end to the other, blowing two of the wall panels to dust, turning framed photographs into clouds of flying glass fragments, hammering the bathroom door off its hinges. The frosted glass of Balazar's shower stall exploded. The March of Dimes trophy Balazar had gotten the year before bonged like a bell as a slug drove through it.

In the movies, people actually kill other people with hand-held rapid-fire weapons. In real life, this rarely happens. If it does, it happens with the first four or five slugs fired (as the unfortunate Dario could have testified, if he had ever been capable of testifying to anything again). After the first four or five, two things happen to a man—even a powerful one—trying to control such a weapon. The muzzle begins to rise, and the shooter himself begins to turn either right or left, depending on which unfortunate shoulder he has decided to bludgeon with the weapon's recoil. In short, only a moron or a movie star would attempt the use of such a gun; it was like trying to shoot someone with a pneumatic drill.

For a moment Eddie was incapable of any action more constructive than staring at this perfect marvel

of idiocy. Then he saw other men crowding through
the door behind Tricks, and raised Roland's revolver.

"*Got him!*" Tricks was screaming with the joyous
hysteria of a man who has seen too many movies to
be able to distinguish between what the script in his
head says should be happening and what really is.
"*Got him! I got him! I g—*"

Eddie pulled the trigger and vaporized Tricks from
the eyebrows up. Judging from the man's behavior,
that was not a great deal.

Jesus Christ, when these things do *shoot, they really
blow holes in things,* he thought.

There was a loud *KA-BLAM* from Eddie's left.
Something tore a hot gouge in his underdeveloped left
bicep. He saw Balazar pointing the Mag at him from
behind the corner of his card-littered desk. His shoulder was a dripping red mass. Eddie ducked as the
Magnum crashed again.

23

Roland managed to get into a crouch, aimed at the
first of the new men coming in through the door, and
squeezed the trigger. He had rolled the cylinder,
dumped the used loads and the duds onto the carpet,
and had loaded this one fresh shell. He had done it
with his teeth. Balazar had pinned Eddie down. *If this
one's a dud, I think we're both gone.*

It wasn't. The gun roared, recoiled in his hand, and
Jimmy Haspio spun aside, the .45 he had been holding
falling from his dying fingers.

Roland saw the other man duck back and then he
was crawling through the splinters of wood and glass
that littered the floor. He dropped his revolver back
into its holster. The idea of reloading again with two
of his right fingers missing was a joke.

Eddie was doing well. The gunslinger measured just

how well by the fact that he was fighting naked. That was hard for a man. Sometimes impossible.

The gunslinger grabbed one of the automatic pistols Claudio Andolini had dropped.

"What are the rest of you guys waiting for?" Balazar screamed. *"Jesus! Eat these guys!"*

Big George Biondi and the other man from the supply room charged in through the door. The man from the supply room was bawling something in Italian.

Roland crawled to the corner of the desk. Eddie rose, aiming toward the door and the charging men. *He knows Balazar's there, waiting, but he thinks he's the only one of us with a gun now,* Roland thought. *Here is another one ready to die for you, Roland. What great wrong did you ever do that you should inspire such terrible loyalty in so many?*

Balazar rose, not seeing the gunslinger was now on his flank. Balazar was thinking of only one thing: finally putting an end to the goddam junkie who had brought this ruin down on his head.

"No," the gunslinger said, and Balazar looked around at him, surprise stamped on his features.

"Fuck y—" Balazar began, bringing the Magnum around. The gunslinger shot him four times with Claudio's automatic. It was a cheap little thing, not much better than a toy, and touching it made his hand feel dirty, but it was perhaps fitting to kill a despicable man with a despicable weapon.

Enrico Balazar died with an expression of terminal surprise on what remained of his face.

"Hi, George!" Eddie said, and pulled the trigger of the gunslinger's revolver. That satisfying crash came again. *No duds in this baby,* Eddie thought crazily. *I guess I must have gotten the good one.* George got off one shot before Eddie's bullet drove him back into the screaming man, bowling him over like a ninepin, but it went wild. An irrational but utterly persuasive feel-

ing had come over him: a feeling that Roland's gun
held some magical, talismanic power of protection.
As long as he held it, he couldn't be hurt.

Silence fell then, a silence in which Eddie could
hear only the man under Big George moaning (when
George landed on Rudy Vechhio, which was this unfortunate fellow's name, he had fractured three of
Vechhio's ribs) and the high ringing in his own ears.
He wondered if he would ever hear right again. The
shooting spree which now seemed to be over made the
loudest rock concert Eddie had ever been to sound like
a radio playing two blocks over by comparison.

Balazar's office was no longer recognizable as a
room of any kind. Its previous function had ceased to
matter. Eddie looked around with the wide, wondering eyes of a very young man seeing something like
this for the first time, but Roland knew the look, and
the look was always the same. Whether it was an open
field of battle where thousands had died by cannon,
rifle, sword, and halberd or a small room where five
or six had shot each other, it was the same place, always the same place in the end: another deadhouse,
stinking of gunpowder and raw meat.

The wall between the bathroom and the office was
gone except for a few struts. Broken glass twinkled
everywhere. Ceiling panels that had been shredded by
Tricks Postino's gaudy but useless M-16 fireworks display hung down like pieces of peeled skin.

Eddie coughed dryly. Now he could hear other
sounds—a babble of excited conversation, shouted
voices outside the bar, and, in the distance, the warble
of sirens.

"How many?" the gunslinger asked Eddie. "Can
we have gotten all of them?"

"Yes, I think—"

"I got something for you, Eddie," Kevin Blake said
from the hallway. "I thought you might want it, like

for a souvenir, you know?'' What Balazar had not been able to do to the younger Dean brother Kevin had done to the elder. He lobbed Henry Dean's severed head through the doorway.

Eddie saw what it was and screamed. He ran toward the door, heedless of the splinters of glass and wood that punched into his bare feet, screaming, shooting, firing the last live shell in the big revolver as he went.

''No, Eddie!'' Roland screamed, but Eddie didn't hear. He was beyond hearing.

He hit a dud in the sixth chamber, but by then he was aware of nothing but the fact that Henry was dead, *Henry*, they had cut off his head, some miserable son of a bitch had cut off Henry's *head*, and that son of a bitch was going to *pay*, oh yes, you could count on that.

So he ran toward the door, pulling the trigger again and again, unaware that nothing was happening, unaware that his feet were red with blood, and Kevin Blake stepped into the doorway to meet him, crouched low, a Llama .38 automatic in his hand. Kevin's red hair stood around his head in coils and springs, and Kevin was smiling.

24

He'll be low, the gunslinger thought, knowing he would have to be lucky to hit his target with this un-trustworthy little toy even if he had guessed right.

When he saw the ruse of Balazar's soldier was going to draw Eddie out, Roland rose to his knees and stead-ied his left hand on his right fist, grimly ignoring the screech of pain making that fist caused. He would have one chance only. The pain didn't matter.

Then the man with the red hair stepped into the doorway, smiling, and as always Roland's brain was gone; his eye saw, his hand shot, and suddenly the redhead was lying against the wall of the corridor with his eyes open and a small blue hole in his forehead. Eddie was standing over him, screaming and sobbing, dry-firing the big revolver with the sandalwood grips again and again, as if the man with the red hair could never be dead enough.

The gunslinger waited for the deadly crossfire that would cut Eddie in half and when it didn't come he knew it was truly over. If there had been other soldiers, they had taken to their heels.

He got wearily to his feet, reeled, and then walked slowly over to where Eddie Dean stood.

"Stop it," he said.

Eddie ignored him and went on dry-firing Roland's big gun at the dead man.

"Stop it, Eddie, he's dead. They're all dead. Your feet are bleeding."

Eddie ignored him and went on pulling the revolver's trigger. The babble of excited voices outside was closer. So were the sirens.

The gunslinger reached for the gun and pulled on it. Eddie turned on him, and before Roland was entirely sure what was happening, Eddie struck him on the side of the head with his own gun. Roland felt a warm gush of blood and collapsed against the wall. He struggled to stay on his feet—they had to get out of here, quick. But he could feel himself sliding down the wall in spite of his every effort, and then the world was gone for a little while in a drift of grayness.

25

He was out for no more than two minutes, and then he managed to get things back into focus and make it to his feet. Eddie was no longer in the hallway. Roland's gun lay on the chest of the dead man with the red hair. The gunslinger bent, fighting off a wave of dizziness, picked it up, and dropped it into its holster with an awkward, cross-body movement.

I want my damned fingers back, he thought tiredly, and sighed.

He tried to walk back into the ruins of the office, but the best he could manage was an educated stagger. He stopped, bent, and picked up all of Eddie's clothes that he could hold in the crook of his left arm. The howlers had almost arrived. Roland believed the men winding them were probably militia, a marshall's posse, something of that sort . . . but there was always the possibility they might be more of Balazar's men.

"Eddie," he croaked. His throat was sore and throbbing again, worse even than the swollen place on the side of his head where Eddie had struck him with the revolver.

Eddie didn't notice. Eddie was sitting on the floor with his brother's head cradled against his belly. He was shuddering all over and crying. The gunslinger looked for the door, didn't see it, and felt a nasty jolt that was nearly terror. Then he remembered. With both of them on this side, the only way to create the door was for him to make physical contact with Eddie.

He reached for him but Eddie shrank away, still weeping. "Don't touch me," he said.

"Eddie, it's over. They're all dead, and your brother's dead, too."

"Leave my brother out of this!" Eddie shrieked childishly, and another fit of shuddering went through him. He cradled the severed head to his chest and rocked it. He lifted his streaming eyes to the gunslinger's face.

"All the times he took care of me, man," he said, sobbing so hard the gunslinger could barely understand him. "All the times. Why couldn't I have taken care of him, just this once, after all the times he took care of me?"

He took care of you, all right, Roland thought grimly. *Look at you, sitting there and shaking like a man who's eaten an apple from the fever-tree. He took care of you just fine.*

"We have to go."

"Go?" For the first time some vague understanding came into Eddie's face, and it was followed immediately by alarm. "I ain't going nowhere. Especially not back to that other place, where those big crabs or whatever they are ate Jack."

Someone was hammering on the door, yelling to open up.

"Do you want to stay here and explain all these bodies?" the gunslinger asked.

"I don't care," Eddie said. "Without Henry, it doesn't matter. Nothing does."

"Maybe it doesn't matter to you," Roland said, "but there are others involved, prisoner."

"Don't call me that!" Eddie shouted.

"I'll call you that until you show me you can walk out of the cell you're in!" Roland shouted back. It hurt his throat to yell, but he yelled just the same. *"Throw that rotten piece of meat away and stop puling!"*

Eddie looked at him, cheeks wet, eyes wide and frightened.

"THIS IS YOUR LAST CHANCE!" an amplified voice said from outside. To Eddie the voice sounded eerily like the voice of a game-show host. *"THE S.W.A.T. SQUAD HAS ARRIVED—I REPEAT: THE S.W.A.T. SQUAD HAS ARRIVED!"*

"What's on the other side of that door for me?" Eddie asked the gunslinger quietly. "Go on and tell me. If you can tell me, maybe I'll come. But if you lie, I'll know."

"Probably death," the gunslinger said. "But before that happens, I don't think you'll be bored. I want you to join me on a quest. Of course, all will probably end in death—death for the four of us in a strange place. But if we should win through . . .'' His eyes gleamed. ''If we win through, Eddie, you'll see something beyond all the beliefs of all your dreams.''

''What thing?''

''The Dark Tower.''

''Where is this Tower?''

''Far from the beach where you found me. How far I know not.''

''What is it?''

''I don't know that, either—except that it may be a kind of . . . of a bolt. A central linchpin that holds all of existence together. All existence, all time, and all size.''

''You said four. Who are the other two?''

''I know them not, for they have yet to be drawn.''

''As I was drawn. Or as you'd like to draw me.''

''Yes.''

From outside there was a coughing explosion like a mortar round. The glass of The Leaning Tower's front window blew in. The barroom began to fill with choking clouds of tear-gas.

''Well?'' Roland asked. He could grab Eddie, force the doorway into existence by their contact, and pummel them both through. But he had seen Eddie risk his life for him; he had seen this hag-ridden man behave with all the dignity of a born gunslinger in spite of his addiction and the fact that he had been forced to fight as naked as the day he was born, and he wanted Eddie to decide for himself.

''Quests, adventures, Towers, worlds to win,'' Eddie said, and smiled wanly. Neither of them turned as fresh tear-gas rounds flew through the windows to explode, hissing, on the floor. The first acrid tendrils of the gas were now slipping into Balazar's office. ''Sounds better than one of those Edgar Rice Burroughs books about Mars Henry used to read me sometimes when we were kids. You only left out one thing.''

''What's that?''

''The beautiful bare-breasted girls.''

The gunslinger smiled. ''On the way to the Dark Tower,'' he said, ''anything is possible.''

Another shudder wracked Eddie's body. He raised Henry's head, kissed one cool, ash-colored cheek, and laid the gore-streaked relic gently aside. He got to his feet.

''Okay,'' he said. ''I didn't have anything else planned for tonight, anyway.''

''Take these,'' Roland said, and shoved the clothes at him. ''Put on your shoes if nothing else. You've cut your feet.''

On the sidewalk outside, two cops wearing plexi-glass faceplates, flak-jackets, and Kelvar vests smashed in The Leaning Tower's front door. In the bathroom, Eddie (dressed in his underpants, his Adidas sneakers, and nothing else) handed the sample packages of Ke-flex to Roland one by one, and Roland put them into the pockets of Eddie's jeans. When they were all safely stowed, Roland slid his right arm around Eddie's neck again and Eddie gripped Roland's left hand again. The door was suddenly there, a rectangle of darkness. Eddie felt the wind from that other world blow his sweaty hair back from his forehead. He heard the waves rolling up that stony beach. He smelled the tang of sour sea-salt. And in spite of everything, all his pain and sorrow, he suddenly wanted to see this Tower of which Roland spoke. He wanted to see it very much. And with Henry dead, what was there in this world for him? Their parents were dead, and there hadn't been a steady girl since he got heavily into the smack three years ago—just a steady parade of sluts, need-lers, and nosers. None of them straight. Fuck that action.

They stepped through, Eddie actually leading a little.

On the other side he was suddenly wracked with fresh shudders and agonizing muscle-cramps—the first symptoms of serious heroin withdrawal. And with them he also had the first alarmed second thoughts.

"Wait!" he shouted. "I want to go back for a minute! His desk! His desk, or the other office! The scag! If they were keeping Henry doped, there's gotta be junk! Heroin! I need it! I need it!"

He looked pleadingly at Roland, but the gunslinger's face was stony.

"That part of your life is over, Eddie," he said. He reached out with his left hand.

"No!" Eddie screamed, clawing at him. *"No, you don't get it, man, I need it! I NEED IT!"*

He might as well have been clawing stone.

The gunslinger swept the door shut.

It made a dull clapping sound that bespoke utter finality and fell backward onto the sand. A little dust puffed up from its edges. There was nothing behind the door, and now no word written upon it. This particular portal between the worlds had closed forever.

"No!" Eddie screamed, and the gulls screamed back at him as if in jeering contempt; the lobstrosities asked him questions, perhaps suggesting he could hear them a little better if he were to come a little closer, and Eddie fell over on his side, crying and shuddering and jerking with cramps.

"Your need will pass," the gunslinger said, and managed to get one of the sample packets out of the pocket of Eddie's jeans, which were so like his own. Again, he could read some of these letters but not all. *Cheeflet*, the word looked like.

Cheeflet.

Medicine from that other world.

"Kill or cure," Roland murmured, and dry-swallowed two of the capsules. Then he took the other three *astin,* and lay next to Eddie, and took him in his arms as well as he could, and after some difficult time, both of them slept.

SHUFFLE

shuffle

The time following that night was broken time for
Roland, time that didn't really exist as time at all.
What he remembered was only a series of images,
moments, conversation without context; images flashing past like one-eyed jacks and treys and nines and
the Bloody Black Bitch Queen of Spiders in a card-
sharp's rapid shuffle.

Later on he asked Eddie how long that time lasted,
but Eddie didn't know either. Time had been destroyed
for both of them. There was no time in hell, and each
of them was in his own private hell: Roland the hell
of the fever and infection, Eddie the hell of withdrawal.

"It was less than a week," Eddie said. "That's all
I know for sure."

"How do you know that?"

"A week's worth of pills was all I had to give you.
After that, you were gonna have to do the one thing
or the other on your own."

"Get well or die."

"Right."

shuffle

There's a gunshot as twilight draws down to dark, a
dry crack impinging on the inevitable and ineluctable
sound of the breakers dying on the desolate beach:
KA-BLAM! He smells a whiff of gunpowder. *Trouble*,
the gunslinger thinks weakly, and gropes for revolvers
that aren't there. *Oh no, it's the end, it's* . . .
But there's no more. as something starts to smell

shuffle

good in the dark. Something, after all this long dark
dry time, something is *cooking*. It's not just the smell.
He can hear the snap and pop of twigs, can see the
faint orange flicker of a campfire. Sometimes, when
the sea-breeze gusts, he smells fragrant smoke as well
as that mouth-watering other smell. *Food,* he thinks.
*My God, am I hungry? If I'm hungry, maybe I'm get-
ting well.*
Eddie, he tries to say, but his voice is all gone. His
throat hurts, hurts so bad. *We should have brought
some* astin, *too,* he thinks, and then tries to laugh: all
the drugs for him, none for Eddie.
Eddie appears. He's got a tin plate, one the gunslinger would know anywhere: it came, after all, from
his own purse. On it are streaming chunks of whitish-
pink meat.
What? he tries to ask, and nothing comes out but a
squeaky little farting sound.
Eddie reads the shape of his lips. "*I* don't know,"
he says crossly. "All I know is it didn't kill me. Eat
it, damn you."
He sees Eddie is very pale, Eddie is shaking, and

he smells something coming from Eddie that is either shit or death, and he knows Eddie is in a bad way. He reaches out a groping hand, wanting to give comfort. Eddie strikes it away.

"I'll feed you," he says crossly. "Fucked if I know why. I ought to kill you. I would, if I didn't think that if you could get through into my world once, maybe you could do it again."

Eddie looks around.

"And if it wasn't that I'd be alone. Except for *them.*"

He looks back at Roland and a fit of shuddering runs through him—it is so fierce that he almost spills the chunks of meat on the tin plate. At last it passes.

"Eat, God damn you."

The gunslinger eats. The meat is more than not bad; the meat is delicious. He manages three pieces and then everything blurs into a new

shuffle

effort to speak, but all he can do is whisper. The cup of Eddie's ear is pressed against his lips, except every now and then it shudders away as Eddie goes through one of his spasms. He says it again. "North. Up . . . up the beach."

"How do you know?"

"Just know," he whispers.

Eddie looks at him. "You're crazy," he says.

The gunslinger smiles and tries to black out but Eddie slaps him, slaps him hard. Roland's blue eyes fly open and for a moment they are so alive and electric Eddie looks uneasy. Then his lips draw back in a smile that is mostly snarl.

"Yeah, you can drone off," he said, "but first you

gotta take your dope. It's time. Sun says it is, anyway.
I guess. I was never no Boy Scout, so I don't know
for sure. But I guess it's close enough for Government
work. Open wide, Roland. Open wide for Dr. Eddie,
you kidnapping fuck.''

The gunslinger opens his mouth like a baby for the
breast. Eddie puts two of the pills in his mouth and
then slops fresh water carelessly into Roland's mouth.
Roland guesses it must be from a hill stream somewhere to the east. It might be poison; Eddie wouldn't
know fair water from foul. On the other hand, Eddie
seems fine himself, and there's really no choice, is
there? No.

He swallows, coughs, and nearly strangles while
Eddie looks at him indifferently.

Roland reaches for him.

Eddie tries to draw away.

The gunslinger's bullshooter eyes command him.

Roland draws him close, so close he can smell the
stink of Eddie's sickness and Eddie can smell the stink
of his; the combination sickens and compels them
both.

"Only two choices here," Roland whispers. "Don't
know how it is in your world, but only two choices
here. Stand and maybe live, or die on your knees with
your head down and the stink of your own armpits in
your nose. Nothing . . ." He hacks out a cough.
"Nothing to me."

"Who are you?" Eddie screams at him.

"Your destiny, Eddie," the gunslinger whispers.

"Why don't you just eat shit and die?" Eddie asks
him. The gunslinger tries to speak, but before he can
he floats off as the cards

shuffle

KA-BLAM!

Roland opens his eyes on a billion stars wheeling through the blackness, then closes them again.

He doesn't know what's going on but he thinks everything's okay. The deck's still moving, the cards still

shuffle

More of the sweet, tasty chunks of meat. He feels better. Eddie looks better, too. But he also looks worried.

"They're getting closer," he says. "They may be ugly, but they ain't completely stupid. They know what I been doing. Somehow they know, and they don't dig it. Every night they get a little closer. It might be smart to move on when daybreak comes, if you can. Or it might be the last daybreak we ever see."

"What?" This is not exactly a whisper but a husk somewhere between a whisper and real speech.

"Them," Eddie says, and gestures toward the beach. *"Dad-a-chack, dum-a-chum,* and all that shit. I think they're like us, Roland—all for eating, but not too big on getting eaten."

Suddenly, in an utter blast of horror, Roland realizes what the whitish-pink chunks of meat Eddie has been feeding him have been. He cannot speak; revulsion robs him of what little voice he has managed to get back. But Eddie sees everything he wants to say on his face.

"What did you think I was doing?" he nearly snarls. "Calling Red Lobster for take-out?"

"They're poison," Roland whispers. "That's why—"

"Yeah, that's why you're *hors de combat*. What I'm trying to keep from you being, Roland my friend, is *h'ors d'oeuvres* as well. As far as poison goes, rattlesnakes are poison, but people eat them. Rattlesnake tastes real good. Like chicken. I read that somewhere. They looked like lobsters to me, so I decided to take a chance. What else were we gonna eat? Dirt? I shot one of the fuckers and cooked the living Christ out of it. There wasn't anything else. And actually, they taste pretty good. I been shooting one a night just after the sun starts to go down. They're not real lively until it gets completely dark. I never saw you turning the stuff down."

Eddie smiles.

"I like to think maybe I got one of the ones that ate Jack. I like to think I'm eating that dink. It, like, eases my mind, you know?"

"One of them ate part of me, too," the gunslinger husks out. "Two fingers, one toe."

"That's also cool," Eddie keeps smiling. His face is pallid, sharklike . . . but some of that ill look has gone now, and the smell of shit and death which has hung around him like a shroud seems to be going away.

"Fuck yourself," the gunslinger husks.

"Roland shows a flash of spirit!" Eddie cries. "Maybe you ain't gonna die after all! Dahling! I think that's *mah-vellous!*"

"Live," Roland says. The husk has become a whisper again. The fishhooks are returning to his throat.

"Yeah?" Eddie looks at him, then nods and answers his own question. "Yeah. I think you mean to. Once I thought you were going and once I thought you were gone. Now it looks like you're going to get better. The antibiotics are helping, I guess, but mostly I think you're *hauling* yourself up. What for? Why the fuck do you keep trying so hard to keep alive on this scuzzy beach?"

Tower, he mouths, because now he can't even manage a husk.

"You and your fucking Tower," Eddie says, starts to turn away, and then turns back, surprised, as Roland's hand clamps on his arm like a manacle.

They look into each other's eyes and Eddie says, "All right. All *right!*"

North, the gunslinger mouths. *North, I told you.* Has he told him that? He thinks so, but it's lost. Lost in the shuffle.

"How do you *know?*" Eddie screams at him in sudden frustration. He raises his fists as if to strike Roland, then lowers them.

I just know—so why do you waste my time and energy asking me foolish questions? he wants to reply, but before he can, the cards

shuffle

being dragged along, bounced and bumped, his head lolling helplessly from one side to the other, bound to some kind of a weird *travois* by his own gunbelts, and he can hear Eddie Dean singing a song which is so weirdly familiar he at first believes this must be a delirium dream:

Heyy Jude . . . don't make it bad . . . take a saaad song . . . and make it better . . . "

Where did you hear that? he wants to ask. *Did you hear me singing it, Eddie? And where are we?*

But before he can ask anything

shuffle

*Cort would bash the kid's head in if he saw that
contraption,* Roland thinks, looking at the *travois* upon
which he has spent the day, and laughs. It isn't much
of a laugh. It sounds like one of those waves dropping
its load of stones on the beach. He doesn't know how
far they have come, but it's far enough for Eddie to be
totally bushed. He's sitting on a rock in the lengthening light with one of the gunslinger's revolvers in his
lap and a half-full water-skin to one side. There's a
small bulge in his shirt pocket. These are the bullets
from the back of the gunbelts—the diminishing supply
of "good" bullets. Eddie has tied these up in a piece
of his own shirt. The main reason the supply of
"good" bullets is diminishing so fast is because one
of every four or five has also turned out to be a dud.

Eddie, who has been nearly dozing, now looks up.
"What are you laughing about?" he asks.

The gunslinger waves a dismissive hand and shakes
his head. Because he's wrong, he realizes. Cort
wouldn't bash Eddie for the *travois,* even though it was
an odd, lame-looking thing. Roland thinks it might
even be possible that Cort might grunt some word of
compliment—such a rarity that the boy to whom it
happened hardly ever knew how to respond; he was
left gaping like a fish just pulled from a cook's barrel.

The man supports were two cottonwood branches of
approximately the same length and thickness. A blow-
down, the gunslinger presumed. He had used smaller
branches as supports, attaching them to the support
poles with a crazy conglomeration of stuff: gunbelts,
the glue-string that had held the devil-powder to his
chest, even the rawhide thong from the gunslinger's hat
and his, Eddie's, own sneaker laces. He had laid the
gunslinger's bedroll over the supports.

Cort would not have struck him because, sick as he was, Eddie had at least done more than squat on his hunkers and bewail his fate. He had made *something*. Had *tried*.

And Cort might have offered one of his abrupt, almost grudging compliments because, crazy as the thing looked, it *worked*. The long tracks stretching back down the beach to a point where they seemed to come together at the rim of perspective proved that.

"You see any of them?" Eddie asks. The sun is going down, beating an orange path across the water, and so the gunslinger reckons he has been out better than six hours this time. He feels stronger. He sits up and looks down to the water. Neither the beach nor the land sweeping to the western slope of the mountains have changed much; he can see small variations of landscape and detritus (a dead seagull, for instance, lying in a little heap of blowing feathers on the sand about twenty yards to the left and thirty or so closer to the water), but these aside, they might as well be right where they started.

"No," the gunslinger says. Then: "Yes. There's one."

He points. Eddie squints, then nods. As the sun sinks lower and the orange track begins to look more and more like blood, the first of the lobstrosities come tumbling out of the waves and begin crawling up the beach.

Two of them race clumsily toward the dead gull. The winner pounces on it, rips it open, and begins to stuff the rotting remains into its maw. *"Did-a-chick?"* it asks.

"Dum-a-chum?" responds the loser. *"Dod-a—"*
KA-BLAM!

Roland's gun puts an end to the second creature's questions. Eddie walks down to it and grabs it by the back, keeping a wary eye on its fellow as he does so.

The other offers no trouble, however; it is busy with
the gull. Eddie brings his kill back. It is still twitching,
raising and lowering its claws, but soon enough it stops
moving. The tail arches one final time, then simply
drops instead of flexing downward. The boxers' claws
hang limp.

"Dinnah will soon be served, mawster," Eddie
says. "You have your choice: filet of creepy-crawler
or filet of creepy-crawler. Which strikes your fancy,
mawster?"

"I don't understand you," the gunslinger said.

"Sure you do," Eddie said. "You just don't have
any sense of humor. What happened to it?"

"Shot off in one war or another, I guess."

Eddie smiles at that. "You look and sound a little
more alive tonight, Roland."

"I am, I think."

"Well, maybe you could even walk for awhile tomorrow. I'll tell you very frankly, my friend, dragging
you is the pits and the shits."

"I'll try."

"You do that."

"You look a little better, too," Roland ventures.
His voice cracks on the last two words like the voice
of a young boy. *If I don't stop talking soon,* he thought,
I won't be able to talk at all again.

"I guess I'll live." He looks at Roland expressionlessly. "You'll never know how close it was a couple
of times, though. Once I took one of your guns and
put it against my head. Cocked it, held it there for
awhile, and then took it away. Eased the hammer down
and shoved it back in your holster. Another night I
had a convulsion. I think that was the second night,
but I'm not sure." He shakes his head and says something the gunslinger both does and doesn't understand.
"Michigan seems like a dream to me now."

Although his voice is down to that husky murmur

again and he knows he shouldn't be talking at all, the gunslinger has to know one thing. "What stopped you from pulling the trigger?"

"Well, this is the only pair of pants I've got," Eddie says. "At the last second I thought that if I pulled the trigger and it was one of those dud shells, I'd never get up the guts to do it again . . . and once you shit your pants, you gotta wash 'em right away or live with the stink forever. Henry told me that. He said he learned it in Nam. And since it was nighttime and Lester the Lobster was out, not to mention all his friends—"

But the gunslinger is laughing, laughing hard, although only an occasional cracked sound actually escapes his lips. Smiling a little himself, Eddie says: "I think maybe you only got your sense of humor shot off up to the elbow in that war." He gets up, meaning to go up the slope to where there will be fuel for a fire, Roland supposes.

"Wait," he whispers, and Eddie looks at him. "Why, really?"

"I guess because you needed me. If I'd killed myself, you would have died. Later on, after you're really on your feet again, I may, like, re-examine my options." He looks around and sighs deeply.

"There may be a Disneyland or Coney Island somewhere in your world, Roland, but what I've seen of it so far really doesn't interest me much."

He starts away, pauses, and looks back again at Roland. His face is somber, although some of the sickly pallor has left it. The shakes have become no more than occasional tremors.

"Sometimes you really don't understand me, do you?"

"No," the gunslinger whispers. "Sometimes I don't."

"Then I'll elucidate. There are people who need

people to need them. The reason you don't understand
is because you're not one of those people. You'd use
me and then toss me away like a paper bag if that's
what it came down to. God fucked you, my friend.
You're just smart enough so it would hurt you to do
that, and just hard enough so you'd go ahead and do
it anyway. You wouldn't be able to help yourself. If I
was lying on the beach there and screaming for help,
you'd walk over me if I was between you and your
goddam Tower. Isn't that pretty close to the truth?''

Roland says nothing, only watches Eddie.

"But not everyone is like that. There are people
who need people to need them. Like the Barbra Strei-
sand song. Corny, but true. It's just another way of
being hooked through the bag.''

Eddie gazes at him.

"But when it comes to that, you're clean, aren't
you?''

Roland watches him.

"Except for your Tower.'' Eddie utters a short
laugh. "You're a Tower junkie, Roland.''

"Which war was it?'' Roland whispers.

"What?''

"The one where you got your sense of nobility and
purpose shot off?''

Eddie recoils as if Roland has reached out and
slapped him.

"I'm gonna go get some water,'' he says shortly.
"Keep an eye on the creepy crawlers. We came a long
way today, but I still don't know if they talk to each
other or not.''

He turns away then, but not before Roland has seen
the last red rays of sunset reflected on his wet cheeks.

Roland turns back to the beach and watches. The
lobstrosities crawl and question, question and crawl,
but both activities seem aimless; they have some in-

telligence, but not enough to pass on information to others of their kind.

God doesn't always dish it in your face, Roland thinks. *Most times, but not always.*

Eddie returns with wood.

"Well?" he asks. "What do you think?"

"We're all right," the gunslinger croaks, and Eddie starts to say something but the gunslinger is tired now and lies back and looks at the first stars peeking through the canopy of violet sky and

shuffle

in the three days that followed, the gunslinger progressed steadily back to health. The red lines creeping up his arms first reversed their direction, then faded, then disappeared. On the next day he sometimes walked and sometimes let Eddie drag him. On the day following he didn't need to be dragged at all; every hour or two they simply sat for a period of time until the watery feeling went out of his legs. It was during these rests and in those times after dinner had been eaten but before the fire had burned all the way down and they went to sleep that the gunslinger heard about Henry and Eddie. He remembered wondering what had happened to make their brothering so difficult, but after Eddie had begun, haltingly and with that sort of resentful anger that proceeds from deep pain, the gunslinger could have stopped him, could have told him: *Don't bother, Eddie. I understand everything.*

Except that wouldn't have helped Eddie. Eddie wasn't talking to help Henry because Henry was dead. He was talking to bury Henry for good. And to remind himself that although Henry was dead, he, Eddie, wasn't.

So the gunslinger listened and said nothing.

The gist was simple: Eddie believed he had stolen his brother's life. Henry also believed this. Henry might have believed it on his own or he might have believed it because he so frequently heard their mother lecturing Eddie on how much both she and Henry had sacrificed for him, so Eddie could be as safe as anyone could be in this jungle of a city, so he could be *happy,* as happy as anyone could be in this jungle of a city, so he wouldn't end up like his poor sister that he didn't even hardly remember but she had been so beautiful, God love her. She was with the angels, and that was undoubtedly a wonderful place to be, but she didn't want Eddie to be with the angels just yet, run over in the road by some crazy drunken driver like his sister or cut up by some crazy junkie kid for the twenty-five cents in his pocket and left with his guts running out all over the sidewalk, and because she didn't think *Eddie* wanted to be with the angels yet, he just better listen to what his big brother said and do what his big brother said to do and always remember that Henry was making a love-sacrifice.

Eddie told the gunslinger he doubted if his mother knew some of the things they had done—filching comic books from the candy store on Rincon Avenue or smoking cigarettes behind the Bonded Electroplate Factory on Cohoes Street.

Once they saw a Chevrolet with the keys in it and although Henry barely knew how to drive—he was six-teen then, Eddie eight—he had crammed his brother into the car and said they were going to New York City. Eddie was scared, crying, Henry scared too and mad at Eddie, telling him to shut up, telling him to stop being such a fuckin baby, he had ten bucks and Eddie had three or four, they could go to the movies all fuckin day and then catch a Pelham train and be back before their mother had time to put supper on the table and wonder where they were. But Eddie kept crying and near the Queensboro Bridge they saw a police car on a side street and although Eddie was pretty sure the cop in it hadn't even been looking their way, he said *Yeah* when Henry asked him in a harsh, quavering voice if Eddie thought that bull had seen them. Henry turned white and pulled over so fast that he had almost amputated a fire hydrant. He was running down the block while Eddie, now in a panic himself, was still struggling with the unfamiliar doorhandle. Henry stopped, came back, and hauled Eddie out of the car. He also slapped him twice. Then they had walked—well, actually they *slunk*—all the way back to Brooklyn. It took them most of the day, and when their mother asked them why they looked so hot and sweaty and tired out, Henry said it was because he'd spent most of the day teaching Eddie how to go one-on-one on the basketball court at the playground around the block. Then some big kids came and they had to run. Their mother kissed Henry and beamed at Eddie. She asked him if he didn't have the bestest big brother in the world. Eddie agreed with her. This was honest agreement, too. He thought he did.

"He was as scared as I was that day," Eddie told Roland as they sat and watched the last of the day dwindle from the water, where soon the only light would be that reflected from the stars. "Scareder, really, because he thought that cop saw us and I knew he didn't. That's why he ran. But he came back. That's the important part. *He came back.*"

Roland said nothing.

"You see that, don't you?" Eddie was looking at Roland with harsh, questioning eyes.

"I see."

"He was always scared, but he always came back."

Roland thought it would have been better for Eddie, maybe better for both of them in the long run, if Henry

had just kept showing his heels that day . . . or on one
of the others. But people like Henry never did. People
like Henry always came back, because people like
Henry *did* know how to use. First they changed trust
into need, then they changed need into a drug, and
once that was done, they—what was Eddie's word for
it?—*push*. Yes. They pushed it.

"I think I'll turn in," the gunslinger said.

The next day Eddie went on, but Roland already
knew it all. Henry hadn't played sports in high school
because Henry couldn't stay after for practice. Henry
had to take care of Eddie. The fact that Henry was
scrawny and uncoordinated and didn't much care for
sports in the first place had nothing to do with it, of
course; Henry would have made a *wonderful* baseball
pitcher or one of those basketball jumpers, their
mother assured them both time and again. Henry's
grades were bad and he needed to repeat a number of
subjects—but that wasn't because Henry was stupid;
Eddie and Mrs. Dean both knew Henry was just as
smart as lickety-split. But Henry had to spend the time
he should have spent studying or doing homework taking care of Eddie (the fact that this usually took place
in the Dean living room, with both boys sprawled on
the sofa watching TV or wrestling around on the floor
somehow seemed not to matter). The bad grades meant
Henry hadn't been able to be accepted into anything
but NYU, and they couldn't afford it because the bad
grades precluded any scholarships, and then Henry got
drafted and then it was Viet Nam, where Henry got
most of his knee blown off, and the pain was bad, and
the drug they gave him for it had a heavy morphine
base, and when he was better they weaned him from
the drug, only they didn't do such a good job because
when Henry got back to New York there was still a
monkey on his back, a hungry monkey waiting to be

fed, and after a month or two he had gone out to see
a man, and it had been about four months later, less
than a month after their mother died, when Eddie first
saw his brother snorting some white powder off a mirror. Eddie assumed it was coke. Turned out it was
heroin. And if you traced it all the way back, whose
fault was it?

Roland said nothing, but heard the voice of Cort in
his mind: *Fault always lies in the same place, my fine
babies: with him weak enough to lay blame.*

When he discovered the truth, Eddie had been
shocked, then angry. Henry had responded not by
promising to quit snorting but by telling Eddie he
didn't blame him for being mad, he knew Nam had
turned him into a worthless shitbag, he was weak, he
would leave, that was the best thing, Eddie was right,
the last thing he needed was a filthy junkie around,
messing up the place. He just hoped Eddie wouldn't
blame him too much. He had gotten weak, he admitted
it; something in Nam had made him weak, had rotted
him out the same way the moisture rotted the laces of
your sneakers and the elastic of your underwear. There
was also something in Nam that apparently rotted out
your heart, Henry told him tearily. He just hoped that
Eddie would remember all the years he had tried to be
strong.

For Eddie.

For Mom.

So Henry tried to leave. And Eddie, of course,
couldn't let him. Eddie was consumed with guilt.
Eddie had seen the scarred horror that had once been
an unmarked leg, a knee that was now more Teflon
than bone. They had a screaming match in the hall,
Henry standing there in an old pair of khakis with his
packed duffle bag in one hand and purple rings under
his eyes, Eddie wearing nothing but a pair of yellowing jockey shorts, Henry saying you don't need me

around, Eddie, I'm poison to you and I know it, and Eddie yelling back You ain't going nowhere, get your ass back inside, and that's how it went until Mrs. McGursky came out of *her* place and yelled *Go or stay, it's nothing to me, but you better decide one way or the other pretty quick or I'm calling the police.* Mrs. McGursky seemed about to add a few more admonishments, but just then she saw that Eddie was wearing nothing but a pair of skivvies. She added: *And you're not decent, Eddie Dean!* before popping back inside. It was like watching a Jack-in-the-box in reverse. Eddie looked at Henry. Henry looked at Eddie. *Look like Angel-Baby done put on a few pounds,* Henry said in a low voice, and then they were howling with laughter, holding onto each other and pounding each other and Henry came back inside and about two weeks later Eddie was snorting the stuff too and he couldn't understand why the hell he had made such a big deal out of it, after all, it was only *snorting,* shit, it got you off, and as Henry (who Eddie would eventually come to think of as the great sage and eminent junkie) said, in a world that was clearly going to hell head-first, what was so low about getting high?

Time passed. Eddie didn't say how much. The gunslinger didn't ask. He guessed that Eddie knew there were a thousand excuses for getting high but no reasons, and that he had kept his habit pretty well under control. And that Henry had also managed to keep *his* under control. Not as well as Eddie, but enough to keep from coming completely unravelled. Because whether or not Eddie understood the truth (down deep Roland believed Eddie did), Henry must have: their positions had reversed themselves. Now Eddie held Henry's hand crossing streets.

The day came when Eddie caught Henry not snorting but skin-popping. There had been another hysterical argument, an almost exact repeat of the first one, except it had been in Henry's bedroom. It ended in almost exactly the same way, with Henry weeping and offering that implacable, inarguable defense that was utter surrender, utter admission: Eddie was right, he wasn't fit to live, not fit to eat garbage from the gutter. He would go. Eddie would never have to see him again. He just hoped he would remember all the . . .

It faded into a drone that wasn't much different from the rocky sound of the breaking waves as they trudged up the beach. Roland knew the story and said nothing. It was *Eddie* who didn't know the story, an Eddie who was really clear-headed for the first time in maybe ten years or more. Eddie wasn't telling the story to Roland; Eddie was finally telling the story to himself.

That was all right. So far as the gunslinger could see, time was something they had a lot of. Talk was one way to fill it.

Eddie said he was haunted by Henry's knee, the twisted scar tissue up and down his leg (of course that was all healed now, Henry barely even limped . . . except when he and Eddie were quarrelling; then the limp always seemed to get worse); he was haunted by all the things Henry had given up for him, and haunted by something much more pragmatic: Henry wouldn't last out on the streets. He would be like a rabbit let loose in a jungle filled with tigers. On his own, Henry would wind up in jail or Bellevue before a week was out.

So he begged, and Henry finally did him the favor of consenting to stick around, and six months after that Eddie also had a golden arm. From that moment things had begun to move in the steady and inevitable downward spiral which had ended with Eddie's trip to the Bahamas and Roland's sudden intervention in his life.

Another man, less pragmatic and more introspective than Roland, might have asked (to himself, if not right out loud), *Why this one? Why this man to start? Why a man who seems to promise weakness or strangeness or even outright doom?*

Not only did the gunslinger never ask the question; it never even formulated itself in his mind. Cuthbert would have asked; Cuthbert had questioned everything, had been poisoned with questions, had died with one in his mouth. Now they were gone, all gone. Cort's last gunslingers, the thirteen survivors of a beginning class that had numbered fifty-six, were all dead. All dead but Roland. He was the last gunslinger, going steadily on in a world that had grown stale and sterile and empty.

Thirteen, he remembered Cort saying on the day before the Presentation Ceremonies. *This is an evil number.* And on the following day, for the first time in thirty years, Cort had not been present at the Ceremonies. His final crop of pupils had gone to his cottage to first kneel at his feet, presenting defenseless necks, then to rise and receive his congratulatory kiss and to allow him to load their guns for the first time. Nine weeks later, Cort was dead. Of poison, some said. Two years after his death, the final bloody civil war had begun. The red slaughter had reached the last bastion of civilization, light, and sanity, and had taken away what all of them had assumed was so strong with the casual ease of a wave taking a child's castle of sand.

So he was the last, and perhaps he had survived because the dark romance in his nature was overset by his practicality and simplicity. He understood that only three things mattered: mortality, *ka,* and the Tower.

Those were enough things to think about.

Eddie finished his tale around four o'clock on the third day of their northward journey up the featureless beach. The beach itself never seemed to change. If a sign of progress was wanted, it could only be obtained by looking left, to the east. There the jagged peaks of the mountains had begun to soften and slump a bit. It was possible that if they went north far enough, the mountains would become rolling hills.

With his story told, Eddie lapsed into silence and they walked without speaking for a half an hour or longer. Eddie kept stealing little glances at him. Roland knew Eddie wasn't aware that he was picking these glances up; he was still too much in himself. Roland also knew what Eddie was waiting for: a response. Some kind of response. *Any* kind. Twice Eddie opened his mouth only to close it again. Finally he asked what the gunslinger had known he would ask.

"So? What do you think?"

"I think you're here."

Eddie stopped, fisted hands planted on his hips. "That's *all?* That's *it?*"

"That's all I know," the gunslinger replied. His missing fingers and toe throbbed and itched. He wished for some of the *astin* from Eddie's world.

"You don't have any opinion on what the hell it all *means?*"

The gunslinger might have held up his subtracted right hand and said, *Think about what* this *means, you silly idiot,* but it no more crossed his mind to say this than it had to ask why it was Eddie, out of all the people in all the universes that might exist. "It's *ka,*" he said, facing Eddie patiently.

"What's *ka?*" Eddie's voice was truculent. "I never heard of it. Except if you say it twice you come out with the baby word for shit."

"I don't know about that," the gunslinger said. "Here it means duty, or destiny, or, in the vulgate, a place you must go."

Eddie managed to look dismayed, disgusted, and amused all at the same time. "Then say it twice, Roland, because words like that sound like shit to this kid.''

The gunslinger shrugged. "I don't discuss philosophy. I don't study history. All I know is what's past is past, and what's ahead is ahead. The second is *ka*, and takes care of itself.''

"Yeah?" Eddie looked northward. "Well all I see ahead is about nine billion miles of this same fucking beach. If *that's* what's ahead, *ka* and kaka are the same thing. We might have enough good shells to pop five or six more of those lobster dudes, but then we're going to be down to chucking rocks at them. So where are we *going?*''

Roland *did* wonder briefly if this was a question Eddie had ever thought to ask his brother, but to ask such a question would only be an invitation to a lot of meaningless argument. So he only cocked a thumb northward and said, "There. To begin with.''

Eddie looked and saw nothing but the same reach of shell- and rock-studded gray shingle. He looked back at Roland, about to scoff, saw the serene certainty on his face, and looked again. He squinted. He shielded the right side of his face from the westering sun with his right hand. He wanted desperately to see something, *anything*, shit, even a mirage would do, but there was nothing.

"Crap on me all you want to," Eddie said slowly, "but I say it's a goddam mean trick. I put my life on the line for you at Balazar's.''

"I know you did." The gunslinger smiled—a rarity that lit his face like a momentary flash of sunlight on a dismal louring day. "That's why I've done nothing but square-deal you, Eddie. It's there. I saw it an hour ago. At first I thought it was only a mirage or wishful thinking, but it's there, all right.''

Eddie looked again, looked until water ran from the corners of his eyes. At last he said, "I don't see anything up ahead but more beach. And I got twenty-twenty vision.''

"I don't know what that means.''

"It means if there was something there to see, I'd *see* it!'' But Eddie wondered. Wondered how much further than his own the gunslinger's blue bullshooter's eyes could see. Maybe a little.

Maybe a *lot.*

"You'll see it,'' the gunslinger said.

"See *what?*''

"We won't get there today, but if you see as well as you say, you'll see it before the sun hits the water. Unless you just want to stand here chin-jawing, that is.''

"Ka,'' Eddie said in a musing voice.

Roland nodded. *"Ka.''*

"Kaka,'' Eddie said, and laughed. "Come on, Roland. Let's take a hike. And if I *don't* see anything by the time the sun hits the water, you owe me a chicken dinner. Or a Big Mac. Or *anything* that isn't lobster.''

"Come on.''

They started walking again, and it was at least a full hour before the sun's lower arc touched the horizon when Eddie Dean began to see the shape in the distance—vague, shimmering, indefinable, but definitely *something.* Something *new.*

"Okay,'' he said. "I see it. You must have eyes like Superman.''

"Who?''

"Never mind. You've got a really incredible case of culture lag, you know it?''

"What?''

Eddie laughed. "Never mind. What is it?''

"You'll see.'' The gunslinger started walking again before Eddie could ask anything else.

Twenty minutes later Eddie thought he *did* see. Fifteen minutes after that he was sure. The object on the beach was still two, maybe three miles away, but he knew what it was. A door, of course. Another door.

Neither of them slept well that night, and they were up and walking an hour before the sun cleared the eroding shapes of the mountains. They reached the door just as the morning sun's first rays, so sublime and so still, broke over them. Those rays lighted their stubbly cheeks like lamps. They made the gunslinger forty again, and Eddie no older than Roland had been when he went out to fight Cort with his hawk David as his weapon.

This door was exactly like the first, except for what was writ upon it:

THE LADY OF SHADOWS

"So," Eddie said softly, looking at the door which simply stood here with its hinges grounded in some unknown jamb between one world and another, one universe and another. It stood with its graven message, real as rock and strange as starlight.

"So," the gunslinger agreed.

"Ka."

"Ka."

"Here is where you draw the second of your three?"

"It seems so."

The gunslinger knew what was in Eddie's mind before Eddie knew it himself. He saw Eddie make his move before Eddie knew he was moving. He could have turned and broken Eddie's arm in two places before Eddie knew it was happening, but he made no move. He let Eddie snake the revolver from his right holster. It was the first time in his life he had allowed one of his weapons to be taken from him without an offer of that weapon having first been made. Yet he made no move to stop it. He turned and looked at Eddie equably, even mildly.

Eddie's face was livid, strained. His eyes showed starey whites all the way around the irises. He held the heavy revolver in both hands and still the muzzle rambled from side to side, centering, moving off, centering again and then moving off again.

"Open it," he said.

"You're being foolish," the gunslinger said in the same mild voice. "Neither of us has any idea where that door goes. It needn't open on your *universe*, let alone upon your world. For all either of us know, the Lady of Shadows might have eight eyes and nine arms, like Suvia. Even if it does open on your world, it might be on a time long before you were born or long after you would have died."

Eddie smiled tightly. "Tell you what, Monty: I'm more than willing to trade the rubber chicken and the shitty seaside vacation for what's behind Door #2."

"I don't understand y—"

"I know you don't. It doesn't matter. Just open the fucker."

The gunslinger shook his head.

They stood in the dawn, the door casting its slanted shadow toward the ebbing sea.

"Open it!" Eddie cried. "I'm going with you! Don't you get it? I'm going *with* you! That doesn't mean I won't come back. Maybe I will. I mean, *probably* I will. I guess I owe you that much. You been square-john with me down the line, don't think I'm not aware of the fact. But while you get whoever this Shadow-Babe is, I'm gonna find the nearest Chicken Delight and pick me up some take-out. I think the Thirty-Piece Family Pak should do for starters."

"You stay here."

"You think I don't mean it?" Eddie was shrill now, close to the edge. The gunslinger could almost see him looking down into the drifty depths of his own damnation. Eddie thumbed back the revolver's ancient hammer. The wind had fallen with the break of the day and the ebb of the tide, and the click of the hammer as Eddie brought it to full cock was very clear. "You just try me."

"I think I will," the gunslinger said.

"*I'll shoot you!*" Eddie screamed.

"*Ka,*" the gunslinger replied stolidly, and turned to the door. He was reaching for the knob, but his heart was waiting: waiting to see if he would live or die.

Ka.

THE LADY OF SHADOWS

CHAPTER 1

DETTA
AND ODETTA

Stripped of jargon, what Adler said was this: the perfect schizophrenic—if there was such a person—would be a man or woman not only unaware of his other persona(e), but one unaware that anything at all was amiss in his or her life.

Adler should have met Detta Walker and Odetta Holmes.

1

"—last gunslinger," Andrew said.

He had been talking for quite awhile, but Andrew always talked and Odetta usually just let it flow over her mind the way you let warm water flow over your hair and face in the shower. But this did more than catch her attention; it snagged it, as if on a thorn.

"I beg pardon?"

"Oh, it was just some column in the paper," Andrew said. "I dunno who wrote it. I didn't notice. One of those political fellas. Prob'ly you'd know, Miz Holmes. I loved him, and I cried the night he was elected—"

She smiled, touched in spite of herself. Andrew said his ceaseless chatter was something he couldn't stop, wasn't responsible for, that it was just the Irish in him coming out, and most of it was nothing—cluckings and chirrupings about relatives and friends she would never meet, half-baked political opinions, weird scientific commentary gleaned from any number of weird sources (among other things, Andrew was a firm believer in flying saucers, which he called *you-foes*)— but this touched her because she had also cried the night he was elected.

"But I didn't cry when that son of a bitch—pardon my French, Miz Holmes—when that son of a bitch Oswald shot him, and I hadn't cried since, and it's been—what, two months?"

Three months and two days, she thought.

"Something like that, I guess."

Andrew nodded. "Then I read this column—in *The Daily News,* it mighta been—yesterday, about how Johnson's probably gonna do a pretty good job, but it won't be the same. The guy said America had seen the passage of the world's last gunslinger."

"I don't think John Kennedy was that at all," Odetta said, and if her voice was sharper than the one Andrew was accustomed to hearing (which it must have been, because she saw his eyes give a startled blink in the rear-view mirror, a blink that was more like a wince), it was because she felt herself touched by this, too. It was absurd, but it was also a fact. There was something about that phrase—*America has seen the passage of the world's last gunslinger*—that rang deeply in her mind. It was ugly, it was untrue—John Kennedy had been a peacemaker, not a leather-slapping Billy the Kid type, that was more in the Goldwater line—but it had also for some reason given her goosebumps.

"Well, the guy said there would be no shortage of shooters in the world," Andrew went on, regarding her nervously in the rear-view mirror. "He mentioned Jack Ruby for one, and Castro, and this fellow in Haiti—"

"Duvalier," she said. "Poppa Doc."

"Yeah, him, and Diem—"

"The Diem brothers are dead."

"Well, he said Jack Kennedy was different, that's all. He said he would draw, but only if someone weaker needed him to draw, and only if there was nothing else to do. He said Kennedy was savvy enough to know that sometimes talking don't do no good. He said Kennedy knew if it's foaming at the mouth you have to shoot it."

His eyes continued to regard her apprehensively.

"Besides, it was just some column I read."

The limo was gliding up Fifth Avenue now, headed toward Central Park West, the Cadillac emblem on the end of the hood cutting the frigid February air.

"Yes," Odetta said mildly, and Andrew's eyes relaxed a trifle. "I understand. I don't agree, but I understand."

You are a liar, a voice spoke up in her mind. This was a voice she heard quite often. She had even named it. It was the voice of The Goad. *You understand perfectly and agree completely. Lie to Andrew if you feel it necessary, but for God's sake don't lie to yourself, woman.*

Yet part of her protested, horrified. In a world which had become a nuclear powder keg upon which nearly a billion people now sat, it was a mistake—perhaps one of suicidal proportions—to believe there was a difference between good shooters and bad shooters. There were too many shaky hands holding lighters near too many fuses. This was no world for gunslingers. If there had ever been a time for them, it had passed.

Hadn't it?

She closed her eyes briefly and rubbed at her temples. She could feel one of her headaches coming on. Sometimes they threatened, like an ominous buildup of thunderheads on a hot summer afternoon, and then blew away . . . as those ugly summer brews sometimes simply slipped away in one direction or another,

to stomp their thunders and lightnings into the ground
of some other place.

She thought, however, that this time the storm was
going to happen. It would come complete with thunder, lightning, and hail the size of golf-balls.

The streetlights marching up Fifth Avenue seemed
much too bright.

"So how was Oxford, Miz Holmes?" Andrew asked
tentatively.

"Humid. February or not, it was very humid." She
paused, telling herself she wouldn't say the words that
were crowding up her throat like bile, that she would
swallow them back down. To say them would be need-
lessly brutal. Andrew's talk of the world's last gunslinger had been just more of the man's endless
prattling. But on top of everything else it was just a
bit too much and it came out anyway, what she had no
business saying. Her voice sounded as calm and as
resolute as ever, she supposed, but she was not fooled:
she knew a blurt when she heard one. "The bail
bondsman came very promptly, of course; he had been
notified in advance. They held onto us as long as they
could nevertheless, and I held on as long as *I* could,
but I guess they won that one, because I ended up
wetting myself." She saw Andrew's eyes wince away
again and she wanted to stop and couldn't stop. "It's
what they want to teach you, you see. Partly because
it frightens you, I suppose, and a frightened person
may not come down to their precious Southland and
bother them again. But I think most of them—even the
dumb ones and they are by all means not all dumb—
know the change will come in the end no matter what
they do, and so they take the chance to degrade you
while they still can. To teach you you *can* be degraded.
You can swear before God, Christ, and the whole company of Saints that you will not, will not, *will not* soil
yourself, but if they hold onto you long enough of

course you do. The lesson is that you're just an animal
in a cage, no more than that, no better than that. Just
an animal in a cage. So I wet myself. I can still smell
dried urine and that damned holding cell. They think
we are descended from the monkeys, you know. And
that's exactly what I smell like to myself right now.

"A monkey."

She saw Andrew's eyes in the rear-view mirror and
was sorry for the way his eyes looked. Sometimes your
urine wasn't the only thing you couldn't hold.

"I'm sorry, Miz Holmes."

"No," she said, rubbing at her temples again. "I
am the one who is sorry. It's been a trying three days,
Andrew."

"I should think *so*," he said in a shocked old-
maidish voice that made her laugh in spite of herself.
But most of her wasn't laughing. She thought she had
known what she was getting into, that she had fully
anticipated how bad it could get. She had been wrong.

A trying three days. Well, that was one way to put
it. Another might be that her three days in Oxford,
Mississippi had been a short season in hell. But there
were some things you couldn't say. Some things you
would die before saying . . . unless you were called
upon to testify to them before the Throne of God the
Father Almighty, where, she supposed, even the truths
that caused the hellish thunderstorms in that strange
gray jelly between your ears (the scientists said that
gray jelly was nerveless, and if *that* wasn't a hoot and
a half she didn't know what was) must be admitted.

"I just want to get home and bathe, bathe, bathe,
and sleep, sleep, sleep. Then I reckon I will be as
right as rain."

"Why, sure! That's just what you're going to be!"
Andrew wanted to apologize for something, and this
was as close as he could come. And beyond this he
didn't want to risk further conversation. So the two of

them rode in unaccustomed silence to the gray Victorian block of apartments on the corner of Fifth and Central Park South, a very exclusive gray Victorian block of apartments, and she supposed that made her a blockbuster, and she *knew* there were people in those poshy-poshy flats who would not speak to her unless they absolutely had to, and she didn't really care. Besides, she was above them, and they *knew* she was above them. It had occurred to her on more than one occasion that it must have galled some of them mightily, knowing there was a nigger living in the penthouse apartment of this fine staid old building where once the only black hands allowed had been clad in white gloves or perhaps the thin black leather ones of a chauffeur. She hoped it *did* gall them mightily, and scolded herself for being mean, for being *unchristian,* but she *did* wish it, she hadn't been able to stop the piss pouring into the crotch of her fine silk imported underwear and she didn't seem to be able to stop this other flood of piss, either. It was mean, it was unchristian, and almost as bad—no, *worse,* at least as far as the Movement was concerned, it was counterproductive. They were going to win the rights they needed to win, and probably this year: Johnson, mindful of the legacy which had been left him by the slain President (and perhaps hoping to put another nail in the coffin of Barry Goldwater), would do more than oversee the passage of the Civil Rights Act; if necessary he would *ram* it into law. So it was important to minimize the scarring and the hurt. There was more work to be done. Hate would not help do that work. Hate would, in fact, hinder it.

But sometimes you went on hating just the same.

Oxford Town had taught her that, too.

2

Detta Walker had absolutely no interest in the Movement and much more modest digs. She lived in the loft of a peeling Greenwich Village apartment building. Odetta didn't know about the loft and Detta didn't know about the penthouse and the only one left who suspected something was not quite right was Andrew Feeny, the chauffeur. He had begun working for Odetta's father when Odetta was fourteen and Detta Walker hardly existed at all.

Sometimes Odetta disappeared. These disappearances might be a matter of hours or of days. Last summer she had disappeared for three weeks and Andrew had been ready to call the police when Odetta called *him* one evening and asked him to bring the car around at ten the next day—she planned to do some shopping, she said.

It trembled on his lips to cry out *Miz Holmes! Where have you been?* But he had asked this before and had received only puzzled stares—*truly* puzzled stares, he was sure—in return. *Right here,* she would say. *Why, right here, Andrew—you've been driving me two or three places every day, haven't you? You aren't starting to go a little mushy in the head, are you?* Then she would laugh and if she was feeling especially good (as she often seemed to feel after her disappearances), she would pinch his cheek.

"Very good, Miz Holmes," he had said. "Ten it is."

That scary time she had been gone for three weeks, Andrew had put down the phone, closed his eyes, and said a quick prayer to the Blessed Virgin for Miz Holmes's safe return. Then he had rung Howard, the doorman at her building.

"What time did she come in?"

"Just about twenty minutes ago," Howard said.

"Who brought her?"

"Dunno. You know how it is. Different car every time. Sometimes they park around the block and I don't see em at all, don't even know she's back until I hear the buzzer and look out and see it's her." Howard paused, then added: "She's got one hell of a bruise on her cheek."

Howard had been right. It sure had been one hell of a bruise, and now it was getting better. Andrew didn't like to think what it might have looked like when it was fresh. Miz Holmes appeared promptly at ten the next morning, wearing a silk sundress with spaghetti-thin straps (this had been late July), and by then the bruise had started to yellow. She had made only a perfunctory effort to cover it with make-up, as if knowing that too much effort to cover it would only draw further attention to it.

"How did you get *that*, Miz Holmes?" he asked.

She laughed merrily. "You know me, Andrew— clumsy as ever. My hand slipped on the grab-handle while I was getting out of the tub yesterday—I was in a hurry to catch the national news. I fell and banged the side of my face." She gauged *his* face. "You're getting ready to start blithering about doctors and examinations, aren't you? Don't bother answering; after all these years I can read you like a book. I won't go, so you needn't bother asking. I'm just as fine as paint. Onward, Andrew! I intend to buy half of Saks', all of Gimbels, and eat everything at Four Seasons in between."

"Yes, Miz Holmes," he had said, and smiled. It was a forced smile, and forcing it was not easy. That bruise wasn't a *day* old; it was a week old, at least . . . and he knew better, anyway, didn't he? He had called her every night at seven o'clock for the last week, because if there was one time when you could catch Miz Holmes in her place, it was when the

Huntley-Brinkley Report came on. A regular junkie
for her news was Miz Holmes. He had done it every
night, that was, except last night. Then he had gone
over and wheedled the passkey from Howard. A con-
viction had been growing on him steadily that she had
had just the sort of accident she had described . . .
only instead of getting a bruise or a broken bone, she
had died, died alone, and was lying up there dead
right now. He had let himself in, heart thumping, feeling like a cat in a dark room criss-crossed with piano
wires. Only there had been nothing to be nervous
about. There was a butter-dish on the kitchen counter,
and although the butter had been covered it had been
out long enough to be growing a good crop of mould.
He got there at ten minutes of seven and had left by
five after. In the course of his quick examination of
the apartment, he had glanced into the bathroom. The
tub had been dry, the towels neatly—even austerely—
arrayed, the room's many grab-handles polished to a
bright steel gleam that was unspotted with water.

He knew the accident she had described had not
happened.

But Andrew had not believed she was lying, either.
She had *believed* what she had told him.

He looked in the rear-view mirror again and saw her
rubbing her temples lightly with the tips of her fingers.
He didn't like it. He had seen her do that too many
times before one of her disappearances.

3

Andrew left the motor running so she could have
the benefit of the heater, then went around to the trunk.
He looked at her two suitcases with another wince.
They looked as if petulant men with small minds and
large bodies had kicked them relentlessly back and
forth, damaging the bags in a way they did not quite

dare damage Miz Holmes herself—the way they might
have damaged *him,* for instance, if he had been there.
It wasn't just that she was a woman; she was a nigger,
an uppity northern nigger messing where she had no
business messing, and they probably figured a woman
like that deserved just what she got. Thing was, she
was also a *rich* nigger. Thing was, she was almost as
well-known to the American public as Medgar Evers
or Martin Luther King. Thing was, she'd gotten her
rich nigger face on the cover of *Time* magazine and it
was a little harder to get away with sticking someone
like that in the 'toolies and then saying *What? No sir,
boss, we sho dint see nobody looked like that down
here, did we, boys?* Thing was, it was a little harder
to work yourself up to hurting a woman who was the
only heir to Holmes Dental Industries when there were
twelve Holmes plants in the sunny South, one of them
just one county over from Oxford Town, Oxford Town.

So they'd done to her suitcases what they didn't dare
do to her.

He looked at these mute indications of her stay in
Oxford Town with shame and fury and love, emotions
as mute as the scars on the luggage that had gone away
looking smart and had come back looking dumb and
thumped. He looked, temporarily unable to move, and
his breath puffed out on the frosty air.

Howard was coming out to help, but Andrew paused
a moment longer before grasping the handles of the
cases. *Who are you, Miz Holmes? Who are you really?
Where do you go sometimes, and what do you do that
seems so bad that you have to make up a false history
of the missing hours or days even to yourself?* And he
thought something else in the moment before Howard
arrived, something weirdly apt: *Where's the rest of
you?*

*You want to quit thinking like that. If anyone around
here was going to do any thinking like that it would be*

Miz Holmes, but she doesn't and so you don't need to, either.

Andrew lifted the bags out of the trunk and handed them to Howard, who asked in a low voice: "Is she all right?"

"I think so," Andrew replied, also pitching his voice low. "Just tired is all. Tired all the way down to her roots."

Howard nodded, took the battered suitcases, and started back inside. He paused only long enough to tip his cap to Odetta Holmes—who was almost invisible behind the smoked glass windows—in a soft and respectful salute.

When he was gone, Andrew took out the collapsed stainless steel scaffolding at the bottom of the trunk and began to unfold it. It was a wheelchair.

Since August 19th, 1959, some five and a half years before, the part of Odetta Holmes from the knees down had been as missing as those blank hours and days.

4

Before the subway incident, Detta Walker had only been conscious a few times—these were like coral islands which look isolated to one above them but are, in fact, only nodes in the spine of a long archipelago which is mostly underwater. Odetta suspected Detta not at all, and Detta had no idea that there was such a person as Odetta . . . but Detta at least had a clear understanding that *something* was wrong, that someone was fucking with her life. Odetta's imagination novelized all sorts of things which had happened when Detta was in charge of her body; Detta was not so clever. She *thought* she remembered things, *some* things, at least, but a lot of the time she didn't.

Detta was at least partially aware of the *blanks*.

She could remember the china plate. She could remember that. She could remember slipping it into the pocket of her dress, looking over her shoulder all the while to make sure the Blue Woman wasn't there, peeking. She had to make sure because the china plate belonged to the Blue Woman. The china plate was, Detta understood in some vague way, a *forspecial*. Detta took it for that why. Detta remembered taking it to a place she knew (although she didn't know how she knew) as The Drawers, a smoking trash-littered hole in the earth where she had once seen a burning baby with plastic skin. She remembered putting the plate carefully down on the gravelly ground and then starting to step on it and stopping, remembered taking off her plain cotton panties and putting them into the pocket where the plate had been, and then carefully slipping the first finger of her left hand carefully against the cut in her at the place where Old Stupid God had joined her and all other girlsandwomen imperfectly, but *something* about that place must be right, because she remembered the jolt, remembered wanting to press, remembered not pressing, remembered how delicious her vagina had been naked, without the cotton panties in the way of it and the world, and she had not pressed, not until her shoe pressed, her black patent leather shoe, not until her shoe pressed down on the plate, *then* she pressed on the cut with her finger the way she was pressing on the Blue Woman's *forspecial* china plate with her foot, she remembered the way the black patent leather shoe covered the delicate blue webbing on the edge of the plate, she remembered the *press*, yes, she remembered pressing in The Drawers, pressing with finger and foot, remembered the delicious promise of finger and cut, remembered that when the plate snapped with a bitter brittle snap a similar brittle pleasure had skewered upward from that cut into her guts like an arrow, she remembered the cry which had broken from her lips, an unpleasant cawing like

the sound of a crow scared up from a cornpatch, she
could remember staring dully at the fragments of the
plate and then taking the plain white cotton panties
slowly out of her dress pocket and putting them on
again, *step-ins,* so she had heard them called in some
time unhoused in memory and drifting loose like
turves on a floodtide, *step-ins,* good, because first you
stepped out to do your business and then you stepped
back in, first one shiny patent leather shoe and then
the other, good, panties were good, she could remember drawing them up her legs so clearly, drawing them
past her knees, a scab on the left one almost ready to
fall off and leave clean pink new babyskin, yes, she
could remember so clearly it might not have been a
week ago or yesterday but only one single moment
ago, she could remember how the waistband had
reached the hem of her party dress, the clear contrast
of white cotton against brown skin, like cream, yes,
like that, cream from a pitcher caught suspended over
coffee, the texture, the panties disappearing under the
hem of the dress, except then the dress was burnt orange and the panties were not going up but down but
they were still white but not cotton, they were nylon,
cheap see-through nylon panties, cheap in more ways
than one, and she remembered stepping out of them,
she remembered how they glimmered on the floormat
of the '46 Dodge DeSoto, yes, how white they were,
how cheap they were, not anything dignified like underwear but cheap panties, the girl was cheap and it
was good to be cheap, good to be on sale, to be on
the block not even like a whore but like a good breed-
sow; she remembered no round china plate but the
round white face of a boy, some surprised drunk fra-
ternity boy, he was no china plate but his face was as
round as the Blue Woman's china plate had been, and
there was webbing on his cheeks, and this webbing
looked as blue as the webbing on the Blue Woman's

forspecial china plate had been, but that was only because the neon was red, the neon was garish, in the
dark the neon from the roadhouse sign made the
spreading blood from the places on his cheeks where
she had clawed him *look* blue, and he had said *Why
did you why did you why did you do,* and then he
unrolled the window so he could get his face outside
to puke and she remembered hearing Dodie Stevens
on the jukebox, singing about tan shoes with pink
shoelaces and a big Panama with a purple hatband,
she remembered the sound of his puking was like
gravel in a cement mixer, and his penis, which moments before had been a livid exclamation point rising
from the tufted tangle of his pubic hair, was collapsing
into a weak white question mark; she remembered the
hoarse gravel sounds of his vomiting stopped and then
started again and she thought *Well I guess he ain't
made enough to lay* this *foundation yet* and laughing
and pressing her finger (which now came equipped
with a long shaped nail) against her vagina which was
bare but no longer bare because it was overgrown with
its own coarse briared tangle, and there had been the
same brittle breaking snap inside her, and it was still
as much pain as it was pleasure (but better, far better,
than nothing at all), and then he was grabbing blindly
for her and saying in a hurt breaking tone *Oh you
goddamned nigger cunt* and she went on laughing just
the same, dodging him easily and snatching up her
panties and opening the door on her side of the car,
feeling the last blind thud of his fingers on the back of
her blouse as she ran into a May night that was redo-
lent of early honeysuckle, red-pink neon light stuttering off the gravel of some postwar parking lot, stuffing
her panties, her cheap slick nylon panties not into the
pocket of her dress but into a purse jumbled with a
teenager's cheerful conglomeration of cosmetics, she
was running, the light was stuttering, and then she was

twenty-three and it was not panties but a rayon scarf, and she was casually slipping it into her purse as she walked along a counter in the Nice Notions section of Macy's—a scarf which sold at that time for $1.99.

Cheap.

Cheap like the white nylon panties.

Cheap.

Like her.

The body she inhabited was that of a woman who had inherited millions, but that was not known and didn't matter—the scarf was white, the edging blue, and there was that same little breaking sense of pleasure as she sat in the back seat of the taxi, and, oblivious of the driver, held the scarf in one hand, looking at it fixedly, while her other hand crept up under her tweed skirt and beneath the leg-band of her white panties, and that one long dark finger took care of the business that needed to be taken care of in a single merciless stroke.

So sometimes she wondered, in a distracted sort of way, where she was when she wasn't *here,* but mostly her needs were too sudden and pressing for any extended contemplation, and she simply fulfilled what needed to be fulfilled, did what needed to be done.

Roland would have understood.

5

Odetta could have taken a limo everywhere, even in 1959—although her father was still alive and she was not as fabulously rich as she would become when he died in 1962, the money held in trust for her had become hers on her twenty-fifth birthday, and she could do pretty much as she liked. But she cared very little for a phrase one of the conservative columnists had coined a year or two before—the phrase was "limousine liberal," and she was young enough not to want to be seen as one even if she really *was* one. Not young enough (or stupid enough!) to believe that a few pairs of faded jeans and the khaki shirts she habitually wore in any real way changed her essential status, or riding the bus or the subway when she could have used the car (but she had been self-involved enough not to see Andrew's hurt and deep puzzlement; he liked her and thought it must be some sort of personal rejection), but young enough to still believe that gesture could sometimes overcome (or at least overset) truth.

On the night of August 19th, 1959, she paid for the gesture with half her legs . . . and half her mind.

6

Odetta had been first tugged, then pulled, and finally caught up in the swell which would eventually turn into a tidal wave. In 1957, when she became involved, the thing which eventually became known as the Movement had no name. She knew some of the background, knew the struggle for equality had gone on not since the Emancipation Proclamation but almost since the first boatload of slaves had been brought to America (to Georgia, in fact, the colony the British founded to get rid of their criminals and debtors), but for Odetta it always seemed to begin in the same place, with the same three words: *I'm not movin.*

The place had been a city bus in Montgomery, Alabama, and the words had been spoken by a black woman named Rosa Lee Parks, and the place from which Rosa Lee Parks was not movin was from the front of the city bus to the back of the city bus, which was, of course, the Jim Crow part of the city bus. Much later, Odetta would sing "We Shall Not Be Moved" with the rest of them, and it always made her think of Rosa Lee Parks, and she never sang it without a sense of shame. It was so easy to sing *we* with your arms linked to the arms of a whole crowd; that was easy even for a woman with no legs. So easy to sing we, so easy to *be* we. There had been no *we* on that bus, that bus that must have stank of ancient leather and years of cigar and cigarette smoke, that bus with the curved ad cards saying things like LUCKY STRIKE L.S.M.F.T. and ATTEND THE CHURCH OF YOUR CHOICE FOR HEAVEN'S SAKE and DRINK OVALTINE! YOU'LL SEE WHAT WE MEAN! and CHESTERFIELD, TWENTY-ONE GREAT TOBACCOS MAKE TWENTY WONDERFUL SMOKES, no *we* under the disbelieving gazes of the motorman, the white passengers among whom she sat, the equally disbelieving stares of the blacks at the back.

No *we*.

No marching thousands.

Only Rosa Lee Parks starting a tidal wave with three words: *I'm not movin.*

Odetta would think *If I could do something like that—if I could be that brave—I think I could be happy for the rest of my life. But that sort of courage is not in me.*

She had read of the Parks incident, but with little interest at first. That came little by little. It was hard to say exactly when or how her imagination had been caught and fired by that at first almost soundless racequake which had begun to shake the south.

A year or so later a young man she was dating more or less regularly began taking her down to the Village, where some of the young (and mostly white) folksingers who performed there had added some new and startling songs to their repertoire—suddenly, in addition to all those old wheezes about how John Henry had taken his hammer and outraced the new steamhammer (killing himself in the process, lawd, lawd) and how Bar'bry Allen had cruelly rejected her lovesick young suitor (and ended up dying of shame, lawd, lawd), there were songs about how it felt to be down and out and ignored in the city, how it felt to be turned away from a job you could do because your skin was the wrong color, how it felt to be taken into a jail cell and whipped by Mr. Charlie because your skin was dark and you had dared, lawd, lawd, to sit in the white folks' section of the lunch-counter at an F.W. Woolworths' in Montgomery, Alabama.

Absurdly or not, it was only then that she had become curious about her own parents, and *their* parents, and *their* parents before them. She would never read *Roots*—she was in another world and time long before that book was written, perhaps even thought of, by Alex Haley, but it was at this absurdly late time in her life when it first dawned upon her that not so many generations back her progenitors had been taken in chains by white men. Surely the *fact* had occurred to her before, but only as a piece of information with no real temperature gradient, like an equation, never as something which bore intimately upon her own life.

Odetta totted up what she knew, and was appalled by the smallness of the sum. She knew her mother had been born in Odetta, Arkansas, the town for which she (the only child) had been named. She knew her father had been a small-town dentist who had invented and patented a capping process which had lain dormant and unremarked for ten years and which had then, suddenly, made him a moderately wealthy man. She knew that he had developed a number of other dental processes during the ten years before and the four years after the influx of wealth, most of them either orthodontic or cosmetic in nature, and that, shortly after moving to New York with his wife and daughter (who had been born four years after the original patent had been secured), he had founded a company called Holmes Dental Industries, which was now to teeth what Squibb was to antibiotics.

But when she asked him what life had been like

during all the years between—the years when she
hadn't been there, and the years when she had, her
father wouldn't tell her. He would say all sorts of
things, but he wouldn't *tell* her anything. He closed
that part of himself off to her. Once her ma, Alice—
he called her ma or sometimes Allie if he'd had a few
or was feeling good—said, "Tell her about the time
those men shot at you when you drove the Ford through
the covered bridge, Dan," and he gave Odetta's ma
such a gray and forbidding look that her ma, always
something of a sparrow, had shrunk back in her seat
and said no more.

Odetta had tried her mother once or twice alone after that night, but to no avail. If she had tried before,
she might have gotten something, but because he
wouldn't speak, she wouldn't speak either—and to him,
she realized, the past—those relatives, those red dirt
roads, those stores, those dirt floor cabins with glassless windows ungraced by a single simple curtsey of a
curtain, those incidents of hurt and harassment, those
neighbor children who went dressed in smocks which
had begun life as flour sacks—all of that was for him
buried away like dead teeth beneath perfect blinding
white caps. He would not speak, perhaps *could* not,
had perhaps willingly afflicted himself with a selective
amnesia; the capped teeth was their life in the Grey-
marl Apartments on Central Park South. All else was
hidden beneath that impervious outer cover. His past
was so well-protected that there had been no gap to
slide through, no way past that perfect capped barrier
and into the throat of revelation.

Detta knew things, but Detta didn't know Odetta
and Odetta didn't know Detta, and so the teeth lay as
smooth and closed as a redan gate there, also.

She had some of her mother's shyness in her as well
as her father's unblinking (if unspoken) toughness, and
the only time she had dared pursue him further on the

subject, to suggest that what he was denying her was a deserved trust fund never promised and apparently never to mature, had been one night in his library. He had shaken his *Wall Street Journal* carefully, closed it, folded it, and laid it aside on the deal table beside the standing lamp. He had removed his rimless steel spectacles and had laid them on top of the paper. Then he had looked at her, a thin black man, thin almost to the point of emaciation, tightly kinked gray hair now drawing rapidly away from the deepening hollows of his temples where tender clocksprings of veins pulsed steadily, and he had said only, *I don't talk about that part of my life, Odetta, or think about it. It would be pointless. The world has moved on since then.*

Roland would have understood.

7

When Roland opened the door with the words THE LADY OF THE SHADOWS written upon it, he saw things he did not understand at all—but he understood they didn't matter.

It was Eddie Dean's world, but beyond that it was only a confusion of lights, people and objects—more objects than he had ever seen in his life. Lady-things, from the look of them, and apparently for sale. Some under glass, some arranged in tempting piles and displays. None of it mattered any more than the movement as that world flowed past the edges of the doorway before them. The doorway was the Lady's eyes. He was looking through them just as he had looked through Eddie's eyes when Eddie had moved up the aisle of the sky-carriage.

Eddie, on the other hand, was thunderstruck. The revolver in his hand trembled and dropped a little. The gunslinger could have taken it from him easily but

did not. He only stood quietly. It was a trick he had
learned a long time ago.

Now the view through the doorway made one of
those turns the gunslinger found so dizzying—but
Eddie found this same abrupt swoop oddly comforting. Roland had never seen a movie. Eddie had seen
thousands, and what he was looking at was like one
of those moving point-of-view shots they did in ones
like *Halloween* and *The Shining*. He even knew what
they called the gadget they did it with. Steadi-Cam.
That was it.

"*Star Wars*, too," he muttered. "Death Star. That
fuckin crack, remember?"

Roland looked at him and said nothing.

Hands—dark brown hands—entered what Roland
saw as a doorway and what Eddie was already starting
to think of as some sort of magic movie screen . . . a
movie screen which, under the right circumstances,
you might be able to walk into the way that guy had
just walked *out* of the screen and into the real world
in *The Purple Rose of Cairo*. Bitchin movie.

Eddie hadn't realized how bitchin until just now.

Except that movie hadn't been made yet on the other
side of the door he was looking through. It was New
York, okay—somehow the very sound of the taxi-cab
horns, as mute and faint as they were—proclaimed
that—and it was some New York department store he
had been in at one time or another, but it was . . .
was . . .

"It's older," he muttered.

"Before your when?" the gunslinger asked.

Eddie looked at him and laughed shortly. "Yeah. If
you want to put it that way, yeah."

"Hello, Miss Walker," a tentative voice said. The
view in the doorway rose so suddenly that even Eddie
was a bit dizzied and he saw a saleswoman who obviously knew the owner of the black hands—knew her

and either didn't like her or feared her. Or both. "Help you today?"

"This one." The owner of the black hands held up a white scarf with a bright blue edge. "Don't bother to wrap it up, babe, just stick it in a bag."

"Cash or ch—"

"Cash, it's always cash, isn't it?"

"Yes, that's fine, Miss Walker."

"I'm so glad you approve, dear."

There was a little grimace on the salesgirl's face—Eddie just caught it as she turned away. Maybe it was something as simple as being talked to that way by a woman the salesgirl considered an "uppity nigger" (again it was more his experience in movie theaters than any knowledge of history or even life on the streets as he had lived it that caused this thought, because this was like watching a movie either set or made in the '60s, something like that one with Sidney Steiger and Rod Poitier, *In the Heat of the Night*), but it could also be something even simpler: Roland's Lady of the Shadows was, black or white, one rude bitch.

And it didn't really matter, did it? None of it made a damned bit of difference. He cared about one thing and one thing only and that was getting the fuck *out*.

That was New York, he could almost *smell* New York.

And New York meant smack.

He could almost smell that, too.

Except there was a hitch, wasn't there?

One big motherfucker of a hitch.

8

Roland watched Eddie carefully, and although he could have killed him six times over at almost any time he wanted, he had elected to remain still and silent and let Eddie work the situation out for himself. Eddie

was a lot of things, and a lot of them were not nice
(as a fellow who had consciously let a child drop to
his death, the gunslinger knew the difference between
nice and not quite well), but one thing Eddie wasn't
was stupid.

He was a smart kid.

He would figure it out.

So he did.

He looked back at Roland, smiled without showing
his teeth, twirled the gunslinger's revolver once on his
finger, clumsily, burlesquing a show-shooter's fancy
coda, and then he held it out to Roland, butt first.

"This thing might as well be a piece of shit for all
the good it can do me, isn't that right?"

You can talk bright when you want to, Roland
thought. *Why do you so often choose to talk stupid,
Eddie? Is it because you think that's the way they
talked in the place where your brother went with his
guns?*

"Isn't that right?" Eddie repeated.

Roland nodded.

"If I *had* plugged you, what would have happened
to that door?"

"I don't know. I suppose the only way to find out
would be to try it and see."

"Well, what do you *think* would happen?"

"I think it would disappear."

Eddie nodded. That was what he thought, too. Poof!
Gone like magic! Now ya see it, my friends, now ya
don't. It was really no different than what would happen if the projectionist in a movie-theater were to draw
a six-shooter and plug the projector, was it?

If you shot the projector, the movie stopped.

Eddie didn't want the picture to stop.

Eddie wanted his money's worth.

"You can go through by yourself," Eddie said
slowly.

"Yes."

"Sort of."

"Yes."

"You wind up in her head. Like you wound up in mine."

"Yes."

"So you can hitchhike into my world, but that's all."

Roland said nothing. *Hitchhike* was one of the words Eddie sometimes used that he didn't exactly understand . . . but he caught the drift.

"But you *could* go through in your body. Like at Balazar's." He was talking out loud but really talking to himself. "Except you'd need me for that, wouldn't you?"

"Yes."

"Then take me with you."

The gunslinger opened his mouth, but Eddie was already rushing on.

"Not now, I don't mean now," he said. "I know it would cause a riot or some goddam thing if we just . . . popped out over there." He laughed rather wildly. "Like a magician pulling rabbits out of a hat, except without any hat, sure I did. We'll wait until she's alone, and—"

"No."

"I'll come back with you," Eddie said. "I swear it, Roland. I mean, I know you got a job to do, and I know I'm a part of it. I know you saved my ass at Customs, but I think I saved yours at Balazar's—now what do you think?"

"I think you did," Roland said. He remembered the way Eddie had risen up from behind the desk, regardless of the risk, and felt an instant of doubt.

But only an instant.

"So? Peter pays Paul. One hand washes the other. All I want to do is go back for a few hours. Grab some take-out chicken, maybe a box of Dunkin Donuts."

Eddie nodded toward the doorway, where things had begun to move again. "So what do you say?"

"No," the gunslinger said, but for a moment he was hardly thinking about Eddie. That movement up the aisle—the Lady, whoever she was, wasn't moving the way an ordinary person moved—wasn't moving, for instance, the way Eddie had moved when Roland looked through his eyes, or (now that he stopped to think of it, which he never had before, any more than he had ever stopped and really noticed the constant presence of his own nose in the lower range of his peripheral vision) the way he moved himself. When one walked, vision became a mild pendulum: left leg, right leg, left leg, right leg, the world rocking back and forth so mildly and gently that after awhile—shortly after you began to walk, he supposed—you simply ignored it. There was none of that pendulum movement in the Lady's walk—she simple moved smoothly up the aisle, as if riding along tracks. Ironically, Eddie had had this same perception . . . only to Eddie it had looked like a SteadiCam shot. He had found this perception comforting because it was familiar.

To Roland it was alien . . . but then Eddie was breaking in, his voice shrill.

"Well why not? Just why the fuck not?"

"Because you don't want chicken," the gunslinger said. "I know what you call the things you want, Eddie. You want to 'fix.' You want to 'score.' "

"So what?" Eddie cried—almost shrieked. "So what if I do? I said I'd come back with you! You got my promise! I mean, you got my fuckin PROMISE! What else do you want? You want me to swear on my mother's name? Okay, I swear on my mother's name! You want me to swear on my brother Henry's name? All right, I swear! I swear! I SWEAR!"

Enrico Balazar would have told him, but the gunslinger didn't need the likes of Balazar to tell him this one fact of life: Never trust a junkie.

Roland nodded toward the door. "Until after the Tower, at least, that part of your life is done. After that I don't care. After that you're free to go to hell in your own way. Until then I need you."

"Oh you fuckin shitass liar," Eddie said softly. There was no audible emotion in his voice, but the gunslinger saw the glisten of tears in his eyes. Roland said nothing. "You know there ain't gonna be no after, not for me, not for her, or whoever the Christ this third guy is. Probably not for you, either—you look as fuckin wasted as Henry did at his worst. If we don't die on the way to your Tower we'll sure as shit die when we get there *so why are you lying to me?*"

The gunslinger felt a dull species of shame but only repeated: "At least for now, that part of your life is done."

"Yeah?" Eddie said. "Well, I got some news for you, Roland. I know what's gonna happen to your *real* body when you go through there and inside of her. I know because I saw it before. I don't need your guns. I got you by that fabled place where the short hairs grow, my friend. You can even turn her head the way you turned mine and watch what I do to the rest of you while you're nothing but your goddam *ka*. I'd like to wait until nightfall, and drag you down by the water. Then you could watch the lobsters chow up on the rest of you. But you might be in too much of a hurry for that."

Eddie paused. The graty breaking of the waves and the steady hollow conch of the wind both seemed very loud.

"So I think I'll just use your knife to cut your throat."

"And close that door forever?"

"You say that part of my life is done. You don't just

mean smack, either. You mean New York, America, my time, *everything*. If that's how it is, I want this part done, too. The scenery sucks and the company stinks. There are times, Roland, when you make Jimmy Swaggart look almost sane.''

''There are great wonders ahead,'' Roland said. ''Great adventures. More than that, there is a quest to course upon, and a chance to redeem your honor. There's something else, too. You could be a gunslinger. I needn't be the last after all. It's in you, Eddie. I see it. I *feel* it.''

Eddie laughed, although now the tears were coursing down his cheeks. ''Oh, wonderful. *Wonderful!* Just what I need! My brother Henry. *He* was a gunslinger. In a place called Viet Nam, that was. It was great for him. You should have seen him when he was on a serious nod, Roland. He couldn't find his way to the fuckin bathroom without help. If there wasn't any help handy, he just sat there and watched *Big Time Wrestling* and did it in his fuckin pants. It's great to be a gunslinger. I can see that. My brother was a doper and you're out of your fucking gourd.''

''Perhaps your brother was a man with no clear idea of honor.''

''Maybe not. We didn't always get a real clear picture of what that was in the Projects. It was just a word you used after Your if you happened to get caught smoking reefer or lifting the spinners off some guy's T-Bird and got ho'ed up in court for it.''

Eddie was crying harder now, but he was laughing, too.

''Your friends, now. This guy you talk about in your sleep, for instance, this dude Cuthbert—''

The gunslinger started in spite of himself. Not all his long years of training could stay that start.

''Did *they* get this stuff you're talking about like a

goddam Marine recruiting sergeant? Adventure, quests, honor?''

"They understood honor, yes," Roland said slowly, thinking of all the vanished others.

"Did it get them any further than gunslinging got my brother?''

The gunslinger said nothing.

"I know you," Eddie said. "I seen lots of guys like you. You're just another kook singing 'Onward Christian Soldiers' with a flag in one hand and a gun in the other. I don't want no honor. I just want a chicken dinner and fix. In that order. So I'm telling you: go on through. You can. But the minute you're gone, I'm gonna kill the rest of you.''

The gunslinger said nothing.

Eddie smiled crookedly and brushed the tears from his cheeks with the backs of his hands. "You want to know what we call this back home?''

"What?''

"A Mexican stand-off.''

For a moment they only looked at each other, and then Roland looked sharply into the doorway. They had both been partially aware—Roland rather more than Eddie—that there had been another of those swerves, this time to the left. Here was an array of sparkling jewelry. Some was under protective glass but because most wasn't, the gunslinger supposed it was trumpery stuff . . . what Eddie would have called costume jewelry. The dark brown hands examined a few things in what seemed an only cursory manner, and then another salesgirl appeared. There had been some conversation which neither of them really noticed, and the Lady (some Lady, Eddie thought) asked to see something else. The salesgirl went away, and that was when Roland's eyes swung sharply back.

The brown hands reappeared, only now they held a purse. It opened. And suddenly the hands were scoop-

ing things—seemingly, almost certainly, at random—
into the purse.

"Well, you're collecting quite a crew, Roland,"
Eddie said, bitterly amused. "First you got your basic
white junkie, and then you got your basic black shop-
lif—"

But Roland was already moving toward the doorway
between the worlds, moving swiftly, not looking at
Eddie at all.

"I mean it!" Eddie screamed. "You go through and
I'll cut your throat, I'll cut your fucking thr—"

Before he could finish, the gunslinger was gone. All
that was left of him was his limp, breathing body lying
upon the beach.

For a moment Eddie only stood there, unable to
believe that Roland had done it, had really gone ahead
and done this idiotic thing in spite of his promise—his
sincere fucking *guarantee,* as far as that went—of what
the consequences would be.

He stood for a moment, eyes rolling like the eyes of
a frightened horse at the onset of a thunderstorm . . .
except of course there was no thunderstorm, except for
the one in the head.

All right. All right, goddammit.

There might only be a moment. That was all the
gunslinger might give him, and Eddie damned well
knew it. He glanced at the door and saw the black
hands freeze with a gold necklace half in and half out
of a purse that already glittered like a pirate's cache of
treasure. Although he could not hear it, Eddie sensed
that Roland was speaking to the owner of the black
hands.

He pulled the knife from the gunslinger's purse and
then rolled over the limp, breathing body which lay
before the doorway. The eyes were open but blank,
rolled up to the whites.

"Watch, Roland!" Eddie screamed. That monotonous, idiotic, never-ending wind blew in his ears. Christ, it was enough to drive anyone bugshit. "Watch very closely! I want to complete your fucking education! I want to show you what happens when you fuck over the Dean brothers!"

He brought the knife down to the gunslinger's throat.

CHAPTER 2
RINGING
THE CHANGES

1

August, 1959:

When the intern came outside half an hour later, he found Julio leaning against the ambulance which was still parked in the emergency bay of Sisters of Mercy Hospital on 23rd Street. The heel of one of Julio's pointy-toed boots was hooked over the front fender. He had changed to a pair of glaring pink pants and a blue shirt with his name written in gold stitches over the left pocket: his bowling league outfit. George checked his watch and saw that Julio's team—The Spics of Supremacy—would already be rolling.

"Thought you'd be gone," George Shavers said. He was an intern at Sisters of Mercy. "How're your guys gonna win without the Wonder Hook?"

"They got Miguel Basale to take my place. He ain't steady, but he gets hot sometimes. They'll be okay." Julio paused. "I was curious about how it came out." He was the driver, a Cubano with a sense of humor George wasn't even sure Julio knew he had. He looked around. Neither of the paramedics who rode with them were in sight.

"Where are they?" George asked.

"Who? The fuckin Bobbsey Twins? Where do you think they are? Chasin Minnesota poontang down in the Village. Any idea if she'll pull through?"

"Don't know."

He tried to sound sage and knowing about the unknown, but the fact was that first the resident on duty and then a pair of surgeons had taken the black woman away from him almost faster than you could say *hail Mary fulla grace* (which had actually been on his lips to say—the black lady really hadn't looked as if she was going to last very long).

"She lost a hell of a lot of blood."

"No shit."

George was one of sixteen interns at Sisters of Mercy, and one of eight assigned to a new program called Emergency Ride. The theory was that an intern riding with a couple of paramedics could sometimes make the difference between life and death in an emergency situation. George knew that most drivers and paras thought that wet-behind-the-ears interns were as likely to kill red-blankets as save them, but George thought maybe it worked.

Sometimes.

Either way it made great PR for the hospital, and although the interns in the program liked to bitch about the extra eight hours (without pay) it entailed each week, George Shavers sort of thought most of them felt the way he did himself—proud, tough, able to take whatever they threw his way.

Then had come the night the T.W.A. Tri-Star crashed at Idlewild. Sixty-five people on board, sixty of them what Julio Estevez referred to as D.R.T.—Dead Right There—and three of the remaining five looking like the sort of thing you might scrape out of the bottom of a coal-furnace . . . except what you scraped out of the bottom of a coal furnace didn't moan and shriek and beg for someone to give them morphine or kill them, did they? *If you can take this*, he thought afterward, remembering the severed limbs lying amid the remains of aluminum flaps and seat-cushions and a ragged chunk of tail with the numbers 17 and a big red letter T and part of a W on it, remembering the eyeball he had seen resting on top of a charred Samsonite suitcase, remembering a child's teddybear with staring shoe-button eyes lying beside a small red sneaker with a child's foot still in it, *if you can take this, baby, you can take anything.* And he had been taking it just fine. He went right on taking it just fine all the way home. He went on taking it just fine through a late supper that consisted of a Swanson's turkey TV dinner. He went to sleep with no problem at all, which proved beyond a shadow of a *doubt* that he was taking it just fine. Then, in some dead dark hour of the morning he had awakened from a hellish nightmare in which the thing resting on top of the charred Samsonite suitcase had not been a teddybear but *his mother's head,* and her eyes had opened, and they had been charred; they were the staring expressionless shoebutton eyes of the teddybear, and her mouth had opened, revealing the broken fangs which had been her dentures up until the T.W.A. Tri-Star was struck by lightning on its final approach, and she had whispered *You couldn't save me, George, we scrimped for you, we saved for you, we went without for you, your dad fixed up the scrape you got into with that girl and you STILL COULDN'T SAVE ME GOD DAMN YOU,* and he had awakened screaming, and he was vaguely aware of someone pounding on the wall, but by then he was already pelting into the bathroom, and he barely made it to the kneeling penitential position before the porcelain altar before dinner came up the express elevator. It came special delivery, hot and steaming and still smelling like processed turkey. He knelt there and looked into the bowl, at the chunks of half-digested turkey and the carrots which had lost none of their original fluorescent brightness, and this word flashed across his mind in large red letters:

ENOUGH

Correct.

It was:

ENOUGH.

He was going to get out of the sawbones business.
He was going to get out because:

ENOUGH WAS ENOUGH

He was going to get out because Popeye's motto was
That's all I can stands and I can't stand nummore,
and Popeye was as right as rain.

He had flushed the toilet and gone back to bed and
fell asleep almost instantly and awoke to discover he
still wanted to be a doctor, and that was a goddam
good thing to know for sure, maybe worth the whole
program, whether you called it Emergency Ride or
Bucket of Blood or Name That Tune.

He *still* wanted to be a doctor.

He knew a lady who did needlework. He paid her
ten dollars he couldn't afford to make him a small,
oldfashioned-looking sampler. It said:

IF YOU CAN TAKE THIS, YOU CAN TAKE
ANYTHING.

Yes. Correct.

The messy business in the subway happened four
weeks later.

2

"That lady was some fuckin weird, you know it?"
Julio said.

George breathed an interior sigh of relief. If Julio
hadn't opened the subject, George supposed he
wouldn't have had the sack. He was an intern, and
someday he was going to be a full-fledged doc, he
really believed that now, but Julio was a *vet,* and you
didn't want to say something stupid in front of a *vet.*
He would only laugh and say *Hell, I seen that shit a
thousand times, kid. Get y'self a towel and wipe off*

whatever it is behind your ears, cause it's wet and drippin down the sides of your face.

But apparently Julio *hadn't* seen it a thousand times, and that was good, because George *wanted* to talk about it.

"She was weird, all right. It was like she was two people."

He was amazed to see that now *Julio* was the one who looked relieved, and he was struck with sudden shame. Julio Estavez, who was going to do no more than pilot a limo with a couple of pulsing red lights on top for the rest of his life, had just shown more courage than he had been able to show.

"You got it, doc. Hunnert per cent." He pulled out a pack of Chesterfields and stuck one in the corner of his mouth.

"Those things are gonna kill you, my man," George said.

Julio nodded and offered the pack.

They smoked in silence for awhile. The paras were maybe chasing tail like Julio had said . . . or maybe they'd just had enough. *George* had been scared, all right, no joke about *that*. But he also knew *he* had been the one who saved the woman, not the paras, and he knew Julio knew it too. Maybe that was really why Julio had waited. The old black woman had helped, and the white kid who had dialed the cops while everyone else (except the old black woman) had just stood around watching like it was some goddam movie or TV show or something, part of a *Peter Gunn* episode, maybe, but in the end it had all come down to George Shavers, one scared cat doing his duty the best way he could.

The woman had been waiting for the train Duke Ellington held in such high regard—that fabled A-train. Just been a pretty young black woman in jeans and a khaki shirt waiting for the fabled A-train so she could go uptown someplace.

Someone had pushed her.

George Shavers didn't have the slightest idea if the police had caught the slug who had done it—that wasn't his business. His business was the woman who had tumbled screaming into the tube of the tunnel in front of that fabled A-train. It had been a miracle that she had missed the third rail; the fabled third rail that would have done to her what the State of New York did to the bad guys up at Sing-Sing who got a free ride on that fabled A-train the cons called Old Sparky.

Oboy, the miracles of electricity.

She tried to crawl out of the way but there hadn't been quite enough time and that fabled A-train had come into the station screeching and squalling and puking up sparks because the motorman had seen her but it was too late, too late for him and too late for her. The steel wheels of that fabled A-train had cut the living legs off her from just above the knees down. And while everyone else (except for the white kid who had dialed the cops) had only stood there pulling their puds (or pushing their pudenda, George supposed), the elderly black woman had jumped down, dislocating one hip in the process (she would later be given a Medal of Bravery by the Mayor), and had used the doorag on her head to cinch a tourniquet around one of the young woman's squirting thighs. The young white guy was screaming for an ambulance on one side of the station and the old black chick was screaming for someone to give her a help, to give her a tie-off for God's sake, anything, anything at all, and finally some elderly white business type had reluctantly surrendered his belt, and the elderly black chick looked up at him and spoke the words which became the headline of the New York *Daily News* the next day, the words which made her an authentic American apple-pie heroine: "Thank you, bro." Then she had noosed the belt around the young woman's left leg halfway between the young woman's crotch and where her left knee had been until that fabled A-train had come along.

George had heard someone say to someone else that the young black woman's last words before passing out had been *"WHO WAS THAT MAHFAH? I GONE HUNT HIM DOWN AND KILL HIS ASS!"*

There was no way to punch holes far enough up for the elderly black woman to notch the belt, so she simply held on like grim old death until Julio, George, and the paras arrived.

George remembered the yellow line, how his mother had told him he must never, never, *never* go past the yellow line while he was waiting for a train (fabled or otherwise), the stench of oil and electricity when he hopped down onto the cinders, remembered how hot it had been. The heat seemed to be baking off him, off the elderly black woman, off the young black woman, off the train, the tunnel, the unseen sky above and hell itself beneath. He remembered thinking incoherently *If they put a blood-pressure cuff on me now I'd go off the dial* and then he went cool and yelled for his bag, and when one of the paras tried to jump down with it he told the para to fuck off, and the para had looked startled, as if he was really seeing George Shavers for the first time, and he *had* fucked off.

George tied off as many veins and arteries as he could tie off, and when her heart started to be-bop he had shot her full of Digitalin. Whole blood arrived. Cops brought it. *Want to bring her up, doc?* one of them had asked and George had told him not yet, and he got out the needle and stuck the juice to her like she was a junkie in dire need of a fix.

Then he let them take her up.

Then they had taken her back.

On the way she had awakened.
Then the weirdness started.

3

George gave her a shot of Demerol when the paras loaded her into the ambulance—she had begun to stir and cry out weakly. He gave her a boost hefty enough for him to be confident she would remain quiet until they got to Sisters of Mercy. He was ninety per cent sure she *would* still be with them when they got there, and that was one for the good guys.

Her eyes began to flutter while they were still six blocks from the hospital, however. She uttered a thick moan.

"We can shoot her up again, doc," one of the paras said.

George was hardly aware this was the first time a paramedic had deigned to call him anything other than George or, worse, Georgie. "Are you nuts? I'd just as soon not confuse D.O.A. and O.D. if it's all the same to you."

The paramedic drew back.

George looked back at the young black woman and saw the eyes returning his gaze were awake and aware.

"What has happened to me?" she asked.

George remembered the man who had told another man about what the woman had supposedly said (how she was going to hunt the motherfucker down and kill his ass, etc., etc.). That man had been white. George decided now it had been pure invention, inspired either by that odd human urge to make naturally dramatic situations even more dramatic, or just race prejudice. This was a cultured, intelligent woman.

"You've had an accident," he said. "You were—"

Her eyes slipped shut and he thought she was going to sleep again. Good. Let someone else tell her she had lost her legs. Someone who made more than $7,600 a year. He had shifted a little to the left, wanting to check her b.p. again, when she opened her eyes once more. When she did, George Shavers was looking at a different woman.

"Fuckah cut off mah laigs. I felt 'em go. Dis d'amblance?"

"Y-Y-Yes," George said. Suddenly he needed something to drink. Not necessarily alcohol. Just something wet. His voice was dry. This was like watching Spencer Tracy in *Dr. Jekyll and Mr. Hyde*, only for real.

"Dey get dat honkey mahfah?"

"No," George said, thinking *The guy got it right, goddam, the guy did actually get it right.*

He was vaguely aware that the paramedics, who had been hovering (perhaps hoping he would do something wrong) were now backing off.

"Good. Honky fuzz jus be lettin him off anyway. I be gittin him. I be cuttin his cock off. Sumbitch! I tell you what I goan do t'dat sumbitch! I tell you one thing, you sumbitch honky! I goan tell you . . . tell . . ."

Her eyes fluttered again and George had thought *Yes, go to sleep,* please *go to sleep, I don't get paid for this, I don't understand this, they told us about shock but nobody mentioned schizophrenia as one of the—*

The eyes opened. The first woman was there.

"What sort of accident was it?" she asked. "I remember coming out of the I—"

"Eye?" he said stupidly.

She smiled a little. It was a painful smile. "The *Hungry I*. It's a coffee house."

"Oh. Yeah. Right."

The other one, hurt or not, had made him feel dirty and a little ill. This one made him feel like a knight in an Arthurian tale, a knight who has successfully rescued the Lady Fair from the jaws of the dragon.

"I remember walking down the stairs to the platform, and after that—"

"Someone pushed you." It sounded stupid, but what was wrong with that? It *was* stupid.

"Pushed me in front of the train?"

"Yes."

"Have I lost my legs?"

George tried to swallow and couldn't. There seemed to be nothing in his throat to grease the machinery.

"Not all of them," he said inanely, and her eyes closed.

Let it be a faint, he thought then, *please let it be a f—*

They opened, blazing. One hand came up and slashed five slits through the air within an inch of his face—any closer and he would have been in the E.R. getting his cheek stitched up instead of smoking Chesties with Julio Estavez.

"YOU AIN'T NUTHIN BUT A BUNCHA HONKY SONSA BITCHES!" she screamed. Her face was monstrous, her eyes full of hell's own light. It wasn't even the face of a human being. *"GOAN KILL EVERY MAHFAHIN HONKY I SEE! GOAN GELD EM FUST! GOAN CUT OFF THEIR BALLS AND SPIT EM IN THEY FACES! GOAN—"*

It was crazy. She talked like a cartoon black woman, Butterfly McQueen gone Loony Tunes. She—or it— also seemed superhuman. This screaming, writhing thing could not have just undergone impromptu surgery by subway train half an hour ago. She bit. She clawed out at him again and again. Snot spat from her nose. Spit flew from her lips. Filth poured from her mouth.

"Shoot her up, doc!" one of the paras yelled. His face was pale. *"Fa crissakes shoot her up!"* The para reached toward the supply case. George shoved his hand aside.

"Fuck off, chickenshit."

George looked back at his patient and saw the calm, cultured eyes of the other one looking at him.

"Will I live?" she asked in a conversational tea-room voice. He thought, *She is unaware of her lapses. Totally unaware.* And, after a moment: *So is the other one, for that matter.*

"I—" He gulped, rubbed at his galloping heart through his tunic, and then ordered himself to get control of this. He had saved her life. Her mental problems were not his concern.

"Are *you* all right?" she asked him, and the genuine concern in her voice made him smile a little—*her* asking *him.*

"Yes, ma'am."

"To which question are you responding?"

For a moment he didn't understand, then did. "Both," he said, and took her hand. She squeezed it, and he looked into her shining lucent eyes and thought *A man could fall in love,* and that was when her hand turned into a claw and she was telling him he was a honky mahfah, and she wadn't just goan *take* his balls, she was goan *chew* on those mahfahs.

He pulled away, looking to see if his hand was bleeding, thinking incoherently that if it was he would have to do something about it, because she was poison, the woman was poison, and being bitten by her would be about the same as being bitten by a copperhead or rattler. There was no blood. And when he looked again, it was the other woman—the first woman.

"Please," she said. "I don't want to die. Pl—" Then she went out for good, and that *was* good. For all of them.

4

"So whatchoo think?" Julio asked.

"About who's gonna be in the Series?" George squashed the butt under the heel of his loafer. "White Sox. I got 'em in the pool."

"Whatchoo think about that lady?"

"I think she might be schizophrenic," George said slowly.

"Yeah, I *know* that. I mean, what's gonna happen to her?"

"I don't know."

"She needs help, man. Who gonna give it?"

"Well, I already gave her one," George said, but his face felt hot, as if he were blushing.

Julio looked at him. "If you already gave her all the help you can give her, you shoulda let her die, doc."

George looked at Julio for a moment, but found he couldn't stand what he saw in Julio's eyes—not accusation but sadness.

So he walked away.

He had places to go.

5

The Time of the Drawing:

In the time since the accident it was, for the most part, still Odetta Holmes who was in control, but Detta Walker had come forward more and more, the thing Detta liked to do best was steal. It didn't matter that her booty was always little more than junk, no more than it mattered that she often threw it away later.

The *taking* was what mattered.

When the gunslinger entered her head in Macy's, Detta screamed in a combination of fury and horror and terror, her hands freezing on the junk jewelry she was scooping into her purse.

　She screamed because when Roland came into her mind, when he *came forward,* she for a moment sensed the *other,* as if a door had been swung open inside of her head.

　And she screamed because the invading raping presence was a honky.

　She could not see but nonetheless *sensed* his whiteness.

　People looked around. A floorwalker saw the screaming woman in the wheelchair with her purse open, saw one hand frozen in the act of stuffing costume jewelry into a purse that looked (even from a distance of thirty feet) worth three times the stuff she was stealing.

　The floorwalker yelled, *"Hey Jimmy!"* and Jimmy Halvorsen, one of Macy's house detectives, looked around and saw what was happening. He started toward the black woman in the wheelchair on a dead run. He couldn't help running—he had been a city cop for eighteen years and it was built into his system—but he was already thinking it was gonna be a shit bust. Little kids, cripples, nuns; they were always a shit bust. Busting them was like kicking a drunk. They cried a little in front of the judge and then took a walk. It was hard to convince judges that cripples could also be slime.

　But he ran just the same.

6

　Roland was momentarily horrified by the snakepit of hate and revulsion in which he found himself . . . and then he heard the woman screaming, saw the big man with the potato-sack belly running toward her/him, saw people looking, and took control.

　Suddenly he *was* the woman with the dusky hands.

He sensed some strange duality inside her, but couldn't think about it now.

He turned the chair and began to shove it forward. The aisle rolled past him/her. People dived away to either side. The purse was lost, spilling Detta's credentials and stolen treasure in a wide trail along the floor. The man with the heavy gut skidded on bogus gold chains and lipstick tubes and then fell on his ass.

7

Shit! Halvorsen thought furiously, and for a moment one hand clawed under his sport-coat where there was a .38 in a clamshell holster. Then sanity reasserted itself. This was no drug bust or armed robbery; this was a crippled black lady in a wheelchair. She was rolling it like it was some punk's drag-racer, but a crippled black lady was all she was just the same. What was he going to do, shoot her? That would be great, wouldn't it? And where was she going to go? There was nothing at the end of the aisle but two dressing rooms.

He picked himself up, massaging his aching ass, and began after her again, limping a little now.

The wheelchair flashed into one of the dressing rooms. The door slammed, just clearing the push-handles on the back.

Got you now, bitch, Jimmy thought. *And I'm going to give you one hell of a scare. I don't care if you got five orphan children and only a year to live. I'm not gonna hurt you, but oh babe I'm gonna shake your dice.*

He beat the floorwalker to the dressing room, slammed the door open with his left shoulder, and it was empty.

No black woman.

No wheelchair.

No nothing.

He looked at the floorwalker, starey-eyed.

"Other one!" the floorwalker yelled. "Other one!"

Before Jimmy could move, the floorwalker had busted open the door of the other dressing room. A woman in a linen skirt and a Playtex Living Bra screamed piercingly and crossed her arms over her chest. She was very white and very definitely not crippled.

"Pardon me," the floorwalker said, feeling hot crimson flood his face.

"Get out of here, you pervert!" the woman in the linen skirt and the bra cried.

"Yes, ma'am," the floorwalker said, and closed the door.

At Macy's, the customer was always right.

He looked at Halvorsen.

Halvorsen looked back.

"What is this shit?" Halvorsen asked. "Did she go in there or not?"

"Yeah, she did."

"So where is she?"

The floorwalker could only shake his head. "Let's go back and pick up the mess."

"You pick up the mess," Jimmy Halvorsen said. "I feel like I just broke my ass in nine pieces." He paused. "To tell you the truth, me fine bucko, I also feel extremely confused."

8

The moment the gunslinger heard the dressing room door bang shut behind him, he rammed the wheelchair around in a half turn, looking for the doorway. If Eddie had done what he had promised, it would be gone.

But the door was open. Roland wheeled the Lady of Shadows through it.

CHAPTER 3

ODETTA ON THE OTHER SIDE

1

Not long after, Roland would think: *Any other woman, crippled or otherwise, suddenly shoved all the way down the aisle of the mart in which she was doing business—monkeybusiness, you may call it if you like— by a stranger inside her head, shoved into a little room while some man behind her yelled for her to stop, then suddenly turned, shoved again where there was by rights no room in which to shove, then finding herself suddenly in an entirely different world . . . I think any other woman, under those circumstances, would have most certainly have asked, "Where am I?" before all else.*

Instead, Odetta Holmes asked almost pleasantly, "What exactly are you planning to do with that knife, young man?"

2

Roland looked up at Eddie, who was crouched with his knife held less than a quarter of an inch over the skin. Even with his uncanny speed, there was no way the gunslinger could move fast enough to evade the blade if Eddie decided to use it.

"Yes," Roland said. "What *are* you planning to do with it?"

"I don't know," Eddie said, sounding completely

258

disgusted with himself. "Cut bait, I guess. Sure doesn't look like I came here to fish, does it?"

He threw the knife toward the Lady's chair, but well to the right. It stuck, quivering, in the sand to its hilt.

Then the Lady turned her head and began, "I wonder if you could please explain where you've taken m—"

She stopped. She had said *I wonder if you* before her head had gotten around far enough to see there was no one behind her, but the gunslinger observed with some real interest that she went on speaking for a moment anyway, because the fact of her condition made certain things elementary truths of her life—if she had moved, for instance, someone must have moved her. But there was no one behind her.

No one at all.

She looked back at Eddie and the gunslinger, her dark eyes troubled, confused, and alarmed, and now she asked. "Where am I? Who pushed me? How can I be here? How can I be dressed, for that matter, when I was home watching the twelve o'clock news in my robe? Who am I? Where is this? Who are you?"

"Who am I?" she asked, the gunslinger thought. *The dam broke and there was a flood of questions; that was to be expected. But that one question—"Who am I?"—even now I don't think she knows she asked it.*

Or when.

Because she had asked *before.*

Even before she had asked who *they* were, she had asked who *she* was.

3

Eddie looked from the lovely young/old face of the black woman in the wheelchair to Roland's face.

"How come she doesn't know?"

"I can't say. Shock, I suppose."

"Shock took her all the way back to her living room,

before she left for Macy's? You telling me the last thing she remembers is sitting in her bathrobe and listening to some blow-dried dude talk about how they found that gonzo down in the Florida Keys with Christa McAuliff's left hand mounted on his den wall next to his prize marlin?''

Roland didn't answer.

More dazed than ever, the Lady said, ''Who is Christa McAuliff? Is she one of the missing Freedom Riders?''

Now it was Eddie's turn not to answer. Freedom Riders? What the hell were *they?*

The gunslinger glanced at him and Eddie was able to read his eyes easily enough: Can't you see she's in shock?

I know what you mean, Roland old buddy, but it only washes up to a point. I felt a little shock myself when you came busting into my head like Walter Payton on crack, but it didn't wipe out my memory banks.

Speaking of shock, he'd gotten another pretty good jolt when she came through. He had been kneeling over Roland's inert body, the knife just above the vulnerable skin of the throat . . . but the truth was Eddie couldn't have used the knife anyway—not then, anyway. He was staring into the doorway, hypnotized, as an aisle of Macy's rushed forward—he was reminded again of *The Shining,* where you saw what the little boy was seeing as he rode his trike through the hallways of that haunted hotel. He remembered the little boy had seen this creepy pair of dead twins in one of those hallways. The end of this aisle was much more mundane: a white door. The words ONLY TWO GARMENTS AT ONE TIME, PLEASE were printed on it in discreet lettering. Yeah, it was Macy's, all right. Macy's for sure.

One black hand flew out and slammed the door open while the male voice (a cop voice if Eddie had ever

heard one, and he had heard many in his time) behind
yelled for her to quit it, that was no way out, she was
only making things a helluva lot worse for herself, and
Eddie caught a bare glimpse of the black woman in
the wheelchair in the mirror to the left, and he remembered thinking *Jesus, he's got her, all right, but she
sure don't look happy about it.*

Then the view pivoted *and Eddie was looking at
himself.* The view rushed toward the viewer and he
wanted to put up the hand holding the knife to shield
his eyes because all at once the sensation of looking
through two sets of eyes was too much, too crazy, it
was going to *drive* him crazy if he didn't shut it out,
but it all happened too fast for him to have time.

The wheelchair came through the door. It was a tight
fit; Eddie heard its hubs squeal on the sides. At the
same moment he heard another sound: a thick *tearing*
sound that made him think of some word

(placental)

that he couldn't quite think of because he didn't
know he knew it. Then the woman was rolling toward
him on the hard-packed sand, and she no longer looked
mad as hell—hardly looked like the woman Eddie had
glimpsed in the mirror at all, for that matter, but he
supposed *that* wasn't surprising; when you all at once
went from a changing-room at Macy's to the seashore
of a godforsaken world where some of the lobsters
were the size of small Collie dogs, it left you feeling
a little winded. That was a subject on which Eddie
Dean felt he could personally give testimony.

She rolled about four feet before stopping, and only
went that far because of the slope and the gritty pack
of the sand. Her hands were no longer pumping the
wheels as they must have been doing *(when you wake
up with sore shoulders tomorrow you can blame them
on Sir Roland, lady,* Eddie thought sourly). Instead

they went to the arms of the chair and gripped them as she regarded the two men.

Behind her, the doorway had already disappeared. Disappeared? That was not quite right. It seemed to *fold in* on itself, like a piece of film run backward. This began to happen just as the store dick came slamming through the other, more mundane door—the one between the store and the dressing room. He was coming hard, expecting the shoplifter would have locked the door, and Eddie thought he was going to take one hell of a splat against the far wall, but Eddie was never going to see it happen or not happen. Before the shrinking space where the door between that world and this disappeared entirely, Eddie saw everything on that side freeze solid.

The movie had become a still photograph.

All that remained now were the dual tracks of the wheelchair, starting in sandy nowhere and running four feet to where it and its occupant now sat.

"Won't somebody please explain where I am and how I got here?" the woman in the wheelchair asked— almost pleaded.

"Well, I'll tell you one thing, Dorothy," Eddie said. "You ain't in Kansas anymore."

The woman's eyes brimmed with tears. Eddie could see her trying to hold them in but it was no good. She began to sob.

Furious (and disgusted with himself as well), Eddie turned on the gunslinger, who had staggered to his feet. Roland moved, but not toward the weeping Lady. Instead he went to pick up his knife.

"Tell her!" Eddie shouted. "You brought her, *so go on and tell her, man!*" And after a moment he added in a lower tone, "And then tell me how come she doesn't remember herself."

4

Roland did not respond. Not at once. He bent, pinched the hilt of the knife between the two remaining fingers of his right hand, transferred it carefully to his left, and slipped it into the scabbard at the side of one gunbelt. He was still trying to grapple with what he had sensed in the Lady's mind. Unlike Eddie, she had fought him, fought him like a cat, from the moment he *came forward* until they rolled through the door. The fight had begun the moment she sensed him. There had been no lapse, because there had been no surprise. He had experienced it but didn't in the least understand it. No surprise at the invading stranger in her mind, only the instant rage, terror, and the commencement of a battle to shake him free. She hadn't come close to winning that battle—could not, he suspected—but that hadn't kept her from trying like hell. He had felt a woman insane with fear and anger and hate.

He had sensed only darkness in her—this was a mind entombed in a cave-in.

Except—

Except that in the moment they burst through the doorway and separated, he had wished—wished *desperately*—that he could tarry a moment longer. One moment would have told so much. Because the woman before them now wasn't the woman in whose mind he had been. Being in Eddie's mind had been like being in a room with jittery, sweating walls. Being in the Lady's had been like lying naked in the dark while venomous snakes crawled all over you.

Until the end.

She had changed at the end.

And there had been something else, something he believed was vitally important, but he either could not understand it or remember it. Something like

(a glance)

the doorway itself, only in her mind. Something about

(you broke the forspecial *it was you)*

some sudden burst of understanding. As at studies, when you finally saw—

"Oh, fuck you," Eddie said disgustedly. "You're nothing but a goddam machine."

He strode past Roland, went to the woman, knelt beside her, and when she put her arms around him, panic-tight, like the arms of a drowning swimmer, he did not draw away but put his own arms around her and hugged her back.

"It's okay," he said. "I mean, it's not great, but it's okay."

"Where are we?" she wept. *"I was sitting home watching TV so I could hear if my friends got out of Oxford alive and now I'm here and I DON'T EVEN KNOW WHERE HERE IS!"*

"Well, neither do I," Eddie said, holding her tighter, beginning to rock her a little, "but I guess we're in it together. I'm from where you're from, little old New York City, and I've been through the same thing—well, a little different, but same principle—and you're gonna be just fine." As an afterthought he added: "As long as you like lobster."

She hugged him and wept and Eddie held her and rocked her and Roland thought, *Eddie will be all right now. His brother is dead but he has someone else to take care of so Eddie will be all right now.*

But he felt a pang: a deep reproachful hurt in his heart. He was capable of shooting—with his left hand, anyway—of killing, of going on and on, slamming with brutal relentlessness through miles and years, even dimensions, it seemed, in search of the Tower. He was capable of survival, sometimes even of protection—he had saved the boy Jake from a slow death at the way station, and from sexual consumption by the Oracle at the foot of the mountains—but in the end, he had let Jake die. Nor had this been by accident; he had committed a conscious act of damnation. He watched the two of them, watched Eddie hug her, assure her it was going to be all right. He could not have done that, and now the rue in his heart was joined by stealthy fear.

If you have given up your heart for the Tower, Roland, you have already lost. A heartless creature is a loveless creature, and a loveless creature is a beast. To be a beast is perhaps bearable, although the man who has become one will surely pay hell's own price in the end, but what if you should gain your object? What if you should, heartless, actually storm the Dark Tower and win it? If there is naught but darkness in your heart, what could you do except degenerate from beast to monster? To gain one's object as a beast would only be bitterly comic, like giving a magnifying glass to an elephaunt. But to gain one's object as a monster . . .

To pay *hell is one thing. But do you want to* own *it?*

He thought of Allie, and of the girl who had once waited for him at the window, thought of the tears he had shed over Cuthbert's lifeless corpse. Oh, then he had loved. Yes. Then.

I do *want to love!* he cried, but although Eddie was also crying a little now with the woman in the wheelchair, the gunslinger's eyes remained as dry as the desert he had crossed to reach this sunless sea.

5

He would answer Eddie's question later. He would do that because he thought Eddie would do well to be on guard. The reason she didn't remember was simple. She wasn't one woman but two.

And one of them was dangerous.

6

Eddie told her what he could, glossing over the shoot-out but being truthful about everything else.

When he was done, she remained perfectly silent for some time, her hands clasped together on her lap.

Little streamlets coursed down from the shallowing mountains, petering out some miles to the east. It was from these that Roland and Eddie had drawn their water as they hiked north. At first Eddie had gotten it because Roland was too weak. Later they had taken turns, always having to go a little further and search a little longer before finding a stream. They grew steadily more listless as the mountains slumped, but the water hadn't made them sick.

So far.

Roland had gone yesterday, and although that made today Eddie's turn, the gunslinger had gone again, shouldering the hide water-skins and walking off without a word. Eddie found this queerly discreet. He didn't want to be touched by the gesture—by anything about Roland, for that matter—and found he was, a little, just the same.

She listened attentively to Eddie, not speaking at all, her eyes fixed on his. At one moment Eddie would guess she was five years older than he, at another he would guess fifteen. There was one thing he didn't have to guess about: he was falling in love with her.

When he had finished, she sat for a moment without saying anything, now not looking at him but beyond him, looking at the waves which would, at nightfall, bring the lobsters and with their alien, lawyerly questions. He had been particularly careful to describe *them*. Better for her to be a little scared now than a lot scared when they came out to play. He supposed she wouldn't want to eat them, not after hearing what they had done to Roland's hand and foot, not after she got a good close look at them. But eventually hunger would win out over *did-a-chick* and *dum-a-chum*.

Her eyes were far and distant.

"Odetta?" he asked after perhaps five minutes had gone by. She had told him her name. Odetta Holmes. He thought it was a gorgeous name.

She looked back at him, startled out of her revery. She smiled a little. She said one word.

"No."

He only looked at her, able to think of no suitable reply. He thought he had never understood until that moment how illimitable a simple negative could be.

"I don't understand," he said finally. "What are you no-ing?"

"All this." Odetta swept an arm (she had, he'd noticed, very strong arms—smooth but very strong), indicating the sea, the sky, the beach, the scruffy foothills where the gunslinger was now presumably searching for water (or maybe getting eaten alive by some new and interesting monster, something Eddie didn't really care to think about). Indicating, in short, this entire world.

"I understand how you feel. I had a pretty good case of the unrealities myself at first."

But *had* he? Looking back, it seemed he had simply accepted, perhaps because he was sick, shaking himself apart in his need for junk.

"You get over it."

"No," she said again. "I believe one of two things has happened, and no matter which one it is, I am still in Oxford, Mississippi. None of this is real."

She went on. If her voice had been louder (or perhaps if he had not been falling in love) it would almost have been a lecture. As it was, it sounded more like lyric than lecture.

Except, he had to keep reminding himself, *bullshit's*

*what it really is, and you have to convince her of that.
For her sake.*

"I may have sustained a head injury," she said.
"They are notorious swingers of axe-handles and billy-
clubs in Oxford Town."

Oxford Town.

That produced a faint chord of recognition far back
in Eddie's mind. She said the words in a kind of rhythm
that he for some reason associated with Henry . . .
Henry and wet diapers. Why? What? Didn't matter
now.

"You're trying to tell me you think this is all some
sort of dream you're having while you're unconscious?"

"Or in a coma," she said. "And you needn't look
at me as though you thought it was preposterous, because it isn't. Look here."

She parted her hair carefully on the left, and Eddie
could see she wore it to one side not just because she
liked the style. The old wound beneath the fall of her
hair was scarred and ugly, not brown but a grayish-
white.

"I guess you've had a lot of hard luck in your time,"
he said.

She shrugged impatiently. "A lot of hard luck and
a lot of soft living," she said. "Maybe it all balances
out. I only showed you because I was in a coma for
three weeks when I was five. I dreamed a lot then. I
can't remember what the dreams were, but I remember
my mamma said they knew I wasn't going to die just
as long as I kept talking and it seemed like I kept
talking all the time, although she said they couldn't
make out one word in a dozen. I *do* remember that the
dreams were very vivid."

She paused, looking around.

"As vivid as this place seems to be. And *you,*
Eddie."

When she said his name his arms prickled. Oh, he had it, all right. Had it bad.

"And *him.*" She shivered. *"He* seems the most vivid of all."

"We ought to. I mean, we *are* real, no matter what you think."

She gave him a kind smile. It was utterly without belief.

"How did that happen?" he asked. "That thing on your head?"

"It doesn't matter. I'm just making the point that what has happened once might very well happen again."

"No, but I'm curious."

"I was struck by a brick. It was our first trip north. We came to the town of Elizabeth, New Jersey. We came in the Jim Crow car."

"What's that?"

She looked at him unbelievingly, almost scornfully. "Where have you been living, Eddie? In a bomb-shelter?"

"I'm from a different time," he said. "Could I ask how old you are, Odetta?"

"Old enough to vote and not old enough for Social Security."

"Well, I guess that puts me in my place."

"But gently, I hope," she said, and smiled that radiant smile which made his arms prickle.

"I'm twenty-three," he said, "but I was born in 1964—the year you were living in when Roland took you."

"That's rubbish."

"No. I was living in 1987 when he took *me.*"

"Well," she said after a moment. "That certainly adds a great deal to your argument for this as reality, Eddie."

"The Jim Crow car . . . was it where the black people had to stay?"

"The *Negros*," she said. "Calling a Negro a black is a trifle rude, don't you think?"

"You'll all be calling yourselves that by 1980 or so," Eddie said. "When I was a kid, calling a black kid a Negro was apt to get you in a fight. It was almost like calling him a nigger."

She looked at him uncertainly for a moment, then shook her head again.

"Tell me about the brick, then."

"My mother's youngest sister was going to be married," Odetta said. "Her name was Sophia, but my mother always called her Sister Blue because it was the color she always fancied. 'Or at least she fancied to fancy it,' was how my mother put it. So I always called her Aunt Blue, even before I met her. It was the most lovely wedding. There was a reception afterward. I remember all the presents."

She laughed.

"Presents always look so wonderful to a child, don't they, Eddie?"

He smiled. "Yeah, you got that right. You never forget presents. Not what you got, not what somebody else got, either."

"My father had begun to make money by then, but all I knew is that we were *getting ahead*. That's what my mother always called it and once, when I told her a little girl I played with had asked if my daddy was rich, my mother told me that was what I was supposed to say if any of my other chums ever asked me that question. That we were *getting ahead*.

"So they were able to give Aunt Blue a lovely china set, and I remember . . ."

Her voice faltered. One hand rose to her temple and rubbed absently, as if a headache were beginning there.

"Remember what, Odetta?"

"I remember my mother gave her a *forspecial*."

"What?"

"I'm sorry. I've got a headache. It's got my tongue tangled. I don't know why I'm bothering to tell you all this, anyway."

"Do you mind?"

"No. I don't mind. I *meant* to say mother gave her a special plate. It was white, with delicate blue tracework woven all around the rim." Odetta smiled a little. Eddie didn't think it was an entirely comfortable smile. Something about this memory disturbed her, and the way its immediacy seemed to have taken precedence over the extremely strange situation she had found herself in, a situation which should be claiming all or most of her attention, disturbed *him*.

"I can see that plate as clearly as I can see you now, Eddie. My mother gave it to Aunt Blue and she cried and cried over it. I think she'd seen a plate like that once when she and my mother were children, only of course their parents could never have afforded such a thing. There was none of them who got anything *forspecial* as kids. After the reception Aunt Blue and her husband left for the Great Smokies on their honeymoon. They went on the train." She looked at Eddie.

"In the Jim Crow car," he said.

"That's right! In the Crow car! In those days that's what Negros rode in and where they ate. That's what we're trying to change in Oxford Town."

She looked at him, almost surely expecting him to insist she was *here*, but he was caught in the webwork of his own memory again: wet diapers and those words. Oxford Town. Only suddenly other words came, just a single line, but he could remember Henry singing it over and over until his mother asked if he couldn't please stop so she could hear Walter Cronkite.

Somebody better investigate soon. Those were the words. Sung over and over by Henry in a nasal monotone. He tried for more but couldn't get it, and was that any real surprise? He could have been no more than three at the time. *Somebody better investigate soon.* The words gave him a chill.

"Eddie, are you all right?"

"Yes. Why?"

"You shivered."

He smiled. "Donald Duck must have walked over my grave."

She laughed. "Anyway, at least I didn't spoil the wedding. It happened when we were walking back to the railway station. We stayed the night with a friend of Aunt Blue's, and in the morning my father called a taxi. The taxi came almost right away, but when the driver saw we were colored, he drove off like his head was on fire and his ass was catching. Aunt Blue's friend had already gone ahead to the depot with our luggage—there was a lot of it, because we were going to spend a week in New York. I remember my father saying he couldn't wait to see my face light up when the clock in Central Park struck the hour and all the animals danced.

"My father said we might as well walk to the station. My mother agreed just as fast as lickety-split, saying that was a fine idea, it wasn't but a mile and it would be nice to stretch our legs after three days on one train just behind us and half a day on another one just ahead of us. My father said yes, and it was gorgeous weather besides, but I think I knew even at five that he was mad and she was embarrassed and both of them were afraid to call another taxi-cab because the same thing might happen again.

"So we went walking down the street. I was on the inside because my mother was afraid of me getting too close to the traffic. I remember wondering if my daddy meant my face would actually start to *glow* or something when I saw that clock in Central Park, and if that might not hurt, and that was when the brick came down on my head. Everything went dark for a while. Then the dreams started. Vivid dreams.''

She smiled.

"Like *this* dream, Eddie.''

"Did the brick fall, or did someone bomb you?''

"They never found anyone. The police (my mother told me this long after, when I was sixteen or so) found the place where they thought the brick had been, but there were other bricks missing and more were loose. It was just outside the window of a fourth-floor room in an apartment building that had been condemned. But of course there were lots of people staying there just the same. Especially at night.''

"Sure,'' Eddie said.

"No one saw anyone leaving the building, so it went down as an accident. My mother said she thought it *had* been, but I think she was lying. She didn't even bother trying to tell me what my father thought. They were both still smarting over how the cab-driver had taken one look at us and driven off. It was that more than anything else that made them believe someone had been up there, just looking out, and saw us coming, and decided to drop a brick on the niggers.''

"Will your lobster-creatures come out soon?''

"No,'' Eddie said. "Not until dusk. So one of your ideas is that all of this is a coma-dream like the ones you had when you got bopped by the brick. Only this time you think it was a billy-club or something.''

"Yes.''

"What's the other one?''

Odetta's face and voice were calm enough, but her head was filled with an ugly skein of images which all added up to Oxford Town, Oxford Town. How did the song go? *Two men killed by the light of the moon,/*

Somebody better investigate soon. Not quite right, but it was close. Close.

"I may have gone insane," she said.

7

The first words which came into Eddie's mind were *If you think you've gone insane, Odetta, you're nuts.*

Brief consideration, however, made this seem an unprofitable line of argument to take.

Instead he remained silent for a time, sitting by her wheelchair, his knees drawn up, his hands holding his wrists.

"Were you really a heroin addict?"

"Am," he said. "It's like being an alcoholic, or 'basing. It's not a thing you ever get over. I used to hear that and go 'Yeah, yeah, right, right,' in my head, you know, but now I understand. I still want it, and I guess part of me will *always* want it, but the physical part has passed."

"What's 'basing?" she asked.

"Something that hasn't been invented yet in your *when.* It's something you do with cocaine, only it's like turning TNT into an A-bomb."

"You did it?"

"Christ, no. Heroin was my thing. I told you."

"You don't seem like an addict," she said.

Eddie actually was fairly spiffy . . . if, that was, one ignored the gamy smell arising from his body and clothes (he could rinse himself and did, could rinse his clothes and did, but lacking soap, he could not really wash either). His hair had been short when Roland stepped into his life (the better to sail through customs, my dear, and what a great big joke *that* had turned out to be), and was still a respectable length. He shaved every morning, using the keen edge of Roland's knife, gingerly at first, but with increasing con-

fidence. He'd been too young for shaving to be part of
his life when Henry left for 'Nam, and it hadn't been
any big deal to Henry back then, either; he never grew
a beard, but sometimes went three or four days before
Mom nagged him into "mowing the stubble." When
he came back, however, Henry was a maniac on the
subject (as he was on a few others—foot-powder after
showering; teeth to be brushed three or four times a
day and followed by a chaser of mouthwash; clothes
always hung up) and he turned Eddie into a fanatic as
well. The stubble was mowed every morning and every
evening. Now this habit was deep in his grain, like the
others Henry had taught him. Including, of course, the
one you took care of with a needle.

"Too clean-cut?" he asked her, grinning.

"Too white," she said shortly, and then was quiet
for a moment, looking sternly out at the sea. Eddie
was quiet, too. If there was a comeback to something
like that, he didn't know what it was.

"I'm sorry," she said. "That was very unkind, very
unfair, and very unlike me."

"It's all right."

"It's *not*. It's like a white person saying something
like 'Jeez, I never would have guessed you were a nigger' to someone with a very light skin."

"You like to think of yourself as more fair-minded,"
Eddie said.

"What we like to think of ourselves and what we
really are rarely have much in common, I should think,
but yes—I like to think of myself as more fair-minded.
So please accept my apology, Eddie."

"On one condition."

"What's that?" she was smiling a little again. That
was good. He liked it when he was able to make her
smile.

"Give *this* a fair chance. That's the condition."

"Give *what* a fair chance?" She sounded slightly

amused. Eddie might have bristled at that tone in someone else's voice, might have felt he was getting boned, but with her it was different. With her it was all right. He supposed with her just about anything would have been.

"That there's a third alternative. That this really is happening. I mean . . ." Eddie cleared his throat. "I'm not very good at this philosophical shit, or, you know, metamorphosis or whatever the hell you call it—"

"Do you mean metaphysics?"

"Maybe. I don't know. I think so. But I know you can't go around disbelieving what your senses tell you. Why, if your idea about this all being a dream is right—"

"I didn't say a *dream*—"

"Whatever you said, that's what it comes down to, isn't it? A false reality?"

If there had been something faintly condescending in her voice a moment ago, it was gone now. "Philosophy and metaphysics may not be your bag, Eddie, but you must have been a hell of a debater in school."

"I was never in debate. That was for gays and hags and wimps. Like chess club. What do you mean, my bag? What's a bag?"

"Just something you like. What do *you* mean, gays? What are *gays?*"

He looked at her for a moment, then shrugged. "Homos. Fags. Never mind. We could swap slang all day. It's not getting us anyplace. What I'm trying to say is that if it's all a dream, it could be mine, not yours. *You* could be a figment of *my* imagination."

Her smile faltered. "You . . . nobody bopped you."

"Nobody bopped *you*, either."

Now her smile was entirely gone. "No one that I *remember*," she corrected with some sharpness.

"Me either!" he said. "You told me they're rough

in Oxford. Well, those Customs guys weren't exactly cheery joy when they couldn't find the dope they were after. One of them could have head-bopped me with the butt of his gun. I could be lying in a Bellevue ward right now, dreaming you and Roland while they write their reports, explaining how, while they were interrogating me, I became violent and had to be subdued."

"It's not the same."

"Why? Because you're this intelligent socially active black lady with no legs and I'm just a hype from Co-Op City?" He said it with a grin, meaning it as an amiable jape, but she flared at him.

"I wish you would stop calling me *black!*"

He sighed. "Okay, but it's gonna take getting used to."

"You should have been on the debate club anyway."

"Fuck," he said, and the turn of her eyes made him realize again that the difference between them was much wider than color; they were speaking to each other from separate islands. The water between was time. Never mind. The word had gotten her attention. "I don't want to debate you. I want to wake you up to the fact that you *are* awake, that's all."

"I might be able to at least operate provisionally according to the dictates of your third alternative as long as this . . . this situation . . . continued to go on, except for one thing: There's a fundamental difference between what happened to you and what happened to me. So fundamental, so large, that you haven't seen it."

"Then show it to me."

"There is no discontinuity in your consciousness. There is a very large one in mine."

"I don't understand."

"I mean you can account for all of your time," Odetta said. "Your story follows from point to point:

the airplane, the incursion by that . . . that . . . by
him—''

She nodded toward the foothills with clear distaste.

"The stashing of the drugs, the officers who took
you into custody, all the rest. It's a fantastic story, it
has no missing links.

"As for myself, I arrived back from Oxford, was
met by Andrew, my driver, and brought back to my
building. I bathed and I wanted sleep—I was getting a
very bad headache, and sleep is the only medicine
that's any good for the really bad ones. But it was close
on midnight, and I thought I would watch the news
first. Some of us had been released, but a good many
more were still in the jug when we left. I wanted to
find out if their cases had been resolved.

"I dried off and put on my robe and went into the
living room. I turned on the TV news. The newscaster
started talking about a speech Krushchev had just
made about the American advisors in Viet Nam. He
said, 'We have a film report from—' and then he was
gone and I was rolling down this beach. You say you
saw me in some sort of magic doorway which is now
gone, and that I was in Macy's, and that I was stealing.
All of this is preposterous enough, but even if it was
so, I could find something better to steal than costume
jewelry. I don't wear jewelry.''

"You better look at your hands again, Odetta,"
Eddie said quietly.

For a very long time she looked from the "diamond" on her left pinky, too large and vulgar to be
anything but paste, to the large opal on the third finger
of her right hand, which was too large and vulgar to
be anything but real.

"None of this is happening," she repeated firmly.

"You sound like a broken record!" He was genuinely angry for the first time. "Every time someone
pokes a hole in your neat little story, you just retreat

to that 'none of this is happening' shit. You have to wise up, 'Detta.''

"Don't call me that! I hate that!" she burst out so shrilly that Eddie recoiled.

"Sorry. Jesus! I didn't know."

"I went from night to day, from undressed to dressed, from my living room to this deserted beach. And what really happened was that some big-bellied redneck deputy hit me upside the head with a club *and that is all!*"

"But your memories don't stop in Oxford," he said softly.

"W-What?" Uncertain again. Or maybe seeing and not wanting to. Like with the rings.

"If you got whacked in Oxford, how come your memories don't stop there?"

"There isn't always a lot of logic to things like this." She was rubbing her temples again. "And now, if it's all the same to you, Eddie, I'd just as soon end the conversation. My headache is back. It's quite bad."

"I guess whether or not logic figures in all depends on what you want to believe. I *saw* you in Macy's, Odetta. I *saw* you stealing. You say you don't do things like that, but you also told me you don't wear jewelry. You told me that even though you'd looked down at your hands several times while we were talking. Those rings were there then, *but it was as if you couldn't see them until I called your attention to them and made you see them.*"

"I don't want to talk about it!" she shouted. "My head hurts!"

"All right. But you know where you lost track of time, and it wasn't in Oxford."

"Leave me alone," she said dully.

Eddie saw the gunslinger toiling his way back with two full water-skins, one tied around his waist and the other slung over his shoulders. He looked very tired.

"I wish I could help you," Eddie said, "but to do that, I guess I'd have to be real."

He stood by her for a moment, but her head was bowed, the tips of her fingers steadily massaging her temples.

Eddie went to meet Roland.

8

"Sit down." Eddie took the bags. "You look all in."

"I am. I'm getting sick again."

Eddie looked at the gunslinger's flushed cheeks and brow, his cracked lips, and nodded. "I hoped it wouldn't happen, but I'm not that surprised, man. You didn't bat for the cycle. Balazar didn't have enough Keflex."

"I don't understand you."

"If you don't take a penicillin drug long enough, you don't kill the infection. You just drive it underground. A few days go by and it comes back. We'll need more, but at least there's a door to go. In the meantime you'll just have to take it easy." But Eddie was thinking unhappily of Odetta's missing legs and the longer and longer treks it took to find water. He wondered if Roland could have picked a worse time to have a relapse. He supposed it was possible; he just didn't see how.

"I have to tell you something about Odetta."

"That's her name?"

"Uh-huh."

"It's very lovely," the gunslinger said.

"Yeah. I thought so, too. What isn't so lovely is the way she feels about this place. She doesn't think she's here."

"I know. And she doesn't like me much, does she?"

No, Eddie thought, *but that doesn't keep her from*

thinking you're one booger *of a hallucination.* He didn't say it, only nodded.

"The reasons are almost the same," the gunslinger said. "She's not the woman I brought through, you see. Not at all."

Eddie stared, then suddenly nodded, excited. That blurred glimpse in the mirror . . . that snarling face . . . the man was right. Jesus Christ, of course he was! That hadn't been Odetta at all.

Then he remembered the hands which had gone pawing carelessly through the scarves and had just as carelessly gone about the business of stuffing the junk jewelry into her big purse—almost, it had seemed, as if she *wanted* to be caught.

The rings had been there.

Same rings.

But that doesn't necessarily mean the same hands, he thought wildly, but that would only hold for a second. He had studied her hands. They *were* the same, long-fingered and delicate.

"No," the gunslinger continued. "She is not." His blue eyes studied Eddie carefully.

"Her hands—"

"Listen," the gunslinger said, "and listen carefully. Our lives may depend on it—mine because I'm getting sick again, and yours because you have fallen in love with her."

Eddie said nothing.

"She is two women in the *same body.* She was one woman when I entered her, and another when I returned here."

Now Eddie *could* say nothing.

"There was something else, something strange, but either I didn't understand it or I did and it's slipped away. It seemed important."

Roland looked past Eddie, looked to the beached

wheelchair, standing alone at the end of its short track from nowhere. Then he looked back at Eddie.

"I understand very little of this, or how such a thing can be, but *you must be on your guard.* Do you understand that?"

"Yes." Eddie's lungs felt as if they had very little wind in them. He understood—or had, at least, a moviegoer's understanding of the sort of thing the gunslinger was speaking of—but he didn't have the breath to explain, not yet. He felt as if Roland had kicked all his breath out of him.

"Good. Because the woman I entered on the other side of the door was as deadly as those lobster-things that come out at night."

CHAPTER 4
DETTA ON THE OTHER SIDE

1

You must be on your guard, the gunslinger said, and Eddie had agreed, but the gunslinger knew Eddie didn't know what he was talking about; the whole back half of Eddie's mind, where survival is or isn't, didn't get the message.

The gunslinger saw this.

It was a good thing for Eddie he did.

2

In the middle of the night, Detta Walker's eyes sprang open. They were full of starlight and clear intelligence.

She remembered everything: how she had fought them, how they had tied her into her chair, how they had taunted her, calling her *niggerbitch, niggerbitch.*

She remembered monsters coming out of the waves, and she remembered how one of the men—the older— had killed one of them. The younger had built a fire and cooked it and then had offered her smoking monster-meat on a stick, grinning. She remembered spitting at his face, remembered his grin turning into an angry honky scowl. He had hit her upside the face, and told her *Well, that's all right, you'll come around, niggerbitch. Wait and see if you don't.* Then he and the Really Bad Man—had laughed and the Really Bad Man had brought out a haunch of beef which he spitted

283

and slowly cooked over the fire on the beach of this
alien place to which they had brought her.

The smell of the slowly roasting beef had been seductive, but she had made no sign. Even when the
younger one had waved a chunk of it near her face,
chanting *Bite for it, niggerbitch, go on and bite for it,*
she had sat like stone, holding herself in.

Then she had slept, and now she was awake, and
the ropes they had tied her with were gone. She was
no longer in her chair but lying on one blanket and
under another, far above the high-tide line, where the
lobster-things still wandered and questioned and
snatched the odd unfortunate gull out of the air.

She looked to her left and saw nothing.

She looked to her right and saw two sleeping men
wrapped in two piles of blankets. The younger one
was closer, and the Really Bad Man had taken off his
gunbelts and laid them by him.

The guns were still in them.

You made a bad mistake, mahfah, Detta thought,
and rolled to her right. The gritty crunch and squeak
of her body on the sand was inaudible under the wind,
the waves, the questioning creatures. She crawled
slowly along the sand (like one of the lobstrosities herself), her eyes glittering.

She reached the gunbelts and pulled one of the guns.

It was very heavy, the grip smooth and somehow
independently deadly in her hand. The heaviness didn't
bother her. She had strong arms, did Detta Walker.

She crawled a little further.

The younger man was no more than a snoring rock,
but the Really Bad Man stirred a little in his sleep and
she froze with a snarl tattooed on her face until he
quieted again.

*He be one sneaky sumbitch. You check, Detta. You
check, be sho.*

She found the worn chamber release, tried to shove

it forward, got nothing, and pulled it instead. The chamber swung open.

Loaded! Fucker be loaded! You goan do this young cocka-de-walk first, and dat Really Bad Man be wakin up and you goan give him one big grin—smile honey-chile so I kin see where you is—and den you goan clean his clock somethin righteous.

She swung the chamber back, started to pull the hammer . . . and then waited.

When the wind kicked up a gust, she pulled the hammer to full cock.

Detta pointed Roland's gun at Eddie's temple.

3

The gunslinger watched all this from one half-open eye. The fever was back, but not bad yet, not so bad that he must mistrust himself. So he waited, that one half-open eye the finger on the trigger of his body, the body which had always been his revolver when there was no revolver at hand.

She pulled the trigger.

Click.

Of course *click.*

When he and Eddie had come back with the water-skins from their palaver, Odetta Holmes had been deeply asleep in her wheelchair, slumped to one side. They had made her the best bed they could on the sand and carried her gently from her wheelchair to the spread blankets. Eddie had been sure she would awake, but Roland knew better.

He had killed, Eddie had built a fire, and they had eaten, saving a portion aside for Odetta in the morning.

Then they had talked, and Eddie had said something which burst upon Roland like a sudden flare of lightning. It was too bright and too brief to be total understanding, but he saw much, the way one may discern the lay of the land in a single lucky stroke of lightning.

He could have told Eddie then, but did not. He understood that he must be Eddie's Cort, and when one of Cort's pupils was left hurt and bleeding by some unexpected blow, Cort's response had always been the same: *A child doesn't understand a hammer until he's mashed his finger at a nail. Get up and stop whining, maggot! You have forgotten the face of your father!*

So Eddie had fallen asleep, even though Roland had told him he must be on his guard, and when Roland was sure they both slept (he had waited longer for the Lady, who could, he thought, be sly), he had reloaded his guns with spent casings, unstrapped them (that caused a pang), and put them by Eddie.

Then he waited.

One hour; two; three.

Halfway through the fourth hour, as his tired and feverish body tried to drowse, he sensed rather than saw the Lady come awake and came fully awake himself.

He watched her roll over. He watched her turn her hands into claws and pull herself along the sand to where his gunbelts lay. He watched her take one of them out, come closer to Eddie, and then pause, her head cocking, her nostrils swelling and contracting, doing more than smelling the air; *tasting* it.

Yes. This was the woman he had brought across.

When she glanced toward the gunslinger he did more than feign sleep, because she would have sensed sham; he *went* to sleep. When he sensed her gaze shift away he awoke and opened that single eye again. He saw her begin to raise the gun—she did this with less effort than Eddie had shown the first time Roland saw him do the same thing—and point it toward Eddie's head. Then she paused, her face filled with an inexpressible cunning.

In that moment she reminded him of Marten.

She fiddled with the cylinder, getting it wrong at first, then swinging it open. She looked at the heads of the shells. Roland tensed, waiting first to see if she would know the firing pins had already been struck, waiting next to see if she would turn the gun, look into the other end of the cylinder, and see there was only emptiness there instead of lead (he had thought of loading the guns with cartridges which had already misfired, but only briefly; Cort had taught them that every gun is ultimately ruled by Old Man Splitfoot, and a cartridge which misfires once may not do so a second time). If she did that, he would spring at once.

But she swung the cylinder back in, began to cock the hammer . . . and then paused again. Paused for the wind to mask the single low click.

He thought: *Here is another. God, she's evil, this one, and she's legless, but she's a gunslinger as surely as Eddie is one.*

He waited with her.

The wind gusted.

She pulled the hammer to full cock and placed it half an inch from Eddie's temple. With a grin that was a ghoul's grimace, she pulled the trigger.

Click.

He waited.

She pulled it again. And again. And again.

Click-Click-Click.

"*MahFAH!*" she screamed, and reversed the gun with liquid grace.

Roland coiled but did not leap. *A child doesn't understand a hammer until he's mashed his finger at a nail.*

If she kills him, she kills you.

Doesn't matter, the voice of Cort answered inexorably.

Eddie stirred. And his reflexes were not bad; he

moved fast enough to avoid being driven unconscious or killed. Instead of coming down on the vulnerable temple, the heavy gun-butt cracked the side of his jaw.

"What . . . Jesus!"

"*MAHFAH! HONKY MAHFAH!*" Detta screamed, and Roland saw her raise the gun a second time. And even though she was legless and Eddie was rolling away, it was as much as he dared. If Eddie hadn't learned the lesson now, he never would. The next time the gunslinger told Eddie to be on his guard, Eddie *would* be, and besides—the bitch was quick. It would not be wise to depend further than this on either Eddie's quickness or the Lady's infirmity.

He uncoiled, flying over Eddie and knocking her backward, ending up on top of her.

"*You want it, mahfah?*" she screamed at him, simultaneously rolling her crotch against his groin and raising the arm which still held the gun above his head. "*You want it? I goan give you what you want, sho!*"

"*Eddie!*" he shouted again, not just yelling now but *commanding.* For a moment Eddie just went on squatting there, eyes wide, blood dripping from his jaw (it had already begun to swell), staring, eyes wide. *Move, can't you move?* he thought, *or is it that you don't want to?* His strength was fading now, and the next time she brought that heavy gun-butt down she was going to break his arm with it . . . that was if he got his arm up in time. If he didn't, she was going to break his *head* with it.

Then Eddie moved. He caught the gun on the downswing and she shrieked, turning toward him, biting at him like a vampire, cursing him in a gutter *patois* so darkly southern that even Eddie couldn't understand it; to Roland it sounded as if the woman had suddenly begun to speak in a foreign language. But Eddie was able to yank the gun out of her hand and with the impending bludgeon gone, Roland was able to pin her.

She did not quit even then but continued to buck and heave and curse, sweat standing out all over her dark face.

Eddie stared, mouth opening and closing like the mouth of a fish. He touched tentatively at his jaw, winced, pulled his fingers back, examined them and the blood on them.

She was screaming that she would kill them both; they could try and rape her but she would kill them with her cunt, they would see, that was one bad son of a bitching cave with teeth around the entrance and if they wanted to try and explore it they would find out.

"What in the hell—" Eddie said stupidly.

"One of my gunbelts," the gunslinger panted harshly at him. "Get it. I'm going to roll her over on top of me and you're going to grab her arms and tie her hands behind her."

"You ain't NEVAH!" Detta shrieked, and sunfished her legless body with such sudden force that she almost bucked Roland off. He felt her trying to bring the remainder of her right thigh up again and again, wanting to drive it into his balls.

"I . . . I . . . she . . ."

"Move, God curse your father's face!" Roland roared, and at last Eddie moved.

4

They almost lost control of her twice during the tying and binding. But Eddie was at last able to slip-knot one of Roland's gunbelts around her wrists when Roland—using all his force—finally brought them together behind her (all the time drawing back from her lunging bites like a mongoose from a snake; the bites he avoided but before Eddie had finished, the gunslinger was drenched with spittle) and then Eddie dragged her off, holding the short leash of the make-shift slip-knot to do it. He did not want to hurt this thrashing screaming cursing thing. It was uglier than the lobstrosities by far because of the greater intelligence which informed it, but he knew it could also be beautiful. He did not want to harm the other person the vessel held somewhere inside it (like a live dove deep inside one of the secret compartments in a magician's magic box).

Odetta Holmes was somewhere inside that screaming screeching thing.

5

Although his last mount—a mule—had died too long ago to remember, the gunslinger still had a piece of its tether-rope (which, in turn, had once been a fine gunslinger's lariat). They used this to bind her in her wheelchair, as she had imagined (or falsely remembered, and in the end they both came to the same thing, didn't they?) they had done already. Then they drew away from her.

If not for the crawling lobster-things, Eddie would have gone down to the water and washed his hands.

"I feel like I'm going to vomit," he said in a voice that jig-jagged up and down the scale like the voice of an adolescent boy.

"Why don't you go on and eat each other's COCKS?" the struggling thing in the chair screeched. *"Why don't you jus go on and do dat if you fraid of a black woman's cunny? You just go on! Sho! Suck on yo each one's candles! Do it while you got a chance, cause Detta Walker goan get outen dis chair and cut dem skinny ole white candles off and feed em to those walkin buzzsaws down there!"*

"*She's* the woman I was in. Do you believe me now?"

"I believed you *before,*" Eddie said. "I *told* you that."

"You *believed* you believed. You believed on the top of your mind. Do you believe it all the way down now? All the way to the bottom?"

Eddie looked at the shrieking, convulsing thing in the chair and then looked away, white except for the slash on his jaw, which was still dripping a little. That side of his face was beginning to look a little like a balloon.

"Yes," he said. "God, yes."

"This woman is a monster."

Eddie began to cry.

The gunslinger wanted to comfort him, could not commit such a sacrilege (he remembered Jake too well), and walked off into the dark with his new fever burning and aching inside him.

6

Much earlier on that night, while Odetta still slept, Eddie said he thought he might understand what was wrong with her. *Might.* The gunslinger asked what he meant.

"She could be a schizophrenic."

Roland only shook his head. Eddie explained what he understood of schizophrenia, gleanings from such films as *The Three Faces of Eve* and various TV programs (mostly the soap operas he and Henry had often watched while stoned). Roland had nodded. Yes. The disease Eddie described sounded about right. A woman with two faces, one light and one dark. A face like the one the man in black had shown him on the fifth Tarot card.

"And they don't know—these schizophrenes—that they have another?"

"No," Eddie said. "But . . ." He trailed off,

moodily watching the lobstrosities crawl and question, question and crawl.

"But what?"

"I'm no shrink," Eddie said, "so I don't really know—"

"Shrink? What is a shrink?"

Eddie tapped his temple. "A head-doctor. A doctor for your mind. They're really called psychiatrists."

Roland nodded. He liked *shrink* better. Because this Lady's mind was too large. Twice as large as it needed to be.

"But I think schizos almost always know *something* is wrong with them," Eddie said. "Because there are blanks. Maybe I'm wrong, but I always got the idea that they were usually two people who thought they had partial amnesia, because of the blank spaces in their memories when the other personality was in control. *She* . . . she says she remembers everything. She *really thinks* she remembers everything."

"I thought you said she didn't believe any of this was happening."

"Yeah," Eddie said, "but forget that for now. I'm trying to say that, no matter what she *believes,* what she *remembers* goes right from her living room where she was sitting in her bathrobe watching the midnight news to here, with no break at all. She doesn't have any sense that some other person took over between then and when you grabbed her in Macy's. Hell, that might have been the next day or even *weeks* later. I know it was still winter, because most of the shoppers in that store were wearing coats—"

The gunslinger nodded. Eddie's perceptions were sharpening. That was good. He had missed the boots and scarves, the gloves sticking out of coat pockets, but it was still a start.

"—but otherwise it's impossible to tell how long Odetta was that other woman because she doesn't know. I think she's in a situation she's never been in before, and her way of protecting both sides is this story about getting cracked over the head.''

Roland nodded.

''And the rings. Seeing those really shook her up. She tried not to show it, but it showed, all right.''

Roland asked: ''If these two women don't know they exist in the same body, and if they don't even suspect that something may be wrong, if each has her own separate chain of memories, partly real but partly made up to fit the times the other is there, what are we to do with her? How are we even to live with her?''

Eddie had shrugged. ''Don't ask me. It's your problem. You're the one who says you need her. Hell, you risked your neck to bring her here.'' Eddie thought about this for a minute, remembered squatting over Roland's body with Roland's knife held just above the gunslinger's throat, and laughed abruptly and without humor. *LITERALLY risked your neck, man,* he thought.

A silence fell between them. Odetta had by then been breathing quietly. As the gunslinger was about to reiterate his warning for Eddie to be on guard and announce (loud enough for the Lady to hear, if she was only shamming) that he was going to turn in, Eddie said the thing which lighted Roland's mind in a single sudden glare, the thing which made him understand at least part of what he needed so badly to know.

At the end, when they came through.

She had changed at the end.

And he had *seen* something, some *thing*—

''Tell you what,'' Eddie said, moodily stirring the remains of the fire with a split claw from this night's kill, ''when you brought her through, I felt like *I* was a schizo.''

''Why?''

Eddie thought, then shrugged. It was too hard to

explain, or maybe he was just too tired. "It's not important."

"Why?"

Eddie looked at Roland, saw he was asking a serious question for a serious reason—or thought he was—and took a minute to think back. "It's really hard to describe, man. It was looking in that door. That's what freaked me out. When you see someone move in that door, it's like you're moving with them. You know what I'm talking about."

Roland nodded.

"Well, I watched it like it was a movie—never mind, it's not important—until the very end. Then you turned her toward *this* side of the doorway and for the first time *I was looking at myself.* It was like . . ." He groped and could find nothing. "I dunno. It should have been like looking in a mirror, I guess, but it wasn't, because . . . because it was like looking at another person. It was like being turned inside out. Like being in two places at the same time. Shit, *I* don't know."

But the gunslinger was thunderstruck. *That* was what he had sensed as they came through; *that* was what had happened to her, no, not just *her, them:* for a moment Detta and Odetta had looked at each other, not the way one would look at her reflection in a mirror but as *separate people;* the mirror became a windowpane and for a moment Odetta had seen Detta and Detta had seen Odetta and had been equally horror-struck.

They each know, the gunslinger thought grimly. *They may not have known before, but they do now. They can try to hide it from themselves, but for a moment they saw, they knew, and that knowing must still be there.*

"Roland?"

"What?"

"Just wanted to make sure you hadn't gone to sleep with your eyes open. Because for a minute you looked like you were, you know, long ago and far away."

"If so, I'm back now," the gunslinger said. "I'm going to turn in. Remember what I said, Eddie: be on your guard."

"I'll watch," Eddie said, but Roland knew that, sick or not, he would have to be the one to do the watching tonight.

Everything else had followed from that.

7

Following the ruckus Eddie and Detta Walker eventually went to sleep again (she did not so much fall asleep as drop into an exhausted state of unconsciousness in her chair, lolling to one side against the restraining ropes).

The gunslinger, however, lay wakeful.

I will have to bring the two of them to battle, he thought, but he didn't need one of Eddie's "shrinks" to tell him that such a battle might be to the death. *If the bright one, Odetta, were to win that battle, all might yet be well. If the dark one were to win it, all would surely be lost with her.*

Yet he sensed that what really needed doing was not killing but *joining.* He had already recognized much that would be of value to him—*them*—in Detta Walker's gutter toughness, and he wanted her—but he wanted her under control. There was a long way to go. Detta thought he and Eddie were monsters of some species she called *Honk Mafahs.* That was only dangerous delusion, but there would be real monsters along the way—the lobstrosities were not the first, nor would they be the last. The fight-until-you-drop woman he had entered and who had come out of hiding again tonight might come in very handy in a fight against such monsters, if she could be tempered by Odetta Holmes's calm humanity—especially now, with him short two fingers, almost out of bullets, and growing more fever.

But that is a step ahead. I think if I can make them acknowledge each other, that would bring them into confrontation. How may it be done?

He lay awake all that long night, thinking, and although he felt the fever in him grow, he found no answer to his question.

8

Eddie woke up shortly before daybreak, saw the gunslinger sitting near the ashes of last night's fire with his blanket wrapped around him Indian-fashion, and joined him.

"How do you feel?" Eddie asked in a low voice. The Lady still slept in her crisscrossing of ropes, although she occasionally jerked and muttered and moaned.

"All right."

Eddie gave him an appraising glance. "You don't look all right."

"Thank you, Eddie," the gunslinger said dryly.

"You're shivering."

"It will pass."

The Lady jerked and moaned again—this time a word that was almost understandable. It might have been *Oxford.*

"God, I hate to see her tied up like that," Eddie murmured. "Like a goddam calf in a barn."

"She'll wake soon. Mayhap we can unloose her when she does."

It was the closest either of them came to saying out loud that when the Lady in the chair opened her eyes, the calm, if slightly puzzled gaze of Odetta Holmes might greet them.

Fifteen minutes later, as the first sunrays struck over the hills, those eyes did open—but what the men saw was not the calm gaze of Odetta Holmes but the mad glare of Detta Walker.

"How many times you done rape me while I was buzzed out?" she asked. "My cunt feel all slick an tallowy, like somebody done been at it with a couple them little bitty white candles you graymeat mahfahs call cocks."

Roland sighed.

"Let's get going," he said, and gained his feet with a grimace.

"I ain't goan nowhere wit *choo,* mahfah," Detta spat.

"Oh yes you are," Eddie said. "Dreadfully sorry, my dear."

"Where you think I'm goan?"

"Well," Eddie said, "what was behind Door Number One wasn't so hot, and what was behind Door Number Two was even worse, so now, instead of quitting like sane people, we're going to go right on ahead and check out Door Number Three. The way things have been going, I think it's likely to be something like Godzilla or Ghidra the Three-Headed Monster, but I'm an optimist. I'm still hoping for the stainless steel cookware."

"I ain't goan."

"You're going, all right," Eddie said, and walked behind her chair. She began struggling again, but the gunslinger had made these knots, and her struggles only drew them tighter. Soon enough she saw this and ceased. She was full of poison but far from stupid. But she looked back over her shoulder at Eddie with a grin which made him recoil a little. It seemed to him the most evil expression he had ever seen on a human face.

"Well, maybe I be goan on a little way," she said, "but maybe not s'far's you think, white boy. And sure-God not s'fast's you think."

"What do you mean?"

That leering, over-the-shoulder grin again.

"You find out, white boy." Her eyes, mad but cogent, shifted briefly to the gunslinger. "You bofe be findin *dat* out."

Eddie wrapped his hands around the bicycle grips at the ends of the push-handles on the back of her wheelchair and they began north again, now leaving not only footprints but the twin tracks of the Lady's chair as they moved up the seemingly endless beach.

9

The day was a nightmare.

It was hard to calculate distance travelled when you were moving along a landscape which varied so little, but Eddie knew their progress had slowed to a crawl.

And he knew who was responsible.

Oh yeah.

You bofe *be findin dat out,* Detta had said, and they hadn't been on the move more than half an hour before the finding out began.

Pushing.

That was the first thing. Pushing the wheelchair up a beach of fine sand would have been as impossible as driving a car through deep unplowed snow. This beach, with its gritty, marly surface, made moving the chair possible but far from easy. It would roll along smoothly enough for awhile, crunching over shells and popping little pebbles to either side of its hard rubber tires . . . and then it would hit a dip where finer sand had drifted, and Eddie would have to shove, grunting, to get it and its solid unhelpful passenger through it. The sand sucked greedily at the wheels. You had to simultaneously push and throw your weight against the handles of the chair in a downward direction, or it and its bound occupant would tumble over face-first onto the beach.

Detta would cackle as he tried to move her without upending her. "You havin a good time back dere, honeychile?" she asked each time the chair ran into one of these drybogs.

When the gunslinger moved over to help, Eddie motioned him away. "You'll get your chance," he said. "We'll switch off." *But I think my turns are going to be a hell of a lot longer than his,* a voice in his head spoke up. *The way he looks, he's going to have his hands full just keeping himself moving before much longer, let alone moving the woman in this chair. No sir, Eddie, I'm afraid this Bud's for you. It's God's revenge, you know it? All those years you spent as a junkie, and guess what? You're finally the pusher!*

He uttered a short out-of-breath laugh.

"What's so funny, white boy?" Detta asked, and although Eddie thought she meant to sound sarcastic, it came out sounding just a tiny bit angry.

Ain't supposed to be any laughs in this for me, he thought. *None at all. Not as far as she's concerned.*

"You wouldn't understand, babe. Just let it lie."

"I be lettin *you* lie before this be all over," she said. "Be lettin you and yo bad-ass buddy there lie in pieces all ovah dis beach. Sho. Meantime you better save yo breaf to do yo pushin with. You already sound like you gettin a little sho't winded."

"Well, you talk for both of us, then," Eddie panted. "You *never* seem to run out of wind."

"I goan *break* wind, graymeat! Goan break it ovah yo dead face!"

"Promises, promises." Eddie shoved the chair out

of the sand and onto relatively easier going—for awhile, at least. The sun was not yet fully up, but he had already worked up a sweat.

This is going to be an amusing and informative day, he thought. *I can see that already.*

Stopping.

That was the next thing.

They had struck a firm stretch of beach. Eddie pushed the chair along faster, thinking vaguely that if he could keep this bit of extra speed, he might be able to drive right through the next sandtrap he happened to strike on pure impetus.

All at once the chair stopped. Stopped dead. The crossbar on the back hit Eddie's chest with a thump. He grunted. Roland looked around, but not even the gunslinger's cat-quick reflexes could stop the Lady's chair from going over exactly as it had threatened to do in each of the sandtraps. It went and Detta went with it, tied and helpless but cackling wildly. She still was when Roland and Eddie finally managed to right the chair again. Some of the ropes had drawn so tight they must be cutting cruelly into her flesh, cutting off the circulation to her extremities; her forehead was slashed and blood trickled into her eyebrows. She went on cackling just the same.

The men were both gasping, out of breath, by the time the chair was on its wheels again. The combined weight of it and the woman in it must have totaled two hundred and fifty pounds, most of it chair. It occurred to Eddie that if the gunslinger had snatched Detta from his own *when,* 1987, the chair might have weighed as much as sixty pounds less.

Detta giggled, snorted, blinked blood out of her eyes.

"Looky here, you boys done opsot me," she said.

"Call your lawyer," Eddie muttered. "Sue us."

"An got yoselfs all tuckered out gittin me back on top agin. Must have taken you ten minutes, too."

The gunslinger took a piece of his shirt—enough of it was gone now so the rest didn't much matter—and reached forward with his left hand to mop the blood away from the cut on her forehead. She snapped at him, and from the savage click those teeth made when they came together, Eddie thought that, if Roland had been only one instant slower in drawing back, Detta Walker would have evened up the number of fingers on his hands for him again.

She cackled and stared at him with meanly merry eyes, but the gunslinger saw fear hidden far back in those eyes. She was afraid of him. Afraid because he was The Really Bad Man.

Why was he The Really Bad Man? Maybe because, on some deeper level, she sensed what he knew about her.

"Almos' got you, graymeat," she said. "Almos' got you that time." And cackled, witchlike.

"Hold her head," the gunslinger said evenly. "She bites like a weasel."

Eddie held it while the gunslinger carefully wiped the wound clean. It wasn't wide and didn't look deep, but the gunslinger took no chances; he walked slowly down to the water, soaked the piece of shirting in the salt water, and then came back.

She began to scream as he approached.

"Doan you be touchin me wid dat thing! Doan you be touchin me wid no water from where them poison things come from! Git it away! Git it *away!*"

"Hold her head," Roland said in the same even voice. She was whipping it from side to side. "I don't want to take any chances."

Eddie held it . . . and squeezed it when she tried to shake free. She saw he meant business and immediately became still, showing no more fear of the damp rag. It had been only sham, after all.

She smiled at Roland as he bathed the cut, carefully washing out the last clinging particles of grit.

"In fact, *you* look *mo* than jest tuckered out," Detta observed. "You look *sick,* graymeat. I don't think you ready fo no long trip. I don't think you ready fo *nuthin* like dat."

Eddie examined the chair's rudimentary controls. It had an emergency hand-brake which locked both wheels. Detta had worked her right hand over there, had waited patiently until she thought Eddie was going fast enough, and then she had yanked the brake, purposely spilling herself over. Why? To slow them down, that was all. There was no reason to do such a thing, but a woman like Detta, Eddie thought, needed no reasons. A woman like Detta was perfectly willing to do such things out of sheer meanness.

Roland loosened her bonds a bit so the blood could flow more freely, then tied her hand firmly away from the brake.

"That be all right, Mister Man," Detta said, offering him a bright smile filled with too many teeth. "That be all right jest the same. There be other ways to slow you boys down. All *sorts* of ways."

"Let's go," the gunslinger said tonelessly.

"You all right, man?" Eddie asked. The gunslinger looked very pale.

"Yes. Let's go."

They started up the beach again.

10

The gunslinger insisted on pushing for an hour, and Eddie gave way to him reluctantly. Roland got her through the first sandtrap, but Eddie had to pitch in and help get the wheelchair out of the second. The gunslinger was gasping for air, sweat standing out on his forehead in large beads.

Eddie let him go on a little further, and Roland was quite adept at weaving his way around the places where the sand was loose enough to bog the wheels, but the chair finally became mired again and Eddie could bear only a few moments of watching Roland struggle to push it free, gasping, chest heaving, while the witch (for so Eddie had come to think of her) howled with laughter and actually threw her body backwards in the chair to make the task that much more difficult—and then he shouldered the gunslinger aside and heaved the chair out of the sand with one angry lurching lunge. The chair tottered and now he saw/sensed her shifting *forward* as much as the ropes would allow, doing this with a weird prescience at the exactly proper moment, trying to topple herself again.

Roland threw his weight on the back of the chair next to Eddie's and it settled back.

Detta looked around and gave them a wink of such obscene conspiracy that Eddie felt his arms crawl up in gooseflesh.

"You almost opsot me *agin,* boys," she said. "You want to look out for me, now. I ain't nuthin but a old crippled lady, so you want to have a care for me now."

She laughed . . . laughed fit to split.

Although Eddie cared for the woman that was the other part of her—was near to loving her just on the basis of the brief time he had seen her and spoken with her—he felt his hands itch to close around her windpipe and choke that laugh, choke it until she could never laugh again.

She peered around again, saw what he was thinking as if it had been printed on him in red ink, and laughed all the harder. Her eyes dared him. *Go on, graymeat. Go on. You want to do it? Go on and do it.*

In other words, don't just tip the chair; tip the

woman, Eddie thought. *Tip her over for good. That's what she wants. For Detta, being killed by a white man may be the only real goal she has in life.*

"Come on," he said, and began pushing again. "We are gonna tour the seacoast, sweet thang, like it or not."

"Fuck you," she spat.

"Cram it, babe," Eddie responded pleasantly.

The gunslinger walked beside him, head down.

11

They came to a considerable outcropping of rocks when the sun said it was about eleven and here they stopped for nearly an hour, taking the shade as the sun climbed toward the roofpeak of the day. Eddie and the gunslinger ate leftovers from the previous night's kill. Eddie offered a portion to Detta, who again refused, telling him she knew what they wanted to do, and if they wanted to do it, they best to do it with their bare hands and stop trying to poison her. That, she said, was the coward's way.

Eddie's right, the gunslinger mused. *This woman has made her own chain of memories. She knows everything that happened to her last night, even though she was really fast asleep.*

She believed they had brought her pieces of meat which smelled of death and putrescence, had taunted her with it while they themselves ate salted beef and drank some sort of beer from flasks. She believed they had, every now and then, held pieces of their own untainted supper out to her, drawing it away at the last moment when she snatched at it with her teeth—and laughing while they did it, of course. In the world (or at least in the mind) of Detta Walker, *Honk Mahfahs* only did two things to brown women: raped them or laughed at them. Or both at the same time.

It was almost funny. Eddie Dean had last seen beef during his ride in the sky-carriage, and Roland had seen none since the last of his jerky was eaten, Gods alone knew how long ago. As far as beer . . . he cast his mind back.

Tull.

There had been beer in Tull. Beer and beef.

God, it would be good to have a beer. His throat ached and it would be so good to have a beer to cool that ache. Better even than the *astin* from Eddie's world.

They drew off a distance from her.

"Ain't I good nough cump'ny for white boys like you?" she cawed after them. "Or did you jes maybe want to have a pull on each other one's little bitty white candle?"

She threw her head back and screamed laughter that frightened the gulls up, crying, from the rocks where they had been met in convention a quarter of a mile away.

The gunslinger sat with his hands dangling between his knees, thinking. Finally he raised his head and told Eddie, "I can only understand about one word in every ten she says."

"I'm way ahead of you," Eddie replied. "I'm getting at least two in every three. Doesn't matter. Most of it comes back to *honky mahfah.*"

Roland nodded. "Do many of the dark-skinned people talk that way where you come from? Her *other* didn't."

Eddie shook his head and laughed. "No. And I'll tell you something sort of funny—at least *I* think it's sort of funny, but maybe that's just because there isn't all that much to laugh at out here. It's not real. It's not real and she doesn't even know it."

Roland looked at him and said nothing.

"Remember when you washed off her forehead, how she pretended she was scared of the water?"

"Yes."

"You knew she was pretending?"

"Not at first, but quite soon."

Eddie nodded. "That was an act, and she *knew* it was an act. But she's a pretty good actress and she fooled both of us for a few seconds. The way she's talking is an act, too. But it's not as good. It's so stupid, so goddam *hokey!*"

"You believe she pretends well only when she knows she's doing it?"

"Yes. She sounds like a cross between the darkies in this book called *Mandingo* I read once and Butterfly McQueen in *Gone with the Wind*. I know you don't know those names, but what I mean is she talks like a cliche. Do you know that word?"

"It means what is always said or believed by people who think only a little or not at all."

"Yeah. I couldn't have said it half so good."

"Ain't you boys done jerkin on dem candles a yours yet?" Detta's voice was growing hoarse and cracked. "Or maybe it's just you can't fine em. Dat it?"

"Come on." The gunslinger got slowly to his feet. He swayed for a moment, saw Eddie looking at him, and smiled. "I'll be all right."

"For how long?"

"As long as I have to be," the gunslinger answered, and the serenity in his voice chilled Eddie's heart.

12

That night the gunslinger used his last sure live cartridge to make their kill. He would start systematically testing the ones he believed to be duds tomorrow night, but he believed it was pretty much as Eddie had said: They were down to beating the damned things to death.

It was like the other nights: the fire, the cooking, the shelling, the eating—eating which was now slow and unenthusiastic. *We're just gassing up*, Eddie thought. They offered food to Detta, who screamed and laughed and cursed and asked how long they was goan take her for a fool, and then she began throwing her body wildly from one side to the other, never minding how her bonds grew steadily tighter, only trying to upset the chair to one side or the other so they would have to pick her up again before they could eat.

Just before she could manage the trick, Eddie grabbed her and Roland braced the wheels on either sides with rocks.

"I'll loosen the ropes a bit if you'll be still," Roland told her.

"Suck shit out my ass, mahfah!"

"I don't understand if that means yes or no."

She looked at him, eyes narrowed, suspecting some buried barb of satire in that calm voice (Eddie also wondered, but couldn't tell if there was or not), and after a moment she said sulkily, "I be still. Too damn hungry to kick up much dickens. You boys goan give me some real food or you jes goan starve me to death? Dat yo plan? You too chickenshit to choke me and I ain't *nev'* goan eat no poison, so dat must be you plan. Starve me out. Well, we see, sho. We goan see. Sho we are."

She offered them her bone-chilling sickle of a grin again.

Not long after she fell asleep.

Eddie touched the side of Roland's face. Roland glanced at him but did not pull away from the touch.

"I'm all right."

"Yeah, you're Jim-dandy. Well, I tell you what, Jim, we didn't get along very far today."

"I know." There was also the matter of having used the last live shell, but that was knowledge Eddie could do without, at least tonight. Eddie wasn't sick, but he was exhausted. Too exhausted for more bad news.

No, he's not sick, not yet, but if he goes too long without rest, gets tired enough, he'll get sick.

In a way, Eddie already was; both of them were. Cold-sores had developed at the corners of Eddie's mouth, and there were scaly patches on his skin. The gunslinger could feel his teeth loosening up in their sockets, and the flesh between his toes had begun to crack open and bleed, as had that between his remaining fingers. They were eating, but they were eating the same thing, day in and day out. They could go on that way for a time, but in the end they would die as surely as if they had starved.

What we have is Shipmate's Disease on dry land, Roland thought. *Simple as that. How funny. We need fruit. We need greens.*

Eddie nodded toward the Lady. "She's going to go right on making it tough."

"Unless the other one inside her comes back."

"That would be nice, but we can't count on it," Eddie said. He took a piece of blackened claw and began to scrawl aimless patterns in the dirt. "Any idea how far the next door might be?"

Roland shook his head.

"I only ask because if the distance between Number Two and Number Three is the same as the distance between Number One and Number Two, we could be in deep shit."

"We're in deep shit right now."

"Neck deep," Eddie agreed moodily. "I just keep wondering how long I can tread water."

Roland clapped him on the shoulder, a gesture of affection so rare it made Eddie blink.

"There's one thing that Lady doesn't know," he said.

"Oh? What's that?"

"We *Honk Mahfahs* can tread water a long time."

Eddie laughed at that, laughed hard, smothering his laughter against his arm so he wouldn't wake Detta up. He'd had enough of her for one day, please and thank you.

The gunslinger looked at him, smiling. "I'm going to turn in," he said. "Be—"

"—on my guard. Yeah. I will."

13

Screaming was next.

Eddie fell asleep the moment his head touched the bunched bundle of his shirt, and it seemed only five minutes later when Detta began screaming.

He was awake at once, ready for anything, some King Lobster arisen from the deep to take revenge for its slain children or a horror down from the hills. It *seemed* he was awake at once, anyway, but the gunslinger was already on his feet, a gun in his left hand.

When she saw they were both awake, Detta promptly quit screaming.

"Jes thought I'd see if you boys on yo toes," she said. "Might be woofs. Looks likely enough country for 'em. Wanted to make sho if I saw me a woof creepin up, I could get you on yo feet in time." But there was no fear in her eyes; they glinted with mean amusement.

"Christ," Eddie said groggily. The moon was up but barely risen; they had been asleep less than two hours.

The gunslinger holstered his gun.

"Don't do it again," he said to the Lady in the wheelchair.

"What *you* goan do if *I* do? Rape me?"

"If we were going to rape you, you would be one

well-raped woman by now," the gunslinger said evenly. "Don't do it again."

He lay down again, pulling his blanket over him.

Christ, dear Christ, Eddie thought, *what a mess this is, what a fucking* . . . and that was as far as the thought went before trailing off into exhausted sleep again and then she was splintering the air with fresh shrieks, shrieking like a firebell, and Eddie was up again, his body flaming with adrenaline, hands clenched, and then she was laughing, her voice hoarse and raspy.

Eddie glanced up and saw the moon had advanced less than ten degrees since she had awakened them the first time.

She means to keep on doing it, he thought wearily. *She means to stay awake and watch us, and when she's sure we're getting down into deep sleep, that place where you recharge, she's going to open her mouth and start bellowing again. She'll do it and do it and do it until she doesn't have any voice left to bellow with.*

Her laughter stopped abruptly. Roland was advancing on her, a dark shape in the moonlight.

"You jes stay away from me, graymeat," Detta said, but there was a quiver of nerves in her voice. "You ain't goan do nothing to me."

Roland stood before her and for a moment Eddie was sure, completely sure, that the gunslinger had reached the end of his patience and would simply swat her like a fly. Instead, astoundingly, he dropped to one knee before her like a suitor about to propose marriage.

"Listen," he said, and Eddie could scarcely credit the silky quality of Roland's voice. He could see much the same deep surprise on Detta's face, only there fear was joined to it. "Listen to me, Odetta."

"Who you callin *O*-Detta? Dat ain my name."

"Shut up, bitch," the gunslinger said in a growl, and then, reverting to that same silken voice: "If you hear me, and if you can control her at all—"

"Why you talkin at me dat way? Why you talkin like you was talkin to somebody else? You quit dat honky jive! You jes quit it now, you hear me?"

"—keep her shut up. I can gag her, but I don't want to do that. A hard gag is a dangerous business. People choke."

"YOU QUIT IT YOU HONKY BULLSHIT VOODOO MAHFAH!"

"Odetta." His voice was a whisper, like the onset of rain.

She fell silent, staring at him with huge eyes. Eddie had never in his life seen such hate and fear combined in human eyes.

"I don't think this bitch would care if she *did* die on a hard gag. She wants to die, but maybe even more, she wants *you* to die. But you *haven't* died, not so far, and I don't think Detta is brand-new in your life. She feels too at home in you, so maybe you can hear what I'm saying, and maybe you can keep some control over her even if you can't come out yet.

"Don't let her wake us up a third time, Odetta."

"I don't want to gag her.

"But if I have to, I will."

He got up, left without looking back, rolled himself into his blanket again, and promptly fell asleep.

She was still staring at him, eyes wide, nostrils flaring.

"Honky voodoo bullshit," she whispered.

Eddie lay down, but this time it was a long time before sleep came to claim him, in spite of his deep tiredness. He would come to the brink, anticipate her screams, and snap back.

Three hours or so later, with the moon now going the other way, he finally dropped off.

Detta did no more screaming that night, either because Roland had frightened her, or because she wanted to conserve her voice for future alarums and excursions, or—possibly, just possibly—because Odetta had heard and had exercised the control the gunslinger had asked of her.

Eddie slept at last but awoke sodden and unrefreshed. He looked toward the chair, hoping against hope that it would be Odetta, please God let it be Odetta this morning—

"Mawnin, whitebread," Detta said, and grinned her sharklike grin at him. "Thought you was goan sleep till noon. You cain't be doin nuthin like *dat,* kin you? We got to bus us some miles here, ain't dat d'fac of d'matter? Sho! An I think *you* the one goan have to do most of de bustin, cause dat other fella, one with de voodoo eyes, he lookin mo peaky all de time, I declare he do! Yes! I doan think he goan be eatin *anything* much longer, not even dat fancy smoked meat you whitebread boys keep fo when you done joikin on each other one's little bitty white candles. So let's go, whitebread! Detta doan want to be d'one keepin you."

Her lids and her voice both dropped a little; her eyes peeked at him slyly from their corners.

"Not f'um startin out, leastways."

Dis goan be a day you 'member, whitebread, those sly eyes promised. *Dis goan be a day you 'member for a long, long time.*

Sho.

14

They made three miles that day, maybe a shade under. Detta's chair upset twice. Once she did it herself, working her fingers slowly and unobtrusively over to that handbrake again and yanking it. The second time Eddie did with no help at all, shoving too hard in one of those goddamned sandtraps. That was near the end of the day, and he simply panicked, thinking he just *wasn't* going to be able to get her out this time, just *wasn't*. So he gave that one last titanic heave with his quivering arms, and of course it had been much too hard, and over she had gone, like Humpty Dumpty falling off his wall, and he and Roland had to labor to get her upright again. They finished the job just in time. The rope under her breasts was now pulled taut across her windpipe. The gunslinger's efficient running slipknot was choking her to death. Her face had gone a funny blue color, she was on the verge of losing consciousness, but still she went on wheezing her nasty laughter.

Let her be, why don't you? Eddie nearly said as Roland bent quickly forward to loosen the knot. *Let her choke! I don't know if she wants to do herself like you said, but I know she wants to do US . . . so let her go!*

Then he remembered Odetta (although their encounter had been so brief and seemed so long ago that memory was growing dim) and moved forward to help.

The gunslinger pushed him impatiently away with one hand. "Only room for one."

When the rope was loosened and the Lady gasping harshly for breath (which she expelled in gusts of her angry laughter), he turned and looked at Eddie critically. "I think we ought to stop for the night."

"A little further." He was almost pleading. "I can go a little further."

"Sho! He be one strong buck He be good fo choppin one mo row cotton and he *still* have enough lef' to give yo little bitty white candle one *fine* suckin-on t'night."

She still wouldn't eat, and her face was becoming

all stark lines and angles. Her eyes glittered in deepening sockets.

Roland gave her no notice at all, only studied Eddie closely. At last he nodded. "A little way. Not far, but a little way."

Twenty minutes later Eddie called it quits himself. His arms felt like Jell-O.

They sat in the shadows of the rocks, listening to the gulls, watching the tide come in, waiting for the sun to go down and the lobstrosities to come out and begin their cumbersome cross-examinations.

Roland told Eddie in a voice too low for Detta to hear that he thought they were out of live shells. Eddie's mouth tightened down a little but that was all. Roland was pleased.

"So you'll have to brain one of them yourself," Roland said. "I'm too weak to handle a rock big enough to do the job . . . and still be sure."

Eddie was now the one to do the studying.

He had no liking for what he saw.

The gunslinger waved his scrutiny away.

"Never mind," he said. "Never mind, Eddie. What is, *is.*"

"*Ka,*" Eddie said.

The gunslinger nodded and smiled faintly. "*Ka.*"

"Kaka," Eddie said, and they looked at each other, and both laughed. Roland looked startled and perhaps even a little afraid of the rusty sound emerging from his mouth. His laughter did not last long. When it had stopped he looked distant and melancholy.

"Dat laffin mean you fine'ly managed to joik each other off?" Detta cried over at them in her hoarse, failing voice. "When you goan get down to de pokin? Dat's what I want to see! Dat pokin!"

15

Eddie made the kill.

Detta refused to eat, as before. Eddie ate half a piece so she could see, then offered her the other half.

"Nossuh!" she said, eyes sparking at him. "No *SUH!* You done put de poison in t'other end. One you trine to give me."

Without saying anything, Eddie took the rest of the piece, put it in his mouth, chewed, swallowed.

"Doan mean a thing," Detta said sulkily. "Leave me alone, graymeat."

Eddie wouldn't.

He brought her another piece.

"*You* tear it in half. Give me whichever you want. I'll eat it, then you eat the rest."

"Ain't fallin fo none o yo honky tricks, Mist' Chahlie. Git away f'um me is what I said, and git away f'um me is what I meant."

16

She did not scream in the night . . . but she was still there the next morning.

17

That day they made only two miles, although Detta made no effort to upset her chair; Eddie thought she might be growing too weak for acts of attempted sabotage. Or perhaps she had seen there was really no need for them. Three fatal factors were drawing inexorably together: Eddie's weariness, the terrain, which after endless days of endless days of sameness, was finally beginning to change, and Roland's deteriorating condition.

There were less sandtraps, but that was cold comfort. The ground was becoming grainier, more and more like cheap and unprofitable soil and less and less like sand (in places bunches of weeds grew, looking almost ashamed to be there), and there were so many large rocks now jutting from this odd combination of sand and soil that Eddie found himself detouring around them as he had previously tried to detour the Lady's chair around the sandtraps. And soon enough, he saw, there would be no beach left at all. The hills, brown and cheerless things, were drawing steadily closer. Eddie could see the ravines which curled between them, looking like chops made by an awkward giant wielding a blunt cleaver. That night, before falling asleep, he heard what sounded like a very large cat squalling far up in one of them.

The beach had seemed endless, but he was coming to realize it had an end after all. Somewhere up ahead, those hills were simply going to squeeze it out of existence. The eroded hills would march down to the sea and then into it, where they might become first a cape or peninsula of sorts, and then a series of archipelagoes.

That worried him, but Roland's condition worried him more.

This time the gunslinger seemed not so much to be burning as *fading*, losing himself, becoming transparent.

The red lines had appeared again, marching relentlessly up the underside of his right arm toward the elbow.

For the last two days Eddie had looked constantly ahead, squinting into the distance, hoping to see the door, the door, the magic door. For the last two days he had waited for Odetta to reappear.

Neither had appeared.

Before falling asleep that night two terrible thoughts came to him, like some joke with a double punchline:

What if there was no door?
What if Odetta Holmes was dead?

18

"Rise and shine, mahfah!" Detta screeched him out
of unconsciousness. "I think it jes be you and me
now, honeychile. Think yo frien done finally passed
on. I think yo frien be pokin the devil down in hell."

Eddie looked at the rolled huddled shape of Roland
and for one terrible moment he thought the bitch was
right. Then the gunslinger stirred, moaned furrily, and
pawed himself into a sitting position.

"Well looky yere!" Detta had screamed so much
that now there were moments when her voice disappeared almost entirely, becoming no more than a weird
whisper, like winter wind under a door. "I thought
you was dead, Mister Man!"

Roland was getting slowly to his feet. He still looked
to Eddie like a man using the rungs of an invisible
ladder to make it. Eddie felt an angry sort of pity, and
this was a familiar emotion, oddly nostalgic. After a
moment he understood. It was like when he and Henry
used to watch the fights on TV, and one fighter would
hurt the other, hurt him terribly, again and again, and
the crowd would be screaming for blood, and *Henry*
would be screaming for blood, but Eddie only sat
there, feeling that angry pity, that dumb disgust; he'd
sat there sending thought-waves at the referee: *Stop it,
man, are you fucking blind? He's dying out there! DY-
ING! Stop the fucking fight!*

There was no way to stop this one.

Roland looked at her from his haunted feverish eyes.
"A lot of people have thought that, Detta." He looked
at Eddie. "You ready?"

"Yeah, I guess so. Are *you?*"

"Yes."

"Can you?"

"Yes."

They went on.

Around ten o'clock Detta began rubbing her temples with her fingers.

"Stop," she said. "I feel sick. Feel like I goan throw up."

"Probably that big meal you ate last night," Eddie said, and went on pushing. "You should have skipped dessert. I told you that chocolate layer cake was heavy."

"I goan throw up! I—"

"Stop, Eddie!" the gunslinger said.

Eddie stopped.

The woman in the chair suddenly twisted galvanically, as if an electric shock had run through her. Her eyes popped wide open, glaring at nothing.

"I BROKE YO PLATE YOU STINKIN OLE BLUE LADY!" she screamed. *"I BROKE IT AND I'M FUCKIN GLAD I D—"*

She suddenly slumped forward in her chair. If not for the ropes, she would have fallen out of it.

Christ, she's dead, she's had a stroke and she's dead, Eddie thought. He started around the chair, remembered how sly and tricksy she could be, and stopped as suddenly as he had started. He looked at Roland. Roland looked back at him evenly, his eyes giving away not a thing.

Then she moaned. Her eyes opened.

Her eyes.

Odetta's eyes.

"Dear God, I've fainted again, haven't I?" she said. "I'm sorry you had to tie me in. My stupid legs! I think I could sit up a little if you—"

That was when Roland's own legs slowly came unhinged and he swooned some thirty miles south of the place where the Western Sea's beach came to an end.

RE SHUFFLE

re-shuffle

1

To Eddie Dean, he and the Lady no longer seemed to be trudging or even walking up what remained of the beach. They seemed to be *flying*.

Odetta Holmes still neither liked nor trusted Roland; that was clear. But she recognized how desperate his condition had become, and responded to that. Now, instead of pushing a dead clump of steel and rubber to which a human body just happened to be attached, Eddie felt almost as if he were pushing a glider.

Go with her. Before, I was watching out for you and that was important. Now I'll only slow you down.

He came to realize how right the gunslinger was almost at once. Eddie pushed the chair; Odetta pumped it.

One of the gunslinger's revolvers was stuck in the waistband of Eddie's pants.

Do you remember when I told you to be on your guard and you weren't?

Yes.

I'm telling you again: Be on your guard. *Every moment. If her* other *comes back, don't wait even a second. Brain her.*

What if I kill her?

Then it's the end. But if she *kills* you, *that's the end, too. And if she comes back she'll try. She'll try.*

Eddie hadn't wanted to leave him. It wasn't just that cat-scream in the night (although he kept thinking

321

about it); it was simply that Roland had become his only touchstone in this world. He and Odetta didn't belong here.

Still, he realized that the gunslinger had been right.

"Do you want to rest?" he asked Odetta. "There's more food. A little."

"Not yet," she answered, although her voice sounded tired. "Soon."

"All right, but at least stop pumping. You're weak. Your . . . your stomach, you know."

"All right." She turned, her face gleaming with sweat, and favored him with a smile that both weakened and strengthened him. He could have died for such a smile . . . and thought he would, if circumstances demanded.

He hoped to Christ circumstances wouldn't, but it surely wasn't out of the question. Time had become something so crucial it screamed.

She put her hands in her lap and he went on pushing. The tracks the chair left behind were now dimmer; the beach had become steadily firmer, but it was also littered with rubble that could cause an accident. You wouldn't have to help one happen at the speed they were going. A really bad accident might hurt Odetta and that would be bad; such an accident could also wreck the chair, and that would be bad for them and probably worse for the gunslinger, who would almost surely die alone. And if Roland died, they would be trapped in this world forever.

With Roland too sick and weak to walk, Eddie had been forced to face one simple fact: there were three people here, and two of them were cripples.

So what hope, what chance was there?

The chair.

The chair was the hope, the whole hope, and nothing *but* the hope.

So help them God.

2

The gunslinger had regained consciousness shortly after Eddie dragged him into the shade of a rock outcropping. His face, where it was not ashy, was a hectic red. His chest rose and fell rapidly. His right arm was a network of twisting red lines.

"Feed her," he croaked at Eddie.

"You—"

"Never mind *me*. I'll be all right. Feed her. She'll eat now, I think. And you'll need her strength."

"Roland, what if she's just *pretending* to be—"

The gunslinger gestured impatiently.

"She's not pretending to be anything, except alone in her body. I know it and you do, too. It's in her face. Feed her, for the sake of your father, and while she eats, come back to me. Every minute counts now. Every *second*."

Eddie got up, and the gunslinger pulled him back with his left hand. Sick or not, his strength was still there.

"And say nothing about the *other*. Whatever she tells you, however she explains, *don't contradict her.*"

"Why?"

"I don't know. I just know it's wrong. Now do as I say and don't waste any more time!"

Odetta had been sitting in her chair, looking out at the sea with an expression of mild and bemused amazement. When Eddie offered her the chunks of lobster left over from the previous night, she smiled ruefully. "I would if I could," she said, "but you know what happens."

Eddie, who had no idea what she was talking about, could only shrug and say, "It wouldn't hurt to try again, Odetta. You need to eat, you know. We've got to go as fast as we can."

She laughed a little and touched his hand. He felt

something like an electric charge jump from her to him. And it was her; Odetta. He knew it as well as Roland did.

"I love you, Eddie. You have tried so hard. Been so patient. So has *he*—" She nodded toward the place where the gunslinger lay propped against the rocks, watching. "—but he is a hard man to love."

"Yeah. Don't I know it."

"I'll try one more time.

"For you."

She smiled and he felt all the world move for her, because of her, and he thought *Please God, I have never had much, so please don't take her away from me again. Please.*

She took the chunks of lobster-meat, wrinkled her nose in a rueful comic expression, and looked up at him.

"Must I?"

"Just give it a shot," he said.

"I never ate scallops again," she said.

"Pardon?"

"I thought I told you."

"You might have," he said, and gave a little nervous laugh. What the gunslinger had said about not letting her know about the *other* loomed very large inside his mind just then.

"We had them for dinner one night when I was ten or eleven. I hated the way they tasted, like little rubber balls, and later I vomited them up. I never ate them again. But . . ." She sighed. "As you say, I'll 'give it a shot.' "

She put a piece in her mouth like a child taking a spoonful of medicine she knows will taste nasty. She chewed slowly at first, then more rapidly. She swallowed. Took another piece. Chewed, swallowed. Another. Now she was nearly *wolfing* it.

"Whoa, slow down!" Eddie said.

"It must be another *kind!* That's it, of *course* it is!" She looked at Eddie shiningly. "We've moved further up the beach and the species has changed! I'm no longer allergic, it seems! It doesn't taste *nasty,* like it did before . . . and I *did* try to keep it down, didn't I?" She looked at him nakedly. "I tried *very* hard."

"Yeah." To himself he sounded like a radio broadcasting a very distant signal. *She thinks she's been eating every day and then upchucking everything. She thinks that's why she's so weak. Christ Almighty.* "Yeah, you tried like hell."

"It tastes—" These words were hard to pick up because her mouth was full. "It tastes so *good!*" She laughed. The sound was delicate and lovely. "It's going to stay down! I'm going to take nourishment! I know it! I *feel* it!"

"Just don't overdo it," he cautioned, and gave her one of the water-skins. "You're not used to it. All that—" He swallowed and there was an audible (audible to him, at least) click in his throat. "All that throwing up."

"Yes. Yes."

"I need to talk to Roland for a few minutes."

"All right."

But before he could go she grasped his hand again.

"Thank you, Eddie. Thank you for being so patient. And thank *him.*" She paused gravely. "Thank him, and don't tell him that he scares me."

"I won't," Eddie had said, and went back to the gunslinger.

3

Even when she wasn't pushing, Odetta was a help. She navigated with the prescience of a woman who has spent a long time weaving a wheelchair through a world that would not acknowledge handicapped people such as she for years to come.

"Left," she'd call, and Eddie would gee to the left, gliding past a rock snarling out of the pasty grit like a decayed fang. On his own, he might have seen it .. or maybe not.

"Right," she called, and Eddie hawed right, barely missing one of the increasingly rare sandtraps.

They finally stopped and Eddie lay down, breathing hard.

"Sleep," Odetta said. "An hour. I'll wake you."

Eddie looked at her.

"I'm not lying. I observed your friend's condition, Eddie—"

"He's not exactly my friend, you kn—"

"—and I know how important time is. I won't let you sleep longer than an hour out of a misguided sense of mercy. I can tell the sun quite well. You won't do that man any good by wearing yourself out, will you?"

"No," he said, thinking: *But you don't understand. If I sleep and Detta Walker comes back—*

"Sleep, Eddie," she said, and since Eddie was too weary (and too much in love) to do other than trust her, he did. He slept and she woke him when she said she would and she was still Odetta, and they went on, and now she was pumping again, helping. They raced up the diminishing beach toward the door Eddie kept frantically looking for and kept not seeing.

4

When he left Odetta eating her first meal in days and went back to the gunslinger, Roland seemed a little better.

"Hunker down," he said to Eddie.

Eddie hunkered.

"Leave me the skin that's half full. All I need. Take her to the door."

"What if I don't—"

"Find it? You'll find it. The first two were there; this one will be, too. If you get there before sundown tonight, wait for dark and then kill double. You'll need to leave her food and make sure she's sheltered as well as she can be. If you don't reach it tonight, kill triple. Here."

He handed over one of his guns.

Eddie took it with respect, surprised as before by how heavy it was.

"I thought the shells were all losers."

"Probably are. But I've loaded with the ones I believe were wetted least—three from the buckle side of the left belt, three from the buckle side of the right. One may fire. Two, if you're lucky. Don't try them on the crawlies." His eyes considered Eddie briefly. "There may be other things out there."

"You heard it too, didn't you?"

"If you mean something yowling in the hills, yes. If you mean the Bugger-Man, as your eyes say, no. I heard a wildcat in the brakes, that's all, maybe with a voice four times the size of its body. It may be nothing you can't drive off with a stick. But there's her to think about. If her *other* comes back, you may have to—"

"I won't kill her, if that's what you're thinking!"

"You may have to wing her. You understand?"

Eddie gave a reluctant nod. Goddam shells probably wouldn't fire anyway, so there was no sense getting his panties in a bunch about it.

"When you get to the door, leave her. Shelter her as well as you can, and come back to me with the chair."

"And the gun?"

The gunslinger's eyes blazed so brightly that Eddie snapped his head back, as if Roland had thrust a flaming torch in his face. "Gods, yes! Leave her with a loaded gun, when her *other* might come back at any time? Are you insane?"

"The shells—"

"*Fuck* the shells!" the gunslinger cried, and a freak drop in the wind allowed the words to carry. Odetta turned her head, looked at them for a long moment, then looked back toward the sea. "Leave it with her not!"

Eddie kept his voice low in case the wind should drop again. "What if something comes down from the brakes while I'm on my way back here? Some kind of cat four times bigger than its voice, instead of the other way around? Something you can't drive off with a stick?"

"Give her a pile of stones," the gunslinger said.

"*Stones!* Jesus wept! Man, you are such a fucking shit!"

"I am *thinking*," the gunslinger said. "Something you seem unable to do. I gave you the gun so you could protect her from the sort of danger you're talking about for half of the trip you must make. Would it please you if I took the gun back? Then perhaps you could *die* for her. Would *that* please you? Very romantic . . . except then, instead of just her, all three of us would go down."

"Very logical. You're still a fucking shit, however."

"Go or stay. Stop calling me names."

"You forgot something," Eddie said furiously.

"What was that?"

"You forgot to tell me to grow up. That's what Henry always used to say. 'Oh grow up, kid.' "

The gunslinger had smiled, a weary, oddly beautiful smile. "I think you *have* grown up. Will you go or stay?"

"I'll go," Eddie said. "What are you going to eat? She scarfed the left-overs."

"The fucking shit will find a way. The fucking shit has been finding one for years."

Eddie looked away. "I . . . I guess I'm sorry I called you that, Roland. It's been—" He laughed suddenly, shrilly. "It's been a very trying day."

Roland smiled again. "Yes," he said. "It has."

5

They made the best time of the entire trek that day, but there was still no door in sight when the sun began to spill its gold track across the ocean. Although she told him she was perfectly capable of going on for another half an hour, he called a halt and helped her out of the chair. He carried her to an even patch of ground that looked fairly smooth, got the cushions from the back of the chair and the seat, and eased them under her.

"Lord, it feels so good to stretch out," she sighed. "But . . . " Her brow clouded. "I keep thinking of that man back there, Roland, all by himself, and I can't really enjoy it. Eddie, who is he? *What* is he?" And, almost as an afterthought: "And why does he *shout* so much?"

"Just his nature, I guess," Eddie said, and abruptly went off to gather rocks. Roland hardly ever shouted. He guessed some of it was this morning—*FUCK the shells!*—but that the rest of it was false memory: the time she *thought* she had been Odetta.

He killed triple, as the gunslinger had instructed, and was so intent on the last that he skipped back from a fourth which had been closing in on his right with only an instant to spare. He saw the way its claws clicked on the empty place which had been occupied by his foot and leg a moment before, and thought of the gunslinger's missing fingers.

He cooked over a dry wood fire—the encroaching

hills and increasing vegetation made the search for good fuel quicker and easier, that was one thing—while the last of the daylight faded from the western sky.

"Look, Eddie!" she cried, pointing up.

He looked, and saw a single star gleaming on the breast of the night.

"Isn't it *beautiful?*"

"Yes," he said, and suddenly, for no reason, his eyes filled with tears. Just where had he been all of his goddamned life? Where had he been, what had he been doing, who had been with him while he did it, and why did he suddenly feel so grimy and abysmally beshitted?

Her lifted face was terrible in its beauty, irrefutable in this light, but the beauty was unknown to its possessor, who only looked at the star with wide wondering eyes, and laughed softly.

"Star light, star bright," she said, and stopped. She looked at him. "Do you know it, Eddie?"

"Yeah." Eddie kept his head down. His voice sounded clear enough, but if he looked up she would see he was weeping.

"Then help me. But you have to look."

"Okay."

He wiped the tears into the palm of one hand and looked up at the star with her.

"Star light—" she looked at him and he joined her. "Star *bright*—"

Her hand reached out, groping, and he clasped it, one the delicious brown of light chocolate, the other the delicious white of a dove's breast.

"First star I see tonight," they spoke solemnly in unison, boy and girl for this now, not man and woman as they would be later, when the dark was full and she called to ask him if he was asleep and he said no and she asked if he would hold her because she was cold; "Wish I may, wish I might—"

They looked at each other, and he saw that tears were streaming down her cheeks. His own came again, and he let them fall in her sight. This was not a shame but an inexpressible relief.

They smiled at each other.

"Have the wish I wish tonight," Eddie said, and thought: *Please, always you.*

"Have the wish I wish tonight," she echoed, and thought *If I must die in this odd place, please let it not be too hard and let this good young man be with me.*

"I'm sorry I cried," she said, wiping her eyes. "I don't usually, but it's been—"

"A very trying day," he finished for her.

"Yes. And you need to eat, Eddie."

"You do, too."

"I just hope it doesn't make me sick again."

He smiled at her.

"I don't think it will."

6

Later, with strange galaxies turning in slow gavotte overhead, neither thought the act of love had ever been so sweet, so full.

7

They were off with the dawn, racing, and by nine Eddie was wishing he had asked Roland what he should do if they came to the place where the hills cut off the beach and there was still no door in sight. It seemed a question of some importance, because the end of the beach *was* coming, no doubt about that. The hills marched ever closer, running in a diagonal line toward the water.

The beach itself was no longer a beach at all, not really; the soil was now firm and quite smooth. Something—run-off, he supposed, or flooding at some rainy season (there had been none since he had been in this world, not a drop; the sky had clouded over a few times, but then the clouds had blown away again)—had worn most of the jutting rocks away.

At nine-thirty, Odetta cried: "Stop, Eddie! Stop!"

He stopped so abruptly that she had to grab the arms of the chair to keep from tumbling out. He was around to her in a flash.

"I'm sorry," he said. "Are you all right?"

"Fine." He saw he had mistaken excitement for distress. She pointed. "Up there! Do you see something?"

He shaded his eyes and saw nothing. He squinted. For just a moment he thought . . . no, it was surely just heat-shimmer rising from the packed ground.

"I don't think so," he said, and smiled. "Except maybe your wish."

"I think I do!" She turned her excited, smiling face to him. "Standing all by itself! Near where the beach ends."

He looked again, squinting so hard this time that his eyes watered. He thought again for just a moment that he saw something. *You did,* he thought, and smiled. *You saw her wish.*

"Maybe," he said, not because he believed it but because she did.

"Let's go!"

Eddie went behind the chair again, taking a moment to massage his lower back where a steady ache had settled. She looked around.

"What are you *waiting* for?"

"You really think you've got it spotted, don't you?"

"Yes!"

"Well then, let's go!"

Eddie started pushing again.

8

Half an hour later he saw it, too. *Jesus,* he thought, *her eyes are as good as Roland's. Maybe better.*

Neither wanted to stop for lunch, but they needed to eat. They made a quick meal and then pushed on again. The tide was coming in and Eddie looked to the right—west—with rising unease. They were still well above the tangled line of kelp and seaweed that marked high water, but he thought that by the time they reached the door they would be in an uncomfortably tight angle bounded by the sea on one side and the slanting hills on the other. He could see those hills very clearly now. There was nothing pleasant about the view. They were rocky, studded with low trees that curled their roots into the ground like arthritic knuckles, keeping a grim grip, and thorny-looking bushes. They weren't really steep, but too steep for the wheelchair. He might be able to carry her up a way, might, in fact, be forced to, but he didn't fancy leaving her there.

For the first time he was hearing insects. The sound was a little like crickets, but higher pitched than that, and with no swing of rhythm—just a steady monotonous *riiiiiiii* sound like power-lines. For the first time he was seeing birds other than gulls. Some were biggies that circled inland on stiff wings. Hawks, he thought. He saw them fold their wings from time to time and plummet like stones. Hunting. Hunting what? Well, small animals. That was all right.

Yet he kept thinking of that yowl he'd heard in the night.

By mid-afternoon they could see the third door clearly. Like the other two, it was an impossibility which nonetheless stood as stark as a post.

"Amazing," he heard her say softly. "How utterly amazing."

It was exactly where he had begun to surmise it would be, in the angle that marked the end of any easy northward progress. It stood just above the high tide line and less than nine yards from the place where the hills suddenly leaped out of the ground like a giant hand coated with gray-green brush instead of hair.

The tide came full as the sun swooned toward the water; and at what might have been four o'clock— Odetta said so, and since she had said she was good at telling the sun (and because she was his beloved), Eddie believed her—they reached the door.

9

They simply looked at it, Odetta in her chair with her hands in her lap, Eddie on the sea-side. In one way they looked at it as they had looked at the evening star the previous night—which is to say, as children look at things—but in another they looked differently. When they wished on the star they had been children of joy. Now they were solemn, wondering, like children looking at the stark embodiment of a thing which only belonged in a fairy tale.

Two words were written on this door.

"What does it mean?" Odetta asked finally.

"I don't know," Eddie said, but those words had brought a hopeless chill; he felt an eclipse stealing across his heart.

"Don't you?" she asked, looking at him more closely.

"No. I . . ." He swallowed. "No."

She looked at him a moment longer. "Push me behind it, please. I'd like to see that. I know you want to get back to him, but would you do that for me?"

He would.

They started around, on the high side of the door.

"Wait!" she cried. "Did you see it?"

"What?"

"Go back! Look! Watch!"

This time he watched the door instead of what might be ahead to trip them up. As they went above it he saw it narrow in perspective, saw its hinges, hinges which seemed to be buried in nothing at all, saw its thickness . . .

Then it was gone.

The thickness of the door was gone.

His view of the water should have been interrupted by three, perhaps even four inches of solid wood (the door looked extraordinarily stout), but there was no such interruption.

The door was gone.

Its shadow was there, but the door was gone.

He rolled the chair back two feet, so he was just south of the place where the door stood, and the thickness was there.

"You see it?" he asked in a ragged voice..

"Yes! It's there again!"

He rolled the chair forward a foot. The door was still there. Another six inches. Still there. Another *two* inches. Still there. Another inch . . . and it was gone. Solid gone.

"Jesus," he whispered. "Jesus Christ."

"Would it open for you?" she asked. "Or me?"

He stepped forward slowly and grasped the knob of the door with those two words upon it.

He tried clockwise; he tried anti-clockwise.

The knob moved not an iota.

"All right." Her voice was calm, resigned. "It's for him, then. I think we both knew it. Go for him, Eddie. Now."

"First I've got to see to you."

"I'll be fine."

"No you won't. You're too close to the high-tide

line. If I leave you here, the lobsters are going to come out when it gets dark and you're going to be din—''

Up in the hills, a cat's coughing growl suddenly cut across what he was saying like a knife cutting thin cord. It was a good distance away, but closer than the other had been.

Her eyes flicked to the gunslinger's revolver shoved into the waistband of his pants for just a moment, then back to his face. He felt a dull heat in his cheeks.

"He told you not to give it to me, didn't he?" she said softly. "He doesn't want me to have it. For some reason he doesn't want me to have it."

"The shells got wet," he said awkwardly. "They probably wouldn't fire, anyway."

"I understand. Take me a little way up the slope, Eddie, can you? I know how tired your back must be, Andrew calls it Wheelchair Crouch, but if you take me up a little way, I'll be safe from the lobsters. I doubt if anything else comes very close to where they are."

Eddie thought, *When the tide's in, she's probably right . . . but what about when it starts to go out again?*

"Give me something to eat and some stones," she said, and her unknowing echo of the gunslinger made Eddie flush again. His cheeks and forehead felt like the sides of a brick oven.

She looked at him, smiled faintly, and shook her head as if he had spoken out loud. "We're not going to argue about this. I saw how it is with him. His time is very, very short. There is no time for discussion. Take me up a little way, give me food and some stones, then take the chair and go."

10

He got her fixed as quickly as he could, then pulled the gunslinger's revolver and held it out to her butt-first. But she shook her head.

"He'll be angry with both of us. Angry with you for giving, angrier at me for taking."

"Crap!" Eddie yelled. "What gave you that idea?"

"I know," she said, and her voice was impervious.

"Well, suppose that's true. Just suppose. *I'll* be angry with you if you *don't* take it."

"Put it back. I don't like guns. I don't know how to use them. If something came at me in the dark the first thing I'd do is wet my pants. The second thing I'd do is point it the wrong way and shoot myself." She paused, looking at Eddie solemnly. "There's something else, and you might as well know it. I don't want to touch anything that belongs to him. Not *anything*. For me, I think his things might have what my Ma used to call a hoodoo. I like to think of myself as a modern woman . . . but I don't want any hoodoo on me when you're gone and the dark lands on top of me."

He looked from the gun to Odetta, and his eyes still questioned.

"Put it *back*," she said, stern as a schoolteacher. Eddie burst out laughing and obeyed.

"Why are you laughing?"

"Because when you said that you sounded like Miss Hathaway. She was my third-grade teacher."

She smiled a little, her luminous eyes never leaving his. She sang softly, sweetly: *"Heavenly shades of night are falling . . . it's twilight time . . ."* She trailed off and they both looked west, but the star they had wished on the previous evening had not yet appeared, although their shadows had drawn long.

"Is there anything else, Odetta?" He felt an urge to

delay and delay. He thought it would pass once he was actually headed back, but now the urge to seize any excuse to remain, seemed very strong.

"A kiss. I could do with that, if you don't mind."

He kissed her long and when their lips no longer touched, she caught his wrist and stared at him intently. "I never made love with a white man before last night," she said. "I don't know if that's important to you or not. I don't even know if it's important to *me*. But I thought you should know."

He considered.

"Not to me," he said. "In the dark, I think we were both gray. I love you, Odetta."

She put a hand over his.

"You're a sweet young man and perhaps I love you, too, although it's too early for either of us—"

At that moment, as if given a cue, a wildcat growled in what the gunslinger had called the brakes. It still sounded four or five miles away, but that was still four or five miles closer than the last time they heard it, and it sounded *big*.

They turned their heads toward the sound. Eddie felt hackles trying to stand up on his neck. They couldn't quite make it. *Sorry, hackles,* he thought stupidly. *I guess my hair's just a little too long now.*

The growl rose to a tortured scream that sounded like a cry of some being suffering a horrid death (it might actually have signalled no more than a successful mating). It held for a moment, almost unbearable, and then it wound down, sliding through lower and lower registers until it was gone or buried beneath the ceaseless cry of the wind. They waited for it to come again, but the cry was not repeated. As far as Eddie was concerned, that didn't matter. He pulled the revolver out of his waistband again and held it out to her.

"Take it and don't argue. If you *should* need to use

it, it won't do shit—that's how stuff like this always works—but take it anyway.''

"Do you want an argument?"

"Oh, you can argue. You can argue all you want."

After a considering look into Eddie's almost-hazel eyes, she smiled a little wearily. "I won't argue, I guess." She took the gun. "Please be as quick as you can."

"I will." He kissed her again, hurriedly this time, and almost told her to be careful . . . but seriously, folks, how careful could she be, with the situation what it was?

He picked his way back down the slope through the deepening shadows (the lobstrosities weren't out yet, but they would be putting in their nightly appearance soon), and looked at the words written upon the door again. The same chill rose in his flesh. They were apt, those words. God, they were so apt. Then he looked back up the slope. For a moment he couldn't see her, and then he saw something move. The lighter brown of one palm. She was waving.

He waved back, then turned the wheelchair and began to run with it tipped up in front of him so the smaller, more delicate front wheels would be off the ground. He ran south, back the way he had come. For the first half-hour or so his shadow ran with him, the improbable shadow of a scrawny giant tacked to the soles of his sneakers and stretching long yards to the east. Then the sun went down, his shadow was gone, and the lobstrosities began to tumble out of the waves.

It was ten minutes or so after he heard the first of their buzzing cries when he looked up and saw the evening star glowing calmly against the dark blue velvet of the sky.

Heavenly shades of night are falling . . . it's twilight time . . .

Let her be safe. His legs were already aching, his

breath too hot and heavy in his lungs, and there was still a third trip to make, this time with the gunslinger as his passenger, and although he guessed Roland must outweigh Odetta by a full hundred pounds and knew he should conserve his strength, Eddie kept running anyway. *Let her be safe, that's my wish, let my beloved be safe.*

And, like an ill omen, a wildcat screeched somewhere in the tortured ravines that cut through the hills . . . only this wildcat sounded as big as a lion roaring in an African jungle.

Eddie ran faster, pushing the untenanted gantry of the wheelchair before him. Soon the wind began to make a thin, ghastly whine through the freely turning spokes of the raised front wheels.

11

The gunslinger heard a reedy wailing sound approaching him, tensed for a moment, then heard panting breath and relaxed. It was Eddie. Even without opening his eyes he knew that.

When the wailing sound faded and the running footsteps slowed, Roland opened his eyes. Eddie stood panting before him with sweat running down the sides of his face. His shirt was plastered against his chest in a single dark blotch. Any last vestiges of the college-boy look Jack Andolini had insisted upon were gone. His hair hung over his forehead. He had split his pants at the crotch. The bluish-purple crescents under his eyes completed the picture. Eddie Dean was a mess.

"I made it," he said. "I'm here." He looked around, then back at the gunslinger, as if he could not believe it. "Jesus Christ, I'm really *here.*"

"You gave her the gun."

Eddie thought the gunslinger looked bad—as bad as

he'd looked before the first abbreviated round of Keflex, maybe a trifle worse. Fever-heat seemed to be coming off him in waves, and he knew he should have felt sorry for him, but for the moment all he could seem to feel was mad as hell.

"I bust my ass getting back here in record time and all you can say is 'You gave her the gun.' Thanks, man. I mean, I expected some expression of gratitude, but this is just over-fucking-*whelming.*"

"I think I said the only thing that matters."

"Well, now that you mention it, I did," Eddie said, putting his hands on his hips and staring truculently down at the gunslinger. "Now you have your choice. You can get in this chair or I can fold it and try to jam it up your ass. Which do you prefer, mawster?"

"Neither." Roland was smiling a little, the smile of a man who doesn't *want* to smile but can't help it. "First you're going to take some sleep, Eddie. We'll see what we'll see when the time for seeing comes, but for now you need sleep. You're done in."

"I want to get back to her."

"I do, too. But if you don't rest, you're going to fall down in the traces. Simple as that. Bad for you, worse for me, and worst of all for *her.*"

Eddie stood for a moment, undecided.

"You made good time," the gunslinger conceded. He squinted at the sun. "It's four, maybe a quarter-past. You sleep five, maybe seven hours, and it'll be full dark—"

"Four. Four hours."

"All right. Until after dark; I think that's the important thing. Then you eat. Then we move."

"You eat, too."

That faint smile again. "I'll try." He looked at Eddie calmly. "Your life is in my hands now; I suppose you know that."

"Yes."

"I kidnapped you."

"Yes."

"Do you want to kill me? If you do, do it now rather than subject any of us to . . ." His breath whistled out softly. Eddie heard his chest rattling and cared very little for the sound. ". . . to any further discomfort," he finished.

"I don't want to kill you."

"Then—" he was interrupted by a sudden harsh burst of coughing "—lie down," he finished.

Eddie did. Sleep did not drift upon him as it sometimes did but seized him with the rough hands of a lover who is awkward in her eagerness. He heard (or perhaps this was only a dream) Roland saying, *But you shouldn't have given her the gun,* and then he was simply in the dark for an unknown time and then Roland was shaking him awake and when he finally sat up all there seemed to be in his body was pain: pain and weight. His muscles had turned into rusty winches and pullies in a deserted building. His first effort to get to his feet didn't work. He thumped heavily back to the sand. He managed it on the second try, but he felt as if it might take him twenty minutes just to perform such a simple act as turning around. And it would hurt to do it.

Roland's eyes were on him, questioning. "Are you ready?"

Eddie nodded. "Yes. Are *you?*"

"Yes."

"Can you?"

"Yes."

So they ate . . . and then Eddie began his third and last trip along this cursed stretch of beach.

12

They rolled a good stretch that night, but Eddie was still dully disappointed when the gunslinger called a halt. He offered no disagreement because he was simply too weary to go on without rest, but he had hoped to get further. The weight. That was the big problem. Compared to Odetta, pushing Roland was like pushing a load of iron bars. Eddie slept four more hours before dawn, woke with the sun coming over the eroding hills which were all that remained of the mountains, and listened to the gunslinger coughing. It was a weak cough, full of rales, the cough of an old man who may be coming down with pneumonia.

Their eyes met. Roland's coughing spasm turned into a laugh.

"I'm not done yet, Eddie, no matter how I sound. Are you?"

Eddie thought of Odetta's eyes and shook his head.

"Not done, but I could use a cheeseburger and a Bud."

"Bud?" the gunslinger said doubtfully, thinking of apple trees and the spring flowers in the Royal Court Gardens.

"Never mind. Hop in, my man. No four on the floor, no T-top, but we're going to roll some miles just the same."

And they did, but when sunset came on the second day following his leave-taking of Odetta, they were still only drawing near the place of the third door. Eddie lay down, meaning to crash for another four hours, but the screaming cry of one of those cats jerked him out of sleep after only two hours, his heart thumping. God, the thing sounded fucking *huge*.

He saw the gunslinger up on one elbow, his eyes gleaming in the dark.

"You ready?" Eddie asked. He got slowly to his feet, grinning with pain.

"Are *you*?" Roland asked again, very softly.

Eddie twisted his back, producing a series of pops like a string of tiny firecrackers. "Yeah. But I could really get behind that cheeseburger."

"I thought chicken was what you wanted."

Eddie groaned. "Cut me a break, man."

The third door was in plain view by the time the sun cleared the hills. Two hours later, they reached it.

All together again, Eddie thought, ready to drop to the sand.

But that was apparently not so. There was no sign of Odetta Holmes. No sign at all.

13

"*Odetta!*" Eddie screamed, and now his voice was broken and hoarse as the voice of Odetta's *other* had been.

There wasn't even an echo in return, something he might at least have mistaken for Odetta's voice. These low, eroded hills would not bounce sound. There was only the crash of the waves, much louder in this tight arrowhead of land, the rhythmic, hollow boom of surf crashing to the end of some tunnel it had dug in the friable rock, and the steady keening of the wind.

"*Odetta!*"

This time he screamed so loudly his voice broke and for a moment something sharp, like a jag of fishbone, tore at his vocal cords. His eyes scanned the hills frantically, looking for the lighter patch of brown that would be her palm, looking for movement as she stood up . . . looking (God forgive him) for bright splashes of blood on roan-colored rock.

He found himself wondering what he would do if he saw that last, or found the revolver, now with deep toothmarks driven into the smooth sandalwood of the grips. The sight of something like that might drive him into hysteria, might even run him crazy, but he looked for it—or something—just the same.

His eyes saw nothing; his ears brought not the faintest returning cry.

The gunslinger, meanwhile, had been studying the third door. He had expected a single word, the word the man in black had used as he turned the sixth Tarot card at the dusty Golgotha where they had held palaver. *Death,* Walter had said, *but not for you, gunslinger.*

There was not one word writ upon this door but two . . . and neither of them was DEATH. He read it again, lips moving soundlessly:

THE PUSHER

Yet it means *death,* Roland thought, and knew it was so.

What made him look around was the sound of Eddie's voice moving away. Eddie had begun to climb the first slope, still calling Odetta's name.

For a moment Roland considered just letting him go.

He might find her, might even find her alive, not too badly hurt, and still herself. He supposed the two of them might even make a life of sorts for themselves here, that Eddie's love for Odetta and hers for him might somehow smother the nightshade who called herself Detta Walker. Yes, between the two of them he supposed it was possible that Detta might simply be squeezed to death. He was a romantic in his own harsh way . . . yet he was also realist enough to know that sometimes love actually *did* conquer all. As for himself? Even if he was able to get the drugs from Eddie's world which had almost cured him before, would they be able to cure him this time, or even make a start? He was now very sick, and he found himself wondering if perhaps things hadn't gone too far. His arms and legs ached, his head thudded, his chest was heavy and full of snot. When he coughed there was a painful grating in his left side, as if ribs were broken there. His left ear flamed. Perhaps, he thought, the time had come to end it; to just cry off.

At this, everything in him rose up in protest.

"Eddie!" he cried, and there was no cough now. His voice was deep and powerful.

Eddie turned, one foot on raw dirt, the other braced on a jutting spar of rock.

"Go on," he said, and made a curious little sweeping gesture with his hand, a gesture that said he wanted to be rid of the gunslinger so he could be about his *real* business, the *important* business, the business of finding Odetta and rescuing her if rescue were necessary. "It's all right. Go on through and get the stuff you need. We'll both be here when you get back."

"I doubt that."

"I have to find her." Eddie looked at Roland and his gaze was very young and completely naked. "I mean, I really *have* to."

"I understand your love and your need," the gunslinger said, "but I want you to come with me this time, Eddie."

Eddie stared at him for a long time, as if trying to credit what he was hearing.

"Come with you," he said at last, bemused. "Come *with* you! Holy God, now I think I really have heard everything. Deedle-deedle-dumpkin *everything*. Last time you were so determined I was gonna stay behind you were willing to take a chance on me cutting your throat. This time you want to take a chance on something ripping *hers* right out."

"That may have already happened," Roland said,

although he knew it hadn't. The Lady might be hurt, but he knew she wasn't dead.

Unfortunately, Eddie did, too. A week or ten days without his drug had sharpened his mind remarkably. He pointed at the door. "You know she's not. If she was, that goddam thing would be gone. Unless you were lying when you said it wasn't any good without all three of us."

Eddie tried to turn back to the slope, but Roland's eyes held him nailed.

"All right," the gunslinger said. His voice was almost as soft as it had been when he spoke past the hateful face and screaming voice of Detta to the woman trapped somewhere behind it. "She's alive. That being so, why does she not answer your calls?"

"Well . . . one of those cats-things may have carried her away." But Eddie's voice was weak.

"A cat would have killed her, eaten what it wanted, and left the rest. At most, it might have dragged her body into the shade so it could come back tonight and eat meat the sun perhaps hadn't yet spoiled. But if that was the case, the door would be gone. Cats aren't like some insects, who paralyze their prey and carry them off to eat later, and you know it."

"That isn't necessarily true," Eddie said. For a moment he heard Odetta saying *You should have been on the debate team, Eddie* and pushed the thought aside. "Could be a cat came for her and she tried to shoot it but the first couple of shells in your gun were misfires. Hell, maybe even the first four or five. The cat gets to her, mauls her, and just before it can kill her . . . *BANG!*" Eddie smacked a fist against his palm, seeing all this so vividly that he might have witnessed it. "The bullet kills the cat, or maybe just wounds it, or maybe just scares it off. What about that?"

Mildly, Roland said: "We would have heard a gunshot."

For a moment Eddie could only stand, mute, able
to think of no counter-argument. Of course they would
have heard it. The first time they had heard one of the
cats yowling, it had to have been fifteen, maybe twenty
miles away. A pistol-shot—

He looked at Roland with sudden cunning. "Maybe
you did," he said. "Maybe *you* heard a gunshot while
I was asleep."

"It would have woken you."

"Not as tired as I am, man. I fall asleep, it's
like—"

"Like being dead," the gunslinger said in that same
mild voice. "I know the feeling."

"Then you understand—"

"But it's not *being* dead. Last night you were out
just like that, but when one of those cats screeched,
you were awake and on your feet in seconds. Because
of your concern for her. There was no gunshot, Eddie,
and you know it. You would have heard it. Because of
your concern for her."

"So maybe she brained it with a rock!" Eddie
shouted. "How the hell do I know when I'm standing
here arguing with you instead of checking out the possibilities? I mean, she could be lying up there someplace hurt, man! Hurt or bleeding to death! How'd you
like it if I *did* come through that door with you and
she died while we were on the other side? How'd you
like to look around once and see that doorway there,
then look around twice and see it gone, just like it
never was, because *she* was gone? Then you'd be
trapped in *my* world instead of the other way around!"
He stood panting and glaring at the gunslinger, his
hands balled into fists.

Roland felt a tired exasperation. Someone—it might
have been Cort but he rather thought it had been his
father—had had a saying: *Might as well try to drink
the ocean with a spoon as argue with a lover.* If any proof

of the saying were needed, there it stood above him, in a posture that was all defiance and defense. *Go on,* the set of Eddie Dean's body said. *Go on, I can answer any question you throw at me.*

"Might not have been a cat that found her," he said now. "This may be your world, but I don't think you've ever been to this part of it any more than I've ever been to Borneo. You don't know what might be running around up in those hills, do you? Could be an ape grabbed her, or something like that."

"Something grabbed her, all right," the gunslinger said.

"Well thank God getting sick hasn't driven all the sense out of your m—"

"And we both know what it was. Detta Walker. That's what grabbed her. Detta Walker."

Eddie opened his mouth, but for some little time— only seconds, but enough of them so both acknowledged the truth—the gunslinger's inexorable face bore all his arguments to silence.

14

"It doesn't *have* to be that way."

"Come a little closer. If we're going to talk, let's talk. Every time I have to shout at you over the waves, it rips another piece of my throat out. That's how it feels, anyway."

"What big eyes you have, grandma," Eddie said, not moving.

"What in hell's name are you talking about?"

"A fairy tale." Eddie did descend a short way back down the slope—four yards, no more. "And fairy tales are what you're *thinking* about if you believe you can coax me close enough to that wheelchair."

"Close enough for *what?* I don't understand," Roland said, although he understood perfectly.

Nearly a hundred and fifty yards above them and perhaps a full quarter of a mile to the east, dark eyes—eyes as full of intelligence as they were lacking in human mercy—watched this tableau intently. It was impossible to tell what they were saying; the wind, the waves, and the hollow crash of the surf digging its underground channel saw to that, but Detta didn't need to hear what they were *saying* to know what they were *talking* about. She didn't need a telescope to see that the Really Bad Man was now also the Really Sick Man, and maybe the Really Bad Man was willing to spend a few days or even a few weeks torturing a legless Negro woman—way things looked around here, entertainment was mighty hard to come by—but she thought the Really Sick Man only wanted one thing, and that was to get his whitebread ass out of here. Just use that magic doorway to haul the fucker out. But before, he hadn't been hauling no ass. Before, he hadn't been hauling nothing. Before, the Really Bad Man hadn't been nowhere but inside *her own head.* She still didn't like to think of how that had been, how it had felt, how easily he had overridden all her clawing efforts to push him out, *away,* to take control of herself again. That had been awful. Terrible. And what made it worse was her lack of understanding. What, exactly, was the real source of her terror? That it wasn't the invasion itself was frightening enough. She knew she might understand if she examined herself more closely, but she didn't want to do that. Such examination might lead her to a place like the one sailors had feared in the ancient days, a place which was no more or less than the edge of the world, a place the cartographers had marked with the legend HERE THERE BE SARPENTS. The hideous thing about the Really Bad Man's invasion had been the sense of *familiarity* that came with it, as if this amazing thing had happened before—not once, but many times. But, frightened or not, she

had denied panic. She had observed even as she
fought, and she remembered looking into that door
when the gunslinger used her hands to pivot the wheelchair toward it. She remembered seeing the body of
the Really Bad Man lying on the sand with Eddie
crouched above it, a knife in his hand.

Would that Eddie had plunged that knife into the
Really Bad Man's throat! Better than a pig-
slaughtering! Better by a country mile!

He hadn't, but she had seen the Really Bad Man's
body. It had been breathing, but *body* was the right
word just the same; it had only been a worthless *thing*,
like a cast-off towsack which some idiot had stuffed
full of weeds or cornshucks.

Detta's mind might have been as ugly as a rat's ass,
but it was even quicker and sharper than Eddie's. *Really Bad Man there used to be full of piss an vinegar.
Not no mo. He know I'm up here and doan want to do
nothin but git away befo I come down an kill his ass.
His little buddy, though—he still be pretty strong, and
he ain't had his fill of hurting on me just yet. Want to
come up here and hunt me down no matter how that
Really Bad Man be. Sho. He be thinkin, One black
bitch widdout laigs no match fo a big ole swingin dick
like me. I doan wan t'run. I want to be huntin that
black quiff down. I give her a poke or two, den we kin
go like you want. That what he be thinkin, and that be
all right. That be jes fine, graymeat. You think you can
take Detta Walker, you jes come on up here in these
Drawers and give her a try. You goan find out when
you fuckin with me, you fuckin wit the best, honey-
bunch! You goan find out—*

But she was jerked from the rat-run of her thoughts
by a sound that came to her clearly in spite of the surf
and wind: the heavy crack of a pistol-shot.

15

"I think you understand better than you let on," Eddie said. "A whole *hell* of a lot better. You'd like for me to get in grabbing distance, that's what I think." He jerked his head toward the door without taking his eyes from Roland's face. Unaware that not far away someone was thinking exactly the same thing, he added: "I know you're sick, all right, but it could be you're pretending to be a lot weaker than you really are. Could be you're laying back in the tall grass just a little bit."

"Could be I am," Roland said, unsmiling, and added: "But I'm not."

He was, though . . . a little.

"A few more steps wouldn't hurt, though, would it? I'm not going to be able to shout much longer." The last syllable turned into a frog's croak as if to prove his point. "And I need to make you think about what you're doing—planning to do. If I can't persuade you to come with me, maybe I can at least put you on your guard . . . again."

"For your precious Tower," Eddie sneered, but he did come skidding halfway down the slope of ground he had climbed, his tattered tennies kicking up listless clouds of maroon dust.

"For my precious Tower and *your* precious health," the gunslinger said. "Not to mention your precious *life.*"

He slipped the remaining revolver from the left holster and looked at it with an expression both sad and strange.

"If you think you can scare me with that—"

"I don't. You know I can't shoot you, Eddie. But I think you do need an object lesson in how things have changed. How much things have changed."

Roland lifted the gun, its muzzle pointing not to-

ward Eddie but toward the empty surging ocean, and
thumbed the hammer. Eddie steeled himself against
the gun's heavy crack.

No such thing. Only a dull click.

Roland thumbed the hammer back again. The cylinder rotated. He squeezed the trigger, and again there
was nothing but a dull click.

"Never mind," Eddie said. "Where I come from,
the Defense Department would have hired you after
the first misfire. You might as well qui—"

But the heavy KA-BLAM of the revolver cut off the
word's end as neatly as Roland had cut small branches
from trees as a target-shooting exercise when he had
been a student. Eddie jumped. The gunshot momentarily silenced the constant *riiiiii* of the insects in the
hills. They only began to tune up again slowly, cautiously, after Roland had put the gun in his lap.

"What in hell does that prove?"

"I suppose that all depends on what you'll listen to
and what you refuse to hear," Roland said a trifle
sharply. "It's *supposed* to prove that not all the shells
are duds. Furthermore, it suggests—*strongly* suggests—that some, maybe even *all,* of the shells in the
gun you gave Odetta may be live."

"Bullshit!" Eddie paused. "Why?"

"Because I loaded the gun I just fired with shells
from the *backs* of my gunbelts—with shells that took
the worst wetting, in other words. I did it just to pass
the time while you were gone. Not that it takes much
time to load a gun, even shy a pair of fingers, you
understand!" Roland laughed a little, and the laugh
turned into a cough he muzzled with an abridged fist.
When the cough had subsided he went on: "But after
you've tried to fire wets, you have to break the machine and clean the machine. *Break the machine, clean
the machine, you maggots*—it was the first thing Cort,
our teacher, drummed into us. I didn't know how long

it would take me to break down my gun, clean it, and put it back together with only a hand and a half, but I thought that if I intended to go on living—and I do, Eddie, I do—I'd better find out. Find out and then learn to do it faster, don't you think so? Come a little closer, Eddie! Come a little closer for your father's sake!''

"All the better to see you with, my child," Eddie said, but did take a couple of steps closer to Roland. *Only* a couple.

"When the first slug I pulled the trigger on fired, I almost filled my pants," the gunslinger said. He laughed again. Shocked, Eddie realized the gunslinger had reached the edge of delirium. "The first slug, but believe me when I say it was the *last* thing I had expected."

Eddie tried to decide if the gunslinger was lying, lying about the gun, and lying about his condition as well. Cat was sick, yeah. But was he really this sick? Eddie didn't know. If Roland was acting, he was doing a great job; as for guns, Eddie had no way of telling because he had no experience with them. He had shot a pistol maybe three times in his life before suddenly finding himself in a firefight at Balazar's place. *Henry* might have known, but Henry was dead—a thought which had a way of constantly surprising Eddie into grief.

"None of the others fired," the gunslinger said, "so I cleaned the machine, re-loaded, and fired around the chamber again. This time I used shells a little further toward the belt buckles. Ones which would have taken even less of a wetting. The loads we used to kill our food, the dry loads, were the ones closest to the buckles."

He paused to cough dryly into his hand, then went on.

"Second time around I hit two live rounds. I broke

my gun down again, cleaned it again, then loaded a third time. You just watched me drop the trigger on the first three chambers of that third loading." He smiled faintly. "You know, after the first two clicks I thought it would be my damned luck to have filled the cylinder with nothing but wets. That wouldn't have been very convincing, would it? Can you come a little closer, Eddie?"

"Not very convincing at all," Eddie said, "and I think I'm just as close to you as I'm going to come, thanks. What lesson am I supposed to take from all this, Roland?"

Roland looked at him as one might look at an imbecile. "I didn't send you out here to die, you know. I didn't send *either* of you out here to die. Great gods, Eddie, where are your brains? She's packing *live iron!*" His eyes regarded Eddie closely. "She's someplace up in those hills. Maybe you think you can track her, but you're not going to have any luck if the ground is as stony as it looks from here. She's lying up there, Eddie, not Odetta but Detta, lying up there with live iron in her hand. If I leave you and you go after her, she'll blow your guts out of your asshole."

Another spasm of coughing set in.

Eddie stared at the coughing man in the wheelchair and the waves pounded and the wind blew its steady idiot's note.

At last he heard his voice say, "You could have held back one shell you *knew* was live. I wouldn't put it past you." And with that said he knew it to be true: he wouldn't put that or anything else past Roland.

His Tower.

His goddamned Tower.

And the slyness of putting the saved shell in the *third* cylinder! It provided just the right touch of reality, didn't it? Made it hard not to believe.

"We've got a saying in my world," Eddie said.

" 'That guy could sell Frigidaires to the Eskimos.'
That's the saying.''

"What does it mean?"

"It means go pound sand."

The gunslinger looked at him for a long time and
then nodded. "You mean to stay. All right. As Detta
she's safer from . . . from whatever wildlife there may
be around here . . . than she would have been as
Odetta, and you'd be safer away from her—at least for
the time being—but I can see how it is. I don't like it,
but I've no time to argue with a fool."

"Does that mean," Eddie asked politely, "that no
one ever tried to argue with you about this Dark Tower
you're so set on getting to?"

Roland smiled tiredly. "A great many did, as a matter of fact. I suppose that's why I recognize you'll not
be moved. One fool knows another. At any rate, I'm
too weak to catch you, you're obviously too wary to
let me coax you close enough to grab you, and time's
grown too short to argue. All I can do is go and hope
for the best. I'm going to tell you one last time before
I do go, and hear me, Eddie: *Be on your guard.*"

Then Roland did something that made Eddie
ashamed of all his doubts (although no less solidly set
in his own decision): he flicked open the cylinder of
the revolver with a practiced flick of his wrist, dumped
all the loads, and replaced them with fresh loads from
the loops closest to the buckles. He snapped the cylinder back into place with another flick of his wrist.

"No time to clean the machine now," he said, "But
'twont matter, I reckon. Now catch, and catch clean—
don't dirty the machine any more than it is already.
There aren't many machines left in my world that work
anymore."

He threw the gun across the space between them. In
his anxiety, Eddie almost *did* drop it. Then he had it
safely tucked into his waistband.

The gunslinger got out of the wheelchair, almost fell when it slid backward under his pushing hands, then tottered to the door. He grasped its knob; in *his* hand it turned easily. Eddie could not see the scene the door opened upon, but he heard the muffled sound of traffic.

Roland looked back at Eddie, his blue bullshooter's eyes gleaming out of a face which was ghastly pale.

16

Detta watched all of this from her hiding place with hungrily gleaming eyes.

17

"Remember, Eddie," he said in a hoarse voice, and then stepped forward. His body collapsed at the edge of the doorway, as if it had struck a stone wall instead of empty space.

Eddie felt an almost insatiable urge to go to the doorway, to look through and see where—and to what *when*—it led. Instead he turned and scanned the hills again, his hand on the gun-butt.

I'm going to tell you one last time.

Suddenly, scanning the empty brown hills, Eddie was scared.

Be on your guard.

Nothing up there was moving.

Nothing he could *see*, at least.

He sensed her all the same.

Not Odetta; the gunslinger was right about that.

It was *Detta* he sensed.

He swallowed and heard a click in his throat.

On your guard.

Yes. But never in his life had he felt such a deadly

need for sleep. It would take him soon enough; if he didn't give in willingly, sleep would rape him.

And while he slept, Detta would come.

Detta.

Eddie fought the weariness, looked at the unmoving hills with eyes which felt swollen and heavy, and wondered how long it might be before Roland came back with the third—The Pusher, whoever he or she was.

"Odetta?" he called without much hope.

Only silence answered, and for Eddie the time of waiting began.

THE
PUSHER

CHAPTER 1

BITTER MEDICINE

1

When the gunslinger entered Eddie, Eddie had experienced a moment of nausea and he had had a sense of being *watched* (this Roland hadn't felt; Eddie had told him later). He'd had, in other words, some vague sense of the gunslinger's presence. With Detta, Roland had been forced to *come forward* immediately, like it or not. She hadn't just sensed him; in a queer way it seemed that she had been *waiting* for him—him or another, more frequent, visitor. Either way, she had been totally aware of his presence from the first moment he had been in her.

Jack Mort didn't feel a thing.

He was too intent on the boy.

He had been watching the boy for the last two weeks.

Today he was going to push him.

2

Even with the back to the eyes from which the gunslinger now looked, Roland recognized the boy. It was the boy he had met at the way station in the desert, the boy he had rescued from the Oracle in the Mountains, the boy whose life he had sacrificed when the choice between saving him or finally catching up with the man in black finally came; the boy who had said *Go then—there are other worlds than these* before

361

plunging into the abyss. And sure enough, the boy had been right.

The boy was Jake.

He was holding a plain brown paper bag in one hand and a blue canvas bag by its drawstring top in the other. From the angles poking against the sides of the canvas, the gunslinger thought it must contain books.

Traffic flooded the street the boy was waiting to cross—a street in the same city from which he had taken the Prisoner and the Lady, he realized, but for the moment none of that mattered. Nothing mattered but what was going to happen or not happen in the next few seconds.

Jake had not been brought into the gunslinger's world through any magic door; he had come through a cruder, more understandable portal: he had been born into Roland's world by dying in his own.

He had been murdered.

More specifically, he had been *pushed*.

Pushed into the street; run over by a car while on his way to school, his lunch-sack in one hand and his books in the other.

Pushed by the man in black.

He's going to do it! He's going to do it right now! That's to be my punishment for murdering him in my world—to see him murdered in this one before I can stop it!

But the rejection of brutish destiny had been the gunslinger's work all his life—it had been his *ka*, if you pleased—and so he *came forward* without even thinking, acting with reflexes so deep they had nearly become instincts.

And as he did a thought both horrible and ironic flashed into his mind: *What if the body he had entered was* itself *that of the man in black? What if, as he rushed forward to save the boy, he saw his* own *hands reach out and push? What if this sense of control was only an illusion, and Walter's final gleeful joke that* Roland himself *should murder the boy?*

3

For one single moment Jack Mort lost the thin strong arrow of his concentration. On the edge of leaping forward and shoving the kid into the traffic, he felt something which his mind mistranslated just as the body may refer pain from one part of itself to another.

When the gunslinger *came forward,* Jack thought some sort of bug had landed on the back of his neck. Not a wasp or a bee, nothing that actually *stung,* but something that bit and itched. Mosquito, maybe. It was on this that he blamed his lapse in concentration at the crucial moment. He slapped at it and returned to the boy.

He thought all this happened in a bare wink; actually, seven seconds passed. He sensed neither the gunslinger's swift advance nor his equally swift retreat, and none of the people around him (going-to-work people, most from the subway station on the next block, their faces still puffy with sleep, their half-dreaming eyes turned inward) noticed Jack's eyes turn from their usual deep blue to a lighter blue behind the prim gold-rimmed glasses he wore. No one noticed those eyes darken to their normal cobalt color either, but when it happened and he refocused on the boy, he saw with frustrated fury as sharp as a thorn that his chance was gone. The light had changed.

He watched the boy crossing with the rest of the sheep, and then Jack himself turned back the way he had come and began shoving himself upstream against the tidal flow of pedestrians.

"Hey, mister! Watch ou—"

Some curd-faced teenaged girl he barely saw. Jack shoved her aside, hard, not looking back at her caw of anger as her own armload of schoolbooks went flying. He went walking on down Fifth Avenue and away from Forty-Third, where he had meant for the boy to die today. His head was bent, his lips pressed together so tightly he seemed to have no mouth at all but only the scar of a long-healed wound above his chin. Once clear of the bottleneck at the corner, he did not slow down but strode even more rapidly along, crossing Forty-Second, Forty-First, Fortieth. Somewhere in the middle of the next block he passed the building where the boy lived. He gave it barely a glance, although he had followed the boy from it every school-morning for the last three weeks, followed him from the building to the corner three and a half blocks further up Fifth, the corner he thought of simply as the Pushing Place.

The girl he bumped was screaming after him, but Jack Mort didn't notice. An amateur lepidopterist would have taken no more notice of a common butterfly.

Jack was, in his way, much like an amateur lepidopterist.

By profession, he was a successful C.P.A.

Pushing was only his hobby.

4

The gunslinger returned to the back of the man's mind and fainted there. If there was relief, it was simply that this man was not the man in black, was not Walter.

All the rest was utter horror . . . and utter realization.

Divorced of his body, his mind—his *ka*—was as healthy and acute as ever, but the sudden *knowing* struck him like a chisel-blow to the temple.

The knowing didn't come when he *went forward* but when he was sure the boy was safe and slipped back

again. He saw the connection between this man and
Odetta, too fantastic and yet too hideously apt to be
coincidental, and understood what the *real* drawing of
the three might be, and *who* they might be.

The third was not this man, this Pusher; the third
named by Walter had been Death.

Death . . . but not for you. That was what Walter,
clever as Satan even at the end, had said. A lawyer's
answer . . . so close to the truth that the truth was
able to hide in its shadow. Death was not for him;
death was *become* him.

The Prisoner, the Lady.

Death was the third.

He was suddenly filled with the certainty that he
himself was the third.

5

Roland *came forward* as nothing but a projectile, a
brainless missile programmed to launch the body he
was in at the man in black the instant he saw him.

Thoughts of what might happen if he stopped the
man in black from murdering Jake did not come until
later—the possible paradox, the fistula in time and dimension which might cancel out everything that had
happened after he had arrived at the way station . . .
for surely if he saved Jake in this world, there would
have been no Jake for him to meet there, and everything which had happened thereafter would change.

What changes? Impossible even to speculate on
them. That one might have been the end of his quest
never entered the gunslinger's mind. And surely such
after-the-fact speculations were moot; if he had seen
the man in black, no consequence, paradox, or or-
dained course of destiny could have stopped him from
simply lowering the head of this body he inhabited and
pounding it straight through Walter's chest. Roland

would have been as helpless to do otherwise as a gun is helpless to refuse the finger that squeezes the trigger and flings the bullet on its flight.

If it sent all to hell, the hell with it.

He scanned the people clustered on the corner quickly, seeing each face (he scanned the women as closely as the men, making sure there wasn't one only *pretending* to be a woman).

Walter wasn't there.

Gradually he relaxed, as a finger curled around a trigger may relax at the last instant. No; Walter was nowhere around the boy, and the gunslinger somehow felt sure that this wasn't the right *when*. Not quite. That *when* was close—two weeks away, a week, maybe even a single day—but it was not quite yet.

So he *went back*.

On the way he *saw* . . .

6

. . . and fell senseless with shock: this man into whose mind the third door opened, had once sat waiting just inside the window of a deserted tenement room in a building full of abandoned rooms—abandoned, that was, except for the winos and crazies who often spent their nights here. You knew about the winos because you could smell their desperate sweat and angry piss. You knew about the crazies because you could smell the stink of their deranged thoughts. The only furniture in this room was two chairs. Jack Mort was using both: one to sit in, one as a prop to keep the door opening on the hallway closed. He expected no sudden interruptions, but it was best not to take chances. He was close enough to the window to look out, but far enough behind the slanted shadow-line to be safe from any casual viewer.

He had a crumbly red brick in his hand.

He had pried it from just outside the window, where a good many were loose. It was old, eroded at the corners, but heavy. Chunks of ancient mortar clung to it like barnacles.

The man meant to drop the brick on someone.

He didn't care who; when it came to murder, Jack Mort was an equal-opportunity employer.

After a bit, a family of three came along the sidewalk below: man, woman, little girl. The girl had been walking on the inside, presumably to keep her safely away from the traffic. There was quite a lot of it this close to the railway station but Jack Mort didn't care about the auto traffic. What he cared about was the lack of buildings directly opposite him; these had already been demolished, leaving a jumbled wasteland of splintered board, broken brick, glinting glass.

He would only lean out for a few seconds, and he was wearing sunglasses over his eyes and an out-of-season knit cap over his blonde hair. It was like the chair under the doorknob. Even when you were safe from expected risks, there was no harm in reducing those unexpected ones which remained.

He was also wearing a sweatshirt much too big for him—one that came almost down to mid-thigh. This bag of a garment would help confuse the actual size and shape of his body (he was quite thin) should he be observed. It served another purpose as well: whenever he "depth-charged" someone (for that was how he always thought of it: as "depth-charging"), he came in his pants. The baggy sweatshirt also covered the wet spot which invariably formed on his jeans.

Now they were closer.

Don't jump the gun, wait, just wait . . .

He shivered at the edge of the window, brought the brick forward, drew it back to his stomach, brought it forward again, withdrew it again (but this time only halfway), and then leaned out, totally cool now. He always was at the penultimate moment.

He dropped the brick and watched it fall.

It went down, swapping one end for the other. Jack saw the clinging barnacles of mortar clearly in the sun. At these moments as at no others everything was clear, everything stood out with exact and geometrically perfect substance; here was a thing which he had pushed into reality, as a sculptor swings a hammer against a chisel to change stone and create some new substance from the brute *caldera;* here was the world's most remarkable thing: logic which was also ecstasy.

Sometimes he missed or struck aslant, as the sculptor may carve badly or in vain, but this was a perfect shot. The brick struck the girl in the bright gingham dress squarely on the head. He saw blood—it was brighter than the brick but would eventually dry to the same maroon color—splash up. He heard the start of the mother's scream. Then he was moving.

Jack crossed the room and threw the chair which had been under the knob into a far corner (he'd kicked the other—the one he'd sat in while waiting—aside as he crossed the room). He yanked up the sweatshirt and pulled a bandanna from his back pocket. He used it to turn the knob.

No fingerprints allowed.

Only Don't Bees left fingerprints.

He stuffed the bandanna into his back pocket again even as the door was swinging open. As he walked down the hall, he assumed a faintly drunken gait. He didn't look around.

Looking around was also only for Don't Bees.

Do Bees knew that trying to see if someone was noticing you was a sure way to accomplish just that. Looking around was the sort of thing a witness *might* remember after an accident. Then some smartass cop *might* decide it was a *suspicious* accident, and there would be an investigation. All because of one nervous glance around. Jack didn't believe anyone could connect him with the crime even if someone decided the "accident" was suspicious and there *was* an investigation, but . . .

Take only acceptable risks. Minimize those which remain. In other words, always prop a chair under the doorknob.

So he walked down the powdery corridor where patches of lathing showed through the plastered walls, he walked with his head down, mumbling to himself like the vags you saw on the street. He could still hear the woman—the mother of the little girl, he supposed—screaming, but that sound was coming from the front of the building; it was faint and unimportant. *All* of the things which happened *after*—the cries, the confusion, the wails of the wounded (if the wounded were still capable of wailing), were not things which mattered to Jack. What mattered was the thing which pushed change into the ordinary course of things and sculpted new lines in the flow of lives . . . and, perhaps, the destinies not only of those struck, but of a widening circle around them, like ripples from a stone tossed into a still pond.

Who was to say that he had not sculpted the cosmos today, or might not at some future time?

God, no wonder he creamed his jeans!

He met no one as he went down the two flights of stairs but he kept up the act, swaying a little as he went but never reeling. A swayer would not be remembered. An ostentatious reeler might be. He muttered but didn't actually say anything a person might understand. Not acting at all would be better than hamming it up.

He let himself out the broken rear door into an alley filled with refuse and broken bottles which twinkled galaxies of sun-stars.

He had planned his escape in advance as he planned everything in advance (take only acceptable risks, minimize those which remain, be a Do Bee in all things); such planning was why he had been marked by his colleagues as a man who would go far (and he *did* intend to go far, but one of the places he did not intend to go was to jail, or the electric chair).

A few people were running along the street into which the alley debouched, but they were on their way to see what the screaming was about, and none of them looked at Jack Mort, who had removed the out-of-season knit cap but not the sunglasses (which, on such a bright morning, did not seem out of place).

He turned into another alley.

Came out on another street.

Now he sauntered down an alley not so filthy as the first two—almost, in fact, a lane. This fed into another street, and a block up there was a bus stop. Less than a minute after he got there a bus arrived, which was also part of the schedule. Jack entered when the doors accordioned open and dropped his fifteen cents into the slot of the coin receptacle. The driver did not so much as glance at him. That was good, but even if he had, he would have seen nothing but a nondescript man in jeans, a man who might be out of work—the sweatshirt he was wearing looked like something out of a Salvation Army grab-bag.

Be ready, be prepared, be a Do-Bee.

Jack Mort's secret for success both at work and at play.

Nine blocks away there was a parking lot. Jack got off the bus, entered the lot, unlocked his car (an unremarkable mid-fifties Chevrolet which was still in fine shape), and drove back to New York City.

He was free and clear.

7

The gunslinger saw all of this in a mere moment. Before his shocked mind could shut out the other images by simply shutting down, he saw more. Not all, but enough. Enough.

8

He saw Mort cutting a piece from page four of *The New York Daily Mirror* with an Exacto knife, being fussily sure to stay exactly upon the lines of the column. NEGRO GIRL COMATOSE FOLLOWING TRAGIC ACCIDENT, the headline read. He saw Mort apply glue to the back of the clipping with the brush attached to the cover of his paste-pot. Saw Mort position it at the center of a blank page of a scrapbook, which, from the bumpy, swelled look of the foregoing pages, contained many other clippings. He saw the opening lines of the piece: "Five-year-old Odetta Holmes, who came to Elizabethtown, N.J., to celebrate a joyous occasion, is now the victim of a cruel freak accident. Following the wedding of an aunt two days ago, the girl and her family were walking toward the railway station when a brick tumbled . . . "

But that wasn't the only time he'd had dealings with her, was it? No. Gods, no.

In the years between that morning and the night when Odetta had lost her legs, Jack Mort had dropped a great many things and pushed a great many people.

Then there had been Odetta again.

The first time he had pushed something *on* her.

The second time he had pushed her *in front* of something.

What sort of man is this that I am supposed to use? What sort of man—

But then he thought of Jake, thought of the push

which had sent Jake into this world, and he thought he heard the laughter of the man in black, and that finished him.

Roland fainted.

9

When he came to, he was looking at neat rows of figures marching down a sheet of green paper. The paper had been ruled both ways, so that each single figure looked like a prisoner in a cell.

He thought: *Something else.*

Not just Walter's laughter. Something—a plan?

No, Gods, no—nothing as complex or hopeful as that.

But an idea, at least. A tickle.

How long have I been out? he thought with sudden alarm. *It was maybe nine o' the clock when I came through the door, maybe a little earlier. How long—?*

He *came forward.*

Jack Mort—who was now only a human doll controlled by the gunslinger—looked up a little and saw the hands of the expensive quartz clock on his desk stood at quarter past one.

Gods, as late as that? As late as that? But Eddie . . . he was so tired, he can never have stayed awake for so l—

The gunslinger turned Jack's head. The door was still there, but what he saw through it was far worse than he would have imagined.

Standing to one side of the door were two shadows, one that of the wheelchair, the other that of a human being . . . but the human being was incomplete, supporting itself on its arms because its lower legs had been snatched away with the same quick brutality as Roland's fingers and toe.

The shadow moved.

Roland whipped Jack Mort's head away at once, moving with the whiplash speed of a striking snake.

She mustn't look in. Not until I am ready. Until then, she sees nothing but the back of this man's head.

Detta Walker would not see Jack Mort in any case, because the person who looked through the open door saw only what the host saw. She could only see Mort's face if he looked into a mirror (although that might lead to its own awful consequences of paradox and repetition), but even then it would mean nothing to either Lady; for that matter, the Lady's face would not mean anything to Jack Mort. Although they had twice been on terms of deadly intimacy, they had never seen each other.

What the gunslinger didn't want was for the Lady to see the *Lady.*

Not yet, at least.

The spark of intuition grew closer to a plan.

But it was late over there—the light had suggested to him that it must be three in the afternoon, perhaps even four.

How long until sunset brought the lobstrosities, and the end of Eddie's life?

Three hours?

Two?

He could go back and try to save Eddie . . . but that was exactly what Detta wanted. She had laid a trap, just as villagers who fear a deadly wolf may stake out a sacrificial lamb to draw it into bowshot. He would go back into his diseased body . . . but not for long. The reason he had seen only her shadow was because she was lying beside the door with one of his revolvers curled in her fist. The moment his Roland-body moved, she would shoot it and end his life.

His ending, because she feared him, would at least be merciful.

Eddie's would be a screaming horror.

He seemed to hear Detta Walker's nasty, giggling voice: *You want to go at me, graymeat? Sho you want to go at me! You ain't afraid of no lil ole cripple black woman, are you?*

"Only one way," Jack's mouth muttered. "Only one."

The door of the office opened, and a bald man with lenses over his eyes looked in.

"How are you doing on that Dorfman account?" the bald man asked.

"I feel ill. I think it was my lunch. I think I might leave."

The bald man looked worried. "It's probably a bug. I heard there's a nasty one going around."

"Probably."

"Well . . . as long as you get the Dorfman stuff finished by five tomorrow afternoon . . ."

"Yes."

"Because you know what a dong he can be—"

"Yes."

The bald man, now looking a little uneasy, nodded. "Yes, go home. You don't seem like your usual self at all."

"I'm not."

The bald man went out the door in a hurry.

He sensed me, the gunslinger thought. *That was part of it. Part, but not all. They're afraid of him. They don't know why, but they're afraid of him. And they're right to be afraid.*

Jack Mort's body got up, found the briefcase the man had been carrying when the gunslinger entered him, and swept all the papers on the surface of the desk into it.

He felt an urge to sneak a look back at the door and

resisted it. He would not look again until he was ready to risk everything and come back.

In the meantime, time was short and there were things which had to be done.

CHAPTER 2
THE HONEYPOT

1

Detta laid up in a deeply shadowed cleft formed by rocks which leaned together like old men who had been turned to stone while sharing some weird secret. She watched Eddie range up and down the rubble-strewn slopes of the hills, yelling himself hoarse. The duck-fuzz on his cheeks was finally becoming a beard, and you might have taken him for a growed man except for the three or four times he passed close to her (once he had come close enough for her to have snaked a hand out and grabbed his ankle). When he got close you saw he wasn't nothing but a kid still, and one who was dog tired to boot.

Odetta would have felt pity; Detta felt only the still, coiled readiness of the natural predator.

When she first crawled in here she had felt things crackling under her hands like old autumn leaves in a woods holler. As her eyes adjusted she saw they weren't leaves but the tiny bones of small animals. Some predator, long gone if these ancient yellow bones told the truth, had once denned here, something like a weasel or a ferret. It had perhaps gone out at night, following its nose further up into The Drawers to where the trees and undergrowth were thicker—following its nose to prey. It had killed, eaten, and brought the remains back here to snack on the following day as it laid up, waiting for night to bring the time of hunting on again.

Now there was a bigger predator here, and at first Detta thought she'd do pretty much what the previous tenant had done: wait until Eddie fell asleep, as he was almost certain to do, then kill him and drag his body up here. Then, with both guns in her possession, she could drag herself back down by the doorway and wait for the Really Bad Man to come back. Her first thought had been to kill the Really Bad Man's body as soon as she had taken care of Eddie, but that was no good, was it? If the Really Bad Man had no body to come back to, there would be no way Detta could get out of here and back to her own world.

Could she make that Really Bad Man take her back?

Maybe not.

But maybe so.

If he knew Eddie was still alive, maybe so.

And that led to a much better idea.

2

She was deeply sly. She would have laughed harshly at anyone daring to suggest it, but she was also deeply insecure. Because of the latter, she attributed the former to anyone she met whose intellect seemed to approach her own. This was how she felt about the gunslinger. She had heard a shot, and when she looked she'd seen smoke drifting from the muzzle of his remaining gun. He had reloaded and tossed this gun to Eddie just before going through the door.

She knew what it was supposed to mean to Eddie: all the shells weren't wet after all; the gun would protect him. She *also* knew what it was supposed to mean to her (for of course the Really Bad Man had known she was watching; even if she had been sleeping when the two of them started chinning, the shot would have awakened her): *Stay away from him. He's packing iron.*

But devils could be subtle.

If that little show had been put on for her benefit, might not that Really Bad Man have had another purpose in mind as well, one *neither* she nor Eddie was supposed to see? Might that Really Bad Man not have been thinking *If she sees* this *one fires good shells, why, she'll think the one she took from Eddie does, too.*

But suppose he had guessed that Eddie would doze off? Wouldn't he know she would be waiting for just that, waiting to filch the gun and creep slowly away up the slopes to safety? Yes, that Really Bad Man might have foreseen all that. He was smart for a honky. Smart enough, anyway, to see that Detta was bound to get the best of that little white boy.

So just maybe that Really Bad Man had purposely loaded this gun with bad shells. He had fooled her once; why not again? This time she had been careful to check that the chambers were loaded with more than empty casings, and yes, they *appeared* to be real bullets, but that didn't mean they were. He didn't even have to take the chance that *one* of them might be dry enough to fire, now did he? He could have fixed them somehow. After all, guns were the Really Bad Man's business. Why would he do that? Why, to trick her into showing herself, of course! Then Eddie could cover her with the gun that really *did* work, and he would not make the same mistake twice, tired or not. He would, in fact, be especially careful not to make the same mistake twice because he *was* tired.

Nice try, honky, Detta thought in her shadowy den, this tight but somehow comforting dark place whose floor was carpeted with the softened and decaying bones of small animals. *Nice try, but I ain't goin fo dat shit.*

She didn't need to shoot Eddie, after all; she only needed to wait.

3

Her one fear was that the gunslinger would return before Eddie fell asleep, but he was still gone. The limp body at the base of the door did not stir. Maybe he was having some trouble getting the medicine he needed—some other kind of trouble, for all she knew. Men like him seemed to find trouble easy as a bitch in heat finds a randy hound.

Two hours passed while Eddie hunted for the woman he called "Odetta" (oh how she hated the sound of that name), ranging up and down the low hills and yelling until he had no voice left to yell with.

At last Eddie did what she had been waiting for: he went back down to the little angle of beach and sat by the wheelchair, looking around disconsolately. He touched one of the chair's wheels, and the touch was almost a caress. Then his hand dropped away and he fetched him a deep sigh.

This sight brought a steely ache to Detta's throat; pain bolted across her head from one side to the other like summer lightning and she seemed to hear a voice calling . . . calling or demanding.

No you don't, she thought, having no idea who she was thinking about or speaking to. *No you don't, not this time, not now. Not now, maybe not ever again.* That bolt of pain ripped through her head again and she curled her hands into fists. Her face made its own fist, twisting itself into a sneer of concentration—an expression remarkable and arresting in its mixture of ugliness and almost beatific determination.

That bolt of pain did not come again. Neither did the voice which sometimes seemed to speak through such pains.

She waited.

Eddie propped his chin on his fists, propping his

head up. Soon it began to droop anyway, the fists sliding up his cheeks. Detta waited, black eyes gleaming.

Eddie's head jerked up. He struggled to his feet,
walked down to the water, and splashed his face with
it.

*Dat's right, white boy. Crine shame there ain't any
No-Doz in this worl or you be takin dat too, ain't dat
right?*

Eddie sat down *in* the wheelchair this time, but ev-
idently found that just a little *too* comfortable. So,
after a long look through the open door *(what you
seein in dere, white boy? Detta give a twenty-dollar
bill to know* dat), he plopped his ass down on the sand
again.

Propped his head with his hands again.

Soon his head began to slip down again.

This time there was no stopping it. His chin lay on
his chest, and even over the surf she could hear him
snoring. Pretty soon he fell over on his side and curled
up.

She was surprised, disgusted, and frightened to feel
a sudden stab of pity for the white boy down there. He
looked like nothing so much as a little squirt who had
tried to stay up until midnight on New Year's Eve and
lost the race. Then she remembered the way he and
the Really Bad Man had tried to get her to eat poison
food and teased her with their own, always snatching
away at the last second . . . at least until they got
scared she might die.

*If they were scared you might die, why'd they try to
get you to eat poison in the first place?*

The question scared her the way that momentary
feeling of pity had scared her. She wasn't used to
questioning herself, and furthermore, the questioning
voice in her mind didn't seem like her voice at all.

Wadn't meanin to kill me wid dat poison food. Jes

*wanted to make me sick. Set there and laugh while I
puked an moaned, I speck.*

She waited twenty minutes and then started down
toward the beach, pulling herself with her hands and
strong arms, weaving like a snake, eyes never leaving
Eddie. She would have preferred to have waited another hour, even another half; it would be better to
have the little mahfah ten miles asleep instead of one
or two. But waiting was a luxury she simply could not
afford. That Really Bad Man might come back anytime.

As she drew near the place where Eddie lay (he was
still snoring, sounded like a buzzsaw in a sawmill
about to go tits up), she picked up a chunk of rock
that was satisfyingly smooth on one side and satisfyingly jagged on the other.

She closed her palm over the smooth side and continued her snake-crawl to where he lay, the flat sheen
of murder in her eyes.

4

What Detta planned to do was brutally simple:
smash Eddie with the jagged side of the rock until he
was as dead as the rock itself. Then she'd take the gun
and wait for Roland to come back.

When his body sat up, she would give him a choice:
take her back to her world or refuse and be killed. *You
goan be quits wid me either way, toots,* she would say,
*and wit yo boyfrien dead, ain't nothin more you can
do like you said you wanted to.*

If the gun the Really Bad Man had given Eddie didn't
work—it was possible; she had never met a man she
hated and feared as much as Roland, and she put no
depth of slyness past him—she would do him just the
same. She would do him with the rock or with her

bare hands. He was sick and shy two fingers to boot.
She could take him.

But as she approached Eddie, a disquieting thought
came to her. It was another question, and again it
seemed to be another voice that asked it.

*What if he knows? What if he knows what you did
the second you kill Eddie?*

*He ain't goan know nuthin. He be too busy gittin his
medicine. Gittin hisself laid, too, for all I know.*

The alien voice did not respond, but the seed of
doubt had been planted. She had heard them talking
when they thought she was asleep. The Really Bad
Man needed to do something. She didn't know what
it was. Had something to do with a tower was all Detta
knew. Could be the Really Bad Man thought this tower
was full of gold or jewels or something like that. He
said he needed her and Eddie and some other one to
get there, and Detta guessed maybe he did. Why else
would these doors be here?

If it was magic and she killed Eddie, he *might* know.
If she killed his way to the tower, she thought she
might be killing the only thing graymeat mahfah was
living for. And if he knew he had nothing to live for,
mahfah might do anything, because the mahfah
wouldn't give a bug-turd for nothin no more.

The idea of what might happen if the Really Bad
Man came back like that made Detta shiver.

But if she couldn't kill Eddie, what was she going
to do? She could take the gun while Eddie was asleep,
but when the Really Bad Man came back, could she
handle both of them?

She just didn't know.

Her eyes touched on the wheelchair, started to move
away, then moved back again, fast. There was a deep
pocket in the leather backrest. Poking out of this was
a curl of the rope they had used to tie her into the
chair.

Looking at it, she understood how she could do everything.

Detta changed course and began to crawl toward the gunslinger's inert body. She meant to take what she needed from the knapsack he called his "purse," then get the rope, fast as she could . . . but for a moment she was held frozen by the door.

Like Eddie, she interpreted what she was seeing in terms of the movies . . . only this looked more like some TV crime show. The setting was a drug-store. She was seeing a druggist who looked scared silly, and Detta didn't blame him. There was a gun pointing straight into the druggist's face. The druggist was saying something, but his voice was distant, distorted, as if heard through sound-baffles. She couldn't tell what it was. She couldn't see who was holding the gun, either, but then, she didn't really need to see the stick-up man, did she? She knew who it was, sho.

It was the Really Bad Man.

Might not look *like him over there, might look like some tubby little sack of shit, might even look like a brother, but inside it* be *him, sho. Didn't take him long to find another gun, did it? I bet it never does. You get movin, Detta Walker.*

She opened Roland's purse, and the faint, nostalgic aroma of tobacco long hoarded but now long gone drifted out. In one way it was very much like a lady's purse, filled with what looked like so much random rickrack at first glance . . . but a closer look showed you the travelling gear of a man prepared for almost any contingency.

She had an idea the Really Bad Man had been on the road to his Tower a good long time. If that was so, just the amount of stuff still left in here, poor as some of it was, was cause for amazement.

You get movin, Detta Walker.

She got what she needed and worked her silent,

snakelike way back to the wheelchair. When she got there she propped herself on one arm and pulled the rope out of the pocket like a fisherwoman reeling in line. She glanced over at Eddie every now and then just to make sure he was asleep.

He never stirred until Detta threw the noose around his neck and pulled it taut.

5

He was dragged backward, at first thinking he was still asleep and this was some horrible nightmare of being buried alive or perhaps smothered.

Then he felt the pain of the noose sinking into his throat, felt warm spit running down his chin as he gagged. This was no dream. He clawed at the rope and tried for his feet.

She yanked him hard with her strong arms. Eddie fell on his back with a thud. His face was turning purple.

"Quit on it!" Detta hissed from behind him. "I ain't goan kill you if you quit on it, but if you don't, I'm goan choke you dead."

Eddie lowered his hands and tried to be still. The running slipknot Odetta had tossed over his neck loosened enough for him to draw a thin, burning breath. All you could say for it was that it was better than not breathing at all.

When the panicked beating of his heart had slowed a little, he tried to look around. The noose immediately drew tight again.

"Nev' mind. You jes go on an take in dat ocean view, graymeat. Dat's all you want to be lookin at right now."

He looked back at the ocean and the knot loosened enough to allow him those miserly burning breaths again. His left hand crept surreptitiously down to the waistband of his pants (but she saw the movement, and although he didn't know it, she was grinning). There was nothing there. She had taken the gun.

She crept up on you while you were asleep, Eddie. It was the gunslinger's voice, of course. *It doesn't do any good to say I told you so now, but . . . I told you so. This is what romance gets you—a noose around your neck and a crazy woman with two guns somewhere behind you.*

But if she was going to kill me, she already would have done it. She would have done it while I was asleep.

And what is it you think *she's going to do, Eddie? Hand you an all-expenses-paid trip for two to Disney World?*

"Listen," he said. "Odetta—"

The word was barely out of his mouth before the noose pulled savagely tight again.

"You doan want to be callin me dat. Nex time you be callin me dat be de las time you be callin anyone *anythin*. My name's *Detta Walker*, and if you want to keep drawin breaf into yo lungs, you little piece of whitewashed shit, you better member it!"

Eddie made choking, gagging noises and clawed at the noose. Big black spots of nothing began to explode in front of his eyes like evil flowers.

At last the choking band around his throat eased again.

"Got dat, honky?"

"Yes," he said, but it was only a hoarse choke of sound.

"Den say it. Say my name."

"Detta."

"Say my *whole* name!" Dangerous hysteria wavered in her voice, and at that moment Eddie was glad he couldn't see her.

"Detta Walker."

"Good." The noose eased a little more. "Now you lissen to me, whitebread, and you do it good, if you want to live til sundown. You don't want to be trine to be cute, like I seen you jus trine t'snake down an git dat gun I took off'n you while you was asleep. You don't want to cause Detta, she got the sight. See what you goan try befo you try it. Sho.

"You don't want to try nuthin cute cause I ain't got no legs, either. I have learned to do a lot of things since I lost em, and now I got *both* o dat honky mah-fah's guns, and dat ought to go for somethin. You think so?"

"Yeah," Eddie croaked. "I'm not feeling cute."

"Well, good. Dat's *real* good." She cackled. "I been one busy bitch while you been sleepin. Got dis bidness all figured out. Here's what I want you to do, whitebread: put yo hands behin you and feel aroun until you find a loop jus like d'one I got roun yo neck. There be three of em. I been braidin while you been sleepin, lazybones!" She cackled again. "When you feel dat loop, you goan put yo wrists right one against t'other an slip em through it.

"Den you goan feel my hand pullin that runnin knot tight, and when you feel *dat,* you goan say 'Dis my chance to toin it aroun on disyere nigger bitch. Right here, while she ain't got her good hold on dat jerk-rope.' But—" Here Detta's voice became muffled as well as a Southern darkie caricature. "—you better take a look aroun befo you go doin anythin *rash."*

Eddie did. Detta looked more witchlike than ever, a dirty, matted thing that would have struck fear into hearts much stouter than his own. The dress she had been wearing in Macy's when the gunslinger snatched her was now filthy and torn. She'd used the knife she had taken from the gunslinger's purse—the one he and Roland had used to cut the masking tape away—to slash her dress in two other places, creating makeshift

holsters just above the swell of her hips. The worn
butts of the gunslinger's revolvers protruded from
them.

Her voice was muffled because the end of the rope
was clenched in her teeth. A freshly cut end protruded
from one side of her grin; the rest of the line, the part
which led to the noose around his neck, protruded
from the other side. There was something so predatory
and barbaric about this image—the rope caught in the
grin—that he was frozen, staring at her with a horror
that only made her grin widen.

"You try to be cute while I be takin care of yo
hans," she said in her muffled voice, "I goan joik yo
win'pipe shut wif my *teef*, graymeat. And *dat* time I
not be lettin up agin. You understan?"

He didn't trust himself to speak. He only nodded.

"Good. Maybe you be livin a little bit longer after
all."

"If I don't," Eddie croaked, "you're never going
to have the pleasure of shoplifting in Macy's again,
Detta. Because he'll know, and then it'll be everybody
out of the pool."

"Hush up," Detta said . . . almost crooned. "You
jes hush up. Leave the thinkin to the folks dat kin do
it. All *you* got to do is be feelin aroun fo dat next
loop."

6

I been braidin while you been sleepin, she had said,
and with disgust and mounting alarm, Eddie discovered she meant exactly what she said. The rope had
become a series of three running slip-knots. The first
she had noosed around his neck as he slept. The second secured his hands behind his back. Then she
pushed him roughly over on his side and told him to
bring his feet up until his heels touched his butt. He

saw where this was leading and balked. She pulled one
of Roland's revolvers from the slit in her dress, cocked
it, and pressed the muzzle against Eddie's temple.

"You do it or *I* do it, graymeat," she said in that
crooning voice. "Only if *I* do it, you goan be dead
when I do. I jes kick some san' over de brains dat
squoit out d'other side yo haid, cover de hole wit yo
hair. He think you be sleepin!" She cackled again.

Eddie brought his feet up, and she quickly secured
the third running slip-knot around his ankles.

"There. Trussed up just as neat as a calf at a ro-
day-o."

That described it as well as anything, Eddie thought.
If he tried to bring his feet down from a position which
was already growing uncomfortable, he would tighten
the slipknot holding his ankles even more. That would
tighten the length of rope between his ankles and his
wrists, which would in turn tighten *that* slipknot, and
the rope between his wrists and the noose she'd put
around his neck, and . . .

She was dragging him, somehow dragging him down
the beach.

"Hey! What—"

He tried to pull back and felt everything tighten—
including his ability to draw breath. He let himself go
as limp as possible (and keep those feet up, don't forget that, asshole, because if you lower your feet enough
you're going to strangle) and let her drag him along
the rough ground. A jag of rock peeled skin away from
his cheek, and he felt warm blood begin to flow. She
was panting harshly. The sound of the waves and the
boom of surf ramming into the rock tunnel were
louder.

*Drown me? Sweet Christ, is that what she means to
do?*

No, of course not. He thought he knew what she
meant to do even before his face plowed through the

twisted kelp which marked the high-tide line, dead salt-stinking stuff as cold as the fingers of drowned sailors.

He remembered Henry saying once, *Sometimes they'd shoot one of our guys. An American, I mean— they knew an ARVN was no good, because wasn't any of us that'd go after a gook in the bush. Not unless he was some fresh fish just over from the States. They'd guthole him, leave him screaming, then pick off the guys that tried to save him. They'd keep doing that until the guy died. You know what they called a guy like that, Eddie?*

Eddie had shaken his head, cold with the vision of it.

They called him a honey-pot, Henry had said. *Something sweet. Something to draw flies. Or maybe even a bear.*

That's what Detta was doing: using him as a honey-pot.

She left him some seven feet below the high-tide line, left him without a word, left him facing the ocean. It was not the tide coming in to drown him that the gunslinger, looking through the door, was supposed to see, because the tide was on the ebb and wouldn't get up this far again for another six hours. And long before then . . .

Eddie rolled his eyes up a little and saw the sun striking a long gold track across the ocean. What was it? Four o'clock? About that. Sunset would come around seven.

It would be dark long before he had to worry about the tide.

And when dark came, the lobstrosities would come rolling out of the waves; they would crawl their questioning way up the beach to where he lay helplessly trussed, and then they would tear him apart.

7

That time stretched out interminably for Eddie Dean. The idea of time itself became a joke. Even his horror of what was going to happen to him when it got dark faded as his legs began to throb with a discomfort which worked its way up the scale of feeling to pain and finally to shrieking agony. He would relax his muscles, all the knots would pull tight, and when he was on the verge of strangling he would manage somehow to pull his ankles up again, releasing the pressure, allowing some breath to return. He was no longer sure he could make it to dark. There might come a time when he would simply be unable to bring his legs back up.

CHAPTER 3
ROLAND TAKES HIS MEDICINE

1

Now Jack Mort knew the gunslinger was here. If he had been another person—an Eddie Dean or an Odetta Walker, for instance—Roland would have held palaver with the man, if only to ease his natural panic and confusion at suddenly finding one's self shoved rudely into the passenger seat of the body one's brain had driven one's whole life.

But because Mort was a monster—worse than Detta Walker ever had been or could be—he made no effort to explain or speak at all. He could hear the man's clamorings—*Who are you? What's happening to me?*—but disregarded them. The gunslinger concentrated on his short list of necessities, using the man's mind with no compunction at all. The clamorings became screams of terror. The gunslinger went right on disregarding them.

The only way he could remain in the worm-pit which was this man's mind was to regard him as no more than a combination atlas and encyclopedia. Mort had all the information Roland needed. The plan he made was rough, but rough was often better than smooth. When it came to planning, there were no creatures in the universe more different than Roland and Jack Mort.

When you planned rough, you allowed room for improvisation. And improvisation at short notice had always been one of Roland's strong points.

2

A fat man with lenses over his eyes, like the bald man who had poked his head into Mort's office five minutes earlier (it seemed that in Eddie's world many people wore these, which his Mortcypedia identified as "glasses"), got into the elevator with him. He looked at the briefcase in the hand of the man who he believed to be Jack Mort and then at Mort himself.

"Going to see Dorfman, Jack?"

The gunslinger said nothing.

"If you think you can talk him out of sub-leasing, I can tell you it's a waste of time," the fat man said, then blinked as his colleague took a quick step backward. The doors of the little box closed and suddenly they were falling.

He clawed at Mort's mind, ignoring the screams, and found this was all right. The fall was controlled.

"If I spoke out of turn, I'm sorry," the fat man said. The gunslinger thought: *This one is afraid, too.* "You've handled the jerk better than anyone else in the firm, that's what I think."

The gunslinger said nothing. He waited only to be out of this falling coffin.

"I say so, too," the fat man continued eagerly. "Why, just yesterday I was at lunch with—"

Jack Mort's head turned, and behind Jack Mort's gold-rimmed glasses, eyes that seemed a somehow different shade of blue than Jack's eyes had ever been before stared at the fat man. "Shut up," the gunslinger said tonelessly.

Color fell from the fat man's face and he took two quick steps backward. His flabby buttocks smacked the fake wood panels at the back of the little moving coffin, which suddenly stopped. The doors opened and the gunslinger, wearing Jack Mort's body like a tight-fitting set of clothes, stepped out with no look back.

The fat man held his finger on the DOOR OPEN button of the elevator and waited inside until Mort was out of sight. *Always did have a screw loose*, the fat man thought, *but this could be serious. This could be a breakdown.*

The fat man found that the idea of Jack Mort tucked safely away in a sanitarium somewhere was very comforting.

The gunslinger wouldn't have been surprised.

3

Somewhere between the echoing room which his Mortcypedia identified as a *lobby,* to wit, a place of entry and exit from the offices which filled this skytower, and the bright sunshine of street (his Mortcypedia identified this street as both *6th Avenue* and *Avenue of the Americas*), the screaming of Roland's host stopped. Mort had not died of fright; the gunslinger felt with a deep instinct which was the same as knowing that if Mort died, their *kas* would be expelled forever, into that void of possibility which lay beyond all physical worlds. Not dead—fainted. Fainted at the overload of terror and strangeness, as Roland himself had done upon entering the man's mind and discovering its secrets and the crossing of destinies too great to be coincidence.

He was glad Mort had fainted. As long as the man's unconsciousness hadn't affected Roland's access to the man's knowledge and memories—and it hadn't—he was glad to have him out of the way.

The yellow cars were public conveyences called *Tack-Sees* or *Cabs* or *Hax*. The tribes which drove them, the Mortcypedia told him, were two: *Spix* and *Mockies*. To make one stop, you held your hand up like a pupil in a classroom.

Roland did this, and after several *Tack-Sees* which

were obviously empty save for their drivers had gone
by him, he saw that these had signs which read *Off-
Duty*. Since these were Great Letters, the gunslinger
didn't need Mort's help. He waited, then put his hand
up again. This time the *Tack-See* pulled over. The gunslinger got into the back seat. He smelled old smoke,
old sweat, old perfume. It smelled like a coach in his
own world.

"Where to, my friend?" the driver asked—Roland
had no idea if he was of the *Spix* or *Mockies* tribe, and
had no intention of asking. It might be impolite in this
world.

"I'm not sure," Roland said.

"This ain't no encounter group, my friend. Time is
money."

Tell him to put his flag down, the Mortcypedia told
him.

"Put your flag down," Roland said.

"That ain't rolling nothing but time," the driver
replied.

Tell him you'll tip him five bux, the Mortcypedia
advised.

"I'll tip you five bucks," Roland said.

"Let's see it," the cabbie replied. "Money talks,
bullshit walks."

*Ask him if he wants his money or if he wants to go
fuck himself,* the Mortcypedia advised instantly.

"Do you want the money, or do you want to go fuck
yourself?" Roland asked in a cold, dead voice.

The cabbie's eyes glanced apprehensively into the
rearview mirror for just a moment, and he said no
more.

Roland consulted Jack Mort's accumulated store of
knowledge more fully this time. The cabbie glanced
up again, quickly, during the fifteen seconds his fare
spent simply sitting there with his head slightly lowered and his left hand spread across his brow, as if he

had an Excedrin Headache. The cabbie had decided to tell the guy to get out or he'd yell for a cop when the fare looked up and said mildly, "I'd like you to take me to Seventh Avenue and Forty-Ninth street. For this trip I will pay you ten dollars over the fare on your taxi meter, no matter what your tribe."

A weirdo, the driver (a WASP from Vermont trying to break into showbiz) thought, *but maybe a* rich *weirdo.* He dropped the cab into gear. "We're there, buddy," he said, and pulling into traffic he added mentally, *And the sooner the better.*

4

Improvise. That was the word.

The gunslinger saw the blue-and-white parked down the block when he got out, and read *Police* as *Posse* without checking Mort's store of knowledge. Two gunslingers inside, drinking something—coffee, maybe—from white paper glasses. Gunslingers, yes—but they looked fat and lax.

He reached into Jack Mort's wallet (except it was much too small to be a *real* wallet; a *real* wallet was almost as big as a purse and could carry all of a man's things, if he wasn't travelling too heavy) and gave the driver a bill with the number 20 on it. The cabbie drove away fast. It was easily the biggest tip he'd make that day, but the guy was so freaky he felt he had earned every cent of it.

The gunslinger looked at the sign over the shop.

CLEMENTS GUNS AND SPORTING GOODS, it said. AMMO, FISHING TACKLE, OFFICIAL FACSIMILES.

He didn't understand all of the words, but one look in the window was all it took for him to see Mort had brought him to the right place. There were wristbands on display, badges of rank . . . and guns. Rifles, mostly, but pistols as well. They were chained, but that didn't matter.

He would know what he needed when—*if*—he saw it.

Roland consulted Jack Mort's mind—a mind exactly sly enough to suit his purposes—for more than a minute.

5

One of the cops in the blue-and-white elbowed the other. "Now that," he said, "is a *serious* comparison shopper."

His partner laughed. "Oh *God*," he said in an effeminate voice as the man in the business suit and gold-rimmed glasses finished his study of the merchandise on display and went inside. "I think he jutht dethided on the *lavender* handcuffths."

The first cop choked on a mouthful of lukewarm coffee and sprayed it back into the styrofoam cup in a gust of laughter.

6

A clerk came over almost at once and asked if he could be of help.

"I wonder," the man in the conservative blue suit replied, "if you have a paper . . ." He paused, appeared to think deeply, and then looked up. "A *chart*, I mean, which shows pictures of revolver ammunition."

"You mean a caliber chart?" the clerk asked.

The customer paused, then said, "Yes. My brother has a revolver. I have fired it, but it's been a good many years. I think I will know the bullets if I see them."

"Well, you may think so," the clerk replied, "but

it can be hard to tell. Was it a .22? A .38? Or maybe—"

"If you have a chart, I'll know," Roland said.

"Just a sec." The clerk looked at the man in the blue suit doubtfully for a moment, then shrugged. Fuck, the customer was always right, even when he was wrong . . . if he had the dough to pay, that was. Money talked, bullshit walked. "I got a *Shooter's Bible*. Maybe that's what you ought to look at."

"Yes." He smiled. *Shooter's Bible*. It was a noble name for a book.

The man rummaged under the counter and brought out a well-thumbed volume as thick as any book the gunslinger had ever seen in his life—and yet this man seemed to handle it as if it were no more valuable than a handful of stones.

He opened it on the counter and turned it around. "Take a look. Although if it's been years, you're shootin' in the dark." He looked surprised, then smiled. "Pardon my pun."

Roland didn't hear. He was bent over the book, studying pictures which seemed almost as real as the things they represented, marvellous pictures the Mortcypedia identified as *Fottergraffs*.

He turned the pages slowly. No . . . no . . . no . . .

He had almost lost hope when he saw it. He looked up at the clerk with such blazing excitement that the clerk felt a little afraid.

"There!" he said. "There! *Right there!*"

The photograph he was tapping was one of a Winchester .45 pistol shell. It was not exactly the same as his own shells, because it hadn't been hand-thrown or hand-loaded, but he could see without even consulting the figures (which would have meant almost nothing to him anyway) that it would chamber and fire from his guns.

"Well, all right, I guess you found it," the clerk

said, "but don't cream your jeans, fella. I mean, they're just *bullets*."

"You have them?"

"Sure. How many boxes do you want?"

"How many in a box?"

"Fifty." The clerk began to look at the gunslinger with real suspicion. If the guy was planning to buy shells, he must know he'd have to show a Permit to Carry photo-I.D. No P.C., no ammo, not for hand-guns; it was the law in the borough of Manhattan. And if this dude had a handgun permit, how come he didn't know how many shells came in a standard box of ammo?

"Fifty!" Now the guy was staring at him with slack-jawed surprise. He was off the wall, all right.

The clerk edged a bit to his left, a bit nearer the cash register . . . and, not so coincidentally, a bit nearer to his own gun, a .357 Mag which he kept fully loaded in a spring clip under the counter.

"Fifty!" the gunslinger repeated. He had expected five, ten, perhaps as many as a dozen, but this . . . this . . .

How much money do you have? he asked the Mort-cypedia. The Mortcypedia didn't know, not exactly, but thought there was at least sixty bux in his wallet.

"And how much does a box cost?" It would be more than sixty dollars, he supposed, but the man might be persuaded to sell him *part* of a box, or—

"Seventeen-fifty," the clerk said. "But, mister—"

Jack Mort was an accountant, and this time there was no waiting; translation and answer came simulta-neously.

"Three," the gunslinger said. "Three boxes." He tapped the *Fotergraff* of the shells with one finger. One hundred and fifty rounds! Ye gods! What a mad store-house of riches this world was!

The clerk wasn't moving.

"You don't have that many," the gunslinger said. He felt no real surprise. It had been too good to be true. A dream.

"Oh, I got Winchester .45s I got .45s up the kazoo." The clerk took another step to the left, a step closer to the cash register and the gun. If the guy was a nut, something the clerk expected to find out for sure any second now, he was soon going to be a nut with an extremely large hole in his midsection. "I got .45 ammo up the old ying-yang. What I want to know, mister, is if *you* got the card."

"Card?"

"A handgun permit with a photo. I can't sell you handgun ammo unless you can show me one. If you want to buy ammo without a P.C., you're gonna hafta go up to Westchester."

The gunslinger stared at the man blankly. This was all gabble to him. He understood none of it. His Mortcypedia had some vague notion of what the man meant, but Mort's ideas were too vague to be trusted in this case. Mort had never owned a gun in his life. He did his nasty work in other ways.

The man sidled another step to the left without taking his eyes from his customer's face and the gunslinger thought: *He's got a gun. He expects me to make trouble . . . or maybe he wants me to make trouble. Wants an excuse to shoot me.*

Improvise.

He remembered the gunslingers sitting in their blue and white carriage down the street. Gunslingers, yes, peacekeepers, men charged with keeping the world from moving on. But these had looked—at least on a passing glance—to be nearly as soft and unobservant as everyone else in this world of lotus-eaters; just two men in uniforms and caps, slouched down in the seats of their carriage, drinking coffee. He might have misjudged. He hoped for all their sakes—that he had not.

"Oh! I understand," the gunslinger said, and drew an apologetic smile on Jack Mort's face. "I'm sorry. I guess I haven't kept track of how much the world has moved on—changed—since I last owned a gun."

"No harm done," the clerk said, relaxing minutely. Maybe the guy was all right. Or maybe he was pulling a gag.

"I wonder if I could look at that cleaning kit?" Roland pointed to a shelf behind the clerk.

"Sure." The clerk turned to get it, and when he did, the gunslinger removed the wallet from Mort's inside jacket pocket. He did this with the flickering speed of a fast draw. The clerk's back was to him for less than four seconds, but when he turned back to Mort, the wallet was on the floor.

"It's a beaut," the clerk said, smiling, having decided the guy was okay after all. Hell, he knew how lousy you felt when you made a horse's ass of yourself. He had done it in the Marines enough times. "And you don't need a goddam permit to buy a cleaning kit, either. Ain't freedom wonderful?"

"Yes," the gunslinger said seriously, and pretended to look closely at the cleaning kit, although a single glance was enough to show him that it was a shoddy thing in a shoddy box. While he looked, he carefully pushed Mort's wallet under the counter with his foot.

After a moment he pushed it back with a passable show of regret. "I'm afraid I'll have to pass."

"All right," the clerk said, losing interest abruptly. Since the guy wasn't crazy and was obviously a looker, not a buyer, their relationship was at an end. Bullshit walks. "Anything else?" His mouth asked while his eyes told blue-suit to get out.

"No, thank you." The gunslinger walked out with a look back. Mort's wallet was deep under the counter. Roland had set out his own honeypot.

Officers Carl Delevan and George O'Mearah had finished their coffee and were about to move on when the man in the blue suit came out of Clements'—which both cops believed to be a powderhorn (police slang for a legal gunshop which sometimes sells guns to independent stick-up men with proven credentials and which does business, sometimes in bulk, to the Mafia), and approached their squad car.

He leaned down and looked in the passenger side window at O'Mearah. O'Mearah expected the guy to sound like a fruit—probably as fruity as his routine about the lavender handcuffths had suggested, but a pouf all the same. Guns aside, Clements' did a lively trade in handcuffs. These were legal in Manhattan, and most of the people buying them weren't amateur Houdinis (the cops didn't like it, but when had what the cops thought on any given subject *ever* changed things?). The buyers were homos with a little taste for s & m. But the man didn't sound like a fag at all. His voice was flat and expressionless, polite but somehow dead.

"The tradesman in there took my wallet," he said.

"*Who?*" O'Mearah straightened up fast. They had been itching to bust Justin Clements for a year and a half. If it could be done, maybe the two of them could finally swap these bluesuits for detectives' badges. Probably just a pipe-dream—this was too good to be true—but just the same . . .

"The tradesman. The—" A brief pause. "The clerk."

O'Mearah and Carl Delevan exchanged a glance.

"Black hair?" Delevan asked. "On the stocky side?"

Again there was the briefest pause. "Yes. His eyes were brown. Small scar under one of them."

There was something about the guy . . . O'Mearah couldn't put his finger on it then, but remembered later on, when there weren't so many other things to think about. The chief of which, of course, was the simple fact that the gold detective's badge didn't matter; it turned out that just holding onto the jobs they had would be a pure brassy-ass miracle.

But years later there was a brief moment of epiphany when O'Mearah took his two sons to the Museum of Science in Boston. They had a machine there—a computer—that played tic-tac-toe, and unless you put your X in the middle square on your first move, the machine fucked you over every time. But there was always a pause as it checked its memory for all possible gambits. He and his boys had been fascinated. But there was something spooky about it . . . and then he remembered Blue-Suit. He remembered because Blue-Suit had had that some fucking habit. Talking to him had been like talking to a robot.

Delevan had no such feeling, but nine years later, when he took his own son (then eighteen and about to start college) to the movies one night, Delevan would rise unexpectedly to his feet about thirty minutes into the feature and scream, *"It's him! That's HIM! That's the guy in the fucking blue suit! The guy who was at Cle—"*

Somebody would shout *Down in front!* but needn't have bothered; Delevan, seventy pounds overweight and a heavy smoker, would be struck by a fatal heart attack before the complainer even got to the second word. The man in the blue suit who approached their cruiser that day and told them about his stolen wallet didn't look like the star of the movie, but the dead delivery of words had been the same; so had been the somehow relentless yet graceful way he moved.

The movie, of course, had been *The Terminator.*

8

The cops exchanged a glance. The man Blue-Suit was talking about wasn't Clements, but almost as good: "Fat Johnny" Holden, Clements' brother-in-law. But to have done something as totally dumb-ass as simply stealing a guy's wallet would be—

—*would be right up that gink's alley,* O'Mearah's mind finished, and he had to put a hand to his mouth to cover a momentary little grin.

"Maybe you better tell us exactly what happened," Delevan said. "You can start with your name."

Again, the man's response struck O'Mearah as a little wrong, a little off-beat. In this city, where it sometimes seemed that seventy per cent of the population believed *Go fuck yourself* was American for *Have a nice day,* he would have expected the guy to say something like, *Hey, that S.O.B. took my wallet! Are you going to get it back for me or are we going to stand out here playing Twenty Questions?*

But there was the nicely cut suit, the manicured fingernails. A guy maybe used to dealing with bureaucratic bullshit. In truth, George O'Mearah didn't care much. The thought of busting Fat Johnny Holden and using him as a lever on Arnold Clements made O'Mearah's mouth water. For one dizzy moment he even allowed himself to imagine using Holden to get Clements and Clements to get one of the really big guys—that wop Balazar, for instance, or maybe Ginelli. That wouldn't be too tacky. Not too tacky at *all.*

"My name is Jack Mort," the man said.

Delevan had taken a butt-warped pad from his back pocket. "Address?"

That slight pause. *Like the machine,* O'Mearah thought again. A moment of silence, then an almost audible click.

"409 Park Avenue South."

Delevan jotted it down.

"Social Security number?"

After another slight pause, Mort recited it.

"Want you to understand I gotta ask you these questions for identification purposes. If the guy *did* take your wallet, it's nice if I can say you told me certain stuff before I take it into my possession. You understand."

"Yes." Now there was the slightest hint of impatience in the man's voice. It made O'Mearah feel a little better about him somehow. "Just don't drag it out any more than you have to. Time passes, and—"

"Things have a way of happening, yeah, I dig."

"Things have a way of happening," the man in the blue suit agreed. "Yes."

"Do you have a photo in your wallet that's distinctive?"

A pause. Then: "A picture of my mother taken in front of the Empire State Building. On the back is written: 'It was a wonderful day and a wonderful view. Love, Mom.'"

Delevan jotted furiously, then snapped his notebook closed. "Okay. That should do it. Only other thing'll be to have you write your signature if we get the wallet back and compare it with the sigs on your driver's license, credit cards, stuff like that. Okay?"

Roland nodded, although part of him understood that, although he could draw on Jack Mort's memories and knowledge of this world as much as he needed, he hadn't a chance in hell of duplicating Mort's signature with Mort's consciousness absent, as it was now.

"Tell us what happened."

"I went in to buy shells for my brother. He has a .45 Winchester revolver. The man asked me if I had a Permit to Carry. I said of course. He asked to see it."

Pause.

"I took out my wallet. I showed him. Only when I turned my wallet around to do that showing, he must have seen there were quite a few—" slight pause "twenties in there. I am a tax accountant. I have a client named Dorfman who just won a small tax refund after an extended—" pause "—litigation. The sum was only eight hundred dollars, but this man, Dorfman, is—" pause "—the biggest prick we handle." Pause. "Pardon my pun."

O'Mearah ran the man's last few words back through his head and suddenly got it. The biggest prick we handle. Not bad. He laughed. Thoughts of robots and machines that played tic-tac-toe went out of his mind. The guy was real enough, just upset and trying to hide it by being cool.

"Anyway, Dorfman wanted cash. He *insisted* on cash."

"You think Fat Johnny got a look at your client's dough," Delevan said. He and O'Mearah got out of the blue-and-white.

"Is that what you call the man in that shop?"

"Oh, we call him worse than that on occasion," Delevan said. "What happened after you showed him your P.C., Mr. Mort?"

"He asked for a closer look. I gave him my wallet but he didn't look at the picture. He dropped it on the floor. I asked him what he did that for. He said that was a stupid question. Then I told him to give me back my wallet. I was mad."

"I bet you were." Although, looking at the man's dead face, Delevan thought you'd never guess this man could get mad.

"He laughed. I started to come around the counter and get it. That was when he pulled the gun."

They had been walking toward the shop. Now they stopped. They looked excited rather than fearful.

"Gun?" O'Mearah asked, wanting to be sure he had heard right.

"It was under the counter, by the cash register," the man in the blue suit said. Roland remembered the moment when he had almost junked his original plan and gone for the man's weapon. Now he told these gunslingers why he hadn't. He wanted to use them, not get them killed. "I think it was in a docker's clutch."

"A *what?*" O'Mearah asked.

A longer pause this time. The man's forehead wrinkled. "I don't know exactly how to say it . . . a thing you put your gun into. No one can grab it but you unless they know how to push—"

"A spring-clip!" Delevan said. "Holy shit!" Another exchange of glances between the partners. Neither wanted to be the first to tell this guy that Fat Johnny had probably harvested the cash from his wallet already, shucked his buns out the back door, and tossed it over the wall of the alley behind the building . . . but a gun in a spring-clip . . . that was different. Robbery was a possible, but all at once a concealed weapons charge looked like a sure thing. Maybe not as good, but a foot in the door.

"What then?" O'Mearah asked.

"Then he told me I didn't have a wallet. He said—" pause "—that I got my picket pocked—my pocket picked, I mean—on the street and I'd better remember it if I wanted to stay healthy. I remembered seeing a police car parked up the block and I thought you might still be there. So I left."

"Okay," Delevan said. "Me and my partner are going in first, and fast. Give us about a minute—a *full* minute—just in case there's some trouble. Then come in, but stand by the door. Do you understand?"

"Yes."

"Okay. Let's bust this motherfucker."

The two cops went in. Roland waited thirty seconds and then followed them.

9

"Fat Johnny" Holden was doing more than protesting. He was bellowing.

"Guy's crazy! Guy comes in here, doesn't even know what he wants, then, when he sees it in the *Shooter's Bible,* he don't know how many comes in a box, how much they cost, and what he says about me wantin' a closer look at his P.C. is the biggest pile of shit I ever heard, because he don't *have* no Permit to—" Fat Johnny broke off. "There he is! There's the creep! Right there! I see you, buddy! I see your face! Next time you see mine you're gonna be fuckin sorry! I guarantee you that! I fuckin guarantee—"

"You don't have this man's wallet?" O'Mearah asked.

"You *know* I don't have his wallet!"

"You mind if we take a look behind this display case?" Delevan countered. "Just to be sure?"

"Jesus-fuckin-jumped-up-Christ-on-a-pony! The case is *glass!* You see any wallets there?"

"No, not *there* . . . I meant *here,*" Delevan said, moving toward the register. His voice was a cat's purr. At this point a chrome-steel reinforcing strip almost two feet wide ran down the shelves of the case. Delevan looked back at the man in the blue suit, who nodded.

"I want you guys out of here right now," Fat Johnny said. He had lost some of his color. "You come back with a warrant, that's different. But for now, I want you the fuck out. Still a free fuckin country, you kn— hey! *hey!* HEY, QUIT THAT!"

O'Mearah was peering over the counter.

"That's illegal!" Fat Johnny was howling. *"That's*

*fuckin illegal, the Constitution . . . my fuckin lawyer
. . . you get back on your side right now or—"*

"I just wanted a closer look at the merchandise,"
O'Mearah said mildly, "on account of the glass in
your display case is so fucking dirty. That's why I
looked over. Isn't it, Carl?"

"True shit, buddy," Delevan said solemnly.

"And look what *I* found."

Roland heard a *click,* and suddenly the gunslinger
in the blue uniform was holding an extremely large
gun in his hand.

Fat Johnny, who had finally realized he was the only
person in the room who would tell a story that differed
from the fairy tale just told by the cop who had taken
his Mag, turned sullen.

"I got a permit," he said.

"To carry?" Delevan asked.

"Yeah."

"To carry concealed?"

"Yeah."

"This gun registered?" O'Mearah asked. "It is,
isn't it?"

"Well . . . I mighta forgot."

"Might be it's hot, and you forgot that, too."

"Fuck you. I'm calling my lawyer."

Fat Johnny started to turn away. Delevan grabbed
him.

"Then there's the question of whether or not you
got a permit to conceal a deadly weapon in a spring-
clip device," he said in the same soft, purring voice.
"That's an interesting question, because so far as I
know, the City of New York doesn't *issue* a permit like
that."

The cops were looking at Fat Johnny; Fat Johnny
was glaring back at them. So none of them noticed
Roland turn the sign hanging in the door from OPEN
to CLOSED.

"Maybe we could start to resolve this matter if we could find the gentleman's wallet," O'Mearah said. Satan himself could not have lied with such genial persuasiveness. "Maybe he just dropped it, you know."

"I told you! I don't know nothing about the guy's wallet! Guy's out of his mind!"

Roland bent down. "There it is," he remarked. "I can just see it. He's got his foot on it."

This was a lie, but Delevan, whose hand was still on Fat Johnny's shoulder, shoved the man back so rapidly that it was impossible to tell if the man's foot *had* been there or not.

It had to be now. Roland glided silently toward the counter as the two gunslingers bent to peer under the counter. Because they were standing side by side, this brought their heads close together. O'Mearah still had the gun the clerk had kept under the counter in his right hand.

"Goddam, it's there!" Delevan said excitedly. "I *see* it!"

Roland snapped a quick glance at the man they had called Fat Johnny, wanting to make sure he was not going to make a play. But he was only standing against the wall—*pushing* against it, actually, as if wishing he could push himself into it—with his hands hanging at his sides and his eyes great wounded O's. He looked like a man wondering how come his horoscope hadn't told him to beware this day.

No problem there.

"Yeah!" O'Mearah replied gleefully. The two men peered under the counter, hands on uniformed knees. Now O'Mearah left his knee and he reached out to snag the wallet. "I see it, t—"

Roland took one final step forward. He cupped Delevan's right cheek in one hand, O'Mearah's left cheek in the other, and all of a sudden a day Fat Johnny Holden believed *had* to have hit rock bottom got a *lot*

---

worse. The spook in the blue suit brought the cops' heads together hard enough to make a sound like rocks wrapped in felt colliding with each other.

The cops fell in a heap. The man in the gold-rimmed specs stood. He was pointing the .357 Mag at Fat Johnny. The muzzle looked big enough to hold a moon rocket.

"We're not going to have any trouble, are we?" the spook asked in his dead voice.

"No sir," Fat Johnny said at once, "not a bit."

"Stand right there. If your ass loses contact with that wall, you are going to lose contact with life as you have always known it. You understand?"

"Yes sir," Fat Johnny said, "I sure do."

"Good."

Roland pushed the two cops apart. They were both still alive. That was good. No matter how slow and unobservant they might be, they were gunslingers, men who had tried to help a stranger in trouble. He had no urge to kill his own.

But he had done it before, hadn't he? Yes. Had not Alain himself, one of his sworn brothers, died under Roland's and Cuthbert's own smoking guns?

Without taking his eyes from the clerk, he felt under the counter with the toe of Jack Mort's Gucci loafer. He felt the wallet. He kicked it. It came spinning out from underneath the counter on the clerk's side. Fat Johnny jumped and shrieked like a goosey girl who spies a mouse. His ass actually *did* lose contact with the wall for a moment, but the gunslinger overlooked it. He had no intention of putting a bullet in this man. He would throw the gun at him and poleaxe him with it before firing a shot. A gun as absurdly big as this would probably bring half the neighborhood.

"Pick it up," the gunslinger said. "Slowly."

Fat Johnny reached down, and as he grasped the wallet, he farted loudly and screamed. With faint amusement the gunslinger realized he had mistaken the sound of his own fart for a gunshot and his time of dying had come.

When Fat Johnny stood up, he was blushing furiously. There was a large wet patch on the front of his pants.

"Put the purse on the counter. Wallet, I mean."

Fat Johnny did it.

"Now the shells. Winchester .45s. And I want to see your hands every second."

"I have to reach into my pocket. For my keys."

Roland nodded.

As Fat Johnny first unlocked and then slid open the case with the stacked cartons of bullets inside, Roland cogitated.

"Give me four boxes," he said at last. He could not imagine needing so many shells, but the temptation to *have* them was not to be denied.

Fat Johnny put the boxes on the counter. Roland slid one of them open, still hardly able to believe it wasn't a joke or a sham. But they were bullets, all right, clean, shining, unmarked, never fired, never reloaded. He held one up to the light for a moment, then put it back in the box.

"Now take out a pair of those wristbands."

"Wristbands—?"

The gunslinger consulted the Mortcypedia. "Handcuffs."

"Mister, I dunno what you want. The cash register's—"

"Do what I say. Now."

Christ, this ain't never *gonna end*, Fat Johnny's mind moaned. He opened another section of the counter and brought out a pair of cuffs.

"Key?" Roland asked.

Fat Johnny put the key to the cuffs on the counter. It made a small click. One of the unconscious cops made an abrupt snoring sound and Johnny uttered a wee screech.

"Turn around," the gunslinger said.

"You ain't gonna shoot me, are you? Say you ain't!"

"Ain't," Roland said tonelessly. "As long as you turn around right now. If you don't do that, I will."

Fat Johnny turned around, beginning to blubber. Of course the guy said he wasn't going to, but the smell of mob hit was getting too strong to ignore. He hadn't even been skimming that much. His blubbers became choked wails.

"Please, mister, for my mother's sake don't shoot me. My mother's old. She's blind. She's—"

"She's cursed with a yellowgut son," the gunslinger said dourly. "Wrists together."

Mewling, wet pants sticking to his crotch, Fat Johnny put them together. In a trice the steel bracelets were locked in place. He had no idea how the spook had gotten over or around the counter so quickly. Nor did he *want* to know.

"Stand there and look at the wall until I tell you it's all right to turn around. If you turn around before then, I'll kill you."

Hope lighted Fat Johnny's mind. Maybe the guy didn't mean to hit him after all. Maybe the guy wasn't crazy, just insane.

"I won't. Swear to God. Swear before all of His saints. Swear before all His angels. Swear before all His *arch*—"

"*I* swear if you don't shut up I'll put a slug through your neck," the spook said.

Fat Johnny shut up. It seemed to him that he stood facing the wall for an eternity. In truth, it was about twenty seconds.

The gunslinger knelt, put the clerk's gun on the floor, took a quick look to make sure the maggot was being good, then rolled the other two onto their backs. Both were good and out, but not dangerously hurt, Roland judged. They were both breathing regularly. A little blood trickled from the ear of the one called Delevan, but that was all.

He took another quick glance at the clerk, then un-buckled the gunslingers' gunbelts and stripped them off. Then he took off Mort's blue suitcoat and buckled the belts on himself. They were the wrong guns, but it still felt good to be packing iron again. *Damned* good. Better than he would have believed.

Two guns. One for Eddie, and one for Odetta . . . when and if Odetta was ready for a gun. He put on Jack Mort's coat again, dropped two boxes of shells into the right pocket and two into the left. The coat, formerly impeccable, now bulged out of shape. He picked up the clerk's .357 Mag and put the shells in his pants pocket. Then he tossed the gun across the room. When it hit the floor Fat Johnny jumped, ut-tered another wee shriek, and squirted a little more warm water in his pants.

The gunslinger stood up and told Fat Johnny to turn around.

10

When Fat Johnny got another look at the geek in the blue suit and the gold-rimmed glasses, his mouth fell open. For a moment he felt an overwhelming certainty that the man who had come in here had become a ghost when Fat Johnny's back was turned. It seemed to Fat Johnny that through the man he could see a figure much more real, one of those legendary gun-fighters they used to make movies and TV shows about when he was a kid: Wyatt Earp, Doc Holliday, Butch Cassidy, one of those guys.

Then his vision cleared and he realized what the crazy nut had done: taken the cops' guns and strapped them around his waist. With the suit and tie the effect should have been ludicrous, but somehow it wasn't.

"The key to the wristbands is on the counter. When the possemen wake up they'll free you."

He took the wallet, opened it, and, incredibly, laid four twenty dollar bills on the glass before stuffing the wallet back into his pocket.

"For the ammunition," Roland said. "I've taken the bullets from your own gun. I intend to throw them away when I leave your store. I think that, with an unloaded gun and no wallet, they may find it difficult to charge you with a crime."

Fat Johnny gulped. For one of the few times in his life he was speechless.

"Now where is the nearest—" Pause. "—nearest drugstore?"

Fat Johnny suddenly understood—or thought he understood—everything. The guy was a junkball, of course. That was the answer. No wonder he was so weird. Probably hopped up to the eyeballs.

"There's one around the corner. Half a block down Forty-Ninth."

"If you're lying, I'll come back and put a bullet in your brain."

"I'm not lying!" Fat Johnny cried. "I swear before God the Father! I swear before all the Saints! I swear on my mother's—"

But then the door was swinging shut. Fat Johnny stood for a moment in utter silence, unable to believe the nut was gone.

Then he walked as rapidly as he could around the counter and to the door. He turned his back to it and fumbled around until he was able to grasp and turn the lock. He fumbled some more until he had managed to shoot the bolt as well.

Only then did he allow himself to slide slowly into a sitting position, gasping and moaning and swearing to God and all His saints and angels that he would go to St. Anthony's this very afternoon, as soon as one of those pigs woke up and let him out of these cuffs, as a matter of fact. He was going to make confession, do an act of contrition, and take communion.

Fat Johnny Holden wanted to get right with God.

This had just been too fucking close.

11

The setting sun became an arc over the Western Sea. It narrowed to a single bright line which seared Eddie's eyes. Looking at such a light for long could put a permanent burn on your retinas. This was just one of the many interesting facts you learned in school, facts that helped you get a fulfilling job like part-time bartender and an interesting hobby like the full-time search for street-skag and the bucks with which to buy it. Eddie didn't stop looking. He didn't think it was going to matter much longer if he got eye-burned or not.

He didn't beg the witch-woman behind him. First, it wouldn't help. Second, begging would degrade him. He had lived a degrading life; he discovered that he had no wish to degrade himself further in the last few minutes of it. Minutes were all he had left now. That's all there would be before that bright line disappeared and the time of the lobstrosities came.

He had ceased hoping that a miraculous change would bring Odetta back at the last moment, just as he ceased hoping that Detta would recognize that his death would almost certainly strand her in this world forever. He had believed until fifteen minutes ago that she was bluffing; now he knew better.

Well, it'll be better than strangling an inch at a time, he thought, but after seeing the loathsome lobster-things night after night, he really didn't believe that was true. He hoped he would be able to die without screaming. He didn't think this would be possible, but he intended to try.

"They be comin fo you, honky!" Detta screeched. "Be comin any minute now! Goan be the best dinner those daddies *evah* had!"

It wasn't just a bluff, Odetta wasn't coming back . . . and the gunslinger wasn't either. This last hurt the most, somehow. He had been sure he and the gunslinger had become—well, partners if not brothers—during their trek up the beach, and Roland would at least make an *effort* to stand by him.

But Roland wasn't coming.

Maybe it isn't that he doesn't want to come. Maybe he can't come. Maybe he's dead, killed by a security guard in a drug store—shit, that'd be a laugh, the world's last gunslinger killed by a Rent-A-Cop—or maybe run over by a taxi. Maybe he's dead and the door's gone. Maybe that's why she's not running a bluff. Maybe there's no bluff to run.

"Goan be any minute now!" Detta screamed, and then Eddie didn't have to worry about his retinas anymore, because that last bright slice of light disappeared, leaving only afterglow.

He stared at the waves, the bright afterimage slowly fading from his eyes, and waited for the first of the lobstrosities to come rolling and tumbling out of the waves.

12

Eddie tried to turn his head to avoid the first one, but he was too slow. It ripped off a swatch of his face with one claw, splattering his left eye to jelly and revealing the bright gleam of bone in the twilight as it asked its questions and the Really Bad Woman laughed . . .

Stop it, Roland commanded himself. *Thinking such thoughts is worse than helpless; it is a distraction. And it need not be. There may still be time.*

And there still was—then. As Roland strode down Forty-Ninth street in Jack Mort's body, arms swinging, bullshooter's eyes fixed firmly upon the sign which read DRUGS, oblivious to the stares he was getting and the way people swerved to avoid him, the sun was still up in Roland's world. Its lower rim would not touch the place where sea met sky for another fifteen minutes or so. If Eddie's time of agony was to come, it was still ahead.

The gunslinger did not know this for a fact, however; he only knew it was later over there than here and while the sun *should* still be up over there, the assumption that time in this world and his own ran at the same speed might be a deadly one . . . especially for Eddie, who would die the death of unimaginable horror that his mind nevertheless kept trying to imagine.

The urge to look back, to see, was almost insurmountable. Yet he dared not. *Must* not.

The voice of Cort interrupted the run of his thoughts sternly: *Control the things you can control, maggot. Let everything else take a flying fuck at you, and if you must go down, go down with your guns blazing.*

Yes.

But it was hard.

Very hard, sometimes.

He would have seen and understood why people were staring at him and then veering away if he had been a little less savagely fixed on finishing his work in this world as soon as he could and getting the hell out, but it would have changed nothing. He strode so rapidly toward the blue sign where, according to the Mortcypedia, he could get the Ke-flex stuff his body needed, that Mort's suitcoat flapped out behind him in spite of the heavy lead weighting in each pocket. The gunbelts buckled across his hips were clearly revealed. He wore them not as their owners had, straight and neat, but as he wore his own, criss-cross, low-hung on his hips.

To the shoppers, boppers, and hawkers on Forty-Ninth, he looked much as he had looked to Fat Johnny: like a desperado.

Roland reached Katz's Drug Store and went in.

13

The gunslinger had known magicians, enchanters, and alchemists in his time. Some had been clever charlatans, some stupid fakes in whom only people more stupid than they were themselves could believe (but there had never been a shortage of fools in the world, so even the stupid fakes survived; in fact most actually thrived), and a small few actually able to do those things of which men whisper—these few could call demons and the dead, could kill with a curse or heal with strange potions. One of these men had been a creature the gunslinger believed to be a demon himself, a creature that pretended to be a man and called itself Flagg. He had seen him only briefly, and that had been near the end, as chaos and the final crash approached his land. Hot on his heels had come two young men who looked desperate and yet grim, men named Dennis and Thomas. These three had crossed only a tiny part of what had been a confused and confusing time in the gunslinger's life, but he would never forget seeing Flagg change a man who had irritated him into a howling dog. He remembered that well enough. Then there had been the man in black.

And there had been Marten.

Marten who had seduced his mother while his father was away, Marten who had tried to author Roland's death but had instead authored his early manhood, Marten who, he suspected, he might meet again before he reached the Tower . . . or at it.

This is only to say that his experience of magic and magicians had led him to expect something quite different than what he did find in Katz's Drug Store.

He had anticipated a dim, candle-lit room full of bitter fumes, jars of unknown powders and liquids and philters, many covered with a thick layer of dust or spun about with a century's cobwebs. He had expected a man in a cowl, a man who might be dangerous. He saw people moving about inside through the transparent plate-glass windows, as casually as they would in any shop, and believed they must be an illusion.

They weren't.

So for a moment the gunslinger merely stood inside the door, first amazed, then ironically amused. Here he was in a world which struck him dumb with fresh wonders seemingly at every step, a world where carriages flew through the air and paper seemed as cheap as sand. And the newest wonder was simply that for these people, wonder had run out: here, in a place of miracles, he saw only dull faces and plodding bodies.

There were thousands of bottles, there were potions, there were philters, but the Mortcypedia identified most as quack remedies. Here was a salve that was supposed to restore fallen hair but would not; there a cream which promised to erase unsightly spots on the hands and arms but lied. Here were cures for things that needed no curing: things to make your bowels run or stop them up, to make your teeth white and your hair black, things to make your breath smell better as if you could not do that by chewing alder-bark. No magic here; only trivialities—although there *was* astin, and a few other remedies which sounded as if they might be useful. But for the most part, Roland was appalled by the place. In a place that promised alchemy but dealt more in perfume than potion, was it any wonder that wonder had run out?

But when he consulted the Mortcypedia again, he discovered that the truth of this place was not just in the things he was looking at. The potions that really worked were kept safely out of sight. One could only obtain these if you had a sorcerer's fiat. In this world, such sorcerers were called DOCKTORS, and they wrote their magic formulae on sheets of paper which the Mortcypedia called REXES. The gunslinger didn't know the word. He supposed he could have consulted further on the matter, but didn't bother. He knew what he needed, and a quick look into the Mortcypedia told him where in the store he could get it.

He strode down one of the aisles toward a high counter with the words PRESCRIPTIONS FILLED over it.

14

The Katz who had opened Katz's Pharmacy and Soda Fountain (Sundries and Notions for Misses and Misters) on 49th Street in 1927 was long in his grave, and his only son looked ready for his own. Although he was only forty-six, he looked twenty years older. He was balding, yellow-skinned, and frail. He knew people said he looked like death on horseback, but none of them understood *why*.

Take this crotch on the phone now. Mrs. Rathbun. Ranting that she would sue him if he didn't fill her goddamned Valium prescription and *right now*, RIGHT THIS VERY INSTANT.

What do you think, lady, I'm gonna pour a stream of blue bombers through the phone? If he did, she would at least do him a favor and shut up. She would just tip the receiver up over her mouth and open wide.

The thought raised a ghostly grin which revealed his sallow dentures.

"You don't understand, Mrs. Rathbun," he interrupted after he had listened to a minute—a full minute, timed it with the sweep second-hand of his watch—of her raving. He would like, just once, to be able to say: *Stop shouting at me, you stupid crotch! Shout at your DOCTOR! He's the one who hooked you on that shit!* Right. Damn quacks gave it out like it was bubblegum, and when they decided to cut off the supply, who got hit with the shit? The sawbones? Oh, no! *He* did!

"What do you mean, I don't understand?" The voice in his ear was like an angry wasp buzzing in a jar. "I understand I do a lot of *business* at your tacky drugstore, I understand I've been a loyal *customer* all these years, I understand—"

"You'll have to speak to—" He glanced at the crotch's Rolodex card through his half-glasses again. "—Dr. Brumhall, Mrs. Rathbun. Your prescription has expired. It's a Federal crime to dispense Valium without a prescription." *And it ought to be one to perscribe it in the first place . . . unless you're going to give the patient you're perscribing it for your unlisted number with it, that is,* he thought.

"*It was an oversight!*" the woman screamed. Now there was a raw edge of panic in her voice. Eddie would have recognized that tone at once: it was the call of the wild Junk-Bird.

"Then call him and ask him to rectify it," Katz said. "He has my number." Yes. They all had his number. That was precisely the trouble. He looked like a dying man at forty-six because of the *fershlugginer* doctors.

And all I have to do to guarantee that the last thin edge of profit I am somehow holding onto in this place will melt away is tell a few of these junkie bitches to go fuck themselves. That's all.

"I CAN'T CALL HIM!" she screamed. Her voice drilled painfully into his ear. *"HIM AND HIS FAG BOY-FRIEND ARE ON VACATION SOMEPLACE AND NO ONE WILL TELL ME WHERE!"*

Katz felt acid seeping into his stomach. He had two ulcers, one healed, the other currently bleeding, and women like this bitch were the reason why. He closed his eyes. Thus he did not see his assistant stare at the man in the blue suit and the gold-rimmed glasses approaching the prescription counter, nor did he see Ralph, the fat old security guard (Katz paid the man a pittance but still bitterly resented the expense; his *father* had never needed a security guard, but his *father,* God rot him, had lived in a time when New York had been a city instead of a toilet-bowl) suddenly come out of his usual dim daze and reach for the gun on his hip. He heard a woman scream, but thought it was because she had just discovered all the Revlon was on sale, he'd been *forced* to put the Revlon on sale because that *putz* Dollentz up the street was undercutting him.

He was thinking of nothing but Dollentz and this bitch on the phone as the gunslinger approached like fated doom, thinking of how wonderful the two of them would look naked save for a coating of honey and staked out over anthills in the burning desert sun. HIS and HERS anthills, wonderful. He was thinking this was the worst it could get, the absolute worst. His father had been so determined that his only son follow in his footsteps that he had refused to pay for anything but a degree in pharmacology, and so he had followed in his father's footsteps, and God rot his father, for this was surely the lowest moment in a life that had been full of low moments, a life which had made him old before his time.

This was the absolute nadir.

Or so he thought with his eyes closed.

"If you come by, Mrs. Rathbun, I could give you a dozen five milligram Valium. Would that be all right?"

"The man sees reason! Thank God, the man sees reason!" And she hung up. Just like that. Not a word of thanks. But when she saw the walking rectum that called itself a doctor again, she would just about fall down and polish the tips of his Gucci loafers with her nose, she would give him a blowjob, she would—

"Mr. Katz," his assistant said in a voice that sounded strangely winded. "I think we have a prob—"

There was another scream. It was followed by the crash of a gun, startling him so badly he thought for a moment his heart was simply going to utter one monstrous clap in his chest and then stop forever.

He opened his eyes and stared into the eyes of the gunslinger. Katz dropped his gaze and saw the pistol in the man's fist. He looked left and saw Ralph the guard nursing one hand and staring at the thief with eyes that seemed to be bugging out of his face. Ralph's own gun, the .38 which he had toted dutifully through eighteen years as a police officer (and which he had only fired from the line of the 23rd Precinct's basement target range; he *said* he had drawn it twice in the line of duty . . . but who knew?), was now a wreck in the corner.

"I want Keflex," the man with the bullshooter eyes said expressionlessly. "I want a lot. Now. And never mind the REX."

For a moment Katz could only look at him, his mouth open, his heart struggling in his chest, his stomach a sickly boiling pot of acid.

Had he thought he had hit rock bottom?

Had he *really*?

15

"You don't understand," Katz managed at last. His voice sounded strange to himself, and there was really nothing very odd about *that*, since his mouth felt like a flannel shirt and his tongue like a strip of cotton batting. "There *is* no cocaine here. It is not a drug which is dispensed under any cir—"

"I did not say cocaine," the man in the blue suit and the gold-rimmed glasses said. "I said *Keflex.*"

That's what I thought *you said*, Katz almost told this crazy *momser*, and then decided that might provoke him. He had heard of drug stores getting held up for speed, for Bennies, for half a dozen other things (including Mrs. Rathbun's precious Valium), but he thought this might be the first penicillin robbery in history.

The voice of his father (God rot the old bastard) told him to stop dithering and gawping and *do* something.

But he could think of nothing *to* do.

The man with the gun supplied him with something.

"Move," the man with the gun said. "I'm in a hurry."

"H-How much do you want?" Katz asked. His eyes flicked momentarily over the robber's shoulder, and he saw something he could hardly believe. Not in *this* city. But it looked like it was happening, anyway. Good luck? Katz actually has some *good* luck? *That* you could put in *The Guinness Book of World Records!*

"I don't know," the man with the gun said. "As much as you can put in a bag. A *big* bag." And with no warning at all, he whirled and the gun in his fist crashed again. A man bellowed. Plate glass blew onto the sidewalk and the street in a sparkle of shards and splinters. Several passing pedestrians were cut, but none seriously. Inside Katz's drugstore, women (and not a few men) screamed. The burglar alarm began its

own hoarse bellow. The customers panicked and stam-
peded toward and out the door. The man with the gun
turned back to Katz and his expression had not changed
at all: his face wore the same look of frightening (but
not inexhaustible) patience that it had worn from the
first. "Do as I say rapidly. I'm in a hurry."

Katz gulped.

"Yes, sir," he said.

16

The gunslinger had seen and admired the curved
mirror in the upper left corner of the shop while he
was still halfway to the counter behind which they kept
the *powerful* potions. The creation of such a curved
mirror was beyond the ability of any craftsman in his
own world as things were now, although there had been
a time when such things—and many of the others he
saw in Eddie and Odetta's world—might have been
made. He had seen the remains of some in the tunnel
under the mountains, and he had seen them in other
places as well . . . relics as ancient and mysterious as
the *Druit* stones that sometimes stood in the places
where demons came.

He also understood the mirror's purpose.

He had been a bit late seeing the guard's move—he
was still discovering how disastrously the lenses Mort
wore over his eyes restricted his peripheral vision—
but he'd still time to turn and shoot the gun out of the
guard's hand. It was a shot Roland thought as nothing
more than routine, although he'd needed to hurry a
little. The guard, however, had a different opinion.
Ralph Lennox would swear to the end of his days that
the guy had made an impossible shot . . . except,
maybe, on those old kiddie Western shows like *Annie
Oakley*.

Thanks to the mirror, which had obviously been

placed where it was to detect thieves, Roland was quicker dealing with the other one.

He had seen the alchemist's eyes flick up and over his shoulder for a moment, and the gunslinger's own eyes had immediately gone to the mirror. In it he saw a man in a leather jacket moving up the center aisle behind him. There was a long knife in his hand and, no doubt, visions of glory in his head.

The gunslinger turned and fired a single shot, dropping the gun to his hip, aware that he might miss with the first shot because of his unfamiliarity with this weapon, but unwilling to injure any of the customers standing frozen behind the would-be hero. Better to have to shoot twice from the hip, firing slugs that would do the job while travelling on an upward angle that would protect the bystanders than to perhaps kill some lady whose only crime had been picking the wrong day to shop for perfume.

The gun had been well cared for. Its aim was true. Remembering the podgy, underexercised looks of the gunslingers he had taken these weapons from, it seemed that they cared better for the weapons they wore than for the weapons they *were*. It seemed a strange way to behave, but of course this was a strange world and Roland could not judge; had no *time* to judge, come to that.

The shot was a good one, chopping through the man's knife at the base of the blade, leaving him holding nothing but the hilt.

Roland stared evenly at the man in the leather coat, and something in his gaze must have made the would-be hero remember a pressing appointment elsewhere, for he whirled, dropped the remains of the knife, and joined the general exodus.

Roland turned back and gave the alchemist his orders. Any more fucking around and blood would flow. When the alchemist turned away, Roland tapped his bony shoulderblade with the barrel of the pistol. The man made a strangled *"Yeeek!"* sound and turned back at once.

"Not you. You stay here. Let your 'prentice do it."

"W-Who?"

"Him." The gunslinger gestured impatiently at the aide.

"What should I do, Mr. Katz?" The remains of the aide's teenage acne stood out brilliantly on his white face.

"Do what he says, you *putz!* Fill the order! Keflex!"

The aide went to one of the shelves behind the counter and picked up a bottle. "Turn it so I may see the words writ upon it," the gunslinger said.

The aide did. Roland *couldn't* read it; too many letters were not of his alphabet. He consulted the Mortcypedia. *Keflex,* it confirmed, and Roland realized even checking had been a stupid waste of time. *He* knew he couldn't read everything in this world, but these men didn't.

"How many pills in that bottle?"

"Well, they're capsules, actually," the aide said nervously. "If it's a cillin drug in pill form you're interested in—"

"Never mind all that. How many doses?"

"Oh. Uh—" The flustered aide looked at the bottle and almost dropped it. "Two hundred."

Roland felt much as he had when he discovered how much ammunition could be purchased in this world for a trivial sum. There had been nine sample bottles of Keflex in the secret compartment of Enrico Balazar's medicine cabinet, thirty-six doses in all, and he had felt well again. If he couldn't kill the infection with *two hundred* doses, it couldn't be killed.

"Give it to me," the man in the blue suit said.

The aide handed it over.

The gunslinger pushed back the sleeve of his jacket,

revealing Jack Mort's Rolex. "I have no money, but
this may serve as adequate compensation. I hope so,
anyway."

He turned, nodded toward the guard, who was still
sitting on the floor by his overturned stool and staring
at the gunslinger with wide eyes, and then walked out.

Simple as that.

For five seconds there was no sound in the drugstore
but the bray of the alarm, which was loud enough to
blank out even the babble of the people on the street.

"God in heaven, Mr. Katz, what do we do now?"
the aide whispered.

Katz picked up the watch and hefted it.

Gold. Solid gold.

He couldn't believe it.

He *had* to believe it.

Some madman walked in off the street, shot a gun
out of his guard's hand and a knife out of another's,
all in order to obtain the most unlikely drug he could
think of.

Keflex.

Maybe sixty dollars' worth of Keflex.

For which he had paid with a $6500 Rolex watch.

"Do?" Katz asked. *"Do?* The first thing you do is
put that wristwatch under the counter. You never saw
it." He looked at Ralph. "Neither did you."

"No sir," Ralph agreed immediately. "As long as
I get my share when you sell it, I never saw that watch
at all."

"They'll shoot him like a dog in the street," Katz
said with unmistakable satisfaction.

"Keflex! And the guy didn't even seem to have the
sniffles," the aide said wonderingly.

CHAPTER 4
THE DRAWING

1

As the sun's bottom arc first touched the Western Sea in Roland's world, striking bright golden fire across the water to where Eddie lay trussed like a turkey, Officers O'Mearah and Delevan were coming groggily back to consciousness in the world from which Eddie had been taken.

"Let me out of these cuffs, would ya?" Fat Johnny asked in a humble voice.

"Where is he?" O'Mearah asked thickly, and groped for his holster. Gone. Holster, belt, bullets, gun. *Gun.*

Oh, shit.

He began thinking of the questions that might be asked by the shits in the Department of Internal Affairs, guys who had learned all they knew about the streets from Jack Webb on *Dragnet*, and the monetary value of his lost gun suddenly became about as important to him as the population of Ireland or the principal mineral deposits of Peru. He looked at Carl and saw Carl had also been stripped of his weapon.

Oh dear Jesus, bring on the clowns, O'Mearah thought miserably, and when Fat Johnny asked again if O'Mearah would use the key on the counter to unlock the handcuffs, O'Mearah said, "I ought to . . ." He paused, because he'd been about to say *I ought to shoot you in the guts instead,* but he couldn't very well shoot Fat Johnny, could he? The guns here were

429

chained down, and the geek in the gold-rimmed glasses, the geek who had seemed so much like a solid citizen, had taken his and Carl's as easily as O'Mearah himself might take a popgun from a kid.

Instead of finishing, he got the key and unlocked the cuffs. He spotted the .357 Magnum which Roland had kicked into the corner and picked it up. It wouldn't fit in his holster, so he stuffed it in his belt.

"Hey, that's mine!" Fat Johnny bleated.

"Yeah? You want it back?" O'Mearah had to speak slowly. His head really ached. At that moment all he wanted to do was find Mr. Gold-Rimmed Specs and nail him to a handy wall. With dull nails. "I hear they like fat guys like you up in Attica, Johnny. They got a saying: 'The bigger the cushion, the better the pushin.' You *sure* you want it back?"

Fat Johnny turned away without a word, but not before O'Mearah had seen the tears welling in his eyes and the wet patch on his pants. He felt no pity.

"Where is he?" Carl Delevan asked in a furry, buzzing voice.

"He left," Fat Johnny said dully. "That's all I know. He left. I thought he was gonna kill me."

Delevan was getting slowly to his feet. He felt tacky wetness on the side of his face and looked at his fingers. Blood. Fuck. He groped for his gun and kept groping, groping and hoping, long after his fingers had assured him his gun and holster were gone. O'Mearah merely had a headache; Delevan felt as if someone had used the inside of his head as a nuclear weapons testing site.

"Guy took my gun," he said to O'Mearah. His voice was so slurry the words were almost impossible to make out.

"Join the club."

"He still here?" Delevan took a step toward O'Mearah, tilted to the left as if he were on the deck of a ship in a heavy sea, and then managed to right himself.

"No."

"How long?" Delevan looked at Fat Johnny, who didn't answer, perhaps because Fat Johnny, whose back was turned, thought Delevan was still talking to his partner. Delevan, not a man noted for even temper and restrained behavior under the best of circumstances, roared at the man, even though it made his head feel like it was going to crack into a thousand pieces: *"I asked you a question, you fat shit! How long has that motherfucker been gone?"'*

"Five minutes, maybe," Fat Johnny said dully. "Took his shells and your guns." He paused. "Paid for the shells. I couldn't believe it."

Five minutes, Delevan thought. The guy had come in a cab. Sitting in their cruiser and drinking coffee, they had seen him get out of it. It was getting close to rush-hour. Cabs were hard to get at this time of day. *Maybe—*

"Come on," he said to George O'Mearah. "We still got a chance to collar him. We'll want a gun from this slut here—"

O'Mearah displayed the Magnum. At first Delevan saw two of them, then the image slowly came together.

"Good." Delevan was coming around, not all at once but getting there, like a prize-fighter who has taken a damned hard one on the chin. "You keep it. I'll use the shotgun under the dash." He started for the door, and this time he did more than reel; he staggered and had to claw the wall to keep his feet.

"You gonna be all right?" O'Mearah asked.

"If we catch him," Delevan said.

They left. Fat Johnny was not as glad about their departure as he had been about that of the spook in the blue suit, but almost. Almost.

2

Delevan and O'Mearah didn't even have to discuss which direction the perp might have taken when he left the gunshop. All they had to do was listen to the radio dispatcher.

"Code 19," she said over and over again. *Robbery in progress, shots fired.* "Code 19, Code 19. Location is 395 West 49th, Katz's Drugs, perpetrator tall, sandy-haired, blue suit—"

Shots fired, Delevan thought, his head aching worse than ever. *I wonder if they were fired with George's gun or mine? Or both? If that shitbag killed someone, we're fucked. Unless we get him.*

"Blast off," he said curtly to O'Mearah, who didn't need to be told twice. He understood the situation as well as Delevan did. He flipped on the lights and the siren and screamed out into traffic. It was knotting up already, rush-hour starting, and so O'Mearah ran the cruiser with two wheels in the gutter and two on the sidewalk, scattering pedestrians like quail. He clipped the rear fender of a produce truck sliding onto Forty-Ninth. Ahead he could see twinkling glass on the sidewalk. They could both hear the strident bray of the alarm. Pedestrians were sheltering in doorways and behind piles of garbage, but residents of the overhead apartments were staring out eagerly, as if this was a particularly good TV show, or a movie you didn't have to pay to see.

The block was devoid of automobile traffic; cabs and commuters alike had scatted.

"I just hope he's still there," Delevan said, and used a key to unlock the short steel bars across the stock and barrel of the pump shotgun under the dashboard. He pulled it out of its clips. "I just hope that rotten-crotch son of a bitch is still there."

What neither understood was that, when you were

dealing with the gunslinger, it was usually better to leave bad enough alone.

3

When Roland stepped out of Katz's Drugs, the big bottle of Keflex had joined the cartons of ammo in Jack Mort's coat pockets. He had Carl Delevan's service .38 in his right hand. It felt so damned good to hold a gun in a whole right hand.

He heard the siren and saw the car roaring down the street. *Them,* he thought. He began to raise the gun and then remembered: they were gunslingers. Gunslingers doing their duty. He turned and went back into the alchemist's shop.

"Hold it, motherfucker!" Delevan screamed. Roland's eyes flew to the convex mirror in time to see one of the gunslingers—the one whose ear had bled—leaning out of the window with a scatter-rifle. As his partner pulled their carriage to a screaming halt that made its rubber wheels smoke on the pavement he jacked a shell into its chamber.

Roland hit the floor.

4

Katz didn't need any mirror to see what was about to happen. First the crazy man, now the crazy cops. *Oy vay.*

"Drop!" he screamed to his assistant and to Ralph, the security guard, and then fell to his knees behind the counter without waiting to see if they were doing the same or not.

Then, a split-second before Delevan triggered the shotgun, his assistant dropped on top of him like an eager tackle sacking the quarterback in a football

game, driving Katz's head against the floor and breaking his jaw in two places.

Through the sudden pain which went roaring through
his head, he heard the shotgun's blast, heard the remaining glass in the windows shatter—along with bottles of aftershave, cologne, perfume, mouthwash,
cough syrup, God knew what else. A thousand conflicting smells rose, creating one hell-stench, and before he passed out, Katz again called upon God to rot
his father for chaining this curse of a drug store to his
ankle in the first place.

5

Roland saw bottles and boxes fly back in a hurricane
of shot. A glass case containing time-pieces disintegrated. Most of the watches inside also disintegrated.
The pieces flew backwards in a sparkling cloud.

*They can't know if there are still innocent people in
here or not,* he thought. *They can't know and yet they
used a scatter-rifle just the same!*

It was unforgivable. He felt anger and suppressed it.
They were gunslingers. Better to believe their brains
had been addled by the head-knocking they'd taken
than to believe they'd done such a thing knowingly,
without a care for whom they might hurt or kill.

They would expect him to either run or shoot.

Instead, he crept forward, keeping low. He lacerated
both hands and knees on shards of broken glass. The
pain brought Jack Mort back to consciousness. He was
glad Mort was back. He would need him. As for Mort's
hands and knees, he didn't care. He could stand the
pain easily, and the wounds were being inflicted on
the body of a monster who deserved no better.

He reached the area just under what remained of the
plate-glass window. He was to the right of the door.

He crouched there, body coiled. He holstered the gun which had been in his right hand.

He would not need it.

6

"What are you doing, Carl?" O'Mearah screamed. In his head he suddenly saw a *Daily News* headline: COP KILLS 4 IN WEST SIDE DRUGSTORE SNAFU.

Delevan ignored him and pumped a fresh shell into the shotgun. "Let's go get this shit."

7

It happened exactly as the gunslinger had hoped it would.

Furious at being effortlessly fooled and disarmed by a man who probably looked to them no more dangerous than any of the other lambs on the streets of this seemingly endless city, still groggy from the head-knocking, they rushed in with the idiot who had fired the scatter-rifle in the lead. They ran slightly bent-over, like soldiers charging an enemy position, but that was the only concession they made to the idea that their adversary might still be inside. In their minds, he was already out the back and fleeing down an alley.

So they came crunching over the sidewalk glass, and when the gunslinger with the scatter-rifle pulled open the glassless door and charged in, the gunslinger rose, his hands laced together in a single fist, and brought it down on the nape of Officer Carl Delevan's neck.

While testifying before the investigating committee, Delevan would claim he remembered nothing at all after kneeling down in Clements' and seeing the perp's wallet under the counter. The committee members thought such amnesia was, under the circumstances, pretty damned convenient, and Delevan was lucky to get off with a sixty-day suspension without pay. Roland, however, would have believed, and, under different circumstances (if the fool hadn't discharged a scatter-rifle into a store which might have been full of innocent people, for instance), even sympathized. When you got your skull busted twice in half an hour, a few scrambled brains were to be expected.

As Delevan went down, suddenly as boneless as a sack of oats, Roland took the scatter-rifle from his relaxing hands.

"Hold it!" O'Mearah screamed, his voice a mixture of anger and dismay. He was starting to raise Fat Johnny's Magnum, but it was as Roland had suspected: the gunslingers of this world were pitifully slow. He could have shot O'Mearah three times, but there was no need. He simply swung the scatter-gun in a strong, climbing arc. There was a flat smack as the stock connected with O'Mearah's left cheek, the sound of a baseball bat connecting with a real steamer of a pitch. All at once O'Mearah's entire face from the cheek on down moved two inches to the right. It would take three operations and four steel pegs to put him together again. He stood there for a moment, unbelieving, and then his eyes rolled up the whites. His knees unhinged and he collapsed.

Roland stood in the doorway, oblivious to the approaching sirens. He broke the scatter-rifle, then worked the pump action, ejecting all the fat red cartridges onto Delevan's body. That done, he dropped the gun itself onto Delevan.

"You're a dangerous fool who should be sent west," he told the unconscious man. "You have forgotten the face of your father."

He stepped over the body and walked to the gunslingers' carriage, which was still idling. He climbed in the door on the far side and slid behind the driving wheel.

8

Can you drive this carriage? he asked the screaming, gibbering thing that was Jack Mort.

He got no coherent answer; Mort just went on screaming. The gunslinger recognized this as hysteria, but one which was not entirely genuine. Jack Mort was having hysterics on purpose, as a way of avoiding any conversation with this weird kidnapper.

Listen, the gunslinger told him. *I only have time to say this—and everything else—once. My time has grown very short. If you don't answer my question, I am going to put your right thumb into your right eye. I'll jam it in as far as it will go, and then I'll pull your eyeball right out of your head and wipe it on the seat of this carriage like a booger. I can get along with one eye just fine. And, after all, it isn't as if it were mine.*

He could no more have lied to Mort than Mort could have lied to him; the nature of their relationship was cold and reluctant on both their parts, yet it was much more intimate than the most passionate act of sexual intercourse would have been. This was, after all, not a joining of bodies but the ultimate meeting of minds.

He meant exactly what he said.

And Mort knew it.

The hysterics stopped abruptly. *I can drive it,* Mort said. It was the first sensible communication Roland had gotten from Mort since he had arrived inside the man's head.

Then do it.

Where do you want me to go?

Do you know a place called "The Village"?

Yes.

Go there.

Where in the Village?

For now, just drive.

We'll be able to go faster if I use the siren.

Fine. Turn it on. Those flashing lights, too.

For the first time since he had seized control of him, Roland pulled back a little and allowed Mort to take over. When Mort's head turned to inspect the dashboard of Delevan's and O'Mearah's blue-and-white, Roland watched it turn but did not initiate the action. But if he had been a physical being instead of only his own disembodied *ka,* he would have been standing on the balls of his feet, ready to leap forward and take control again at the slightest sign of mutiny.

There was none, though. This man had killed and maimed God knew how many innocent people, but he had no intention of losing one of his own precious eyes. He flicked switches, pulled a lever, and suddenly they were in motion. The siren whined and the gunslinger saw red pulses of light kicking off the front of the carriage.

Drive fast, the gunslinger commanded grimly.

9

In spite of lights and siren and Jack Mort beating steadily on the horn, it took them twenty minutes to reach Greenwich Village in rush-hour traffic. In the gunslinger's world Eddie Dean's hopes were crumbling like dykes in a downpour. Soon they would collapse altogether.

The sea had eaten half the sun.

Well, Jack Mort said, *we're here.* He was telling the truth (there was no way he could lie) although to Roland everything here looked just as it had everywhere else: a choke of buildings, people, and carriages. The carriages choked not only the streets but the air itself—with their endless clamor and their noxious fumes. It came, he supposed, from whatever fuel it was they burned. It was a wonder these people could live at all, or the women give birth to children that were not monsters, like the Slow Mutants under the mountains.

Now where do we go? Mort was asking.

This would be the hard part. The gunslinger got ready—as ready as he could, at any rate.

Turn off the siren and the lights. Stop by the sidewalk.

Mort pulled the cruiser up beside a fire hydrant.

There are underground railways in this city, the gunslinger said. *I want you to take me to a station where these trains stop to let passengers on and off.*

Which one? Mort asked. The thought was tinged with the mental color of panic. Mort could hide nothing from Roland, and Roland nothing from Mort— not, at least, for very long.

Some years ago—I don't know how many—you pushed a young woman in front of a train in one of those underground stations. That's the one I want you to take me to.

There ensued a short, violent struggle. The gunslinger won, but it was a surprisingly hard go. In his way, Jack Mort was as divided as Odetta. He was not a schizophrenic as she was; he knew well enough what he did from time to time. But he kept his secret self— the part of him that was The Pusher—as carefully locked away as an embezzler might lock away his secret skim.

Take me there, you bastard, the gunslinger repeated. He slowly raised the thumb toward Mort's right eye again. It was less than half an inch away and still moving when he gave in.

Mort's right hand moved the lever by the wheel again and they rolled toward the Christopher Street station where that fabled A-train had cut off the legs of a

woman named Odetta Holmes some three years before.

10

"Well looky there," foot patrolman Andrew Staunton said to *his* partner, Norris Weaver, as Delevan's
and O'Mearah's blue-and-white came to a stop halfway down the block. There were no parking spaces,
and the driver made no effort to find one. He simply
double-parked and let the clog of traffic behind him
inch its laborious way through the loophole remaining,
like a trickle of blood trying to serve a heart hopelessly clogged with cholesterol.

Weaver checked the numbers on the side by the right
front headlight. 744. Yes, that was the number they'd
gotten from dispatch, all right.

The flashers were on and everything looked ko-
sher—until the door opened and the driver stepped out.
He was wearing a blue suit, all right, but not the kind
that came with gold buttons and silver badge. His shoes
weren't police issue either, unless Staunton and Weaver
had missed a memo notifying officers that duty foot-
wear would henceforth come from Gucci. That didn't
seem likely. What seemed likely was that this was the
creep who had hijacked the cops uptown. He got out
oblivious to the honkings and cries of protest from the
drivers trying to get by him.

"Goddam," Andy Staunton breathed.

Approach with extreme caution, the dispatcher had
said. *This man is armed and* extremely *dangerous.*
Dispatchers usually sounded like the most bored human beings on earth—for all Andy Staunton knew, they
were—and so the almost awed emphasis this one put
on the word *extremely* had stuck to his consciousness
like a burr.

He drew his weapon for the first time in his four

years on the force, and glanced at Weaver. Weaver had
also drawn. The two of them were standing outside a
deli about thirty feet from the IRT stairway. They had
known each other long enough to be attuned to each
other in a way only cops and professional soldiers can
be. Without a word between them they stepped back
into the doorway of the delicatessen, weapons pointing upward.

"Subway?" Weaver asked.

"Yeah." Andy took one quick glance at the entrance. Rush hour was in high gear now, and the
subway stairs were clogged with people heading for
their trains. "We've got to take him right now, before
he can get close to the crowd."

"Let's do it."

They stepped out of the doorway in perfect tandem,
gunslingers Roland would have recognized at once as
adversaries much more dangerous than the first two.
They were younger, for one thing; and although he
didn't know it, some unknown dispatcher had labelled
him *extremely* dangerous, and to Andy Staunton and
Norris Weaver, that made him the equivalent of a rogue
tiger. *If he doesn't stop the second I tell him to, he's
dead,* Andy thought.

"*Hold it!*" he screamed, dropping into a crouch
with his gun held out before him in both hands. Beside
him, Weaver had done the same. "*Police! Get your
hands on your he—*"

That was as far as he got before the guy ran for the
IRT stairway. He moved with a sudden speed that was
uncanny. Nevertheless, Andy Staunton was wired, all
his dials turned up to the max. He swivelled on his
heels, feeling a cloak of emotionless coldness drop
over him—Roland would have known this, too. He had
felt it many times in similar situations.

Andy led the running figure slightly, then squeezed
the trigger of his .38. He saw the man in the blue suit

spin around, trying to keep his feet. Then he fell to the pavement as commuters who, only seconds ago, had been concentrating on nothing but surviving another trip home on the subway, screamed and scattered like quail. They had discovered there was more to survive than the uptown train this afternoon.

"Holy fuck, partner," Norris Wheaton breathed, "you blew him away."

"I know," Andy said. His voice didn't falter. The gunslinger would have admired it. "Let's go see who he was."

11

I'm dead! Jack Mort was screaming. *I'm dead, you've gotten me killed, I'm dead, I'm—*

No, the gunslinger responded. Through slitted eyes he saw the cops approaching, guns still out. Younger and faster than the ones who had been parked near the gun-shop. Faster. And at least one of them was a hell of a shot. Mort—and Roland along with him—*should* have been dead, dying, or seriously wounded. Andy Staunton had shot to kill, and his bullet had drilled through the left lapel of Mort's suit-coat. It had likewise punched through the pocket of Mort's Arrow shirt—but that was as far as it went. The life of both men, the one inside and the one outside, were saved by Mort's lighter.

Mort didn't smoke, but his boss—whose job Mort had confidently expected to have himself by this time next year—did. Accordingly, Mort had bought a two hundred dollar silver lighter at Dunhill's. He did not light *every* cigarette Mr. Framingham stuck in his gob when the two of them were together—that would have made him look too much like an ass-kisser. Just once in awhile . . . and usually when someone even higher up was present, someone who could appreciate a.) Jack Mort's quiet courtesy, and b.) Jack Mort's good taste.

Do-Bees covered all the bases.

This time covering the bases saved his life and Roland's. Staunton's bullet smashed the silver lighter instead of Mort's heart (which was generic; Mort's passion for brand names—*good* brand names—stopped mercifully at the skin).

He was hurt just the same, of course. When you were hit by a heavy-caliber slug, there was no such thing as a free ride. The lighter was driven against his chest hard enough to create a hollow. It flattened and then smashed apart, digging shallow grooves in Mort's skin; one sliver of shrapnel sliced Mort's left nipple almost in two. The hot slug also ignited the lighter's fluid-soaking batting. Nevertheless, the gunslinger lay still as they approached. The one who had not shot him was telling people to stay back, just stay back, goddammit.

I'm on fire! Mort shrieked. *I'm on fire, put it out! Put it out! PUT IT OWWWWWW—*

The gunslinger lay still, listening to the grit of the gunslingers' shoes on the pavement, ignoring Mort's shrieks, *trying* to ignore the coal suddenly glowing against his chest and the smell of frying flesh.

A foot slid beneath his ribcage, and when it lifted, the gunslinger allowed himself to roll boneless onto his back. Jack Mort's eyes were open. His face was slack. In spite of the shattered, burning remains of the lighter, there was no sign of the man screaming inside.

"God," someone muttered, "did you shoot him with a tracer, man?"

Smoke was rising from the hole in the lapel of Mort's coat in a neat little stream. It was escaping around the edge of the lapel in more untidy blotches. The cops could smell burning flesh as the wadding in the smashed lighter, soaked with Ronson lighter fluid, really began to blaze.

Andy Staunton, who had performed faultlessly thus far, now made his only mistake, one for which Cort would have sent him home with a fat ear in spite of his earlier admirable performance, telling him one mistake was all it took to get a man killed most of the time. Staunton had been able to shoot the guy—a thing no cop really knows if he can do until he's faced with a situation where he must find out—but the idea that his bullet had somehow *set the guy on fire* filled him with unreasoning horror. So he bent forward to put it out without thinking, and the gunslinger's feet smashed into his belly before he had time to do more than register the blaze of awareness in eyes he would have sworn were dead.

Staunton went flailing back into his partner. His pistol flew from his hand. Wheaton held onto his own, but by the time he had gotten clear of Staunton, he heard a shot and his gun was magically gone. The hand it had been in felt numb, as if it had been struck with a very large hammer.

The guy in the blue suit got up, looked at them for a moment and said, "You're good. Better than the others. So let me advise you. Don't follow. This is almost over. I don't want to have to kill you."

Then he whirled and ran for the subway stairs.

12

The stairs were choked with people who had reversed their downward course when the yelling and shooting started, obsessed with that morbid and somehow unique New Yorkers' curiosity to see how bad, how many, how much blood spilled on the dirty concrete. Yet somehow they still found a way to shrink back from the man in the blue suit who came plunging down the stairs. It wasn't much wonder. He was holding a gun, and another was strapped around his waist.

Also, he appeared to be on fire.

13

Roland ignored Mort's increasing shrieks of pain as his shirt, undershirt, and jacket began to burn more briskly, as the silver of the lighter began to melt and run down his midsection to his belly in burning tracks.

He could smell dirty moving air, could hear the roar of an oncoming train.

This was almost the time; the moment had almost come around, the moment when he would draw the three or lose it all. For the second time he seemed to feel worlds tremble and reel about his head.

He reached the platform level and tossed the .38 aside. He unbuckled Jack Mort's pants and pushed them casually down, revealing a pair of white underdrawers like a whore's panties. He had no time to reflect on this oddity. If he did not move fast, he could stop worrying about burning alive; the bullets he had purchased would get hot enough to go off and this body would simply explode.

The gunslinger stuffed the boxes of bullets into the underdrawers, took out the bottle of Keflex, and did the same with it. Now the underdrawers bulged grotesquely. He stripped off the flaming suit-jacket, but made no effort to take off the flaming shirt.

He could hear the train roaring toward the platform, could see its light. He had no way of knowing it was a train which kept the same route as the one which had run over Odetta, but all the same he *did* know. In matters of the Tower, fate became a thing as merciful as the lighter which had saved his life and as painful as the fire the miracle had ignited. Like the wheels of the oncoming train, it followed a course both logical and crushingly brutal, a course against which only steel and sweetness could stand.

He hoicked up Mort's pants and began to run again, barely aware of the people scattering out of his way. As more air fed the fire, first his shirt collar and then his hair began to burn. The heavy boxes in Mort's underdrawers slammed against his balls again and again, mashing them; excruciating pain rose into his gut. He jumped the turnstile, a man who was becoming a meteor. *Put me out!* Mort screamed. *Put me out before I burn up!*

You ought to burn, the gunslinger thought grimly. *What's going to happen to you is more merciful than you deserve.*

What do you mean? WHAT DO YOU MEAN?

The gunslinger didn't answer; in fact turned him off entirely as he pelted toward the edge of the platform. He felt one of the boxes of shells trying to slip out of Mort's ridiculous panties and held it with one hand.

He sent out every bit of his mental force toward the Lady. He had no idea if such a telepathic command could be heard, or if the hearer could be compelled to obey, but he sent it just the same, a swift, sharp arrow of thought:

THE DOOR! LOOK THROUGH THE DOOR! NOW! NOW!

Train-thunder filled the world. A woman screamed *"Oh my God he's going to jump!"* A hand slapped at his shoulder trying to pull him back. Then Roland pushed the body of Jack Mort past the yellow warning line and dove over the edge of the platform. He fell into the path of the oncoming train with his hands cupping his crotch, holding the luggage he would bring back . . . if, that was, he was fast enough to get out of Mort at just the right instant. As he fell he called her—*them*—again:

ODETTA HOLMES! DETTA WALKER! LOOK NOW!

As he called, as the train bore down upon him, its wheels turning with merciless silver speed, the gunslinger finally turned his head and looked back through the door.

And directly into her face.

Faces!

Both of them, I see both of them at the same time—

NOO—! Mort shrieked, and in the last split second before the train ran him down, cutting him in two not above the knees but at the waist, Roland lunged at the door . . . and through it.

Jack Mort died alone.

The boxes of ammunition and the bottle of pills appeared beside Roland's physical body. His hands clenched spasmodically at them, then relaxed. The gunslinger forced himself up, aware that he was wearing his sick, throbbing body again, aware that Eddie Dean was screaming, aware that Odetta was shrieking in two voices. He looked—only for a moment—and saw exactly what he had heard: not one woman but two. Both were legless, both dark-skinned, both women of great beauty. Nonetheless, one of them was a hag, her interior ugliness not hidden by her outer beauty but enhanced by it.

Roland stared at these twins who were not really twins at all but negative and positive images of the same woman. He stared with a feverish, hypnotic intensity.

Then Eddie screamed again and the gunslinger saw the lobstrosities tumbling out of the waves and strutting toward the place where Detta had left him, trussed and helpless.

The sun was down. Darkness had come.

14

Detta saw herself in the doorway, saw herself through her eyes, saw herself through the *gunslinger's* eyes, and her sense of dislocation was as sudden as Eddie's, but much more violent.

She was here.

She was *there,* in the gunslinger's eyes.

She heard the oncoming train.

Odetta! she screamed, suddenly understanding everything: what she was and when it had happened.

Detta! she screamed, suddenly understanding everything: what she was and who had done it.

A brief sensation of being turned inside out . . . and then a much more agonizing one.

She was being torn apart.

15

Roland shambled down the short slope to the place where Eddie lay. He moved like a man who has lost his bones. One of the lobster-things clawed at Eddie's face. Eddie screamed. The gunslinger booted it away. He bent rustily and grabbed Eddie's arms. He began to drag him backwards, but it was too late, his strength was too little, they were going to get Eddie, hell, both of them—

Eddie screamed again as one of the lobstrosities asked him *did-a-chick?* and then tore a swatch of his pants and a chunk of meat to go along with it. Eddie tried another scream, but nothing came out but a choked gargle. He was strangling in Detta's knots.

The things were all around them, closing in, claws clicking eagerly. The gunslinger threw the last of his strength into a final yank . . . and tumbled backwards. He heard them coming, them with their hellish questions and clicking claws. Maybe it wasn't so bad, he thought. He had staked everything, and that was all he had lost.

The thunder of his own guns filled him with stupid wonder.

16

The two women lay face to face, bodies raised like snakes about to strike, fingers with identical prints locked around throats marked with identical lines.

The woman was trying to kill her but the woman was not real, no more than the girl had been real; she was a dream created by a falling brick . . . but now the dream was real, the dream was clawing her throat and trying to kill her as the gunslinger tried to save his friend. The dream-made-real was screeching obscenities and raining hot spittle into her face. "I took the blue plate because that woman landed me in the hospital and besides I didn't get no forspecial *plate an I bust it cause it* needed *bustin an when I saw a white boy I could bust why I bust him too I hurt the white boys because they needed hurtin I stole from the stores that only sell things that are* forspecial *to whitefolks while the brothers and sisters go hungry in Harlem and the rats eat their babies, I'm the one, you bitch, I'm the one, I . . . I . . . I!*

Kill her, Odetta thought, and knew she could not.

She could no more kill the hag and survive than the hag could kill *her* and walk away. They could choke each other to death while Eddie and the

(Roland)/(Really Bad Man)

one who had called them were eaten alive down there by the edge of the water. That would finish all of them. Or she could

(love)/(hate)

let go.

Odetta let go of Detta's throat, ignored the fierce

hands throttling her, crushing her windpipe. Instead of using her own hands to choke, she used them to embrace the other.

"No, you bitch!" Detta screamed, but that scream was infinitely complex, both hateful and grateful. *"No, you leave me lone, you jes leave me—"*

Odetta had no voice with which to reply. As Roland kicked the first attacking lobstrosity away and as the second moved in to lunch on a chunk of Eddie's arm, she could only whisper in the witch-woman's ear: *"I love you."*

For a moment the hands tightened into a killing noose . . . and then loosened.

Were gone.

She was being turned inside out again . . . and then, suddenly, blessedly, she was *whole*. For the first time since a man named Jack Mort had dropped a brick on the head of a child who was only there to be hit because a white taxi driver had taken one look and driven away (and had not her father, in his pride, refused to try again for fear of a second refusal), she was *whole*. She was Odetta Holmes, but the other—?

Hurry up, bitch! Detta yelled . . . but it was still her own voice; she and Detta had merged. She had been one; she had been two; now the gunslinger had drawn a third from her. *Hurry up or they gonna be dinner!*

She looked at the shells. There was no time to use them; by the time she had his guns reloaded it would be over. She could only hope.

But is there anything else? she asked herself, and drew.

And suddenly her brown hands were full of thunder.

17

Eddie saw one of the lobstrosities loom over his face, its rugose eyes dead yet hideously sparkling with hideous life. Its claws descended toward his face.

Dod-a—, it began, and then it was smashed backward in chunks and splatters.

Roland saw one skitter toward his flailing left hand and thought *There goes the other hand* . . . and then the lobstrosity was a splatter of shell and green guts flying into the dark air.

He twisted around and saw a woman whose beauty was heartstopping, whose fury was heart-freezing. *"COME ON, MAHFAHS!"* she screamed. *"YOU JUST COME ON! YOU JUST COME FOR EM! I'M GONNA BLOW YO EYES RIGHT BACK THROUGH YO FUCKIN ASSHOLES!"*

She blasted a third one that was crawling rapidly between Eddie's spraddled legs, meaning to eat on him and neuter him at the same time. It flew like a tiddly-wink.

Roland had suspected they had some rudimentary intelligence; now he saw the proof.

The others were retreating.

The hammer of one revolver fell on a dud, and then she blew one of the retreating monsters into gobbets.

The others ran back toward the water even faster. It seemed they had lost their appetite.

Meanwhile, Eddie was strangling.

Roland fumbled at the rope digging a deep furrow into his neck. He could see Eddie's face melting slowly from purple to black. Eddie's strugglings were weakening.

Then his hands were pushed away by stronger ones.

"I'll take care of it." There was a knife in her hand . . . *his* knife.

Take care of what? he thought as his consciousness

faded. *What is it you'll take care of, now that we're both at your mercy?*

"Who are you?" he husked, as darkness deeper than night began to take him down.

"I am three women," he heard her say, and it was as if she were speaking to him from the top of a deep well into which he was falling. "I who was; I who had no right to be but was; I am the woman who you have saved.

"I thank you, gunslinger."

She kissed him, he knew that, but for a long time after, Roland knew only darkness.

FINAL
SHUFFLE

final shuffle

1

For the first time in what seemed like a thousand years, the gunslinger was not thinking about the Dark Tower. He thought only about the deer which had come down to the pool in the woodland clearing.

He sighted over the fallen log with his left hand.

Meat, he thought, and fired as saliva squirted warmly into his mouth.

Missed, he thought in the millisecond following the shot. *It's gone. All my skill . . . gone.*

The deer fell dead at the edge of the pool.

Soon the Tower would fill him again, but now he only blessed what gods there were that his aim was still true, and thought of meat, and meat, and meat. He re-holstered the gun—the only one he wore now— and climbed over the log behind which he had patiently lain as late afternoon drew down to dusk, waiting for something big enough to eat to come to the pool.

I am getting well, he thought with some amazement as he drew his knife. *I am really getting well.*

He didn't see the woman standing behind him, watching with assessing brown eyes.

2

. They had eaten nothing but lobster-meat and had drunk nothing but brackish stream water for six days following the confrontation at the end of the beach. Roland remembered very little of that time; he had been raving, delirious. He sometimes called Eddie Alain, sometimes Cuthbert, and always he called the woman Susan.

His fever had abated little by little, and they began the laborious trek into the hills. Eddie pushed the woman in the chair some of the time, and sometimes Roland rode in it while Eddie carried her piggyback, her arms locked loosely around his neck. Most of the time the way made it impossible for either to ride, and that made the going slow. Roland knew how exhausted Eddie was. The woman knew, too, but Eddie never complained.

They had food; during the days when Roland lay between life and death, smoking with fever, reeling and railing of times long past and people long dead, Eddie and the woman killed again and again and again. Bye and bye the lobstrosities began staying away from their part of the beach, but by then they had plenty of meat, and when they at last got into an area where weeds and slutgrass grew, all three of them ate compulsively of it. They were starved for greens, any greens. And, little by little, the sores on their skins began to fade. Some of the grass was bitter, some sweet, but they ate no matter what the taste . . . except once.

The gunslinger had wakened from a tired doze and seen the woman yanking at a handful of grass he recognized all too well.

"No! Not that!" he croaked. "Never that! Mark it, and remember it! Never that!"

She looked at him for a long moment and put it aside without asking for an explanation.

The gunslinger lay back, cold with the closeness of it. Some of the other grasses might kill them, but what the woman had pulled would damn her. It had been devil-weed.

The Keflex had brought on explosions in his bowels, and he knew Eddie had been worried about that, but eating the grasses had controlled it.

Eventually they had reached real woods, and the sound of the Western Sea diminished to a dull drone they heard only when the wind was right.

And now . . . *meat.*

3

The gunslinger reached the deer and tried to gut it with the knife held between the third and fourth fingers of his right hand. No good. His fingers weren't strong enough. He switched the knife to his stupid hand, and managed a clumsy cut from the deer's groin to its chest. The knife let out the steaming blood before it could congeal in the meat and spoil it . . . but it was still a bad cut. A puking child could have done better.

You are going to learn to be smart, he told his left hand, and prepared to cut again, deeper.

Two brown hands closed over his one and took the knife.

Roland looked around.

"I'll do it," Susannah said.

"Have you ever?"

"No, but you'll tell me how."

"All right."

"Meat," she said, and smiled at him.

"Yes," he said, and smiled back. "Meat."

"What's happening?" Eddie called. "I heard a shot."

"Thanksgiving in the making!" she called back. "Come help!"

Later they ate like two kings and a queen, and as the gunslinger drowsed toward sleep, looking up at the stars, feeling the clean coolness in this upland air, he thought that this was the closest he had come to contentment in too many years to count.

He slept. And dreamed.

4

It was the Tower. The Dark Tower.

It stood on the horizon of a vast plain the color of blood in the violent setting of a dying sun. He couldn't see the stairs which spiraled up and up and up within its brick shell, but he could see the windows which spiraled up along that staircase's way, and saw the ghosts of all the people he had ever known pass through them. Up and up they marched, and an arid wind brought him the sound of voices calling his name.

Roland . . . come . . . Roland . . . come . . . come . . . come . . .

"I come," he whispered, and awoke sitting bolt upright, sweating and shivering as if the fever still held his flesh.

"Roland?"

Eddie.

"Yes."

"Bad dream?"

"Bad. Good. *Dark.*"

"The Tower?"

"Yes."

They looked toward Susannah, but she slept on, undisturbed. Once there had been a woman named Odetta Susannah Holmes; later, there had been another named

Detta Susannah Walker. Now there was a third: Susannah Dean.

Roland loved her because she would fight and never give in; he feared for her because he knew he would sacrifice her—Eddie as well—without a question or a look back.

For the Tower.

The God-Damned Tower.

"Time for a pill," Eddie said.

"I don't want them anymore."

"Take it and shut up."

Roland swallowed it with cold stream-water from one of the skins, then burped. He didn't mind. It was a *meaty* burp.

Eddie asked, "Do you know where we're going?"

"To the Tower."

"Well, yeah," Eddie said, "but that's like me being some ignoramus from Texas without a road-map saying he's going to Achin' Asshole, Alaska. Where is it? Which direction?"

"Bring me my purse."

Eddie did. Susannah stirred and Eddie paused, his face red planes and black shadows in the dying embers of the campfire. When she rested easy again, he came back to Roland.

Roland rummaged in the purse, heavy now with shells from that other world. It was short enough work to find what he wanted in what remained of his life.

The jawbone.

The jawbone of the man in black.

"We'll stay here awhile," he said, "and I'll get well."

"You'll know when you are?"

Roland smiled a little. The shakes were abating, the sweat drying in the cool night breeze. But still, in his mind, he saw those figures, those knights and friends and lovers and enemies of old, circling up and up,

seen briefly in those windows and then gone; he saw
the shadow of the Tower in which they were pent struck
black and long across a plain of blood and death and
merciless trial.

"*I* won't," he said, and nodded at Susannah. "But
she will."

"And then?"

Roland held up the jawbone of Walter. "This once
spoke."

He looked at Eddie.

"It will speak again."

"It's dangerous." Eddie's voice was flat.

"Yes."

"Not just to you."

"No."

"I love her, man."

"Yes."

"If you hurt her—"

"I'll do what I need to," the gunslinger said.

"And we don't matter? Is that it?"

"I love you both." The gunslinger looked at Eddie,
and Eddie saw that Roland's cheeks glistened red in
what remained of the campfire's embered dying glow.
He was weeping.

"That doesn't answer the question. You'll go on,
won't you?"

"Yes."

"To the very end."

"Yes. To the very end."

"No matter what." Eddie looked at him with love
and hate and all the aching dearness of one man's dying hopeless helpless reach for another man's mind
and will and need.

The wind made the trees moan.

"You sound like Henry, man." Eddie had begun to
cry himself. He didn't want to. He hated to cry. "He
had a tower, too, only it wasn't dark. Remember me

telling you about Henry's tower? We were brothers, and I guess we were gunslingers. We had this White Tower, and he asked me to go after it with him the only way he could ask, so I saddled up, because he was my brother, you dig it? We got there, too. Found the White Tower. But it was poison. It killed him. It would have killed me. You saw me. You saved more than my life. You saved my fuckin *soul*."

Eddie held Roland and kissed his cheek. Tasted his tears.

"So what? Saddle up again? Go on and meet the man again?"

The gunslinger said not a word.

"I mean, we haven't seen many people, but I know they're up ahead, and whenever there's a Tower involved, there's a man. You wait for the man because you gotta meet the man, and in the end money talks and bullshit walks, or maybe here it's bullets instead of bucks that do the talking. So is that it? Saddle up? Go to meet the man? Because if it's just a replay of the same old shitstorm, you two should have left me for the lobsters." Eddie looked at him with dark-ringed eyes. "I been dirty, man. If I found out anything, it's that I don't want to die dirty."

"It's not the same."

"No? You gonna tell me you're not hooked?"

Roland said nothing.

"Who's gonna come through some magic door and save *you*, man? Do you know? *I* do. No one. You drew all you could draw. Only thing you can draw from now on is a fucking gun, because that's all you got left. Just like Balazar."

Roland said nothing.

"You want to know the only thing my brother ever had to teach me?" His voice was hitching and thick with tears.

"Yes," the gunslinger said. He leaned forward, his eyes intent upon Eddie's eyes.

"He taught me if you kill what you love, you're damned."

"I am damned already," Roland said calmly. "But perhaps even the damned may be saved."

"Are you going to get all of us killed?"

Roland said nothing.

Eddie seized the rags of Roland's shirt. *"Are you going to get her killed?"*

"We all die in time," the gunslinger said. "It's not just the world that moves on." He looked squarely at Eddie, his faded blue eyes almost the color of slate in this light. *"But we will be magnificent."* He paused. "There's more than a world to win, Eddie. I would not risk you and her—I would not have allowed the boy to die—if that was all there was."

"What are you talking about?"

"Everything there is," the gunslinger said calmly. "We are going to go, Eddie. We are going to fight. We are going to be hurt. *And in the end we will stand.*"

Now it was Eddie who said nothing. He could think of nothing to say.

Roland gently grasped Eddie's arm. "Even the damned love," he said.

5

Eddie eventually slept beside Susannah, the third Roland had drawn to make a new three, but Roland sat awake and listened to voices in the night while the wind dried the tears on his cheeks.

Damnation?

Salvation?

The Tower.

He would come to the Dark Tower and there he

would sing their names; there he would sing their names; there he would sing all their names.

The sun stained the east a dusky rose, and at last Roland, no longer the last gunslinger but one of the last three, slept and dreamed his angry dreams through which there ran only that one soothing blue thread:

There I will sing all their names!

AFTERWORD

This completes the second of six or seven books which make up a long tale called *The Dark Tower*. The third, *The Waste Lands,* details half of the quest of Roland, Eddie, and Susannah to reach the Tower; the fourth, *Wizard and Glass,* tells of an enchantment and a seduction but mostly of those things which befell Roland before his readers first met him upon the trail of the man in black.

My surprise at the acceptance of the first volume of this work, which is not at all like the stories for which I am best known, is exceeded only by my gratitude to those who have read it and liked it. This work seems to be my own Tower, you know; these people haunt me, Roland most of all. Do I really know what that Tower is, and what awaits Roland there (should he reach it, and you must prepare yourself for the very real possibility that he will not be the one to do so)? Yes . . . and no. All I know is that the tale has called to me again and again over a period of seventeen years. This longer second volume still leaves many questions unanswered and the story's climax far in the future, but I feel that it is a much more complete volume than the first.

And the Tower is closer.

—Stephen King
December 1st, 1986

The First Volume in an Epic Series ...

THE GUNSLINGER

This heroic fantasy is set in a world of ominous landscape and macabre menace that is a dark mirror of our own. A spellbinding tale of good versus evil, it features one of Stephen King's most powerful creations— The Gunslinger, a haunting figure who embodies the qualities of the lone hero through the ages, from ancient myth to frontier western legend.

The Gunslinger's quest involves the pursuit of The Man in Black, a liaison with the sexually ravenous Alice, and a friendship with the kid from Earth called Jake. Both grippingly realistic and eerily dreamlike, here is stunning proof of Stephen King's storytelling sorcery.

> **"A compelling whirlpool of a story that draws one irretrievably to its center."**
> **—*Milwaukee Sentinel***

W⊕RKS BY ST⊕PH⊕N KING

NOVELS

Carrie
'Salem's Lot
The Shining
The Stand
The Dead Zone
Firestarter
Cujo
THE DARK TOWER I:
The Gunslinger
Christine
Pet Sematary
Cycle of the Werewolf
The Talisman
(with Peter Straub)
It
Eyes of the Dragon

Misery
The Tommyknockers
THE DARK TOWER II:
*The Drawing
of the Three*
THE DARK TOWER III:
The Waste Lands
The Dark Half
Needful Things
Gerald's Game
Dolores Claiborne
Insomnia
Rose Madder
Desperation
The Green Mile
THE DARK TOWER IV:
Wizard and Glass

AS RICHARD BACHMAN

Rage
The Long Walk
Roadwork
The Running Man
Thinner
The Regulators

COLLECTIONS
Night Shift
Different Seasons
Skeleton Crew
Four Past Midnight
Nightmares and
Dreamscapes

NONFICTION
Danse Macabre

SCREENPLAYS
Creepshow
Cat's Eye
Silver Bullet
Maximum Overdrive
Pet Sematary
Golden Years
Sleepwalkers
The Stand
The Shining

THE
DARK
TOWER
THE GUNSLINGER

by

STEPHEN KING

Ⓞ
A SIGNET BOOK

SIGNET
Published by the Penguin Group
Penguin Putnam Inc.,
375 Hudson Street, New York, New York 10014, U.S.A.
Penguin Books Ltd, 27 Wrights Lane, London W8 5TZ, England
Penguin Books Australia Ltd, Ringwood, Victoria, Australia
Penguin Books Canada Ltd, 10 Alcorn Avenue,
Toronto, Ontario, Canada M4V 3B2
Penguin Books (N.Z.) Ltd, 182–190 Wairau Road, Auckland 10, New Zealand

Penguin Books Ltd, Registered Offices: Harmondsworth, Middlesex, England

Published by Signet, an imprint of Dutton NAL, a member of Penguin Putnam Inc.

The Gunslinger previously appeared in a limited edition
published by Donald M. Grant, Publisher, Inc., West Kingston,
Rhode Island, and in a Plume edition published by New American Library.

First Signet Printing, July, 1989
40 39 38 37 36 35 34

ACKNOWLEDGMENTS

The Gunslinger, copyright 1978 by Mercury Press, Inc., for *The Magazine of
Fantasy and Science Fiction,* October 1978.
The Way Station, copyright 1980 by Mercury Press, Inc., for *The Magazine of
Fantasy and Science Fiction,* April 1980.
The Oracle and the Mountain, copyright 1981 by Mercury Press, Inc., for *The
Magazine of Fantasy and Science Fiction,* February 1981.
The Slow Mutants, copyright 1981 by Mercury Press, Inc., for *The Magazine
of Fantasy and Science Fiction,* July 1981.
The Gunslinger and the Dark Man, copyright 1981 by Mercury Press, Inc., for
The Magazine of Fantasy and Science Fiction, November 1981.

 REGISTERED TRADEMARK—MARCA REGISTRADA

Printed in the United States of America

To

ED FERMAN

who took a chance on these stories,
one by one

CONTENTS

THE
GUNSLINGER

The man in black fled across the desert, and the gunslinger followed.

The desert was the apotheosis of all deserts, huge, standing to the sky for what might have been parsecs in all directions. White; blinding; waterless; without feature save for the faint, cloudy haze of the mountains which sketched themselves on the horizon and the devil-grass which brought sweet dreams, nightmares, death. An occasional tombstone sign pointed the way, for once the drifted track that cut its way through the thick crust of alkali had been a highway and coaches had followed it. The world had moved on since then. The world had emptied.

The gunslinger walked stolidly, not hurrying, not loafing. A hide waterbag was slung around his middle like a bloated sausage. It was almost full. He had progressed through the *khef* over many years, and had reached the fifth level. At the seventh or eighth, he would not have been thirsty; he could have watched his own body dehydrate with clinical, detached attention, watering its crevices and dark inner hollows only when his logic told him it must be done. He was not seventh or eighth. He was fifth. So he was thirsty, although he had no particular urge to drink. In a vague way, all this pleased him. It was romantic.

Below the waterbag were his guns, finely weighted to his hand. The two belts crisscrossed above his crotch. The holsters were oiled too deeply for even this Philistine sun to crack. The stocks of the guns were sandalwood, yellow and finely grained. The holsters were tied down with rawhide cord, and they swung heavily against his hips. The brass casings of the cartridges looped into the gunbelts twinkled and flashed and heliographed in the sun. The leather made subtle creaking noises. The guns themselves made no noise. They had spilled blood. There was no need to make noise in the sterility of the desert.

His clothes were the no-color of rain or dust. His shirt was open at the throat, with a rawhide thong dangling loosely in hand-punched eyelets. His pants were seam-stretched dungarees.

He breasted a gently rising dune (although there was no sand here; the desert was hardpan, and even the harsh winds that blew when dark came raised only an aggravating harsh dust like scouring powder) and saw the kicked remains of a tiny campfire on the lee side, the side which the sun would quit earliest. Small signs like this, once more affirming the man in black's essential humanity, never failed to please him. His lips stretched in the pitted, flaked remains of his face. He squatted.

He had burned the devil-grass, of course. It was the only thing out here that *would* burn. It burned with a greasy, flat light, and it burned slow. Border dwellers had told him that devils lived even in the flames. They burned it but would not look into the light. They said the devils hypnotized, beckoned, would eventually draw the one who looked into the fires. And the next man foolish enough to look into the fire might see you.

The burned grass was crisscrossed in the now-familiar ideographic pattern, and crumbled to gray senselessness before the gunslinger's prodding hand. There was nothing in the remains but a charred scrap of bacon, which he ate thoughtfully. It had always been this way. The gunslinger had followed the man in black across the desert for two months now, across the endless, screamingly monotonous purgatorial wastes, and had yet to find spoor other than the hygienic sterile ideographs of the man in black's campfires. He had not found a can, a bottle, or a waterbag (the gunslinger had left four of those behind, like dead snakeskins).

—Perhaps the campfires are a message, spelled out letter by letter. *Take a powder.* Or, *the end draweth nigh.* Or maybe even, *Eat at Joe's.* It didn't matter. He had no understanding of the ideograms, if they were ideograms. And the remains were as cold as all the others. He knew he was closer, but did not know how he knew. That didn't matter either. He stood up, brushing his hands.

No other trace; the wind, razor-sharp, had of course filed away even what scant tracks the hardpan held. He had never even been able to find his quarry's droppings. Nothing. Only these cold campfires along the ancient highway and the relentless range-finder in his own head.

He sat down and allowed himself a short pull from the waterbag. He scanned the desert, looked up at the sun, which was now sliding down the far quadrant of the sky. He got up, removed his gloves from his belt, and began to pull devil-grass for his own fire, which he laid over the ashes the man in black had left. He found the irony, like the romance of his thirst, bitterly appealing.

He did not use the flint and steel until the remains of the day were only the fugitive heat in the ground beneath him and a sardonic orange line on the monochrome western horizon. He watched the south patiently, toward the mountains, not hoping or expecting to see the thin straight line of smoke from a new campfire, but merely watching because that was a part of it. There was nothing. He was close, but only relatively so. Not close enough to see smoke at dusk.

He struck his spark to the dry, shredded grass and lay down upwind, letting the dreamsmoke blow out toward the waste. The wind, except for occasional gyrating dust-devils, was constant.

Above, the stars were unwinking, also constant. Suns and worlds by the million. Dizzying constellations, cold fire in every primary hue. As he watched, the sky washed from violet to ebony. A meteor etched a brief, spectacular arc and winked out. The fire threw strange shadows as the devilgrass burned its slow way down into new patterns— not ideograms but a straightforward crisscross vaguely frightening in its own no-nonsense surety. He had laid his fuel in a pattern that was not artful but only workable. It spoke of blacks and whites. It spoke of a man who might straighten bad pictures in strange hotel rooms. The fire burned its steady, slow flame, and phantoms danced in its incandescent core. The gunslinger did not see. He slept. The two patterns, art and craft, were welded together. The wind moaned. Every now and then a perverse downdraft would make the smoke whirl and eddy toward him, and sporadic whiffs of the smoke touched him. They built dreams in the same way that a small irritant may build a pearl in an oyster. Occasionally the gunslinger moaned with the wind. The stars were as indifferent to this as they were to wars, crucifixions, resurrections. This also would have pleased him.

II

He had come down off the last of the foothills leading the donkey, whose eyes were already dead and bulging with the heat. He had passed the last town three weeks before, and since then there had only been the deserted coach track and an occasional huddle of border dwellers' sod dwellings. The huddles had degenerated into single dwellings, most inhabited by lepers or madmen. He found the madmen better company. One had given him a stainless steel Silva compass and bade him give it to Jesus. The gunslinger took it gravely. If he saw Him, he would turn over the compass. He did not expect to.

Five days had passed since the last hut, and he had begun to suspect there would be no more when he topped the last eroded hill and saw the familiar low-backed sod roof.

The dweller, a surprisingly young man with a wild shock of strawberry hair that reached almost to his waist, was weeding a scrawny stand of corn with zealous abandon. The mule let out a wheezing grunt and the dweller looked up, glaring blue eyes coming target-center on the gunslinger in a moment. He raised both hands in curt salute and then bent to the corn again, humping up the row next to his hut with back bent, tossing devil-grass and an occasional stunted corn plant over his shoulder. His hair flopped and flew in the wind that now came directly from the desert, with nothing to break it.

The gunslinger came down the hill slowly, leading the donkey on which his waterskins sloshed. He paused by the edge of the lifeless-looking cornpatch, drew a drink from one of his skins to start the saliva, and spat into the arid soil.

"Life for your crop."

"Life for your own," the dweller answered and stood up. His back popped audibly. He surveyed the gunslinger without fear. The little of his face visible between beard and hair seemed unmarked by the rot, and his eyes, while a bit wild, seemed sane.

"I don't have anything but corn and beans," he said. "Corn's free, but you'll have to kick something in for the beans. A man brings them out once in a while. He don't stay long." The dweller laughed shortly. "Afraid of spirits."

"I expect he thinks you're one."

"I expect he does."

They looked at each other in silence for a moment.

The dweller put out his hand. "Brown is my name."

The gunslinger shook his hand. As he did so, a scrawny raven croaked from the low peak of the sod roof. The dweller gestured at it briefly:

"That's Zoltan."

At the sound of its name the raven croaked again and flew across to Brown. It landed on the dweller's head and roosted, talons firmly twined in the wild thatch of hair.

"Screw you," Zoltan croaked brightly. "Screw you and the horse you rode in on."

The gunslinger nodded amiably.

"Beans, beans, the musical fruit," the raven recited, inspired. "The more you eat, the more you toot."

"You teach him that?"

"That's all he wants to learn, I guess," Brown said. "Tried to teach him The Lord's Prayer once." His eyes traveled out beyond the hut for a moment, toward the gritty, featureless hardpan. "Guess this ain't Lord's Prayer country. You're a gunslinger. That right?"

"Yes." He hunkered down and brought out his makings. Zoltan launched himself from Brown's head and landed, flittering, on the gunslinger's shoulder.

"After the other one, I guess."

"Yes." The inevitable question formed in his mouth: "How long since he passed by?"

Brown shrugged. "I don't know. Time's funny out here. More than two weeks. Less than two months. The bean man's been twice since he passed. I'd guess six weeks. That's probably wrong."

"The more you eat, the more you toot," Zoltan said.

"Did he stop off?" the gunslinger asked.

Brown nodded. "He stayed supper, same as you will, I guess. We passed the time."

The gunslinger stood up and the bird flew back to the roof, squawking. He felt an odd, trembling eagerness. "What did he talk about?"

Brown cocked an eyebrow at him. "Not much. Did it ever rain and when did I come here and had I buried my wife. I did most of the talking, which ain't usual." He paused, and the only sound was the stark wind. "He's a sorcerer, ain't he?"

"Yes."

Brown nodded slowly. "I knew. Are you?"

"I'm just a man."

"You'll never catch him."

"I'll catch him."

They looked at each other, a sudden depth of feeling between them, the dweller upon his dust-puff-dry ground, the gunslinger on the hardpan that shelved down to the desert. He reached for his flint.

"Here." Brown produced a sulfur-headed match and struck it with a grimed nail. The gunslinger pushed the tip of his smoke into the flame and drew.

"Thanks."

"You'll want to fill your skins," the dweller said, turning away. "Spring's under the eaves in back. I'll start dinner."

The gunslinger stepped gingerly over the rows of corn and went around back. The spring was at the bottom of a hand-dug well, lined with stones to keep the powdery earth from caving. As he descended the rickety ladder, the gunslinger reflected that the stones must represent two years' work easily—hauling, dragging, laying. The water was clear but slow-moving, and filling the skins was a long chore. While he was topping the second, Zoltan perched on the lip of the well.

"Screw you and the horse you rode in on," he advised.

He looked up, startled. The shaft was about fifteen feet deep: easy enough for Brown to drop a rock on him, break his head, and steal everything on him. A crazy or a rotter wouldn't do it;

Brown was neither. Yet he liked Brown, and so he pushed the thought out of his mind and got the rest of his water. What came, came.

When he came through the hut's door and walked down the steps (the hovel proper was set below ground level, designed to catch and hold the coolness of the nights), Brown was poking ears of corn into the embers of a tiny fire with a hardwood spatula. Two ragged plates had been set at opposite ends of a dun blanket. Water for the beans was just beginning to bubble in a pot hung over the fire.

"I'll pay for the water, too."

Brown did not look up. "The water's a gift from God. Pappa Doc brings the beans."

The gunslinger grunted a laugh and sat down with his back against one rude wall, folded his arms and closed his eyes. After a little, the smell of roasting corn came to his nose. There was a pebbly rattle as Brown dumped a paper of dry beans into the pot. An occasional *tak-tak-tak* as Zoltan walked restlessly on the roof. He was tired; he had been going sixteen and sometimes eighteen hours a day between here and the horror that had occurred in Tull, the last village. And he had been afoot for the last twelve days; the mule was at the end of its endurance.

Tak-tak-tak.

Two weeks, Brown had said, or as much as six. Didn't matter. There had been calendars in Tull, and they had remembered the man in black because of the old man he had healed on his way through. Just an old man dying with the weed. An old man of thirty-five. And if Brown was right, the man in black had lost ground since then. But the desert was next. And the desert would be hell.

Tak-tak-tak.

—Lend me your wings, bird. I'll spread them and fly on the thermals.

He slept.

III

Brown woke him up five hours later. It was dark. The only light was the dull cherry glare of the banked embers.

"Your mule has passed on," Brown said. "Dinner's ready."

"How?"

Brown shrugged. "Roasted and boiled, how else? You picky?"

"No, the mule."

"It just laid over, that's all. It looked like an old mule." And with a touch of apology: "Zoltan et the eyes."

"Oh." He might have expected it. "All right."

Brown surprised him again when they sat down to the blanket that served as a table by asking a brief blessing: Rain, health, expansion to the spirit.

"Do you believe in an afterlife?" The gunslinger asked him as Brown dropped three ears of hot corn onto his plate.

Brown nodded. "I think this is it."

IV

The beans were like bullets, the corn tough. Outside, the prevailing wind snuffled and whined around the ground-level eaves. He ate quickly, ravenously, drinking four cups of water with the meal. Halfway through, there was a machine-gun rapping at the door. Brown got up and let Zoltan in. The bird flew across the room and hunched moodily in the corner.

"Musical fruit," he muttered.

After dinner, the gunslinger offered his tobacco.

—Now. Now the questions will come.

But Brown asked no questions. He smoked

and looked at the dying embers of the fire. It was already noticeably cooler in the hovel.

"Lead us not into temptation," Zoltan said suddenly, apocalyptically.

The gunslinger started as if he had been shot at. He was suddenly sure that it was an illusion, all of it (not a dream, no; an enchantment), that the man in black had spun a spell and was trying to tell him something in a maddeningly obtuse, symbolic way.

"Have you been through Tull?" he asked suddenly.

Brown nodded. "Coming here, and once to sell corn. It rained that year. Lasted maybe fifteen minutes. The ground just seemed to open and suck it up. An hour later it was just as white and dry as ever. But the corn—God, the corn. You could see it grow. That wasn't so bad. But you could *hear* it, as if the rain had given it a mouth. It wasn't a happy sound. It seemed to be sighing and groaning its way out of the earth." He paused. "I had extra, so I took it and sold it. Pappa Doc said he'd do it, but he would have cheated me. So I went."

"You don't like town?"

"No."

"I almost got killed there," the gunslinger said abruptly.

"That so?"

"I killed a man that was touched by God," the gunslinger said. "Only it wasn't God. It was the man in black."

"He laid you a trap."

"Yes."

They looked at each other across the shadows, the moment taking on overtones of finality.

—*Now* the questions will come.

But Brown had nothing to say. His smoke was a smoldering roach, but when the gunslinger tapped his poke, Brown shook his head.

Zoltan shifted restlessly, seemed about to speak, subsided.

"May I tell you about it?" the gunslinger asked.

"Sure."

The gunslinger searched for words to begin and found none. "I have to flow," he said.

Brown nodded. "The water does that. The corn, please?"

"Sure."

He went up the stairs and out into the dark. The stars glittered overhead in a mad splash. The wind pulsed steadily. His urine arched out over the powdery cornfield in a wavering stream. The man in black had sent him here. Brown might even be the man in black himself. It might be—

He shut the thoughts away. The only contingency he had not learned how to bear was the possibility of his own madness. He went back inside.

"Have you decided if I'm an enchantment yet?" Brown asked, amused.

The gunslinger paused on the tiny landing, startled. Then he came down slowly and sat.

"I started to tell you about Tull."

"Is it growing?"

"It's dead," the gunslinger said, and the words hung in the air.

Brown nodded. "The desert. I think it may strangle everything eventually. Did you know that there was once a coach road across the desert?"

The gunslinger closed his eyes. His mind whirled crazily.

"You doped me," he said thickly.

"No. I've done nothing."

The gunslinger opened his eyes warily.

"You won't feel right about it unless I invite you," Brown said. "And so I do. Will you tell me about Tull?"

The gunslinger opened his mouth hesitantly and was surprised to find that this time the words were there. He began to speak in flat bursts that slowly spread into an even, slightly toneless narrative. The doped feeling left him, and he found himself oddly excited. He talked deep into the night. Brown did not interrupt at all. Neither did the bird.

V

He had bought the mule in Pricetown, and when he reached Tull, it was still fresh. The sun had set an hour earlier, but the gunslinger had continued traveling, guided by the town glow in the sky, then by the uncannily clear notes of a honky-tonk piano playing *Hey Jude*. The road widened as it took on tributaries.

The forests had been gone long now, replaced by the monotonous flat country: endless, desolate fields gone to timothy and low shrubs, shacks, eerie, deserted estates guarded by brooding, shadowed mansions where demons undeniably walked; leering, empty shanties where the people had either moved on or had been moved along, an occasional dweller's hovel, given away by a single flickering point of light in the dark, or by sullen, inbred clans toiling silently in the fields by day. Corn was the main crop, but there were beans and also some peas. An occasional scrawny cow stared at him lumpishly from between peeled alder poles. Coaches had passed him four times, twice coming and twice going, nearly empty as they came up on him from behind and bypassed him and his mule, fuller as they headed back toward the forests of the north.

It was ugly country. It had showered twice since he had left Pricetown, grudgingly both times. Even the timothy looked yellow and dispirited. Ugly country. He had seen no sign of the man in black. Perhaps he had taken a coach.

The road made a bend, and beyond it the gunslinger clucked the mule to a stop and looked down at Tull. It was at the floor of a circular, bowl-shaped hollow, a shoddy jewel in a cheap setting. There were a number of lights, most of them clustered around the area of the music. There looked to be four streets, three running at right angles to the coach road, which was the main avenue of the town. Perhaps there would be a restaurant. He doubted it, but perhaps. He clucked at the mule.

More houses sporadically lined the road now, most of them still deserted. He passed a tiny graveyard with moldy, leaning wooden slabs overgrown and choked by the rank devil-grass. Perhaps five hundred feet further on he passed a chewed sign which said: TULL

The paint was flaked almost to the point of illegibility. There was another further on, but the gunslinger was not able to read that one at all.

A fool's chorus of half-stoned voices was rising in the final protracted lyric of *Hey Jude*—"Naa-naa-naa naa-na-na-na ... hey, Jude ..."—as he entered the town proper. It was a dead sound, like the wind in the hollow of a rotted tree. Only the prosaic thump and pound of the honky-tonk piano saved him from seriously wondering if the man in black might not have raised ghosts to inhabit a deserted town. He smiled a little at the thought.

There were a few people on the streets, not many, but a few. Three ladies wearing black slacks and identical middy blouses passed by on the opposite boardwalk, not looking at him with pointed curiosity. Their faces seemed to swim above their all-but-invisible bodies like huge, pallid baseballs with eyes. A solemn old man with a straw hat perched firmly on top of his head watched him from the steps of a boarded-up grocery store. A scrawny tailor with a late customer paused to watch him by; he held up the lamp in his window for a better look. The gunslinger nodded. Neither the tailor nor his customer nodded back. He could feel their eyes resting heavily against the low-slung holsters that lay against his hips. A young boy, perhaps thirteen, and his girl crossed the street a block up, pausing imperceptibly. Their footfalls raised little hanging clouds of dust. A few of the streetside lamps worked, but their glass sides were cloudy with congealed oil. Most had been crashed out. There was a livery, probably depending on the coach line for its survival. Three boys were crouched silently around a marble ring drawn in the dust to one side of the barn's gaping maw, smoking cornshuck cigarettes. They made long shadows in the yard.

The gunslinger led his mule past them and looked into the dim depths of the barn. One lamp glowed sunkenly, and a shadow jumped and flickered as a gangling old man in bib overalls forked loose timothy hay into the hay loft with huge, grunting swipes of his fork.

"Hey!" the gunslinger called.

The fork faltered and the hostler looked around waspishly. "Hey yourself!"

"I got a mule here."

"Good for you."

The gunslinger flicked a heavy, unevenly milled

gold piece into the semidark. It rang on the old, chaff-drifted boards and glittered.

The hostler came forward, bent, picked it up, squinted at the gunslinger. His eyes dropped to the gunbelts and he nodded sourly.

"How long you want him put up?"

"A night. Maybe two. Maybe longer."

"I ain't got no change for gold."

"I'm not asking for any."

"Blood money," the hostler muttered.

"What?"

"Nothing." The hostler caught the mule's bridle and led him inside.

"Rub him down!" the gunslinger called. The old man did not turn.

The gunslinger walked out to the boys crouched around the marble ring. They had watched the entire exchange with contemptuous interest.

"How they hanging?" the gunslinger asked conversationally.

No answer.

"You dudes live in town?"

No answer.

One of the boys removed a crazily tilted twist of cornshuck from his mouth, grasped a green cat's-eye marble, and squirted it into the dirt circle. It struck a croaker and knocked it outside.

He picked up the cat's-eye and prepared to shoot again.

"There a restaurant in this town?" the gunslinger asked.

One of them looked up, the youngest. There was a huge cold-sore at the corner of his mouth, but his eyes were still ingenuous. He looked at the gunslinger with hooded brimming wonder that was touching and frightening.

"Might get a burger at Sheb's."

"That the honky-tonk?"

The boy nodded but didn't speak. The eyes of his playmates had turned ugly and hostile.

The gunslinger touched the brim of his hat. "I'm grateful. It's good to know someone in this town is bright enough to talk."

He walked past, mounted the boardwalk and started down toward Sheb's, hearing the clear, contemptuous voice of one of the others, hardly more than a childish treble: "Weed-eater! How long you been screwin' your sister, Charlie? Weed-eater!"

There were three flaring kerosene lamps in front of Sheb's, one to each side and one nailed above the drunk-hung batwing doors. The chorus of *Hey Jude* had petered out, and the piano was plinking some other old ballad. Voices murmured like broken threads. The gunslinger paused outside for a moment, looking in. Sawdust floor, spittoons by the tipsy-legged tables. A plank bar on sawhorses. A gummy mirror behind it, reflecting the piano player, who wore an inevitable piano-stool slouch. The front of the piano had been removed so you could watch the wooden keys whonk up and down as the contraption was played. The bartender was a straw-haired woman wearing a dirty blue dress. One strap was held with a safety pin. There were perhaps six townies in the back of the room, juicing and playing Watch Me apathetically. Another half-dozen were grouped loosely about the piano. Four or five at the bar. And an old man with wild gray hair collapsed at a table by the doors. The gunslinger went in.

Heads swiveled to look at him and his guns. There was a moment of near silence, except for the oblivious piano player, who continued to tinkle. Then the woman mopped at the bar, and things shifted back.

"Watch me," one of the players in the corner said and matched three hearts with four spades, emptying his hand. The one with the hearts swore, handed over his bet, and the next was dealt.

The gunslinger approached the bar. "You got hamburger?" he asked.

"Sure." She looked him in the eye, and she might have been pretty when she started out, but now her face was lumpy and there was a livid scar corkscrewed across her forehead. She had powdered it heavily, but it called attention rather than camouflaging. "It's dear, though."

"I figured. Gimme three burgers and a beer."

Again that subtle shift in tone. Three hamburgers. Mouths watered and tongues licked at saliva with slow lust. Three hamburgers.

"That would go you five bucks. With the beer."

The gunslinger put a gold piece on the bar.

Eyes followed it.

There was a sullenly smoldering charcoal brazier behind the bar and to the left of the mirror. The woman disappeared into a small room behind it and returned with meat on a paper. She scrimped out three patties and put them on the fire. The smell that arose was maddening. The gunslinger stood with stolid indifference, only peripherally aware of the faltering piano, the slowing of the card game, the sidelong glances of the barflies.

The man was halfway up behind him when the gunslinger saw him in the mirror. The man was almost completely bald, and his hand was wrapped around the haft of a gigantic hunting knife that was looped onto his belt like a holster.

"Go sit down," the gunslinger said quietly.

The man stopped. His upper lip lifted unconsciously, like a dog's, and there was a moment of silence. Then he went back to his table, and the atmosphere shifted back again.

His beer came in a cracked glass schooner. "I ain't got change for gold," the woman said truculently.

"Don't expect any."

She nodded angrily, as if this show of wealth, even at her benefit, incensed her. But she took his gold, and a moment later the hamburgers came on a cloudy plate, still red around the edges.

"Do you have salt?"

She gave it to him from underneath the bar. "Bread?"

"No." He knew she was lying, but he didn't push it. The bald man was staring at him with cyanosed eyes, his hands clenching and unclenching on the splintered and gouged surface of his table. His nostrils flared with pulsating regularity.

The gunslinger began to eat steadily, almost blandly, chopping the meat apart and forking it into his mouth, trying not to think of what might have been added to cut the beef.

He was almost through, ready to call for another beer and roll a smoke, when the hand fell on his shoulder.

He suddenly became aware that the room had gone silent again, and he tasted thick tension in the air. He turned around and stared into the face of the man who had been asleep by the door when he entered. It was a terrible face. The odor of the devil-grass was a rank miasma. The eyes were damned, the staring, glaring eyes of those who see but do not see, eyes ever turned inward to the sterile hell of dreams beyond control, dreams unleashed, risen out of the stinking swamps of the unconscious.

The woman behind the bar made a small moaning sound.

The cracked lips writhed, lifted, revealing the green, mossy teeth, and the gunslinger thought: —He's not even smoking it anymore. He's chewing it. He's really *chewing* it.

And on the heels of that:—He's a dead man. He should have been dead a year ago.

And on the heels of that:—The man in black.

They stared at each other, the gunslinger and the man who had gone around the rim of madness.

He spoke, and the gunslinger, dumbfounded, heard himself addressed in the High Speech:

"The gold for a favor, gunslinger. Just one? For a pretty."

The High Speech. For a moment his mind refused to track it. It had been years—God! —centuries, millenniums; there was no more High Speech, he was the last, the last gunslinger. The others were—

Numbed, he reached into his breast pocket and produced a gold piece. The split, scrabbed hand reached for it, fondled it, held it up to reflect the greasy glare of the kerosene lamps. It threw off its proud civilized glow; golden, reddish, bloody.

"Ahhhhhh . . ." An inarticulate sound of pleasure. The old man did a weaving turn and began moving back to his table, holding the coin at eye level, turning it, flashing it.

The room was emptying rapidly, the batwings shuttling madly back and forth. The piano player closed the lid of his instrument with a bang and exited after the others in long, comic-opera strides.

"Sheb!" The woman screamed after him, her voice an odd mixture of fear and shrewishness, "Sheb, you come back here! Goddammit!"

The old man, meanwhile, had gone back to his table. He spun the gold piece on the gouged wood, and the dead-alive eyes followed it with empty fascination. He spun it a second time, a third, and his eyelids drooped. The fourth time, and his head settled to the wood before the coin stopped.

"There," she said softly, furiously. "You've driven out my trade. Are you satisfied?"

"They'll be back," the gunslinger said.

"Not tonight they won't."

"Who is he?" He gestured at the weed-eater.

"Go—" She completed the command by describing an impossible act of masturbation.

"I have to know," the gunslinger said patiently. "He—"

"He talked to you funny," she said. "Nort never talked like that in his life."

"I'm looking for a man. You would know him."

She stared at him, the anger dying. It was replaced with speculation, then with a high, wet gleam that he had seen before. The rickety building ticked thoughtfully to itself. A dog barked brayingly, far away. The gunslinger waited. She saw his knowledge and the gleam was replaced by hopelessness, by a dumb need that had no mouth.

"You know my price," she said.

He looked at her steadily. The scar would not show in the dark. Her body was lean enough so the desert and grit and grind hadn't been able to sag everything. And she'd once been pretty, maybe even beautiful. Not that it mattered. It would not have mattered if the grave-beetles had nested in the arid blackness of her womb. It had all been written.

Her hands came up to her face and there was still some juice left in her—enough to weep.

"Don't *look!* You don't have to look at me so mean!"

"I'm sorry," the gunslinger said. "I didn't mean to be mean."

"None of you mean it!" She cried at him.

"Put out the lights."

She wept, hands at her face. He was glad she had her hands at her face. Not because of the scar but because it gave her back her maidenhood, if not head. The pin that held the strap of her dress glittered in the greasy light.

"Put out the lights and lock up. Will he steal anything?"

"No," she whispered.

"Then put out the lights."

She would not remove her hands until she was behind him and she doused the lamps one by one, turning down the wicks and then breathing the flames into extinction. Then she took his hand in the dark and it was warm. She led him upstairs. There was no light to hide their act.

VI

He made cigarettes in the dark, then lit them and passed one to her. The room held her scent, fresh lilac, pathetic. The smell of the desert had overlaid it, crippled it. It was like the smell of the sea. He realized he was afraid of the desert ahead.

"His name is Nort," she said. No harshness had been worn out of her voice. "Just Nort. He died."

The gunslinger waited.

"He was touched by God."

The gunslinger said, "I have never seen Him."

"He was here ever since I can remember—Nort, I mean, not God." She laughed jaggedly into the dark. "He had a honeywagon for a while. Started to drink. Started to smell the grass. Then to smoke it. The kids started to follow him around and sic their dogs onto him. He wore old green pants that stank. Do you understand?"

"Yes."

"He started to chew it. At the last he just sat in there and didn't eat anything. He might have been a king, in his mind. The children might have been his jesters, and the dogs his princes."

"Yes."

41

"He died right in front of this place," she said. "He came clumping down the boardwalk—his boots wouldn't wear out, they were engineer boots—with the children and dogs behind him. He looked like wire clothes hangers all wrapped and twirled together. You could see all the lights of hell in his eyes, but he was grinning, just like the grins the children carve into their pumpkins on All-Saints Eve. You could smell the dirt and the rot and the weed. It was running down from the corners of his mouth like green blood. I think he meant to come in and listen to Sheb play the piano. And right in front, he stopped and cocked his head. I could see him, and I thought he heard a coach, although there was none due. Then he puked, and it was black and full of blood. It went right through that grin like sewer water through a grate. The stink was enough to make you want to run mad. He raised up his arms and just threw over. That was all. He died with that grin on his face, in his own vomit."

She was trembling beside him. Outside, the wind kept up its steady whine, and somewhere far away a door was banging, like a sound heard in a dream. Mice ran in the walls. The gunslinger thought in the back of his mind that it was probably the only place in town prosperous enough to support mice. He put a hand on her belly and she started violently, then relaxed.

"The man in black," he said.

"You have to have it, don't you!"

"Yes."

"All right. I'll tell you." She grasped his hand in both of hers and told him.

VII

He came in the late afternoon of the day Nort died, and the wind was whooping up, pulling away the loose topsoil, sending sheets of grit and uprooted stalks of corn windmilling past. Kennerly had padlocked the livery, and the other few merchants had shuttered their windows and laid boards across the shutters. The sky was the yellow color of old cheese and the clouds moved flyingly across it, as if they had seen something horrifying in the desert wastes where they had so lately been.

He came in a rickety rig with a rippling tarp tied across its bed. They watched him come, and old man Kennerly, lying by the window with a bottle in one hand and the loose, hot flesh of his second-eldest daughter's left breast in the other, resolved not to be there if he should knock.

But the man in black went by without hawing the bay that pulled his rig, and the spinning wheels spumed up dust that the wind clutched eagerly. He might have been a priest or a monk; he wore a black cassock that had been floured with dust, and a loose hood covered his head and obscured his features. It rippled and flapped. Beneath the garment's hem, heavy buckled boots with square toes.

He pulled up in front of Sheb's and tethered the horse, which lowered its head and grunted at the ground. Around the back of the rig he untied one flap, found a weathered saddlebag, threw it over his shoulder, and went in through the batwings.

Alice watched him curiously, but no one else noticed his arrival. The rest were drunk as lords. Sheb was playing Methodist hymns ragtime, and the grizzled layabouts who had come in early to avoid the storm and to attend Nort's wake had sung themselves hoarse. Sheb, drunk nearly to the point of senselessness, intoxicated and horny with his own continued existence, played with hectic, shuttlecock speed, fingers flying like looms.

Voices screeched and hollered, never overcoming the wind but sometimes seeming to challenge it. In the corner Zachary had thrown Amy Feldon's skirts over her head and was painting zodiac signs on her knees. A few other women circulated. A fervid glow seemed to be on all of them. The dull stormglow that filtered through the batwings seemed to mock them, however.

Nort had been laid out on two tables in the center of the room. His boots made a mystical V. His mouth hung open in a slack grin, although someone had closed his eyes and put slugs on them. His hands had been folded on his chest with a sprig of devil-grass in them. He smelled like poison.

The man in black pushed back his hood and came to the bar. Alice watched him, feeling trepidation mixed with the familiar want that hid within her. There was no religious symbol on him, although that meant nothing by itself.

"Whiskey," he said. His voice was soft and pleasant. "Good whiskey."

She reached under the counter and brought out a bottle of Star. She could have palmed off the local popskull on him as her best, but did not. She poured, and the man in black watched her. His eyes were large, luminous. The shadows were too thick to determine their color exactly. Her need intensified. The hollering and whooping went on behind, unabated. Sheb, the worthless gelding, was playing about the Christian Soldiers and somebody had persuaded Aunt Mill to sing. Her voice, warped and distorted, cut through the babble like a dull ax through a calf's brain.

"Hey, Allie!"

She went to serve, resentful of the stranger's silence, resentful of his no-color eyes and her own restless groin. She was afraid of her needs. They were capricious and beyond her control. They might be the signal of the change, which would in turn signal the beginning of her old age—a condition which in Tull was usually as short and bitter as a winter sunset.

She drew beer until the keg was empty, then broached another. She knew better than to ask Sheb; he would come willingly enough, like the dog he was, and would either chop off his own fingers or spume beer all over everything. The stranger's eyes were on her as she went about it; she could feel them.

"It's busy," he said when she returned. He had not touched his drink, merely rolled it between his palms to warm it.

"Wake," she said.

"I noticed the departed."

"They're bums," she said with sudden hatred. "All bums."

"It excites them. He's dead. They're not."

"He was their butt when he was alive. It's not right that he should be their butt now. It's . . ." She trailed off, not able to express what it was, or how it was obscene.

"Weed-eater?"

"Yes! What else did he have?"

Her tone was accusing, but he did not drop his eyes, and she felt the blood rush to her face. "I'm sorry. Are you a priest? This must revolt you."

"I'm not and it doesn't." He knocked the whiskey back neatly and did not grimace. "Once more, please."

"I'll have to see the color of your coin first. I'm sorry."

"No need to be."

He put a rough silver coin on the counter, thick on one edge, thin on the other, and she said as she would say later: "I don't have change for this."

He shook his head, dismissing it, and watched absently as he poured again.

"Are you only passing through?" she asked.

He did not reply for a long time, and she was about to repeat when he shook his head impatiently. "Don't talk trivialities. You're here with death."

She recoiled, hurt and amazed, her first thought being that he had lied about his holiness to test her.

"You cared for him," he said flatly. "Isn't that true?"

"Who? Nort?" She laughed, affecting annoyance to cover her confusion. "I think you better—"

"You're soft-hearted and a little afraid," he went on, "and he was on the weed, looking out hell's back door. And there he is, and they've even slammed the door now, and you don't think they'll open it until it's time for you to walk through, isn't it so?"

"What are you, drunk?"

"Mistuh Norton, he dead," the man in black intoned sardonically. "Dead as anybody. Dead as you or anybody."

"Get out of my place." She felt a trembling loathing spring up in her, but the warmth still radiated from her belly.

"It's all right," he said softly. "It's all right. Wait. Just wait."

The eyes were blue. She felt suddenly easy in her mind, as if she had taken a drug.

"See?" he asked her. "Do you see?"

She nodded dumbly and he laughed aloud—a fine, strong, untainted laugh that swung heads around. He whirled and faced them, suddenly made the center of attention by some unknown alchemy. Aunt Mill faltered and subsided, leaving a cracked high note bleeding on the air. Sheb struck a discord and halted. They looked at the stranger uneasily. Sand rattled against the sides of the building.

The silence held, spun itself out. Her breath had clogged in her throat and she looked down and saw both hands pressed to her belly beneath the bar. They all looked at him and he looked at them. Then the laugh burst forth again, strong, rich, beyond denial. But there was no urge to laugh along with him.

"I'll show you a wonder!" he cried at them. But they only watched him, like obedient children taken to see a magician in whom they have grown too old to believe.

The man in black sprang forward, and Aunt Mill drew away from him. He grinned fiercely and slapped her broad belly. A short, unwitting cackle was forced out of her, and the man in black threw back his head.

"It's better, isn't it?"

Aunt Mill cackled again, suddenly broke into sobs, and fled blindly through the doors. The others watched her go silently. The storm was beginning; shadows followed each other, rising and falling on the white cyclorama of the sky. A man near the piano with a forgotten beer in one hand made a groaning, grinning sound.

The man in black stood over Nort, grinning down at him. The wind howled and shrieked and thrummed. Something large struck the side of the building and bounced away. One of the men at the bar tore himself free and exited in looping, grotesque strides. Thunder racketed in sudden dry vollies.

"All right," the man in black grinned. "All right, let's get down to it."

He began to spit into Nort's face, aiming carefully. The spittle gleamed on his forehead, pearled down the shaven beak of his nose.

Under the bar, her hands worked faster.

Sheb laughed, loon-like, and hunched over. He began to cough up phlegm, huge and sticky gobs of it, and let fly. The man in black roared approval and pounded him on the back. Sheb grinned, one gold tooth twinkling.

Some fled. Others gathered in a loose ring around Nort. His face and the dewlapped rooster-wrinkles of his neck and upper chest gleamed with liquid—liquid so precious in this dry country. And suddenly it stopped, as if on signal. There was ragged, heavy breathing.

The man in black suddenly lunged across the body, jackknifing over it in a smooth arc. It was pretty, like a flash of water. He caught himself on his hands, sprang to his feet in a twist, grinning, and went over again. One of the watchers forgot himself, began to applaud, and suddenly backed away, eyes cloudy with terror. He slobbered a hand across his mouth and made for the door.

Nort twitched the third time the man in black went across.

A sound went through the watchers—a grunt— and then they were silent. The man in black threw his head back and howled. His chest moved in a quick, shallow rhythm as he sucked air. He began to go back and forth at a faster clip, pouring over Nort's body like water poured from one glass to another glass. The only sound in the room was the tearing rasp of his respiration and the rising pulse of the storm.

Nort drew a deep, dry breath. His hands rattled and pounded aimlessly on the table. Sheb screeched and exited. One of the women followed him.

The man in black went across once more, twice, thrice. The whole body was vibrating now, trembling and rapping and twitching. The smell of rot and excrement and decay billowed up in choking waves. His eyes opened.

Alice felt her feet propelling her backward. She struck the mirror, making it shiver, and blind panic took over. She bolted like a steer.

"I've given it to you," the man in black called after her, panting. "Now you can sleep easy. Even *that* isn't irreversible. Although it's ... so ... goddamned ... *funny!*" And he began to laugh again. The sound faded as she raced up the stairs, not stopping until the door to the three rooms above the bar was bolted.

She began to giggle then, rocking back and forth on her haunches by the door. The sound rose to a keening wail that mixed with the wind.

Downstairs, Nort wandered absently out into the storm to pull some weed. The man in black, now the only patron of the bar, watched him go, still grinning.

When she forced herself to go back down that evening, carrying a lamp in one hand and a heavy stick of stovewood in the other, the man in black was gone, rig and all. But Nort was there, sitting at the table by the door as if he had never been away. The smell of the weed was on him, but not as heavily as she might have expected.

He looked up at her and smiled tentatively. "Hello, Allie."

"Hello, Nort." She put the stovewood down

and began lighting the lamps, not turning her back to him.

"I been touched by God," he said presently. "I ain't going to die no more. He said so. It was a promise."

"How nice for you, Nort." The spill she was holding dropped through her trembling fingers and she picked it up.

"I'd like to stop chewing the grass," he said. "I don't enjoy it no more. It don't seem right for a man touched by God to be chewing the weed."

"Then why don't you stop?"

Her exasperation startled her into looking at him as a man again, rather than an infernal miracle. What she saw was a rather sad-looking specimen only half-stoned, looking hangdog and ashamed. She could not be frightened by him anymore.

"I shake," he said. "And I want it. I can't stop. Allie, you was always so good to me—" he began to weep. "I can't even stop peeing myself."

She walked to the table and hesitated there, uncertain.

"He could have made me not want it," he said through the tears. "He could have done that if he could have made me be alive. I ain't complaining ... I don't want to complain ..." He stared around hauntedly and whispered, "He might strike me dead if I did."

"Maybe it's a joke. He seemed to have quite a sense of humor."

Nort took his poke from where it dangled inside his shirt and brought out a handful of grass. Unthinkingly she knocked it away and then drew her hand back, horrified.

"I can't help it, Allie, I can't—" and he made a crippled dive for the poke. She could have stopped him, but she made no effort. She went back to lighting the lamps, tired although the evening had barely begun. But nobody came in that night except old man Kennerly, who had missed everything. He did not seem particularly surprised to see Nort. He ordered beer, asked where Sheb was, and pawed her. The next day things were almost normal, although none of the children followed Nort. The day after that, the catcalls resumed. Life had gotten back on its own sweet keel. The uprooted corn was gathered together by the children, and a week after Nort's resurrection, they burned it in the middle of the street. The fire was momentarily bright and most of the barflies stepped or staggered out to watch. They looked primitive. Their faces seemed to float between the flames and the ice-chip brilliance of the sky. Allie watched them and felt a pang of fleeting despair for the sad times of the world. Things had stretched apart. There was no glue at the center of things anymore. She had never seen the ocean, never would.

"If I had *guts,*" she murmured, "If I had guts, guts, *guts* . . ."

Nort raised his head at the sound of her voice and smiled emptily at her from hell. She had no guts. Only a bar and a scar.

The fire burned down rapidly and her customers came back in. She began to dose herself with the Star Whiskey, and by midnight she was blackly drunk.

VIII

She ceased her narrative, and when he made no immediate comment, she thought at first that the story had put him to sleep. She had begun to drowse herself when he asked: "That's all?"

"Yes. That's all. It's very late."

"Um." He was rolling another cigarette.

"Don't go getting your tobacco dandruff in my bed," she told him, more sharply than she had intended.

"No."

Silence again. The tip of his cigarette winked off and on.

"You'll be leaving in the morning," she said dully.

"I should. I think he's left a trap for me here."

"Don't go," she said.

"We'll see."

He turned on his side away from her, but she was comforted. He would stay. She drowsed.

On the edge of sleep she thought again about the way Nort had addressed him, in that strange talk. She had not seen him express emotion before or since. Even his lovemaking had been a silent thing, and only at the last had his breathing roughened and then stopped for a minute. He was like something out of a fairytale or a myth, the last of his breed in a world that was writing the last page of its book. It didn't matter. He would stay for a while. Tomorrow was time enough to think, or the day after that. She slept.

IX

In the morning she cooked him grits which he ate without comment. He shoveled them into his mouth without thinking about her, hardly seeing her. He knew he should go. Every minute he sat here the man in black was further away—probably into the desert by now. His path had been undeviatingly south.

"Do you have a map?" he asked suddenly, looking up.

"Of the town?" she laughed. "There isn't enough of it to need a map."

"No. Of what's south of here."

Her smile faded. "The desert. Just the desert. I thought you'd stay for a little."

"What's south of the desert?"

"How would I know? Nobody crosses it. Nobody's tried since I was here." She wiped her hands on her apron, got potholders, and dumped the tub of water she had been heating into the sink, where it splashed and steamed.

He got up.

"Where are you going?" She heard the shrill fear in her voice and hated it.

"To the stable. If anyone knows, the hostler will." He put his hands on her shoulders. The hands were warm. "And to arrange for my mule. If I'm going to be here, he should be taken care of. For when I leave."

But not yet. She looked up at him. "But you

watch that Kennerly. If he doesn't know a thing, he'll make it up."

When he left she turned to the sink, feeling the hot, warm drift of her grateful tears.

X

Kennerly was toothless, unpleasant, and plagued with daughters. Two half-grown ones peeked at the gunslinger from the dusty shadows of the barn. A baby drooled happily in the dirt. A full-grown one, blonde, dirty, sensual, watched with a speculative curiosity as she drew water from the groaning pump beside the building.

The hostler met him halfway between the door to his establishment and the street. His manner vacillated between hostility and a craven sort of fawning—like a stud mongrel that has been kicked too often.

"It's bein' cared for," he said, and before the gunslinger could reply, Kennerly turned on his daughter: "You get in, Soobie! You get right the hell in!"

Soobie began to drag her bucket sullenly toward the shack appended to the barn.

"You meant my mule," the gunslinger said.

"Yes, sir. Ain't seen a mule in quite a time. Time was they used to grow up wild for want of 'em, but the world has moved on. Ain't seen nothin' but a few oxen and the coach horses and ... Soobie, I'll whale you, 'fore God!"

"I don't bite," the gunslinger said pleasantly.

Kennerly cringed a little. "It ain't you. No, sir, it ain't *you*." He grinned loosely. "She's just naturally gawky. She's got a devil. She's wild." His eyes darkened. "It's coming to Last Times, mister. You know how it says in the Book. Children won't obey their parents, and a plague'll be visited on the multitudes."

The gunslinger nodded, then pointed south. "What's out there?"

Kennerly grinned again, showing gums and a few sociable yellow teeth. "Dwellers. Weed. Desert. What else?" He cackled, and his eyes measured the gunslinger coldly.

"How big is the desert?"

"Big." Kennerly endeavored to look serious. "Maybe three hundred miles. Maybe a thousand. I can't tell you, mister. There's nothing out there but devil-grass and maybe demons. That's the way the other fella went. The one who fixed up Norty when he was sick."

"Sick? I heard he was dead."

Kennerly kept grinning. "Well, well. Maybe. But we're growed-up men, ain't we?"

"But you believe in demons."

Kennerly looked affronted. "That's a lot different."

The gunslinger took off his hat and wiped his forehead. The sun was hot, beating steadily. Kennerly seemed not to notice. In the thin shadow by the livery, the baby girl was gravely smearing dirt on her face.

"You don't know what's after the desert?"

Kennerly shrugged. "Some might. The coach ran through part of it fifty years ago. My pap said so. He used to say 'twas mountains. Others say an ocean . . . a green ocean with monsters. And some say that's where the world ends. That there ain't nothing but lights that'll drive a man blind and the face of God with his mouth open to eat them up."

"Drivel," the gunslinger said shortly.

"Sure it is," Kennerly cried happily. He cringed again, hating, fearing, wanting to please.

"You see my mule is looked after." He flicked Kennerly another coin, which Kennerly caught on the fly.

"Surely. You stayin' a little?"

"I guess I might."

"That Allie's pretty nice when she wants to be, ain't she?"

"Did you say something?" the gunslinger asked remotely.

Sudden terror dawned in Kennerly's eyes, like twin moons coming over the horizon. "No, sir, not a word. And I'm sorry if I did." He caught sight of Soobie leaning out a window and whirled on her. "I'll whale you now, you little slut-face! 'Fore God! I'll—"

The gunslinger walked away, aware that Kennerly had turned to watch him, aware of the fact that he could whirl and catch the hostler with some true and untinctured emotion distilled on his face. He let it slip. It was hot. The only sure thing about the desert was its size. And it wasn't all played out in this town. Not yet.

XI

They were in bed when Sheb kicked the door open and came in with the knife.

It had been four days, and they had gone by in a blinking haze. He ate. He slept. He made sex with Allie. He found that she played the fiddle and he made her play it for him. She sat by the window in the milky light of daybreak, only a profile, and played something haltingly that might have been good if she had been trained. He felt a growing (but strangely absent-minded) affection for her and thought this might be the trap the man in black had left behind. He read dry and tattered back issues of magazines with faded pictures. He thought very little about everything.

He didn't hear the little piano player come up—his reflexes had sunk. That didn't seem to matter either, although it would have frightened him badly in another time and place.

Allie was naked, the sheet below her breasts, and they were preparing to make love.

"Please," she was saying. "Like before, I want that, I want—"

The door crashed open and the piano player made his ridiculous, knock-kneed run for the sun. Allie did not scream, although Sheb held an eight-inch carving knife in his hand. Sheb was making a noise, an inarticulate blabbering. He sounded like a man being drowned in a bucket of mud. Spittle flew. He brought the knife down with both hands, and the gunslinger caught his wrists and turned them. The knife went flying. Sheb made a high screeching noise, like a rusty screen door. His hands fluttered in marionette movements, both wrists broken. The wind gritted against the window. Allie's glass on the wall, faintly clouded and distorted, reflected the room.

"She was mine!" He wept. "She was mine first! Mine!"

Allie looked at him and got out of bed. She put on a wrapper, and the gunslinger felt a moment of empathy for a man who must be seeing himself coming out on the far end of what he once had. He was just a little man, and gelded.

"It was for you," Sheb sobbed. "It was only for you, Allie. It was you first and it was all for you. I—ah, oh God, dear God—" The words dissolved into a paroxysm of unintelligibilities, finally to tears. He rocked back and forth, holding his broken wrists to his belly.

"Shhh. Shhh. Let me see." She knelt beside him. "Broken. Sheb, you ass. Didn't you know you were never strong?" She helped him to his feet. He tried to hold his hands to his face, but they would not obey, and he wept nakedly. "Come on over to the table and let me see what I can do."

She led him to the table and set his wrists with slats of kindling from the fire box. He wept weakly and without volition, and left without looking back.

She came back to the bed. "Where were we?"

"No," he said.

She said patiently, "You knew about that. There's nothing to be done. What else is there?" She touched his shoulder. "Except I'm glad that you are so strong."

"Not now," he said thickly.

"I can make you strong——"

"No," he said. "You can't do that."

XII

The next night the bar was closed. It was whatever passed for the Sabbath in Tull. The gunslinger went to the tiny, leaning church by the graveyard while Allie washed tables with strong disinfectant and rinsed kerosene lamp chimneys in soapy water.

An odd purple dusk had fallen, and the church, lit from the inside, looked almost like a blast furnace from the road.

"I don't go," Allie had said shortly. "The woman who preaches has poison religion. Let the respectable ones go."

He stood in the vestibule, hidden in a shadow, looking in. The pews were gone and the congregation stood (he saw Kennerly and his brood;

Castner, owner of the town's scrawny dry-goods emporium and his slat-sided wife; a few barflies; a few "town" women he had never seen before; and, surprisingly, Sheb). They were singing a hymn raggedly, *a cappella*. He looked curiously at the mountainous woman at the pulpit. Allie had said: "She lives alone, hardly ever sees anybody. Only comes out on Sunday to serve up the hellfire. Her name is Sylvia Pittston. She's crazy, but she's got the hoodoo on them. They like it that way. It suits them."

No description could take the measure of the woman. Breasts like earthworks. A huge pillar of a neck overtopped by a pasty white moon of a face, in which blinked eyes so large and so dark that they seemed to be bottomless tarns. Her hair was a beautiful rich brown and it was piled atop her head in a haphazard, lunatic sprawl, held by a hairpin big enough to be a meat skewer. She wore a dress that seemed to be made of burlap. The arms that held the hymnal were slabs. Her skin was creamy, unmarked, lovely. He thought that she must top three hundred pounds. He felt a sudden red lust for her that made him feel shaky, and he turned his head and looked away.

"Shall we gather at the river,
The beautiful, the beautiful,

The riiiiver,
Shall we gather at the river,
That flows by the kingdom of God."

The last note of the last chorus faded off, and there was a moment of shuffling and coughing.

She waited. When they were settled, she spread her hands over them, as if in benediction. It was an evocative gesture.

"My dear little brothers and sisters in Christ."

It was a haunting line. For a moment the gunslinger felt mixed feelings of nostalgia and fear, stitched in with an eerie feeling of *déjà vu*— he thought: I dreamed this. When? He shook it off. The audience—perhaps twenty-five all told— had become dead silent.

"The subject of our meditation tonight is The Interloper." Her voice was sweet, melodious, the speaking voice of a well-trained soprano.

"A little rustle ran through the audience.

"I feel," Sylvia Pittston said reflectively, "I feel that I know everyone in The Book personally. In the last five years I have worn out five Bibles, and uncountable numbers before that. I love the story, and I love the players in that story. I have walked arm in arm in the lion's den with Daniel. I stood with David when he was tempted by Bathsheba as she bathed at the pool. I have been in the fiery

furnace with Shadrach, Meshach, and Abednego.
I slew two thousand with Samson and was blinded
with St. Paul on the road to Damascus. I wept
with Mary at Golgotha."

A soft, shurring sigh in the audience.

"I have known and loved them. There is only
one—*one*—" she held up a finger—"only one
player in the greatest of all dramas that I do not
know. Only *one* who stands outside with his face
in the shadow. Only *one* that makes my body
tremble and my spirit quail. I fear him. I don't
know his mind and I fear him. I fear The
Interloper."

Another sigh. One of the women had put a
hand over her mouth as if to stop a sound and
was rocking, rocking.

"The Interloper who came to Eve as a snake
on its belly, grinning and writhing. The Interloper who walked among the Children of Israel
while Moses was up on the Mount, who whispered
to them to make a golden idol, a golden calf,
and to worship it with foulness and fornication."

Moans, nods.

"The Interloper! He stood on the balcony with
Jezebel and watched as King Ahaz fell screaming
to his death, and he and she grinned as the dogs
gathered and lapped up his life's blood. Oh, my

little brothers and sisters, watch thou for The Interloper."

"Yes, O Jesus—" The man the gunslinger had first noticed coming into town, the one with the straw hat.

"He's always been there, my brothers and sisters. But I don't know his mind. And you don't know his mind. Who could understand the awful darkness that swirls there, the pride like pylons, the titanic blasphemy, the unholy glee? And the madness! The cyclopean, gibbering madness that walks and crawls and wriggles through men's most awful wants and desires?"

"O Jesus Savior—"

"It was *him* who took our Lord up on the mountain—"

"Yes—"

"It was *him* that tempted him and shewed him all the world and the world's pleasures—"

"*Yesss—*"

"It's *him* that will come back when Last Times come on the world ... and they are coming, my brothers and sisters, can't you feel they are?"

"*Yesss—*"

Rocking and sobbing, the congregation became a sea; the woman seemed to point at all of them, none of them.

"It's *him* that will come as the Antichrist, to lead men into the flaming bowels of perdition, to the bloody end of wickedness, as Star Wormword hangs blazing in the sky, as gall gnaws at the vitals of the children, as women's wombs give forth monstrosities, as the works of men's hands turn to blood—"

"Ahhh—"

"Ah, God—"

"Gawwwwwwww—"

A woman fell on the floor, her legs crashing up and down against the wood. One of her shoes flew off.

"It's *him* that stands behind every fleshly pleasure ... *him!* The Interloper!"

"Yes, Lord!"

A man fell on his knees, holding his head and braying.

"When you take a drink, who holds the bottle?"

"The Interloper!"

"When you sit down to a faro or a Watch Me table, who turns the cards?"

"The Interloper!"

"When you riot in the flesh of another's body, when you pollute yourself, who are you selling your soul to?"

"In—"

"The—"

"Oh, Jesus ... Oh—"

"—loper—"

"—Aw ... Aw ... Aw ..."

"And who is he?" she screamed (but calm within, he could sense the calmness, the mastery, the control, the domination. He thought suddenly, with terror and absolute surety: he has left a demon in her. She is haunted. He felt the hot ripple of sexual desire again through his fear).

The man who was holding his head crashed and blundered forward.

"I'm in hell!" he screamed up at her. His face twisted and writhed as if snakes crawled beneath his skin. "I done fornications! I done gambling! I done weed! I done *sins!* I—" But his voice rose skyward in a dreadful, hysterical wail that drowned articulation. He held his head as if it would burst like an overripe cantaloupe at any moment.

The audience stilled as if a cue had been given, frozen in their half-erotic poses of ecstasy.

Sylvia Pittston reached down and grasped his head. The man's cry ceased as her fingers, strong and white, unblemished and gentle, worked through his hair. He looked up at her dumbly.

"Who was with you in sin?" she asked. Her

eyes looked into his, deep enough, gentle enough, cold enough to drown in.

"The ... the Interloper."

"Called who?"

"Called Satan." Raw, oozing whisper.

"Will you renounce?"

Eagerly: "Yes! Yes! Oh, my Jesus Savior!"

She rocked his head; he stared at her with the blank, shiny eyes of the zealot. "If he walked through that door—" she hammered a finger at the vestibule shadows where the gunslinger stood—"would you renounce him to his face?"

"On my mother's name!"

"Do you believe in the eternal love of Jesus?"

He began to weep. "Your fucking-A I do—"

"He forgives you that, Jonson."

"Praise God," Jonson said, still weeping.

"I know he forgives you just as I know he will cast out the unrepentant from his palaces and into the place of burning darkness."

"*Praise God.*" The congregation drained, spoke it solemnly.

"Just as I know this Interloper, this Satan, this Lord of Flies and Serpents will be cast down and crushed ... will you crush him if you see him, Jonson?"

"Yes and praise God!" Jonson wept.

"Will you crush him if you see him, brothers and sisters?"

"Yess ..." Sated.

"If you see him sashaying down Main St. tomorrow?"

"Praise God ..."

The gunslinger, unsettled, at the same time, faded back out the door and headed for town. The smell of the desert was clear in the air. Almost time to move on. Almost.

XIII

In bed again.

"She won't see you," Allie said. She sounded frightened. "She doesn't see anybody. She only comes out on Sunday evenings to scare the hell out of everybody."

"How long has she been here?"

"Twelve years or so. Let's not talk about her."

"Where did she come from? Which direction?"

"I don't know." Lying.

"Allie?"

"I don't know!"

"Allie?"

"All right! All right! She came from the dwellers! From the desert!"

"I thought so." He relaxed a little. "Where does she live?"

Her voice dropped a notch. "If I tell you, will you make love to me?"

"You know the answer to that."

She sighed. It was an old, yellow sound, like turning pages. "She has a house over the knoll in back of the church. A little shack. It's where the ... the real minister used to live until he moved out. Is that enough? Are you satisfied?"

"No. Not yet." And he rolled on top of her.

XIV

It was the last day, and he knew it.

The sky was an ugly, bruised purple, weirdly lit from above with the first fingers of dawn. Allie moved about like a wraith, lighting lamps, tending the corn fritters that spluttered in the skillet. He had loved her hard after she had told him what he had to know, and she had sensed the coming end and had given more than she had ever given, and she had given it with desperation against the coming of dawn, given it with the tireless energy of sixteen. But she was pale this morning, on the brink of menopause again.

She served him without a word. He ate rapidly, chewing, swallowing, chasing each bite with hot coffee. Allie went to the batwings and stood staring out at the morning, at the silent battalions of slow-moving clouds.

"It's going to dust up today."

"I'm not surprised."

"Are you ever?" she asked ironically, and turned to watch him get his hat. He clapped it on his head and brushed past her.

"Sometimes," he told her. He only saw her once more alive.

XV

By the time he reached Sylvia Pittston's shack, the wind had died utterly and the whole world seemed to wait. He had been in desert country long enough to know that the longer the lull, the harder the wind would blow when it finally decided to start up. A queer, flat light hung over everything.

There was a large wooden cross nailed to the door of the place, which was leaning and tired.

He rapped and waited. No answer. He rapped again. No answer. He drew back and kicked in the door with one hard shot of his right boot. A small bolt on the inside ripped free. The door banged against a haphazardly planked wall and scared rats into skittering flight. Sylvia Pittston sat in the hall, sat in a mammoth darkwood rocker, and looked at him calmly with those great and dark eyes. The stormlight fell on her cheeks in terrifying half-tones. She wore a shawl. The rocker made tiny squeaking noises.

They looked at each other for a long, clockless moment.

"You will never catch him," she said. "You walk in the way of evil."

"He came to you," the gunslinger said.

"And to my bed. He spoke to me in the Tongue. He—"

"He screwed you."

She did not flinch. "You walk an evil way, gunslinger. You stand in shadows. You stood in the shadows of the holy place last night. Did you think I couldn't see you?"

"Why did he heal the weed-eater?"

"He was an angel of God. He said so."

"I hope he smiled when he said it."

She drew her lip back from her teeth in an

unconsciously feral gesture. "He told me you would follow. He told me what to do. He said you are the Antichrist."

The gunslinger shook his head. "He didn't say that."

She smiled up at him lazily. "He said you would want to bed me. Do you?"

"Yes."

"The price is your life, gunslinger. He has got me with child ... the child of an angel. If you invade me—" She let the lazy smile complete her thought. At the same time she gestured with her huge, mountainous thighs. They stretched beneath her garment like pure marble slabs. The effect was dizzying.

The gunslinger dropped his hands to the butts of his pistols. "You have a demon, woman. I can remove it."

The effect was instantaneous. She recoiled against the chair, and a weasel look flashed on her face. "Don't touch me! Don't come near me! You dare not touch the Bride of God!"

"Want to bet?" the gunslinger said, grinning. He stepped toward her.

The flesh on the huge frame quaked. Her face had become a caricature of crazed terror, and she stabbed the sign of the Eye at him with pronged fingers.

"The desert," the gunslinger said. "What after the desert?"

"You'll never catch him! Never! Never! You'll burn! He told me so!"

"I'll catch him," the gunslinger said. "We both know it. What is beyond the desert?"

"No!"

"Answer me!"

"No!"

He slid forward, dropped to his knees, and grabbed her thighs. Her legs locked like a vise. She made strange, lustful keening noises.

"The demon, then," he said.

"No—"

He pried the legs apart and unholstered one of his guns.

"No! No! No!" Her breath came in short, savage grunts.

"Answer me."

She rocked in the chair and the floor trembled. Prayers and garbled bits of jargon flew from her lips.

He rammed the barrel of the gun forward. He could feel the terrified wind sucked into her lungs more than he could hear it. Her hands beat at his head; her legs drummed against the floor. And at the same time the huge body tried to take the invader and enwomb it. Outside nothing watched them but the bruised sky.

She screamed something, high and inarticulate.

"What?"

"Mountains!"

"What about them?"

"He stops ... on the other side ... s-s-sweet *Jesus!* ... to m-make his strength. Med-m-meditation, do you understand? Oh ... I'm ... I'm ..."

The whole huge mountain of flesh suddenly strained forward and upward, yet he was careful not to let her secret flesh touch him.

Then she seemed to wilt and grow smaller, and she wept with her hands in her lap.

"So," he said, getting up. "The demon is served, eh?"

"Get out. You've killed the child. Get out. Get out."

He stopped at the door and looked back. "No child," he said briefly. "No angel, no demon."

"Leave me alone."

He did.

XVI

By the time he arrived at Kennerly's, a queer obscurity had come over the northern horizon and he knew it was dust. Over Tull the air was still dead quiet.

Kennerly was waiting for him on the chaff-strewn stage that was the floor of his barn. "Leaving?" He grinned abjectly at the gunslinger.

"Yes."

"Not before the storm?"

"Ahead of it."

"The wind goes faster than a man on a mule. In the open it can kill you."

"I'll want the mule now," the gunslinger said simply.

"Sure." But Kennerly did not turn away, merely stood as if searching for something further to say, grinning his groveling, hate-filled grin, and his eyes flicked up and over the gunslinger's shoulder.

The gunslinger sidestepped and turned at the same time, and the heavy stick of stovewood that the girl Soobie held swished through the air, grazing his elbow only. She lost hold of it with the force of her swing and it clattered over the floor. In the explosive height of the loft, barnswallows took shadowed wing.

The girl looked at him bovinely. Her breasts thrust with overripe grandeur at the wash-faded shirt she wore. One thumb sought the haven of her mouth with dreamlike slowness.

The gunslinger turned back to Kennerly. Kennerly's grin was huge. His skin was waxy yellow. His eyes rolled in their sockets. "I—" he began in a phlegm-filled whisper and could not continue.

"The mule," the gunslinger prodded gently.

"Sure, sure, sure," Kennerly whispered, the grin now touched with incredulity. He shuffled after it.

He moved to where he could watch Kennerly. The hostler brought the mule back and handed him the bridle. "You get in an' tend your sister," he said to Soobie.

Soobie tossed her head and didn't move.

The gunslinger left them there, staring at each other across the dusty, droppings-strewn floor, he with his sick grin, she with dumb, inanimate defiance. Outside the heat was still like a hammer.

XVII

He walked the mule up the center of the street, his boots sending up squirts of dust. His waterbags were strapped across the mule's back.

He stopped at Sheb's, and Allie was not there. The place was deserted, battened for the storm, but still dirty from the night before. She had not begun her cleaning and the place was as fetid as a wet dog.

He filled his tote sack with corn meal, dried and roasted corn, and half of the raw hamburg in the cooler. He left four gold pieces stacked on the planked counter. Allie did not come down. Sheb's piano bid him a silent, yellow-toothed good-by. He stepped back out and cinched the tote sack across the mule's back. There was a tight feeling in his throat. He might still avoid the trap, but the chances were small. He was, after all, the interloper.

He walked past the shuttered, waiting buildings, feeling the eyes that peered through cracks and chinks. The man in black had played God in Tull. Was it only a sense of the cosmic comic, or a matter of desperation? It was a question of some importance.

There was a shrill, harried scream from behind

him, and doors suddenly threw themselves open. Forms lunged. The trap was sprung, then. Men in longhandles and men in dirty dungarees. Women in slacks and in faded dresses. Even children, tagging after their parents. And in every hand there was a chunk of wood or a knife.

His reaction was automatic, instantaneous, in-bred. He whirled on his heels while his hands pulled the guns from their holsters, the hafts heavy and sure in his hands. It was Allie, and of course it had to be Allie, coming at him with her face distorted, the scar a hellish purple in the lowering light. He saw that she was held hostage; the distorted, grimacing face of Sheb peered over her shoulder like a witch's familiar. She was his shield and sacrifice. He saw it all, clear and shad-owless in the frozen deathless light of the sterile calm, and heard her:

"He's got me O Jesus don't shoot don't don't *don't*—"

But the hands were trained. He was the last of his breed and it was not only his mouth that knew the High Speech. The guns beat their heavy, atonal music into the air. Her mouth flapped and she sagged and the guns fired again. Sheb's head snapped back. They both fell into the dust.

Sticks flew through the air, rained on him. He

staggered, fended them off. One with a nail pounded raggedly through it ripped at his arm and drew blood. A man with a beard stubble and sweat-stained armpits lunged flying at him with a dull kitchen knife held in one paw. The gunslinger shot him dead and the man thumped into the street. His teeth clicked audibly as his chin struck.

"SATAN!" Someone was screaming: "THE ACCURSED! BRING HIM DOWN!"

"THE INTERLOPER!" another voice cried. Sticks rained on him. A knife struck his boot and bounced. "THE INTERLOPER! THE ANTI-CHRIST!"

He blasted his way through the middle of them, running as the bodies fell, his hands picking the targets with dreadful accuracy. Two men and a woman went down, and he ran through the hole they left.

He led them a feverish parade across the street and toward the rickety general store/barber shop that faced Sheb's. He mounted the boardwalk, turned again, and fired the rest of his loads into the charging crowd. Behind them, Sheb and Allie and the others lay crucified in the dust.

They never hesitated or faltered, although every shot he fired found a vital spot and although they had probably never seen a gun except for pictures in old magazines.

He retreated, moving his body like a dancer to avoid the flying missiles. He reloaded as he went, with a rapidity that had also been trained into his fingers. They shuttled busily between gunbelts and cylinders. The mob came up over the board-walk and he stepped into the general store and rammed the door closed. The large display window to the right shattered inward and three men crowded through. Their faces were zealously blank, their eyes filled with bland fire. He shot them all, and the two that followed them. They fell in the window, hung on the jutting shards of glass, choking the opening.

The door crashed and shuddered with their weight and he could hear *her* voice: "THE KILLER! YOUR SOULS! THE CLOVEN HOOF!"

The door ripped off its hinges and fell straight in, making a flat handclap. Dust puffed up from the floor. Men, women, and children charged him. Spittle and stovewood flew. He shot his guns empty and they fell like ninepins. He retreated, shoving over a flour barrel, rolling it at them, into the barber shop, throwing a pan of boiling water that contained two nicked straight-razors. They came on, screaming with frantic incoherency. From somewhere, Sylvia Pittston exhorted them, her voice rising and falling on blind inflections. He pushed shells into hot chambers, smelling the smells of shave and tonsure, smelling his own flesh as the calluses at the tips of his fingers singed.

He went through the back door and onto the porch. The flat scrubland was at his back now, flatly denying the town that crouched against its huge haunch. Three men hustled around the corner, with large betrayer grins on their faces. They saw him, saw him seeing them, and the grins curdled in the second before he mowed them down. A woman had followed them, howling. She was large and fat and known to the patrons of Sheb's as Aunt Mill. The gunslinger blew her backwards and she landed in a whorish sprawl, her skirt kinked up between her thighs.

He went down the steps and walked backwards into the desert, ten paces, twenty. The back door of the barber shop flew open and they boiled out. He caught a glimpse of Sylvia Pittston. He opened up. They fell in squats, they fell backwards, they tumbled over the railing into the dust. They cast no shadows in the deathless purple light of the day. He realized he was screaming. He had been screaming all along. His eyes felt like cracked ball bearings. His balls had drawn up against his belly. His legs were wood. His ears were iron.

The guns were empty and they boiled at him, transmogrified into an Eye and a Hand, and he stood, screaming and reloading, his mind far away and absent, letting his hands do their reloading trick. Could he hold up a hand, tell them he had spent twenty-five years learning this trick and others, tell them of the guns and the blood that had blessed them? Not with his mouth. But his hands could speak their own tale.

They were in throwing range as he finished reloading, and a stick struck him on the forehead and brought blood in abraded drops. In two seconds they would be in gripping distance. In the forefront he saw Kennerly; Kennerly's younger daughter, perhaps eleven; Soobie; two male barflies; a female barfly named Amy Feldon. He let them all have it, and the ones behind them. Their bodies thumped like scarecrows. Blood and brains flew in streamers.

They halted for a moment, startled, the mob face shivering into individual, bewildered faces. A man ran in a large, screaming circle. A woman with blisters on her hands turned her head up and cackled feverishly at the sky. The man whom he had first seen sitting gravely on the steps of the mercantile store made a sudden and amazing load in his pants.

He had time to reload one gun.

Then it was Sylvia Pittston, running at him, waving a wooden cross in each hand. "DEVIL! DEVIL! DEVIL! CHILD-KILLER! MONSTER! DESTROY HIM, BROTHERS AND SISTERS! DESTROY THE CHILDKILLING INTER-LOPER!"

He put a shot into each of the crosspieces, blowing the roods to splinters, and four more into the woman's head. She seemed to accordion into herself and waver like a shimmer of heat.

They all stared at her for a moment in tableau, while the gunslinger's fingers did their reloading trick. The tips of his fingers sizzled and burned. Neat circles were branded into the tips of each one.

There were less of them, now; he had run through them like a mower's scythe. He thought they would break with the woman dead, but someone threw a knife. The hilt struck him squarely between the eyes and knocked him over. They ran at him in a reaching, vicious clot. He fired his guns empty again, lying in his own spent shells. His head hurt and he saw large brown circles in front of his eyes. He missed one shot, downed eleven.

But they were on him, the ones that were left. He fired the four shells he had reloaded, and then they were beating him, stabbing him. He threw a pair of them off his left arm and rolled away. His hands began doing their infallible trick. He was stabbed in the shoulder. He was stabbed in the back. He was hit across the ribs. He was stabbed in the ass. A small boy squirmed at him and made the only deep cut, across the bulge of his calf. The gunslinger blew his head off.

They were scattering and he let them have it again. The ones left began to retreat toward the sand-colored, pitted buildings, and still the hands did their trick, like overeager dogs that want to do their rolling-over trick for you not once or twice but all night, and the hands were cutting them down as they ran. The last one made it as far as the steps of the barber shop's back porch, and then the gunslinger's bullet took him in the back of the head.

Silence came back in, filling jagged spaces.

The gunslinger was bleeding from perhaps twenty different wounds, all of them shallow except for the cut across his calf. He bound it with a strip of shirt and then straightened and examined his kill.

They trailed in a twisted, zigzagging path from the back door of the barber shop to where he stood. They lay in all positions. None of them seemed to be sleeping.

He followed them back, counting as he went. In the general store one man lay with his arms wrapped lovingly around the cracked candy jar he had dragged down with him.

He ended up where he had started, in the middle of the deserted main street. He had shot and killed thirty-nine men, fourteen women, and five children. He had shot and killed everyone in Tull.

A sickish-sweet odor came to him on the first of the dry, stirring wind. He followed it, then looked up and nodded. The decaying body of Nort was spread-eagled atop the plank roof of Sheb's, crucified with wooden pegs. Mouth and eyes were open. A large and purple cloven hoof had been pressed into the skin of his grimy forehead.

He walked out of town. His mule was standing in a clump of weed about forty yards out along the remnant of the coach road. The gunslinger led it back to Kennerly's stable. Outside, the wind was playing a jagtime tune. He put the mule up and went back to Sheb's. He found a ladder in the back shed, went up to the roof, and cut Nort down. The body was lighter than a bag of sticks. He tumbled it down to join the common people. Then he went back inside, ate hamburgers and drank three beers while the light failed and the sand began to fly. That night he slept in the bed where he and Allie had lain. He had no dreams. The next morning the wind was gone and the sun was its usual bright and forgetful self. The bodies had gone south like tumbleweeds with the wind. At midmorning, after he had bound all his cuts, he moved on as well.

XVIII

He thought Brown had fallen asleep. The fire was down to a spark and the bird, Zoltan, had put his head under his wing.

Just as he was about to get up and spread a pallet in the corner, Brown said, "There. You've told it. Do you feel better?"

The gunslinger started. "Why would I feel bad?"

"You're human, you said. No demon. Or did you lie?"

"I didn't lie." He felt the grudging admittance

in him: he liked Brown. Honestly did. And he hadn't lied to the dweller in any way. "Who are you, Brown? Really, I mean."

"Just me," he said, unperturbed. "Why do you have to think you're such a mystery?"

The gunslinger lit a smoke without replying.

"I think you're very close to your man in black," Brown said. "Is he desperate?"

"I don't know."

"Are you?"

"Not yet," the gunslinger said. He looked at Brown with a shade of defiance. "I do what I have to do."

"That's good then," Brown said and turned over and went to sleep.

XIX

In the morning Brown fed him and sent him on his way. In the daylight he was an amazing figure with his scrawny, burnt chest, pencil-like collarbones and ringleted shock of red hair. The bird perched on his shoulder.

"The mule?" The gunslinger asked.

"I'll eat it," Brown said.

"Okay."

Brown offered his hand and the gunslinger shook it. The dweller nodded to the south. "Walk easy."

"You know it."

They nodded at each other and then the gunslinger walked away, his body festooned with guns and water. He looked back once. Brown was rooting furiously at his little cornbed. The crow was perched on the low roof of his dwelling like a gargoyle.

XX

The fire was down, and the stars had begun to pale off. The wind walked restlessly. The gunslinger twitched in his sleep and was still again. He dreamed a thirsty dream. In the darkness the shape of the mountains was invisible. The thoughts of guilt had faded. The desert had baked them out. He found himself thinking more and more about Cort, who had taught him to shoot, instead. Cort had known black from white.

He stirred again and awoke. He blinked at the dead fire with its own shape superimposed over the other, more geometrical one. He was a romantic, he knew it, and he guarded the knowledge jealously.

That, of course, made him think of Cort again. He didn't know where Cort was. The world had moved on.

The gunslinger shouldered his tote sack and moved on with it.

THE
WAY STATION

A nursery rhyme had been playing itself through his mind all day, the maddening kind of thing that will not let go, that stands mockingly outside the apse of the conscious mind and makes faces at the rational being inside. The rhyme was:

The rain in Spain falls mainly on the plain.
There is joy and also pain
but the rain in Spain falls mainly on the plain.

Pretty-plain, loony-sane
The ways of the world all will change
and all the ways remain the same

but if you're mad or only sane
the rain in Spain falls mainly on the plain.

We walk in love but fly in chains
And the planes in Spain fall mainly in the rain.

He knew why the rhyme had occurred to him.
There had been the recurring dream of his room
in the castle and of his mother, who had sung it
to him as he lay solemnly in the tiny bed by the
window of many colors. She did not sing it at
bedtimes because all small boys born to the High
Speech must face the dark alone, but she sang to
him at naptimes and he could remember the
heavy gray rainlight that shivered into colors on
the counterpane; he could feel the coolness of
the room and the heavy warmth of blankets, love
for his mother and her red lips, the haunting melody
of the little nonsense lyric, and her voice.

Now it came back maddeningly, like prickly
heat, chasing its own tail in his mind as he walked.
All his water was gone, and he knew he was very
likely a dead man. He had never expected it to
come to this, and he was sorry. Since noon he had
been watching his feet rather than watching the
way ahead. Out here even the devil-grass had
grown stunted and yellow. The hardpan had dis-

integrated in places to mere rubble. The mountains were not noticeably clearer, although sixteen days had passed since he had left the hut of the last homesteader, a loony-sane young man on the edge of the desert. He had had a raven, the gunslinger remembered, but he couldn't remember the raven's name.

He watched his feet move up and down, listened to the nonsense rhyme sing itself into a pitiful garble in his mind, and wondered when he would fall down for the first time. He didn't want to fall, even though there was no one to see him. It was a matter of pride. A gunslinger knows pride—that invisible bone that keeps the neck stiff.

He stopped and looked up suddenly. It made his head buzz and for a moment his whole body seemed to float. The mountains dreamed against the far horizon. But there was something else up ahead, something much closer. Perhaps only five miles away. He squinted at it, but his eyes were sandblasted and going glareblind. He shook his head and began to walk again. The rhyme circled and buzzed. About an hour later he fell down and skinned his hands. He looked at the tiny beads of blood on his flaked skin with unbelief. The blood looked no thinner; it looked mutely viable. It seemed almost as smug as the desert. He dashed the drops away, hating them blindly. Smug? Why not? The blood was not thirsty. The blood was being served. The blood was being made sacrifice unto. Blood sacrifice. All the blood needed to do was run ... and run ... and run.

He looked at the splotches that had landed on the hardpan and watched as they were sucked up with uncanny suddenness. How do you like that, blood? How does that grab you?

O Jesus, you're far gone.

He got up, holding his hands to his chest and the thing he had seen earlier was almost in front of him, startling a cry out of him—a dust-choked crow-croak. It was a building. No; two buildings, surrounded by a fallen rail fence. The wood seemed old, fragile to the point of elvishness; it was wood being transmogrified into sand. One of the buildings had been a stable—the shape was clear and unmistakable. The other was a house, or an inn. A way station for the coach line. The tottering sand-house (the wind had crusted the wood with grit until it looked like a sand castle that the sun had beat upon at low tide and hardened to a temporary abode) cast a thin line of shadow, and someone sat in the shadow, leaning against the building. And the building seemed to lean with the burden of his weight.

Him, then. At last. The man in black.

The gunslinger stood with his hands to his chest, unaware of his declamatory posture, and gawped. And instead of the tremendous winging excitement he had expected (or perhaps fear, or awe), there was nothing but the dim, atavistic guilt for the sudden, raging hate of his own blood moments earlier and the endless ring-a-rosy of the childhood song:

... the rain in Spain ...

He moved forward, drawing one gun.

... falls mainly on the plain.

He came the last quarter mile at the run, not trying to hide himself; there was nothing to hide behind. His short shadow raced him. He was not aware that his face had become a gray and grinning deathmask of exhaustion; he was aware of nothing but the figure in the shadow. It did not occur to him until later that the figure might even have been dead.

He kicked through one of the leaning fence rails (it broke in two without a sound, almost apologetically) and lunged across the dazzled and silent stable yard, bringing the gun up.

"You're covered! You're covered! You're—"

The figure moved restlessly and stood up. The gunslinger thought: My God, he is worn away to nothing, what's happened to him? Because the man in black had shrunk two full feet and his hair had gone white.

He paused, struck dumb, his head buzzing tunelessly. His heart was racing at a lunatic rate and he thought, I'm dying right here—

He sucked the white-hot air into his lungs and hung his head for a moment. When he raised it again, he saw it wasn't the man in black but a small boy with sun-bleached hair, regarding him with eyes that did not even seem interested. The gunslinger stared at him blankly and then shook his head in negation. But the boy survived his refusal to believe; he was still there, wearing blue jeans with a patch on one knee and a plain brown shirt of rough weave.

The gunslinger shook his head again and started for the stable with his head lowered, gun still in hand. He couldn't think yet. His head was filled with motes and there was a huge, thrumming ache building in it.

The inside of the stable was silent and dark and exploding with heat. The gunslinger stared around himself with huge, floating walleyes. He made a drunken about-face and saw the boy standing in the ruined doorway, staring at him. A huge lancet of pain slipped dreamily into his head, cutting from temple to temple, dividing his brain like an orange. He reholstered his gun, swayed, put out his hands as if to ward off phantoms, and fell over on his face.

When he woke up, he was on his back, and there was a pile of light, odorless hay beneath his head. The boy had not been able to move him, but he had made him reasonably comfortable. And he was cool. He looked down at himself and saw that his shirt was dark with moisture. He licked at his face and tasted water. He blinked at it.

The boy was hunkered down beside him. When he saw the gunslinger's eyes were open, he reached behind him and gave the gunslinger a dented tin can filled with water. He grasped it with trembling hands and allowed himself to drink a little—just a little. When that was down and sitting in his belly, he drank a little more. Then he spilled the rest over his face and made shocked blowing noises. The boy's pretty lips curved in a solemn little smile.

"Want something to eat?"

"Not yet," the gunslinger said. There was still a sick ache in his head from the sunstroke, and the water sat uneasily in his stomach, as if it did not know where to go. "Who are you?"

"My name is John Chambers. You can call me Jake."

The gunslinger sat up, and the sick ache became hard and immediate. He leaned forward and lost a brief struggle with his stomach.

"There's more," Jake said. He took the can and walked toward the rear of the stable. He paused and smiled back at the gunslinger uncertainly. The gunslinger nodded at him and then put his head down and propped it with his hands. The boy was well-made, handsome, perhaps nine. There had been a shadow on his face, but there were shadows on all faces now.

A strange, thumping hum began at the rear of the stable, and the gunslinger raised his head alertly, hands going to gunbutts. The sound lasted for perhaps fifteen seconds and then quit. The boy came back with the can—filled now.

The gunslinger drank sparingly again, and this time it was a little better. The ache in his head was fading.

"I didn't know what to do with you when you fell down," Jake said. "For a couple of seconds there, I thought you were going to shoot me."

"I thought you were somebody else."

"The priest?"

The gunslinger looked up sharply. "What priest?"

The boy looked at him, frowning lightly. "The priest. He camped in the yard. I was in the house over there. I didn't like him, so I didn't come out. He came in the night and went on the next day. I would have hidden from you, but I was sleepin' when you came." He looked darkly over the gunslinger's head. "I don't like people. They fuck me up."

"What did the priest look like?"

The boy shrugged. "Like a priest. He was wearing black things."

"Like a hood and a cassock?"

"What's a cassock?"

"A robe."

The boy nodded. "A robe and a hood."

The gunslinger leaned forward, and something in his face made the boy recoil a little. "How long ago?"

"I—I—"

Patiently, the gunslinger said, "I'm not going to hurt you."

"I don't know. I can't remember time. Every day is the same."

For the first time the gunslinger wondered

consciously how the boy had come to this place, with dry and man-killing leagues of desert all around it. But he would not make it his concern; not yet, at least. "Make a guess. Long ago?"

"No. Not long. I haven't been here long."

The fire lit in him again. He grabbed the can and drank from it with hands that trembled the smallest bit. A snatch of the cradle song recurred, but this time, instead of his mother's face, he saw the scarred face of Alice, who had been his woman in the now-defunct town of Tull. "How long? A week? Two? three?"

The boy looked at him distractedly. "Yes."

"Which one?"

"A week. Or two. I didn't come out. He didn't even drink. I thought he might be the ghost of a priest. I was scared. I've been scared almost all the time." His face quivered like crystal on the edge of the ultimate, destructive high note. "He didn't even build a fire. He just sat there. I don't even know if he went to sleep."

Close! He was closer than he had ever been. In spite of his extreme dehydration, his hands felt faintly moist; greasy.

"There's some dried meat," the boy said.

"All right." The gunslinger nodded. "Good."

The boy got up to fetch it, his knees popping

slightly. He made a fine straight figure. The desert had not yet sapped him. His arms were thin, but the skin, although tanned, had not dried and cracked. He's got juice, the gunslinger thought. He drank from the can again. He's got juice and he didn't come from this place.

Jake came back with a pile of dried jerky on what looked like a sun-scoured breadboard. The meat was tough, stringy, and salty enough to make the cankered lining of the gunslinger's mouth sing. He ate and drank until he felt logy, and then settled back. The boy ate only a little.

The gunslinger regarded him steadily, and the boy looked back at him. "Where did you come from, Jake?" He asked finally.

"I don't know." The boy frowned. "I did know. I knew when I came here, but it's all fuzzy now, like a bad dream when you wake up. I have lots of bad dreams."

"Did somebody bring you?"

"No," the boy said. "I was just here."

"You're not making any sense," the gunslinger said flatly.

Quite suddenly the boy seemed on the verge of tears. "I can't help it. I was just here. And now you'll go away and I'll starve because you ate up almost all my food. I didn't ask to be here. I don't like it. It's spooky."

"Don't feel so sorry for yourself. Make do."

"I didn't ask to be here," the boy repeated with bewildered defiance.

The gunslinger ate another piece of the meat, chewing the salt out of it before swallowing. The boy had become part of it, and the gunslinger was convinced he told the truth—he had not asked for it. It was too bad. He himself ... *he* had asked for it. But he had not asked for the game to become this dirty. He had not asked to be allowed to turn his guns on the unarmed populace of Tull; had not asked to shoot Allie, her face marked by that strange, shining scar; had not asked to be faced with a choice between the obsession of his duty and his quest and criminal amorality. The man in black had begun to pull bad strings in his desperation, if it was the man in black who had pulled this particular string. It was not fair to ring in innocent bystanders and make them speak lines they didn't understand on a strange stage. Allie, he thought, Allie at least had been into the world in her own self-illusory way. But this *boy* ... this God-damned *boy*. . . .

"Tell me what you can remember," he told Jake.

"It's only a little. It doesn't seem to make any sense anymore."

"Tell me. Maybe I can pick up the sense."

"There was a place ... the one before this one. A high place with lots of rooms and a patio where you could look at tall buildings and water. There was a statue that stood in the water."

"A statue in the water?"

"Yes. A lady with a crown and a torch."

"Are you making this up?"

"I guess I must be," the boy said hopelessly. "There were things to ride in on the streets. Big ones and little ones. Yellow ones. A lot of yellow ones. I walked to school. There were cement paths beside the streets. Windows to look in and more statues wearing clothes. The statues sold the clothes. I know it sounds crazy, but the statues sold the clothes."

The gunslinger shook his head and looked for a lie on the boy's face. He saw none.

"I walked to school," the boy repeated fixedly. "And I had a—" His eyes tilted closed and his lips moved gropingly. "—a brown ... book ... bag. I carried a lunch. And I wore—" the groping again, agonized groping "—a tie."

"A what?"

"I don't know." The boy's fingers made a slow,

unconscious clinching motion at his throat—a gesture the gunslinger associated with hanging. "I don't know. It's just all gone." And he looked away.

"May I put you to sleep?" the gunslinger asked.

"I'm not sleepy."

"I can make you sleepy, and I can make you remember."

Doubtfully, Jake asked, "How could you do that?"

"With this."

The gunslinger removed one of the shells from his gunbelt and twirled it in his fingers. The movement was dexterous, as flowing as oil. The shell cartwheeled effortlessly from thumb and index to index and second, to second and ring, to ring and pinky. It popped out of sight and reappeared; seemed to float briefly, and then reversed. The shell walked across the gunslinger's fingers. The fingers themselves moved like a beaded curtain in a breeze. The boy watched, his initial doubt replaced with plain delight, then by raptness, then by a dawning mute blankness. The eyes slipped shut. The shell danced back and forth. Jake's eyes opened again, caught the steady, limpid dance between the gunslinger's fingers for a while longer, and then his eyes closed once more. The gunslinger continued, but Jake's eyes did not open again. The boy breathed with steady, bovine calmness. Was this part of it? Yes. There was a certain beauty, a logic, like the lacy frettings that fringe hard blue ice-packs. He seemed to hear the sound of wind-chimes. Not for the first time the gunslinger tasted the smooth, loden taste of soul-sickness. The shell in his fingers, manipulated with such unknown grace, was suddenly undead, horrific, the spoor of a monster. He dropped it into his palm and closed it into a fist with painful force. There were such things as rape in the world. Rape and murder and unspeakable practices, and all of them were for the good, the bloody good, for the myth, for the grail, for the Tower. Ah, the Tower stood somewhere, rearing its black bulk to the sky, and in his desert-scoured ears, the gunslinger heard the faint sweet sound of wind-chimes.

"Where are you?" he asked.

Jake Chambers is going downstairs with his bookbag. There is Earth Science, there is Economic Geography, there is a notepad, a pencil, a lunch his mother's cook, Mrs. Greta Shaw, has made for him in the chrome-and-formica kitchen where a fan whirrs eter-

nally, sucking up alien odors. In his lunch sack he has a peanut butter and jelly sandwich, a bologna, lettuce, and onion sandwich, and four Oreo cookies. His parents do not hate him, but they seem to have overlooked him. They have abdicated and left him to Mrs. Greta Shaw, to nannies, to a tutor in the summer and The School (which is Private and Nice, and most of all, White) the rest of the time. None of these people have ever pretended to be more than what they are—professional people, the best in their fields. None have folded him to a particularly warm bosom as usually happens in the historical novels his mother reads and which Jake has dipped into, looking for the "hot parts." Hysterical novels, his father sometimes calls them, and sometimes, "bodice-rippers." You should talk, his mother says with infinite scorn from behind some closed door where Jake listens. His father works for The Network, and Jake could pick him out of a line-up. Probably.

Jake does not know that he hates all the professional people, but he does. People have always bewildered him. He likes stairs and will not use the self-service elevator in his building. His mother, who is scrawny in a sexy way, often goes to bed with sick friends.

Now he is on the street, Jake Chambers is on the street, he has "Hit the bricks." He is clean and well-mannered, comely, sensitive. He has no friends;

only acquaintances. He has never bothered to think about this, but it hurts him. He does not know or understand that a long association with professional people has caused him to take many of their traits. Mrs. Greta Shaw makes very professional sandwiches. She quarters them and cuts off the breadcrusts so that when he eats in the gym period four he looks like he ought to be at a cocktail party with a drink in his other hand instead of a sports novel from the school library. His father makes a great deal of money because he is a master of "the kill"—that is, placing a stronger show on his Network against a weaker show on a rival Network. His father smokes four packs of cigarettes a day. His father does not cough, but he has a hard grin, like the steak knives they sell in supermarkets.

Down the street. His mother leaves cab fare, but he walks every day it doesn't rain, swinging his bookbag, a small boy who looks very American with his blonde hair and blue eyes. Girls have already begun to notice him (with their mother's approval), and he does not shy away with skittish little-boy arrogance. He talks to them with unknowing professionalism and puzzles them away. He likes geography and bowls in the afternoon. His father owns stock in a company that makes automatic pin-setting machinery, but the bowling alley Jake patronizes does not use his father's brand. He does not think he has thought about this, but he has.

Walking down the street, he passes Brendio's where the models stand dressed in fur coats, in six-button Edwardian suits, some in nothing at all; some are "barenaked." These models—these mannequins— are perfectly professional, and he hates all profession-alism. He is too young to have learned to hate himself yet, but that seed is already there; it has been planted in the bitter cleft of his heart.

He comes to the corner and stands with his bookbag at his side. Traffic roars by—grunting busses, taxis, Volkswagens, a large truck. He is just a boy, but not average, and he sees the man who kills him out of the corner of his eye. It is the man in black, and he doesn't see the face, only the swirling robe, the outstretched hands. He falls into the street with his arms outstretched, not letting go of the bookbag which contains Mrs. Greta Shaw's extremely profes-sional lunch. There is a brief glance through a po-larized windshield at the horrified face of a businessman wearing a dark-blue hat in the band of which is a small, jaunty feather. An old woman on the far curb screams—she is wearing a black hat with a net. Nothing jaunty about that black net; it is like a mourner's veil. Jake feels nothing but surprise and his usual sense of headlong bewilderment—is this how it ends? He lands hard in the street and looks at an asphalt-sealed crack some two inches from his eyes. The bookbag is jolted from his hand. He is wondering if he has skinned his knees when the car of the businessman wearing the blue hat with the jaunty feather passes over him. It is a big blue 1976 Cadillac with sixteen-inch wheels. It is almost exactly the same color as the businessman's hat. It breaks Jake's back, mushes his stomach, and sends blood from his mouth in a high-pressure jet. He turns his head and sees the Cadillac's gaming taillights and smoke spurting from beneath its locked rear wheels. The car has also run over his bookbag and left a wide black tread on it. He turns his head the other way and sees a large yellow Ford screaming to a stop inches from his body. A black fellow who has been selling pretzels and sodas from a pushcart is coming toward him on the run. Blood runs from Jake's nose, ears, eyes, rectum. His genitals have been squashed. He wonders irritably how badly he has skinned his knees. Now the driver of the Cadillac is running toward him, babbling. Somewhere a terrible, calm voice, the voice of doom, says: "I am a priest. Let me through. An act of Contrition—"

He sees the black robe and knows sudden horror. It is him, the man in black. He turns his face away

with the last of his strength. Somewhere a radio is
playing a song by the rock group Kiss. He sees his
own hand trailing on the pavement, small, white,
shapely. He has never bitten his nails.

Looking at his hand, Jake dies.

The gunslinger sat in frowning thought. He
was tired and his body ached and the thoughts
came with aggravating slowness. Across from him
the amazing boy slept with his hands folded in
his lap, still breathing calmly. He had told his tale
without much emotion, although his voice had
trembled near the end, when he had come to the
part about the "priest" and the "Act of Contrition."
He had not, of course, told the gunslinger about his
family and his own sense of bewildered dichotomy,
but that had seeped through anyway—enough had
seeped through to make out its shape. The fact
that there had never been such a city as the boy
described (or, if so, it had only existed in the myth
of prehistory) was not the most upsetting part of
the story, but it was disturbing. It was all disturbing. The gunslinger was afraid of the implications.

"Jake?"

"Uh-huh?"

"Do you want to remember this when you
wake up, or forget it?"

"Forget it," the boy said promptly. "I bled."

"All right. You're going to sleep, understand? Go ahead and lie over."

Jake laid over, looking small and peaceful and harmless. The gunslinger did not believe he was harmless. There was a deadly feeling about him, and the stink of predestination. He didn't like the feeling, but he liked the boy. He liked him a great deal.

"Jake?"

"Shhh. I want to sleep."

"Yes. And when you wake up you won't remember any of this."

"Kay."

The gunslinger watched him for a brief time, thinking of his own boyhood, which usually seemed to have happened to another person—to a person who had jumped through some osmotic lens and become someone else—but which now seemed poignantly close. It was very hot in the stable of the way station, and he carefully drank some more water. He got up and walked to the back of the building, pausing to look into one of the horse stalls. There was a small pile of white hay in the corner, and a neatly folded blanket, but there was no smell of horse. There was no smell of anything in the stable. The sun had bled away every smell and left nothing. The air was perfectly neutral.

At the back of the stable was a small, dark room with a stainless steel machine in the center. It was untouched by rust or rot. It looked like a butter churn. At the left, a chrome pipe jutted from it, terminating over a drain in the floor. The gunslinger had seen pumps like it in other dry places, but never one so big. He could not contemplate how deep they must have drilled before they struck water, secret and forever black under the desert.

Why hadn't they removed the pump when the way station had been abandoned?

Demons, perhaps.

He shuddered abruptly, an abrupt twisting of his back. Heatflesh poked out on his skin, then receded. He went to the control switch and pushed the ON button. The machine began to hum. After perhaps half a minute, a stream of cool, clear water belched from the pipe and went down the drain to be recirculated. Perhaps three gallons flowed out of the pipe before the pump shut itself down with a final click. It was a thing as alien to this place and time as true love, and yet as concrete as a Judgment, a silent reminder of the time when the world had not yet moved on. It probably ran on an atomic slug, as there was no electricity within a thousand miles of here and even dry batteries would have lost their charge long ago. The gunslinger didn't like it.

He went back and sat down beside the boy, who had put one hand under his cheek. Nice-looking boy. The gunslinger drank some more water and crossed his legs so he was sitting Indian fashion. The boy, like the squatter on the edge of the desert who kept the bird (Zoltan, the gunslinger remembered abruptly, the bird's name was Zoltan), had lost his sense of time, but the fact that the man in black was closer seemed beyond doubt. Not for the first time, the gunslinger wondered if the man in black was letting him catch up for some reason of his own. Perhaps the gunslinger was playing into his hands. He tried to imagine what the confrontation might be like, and could not.

He was very hot, but he no longer felt sick. The nursery rhyme occurred to him again, but this time instead of his mother, he thought of Cort—Cort, with his face hem-stitched with the scars of bricks and bullets and blunt instruments. The scars of war. He wondered if Cort had ever had a love to match those monumental scars. He doubted it. He thought of Aileen, and of Marten, that incomplete enchanter.

The gunslinger was not a man to dwell on the past; only a shadowy conception of the future and of his own emotional make-up saved him from being a creature without imagination, a dullard. His present run of thought therefore rather amazed him. Each name called up others—Cuthbert, Paul, the old man Jonas; and Susan, the lovely girl at the window.

The piano player in Tull (also dead, all dead in Tull, and by his hand) had been fond of the old songs, and the gunslinger hummed one tunelessly under his breath:

Love o love o careless love
See what careless love has done.

The gunslinger laughed, bemused. *I am the last of that green and warm-hued world.* And for all his nostalgia, he felt no self-pity. The world had moved on mercilessly, but his legs were still strong, and the man in black was closer. The gunslinger nodded out.

When he woke up it was almost dark and the boy was gone.

The gunslinger got up, hearing his joints pop, and went to the stable door. There was a small flame dancing in darkness on the porch of the inn. He walked toward it, his shadow long and black and trailing in the ochre light of the sunset.

Jake was sitting by a kerosene lamp. "The oil was in a drum," he said, "but I was scared to burn it in the house. Everything's so dry—"

"You did just right." The gunslinger sat down, seeing but not thinking about the dust of years that puffed up around his rump. The flame from the lamp shadowed the boy's face with delicate tones. The gunslinger produced his poke and rolled a cigarette.

"We have to talk," he said.

Jake nodded.

"I guess you know I'm on the prod for that man you saw."

"Are you going to kill him?"

"I don't know. I have to make him tell me something. I may have to make him take me someplace."

"Where?"

"To find a tower," the gunslinger said. He held his cigarette over the chimney of the lamp and drew on it; the smoke drifted away on the rising night breeze. Jake watched it. His face showed neither fear nor curiosity, certainly not enthusiasm.

"So I'm going on tomorrow," the gunslinger

said. "You'll have to come with me. How much of that meat is left?"

"Only a handful."

"Corn?"

"A little."

The gunslinger nodded. "Is there a cellar?"

"Yes." Jake looked at him. The pupils of his eyes had grown to a huge, fragile size. "You pull up on a ring in the floor, but I didn't go down. I was afraid the ladder would break and I wouldn't be able to get up again. And it smells bad. It's the only thing around here that smells at all."

"We'll get up early and see if there's anything down there worth taking. Then we'll bug out."

"All right." The boy paused and then said, "I'm glad I didn't kill you when you were sleeping. I had a pitchfork and I thought about doing it. But I didn't, and now I won't have to be afraid to go to sleep."

"What would you be afraid of?"

The boy looked at him ominously. "Spooks. Of *him* coming back."

"The man in black," the gunslinger said. Not a question.

"Yes. Is he a bad man?"

"That depends on where you're standing," the gunslinger said absently. He got up and pitched his cigarette out onto the hardpan. "I'm going to sleep."

The boy looked at him timidly. "Can I sleep in the stable with you?"

"Of course."

The gunslinger stood on the steps, looking up, and the boy joined him. Polaris was up there, and Mars. It seemed to the gunslinger that, if he closed his eyes he would be able to hear the croaking of the first spring peepers, smell the green and almost-summer smell of the court lawns after their first cutting (and hear, perhaps, the indolent click of croquet balls as the ladies of the East Wing, attired only in their shifts as dusk glimmered toward dark, played at Points), could almost see Aileen as she came through the break in the hedges—

It was not like him to think so much of the past.

He turned back and picked up the lamp. "Let's go to sleep," he said.

They crossed to the stable together.

The next morning he explored the cellar.

Jake was right; it smelled bad. It had a wet, swampy smell that made the gunslinger feel nauseous and a little lightheaded after the antiseptic odorlessness of the desert and the stable. The cellar smelled of cabbages and turnips and potatoes with long, sightless eyes gone to everlasting rot. The ladder, however, seemed quite sturdy, and he climbed down.

The floor was earthen, and his head almost touched the overhead beams. Down here spiders still lived, disturbingly big ones with mottled gray bodies. Many of them had mutated. Some had eyes on stalks, some had what might have been as many as sixteen legs.

The gunslinger peered around and waited for his nighteyes.

"You all right?" Jake called down nervously.

"Yes." He focused on the corner. "There are cans. Wait."

He went carefully to the corner, ducking his head. There was an old box with one side folded down. The cans were vegetables—green beans, yellow beans ... and three cans of corned beef.

He scooped up an armload and went back to the ladder. He climbed halfway up and handed them to Jake, who knelt to receive them. He went back for more.

It was on the third trip that he heard the groaning in the foundations.

He turned, looked, and felt a kind of dreamy

terror wash over him, a feeling both languid and repellent, like sex in the water—one drowning within another.

The foundation was composed of huge sandstone blocks that had probably been evenly cornered when the way station was new, but which were now at every zigzag, drunken angle. It made the wall look as if it were inscribed with strange, meandering hieroglyphics. And from the joining of two of these abstruse cracks, a thin spill of sand was running, as if something on the other side was digging itself through with slobbering, agonized intensity.

The groaning rose and fell, becoming louder, until the whole cellar was full of the sound, an abstract noise of ripping pain and dreadful effort.

"Come up!" Jake screamed. "O Jesus, mister, come up!"

"Go away," the gunslinger said calmly.

"Come up!" Jake screamed again.

The gunslinger did not answer. He pulled leather with his right hand.

There was a hole in the wall now, a hole as big as a coin. He could hear, through the curtain of his own terror, Jake's pattering feet as the boy ran. Then the spill of sand stopped. The groaning ceased, but there was a sound of steady, labored breathing.

"Who are you?" The gunslinger asked.

No answer.

And in the High Speech, his voice filling with the old thunder of command, Roland demanded: "Who are you, Demon? Speak, if you would speak. My time is short; my hands lose patience."

"Go slow," a dragging, clotted voice said from within the wall. And the gunslinger felt the dream-like terror deepen and grow almost solid. It was the voice of Alice, the woman he had stayed with in the town of Tull. But she was dead; he had seen her go down himself, a bullet hole between her eyes. Fathoms seemed to swim by his eyes, descending. "Go slow past the Drawers, gunslinger. While you travel with the boy, the man in black travels with your soul in his pocket."

"What do you mean? Speak on!"

But the breathing was gone.

The gunslinger stood for a moment, frozen, and then one of the huge spiders dropped on his arm and scrambled frantically up to his shoulder. With an involuntary grunt he brushed it away and got his feet moving. He did not want to do it, but custom was strict, inviolable. The dead from the dead, as the old proverb has it; only a corpse may speak. He went to the hole and punched at it. The sandstone crumbled easily at the edges, and with a bare stiffening of muscles, he thrust his hand through the wall.

And touched something solid, with raised and fretted knobs. He drew it out. He held a jaw-bone, rotted at the far hinge. The teeth leaned this way and that.

"All right," he said softly. He thrust it rudely into his back pocket and went back up the ladder, carrying the last cans awkwardly. He left the trapdoor open. The sun would get in and kill the spiders.

Jake was halfway across the stable yard, cowering on the cracked, rubbly hardpan. He screamed when he saw the gunslinger, backed away a step or two, and then ran to him, crying.

"I thought it got you, that it got you. I thought—"

"It didn't." He held the boy to him, feeling his face, hot against his chest, and his hands, dry against his ribcage. It occurred to him later that this was when he began to love the boy—which was, of course, what the man in black must have planned all along.

"Was it a demon?" The voice was muffled.

"Yes. A speaking-demon. We don't have to go back there anymore. Come on."

They went to the stable, and the gunslinger made a rough pack from the blanket he had slept under—it was hot and prickly, but there was nothing else. That done, he filled the waterbags from the pump.

"You carry one of the waterbags," the gunslinger said. "Wear it around your shoulders—like a fakir carries his snake. See?"

"Yes." The boy looked up at him worshipfully. He slung one of the bags.

"Is it too heavy?"

"No. It's fine."

"Tell me the truth, now. I can't carry you if you get a sunstroke."

"I won't have a sunstroke. I'll be okay."

The gunslinger nodded.

"We're going to the mountains, aren't we?"

"Yes."

They walked out into the steady smash of the sun. Jake, his head as high as the swing of the gunslinger's elbows, walked to his right and a little ahead, the rawhide-wrapped ends of the waterbag hanging nearly to his shins. The gunslinger had crisscrossed two more waterbags across his shoulders and carried the sling of food in his armpit, his left arm holding it against his body.

They passed through the far gate of the way

station and found the blurred ruts of the stage track again. They had walked perhaps fifteen minutes when Jake turned around and waved at the two buildings. They seemed to huddle in the titanic space of the desert.

"Goodbye!" Jake cried. "Goodbye!"

They walked. The stage track breasted a frozen sand drumlin, and when the gunslinger looked around, the way station was gone. Once again there was the desert, and that only.

They were three days out of the way station; the mountains were deceptively clear now. They could see the rise of the desert into foothills, the first naked slopes, the bedrock bursting through the skin of the earth in sullen, eroded triumph. Further up, the land gentled off briefly again, and for the first time in months or years the gunslinger could see green—real, living green. Grass, dwarf spruces, perhaps even willows, all fed by snow runoff from further up. Beyond that the rock took over again, rising in cyclopean, tumbled splendor to the blinding snowcaps. Off to the left, a huge slash showed the way to the smaller, eroded sandstone cliffs and mesas and buttes on the far side. This draw was obscured in the almost continual gray membrane of showers. At night, Jake would sit fascinated for the few minutes before he fell into sleep, watching the brilliant swordplay of the far-off lightning, white and purple, startling in the clarity of the night air.

The boy was fine on the trail. He was tough, but more than that, he seemed to fight exhaustion with a calm and professional reservoir of will which the gunslinger fully appreciated. He did not talk much and he did not ask questions, not even about the jawbone, which the gunslinger turned over and over in his hands during his evening smoke. He caught a sense that the boy felt highly flattered by the gunslinger's companionship—perhaps even exalted by it—and this disturbed him. The boy had been placed in his path—*While you travel with the boy, the man in black travels with your soul in his pocket*—and the fact that Jake was not slowing him down only opened the way to more sinister possibilities.

They passed the symmetrical campfire leavings of the man in black at regular intervals, and it seemed to the gunslinger that these leavings were much fresher now. On the third night, the gunslinger was sure that he could see the distant spark of another campfire, somewhere in the first rising swell of the foothills.

Near two o'clock on the fourth day out from the way station, Jake reeled and almost fell.

"Here, sit down," the gunslinger said.

"No, I'm okay."

"Sit down."

The boy sat obediently. The gunslinger squatted close by, so Jake would be in his shadow.

"Drink."

"I'm not supposed to until—"

"Drink."

The boy drank, three swallows. The gunslinger wet the tail of the blanket, which was lighter now, and applied the damp fabric to the boy's wrists and forehead, which were fever-dry.

"From now on we rest every afternoon at this time. Fifteen minutes. Do you want to sleep?"

"No." The boy looked at him with shame. The gunslinger looked back blandly. In an abstracted way he withdrew one of the bullets from his belt and began to twirl it between his fingers. The boy watched, fascinated.

"That's neat," he said.

The gunslinger nodded. "Sure it is." He paused. "When I was your age, I lived in a walled city, did I tell you that?"

The boy shook his head sleepily.

"Sure. And there was an evil man—"

"The priest?"

"No," the gunslinger said, "but the two of

them had some relationship, I think now. Maybe even half-brothers. Marten was a wizard ... like Merlin. Do they tell of Merlin where you come from, Jake?"

"Merlin and Arthur and the knights of the round table," Jake said dreamily.

The gunslinger felt a nasty jolt go through him. "Yes," he said. "I was very young, ..."

But the boy was asleep sitting up, his hands folded neatly in his lap.

"When I snap my fingers, you'll wake up. You'll be rested and fresh. Do you understand?"

"Yes."

"Lie over, then."

The gunslinger got makings from his poke and rolled a cigarette. There was something missing. He searched for it in his diligent, careful way and located it. The missing thing was that maddening sense of hurry, the feeling that he might be left behind at any time, that the trail would die out and he would be left with only a broken piece of string. All that was gone now, and the gunslinger was slowly becoming sure that the man in black wanted to be caught.

What would follow?

The question was too vague to catch his interest. Cuthbert would have found interest in it, lively interest, but Cuthbert was gone, and the gunslinger could only go forward in the way he knew.

He watched the boy as he smoked, and his mind turned back on Cuthbert, who had always laughed—to his death he had gone laughing—and Cort, who never laughed, and on Marten, who sometimes smiled—a thin, silent smile that had its own disquieting gleam ... like an eye that slips open in the dark and discloses blood. And there had been the falcon, of course. The falcon was named David, after the legend of the boy with the sling. David, he was quite sure, knew nothing but the need for murder, rending, and terror. Like the gunslinger himself. David was no dilettante; he played the center of the court.

Perhaps, though, in some final accounting, David the falcon had been closer to Marten than to anyone else ... and perhaps his mother, Gabrielle, had known it.

The gunslinger's stomach seemed to rise painfully against his heart, but his face didn't change. He watched the smoke of his cigarette rise into the hot desert air and disappear, and his mind went back.

II

The sky was white, perfectly white, and the smell of rain was in the air. The smell of hedges and growing green was strong and sweet. It was deep spring.

David sat on Cuthbert's arm, a small engine of destruction with bright golden eyes that glared outward at nothing. The rawhide leash attached to his jesses was looped carelessly about Cuthbert's arm.

Cort stood aside from the two boys, a silent figure in patched leather trousers and a green cotton shirt that had been cinched high with his old, wide infantry belt. The green of his shirt merged with the hedges and the rolling turf of the Back Courts, where the ladies had not yet begun to play at Points.

"Get ready," Roland whispered to Cuthbert.

"We're ready," Cuthbert said confidently. "Aren't we, Davey?"

They spoke the low speech, the language of both scullions and squires; the day when they would be allowed to use their own tongue in the presence of others was still far. "It's a beautiful day for it. Can you smell the rain? It's—"

Cort abruptly raised the trap in his hands and

let the side fall open. The dove was out and up, trying for the sky in a quick, fluttering blast of its wings. Cuthbert pulled the leash, but he was slow; the hawk was already up and his takeoff was awkward. With a brief twitch of its wings the hawk had recovered. It struck upward, gaining altitude over the dove, moving bullet-swift.

Cort walked over to where the boys stood, casually, and swung his huge and twisted fist at Cuthbert's ear. The boy fell over without a sound, although his lips writhed back from his gums. A trickle of blood flowed slowly from his ear and onto the rich green grass.

"You were slow," he said.

Cuthbert was struggling to his feet. "I'm sorry, Cort. It's just that I—"

Cort swung again, and Cuthbert fell over again. The blood flowed more swiftly now.

"Speak the High Speech," he said softly. His voice was flat, with a slight, drunken rasp. "Speak your act of contrition in the speech of civilization for which better men than you will ever be have died, maggot."

Cuthbert was getting up again. Tears stood brightly in his eyes, but his lips were pressed tightly together in a bright line of hate which did not quiver.

"I grieve," Cuthbert said in a voice of breathless control. "I have forgotten the face of my father, whose guns I hope someday to bear."

"That's right, brat," Cort said. "You'll consider what you did wrong, and bookend your reflections with hunger. No supper. No breakfast."

"Look!" Roland cried. He pointed up.

The hawk had climbed above the soaring dove. It glided for a moment, its stubby, muscular wings outstretched and without movement on the still, white spring air. Then it folded its wings and dropped like a stone. The two bodies came together, and for a moment Roland fancied he could see blood in the air ... but it might have been his imagination. The hawk gave a brief scream of triumph. The dove fluttered, twisting, to the ground, and Roland ran toward the kill, leaving Cort and the chastened Cuthbert behind him.

The hawk had landed beside its prey and was complacently tearing into its plump white breast. A few feathers seesawed slowly downward.

"David!" The boy yelled, and tossed the hawk a piece of rabbit flesh from his poke. The hawk caught it on the fly, ingested it with an upward shaking of its back and throat, and Roland attempted to re-leash the bird.

The hawk whirled, almost absentmindedly, and ripped skin from Roland's arm in a long, dangling gash. Then it went back to its meal.

With a grunt, Roland looped the leash again, this time catching David's diving, slashing beak on the leather gauntlet he wore. He gave the hawk another piece of meat, then hooded it. Docilely, David climbed onto his wrist.

He stood up proudly, the hawk on his arm.

"What's this?" Cort asked, pointing to the dripping slash on Roland's forearm. The boy stationed himself to receive the blow, locking his throat against any possible cry, but no blow fell.

"He struck me," Roland said.

"You pissed him off," Cort said. "The hawk does not fear you, boy, and the hawk never will. The hawk is God's gunslinger."

Roland merely looked at Cort. He was not an imaginative boy, and if Cort had intended to imply a moral, it was lost on him; he was pragmatic enough to believe that it might have been one of the few foolish statements he had ever heard Cort make.

Cuthbert came up behind them and stuck his tongue out at Cort, safely on his blind side. Roland did not smile, but nodded to him.

"Go in now," Cort said, taking the hawk. He

pointed at Cuthbert. "But remember your reflection, maggot. And your fast. Tonight and tomorrow morning."

"Yes," Cuthbert said, stiltedly formal now. "Thank you for this instructive day."

"You learn," Cort said, "but your tongue has a bad habit of lolling from your stupid mouth when your instructor's back is turned. Mayhap the day will come when it and you will learn their respective places." He struck Cuthbert again, this time solidly between the eyes and hard enough so that Roland heard a dull thud—the sound a mallet makes when a scullion taps a keg of beer. Cuthbert fell backward onto the lawn, his eyes cloudy and dazed at first. Then they cleared and he stared burningly up at Cort, his hatred unveiled, a pinprick as bright as the dove's blood in the center of each eye.

Cuthbert nodded and parted his lips in a scarifying smile that Roland had never seen.

"Then there's hope for you," Cort said. "When you think you can, you come for me, maggot."

"How did you know?" Cuthbert said between his teeth.

Cort turned toward Roland so swiftly that Roland almost fell back a step—and then both of them would have been on the grass, decorating the new green with their blood. "I saw it reflected in this maggot's eyes," he said. "Remember it, Cuthbert. Last lesson for today."

Cuthbert nodded again, the same frightening smile on his face. "I grieve," he said. "I have forgotten the face—"

"Cut that shit," Cort said, losing interest. He turned to Roland. "Go on, now. The both of you. If I have to look at your stupid maggot faces any longer I'll puke my guts."

"Come on," Roland said.

Cuthbert shook his head to clear it and got to his feet. Cort was already walking down the hill in his squat, bowlegged stride, looking powerful and somehow prehistoric. The shaved and grizzled spot at the top of his head loomed at a slant, hunched.

"I'll kill the son of a bitch," Cuthbert said, still smiling. A large goose egg, purple and knotted, was rising mystically on his forehead.

"Not you or me," Roland said, suddenly bursting into a grin. "You can have supper in the west kitchen with me. Cook will give us some."

"He'll tell Cort."

"He's no friend of Cort's," Roland said, and then shrugged. "And what if he did?"

Cuthbert grinned back. "Sure. Right. I always

wanted to know how the world looked when your head was on backwards and upside down."

They started back together over the green lawns, casting shadows in the fine white springlight.

The cook in the west kitchen was named Hax. He stood huge in foodstained whites, a man with a crude-oil complexion whose ancestry was a quarter black, a quarter yellow, a quarter from the South Islands, now almost forgotten (the world had moved on), and a quarter God knew what. He shuffled about three high-ceilinged steamy rooms like a tractor in low gear, wearing huge, Caliph-like slippers. He was one of those quite rare adults who communicate with small children fairly well and who love them all impartially—not in a sugary way but in a businesslike fashion that may sometimes entail a hug, in the same way that closing a big business deal may call for a handshake. He even loved the boys who had begun The Training, although they were different from other children—not always demonstrative and somehow dangerous, not in an adult way, but rather as if they were ordinary children with a slight touch of madness—and Cuthbert was not the first of Cort's students whom he had fed on the sly. At this moment he stood in front of his huge, rambling electric stove—one of six working appliances left on the whole estate. It was his personal domain, and he stood there watching the two boys bolt the gravied meat scraps he had produced. Behind, before, and all around, cookboys, scullions, and various underlings rushed through the foaming, humid air, rattling pans, stirring stew, slaving over potatoes and vegetables in nether regions. In the dimly lit pantry alcove, a washerwoman with a doughy, miserable face and hair caught up in a rag splashed water around on the floor with a mop.

One of the scullery boys rushed up with a man from the Guards in tow. "This man, he wantchoo, Hax."

"All right." Hax nodded to the Guard, and he nodded back. "You boys," he said. "Go over to Maggie, she'll give you some pie. Then scat."

They nodded and went over to Maggie, who gave them huge wedges of pie on dinner plates ... but gingerly, as if they were wild dogs that might bite her.

"Let's eat it on the stairs," Cuthbert said.

"All right."

They sat behind a huge, sweating stone colonnade, out of sight of the kitchen, and gobbled their pie with their fingers. It was only moments later that they saw shadows fall on the far curving wall of the wide staircase. Roland grabbed Cuthbert's arm. "Come on," he said. "Someone's coming." Cuthbert looked up, his face surprised and berry-stained.

But the shadows stopped, still out of sight. It was Hax and the man from the Guards. The boys sat where they were. If they moved now, they might be heard.

"... the good man," the Guard was saying.

"In Farson?"

"In two weeks," the Guard replied. "Maybe three. You have to come with us. There's a shipment from the freight depot...." A particularly loud crash of pots and pans and a volley of catcalls directed at the hapless potboy who had dropped them blotted out some of the rest; then the boys heard the Guard finish: "... poisoned meat."

"Risky."

"Ask not what the good man can do for you—" the Guard began.

"—but what you can do for him," Hax sighed. "Soldier, ask not."

"You know what it could mean," the Guard said quietly.

"Yes. And I know my responsibilities to him;

you don't need to lecture me. I love him just as you do."

"All right. The meat will be marked for short-term storage in your coldrooms. But you'll have to be quick. You must understand that."

"There are children in Farson?" The cook asked sadly. It was not really a question.

"Children everywhere," the Guard said gently. "It's the children we—and he—care about."

"Poisoned meat. Such a strange way to care for children." Hax uttered a heavy, whistling sigh. "Will they curdle and hold their bellies and cry for their mammas? I suppose they will."

"It will be like a going to sleep," the Guard said, but his voice was too confidently reasonable.

"Of course," Hax said, and laughed.

"You said it yourself. 'Soldier, ask not.' Do you enjoy seeing children under the rule of the gun, when they could be under his hands, who makes the lion lie down with the lamb?"

Hax did not reply.

"I go on duty in twenty minutes," the Guard said, his voice once more calm. "Give me a joint of mutton and I will pinch one of your girls and make her giggle. When I leave—"

"My mutton will give no cramps to your belly, Robeson."

"Will you ..." But the shadows moved away and the voices were lost.

I could have killed them, Roland thought, frozen and fascinated. I could have killed them both with my knife, slit their throats like hogs. He looked at his hands, now stained with gravy and berries as well as dirt from the day's lessons.

"Roland."

He looked at Cuthbert. They looked at each other for a long moment in the fragrant semi-darkness, and a taste of warm despair rose in Roland's throat. What he felt might have been a sort of death—something as brutal and final as the death of the dove in the white sky over the games field. Hax? he thought, bewildered. Hax who put a poultice on my leg that time? *Hax?* And then his mind snapped closed, cutting the subject off.

What he saw, even in Cuthbert's humorous, intelligent face, was nothing—nothing at all. Cuthbert's eyes were flat with Hax's doom. In Cuthbert's eyes, it had already happened. He had fed them and they had gone to the stairs to eat and then Hax had brought the Guard named Robeson to the wrong corner of the kitchen for their treasonous little *tête-à-tête*. That was all. In Cuthbert's eyes Roland saw that Hax would die for his treason as a viper dies in a pit. That, and nothing else. Nothing at all.

They were gunslinger's eyes.

Roland's father was only just back from the uplands, and he looked out of place amid the drapes and the chiffon fripperies of the main receiving hall that the boy had only lately been granted access to, as a sign of his apprenticeship. His father was dressed in black jeans and a blue work shirt. His cloak, dusty and streaked, torn to the lining in one place, was slung carelessly over his shoulder with no regard for the way it and he clashed with the elegance of the room. He was desperately thin and the heavy handlebar mustache below his nose seemed to weight his head as he looked down at his son. The guns crisscrossed over the wings of his hips hung at the perfect angle for his hands, the worn sandalwood handles looking dull and sleepy in this languid indoor light.

"The head cook," his father said softly. "Imagine it! The tracks that were blown upland at the railhead. The dead stock in Hendrickson. And perhaps even ... imagine! Imagine!"

He looked more closely at his son.

"It preys on you."

"Like the hawk," Roland said. "It preys on you." He laughed—at the startling appropriateness of the image rather than at any lightness in the situation.

His father smiled.

"Yes," Roland said. "I guess it ... it preys on me."

"Cuthbert was with you," his father said. "He will have told his father by now."

"Yes."

"He fed both of you when Cort—"

"Yes."

"And Cuthbert. Does it prey on him, do you think?"

"I don't know." Such an avenue of comparison did not really interest him. He was not concerned with how his feelings compared with those of others.

"It preys on you because you feel you've killed?"

Roland shrugged unwillingly, all at once not content with this probing of his motivations.

"Yet you told. Why?"

The boy's eyes widened. "How could I not? Treason was—"

His father waved a hand curtly. "If you did it for something as cheap as a schoolbook idea, you did it unworthily. I would rather see all of Farson poisoned."

"I didn't!" The words jerked out of him violently. "I wanted to kill him—both of them! Liars! Snakes! They—"

"Go ahead."

"They hurt me," he finished, defiant. "They did something to me. Changed something. I wanted to kill them for it."

His father nodded. "That is worthy. Not moral, but it is not your place to be moral. In fact . . ." He peered at his son. "Morals may always be beyond you. You are not quick, like Cuthbert or Wheeler's boy. It will make you formidable."

The boy, impatient before this, felt both pleased and troubled. "He will—"

"Hang."

The boy nodded. "I want to see it."

Roland the elder threw his head back and roared laughter. "Not as formidable as I thought . . . or perhaps just stupid." He closed his mouth abruptly. An arm shot out like a bolt of lightning and grabbed the boy's upper arm painfully. He grimaced but did not flinch. His father peered at him steadily, and the boy looked back, although it was more difficult than hooding the hawk had been.

"All right," he said, and turned abruptly to go.

"Father?"

"What?"

"Do you know who they were talking about? Do you know who the good man is?"

His father turned back and looked at him speculatively. "Yes. I think I do."

"If you caught him," Roland said in his thoughtful, near-plodding way, "no one else like Cook would have to . . . have to be neck-popped."

His father smiled thinly. "Perhaps not for a while. But in the end, someone always has to have his or her neck popped, as you so quaintly put it. The people demand it. Sooner or later, if there isn't a turncoat, the people make one."

"Yes," Roland said, grasping the concept instantly—it was one he never forgot. "But if you got him—"

"No," his father said flatly.

"Why?"

For a moment his father seemed on the verge of saying why, but he bit it back. "We've talked enough for now, I think. Go out from me."

He wanted to tell his father not to forget his promise when the time came for Hax to step through the trap, but he was sensitive to his father's moods. He suspected his father wanted to fuck. He closed that door quickly. He was aware that his mother and father did that ... that thing together, and he was reasonably well informed as to what that act was, but the mental picture that always condensed with the thought made him feel both uneasy and oddly guilty. Some years later, Susan would tell him the story of Oedipus, and he would absorb it in quiet thoughtfulness, thinking of the odd and bloody triangle formed by his father, his mother, and by Marten—known in some quarters as the good man. Or perhaps it was a quadrangle, if one wished to add himself.

"Good night, father," Roland said.

"Good night, son," his father said absently, and began unbuttoning his shirt. In his mind, the boy was already gone. Like father, like son.

Gallows Hill was on the Farson Road, which was nicely poetic—Cuthbert might have appreciated this, but Roland did not. He did appreciate the splendidly ominous scaffold which climbed into the brilliantly blue sky, a black and angular silhouette which overhung the coach road.

The two boys had been let out of Morning Exercises—Cort had read the notes from their fathers laboriously, lips moving, nodding here and there. When he finished with them both, he had looked up at the blue-violet dawn sky and had nodded again.

"Wait here," he said, and went toward the leaning stone hut that was his living quarters. He came back with a slice of rough, unleavened bread, broke it in two, and gave half to each.

"When it's over, each of you will put this beneath his shoes. Mind you do exactly as I say, or I'll clout you into next week."

They had not understood until they arrived, riding double on Cuthbert's gelding. They were the first, fully two hours ahead of anyone else and four hours before the hanging, and Gallows Hill stood deserted—except for the rooks and ravens. The birds were everywhere, and of course they were all black. They roosted noisily on the hard, jutting bar that overhung the trap—the armature of death. They sat in a row along the edge of the platform, they jostled for position on the stairs.

"They leave them," Cuthbert muttered. "For the birds."

"Let's go up," Roland said.

Cuthbert looked at him with something like horror. "Do you think——"

Roland cut him off with a gesture of his hands. "We're *years* early. No one will come."

"All right."

They walked slowly toward the gibbet, and the birds took indignant wing, cawing and circling like a mob of angry dispossessed peasants. Their bodies were flat and black against the pure dawnlight of the sky.

For the first time Roland felt the enormity of his responsibility in the matter; this wood was not noble, not part of the awesome machine of Civilization, but merely warped pine covered with splattered white bird droppings. It was splashed everywhere—stairs, railing, platform—and it stank.

The boy turned to Cuthbert with startled, terrified eyes and saw Cuthbert looking back at him with the same expression.

"I can't," Cuthbert whispered. "I can't watch it."

Roland shook his head slowly. There was a lesson here, he realized, not a shining thing but something that was old and rusty and misshapen. It was why their fathers had let them come. And with his usual stubborn and inarticulate doggedness, Roland laid mental hands on whatever it was.

"You can, Bert."

"I won't sleep tonight."

"Then you won't," Roland said, not seeing what that had to do with it.

Cuthbert suddenly seized Roland's hand and

looked at him with such mute agony that Roland's own doubt came back, and he wished sickly that they had never gone to the west kitchen that night. His father had been right. Better every man, woman, and child in Farson than this.

But whatever the lesson was, rusty, half-buried thing, he would not let it go or give up his grip on it.

"Let's not go up," Cuthbert said. "We've seen everything."

And Roland nodded reluctantly, feeling his grip on that thing—whatever it was—weaken. Cort, he knew, would have knocked them both sprawling and then forced them up to the platform step by cursing step ... and sniffing fresh blood back up their noses as they went. Cort would probably have looped new hemp over the yardarm itself and put the noose around each of their necks in turn, would have made them stand on the trap to feel it; and Cort would have been ready to strike them again if either wept or lost control of his bladder. And Cort, of course, would have been right. For the first time in his life, Roland found himself hating his own childhood. He wished for the size and calluses and sureness of age.

He deliberately pried a splinter from the railing and placed it in his breast pocket before turning away.

"Why did you do that?" Cuthbert asked.

He wished to answer something swaggering: *Oh, the luck of the gallows* ... but he only looked at Cuthbert and shook his head. "Just so I'll have it," he said. "Always have it."

They walked away from the gallows, sat down, and waited. In an hour or so the first of them began to gather, mostly families who had come in broken-down wagons and shays, carrying their breakfasts with them—hampers of cold pancakes folded over fillings of wild strawberry jam. Roland felt his stomach growl hungrily and wondered again, with despair, where the honor and the nobility of it was. It seemed to him that Hax in his dirty whites, walking around and around his steaming, subterranean kitchen, had more honor than this. He fingered the splinter from the gallows tree with sick bewilderment. Cuthbert lay beside him with his face made impassive.

In the end it was not so much, and Roland was glad. Hax was carried in an open cart, but only his huge girth gave him away; he had been blindfolded with a wide black cloth that hung down over his face. A few threw stones, but most merely continued with their breakfasts.

A gunslinger whom the boy did not know (he was glad his father had not drawn the lot) led the fat cook carefully up the steps. Two Guards of the Watch had gone ahead and stood on either side of the trap. When Hax and the gunslinger reached the top, the gunslinger threw the noosed rope over the crosstree and then put it over the cook's head, dropping the knot until it lay just below the left ear. The birds had all flown, but Roland knew they were waiting.

"Do you wish to make confession?" the gunslinger asked.

"I have nothing to confess," Hax said. His words carried well, and his voice was oddly dignified in spite of the muffle of cloth which hung over his lips. The cloth ruffled slightly in the faint, pleasant breeze that had blown up. "I have not forgotten my father's face; it has been with me through all."

Roland glanced sharply at the crowd and was disturbed by what he saw there—a sense of sympathy? Perhaps admiration? He would ask his father. When traitors are called heroes (or heroes traitors, he supposed in his frowning way), dark times must have fallen. He wished he understood better. His mind flashed to Cort and the bread Cort had given them. He felt contempt; the day was coming when Cort would serve him. Perhaps not Cuthbert; perhaps Cuthbert would buckle under Cort's steady fire and remain a page or a horseboy (or infinitely worse, a perfumed diplomat, dallying in receiving chambers or looking into bogus crystal balls with doddering kings and princes), but he would not. He knew it.

"Roland?"

"I'm here." He took Cuthbert's hand, and their fingers locked together like iron.

The trap dropped. Hax plummeted through. And in the sudden stillness, there was a sound: that sound an exploding pineknot makes on the hearth during a cold winter night.

But it was not so much. The cook's legs kicked out once in a wide Y; the crowd made a satisfied whistling noise; the Guards of the Watch dropped their military pose and began to gather things up negligently. The gunslinger walked back down the steps slowly, mounted his horse, and rode off, cutting roughly through one gaggle of picnickers, making them scurry.

The crowd dispersed rapidly after that, and in forty minutes the two boys were left alone on the small hill they had chosen. The birds were returning to examine their new prize. One lit on Hax's shoulder and sat there chummily, darting its beak at the bright and shiny hoop Hax had always worn in his right ear.

"It doesn't look like him at all," Cuthbert said.

"Oh, yes, it does," Roland said confidently as they walked toward the gallows, the bread in their hands. Cuthbert looked abashed.

They paused beneath the crosstree, looking up at the dangling, twisting body. Cuthbert reached up and touched one hairy ankle, defiantly. The body started on a new, twisting arc.

Then, rapidly, they broke the bread and spread the crumbs beneath the dangling feet. Roland looked back just once as they rode away. Now there were thousands of birds. The bread—he grasped this only dimly—was symbolic, then.

"It was good," Cuthbert said suddenly. "It . . . I . . . I liked it. I did."

Roland was not shocked by this, although he had not particularly cared for the scene. But he thought he could perhaps understand it.

"I don't know about that," he said, "but it was something. It surely was."

The land did not fall to the good man for another ten years, and by that time he was a gunslinger, his father was dead, he himself had become a matricide—and the world had moved on.

III

"Look," Jake said, pointing upward.

The gunslinger looked up and felt an obscure joint in his back pop. They had been in the foothills two days now, and although the waterskins were almost empty again, it didn't matter now. There would soon be all the water they could drink.

He followed the vector of Jake's finger upward, past the rise of the green plain to the naked and flashing cliffs and gorges above it ... and on up toward the snowcap itself.

Faint and far, nothing but a tiny dot (it might have been one of those motes that dance perpetually in front of the eyes, except for its constancy), the gunslinger beheld the man in black, moving up the slopes with deadly progress, a minuscule fly on a huge granite wall.

"Is that him?" Jake asked.

The gunslinger looked at the depersonalized mote doing its faraway acrobatics, feeling nothing but a premonition of sorrow.

"That's him, Jake."

"Do you think we'll catch him?"

"Not on this side. On the other. And not if we stand here talking about it."

"They're so high," Jake said. "What's on the other side?"

"I don't know," the gunslinger said. "I don't think anybody does. Maybe they did once. Come on, boy."

They began to move upward again, sending small runnels of pebbles and sand down toward the desert that washed away behind them in a flat bake-sheet that seemed to never end. Above them, far above, the man in black moved up and up and up. It was impossible to see if he looked back. He seemed to leap across impossible gulfs, to scale sheer faces. Once or twice he disappeared, but always they saw him again, until the violet curtain of dusk shut him out of their view. When they made their camp for the evening, the boy spoke little, and the gunslinger wondered if the boy knew what he had already intuited. He thought of Cuthbert's face, hot, dismayed, excited. He thought of the crumbs. He thought of the birds. It ends this way, he thought. Again and again it ends this way. There are quests and roads that lead ever onward, and all of them end in the same place—upon the killing ground.

Except, perhaps, the road to the Tower.

The boy, the sacrifice, his face innocent and very young in the light of their tiny fire, had fallen asleep over his beans. The gunslinger covered him with the horse blanket and then curled up to sleep himself.

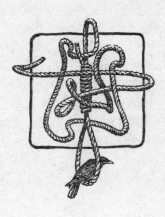

THE ORACLE AND THE MOUNTAINS

The boy found the oracle and it almost destroyed him.

Some thin instinct brought the gunslinger up from sleep to the velvet darkness, which had fallen on them at dusk like a shroud of well water. That had been when he and Jake reached the grassy, nearly level oasis above the first rise of tumbled foothills. Even on the hardscrabble below, where they had toiled and fought for every foot in the killer sun, they had been able to hear the sound of crickets rubbing their legs seductively together in the perpetual green of willow groves above them. The gunslinger remained calm in his mind, and the boy had kept up at least the pretense of a facade, and that had made the gunslinger proud. But Jake hadn't been able to hide the wildness in his eyes, which were white and starey, the eyes of a horse scenting water and held back from bolting only by the tenuous chain of its master's mind; like a horse at the point where only understanding, not the spur, could hold it steady. The gunslinger could gauge the need in Jake by the madness the sounds of the crickets bred in his own body. His arms seemed to seek out shale to scrape on, and his knees seemed to beg to be ripped in tiny, maddening, salty gashes.

The sun trampled down on them all the way; even when it turned a swollen, feverish red with sunset, it shone perversely through the knife-cut in the hills off to their left, blinding them and making every teardrop of sweat into a prism of pain.

Then there was grass: at first only yellow scrub, clinging to the bleak soil where the last of the runoff reached with gruesome vitality. Further up there was witchgrass, sparse, then green and rank ... then the first sweet smell of real grass, mixed with timothy and shaded by the first of the dwarfed firs. There the gunslinger saw an arc of brown movements in the shadows. He drew, fired, and felled the rabbit all before Jake could begin to cry out his surprise. A moment later he had reholstered the gun.

"Here," the gunslinger said. Up ahead the grass deepened into a jungle of green willows that was shocking after the parched sterility of the endless hardpan. There would be a spring, perhaps several of them, and it would be even cooler, but it was better out here in the open. The boy had pushed every step he could push, and there might be suckerbats in the deeper shadows of the grove. The bats might break the boy's sleep, no matter how deep it was, and if they were vampires, neither of them might awaken ... at least, not in this world.

The boy said, "I'll get some wood."

The gunslinger smiled. "No, you won't. Sit yourself, Jake." Whose phrase had that been? Some woman.

The boy sat. When the gunslinger got back, Jake was asleep in the grass. A large praying mantis was performing ablutions on the springy stem of Jake's cowlick. The gunslinger set the fire and went after water.

The willow jungle was deeper than he had suspected, and confusing in the failing light. But he found a spring, richly guarded by frogs and peepers. He filled one of their waterskins ... and paused. The sounds that filled the night awoke an uneasy sensuality in him, a feeling that not even Allie, the woman he had bedded with in Tull, had been able to bring to the fore. Sensuality and fucking are, after all, cousins of the most tenuous relation. He chalked it up to the sudden blinding change from the desert. The softness of the dark seemed nearly decadent.

He returned to the camp and skinned the rabbit while water boiled over the fire. Mixed with the last of their canned food, the rabbit made an excellent stew. He woke Jake and watched him as he ate, bleary but ravenous.

"We stay here tomorrow," the gunslinger said.

"But that man you're after ... that priest."

"He's no priest. And don't worry. We've got him."

"How do you know that?"

The gunslinger could only shake his head. The knowledge was strong in him ... but it was not a good knowledge.

After the meal, he rinsed the cans they had eaten from (marveling again at his own water extravagance), and when he turned around, Jake was asleep again. The gunslinger felt the now-familiar rising and falling in his chest that he could only identify with Cuthbert. Cuthbert had been Roland's own age, but he had seemed so much younger.

His cigarette drooped toward the grass, and he tossed it into the fire. He looked at it, the clear yellow burn so different, so much cleaner, from the way the devil-grass burned. The air was wonderfully cool, and he lay down with his back to the fire. Far away, through the gash that led the way into the mountains, he heard the thick mouth of the perpetual thunder. He slept. And dreamed.

Susan, his beloved, was dying before his eyes:

As he watched, his arms held by two villagers on each side, his neck dog-caught in a huge, rusty iron collar, she was dying. Even through the thick stench of the fire Roland could smell the dankness of the pits . . . and he could see the color of his own madness. Susan, lovely girl at the window, horse-drover's daughter. She was turning black in the flames, her skin cracking open.

"The boy!" she was screaming. "Roland, the boy!"

He whirled, pulling his captors with him. The collar ripped at his neck and he heard the hitching, strangled sounds that were coming from his own throat. There was a sickish-sweet smell of barbecuing meat on the air.

The boy was looking down at him from a window high above the courtyard, the same window where Susan, who had taught him to be a man, had once sat and sung the old songs; "Hey Jude" and "Ease on Down the Road" and "A Hundred Leagues to Banberry Cross." He looked out from the window like the statue of an alabaster saint in a cathedral. His eyes were marble. A spike had been driven through Jake's forehead.

The gunslinger felt the strangling, ripping scream that signaled the beginning of his lunacy pull up from the root of his belly.

"Nnnnnnnnnn—"

Roland grunted a cry as he felt the fire singe him. He sat bolt upright in the dark, still feeling the dream around him, strangling him like the collar he had worn. In his twistings and turnings he had thrown one hand against the dying coals of the fire. He put the hand to his face, feeling the dream flee, leaving only the stark picture of Jake, plaster-white, a saint for demons.

"Nnnnnnnnnn—"

He glared around at the mystic darkness of the willow grove, both guns out and ready. His eyes were red loopholes in the last glow from the fire.

"Nnnnnn-nnn—"

Jake.

The gunslinger was up and on the run. A bitter circle of moon had risen and he could follow the boy's track in the dew. He ducked under the first of the willows, splashed through the spring, and legged up the far bank, skidding in the dampness (even now his body could relish it). Willow withes slapped at his face. The trees were thicker here, and the moon was blotted out. Treetrunks rose in lurching shadows. The grass, now knee-high, slapped against him. Half-rotted dead branches reached for his shins, his *cojones*. He paused for a moment, lifting his head and scenting at the air. A ghost of a breeze helped him. The boy did not smell good, of course; neither of them did. The gunslinger's nostrils flared like those of an ape. The odor of sweat was faint, oily, unmistakable. He crashed over a dead-fall of grass and bramble and downed branches, sprinted down a tunnel of overhanging willow and sumac. Moss struck his shoulders. Some clung in sighing gray tendrils.

He clawed through a last barricade of willows and came to a clearing that looked up at the stars and the highest peak of the range, gleaming skull-white at an impossible altitude.

There was a ring of tall, black stones which

looked like some sort of surreal animal-trap in the moonlight. In the center was a table of stone ... an altar. Very old, rising out of the ground on a powerful arm of basalt.

The boy stood before it, trembling back and forth. His hands shook at his sides as if infused with static electricity. The gunslinger called his name sharply, and Jake responded with that inarticulate sound of negation. The faint smear of face, almost hidden by the boy's left shoulder, looked both terrified and exalted. And there was something else.

The gunslinger stepped inside the ring and Jake screamed, recoiling and throwing up his arms. Now his face could be seen clearly, and indexed. The gunslinger saw fear and terror warring with an almost excruciating grimace of pleasure.

The gunslinger felt it touch him—the spirit of the oracle, the succubus. His loins were suddenly filled with rose light, a light that was soft yet hard. He felt his head twisting, his tongue thickening and becoming excruciatingly sensitive to even the spittle that coated it.

He did not think when he pulled the half-rotted jawbone from the pocket where he had carried it since he found it in the lair of the

Speaking Demon at the way station. He did not think, but it did not frighten him to operate on pure instinct. He held the jawbone's frozen, prehistoric grin up in front of him, holding his other arm out stiffly, first and last fingers poked out in the ancient forked talisman, the ward against the evil eye.

The current of sensuality was whipped away from him like a drape.

Jake screamed again.

The gunslinger walked to him, and held the jawbone in front of Jake's warring eyes. A wet sound of agony. The boy tried to pull his gaze away, could not. And suddenly both eyes rolled up to show the whites. Jake collapsed. His body struck the earth limply, one hand almost touching the altar. The gunslinger dropped to one knee and picked him up. He was amazingly light, as dehydrated as a November leaf from their long walk through the desert.

Around him Roland could feel the presence that dwelt in the circle of stones, whirring with a jealous anger—its prize had been taken from it. When the gunslinger passed out of the circle, the sense of frustrated jealousy faded. He carried Jake back to their camp. By the time they got there, the boy's twitching unconsciousness had become deep sleep. The gunslinger paused for a moment above the gray ruin of the fire. The moonlight on Jake's face reminded him again of a church saint, alabaster purity all unknown. He suddenly hugged the boy, knowing that he loved him. And it seemed that he could almost feel the laughter from the man in black, someplace far above them.

Jake was calling him; that was how he awoke. He had tied the boy firmly to one of the tough bushes that grew nearby, and the boy was hungry and upset. By the sun, it was almost nine-thirty.

"Why'd you tie me up?" Jake asked indignantly as the gunslinger loosened the thick knots in the blanket. "I wasn't going to run away!"

"You did run away," the gunslinger said, and the expression on Jake's face made him smile. "I had to go out and get you. You were sleepwalking."

"I was?" Jake looked at him suspiciously.

The gunslinger nodded and suddenly produced the jawbone. He held it in front of Jake's face and Jake flinched away from it, raising his arm.

"See?"

Jake nodded, bewildered.

"I have to go off for a while now. I may be gone the whole day. So listen to me, boy. It's important. If sunset comes and I'm not back—"

Fear flashed on Jake's face. "You're leaving me!"

The gunslinger only looked at him.

"No," Jake said after a moment. "I guess you're not."

"I want you to stay right here while I'm gone. And if you feel strange—funny in any way—you pick up this bone and hold it in your hands."

Hate and disgust crossed Jake's face, mixed with bewilderment. "I couldn't. I ... I just couldn't."

"You can. You may have to. Especially after midday. It's important. Dig?"

"Why do you have to go away?" Jake burst out.

"I just do."

The gunslinger caught another fascinating glimpse of the steel that lay under the boy's surface, as enigmatic as the story he had told about coming from a city where the buildings were so tall they actually scraped the sky.

"All right," Jake said.

The gunslinger laid the jawbone carefully on the ground next to the ruins of the fire, where it grinned up through the grass like some eroded fossil that has seen the light of day after a night of five thousand years. Jake would not look at it. His face was pale and miserable. The gunslinger wondered if it would profit them for him to put the boy to sleep and question him, but he decided there would be little gain. He knew well enough that the spirit of the stone circle was surely a demon, and very likely an oracle as well. A demon with no shape, only a kind of unformed sexual glare with the eye of prophecy. He wondered sardonically if it might not be the soul of Sylvia Pittston, the giant woman whose religious hucksterING had led to the final showdown in Tull ... but knew it was not. The stones in the circle had been ancient, this particular demon's territory staked out long before the earliest shade of pre-history. But the gunslinger knew the forms of speaking quite well and did not think the boy would have to use the jawbone mojo. The voice and mind of the oracle would be more than occupied with him. And the gunslinger needed to know things, in spite of the risk ... and the risk was high. For both Jake and himself, he needed desperately to know.

The gunslinger opened his tobacco poke and pawed through it, pushing the dry strands of leaf aside until he came to a minuscule object wrapped in a fragment of white paper. He hefted it in his hand, looking absently up at the sky. Then he unwrapped it and held the contents—a tiny white pill with edges that had been much worn with traveling—in his hand.

Jake looked at it curiously. "What's that?"

The gunslinger uttered a short laugh. "The philosopher's stone," he said. "The story that Cort used to tell us was that the Old Gods pissed over the desert and made mescaline."

Jake only looked puzzled.

"A drug," the gunslinger said. "But not one that puts you to sleep. One that wakes you up all the way for a little while."

"Like LSD," the boy agreed instantly and then looked puzzled.

"What's that?"

"I don't know," Jake said. "It just popped out. I think it came from ... you know, before."

The gunslinger nodded, but he was doubtful. He had never heard of mescaline referred to as LSD, not even in Marten's old books.

"Will it hurt you?" Jake asked.

"It never has," the gunslinger said, conscious of the evasion.

"I don't like it."

"Never mind."

The gunslinger squatted in front of the waterskin, took a mouthful, and swallowed the pill. As al-

STEPHEN KING

ways, he felt an immediate reaction in his mouth; it seemed overloaded with saliva. He sat down before the dead fire.

"When does something happen to you?" Jake asked.

"Not for a little while. Be quiet."

So Jake was quiet, watching with open suspicion as the gunslinger went calmly about the ritual of cleaning his guns.

He reholstered them and said, "Your shirt, Jake. Take it off and give it to me."

Jake pulled his faded shirt reluctantly over his head and gave it to the gunslinger.

The gunslinger produced a needle that had been threaded into the side-seam of his jeans, and thread from an empty cartridge-loop in his gunbelt. He began to sew up a long rip in one of the sleeves of the boy's shirt. As he finished and handed the shirt back, he felt the mesc beginning to take hold—there was a tightening in his stomach and a feeling that all the muscles in his body were being cranked up a notch.

"I have to go," he said, getting up.

The boy half rose, his face a shadow of concern, and then he settled back. "Be careful," he said. "Please."

"Remember the jawbone," the gunslinger said.

He put his hand on Jake's head as he went by and tousled the corn-colored hair. The gesture startled him into a short laugh. Jake watched after him with a troubled smile until he was gone into the willow jungle.

The gunslinger walked deliberately toward the circle of stones, pausing once to get a cool drink from the spring. He could see his own reflection in a tiny pool edged with moss and lilypads, and he looked at himself for a moment, as fascinated as Narcissus. The mind-reaction was beginning to settle in, slowing down his chain of thought by seeming to increase the connotations of every idea and every bit of sensory input. Things began to take on weight and thickness that had been heretofore invisible. He paused, getting to his feet again, and looked through the tangled snarl of willows. Sunlight slanted through in a golden, dusty bar, and he watched the interplay of motes and tiny flying things for a moment before going on.

The drug often had disturbed him: his ego was too strong (or perhaps just too simple) to enjoy being eclipsed and peeled back, made a target for more sensitive emotions—they tickled at him like a cat's whiskers. But this time he felt fairly calm. That was good.

He stepped into the clearing and walked straight into the circle. He stood, letting his mind run free. Yes, it was coming harder now, faster. The grass screamed green at him; it seemed that if he bent over and rubbed his hands in it he would stand up with green paint all over his fingers and palms. He resisted a puckish urge to try the experiment.

But there was no voice from the oracle. No sexual stirring.

He went to the altar, stood beside it for a moment. Coherent thought was now almost impossible. His teeth felt strange in his head. The world held too much light. He climbed up on the altar and lay back. His mind was becoming a jungle full of strange thought-plants that he had never seen or suspected before, a willow-jungle that had grown up around a mescaline spring. The sky was water and he hung suspended over it. The thought gave him a vertigo that seemed faraway and unimportant.

A line of old poetry occurred to him, not a nursery verse now, no; his mother had feared the drugs and the necessity of them (as she had feared Cort and the necessity for this beater of boys); this verse came from one of the Dens to the north of the desert, where men still lived among the machines that usually didn't work ... and which sometimes ate the men when they did. The lines played again and again, reminding him (in an unconnected way that was typical of the mescaline rush) of snow falling in a globe he had owned as a child, mystic and half fantastical:

Beyond the reach of human range
A drop of hell, a touch of strange ...

The trees which overhung the altar contained faces. He watched them with abstracted fascination: Here was a dragon, green and twitching. Here a wood-nymph with beckoning branch arms. Here a living skull overgrown with slime. Faces. Faces.

The grasses of the clearing suddenly whipped and bent.

I come.

I come.

Vague stirrings within his flesh. How far I have come, he thought. From couching with Susan in sweet hay to this.

She pressed over him, a body made of the wind, a breast of sudden fragrant jasmine, rose, and honeysuckle.

"Make your prophecy," he said. His mouth felt full of metal.

A sigh. A faint sound of weeping. The gunslinger's genitals felt drawn and hard. Over him and beyond the faces in the leaves, he could see the mountains—hard and brutal and full of teeth.

The body moved against him, struggled with him. He felt his hands curl into fists. She had sent him a vision of Susan. It was Susan above him, lovely Susan at the window, waiting for him with her hair spilled down her back and over her shoulders. He tossed his head, but her face followed.

Jasmine, rose, honeysuckle, old hay . . . the smell of love. Love me.

"Speak prophecy," he said.

Please, the oracle wept. *Don't be cold. It is always so cold here—*

Hands slipping over his flesh, manipulating, lighting him on fire. Pulling him. Drawing. A black crevice. The ultimate wanton. Wet and warm—

No. Dry. Cold. Sterile.

Have a touch of mercy, gunslinger. Ah, please, I beg your favor! Mercy!

Would you have mercy on the boy?

What boy? I know no boy. It's not boys I need. O please.

Jasmine, rose, honeysuckle. Dry hay with its ghost

*of summer clover. Oil decanted from ancient urns. A
riot for flesh.*

"After," he said.

Now. Please. Now.

He let his mind coil out at her, the antithesis of
emotion. The body that hung over him froze and
seemed to scream. There was a brief, vicious
tug-of-war between his temples—his mind was
the rope, gray and fibrous. For long moments
there was no sound but the quiet hush of his
breathing and the faint breeze which made the
green faces in the trees shift, wink, and grimace.
No bird sang.

Her hold loosened. Again there was the sound
of sobbing. It would have to be quick, or she
would leave him. To stay now meant attenuation;
perhaps her own kind of death. Already he felt her
drawing away to leave the circle of stones. Wind
rippled the grass in tortured patterns.

"Prophecy," he said—a bleak noun.

A weeping, tired sigh. He could almost have
granted the mercy she begged, but—there was
Jake. He would have found Jake dead or insane
if he had been any later last night.

Sleep, then.

"No."

Then half-sleep.

The gunslinger turned his eyes up to the faces in the leaves. A play was being enacted there for his amusement. Worlds rose and fell before him. Empires were built across shining sands where forever machines toiled in abstract electronic frenzies. Empires declined and fell. Wheels that had spun like silent liquid moved more slowly, began to squeak, began to scream, stopped. Sand choked the stainless steel gutters of concentric streets below dark skies full of stars like beds of cold jewels. And through it all, a dying wind of change blew, bringing with it the cinnamon smell of late October. The gunslinger watched as the world moved on.

And half-slept.

Three. This is the number of your fate.

Three?

Yes, three is mystic. Three stands at the heart of the mantra.

Which three?

'We see in part, and thus is the mirror of prophecy darkened.'

Tell me what you can.

The first is young, dark-haired. He stands on the brink of robbery and murder. A demon has infested him. The name of the demon is HEROIN.

Which demon is that? I know it not, even from nursery stories.

'We see in part, and thus is the mirror of prophecy darkened.' *There are other worlds, gunslinger, and other demons. These waters are deep.*

The second?

She comes on wheels. Her mind is iron but her heart and eyes are soft. I see no more.

The third?

In chains.

The man in black? Where is he?

Near. You will speak with him.

Of what will we speak?

The Tower.

The boy? Jake?

. . .

Tell me of the boy!

The boy is your gateway to the man in black. The man in black is your gate to the three. The three are your way to the Dark Tower.

How? How can that be? Why must it be?

'We see in part, and thus is the mirror—'

God damn you.

No god damned me.

"Don't patronize me, Thing. I'm stronger than you.

. . .

What do they call you, then? Star-slut? Whore of the Winds?

Some live on love that comes to the ancient places ... even in these sad and evil times. Some, gunslinger live on blood. Even, I understand, on the blood of young boys.

May he not be spared?

Yes.

How?

Cease, gunslinger. Strike your camp and turn west. In the west there is still a need for men who live by the bullet.

I am sworn by my father's guns and by the treachery of Marten.

Marten is no more. The man in black has eaten his soul. This you know.

I am sworn.

Then you are damned.

Have your way with me, bitch.

Eagerness.

The shadow swung over him, enfolded him. Suddenly ecstasy broken only by a galaxy of pain, as faint and bright as ancient stars gone red with collapse. Faces came to him unbidden at the climax of their coupling: Sylvia Pittston, Alice, the woman from Tull, Susan, Aileen, a hundred others.

And finally, after an eternity, he pushed her away from him, once again in his right mind, bone-weary and disgusted.

No! It isn't enough! It—

"Let me be," the gunslinger said. He sat up and almost fell off the altar before regaining his feet. She touched him tentatively

(honeysuckle, jasmine, sweet attar)

and he pushed her violently, falling to his knees.

He staggered up and made his drunken way to the perimeter of the circle. He staggered through, feeling a huge weight fall from his shoulders. He drew a shuddering, weeping breath. As he started away he could feel her standing at the bars of her prison, watching him go from her. He wondered how long it might be before someone else crossed the desert and found her, hungry and alone. For a moment he felt dwarfed by the possibilities of time.

"You're sick!"

Jake stood up fast when the gunslinger shambled back through the last trees and came into camp. Jake had been huddled by the ruins of the tiny fire, the jawbone across his knees, gnawing disconsolately on the bones of the rabbit. Now he ran toward the gunslinger with a look of distress that made Roland feel the full, ugly weight of a coming betrayal—one he sensed which might only be the first of many.

"No," he said. "Not sick. Just tired. I'm whipped." He gestured absently at the jawbone. "You can throw that away."

Jake threw it quickly and violently, rubbing his hands across his shirt after doing it.

The gunslinger sat down—almost fell down—feeling the aching joints and the pummeled, thick mind that was the unlovely afterglow of mescaline. His crotch also pulsed with a dull ache. He rolled a cigarette with careful, unthinking slowness. Jake watched. The gunslinger had a sudden impulse to tell him what he had learned, then thrust the idea away with horror. He wondered if a part of him—mind or soul—might not be disintegrating.

"We sleep here tonight," the gunslinger said. "Tomorrow we climb. I'll go out a little later and see if I can't shoot something for supper. I've got to sleep now. Okay?"

"Sure."

The gunslinger nodded and lay back. When he woke up the shadows were long across the small grass clearing. "Build up the fire," he told Jake and tossed him his flint and steel. "Can you use that?"

"Yes, I think so."

The gunslinger walked toward the willow grove and then turned left, skirting it. At a place where the ground opened out and upward in heavy open grass, he stepped back into the shadows and stood silently. Faintly, clearly, he could hear the *clik-clink-clik-clink* of Jake striking sparks. He stood without moving for ten minutes, fifteen, twenty. Three rabbits came, and the gunslinger pulled leather. He took down the two plumpest, skinned them and gutted them, brought them back to the camp. Jake had the fire going and the water was already steaming over it.

The gunslinger nodded to him. "That's a good piece of work."

Jake flushed with pleasure and silently handed back the flint and steel.

While the stew cooked, the gunslinger used the last of the light to go back into the willow grove. Near the first pool he began to hack at the tough vines that grew near the water's marshy verge. Later, as the fire burned down to coals and Jake slept, he would plait them into ropes that might be of some limited use later. But he did not think somehow that the climb would be a particularly difficult one. He felt a sense of fate that he no longer even considered odd.

The vines bled green sap over his hands as he carried them back to where Jake waited.

They were up with the sun and packed in half an hour. The gunslinger hoped to shoot another rabbit in the meadow as they fed, but time was short and no rabbit showed itself. The bundle of their remaining food was now so small and light that Jake carried it easily. He had toughened up, this boy; you could see it.

The gunslinger carried their water, freshly drawn from one of the springs. He looped his three vine ropes around his belly. They gave the circle of stones a wide berth (the gunslinger was afraid the boy might feel a recurrence of fear, but when they passed above it on a stony rise, Jake only offered it a passing glance and then looked at a bird that hovered upwind). Soon enough, the trees began to lose their height and lushness. Trunks were twisted and roots seemed to struggle with the earth in a tortured hunt for moisture.

"It's all so old," Jake said glumly when they paused for a rest. "Isn't there anything young?"

The gunslinger smiled and gave Jake an elbow. "You are," he said.

"Will it be a hard climb?"

The gunslinger looked at him, curious. "The

mountains are high. Don't you think it will be a hard climb?"

Jake looked back at him, his eyes clouded, puzzled.

"No."

They went on.

The sun climbed to its zenith, seemed to hang there more briefly than it ever had during the desert crossing, and then passed on, giving them back their shadows. Shelves of rock protruded from the rising land like the arms of giant easychairs buried in the earth. The scrub grass turned yellow and sere. Finally they were faced with a deep, chimneylike crevasse in their path and they scaled a short, peeling rise of rock to get around and above it. The ancient granite had faulted on lines that were steplike, and as they had both intuited, the climb was an easy one. They paused on the four-foot-wide scarp at the top and looked back over the falling land to the desert, which curled around the upland like a huge yellow paw. Further off it gleamed at them in a white shield that dazzled the eye, receding into dim waves of rising heat. The gunslinger felt faintly amazed at the realization that this desert had nearly murdered him. From where they stood, in a new coolness, the desert certainly appeared momentous, but not deadly.

STEPHEN KING

They turned back to the business of the climb, scrambling over jackstraw falls of rock and crouch-walking up inclined planes of stone shot with glitters of quartz and mica. The rock was pleasantly warm to the touch, but the air was definitely cooler. In the late afternoon the gunslinger heard the faint sound of thunder. The rising line of the mountains obscured the sight of the rain on the other side, however.

When the shadows began to turn purple, they camped in the overhang of a jutting brow of rock. The gunslinger anchored their blanket above and below, fashioning a kind of shanty lean-to. They sat at the mouth of it, watching the sky spread a cloak over the world. Jake dangled his feet over the drop. The gunslinger rolled his evening smoke and eyed Jake half humorously. "Don't roll over in your sleep," he said, "or you may wake up in hell."

"I won't," Jake replied seriously. "My mother says—" He broke it off.

"She says what?"

"That I sleep like a dead man," Jake finished. He looked at the gunslinger, who saw that the boy's mouth was trembling as he strove to keep back tears—*only a boy,* he thought, and pain smote him, like the icepick that too much cold

190

water can sometimes plant in the forehead. *Only a boy. Why?* Silly question. When a boy, wounded in body or spirit, called that question out to Cort, that ancient, scarred battle-engine whose job it was to teach the sons of gunslingers the beginning of what they had to know, Cort would answer: *Why is a crooked letter and can't be made straight ... never mind why, just get up, pus-head! Get up! The day's young!*

"Why am I here?" Jake asked. "Why did I forget everything from before?"

"Because the man in black has drawn you here," the gunslinger said. "And because of the Tower. The Tower stands at a kind of ... power-nexus. In time."

"I don't understand that!"

"Nor do I," the gunslinger said. "But something has been happening. Just in my own time. 'The world has moved on,' we say ... we've always said. But it's moving on faster now. Something has happened to time."

They sat in silence. A breeze, faint but with an edge, picked at their legs. Somewhere it made a hollow *whooooo* in a rock fissure.

"Where do you come from?" Jake asked.

"From a place that no longer exists. Do you know the Bible?"

"Jesus and Moses. Sure."

The gunslinger smiled. "That's right. My land had a Biblical name—New Canaan, it was called. The land of milk and honey. In the Bible's Canaan, there were supposed to be grapes so big that men had to carry them on sledges. We didn't grow them that big, but it was a sweet land."

"I know about Ulysses," Jake said hesitantly. "Was he in the Bible?"

"Maybe," the gunslinger said. "The Book is lost now—all except the parts I was forced to memorize."

"But the others—"

"No others," the gunslinger said. "I'm the last."

A tiny wasted moon began to rise, casting its slitted gaze down into the tumble of rocks where they sat.

"Was it pretty? Your country . . . your land?"

"It was beautiful," the gunslinger said absently. "There were fields and rivers and mists in the morning. But that's only pretty. My mother used to say that . . . and that the only real beauty is order and love and light."

Jake made a noncommittal noise.

The gunslinger smoked and thought of how it had been—the nights in the huge central hall, hundreds of richly clad figures moving through the slow, steady waltz steps or the faster, light ripples of the *pol-kam,* Aileen on his arm, her eyes brighter than the most precious gems, the light of the crystal-enclosed electric lights making highlights in the newly done hair of the courtesans and their half-cynical amours. The hall had been huge, an island of light whose age was beyond telling, as was the whole Central Place, which was made up of nearly a hundred stone castles. It had been twelve years since he had seen it, and leaving for the last time, Roland had ached as he turned his face away from it and began his first cast for the trail of the man in black. Even then, twelve years ago, the walls had fallen, weeds grew in the courtyards, bats roosted amongst the great beams of the central hall, and the galleries echoed with the soft swoop and whisper of swallows. The fields where Cort had taught them archery and gunnery and falconry were gone to hay and timothy and wild vines. In the huge and echoey kitchen where Hax had once held his own fuming and aromatic court, a grotesque colony of Slow Mutants nested, peering at him from the merciful darkness of pantries and shadowed pillars. The warm steam that had been filled with the pungent odors of roasting beef and pork had been transmuted to the clammy damp of moss and huge white toadstools grew in corners where not even the Slow Muties dared to encamp. The huge oak subcellar bulkhead stood open, and the most poignant smell of all had issued from that, an odor that seemed to symbolize with a flat finality all the hard facts of dissolution and decay: the high sharp odor of wine gone to vinegar. It had been no struggle to turn his face to the south and leave it behind—but it had hurt his heart.

"Was there a war?" Jake asked.

"Even better," the gunslinger said and pitched the last smoldering ember of his cigarette away. "There was a revolution. We won every battle, and lost the war. No one won the war, unless maybe it was the scavengers. There must have been rich pickings for years after."

"I wish I'd lived there," Jake said wistfully.

"It was another world," the gunslinger said. "Time to turn in."

The boy, now only a dim shadow, turned on his side and curled up with the blanket tossed loosely over him. The gunslinger sat sentinel over him for perhaps an hour after, thinking his long, sober thoughts. Such meditation was a new thing for him, novel, sweet in a melancholy sort of way, but still utterly without practical value: there was no solution to the problem of Jake other than the

one the Oracle had offered—and that was simply
not possible. There might have been tragedy in
the situation, but the gunslinger did not see that;
he saw only the predestination that had always
been there. And finally, his more natural character reasserted itself and he slept deeply, with no
dreams.

The climb became grimmer on the following
day as they continued to angle toward the narrow
V of the pass through the mountains. The gunslinger pushed slowly, still with no sense of hurry.
The dead stone beneath their feet left no trace of
the man in black, but the gunslinger knew he
had been this way before them—and not only
from the path of his climb as he and Jake had
observed him, tiny and bug-like, from the foothills. His aroma was printed on every cold downdraft of air. It was an oily, sardonic odor, as
bitter to his nose as the aroma of devil-grass.

Jake's hair had grown much longer, and it
curled slightly at the base of his sunburned neck.
He climbed tough, moving with sure-footedness
and no apparent acrophobia as they crossed gaps
or scaled their way up ledged facings. Twice
already he had gone up in places the gunslinger
could not have managed. Jake had anchored one

of the ropes so that the gunslinger could climb up hand over hand.

The following morning they climbed through a coldly damp snatch of cloud that began blotting out the tumbled slopes below them. Patches of hard, granulated snow began to appear nestled in some of the deeper pockets of stone. It glittered like quartz and its texture was as dry as sand. That afternoon they found a single footprint in one of these snowpatches. Jake stared at it for a moment with awful fascination, then looked up frightfully, as if expecting to see the man in black materialize into his own footprint. The gunslinger tapped him on the shoulder then and pointed ahead. "Go. The day's getting old."

Later, they made camp in the last of the daylight on a wide, flat ledge to the east and north of the cut that slanted into the heart of the mountains. The air was frigid; they could see the puffs of their breath, and the humid sound of thunder in the red-and-purple afterglow of the day was surreal, slightly lunatic.

The gunslinger thought the boy might begin to question him, but there were no questions from Jake. The boy fell almost immediately into sleep. The gunslinger followed his example. He dreamed again of the dark place in the earth, the dungeon, and again of Jake as an alabaster saint with a nail through his forehead. He awoke with a gasp, instinctively reaching for the jawbone that was no longer there, expecting to feel the grass of that ancient grove. He felt rock instead, and the cold thinness of altitude in his lungs. Jake was asleep beside him, but his sleep was not easy: he twisted and mumbled inarticulate words to himself, chasing his own phantoms. The gunslinger lay over uneasily, and slept again.

They were another week before they reached the end of the beginning—for the gunslinger, a twisted prologue of twelve years, from the final crash of his native place and the gathering of the other three. For Jake, the gateway had been a strange death in another world. For the gunslinger it had been a stranger death yet—the endless hunt for the man in black through a world with neither map nor memory. Cuthbert and the others were gone, all of them gone: Randolph, Jamie de Curry, Aileen, Susan, Marten (yes, they had dragged him down, and there had been gunplay, and even that grape had been bitter). Until finally only three remained of the old world, three like dreadful cards from a terrible deck of tarot cards: gunslinger, man in black, and the Dark Tower.

A week after Jake saw the footstep, they faced the man in black for a brief moment of time. In that moment, the gunslinger felt he could almost understand the gravid implication of the Tower itself, for that moment seemed to stretch out forever.

They continued southwest, reaching a point perhaps halfway through the Cyclopean mountain range, and just as the going seemed about to become really difficult for the first time (above them, seeming to lean out, the icy ledges and screaming buttes made the gunslinger feel an unpleasant reverse vertigo), they began to descend again along the side of the narrow pass. An angular, zigzagging path led them toward a canyon floor where an ice-edged stream boiled with slaty, headlong power from higher country still.

On that afternoon the boy paused and looked back at the gunslinger, who had paused to wash his face in the stream.

"I smell him," Jake said.

"So do I."

Ahead of them the mountain threw up its final defense—a huge slab of insurmountable granite facing that climbed into cloudy infinity. At any moment the gunslinger expected a twist in the stream to bring them upon a high waterfall and the insurmountable smoothness of rock—dead end. But the air here had that odd magnifying quality that is common to high places, and it was another day before they reached that great granite face.

The gunslinger began to feel the dreadful tug of anticipation again, the feeling that it was all finally in his grasp. Near the end, he had to fight himself to keep from breaking into a trot.

"Wait!" The boy had stopped suddenly. They faced a sharp elbow-bend in the stream; it boiled and frothed with high energy around the eroded hang of a giant sandstone boulder. All that morning they had been in the shadow of the mountains as the canyon narrowed.

Jake was trembling violently and his face had gone pale.

"What's the matter?"

"Let's go back," Jake whispered. "Let's go back quick."

The gunslinger's face was wooden.

"Please?" The boy's face was drawn, and his jawline shook with suppressed agony. Through the heavy blanket of stone they still heard thunder, as steady as machines in the earth. The slice of sky they could see had itself assumed a turbulent, gothic gray above them as warm and cold currents met and warred.

"Please, *please!*" The boy raised a fist, as if to strike the gunslinger's chest.

"No."

The boy's face took on wonder. "You're going to kill me. He killed me the first time and you are going to kill me now."

The gunslinger felt the lie on his lips. He spoke it: "You'll be all right." And a greater lie. "I'll take care."

Jake's face went gray, and he said no more. He put an unwilling hand out, and he and the gunslinger went around the elbow-bend. They came face to face with that final rising wall and the man in black.

He stood no more than twenty feet above them, just to the right of the waterfall that crashed and spilled from a huge ragged hole in the rock. Unseen wind rippled and tugged at his hooded robe. He held a staff in one hand. The other hand he held out to them in a mocking gesture of welcome. He seemed a prophet, and below that rushing sky, mounted on a ledge of rock, a prophet of doom, his voice the voice of Jeremiah.

"Gunslinger! How well you fulfill the prophecies of old! Good day and good day and good day!" He laughed, the sound echoing ever over the bellow of the falling water.

Without a thought and seemingly without a click of motor relays, the gunslinger had drawn his pistols. The boy cowered to his right and behind, a small shadow.

Roland fired three times before he could gain control of his traitor hands—the echoes bounced their bronze tones against the rock valley that rose around them, over the sound of the wind and water.

A spray of granite puffed over the head of the man in black; a second to the left of his hood; a third to the right. He had missed cleanly all three times.

The man in black laughed—a full, hearty laugh that seemed to challenge the receding echo of gunshots. "Would you kill all your answers so easily, gunslinger?"

"Come down," the gunslinger said. "Answers all around."

Again that huge, derisive laugh. "It's not your bullets I fear, Roland. It's your idea of answers that scares me."

"Come down."

"The other side, I think," the man in black said. "On the other side we will hold much council."

His eyes flicked to Jake and he added:

"Just the two of us."

Jake flinched away from him with a small, whining cry, and the man in black turned, his robe swirling in the gray air like a batwing. He disappeared into the cleft in the rock from which the water spewed at full force. The gunslinger exercised grim will and did not send a bullet after him—*would you kill all your answers so easily, gunslinger?*

There was only the sound of wind and water, sounds that had been in this place of desolation for a thousand years. Yet the man in black had been here. After these twelve years, Roland had seen him close-up, spoken to him. And the man in black had laughed at him.

On the other side we will hold much council.

The boy looked up at him with dumbly submissive sheep's eyes, his body trembling. For a moment the gunslinger saw the face of Alice, the girl from Tull, superimposed over Jake's, the scar standing out on her forehead like a mute accusation, and felt brute loathing for them both (it would not occur to him until much later that both the scar on Alice's forehead and the nail he saw spiked through Jake's forehead in his dreams were in the same place). Jake seemed to catch a whiff of his thought and a moan was dragged from his throat. But it was short; he twisted his lips shut over it. He held the makings of a fine man, perhaps a gunslinger in his own right if given time.

Just the two of us.

The gunslinger felt a great and unholy thirst in some deep unknown pit of his body, a thirst no wine could touch. Worlds trembled, almost within reach of his fingers, and in some instinctual way he strove not to be corrupted, knowing in his colder mind that such strife was vain and always would be.

It was noon. He looked up, letting the cloudy, unsettled daylight shine for the last time on the all-too-vulnerable sun of his own righteousness. No one ever really pays for it in silver, he thought. The price of any evil—necessary or otherwise—comes due in flesh.

"Come with me or stay," the gunslinger said.

The boy only looked at him mutely. And to the gunslinger, in that final and vital moment of uncoupling from a moral principle, he ceased to be Jake and became only the boy, an impersonality to be moved and used.

Something screamed in the windy stillness; he and the boy both heard.

The gunslinger began, and after a moment

Jake came after. Together they climbed the tumbled rock beside the steely-cold falls, and stood where the man in black had stood before them. And together they entered in where he had disappeared. The darkness swallowed them.

THE
SLOW
MUTANTS

The gunslinger spoke slowly to Jake in the rising and falling inflections of a dream:

"There were three of us: Cuthbert, Jamie, and I. We weren't supposed to be there, because none of us had passed from the time of children. If we had been caught, Cort would have striped us. But we weren't. I don't think any of the ones that went before us were caught, either. Boys must put on their fathers' pants in private, strut them in front of the mirror, and then sneak them back on their hangers; it was like that. The father pretends he doesn't notice the new way they are hung up, or the traces of boot-polish mustaches still under their noses. Do you see?"

The boy said nothing. He had said nothing since they had relinquished the daylight. The gunslinger had talked hectically, feverishly, to fill his silence. He had not looked back at the lights as they passed into the lightlessness beneath the mountains, but the boy had. The gunslinger had read the failing of day in the soft mirror of Jake's cheek: Now faint rose; now milk-glass; now pallid silver; now the last dusk-glow touch of evening; now nothing. The gunslinger had struck a false light and they had gone on.

Now they were camped. No echo from the man in black returned to them. Perhaps he had stopped to rest, too. Or perhaps he floated onward and without running-lights, through nighted chambers.

"It was held once a year in the Great Hall," the gunslinger went on. "We called it The Hall of Grandfathers. But it was only the Great Hall."

The sound of dripping water came to their ears.

"A courting rite." The gunslinger laughed deprecatingly, and the insensate walls made the sound into a loonlike wheeze. "In the old days, the books say, it was the welcoming of spring. But civilization, you know...."

He trailed off, unable to describe the change inherent in that mechanized noun, the death of the romantic and its sterile, carnal revenant, living only a forced respiration of glitter and ceremony; the geometric steps of courtship during the Easter-night dance at the Great Hall which had replaced the mad scribble of love which he could only intuit dimly—hollow grandeur in the place of mean and sweeping passions which might once have erased souls.

"They made something decadent out of it," the gunslinger said. "A play. A game." In his voice was all the unconscious distaste of the ascetic. His face, had there been stronger light to illumine it, would have shown change—harshness and sorrow. But his essential force had not been cut or diluted. The lack of imagination that still remained in that face was remarkable.

"But the Ball," the gunslinger said. "The Ball ..." The boy did not speak.

"There were five crystal chandeliers, heavy glass with electric lights. It was all light, it was an island of light.

"We had sneaked into one of the old balconies, the ones that were supposed to be unsafe. But we were still boys. We were above everything, and we could look down on it. I don't remember that any of us said anything. We only looked, and we looked for hours.

"There was a great stone table where the gunslingers and their women sat, watching the dancers. A few of the gunslingers danced, but only a few. And they were the young ones. The other ones only sat, and it seemed to me they were half embarrassed in all that light, that civilized light. They were revered ones, the feared ones, the guardians, but they seemed like hostlers in that crowd of cavaliers with their soft women. . . .

"There were four circular tables loaded with food, and they turned all the time. The cooks' boys never stopped coming and going from seven until three the next morning. The tables rotated like clocks, and we could smell roast pork, beef, lobster, chickens, baked apples. There were ices and candies. There were great flaming skewers of meat.

"And Marten sat next to my mother and father—I knew them even from so high above—and once she and Marten danced, slowly and revolvingly, and the others cleared the floor for them and clapped when it was over. The gunslingers did not clap, but my father stood slowly and held his hands out to her. And she went, smiling.

"It was a moment of passage, boy. A time such as must be at the Tower itself, when things come together and hold and make power in time. My father had taken control, had been acknowledged and singled out. Marten was the acknowledger; my father was the mover. And his wife my mother, went to him, the connection between them. Betrayer.

"My father was the last lord of light."

The gunslinger looked down at his hands. The boy still said nothing. His face was only thoughtful.

"I remember how they danced," the gunslinger said softly. "My mother and Marten the enchanter. I remember how they danced, revolving slowly together and apart, in the old steps of courtship."

He looked at the boy, smiling. "But it meant nothing, you know. Because power had been passed in some way that none of them knew but all understood, and my mother was locked root and rind to the holder and wielder of that power. Was it not so? She went to him when the dance was over, didn't she? And clasped his hand? Did they applaud? Did the hall ring with it as those pansy-boys and their soft ladies applauded and lauded him? Did it? Did it?"

Bitter water dripped distantly in the darkness. The boy said nothing.

"I remember how they danced," the gunslinger said softly. "I remember how they danced. . . ." He looked up at the unseeable stone roof and it seemed for a moment that he might scream at it, rail at it, challenge it blindly—those dumb tonnages of insensible granite that bore their tiny lives in its stone intestine.

"What hand could have held the knife that did my father to his death?"

"I'm tired," the boy said wistfully.

The gunslinger lapsed into silence, and the boy laid over and put one hand between his cheek and the stone. The little flame in front of them guttered. The gunslinger rolled a smoke. It seemed he could see the crystal light still, in the sardonic hall of his memory; hear the shout of accolade, empty in a husked land that stood even then hopeless against a gray ocean of time. The island of light hurt him bitterly, and he wished he had never held witness to it, or to his father's cuckoldry.

He passed smoke between his mouth and nostrils, looking down at the boy. How we make large circles in earth for ourselves, he thought. How long before the daylight again?

He slept.

After the sound of his breathing had become long and steady and regular, the boy opened his eyes and looked at the gunslinger with an expression that was very much like love. The last light of the fire caught in one pupil for a moment and was drowned there. He went to sleep.

The gunslinger had lost most of his time sense in the desert, which was changeless; he lost the rest of it here in these chambers under the mountains, which were lightless. Neither of them had any means of telling time, and the concept of hours became meaningless. In a sense, they stood outside of time. A day might have been a week, or a week a day. They walked, they slept, they ate thinly. Their only companion was the steady thundering rush of the water, drilling its auger path through the stone. They followed it, drank from its flat, mineral-salted depth. At times the gunslinger thought he saw fugitive drifting lights like corpse-lamps beneath its surface, but supposed they were only projections of his brain, which had not forgotten the light. Still, he cautioned the boy not to put his feet in the water.

The range finder in his head took them on steadily.

The path beside the river (for it was a path; smooth, sunken to a slight concavity) led always upward, toward the river's head. At regular intervals they came to curved stone pylons with sunken ringbolts; perhaps once oxen or stage-horses had tethered there. At each was a steel flagon holding an electric torch, but these were all barren of life and light.

During the third period of rest-before-sleep, the boy wandered away a little. The gunslinger could hear small conversation of rattled pebbles as he moved cautiously.

"Careful," he said. "You can't see where you are."

"I'm crawling. It's ... say!"

"What is it?" The gunslinger half crouched, touching the haft of one gun.

There was a slight pause. The gunslinger strained his eyes uselessly.

"I think it's a railroad," the boy said dubiously.

The gunslinger got up and walked slowly toward the sound of Jake's voice, leading with one foot lightly to test for pitfalls.

"Here." A hand reached out and cat's-pawed the gunslinger's face. The boy was very good in the dark, better than the gunslinger himself. His eyes seemed to dilate until there was no color left in them: the gunslinger saw this as he struck a meager light. There was no fuel in this rock womb, and what they had brought with them was going rapidly to ash.

At times the urge to strike a light was well-nigh insatiable.

The boy was standing beside a curved rock wall that was lined with parallel metal staves off into the darkness. Each carried black bulbs that might once have been conductors of electricity. And beside and below, set only inches off the stone floor, were tracks of bright metal. What might have run on those tracks at one time? The gunslinger could only imagine black electric bullets, flying through this forever night with affrighted searchlight eyes going before. He had never heard of such things. But there were skeletons in the world, just as there were demons. He had once come upon a hermit who had gained a quasi-religious power over a miserable flock of kine-keepers by possession of an ancient gasoline pump. The hermit crouched beside it, one arm wrapped possessively around it, and preached wild, guttering, sullen sermons. He occasionally placed the still-bright steel nozzle, which was attached to a rotted rubber hose, between his legs. On the pump, in perfectly legible (although rust-clotted) letters, was a legend of unknown meaning: *AMOCO. Lead Free.* Amoco had become the totem of a thundergod, and they had worshipped Him with the half-mad slaughter of sheep.

215

Hulks, the gunslinger thought. Only meaningless hulks in sands that once were seas.

And now a railroad.

"We'll follow it," he said.

The boy said nothing.

The gunslinger extinguished the light and they slept. When the gunslinger awoke the boy was up before him, sitting on one of the rails and watching him sightlessly in the dark.

They followed the rails like blindmen, the gunslinger leading, the boy following. They slipped their feet along one rail always, also like blindmen. The steady rush of the river off to the right was their companion. They did not speak, and this went on for three periods of waking. The gunslinger felt no urge to think coherently, or to plan. His sleep was dreamless.

During the fourth period of waking and walking, they literally stumbled on a handcar.

The gunslinger ran into it chest-high, and the boy, walking on the other side, struck his forehead and went down with a cry.

The gunslinger made a light immediately. "Are you all right?" The words sounded sharp, almost waspish, and he winced at them.

"Yes." The boy was holding his head gingerly. He shook it once to make sure he had told the truth. They turned to look at what they had run into.

It was a flat square of metal that sat mutely on the tracks. There was a seesaw handle in the center of the square. The gunslinger had no immediate sense of it, but the boy knew immediately.

"It's a handcar."

"What?"

"Handcar," the boy said impatiently, "like in the old movies. Look."

He pulled himself up and went to the handle. He managed to push it down, but it was necessary to hang all his weight on the handle. He grunted briefly. The handcar moved a foot, with silent timelessness, on the rails.

"It works a little hard," the boy said, as if apologizing for it.

The gunslinger pulled himself up and pushed the handle down. The handcar moved forward obediently, then stopped. He could feel a driveshaft turn beneath his feet. The operation pleased him—it was the first old machine other than the pump at the way station that he had seen in years which still worked well—but it disquieted him, too. It would take them to their destination that much quicker. The curse-kiss again, he thought, and knew the man in black had meant them to find this, too.

"Neat, huh?" the boy said, and his voice was full of loathing.

"What are movies?" the gunslinger asked again.

Jake still did not answer and they stood in a black silence, like in a tomb where life had fled. The gunslinger could hear his organs at work inside his body and the boy's respiration. That was all.

"You stand on one side. I stand on the other side," Jake said. "You'll have to push by yourself until it gets rolling good. Then I can help. First you push, then I push. We'll go right along. Get it?"

"I get it," the gunslinger said. His hands were in helpless, despairing fists.

"But you'll have to push by yourself until it gets rolling good," the boy repeated, looking at him.

The gunslinger had a sudden vivid picture of the Great Hall a year after the spring Ball, in the shattered, hulked shards of revolt, civil strife, and invasion. It was followed with the memory of Allie, the woman from Tull with the scar, pushed and pulled by the bullets that were killing her in reflex. It was followed by Jamie's face, blue in death, by Susan's, twisted and weeping. All my old friends, the gunslinger thought, and smiled hideously.

"I'll push," the gunslinger said.

He began to push.

They rolled on through the dark, faster now, no longer having to feel their way. Once the awkwardness of a buried age had been run off the handcar, it went smoothly. The boy tried to do his share, and the gunslinger allowed him small shifts—but mostly he pumped by himself, in large and chest-stretching rises and fallings. The river was their companion, sometimes closer on their right, sometimes further away. Once it took on huge and thunderous hollowness, as if passing through a prehistoric cathedral narthex. Once the sound of it disappeared almost altogether.

The speed and the made wind against their faces seemed to take the place of sight and to put them once again in a frame of time and reference. The gunslinger estimated they were making anywhere from ten to fifteen miles an hour, always on a shallow, almost imperceptible uphill grade that wore him out deceptively. When they stopped he slept like the stone itself. Their food was almost gone again. Neither of them worried about it.

For the gunslinger, the tenseness of a coming climax was as imperceivable but as real and as accretive as the fatigue of propelling the handcar. They were close to the end of the beginning. He felt like a performer placed on center stage minutes before the rise of the curtain; settled in position with his first line held in his mind, he heard the unseen audience rattling programs and settling in seats. He lived with a tight, tidy ball of unholy anticipation in his belly and welcomed the exercise that let him sleep.

The boy spoke less and less; but at their stopping place one sleep-period before they were attacked by the Slow Mutants, he asked the gunslinger almost shyly about his coming of age.

The gunslinger had been leaning against the handle, a cigarette from his dwindling supply of tobacco clamped in his mouth. He had been on the verge of his usual unthinking sleep when the boy asked his question.

"Why would you want to know that?" He asked.

The boy's voice was curiously stubborn, as if hiding embarrassment. "I just do." And after a pause, he added: "I always wondered about growing up. It's mostly lies."

"It wasn't growing up," the gunslinger said. "I

never grew up all at once. I did it one place and another along the way. I saw a man hung once. That was part of it, though I didn't know it then. I left a girl in a place called King's Town twelve years ago. That was another part. I never knew any of the parts when they happened. Only later I knew that."

He realized with some unease that he was avoiding.

"I suppose the coming of age was part, too," he said, almost grudgingly. "It was formal. Almost stylized; like a dance." He laughed unpleasantly. "Like love.

"Love and dying have been my life."

The boy said nothing.

"It was necessary to prove one's self in battle," the gunslinger began.

Summer and hot.

August had come to the land like a vampire lover, killing the land and the crops of the tenant farmers, turning the fields of the castle-city white and sterile. In the west, some miles distant and near the borders that were the end of the civilized world, fighting had already begun. All reports were bad, and all of them palled before the heat that rested over this place of the center.

Cattle lolled empty-eyed in the pens of the stockyards. Pigs grunted listlessly, unmindful of knives whetted for the coming fall. People whined about taxes and conscription, as they always have; but there was an emptiness beneath the apathetic passion play of politics. The center had frayed like a rag rug that had been washed and walked on and shaken and hung and dried. The lines and nets of mesh which held the last jewel at the breast of the world were unraveling. Things were not holding together. The earth drew in its breath in the summer of the coming eclipse.

The boy idled along the upper corridor of this stone place which was home, sensing these things, not understanding. He was also empty and dangerous.

It had been three years since the hanging of the cook who had always been able to find snacks for hungry boys, and he had filled out. Now, dressed only in faded denim pants, fourteen years old, he had already come to the widened chestspan and lengthening legs that would characterize his manhood. He was still unbedded, but two of the younger slatterns of a West-Town merchant had cast eyes on him. He had felt a response and felt it more strongly now. Even in the coolness of the passage, he felt sweat on his body.

Ahead were his mother's apartments and he approached them incuriously, meaning only to pass them and go upward to the roof, where a thin breeze and the pleasure of his hand awaited.

He had passed the door when a voice called him: "You. Boy."

It was Marten, the enchanter. He was dressed with a suspicious, upsetting casualness—black whipcord trousers almost as tight as leotards, and a white shirt open halfway down his chest. His hair was tousled.

The boy looked at him silently.

"Come in, come in! Don't stand in the hall! Your mother wants to speak to you." He was smiling with his mouth, but the lines of his face held a deeper, more sardonic humor. Beneath that there was only coldness.

But his mother did not seem to want to see him. She sat in the low-backed chair by the large window in the central parlor of her apartments, the one which overlooked the hot blank stone of the central courtyard. She was dressed in a loose, informal gown and looked at the boy only once— a quick, glinting rueful smile, like autumn sun on stream water. During the rest of the interview she studied her hands.

He saw her seldom now, and the phantom of

cradle songs had almost faded from his brain. But she was a beloved stranger. He felt an amorphous fear, and an uncoalesced hatred for Marten, his father's right-hand man (or was it the other way around?), was born.

And, of course, there had already been some backstreet talk—talk which he honestly thought he hadn't heard.

"Are you well?" she asked him softly, studying her hands. Marten stood beside her, a heavy, disturbing hand near the juncture of her white shoulder and white neck, smiling on them both. His brown eyes were dark to the point of blackness with smiling.

"Yes," he said.

"Your studies go well?"

"I'm trying," he said. They both knew he was not flashingly intelligent like Cuthbert, or even quick, like Jamie. He was a plodder and a bludgeoner.

"And David?" She knew his affection for the hawk.

The boy looked up at Marten, still smiling paternally down on all this. "Past his prime."

His mother seemed to wince; for a moment Marten's face seemed to darken, his grip on her shoulder tighten. Then she looked out into the hot whiteness of the day, and all was as it had been.

It's a charade, he thought. A game. Who is playing with whom?

"You have a scar on your forehead," Marten said, still smiling. "Are you going to be a fighter like your father or are you just slow?"

This time she did wince.

"Both," the boy said. He looked steadily at Marten and smiled painfully. Even in here, it was very hot.

Marten stopped smiling abruptly. "You can go to the roof now, boy. I believe you have business there."

But Marten had misunderstood, underestimated. They had been speaking in the low tongue, a parody of informality. But now the boy flashed into High Speech:

"My mother has not yet dismissed me, bondsman!"

Marten's face twisted as if quirt-lashed. The boy heard his mother's dreadful, woeful gasp. She spoke his name.

But the painful smile remained intact on the boy's face and he stepped forward. "Will you give me a sign of fealty, bondsman? In the name of my father whom you serve?"

Marten stared at him, rankly unbelieving.

"Go," Marten said gently. "Go and find your hand."

Smiling, the boy went.

As he closed the door and went back the way he came, he heard his mother wail. It was a banshee sound.

Then he heard Marten's laugh.

The boy continued to smile as he went to his test.

Jamie had come from the shop-wives, and when he saw the boy crossing the exercise yard, he ran to tell Roland the latest gossips of bloodshed and revolt to the west. But he fell aside, the words all unspoken. They had known each other since the time of infancy, and as boys they had dared each other, cuffed each other, and made a thousand explorations of the walls within which they had both been birthed.

The boy strode past him, staring without seeing, grinning his painful grin. He was walking toward Cort's cottage, where the shades were drawn to ward off the savage afternoon heat. Cort napped in the afternoon so that he could enjoy his evening tomcat forays into the mazed and filthy brothels of the lower town to the fullest extent.

Jamie knew in a flash of intuition, knew what

was to come, and in his fear and ecstasy he was torn between following Roland and going after the others.

Then his hypnotism was broken and he ran toward the main buildings, screaming, "Cuthbert! Allen! Thomas!" His screams sounded puny and thin in the heat. They had known, all of them, in that invisible way boys have, that the boy would be the first of them to try the line. But this was too soon.

The hideous grin on Roland's face galvanized him as no news of wars, revolts, and witchcrafts could have done. This was more than words from a toothless mouth given over fly-specked heads of lettuce.

Roland walked to the cottage of his teacher and kicked the door open. It slammed backward, hit the plain rough plaster of the wall and rebounded.

He had never been here before. The entrance opened on an austere kitchen that was cool and brown. A table. Two straight chairs. Two cabinets. A faded linoleum floor, tracked in black paths from the cooler set in the floor to the counter where knives hung, to the table.

A public man's privacy here. The last faded sobriety of a violent midnight carouser who had loved the boys of three generations roughly, and made some of them into gunslingers.

"Cort!"

He kicked the table, sending it across the room and into the counter. Knives from the wall rack fell in twinkling jackstraws.

There was thick stirring in the other room, a half-sleep clearing of the throat. The boy did not enter, knowing it was sham, knowing that Cort had awakened immediately in the cottage's other room and stood with one glittering eye beside the door, waiting to break the intruder's unwary neck.

"Cort, I want you, bondsman!"

Now he spoke the High Speech, and Cort swung the door open. He was dressed only in thin underwear shorts, a squat man with bow legs, runneled with scars from top to toe, thick with twists of muscle. There was a round, bulging belly. The boy knew from experience that it was spring steel. The one good eye glared at him from the bashed and dented hairless head.

The boy saluted formally. "Teach me no more, bondsman. Today I teach you."

"You are early, puler," he said casually, but he also spoke the High Speech. "Five years early, I should judge. I will ask only once. Will you renege?"

The boy only smiled his hideous, painful smile. For Cort, who had seen the smile on a score of bloodied, scarlet-skied fields of honor and dishonor, it was answer enough—perhaps the only answer he would have believed.

"It's too bad," the teacher said absently. "You have been a most promising pupil—the best in two dozen years, I should say. It will be sad to see you broken and set upon a blind path. But the world has moved on. Bad times are on horseback."

The boy still did not speak (and would have been incapable of any coherent explanation, had it been required), but for the first time the awful smile softened a little.

"Still, there is the line of blood," Cort said somberly, "revolt and witchcraft to the west or no. I am your bondsman, boy. I recognize your command and bow to it now—if never again—with my heart."

And Cort, who had cuffed him, kicked him, bled him, cursed him, made mock of him and called him the very eye of syphilis, bent to one knee and bowed his head.

The boy touched the leathery, vulnerable flesh of his neck with wonder, "Rise, bondsman. In love."

Cort stood slowly, and there might have been

pain behind the impassive mask of his reamed features. "This is waste. Renege, boy. I break my own oath. Renege, and wait!"

The boy said nothing.

"Very well." Cort's voice became dry and businesslike. "One hour. And the weapon of your choice."

"You will bring your stick?"

"I always have."

"How many sticks have been taken from you, Cort?" Which was tantamount to asking: How many boys have entered the square yard beyond the Great Hall and returned as gunslinger apprentices?

"No stick will be taken from me today," Cort said slowly. "I regret it. There is only the once, boy. The penalty for overeagerness is the same as the penalty for unworthiness. Can you not wait?"

The boy recalled Marten standing over him, tall as mountains. "No."

"Very well. What weapon do you choose?"

The boy said nothing.

Cort's smile showed a jagged ring of teeth. "Wise enough to begin. In an hour. You realize you will in all probability never see the others, or your father, or this place again?"

"I know what exile means," he said softly.

"Go now."

The boy went, without looking back.

The cellar of the barn was spuriously cool, dank, smelling of cobwebs and earthwater. It was lit from the ubiquitous sun, but felt none of the day's heat; the boy kept the hawk here and the bird seemed comfortable enough.

David was old, now, and no longer hunted the sky. His feathers had lost the radiant animal brightness of three years ago, but the eyes were still as piercing and motionless as ever. You cannot friend a hawk, they said, unless you are a hawk yourself, alone and only a sojourner in the land, without friends or the need of them. The hawk pays no coinage to morals.

David was an old hawk now. The boy hoped (or was he too unimaginative to hope? Did he only know?) that he himself was a young one.

"Hai," he said softly and extended his arm to the tethered perch.

The hawk stepped onto the boy's arm and stood motionless, unhooded. With his other hand the boy reached into his pocket and fished out a bit of dried jerky. The hawk snapped it deftly from between his fingers and made it disappear.

The boy began to stroke David very carefully. Cort most probably would not have believed it if he had seen it, but Cort did not believe the boy's time had come, either.

"I think you die today," he said, continuing to stroke. "I think you will be made sacrifice, like all those little birds we trained you on. Do you remember? No? It doesn't matter. After today, I am the hawk."

David stood on his arm, silent and unblinking, indifferent to his life or death.

"You are old," the boy said reflectively. "And perhaps not my friend. Even a year ago you would have had my eyes instead of that little string of meat, isn't it so? Cort would laugh. But if we get close enough ... which is it, bird? Age or friendship?"

David did not say.

The boy hooded him and found the jesses, which were looped at the end of David's perch. They left the barn.

The yard behind the Great Hall was not really a yard at all, but only a green corridor whose walls were formed by tangled, thick-grown hedges. It had been used for the rite of coming of age since time out of mind, long before Cort and his predecessor, who had died of a stab-wound from an overzealous hand in this place. Many boys had left the corridor from the east end, where the teacher always entered, as men. The east end faced the Great Hall and all the civilization and intrigue of the lighted world. Many more had slunk away, beaten and bloody, from the west end, where the boys always entered, as boys forever. The west end faced the mountains and the hut-dwellers; beyond that, the tangled barbarian forests; and beyond that the desert. The boy who became a man progressed from darkness and unlearning to light and responsibility. The boy who was beaten could only retreat, forever and forever. The hallway was as smooth and green as a gaming field. It was exactly fifty yards long.

Each end was usually clogged with tense spectators and relatives, for the ritual was usually forecast with great accuracy—eighteen was the most common age (those who had not made their test by the age of twenty-five usually slipped into obscurity as freeholders, unable to face the brutal all-or-nothing fact of the field and the test). But on this day there were none but Jamie, Cuthbert, Allen, and Thomas. They clustered at the boy's end, gape-mouthed and frankly terrified.

"Your weapon, stupid!" Cuthbert hissed, in agony. "You forgot your weapon!"

"I have it," the boy said distantly. Dimly he wondered if the news of this had reached yet to the central buildings, to his mother—and Marten. His father was on a hunt, not due back for weeks. In this he felt a sense of shame, for he felt that in his father he would have found understanding, if not approval. "Has Cort come?"

"Cort is here." The voice came from the far end of the corridor, and Cort stepped into view, dressed in a short singlet. A heavy leather band encircled his forehead to keep sweat from his eyes. He held an ironwood stick in one hand, sharp on one end, heavily blunted and spatulate on the other. He began the litany which all of them, chosen by the blind blood of their fathers, had known since early childhood, learned against the day when they would, perchance, become men.

"Have you come here for a serious purpose, boy?"

"I have come for a serious purpose, teacher."

"Have you come as an outcast from your father's house?"

"I have so come, teacher." And would remain outcast until he had bested Cort. If Cort bested him, he would remain outcast forever.

234

"Have you come with your chosen weapon?"

"I have so come, teacher."

"What is your weapon?" This was the teacher's advantage, his chance to adjust his plan of battle to the sling or the spear or the net.

"My weapon is David, teacher."

Cort halted only briefly.

"So then have you at me, boy?"

"I do."

"Be swift, then."

And Cort advanced into the corridor, switching his pike from one hand to the other. The boys sighed flutteringly, like birds, as their compatriot stepped to meet him.

My weapon is David, teacher.

Did Cort remember? Had he fully understood? If so, perhaps it was all lost. It turned on surprise—and on whatever stuff the hawk had left in him. Would he only sit, disinterested, on the boy's arm, while Cort struck him brainless with the ironwood? Or seek the high, hot sky?

They drew close together, and the boy loosened the hawk's hood with nerveless fingers. It dropped to the green grass, and the boy halted in his tracks. He saw Cort's eyes drop to the bird and widen with surprise and slow-dawning comprehension.

Now, then.

"At him!" the boy cried and raised his arm.

And David flew like a silent brown bullet, stubby wings pumping once, twice, three times, before crashing into Cort's face, talons and beak searching.

"Hai! Roland!" Cuthbert screamed deliriously.

Cort staggered backwards, off balance. The ironwood staff rose and beat futilely at the air about his head. The hawk was an undulating, blurred bundle of feathers.

The boy arrowed forward, his hand held out in a straight wedge, his elbow locked.

Still, Cort was almost too quick for him. The bird had covered ninety percent of his vision, but the ironwood came up again, spatulate end forward, and Cort coldbloodly performed the only action that could turn events at that point. He beat his own face three times, biceps flexing mercilessly.

David fell away, broken and twisted. One wing flapped at the ground frantically. His cold, predator's eyes stared fiercely into the teacher's bloody, streaming face. Cort's bad eye now bulged blindly from its socket.

The boy delivered a kick to Cort's temple, connecting solidly. It should have ended it; his leg had been numbed by Cort's only blow, but it still should have ended it. It did not. For a moment Cort's face went slack, and then he lunged, grabbing for the boy's foot.

The boy skipped back and tripped over his own feet. He went down asprawl. He heard, from far away, the sound of Jamie's scream.

Cort was up, ready to fall on him and finish it. He had lost his advantage. For a moment they looked at each other, the teacher standing over the pupil, with gouts of blood pouring from the left side of his face, the bad eye now closed except for a thin slit of white. There would be no brothels for Cort this night.

Something ripped jaggedly at the boy's hand. It was the hawk, David, tearing blindly. Both wings were broken. It was incredible that he still lived.

The boy grabbed him like a stone, unmindful of the jabbing, diving beak that was taking the flesh from his wrist in ribbons. As Cort flew at him, all spread-eagled, the boy threw the hawk upward.

"Hai! David! Kill!"

Then Cort blotted out the sun and came down atop of him.

The bird was smashed between them, and the

boy felt a calloused thumb probe for the socket of his eye. He turned it, at the same time bringing up the slab of his thigh to block Cort's crotch-seeking knee. His own hand flailed against the tree of Cort's neck in three hard chops. It was like hitting ribbed stone.

Then Cort made a thick grunting. His body shuddered. Faintly, the boy saw one hand flailing for the dropped stick, and with a jackknifing lunge, he kicked it out of reach. David had hooked one talon into Cort's right ear. The other battered mercilessly at the teacher's cheek, making it a ruin. Warm blood splattered the boy's face, smelling of sheared copper.

Cort's fist struck the bird once, breaking its back. Again, and the neck snapped away at a crooked angle. And still the talon clutched. There was no ear now; only a red hole tunneled into the side of Cort's skull. The third blow sent the bird flying, clearing Cort's face.

The boy brought the edge of his hand across the bridge of Cort's nose, breaking the thin bone. Blood sprayed.

Cort's grasping, unseeing hand ripped at the boy's buttocks and Roland rolled away blindly, finding Cort's stick, rising to his knees.

Cort came to his own knees, grinning. His face

was curtained with gore. The one seeing eye rolled madly in its socket. The nose was smashed over to a haunted, leaning angle. Both cheeks hung in flaps.

The boy held his stick like a baseball player waiting for the pitch.

Cort double-feinted, then came directly at him.

The boy was ready. The ironwood swung in a flat arc, striking Cort's skull with a dull thudding noise. Cort fell on his side, looking at the boy with a lazy unseeing expression. A tiny trickle of spit came from his mouth.

"Yield or die," the boy said. His mouth was filled with wet cotton.

And Cort smiled. Nearly all consciousness was gone, and he would remain tended in his cottage for a week afterward, wrapped in the blackness of coma, but now he held on with all the strength of his pitiless, shadowless life.

"I yield, gunslinger. I yield smiling."

Cort's clear eye closed.

The gunslinger shook him gently, but with persistence. The others were around him now, their hands trembling to thump his back and hoist him to their shoulders; but they held back, afraid, sensing a new gulf. Yet it was not as strange as it could have been, because there had always been a gulf between this one and the rest.

Cort's eye fluttered open again, weakly.

"The key," the gunslinger said. "My birthright, teacher. I need it."

His birthright was the guns—not the heavy ones of his father, weighted with sandalwood— but guns, all the same. Forbidden to all but a few. The ultimate, the final weapon. In the heavy vault under the barracks where he by ancient law was now required to abide, away from his mother's breast, hung his apprentice weapons, heavy cumbersome things of steel and nickel. Yet they had seen his father through his apprenticeship, and his father now ruled—at least in name.

"Is it so fearsome, then?" Cort muttered, as if in his sleep. "So pressing? I feared so. And yet you won."

"The key."

"The hawk ... a fine ploy. A fine weapon. How long did it take you to train the bastard?"

"I never trained David. I friended him. The key."

"Under my belt, gunslinger." The eye closed again.

The gunslinger reached under Cort's belt, feeling the heavy press of his belly, the huge muscles there now slack and asleep. The key was on a brass ring. He clutched it in his hand, restraining the mad urge to thrust it up to the sky in a salutation of victory.

He got to his feet and was finally turning to the others when Cort's hand fumbled for his foot. For a moment the gunslinger feared some last attack and tensed, but Cort only looked up at him and beckoned with one crusted finger.

"I'm going to sleep now," Cort whispered calmly. "Perhaps forever, I don't know. I teach you no more, gunslinger. You have surpassed me, and two years younger than your father, who was the youngest. But let me counsel."

"What?" Impatiently.

"Wait."

"Huh?" The word was startled out of him.

"Let the word and the legend go before you. There are those who will carry both." His eyes flicked over the gunslinger's shoulder. "Fools, perchance. Let the word go before you. Let your shadow grow. Let it grow hair on its face. Let it become dark." He smiled grotesquely. "Given time, words may even enchant an enchanter. Do you take my meaning, gunslinger?"

"Yes."

"Will you take my last counsel?"

The gunslinger rocked back on his heels, a hunkered, thinking posture that foreshadowed the man. He looked at the sky. It was deepening, purpling. The heat of the day was failing and thunderheads in the west foretold rain. Lightning tines jabbed the placid flank of the rising foothills miles distant. Beyond that, the mountains. Beyond that, the rising fountains of blood and unreason. He was tired, tired into his bones and beyond.

He looked back at Cort. "I will bury my hawk tonight, teacher. And later go into lower town to inform those in the brothels that will wonder about you."

Cort's lips parted in a pained smile. And then he slept.

The gunslinger got to his feet and turned to the others. "Make a litter and take him to his house. Then bring a nurse. No, two nurses. Okay?"

They still watched him, caught in a bated moment that was not yet able to be broken. They still looked for a corona of fire, or a werewolf change of features.

"Two nurses," the gunslinger repeated, and then smiled. They smiled.

"You god-damned horse drover!" Cuthbert suddenly yelled, grinning. "You haven't left enough meat for the rest of us to pick off the bone!"

"The world won't move on tomorrow," the

gunslinger said, quoting the old adage with a smile. "Allen, you butter-ass. Move your freight."

Allen set about making the litter; Thomas and Jamie went together to the main hall and the infirmary.

The gunslinger and Cuthbert looked at each other. They had always been the closest—or as close as they could be under the particular shades of their characters. There was a speculative, open light in Cuthbert's eyes, and the gunslinger controlled only with great difficulty the need to tell him not to call for the test for a year or even eighteen months, lest he go west. But they had been through a great deal together, and the gunslinger did not feel he could risk it without an expression that might be taken for patronization. I've begun to scheme, he thought, and was a little dismayed. Then he thought of Marten, of his mother, and he smiled a deceiver's smile at his friend.

I am to be the first, he thought, knowing it for the first time, although he had thought of it (in a bemused way) many times before. I am to be first.

"Let's go," he said.

"With pleasure, gunslinger."

They left by the east end of the hedge-bordered

corridor; Thomas and Jamie were returning with the nurses already. They looked like ghosts in their heavy white robes, crossed at the breast with red.

"Shall I help you with the hawk?" Cuthbert asked.

"Yes," the gunslinger said.

And later, when darkness had come and the rushing thundershowers with it; while huge, phantom caissons rolled across the sky and lightning washed the crooked streets of the lower town in blue fire; while horses stood at hitching rails with their heads down and their tails drooping, the gunslinger took a woman and lay with her.

It was quick and good. When it was over and they lay side by side without speaking, it began to hail with a brief, rattling ferocity. Downstairs and far away, someone was playing *Hey Jude* ragtime. The gunslinger's mind turned reflectively inward. It was in that hail-splattered silence, just before sleep overtook him, that he first thought that he might also be the last.

The gunslinger did not, of course, tell the boy all of this, but perhaps most of it had come through anyway. He had already realized that this was an extremely perceptive boy, not so different from Cuthbert, or even Jamie.

"You asleep?" the gunslinger asked.

"No."

"Did you understand what I told you?"

"Understand it?" The boy asked, with cautious scorn. "Understand it? Are you kidding?"

"No." But the gunslinger felt defensive. He had never told anyone about his coming of age before, because he felt ambivalent about it. Of course, the hawk had been a perfectly acceptable weapon, yet it had been a trick, too. And a betrayal. The first of many: *Am I readying to throw this boy at the man in black?*

"I understood it," the boy said. "It was a game, wasn't it? Do grown men always have to play games? Does everything have to be an excuse for another kind of game? Do any men grow up or do they only come of age?"

"You don't know everything," the gunslinger said, trying to hold his slow anger.

"No. But I know what I am to you."

"And what is that?" the gunslinger asked tightly.

"A poker chip."

The gunslinger felt an urge to find a rock and brain the boy. Instead, he held his tongue.

"Go to sleep," he said. "Boys need their sleep."

And in his mind he heard Marten's echo: *Go and find your hand.*

He sat stiffly in the darkness, stunned with horror and terrified (for the first time in his existence; of anything) of the self-loathing that might come.

During the next period of waking, the railway angled closer to the underground river, and they came upon the Slow Mutants.

Jake saw the first one and screamed aloud.

The gunslinger's head, which had been fixed straight forward as he pumped the handcar, jerked to the right. There was a rotten jack-o-lantern greenness below and away from them, circular and pulsating faintly. For the first time he became aware of odor—faint, unpleasant, wet.

The greenness was a face, and the face was abnormal. Above the flattened nose was an insectile node of eyes, looking at them expressionlessly. The gunslinger felt an atavistic crawl in his intestines and privates. He stepped up the rhythm of arms and handcar handle slightly.

The glowing face faded.

"What was it?" the boy asked, crawling. "What—" The words stopped dumb in his throat as they came up upon and passed a group of three faintly glowing forms, standing between the rails and the invisible river, watching them, motionless.

"They're Slow Mutants," the gunslinger said. "I don't think they'll bother us. They're probably just as frightened of us as we are of—"

One of the forms broke free and shambled toward them, glowing and changing. The face was that of a starving idiot. The faint naked body had been transformed into a knotted mess of tentacular limbs with suckers.

The boy screamed again and crowded against the gunslinger's leg like an affrighted dog.

One of the tentacles pawed across the flat platform of the handcar. It reeked of the wet and the dark and of strangeness. The gunslinger let loose of the handle and drew. He put a bullet through the forehead of the starving idiot face. It fell away, its faint swamp-fire glow fading, an eclipsed moon. The gunflash lay bright and branded on their dark retinas, fading only reluctantly. The smell of expended powder was hot and savage and alien in this buried place.

There were others, more of them. None moved against them overtly, but they were closing in on the tracks, a silent, hideous party of rubberneckers.

"You may have to pump for me," the gunslinger said. "Can you?"

"Yes."

"Then be ready."

The boy stood close to him, his body poised. His eyes took in the Slow Mutants only as they passed, not traversing, not seeing more than they had to. The boy assumed a psychic bulge of terror, as if his very id had somehow sprung out through his pores to form a telepathic shield.

The gunslinger pumped steadily but did not increase his speed. The Slow Mutants could smell their terror, he knew that, but he doubted if terror would be enough for them. He and the boy were, after all, creatures of the light, and whole. How they must hate us, he thought, and wondered if they had hated the man in black in the same way. He thought not, or perhaps he had passed among them and through their pitiful hive colony unknown, only the shadow of a dark wing.

The boy made a noise in his throat and the gunslinger turned his head almost casually. Four of them were charging the handcar in a stumbling way—one of them in the process of finding a handgrip.

The gunslinger let go of the handle and drew again, with the same sleepy casual motion. He shot the lead mutant in the head. The mutant made a sighing, sobbing noise and began to grin.

Its hands were limp and fishlike, dead; the fingers clove to one another like the fingers of a glove long immersed in drying mud. One of these corpse-hands found the boy's foot and began to pull.

The boy shrieked aloud in the granite womb.

The gunslinger shot the mutant in the chest. It began to slobber through the grin. Jake was going off the side. The gunslinger caught one of his arms and was almost pulled off balance himself. The thing was amazingly strong. The gunslinger put another bullet in the mutant's head. One eye went out like a candle. Still it pulled. They engaged in a silent tug of war for Jake's jerking, wriggling body. They yanked on him like a wishbone.

The handcar was slowing down. The others began to close in—the lame, the halt, the blind. Perhaps they only looked for a Jesus to heal them, to raise them Lazarus-like from the darkness.

It's the end for the boy, the gunslinger thought with perfect coldness. This is the end he meant. Let go and pump or hold on and be buried. The end for the boy.

He gave a tremendous yank on the boy's arm and shot the mutant in the belly. For one frozen moment its grip grew even tighter and Jake began to slide off the edge again. Then the dead mud-hands loosened, and the Slow Mutie fell on its face between the tracks behind the slowing handcar, still grinning.

"I thought you'd leave me," the boy was sobbing. "I thought . . . I thought. . . ."

"Hold onto my belt," the gunslinger said. "Hold on just as tight as you can."

The hand worked into his belt and clutched there; the boy was breathing in great convulsive, silent gasps.

The gunslinger began to pump steadily again, and the handcar picked up speed. The Slow Mutants fell back a step and watched them go with faces hardly human (or pathetically so), faces that generated the weak phosphorescence common to those weird deep-sea fishes that live under incredible black pressure, faces that held no anger or hate on their senseless orbs, but only what seemed to be a semiconscious, idiot regret.

"They're thinning," the gunslinger said. The drawn-up muscles of his lower belly and privates relaxed the smallest bit. "They're—"

The Slow Mutants had put rocks across the track. The way was blocked. It had been a quick, poor job, perhaps the work of only a minute to clear, but they were stopped. And someone would have to get down and move them. The boy moaned and shuddered closer to the gunslinger. The gunslinger let go of the handle and the handcar coasted noiselessly to the rocks, where it thumped to rest.

The Slow Mutants began to close in again, almost casually, almost as if they had been passing by, lost in a dream of darkness, and had found someone of whom to ask directions. A street-corner congregation of the damned beneath the ancient rock.

"Are they going to get us?" The boy asked calmly.

"No. Be quiet a second."

He looked at the rocks. The mutants were weak, of course, and had not been able to drag any of the boulders to block their way. Only small rocks. Only enough to stop them, to make someone get down.

"Get down," the gunslinger said. "You'll have to move them. I'll cover you."

"No," the boy whispered. "Please."

"I can't give you a gun and I can't move the rocks and shoot too. You have to get down."

Jake's eyes rolled terribly; for a moment his body shuddered in tune with the turnings of his mind, and then he wriggled over the side and began to throw rocks to the right and the left madly, not looking.

The gunslinger drew and waited.

Two of them, lurching rather than walking, went for the boy with arms like dough. The guns did their work, stitching the darkness with red-white lances of light that pushed needles of pain into the gunslinger's eyes. The boy screamed and continued to throw away rocks. Witch-glow leaped and danced. Hard to see, now, that was the worst. Everything had gone to shadows.

One of them, glowing hardly at all, suddenly reached for the boy with rubber boogeyman arms. Eyes that ate up half the mutie's head rolled wetly.

Jake screamed again and turned to struggle.

The gunslinger fired without allowing himself to think, before his spotty vision could betray his hands into a terrible quiver; the two heads were only inches apart. It was the mutie who fell, slitheringly.

Jake threw rocks wildly. The mutants milled just outside the invisible line of trespass, closing a little at a time, now very close. Others had caught up, swelling their number.

"All right," the gunslinger said. "Get on. Quick."

When the boy moved, the mutants came at

them. Jake was over the side and scrambling to his feet; the gunslinger was already pumping again, all out. Both guns were holstered now. They must run.

Strange hands slapped the metal plane of the car's surface. The boy was holding his belt with both hands now, his face pressed tightly into the small of the gunslinger's back.

A group of them ran onto the tracks, their faces full of that mindless, casual anticipation. The gunslinger was pumped full of adrenalin; the car was flying along the tracks into the darkness. They struck the four or five pitiful hulks full force. They flew like rotten bananas struck from the stem.

On and on, into the soundless, flying, banshee darkness.

After an age, the boy raised his face into the made wind, dreading and yet needing to know. The ghost of gun-flashes still lingered on his retinas. There was nothing to see but the darkness and nothing to hear but the rumble of the river.

"They're gone," the boy said, suddenly fearing an end to the tracks in the darkness, and the wounding crash as they jumped the rails and plunged to twisted ruin. He had ridden in cars;

once his humorless father had driven at ninety on the New Jersey Turnpike and had been stopped. But he had never ridden like this, with the wind and the blindness and the terrors behind and ahead, with the sound of the river like a chuckling voice—the voice of the man in black. The gunslinger's arms were pistons in a lunatic human factory.

"They're gone," the boy said timidly, the words ripped from his mouth by the wind. "You can slow down now. We left them behind."

But the gunslinger did not hear. They careened onward into the strange dark.

They went on three periods of waking and sleeping without incident.

During the fourth period of waking (halfway through? three-quarters? they didn't know—only that they weren't tired enough yet to stop) there was a sharp thump beneath them, the handcar swayed, and their bodies immediately leaned to the right with gravity as the rails took a gradual turn to the left.

There was a light ahead—a glow so faint and alien that it seemed at first to be a totally new element, neither earth, air, fire, or water. It had no color and could only be discerned by the fact that they had regained their hands and faces in a dimension beyond that of touch. Their eyes had become so light-sensitive that they noticed the glow over five miles before they approached it.

"The end," the boy said tightly. "It's the end."

"No." The gunslinger spoke with odd assurance. "It isn't."

And it was not. They reached light but not day.

As they approached the source of the glow, they saw for the first time that the rock wall to the left had fallen away and their tracks had been joined by others which crossed in a complex spiderweb. The light laid them in burnished vectors. On some of them there were dark boxcars, passenger coaches, a stage that had been adapted to rails. They made the gunslinger nervous, like ghost galleons trapped in an underground Sargasso.

The light grew stronger, hurting their eyes a little, but growing slowly enough to allow them to adapt. They came from dark to light like divers coming up from deep fathoms in slow stages.

Ahead, drawing nearer, was a huge hangar stretching up into the dark. Cut into it, showing yellow squares of light, were a series of perhaps twenty-four entranceways, growing from the size of toy windows to a height of twenty feet as they drew closer. They passed inside through one of the middle ways. Written above were a series of characters, in various languages, the gunslinger presumed. He was astounded to find that he could read the last one; it was an ancient root of the High Speech itself and said:

TRACK 10 TO SURFACE AND POINTS WEST

The light inside was brighter; the tracks met and merged through a series of switchings. Here some of the traffic lanterns still worked, flashing eternal reds and greens and ambers.

They rolled between rising stone piers caked black with the passage of thousands of vehicles, and then they were in some kind of central terminal. The gunslinger let the handcar coast slowly to a stop, and they peered around.

"It's like the subway," the boy said.

"Subway?"

"Never mind."

The boy climbed up and onto the hard cement. They looked at silent, deserted booths where newspapers and books had once been vended; an ancient bootery; a weapon shop (the gunslinger, with a sudden burst of excitement, saw revolvers and rifles; closer inspection showed that their barrels had been filled with lead; he did, however, pick out a bow, which he slung over his back, and a quiver of almost useless, badly weighted arrows); a women's apparel shop. Somewhere a converter was turning the air over and over, as it had for thousands of years—but perhaps not for much longer. It had a grating noise somewhere in the middle of its cycle which served to remind that perpetual motion, even under strictly controlled conditions, is still a fool's dream. The air had a mechanized taste. Their shoes made flat echoes.

The boy cried out: "Hey! Hey...."

The gunslinger turned around and went to him. The boy was standing, transfixed, at the book stall. Inside, sprawled in the far corner, was a mummy. The mummy was wearing a blue uniform with gold piping—a trainman's uniform by the look. There was an ancient, perfectly preserved newspaper on the mummy's lap, which crumbled to dust when the gunslinger attempted to look at it. The mummy's face was like an old, shriveled apple. Cautiously, the gunslinger touched the cheek. There was a small puff of dust, and they looked through the cheek and into the mummy's mouth. A gold tooth twinkled.

"Gas," the gunslinger murmured. "They used to be able to make a gas that would do this."

"They fought wars with it," the boy said darkly.
"Yes."

There were other mummies, not a great many, but a few. They were all wearing blue and gold ornamental uniforms. The gunslinger supposed that the gas had been used when the place was empty of all incoming and outgoing traffic. Perhaps, in some dim day, the station had been a military objective of some long-gone army and cause.

The thought depressed him.

"We had better go on," he said, and started toward Track 10 and the handcar again. But the boy stood rebelliousy behind him.

"Not going."

The gunslinger turned back, surprised.

The boy's face was twisted and trembling. "You won't get what you want until I'm dead. I'll take my chances by myself."

The gunslinger nodded noncommittally, hating himself. "Okay." He turned around and walked across to the stone piers and leaped easily down onto the handcar.

"You made a deal!" the boy screamed after him. "I know you did!"

The gunslinger, not replying, carefully put the bow in front of the T-post rising out of the handcar's floor, out of harm's way.

The boy's fists were clenched, his features drawn in agony.

How easily you bluff this young boy, the gunslinger told himself dryly. Again and again his intuition has led him to this point, and again and again you have led him on by the nose—after all, he has no friends but you.

In a sudden, simple thought (almost a vision) it came to him that all he had to do was give it over, turn around, take the boy with him, make him the center of a new force. The Tower did not have to be obtained in this humiliating, nose-rubbing way. Let it come after the boy had a growth of years, when the two of them could cast the man in black aside like a cheap wind-up toy.

Surely, he thought cynically. Surely.

He knew with sudden coldness that going backward would mean death for both of them—death or worse: entombment with the living dead behind them. Decay of all the faculties. With, perhaps, the guns of his father living long after both of them, kept in rotten splendor as totems not unlike the unforgotten gas pump.

Show some guts, he told himself falsely.

He reached for the handle and began to pump it. The handcar moved away from the stone piers.

The boy screamed: *"Wait!"* And began running on the diagonal, toward where the handcar would emerge toward the darkness ahead. The gunslinger had an impulse to speed up, to leave the boy alone yet at least with an uncertainty.

Instead, he caught him as he leaped. The heart beneath the thin shirt thrummed and fluttered as Jake clung to him. It was like the beat of a chicken's heart.

It was very close now.

The sound of the river had become very loud, filling even their dreams with its steady thunder. The gunslinger, more as a whim than anything else, let the boy pump them ahead while he shot a number of arrows into the dark, tethered by fine white lengths of thread.

The bow was very bad, incredibly preserved but with a terrible pull and aim despite that, and the gunslinger knew that very little would improve it. Even re-stringing would not help the tired wood. The arrows would not fly far into the dark, but the last one he sent out came back wet and slick. The gunslinger only shrugged when the boy asked him how far, but privately he didn't think the arrow could have traveled more than a hundred yards from the rotted bow—and lucky to get that.

And still the sound grew louder.

During the third waking period after the station, a spectral radiance began to grow again. They had entered a long tunnel of some weird phosphorescent rock, and the wet walls glittered and twinkled with thousands of minute starbursts. They saw things in a kind of eerie, horror-house surreality.

The brute sound of the river was channeled to them by the confining rock, magnified in its own natural amplifier. Yet the sound remained oddly constant, even as they approached the crossing point the gunslinger was sure lay ahead, because the walls were widening, drawing back. The angle of their ascent became more pronounced.

The tracks arrowed straight ahead in the new light. To the gunslinger they looked like the captive tubes of swamp gas sometimes sold for a pretty at the Feast of Joseph fairtime; to the boy they looked like endless streamers of neon tubing. But in its glow they could both see that the rock that had enclosed them so long ended up ahead in ragged twin peninsulas that pointed toward a gulf of darkness ahead—the chasm over the river.

The tracks continued out and over the unknowable drop, supported by a trestle aeons old. And beyond, what seemed an incredible distance, was a tiny pinprick of light; not phosphorescence or fluorescence, but the hard, true light of day. It was as tiny as a needle-prick in a dark cloth, yet weighted with frightful meaning.

Stop," the boy said. "Stop for a minute. Please."

Unquestioning, the gunslinger let the handcar coast to a rest. The sound of the river was a steady, booming roar, coming from beneath and ahead. The artificial glow from the wet rock was suddenly hateful. For the first time he felt a claustrophobic hand touch him, and the urge to get out, to get free of this living burial, was strong and nearly undeniable.

"We'll go through," the boy said. "Is that what he wants? For us to drive the handcar out over ... that ... and fall down?"

The gunslinger knew it was not but said: "I don't know what he wants."

"We're close now. Can't we walk?"

They got down and approached the lip of the drop carefully. The stone beneath their feet continued to rise until, with a sudden, angling drop, the floor fell away from the tracks and the tracks continued alone, across blackness.

The gunslinger dropped to his knees and peered down. He could dimly make out a complex, nearly incredible webwork of steel girders and struts, disappearing down toward the roar of the river, all in support of the graceful arch of the tracks across the void.

In his mind's eye he could imagine the work of time and water on the steel, in deadly tandem. How much support was left? Little? Hardly any? None? He suddenly saw the face of the mummy again, and the way the flesh, seemingly solid, had crumbled effortlessly to powder at the bare touch of his finger.

"We'll walk," the gunslinger said.

He half expected the boy to balk again, but he preceded the gunslinger calmly out onto the rails, crossing on the welded steel slats calmly, with sure feet. The gunslinger followed him, ready to catch him if Jake should put foot wrong.

They left the handcar behind them and walked precariously out over darkness.

The gunslinger felt a fine slick of sweat cover his skin. The trestle was rotten, very rotten. It thrummed beneath his feet with the heady motion of the river far beneath, swaying a little on unseen guy wires. We're acrobats, he thought. Look, mother, no net. I'm flying. He knelt once and examined the crossties they were walking on. They were caked and pitted with rust (he could feel the reason on his face; fresh air, the friend of corruption: very close to the surface now), and a strong blow of the fist made the metal quiver sickly. Once he heard a warning groan beneath his feet and felt the steel settle preparatory to giving way, but he had already moved on.

The boy, of course, was over a hundred pounds lighter and safe enough, unless the going became progressively worse.

Behind them, the handcar had melted into the general gloom. The stone pier on the left extended out perhaps twenty feet. Further than the one on the right, but this was also left behind and they were alone over the gulf.

At first it seemed that the tiny prick of daylight remained mockingly constant (perhaps drawing away from them at the exact pace they approached it—that would be wonderful magic indeed), but gradually the gunslinger realized that it was widening, becoming more defined. They were still below it, but the tracks were still rising.

The boy gave a surprised grunt and suddenly lurched to the side, arms pinwheeling in slow, wide revolutions. It seemed that he tottered on the brink for a very long time indeed before stepping forward again.

"It almost went on me," he said softly, without emotion. "Step over."

The gunslinger did so. The crosstie the boy had stepped on had given way almost entirely and flopped downward lazily, swinging easily on a disintegrating rivet, like a shutter on a haunted window.

Upward, still upward. It was a nightmare walk and so seemed to go on much longer than it did; the air itself seemed to thicken and become like taffy, and the gunslinger felt as if he might be swimming rather than walking. Again and again his mind tried to turn itself to thoughtful, lunatic consideration of the awful space between this trestle and the river below. His brain viewed it in spectacular detail, and how it would be: The scream of twisting metal, the lurch as his body slid off to the side, the grabbing for nonexistent handholds with the fingers, the swift rattle of bootheels on treacherous, rotted steel—and then down, turning over and over, the warm spray in his crotch as his bladder let go, the rush of wind against his face, rippling his hair up in cartoon fright, pulling his eyelids back, the dark water rushing to meet him, faster, outstripping even his own scream—

Metal screamed beneath him and he stepped past it unhurriedly, shifting his weight, not thinking of the drop, or of how far they had come, or of how far was left. Not thinking that the boy was expendable and that the sale of his honor was now, at last, nearly negotiated.

"Three ties out here," the boy said coolly. "I'm going to jump. Here! Here!"

The gunslinger saw him silhouetted for a moment against the daylight, an awkward, hunched spread-eagle. He landed and the whole edifice swayed drunkenly. Metal beneath them protested and something far below fell, first with a crash, then with the sound of deep water.

"Are you over?" The gunslinger asked.

"Yes," the boy said remotely, "but it's very rotten. I don't think it will hold you. Me, but not you. Go back now. Go back now and leave me alone."

His voice was hysterical, cold but hysterical.

The gunslinger stepped over the break. One large step did it. The boy was shuddering helplessly. "Go back. I don't want you to kill me."

"For Christ's sake, walk," the gunslinger said roughly. "It's going to fall down."

The boy walked drunkenly now, his hands held out shudderingly before him, fingers splayed.

They went up.

Yes, it was much more rotten now. There were frequent breaks of one, two, even three ties, and the gunslinger expected again and again that they would find the long empty space between rails that would either force them back or make them walk on the rails themselves, balanced giddily over the chasm.

He kept his eyes fixed on the daylight.

The glow had taken on a color—blue—and as it came closer it became softer, paling the radiance of the phosphor as it mixed with it. Fifty yards or a hundred? He could not say.

They walked, and now he looked at his feet, crossing from tie to tie. When he looked again, the glow had grown to a hole, and it was not a light but a way out. They were almost there.

Thirty yards, yes. Ninety short feet. It could be done. Perhaps they would have the man in black yet. Perhaps, in the bright sunlight the evil flowers in his mind would shrivel and anything would be possible.

The sunlight was blocked out.

He looked up, startled, staring, and saw a silhouette filling the light, eating it up, allowing only chinks of mocking blue around the outline of shoulders, the fork of crotch.

"Hello, boys!"

The man in black's voice echoed to them, amplified in this natural throat of stone, the sarcasm taking on mighty overtones. Blindly, the gunslinger sought the jawbone, but it was gone, lost somewhere, used up.

He laughed above them and the sound crashed around them, reverberating like surf in a filling cave. The boy screamed and tottered, a windmill again, arms gyrating through the scant air.

Metal ripped and sloughed beneath them; the rails canted through a slow and dreamy twisting. The boy plunged, and one hand flew up like a gull in the darkness, up, up, and then he hung over the pit; he dangled there, his dark eyes staring up at the gunslinger in final blind lost knowledge.

"Help me."

Booming, racketing: "Come now, gunslinger. Or catch me never."

All chips on the table. Every card up but one. The boy dangled, a living Tarot card, the hanged man, the Phoenician sailor, innocent lost and barely above the wave of a stygian sea.

Wait then, wait awhile.

"Do I go?" The voice so loud, he makes it hard to think, the power to cloud men's minds....

Don't make it bad, take a sad song and make it better....

"Help me."

The trestle had begun to twist further, scream-ing, pulling loose from itself, giving—

"Then I shall leave you."

"No!"

His legs carried him in a sudden leap through the entropy that held him, above the dangling boy, into a skidding, plunging rush toward the light that offered, the Tower frozen on the retina of his mind's eye in a black frieze, suddenly silence, the silhouette gone, even the beat of his heart gone as the trestle settled further, beginning its final slow dance to the depths, tearing loose, his hand finding the rocky, lighted lip of damna-tion; and behind him, in the dreadful silence, the boy spoke from too far beneath him.

"Go then. There are other worlds than these."

It tore away from him, the whole weight of it; and as he pulled himself up and through to the light and the breeze and the reality of a new karma *(we all shine on),* he twisted his head back, for a moment in his agony striving to be Janus— but there was nothing, only plummeting silence, for the boy made no sound.

Then he was up, pulling his legs through onto the rocky escarpment that looked toward a grassy plain at the descending foot, toward where the man in black stood spread-legged, with arms crossed.

The gunslinger stood drunkenly, pallid as a ghost, eyes huge and swimming beneath his forehead, shirt smeared with the white dust of his final, lunging crawl. It came to him that he would always flee murder. It came to him that there would be further degradations of the spirit ahead that might make this one seem infinitesimal, and yet he would still flee it, down corridors and through cities, from bed to bed; he would flee the boy's face and try to bury it in cunts or even in further destruction, only to enter one final room and find it looking at him over a candle flame. He had become the boy; the boy had become him. He was a *wurderlak,* lycanthropus of his own making, and in deep dreams he would become the boy and speak strange tongues.

This is death. Is it? Is it?

He walked slowly, drunkenly down the rocky hill toward where the man in black waited. Here the tracks had been worn away, under the sun of reason, and it was as if they had never been.

The man in black pushed his hood away with the backs of both hands, laughing.

"So!" he cried. "Not an end, but the end of the beginning, eh? You progress, gunslinger! You progress! Oh, how I admire you!"

The gunslinger drew with blinding speed and

fired twelve times. The gun-flashes dimmed the sun itself, and the pounding of the explosions slammed back from the rock-faced escarpments behind them.

"Now," the man in black said, laughing. "Oh, now. We make great magic together, you and I. You kill me no more than you kill yourself."

He withdrew, walking backwards, facing the gunslinger, grinning. "Come. Come. Come."

The gunslinger followed him in broken boots to the place of counseling.

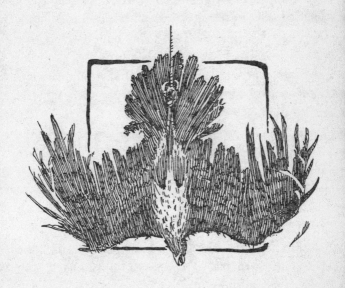

THE GUNSLINGER AND THE DARK MAN

The man in black led him to an ancient killing ground to make palaver. The gunslinger knew it immediately; a golgotha, place-of-the-skull. And bleached skulls stared blandly up at them—cattle, coyotes, deer, rabbits. Here the alabaster xylophone of a hen pheasant killed as she fed; there the tiny, delicate bones of a mole, perhaps killed for pleasure by a wild dog.

The golgotha was a bowl indented into the descending slope of the mountain, and below, in easier altitudes, the gunslinger could see Joshua trees and scrub firs. The sky overhead was a softer blue than he had seen for a twelve-month, and there was an indefinable something that spoke of the sea in the not-too-great distance.

I am in the West, Cuthbert, he thought wonderingly.

And of course in each skull, in each rondure of vacated eye, he saw the boy's face.

The man in black sat on an ancient ironwood log. His boots were powdered white with dust and the uneasy bonemeal of this place. He had put his hood up again, but the gunslinger could see the square shape of his chin clearly, and the shading of his jaw.

The shadowed lips twitched in a smile. "Gather wood, gunslinger. This side of the mountains is gentle, but at this altitude, the cold still may put a knife in one's belly. And this is a place of death, eh?"

"I'll kill you," the gunslinger said.

"No you won't. You can't. But you can gather wood to remember your Isaac."

The gunslinger had no understanding of the reference. He went wordlessly and gathered wood like a common cook's boy. The pickings were slim. There was no devil-grass on this side and the ironwood would not burn. It had become stone. He returned finally with a large armload, powdered and dusted with disintegrated bone, as if dipped in flour. The sun had sunk beyond the highest Joshua trees and had taken on a reddish glow and peered at them with baleful indifference through the black, tortured branches.

"Excellent," the man in black said. "How exceptional you are! How methodical! I salute you!" He giggled, and the gunslinger dropped the wood at his feet with a crash that ballooned up bone dust.

The man in black did not start or jump; he merely began laying the fire. The gunslinger watched, fascinated, as the ideogram (fresh, this time) took shape. When it was finished, it resembled a small and complex double chimney about two feet high. The man in black lifted his hand skyward, shaking back the voluminous sleeve from a tapered, handsome hand, and brought it down rapidly, index and pinky fingers forked out in the traditional sign of the evil eye. There was a blue flash of flame, and their fire was lighted.

"I have matches," the man in black said jovially, "but I thought you might enjoy the magic. For a pretty, gunslinger. Now cook our dinner."

The folds of his robe shivered, and the plucked and gutted carcass of a plump rabbit fell on the dirt.

The gunslinger spitted the rabbit wordlessly and roasted it. A savory smell drifted up as the sun went down. Purple shadows drifted hungrily over the bowl where the man in black had chosen to finally face him. The gunslinger felt hunger begin to rumble endlessly in his belly as the rabbit browned; but when the meat was cooked and its juices sealed in, he handed the entire skewer wordlessly to the man in black, rummaged in his own nearly flat knapsack, and withdrew the last of his jerky. It was salty, painful to his mouth, and tasted like tears.

"That's a worthless gesture," the man in black said, managing to sound angry and amused at the same time.

"Nevertheless," the gunslinger said. There were tiny sores in his mouth, the result of vitamin deprivation, and the salt taste made him grin bitterly.

"Are you afraid of enchanted meat?"

"Yes."

The man in black slipped his hood back.

The gunslinger looked at him silently. In a way, the face of the man in black was an uneasy disappointment. It was handsome and regular, with none of the marks and twists which indicate a person who has been through awesome times and who has been privy to great and unknown secrets. His hair was black and of a ragged, matted length. His forehead was high, his eyes dark and brilliant. His nose was nondescript. The lips were full and sensual. His complexion was pallid, as was the gunslinger's own.

He said finally, "I expected an older man."

"Not necessary. I am nearly immortal. I could have taken a face that you more expected, of course, but I elected to show you the one I was—ah—born with. See, gunslinger, the sunset."

The sun had departed already, and the western sky was filled with a sullen furnace light.

"You won't see another sunrise for what may seem a very long time," the man in black said softly.

The gunslinger remembered the pit under the mountains and then looked at the sky, where the constellations sprawled in clockspring profusion.

"It doesn't matter," he said softly, "now."

The man in black shuffled the cards with flying, merging rapidity. The deck was huge, the design on the backs of the cards convoluted. "These are tarot cards," the man in black was saying, "a mixture of the standard deck and a selection of my own development. Watch closely gunslinger."

"Why?"

"I'm going to tell your future, Roland. Seven cards must be turned, one at a time, and placed in conjunction with the others. I've not done this for over three hundred years. And I suspect I've never read one quite like yours." The mocking note was creeping in again, like a Kuvian night-soldier with a killing knife gripped in one hand. "You are the world's last adventurer. The last crusader. How that must please you, Roland! Yet you have no idea how close you stand to the Tower now, how close in time. Worlds turn about your head."

"Read my fortune then," he said harshly.

The first card was turned.

"The Hanged Man," the man in black said. The darkness had given him back his hood. "Yet here, in conjunction with nothing else, it signifies strength and not death. You, gunslinger, are the Hanged Man, plodding ever onward toward your goal over all the pits of Hades. You have already dropped one co-traveler into the pit, have you not?"

He turned the second card. "The Sailor. Note the clear brow, the hairless cheeks, the wounded eyes. He drowns, gunslinger, and no one throws out the line. The boy Jake."

The gunslinger winced, said nothing.

The third card was turned. A baboon stood grinningly astride a young man's shoulder. The young man's face was turned up, a grimace of stylized dread and horror on his features. Looking more closely, the gunslinger saw the baboon held a whip.

"The Prisoner," the man in black said. The fire cast uneasy, flickering shadows over the face of the ridden man, making it seem to move and writhe in wordless terror. The gunslinger flicked his eyes away.

"A trifle upsetting, isn't he?" The man in black said, and seemed on the verge of sniggering.

He turned the fourth card. A woman with a shawl over her head sat spinning at a wheel. To the gunslinger's dazed eyes, she appeared to be smiling craftily and sobbing at the same time.

"The Lady of Shadows," the man in black remarked. "Does she look two-faced to you, gunslinger? She is. A veritable Janus."

"Why are you showing me these?"

"Don't ask!" the man in black said sharply, yet he smiled. "Don't ask. Merely watch. Consider this only pointless ritual if it eases you and cools you to do so. Like church."

He tittered and turned the fifth card.

A grinning reaper clutched a scythe with bony fingers. "Death," the man in black said simply. "Yet not for you."

The sixth card.

The gunslinger looked at it and felt a strange, crawling anticipation in his guts. The feeling was mixed with horror and joy, and the whole of the emotion was unnamable. It made him feel like throwing up and dancing at the same time.

"The Tower," the man in black said softly.

The gunslinger's card occupied the center of the pattern; each of the following four stood at one corner, like satellites circling a star.

"Where does that one go?" the gunslinger asked.

The man in black placed the Tower over the Hanged Man, covering it completely.

"What does that mean?" the gunslinger asked.

The man in black did not answer.

"What does that mean?" he asked raggedly.

The man in black did not answer.

"God damn you!"

No answer.

"Then what's the seventh card?"

The man in black turned the seventh. A sun rose in a luminously blue sky. Cupids and sprites sported around it.

"The seventh is Life," the man in black said softly. "But not for you."

"Where does it fit the pattern?"

"That is not for you to know," the man in black said. "Or for me to know." He flipped the card carelessly into the dying fire. It charred, curled and flashed to flame. The gunslinger felt his heart quail and turn icy in his chest.

"Sleep now," the man in black said carelessly. "Perchance to dream and that sort of thing."

"I'm going to choke you dead," the gunslinger said. His legs coiled with savage, splendid suddenness, and he flew across the fire at the other. The man in black, smiling, swelled in his vision and then retreated down a long and echoing corridor filled with obsidian pylons. The world filled with the sound of sardonic laughter, he was falling, dying, sleeping.

He dreamed.

The universe was void. Nothing moved. Nothing was.

The gunslinger drifted, bemused.

"Let us have light," the voice of the man in black said nonchalantly, and there was light. The gunslinger thought in a detached way that the light was good.

"Now darkness overhead with stars in it. Water down below." It happened. He drifted over endless seas. Above, the stars twinkled endlessly.

"Land," the man in black invited. There was; it heaved itself out of the water in endless, galvanic convulsions. It was red, arid, cracked and glazed with sterility. Volcanoes blurted endless magma like giant pimples on some ugly adolescent's baseball head.

"Okay," the man in black was saying. "That's a start. Let's have some plants. Trees. Grass and fields."

There was. Dinosaurs rambled here and there, growling and whoofing and eating each other and getting stuck in bubbling, odiferous tarpits. Huge tropical rain-forests sprawled everywhere. Giant ferns waved at the sky with serated leaves. Beetles with two heads crawled on some of them. All this the gunslinger saw. And yet he felt big.

"Now man," the man in black said softly, but the gunslinger was falling ... falling up. The horizon of this vast and fecund earth began to curve. Yes, they had all said it had curved, his teachers, they had claimed it had been proved long before the world had moved on. But this—

Further and further. Continents took shape before his amazed eyes, and were obscured with clocksprings of clouds. The world's atmosphere held it in a placental sac. And the sun, rising beyond the earth's shoulder—

He cried out and threw an arm before his eyes.

"Let there be light!" The voice that cried was no longer that of the man in black. It was gigantic, echoing. It filled space, and the spaces between spaces.

"Light!"

Falling, falling.

The sun shrank. A red planet crossed with canals whirled past him, two moons circling it furiously. A whirling belt of stones. A gigantic planet that seethed with gasses, too huge to support itself, oblate in consequence. A ringed world that glittered with its engirdlement of icy spicules.

"Light! Let there be—"

Other worlds, one, two, three. Far beyond the last, one lonely ball of ice and rock twirling in dead darkness about a sun that glittered no brighter than a tarnished penny.

Darkness.

"No," the gunslinger said, and his words were flat and echoless in the darkness. It was darker than dark. Beside it the darkest night of a man's soul was noonday. The darkness under the mountains was a mere smudge on the face of Light. "No more, please, no more now. No more—"

"LIGHT!"

"No more. No more, please—"

The stars themselves began to shrink. Whole nebulae drew together and became mindless smudges. The whole universe seemed to be drawing around him.

"Jesus no more no more no more—"

The voice of the man in black whispered silkily in his ear: "Then renege. Cast away all thoughts of the Tower. Go your way, gunslinger, and save your soul."

He gathered himself. Shaken and alone, enwrapt in the darkness, terrified of an ultimate meaning rushing at him, he gathered himself and uttered the final, flashing imperative:

"NO! NEVER!"

"THEN LET THERE BE LIGHT!"

And there was light, crashing in on him like a hammer, a great and primordial light. In it, consciousness perished—but before it did, the gunslinger saw something of cosmic importance. He clutched it with agonized effort and sought himself.

He fled the insanity the knowledge implied, and so came back to himself.

It was still night—whether the same or another, he had no way of knowing. He pushed himself up from where his demon spring at the man in black had carried him and looked at the ironwood where the man in black had been sitting. He was gone.

A great sense of despair flooded him—God, all that to do over again—and then the man in black said from behind him: "Over here, gunslinger. I don't like you so close. You talk in your sleep." He tittered.

The gunslinger got groggily to his knees and turned around. The fire had burned down to red embers and gray ashes, leaving the familiar decayed pattern of exhausted fuel. The man in black was seated next to it, smacking his lips over the greasy remains of the rabbit.

"You did fairly well," the man in black said. "I never could have sent that vision to Marten. He would have come back drooling."

"What was it?" the gunslinger asked. His words were blurred and shaky. He felt that if he tried to rise, his legs would buckle.

"The universe," the man in black said carelessly. He burped and threw the bones into the fire where they glistened with unhealthy whiteness. The wind above the cup of the golgotha whistled with keen unhappiness.

"Universe," the gunslinger said blankly.

"You want the Tower," the man in black said. It seemed to be a question.

"Yes."

"But you shan't have it," the man in black said, and smiled with bright cruelty. "I have an idea of how close to the edge that last pushed you. The Tower will kill you half a world away."

"You know nothing of me," the gunslinger said quietly, and the smile faded from the other's lips.

"I made your father and I broke him," the man in black said grimly. "I came to your mother through Marten and took her. It was written, and it was. I am the furthest minion of the Dark Tower. Earth has been given into my hand."

"What did I see?" the gunslinger asked. "At the end? What was it?"

"What did it seem to be?"

The gunslinger was silent, thoughtful. He felt for his tobacco, but there was none. The man in black did not offer to refill his poke by either black magic or white.

"There was light," the gunslinger said finally. "Great white light. And then—" He broke off and stared at the man in black. He was leaning forward, and an alien emotion was stamped on his face, writ too large for lies or denial. Wonder.

"You don't know," he said, and began to smile. "O great sorcerer who brings the dead to life. You don't know."

"I know," the man in black said. "But I don't know ... what."

"White light," the gunslinger repeated. "And then—a blade of grass. One single blade of grass that filled everything. And I was tiny. Infinitesimal."

"Grass." The man in black closed his eyes. His face looked drawn and haggard. "A blade of grass. Are you sure?"

"Yes." The gunslinger frowned. "But it was purple."

And so the man in black began to speak.

The universe (he said) offers a paradox too great for the finite mind to grasp. As the living brain cannot conceive of a nonliving brain—although it may think it can—the finite mind cannot grasp the infinite.

The prosaic fact of the universe's existence single-handedly defeats the pragmatist and the cynic. There was a time, yet a hundred generations before the world moved on, when mankind had achieved enough technical and scientific prowess to chip a few splinters from the great stone pillar of reality. Even then, the false light of science (knowledge, if you like) shone in only a few developed countries.

Yet, despite a tremendous increase in available facts, there were remarkably few insights. Gunslinger, our fathers conquered the-disease-which-rots, which we call cancer, almost conquered aging, went to the moon—

("I don't believe that," the gunslinger said flatly, to which the man in black merely smiled and answered, "You needn't.")

—and made or discovered a hundred other marvelous baubles. But this wealth of information produced little or no insight. There were no great odes written to the wonders of artificial insemination—

("What?" "Having babies from frozen mansperm." "Bullshit." "As you wish ... although not even the ancients could produce children from that material.")

—or to the car-which-moves. Few if any seemed to have grasped the Principle of Reality; new knowledge leads always to yet more awesome mysteries. Greater physiological knowledge of the brain makes the existence of the soul less possible yet more probable by the nature of the search. Do you see? Of course you don't. You are surrounded by your own romantic aura, you lie cheek and jowl daily with the arcane. Yet now you approach the limits—not of belief, but of comprehension. You face reverse entropy of the soul.

But to the more prosaic:

The greatest mystery the universe offers is not life but Size. Size encompasses life, and the Tower encompasses Size. The child, who is most at home with wonder, says: Daddy, what is above the sky? And the father says: The darkness of space. The child: What is beyond space? The father: The galaxy. The child: Beyond the galaxy? The father: Another galaxy. The child: Beyond the other galaxies? The father: No one knows.

You see? Size defeats us. For the fish, the lake in which he lives is the universe. What does the fish think when he is jerked up by the mouth through the silver limits of existence and into a new universe where the air drowns him and the light is blue madness? Where huge bipeds with no gills stuff it into a suffocating box and cover it with wet weeds to die?

Or one might take the point of a pencil and magnify it. One reaches the point where a stunning realization strikes home: The pencil point is not solid; it is composed of atoms which whirl and revolve like a trillion demon planets. What seems solid to us is actually only a loose net held together by gravitation. Shrunk to the correct size, the distances between these atoms might become leagues, gulfs, aeons. The atoms themselves are composed of nuclei and revolving protons and electrons. One may step down further to subatomic particles. And then to what? Tachyons? Nothing? Of course not. Everything in the universe denies nothing; to suggest conclusions to things is one impossibility.

If you fell outward to the limit of the universe, would you find a board fence and signs reading DEAD END? No. You might find something hard and rounded, as the chick must see the egg from the inside. And if you should peck through that shell, what great and torrential light might shine through your hole at the end of space? Might you look through and discover our entire universe is but part of one atom on a blade of grass? Might you be forced to think that by burning a twig you incinerate an eternity of eternities? That existence rises not to one infinite but to an infinity of them?

Perhaps you saw what place our universe plays in the scheme of things—as an atom in a blade of grass. Could it be that everything we can perceive, from the infinitesimal virus to the distant Horsehead Nebula, is contained in one blade of grass ... a blade that may have existed for only a day or two in an alien time-flow? What if that blade should be cut off by a scythe? When it began to die, would the rot seep into our own universe and our own lives, turning everything yellow and brown and desiccated? Perhaps it's already begun to happen. We say the world has moved on; maybe we really mean that it has begun to dry up.

Think how small such a concept of things makes us, gunslinger! If a God watches over it all, does He actually mete out justice for a race of gnats among an infinitude of races of gnats? Does his eye see the sparrow fall when the sparrow is less than a speck of hydrogen floating disconnected in the depth of space? And if He does see ... what must the nature of such a God be? Where does He live? How is it possible to live beyond infinity?

Imagine the sand of the Mohaine Desert, which you crossed to find me, and imagine a trillion universes—not worlds but universes—encapsulated in each grain of that desert; and within each universe an infinity of others. We tower over these universes from our pitiful grass vantage point; with one swing of your boot you may knock a billion billion worlds flying off into darkness, in a chain never to be completed.

Size, gunslinger ... Size....

Yet suppose further. Suppose that all worlds, all universes, met in a single nexus, a single pylon, a Tower. A stairway, perhaps, to the Godhead itself. Would you dare, gunslinger? Could it be that somewhere above all of endless reality, there exists a Room ... ?

You dare not.

You dare not.

"Someone has dared," the gunslinger said.

"Who would that be?"

"God," the gunslinger said softly. His eyes gleamed. "God has dared ... or is the room empty, seer?"

"I don't know." Fear passed over the man in black's bland face, as soft and dark as a buzzard's wing. "And, furthermore, I don't ask. It might be unwise."

"Afraid of being struck dead?" The gunslinger asked sardonically.

"Perhaps afraid of an accounting," the man in black replied, and there was silence for a while. The night was very long. The Milky Way sprawled above them in great splendor, yet terrifying in its emptiness. The gunslinger wondered what he would feel if that inky sky should split open and let in a torrent of light.

"The fire," he said. "I'm cold."

The gunslinger drowsed and awoke to see the man in black regarding him avidly, unhealthily.

"What are you staring at?"

"You, of course."

"Well, don't." He poked up the fire, ruining the precision of the ideogram. "I don't like it." He looked to the east to see if there was the beginning of light, but this night went on and on.

"You seek the light so soon?"

"I was made for light."

"Ah, so you were! And so impolite of me to forget the fact! Yet we have much to discuss yet, you and I. For so has it been told to me by my master."

"Who?"

The man in black smiled. "Shall we tell the truth then, you and I? No more lies? No more glammer?"

"Glammer? What does that mean?"

But the man in black persisted: "Shall there be truth between us, as two men? Not as friends, but as enemies and equals? There is an offer you will get rarely, Roland. Only enemies speak the truth. Friends and lovers lie endlessly, caught in the web of duty."

"Then we'll speak the truth." He had never spoken less on this night. "Start by telling me what glammer is."

"Glammer is enchantment, gunslinger. My master's enchantment has prolonged this night and will prolong it still . . . until our business is done."

"How long will that be?"

"Long. I can tell you no better. I do not know myself." The man in black stood over the fire, and the glowing embers made patterns on his face. "Ask. I will tell you what I know. You have caught me. It is fair; I did not think you would. Yet your quest has only begun. Ask. It will lead us to business soon enough."

"Who is your master?"

"I have never seen him, but you must. In order to reach the Tower you must reach this one first, the Ageless Stranger." The man in black smiled spitelessly. "You must slay him, gunslinger. Yet I think it is not what you wished to ask."

"If you've never seen him, how do you know him?"

"He came to me once in a dream. As a stripling he came to me, when I lived in a far land. A thousand years ago, or five or ten. He came to me in days before the old ones had yet to cross the sea. In a land called England. A sheaf of centuries ago he imbued me with my duty, although there were errands in between my youth and my apotheosis. You are that, gunslinger." He tittered. "You see, someone has taken you seriously."

"This Stranger has no name?"

"O, he is named."

"And what is his name?"

"Maerlyn," the man in black said softly, and somewhere in the easterly darkness where the mountains lay a rockslide punctuated his words and a puma screamed like a woman. The gunslinger shivered and the man in black flinched. "Yet I do not think that is what you wished to ask, either. It is not your nature to think so far ahead."

The gunslinger knew the question; it had gnawed him all this night, and he thought, for years before. It trembled on his lips but he didn't ask it ... not yet.

"This Stranger, this Maerlyn, is a minion of the Tower? Like yourself?"

"Much greater than I. It has been given to him to live backward in time. He *darkles*. He *tincts*. He is in all times. Yet there is one greater than he."

"Who?"

"The Beast," the man in black whispered fearfully. "The keeper of the Tower. The originator of all *glammer*."

"What is it? What does this Beast—"

"Ask me no more!" The man in black cried. His voice aspired to sternness and crumbled into beseechment. "I know not! I do not wish to know. To speak of the Beast is to speak of the ruination of one's own soul. Before It, Maerlyn is as I am to him."

"And beyond the Beast is the Tower and whatever the Tower contains?"

"Yes," whispered the man in black. "But none of these things are what you wish to ask."

True.

"All right," the gunslinger said, and then asked the world's oldest question. "Do I know you? Have I seen you somewhere before?"

"Yes."

"Where?" The gunslinger leaned forward urgently. This was a question of his destiny.

The man in black clapped his hands to his mouth and giggled through them like a small child. "I think you know."

"Where!" He was on his feet; his hands had dropped to the worn butts of his guns.

"Not with those, gunslinger. Those do not open doors; those only close them forever."

"Where?" The gunslinger reiterated.

"Must I give him a hint?" The man in black asked the darkness. "I believe I must." He looked at the gunslinger with eyes that burned. "There was a man who gave you advice," he said. "Your teacher—"

"Yes, Cort," the gunslinger interrupted impatiently.

"The advice was to wait. It was bad advice. For even then Marten's plans against your father had proceeded. And when your father returned—"

"He was killed," the gunslinger said emptily.

"And when you turned and looked, Marten was gone ... gone west. Yet there was a man in Marten's entourage, a man who affected the dress of a monk and the shaven head of a penitent—"

"Walter," the gunslinger whispered. "You ... you're not Marten at all. You're *Walter!*"

The man in black tittered. "At your service."

"I ought to kill you now."

"That would hardly be fair. After all, it was I who delivered Marten into your hands three years later, when—"

"Then you've controlled me."

"In some ways, yes. But no more, gunslinger.

Now comes the time of sharing. Then, in the morning, I will cast the runes. Dreams will come to you. And then your real quest must begin."

"Walter," the gunslinger repeated, stunned.

"Sit," the man in black invited. "I tell you my story. Yours, I think, will be much longer."

"I don't talk of myself," the gunslinger muttered.

"Yet tonight you must. So that we may understand."

"Understand what? My purpose? You know that. To find the Tower is my purpose. I'm sworn."

"Not your purpose, gunslinger. Your mind. Your slow, plodding, tenacious mind. There has never been one quite like it, in all the history of the world. Perhaps in the history of creation.

"This is the time of speaking. This is the time of histories."

"Then speak."

The man in black shook the voluminous arm of his robe. A foil-wrapped package fell out and caught the dying embers in many reflective folds.

"Tobacco, gunslinger. Would you smoke?"

He had been able to resist the rabbit, but he could not resist this. He opened the foil with eager fingers. There was fine crumbled tobacco inside, and green leaves to wrap it in, amazingly moist. He had not seen such tobacco for ten years.

He rolled two cigarettes and bit the ends of each to release flavor. He offered one to the man in black, who took it. Each of them took a burning twig from the fire.

The gunslinger lit his cigarette and drew the aromatic smoke deep into his lungs, closing his eyes to concentrate the senses. He blew out with long, slow satisfaction.

"Is it good?" the man in black enquired.

"Yes. Very good."

"Enjoy it. It may be the last smoke for you in a very long time."

The gunslinger took this impassively.

"Very well," the man in black said. "To begin then:

"You must understand that the Tower has always been, and there have always been boys who know of it and lust for it, more than power or riches or women. . . ."

There was talk then, a night's worth of talk and God alone knew how much more, but the Gunslinger remembered little of it later . . . and to his oddly practical mind, little of it seemed to matter. The man in black told him that he must go to the sea, which lay no more than twenty easy miles to the west, and there he would be invested with the power of *drawing*.

"But that's not exactly right, either," the man in black said, pitching his cigarette into the remains of the campfire. "No one wants to invest you with a power of any kind, gunslinger; it is simply in you, and I am compelled to tell you, partly because of the sacrifice of the boy, and partly because it is the law; the natural law of things. Water must run downhill, and you must be told. You will draw three, I understand ... but I don't really care, and I don't really want to know."

"The three," the gunslinger murmured, thinking of the Oracle.

"And then the fun begins. But, by then, I'll be long gone. Good-bye, gunslinger. My part is done now. The chain is still in your hands. Beware it doesn't wrap itself around your neck."

Compelled by something outside him, Roland said, "You have one more thing to say, don't you?"

"Yes," the man in black said, and he smiled at the gunslinger with his depthless eyes and stretched one of his hands out toward him. "Let there be light."

And there was light.

Roland awoke by the ruins of the campfire to find himself ten years older. His black hair had thinned at the temples and gone the gray of cobwebs at the end of autumn. The lines in his face were deeper, his skin rougher.

The remains of the wood he had carried had turned to ironwood, and the man in black was a laughing skeleton in a rotting black robe, more bones in this place of bones, one more skull in golgotha.

The gunslinger stood up and looked around. He looked at the light and saw that the light was good.

With a sudden quick gesture he reached toward the remains of his companion of the night before ... a night that had somehow lasted ten years. He broke off Walter's jawbone and jammed it carelessly into the left hip pocket of his jeans—a fitting enough replacement for the one lost under the mountains.

The Tower. Somewhere ahead, it waited for him—the nexus of Time, the nexus of Size.

He began west again, his back set against the sunrise, heading toward the ocean, realizing that a great passage of his life had come and gone. "I loved you, Jake," he said aloud.

The stiffness wore out of his body and he began to walk more rapidly. By that evening he had come to the end of the land. He sat on a beach which stretched left and right forever, deserted. The waves beat endlessly against the shore, pounding and pounding. The setting sun painted the water in a wide strip of fool's gold.

There the gunslinger sat, his face turned up into the fading light. He dreamed his dreams and watched as the stars came out; his purpose did not flag, nor did his heart falter; his hair, finer now and gray, blew around his head, and the sandalwood-inlaid guns of his father lay smooth and deadly against his hips, and he was lonely but did not find loneliness in any way a bad or ignoble thing. The dark came down on the world and the world moved on. The gunslinger waited for the time of the *drawing* and dreamed his long dreams of the Dark Tower, to which he would some day come at dusk and approach, winding his horn, to do some unimaginable final battle.

AFTERWORD

The foregoing tale, which is almost (but not quite!) complete in itself, is the first stanza in a much longer work called *The Dark Tower*. Some of the work beyond this segment has been completed, but there is much more to be done—my brief synopsis of the action to follow suggests a length approaching 3000 pages, perhaps more. That probably sounds as if my plans for the story have passed beyond mere ambition and into the land of lunacy . . . but ask your favorite English teacher sometime to tell you about the plans Chaucer had for *The Canterbury Tales*—now *Chaucer* might have been crazy.

At the speed which the work entire has progressed so far, I would have to live approximately 300 years to complete the tale of the Tower; this segment, "The Gunslinger and the Dark Tower," was written over a period of twelve years. It is by far the longest I've taken with any work ... and it might be more honest to put it another way: it is the longest that any of my unfinished works has remained alive and viable in my own mind, and if a book is not alive in the writer's mind, it is as dead as year-old horseshit even if words continue to march across the page.

The Dark Tower began, I think, because I inherited a ream of paper in the spring semester of my senior year in college. It wasn't a ream of your ordinary garden-variety bond paper, not even a ream of those colorful "second sheets" that many struggling writers use because those reams of colored sheets (often with large chunks of undissolved wood floating in them) are three or four dollars cheaper.

The ream of paper I inherited was bright green, nearly as thick as cardboard, and of an extremely eccentric size—about seven inches wide by about ten inches long, as I recall. I was working at the University of Maine library at the time, and several reams of this stuff, in various hues, turned up one day, totally unexplained and unaccounted for. My wife-to-be, the then Tabitha Spruce, took one of these reams of paper (robin's egg blue) home with her; the fellow she was then going with took home another (Roadrunner yellow). I got the green stuff.

As it happened, all three of us turned out to be real writers—a coincidence almost too large to be termed mere coincidence in a society where literally tens of thousands (maybe hundreds of thousands) of college students aspire to the writer's trade and where bare hundreds actually break through. I've gone on to publish half a dozen novels or so, my wife has published one *(Small World)* and is hard at work on an even better one, and the fellow she was going with back then, David Lyons, has developed into a fine poet and the founder of Lynx Press in Massachusetts.

Maybe it was the paper, folks. Maybe it was *magic* paper. You know, like in a Stephen King novel.

Anyway, all of you out there reading this may not understand how fraught with possibility those five hundred sheets of blank paper seemed to be, although I'd guess there are plenty of you who are nodding in perfect understanding right now. Publishing writers can, of course, have all the blank paper they want; it is their stock-in-trade. It's even tax deductible. They can have so much, in fact, that all of those blank sheets can actually begin to cast a malign spell—better writers than

I have talked about the mute challenge of all that white space, and God knows some of them have been intimidated into silence by it.

The other side of the coin, particularly to a young writer, is almost unholy exhilaration all that blank paper can bring on; you feel like an alcoholic contemplating a fifth of whiskey with the seal unbroken.

I was at that time living in a scuzzy riverside cabin not far from the University, and I was living all by myself—the first third of the foregoing tale was written in a ghastly, unbroken silence which I now, with a houseful of rioting children, two secretaries, and a housekeeper who always thinks I look ill, find hard to remember. The three roommates with whom I had begun the year had all flunked out. By March, when the ice went out of the river, I felt like the last of Agatha Christie's ten little Indians.

Those two factors, the challenge of that blank green paper, and the utter silence (except for the trickle of the melting snow as it ran downhill and into the Stillwater), were more responsible than anything else for the opening lay of *The Dark Tower*. There was a third factor, but without the first two, I don't believe the story ever would have been written.

That third element was a poem I'd been assigned two years earlier, in a sophomore course covering the earlier romantic poets (and what better time to study romantic poetry than in one's sophomore year?). Most of the other poems had fallen out of my consciousness in the period between, but that one, gorgeous and rich and inexplicable, remained ... and it remains still. That poem was "Childe Roland," by Robert Browning.

I had played with the idea of trying a long romantic novel embodying the feel, if not the exact sense, of the Browning poem. Play was as far as things had gone because I had too many other things to write—poems of my own, short stories, newspaper columns, God knows what.

But during that spring semester, a sort of hush fell over my previously busy creative life—not a writer's block, but a sense that it was time to stop goofing around with a pick and shovel and get behind the controls of one big great God a'mighty steamshovel, a sense that it was time to try and dig something big out of the sand, even if the effort turned out to be an abysmal failure.

And so, one night in March of 1970, I found myself sitting at my old office-model Underwood with the chipped 'm' and the flying capital 'O' and writing the words that begin this story: *The man in black fled across the desert and the gunslinger followed.*

In the years since I typed that sentence, with Johnny Winter on the stereo not quite masking the sound of melting snow running downhill outside, I have started to go gray, I have begotten children, I have buried my mother, I have gone on drugs and gone off them, and I've learned a few things about myself—some of them rueful, some of them unpleasant, most of them just plain funny. As the gunslinger himself would probably point out, the world has moved on.

But I've never completely left the gunslinger's world in all that time. The thick green paper got lost somewhere along the way, but I still have the original forty or so pages of typescript, comprising the sections titled "The Gunslinger" and "The Way Station." It was replaced by a more legitimate-looking paper, but I remember those funny green sheets with more affection than I could ever convey in words. I came back to the gunslinger's world when *'Salem's Lot* was going badly ("The Oracle and the Mountains") and wrote of the boy Jake's sad ending not long after I had seen another boy, Danny Torrance, escape another bad place in *The Shining*. In fact, the only time when my thoughts did not turn at least occasionally to the gunslinger's dry and yet somehow gorgeous world (at least it has always seemed gorgeous to me) was when I was inhabiting another that seemed every bit as real—the post-apocalypse world of *The Stand*. The final segment presented here, "The Gunslinger and the Man in Black," was written less than eighteen months ago, in western Maine.

I believe that I probably owe readers who have come this far with me some sort of synopsis ("the argument," those great old romantic poets would have called it) of what is to come, since I'll almost surely die before completing the entire novel . . . or epic . . . or whatever you'd call it. The sad fact is that I can't really do that. People who know me understand that I am not an intellectual ball of fire, and people who have read my work with some critical approval (there are a few; I bribe them) would probably agree that the best of my stuff has come more from the heart than from the head . . . or from the gut, which is the place from which the strongest emotional writing originates.

All of which is just a way of saying that I'm never completely sure where I'm going, and in this story that is even more true than usual. I know from Roland's vision near the end that his world is indeed moving on because Roland's universe exists within a single molecule of a weed dying in some cosmic vacant lot (I think I probably got this idea from Clifford D. Simak's *Ring Around the Sun;* please don't sue me, Cliff!), and I know that the *drawing* involves calling three people from our own world (as Jake himself was called by the man in black) who will join Roland in his quest for the Dark Tower—I know that because segments of the second cycle of stories (called "The Drawing of the Three") have already been written.

But what of the gunslinger's murky past? God, I know so little. The revolution that topples the gunslinger's "world of light"? I don't know. Roland's final confrontation with Marten, who seduces his mother and kills his father? Don't know. The deaths of Roland's compatriots, Cuthbert and Jamie, or his adventures during the years between his coming of age and his first appearance to us in the desert? I don't know that, either. And there's this girl, Susan. Who is she? Don't know.

Except somewhere inside, I do. Somewhere inside I know all of those things, and there is no need of an argument, or a synopsis, or an outline (outlines are the last resource of bad fiction writers who wish to God they were writing masters' theses). When it's time, those things—and their relevance to the gunslinger's quest—will roll out as naturally as tears or laughter. And if they never get around to rolling out, well, as Confucius once said, five hundred million Red Chinese don't give a shit.

I do know this: at some point, at some magic time, there will be a purple evening (an evening made for romance!) when Roland will come to his dark tower, and approach it, winding his horn ... and if I should ever get there, you'll be the first to know.

Stephen King
Bangor, Maine